The Leopard

Jo Nesbo

The Leopard

TRANSLATED

FROM THE NORWEGIAN

BY

Don Bartlett

Harvill Secker
LONDON

Published by Harvill Secker 2010

2 4 6 8 10 9 7 5 3

Copyright © Jo Nesbo 2009
English translation copyright © Don Bartlett 2011

First published with the title *Panserhjerte* in 2009
by H. Aschehoug & Co. (W. Nygaard), Oslo

First published in Great Britain in 2010 by
HARVILL SECKER
Random House
20 Vauxhall Bridge Road
London SW1V 2SA

www.rbooks.co.uk

Addresses for companies within The Random House Group Limited can be found at:
www.randomhouse.co.uk/offices.htm

The Random House Group Limited Reg. No. 954009

A CIP catalogue record for this book is available from the British Library

ISBN 9781846554001 (hardback)
ISBN 9781846554018 (trade paperback)

This translation has been published with the financial support of NORLA

Typeset in Minion by Palimpsest Book Production Limited,
Falkirk, Stirlingshire

Printed and bound in Great Britain by
Clays Ltd, St Ives plc

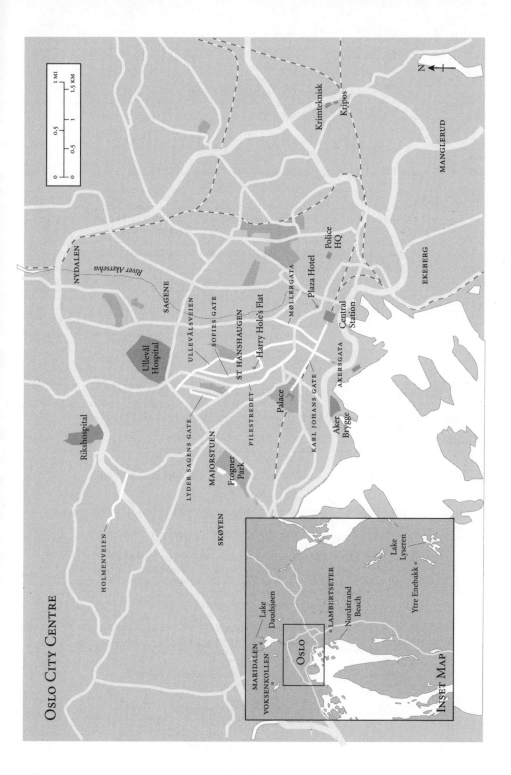

PART ONE

1

The Drowning

SHE AWOKE. BLINKED IN THE PITCH DARKNESS. YAWNED, and breathed through her nose. She blinked again. Felt a tear run down her face, felt it dissolve the salt of other tears. But saliva was no longer entering her throat; her mouth was dry and hard. Her cheeks were forced out by the pressure from inside. The foreign body in her mouth felt as though it would explode her head. But what was it? What was it? The first thing she thought when she awoke was that she wanted to go back. Back into the dark, warm depths that had enveloped her. The injection he had given her had not worn off yet, but she knew pain was on the way, felt it coming in the slow, dull beat of her pulse and the jerky flow of blood through her brain. Where was he? Was he standing right behind her? She held her breath, listened. She couldn't hear anything, but she could sense a presence. Like a leopard. Someone had told her leopards made so little noise they could sneak right up to their prey in the dark. They could regulate their breathing so that it was in tune with yours. Could hold their breath when you held yours. She was certain she could feel his body heat. What was he waiting for? She exhaled again. And at that same moment was sure she had felt breath on her neck. She whirled round, hit out, but was met by air. She hunched up, tried to make herself small, to hide. Pointless.

How long had she been unconscious?

The drug wore off. The sensation lasted only for a fraction of a second.

But it was enough to give her the foretaste, the promise. The promise of what was to come.

The foreign body placed on the table in front of her had been the size of a billiard ball, made of shiny metal with punched-out small holes and figures and symbols. From one of the holes protruded a red wire with a looped end, which instantly made her think of the Christmas tree that would need decorating at her parents' house on 23 December, in seven days. With shiny balls, Christmas pixies, hearts, candles and Norwegian flags. In eight days they would be singing a traditional Christmas carol, and she would see the twinkling eyes of her nephews and nieces as they opened their presents. All the things she should have done differently. All the days she should have lived to the full, avoiding escapism, should have filled with happiness, breath and love. The places she had merely travelled through, the places she was planning to visit. The men she had met, the man she had still not met. The foetus she had got rid of when she was seventeen, the children she had not yet had. The days she had wasted for the days she thought she would have.

Then she had stopped thinking about anything except the knife that had been brandished before her. And the gentle voice that had told her to put the ball in her mouth. She had done so, of course she had. With her heart thumping she had opened her mouth as wide as she could and pushed the ball in with the wire left hanging outside. The metal tasted bitter and salty, like tears. Then her head had been forced back, and the steel burned against her skin as the knife was laid flat against her throat. The ceiling and the room were illuminated by a standard lamp leaning against the wall in one of the corners. Bare, grey concrete. Apart from the lamp, the room contained a white plastic camping table, two chairs, two empty beer bottles and two people. Him and her. She smelt a leather glove as a finger had tugged lightly at the red loop hanging from her mouth. And the next moment her head had seemed to explode.

The ball had expanded and forced itself against the inside of her mouth. But however wide she opened her jaws, the pressure was constant. He had examined her with a concentrated, engaged expression, like a dentist checking to see whether the orthodontic brace was sitting as it should. A little smile intimated satisfaction.

With her tongue she could feel circular ridges around the holes in the ball and that was what was pressing against her palate, against the soft flesh of her tongue, against her teeth, against the uvula. She had tried to say something. He had listened patiently to the inarticulate sounds emerging from her mouth. Had nodded when she gave up, and had taken out a syringe. The drop on the tip had glinted in the torchlight. He had whispered something in her ear: 'Don't touch the wire.'

Then he had injected her in the neck. She was out in seconds.

She listened to her own terrified breathing as she blinked in the darkness.

She had to do something.

She placed her palms on the chair seat, which was clammy from her perspiration, and pushed herself up. No one stopped her.

She advanced with tiny steps until she hit a wall. Groped her way along to a smooth, cold surface. The metal door. She pulled at the bolt. It didn't budge. Locked. Of course it was locked. What had she been thinking? Was that laughter she could hear, or was the sound coming from inside her head? Where was he? Why was he playing with her like this?

Do something. Think. But to think, she would first have to get rid of this metal ball before the pain drove her insane. She put her thumb and first finger in the corners of her mouth. Felt the ridges. Tried in vain to get her fingers under one of them. Had a coughing fit and a panic attack when she couldn't breathe. She realised that the ridges had made the flesh around her windpipe swell, that soon she would be in danger of suffocating. She kicked the metal door, tried to scream, but the ball stifled the sound. She gave up again. Leaned against the wall. Listened. Was that his wary tread she could hear? Was he moving around the room? Was he playing blind man's buff with her? Or was it her blood throbbing past her ears? She steeled herself against the pain and forced her mouth shut. The ridges were hardly down before they sprang back and forced her mouth open again. The ball seemed to be pulsating now, as though it had become an iron heart, a part of her.

Do something. Think.

Springs. The ridges were spring-loaded.

They had jumped up when he pulled the wire.

'Don't touch the wire,' he had said.

Why not? What would happen?

She slid down the wall until she was sitting. Cold damp rose from the concrete floor. She wanted to scream again, but she couldn't. Quiet. Silence.

All the things she should have said to those she loved, instead of the words that had served to fill the silence with those to whom she was indifferent.

There was no way out. There was just her and this unbelievable pain, her head exploding.

'Don't touch the wire.'

If she pulled it, the ridges might retract into the ball, and she would be spared the pain.

Her thoughts ran in the same circles. How long had she been here? Two hours? Eight hours? Twenty minutes?

If all you had to do was pull the wire, why hadn't she already done it? Because the warning had been given by an obvious sicko? Or was this part of the game? Being tricked into resisting the temptation to stop this quite unnecessary pain? Or was the game about defying the warning and pulling the wire, causing ... causing something dreadful to happen? What would happen? What was this ball?

Yes, it was a game, a brutal game. And she had to play. The pain was intolerable, her throat was swelling, soon she would suffocate.

She tried to scream again, but it subsided into a sob, and she blinked and blinked, without producing any further tears.

Her fingers found the string hanging from her lips. She pulled tentatively until it was taut.

There was so much she regretted not having done, naturally. But if a

6

life of self-denial would had placed her anywhere else than here, right now, she would have chosen that. She just wanted to live. Any sort of life. As simple as that.

She pulled the wire.

The needles shot out of the circular ridges. They were seven centimetres long. Four burst through her cheeks on each side, three into the sinuses, two up the nasal passages and two out through the chin. Two needles pierced the windpipe and one the right eye, one the left. Several needles penetrated the rear part of the palate and reached the brain. But that was not the direct cause of her death. Because the metal ball impeded movement, she was unable to spit out the blood pouring from the wounds into her mouth. Instead it ran down her windpipe and into her lungs, not allowing oxygen to be absorbed into her bloodstream, which in turn led to a cardiac arrest and what the pathologist would call in his report cerebral hypoxia, that is, lack of oxygen to her brain. In other words, Borgny Stem-Myhre drowned.

2

The Illuminating Darkness

18 December

The days are short. It's still light outside, but here in my cutting room there is eternal darkness. In the light from my work lamp the people in the pictures on the wall look so irritatingly happy and unsuspecting. So full of expectations, as though they take it for granted that all life lies before them, a perfectly calm ocean of time, smooth and unruffled. I have taken cuttings from the newspaper, snipped off all the lachrymose stories about the shocked family, edited out the gory details about the finding of the body. Contented myself with the inevitable photo a relative or a friend has given a persistent journalist, the picture of when she was in her prime, smiling as though immortal.

The police don't know a lot. Not yet. But soon they will have more to work with.

What is it, where is it, whatever it is that makes a murderer? Is it innate, is it in a gene, inherited potential that some have and others do not? Or is it shaped by need, developed in a confrontation with the world, a survival strategy, a life-saving sickness, rational insanity? For just as sickness is a fevered bombardment of the body, insanity is a vital retreat to a place where one can entrench oneself anew.

For my part, I believe that the ability to kill is fundamental to any healthy person. Our existence is a fight for gain, and whoever cannot kill his neighbour has no right to an existence. Killing is, after all, only hastening the inevitable. Death allows no exceptions, which is good because life is pain and suffering. In that sense, every murder is an act of charity. It just doesn't seem like that when the sun warms your skin or water wets your lips and you recognise your idiotic lust for life in every heartbeat and are ready to buy mere crumbs of time with everything you have accrued through life: dignity, status, principles. That is when you have to dig deep, to give a wide berth to the confusing, blinding light. Into the cold illuminating darkness. And perceive the hard kernel. The truth. For that is what I had to find. That is what I found. Whatever it is that makes a person into a murderer.

What about my life? Do I also believe it is a calm, unruffled ocean of time?

Not at all. Before long I too will be lying on death's refuse heap, together with all the other role players in this little drama. But whatever stage of decay my body may attain, even if all that remains is the skeleton, it will have a smile on its lips. This is what I live for now, my right to exist, my chance to be cleansed, to be cleared of all dishonour.

But this is only the beginning. Now I am going to switch off the lamp and go out into the light of day. The little that is left.

3

Hong Kong

THE RAIN DID NOT STOP FIRST THING. NOR SECOND THING. In fact, it didn't stop at all. It was mild and wet week upon week. The ground was saturated, European motorways caved in, migratory birds did not migrate and there were reports of insects hitherto unseen in northern climes. The calendar showed that it was winter, but Oslo's parkland was not just snowless, it was not even brown. It was as green and inviting as the artificial pitch in Sogn where despairing keep-fit fans had resorted to jogging in their Bjørn Dæhlie tights as they waited in vain for conditions around Lake Sognsvann to allow skiing. On New Year's Eve the fog was so thick that the sound of rockets carried from the centre of Oslo right out to suburban Asker, but you couldn't see a thing, even if you set them off on your back lawn. Nevertheless, that night Norwegians burned fireworks amounting to six hundred kroner per household, according to a consumer survey, which also revealed that the number of Norwegians who realised their dream of a white Christmas on Thailand's white beaches had doubled in just three years. However, also in South-East Asia, it seemed as if the weather had run amok: ominous symbols usually seen only on weather charts in the typhoon season were now lined up across the China Sea. In Hong Kong, where February tends to be one of the driest months of the year, rain was bucketing down and poor visibility meant that Cathay Pacific flight number 731 from London had to circle again before coming in to land at Chek Lap Kok Airport.

'You should be happy we don't have to land at the old airport,' said the Chinese-looking passenger next to Kaja Solness, who was squeezing the armrests so hard her knuckles were white. 'It was in the centre of town. We would have flown straight into one of the skyscrapers.'

Those were the first words the man had uttered since they had taken off twelve hours earlier. Kaja eagerly grabbed the chance to focus on something other than the fact that they were temporarily caught in turbulence.

'Thank you, sir, that was reassuring. Are you English?'

He recoiled as if someone had slapped him, and she realised she had offended him mortally by suggesting that he belonged to the previous colonialists: 'Erm . . . Chinese perhaps?'

He shook his head firmly. 'Hong Kong Chinese. And you, miss?'

Kaja Solness wondered for a moment if she should reply Hokksund Norwegian, but confined herself to 'Norwegian', which the Hong Kong Chinese man mused on for a while then delivered a triumphant 'Aha!' before amending it to 'Scandinavian' and asked her what her business was in Hong Kong.

'To find a man,' she said, staring down at the bluish-grey clouds in the hope that terra firma would soon reveal itself.

'Aha!' repeated the Hong Kong Chinese. 'You are very beautiful, miss. And don't believe all you hear about the Chinese only marrying other Chinese.'

She managed a weary smile. 'Hong Kong Chinese, do you mean?'

'Particularly Hong Kong Chinese,' he nodded with enthusiasm, holding up a ringless hand. 'I deal in microchips. The family has factories in China and South Korea. What are you doing tonight?'

'Sleeping, I hope,' Kaja yawned.

'What about tomorrow evening?'

'I hope by then I'll have found him and I'll be on my way back home.'

The man frowned. 'Are you in such a hurry, miss?'

Kaja refused the man's offer of a lift and caught a bus, a double-decker, to the city centre. One hour later she was standing alone in a corridor at the Empire Kowloon Hotel, taking deep breaths. She had put the key card into the door of the room she had been allocated and now all that remained was to open it. She forced her hand to press down the handle. Then she jerked the door open and stared into the room.

No one there.

Of course there wasn't.

She entered, wheeled her bag to the side of the bed, stood by the window and looked out. First, down at the swarm of people in the street seventeen floors below, then at the skyscrapers that in no way resembled their graceful or, at any rate pompous, sisters in Manhattan, Kuala Lumpur or Tokyo. These looked like termite anthills, terrifying and impressive at the same time, like a grotesque testimony to how humankind is capable of adapting when seven million inhabitants have to find room in not much more than a hundred square kilometres. Kaja felt exhaustion creeping up on her, kicked off her shoes and fell back on the bed. Even though it was a double room and the hotel sported four stars, the 120-centimetre-wide bed occupied all the floor space. And it hit home that from among all these anthills she now had to find one particular person, a man who, all the evidence suggested, had no particular wish to be found.

For a moment or two she weighed up the options: closing her eyes or springing into action. Then she pulled herself together and got to her feet. Took off her clothes and went into the shower. Afterwards she stood in front of the mirror and confirmed without a hint of self-satisfaction that the Hong Kong Chinese man was right: she was beautiful. This was not her opinion, it was as close to being a fact as beauty can be. The face with the high cheekbones, the pronounced raven-black but finely formed eyebrows above the almost childlike wide eyes with green irises that shone with the intensity of a mature young woman. The honey-brown hair, the full lips that seemed to be kissing each other in her somewhat broad mouth. The long, slim neck, the equally slim body with the small breasts that were no more than mounds, swells on a sea of perfect, though winter-pale, skin. The gentle curve of her hips. The long legs that persuaded two Oslo modelling agencies to make the trip to her school in Hokksund, only to have to accept her refusal with a rueful shake of the head. And what had pleased her most was when one of them said

12

as he left: 'OK, but remember, my dear: you are not a *perfect* beauty. Your teeth are small and pointed. You shouldn't smile so much.'

After that she had smiled with a lighter heart.

Kaja put on a pair of khaki trousers, a thin waterproof jacket and floated weightlessly and soundlessly down to reception.

'Chungking Mansion?' the receptionist asked, unable to refrain from cocking an eyebrow, and pointed. 'Kimberley Road, up to Nathan Road, then left.'

All hostels and hotels in Interpol member countries are legally obliged to register foreign guests, but when Kaja had rung the Norwegian ambassador's secretary to check where the man she was looking for had last registered, the secretary had explained that Chungking Mansion was neither a hotel nor a mansion, in the sense of a wealthy residence. It was a collection of shops, takeaways, restaurants and probably more than a hundred classified and non-classified hostels with everything from two to twenty rooms spread over four large tower blocks. The rooms for rent could be characterised as everything from simple, clean and cosy to ratholes and one-star prison cells. And most important of all: at Chungking Mansion a man with modest demands of life could sleep, eat, live, work and propagate without ever leaving the anthill.

Kaja found the entrance to Chungking in Nathan Road, a busy shopping street with branded goods, polished shopfronts and tall display windows. She went in. To the cooking fumes from fast-food outlets, hammering from cobblers, radio broadcasts of Muslim prayer meetings and tired looks in used clothes shops. She flashed a quick smile at a bewildered backpacker with a *Lonely Planet* guidebook in his hand and frozen white legs sticking out of over-optimistic camouflage shorts.

A uniformed guard looked at the note Kaja showed him, said 'Lift C' and pointed down a corridor.

The queue in front of the lift was so long that she didn't get in until the third attempt, when they were squeezed up tight in a creaky, juddering iron chest that made Kaja think of the gypsies who buried their dead vertically.

The hostel was owned by a turban-clad Muslim who immediately, and with great enthusiasm, showed her a tiny box of a room where by some miracle they had found space for a wall-mounted TV at the foot of the bed and a gurgling A/C unit above the bedhead. The owner's enthusiasm waned when she interrupted his sales spiel to produce a photo of a man with his name spelt as it would have been in his passport, and asked where he was now.

On seeing the reaction, she hastened to inform him that she was his wife. The embassy secretary had explained to her that waving an official ID card around in Chungking would be, quote, counterproductive. And when Kaja added, for safety's sake, that she and the man in the photo had five children together, the hostel owner's attitude underwent a dramatic change. A young Western heathen who had already brought so many children into the world earned his respect. He expelled a heavy sigh, shook his head and said in mournful, staccato English, 'Sad, sad, lady. They come and take his passport.'

'Who did?'

'Who? The Triad, lady. It's always the Triad.'

Naturally enough, she was aware of the organisation, but she had some vague notion that the Chinese mafia primarily belonged to the world of cartoons and kung fu films.

'Sit yourself down, lady.' He quickly found a chair, onto which she slumped. 'They were after him, he was out, so they took his passport.'

'Passport? Why?'

He hesitated.

'Please, I have to know.'

'Your husband bet on horses, I am sorry to say.'

'Horses?'

'Happy Valley. Racecourse. It is an abomination.'

'Does he owe money? To the Triad?'

He nodded and shook his head several times to confirm and regret, alternately, this fact of life.

'And they took his passport?'

'He will have to pay back the debt if he wants to leave Hong Kong.'

'He can only get a new passport from the Norwegian embassy.'

The turban waggled from side to side. 'Ah, you can get a false passport here in Chungking for eighty American dollars. But this is not the problem. The problem is Hong Kong is an island, lady. How did you get here?'

'Plane.'

'And how will you leave?'

'Plane.'

'One airport. Tickets. All names on computer. Many control points. Many at airport who get money from the Triad to recognise faces. Understand?'

She nodded slowly. 'It's difficult to escape.'

The hostel owner shook his head with a guffaw. 'No, lady. It's *impossible* to escape. But you can hide in Hong Kong. Seven million people. Easy to go underground.'

Lack of sleep was catching up on Kaja, and she closed her eyes. The owner must have misunderstood because he laid a consoling hand on her shoulder and mumbled, 'There, there.'

He wavered, then leaned forward and whispered, 'I think he still here, lady.'

'Yes, I know he is.'

'No, I mean here in Chungking. I see him.'

She raised her head.

'Twice,' he said. 'At Li Yuan's. He eat there. Cheap rice. Don't tell anyone I said. Your husband is good man. But trouble.' He rolled his eyes so that they almost disappeared into his turban. 'Lots of trouble.'

Li Yuan's comprised a counter, four plastic tables and a Chinese man who sent her an encouraging smile when after six hours, two portions of fried rice, three coffees and two litres of water she awoke with a jolt, lifted her head from the greasy table and looked at him.

'Tired?' he laughed, revealing an incomplete set of front teeth.

Kaja yawned, ordered her fourth cup of coffee and continued to wait. Two Chinese men came and sat at the counter without speaking or ordering. They didn't even spare her a glance, for which she was glad. Her body was so stiff from sitting on the plane that pain shot through her whatever sedentary position she adopted. She rolled her head from side to side to try to stimulate circulation. Then backwards. Her neck cracked. She stared at the bluish-white neon tubes in the ceiling before lowering her head. And stared straight into a pale, hunted face. He had stopped in front of the closed steel shutters in the corridor and scanned Li Yuan's tiny establishment. His gaze rested on the two Chinese men by the counter. Then he hurried on.

Kaja got to her feet, but one leg had gone to sleep and gave way under her weight. She grabbed her bag and limped after the man as fast as she could.

'Come back soon,' she heard Li Yuan shout after her.

He had looked so thin. In the photographs he had been a broad, tall figure, and on the TV talk show he had made the chair he was sitting on look like it had been manufactured for pygmies. But she had not the slightest doubt it was him: the dented, shaven skull, the prominent nose, the eyes with the spider's web of blood vessels and the alcoholic's washed-out, pale blue irises. The determined chin with the surprisingly gentle, almost beautiful mouth.

She stumbled into Nathan Road. In the gleam of the neon light she caught sight of a leather jacket towering above the crowd. He didn't appear to be walking fast, yet she had to quicken her pace to keep up. From the busy shopping parade he turned off and she let the distance between them increase as they came into narrower, less populated streets. She registered a sign saying 'Melden Row'. It was tempting to go and introduce herself, get it all over with. But she had decided to stick to the plan: to find out where he lived. It had stopped raining, and all of a sudden a scrap of cloud was drawn aside and the sky behind was high and velvet black, with glittering, pinhole stars.

After walking for twenty minutes he came to a sudden halt at a corner, and Kaja was afraid she had been rumbled. However, he didn't turn round, just took something from his jacket pocket. She stared in amazement. A baby's bottle?

He disappeared round the corner.

Kaja followed and came into a large, open square packed with people, most of them young. At the far end of the square, above wide glass doors, shone a sign written in English and Chinese. Kaja recognised the titles of some of the new films she would never see. Her eyes found his leather jacket, and she saw him put the bottle down on the low plinth of a bronze sculpture representing a gallows with an empty noose. He continued past two fully occupied benches and took a seat on the third where he picked up a newspaper. After about twenty seconds he got up again, walked back to the sculpture, grabbed the bottle as he passed, put it into his pocket and returned the same way he had come.

It had started to rain when she saw him enter Chungking Mansion. She slowly began to prepare her speech. There was no longer a queue by the lifts; nevertheless he ascended a staircase, turned right and went through a swing door. She hurried after him and suddenly found herself in a deserted, run-down stairwell with an all-permeating smell of cat piss and wet concrete. She held her breath, but all she could hear were dripping sounds. As she took the decision to go on up, she heard a door bang beneath her. She sprinted down the stairs and found the only thing that could have made a bang: a dented metal door. She held the handle, felt the trembling come, closed her eyes and cursed to herself. Then she ripped open the door and stepped into the darkness. That is to say: out.

Something ran across her feet, but she neither screamed nor moved.

At first she thought she had entered a lift shaft. But when she looked up, she glimpsed blackened brick walls covered with a tangled mass of water pipes, cables, distorted chunks of metal and collapsed, rusty iron scaffolding. It was a courtyard, a few square metres of space between tower blocks. The only light came from a small square of stars high above.

Although there wasn't a cloud in the sky, water was splashing down onto the tarmac and her face, and she realised it was condensed water from the small, rusty A/C units protruding from the front of the buildings. She retreated and leaned back against the iron door.

Waited.

And, eventually, from the dark, she heard: 'What do you want?'

She had never heard his voice before. Well, she had heard it on the talk show when they were discussing serial killers, but hearing it in reality was quite different. There was a worn hoarse quality that made him sound older than the forty years she knew he had just turned. But at the same time there was a secure, self-assured calm which belied the hunted face she had seen outside Li Yuan's. Deep, warm.

'I'm Norwegian,' she said.

There was no response. She swallowed. She knew that her first words would be the most important.

'My name is Kaja Solness. I have been tasked with finding you. By Gunnar Hagen.'

No reaction to the name of his Crime Squad boss. Had he gone?

'I work as a detective on murder investigations for Hagen,' she said into the blackness.

'Congratulations.'

'No congratulations necessary. Not if you've been reading Norwegian papers for the last months.' She could have bitten her tongue. Was she trying to be funny? Had to be the lack of sleep. Or nerves.

'I mean congratulations on a well-accomplished mission,' said the voice. 'I have been found. Now you can go back.'

'Wait!' she shouted. 'Don't you want to hear what I have to say?'

'I'd prefer not to.'

But the words she had jotted down and practised rolled out. 'Two women have been killed. Forensic evidence suggests it's the same perp. Beyond that we don't have any leads. Even though the press has been given minimal info, they've been screaming for ages that another serial killer is on the loose. Some commentators have written that he may have been inspired by the Snowman. We've called in experts from Interpol, but they haven't made any headway. The pressure from the media and authorities –'

'By which I mean no,' the voice said.

A door slammed.

'Hello? Hello? Are you there?'

She fumbled her way forward and found a door. Opened it before terror managed to gain a foothold and she was in another darkened stairwell. She glimpsed light further up and climbed three steps at a time. The light was coming through the glass of a swing door, and she pushed it open. Entered a plain, bare corridor in which attempts to patch the peeling plaster had been given up, and damp steamed off the walls like bad breath. Leaning against the wall were two men with cigarettes hanging from the corners of their mouths, and a sweet stench drifted towards her. They appraised her through sluggish eyes. Too sluggish to move, she hoped. The smaller of the two was black, of African origin, she assumed. The big one was white and had a pyramid-shaped scar on his forehead, like a warning triangle. She had read in *The Police* magazine that Hong Kong had almost thirty thousand officers on the street and was reckoned to be the world's safest metropolis. But then that was on the street.

'Looking for hashish, lady?'

She shook her head, tried to flash a confident smile, tried to act as she had advised young girls to do when she had been going around schools: to look like someone who knew where she was going, not like someone who had lost the flock. Like prey.

They returned her smile. The only other doorway in the corridor had been bricked up. They took their hands out of their pockets, the cigarettes from their mouths.

'Looking for fun then?'

'Wrong door, that's all,' she said, turning to go back out. A hand closed around her wrist. Her terror tasted like tinfoil in her mouth. In theory, she knew how to get out of this. Had practised it on a rubber mat in an illuminated gym with an instructor and colleagues gathered around her.

'Right door, lady. Right door. Fun is this way.' The breath in her face stank of fish, onions and marijuana. In the gym there had only been one adversary.

'No, thanks,' she said, struggling to keep her voice steady.

The black man sidled up, grabbed her other wrist and said in a voice that slipped in and out of falsetto: 'We'll show you the way.'

'Only there's not much to see, is there.'

All three turned towards the swing door.

She knew it said one ninety-two in his passport, but standing there in the doorway that had been built to Hong Kong measurements he looked at least two ten. And twice as wide as only an hour ago. His arms hung down by his sides, slightly away from his body, but he didn't move, didn't stare, didn't snarl, just looked calmly at the white man and repeated: 'Is there, *jau-ye?*'

She felt the white man's fingers tense and relax around her wrist, noticed the black man shift weight from foot to foot.

'*Ng-goy,*' said the man in the doorway.

She felt their hands hesitantly let go.

'Come on,' he said, lightly taking her arm.

She felt the heat in her flushed cheeks as they walked out. Heat produced by tension and shame. Shame at how relieved she was, how tardily her brain had functioned in the situation, how willing she had been to let him sort out two harmless drug dealers who only wanted to ruffle her a little.

He accompanied her up two floors and in through the swing door where he positioned her in front of a lift, pressed the arrow for down, stood beside her and focused his gaze on the luminous figure 11 above the lift door. 'Guest workers,' he said. 'They're alone and bored.'

'I know,' she said defiantly.

'Press G for ground floor, turn right and go straight ahead until you're in Nathan Road.'

'Please listen to me. You are the only person in Crime Squad with the appropriate expertise to catch serial killers. After all, it was you who caught the Snowman.'

'True,' he said. She registered a movement in his eyes, and he ran a finger along his jaw under his right ear. 'And then I resigned.'

'Resigned? Went on leave, you mean.'

'Resigned. As in *finished.*'

It was only now that she noticed the unnatural protrusion of his right jawbone.

'Gunnar Hagen says that when you left Oslo he agreed to give you leave until further notice.'

The man smiled, and Kaja saw how it changed his face completely. 'That's because Hagen can't get it into his head . . .' He paused, and the smile vanished. His eyes were directed towards the light above the lift that now read '5'. 'Nonetheless, I don't work for the police any longer.'

'We need you . . .' She inhaled. Knew that she was skating on thin ice, but that she had to act before she lost sight of him again. 'And you need us.'

His eyes shifted back to her. 'What on earth makes you think that?'

'You owe the Triad money. You buy dope off the street in a baby's bottle. You live . . .' She grimaced. '. . . here. And you don't have a passport.'

'I'm enjoying myself here. What do I need a passport for?'

The lift pinged, the door creaked open, and hot, stinking air rose off the bodies inside.

'I'm not going!' Kaja said, louder than she had anticipated, and noticed the faces looking at her with a mixture of impatience and obvious curiosity.

'Yes, you are,' he said, placing a hand in the middle of her back and pushing her gently but firmly inside. She was immediately surrounded by human bodies closing in on her and making it impossible for her to move or even turn. She twisted her head in time to see the doors gliding to.

'Harry!' she shouted.

But he had already gone.

4

Sex Pistols

THE OLD HOSTEL OWNER PLACED A THOUGHTFUL FINGER ON his forehead under the turban and looked at her long and hard. Then he picked up the telephone and dialled a number. He said a few words in Arabic and rang off. 'Wait,' he said. 'Maybe, maybe not.'

Kaja smiled and nodded.

They sat observing each other from either side of the narrow table that served as a reception desk.

Then the phone rang. He picked it up, listened and put it down without a word.

'One hundred and fifty thousand dollars,' he said.

'One hundred and fifty?' she repeated in utter disbelief.

'Hong Kong dollars, lady.'

Kaja did some mental arithmetic. That would be about one hundred and thirty thousand Norwegian kroner. Roughly double what she had been authorised to pay.

It was past midnight, and almost forty hours since she had slept, when she found him. She had trawled H-Block for three hours. Had sketched out a map of the interior as she moved through hostels, cafes, snack bars, massage clubs and prayer rooms until she arrived at the cheapest rooms and dormitories where the imported labour force from Africa and Pakistan stayed, those who had no rooms, just cubicles without doors,

22

without TVs, without air conditioning and without a private life. The black night porter who admitted Kaja looked at the photo for a long time and at the hundred-dollar bill she was holding for even longer before he took it and pointed to one of the cubicles.

Harry Hole, she thought. Gotcha.

He was lying supine on a mattress, breathing almost without sound. He had a deep frown on his forehead, and the prominent jawbone under his right ear was even more defined now that he was asleep. From the other cubicles she heard men coughing and snoring. Water dripped from the ceiling, hitting the brick floor with deep, disgruntled sighs. The opening to the cubicle let in a cold, blue stripe of light from the neon tubes in reception. She saw a clothes cupboard in front of the window, a chair and a plastic bottle of water beside the mattress. There was a bitter-sweet smell, like burned rubber. Smoke rose from a cigarette end in an ashtray beside the baby's bottle on the floor. She sat down on the chair and discovered that he was holding something in his hand. A greasy, yellowish-brown clump. Kaja had seen enough hash the year she worked in a patrol car to know this was not hash.

It was almost two o'clock when he awoke.

She heard a tiny change in the rhythm of his breathing, and then the whites of his eyes shone in the dark.

'Rakel?' He whispered it. And went back to sleep.

Half an hour later he opened his eyes wide, gave a start, cast around and made a grab for something under the mattress.

'It's me,' Kaja whispered. 'Kaja Solness.'

The body at her feet stopped in mid-movement. Then it collapsed and fell back on the mattress.

'What the hell are you doing here?' he groaned, his voice still thick with sleep.

'Fetching you,' she said.

He chuckled, his eyes closed. 'Fetching me? Still?'

She took out an envelope, leaned forward and held it up in front of him. He opened one eye.

'Plane ticket,' she said. 'To Oslo.'

The eye closed again. 'Thanks, but I'm staying here.'

23

'If I can find you, it's only a matter of time before they do, too.'

He didn't answer. She waited while listening to his breathing and the water that dripped and sighed. Then he opened his eyes again, rubbed under his right ear and hoisted himself up onto his elbows.

'Got a smoke?'

She shook her head. He threw off the sheet, stood up and went over to the cupboard. He was surprisingly pale considering he had been living in a subtropical climate, and so lean that his ribs showed, even on his back. His build suggested that at one time he had been athletic, but now the wasted muscles appeared as sharp shadows under the white skin. He opened the cupboard. She was amazed to see that his clothes lay folded in neat piles. He put on a T-shirt and a pair of jeans, the ones he had been wearing the day before, and with some difficulty tugged a creased packet of cigarettes out from his pocket.

He slipped into a pair of flip-flops and edged past her with a click of his lighter.

'Come on,' he said softly as he passed. 'Supper.'

It was nearly three in the morning. Grey iron shutters had been pulled down over shops and restaurants in Chungking. Apart from at Li Yuan's.

'So how did you wind up in Hong Kong?' Kaja asked, looking at Harry, who, in an inelegant but effective way, was shovelling shiny glass noodles into his mouth from the white soup bowl.

'I flew. Are you cold?'

Kaja automatically removed her hands from under her thighs. 'But why here?'

'I was on my way to Manila. Hong Kong was only supposed to be a stopover.'

'The Philippines. What were you going to do there?'

'Throw myself into a volcano.'

'Which one?'

'Well, which ones can you name?'

'None. I've just read that there are loads of them. Aren't some of them in . . . er, Luzon?'

'Not bad. There are eighteen volcanoes in all, and three of them are in Luzon. I wanted to go up Mount Mayon. Two and a half thousand metres. A stratovolcano.'

'Volcano with steep sides formed by layer upon layer of lava after an eruption.'

Harry stopped chewing and looked at her. 'Any eruptions in modern times?'

'Loads. Thirty?'

'Records say forty-seven since 1616. Last one in 2002. Can be held to account for at least three thousand murders.'

'What happened?'

'The pressure built up.'

'I mean to you.'

'I'm talking about me.' She fancied she saw a hint of a smile. 'I exploded and started drinking on the plane. I was ordered off in Hong Kong.'

'There are several flights to Manila.'

'I realised that apart from volcanoes Manila has nothing that Hong Kong doesn't have.'

'Such as?'

'Such as distance from Norway.'

Kaja nodded. She had read the reports on the Snowman case.

'And most importantly,' he said, pointing with a chopstick, 'Hong Kong's got Li Yuan's glass noodles. Try them. That's reason enough to apply for citizenship.'

'That and opium?'

It was not her style to be so direct, but she knew she would have to swallow her natural shyness. This was her one shot at achieving what she had come to do.

He shrugged and concentrated on the noodles.

'Do you smoke opium regularly?'

'Irregularly.'

'And why do you do that?'

He answered with food in his mouth. 'So that I don't drink. I'm an alkie. There, for example, is another advantage of Hong Kong compared with Manila. Lower sentences for dope. And cleaner prisons.'

'I knew about your alcoholism, but are you a drug addict?'

'Define drug addict.'

'Do you *have* to take drugs?'

'No, but I want to.'

'Why?'

'To numb the senses. This sounds like a job interview for a job I don't want, Solness. Have you ever smoked opium?'

Kaja shook her head. She had tried marijuana a few times backpacking around South America but had not been particularly fond of it.

'But the Chinese have. Two hundred years ago the British imported opium from India to improve the trade balance. They turned half of China into junkies just like that.' He flicked the fingers of his free hand. 'And when, sensibly enough, the Chinese authorities banned opium, the British went to war for their right to drug China into submission. Imagine Colombia bombing New York because the Americans confiscated a bit of cocaine on the border.'

'What's your point?'

'I see it as my duty, as a European, to smoke some of the shit we have imported into this country.'

Kaja could hear herself laughing. She really needed to get some sleep.

'I was tailing you when you did the deal,' she said. 'I saw how you do it. There was money in the bottle when you put it down. And opium afterwards. Isn't that right?'

'Mm,' Harry said with a mouth full of noodles. 'Have you worked at the Narc Unit?'

She shook her head. 'Why the baby's bottle?'

Harry stretched his arms above his head. The soup bowl in front of him was empty. 'Opium stinks something awful. If you've got a ball of it in your pocket or in foil, the narco dogs can sniff you out even in a huge crowd. There is no money back on baby's bottles, so no chance of some kid or some drunk nicking it during a handover. That has happened.'

Kaja nodded slowly. He had started to relax, it was just a question of persisting. Anyone who hasn't spoken their mother tongue for a while gets chatty when they meet a compatriot. It's natural. Keep going.

'You like horses?'

He was chewing on a toothpick. 'Not really. They're so bloody moody.'

'But you like betting on them?'

'I like it, but compulsive gambling is not one of my vices.'

He smiled, and again it struck her how his smile transformed him, made him human, accessible, boyish. And she was reminded of the glimpse of open sky she had caught over Melden Row.

'Gambling is a poor winning strategy long term. But if you have nothing left to lose, it's the only strategy. I bet everything I had, plus a fair bit I didn't have, on one single race.'

'You put everything you had on one horse?'

'Two. A quinella. You pick out the two horses to come first and second, regardless which of the two is the winner.'

'And you borrowed money from the Triad?'

For the first time she saw astonishment in Harry's eyes.

'What makes a serious Chinese gangster cartel lend money to an opium-smoking foreigner who has nothing to lose?'

'Well,' Harry said, producing a cigarette, 'as a foreigner you have access to the VIP box at Happy Valley racecourse for the first three weeks after your passport has been stamped.' He lit his cigarette and blew smoke at the ceiling fan, which was turning so slowly that the flies were taking rides on it. 'There are dress codes, so I had a suit made. The first two weeks were enough to give me a taste for it. I met Herman Kluit, a South African who earned himself a fortune in minerals in Africa. He taught me how to lose quite a lot of money in style. I simply loved the concept. The evening before race day in the third week Kluit invited me to dinner, at which he entertained the guests by exhibiting his collection of African torture instruments from Goma. And that was where I got insider info from Kluit's chauffeur. The favourite for one of the races was injured, but this titbit was being kept secret because it was going to run anyway. The point was that it was such a clear favourite that a minus pool came into question, that is, it would be impossible to earn any money by betting on it. However, there was money to be earned by hedging your bets with several of the others. For example, with quinellas. But, of course, that would require quite a bit of capital if you were going to earn anything. I was given a loan by Kluit on the basis of my honest face. And a made-to-measure suit.' Harry studied the glow of his cigarette and seemed to be smiling at the thought.

'And?' Kaja asked.

'And the favourite won by six lengths.' Harry shrugged. 'When I explained to Kluit that I didn't own a bean he seemed genuinely sorry and explained politely that, as a businessman, he was obliged to stick to his business principles. He assured me that these did not include the use of Congolese torture weapons, but quite simply selling debts to the Triad with a discount. Which, he conceded, was not a lot better. But in my case he would wait thirty-six hours before he sold so that I could get out of Hong Kong.'

'But you didn't go?'

'Sometimes I'm a bit slow on the uptake.'

'And afterwards?'

Harry opened his hands. 'This. Chungking.'

'Future plans?'

Harry shrugged and went to stub out his cigarette. And Kaja was reminded of the record cover Even had shown her with the picture of Sid Vicious from the Sex Pistols. And the music playing in the background, 'No fu-ture, no fu-ture.'

He stubbed out his cigarette. 'You've heard what you need, Kaja Solness.'

'Need?' She frowned. 'I don't understand.'

'Don't you?' He stood up. 'Do you think I babble on about opium and debts because I'm one lonely Norwegian meeting another?'

She didn't answer.

'It's because I want you to appreciate that I am not the man you all need. So that you can go back without feeling you haven't done your job. So that you don't get into trouble in stairwells, and I can sleep in peace without wondering whether you will lead my creditors straight to me.'

She looked at him. There was something severe, ascetic, about him, yet this was contradicted by the amusement dancing in his eyes, saying that you didn't need to take everything so seriously. Or to be more exact: that he didn't give a flying fuck.

'Wait.' Kaja opened her bag and took out a small, red booklet, passed it to him and observed the reaction. Saw incredulity spread across his face as he flicked through it.

'Shit, looks just like my passport.'

'It is.'

'I doubt Crime Squad had the budget for this.'

'Your debts have sunk in value,' she lied. 'I got a discount.'

'I hope for your sake you did because I have no intention of returning to Oslo.'

Kaja subjected him to a long stare. Dreading it. There was no way out now. She was being forced to play her final card, the one Gunnar Hagen had said she should leave to last if the old bastard proved obdurate.

'There is one more thing,' Kaja said, bracing herself.

One of Harry's eyebrows shot into the air; perhaps he detected something in her intonation.

'It's about your father, Harry.' She could hear that she had instinctively used his first name. Convinced herself it was meant sincerely, not just for effect.

'My father?' He said this as if it came as something of a surprise that he had one.

'Yes. We contacted him to find out if he knew where you were living. The long and short of it is he's ill.'

She looked down at the table.

Heard him exhale. The drowsiness was back in his voice. 'Seriously ill?'

'Yes. And I'm sorry to be the one to have to tell you this.'

She still did not dare to raise her gaze. Ashamed. Waited. Listened to the machine-gun sounds of Cantonese on the TV behind Li Yuan's counter. Swallowed and waited. She would have to sleep soon.

'When does the plane go?'

'At eight,' she said. 'I'll pick you up in three hours outside here.'

'I'll get there under my own steam. There are a couple of things I have to fix first.'

He held out his palm. She questioned him with her eyes.

'For that I need the passport. And then you should eat. Get a bit of meat on your bones.'

She wavered. Then she handed him the passport and the ticket.

'I trust you,' she said.

He sent her a blank look.

Then he was gone.

The clock above gate C4 in Chek Lap Kok Airport showed a quarter to eight, and Kaja had given up. Of course he wasn't coming. It was a natural reflex for animals and humans to hide when hurt. And Harry Hole was definitely hurt. Reports on the Snowman case had described in detail the murders of all the women. But Gunnar Hagen had added what had not been included. How Harry Hole's ex-partner, Rakel, and her son, Oleg, had ended up in the clutches of the deranged killer. How she and her son had fled the country as soon as the case was over. And how Harry had handed in his resignation and slung his hook. He had been more hurt than she had realised.

Kaja had already handed in her boarding card, was on her way up to the boarding bridge and beginning to consider the formulation of her report on the failed mission when she saw him jogging through the slanted sunbeams that penetrated the terminal building. He was carrying a plain holdall over his shoulder, a tax-free bag and was puffing away furiously at a cigarette. He stopped at the gate. But instead of giving the waiting personnel his boarding card he put down his bag and sent Kaja a despairing look.

She went back to the gate.

'Problems?' she asked.

'Sorry,' he said. 'Can't come.'

'Why not?'

He pointed to the tax-free bag. 'Just remembered that in Norway the allowance per person is one carton of cigarettes. I've got two. So unless . . .' He didn't bat an eyelid.

She rolled her eyes heavenwards, trying not to look relieved. 'Give it here.'

'Thank you very much,' he said, opening the bag, which she happened to notice did not contain any bottles, and passing her an opened carton of Camel with one pack already gone.

She walked in front of him to the plane so that he would not be able to see her smiles.

Kaja stayed awake long enough to catch take-off, Hong Kong disappearing beneath them and Harry's eyes watching the trolley as it approached fitfully with its joyful clink of bottles. And him closing his eyes and answering the stewardess with a barely audible 'No, thank you.'

She wondered whether Gunnar Hagen was right, whether the man beside her was really what they needed.

Then she was gone, unconscious, dreaming that she was standing in front of a closed door. She heard a lone, frozen bird-call from the forest and it sounded so strange because the sun was shining high in the sky. She opened the door . . .

She woke with her head lolling on his shoulder and dried saliva at the corners of her mouth. The captain's voice announced that they were approaching the runway at London Heathrow.

5

The Park

MARIT OLSEN LIKED TO SKI IN THE MOUNTAINS. BUT SHE hated jogging. She hated her wheezing gasps after only a hundred metres, the tremor-like vibrations in the ground as she planted her foot, the slightly bemused looks from walkers and the images that appeared when she saw herself through their eyes: the quivering chins, the flab that bounced around in the stretched tracksuit and the help-less, open-mouthed, fish-out-of-water expression she herself had seen on very overweight people training. That was one of the reasons she scheduled her three runs per week in Frogner Park for ten o'clock at night: the place was as good as deserted. The people who were there saw as little as possible of her as she puffed her way through the pitch dark between the few lamps illuminating the paths which criss-crossed Oslo's largest park. And of those few who saw her there were fewer who recognised the Socialist MP for Finnmark. Forget 'recognised'. There were few people who had ever seen Marit Olsen. When she spoke – usually on behalf of her home region – she did not attract the atten-tion that others, her more photogenic colleagues, did. In addition, she had not said or done anything wrong in the course of the two sessions she had been sitting as a Stortinget representative. At least that was how she explained it to herself. The *Finnmark Dagblad* editor's explan-ation, that she was a political lightweight, was no more than malicious wordplay on her physical appearance. The editor had not, however, ruled out the possibility that one day she might be seen in a Socialist government, as she fulfilled the most telling requirements: she was not educated, not male and not from Oslo.

Well, he might have been right that her strengths did not lie in large, complicated castles in the air. But she had a common touch, she was folksy enough to know the opinions of ordinary men and women, and she could be their voice here among all the self-centred, self-satisfied voters in the capital. For Marit Olsen shot from the hip. That was her real qualification, that was what had taken her to where she was, after all. With her verbal intelligence and wit – which southerners liked to call 'northern Norwegian' and 'gritty' – she was a sure winner in the few debates in which she had been allowed to participate. It was just a question of time before they would have to take note of her. So long as she could get rid of these kilos. Surveys proved that people had less confidence in overweight public figures; they were subconsciously perceived to be lacking in self-control.

She came to an incline, clenched her teeth and slowed her pace, went into what seemed very much like a walk, if she was honest. Power-walk. Yes, that's what it was. The march towards power. Her weight was decreasing, her eligibility for office increasing.

She heard the crunch of gravel behind her and automatically her back went rigid, her pulse rose a few further notches. It was the same sound she had heard while out jogging three days ago. And two days before that. Both times someone had been running behind her for close on two minutes before the sound had gone. Marit had turned round on the previous occasion and seen a black tracksuit and a black hood, as though it were a commando training behind her. Except that no one, and especially not a commando, could find any purpose in jogging as slowly as Marit.

Of course, she could not be sure that this was the same person, but something about the sound of the footsteps told her it was. There was just a bit of the slope up to the Monolith, then it was an easy downhill run home, to Skøyen, her husband and a reassuringly unprepossessing, overfed Rottweiler. The steps came closer. And now it was not so wonderful that it was ten at night and the park was dark and deserted. Marit Olsen was frightened of several things, but primarily she was frightened of foreigners. Yes, indeed, she knew it was xenophobia and ran counter to party policy, but fearing whatever is alien nevertheless constitutes a sensible survival strategy. Right now she wished she had voted against all the immigrant-friendly bills her party had pushed, and that she had shot from her notorious hip a bit more.

Her body was moving all too slowly, her thigh muscles ached, her lungs were screaming for air, and she knew that soon she would not be able to move at all. Her brain tried to combat the fear, tried to tell her she was not exactly an obvious victim for rape.

Fear had borne her aloft, she could see over the hill now, down to Madserud allé. A car was reversing out of a garden gate. She could make it, there was little more than a hundred metres left. Marit Olsen ran onto the slippery grass, down the slope, only just managing to stay on her feet. She could no longer hear the steps behind her, everything was drowned out by her panting. The car had backed onto the road now, there was a crash of gears as the driver went from reverse to first. Marit was nearing the bottom, only a few metres left to the road, to the blessed cones of light emitted by the headlamps. Her considerable body weight had a slight start on her in the descent, and now it was relentlessly pulling her forward. Such that her legs could no longer keep up. She fell headlong, into the road, into the light. Her stomach, encased in sweaty polyester, hit the tarmac, and she half slid, half rolled forward. Then Marit lay still, the bitter taste of road dust in her mouth and her grazed palms stinging from contact with gravel.

Someone was standing over her. Grabbed her shoulders. With a groan she rolled onto her side and held her arms over her face in defence. Not a commando, just an elderly man wearing a hat. The car door behind him was open.

'Are you alright, frøken?' he enquired.

'What d'you think?' said Marit Olsen, feeling the anger boil inside her.

'Hang on! I've seen you somewhere before.'

'Well, that's a turn-up,' she said, waving away his helping hand and struggling noisily to her feet.

'Aren't you in that comedy programme?'

'You ...' she said, staring into the dark, silent void of the park and massaging her notorious hip, '... mind your own bloody business, grandpa.'

6

Homecoming

A Volvo Amazon, the last to roll out of the Volvo factory in 1970, had stopped in front of the pedestrian crossing by the arrivals terminal at Gardemoen Airport in Oslo.

A crocodile of nursery children paraded past the car in chafing rain gear. Some of them glanced with curiosity at the strange old car with rally stripes along the bonnet, and at the two men behind the windscreen wipers swishing away the morning rain.

The man in the passenger seat, *Politioverbetjent*, shortened to POB, Gunnar Hagen, knew that the sight of children walking in hand in hand ought to make him smile and think of solidarity, consideration for others and a society where everyone looked after everyone else. But Hagen's first association was a search party hunting for a person they expected to find dead. That was what working as the head of Crime Squad did to you. Or, as some wit had written in English on Harry Hole's office door: I see dead people.

'What the heck's a nursery class doing at an airport?' asked the man in the driver's seat. His name was Bjørn Holm, and the Amazon was his dearest possession. The mere smell of the noisy but uncannily efficient heater, the sweat-ingrained imitation leather and the dusty rear shelf gave him inner peace. Especially if it was accompanied by the engine at the right revs, that is about eighty kilometres an hour on the flat, and Hank Williams on the cassette player. Bjørn Holm from Krimteknisk, the Forensics Unit in Bryn, was a hillbilly from Skreia with snakeskin cowboy boots, a moon face and bulging eyes which lent him a constantly surprised expression. This face had caused more than one leader of an investigation to misjudge Bjørn Holm. The truth was that he was the greatest crime-scene talent since the glory days of Weber. Holm was wearing a soft suede jacket with fringes and a knitted Rastafarian hat from under which grew the most vigorous, intensely red sideburns Hagen had seen this side of the North Sea and they as good as covered his cheeks.

Holm swung the Amazon into the short-term car park where it stopped with a gasp, and the two men got out. Hagen turned up his coat collar, which of course did nothing to prevent the rain from bombarding his shiny pate. It was, by the way, wreathed by black hair so thick and so fertile that some suspected Gunnar Hagen of having perfectly normal hairgrowth but an eccentric hairdresser.

'Tell me, is that jacket really waterproof?' Hagen asked as they strode towards the entrance.

'Nope,' said Holm.

Kaja Solness had called them while they were in the car and informed them that the Scandinavian Airlines plane had landed ten minutes early. And that she had lost Harry Hole.

After entering through the swing doors, Gunnar Hagen looked around, saw Kaja sitting on her suitcase by the taxi counter, signalled with a brief nod and headed for the door to the customs hall. He and Holm slipped in as it opened for passengers leaving. A guard made to stop them, but nodded, indeed almost bowed, when Hagen held up his ID card and barked a curt 'Police'.

Hagen turned right and walked straight past the customs officials and their dogs, past the metal counters that reminded him of the trolleys at the Pathology Institute, and into the cubicle behind.

There he came to such a sudden halt that Holm walked into him from behind. A familiar voice wheezed between clenched teeth. 'Hi, boss. Regretfully, I'm unable to stand to attention right now.'

Bjørn Holm peered over the unit leader's shoulder.

It was a sight that would haunt him for years.

Bent over the back of a chair was the man who was a living legend not just at Oslo Police HQ but in every police station across Norway, for good or ill. A man with whom Holm himself had worked closely. But not as closely as the male customs official standing behind the legend with a latex-clad hand partially obscured by the legend's pale white buttocks.

'He's mine,' Hagen said to the official, waving his ID card. 'Let him go.'

The official stared at Hagen and seemed reluctant to release him, but when an older officer with gold stripes on his epaulettes came in and nodded briefly with closed eyes, the customs official twisted his hand round one last time and removed it. The victim gave a loud groan.

'Get your pants on, Harry,' Hagen said and turned away.

Harry pulled up his trousers and said to the official peeling off the latex glove, 'Was it good for you, too?'

Kaja Solness rose from the suitcase when her three colleagues came back through the door. Bjørn Holm went to drive the car round while Gunnar Hagen went to get something to drink from the kiosk.

'Are you often checked?' Kaja asked.

'Every time,' Harry said.

'Don't think I've ever been stopped at customs.'

'I know.'

'How do you know?'

'Because there are a thousand small telltale signs they look for, and you have none of them. Whereas I have at least half.'

'Do you think customs officers are so prejudiced?'

'Well, have you ever smuggled anything?'

'No.' She laughed. 'OK then, I have. But if they're so good, they should have seen that you're also a policeman. And let you through.'

'They did see.'

'Come on. That only happens in films.'

'They saw alright. They saw a fallen policeman.'

'Oh yes?' said Kaja.

Harry rummaged for his pack of cigarettes. 'Let your eyes drift over to the taxi counter. There's a man with narrow eyes, a bit slanted. See him?'

She nodded.

'He's tugged at his belt twice since we came out. As if there was something heavy hanging from it. A pair of handcuffs or a truncheon. An automatic reaction if you've been in patrol cars or in the custody block for a few years.'

'I've worked in patrol cars, and I've never –'

'He's working for Narc now and keeps an eye open for people who look a bit too relieved after passing through customs. Or go straight to the toilet because they can't stand having the goods up their rectum any longer. Or suitcases that change hands between a naive, helpful passenger and the smuggler who got the idiot to carry the luggage containing all the dope through customs.'

She tilted her head and squinted at Harry with a little smile playing on her lips. 'Or he might be a normal guy whose pants keep slipping down, and he's waiting for his mother. And you're mistaken.'

'Certainly,' said Harry, looking at his watch and the clock on the wall. 'I'm always making mistakes. Is that really the time?'

The Volvo Amazon glided onto the motorway as the street lights came on.

In the front seats Holm and Solness were deep in conversation as Townes van Zandt sang in controlled sobs on the cassette player. On the back seat, Gunnar Hagen was stroking the smooth pig-leather briefcase he was holding on his lap.

'I wish I could say you looked good,' he said in a low voice.

'Jet lag, boss,' Harry said, who was lying more than sitting.

'What happened to your jaw?'

'It's a long, boring story.'

'Anyway, welcome back. Sorry about the circumstances.'

'I thought I had handed in my resignation.'

'You've done that before.'

'So how many times do you want it?'

Gunnar Hagen looked at his former inspector and lowered his eyebrows and voice even further. 'As I said, I'm sorry about the circumstances. And I appreciate that the last case took a lot out of you. That you and your loved ones were involved in a way which . . . well, could make anyone wish for a different life. But this is your job, Harry, this is what you're good at.'

Harry sniffed as though he had already contracted the typical homecoming cold.

'Two murders, Harry. We're not even sure how they've been carried out, only that they're identical. But thanks to recent dearly bought experiences, we know what we're facing.' The POB paused.

'Doesn't hurt to say the words, boss.'

'I'm not so sure about that.'

Harry looked out at the snow-free, rolling, brown countryside. 'People have cried wolf a number of times, but events have shown that a serial killer is a rare beast.'

'I know,' Hagen nodded. 'The Snowman is the only one we've seen in this country during my period of office. But we're pretty certain this time. The victims have nothing to do with each other, and the sedative found in their blood is identical.'

'That's something. Good luck.'

'Harry . . .'

'Find someone qualified for the job, boss.'

'*You're* qualified.'

'I've gone to pieces.'

Hagen took a deep breath. 'Then we'll put you together again.'

'Beyond repair,' Harry said.

'You're the only person in this country with the skills and the experience to deal with a serial killer.'

'Fly in an American.'

'You know very well things don't work like that.'

'Then I'm sorry.'

'Are you? Two people dead so far, Harry. Young women . . .'

Harry waved a dismissive hand when Hagen opened his briefcase and pulled out a brown file.

'I mean it, boss. Thank you for buying my passport and all that, but I've finished with photos and reports full of blood and gore.'

Hagen sent Harry a wounded expression, but still kept the file on his lap.

'Peruse this, that's all I'm asking. And don't tell anyone we're working on this case.'

'Oh? Why's that?'

'It's complicated. Just don't mention it to anyone, OK?'

The conversation at the front of the car had died, and Harry focused on the back of Kaja's head. As Bjørn Holm's Amazon had been made long before anyone used the term 'whiplash', there was no headrest, and Harry could see her slim neck, since her hair had been pinned up, see the white down on her skin, and he mused on how vulnerable she was, how quickly things changed, how much could be destroyed in a matter of seconds. That was what life was: a process of destruction, a disintegration from what at the outset was perfect. The only suspense involved was whether we would be destroyed in one sudden act or slowly. It was a sad thought. Yet he clung to it. Until they were through Ibsen Tunnel, a grey, anonymous component of the capital's traffic machinery that could have been in any city in the world. Nevertheless it was at that particular moment that he felt it. A huge, unalloyed pleasure at being here. In Oslo. Home. The feeling was so overwhelming that for a few seconds he was oblivious to why he had returned.

Harry gazed at Sofies gate 5 as the Amazon sailed out of view behind him. There was more graffiti on the front of the building than when he had left, but the blue paint beneath was the same.

So, he had refused to take the case. He had a father lying in the hospital. That was the only reason he was here. What he didn't tell them was that if he'd had the choice of knowing about his father's illness or not, he would have chosen not to know. Because he hadn't returned out of love. He had returned out of shame.

Harry peered up at the two black windows on the second floor that were his.

Then he opened the door and walked into the backyard. The rubbish container was standing where it always did. Harry pushed open the lid. He had promised Hagen he would take a look at the case file. Mostly so that his boss would not lose face – after all, the passport had cost Crime Squad quite a few kroner. Harry dropped the file onto the burst plastic bags leaking coffee grounds, nappies, rotten fruit and potato peelings. He inhaled and wondered at how surprisingly international the smell of rubbish was.

Nothing had been touched in his two-room flat, yet something was different. A powder-grey hue, as though someone had just left but their frosty breath was still there. He went into the bedroom, put down his bag and fished out the unopened carton of cigarettes. Everything was the same there, grey as the skin of a two-day-old corpse. He fell back onto the bed. Closed his eyes. Greeted the familiar sounds. Such as the drip from the hole in the gutter onto the lead flashing around the window frame. It wasn't the slow, comforting drip-drip from the ceiling in Hong Kong, but a feverish drumming, somewhere in the transition between dripping and running water, like a reminder that time was passing, the seconds were racing, the end of a number line was approaching. It had made him think of La Linea, the Italian cartoon figure who after four minutes always ended up falling off the edge of the cartoonist's line into oblivion.

Harry knew that there was a half-full bottle of Jim Beam in the cupboard under the sink. Knew that he could start where he had left off in this flat. Shit, he had been wrecked even before he got into the taxi to the airport that day several months ago. No wonder he had not managed to drag himself to Manila.

He could go straight into the kitchen now and pour the contents down the sink.

Harry groaned.

Wondering who she resembled was so much nonsense. He knew who she resembled. She resembled Rakel. They all resembled Rakel.

7

Gallows

'BUT I'M SCARED, RASMUS,' SAID MARIT OLSEN. 'THAT'S WHAT I am!'

'I know,' said Rasmus Olsen, in that muted, congenial voice that had accompanied and comforted his wife for more than twenty-five years through political decisions, driving tests, bouts of fury and the odd panic attack. 'It's just natural,' he said, putting his arm round her. 'You work hard, you have a lot on your mind. Your brain doesn't have any spare capacity to shut out that kind of thought.'

'That kind of thought?' she said, turning to face him on the sofa. She had lost interest in the DVD they were watching – *Love Actually* – a long time before. 'That kind of thought, that kind of rubbish, is that what you mean?'

'The important thing is not what I think,' he said, his fingertips poised to touch. 'The important—'

'—thing is what *you* think,' she mimicked. 'For Christ's sake, Rasmus, you've gotta stop watching that Dr Phil show.'

He released a silky smooth chuckle. 'I'm just saying that you, as a member of Stortinget, can obviously ask for a bodyguard to accompany you if you feel threatened. But is that what you want?'

'Mmm,' she purred as his fingers began to massage the exact spot where she knew he knew she loved it. 'What do you mean by *what you want*?'

'Give it some thought. What do you imagine is going to happen?'

Marit Olsen gave it some thought. Closed her eyes and felt his fingers massaging calm and harmony into her body. She had met Rasmus when she had been working at the Norwegian Employment Service in Alta, in Finnmark. She had been elected as an official for NTL, a union for state employees, and they had sent her south on a training course to the Sørmarka conference centre. There a thin man with vivid blue eyes beneath a fast-receding hairline had approached her the first evening. He had talked in a way that was reminiscent of redemption-happy Christians at the youth club in Alta. Except that he was talking politics. He worked in the secretariat for the Socialist Party, helping MPs with practical office jobs, travel, the press and even, on the odd occasion, writing a speech for them.

Rasmus had bought her a beer, asked if she wanted to dance and after four increasingly slow evergreen numbers with increasingly close physical contact had asked if she wanted to join him. Not in his room, but in the party.

After returning home she had started going to party meetings in Alta, and in the evenings she and Rasmus had long telephone conversations about what they had done and thought that day. Of course, Marit had never said it aloud: that sometimes she thought the best time they had spent together was when they were two thousand kilometres apart. Then the Appointments Committee had rung, put her on a list and, hey presto, she was elected to Alta Town Council. Two years later she was the vice chairperson of Alta Socialist Party, the year after she was sitting on the County Council, and then there was another telephone call, and this time it was the Appointments Committee for Stortinget.

And now she had a tiny office in Stortinget, a partner who helped her with her speeches, and prospects of climbing the ladder so long as everything went to plan. And she avoided blunders.

'They'll detail a policeman to keep an eye on me,' she said. 'And the press will want to know why a woman MP no one has ever heard of should be walking around with a bloody bodyguard at the taxpayer's expense. And when they find out why – she *suspected* someone had been following her in the park – they will write that with *that* kind of reasoning every woman in Oslo will be asking for state-subsidised police protection. I don't want any protection. Drop it.'

Rasmus laughed silently and used his fingers to massage his approval.

*   *   *

The wind howled through the leafless trees in Frogner Park. A duck with its head drawn deep into its plumage drifted across the pitch-black surface of the lake. Rotting leaves stuck to the tiles of the empty pools at Frogner Lido. The place seemed abandoned for all eternity, a lost world. The wind blew up a storm in the deep pool and sang its monotonous lament beneath the ten-metre-high diving tower that stood out against the night sky like a gallows.

8

Snow Patrøl

It was three o'clock in the afternoon when Harry awoke. He opened his bag, put in a set of clean clothes, found a woollen coat in the wardrobe and went out. The drizzle roused Harry enough for him to look moderately sober as he entered the brown, smoky rooms of Schrøder's. His table was taken, so he went into the corner, under the TV.

He looked around. He spotted a couple of faces he hadn't seen before, hunched over beer glasses, otherwise time had stood still. Rita came and placed a white mug and a steel jug of coffee in front of him.

'Harry,' she said. Not as a form of welcome, but to confirm that it was indeed he.

Harry nodded. 'Hi, Rita. Old newspapers?'

Rita scuttled off to the back room and returned with a pile of yellowing papers. Harry had never been given a clear explanation as to why they kept newspapers at Schrøder's, but he had benefited from this arrangement on more than one occasion.

'Been a long time,' said Rita and was gone. And Harry remembered what he liked about Schrøder's, apart from its being the closest taproom to his flat. The short sentences. And respect for your private life. Your return was noted; no elucidation was required.

Harry downed two mugs of the surprisingly unpleasant coffee while flicking through the newspapers in a fast-forward kind of way to furnish himself with a general perspective of what had happened in the kingdom over the last months. Not much, as usual. Which was what he liked best about Norway.

Someone had won *Norwegian Idol,* a celeb had been eliminated from a dance competition, a footballer in the third division had been caught taking cocaine, and Lene Galtung, daughter of the shipping magnate Anders Galtung, had pre-inherited some of the millions and got engaged to a better-looking but presumably less affluent investor called Tony. The editor of *Liberal,* Arve Støp, wrote that for a nation wanting to stand out as a social-democratic model, it was beginning to be embarrassing that Norway was still a monarchy. Nothing had changed.

In the December newspapers Harry saw the first articles about the murders. He recognised Kaja's description of the crime scene, a basement in an office complex under construction in Nydalen. The cause of death was unclear, but the police suspected foul play.

Harry thumbed through, preferring to read about a politician who boasted that he was standing down to spend more time with his family.

Schrøder's newspaper archives were by no means complete, but the second murder appeared in a paper dated a couple of weeks later.

The woman had been found behind a wrecked Datsun dumped at the edge of a wood by Lake Daudsjøen in Maridalen. The police did not rule out a 'criminal act', but nor did they reveal any details about the cause of death.

Harry's eyes scanned the article and established that the reason for police silence was the usual: they had no leads, *nada,* the radar was sweeping across an open sea of nothingness.

Only two murders. Yet Hagen had seemed so certain of his facts when he said this was a serial killer. So, what was the connection? What was it that the press didn't say? Harry could feel his brain beginning to pursue the old, familiar paths; he cursed himself for his inability to refrain and continued to leaf through.

When the steel coffee jug was empty, he left a crumpled banknote on the table and went into the street. Tightened his coat around him and squinted up at the grey sky.

He hailed an unoccupied taxi, which pulled into the kerb. The driver leaned across and the rear door swung open. A trick you rarely saw nowadays, and one Harry decided to reward with a tip. Not just because he could step right in, but because the window in the door had reflected a face at the wheel of a car parked behind Harry.

'Rikshospital,' Harry said, wriggling to the middle of the back seat.

'Righto,' said the driver.

Harry studied the rear-view mirror as they drove off from the kerb. 'Oh, could you go to Sofies gate 5 first, please?'

In Sofies gate the taxi waited, its diesel engine clattering away, while Harry mounted the staircase with long, quick strides and his brain assessed the range of possibilities. The Triad? Herman Kluit? Or good old paranoia. The gear lay where he had left it before taking off, in the toolbox in the food cupboard. The old, expired ID card. Two sets of Hiatt handcuffs with a spring-loaded arm for speed-cuffing. And the service revolver, a. 38 calibre Smith & Wesson.

Returning to the street, he looked neither left nor right, just jumped straight into the taxi.

'Rikshospital?' asked the driver.

'Drive in that direction at any rate,' Harry answered, studying the mirror as they turned up Stensbergata and then Ullevålsveien. He saw nothing. Which meant one of two things. It was good old paranoia. Or the guy was a pro.

Harry hesitated, then said finally, 'Rikshospital.'

He continued to keep an eye on the mirror as they passed Vestre Aker Church and Ullevål Hospital. Whatever he did, he mustn't lead them straight to where he was most vulnerable. Where they would always try to strike. The family.

The country's biggest hospital was situated high above the town.

Harry paid the driver, who thanked him for the tip and repeated the trick with the rear door.

The facades of the buildings rose in front of Harry and the low cloud cover seemed to sweep away the roofs.

He took a deep breath.

Olav Hole's smile from the hospital pillow was so gentle and frail that Harry had to swallow.

47

'I was in Hong Kong,' Harry replied. 'I had to do some thinking.'

'Did you get it done?'

Harry shrugged. 'What do the doctors say?'

'As little as possible. Hardly a good sign, but I've noticed that I prefer it like that. Tackling life's realities has, as you know, never been our family's strong suit.'

Harry wondered whether they would talk about Mum. He hoped not.

'Have you got a job?'

Harry shook his head. His father's hair hung over his forehead, so tidy and white that Harry assumed it wasn't his hair but an accessory that had been handed out with the pyjamas and slippers.

'Nothing?' his father said.

'I've had an offer to lecture at a police college.'

It was almost the truth. Hagen had offered him that after the Snowman case, as a kind of leave of absence.

'Teacher?' His father chuckled cautiously, as if any further effort would be the end of him. 'I thought one of your principles was never to do anything I had done.'

'It was never like that.'

'That's alright. You've always done things your way. This police stuff . . . Well, I suppose I should just be grateful you haven't done what I did. I'm no model for anyone to follow. You know, after your mother died . . .'

Harry had been sitting in the white hospital room for twenty minutes and already felt a desperate urge to flee.

'After your mother died, I struggled to make sense of anything. I retreated into my shell, found no joy in anyone's company. It was as though loneliness brought me closer to her, or so I thought. But it's a mistake, Harry.' His father's smile was as gentle as an angel's. 'I know losing Rakel hit you hard, but you mustn't do what I did. You mustn't hide, Harry. You mustn't lock the door and throw away the key.'

Harry looked down at his hands, nodded and felt ants crawling all over his body. He had to have something, anything.

A nurse came in, introduced himself as Altman, held up a syringe and said, with a slight lisp, that he was going to give 'Olav' something to help him sleep. Harry felt like asking if he had something for him, too.

His father lay on his side, the skin on his face sagging; he looked older than he had on his back. He gazed at Harry with heavy, blank eyes.

Harry stood up so abruptly that the chair legs scraped loudly on the floor.

'Where are you going?' Olav asked.

'Out for a smoke,' Harry said. 'I won't be long.'

Harry sat on a low brick wall with a view of the car park and lit up a Camel. On the other side of the motorway he could see Blindern and the university buildings where his father had studied. There were those who asserted that sons always became, to some degree or other, disguised variants of their fathers, that the experience of breaking out was never more than an illusion; you returned; the gravity of blood was not only stronger than your willpower, it was your willpower. To Harry it had always seemed he was evidence of the contrary. So why had seeing his father's naked, ravaged face on the pillow been like looking into a mirror? Listening to him speak like hearing himself? Hearing him think, the words . . . like a dentist's drill that found Harry's nerves with unerring accuracy. Because he was a copy. Shit! Harry's searching gaze had found a white Corolla in the car park.

Always white, that's the most anonymous colour. The colour of the Corolla outside Schrøder's, the one with the face behind the wheel, the same face that had been staring at him with its narrow, slanting eyes less than twenty-four hours before.

Harry tossed away his cigarette and hurried inside. Slackened his pace when he entered the corridor leading to his father's room. He turned where the corridor widened to an open waiting area and pretended to search through a pile of magazines on the table while scanning the people sitting there from the corner of his eye.

The man had hidden himself behind a copy of *Liberal*.

Harry picked up a *Se og Hør* gossip rag with a picture of Lene Galtung and her fiancé and left.

Olav Hole was lying with his eyes closed. Harry bent down and put his ear to Olav's mouth. He was breathing so lightly it was barely audible, but Harry felt a current of air on his cheek.

He sat for a while on the chair beside the bed watching his father as his mind played back poorly edited childhood memories in arbitrary order and with no other central theme than that they were things he remembered clearly.

Then he placed the chair by the door, which he opened a crack, and waited.

It was half an hour before he saw the man come from the waiting area and walk down the corridor. Harry noticed that the squat, robust-looking man was unusually bow-legged; he seemed to be walking with a beach ball stuck between his knees. Before entering a door marked with the international sign for the men's toilet, he plucked at his belt. As if something heavy was hanging from it.

Harry got up and followed.

Stopped outside the toilet and breathed in. It had been a long time. Then he pushed open the door and slipped in.

The toilet was like the whole hospital: clean, nice, new and too big. Along the main wall there were six cubicle doors, none with a red square above the lock. On the shorter wall four basins, and on the other long wall four porcelain urinals at hip height. The man was standing at a urinal, with his back to Harry. On the wall above him ran a horizontal pipe. It looked solid. Solid enough. Harry took out his revolver and handcuffs. International etiquette in men's toilets is not to look at each other. Eye contact, even unintentional, is cause for murder. Accordingly, the man didn't turn to look at Harry. Not when Harry locked the outside door with infinite care, not when he walked over slowly and not when he placed the gun barrel against the roll of fat between the man's neck and head and whispered what a colleague used to claim all police officers should be allowed to say at least once in their careers: 'Freeze.'

The man did exactly that. Harry could see the gooseflesh appear on the roll of fat as the man stiffened.

'Hands up.'

The man lifted a couple of short, powerful arms above his head.

Harry leaned forward. And realised at that moment it had been a blunder. The man's speed was breathtaking. Harry knew from the hours spent swotting up on hand-to-hand combat techniques that knowing how to take a beating was as important as giving one. The art was to let your muscles relax, to appreciate that punishment cannot be avoided, only reduced. So, when the man spun round, with his knee raised, as supple as a dancer, Harry reacted by following the movement. He moved his body in the same direction as the kick. The foot hit him above the hip. Harry lost balance, fell and slid along the tiled floor until he was out of range. He remained there, sighed and looked at the ceiling as he took out his pack of cigarettes. He poked one in his mouth.

'Speed-cuffing,' Harry said. 'Learned it the year I did an FBI course in Chicago. Cabrini Green, digs were the pits. For a white man, there was nothing to do in the evenings unless you wanted to go out and get yourself robbed. So I sat indoors practising two things. Loading and unloading my service pistol as fast as I could in the dark. And speed-cuffing on a table leg.'

Harry levered himself up onto his elbows.

The man was still standing with his short arms stretched up above his head. His wrists were shackled to the handcuffs on either side of the pipe. He stared blankly at Harry.

'Mr Kluit send you?' Harry asked, in English.

The man held Harry's gaze without blinking.

'The Triad? I've paid my debts, haven't you heard?' Harry studied the man's expressionless face. The features could have been Asian, but he didn't have a Chinese face or complexion. Mongolian maybe? 'So what do you want from me?'

No answer. Which was bad news, as the man had most probably not come to ask for anything, but to do something.

Harry stood up and walked in a semicircle so that he could approach him from the side. He held the revolver to the man's temple while slipping his left hand inside the man's suit jacket. His hand ran over the cold steel of a weapon, then found a wallet and plucked it out.

Harry stepped back three paces.

'Let's see . . . Mr Jussi Kolkka.' Harry held an American Express card up to the light. 'Finnish? I suppose you know some Norwegian then?'

No answer.

'You've been a policeman, haven't you. When I saw you in arrivals at Gardemoen, I thought you were an undercover narco cop. How did you know I was catching that particular flight, Jussi? It's alright if I call you Jussi, isn't it? It feels sort of natural to address a guy with his schlong hanging out by his first name.'

There was a brief throaty noise before a gobbet of spit came whirling through the air, rotating on its axis, and landed on Harry's chest.

Harry looked down at his T-shirt. The black snus-spit had drawn a diagonal line through the second 'o' and it now read 'Snow Patrøl'.

'So you do understand Norwegian,' Harry said. 'Who do you work for then, Jussi? And what do you want?'

Not a muscle stirred in Jussi's face. Someone shook the door handle outside, swore and went away.

Harry sighed. Then he raised his revolver until it was level with the Finn's forehead and cocked it.

'You might suppose, Jussi, that I'm a normal, sane person. Well, this is how sane I am. My father is lying helpless in his sickbed in there. You've found out, and that presents me with a problem. There's only one way to solve it. Fortunately, you're armed so I can tell the police it was self-defence.'

Harry pressed the hammer back still further. And felt the familiar nausea.

'Kripos.'

Harry stopped the hammer. 'Repeat.'

'I'm in Kripos,' he hissed in Swedish, with the Finnish accent of which witty speech-makers at Norwegian wedding receptions are so fond.

Harry stared at the man. He didn't have a second's doubt that he was telling the truth. Yet it was totally incomprehensible.

'In my wallet,' the Finn snarled, not letting the fury in his voice reach his eyes.

Harry opened the wallet and checked inside. Removed a laminated ID card. There wasn't much information, but it was adequate. The man in front of Harry was employed by Krimpolitisentralen, Kripos for short, the central crime unit in Oslo that assisted in – and usually led – the investigations into murder cases affecting the whole of the country.

'What the hell does Kripos want with me?'

'Ask Bellman.'

'Who's Bellman?'

The Finn uttered a brief sound; it was difficult to determine whether it was a cough or laughter. 'POB Bellman, you poor sod. My chief. Let me go now, handsome.'

'Fuck,' Harry said, inspecting the card again. 'Fuck, fuck, fuck.' He dropped the wallet on the floor and made for the door.

'Hey! Hey!'

The Finn's shouts faded as the door slid to behind Harry and he walked down the corridor to the exit. The nurse who had been with his father was coming from the opposite direction and nodded with a smile when they were close enough. Harry tossed the tiny key for the handcuffs up in the air.

'There's a flasher in the boys' room, Altman.'

Out of instinct, the nurse caught the key with both hands. Harry could feel the open-mouthed stare on his back until he was out of the door.

9

The Dive

IT WAS A QUARTER TO ELEVEN AT NIGHT. NINE DEGREES centigrade, and Marit Olsen remembered that the weather forecaster had said it would be even milder tomorrow. In Frogner Park there wasn't a soul to be seen. Something about the lido made her think of laid-up ships, of abandoned fishing villages with the wind whispering through house walls, and fairgrounds out of season. Fragmented memories of her childhood. Like the drowned fishermen who haunted Tronholmen, who emerged from the sea at night, with seaweed in their hair and fish in their mouths and nostrils. Ghosts without breath, but who were wont to scream cold, hoarse seagull cries. The dead with their swollen limbs, which snagged on branches and were wrenched off with a ripping sound, not that this halted their advance towards the isolated house in Tronholmen. Tronholmen where Grandma and Grandpa lived. Where she herself lay trembling in the children's room. Marit Olsen breathed out. Kept breathing out.

Down there the wind was still, but up here at the top of the ten-metre-high diving platform you could feel the air moving. Marit felt her pulse throbbing in her temples, in her throat, in her groin, blood streaming through every limb, fresh and life-giving. Living was wonderful. Being alive. She had hardly been out of breath after scaling all the steps of the tower, had just felt her heart, that loyal muscle, racing wildly. She stared down at the empty diving pool beneath her, to which the moonlight lent an almost unnatural bluish sheen. Further away, at the end of the pool, she could see the large clock. The hand had stopped at ten past five. Time stood still. She could hear the city, see car lights in Kirkeveien. So close. And yet too far. Too far away for anyone to hear her.

She was breathing. And was dead nonetheless. She had a rope as thick as a hawser around her neck and could hear the gulls screaming, ghosts she would soon be joining. But she was not thinking about death. She was thinking about life, how much she would have liked to live. All the small things, and the big things, she would like to have done. She would have travelled to countries she hadn't seen, watched her nephews and nieces grow, seen the world come to its senses.

It had been a knife; the blade had glistened in the light from the street lamp, and it had been held to her throat. Fear is said to release energy. Not in her case, it had stolen all her energy, deprived her of the power to act. The thought of steel cutting into her flesh had turned her into a quivering bundle of helplessness. So when she had been told to climb over the fence, she had not been able to and had fallen to the ground and lain there like a beanbag, tears streaming down her cheeks. Because she knew what was going to happen. She would do everything she could not to be cut and knew she would not be able to prevent it. Because she wanted so much to live. A few more years, a few more minutes, it was the same crazy, blind rationality that drove everyone.

She had started to explain that she couldn't climb over; she had forgotten that he had told her to keep her mouth shut. The knife had writhed like a snake, sliced her mouth, twisted round, crunched against her teeth and then been pulled out. The blood had gushed at once. The voice had whispered something behind the mask and nudged her forward along the fence. To a place in the bushes where she was pushed through a gap in the fence.

Marit Olsen swallowed the blood that continued to fill her mouth and looked down at the spectator stands beneath her; they, too, were bathed in the blue moonlight. They were so empty, it was a courtroom without spectators or jury, just a judge. An execution without a mob, just the executioner. A final public appearance which no one had considered worth attending. It struck Marit that she lacked as much appeal in death as in life. And now she couldn't speak, either.

55

'Jump.'

She saw how beautiful the park was, even now in winter. She wished the clock at the end of the pool were working so that she could see the seconds of life she was stealing.

'Jump,' the voice repeated. He must have removed his mask, for his voice had changed, she recognised it now. She turned her head and stared in shock. Then she felt a foot on her back. She screamed. She no longer had ground beneath her feet; for one astonishing moment she was weightless. But the ground was pulling her down, her body accelerated and she registered that the bluish-white porcelain of the pool was racing towards her, to smash her into pieces.

Three metres above the bottom of the pool the rope tightened around Marit Olsen's neck and throat. The rope was an old-fashioned type, made of linden and elm, and had no elasticity. Marit Olsen's stout body was not checked to any appreciable degree; it detached itself from the head and hit the base of the pool with a dull thud. The head and the neck were left in the rope. There wasn't much blood. Then the head tipped forward, slipped out of the noose, fell onto Marit Olsen's blue tracksuit top and rolled across the tiles with a rumble.

Then the lido was still again.

PART TWO

10

Reminders

AT THREE O'CLOCK IN THE MORNING HARRY ABANDONED his attempts to sleep and got up. He turned on the tap in the kitchen and put a glass underneath, held it there until the water overflowed and trickled down his wrist, cold. His jaw ached. His attention was held by two photographs pinned up over the kitchen worktop.

One, with a couple of disfiguring creases, showed Rakel in a light blue summer dress. But it wasn't summer, the leaves behind her were autumnal. Her dark brown hair cascaded down onto her bare shoulders. Her eyes seemed to be searching for something behind the lens, perhaps the photographer. Had he taken the photo himself? Strange that he couldn't remember.

The other was of Oleg. Taken with Harry's mobile phone camera at Valle Hovin skating rink during a training session last winter. At that time, a delicate young boy, but if he had continued his training he would have soon filled out that red skinsuit of his. What was he doing now? Where was he? Had Rakel managed to create a home for them wherever they were, a home that felt safer than the one they had in Oslo? Were there new people in her life? When Oleg became tired, or lost concentration, did he still refer to Harry as 'Dad'?

Harry turned off the tap. He was conscious of the cupboard door against his knees. Jim Beam was whispering his name from inside.

Harry pulled on a pair of trousers and a T-shirt, went into the sitting room and put on Miles Davis's *Kind of Blue*. It was the original, the one where they didn't compensate for the reel tape in the studio running a tiny bit slow, so the whole record was an almost imperceptible displacement of reality.

He listened for a while before increasing the volume to drown the whispering from the kitchen. Closed his eyes.

Kripos. Bellman.

He had never heard the name. He could, of course, have rung Hagen and enquired, but he couldn't be bothered. Because he had a feeling he knew what this might be about. Best to let sleeping dogs lie.

Harry had come to the last track, 'Flamenco Sketches', then he gave up. He got to his feet and left the sitting room for the kitchen. In the hall he turned left, emerged wearing Doc Martens boots and went out.

He found it under a split plastic bag. Something akin to dried pea soup coated the front of the file.

Back in his sitting room he sat down in the green wing chair and began to read with a shiver.

The first woman was Borgny Stem-Myhre, thirty-three years old, originally from Levanger, in the north. Single, no children, resident of Sagene in Oslo. Worked as a hairstylist, had a large circle of acquaintances, particularly among hairdressers, photographers and people in the fashion press. She frequented several of Oslo's restaurants, and not just the coolest. Besides that, she was keen on the outdoors and liked walking or skiing from mountain cabin to mountain cabin.

'You can take the woman out of Levanger, but you can't take Levanger out of the woman,' was the general summary of interviews with her colleagues. Harry assumed the remark came from colleagues who had succeeded in erasing their own small-town upbringings.

'We all liked her. In this line of business she was one of the few who was genuine.'

'It's incomprehensible. We can't understand how anyone could take her life.'

'She was too nice. And sooner or later all the men she fell for exploited her. She became a toy for them. She aimed too high, that was basically the problem.'

Harry studied a photograph of her. One in the file of when she was still alive. Blonde, maybe not natural. Run-of-the-mill looker, no obvious beauty, but she was smartly dressed in a military jacket and a Rastafarian hat. Smartly dressed and too nice – did they go together?

She had been to Mono restaurant for the monthly launch and preview of the fashion magazine *Sheness*. That had been between seven and eight, and Borgny had told a colleague slash friend that she would be at home preparing for a photo shoot the day after, at which the photographer had wanted a 'jungle meets punk meets eighties look'.

They assumed she would go to the nearest taxi rank, but none of the taxi drivers in the vicinity at the time in question (computerised lists from Norgestaxi and Oslotaxi attached) had recognised the photograph of Borgny Stem-Myhre or had driven to Sagene. In short, no one had seen her after she left Mono. Until two Polish brickies had showed up for work, noticed the padlock on the iron bomb shelter door had been snapped, and gone in. Borgny had been lying in the middle of the floor, in a contorted position, with all her clothes on.

Harry examined the photo. The same military jacket. The face looked as if it had been made up with white foundation. The flash cast sharp shadows against the cellar wall. Photo shoot. Smart.

The pathologist had determined that Borgny Stem-Myhre died some-where between ten and eleven o'clock at night. Traces of the drug keta-nome were found in her blood, a strong anaesthetic that worked fast even when injected intramuscularly. But the direct cause of death was drowning, triggered by blood from wounds in the mouth. And this was where the most disturbing elements came in. The pathologist found twenty-four stab wounds in the mouth, symmetrically distributed and at the same depth, seven centimetres, those that did not pierce the face, that is. But the police were at a loss as to what kind of weapon or instru-ment had been used. They had simply never seen anything like it. There were absolutely no forensic clues: no fingerprints, no DNA, not even shoe or boot prints, as the concrete floor had been cleaned the day before in preparation for heating cables and floor covering. In the report collated by Kim Erik Lokker, a forensics officer who must have been appointed after Harry's time, there was a photograph of two grey-black pebbles found on the floor which did not originate from the gravel around the crime scene. Lokker pointed out that small stones often got stuck in boots with heavy-duty tread, and came loose when worn on firmer ground, such as this concrete floor. Furthermore, these stones were so unusual that if they turned up later in the investigation, for example in a gravel path, they might well find a match. There was one addition to the report after it had been signed and dated: small traces of iron and coltan had been found on two molars.

Harry could already guess the conclusion. He flicked through.

The other woman's name was Charlotte Lolles. French father, Norwegian mother. Resident of Lambertseter, in Oslo. Twenty-nine years old. Qualified lawyer. Lived alone, but had a boyfriend: one Erik Fokkestad who had been quickly eliminated from inquiries. He had been at a geology seminar in Yellowstone National Park in Wyoming, USA. Charlotte should have joined him, but had prioritised a serious property dispute on which she had been working.

Colleagues had last seen her at the office on Monday evening at around nine. She had probably never returned home. Her briefcase of papers had been found next to her body behind the abandoned car by the wood in Maridalen. In addition, both parties in the property dispute had been eliminated. The post-mortem report highlighted bits of paint and rust found under Charlotte Lolles's nails, which fitted with the crime scene report's mention of scrape marks around the car-boot lock, as though she had been trying to get it open. Closer examination of the lock revealed that it had been picked at least once. But hardly by Charlotte Lolles. Harry formed a mental image of her chained to something locked inside the boot and speculated that that was why she had been trying to escape. Something the killer had taken with him afterwards. But what? And how? And why?

Records of the interview with a female colleague from the law firm included a quote: 'Charlotte was an ambitious person and always worked late. Although how efficient she was, I don't know. Always gentle, but not as outgoing as her smiles and Mediterranean appearance would have suggested. Quite private, basically. She never talked about her partner, for example. But my bosses liked her very much.'

Harry could imagine the female colleague serving up one intimate revelation after another about her boyfriend, without getting more than a smile from Charlotte in return. His investigative brain was on autopilot now: perhaps Charlotte had held back from embracing a clingy sister-hood, perhaps she had had something to hide. Perhaps . . .

Harry studied the photographs. Hard-ish but attractive features. Dark eyes, she looked like . . . Shit! He closed his eyes. Opened them again. Flicked through to the pathologist's report. Skimmed through the document.

He had to check Charlotte's name at the top to make sure he wasn't reading the report on Borgny for a second time. Anaesthetic. Twenty-four wounds to the mouth. Drowning. No external violence, no signs of sexual interference. The only difference was that the time of death was between eleven and midnight. However, this report had an additional note as well, concerning traces of iron and coltan found on the victim's teeth. Presumably because Krimteknisk had later realised that it might be relevant since it was found on both victims. Coltan. Wasn't Schwarzenegger's Terminator made of that?

Harry realised he was wide awake now and found himself perching on the edge of the chair. He felt the stirrings, the excitement. And the nausea. Like when he took his first drink, the one that made his stomach turn, the one his body desperately rejected. And soon he would be begging for more. More and more. Until it destroyed him and everyone around him. As this was doing. Harry jumped up so quickly he went dizzy, grabbed the file, knew it was too thick, but still managed to tear it in two.

He picked up the bits of paper and took them back to the refuse container. Let them fall down the side and lifted the plastic bags so that the documents slipped right down, to the very bottom. The dustcart would be round tomorrow or the day after, he hoped.

Harry went back and sat down in the green chair.

As night softened into a greyish hue, he heard the first sounds of a waking town. But over the regular drone of the first rush-hour traffic in Pilestredet, he could also hear a distant, reedy police siren gyrating through the frequencies. Could be anything. He heard another siren winding up. Anything. And then another. No, not anything.

The landline telephone rang.

Harry lifted the receiver.

'Hagen speaking. We've just received a mess—'

Harry put down the phone.

It rang again. Harry looked out of the window. He hadn't rung Sis. Why not? Because he didn't want to show himself to his little sister – his most enthusiastic, most unconditional admirer. The woman who had what she called 'a touch of Down's syndrome' and still coped with her life immeasurably better than he did his own. She was the only person he could not allow himself to disappoint.

The telephone stopped ringing. And started again.

Harry snatched at the phone. 'No, boss. The answer is no, I don't want the job.'

The other end of the line was quiet for a second. Then an unfamiliar voice said, 'Oslo Energy here. Herr Hole?'

Harry cursed to himself. 'Yes?'

'You haven't paid the bills we sent you, and you haven't responded to our final demands. I'm ringing to say we are cutting off the electricity supply to Sofies gate 5 from midnight tonight.'

Harry didn't answer.

'We will only reconnect when we've received the outstanding amount.'

'And that is?'

'With fees for reminders and disconnection, plus interest, it's fourteen thousand, four hundred and sixty-three kroner.'

Silence.

'Hello?'

'I'm here. I'm a bit out of pocket right now.'

'The outstanding amount will be recovered by our debt collection agency. In the meantime we'll have to hope the temperature doesn't fall below zero. Won't we?'

'We will,' Harry confirmed, and rang off.

The sirens outside rose and fell.

Harry went for a lie-down. He lay there for a quarter of an hour with his eyes closed before giving up, getting dressed again and leaving the flat to catch a tram to Rikshospital.

11

Print

When I woke up this morning, I knew I had been there again. In the dream it is always like that: we are lying on the ground, blood is flowing, and when I glance to the side, she's there looking at us. She looks at me with sorrow in her eyes, as if it is only now that she has discovered who I am, only now that she has unmasked me, seen that I am not the man she wants.

Breakfast was excellent. It's on teletext. 'Woman MP found dead in diving pool at Frogner Lido.' The news sites are full of it. Print out, snip, snip.

Before very long the first websites will publish the name. Thus far the so-called police investigation has been such a ridiculous farce that it has been irritating rather than exciting. But this time they will invest all their resources, they won't play at investigation the way they did with Borgny and Charlotte. After all, Marit Olsen was an MP. It's time this was stopped. Because I have appointed the next victim.

12

Crime Scene

HARRY WAS SMOKING A CIGARETTE OUTSIDE THE HOSPITAL entrance. Above him the sky was pale blue, but beneath him, the town, lying in a dip between low, green mountain ridges, was wreathed in mist. The sight reminded him of his childhood in Oppsal when he and Øystein had skipped the first lesson at school and gone to the German bunkers in Nordstrand. From there they had looked down on the pea-souper enveloping Oslo city centre. But with the years the morning fog had gradually drifted away from Oslo, along with industry and wood-burning.

Harry crushed the cigarette with his heel.

Olav Hole looked better. Or perhaps it was merely the light. He asked why Harry was smiling. And what had actually happened to his jaw.

Harry said something about being clumsy and wondered at what age the change took place, when children started protecting parents from reality. Around the age of ten, he concluded.

'Your little sister was here,' Olav said.

'How is she?'

'Fine. When she heard you were back, she said that now she would look after you. Because she's big now. And you're small.'

'Mm. Smart girl. How are you today?'

'Well. Very well, actually. Think it's about time I got out of here.'

He smiled, and Harry smiled back.

'What do the doctors say?'

Olav Hole was still smiling. 'Far too much. Shall we talk about something else?'

'Of course. What would you like to talk about?'

Olav Hole reflected. 'I'd like to talk about her.'

Harry nodded. And sat silently listening to his father tell him about how he and Harry's mother had met. Got married. About her illness when Harry was a boy.

'Ingrid helped me all the time. All the time. But she needed me so rarely. Until she fell ill. Sometimes I thought the illness was a blessing.'

Harry flinched.

'It gave me the chance to repay, you understand. And I did. Everything she asked me, I did.' Olav Hole fixed his eyes on his son. 'Everything, Harry. Almost.'

Harry nodded.

His father kept talking. About Sis and Harry, how wonderfully gentle Sis had been. And what willpower Harry had possessed. How frightened he had been but kept it to himself. When he and Ingrid had listened at the door, they had heard Harry crying and cursing invisible monsters in turn. However, they knew they shouldn't go in to console and reassure him. He would become furious, shout that they were ruining everything and tell them to get out.

'You always wanted to fight the monsters on your own, you did, Harry.'

Olav Hole told the ancient story about Harry not speaking until he was nearly five. And then – one day – whole sentences just flowed out of him. Slow, earnest sentences with adult words; they had no idea where he had learned them.

'But your sister is right,' Olav smiled. 'You're a small boy again. You don't speak.'

'Mm. Do you want me to speak?'

Olav shook his head. 'You have to listen. But that's enough for now. You'll have to come back another day.'

Harry squeezed his father's left hand with his right and stood up. 'Is it OK if I stay in Oppsal for a few days?'

'Thanks for the offer. I didn't want to hassle you, but the house does need to be looked after.'

Harry dropped his plan to tell him that the power was going to be cut off in his flat.

Olav rang a bell and a young, smiling nurse came in and used his father's first name in an innocent, flirty way. And Harry noted how his father deepened his voice as he explained that Harry needed the suitcase containing the keys. He saw the way the sick man in the bed tried to fluff his plumage for her. And for some reason it didn't seem pathetic; it was the way it should be.

In parting, his father repeated: 'Everything she asked me.' And whispered: 'Bar one thing.'

Leading him to the storage room, the nurse told Harry the doctor wanted to have a couple of words with him. After locating the keys in the suitcase, Harry knocked on the door the nurse had indicated.

The doctor nodded to a seat, leaned back on his swivel chair and pressed his fingertips together. 'Good thing you came home. We had been trying to get hold of you.'

'I know.'

'The cancer has spread.'

Harry nodded. Someone had once told him that was a cancer cell's function: to spread.

The doctor studied him, as though considering his next move.

'OK,' Harry said.

'OK?'

'OK, I'm ready to hear the rest.'

'We don't usually say how much time a person has left. The errors of judgement and the psychological strain that ensue are too great for that. However, in this case, I think it is appropriate to tell you he is already living on borrowed time.'

Harry nodded. Gazed out the window. Fog was still as thick down below.

'Have you got a mobile number we can contact you on should anything happen?'

Harry shook his head. Was that a siren he heard down in the fog?

'Anyone you know who can pass on a message?'

Harry shook his head again. 'Not a problem. I'll ring in and visit him every day. OK?'

The doctor nodded and watched Harry get up and stride out.

It was nine by the time Harry got to Frogner Lido. The whole of Frogner Park measures about fifty hectares, but since the public lido constitutes a small fraction of this and, furthermore, is fenced in, the police had an easy job cordoning off the crime scene; they had simply run a cordon round the entire fence and put a guard in the ticket office. The kettle of crime-correspondent vultures was in flight and they swooped in, stood cackling outside the gate wondering when they would gain access to the cadaver. For Christ's sake, this was a bona fide MP, didn't the public have a right to photos of such a prominent corpse?

Harry bought an americano at Kaffepikene. They had chairs and tables on the pavement throughout February, and Harry took a seat, lit a cigarette and watched the flock in front of the ticket booth.

A man sat down on the chair next to him.

'Harry Hole himself. Where have you been?'

Harry looked up. Roger Gjendem, the *Aftenposten* crime correspondent, lit a cigarette and gestured towards Frogner Park. 'At last Marit Olsen gets what she wants. By eight this evening she'll be a celeb. Hanging herself from the diving tower? Good career move.' He turned to Harry and grimaced. 'What happened to your jaw? You look dreadful.'

Harry didn't answer. Just sipped his coffee and said nothing to alleviate the embarrassing silence in the futile hope that the journalist would twig that he was not desirable company. From the bank of fog above them came the noise of whirring rotors. Roger Gjendem peered up.

'Gotta be *Verdens Gang*. Typical of that tabloid to hire a helicopter. Hope the fog doesn't lift.'

'Mm. Better that no one gets photos than *VG* does?'

'Right. What do you know?'

'I'm sure less than you,' said Harry. 'The body was found by one of the nightwatchmen at dawn, and he rang the police straight away. And you?'

'Head torn off. Woman jumped from the top of the tower with a rope around her neck, it seems. And she was pretty hefty, as you know. Over a hundred kilos.

'They've found threads that may match her tracksuit on the fence

69

where they reckon she entered. They didn't find any other clues, so they think she was alone.'

Harry inhaled the cigarette smoke. *Head torn off.* They spoke how they wrote, these journalists, the inverted pyramid, as they called it: the most important information first.

'Must have happened in the early hours, I suppose?' Harry fished.

'Or in the evening. According to Marit Olsen's husband, she left home at a quarter to ten to go jogging.'

'Late for a jog.'

'Must have been when she usually jogged. Liked having the park to herself.'

'Mm.'

'By the way, I tried to track down the nightwatchman who found her.'

'Why?'

Gjendem sent Harry a surprised look. 'To get a first-hand account, of course.'

'Of course,' Harry said, sucking on his cigarette.

'But he seems to have gone into hiding. He's not here or at home. Must be in shock, poor fella.'

'Well, it's not the first time he's found bodies in the pool. I assume the detective leading the investigation has seen to it that you can't lay your hands on him.'

'What do you mean, it's not the first time?'

Harry shrugged. 'I've been called here two or three times before. Young lads sneaking in during the night. One time it was suicide, another an accident. Four drunken friends on their way home from a party wanted to play, see who dared to stand closest to the edge of the diving board. The boy who won the dare was nineteen. The oldest was his brother.'

'Bloody hell,' Gjendem said dutifully.

Harry checked his watch as if he had to hurry off.

'Must have been some strength in that rope,' Gjendem said. 'Head torn off. Ever heard the like?'

'Tom Ketchum,' said Harry, draining the rest of his coffee in one swig and getting up.

'Ketchup?'

70

'Ketchum. Hole-in-the-Wall gang. Hanged in New Mexico Territory in 1901. Standard gallows, they just used too much rope.'

'Oh. How much?'

'Just over two metres.'

'Not more? He must have been a fat lump.'

'Nope. Tells you how easy it is to lose your head, doesn't it.'

Gjendem shouted something after him, but Harry didn't catch it. He crossed the car park north of the lido, continued across the grass and took a left over the bridge to the main gate. The fence was more than two and a half metres high all the way round. *Over a hundred kilos.* Marit Olsen might have tried, but she did not get over the lido fence unaided.

On the other side of the bridge, Harry turned left so that he could approach the lido from the opposite angle. He stepped over the orange police cordon and stopped at the top of the slope by a shrub. Harry had forgotten an alarming amount over recent years. But the cases stuck. He could still remember the names of the four boys on the diving tower. The older brother's distant eyes as he answered Harry's questions in a monotone. And the hand pointing to the place where they had got in.

Harry chose his steps carefully, not wishing to destroy possible clues, and bent the shrub to one side. Oslo Parks' maintenance planned well in advance. If they planned at all. The tear in the fence was still there.

Harry crouched down and studied the jagged edges of the tear. He could see dark threads. Someone who had not sneaked in, but had forced her way through here. Or was pushed. He looked for other evidence. From the top of the tear hung a long black piece of wool. The tear was so high that the person must have been standing upright to touch the fence at that point. The head. Wool made sense, a woollen hat. Had Marit Olsen been wearing a woollen hat? According to Roger Gjendem, Marit Olsen had left home at a quarter to ten to jog in the park. As usual, he had surmised.

Harry tried to visualise it. He imagined an abnormally mild evening in the park. He saw a large, sweaty woman jogging. He didn't see a woollen hat. He couldn't see anyone else wearing a woollen hat, either.

Not because it was cold at any rate. But perhaps so as not to be seen or recognised. Black wool. A balaclava maybe.

He stepped out of the bushes with care.

He hadn't heard them coming.

One man held a pistol – probably a Steyr, Austrian, semi-automatic. It was pointed at Harry. The man behind it had blond hair, an open mouth with a powerful underbite, and when he emitted a grunt of a laugh, Harry remembered the nickname belonging to Truls Berntsen from Kripos. Beavis. As in Beavis and Butt-Head.

The second man was short, unusually bow-legged and had his hands in the pockets of a coat that Harry knew concealed a gun and an ID card bearing a Finnish-sounding name. But it was the third man, the one in an elegant grey trench coat, who attracted Harry's attention. He stood to the side of the other two, but there was something about the gunman and the Finn's body language, the way they partly addressed Harry, partly this man. As though they were an extension of him, as though this man was *actually* holding the gun. What struck Harry about the man was not his almost feminine good looks. Nor that his eyelashes were so clearly visible above and below his eyes, incurring suspicions he used make-up. Nor the nose, the chin, the fine shape of his cheeks. Nor that his hair was thick, dark, grey, elegantly cut and a great deal longer than was standard for the force. Nor the many tiny colourless blemishes in the suntanned skin that made him look as if he had been exposed to acid rain. No, what struck Harry was the hatred. The hatred in the eyes that bored into him, a hatred so fierce that Harry seemed to sense it physically, as something white and hard.

The man was cleaning his teeth with a toothpick. His voice was higher and softer than Harry would have imagined. 'You've trespassed into territory that has been cordoned off for an investigation, Hole.'

'An incontrovertible fact,' Harry said, looking around him.

'Why?'

Harry eyed the man, quietly rejecting one potential answer after the other until he realised he simply didn't have one.

'Since you appear to know me,' Harry said, 'who do I have the pleasure of meeting?'

'I doubt it will be much of a pleasure for either of us, Hole. So I suggest you leave the area now and never show your face near a Kripos crime scene again. Is that understood?'

'Well, received but not completely understood. What about if I can help the police in the form of a tip about how Marit Olsen—'

'The only help you've given the police', the gentle voice interrupted, 'has been to besmirch its reputation. In my book, you're a drunk, a lawbreaker and vermin, Hole. So my advice to you is this: crawl back under the stone you came from before someone crushes you with their heel.'

Harry looked at the man, and his gut instinct and his brain concurred: Take it. Withdraw. You have no ammunition to counter with. Be smart.

And he really wished he was smart; he would really have appreciated that quality. Harry took out his pack of cigarettes.

'And that someone would be you, would it, Bellman? You are Bellman, aren't you? The genius who sent the sauna-ape after me?' Harry nodded towards the Finn. 'Judging from that attempt, I doubt you would be able to crush ... er ... er ...' Harry struggled feverishly to remember the analogy, but it wouldn't come. Bloody jet lag.

Bellman interceded. 'Piss off now, Hole.' The POB jerked his thumb behind him. 'Come on. Hop it.'

'I—' Harry began.

'That's it,' Bellman said with a broad smile. 'You're under arrest, Hole.'

'What?!'

'You've been told three times to vacate the crime scene and you haven't complied. Hands behind your back.'

'Now listen here!' Harry snarled with a niggling feeling that he was a very predictable rat caught in the laboratory maze. 'I just want—'

Berntsen, alias Beavis, jogged his arm, knocking the cigarette out of his mouth and onto the wet ground. Harry bent down to pick it up, but got Jussi's boot in his backside and toppled forwards. He banged his head on the ground and tasted earth and bile. And heard Bellman's soft voice in his ear.

'Resisting arrest, Hole? I told you to put your hands behind your back, didn't I? Told you to put them here ...'

Bellman placed his hand lightly on Harry's bottom. Harry breathed hard through his nose without moving. He knew exactly what Bellman was after. Assault on a police officer. Two witnesses. Paragraph 127. Sentence: five years. Game over. And even though this was already as clear as day to Harry, he knew that Bellman would get what he wanted before long. So he concentrated on something else, excluded Beavis's grunted laugh and Bellman's eau de cologne from his mind. He thought about her. About Rakel. He put his hands behind his back, on top of Bellman's hand and turned his head. Now the wind had blown away the fog hanging over them and he could see the slim, white diving tower outlined against the grey sky. Something was dangling aloft, from the platform, a rope perhaps.

The handcuffs clicked gently into place.

Bellman stood in the car park by Middelthunsgate watching them as they drove away. The wind was tugging gently at his coat.

The custody officer was reading the newspaper when he noticed the three men in front of the counter.

'Hi, Tore,' Harry said. 'Got a non-smoker with a view?'

'Hi, Harry. Long time no see.' The officer picked up a key from the cupboard behind him and passed it to Harry. 'Honeymoon suite.'

Harry saw the confusion on Tore's face when Beavis leaned forward, grabbed the key and snarled, 'He's the prisoner, you old git.'

Harry grimaced an apology to Tore as Jussi frisked him and turned up some keys and a wallet.

'Would you mind ringing Gunnar Hagen, Tore? He—'

Jussi snatched at the handcuffs, cutting into Harry's skin, and Harry tumbled backwards after the two men heading for the custody block.

Once they had locked him in the two-and-a-half by one-and-a-half-metre cell, Jussi went back to Tore to sign the papers while Beavis stood outside the barred door, peering in at Harry. Harry could see he had something on his chest and waited. And at last it came, in a voice shaking with suppressed fury.

'How does it feel, eh? You being such a bloody hotshot, catching two serial killers, being on TV and all that? And here you are now, looking at bars from the inside, eh?'

'What are you so angry about, Beavis?' Harry asked softly and closed his eyes. He could feel the swell in his body as if he had just come ashore after a long voyage.

'I'm not angry. But as far as punks shooting good policemen are concerned, I'm furious with them.'

'Three mistakes in one sentence,' Harry said, lying down on the cell bed. 'First of all, it's "is" not "are", secondly Inspector Waaler was not a good policeman and thirdly I didn't shoot him. I pulled off his arm. Here, up by the shoulder.' Harry demonstrated.

Beavis's mouth opened and shut, but nothing emerged.

Harry closed his eyes again.

13

Office

THE NEXT TIME HARRY OPENED HIS EYES, HE HAD BEEN lying in the cell for two hours, and Gunnar Hagen was standing outside struggling to open the door with the key.

'Sorry, Harry, I was in a meeting.'

'Suited me fine, boss,' Harry said, stretching on the bed with a yawn. 'Am I being released?'

'I spoke to the police lawyer, who said it was OK. Custody is detention, not a punishment. I heard two Kripos men brought you in. What happened?'

'I'm hoping you can tell me.'

'I can tell you?'

'Ever since I landed in Oslo I've been followed by Kripos.'

'Kripos?'

Harry sat up and ran a hand through the brush-like bristles on his head. 'They tracked me down to Rikshospital. They arrested me on a formality. What's going on, boss?'

Hagen raised his chin and stroked the skin over his larynx. 'Hell, I should have anticipated this.'

'Anticipated what?'

'That it would leak out that we were trying to run you to earth. That Bellman would try to stop us.'

'A few main clauses would be nice.'

'It's pretty complicated, as I told you. It's all about cuts and rationalisation in the force. About jurisdiction. The old fight, Crime Squad versus Kripos. Whether there are enough resources for two specialist branches with parallel expertise in a small country. The discussion flared up when Kripos got a new second in command, one Mikael Bellman.'

'Tell me about him.'

'Bellman? Police College, brief period of service in Norway before washing up in Europol in The Hague. Came back to Kripos a wonder boy, ready to move upwards and onwards. Nothing but grief from day one when he wanted to employ an ex-colleague from Interpol, a foreigner.'

'Not Finnish, by any chance, was he?'

Hagen nodded. 'Jussi Kolkka. Police training in Finland, but has none of the formal qualifications required for police status in Norway. The trade union went ballistic. The solution was, of course, that Kolkka would be temporarily employed on an exchange. Bellman's next initiative was to make it clear that the rules should be interpreted in such a way that on bigger murder investigations Kripos would decide whether it was their case or the police district's, not vice versa.'

'And?'

'And that is quite unacceptable, goes without saying. We have the country's largest murder unit here at Police HQ, we decide which cases we take within the Oslo district, what we need help with and where we request Kripos to take control. Kripos was established to offer their know-how to police districts running murder cases, but Bellman has, at the drop of a hat, endowed the department with his emperor status. The Ministry of Justice was drawn into the matter. And they soon saw their chance to do what we have managed to keep a lid on for so long: to centralise murder investigations so that there is one centre of expertise. They don't give two hoots about our arguments concerning the dangers of standardisation and inbreeding, the importance of local knowledge and the spread of skills, recruitment and—'

'Thank you, you're preaching to the converted.'

Hagen held up a hand. 'Fine, but the Ministry of Justice is working now on an appointment . . .'

'And . . . ?'

'They say they're going to be pragmatic. It's all about exploiting scarce resources in the most cost-effective way. If Kripos can show that they achieve their best results by being unencumbered by police districts—'

'—then all the power goes to Kripos HQ in Bryn,' Harry said. 'Big office for Bellman and bye-bye Crime Squad.'

Hagen hunched his shoulders. 'Something of that nature. When Charlotte Lolles was found dead behind the Datsun and we saw the similarities with the girl murdered in the cellar of the new building, there was a head-on collision. Kripos said that even though the bodies were found in Oslo, a double murder is a matter for Kripos, not Oslo Police District, and started their own independent investigation. They've realised that the battle for the ministry's support will stand or fall on this case.'

'So it's just a question of solving the case before Kripos?'

'As I said, it's complicated. Kripos refuses to share info with us even though they've made no headway. Instead they went to the ministry. The Chief Constable here received a call to say that the ministry *would like to see* Kripos being allowed to run this case until they've made up their mind about how to allocate areas of responsibility in the future.'

Harry shook his head slowly. 'It's beginning to sink in. You all got desperate . . .'

'I wouldn't use that word.'

'Desperate enough to dig up the old serial-killer hunter, Hole. An outsider no longer on the payroll, who could investigate the matter on the q.t. That was why I couldn't say anything to anyone.'

Hagen sighed. 'Bellman found out anyway, obviously. And stuck a tail on you.'

'To see whether you seemed to be complying with the ministry's request. To catch me in flagrante delicto reading old reports or questioning old witnesses.'

'Or even more effective: to disqualify you from the game. Bellman knows one single mistake would be enough to have you suspended, one single beer while on duty, one single breach of service rules.'

'Mm. Or resisting arrest. He's thinking of taking the case further, the prick.'

'I'll talk to him. He'll drop it when I tell him you don't want the case anyway. We don't dump police officers in the shit when there's no point.' Hagen glanced at his watch. 'I've got work waiting for me. Let's get you out.'

They walked out of the custody block, across the car park and stopped at the entrance to Police HQ, a tower of concrete and steel presiding over the park. Beside them, attached to Police HQ by an underground culvert, stood the old grey walls of Botsen, Oslo District Prison. Beneath them, the area of Grønland stretched down to the fjord and harbour. The facades were winter-pale and filthy as though ash had rained down on them. The cranes by the harbour stood like gallows outlined against the sky.

'Not a pretty sight, eh?'

'No,' Harry said, breathing in.

'But there's something about this town nonetheless.'

Harry nodded. 'There is that.'

They stood there for a while, rocking back on their heels, hands in pockets.

'Chilly,' Harry said.

'Not really.'

'S'pose not, but my thermostat is still set to Hong Kong temperatures.'

'I see.'

'You've got a cup of coffee waiting for you upstairs, have you?' Harry motioned to the sixth floor. 'Or was it work? The Marit Olsen case?'

Hagen didn't answer.

'Mm,' Harry said. 'So Bellman and Kripos have got that, too.'

Harry received the odd measured nod on his way through the corridors of the red zone on the sixth floor. A legend in the building he might have been, but he had never been a popular man.

They passed an office door on which someone had glued an A4 piece of paper saying 'I SEE DEAD PEOPLE'.

Hagen cleared his throat. 'I had to let Magnus Skarre take over your office. Everywhere else is bursting at the seams.'

'No worries,' Harry said.

They each took their paper cup of the infamous percolated coffee from the kitchenette.

Inside Hagen's office Harry settled in the chair facing the POB's desk, where he had sat so many times.

'You've still got it, I see,' Harry said, pointing with his head to the memento on the desk that, at first sight, resembled a white exclamation mark. It was a stuffed little finger. Harry knew it had once belonged to a Japanese Second World War commander. In retreat, the commander had cut off his finger in front of his men to apologise for not being able to return and pick up their dead. Hagen loved to use the story when he was teaching middle management about leadership.

'And you still haven't.' Hagen nodded towards the hand, minus middle finger, Harry was using to hold the paper cup.

Harry conceded the point and drank. The coffee hadn't changed, either. Liquefied tarmac.

Harry grimaced. 'I need a team of three.'

Hagen drank slowly and put down the cup. 'Not more?'

'You always ask that. You know I don't work with large teams of detectives.'

'In that case I won't complain. Fewer people means less chance of Kripos and the Ministry of Justice catching wind of our investigations into the double murder.'

'Triple murder,' Harry said with a yawn.

'Hold on, we don't know if Marit Olsen—'

'Woman alone at night, abducted, murdered in an unconventional manner. The third time in little old Oslo. Triple. Believe me. But however many there are of us, you can take it from me that we will take bloody good care that our paths don't cross those of Kripos.'

'Yes,' Hagen said. 'I do know that. That's why it's a condition that if the investigation were to be brought to light, it has nothing to do with Crime Squad.'

Harry closed his eyes. Hagen went on.

'Of course we will regret that some of our employees have been involved, but make it clear that this is something the notorious maverick Harry Hole initiated off his own bat, without the knowledge of the unit head. And you will confirm that version of events.'

Harry opened his eyes again and stared at Hagen.

Hagen met his stare. 'Any questions?'

'Yes.'

'Shoot.'

'Where's the leak?'

'Pardon?'

'Who's informing Bellman?'

Hagen rolled his shoulders. 'I don't have the impression that he has any systematic access to what we're doing. He could have caught a sniff of your return in lots of places.'

'I know Magnus Skarre has a habit of talking anywhere and anyhow.'

'Don't ask me any more questions, Harry.'

'OK. Where should we set up shop?'

'Right. Right.' Gunnar Hagen nodded several times as if that were something they had already discussed. 'As far as an office is concerned . . .'

'Yes?'

'As I said, the place is full to bursting, so we'll have to find somewhere outside, but not too far away.'

'Fine. Where then?'

Hagen looked out of the window. At the grey walls of Botsen.

'You're kidding,' Harry said.

14

Recruitment

BJØRN HOLM ENTERED THE CONFERENCE ROOM AT KRIMTEKNISK in the Bryn district of Oslo. Outside the windows, the sun was relinquishing its grip on the house fronts and casting the town into afternoon gloom. The car park was packed, and in front of the entrance to Kripos, across the road, there was a white bus with a soup dish on the roof and the Norwegian Broadcasting Company logo on its side.

The only person in the room was his boss, Beate Lønn, an unusually pale, petite and quiet-mannered woman. Had one not known any better, one might have thought a person like this would have problems leading a group of experienced, professional, self-aware, always quirky and seldom conflict-shy forensics officers. Had one known better, one would have realised she was the only person who could deal with them. Not primarily because they respected the fact that she stood erect and proud despite losing two policemen to the eternity shift, first her father and later the father of her child. But because, in their group, she was the best, and radiated such unimpeachability, integrity and gravity that when Beate Lønn whispered an order with downcast gaze and flushed cheeks, it was carried out on the spot. So Bjørn Holm had come as soon as he was informed.

She was sitting in a chair drawn up close to the TV monitor.

'They're recording live from the press conference,' she said without turning. 'Take a seat.'

Holm immediately recognised the people on the screen. How strange it was, it struck him, to be watching signals that had travelled thousands of kilometres out into space and back, just to show him what was happening right now on the opposite side of the street.

Beate Lønn turned up the volume.

'You have understood correctly,' said Mikael Bellman, leaning towards the microphone on the table in front of him. 'For the present we have neither leads nor suspects. And to repeat myself once again: we have not ruled out the possibility of suicide.'

'But you said—' began a voice from the body of journalists present.

Bellman cut her off. 'I said we regard the death as *suspicious*. I am sure you're familiar with the terminology. If not, you should . . .' He left the end of the sentence hanging in the air and pointed to a person behind the camera.

'*Stavanger Aftenblad*,' came the slow bleat of the Rogaland dialect. 'Do the police see a connection between this death and the two in—?'

'No! If you'd been following, you would have heard me say that we *do not rule out* a connection.'

'I caught that,' continued the slow, imperturbable dialect. 'But those of us here are more interested in what you think rather than what you *don't rule out*.'

Bjørn Holm could see Bellman giving the man the evil eye as impatience strained at the corners of his mouth. A uniformed woman officer at Bellman's side placed her hand over the microphone, leaned in to him and whispered something. The POB's face darkened.

'Mikael Bellman is getting a crash course in how to deal with the media,' said Bjørn Holm. 'Lesson one, stroke the ones *with* hair, especially the provincial newspapers.'

'He's new to the job,' Beate Lønn said. 'He'll learn.'

'Think so?'

'Yes. Bellman's the type to learn.'

'Humility's hard to learn, I've heard.'

'Genuine humility, that's true. But to grovel when it suits you is basic to modern communication. That's what Ninni's telling him. And Bellman's smart enough to appreciate that.'

On-screen, Bellman coughed, forced an almost boyish smile and leaned into the microphone. 'I apologise if I sounded a bit brusque, but it's been a long day for all of us, and I hope you understand that we are simply impatient to get back to the investigation into this tragic case. We have to finish here, but if any of you have any further questions, please direct them to Ninni, and I promise I will try to return to you later this evening. Before the deadline. Is that OK?'

'What did I say?' Beate laughed triumphantly.

'A star is born,' Bjørn said.

The picture imploded and Beate Lønn turned. 'Harry called. He wants me to hand you over.'

'Me?' said Bjørn Holm. 'To do what?'

'You know very well what. I heard you were with Gunnar Hagen at the airport when Harry arrived.'

'Whoops.' Holm smiled, revealing both top and bottom sets of teeth.

'I assume Hagen wanted to use you in Operation Persuasion since he knows you are one of the few people Harry likes working with.'

'We never got that far, and Harry turned down the job.'

'But now it seems he has changed his mind.'

'Uh-huh? What made him do that?'

'He didn't say. He just said he thought it was right to go through me.'

'Sure. You're the boss here.'

'You can take nothing for granted where Harry is concerned. I know him pretty well, as you're aware.'

Holm nodded. He was aware. Knew Jack Halvorsen, Beate's partner and soon-to-be father of their child, had been killed while working for Harry. One freezing cold winter's day, in broad daylight, in Grünerløkka, stabbed in the chest. Holm had arrived straight afterwards. Hot blood soaking down into the blue ice. A policeman's death. No one had blamed Harry. Apart from Harry, that is.

He scratched his sideburns. 'So what did you say?'

Beate took a deep breath and watched the journalists and photographers hurrying out of the Kripos building. 'The same as I'm going to tell you now. The Ministry of Justice has let it be known that Kripos has priority, and accordingly there is no chance that I can pass on forensics officers to anyone other than Bellman for this case.'

84

'But?'

Beate Lønn drummed a Bic pen on the table, hard. 'But there are other cases besides this double murder.'

'Triple murder,' Holm said, and after a sharp look from Beate, he added, 'Believe me.'

'I don't know exactly what Inspector Hole is investigating, but it is definitely not any of these murder cases. He and I are totally agreed on that,' Beate said. 'And you are thereby transferred to that case or those cases – of which I know nothing. For two weeks. Copy of first report on whatever you do to be on my desk five working days from now. Understood?'

Inwardly, Kaja Solness was beaming like a sun and felt an almost irresistible desire to do a couple of spins in her swivel chair.

'If Hagen says OK, of course I'll join you,' she said, trying to contain herself, but she could hear the exultation in her voice.

'Hagen says OK,' said the man leaning against the door frame with his arm over his head, forming a diagonal in her doorway. 'So it's just Holm, you and me. And the case we're working on is confidential. We start tomorrow. Meet at seven in my office.'

'Er . . . seven?'

'*Sieben*. Seven. O seven hundred hours.'

'I see. Which office?'

The man grinned and explained.

She looked at him in disbelief. 'We've got an office in the prison?'

The diagonal in the doorway relaxed. 'Meet up, all systems go. Questions?'

Kaja had several, but Harry had already left.

The dream has begun to appear in the daytime, too, now. A long way off I can still hear the band playing 'Love Hurts'. I notice a few boys standing around us, but they don't move in. Good. As for me, I'm looking at her. See what you've done, I try to say. Look at him now. Do you still want him?

My God, how I hate her, how I want to tear the knife out of my mouth and stick it in her, stab holes in her, see it gush out: blood, guts, the lie, the stupidity, her idiotic self-righteousness. Someone should show her how ugly she is on the inside.

I saw the press conference on TV. Incompetent oafs! No clues. No suspects! The golden first forty-eight hours, the sands are running out, hurry, hurry. What do you want me to do? Write it on the wall in blood?

It's you who are allowing this killing to go on.

The letter is finished.

Hurry.

15

Strobe Lights

STINE EYED THE BOY WHO HAD JUST SPOKEN TO HER. HE had a beard, blond hair and a woollen hat. Indoors. And this was no indoor hat, but a thick hat to keep your ears warm. A snowboarder? Anyway, when she took a closer look, this was no boy, but a man. Over thirty. At any rate, there were white wrinkles in the brown skin.

'So?' she shouted over the music booming out through the stereo system at Krabbe. The recently opened restaurant had proclaimed it was the new hangout for Stavanger's young avant-garde musicians, film-makers and writers, of whom there were quite a few in this otherwise business-orientated, dollar-counting oil town. It would turn out that the in-crowd had not yet decided whether Krabbe deserved their favour or not. As indeed Stine had not yet decided whether this boy – man – deserved hers.

'It's just I think you should let me tell you about it,' he said with a confident smile and looked at her with a pair of eyes that seemed much too pale blue to her. But perhaps that was the lighting in here? Strobe lights? Was that cool? Time would tell. He turned the beer glass in his hand and leaned back against the bar so that she had to lean forward if she wanted to hear what he was saying, but she didn't fall for that one. He was wearing a thick puffa jacket, yet there was not a drop of sweat to be seen on his face under that ridiculous hat. Or was that cool?

'There are very few people who've biked through the delta district of Burma and returned sufficiently alive to tell the tale,' he said.

Sufficiently alive. A talker, then. She liked that up to a point. He looked like someone. Some American action hero from an old film or a TV show from the eighties.

'I promised myself that if I got back to Stavanger I would go out, buy myself a beer and accost the most attractive girl I could see and say what I am saying now.' He thrust out his arms and wore a big white smile. 'I think you're the girl by the blue pagoda.'

'What?'

'Rudyard Kipling, missie. You're the girl waiting for the English soldier by the old blue Moulmein pagoda. So what do you say? Will you join me and walk barefoot on the marble in Shwedagon? Eat cobra meat in Bago? Sleep till the Muslims' call to prayers in Rangoon and wake to the Buddhists in Mandalay?'

He breathed in. She bent forward. 'So I'm the most attractive girl in here, am I?'

He looked around. 'No, but you've got the biggest boobs. You're good-looking, but the competition is too fierce for you to be the best-looking of *the lot*. Shall we be off?'

She laughed and shook her head. Didn't know whether he was fun or just mad.

'I'm with some girls. You can try that trick on someone else.'

'Elias.'

'What?'

'You were wondering what my name was. In case we meet again. And my name's Elias. Skog. You'll forget that, but you'll remember Elias. And we'll meet again. Before you imagine, actually.'

She slanted her head. 'Oh yes?'

Then he drained his glass, put it on the bar, smiled at her and left.

'Who was he?'

It was Mathilde.

'Don't know,' Stine said. 'He was quite nice. But weird. Talked like he came from eastern Norway.'

'Weird?'

'There was something odd about his eyes. And teeth. Are there strobe lights in here?'

88

'Strobe lights?'

Stine laughed. 'No, it's that toothpaste-coloured solarium light. Makes your face look like a zombie's.'

Mathilde shook her head. 'You need a drink. Come on.'

Stine turned towards the exit as she followed. She thought she had seen a face against a pane, but no one was there.

16

Speed King

It was nine o'clock at night, and Harry was walking through Oslo city centre. He had spent the morning humping chairs and tables into the new office. In the afternoon he had gone up to Rikshospital, but his father was undergoing some tests. So he had doubled back, copied reports, made a few calls, booked a ticket to Bergen, nipped down to the shops and bought a SIM card the size of a cigarette end.

Harry strode out. He had always enjoyed moving from east to west in this compact town, seeing the gradual but obvious changes in people, fashion, ethnicity, architecture, shops, cafes and bars. He popped into a McDonald's, had a hamburger, stuffed three straws in his coat pocket and continued his journey.

Half an hour after standing in the ghetto-like Pakistani Grønland, he found himself in neat, slightly sterile and very white West End land. Kaja Solness's address was in Lyder Sagens gate and turned out to be one of those large old timber houses that attracted a long queue of Oslo-ites on the rare occasions one of them was for sale. Not to buy – very few could afford that – but to see, dream about and receive confirmation that Fagerborg really was what it purported to be: a neighbourhood where the rich were not too rich, the money was not too new, and no one had a swimming pool, electric garage doors or any other vulgar modern invention. For the Fagerborger, quite liter-ally the fine burghers, did as they always had done here. In the summer they sat under apple trees in their large shaded gardens on the garden furniture that was as old, impractically large and stained black as the houses from which it had been carried. And when it was transported back and the days became shorter, candles were lit behind the leaded windows. In Lyder Sagens gate there was a Yuletide atmosphere from October through to March.

The gate gave a screech so loud that it made any need for a dog superfluous, Harry hoped. The gravel crunched beneath his boots. He had been as happy as a child to be reunited with his boots when he found them in the wardrobe, but now they were drenched right through.

He went up the porch steps and pressed the bell without a nameplate.

In front of the door was a pair of pretty ladies' shoes and a pair of men's shoes. Size forty-six, Harry estimated. Kaja's husband was big, they seemed to suggest. For, naturally, she had a husband; he didn't know why he had thought any differently. Because he had, hadn't he? It was of no consequence. The door opened.

'Harry?' She was wearing an open and much too large woollen jacket, faded jeans and felt slippers that were so old Harry could swear they had liver spots. No make-up. Just a surprised smile. Nevertheless she seemed to have been expecting him. Expected that he would like to see her this way. Of course, he had already seen it in her eyes in Hong Kong, the fascination so many women have for any man with a reputation, good or bad. Though he had not made a comprehensive analysis of every single thought process that, in concert, had led him to this door. Just as well he had saved himself the effort. Size forty-six shoes. Or forty-six and a half.

'I got your address from Hagen,' Harry said. 'You live within walking distance of my flat so I thought I would drop by instead of ringing.'

She smirked. 'You haven't got a mobile.'

'Wrong.' Harry produced a red phone from his pocket. 'I was given this by Hagen, but I've already forgotten the PIN. Am I disturbing?'

'No, no.' She opened the door wide and Harry stepped in.

It was pathetic, but his heart had been beating a bit faster while he waited for her. Fifteen years ago that would have annoyed him, but he

91

had resigned himself and accepted the banal fact that a woman's beauty would always have this modicum of power over him.

'I'm making coffee. Would you like some?'

They had moved into the living room. The walls were covered with pictures and shelves with so many books he doubted she could have read them all herself. The room had a distinctly masculine character. Large, angular furniture, a globe, a hookah, vinyl records on more shelves, maps and photographs of high, snow-covered mountains on the walls. Harry concluded that he was a great deal older than her. A TV was on, but without the volume.

'Marit Olsen is the main item on all the news broadcasts,' Kaja said, lifting the remote and switching off the TV. 'Two of the Opposition leaders stood up and demanded quick results. They said the government had been systematically dismantling the police force. Kripos won't get much peace for the next few days.'

'Yes please to the coffee,' Harry said, and Kaja scurried into the kitchen.

He sat on the sofa. An open John Fante book lay face down on the coffee table, beside a pair of ladies' reading glasses. Beside it were photos of Frogner Lido. Not of the crime scene itself, but of the people who had gathered outside the cordon to rubberneck. Harry gave a grunt of satisfaction. Not only because she had taken work home, but because crime scene officers continued to take these photos. It had been Harry who insisted they always photograph the crowd. It was something he had learned on the FBI course about serial killings; the killer returning to the scene of a crime was no myth. The King brothers in San Antonio and the K-Mart man had been arrested precisely because they couldn't restrain themselves from returning to admire their handiwork, to see all the commotion they had caused, to feel how invulnerable they were. The photographers at Krimteknisk called it Hole's sixth commandment. And, yes, there were nine other commandments. Harry riffled through the photos.

'You don't take milk, do you?' Kaja shouted from the kitchen.

'Yes.'

'Do you? At Heathrow—'

'I mean yes, as in yes, you're right, I don't take milk.'

'Aha. You've gone over to the Cantonese system.'

'What?'

'You've stopped using double negatives. Cantonese is more logical. You like logical.'

'Is that right? About Cantonese?'

'I don't know,' she laughed from the kitchen. 'I'm just trying to sound clever.'

Harry could see that the photographer had been discreet, he'd shot from hip height, no flash. The spectators' attention was directed towards the diving tower. Dull eyes, half-open mouths, as if they were bored of waiting for a glimpse of something dreadful, something for their albums, something with which they could scare the neighbours out of their wits. A man holding a mobile phone up in the air; he was definitely taking photos. Harry took the magnifying glass lying on the pile of reports, and scrutinised their faces, one by one. He didn't know what he was looking for, his brain was empty; it was the best way, so as not to miss whatever might be there.

'Can you see anything?' She had taken up a position behind his chair and bent down to see. He caught a mild fragrance of lavender soap, the same he had smelt on the plane when she had fallen asleep on his shoulder.

'Mm. Do you think there's anything to see here?' he asked, taking the coffee mug.

'No.'

'So why did you bring the photos home?'

'Because ninety-five per cent of all police work is searching in the wrong place.'

She had just quoted Harry's third commandment.

'And you have to learn to enjoy the ninety-five per cent, too. Otherwise you'll go mad.'

Fourth commandment.

'And the reports?' Harry asked.

'All we have are the reports on the murders of Borgny and Charlotte, and there's nothing in them. No forensic leads, no accounts of unusual activities. No tip-offs about bitter enemies, jealous lovers, greedy heirs, deranged stalkers, impatient drug dealers or other creditors. In short—'

'No leads, no apparent motives, no murder weapons. I would have liked to start interviewing people in the Marit Olsen case, but, as you know, we're not working on it.'

Kaja smiled. 'Of course not. By the way, I spoke to a political journalist from *VG* today. He said none of the journalists at Stortinget knew anything about Marit Olsen having depression, personal crises or suicidal thoughts. Or enemies, in her professional or her private life.'

'Mm.'

Harry skimmed the row of spectators' faces. A woman with sleep-walker eyes and a child on her arm.

'What do these people want?' Behind them: the back of a man leaving. Puffa jacket, woollen hat. 'To be shocked. Shaken. Entertained. Purified . . .'

'Incredible.'

'Mm. And so you're reading John Fante. You like older things, do you?' He nodded towards the room, the house. And he meant the room, the house. But reckoned she would drop in a comment about the husband if he was a lot older than her, as Harry guessed he was.

She looked at him with enthusiasm. 'Have you read Fante?'

'When I was young and was going through my Bukowski period I read one whose title eludes me. I bought them mostly because Charles Bukowski was an ardent fan.' He made a show of checking his watch. 'Whoops, time to go home.'

Kaja looked at him in amazement and then at the untouched cup of coffee.

'Jet lag,' Harry smiled, getting to his feet. 'We can talk tomorrow at the meeting.'

'Of course.'

Harry patted his trouser pocket. 'By the way, I've run out of cigarettes. The tax-free Camel cigarettes you took through customs for me . . .'

'Just a minute,' she smiled.

When she came back with the carton Harry was standing in the hall, with his jacket and shoes already on.

'Thank you,' he said, taking out one of the packs and opening it.

When he was outside on the steps, she leaned against the door frame.

'Perhaps I shouldn't say this, but I have a feeling that this was some kind of test.'

'Test?' Harry said, lighting a cigarette.

'I won't ask what the test was for, but did I pass?'

Harry chuckled. 'It was just this.' He walked down the steps waving the carton. 'O seven hundred hours.'

Harry let himself into his flat. Pressed the light switch and established that the electricity had not been disconnected. Took off his coat, went into the sitting room, put on Deep Purple, his top favourite band in the category can't-help-being-funny, but-brilliant-anyway. 'Speed King'. Ian Paice on drums. He sat down on the sofa and pressed his fingertips against his forehead. The dogs were yanking at the chains. Howling, snarling, barking, their teeth tearing at his innards. If he let them loose, there would be no way back. Not this time. Before, there had always been good enough reasons to stop drinking again. Rakel, Oleg, the job, perhaps even Dad. He didn't have any of them any more. It couldn't happen. Not with alcohol. So he had to have an alternative intoxicant. He could control intoxication. Thank you, Kaja. Was he ashamed? Of course he was. But pride was a luxury he couldn't always afford.

He tore the plastic wrapping from the carton. Took out the bottom pack. You could hardly see that the seal on the pack had been broken. It was a fact that women like Kaja were never checked at customs. He opened the pack and pulled out the tinfoil. Unfolded it and looked at the brown ball. Inhaled the sweet smell.

Then he set about his preparations.

Harry had seen all possible ways of smoking opium, everything from the complicated, ritual procedures of opium dens, which were nothing less than Chinese tea ceremonies, through all sorts of pipe arrangements to the simplest: lighting the ball, placing a straw over it and inhaling for all you were worth as the goods literally went up in smoke. Whatever method you chose, the principle was the same: to get the substances – morphine, thebaine, codeine and a whole bouquet of other chemical friends – into your bloodstream. Harry's method was straightforward. He taped a steel spoon to the end of the table, placed a tiny particle of the lump, no bigger than the head of a matchstick, in the spoon and heated it with a lighter. When the opium began to burn he held an ordinary glass over it to collect the smoke. Then he put a drinking straw, one with a flexible joint, in the glass and inhaled. Harry noted that his fingers worked without a hint of a tremble. In Hong Kong he had regularly kept a check on his dependency level; seen in that light, he was the most disciplined drug abuser he knew. He could predetermine his dose of alcohol and stop there, however plastered he was. In Hong Kong he had cut out opium for a week or two and only taken a couple of analgesic tablets, which would not have prevented withdrawal symptoms from materialising anyway, but which perhaps had a psychological effect since he knew they contained a tiny amount of morphine. He was not hooked. On drugs in general he was, but on opium in particular: no. Though it is a sliding scale of course. Because while he was taping the spoon into position he could already feel the dogs calming down. For they knew now, knew they would soon be fed.

And could be at peace. Until the next time.

The burning hot lighter was already scorching Harry's fingers. On the table were the straws from McDonald's.

A minute later he had taken the first drag.

The effect was immediate. The pains, even those he didn't know he had, vanished. The associations, the images, appeared. He would be able to sleep tonight.

Bjørn Holm couldn't sleep.

He had tried reading Escott's *Hank Williams: The Biography*, about the country legend's short life and long death, listening to a bootleg Lucinda Williams CD of a concert in Austin and counting Texas longhorns, but to no avail.

A dilemma. That's exactly what it was. A problem without a proper solution. Forensics Officer Holm hated that type of problem.

He huddled up on the slightly too short sofa bed that had been among the goods he'd brought from Skreia, along with his vinyl collection of Elvis, the Sex Pistols, Jason & the Scorchers, three hand-sewn suits from

Nashville, an American Bible and a dining-room suite that had survived three generations of Holms. But he couldn't concentrate.

The dilemma was that he had made an interesting discovery while examining the rope with which Marit Olsen had been hung – or to be more precise, beheaded. It wasn't a clue that would necessarily produce anything, but nonetheless the dilemma remained the same: would it be right to pass the information on to Kripos or to Harry? Bjørn Holm had identified the tiny shells on the rope during the time he was still working for Kripos. When he was talking to a freshwater biologist at the Biological Institute, Oslo University. But then Beate Lønn had transferred him to Harry's unit before the report had been written and, sitting down at the computer tomorrow to write it, he would in fact be reporting to Harry.

OK, technically perhaps it wasn't a dilemma, the information belonged to Kripos. Giving it to anyone else would be regarded as a dereliction of duty. And what did he owe Harry Hole actually? He had never given him anything but aggro. He was quirky and inconsiderate at work. Positively dangerous when on the booze. But on the level when sober. You could rely on him turning up and there would be no messing and no 'you owe me'. An irksome enemy, but a good friend. A good man. A bloody good man. A bit like Hank, in fact.

Bjørn Holm groaned and rolled over to face the wall.

Stine woke with a start.

In the dark she heard a grinding sound. She rolled onto her side. The ceiling was dimly lit; the light came from the floor beside the bed. What was the time? Three o'clock in the morning? She stretched and grabbed her mobile phone.

'Yes?' she said with a voice that made her seem more sleepy than she was.

'After the delta I was sick of snakes and mozzies, and me and the motorbike headed north along the Burmese coast to Arakan.'

She recognised the voice straight away.

'To the island of Sai Chung,' he said. 'There's an active mud volcano I heard was about to explode. And on the third night I was there, it erupted. I thought there would just be mud, but, you know, it spewed good old-fashioned lava as well. Thick lava that flowed so slowly through the town that we could blithely walk away from it.'

'It's the middle of the night,' she yawned.

'Yet still it wouldn't stop. Apparently they call it cold lava when it's so sticky, but it consumed everything in its path. Trees with fresh green leaves were like Christmas trees for four seconds until they were turned to ashes and were gone. The Burmese tried to escape in cars loaded with the chattels they had snatched, but they had spent too much time packing. The lava was moving that fast after all! When they emerged with the TV set, the lava was already up to their walls. They threw themselves inside their cars, but the heat punctured the tyres. Then the petrol caught fire and they clambered out like human torches. Do you remember my name?'

'Listen, Elias—'

'I said you would remember.'

'I have to sleep. I've got classes tomorrow.'

'I am such an eruption, Stine. I'm cold lava. I move slowly, but I'm unstoppable. I'm coming to where you are.'

She tried to remember if she had told him her name. And automatically directed her gaze to the window. It was open. Outside, the wind soughed, peaceful, reassuring.

His voice was low, a whisper. 'I saw a dog entangled in barbed wire, trying to flee. It was in the path of the lava. But then the stream veered left, it would pass right by. A merciful God, I supposed. But the lava brushed against it. Half the dog simply vanished, evaporated. Before the rest burned up. So it was ashes, too. Everything turns to ashes.'

'Yuk, I'm ringing off.'

'Look outside. Look, I'm already up against the house.'

'Stop it!'

'Relax, I'm only teasing.' His loud laughter pealed in her ears.

Stine shuddered. He must have been drunk. Or he was mad. Or both.

'Sleep tight, Stine. See you soon.'

He broke the connection. Stine stared at the phone. Then she switched it off and threw it to the foot of her bed. Cursed because she already knew. She would get no more sleep that night.

17

Fibres

It was 6.58. Harry Hole, Kaja Solness and Bjørn Holm were walking through the culvert, a three-hundred-metre-long subterranean corridor connecting Police HQ and Oslo District Prison. Now and then it was used to transport prisoners to Police HQ for questioning, sometimes for sports training sessions in the winter and in the bad old days for extremely unofficial beatings of particularly intractable prisoners.

Water from the ceiling dripped onto the concrete with wet kisses that echoed down the dimly lit corridor.

'Here,' Harry said as they reached the end.

'HERE?' asked Bjørn Holm.

They had to bend their heads to pass under the stairs leading to the prison cells. Harry turned the key in the lock and opened the iron door. The musty smell of heated dank air hit him.

He pressed the light switch. Cold, blue light from neon tubes enveloped a square concrete room with grey-blue lino on the floor and nothing on the walls.

The room had no windows, no radiators, none of the facilities you expect in a space supposed to function as an office for three people.

Apart from desks with chairs and a computer each. On the floor there was a coffee machine stained brown and a water cooler.

'The boilers heating the whole prison are in the adjacent room,' Harry said. 'That's why it's so hot in here.'

'Basically not very homely,' Kaja said, sitting at one of the desks.

'Right, bit reminiscent of hell,' Holm said, pulling off his suede jacket and undoing one shirt button. 'Is there mobile coverage here?'

'Just about,' Harry said. 'And an Internet connection. We have everything we need.'

'Apart from coffee cups,' Holm said.

Harry shook his head. From his jacket pocket he produced three white cups, and he placed one on each of the three desks. Then he pulled a bag of coffee from his inside pocket and went over to the machine.

'You've taken them from the canteen,' Bjørn said, raising the cup Harry had put down in front of him. 'Hank Williams?'

'Written with a felt pen, so be careful,' Harry said, tearing open the coffee pouch with his teeth.

'John Fante?' Kaja read on her cup. 'What have you got?'

'For the time being, nothing,' Harry said.

'And why not?'

'Because it will be the name of our main suspect of the moment.'

Neither of the other two said anything. The coffee machine slurped up the water.

'I want three names on the table by the time this is ready,' Harry said.

They were well down their second cup of coffee and into the sixth theory when Harry interrupted the session.

'OK, that was the warm-up, just to get the grey matter working.'

Kaja had just launched the idea that the murders were sexually motivated and that the killer was an ex-con with a record for similar crimes who knew that the police had his DNA and therefore did not spill his seed on the ground, but masturbated into a bag or some such receptacle before leaving the scene. Accordingly, she said, they should start going through criminal records and talking to staff in the Sexual Offences Unit.

'But don't you believe we're onto something?' she said.

'I don't believe anything,' Harry answered. 'I'm trying to keep my brain clear and receptive.'

100

'But you must believe something?'

'Yes, I do. I believe the three murders have been carried out by the same person or persons. And I believe it's possible to find a connection which in turn might lead us to a motive which in turn – if we're very, very lucky – will lead us to the guilty party or parties.'

'Very, very lucky. You make it sound as if the odds are not good.'

'Well.' Harry leaned back on his chair with his hands behind his head. 'Several metres of specialist books have been written about what characterises serial killers. In films, the police call in a psychologist who, after reading a couple of reports, gives them a profile which invariably fits. People believe that *Henry: Portrait of a Serial Killer* is a general description. But in reality serial killers are, sad to say, as different from each other as everyone else. There is only one thing which distinguishes them from other criminals.'

'And that is?'

'They don't get caught.'

Bjørn Holm laughed, realised it was inappropriate, and shut up.

'That's not true, is it?' Kaja said. 'What about . . . ?'

'You're thinking of the cases where a pattern emerged and they caught the person. But don't forget all the unsolved murders we still think are one-offs, where a connection was never found. Thousands.'

Kaja glanced at Bjørn who was nodding meaningfully.

'You believe in connections?' she said.

'Yep,' Harry said. 'And we have to find one without going down the path of interviewing people, which might give us away.'

'So?'

'When we predicted potential threats in the Security Service we did nothing but look for possible connections, without talking to a living soul. We had a NATO-built search engine long before anyone had heard of Yahoo or Google. With it we could sneak in anywhere and scan practically everything with any connection to the Net. That's what we have to do here as well.' He glanced at his watch. 'And that's why in one and a half hours I'll be sitting on a plane to Bergen. And in three hours I'll be talking to an unemployed colleague who I hope can help us. So let's finish up here, shall we? Kaja and I have talked a fair bit, Bjørn. What have you got?'

Bjørn Holm jerked in his chair as if roused from sleep.

'Me? Er . . . not much, I'm afraid.'

Harry rubbed his jaw carefully. 'You've got something.'

'Nope. Neither forensics nor the detectives on the case have got so much as a lump of fly shit. Not in the Marit Olsen case, nor in either of the other two.'

'Two months,' Harry said. 'Come on.'

'I can give you a summary,' said Bjørn Holm. 'For two months we have analysed, X-rayed and stared ourselves stupid at photos, blood samples, strands of hair, nails, all sorts. We've gone through twenty-four theories of how and why he's stabbed twenty-four holes in the mouths of the first two victims in such a way that all the wounds point inwards to the same central point. With no result. Marit Olsen also had wounds to the mouth, but they were inflicted with a knife and were sloppy, brutal. In short: *nada*.'

'What about those small stones in the cellar where Borgny was found?'

'Analysed. Lots of iron and magnesium, bit of aluminium and silica. So-called basalt rock. Porous and black. Any the wiser?'

'Both Borgny and Charlotte had iron and coltan on the insides of their molars. What does that tell us?'

'That they were killed with the same goddam instrument, but that doesn't get us any closer to what it was.'

Silence.

Harry coughed. 'OK, Bjørn, out with it.'

'Out with what?'

'What you've been brooding about ever since we got here.'

The forensics officer scratched his sideburns while eyeballing Harry. Coughed once. Twice. Glanced at Kaja as if to solicit help there. Opened his mouth, closed it.

'Fine,' Harry said. 'Let's move on to—'

'The rope.'

The other two stared at Bjørn.

'I found shells on it.'

'Oh yes?' Harry said.

'But no salt.'

They were still staring at him.

'That's pretty unusual,' Bjørn went on. 'Shells. In fresh water.'

'So?'

'So I checked it out with a freshwater biologist. This particular mollusc is called a Jutland mussel, it's the smallest of the pool mussels and has been observed in only two lakes in Norway.'

'And the nominations are?'

'Øyeren and Lyseren.'

'Østfold,' Kaja said. 'Neighbouring lakes. Big ones.'

'In a densely populated region,' Harry said.

'Sorry,' Holm said.

'Mm. Any marks on the rope that tell us where it might have been bought?'

'No, that's the point,' Holm said. 'There are no marks. And it doesn't look like any rope I've seen before. The fibre is one hundred per cent organic, there's no nylon or any other synthetic materials.'

'Hemp,' Harry said.

'What?' Holm said.

'Hemp. Rope and hash are made from the same material. If you fancy a joint, you can just stroll down to the harbour and light up the mooring ropes of the Danish ferry.'

'It's not hemp,' Bjørn Holm said over Kaja's laughter. 'The fibre's made from the elm and the linden tree. Mostly elm.'

'Home-made Norwegian rope,' Kaja said. 'They used to make rope on farms long ago.'

'On farms?' Harry queried.

Kaja nodded. 'As a rule every village had at least one rope-maker. You just soaked the wood in water for a month, peeled off the outer bark and used the bast inside. Twined it into rope.'

Harry and Bjørn swivelled round to face Kaja.

'What's the matter?' she asked hesitantly.

'Well,' Harry said, 'is this general knowledge everyone ought to possess?'

'Oh, I see,' Kaja said. 'My grandfather made rope.'

'Aha. And for rope-making you need elm and linden?'

'In principle you can use bast fibres from any kind of tree.'

'And the composition?'

Kaja shrugged. 'I'm no expert, but I think it's unusual to use bast from several different trees for the same rope. I remember that Even, my big brother, said that Grandad used only linden because it absorbs very little water. So he didn't need to tar his.'

'Mm. What do you think, Bjørn?'

'If the compositon is unusual, it will be easier to trace where it was made, of course.'

Harry stood up and began to pace back and forth. There was a heavy sigh every time his rubber soles relinquished the lino. 'Then we can assume production was limited and sales were local. Do you think that sounds reasonable, Kaja?'

'Guess so, yes.'

'And we can also assume that the centres of production and consumption were in close proximity. These home-made ropes would hardly have travelled far.'

'Still sounds reasonable, but . . .'

'So let's take that as our starting point. You two begin mapping out local rope-makers near lakes Øyeren and Lyseren.'

'But no one makes ropes like that any more,' Kaja protested.

'Do the best you can,' Harry said, looked at his watch, grabbed his coat from the back of the chair and walked to the door. 'Find out where the rope was made. I presume Bellman knows nothing about these Jutland mussels. That right, Bjørn?'

Bjørn Holm forced a smile by way of answer.

'Is it OK if I follow up the theory of a sexually motivated murder?' Kaja asked. 'I can talk to someone I know at Sexual Offences.'

'Negative,' Harry said. 'The general order to keep your trap shut about what we're doing applies in particular to our dear colleagues at Police HQ. There seems to be some seepage between HQ and Kripos, so the only person we speak to is Gunnar Hagen.'

Kaja had opened her mouth, but a glance from Bjørn was enough to make her close it again.

'But what you can do', Harry said, 'is get hold of a volcano expert. And send him the test results of the small stones.'

Bjørn's fair eyebrows rose a substantial way up his forehead.

'Porous, black stone, basalt rock,' Harry said. 'I would reckon lava. I'll be back from Bergen at fourish.'

'Say hello to Baa-baargen Police HQ,' Bjørn bleated and raised his coffee cup.

'I won't be going to the police station,' Harry said.

'Oh? Where then?'

'Sandviken Hospital.'

'Sand—'

The door slammed behind Harry. Kaja watched Bjørn Holm, who was staring at the closed door with a stunned expression on his face.

'What's he going to do there?' she asked. 'See a pathologist?'

Bjørn shook his head. 'Sandviken Hospital is a mental hospital.'

'Really? So he's going to meet a psychologist with serial killings as a speciality, is he?'

'I knew I should have said no,' Bjørn whispered, still staring at the door. 'He's clean out of his mind.'

'Who's out of his mind?'

'We're working in a prison,' Bjørn said. 'We're risking our jobs if the boss finds out what we're up to, and the colleague in Bergen . . .'

'Yes?'

'She is seriously out of her mind.'

'You mean she's . . . ?'

'Sectioned out of her mind.'

18

The Patient

FOR EVERY STEP THE TALL POLICEMAN TOOK, KJERSTI Rødsmoen had to take two. Even so, she was left behind as they walked along the corridor of Sandviken Hospital. The rain was pouring down outside the high, narrow windows facing the fjord where the trees were so green you would have thought spring had arrived before winter.

The day before, Kjersti Rødsmoen had recognised the policeman's voice at once. As though she had been waiting for him to ring. And to make the very request he did: to talk to the Patient. The Patient had come to be called the Patient to give her maximum anonymity after the strain of her most recent murder case as a detective had sent her right back to square one: the psychiatric ward. In fact, she had recovered with remarkable speed, had moved back home, but the press – which was still hysterically pursuing the Snowman case long after it had been cleared up – had not left her in peace. And one evening, a few months ago, the Patient had called Rødsmoen and asked if she could return.

'So she's in serviceable shape?' the police officer asked. 'On medication?'

'Yes to the first,' Kjersti Rødsmoen said. 'The second is confidential.' The truth was the Patient was so well that neither medicine nor hospitalisation was required any longer. Nevertheless Rødsmoen had wondered whether she should let him visit her; he had been on the Snowman case and could cause old issues to emerge. Kjersti Rødsmoen had, in her time as a psychologist, come to believe more and more in repression, in shutting things off, in oblivion. It was an unfashionable view within the profession. On the other hand, meeting a person who had been on that particular case might be a good test of how robust the Patient had become.

'You've got half an hour,' Rødsmoen said before opening the door to the common room. 'And don't forget that the mind is tender.'

The last time Harry had seen Katrine Bratt she had been unrecognisable. The attractive young woman with the dark hair and the glowing skin and eyes had gone, to be replaced by someone who reminded him of a dried flower: lifeless, frail, delicate, wan. He had had a feeling he might crush her hand if he squeezed too hard.

So it was a relief to see her now. She looked older, or perhaps she was just tired. But the gleam in her eyes returned as she smiled and got up.

'Harry H,' she said, giving him a hug. 'How's it going?'

'Fair to middling,' Harry said. 'And you?'

'Dreadful,' she said. 'But a lot better.'

She laughed, and Harry knew she was back. Or that enough of her was back.

'What happened to your jaw? Does it hurt?'

'Only when I speak and eat,' Harry said. 'And when I'm awake.'

'Sounds familiar. You're uglier than I remember, but I'm glad to see you anyway.'

'Same to you.'

'You mean same to me, except for the ugly bit?'

Harry smiled. 'Naturally.' He looked around. The other patients in the room were sitting and staring out of the window, at their laps or straight at the wall. But no one seemed interested in him or Katrine.

Harry told her what had happened since the last time they'd seen each other. About Rakel and Oleg, who had moved to an unnamed destination abroad. About Hong Kong. About his father's illness. About the case he had taken on. She even laughed when he said she mustn't tell anyone.

'What about you?' Harry asked.

'They want me out of here really; they think I'm well and I'm taking up someone else's place. But I like it here. The room service stinks, but it's safe. I've got TV and can come and go as I want. In a month or two I'll move back home maybe, who knows.'

'Who knows?'

'No one. The madness is intermittent. What do you want?'

'What do you want me to want?'

She gave him a long, hard look before answering. 'Apart from wanting you to have a burning desire to fuck me, I want you to have some use for me.'

'And that's exactly what I have.'

'A desire to fuck me?'

'Some use for you.'

'Shit. Well, OK. What's it about?'

'Have you got a computer with Internet access here?'

'We have a communal computer in the Hobbies Room, but it isn't connected to the Net. They wouldn't risk that. The only thing it's used for is playing solitaire. But I've got my own computer in my room.'

'Use the communal one.' Harry put his hand in his pocket and tossed a dongle across the table. 'This is a mobile office as they called it in the shop. You just plug it into—'

'—one of the USB ports,' Katrine said, taking the device and pocketing it. 'Who pays the subscription?'

'I do. That is, Hagen does.'

'Yippee, there's gonna be some surfing tonight. Any hot new porno sites I should know about?'

'Probably.' Harry pushed a file across the table. 'Here are the reports. Three murders, three names. I want you to do the same as you did on the Snowman case. Find connections we've missed. Do you know about the case?'

'Yes,' Katrine Bratt said without looking at the file. 'They were women. That's the connection.'

'You read newspapers . . .'

'Barely. Why do you believe they're any more than random victims?'

'I don't believe anything, I'm looking.'

'But you don't know what you're looking for?'

'Correct.'

'But you're sure Marit Olsen's killer is the same person who killed the other two? The method was completely different, I understand.'

Harry smiled. Amused by Katrine's attempt to hide the fact that she had scrutinised every detail in the papers. 'No, Katrine, I'm not sure. But I can hear you've drawn the same conclusion as I have.'

'Course. We were soulmates, remember?'

She laughed, and at a stroke she was Katrine again, and not the skeleton of the brilliant, eccentric detective he had only just got to know before everything crumbled. Harry felt, to his surprise, a lump in his throat. Sodding jet lag.

'Can you help me, do you think?'

'To find something Kripos have spent two months not finding? With an outdated computer in the Hobbies Room of a mental institution? I don't even know why you're asking me. There are folk at Police HQ who are a lot more computer-savvy than me.'

'I know, but I have something they don't. And cannot give them.'

'The password to the underground.'

She fixed him with an uncomprehending stare. Harry checked no one was within earshot.

'When I was working for the Security Service, POT, on the Redbreast case, I gained access to the search engine they were using to trace terrorists. They use secret back doors on the Net like MILNET, the American military Internet, made before they released the Net for commercial purposes through ARPANET in the eighties. ARPANET became, as you know, the Internet, but the back doors are still there. The search engines use Trojan Horses that update the passwords, codes and upgrades at the first entry point. Plane ticket bookings, hotel reservations, road tolls, Internet banking, these engines can see the lot.'

'I'd heard rumours of the search engines, but I honestly thought they were non-existent,' Katrine said.

'They do exist. They were set up in 1984. The Orwellian nightmare come true. And best of all, my password is still valid. I checked it.'

'So what do you need me for? You can do this yourself, can't you.'

'Only POT is allowed to use the system, and only in emergency situations. Like Google, your searches can be traced back to the user. If it's discovered that I or anyone else at Police HQ have been using the search engines, we risk a prison sentence. But if the search were traced and led back to a communal computer in a psychiatric hospital . . .'

Katrine Bratt laughed. Her other laugh, the evil witch variety. 'I'm beginning to see. Katrine Bratt, the brilliant detective, is not my strongest qualification here, but . . .' She threw up her hands. 'Katrine Bratt the patient is. Because she, being of unsound mind, cannot be prosecuted.'

'Correct,' Harry smiled. 'And you're one of the few people I can trust to keep your mouth shut. And if you're not a genius, you're definitely smarter than the average detective.'

'Three smashed nicotine-stained fingers up your tiny little arsehole.'

'No one can find out what we're up to. But I promise you we're the Blues Brothers here.'

'On a mission from God?' she quoted.

'I've written the password on the back of the SIM card inside the dongle.'

'What makes you think I know how to use the search engines?'

'It's like googling. Even I worked that out when I was at POT.' He gave a wry smile. 'After all, the engines were created for the police.'

She released a deep sigh.

'Thank you,' Harry said.

'I didn't *say* anything.'

'When can you have something for me, do you reckon?'

'Fuck you!' She banged the table with her hand. Harry noticed a nurse glance in their direction. Harry held Katrine's wild stare. Waited.

'I don't know,' she whispered. 'I don't think I should be sitting in the Hobbies Room using illegal search engines in broad daylight, if I can put it like that.'

Harry got up. 'OK, I'll contact you in three days.'

'Haven't you forgotten something?'

'What?'

'To tell me what's in it for me?'

'Well,' Harry said, buttoning up his coat, 'now I know what you want.'

'What I want . . .' The surprise on her face gave way to amazement as the meaning dawned on her, and she shouted after Harry, who was already on his way to the door: 'You cheeky bastard! And presumptuous with it!'

Harry got into the taxi, said 'Airport', removed his mobile phone and saw three missed calls from one of the only two numbers he had in his contacts. Good, that meant they had something.

He called back.

'Lake Lyseren,' Kaja said. 'Rope-making business there. Closed down fifteen years ago. The County Officer responsible for Ytre Enebakk can show us the place this afternoon. He had a couple of persistant criminals in the area, but small beer: break-ins and car theft. Plus one who had done time for beating up his wife. He's sent us a list of men, though, and I'm going to run a check with Criminal Records right now.'

'Good. Pick me up from Gardemoen on the way to Lyseren.'

'It's not on the way.'

'You're right. Pick me up anyway.'

19

The White Bride

DESPITE THE SLOW SPEED, BJØRN HOLM'S VOLVO AMAZON was rolling and pitching on the narrow road that snaked between Østfold's meadows and fields.

Harry was asleep on the back seat.

'So no sex offenders around Lake Lyseren,' Bjørn said.

'None that have been caught,' Kaja corrected. 'Didn't you see the survey in *VG*? One in twenty say they have committed what might be termed sexual abuse.'

'Do people really answer that sort of questionnaire honestly? If I'd pushed a girl too far I think my brain would've goddam rationalised it away afterwards.'

'Is that what you did?'

'Me?' Bjørn swung out and overtook a tractor. 'Nope. I'm one of the nineteen. Ytre Enebakk. Christ, what's the name of that comic who hails from these parts? The bumpkin with the cracked glasses and moped. What's his face from Ytre Enebakk. Hilarious parody.'

Kaja shrugged. Bjørn looked into the mirror, but found himself looking down Harry's open mouth.

The County Officer for Ytre Enebakk was standing by the treatment plant on the Vøyentangen peninisula waiting for them as arranged. They parked, he introduced himself as Skai – the Norwegian name for the synthetic leather that Bjørn Holm seemed to hold in such high regard – and they accompanied him to a jetty where a dozen boats bobbed up and down in the calm waters.

'Early to have boats in the lake, isn't it?' Kaja said.

'There hasn't been any ice this year, won't be either,' the officer said. 'First time since I was born.'

They stepped into a broad, flat-bottomed boat, Bjørn with greater caution than the others.

'It's green here,' Kaja said as the officer pushed off from the jetty with a pole.

'Yes,' he said, peering down into the water and pulling the cord to start the engine. 'The ropery is over there, on the deep side. There's a path, but the terrain is so steep that it's best to go by boat.' He flicked the handle on the side of the engine forwards. A bird of indeterminate species took off from a tree inside the bare forest and shrieked a warning.

'I hate the sea,' Bjørn said to Harry, who could just hear his colleague above the hacking sound of the two-stroke outboard motor. They slipped through the grey afternoon light in a channel between the two-metre-high rushes. Crept past a pile of twigs that Harry assumed must have been a beaver's nest and out through an avenue of mangrove-like trees.

'This is a lake,' Harry said. 'Not the sea.'

'Same shit,' Bjørn said, shifting closer to the middle of the seat. 'Give me inland, cow muck and rocky mountains.'

The channel widened and there it lay in front of them: Lake Lyseren. They chugged past islands and islets from which winter-abandoned cabins with black windows seemed to be staring at them through wary eyes.

'Basic cabins,' the officer said. 'Here you're free from the stress down on the gold coast where you have to compete with your neighbour for the biggest boat or the most attractive cabin extension.' He spat into the water.

'What's the name of that TV comic from Ytre Enebakk?' Bjørn shouted over the drone of the motor. 'Cracked glasses and moped.'

The officer sent Holm a blank look and shook his head slowly.

'The ropery,' he said.

In front of the bow, right down by the lake, Harry saw an old wooden building, oblong in shape, standing alone at the foot of a steep slope, dense forest on both sides. Beside the building, steel rails ran down the mountainside and disappeared into the black water. The red paint was peeling off the walls with gaping spaces for windows and doors. Harry squinted. In the fading light it looked as if there was a person in white standing at a window staring at them.

'Jeez, the ultimate haunted house,' Bjørn laughed.

'That's what they say,' said County Officer Skai, cutting the engine.

In the sudden silence they could hear the echo of Bjørn's laughter from the other side and a lone sheep bell reaching them from far across the lake.

Kaja took the rope, jumped onto the shore and, being of a nautical bent herself, tied a half-hitch around a rotten green pole protruding between the water lilies.

The others got out of the boat, onto the huge rocks serving as a wharf. Then they entered through the doorway and found themselves in a deserted narrow, rectangular room smelling of tar and urine. It hadn't been so easy to discern from the outside because the extremities of the building merged into the dense forest, but while the room was barely two metres across it must have been more than sixty metres from end to end.

'They stood at opposite ends of the building and twined the rope,' Kaja explained before Harry could ask.

In one corner lay three empty bottles and signs of attempts to light a fire. On the facing wall, a net hung in front of a couple of loose boards.

'No one wanted to take over after Simonsen,' Skai said, looking around. 'It's been empty ever since.'

'What are the rails at the side of the building for?' Harry asked.

'Two things. To raise and lower the boat he used to collect timber. And to hold the sticks under water while they soaked. He tied the sticks to the iron carriage, which must be up in the boathouse. Then he cranked the carriage down under the water and wound it back up after a few weeks when the wood was ready. Practical fellow, Simonsen.'

They all gave a start at the sudden noise from the forest outside.

'Sheep,' the officer said. 'Or deer.'

They followed him up a narrow wooden staircase to the first floor. An enormously long table stood in the centre of the room. The margins of the room were enshrouded in darkness. The wind blew in through the windows – with borders of jagged glass set in the frames – making a low whistling sound, and it caused the woman's bridal veil to flap. She stood looking out over the lake. Beneath the head and torso was the skeleton: a black iron stand on wheels.

'Simonsen used her as a scarecrow,' Skai said, nodding towards the shop dummy.

'Pretty creepy,' Kaja said, taking up a position beside Skai and shivering inside her coat.

He cast a sideways glance, plus a crooked smile. 'The kids round here were terrified of her. The adults said that at full moon she walked around the district chasing the man who had jilted her on her wedding day. And you could hear the rusty wheels as she approached. I grew up right behind here, in Haga, you see.'

'Did you?' asked Kaja, and Harry smothered a grin.

'Yes,' said Skai. 'By the way, this was the only woman known to be in Simonsen's life. He was a bit of a recluse. But he could certainly make rope.'

Behind them Bjørn Holm took down a coil of rope hanging from a nail.

'Did I say you could touch anything?' the officer said without turning.

Bjørn hurriedly put back the rope.

'OK, boss,' Harry said, sending Skai a closed smile. 'Can we touch anything?'

The officer weighed Harry up. 'You still haven't told me what kind of case this is.'

'It's confidential,' Harry said. 'Sorry. Fraud Squad. You know.'

'That right? If you're the Harry Hole I think you are, you used to work on murders.'

'Well,' Harry said, 'now it's insider trading, tax evasion and fraud. One moves upwards in life.'

Officer Skai pinched an eye shut. A bird shrieked.

'Of course, you're right, Skai,' Kaja said with a sigh. 'But I'm the person who has to deal with the red tape for the search warrant from the police solicitor. As you know, we're understaffed and it would save me a lot of time if we could just ...' She smiled with her tiny, pointed teeth and gestured towards the coil of rope.

Skai looked at her. Rocked to and fro on his rubber heels a couple of times. Then he nodded.

'I'll wait in the boat,' he said.

Bjørn set to work immediately. He placed the coil on the long table, opened the little rucksack he had with him, switched on a torch attached to a cord with a fish hook on the end and secured it into position between two boards in the ceiling. He took out his laptop and a portable microscope shaped like a hammer, plugged the microscope into the USB port on the laptop, checked it was transmitting pictures to the screen and clicked on an image he had transferred to the laptop before they departed.

Harry stood beside the bride and gazed down at the lake. In the boat he could see the glow of a cigarette. He eyed the rails that went down into the water. The deep end. Harry had never liked swimming in fresh water, especially after the time he and Øystein had skipped school, gone to Lake Hauktjern in Østmarka and jumped off the Devil's Tip, which people said was twelve metres high. And Harry – seconds before he hit the water – had seen a viper gliding through the depths beneath him. Then he was enveloped by the freezing cold, bottle-green water and in his panic he swallowed half the lake and was sure he would never see daylight or breathe air again.

Harry smelt the fragrance that told him Kaja was standing behind him.

'Bingo,' he heard Bjørn Holm whisper.

Harry turned. 'Same type of rope?'

'No doubt about it,' Bjørn said, holding the microscope against the rope end and pressing a key for high-resolution images. 'Linden and elm. Same thickness and length of fibre. But the *bingo* is reserved for the recently sliced rope end.'

'What?'

Bjørn Holm pointed to the screen. 'The photo on the left is the one I brought with me. It shows the rope from Frogner Lido, magnified twenty-five times. And on this rope I have a perfect ...'

Harry closed his eyes so as to relish to the full the word he knew was coming.

'. . . match.'

He kept his eyes closed. The rope Marit Olsen was hung with had not only been made here, it had been cut from the rope they had before them. And it was a recent cut. Not so long ago he had been standing where they were standing. Harry sniffed the air.

An all-embracing darkness had fallen. Harry could hardly make out anything white in the window as they left.

Kaja sat at the front of the boat with him. She had to lean close so that he could hear her over the drone of the motor.

'The person who collected the rope must have known his way around this area. And there can't be many links in the chain between that person and the killer . . .'

'I don't think there are any links at all,' Harry said. 'The cut was recent. And there are not many reasons for rope to change hands.'

'Local knowledge, lives nearby or has a cabin here,' Kaja mused aloud. 'Or he grew up here.'

'But why come all the way to a disused ropery to get a few metres of rope?' Harry asked. 'How much does a long rope cost in a shop? A couple of hundred kroner?'

'Perhaps he happened to be in the vicinity and knew the rope was there.'

'OK, but *in the vicinity* would mean he must have been staying in one of the nearby cabins. For everyone else it's a fair old boat trip. Are you making . . . ?'

'Yes, I'm making a list of the closest neighbours. By the way, I tracked down the volcano expert you asked for. A nerd up at the Geological Institute. Felix Røst. He seems to do a bit of volcano-spotting. Travelling all over the world to look at volcanoes and eruptions and that sort of thing.'

'Did you talk to him?'

'Just his sister, who lives with him. She asked me to email or text. He doesn't communicate in any other way, she said. Anyway, he was out playing chess. I sent him the stones and the information.'

They advanced at a snail's pace through the shallow channel to the pontoon. Bjørn held up the torch as a lantern to light their way through the hazy mist drifting across the water. The officer cut the motor.

'Look!' whispered Kaja, leaning even closer to Harry. He could smell her scent as he followed her index finger. From the rushes behind the jetty emerged a large, lone, white swan through the veil of mist into the torchlight.

'Isn't it just . . . beautiful,' she whispered, entranced, then laughed and fleetingly squeezed his hand.

Skai accompanied them to the treatment plant. Then they got into the Volvo Amazon and were about to set off when Bjørn feverishly wound down the window and shouted to the officer: 'FRITJOF!'

Skai stopped and turned slowly. The light from a street lamp fell onto his heavy, expressionless face.

'The funny guy on TV,' Bjørn shouted. 'Fritjof from Ytre Enebakk.'

'Fritjof?' Skai said and spat. 'Never heard of him.'

As the Amazon turned onto the E-road by the incinerator in Grønmo twenty-five minutes later, Harry had made a decision.

'We must leak this information to Kripos,' he said.

'What?!' Bjørn and Kaja said in unison.

'I'll talk to Beate, then she'll pass the message on so that it looks like her people at Krimteknisk have discovered the business with the rope and not us.'

'Why?' Kaja asked.

'If the killer lives in the Lyseren area, there'll have to be a door-to-door search. We don't have the means or the manpower for that.'

Bjørn Holm smacked the steering wheel.

'I know,' Harry said. 'But the most important thing is that he's caught, not who catches him.'

They drove on in silence with the false ring of the words hanging in the air.

20

Øystein

No electricity. Harry stood in the dark hall flipping the light switch on and off. Did the same in the sitting room.

Then he sat down in the wing chair staring into the black void.

After he had sat there for a while, his mobile rang.

'Hole.'

'Felix Røst.'

'Mm?' Harry said. The voice sounded as if it belonged to a slender, petite woman.

'Frida Larsen, his sister. He asked me to ring and say that the stones you found are mafic, basalt lava. Alright?'

'Just a minute. What does that mean? Mafic?'

'It's hot lava, over a thousand degrees C, low viscosity, which thins it and allows it to spread over a wide distance on eruption.'

'Could it have come from Oslo?'

'No.'

'Why not? Oslo is built on lava.'

'Old lava. This lava is recent.'

'How recent?'

He heard her put her hand over the phone and speak. But he couldn't hear any other voices. She must have received an answer though, because soon afterwards she was back.

'He says anything from five to fifty years. But if you were thinking of establishing which volcano it comes from, you've got quite a job on your hands. There are over one and a half thousand active volcanoes in the world. And that's just the ones we know about. If there are any other queries, Felix can be contacted by email. Your assistant has got the address.'

'But . . .'

She had already rung off.

He considered calling back, but changed his mind and punched in another number.

'Oslotaxi.'

'Hi, Øystein, this is Harry H.'

'You're kidding. Harry H is dead.'

'Not quite.'

'OK, then I must be dead.'

'Feel like driving me from Sofies gate to my childhood home?'

'No, but I'll do it anyway. Just have to do this trip.' Øystein's laugh morphed into a cough. 'Harry H! Bloody hell . . . Call you when I'm there.'

Harry rang off, went into the bedroom, packed a bag in the light from the street lamp outside the window and chose a couple of CDs from the sitting room in the light from his mobile. Carton of smokes, handcuffs, service pistol.

He sat in the wing chair, making use of the dark to repeat the revolver exercise. Started the stopwatch on his wrist, flicked out the cylinder of his Smith & Wesson, emptied and loaded. Four cartridges out, four in, without a speed-loader, just nimble fingers. Flicked the cylinder back in so that the first cartridge was first in line. Stop. Nine sixty-six. Almost three seconds over the record. He opened the cylinder. He had messed up. The first chamber ready to fire was one of the two empty ones. He was dead. He repeated the exercise. Nine fifty. And dead again. When Øystein rang, after twenty minutes, he was down to eight seconds and had died six times.

'Coming,' Harry said.

He walked into the kitchen. Looked at the cupboard under the sink. Hesitated. Then he took down the photos of Rakel and Oleg and put them in his inside pocket.

* * *

120

'Hong Kong?' sniffed Øystein Eikeland. He turned his bloated alky face with huge hooter and sad drooping moustache to Harry in the seat next to him. 'What the hell d'you do there?'

'You know me,' Harry said as Øystein stopped on red outside the Radisson SAS Hotel.

'I bloody do not,' Øystein said, sprinkling tobacco into his roll-up. 'How would I?'

'Well, we grew up together. Do you remember?'

'So? You were already a sodding enigma then, Harry.'

The rear door was torn open and a man wearing a coat got in. 'Airport express, main station. Quick.'

'Taxi's taken,' Øystein said without turning.

'Nonsense, the sign on the roof's lit.'

'Hong Kong sounds groovy. Why d'you come home actually?'

'I beg your pardon,' said the man on the back seat.

Øystein poked the cigarette between his lips and lit up. 'Tresko rang to invite me to a get-together tonight.'

'Tresko hasn't got any friends,' Harry said.

'He hasn't, has he. So I asked him, "Who are your friends then?" "*You*", he said, and asked me, "And yours, Øystein?" "*You*," I answered. "So it's just us two." We'd forgotten all about you, Harry. That's what happens when you go to . . .' He funnelled his lips and, in a staccato voice, said, 'Hong Kong!'

'Hey!' came a shout from the back seat. 'If you've finished, perhaps we might . . .'

The lights changed to green, and Øystein accelerated away.

'Are you coming then? It's at Tresko's place.'

'Stinks of toe-fart there, Øystein.'

'He's got a full fridge.'

'Sorry, I'm not in a party mood.'

'Party mood?' Øystein snorted, smacking the wheel with his hand. 'You don't know what a party mood is, Harry. You always backed off parties. Do you remember? We'd bought some beers, intending to go to some fancy address in Nordstrand with loads of women. And you suggested you, me and Tresko went to the bunkers instead and drank on our own.'

'Hey, this isn't the way to the airport express!' came a whine from the back seat.

Øystein braked for red again, tossed his wispy shoulder-length hair to the side and addressed the back seat. 'And that was where we ended up. Got rat-arsed and that fella started singing "No Surrender" until Tresko chucked empty bottles at him.'

'Honest to God!' the man sobbed, tapping his forefinger on the glass of a TAG Heuer watch. 'I just *have* to catch the last plane to Stockholm.'

'The bunkers are great,' Harry said. 'Best view in Oslo.'

'Yep,' Øystein said. 'If the Allies had attacked there, the Germans would've shot them to bits.'

'Right,' Harry grinned.

'You know, we had a standing agreement, him and me and Tresko,' Øystein said, but the suit was now desperately scanning the rain for vacant taxis. 'If the sodding Allies come, we'll bloody shoot the meat off their carcasses. Like this.' Øystein pointed an imaginary machine gun at the suit and fired a salvo. The suit stared in horror at the crazy taxi driver whose chattering noises were causing small, foam-white drops of spit to land on his dark, freshly ironed suit trousers. With a little gasp he managed to open the car door and stumble out into the rain.

Øystein burst into coarse, hearty laughter.

'You were missing home,' Øystein said. 'You wanted to dance with Killer Queen at Ekeberg restaurant again.'

Harry chuckled and shook his head. In the wing mirror he saw the man charging madly towards the National Theatre station. 'It's my father. He's ill. He hasn't got long left.'

'Oh shit.' Øystein pressed the accelerator again. 'Good man, too.'

'Thank you. Thought you would want to know.'

'Course I bloody do. Have to tell my folks.'

'So, here we are,' Øystein said, parking outside the garage and the tiny, yellow timber house in Oppsal.

'Yup,' Harry said.

Øystein inhaled so hard the cigarette seemed to be catching fire, held the smoke down in his lungs and let it out again with a long, gurgling wheeze. Then he tilted his head slightly and flicked the ash into the ashtray. Harry experienced a sweet pain in his heart. How many times had he seen Øystein do exactly that, seen him lean to the side as though the cigarette were so heavy that he would lose balance. Head tilted. The ash on the ground in a smokers' shed at school, in an empty beer bottle at a party they had gatecrashed, on cold, damp concrete in a bunker.

'Life's bloody unfair,' Øystein said. 'Your father was sober, went walking on Sundays and worked as a teacher. While my father drank, worked at the Kadok factory, where everyone got asthma and weird rashes, and didn't move a millimetre once he was ensconced on the sofa at home. And the guy's as fit as a fuckin' fiddle.'

Harry remembered the Kadok factory. Kodak backwards. The owner, from Sunnmøre, had read that Eastman had called his camera factory Kodak because it was a name that could be remembered and pronounced all over the world. But Kadok was forgotten and it shut down several years ago.

'All things pass,' Harry said.

Øystein nodded as though he had been following his train of thought.

'Ring if you need anything, Harry.'

'Yep.'

Harry waited until he heard the wheels crunching on the gravel behind him and the car was gone before he unlocked the door and entered. He switched on the light and stood still as the door fell to and clicked shut. The smell, the silence, the light falling on the coat cupboard, everything spoke to him, it was like sinking into a pool of memories. They embraced him, warmed him, made his throat constrict. He removed his coat and kicked off his shoes. Then he started to walk. From room to room. From year to year. From Mum and Dad to Sis, and then to himself. The boy's room. The Clash poster, the one where the guitar is about to be smashed on the floor. He lay on his bed and breathed in the smell of the mattress. And then came the tears.

21

Snow White

IT WAS TWO MINUTES TO EIGHT IN THE EVENING WHEN Mikael Bellman was walking up Karl Johans gate, one of the world's more modest parades. He was in the middle of the kingdom of Norway, at the mid-point of the axis. To the left, the university and knowledge; to the right, the National Theatre and culture. Behind him, in the Palace Gardens, the Royal Palace situated upon high. And right in front of him: power. Three hundred paces later, at exactly eight o'clock, he mounted the stone steps to the main entrance of Stortinget. The parliament building, like most of Oslo, was not particularly big or impressive. And security was minimal. There were only two lions carved from Grorud granite standing on either side of the slope which led to the entrance.

Bellman went up to the door, which opened noiselessly before he had a chance to push. He arrived at reception and stood looking around. A security guard appeared in front of him with a friendly but firm nod towards a Gilardoni X-ray machine. Ten seconds later it had revealed that Mikael Bellman was unarmed, there was metal in his belt, but that was all.

Rasmus Olsen was waiting for him, leaning against the reception desk. Marit Olsen's thin widower shook hands with Bellman and walked ahead as he automatically switched on his guide voice.

'Stortinget, three hundred and eighty employees, a hundred and sixty-nine MPs. Built in 1866, designed by Emil Victor Langlet. A Swede, by the way. This is the hall known as Trappehallen. The stone mosaics are called *Society*, Else Hagen, 1950. The king's portrait was painted . . .'

They emerged into Vandrehallen, which Mikael recognised from the TV. A couple of faces, neither familiar, flitted past. Rasmus explained to him that there had just been a committee meeting, but Bellman was not listening. He was thinking that these were the corridors of power. He was disappointed. Fine to have all the gold and red, but where was the magnificence, the stateliness, that was supposed to instil awe at the feet of those who ruled? This damned humble sobriety; it was like a weakness, of which this tiny and, not so long ago, poor democracy in Northern Europe could not rid itself. Yet he had returned. If he had not been able to reach the top where he had tried first, among the wolves of Europol, he would certainly succeed here, in competition with midgets and second-raters.

'This entire room was Reichskommissar Terboven's office during the war. No one has such a large office nowadays.'

'What was your marriage like?'

'I beg your pardon?'

'You and Marit. Did you row?'

'Er . . . no.' Rasmus Olsen looked shaken, and he started walking faster. As if to leave the policeman behind, or at least to move beyond the hearing range of others. It was only when they were sitting behind the closed office door in the group secretariat that he released his trembling breath. 'Of course we had our ups and downs. Are you married, Bellman?'

Mikael Bellman nodded.

'Then you know what I mean.'

'Was she unfaithful?'

'No. I think I can count that one out.'

Since she was so fat? Bellman felt like asking, but he dropped it. He had what he was after. The hesitation, the twitch at the corner of his eye, the almost imperceptible contraction of the pupil.

'And you, Olsen, have you been unfaithful?'

Same reaction. Plus a certain flush to the forehead under the receding hairline. The answer was brief and resolute. 'No, in fact I haven't.'

Bellman angled his head. He didn't suspect Rasmus Olsen. So why torment the man with this type of question? The answer was as simple as it was exasperating. Because he had no one else to question, no other leads to follow. He was merely taking out his frustration on this poor man.

'What about you?'

'What about me?' Bellman, said, stifling a yawn.

'Are you unfaithful?'

'My wife is too beautiful,' Bellman smiled. 'Furthermore, we have two children. You and your wife were childless, and that encourages a little more . . . fun. I was talking to a source who said that you and your wife were having problems a while ago.'

'I assume that's the next-door neighbour. Marit chatted quite a bit with her, yes. There was a jealous patch some months ago. I had recruited a young girl to the party on a shop-steward course. That was how I met Marit, so she . . .'

Rasmus Olsen's voice disintegrated, and Bellman saw that tears were welling up in his eyes.

'It was nothing. But Marit went to the mountains for a couple of days to think things over. Afterwards everything was fine again.'

Bellman's phone rang. He took it out, saw the name on the display and answered with a curt 'yes'. And felt his pulse and fury increase as he listened to the voice.

'Rope?' he repeated. 'Lyseren? That's . . . Ytre Enebakk? Thanks.'

He stuffed the phone in his coat pocket. 'I have to be off, Olsen. Thank you for your time.'

On his way out Bellman briefly stopped and looked around the room Terboven, the German Nazi, had occupied.

It was one o'clock in the morning and Harry was sitting in the living room listening to Martha Wainwright singing 'Far Away', '. . . Whatever remains is yet to be found'.

He was exhausted. In front of him on the coffee table was his mobile phone, the lighter and the silver foil containing the brown clump. He hadn't touched it. But he had to sleep soon, find a rhythm, have a break. In his hand he was holding a photo of Rakel. Blue dress. He closed his eyes. Smelt her scent. Heard her voice. 'Look!' Her hand exerted a light squeeze. The water around them was black and deep, and she floated, white, soundless, weightless on the surface. The wind raised her veil and showed the white feathers beneath. Her long, slim neck formed a question mark. Where? She stepped ashore, a black iron skeleton with chafing, wailing wheels. She entered the house and vanished from sight. And reappeared on the first floor. She had a noose around her neck and there was a man by her side wearing a black suit with a white flower on his lapel. In front, with his back to them, stood a priest in a white cloak. He was reading slowly. Then he turned. His face and hands were white. Made of snow.

Harry awoke with a start.

Blinked in the dark. Sound. But not Martha Wainwright. Harry grabbed the luminous, vibrating phone on the coffee table.

'Yes,' he said with a voice like sludge.

'I've got it.'

He sat up. 'You've got what?'

'The link. And there aren't three dead. There are four.'

22

Search Engine

'First of all, I tried the three names you gave me,' said Katrine Bratt. 'Borgny Stem-Myhre, Charlotte Lolles and Marit Olsen. But the search didn't produce anything sensible. So I put in all the missing persons in Norway over the last twelve months as well. And then I had something to work with.'

'Wait,' Harry said. He was wide awake now. 'Where the hell did you get the missing persons from?'

'Intranet at Missing Persons Unit, Oslo Police District. What did you think?'

Harry groaned, and Katrine went on.

'There was one name that in fact linked the other three. Are you ready?'

'Well . . .'

'The missing woman is called Adele Vetlesen, twenty-three years old, living in Drammen. She was reported missing by her partner in November. A connection appeared on the NSB ticketing system. On the 7th of November Adele Vetlesen booked a train ticket online from Drammen to Ustaoset. The same day Borgny Stem-Myhre bought a train ticket from Kongsberg to the same place.'

'Ustaoset's not exactly the centre of the universe,' Harry said.

'It's not a place, it's a chunk of mountain. Where Bergen families have built their mountain cabins with old money and the Tourist Association has built cabins on the peaks, so that Norwegians can preserve Amundsen and Nansen's heritage and trudge from cabin to cabin with skis on their feet, twenty-five kilos on their backs and a taste of mortal fear in the hinterland of the mind. Adds spice to life, you know.'

'Sounds like you've been there.'

'My ex-husband's family has a cabin in the mountains. They're so rich and revered that they have neither electricity nor running water. Only social climbers have a sauna and a jacuzzi.'

'The other connections?'

'There wasn't a train ticket in the name of Marit Olsen. However, a payment was registered on the cash dispenser in the restaurant car on the corresponding train the day before. At 14.13. According to the railway timetable that would be somewhere between Ål and Geilo, in other words before Ustaoset.'

'Less convincing,' Harry said. 'The train goes right through to Bergen. Perhaps she was going there.'

'Do you think . . . ?' Katrine Bratt started, then faltered, waited and went on in hushed tones. 'You think I'm stupid? The hotel at Ustaoset booked an overnight stay in a double room for one Rasmus Olsen who, according to the Civil Registration System, is resident at the same address as Marit Olsen. So I assumed that—'

'Yes, that's her husband. Why are you whispering?'

'Because the night porter just walked past, OK? Listen, we've placed two murder victims and one missing person in Ustaoset on the same day. What do you reckon?'

'Well, it's a significant coincidence, but we can't exclude the possibility that it's pure chance.'

'Agreed. So here's the rest. I searched for Charlotte Lolles plus Ustaoset, but didn't get a hit. So I concentrated on the date to see where Charlotte Lolles might have been when the other three were in Ustaoset. Two days before, Charlotte had paid for diesel at a petrol station outside Hønefoss.'

'That's a long way from Ustaoset.'

'But it's in the right direction from Oslo. I tried to find a car registered in her name or a possible partner's. If they have an AutoPASS and have driven through several toll stations you can follow their movements.'

'Mm.'

'The problem is that she had neither a car nor a live-in partner, not officially anyway.'

'She had a boyfriend.'

'It's possible. But the search engine found a car in a Europark garage in Geilo, paid for by an Iska Peller.'

'That's just a few kilometres away. But who's . . . er, Iska Peller?'

'According to the credit card info she's a resident of Bristol, Sydney, Australia. The point is that she scores high on a relational search with Charlotte Lolles.'

'Relational search?'

'It works like this, OK. Based on the last few years, names come up for people paying with a card at the same restaurant at the same time, which suggests that they have eaten together and split the bill. Or for people who are members of the same gym with matching enrolment dates or have plane seats next to each other more than once. You get the picture.'

'I get the picture,' Harry repeated, copying her Bergensian intonation. 'And I'm sure you've checked out the make of car and whether it uses—'

'Yes, I have, and it uses diesel,' Katrine answered sharply. 'Do you want to hear the rest or not?'

'By all means.'

'You can't pre-book beds in these self-service Tourist Association cabins. If all the beds are taken when you arrive, you just have to doss down on the floor, on a mattress or in a sleeping bag with your own mat. It only costs a hundred and seventy a night, and you can either put cash into a box at the cabin, or leave an envelope with an authorisation to charge your account.'

'In other words you can't see who has been in which cabins when?'

'Not if they pay cash. But if they've left an authorisation, afterwards there would be a transaction on their account between them and the Tourist Association. Mentioning the cabin used and the date the payment was for.'

'I seem to remember it's a pain searching through bank transactions.'

'Not if the engine is given the right criteria by a sharp human brain.'

'Which is the case, I take it?'

'That's the general idea. Iska Peller's account was charged for two beds at four of the Tourist Association cabins on the 20th of November, each a day's march from the next.'

'A four-day skiing trip.'

'Yes. And they stayed at the last one, the Håvass cabin, on the 7th of November. It's only half a day's walk from Ustaoset.'

'Interesting.'

'What's really interesting is that there are two other accounts that were charged for overnight stays at the Håvass cabin on the 7th of November. Guess whose?'

'Well, it'll hardly be Marit Olsen's or Borgny Stem-Myhre's since I assume Kripos would have found out that two of the murder victims had recently stayed at the same place the same night. So it must be the missing girl's. What was her name?'

'Adele Vetlesen. And you're spot on. She paid for two people, but there's no way of knowing who the other person was.'

'Who's the other person who paid with an authorisation slip?'

'Not so interesting. From Stavanger.'

Nevertheless Harry picked up a pen and noted the name and address of the individual concerned and also of Iska Peller in Sydney. 'Sounds like you rate search engines,' he said.

'Yep,' she said. 'It's like flying an old bomber. Bit rusty and slow to get going, but when you're in the air . . . my goodness. What do you think of the results?'

Harry pondered.

'What you've done', he said, 'is to locate one missing woman and a woman who presumably has nothing to do with the case at the same place at the same time. In itself, nothing to shout about. But you've made it more likely that one of the murder victims – Charlotte Lolles – was with her. And you've located two of the murder victims – Borgny Stem-Myhre and Marit Olsen – in the immediate vicinity of Ustaoset. So . . .'

'So?'

'So, my congratulations. You've kept your part of the bargain. Now, as for mine . . .'

'Save your breath and wipe that grin off your face. I didn't mean it. I'm of unsound mind, didn't you realise?'

She smacked down the receiver.

23

Passenger

SHE WAS ALONE ON THE BUS. STINE RESTED HER FOREHEAD against the window so that she wouldn't see her reflection. Stared out into the deserted, pitch-black bus station. Hoping someone would come. Hoping no one would come.

He had been sitting by a window in Krabbe with a beer in front of him staring at her, motionless. Woollen hat, blond hair and those wild blue eyes. His eyes laughed, penetrated, implored, called her name. In the end she had told Mathilde that she wanted to go home. But Mathilde had just started a conversation with an American oil guy and wanted to stay a bit longer. So Stine had grabbed her coat, run from Krabbe to the bus station and got on a bus to Våland.

She looked at the red numbers on the digital clock above the driver. Hoping the doors would shut and the bus would start moving. One minute left.

She didn't raise her eyes, not even when she heard the running foot-steps, heard the breathless voice request a ticket from the driver at the front, nor when he sat down on the seat beside her.

'Hey, Stine,' he said. 'I think you're avoiding me.'

'Oh, hi, Elias,' she said without shifting her gaze from the rain-wet tarmac. Why had she sat so far back in the bus, so far from the driver?

'You shouldn't be out alone on a night like this, you know.'

'Shouldn't I?' she mumbled, hoping someone would come, anyone.

'Don't you read the newspapers? Those two girls in Oslo. And now, the other day, that MP. What was her name again?'

'No idea,' Stine lied, feeling her heart rate gallop.

'Marit Olsen,' Elias said. 'Socialist Party. The other two were Borgny and Charlotte. Sure you don't recognise the names, Stine?'

'I don't read newspapers,' Stine said. Someone had to come soon.

'Great girls, all three of them,' he said.

'Course, you knew them, didn't you?' Stine regretted the sarcastic tone immediately. It was fear.

'Not well though,' Elias said. 'But the first impression was good. I'm – as you know – the kind who attaches a lot of importance to first impressions.'

She stared at the hand he cautiously placed on her knee.

'You . . .' she said, and even in that one syllable she could hear herself begging.

'Yes, Stine?'

She looked up at him. His face was as open as a child's, his eyes genuinely curious. She wanted to scream, jump up, when she heard the steps and voice up by the driver. A passenger. A man. He came to the back of the bus. Stine tried to catch his eye, to make him understand, but the brim of his hat covered the upper half of his face, and he was busy checking his change and putting the ticket in his wallet. Her breathing was lighter when he took a seat right behind them.

'It's incredible that the police haven't discovered the connection between them,' Elias said. 'It shouldn't be so difficult. They must know that all three women liked to go cross-country skiing in the mountains. They stayed at the cabin in Håvass on the same night. Do you think I should tell them?'

'Maybe,' Stine whispered. If she was quick perhaps she could squeeze past Elias and jump off the bus. But she had hardly articulated the thought in her mind before the hydraulics hissed, the doors slid shut and the bus set off. She closed her eyes.

'I just don't want to be involved. I hope you can understand that, Stine.'

She nodded slowly, her eyes still closed.

'Good. Then I can tell you about someone else who was there. Someone I'm sure you know.'

PART THREE

24

Stavanger

'IT SMELLS OF . . .' KAJA SAID.

'Shit,' Harry said. 'Cow variety. Welcome to the district of Jæren.'

The dawn light leaked from the clouds sweeping across the spring-green fields. From behind stone walls cows stared mutely at their taxi. They were on their way from Sola Airport to Stavanger city centre.

Harry leaned forward between the front seats. 'Could you put your foot down, driver?' He held up his ID card. The driver beamed, gave it some gas, and they accelerated onto the motorway.

'Are you afraid we're too late?' Kaja asked as Harry fell back.

'Didn't answer the phone, didn't turn up for work,' Harry said, not needing to complete his reasoning.

After he had spoken to Katrine Bratt the night before, Harry had skimmed over what he had noted down. He had the names, telephone numbers and addresses of two living persons who had probably stayed in a cabin in November with the three murder victims. He had checked his watch, worked out it was early morning in Sydney and rung Iska Peller's number. She had answered and sounded very surprised when Harry broached the topic of the Håvass cabin. She hadn't been able to tell Harry much about the overnight stay because she had been stuck in a bedroom with a high temperature. Perhaps because she had been wearing wet, sweaty clothes for too long, perhaps because skiing from cabin to cabin had been a baptism of fire for an inexperienced langlaufer like herself. Or perhaps simply because flu strikes at random. At any rate, she had only just managed to drag herself to Håvass, where she had been ordered straight to bed by her companion Charlotte Lolles. There, Iska Peller had drifted in and out of dream-filled sleep as her body ached, sweated and froze in turn. Whatever had gone on between the others in the cabin, whoever they were, well, she hadn't picked up anything, as she and Charlotte had been the first to arrive. The next day she had stayed in bed until the others had left, and she and Charlotte were collected on a snow scooter by a local policeman Charlotte had managed to contact. He had driven them to his place where he had invited them to stay overnight as the only hotel was full, so he informed them. They had accepted, but that night they changed their minds and caught a late train to Geilo to stay at a hotel there. Charlotte hadn't told Iska anything in particular about the night in the Håvass cabin. An uneventful night, apparently.

Five days after the skiing trip Iska had left Oslo for Sydney, still with a temperature, and had kept in regular email contact with Charlotte but hadn't noticed anything out of the ordinary. Until she received the shocking news that her friend had been found dead behind a wrecked car on the edge of a wood by Lake Daudsjøen, just outside the urban sprawl of Oslo.

Harry had explained to Iska Peller with some care, but without beating around the bush, that they were worried about the people who had been in the cabin on the night of the 7th of November and that, after ringing off, he would call the head of Crime Squad in Sydney South Police District, Neil McCormack, whom Harry had worked for on one occasion. McCormack, he said, would require further details from her and – even though Australia was a long way from Oslo – provide police protection until further notice. Iska Peller seemed to accept this with equanimity.

Then Harry had rung the second number he had been given, the number in Stavanger. He had tried four times, but no one had answered. He knew, of course, that this did not mean anything in itself. Not everyone slept with their mobile switched on beside them. But Kaja Solness clearly did. She answered on the second ring, and when Harry said they were going to Stavanger on the first flight and that she should be on the airport express by five past six, she had uttered one word: 'OK.'

They had arrived at Oslo's Gardemoen Airport at half past six and Harry had tried the number again, without success. An hour later they had landed at Sola Airport, and Harry rang with the same result. On their way to the taxi queue, Kaja managed to contact the employer, who said that the person they were looking for had not turned up for work at the usual time. She had informed Harry, and he had gently placed his hand on the small of her back and led her firmly past the taxi queue and into a taxi in the face of loud protests, which he met with: 'Thanking you, and may you have a wonderful day, folks.'

It was exactly 8.16 when they arrived at the address, a white timber house in Våland. Harry let Kaja pay, got out and left the door open. Studied the house front, which revealed nothing. Inhaled the damp, fresh, though still mild Vestland air. Braced himself. Because he already knew. He might be mistaken, of course, but he knew with the same certainty that he knew Kaja would say 'Thank you' after being given the receipt.

'Thank you.' The car door closed.

The name was next to the middle of the three bells, by the front door.

Harry pressed the button and heard the bell ring somewhere in the house's innards.

One minute and three attempts later he pressed the bottom bell.

The old lady who opened the door smiled at them.

Harry noted that Kaja instinctively knew who should speak. 'Hello, I'm Kaja Solness. We're from the police. The floor above you isn't answering. Do you know if anyone is at home?'

'Probably. Even though it's been quiet there this morning,' the lady said. And, on seeing Harry's elevated eyebrows, hastened to add: 'You can hear everything here, and I heard people last night. Since I rent out the flat I think I ought to keep an ear open.'

'Keep an ear open?' Harry queried.

'Yes, but I don't stick . . .' The lady's cheeks flushed pink. 'There's nothing wrong, I trust? I mean, I've never had any problems at all with—'

'We don't know,' Harry said.

'The best thing to do would be to check,' Kaja said. 'So if you have a key . . .' Harry knew a variety of set phrases would be whirring around Kaja's brain now, and waited for the continuation with interest. '. . . then we would like to assist you in ensuring that everything is in order.'

Kaja Solness was a bright woman. If the house owner agreed to the proposal and they found something, the report would say they were summoned. There was no question of them having forced their way in or having ransacked the place without a warrant.

The woman hesitated.

'But you can also let yourself in after we've gone,' Kaja smiled. 'And then call the police. Or the ambulance. Or . . .'

'I think it's best if you come with me,' the woman said after a deep furrow of concern entrenched itself in her brow. 'Wait here and I'll fetch the keys.'

The flat they entered one minute later was clean, tidy and almost completely unfurnished. At once Harry recognised the silence that is so present, so oppressive, in bare flats in the morning, when the hustle and bustle of the working day is a scarcely audible noise on the outside. But there was also a smell he recognised. Glue. He spotted a pair of shoes, though no outdoor clothing.

In the kitchenette there was a large teacup in the sink, and on the shelf above tins proclaiming they contained teas of unknown origin to Harry: oolong, Anji Bai Cha. They advanced through the flat. On the sitting-room wall was a picture Harry thought was K2, the popular killing machine of a mountain in the Himalayas.

'Check that one, will you?' Harry asked, nodding to the door with a heart on it and walked to what he assumed must be the bedroom door. He took a deep breath, pressed down the handle and pushed open the door.

The bed was made. The room tidy. A window was ajar, no smell of glue, air as fresh as a child's breath. Harry heard the landlady take up a position in the doorway behind him.

'So odd,' she said. 'I heard them last night, I did. But there was only one person's steps.'

'Them?' Harry said. 'You're sure there was more than one person?'

'Yes, I heard voices.'

'How many?'

'Three, I would say.'

Harry peered into the wardrobe. 'Men? Women?'

'You can't hear absolutely everything, I'm afraid.'

Clothes. A sleeping bag and a rucksack. More clothes.

'Why would you say there were three?'

'After one left, I heard noises from up here.'

'What sort of noises?'

The landlady's cheeks flushed again. 'Banging. As if . . . well, you know.'

'But no voices?'

The landlady considered the question. 'No, no voices.'

Harry walked out of the room. And to his surprise saw that Kaja was still standing in the hall by the bathroom door. There was something about the way she was standing – as though facing a strong headwind.

'Something up?'

'Not at all,' Kaja said quickly, lightly. Too lightly.

Harry went over and stood beside her.

'What is it?' he asked in a whisper.

'I . . . just have a tiny problem with closed doors.'

'OK,' Harry said.

'That's . . . that's just how I am.'

Harry nodded. And that was when he heard the sound. The sound of allotted time, of a line running out, of seconds disappearing, a quick, hectic drumming of water that doesn't quite flow and doesn't quite drip. A tap on the other side of the door. And he knew he had not been mistaken.

'Wait here,' Harry said. He pushed open the door.

The first thing he noticed was that the smell of glue was even stronger inside.

The second was that a jacket, a pair of jeans, pants, a T-shirt, two black socks, a hat and a thin wool jumper were lying on the floor.

The third was that water was dripping in an almost continuous line from the tap into a bathtub filled so full that water was escaping down the overflow at the side.

The fourth was that the water in the bath was red, blood from what he could tell.

The fifth was that the glazed eyes above the taped mouth of the naked, corpse-white person lying at the bottom of the bath faced the side. As if trying to glimpse something in the blind spot, something he hadn't seen coming.

The sixth was that he couldn't see any indications of violence, no external injuries that would explain all the blood.

Harry cleared his throat and wondered how he could ask the land-lady in the most considerate way possible to come in and identify her lodger.

But he didn't have to; she was already at the door.

'OhmyGod!' she groaned. And then – stressing every single syllable: 'Oh my God!' And, finally, in a wailing tone invoking even greater emphasis: 'Oh my Lord God Almighty . . .'

'Is it . . . ?' Harry began.

'Yes,' the woman said with a tear-filled voice. 'That's him. That's Elias. Elias Skog.'

25

Territory

THE WOMAN HAD CLASPED HER HANDS IN FRONT OF HER mouth, and mumbled through her fingers. 'But what have you done, dear Elias? A vein?'

'I'm not sure he did anything,' Harry said, leading her from the bathroom to the front door of the flat. 'Could I ask you to ring the police station in Stavanger and tell them to send forensics officers? Tell them we have a crime scene here.'

'Crime scene?' Her eyes were large and black with shock.

'Yes, say that. Use the emergency number, 112, if you like. OK?'

'Y-yes.'

They heard the woman stomping down the stairs to her flat.

'We've got about a quarter of an hour before they get here,' Harry said. They removed their shoes, put them in the hall and walked into the bathroom in stockinged feet. Harry looked around. The sink was full of long blond hair, and on the bench a tube was squeezed flat.

'That looks like toothpaste,' Harry said, bending over the tube, trying not to touch it.

Kaja went closer. 'Superglue,' she stated. 'Strongest there is.'

'That's the stuff you shouldn't get on your fingers, isn't it?'

'Works in no time. If your fingers are pressed together for too long, they'll be stuck. Then you'll either have to cut them apart or tug until the skin comes off.'

Harry stared first at Kaja. Then at the body in the bath.

'Bloody hell,' he said slowly. 'This can't be true . . .'

POB Gunnar Hagen had had his doubts. Perhaps it was the most stupid thing he had done since he came to Police HQ. Forming a group to run an investigation against the ministry's orders could get him into trouble. Making Harry Hole the leader was asking for trouble. And trouble had just knocked on the door and walked in. Now it was standing in front of him in the shape of Mikael Bellman. And as Hagen listened, he noticed the strange marks on the Kripos POB's face shining whiter than usual, as if they were illuminated by something red hot inside, cooled fission in a nuclear reactor, a potential explosion that was under control for the moment.

'I know for certain that Harry Hole and two of his colleagues have been to Lake Lyseren to investigate the murder of Marit Olsen. Beate Lønn from Krimteknisk asked us to carry out a cabin-to-cabin search in the area around an old ropery. One of her officers was said to have found out that the rope used to hang Marit Olsen originates from there. So far so good . . .'

Mikael Bellman rocked back on his heels. He hadn't even taken off his floor-length trench coat. Gunnar Hagen steeled himself for what was to follow. Which came in painfully protracted form, with somewhat perplexed intonation.

'But when we spoke to the officer in Ytre Enebakk, he told me that the herostratic Harry Hole was one of three officers involved in the investigation. Hence, one of your men, Hagen.'

Hagen didn't answer.

'I assume you are aware of the consequences of placing yourself above Ministry of Justice orders, Hagen.'

Hagen still didn't answer, but he met Bellman's glare.

'Listen,' Bellman said, loosening a button on his coat and sitting down after all. 'I like you, Hagen. I think you're a good policeman, and I will need good men.'

'When Kripos has total power, you mean?'

'Exactly. I could benefit from having someone like you in a prominent position. You have a military academy background, you know the importance of thinking tactically, of avoiding battles you can't win, of realising when retreat is the best way to win ...'

Hagen nodded slowly.

'Good,' Bellman said, rising to his feet. 'Let's say Harry Hole inadvertently found himself by Lake Lyseren; it was a coincidence, had nothing to do with Marit Olsen. And such coincidences are hardly likely to reoccur. Can we agree on that ... Gunnar?'

Hagen flinched involuntarily when he heard his first name in the other man's mouth, like an echo of a first name he himself had once spoken, his predecessor's, in an attempt to create a joviality for which there was no basis. But he let it go. For he knew that this was the kind of battle Bellman had been talking about. And that, furthermore, he was about to lose the war. And that the conditions of surrender which Bellman had offered him could have been worse. A lot worse.

'I'll have a word with Harry,' he said and took Bellman's outstretched hand. It was like squeezing marble: hard, cold and lifeless.

Harry took a swig and unhooked the final joint of his forefinger from the handle of the landlady's translucent coffee cup.

'So you're Inspector Harry Hole from Oslo Police District,' said the man sitting on the opposite side of the landlady's coffee table. He had introduced himself as Inspector Colbjørnsen, with a 'c', and now he repeated Harry's title, name and affiliation with the stress on Oslo. 'And what brings Oslo Police to Stavanger, herr Hole?'

'The usual,' Harry said. 'Fresh air, beautiful mountains.'

'Oh yes?'

'The fjord. Base jumping from Pulpit Rock, if we have time.'

'So Oslo have sent us a comedian, have they? You're participating in an extreme sport, I can tell you that much. Any good reason why we were not informed of this visit?'

Inspector Colbjørnsen's smile was as thin as his moustache. He was sporting one of those funny little hats only very old men and super-self-aware hipsters have. Harry was reminded of Popeye Doyle in *The French*

Connection. And guessed that Colbjørnsen would not shy away from sucking a lollipop or stopping on his way out of the door with an 'Oh, just one more thing'.

'I reckon there must be a fax at the bottom of the in tray,' Harry said, looking up at the man in the white outfit as he came in. The material of the forensics officer's overalls rustled as he took off the white hood and plumped down into a chair. He looked straight at Colbjørnsen and muttered a local profanity.

'Well?' asked Colbjørnsen.

'He's right,' the crime scene officer said and nodded in Harry's direction, without glancing at him. 'The lad up there has been stuck to the bottom of the bath with superglue.'

'Has been?' said Colbjørnsen, looking at his subordinate with a quizzical eyebrow. 'Passive form. Aren't you a bit premature in ruling out the possibility that Elias Skog did it himself?'

'And managed to turn on the tap so he would drown in the slowest, most painful manner conceivable?' Harry suggested. 'After taping up his mouth so that he couldn't scream?'

Colbjørnsen sent Harry another razor-thin smile. 'I'll tell you when you can interrupt, *Oslo*.' ·

'Stuck fast from top to toe,' the officer continued. 'The back of his head was shaved and smeared with glue. The same with his shoulders and back. Buttocks. Arms. Both legs. In other words—'

'In other words,' Harry said, 'when the killer was finished with the glueing job, Elias had been lying there for a while and the adhesive had been hardening. He turned the tap a little way and left Elias Skog to a slow death by drowning. And Elias began his fight against time and death. The water rose slowly but his strength was ebbing away. Until mortal fear had him in its grip and gave him the energy for a last desperate attempt to pull himself free. And he did. He freed the strongest of his limbs from the bottom of the bathtub. His right leg. He simply tore it off and you can see the skin left on the bath surface. Blood spurted into the water as Elias banged his foot to rouse the landlady downstairs. And she heard the banging.'

Harry nodded towards the kitchen where Kaja was trying to calm and console the elderly lady. They could hear her bitter sobs.

'But she misunderstood. She thought her lodger was bonking a girl who had accompanied him home.'

He looked at Colbjørnsen, who had turned pale and no longer exhibited any signs of wanting to interrupt.

'And all the time Elias was losing blood. A lot of blood. All the skin from his leg was gone. He became weaker, more tired. In the end, his determination began to fade. He gave up. Perhaps he was already unconscious from loss of blood as the water rose into his nostrils.' Harry fixed his eyes on Colbjørnsen. 'Or perhaps not.'

Colbjørnsen's Adam's apple was running a shuttle service.

Harry looked down at the dregs in the coffee cup. 'And now I think Detective Solness and I should thank you for your hospitality and return to *Oslo*. Should you have any more questions, you can reach me here.' Harry jotted down a number in the margin of a newspaper, tore off a section and passed it over the table. Then he got to his feet.

'But . . .' said Colbjørnsen, getting to his feet as well. Harry towered twenty centimetres over him. 'What was it you wanted with Elias Skog?'

'To save him,' Harry said, buttoning up his coat.

'Save? Was he mixed up in something? Wait, Hole, we have to get to the bottom of this.' But there was no longer the same authority in Colbjørnsen's use of the imperative form.

'I'm sure you officers in the Stavanger force are perfectly capable of working this out for yourselves,' Harry said, walking to the kitchen door and motioning to Kaja that they were leaving. 'If not, I can recommend Kripos. Say hello to Mikael Bellman from me, if you have to.'

'Save him from what?'

'From what we were unable to save him from,' Harry said.

In the taxi on the way to Sola, Harry stared out of the window at the rain hammering down on the unnaturally green fields. Kaja didn't say a word. For which he was grateful.

26

The Needle

GUNNAR HAGEN WAS IN HARRY'S CHAIR WAITING FOR THEM when Harry and Kaja stepped into the hot, damp office.

Bjørn Holm, who was sitting behind Hagen, shrugged and gestured that he didn't know what the POB wanted.

'Stavanger, I hear,' Hagen said, getting up.

'Yes,' Harry said. 'Don't get up, boss.'

'It's your chair. I'll be going soon.'

'Uh-uh?'

Harry inferred that it was bad news. Bad news of a certain significance. Bosses don't hasten down the culvert to Botsen Prison to tell you your travel invoice has been completed incorrectly.

Hagen remained standing, so Holm was the only person in the room to be seated.

'I'm afraid I have to inform you that Kripos has already discovered that you are working on the murders. And I have no choice but to close the investigation.'

In the ensuing silence Harry could hear the boiler rumbling in the adjacent room. Hagen ran his eyes over them, meeting each gaze in turn and stopping at Harry. 'I can't say this is an honourable discharge, either. I gave you clear instructions that this was to be a discreet operation.'

'Well,' Harry said, 'I asked Beate Lønn to leak information about a certain ropery to Kripos, but she promised she would do it in a way that made Krimteknisk appear to be the source.'

'And I'm sure she did,' Hagen said. 'It was the County Officer in Ytre Enebakk who gave you away, Harry.'

Harry rolled his eyes and uttered a low curse.

Hagen clapped his hands together and a dry bang resounded between the brick walls. 'So that's why, sadly, I have to command you to drop all investigative work with immediate effect. And to clear this office within forty-eight hours. *Gomen nasai.*'

Harry, Kaja and Bjørn looked at one another as the iron door closed and Hagen's hurried footsteps faded down the culvert.

'Forty-eight hours,' Bjørn said at length. 'Anyone want fresh coffee?'

Harry kicked the bin beside the desk. It hit the wall with a crash, spilling its modest contents and rolling back towards him.

'I'll be at Rikshospital,' he said and strode towards the door.

Harry had positioned the hard wooden chair by the window and listened to his father's regular breathing as he flicked through the newspaper. A wedding and a funeral side by side. On the left, pictures of Marit Olsen's funeral, showing the Norwegian Prime Minister's serious, compassionate face, party colleagues' black suits, and the husband, Rasmus Olsen, behind a pair of large, unbecoming sunglasses. On the right, an article announcing that the shipping magnate's daughter, Lene, would get her Tony in the spring, with photos of the (A-list) wedding guests who would all be flown in to St Tropez. On the back page, it said that the sun would go down today at precisely 16.58 in Oslo. Harry looked at his watch and established that it was in fact doing that now, behind the low clouds that would not release either rain or snow. He watched the lights coming on in all the homes on the side of the ridge around what had once been a volcano. In a way, it was a liberating thought that the volcano would open beneath them one day, swallow them up and remove all traces of what had once been a contented, well-organised and slightly sad town.

Forty-eight hours. Why? It wouldn't take them more than two hours to clear their so-called office.

Harry closed his eyes and considered the case. Wrote a last mental report for his personal archive.

Two women killed in the same way, drowning in their own blood, with ketanome in the bloodstream. One woman hanged from a diving tower, with a rope taken from an old ropery. One man drowned in his own bathtub. All the victims had probably been in the same cabin at the same time. They didn't know yet who else had been there, what the motive behind the murders could be or what had gone on in the Håvass cabin that day or night. There was just effect, no cause. Case closed.

'Harry . . .'

He hadn't heard his father wake, and he turned.

Olav Hole looked renewed, but perhaps that was because of the colour in his cheeks and the feverish glow in his eyes. Harry got up and moved his chair over to his father's bedside.

'Have you been here long?'

'Ten minutes,' Harry lied.

'I've slept so well,' Olav said. 'And had such wonderful dreams.'

'I can see. You look like you're ready to get up and leave.'

Harry plumped his pillow, and his father let him do it even though they both knew that it wasn't necessary.

'How's the house?'

'Fine,' Harry said. 'It will stand for ever.'

'Good. There's something I want to talk to you about, Harry.'

'Mm?'

'You're a grown man now. You'll lose me in a natural way. That's how it should be. Not how you lost your mother. You were on the verge of going insane.'

'Was I?' Harry said, straightening the pillowslip.

'You demolished your room. You wanted to kill the doctors, those that had infected her, and even me. Because I had . . . well, because I hadn't discovered it earlier, I suppose. You were so full of love.'

'Of hatred, you mean?'

'No, of love. It's the same currency. Everything starts with love. Hatred is just the other side of the coin. I've always thought that your mother's death is what drove you to drink. Or rather the love for your mother.'

'Love is a killer,' Harry mumbled.

'What?'

'Just something someone once said to me.'

'I did everything your mother asked me to do. Apart from one thing. She asked me to help her when the time came.'

It felt as if someone had injected ice-cold water into Harry's chest.

'But I couldn't. And do you know what, Harry? It has given me night-mares. Not a day has passed when I haven't thought about not being able to fulfil that wish for her, for the woman I loved above all else on this earth.'

The thin wooden chair creaked as Harry jumped up. He walked over to the window. He heard his father draw breath a couple of times behind him, deep, trembling. Then it came.

'I know that this is a heavy burden to impose on you, son. But I also know that you're like me – it will haunt you if you don't. So let me explain what you do . . .'

'Dad,' Harry said.

'Can you see this hypodermic needle?'

'Dad! Stop!'

Everything went quiet behind him. Except for the rasp of his breathing. Outside, Harry saw the black-and-white film of a town with face-like clouds pressing their blurred, leaden-grey features against the rooftops.

'I want to be buried in Åndalsnes,' his father said.

Buried. The word sounded like an echo from Easters with Mum and Dad in Lesja when Olav Hole, with great earnestness, explained to Harry and Sis what they should do if they were buried in an avalanche and they had constrictive pericarditis, a hardened sac around the heart that prevented it from expanding. An armoured heart. Around them were flat fields and gently sloping ridges; it was a bit like when air hostesses on domestic flights over Inner Mongolia explain how to use life jackets. Absurd, but nevertheless: it gave them a feeling of security, the sense that they would all survive if they just did the right things. And now Dad was saying that wasn't true, after all.

Harry coughed. 'Åndalsnes . . . to be with Mum . . . ?'

Harry fell quiet.

'And I want to lie alongside my fellow villagers.'

'You don't know them.'

'Well, who do we know? At least they and I are from the same place. Perhaps ultimately that's what it's about. The tribe. We want to be with our tribe.'

'Do we?'

'Yes, we do. Whether we are aware of it or not, that's what we want.'

The nurse with the badge bearing the name Altman came in, flashed a quick smile at Harry and tapped his watch.

Harry went downstairs and met two uniformed policemen on their way up. He nodded automatically; it was a convention. They stared at him in silence, as though he were a stranger.

Usually Harry longed for solitude and all the benefits that came with it: peace, calm, freedom. But standing at the tram stop, suddenly he didn't know where to go. Or what to do. He just knew that being alone in the house in Oppsal would be unbearable right now.

He dialled Øystein's number.

Øystein was on a long trip to Fagernes, but suggested a beer at Lompa at around midnight to celebrate the relatively satisfactory completion of another day in Øystein Eikeland's life. Harry reminded Øystein that Harry was an alcoholic, and received the response that even an alcoholic had to go on a bender once in a while, didn't he.

Harry wished Øystein a safe journey and rang off. Glanced at his watch. And the question arose again. Forty-eight hours. Why?

A tram stopped in front of him and the doors banged open. Harry peered into the invitingly warm, lit carriage. Then he turned and began to walk down towards town.

27

Kind, Light-Fingered and Tight-Fisted

'I WAS IN THE VICINITY,' HARRY SAID. 'BUT I SUPPOSE YOU'RE on your way out.'

'Not at all,' smiled Kaja, who was standing in the doorway with a thick puffa jacket on. 'I was sitting on the veranda. Come in. Take the slippers over there.'

Harry removed his shoes and followed her through the living room. They each sat down on an enormous wooden chair on the covered veranda. It was quiet and deserted in Lyder Sagens gate, only one parked car. But on the first floor of the house over the road Harry could see the outline of a man in an illuminated window.

'That's Greger,' Kaja said. 'He's eighty now. He's sat like that and followed everything that's happened on the street since the war, I think. I like to believe he looks after me.'

'Yes, we need that,' Harry said, taking out a pack of cigarettes. 'To believe someone is looking after us.'

'Have you got a Greger as well?'

'No,' Harry said.

'Can I have one?'

'A cigarette?'

She laughed. 'I smoke occasionally. It makes me . . . calmer, I think.'

'Mm. Thought about what you're going to do? After these forty-eight hours, I mean.'

She shook her head. 'Back to Crime Squad. Feet on the table. Wait for a murder that is trivial enough for Kripos not to whisk it away from under our noses.'

Harry tapped out two cigarettes, put them between his lips, lit both and passed her one.

'*Now, Voyager*,' she said. 'Hen . . . Hen . . . What was the name of the man who did that?'

'Henreid,' Harry said. 'Paul Henreid.'

'And the woman whose cigarette he lit?'

'Bette Davis.'

'Killer film. Would you like to borrow a thicker jacket?'

'No, thanks. Why are you sitting on the veranda by the way? It's not exactly a tropical night.'

She held up a book. 'My brain is sharper in cold air.'

Harry read the front cover. '*Materialistic Monism*. Hm. Long-forgotten fragments from philosophy studies spring to mind.'

'Right. Materialism holds that everything is matter and energy. Everything that happens is a part of a larger calculation, a chain reaction, consequences of something that has already happened.'

'And free will is illusory?'

'Yep. Our actions are determined by our brain's chemical composition, which is determined by who chose to have children with whom, who in turn are determined by their brain chemistry. And so on. Everything can be taken back to the big bang, for example, and even further back. Including the fact that this book came to be written, and what you're thinking right now.'

'I remember that bit,' Harry nodded and blew smoke into the winter night. 'Made me think of the meteorologist who said that if only he had all the relevant variables he could forecast all future weather.'

'And we could prevent murders before they took place.'

'And predict that cigarette-cadging policewomen would sit on cold verandas with expensive philosophy books.'

She laughed. 'I didn't buy the book myself, I found it on the shelf here.' She pouted and sucked at the cigarette, and got smoke in her eyes. 'I never buy books, I only borrow them. Or steal them.'

'I don't exactly see you as a thief.'

'No one does, that's why I'm never caught,' she said, resting the cigarette on the ashtray.

Harry coughed. 'And why do you pilfer?'

'I only steal from people I know and who can afford it. Not because I'm greedy, but because I'm a bit tight. When I was studying, I nicked loo rolls from the university toilet. By the way, have you thought of the title of the Fante book that was so good?'

'No.'

'Text me when you remember it.'

Harry chuckled. 'Sorry, I don't text.'

'Why not?'

Harry shrugged. 'I don't know. I don't like the concept. Like Aborigines who don't want their photo taken because they think they'll lose a bit of their souls, maybe.'

'I know!' she said with enthusiasm. 'You don't want to leave traces. Tracks. Irrefutable evidence of who you are. You want to know that you are going to disappear, utterly and totally.'

'You've hit the nail on the head,' Harry said drily, and inhaled. 'Do you want to go back in?' He nodded towards her hands which she had put between her thighs and the chair.

'No, it's just my hands that are cold,' she smiled. 'Warm heart though. What about you?'

Harry gazed across the garden fence, onto the road. At the car standing there. 'What about me?'

'Are you like me? Kind, light-fingered and tight-fisted?'

'No, I'm evil, honest and tight-fisted. What about your husband?'

It came out harder than Harry had intended, as though he wanted to put her in her place because she . . . because she what? Because she was sitting here and was beautiful and liked the same things as he did and lent him slippers belonging to a man she pretended didn't exist.

'What about him?' she asked with a tiny smile.

'Well, he's got big feet,' Harry heard himself say, feeling an urgent desire to bang his head on the table.

She laughed out loud. The laughter trilled into the dark Fagerborg silence that lay over the houses, gardens and garages. The garages.

Everyone had a garage. There was only one car parked in the street. Of course there could be a thousand reasons for it being there.

'I don't have a husband,' she said.

'So . . .'

'So it's a pair of my brother's slippers you're wearing on your feet.'

'And the shoes on the steps . . . ?'

'. . . are also my brother's, and are there because I suspect that men's size forty-six and a half shoes have a deterrent effect on evil men with sinister plans.'

She sent Harry a meaningful look. He chose to believe the ambiguity was not intended.

'So your brother lives here?'

She shook her head. 'He died. Ten years ago. It's Daddy's house. In the last years, when Even was studying at Blindern, he and Daddy lived here.'

'And Daddy?'

'He died soon after Even. And as I was already living here, I took over the house.'

Kaja drew her legs up onto the chair and rested her head on her knees. Harry gazed at the slim neck, the hollow where her pinned-up hair was taut and a few loose strands fell back onto her skin.

'Do you often think about them?' Harry asked.

She raised her head from her knees.

'Mostly about Even,' she said. 'Daddy moved out when we were small, and Mummy lived in her own bubble, so Even became sort of both parents in one for me. He looked after me, encouraged me, brought me up, he was my role model. He could do no wrong in my eyes. When you've been as close to someone as Even and I were to each other, that closeness never wears off. Never.'

Harry nodded.

With a tentative cough, Kaja said: 'How's your father?'

Harry studied the cigarette glow.

'Don't you think it's odd?' he said. 'Hagen giving us forty-eight hours. We could have cleared the office in two with ease.'

'I suppose. Now you say so.'

'Maybe he thought we could spend our final two days doing something useful.'

Kaja looked at him.

'Not investigating the present murder case, of course. We'll have to leave that to Kripos. But the Missing Persons Unit needs help, I hear.'

'What do you mean?'

'Adele Vetlesen is a young woman who, to my knowedge, is not connected with any murder case.'

'You think we should . . . ?'

'I think we should meet for work at seven tomorrow morning,' Harry said. 'And see if we can do something useful.'

Kaja Solness sucked on the cigarette again. Harry stubbed his out.

'Time to go,' he said. 'Your teeth are chattering.'

On his way out he tried to see if there was anyone in the parked car, but it was impossible without going closer. And he chose not to go any closer.

In Oppsal the house was waiting for him. Big, empty and full of echoes.

He went to bed in the boy's room and closed his eyes.

And dreamed the dream he so often had. He is standing by a marina in Sydney, a chain is hauled up, a poisonous jellyfish rises to the surface, it is not a jellyfish but red hair floating around a white face. Then came the second dream. The new one. It had first appeared in Hong Kong, just before Christmas. He is on his back staring up at a nail protruding from the wall, a face is impaled on it, a face, a sensitive-looking face with a neatly trimmed moustache. In the dream Harry has something in his mouth, something that feels as if it would blow his head to pieces. What was it, what was it? It was a promise. Harry twitched. Three times. Then he fell asleep.

28

Drammen

'So it was you who reported Adele Vetlesen missing,' Kaja confirmed.

'Yes,' said the young man sitting in front of her at People & Coffee. 'We lived together. She didn't come home. I felt I had to do something.'

'Of course,' Kaja said with a glance at Harry. It was half past eight. It had taken them thirty minutes to drive from Oslo to Drammen after the trio's morning meeting which had ended in Harry discharging Bjørn Holm. Holm hadn't said much, had expelled a deep sigh, washed his coffee cup and then driven back to Krimteknisk in Bryn to resume his work there.

'Have you heard anything from Adele?' the man asked, looking from Kaja to Harry.

'No,' Harry said. 'Have you?'

The man shook his head and peered over his shoulder, at the counter, to make sure there weren't any customers waiting. They perched on high bar stools in front of the window facing one of Drammen's many squares, that is, an open area that was used as a car park. People & Coffee sold coffee and cakes at airport prices and tried to give the impression they belonged to an American chain, and indeed perhaps they did. The man Adele Vetlesen lived with, Geir Bruun, appeared to be around thirty, was unusually white with a shiny, perspiring crown and constantly wandering blue eyes. He worked at the place as a 'barista', a title that had attracted awe-inspiring respect in the nineties when coffee bars had first invaded Oslo. And it also involved making coffee, an art form which – the way Harry saw it – was primarily about avoiding obvious pitfalls. As a policeman, Harry used people's intonation, diction, vocabulary and grammatical solecisms to place them. Geir Bruun neither dressed, nor combed his hair, nor behaved like a homosexual, but as soon as he opened his mouth, it was impossible to think of anything else. There was something about the rounding of the vowels, the tiny redundant lexical embellishments, the lisping that almost seemed feigned. Harry knew that the guy could be a die-hard hetero, but he had already decided that Katrine had jumped to a premature conclusion when she described Adele Vetlesen and Geir Bruun as living togther. They were just two people who had shared a city-centre flat in Drammen for economic reasons.

'Yes, I have,' Geir Bruun said in answer to Harry's question. 'I remember she went to some kind of mountain cabin in the autumn.' He uttered this as though it were a concept he found fairly alien. 'But that wasn't where she disappeared.'

'We know that,' Kaja said. 'Did she go there with anyone, and if so, do you know who?'

'No idea. We didn't talk about that sort of thing – it was enough to share a bathroom, if you know what I mean. She had her private life, I had mine. But I doubt she would have gone into the wilds on her own, if I may put it like that.'

'Oh?'

'Adele did very little on her own. I don't see her in a cabin without a guy. But impossible to say who. She was – if I may be frank – a bit promiscuous. She had no female friends, though she compensated with male friends. Whom she kept apart. Adele didn't live a double life so much as a quadruple life. Or thereabouts.'

'So she was dishonest?'

'Not necessarily. I remember she gave me advice on honest ways to finish with someone. She said that once while she was being shagged from behind she took a photo over her shoulder with her mobile, wrote the name of the guy, sent the photo and deleted the addressee. All in one swift operation.' Geir Bruun's face was expressionless.

'Impressive,' Harry said. 'We know she paid for two people in the mountains. Could you give us the name of a male friend, so we could start our enquiries there?'

''Fraid I can't,' Geir Bruun said, 'but when I reported her missing, you lot checked who she'd been talking to on the phone over the last few weeks.'

'Which officers precisely?'

'I don't remember any names. Local police.'

'Fine, we have a meeting at the police station now,' Harry said, looking at his watch and getting up.

'Why', asked Kaja, who hadn't moved, 'did the police stop investigating the case? I don't even recall reading about it in the newspapers.'

'Don't you know?' the man said, signalling to two women with a pram that he would attend to them immediately. 'She sent a postcard.'

'Postcard?' Harry said.

'Yes. From Rwanda. Down in Africa.'

'What did she write?'

'It was very brief. She'd met her dream guy, and I would have to pay the rent on my own until she was back in March. The bitch.'

It was walking distance to the police station. An inspector with a squat pumpkin head and a name Harry forgot as soon as he heard it received them in a smoke-infested office, served them coffee in plastic cups that burned their fingers, and cast long looks at Kaja every time he considered himself unobserved.

He began by delivering a lecture about there being somewhere between five hundred and a thousand missing Norwegians at any one time. Sooner or later they would all turn up. If the police were to investigate every missing person case whenever there was suspicion of a criminal act or an accident, they wouldn't have time for anything else. Harry stifled a yawn.

In Adele Vetlesen's case they had even received a sign of life; they had it somewhere. The inspector got up and stuck his pumpkin head into a drawer of hanging files and reappeared with a postcard, which he laid before them. There was a photo of a conical mountain with a cloud around the peak, but no text to explain what the mountain was called or where in the world it was. The handwriting was scratchy, dreadful. Harry could just decipher the signature. Adele. There was a stamp bearing the name Rwanda and the envelope was postmarked Kigali, which Harry seemed to recall was the capital.

'Her mother confirmed it was her daughter's handwriting,' the inspector said and explained that at the mother's insistence they had checked and found Adele Vetlesen's name on the passenger list of a Brussels Airlines flight to Kigali via Entebbe in Uganda on the 25th of November. Furthermore, they had carried out a hotel search through Interpol, and a hotel in Kigali – the inspector read out his notes: the Gorilla Hotel! – had indeed had an Adele Vetlesen down as a guest the same night she arrived by plane. The only reason Adele Vetlesen was still on the missing persons list was that they didn't know precisely where she was now, and that a postcard from abroad did not technically change her status as missing.

'Besides, we're not exactly talking about the civilised part of the world here,' the inspector said, throwing up his arms. 'Huti, Tutsu, or whatever they're called. Machetes. Two million dead. Get me?'

Harry saw Kaja close her eyes as the inspector with the schoolmaster's voice and a string of interpolated dependent clauses explained how little life was worth in Africa, where human trafficking was hardly an unknown phenomenon, and how in theory Adele could have been abducted and forced to write a postcard, since blacks would pay a year's salary to sink their teeth into a blonde Norwegian girl, wouldn't they.

Harry examined the postcard and tried to block out the pumpkin man's voice. A conical mountain with a cloud around the peak. He glanced up when the inspector with the forgettable name cleared his throat.

'Yes, now and then you can understand them, can't you?' he said with a conspiratorial smile directed at Harry.

Harry got up and said work was waiting in Oslo. Would Drammen be so kind as to scan the postcard and email it on for them?

'To a handwriting expert?' the inspector asked, clearly displeased, and studied the address Kaja had noted down for him.

'Volcano expert,' Harry said. 'I'd like you to send him the picture and ask if he can identify the mountain.'

'*Identify the mountain?*'

'He's a specialist. He travels around examining them.'

The inspector shrugged, but nodded. Then he accompanied them to the main door. Harry asked if they had checked whether there had been any calls on Adele's mobile phone since she left.

'We know our job, Hole,' the inspector said. 'No outgoing calls. But you can imagine the mobile network in a country like Rwanda . . .'

'Actually I can't,' Harry said. 'But then I've never been there.'

'A postcard!' Kaja groaned when they were standing on the square by the unmarked police car they had requisitioned from Police HQ. 'Plane ticket and hotel record in Rwanda! Why couldn't your computer freak in Bergen have found that, so we wouldn't have had to waste half a day in fucking Drammen?'

'Thought that would put you in a great mood,' Harry said, unlocking the door. 'Got yourself a new friend, and perhaps Adele isn't dead after all.'

'Are *you* in a great mood?' Kaja asked.

Harry looked at the car keys. 'Feel like driving?'

'Yes!'

Strangely enough, none of the speed boxes flashed, and they were back in Oslo in twenty minutes flat.

They agreed they would take the light things, the office equipment and the desk drawers, to Police HQ first, and wait with the heavy things until the day after. They put them on the same trolley Harry had used when they were fitting out their office.

'Have you been given an office yet?' Kaja asked when they were halfway down the culvert. Her voice cast long echoes.

Harry shook his head. 'We'll put the things in yours.'

'Have you applied for an office?' she asked, and stopped.

Harry kept going.

'Harry!'

He stopped.

'You asked about my father,' he said.

'I didn't mean to . . .'

'No, of course not. But he hasn't got much time left. OK? After that I'll be off again. I just wanted to . . .'

'Wanted to what?'

'Have you heard of the Dead Policemen's Society?'

'What is it?'

'People who worked at Crime Squad. People I cared about. I don't know if I owe them something, but that's the tribe.'

'What?'

'It's not much, but it's all I have, Kaja. They're the only ones I have any reason to feel loyalty towards.'

'A police unit?'

Harry started walking. 'I know, and it'll probably pass. The world will go on. It's just restructuring, isn't it? The stories are in the walls, and now the walls are coming down. You and yours will have to make new stories, Kaja.'

'Are you drunk?'

Harry laughed. 'I'm just beaten. Finished. And it's fine. Absolutely fine.'

His phone rang. It was Bjørn.

'I left my Hank biography on my desk,' he said.

'I've got it here,' Harry said.

'What a sound. Are you in a church?'

'The culvert.'

'Jeez, you've got coverage there?'

'Seems we've got a better phone network than Rwanda. I'll leave the book in reception.'

'That's the second time I've heard Rwanda and mobile phones mentioned in the same breath today. Tell them I'll pick it up tomorrow, OK?'

'What did you hear about Rwanda?'

'It was something Beate said. About coltan – you know the bits of metal we found on the teeth of the two with the stab wounds in their mouths.'

'The Terminator.'

'Eh?'

'Nothing. What's that got to do with Rwanda?'

'Coltan's used in mobile phones. It's a rare metal and the Democratic Republic of the Congo has almost the entire world supply. Snag is that the deposits are in the war zone where no one keeps an eye on it, so smart operators are pinching it in all the chaos and shipping it over to Rwanda.'

'Mm.'

'See you.'

Harry was about to pocket his phone when he noticed he had an unread text message. He opened it.

Mt Nyiragongo. Last eruption 2002. One of few volcanoes with lava lake in crater. In DR Congo by Goma. Felix.

Goma. Harry stood watching the drips from a pipe in the ceiling. That was where Kluit's instruments of torture originated.

'What's up?' Kaja asked.

'Ustaoset,' Harry said. 'And the Congo.'

'And what's that supposed to mean?'

'I don't know,' Harry said. 'But I'm a non-believer as far as coincidences are concerned.' He grabbed the trolley and swung it round.

'What are you doing?' Kaja asked.

'U-turn,' Harry said. 'We've still got more than twenty-four hours left.'

29

Kluit

IT WAS AN UNUSUALLY MILD EVENING IN HONG KONG. THE skyscrapers cast long shadows over The Peak, some almost as far as the house where Herman Kluit was sitting on the terrace with a blood-red Singapore sling in one hand and the telephone in the other. He was listening while watching the lights in the queues of traffic twisting and turning like fireworms way below.

He liked Harry Hole, had liked him from the first moment he had clapped eyes on the tall, athletic, but obviously alcoholic Norwegian stepping into Happy Valley to put his last money on the wrong horse. There was something about the aggressive expression, the arrogant bearing, the alert body language that reminded him of himself as a young mercenary soldier in Africa. Herman Kluit had fought everywhere, on all sides, serving the paymasters. In Angola, Zambia, Zimbabwe, Sierra Leone, Liberia. All countries with dark pasts and even darker futures. But nowhere darker than the country about which Harry had asked. The Congo. That was where they had eventually found the vein of gold. In the form of diamonds. And cobalt. And coltan. The village chief belonged to the Mai Mai, who thought water made them invulnerable. But otherwise he was a sensible man. There was nothing you couldn't fix in Africa with a bundle of notes or – at a pinch – a supply of Kalashnikovs. In the course of one year Herman Kluit became a rich man. In the course of three he was wealthy beyond anyone's wildest dreams. Once a month they had travelled to the closest town, Goma, and slept in beds instead of on the jungle floor where a carpet of mysterious bloodsucking flies emerged from holes every night and you woke up like a half-eaten corpse. Goma. Black lava, black money, black beauties, black sins. Half of the men in the jungle had contracted malaria, the rest sicknesses with which no white doctor was conversant and which were subsumed under the generic term 'jungle fever'. That was the affliction Herman Kluit suffered from, and even though it left him in peace for long periods, he was never completely free. The only remedy Herman Kluit knew of was Singapore sling. He had been introduced to the drink in Goma by a Belgian who owned a fantastic house that had reportedly been built by King Leopold in the period when the country was known as the Congo Free State and was the monarch's private playpen and treasure chest. The house was situated down by the banks of Lake Kivu with women and sunsets so beautiful that for a while you could forget the jungle, Mai Mai and earth flies.

It was the Belgian who had shown Herman Kluit the king's little treasury in the cellar. There he had collected everything, from the world's most advanced clocks, rare weapons and imaginative instruments of torture to gold nuggets, unpolished diamonds and preserved human heads. That was where Herman Kluit had first come face to face with what they called a Leopold's apple. By all accounts it had been developed by one of the king's Belgian engineers to use on recalcitrant tribal chiefs who would not say where they found their diamonds. The earlier method had been to use buffaloes. They covered the chief in honey, tied him to a tree and brought along a captured forest buffalo, which began to lick off the honey. The point of this was that the buffalo's tongue was so coarse that it licked off skin and flesh with it. But it took time to catch a buffalo, and they could be hard to stop once they had started. Hence Leopold's apple. Not that it was particularly effective from a torturer's angle – after all, the apple prevented the prisoner from speaking. But the effect on the natives who witnessed what happened when the interrogator pulled the string for the second time was exemplary. The next man asked to open wide couldn't speak fast enough.

Herman Kluit nodded to his Filipina housemaid for her to take away the empty glass.

166

'You remember rightly, Harry,' Herman Kluit said. 'It's still on my mantelpiece. Fortunately I do not know if it has ever been used. A souvenir. It reminds me of what there is in the heart of darkness. That's always useful, Harry. No, I've neither seen it nor heard of it being used anywhere else. It's a complicated piece of technology, you know, with all these springs and needles. Requires a special alloy. Coltan is correct. Yes indeed. Very rare. The person from whom I purchased my apple, Eddie Van Boorst, claimed only twenty-four had been made, and that he had twenty-two of them, one of which was twenty-four-carat gold. That's right, there are twenty-four needles as well. How did you know? Apparently the number twenty-four had something to do with the engineer's sister, I don't recall what. But that may also have been something Van Boorst said to push up the price. He's Belgian, isn't he.'

Kluit's laughter transmuted into coughing. Damned fever.

'However, he ought to have some idea of where the apples are. He lived in a splendid house in Goma, in north Kivu, by the border to Rwanda. The address?' Kluit coughed again. 'Goma gets a new street every day, and now and then half the town is buried under lava, so addresses don't exist, Harry. But the post office has a list of all the whites. No, I have no idea if he still lives in Goma. Or whether he is still alive, for that matter. Life expectancy in the Congo is thirty-something, Harry. For whites also. Besides, the town is as good as under siege. Exactly. No, of course you haven't heard of the war. No one has.'

Dumbfounded, Gunnar Hagen stared at Harry and leaned across his desk.

'You want to go to Rwanda?' he said.

'Just a flying visit,' Harry said. 'Two days including the flights.'

'To investigate what?'

'What I said. A missing persons case. Adele Vetlesen. Kaja will go to Ustaoset to see if she can find out who Adele was travelling with before she disappeared.'

'Why can't you just ring up and ask them to check the guest book?'

'Because the cabin in Håvass is self-service,' said Kaja, who had settled in the chair next to Harry's. 'But anyone who stays in a Tourist Association cabin has to sign the guest book and state their destination. It's compulsory because if anyone's reported missing in the mountains, the search party will know where to concentrate their efforts. I'm hoping Adele and her companion gave a full name and address.'

Gunnar Hagen scratched his wreath of hair with both hands. 'And none of this has anything to do with the other murders?'

Harry stuck out his bottom lip. 'Not as far as I can see, boss. Can you?'

'Hm. And why should I decimate the travel budget for such an extravagant trip?'

'Because human trafficking is a priority,' Kaja said. 'Hence the Minister of Justice's statement to the press earlier this week.'

'Anyway,' Harry said, stretching upwards and entwining his fingers behind his head, 'it may well be that other things come to light in the process, things which might lead to us cracking other cases.'

Gunnar Hagen scrutinised his inspector thoughtfully.

'Boss,' Harry added.

30

Guest Book

A SIGN ON AN UNASSUMING YELLOW STATION BUILDING announced that they were in Ustaoset. Kaja checked that they had arrived on schedule, 10.44. She looked out. The sun was shining on the snow-covered plains and porcelain-white mountains. Apart from a clump of houses and a two-storey hotel, Ustaoset was bare rock. To be fair, there were small cabins dotted around and the odd confused shrub, but it was still a wilderness. Beside the station building, almost on the platform itself, stood a lonely SUV with the engine idling. From the train it had seemed as if there wasn't a breath of wind. But when Kaja alighted, the wind seemed to pierce right through her clothing: special thermal under-wear, anorak, ski boots.

A figure jumped out of the SUV and came towards her. He had the low winter sun behind him. Kaja squinted. Light, confident walk, a brilliant smile and an outstretched hand. She stiffened. It was Even.

'Aslak Krongli,' the man said, giving her hand a firm squeeze. 'County Officer.'

'Kaja Solness.'

'It's cold, yes? Not like in the lowlands, eh?'

'Exactly,' Kaja said, returning the smile.

'I can't join you at the cabin today. There's been an avalanche. A tunnel's closed, and we have to redirect traffic.' Without asking he took her skis, swung them over his shoulder and began to walk towards the

SUV. 'But I've got the man who keeps an eye on the mountain cabins to drive you there. Odd Utmo. Is that alright?'

'Fine,' said Kaja, who was only too pleased. It meant perhaps she could escape all the questions about why Oslo Police were suddenly interested in a missing persons case from Drammen.

Krongli drove her the five hundred metres or so to the hotel. There was a man sitting on a yellow snowmobile in the icy square in front of the entrance. He was wearing a red snowsuit, a leather hat with ear flaps, a scarf around his mouth and large goggles.

When he pushed up the goggles and mumbled his name, Kaja saw that one eye was a white, transparent membrane, as though there had been a milk spillage. The other eye studied her from top to toe without embarrassment. The man's erect posture could have belonged to a youngster, but his face was old.

'Kaja. Thanks for turning up at such short notice,' she said.

'I'm paid,' Odd Utmo said, looked at his watch, pulled down the scarf and spat. Kaja saw the glint of an orthodontic brace between the snus-stained teeth. The gobbet of tobacco made a black star on the ice.

'Hope you've had a bite to eat and a piss.'

Kaja laughed, but Utmo had already straddled the snowmobile and turned his back on her.

She looked at Krongli, who in the meantime had firmly stowed the skis and poles under the straps so they now spanned the length of the snowmobile, together with Utmo's skis and a bundle of what looked like red sticks of dynamite plus a rifle with telescopic sights.

Krongli shrugged and flashed his boyish smile again. 'Good luck, hope you find . . .'

The rest was drowned by the roar of the engine. Kaja quickly mounted. To her relief she saw handles she could hold on to, so that she wouldn't have to cling to the white-eyed old man. The exhaust fumes surrounded them; then they started with a jerk.

Utmo stood with his knees like shock absorbers and used his body weight to balance the snowmobile, which he guided past the hotel, over a snowdrift into the soft snow and diagonally up the first gentle slope.

On reaching the top with a view to the north, Kaja saw a boundless expanse of white spread out before them. Utmo turned with an enquiring nod. Kaja nodded back that everything was OK. Then he accelerated. Kaja watched the buildings disappear through the fountain of snow spraying off the drive belts.

Kaja had often heard people say that snowy plains made them think of deserts. It made her think of the days and nights with Even on his ocean racer.

The snowmobile sliced through the vast, empty landscape. The combination of snow and wind had erased, smoothed over, levelled the contours until they were one huge ocean in which the tall mountain, Hallingskarvet, towered like a menacing monster wave. There were no sudden movements; the weight of the snowmobile and the softness of the snow made all movements gentle, cushioned. Kaja rubbed her nose and cheeks carefully to ensure enough blood was circulating. She had seen what even relatively minor frostbite could do to faces. The engine's monotonous roar and the terrain's reassuring uniformity had lulled her into a drowsy state until the engine died and they came to a stand-still. She woke up and looked at her watch. Her first thought was that the engine had cut out and they were at least a forty-five-minute drive from civilisation. How far was it on skis? Three hours? Five? She had no idea. Utmo had already jumped off and was loosening the skis from the scooter.

'Is there something wrong . . . ?' she began, but stopped when Utmo stood up and pointed to the little valley in front of them.

'Håvass cabin,' he said.

Kaja squinted through her sunglasses. And, indeed, at the foot of the mountain face she saw a small, black cabin.

'Why don't we drive . . . ?'

'Because people are stupid, and that's why we have to creep up on the cabin.'

'Creep?' Kaja said, hurriedly clipping on her skis as Utmo had done.

He pointed the pole to the side of the mountain. 'If you drive the scooter into such a narrow valley, sound ricochets to and fro. Loosens new snow . . .'

'Avalanche,' Kaja said. She remembered something her father had told her after one of his trips to the Alps. More than sixty thousand troops had died in avalanches there during the Second World War, and most of them had been caused by sound waves from artillery fire.

Utmo stopped for a moment and faced her. 'These nature freaks from town think they're being clever when they build cabins in sheltered areas. But it's just a question of time before they're covered in snow, too.'

'Too?'

'The Håvass cabin has been here only three years. This year is the first winter with decent avalanche snow. And soon there's going to be more.'

He pointed westwards. Kaja shielded her eyes. On the snowy horizon she could see what he meant. Heavy, grey-white cumulus clouds were building giant mushroom formations against the blue background.

'Going to snow all week,' said Utmo, unhitching the rifle from the snowmobile and hanging it over his shoulder. 'If I were you, I'd hurry. And don't shout.'

They entered the valley in silence, and Kaja felt the temperature fall as they reached the shade and the cold filled the depressions in the ground.

They undid their skis by the black timber cabin, rested them against the wall, and Utmo took a key from his pocket and inserted it into the lock.

'How do overnight guests get in?' Kaja asked.

'They buy a skeleton key. Fits all four hundred and fifty Tourist Association cabins nationwide.' He twisted the key, pressed down the handle and pushed the door. Nothing happened. He cursed under his breath, placed his shoulder against the door and shoved. It came away from the frame with a shrill scream.

'Cabins shrink in the cold,' he muttered.

Inside it was pitch black and smelt of paraffin and a wood-burning stove. Kaja inspected the cabin. She knew the lodging arrangements were very simple. You came, entered details in the guest book, took a bed, or a mattress if it was crowded, lit the fire, cooked your own food in the kitchen where there was a stove and cooking utensils, or – if you used the food provided in the cupboards, you put some money in a tin. You paid for your stay in the same tin or you filled in a bank authorisation slip. All payments were a matter for your own conscience and moral integrity.

The cabin had four north-facing bedrooms with four bunk beds in each. The sitting room faced south and was kitted out in traditional manner, that is, with solid pine furniture. There was a large open fireplace for a homely effect and a wood burner for more efficient heating. Kaja calculated that there was seating space for twelve to fifteen people around the table, and sleeping space for double that if people squeezed up and used the floor and mattresses. She visualised the light from candles and the fire flickering over familiar and unfamiliar faces as conversation covered the day's skiing and the morrow's plans over a beer or a glass of wine. Even's ruddy complexion smiled at her, and he toasted her from one of the darkened corners.

'The guest book's in the kitchen,' Utmo said, pointing to one of the doors. Still standing by the front door with hat and gloves on, he seemed impatient. Kaja was holding the door handle and about to press when an image flashed into her mind. County Officer Krongli. He had looked similar. She had known the thought would reappear, she just hadn't known when.

'Can you open the door for me?' she said.

'Eh?'

'It's stuck,' Kaja said. 'The cold.'

She closed her eyes as she listened to him approach, heard the door open without a sound, felt his astonished gaze on her. Then she opened her eyes and went in.

There was a smell of slightly rancid fat in the kitchen. Her pulse raced as her eyes skimmed over the surfaces, cupboards. She spotted the black, leather-bound register on the worktop under the window. It was attached to the wall by a blue nylon cord.

Kaja breathed in. She walked over to the book. Flicked through.

Page after page of handwritten names, scribbled by the guests. Most had observed the rule and noted down their next destination.

'In fact, I'd been going to come here over the weekend to check the book for you,' she heard Utmo say behind her. 'But obviously the police couldn't wait, could they.'

'No,' said Kaja, thumbing through the dates. November. 6 November. 8 November. She flicked back. And forward again. It wasn't there. 7 November was gone. She laid the book flat. The jagged edges of the torn sheet stood upright. Someone had taken it.

31

Kigali

THE AIRPORT AT KIGALI, RWANDA, WAS SMALL, MODERN and surprisingly well organised. However, it was Harry's experience that international airports said little or nothing about the country in which they were situated. In Mumbai, India, there was total calm and efficiency; at JFK in New York, paranoia and chaos. The passport queue took a tiny lurch forward, and Harry followed. Despite the pleasant temperature, he could feel sweat trickling down between his shoulder blades under the thin cotton shirt. He thought again about the figures he had seen at Schiphol Airport in Amsterdam where the delayed Oslo plane had landed. Harry had worked up a sweat running through the corridors, the alphabet and the ever larger numbers of the gates to catch the flight to Kampala, Uganda. As corridors crossed he had seen something out of the corner of his eye. A figure that had seemed vaguely familiar. He had been looking into the light and the figure was too far away for him to make out the face. Once on board the plane, the last passenger, Harry had concluded the patently obvious: it had not been her. What were the chances of it happening? There was no chance the boy next to her had been Oleg. He couldn't have grown that much.

'Next.'

Harry stepped forward to the window, presented his passport, landing card, copy of the visa application he had printed off the Net and the crisp sixty dollars the visa had cost.

'Business?' the passport official asked, and Harry met his eyes. The man was tall, thin and his skin so dark that it reflected light. Probably Tutsi, Harry thought. They controlled the national borders now.

'Yes.'

'Where?'

'The Congo,' Harry said, then used the local name to distinguish the two Congo countries.

'Congo Kinshasa,' the passport official corrected.

He pointed to the landing card Harry had filled in on the plane. 'Says here you're staying at Gorilla Hotel in Kigali.'

'Just tonight,' Harry said. 'Then I'm going to the Congo tomorrow, one night in Goma and then back here and home. It's a shorter drive than from Kinshasa.'

'Have a pleasant stay in the Congo, busy man,' the uniformed official said with a hearty laugh, smacked the stamp down on the passport and returned it.

Half an hour later Harry filled in the hotel registration card at Gorilla, signed it and was given a key attached to a wooden gorilla. When Harry went to bed it was eighteen hours since he had left his at home in Oppsal. He stared at the fan howling at the foot of the bed. It provided hardly a puff of air even though the blades were rotating at a hysterical speed. He wasn't going to be able to sleep.

The driver asked Harry to call him Joe. Joe was Congolese, spoke fluent French and rather more halting English. He had been hired by contacts at a Norwegian aid organisation based in Goma.

'Eight hundred thousand,' Joe said, guiding the Land Rover along a potholed but perfectly navigable tarmac road winding between green meadows and mountain slopes cultivated from top to bottom. Occasionally, he was charitable and braked so as not to run down people walking, cycling, wheeling and carrying goods at the edge of the road, but as a rule they made a life-saving leap at the very last second.

'They kill eight hundred thousand in just few weeks in 1994. The

Hutus invade their kind, old neighbours and cut them down with machetes because they Tutsis. The propaganda on the radio say that if your husband is Tutsi it is your duty as Hutu to kill him. Cut down the tall trees. Many flee along this road . . .' Joe pointed out of the window. 'Bodies pile up. Some places it is impossible to pass. Good times for vultures.'

They drove on in silence.

They passed two men carrying a big cat bound to a pole by its legs. Children were dancing and cheering beside it and sticking pins into the dead animal. The coat was sun-coloured with patches of shade.

'Hunters?' Harry asked.

Joe shook his head, glanced in the mirror and answered in a mixture of English and French: 'Hit by car, *je crois*. That one is almost impossible to hunt. It is rare, has large territory, only hunts at night. Hides and blends into environs during the day. I think it is very lonely animal, Harry.'

Harry watched men and women working in the fields. At several points there was heavy machinery and men repairing the road. Down in a valley he saw a motorway under construction. In a field children in blue school uniforms were kicking a football about and shouting.

'Rwanda is good,' Joe said.

Two and a half hours later Joe pointed through the windscreen. 'Lake Kivu. Very nice, very deep.'

The surface of the huge expanse of water seemed to reflect a thousand suns. The country on the other side was the Democratic Republic of the Congo. Mountains rose on all sides. A single white cloud encircled the peak of one of them.

'Not much cloud,' Joe said as if intuiting what Harry was thinking. 'The killer mountain. Nyiragongo.'

Harry nodded.

An hour later they had passed the border and were driving into Goma. On the roadside an emaciated man in a torn jacket was sitting and staring ahead through desperate, crazed eyes. Joe steered the vehicle carefully between the craters in the muddy path. A military jeep was in front of them. The swaying soldier manning the machine gun looked at them with cold, weary eyes. Above them roared aeroplane engines.

'UN,' Joe said. 'More guns and grenades. Nkunda come closer to the city. Very strong. Many people escape now. Refugees. Maybe Monsieur Van Boorst, too, eh? I not see him long time.'

'You know him?'

'Everybody know Mr Van. But he has Ba-Maguje in him.'

'Ba-what?'

'*Un mauvais ésprit*. A demon. He makes you thirsty for alcohol. And take away your emotions.'

The air-conditioning unit was blowing cold air. The sweat was running down between Harry's shoulder blades.

They had stopped midway between two rows of shacks, in what Harry realised was a kind of city centre in Goma. People hastened to and fro on the almost impassable path between the shops. Black boulders were piled up alongside the houses and served as foundations. The ground looked like stiffened black icing and grey dust whirled up in the air that stank of rotten fish.

'*Là,*' Joe said, pointing to the door of the only brick house in the row. 'I wait in the car.'

Harry noticed a couple of men stop in the street as he exited the car. They gave him the neutral, dangerous gaze that relayed no warning. Men who knew that acts of aggression were more effective without a warning. Harry headed straight for the door without looking either side, showed that he knew what he was doing there, where he should go. He knocked. Once. Twice. Three times. Bollocks! Bloody long way to come just to—

The door opened a fraction.

A wrinkled white face with questioning eyes stared at him.

'Eddie Van Boorst?' Harry asked.

'*Il est mort,*' said the man in a voice so hoarse it sounded like a death rattle.

Harry remembered enough school French to understand that the man was claiming Van Boorst was dead. He tried in English. 'My name is Harry Hole. I was given Van Boorst's name by Herman Kluit in Hong Kong. I'm interested in a Leopold's apple.'

The man blinked twice. Stuck his head out of the door and looked left and right. Then he opened the door a little more. '*Entrez*,' he said, motioning Harry in.

Harry ducked beneath the low door frame and just managed to bend his knees in time; the floor inside was twenty centimetres lower.

There was a smell of incense. As well as something else, familiar – the sweet stench of an old man who had been drinking for several days.

Harry's eyes became used to the dark, and he discovered that the small, frail old man was wearing an elegant, burgundy silk dressing gown.

'Scandinavian accent,' said Van Boorst in Hercule Poirot English and placed a cigarette in a yellowing holder between his thin lips. 'Let me guess. Definitely not Danish. Could be Swedish. But I think Norwegian. Yes?'

A cockroach showed its antennae through a crack in the wall behind him.

'Mm. An expert on accents?'

'A mere pastime,' said Van Boorst, flattered, pleased. 'For small nations like Belgium you have to learn to look outwards, not inwards. And how is Herman?'

'Fine,' Harry said, turning to his right and seeing two pairs of bored eyes looking at him. One from a photo above the bed in the corner. A framed portrait of a person with a long grey beard, powerful nose, short hair, epaulettes, chain and sword. King Leopold, unless Harry was much mistaken. The other pair of eyes belonged to the woman lying on her side in the bed with only a blanket draped over her hips. The light from the window above her fell on her small, supple young girl's breasts. She responded to Harry's nod with a fleeting smile that revealed a large gold tooth among all the white ones. She couldn't have been more than twenty. On the wall behind the slim waist Harry glimpsed a bolt hammered into the cracked plaster. From the bolt dangled a pair of pink handcuffs.

'My wife,' said the little Belgian. 'Well, one of them.'

'Mistress Van Boorst?'

'Something of that kind. You want to buy? You have money?'

'First I want to see what you've got,' Harry said.

Eddie Van Boorst went to the door, opened it a crack and peered outside. Shut it and locked up. 'Only got your driver with you?'

'Yes.'

Van Boorst puffed on his cigarette while studying Harry through the folds of skin that gathered when he squinted.

Then he went to a corner of the room, kicked away the carpet, bent down and pulled at an iron ring. A trapdoor opened. The Belgian waved Harry down into the cellar first. Harry assumed it was a precaution based on experience, and did as he was told. A ladder led into pitch darkness. Harry reached solid ground after only the seventh rung. Then a light was switched on.

Harry looked around the room; the ceiling was full height and there was a level cement floor. Shelves and cupboards covered three of the walls. On the shelves were the day-to-day products: well-used Glock pistols, his Smith & Wesson .38, boxes of ammunition, a Kalashnikov. Harry had never held the famous Russian automatic rifle known officially as the AK-47. He stroked the wooden stock.

'An original from the first year of production, 1947,' Van Boorst said.

'Seems like everyone down here has got one,' Harry said. 'The most popular cause of death in Africa, I've heard.'

Van Boorst nodded. 'For two simple reasons. Firstly when the Communist countries started exporting the Kalashnikov here after the Cold War, the gun cost as much as a fat chicken in peacetime. And no more than a hundred dollars in wartime. Secondly, it works, no matter what you do with it, and that's important in Africa. In Mozambique they like their Kalashnikovs so much it's on their national flag.'

Harry's eyes stopped at the letters discreetly stamped on a black case.

'Is that what I think it is?' Harry asked.

'Märklin,' said Van Boorst. 'A rare rifle. It was manufactured in very limited numbers as it was a fiasco. Much too heavy and large a calibre. Used to hunt elephants.'

'And humans,' Harry said softly.

'Do you know the weapon?'

'World's best telescopic sights. Not exactly something you need to hit an elephant at a hundred metres. Perfect for an assassination.' Harry ran his fingers along the case as the memories streamed back. 'Yes, I know it.'

'You can have it cheap. Thirty thousand euros.'

'I'm not after a rifle this time.' Harry turned to the shelving unit in the middle of the room. Grotesque white wooden masks grimaced at him from the shelves.

'The Mai Mai tribe's spiritual masks,' said Van Boorst. 'They think that if they dip themselves in holy water, the enemy's bullets cannot hurt them. Because the bullets will also turn to H_2O. The Mai Mai guerrillas went to war against the government army with bows and arrows, shower hats on their heads and bath plugs as amulets. I am not kidding you, monsieur. Naturally, they were mown down. But they like water, the Mai Mai do. And white masks. And their enemies' hearts and kidneys. Lightly grilled with mashed corn.'

'Mm,' Harry said. 'I hadn't expected that such a basic house would have such a full cellar.'

Van Boorst chuckled. 'Cellar? This is the ground floor. Or was. Before the eruption three years ago.'

Everything fell into place for Harry. Black boulders, black icing. The floor upstairs that was lower than the street.

'Lava,' Harry said.

Van Boorst nodded. 'It flowed straight through the centre and took my house by Lake Kivu. All the wooden houses around here burned to the ground; this brick house was the only one left standing, but was half buried in lava.' He pointed to the wall. 'There you can see the front door to what was street level three years ago. I bought the house and just put in a new door where you entered.'

Harry nodded. 'Lucky the lava didn't burn down the door and fill this floor too.'

'As you can see, the windows and doors are in the wall facing away from Nyiragongo. It's not the first time. The bloody volcano spews lava on this town every ten or twenty years.'

Harry cocked an eyebrow. 'And still people move back?'

Van Boorst shrugged. 'Welcome to Africa. But the volcano is bloody useful. If you want to get rid of a troublesome corpse – which is a fairly normal problem in Goma – you can of course sink it in Lake Kivu. But it is *still* down there. Whereas if you use Nyiragongo . . . People often think that volcanoes have these red-hot, bubbling lava lakes at the bottom, but they do not. None of them. Apart from Nyiragongo. A thousand degrees centigrade. Drop something down there and, pouf, it is gone. It returns as a gas. It is the only chance anyone in Goma has to reach heaven.' He broke into a hacking laugh. 'I witnessed an over-enthusiastic coltan-hunter drop a tribal chief's daughter on a chain into the crater up there once. The chief wouldn't sign the papers giving the hunters the right to mine on their territory. Her hair caught fire at twenty metres above the lava. At ten metres above, the girl was burning like a candle. And five metres further down she was dripping. I am not exaggerating. Skin, flesh, it flowed off her bones . . . Is this what you were interested in?' Van Boorst had opened a cupboard and taken out a metal ball. It was shiny, perforated with tiny apertures and smaller than a tennis ball. From a slightly larger opening there hung a wire loop. It was the same instrument Harry had seen at Herman Kluit's house.

'Does it work?' Harry asked.

Van Boorst sighed. He stuck his little finger in the loop and pulled. There was a loud bang and the ball jumped in the Belgian's hand. Harry stared. From the holes in the ball were protruding what looked like antennae.

'May I?' he asked, and put out his hand. Van Boorst passed him the ball and watched with great vigilance as Harry counted the antennae.

Harry nodded. 'Twenty-four,' he said.

'Same as the number of apples made,' said Van Boorst. 'The number had some symbolic value for the engineer who designed and made it. It was the age of his sister when she took her own life.'

'And how many of them have you got in your cupboard?'

'Only eight. Including this *pièce de résistance* in gold.' He took out a ball which gleamed matt in the light from the electric bulb, then returned it to the cupboard. 'But it is not for sale. You would have to kill me to get your paws on that one.'

'So you've sold thirteen since Kluit bought his?'

'And for ever increasing sums. It is a guaranteed investment, Monsieur Hole. Old instruments of torture have a loyal body of followers who are keen to pay, *croyez-moi*.'

'I believe you,' Harry said, trying to press down one of the antennae.

'Spring-loaded,' Van Boorst said. 'Once the wire has been pulled, the victim will not be able to remove the apple from their mouth. Nor will anyone else for that matter. Do not take step two if you want to retract the circular ridges. Don't pull the wire, please.'

'Step two?'

'Give it to me.'

Harry passed Van Boorst the ball. The Belgian carefully threaded a biro through the loop, held it horizontal and at the same height as the ball and then let go of the ball. As the wire became taut there was another bang. The Leopold's apple jiggled fifteen centimetres below the biro and the sharp needles sticking out of each of the antennae glistened.

'*Å faen*,' Harry swore in Norwegian.

The Belgian smiled. 'The Mai Mai called the device "Blood of the Sun". This sweet child has several names.' He placed the apple on the table, put the biro in the opening where the wire came from, pushed hard, and the needles and antennae retracted with a bang, and the royal apple regained its smooth round shape.

'Impressive,' Harry said. 'How much?'

'Six thousand dollars,' Van Boorst said. 'Usually I add a bit each time, but you can have it for the same price I sold the last one.'

'Why's that?' Harry asked, running his forefinger over the sleek metal.

'Because you have come a long way,' Van Boorst said, blowing cigarette smoke into the room. 'And because I like your accent.'

'Mm. And who was the last buyer?'

Van Boorst chuckled. 'Just as no one will ever find out that you have been here, I will not tell you about my other customers. Does that not sound reassuring, monsieur . . . ? See, I have already forgotten your name.'

Harry nodded. 'Six hundred,' he said.

'I beg your pardon?'

'Six hundred dollars.'

Van Boorst emitted the same brief chuckle. 'Ridiculous. But the price you mention happens to be the price of a three-hour guided tour of the nature reserve where there are mountain gorillas. Would you prefer that, Monsieur Hole?'

'You can keep the royal apple,' Harry said, taking out a slim wad of twenty-dollar bills from his back pocket. 'I'm offering you six hundred for information about who bought apples from you.'

He placed the wad on the table in front of Van Boorst. And on the top an ID card.

'Norwegian police,' Harry said. 'At least two women have been killed by the product over which you have a monopoly.'

Van Boorst bent over the money and studied the ID card without touching either.

'If that is the case I am truly sorry,' he said, and it sounded as if his voice had become even more gravelly. 'Believe me. But my personal security is probably worth more than six hundred dollars. If I were to talk openly about all the people who have shopped here my life expectancy would be . . .'

'You should worry more about your life expectancy in a Congolese prison,' Harry said.

Van Boorst laughed again. 'Nice try, Hole. But the Chief of Police in Goma happens to be a personal acquaintance of mine, and anyway –' he threw his arms in the air – 'what have I done after all?'

'What you have done is less interesting,' Harry said, taking a photo out of his breast pocket. 'The Norwegian state is one of the most important providers of aid to the Congo. If the Norwegian authorities ring Kinshasa, name you as a non-cooperative source of the murder weapon in a Norwegian double murder, what do you think will happen?'

Van Boorst was no longer smiling.

'You won't be falsely convicted of anything, gracious, no,' Harry said. 'You'll just be on remand, which should not be confused with punishment. It's the judicious confinement of a person while a case is being investigated and perhaps there are fears that evidence may have been tampered with. But it is prison nevertheless. And this investigation could take a long time. Have you ever seen the inside of a Congolese prison, Van Boorst? No, I suppose there are not many white men who have.'

Van Boorst pulled the dressing gown round him tighter. Eyed Harry while gnawing at the cigarette holder. 'OK,' he said, 'a thousand dollars.'

'Five hundred,' Harry said.

'Five? But you—'

'Four,' Harry said.

'Done!' Van Boorst shouted, raising his arms into the air. 'What do you want to know?'

'Everything,' Harry said, leaning against the wall and producing a pack of cigarettes.

When, half an hour later, Harry stepped out of Van Boorst's house and into Joe's Land Rover, darkness had fallen.

'The hotel,' Harry said.

The hotel turned out to be right down by the lake. Joe warned Harry against swimming. Not because of the guinea parasite he would be unlikely to discover until one day a thin worm began to wriggle under his skin, but because of the methane gas that rose from the bottom in the form of large bubbles that could render him unconscious and precip-itate drowning.

Harry sat on the balcony, looking down on two long-legged creatures walking stilt-like over the illuminated lawn. They looked like flamingos in peacock costume. On the floodlit tennis court two young black boys were playing with just two balls, both so ragged that they looked like rolled-up socks sailing to and fro across the semi-torn net. Every now and then aeroplanes thundered across the sky, above the hotel roof.

Harry heard the clink of bottles at the bar. It was exactly sixty-eight paces from where he was sitting. He had counted when he entered. He took out his phone and rang Kaja's number.

She sounded happy to hear his voice. Happy anyway.

'I'm snowbound in Ustaoset,' she said. 'It's coming down horses and cows here, not cats and dogs. But at least I've been invited to dinner. And the guest book was interesting.'

'Oh yes?'

'The page for the day we're interested in was missing.'

'There you go. Did you check if—'

'Yes, I checked if there were any fingerprints or if the writing had gone through to the next page.' She giggled, and Harry guessed that she had had a couple of glasses of wine.

'Mm. I was thinking more of—'

'Yes, I checked what had been written the day before and after. But almost no one stays more than one night in such basic accommodation. Unless they're snowed in. And the weather was clear on the 7th of November. But the officer up here has promised me that he'll check the guest books at the surrounding cabins on the days before and after to see which guests might have stayed over at Håvass on their trek.'

'Good. Sounds like we're getting warmer.'

'Maybe. How about you?'

'Bit cooler here, I'm afraid. I've found Van Boorst, but none of the fourteen customers he dealt with were Scandinavian. He was fairly sure. I have six names and addresses, but they're all known collectors. Otherwise there were a few names he half remembered, a few descriptions, that's all. There are two more apples, but Van Boorst happened to know they were still in the hands of a collector in Caracas. Did you check out Adele and her visa?'

'I called the Rwandan consulate in Sweden. I have to confess I expected chaos but everything was bang on the button.'

'The Congo's small, straightforward big brother.'

'They had a copy of Adele's visa application, and the dates matched. The period covered by the visa is well out of date now, but of course they had no idea where she was. They told me to contact the immigration authorities in Kigali. I was given a number, tried it and was bounced around between offices like a pinball, until I was put through to an English-speaking know-all who pointed out that there was no cooperation agreement with Rwanda in that area, regretted politely that he would have to decline my request and wished me and my family a long and happy life. You haven't got a sniff of anything, either?'

'No. I showed Van Boorst the photo of Adele. He said the only woman who had bought anything off him was a woman with big rust-red curls and an East German accent.'

'*East* German accent? Does such a thing exist?'

'I don't know, Kaja. This man walks around in a dressing gown, has a cigarette holder, is an alcoholic and a specialist in accents. I'm trying to keep my mind on the case and then get out.'

She laughed. White wine, Harry wagered. Red-wine drinkers don't laugh as much.

'But I have an idea,' he said. 'Landing cards.'

'Yes?'

'You have to give the address of where you plan to stay on your first night. If they hold onto the cards in Kigali and there is further info, such as a forwarding address, perhaps I can find out where Adele went. That might be a lead. For all we know she may be the only person alive who knows who was at the Håvass cabin that night.'

'Good luck, Harry.'

'Good luck to you, too.'

He rang off. Of course he could have asked her who she was having dinner with, but if that had been relevant to the investigation she would probably have told him.

Harry sat on the balcony until the bar closed and the clinking of bottles stopped, to be replaced by the sounds of lovemaking from an open window above. Throaty, monotonous cries. They reminded him of the gulls at Åndalsnes when he and his grandfather used to get up at the crack of dawn to go fishing. His father never went with him. Why not? And why had Harry never thought about it, why hadn't he instinctively known that Olav didn't feel at home in a fishing boat? Had he already understood, as a five-year-old, that his father had opted for an education and left the farm precisely so that he wouldn't have to sit in boat? Nevertheless, his father wanted to return and spend eternity there. Life was strange. Death, at any rate.

Harry lit up a cigarette. The sky was starless and black apart from above the Nyiragongo crater, where a red glow smouldered. Harry felt a smarting pain as an insect stung him. Malaria. Methane gas. Lake Kivu glittered in the distance. Very nice, very deep.

A boom resounded from the mountains, and the sound rolled across the lake. Vocanic eruption or just thunder? Harry looked up. Another clap; the echo rang between the mountains. And another echo, distant, reached Harry at the same time.

Very deep.

He stared, wide-eyed, into the darkness, hardly noticing that the heavens were opening and the rain was hammering down and drowning the gull cries.

32

Police

'I'M GLAD YOU GOT AWAY FROM THE HÅVASS CABIN BEFORE this swept in,' Officer Krongli said. 'You could have been stranded there for several days.' He nodded towards the hotel restaurant's large panoramic window. 'But it's wonderful to see, don't you think?'

Kaja looked out at the heavy snowfall. Even had been like that, too; he was excited by the power of nature, regardless of whether it was working for or against him.

'I hope my train will finally get through,' she said.

'Yes, of course,' Krongli said, fingering his wine glass in a way that suggested to Kaja that wining and dining was not something he did that often. 'We'll make sure it does. And sort out the guest books from the other cabins.'

'Thank you,' Kaja said.

Krongli ran a hand through his unruly locks and put on a wry smile. Chris de Burgh with 'Lady in Red' oozed like syrup through the loud-speakers.

There were only two other guests in the restaurant, two men in their thirties, each sitting at a table with a white cloth, each with a beer in front of them, staring at the snow, waiting for something that wasn't going to happen.

'Doesn't it get lonely here sometimes?' Kaja asked.

'Depends,' the rural policeman said, following her glance. 'If you don't have a wife or family, it means you tend to gather at places like this.'

'To be lonely together,' Kaja said.

'Yep,' Krongli said, pouring more wine into their glasses. 'But I suppose it's the same in Oslo, too?'

'Yes,' Kaja said. 'It is. Have you got any family?'

Krongli shrugged. 'I did live with someone. But she found life too empty here, so she moved down to where you live. I can understand her. You have to have an interesting job in a place like this.'

'And you do?'

'I think so. I know everyone here, and they know me. We help each other. I need them and they . . . well . . .' He twirled the glass.

'They need you,' Kaja said.

'I believe so, yes.'

'And that's important.'

'Yes, it is,' Krongli said firmly, looking up at her. Even's eyes. Which had the embers of laughter in them; something amusing or something to be happy about always seemed to have just happened. Even if it hadn't. Especially when it hadn't.

'What about Odd Utmo?' Kaja said.

'What about him?'

'He left as soon as he had dropped me off. What does he do on an evening like tonight?'

'How do you know he isn't sitting at home with his wife and children?'

'If I've ever met a recluse, Officer—'

'Call me Aslak,' he said, laughing and tipping back his glass. 'And I can see that you're a real detective. But Utmo hasn't always been like that.'

'He hasn't?'

'Before his son went missing he was apparently pretty approachable. Yes, now and then he was nothing less than affable. But I suppose he's always had a dangerous temper.'

'I would have thought a man like Utmo would be single.'

'His wife was good-looking, too. When you consider how ugly he is. Did you see his teeth?'

'I saw he was wearing an orthodontic brace, yes.'

'He says it's so that his teeth don't go crooked.' Aslak Krongli shook his head, with laughter in his eyes, though not in his voice. 'But it's the only way to make sure they don't fall out.'

'Tell me, was that really *dynamite* he was carrying on his snow-mobile?'

'*You* saw it,' Krongli said. 'Not me.'

'What do you mean?'

'There are lots of residents up here who can't quite see the romanti-cism of sitting for hours with a fishing rod by the mountain lakes, but who would like to have the fish they regard as their own on the dinner table.'

'They chuck dynamite in the lakes?'

'As soon as the ice has gone.'

'Isn't that somewhat illegal?'

Krongli held up his hands in defence. 'As I said, I didn't see anything.'

'No, that's true, you only live here. Have you got dynamite, too, by any chance?'

'Just for the garage. Which I'm planning to build.'

'Right. What about Utmo's gun? Looked modern with the telescopic sights and so on.'

'Certainly is. Utmo was good at hunting bears. Until he went half blind.'

'I saw his eye. What happened?'

'Apparently his boy spilt a glass of acid on him.'

'Apparently?'

Krongli rolled his shoulders. 'Utmo is the only person left who knows what happened. His son went missing when he was fifteen. Soon after-wards his wife disappeared as well. But that was eighteen years ago, before I moved up here. Since then Utmo has lived alone in the mountains, no TV, no radio, doesn't even read the papers.'

'How did they disappear?'

'You tell me. There are lots of sheer drops around Utmo's farm where you might fall. And the snow. The son's shoe was found after an avalanche, but there was no sign of him after the snow melted that year, and it was strange to lose a shoe like that up in the snow. Some thought it was a bear. Though, as far as I know, there weren't any bears up here eighteen years ago. And then there were those who reckoned it was Utmo.'

'Oh? Why's that?'

'We-ell,' Aslak said, dragging it out, 'the boy had a bad scar on his chest. Folk reckoned he'd got that from his father. It was something to do with the mother, Karen.'

'How so?'

'They were competing for her.'

Aslak shook his head at the question in Kaja's eyes. 'This was before my time. And Roy Stille, who has been an officer here since the dawn of time, went to the house, but only Odd and Karen were there. And they both said the same. The boy had gone out hunting and hadn't returned. But this was in April.'

'Not hunting season?'

Aslak shook his head. 'And since then no one has seen him. The following year, Karen went missing. Folk here believe it was the grief that broke her and she took a one-way ticket off a cliff.'

Kaja thought she detected a little quiver in the officer's voice, but concluded it must have been the wine.

'What do you believe?' she asked.

'I believe it's true. The boy was caught by an avalanche. He suffocated under the snow. The snow melted and he was carried into a lake and that's where he is. With his mother, let's hope.'

'Sounds nicer than the bear story, anyway.'

'Well, it isn't.'

Kaja looked up at Aslak. There was no laughter in his eyes now.

'Buried alive in an avalanche,' he said, and his gaze wandered out of the window, to the drifting snow. 'The darkness. The loneliness. You can't move, it holds you in its iron grip, laughs at your attempts to free yourself. The certainty that you're going to die. The panic, the mortal fear when you can't breathe. There's no worse way to go.'

Kaja took a gulp of wine. She put down the glass. 'How long were you lying there?' she asked.

'I thought it was three, maybe four hours,' Aslak said. 'When they dug me out, they said I had been trapped for fifteen minutes. Another five and I would have been dead.'

The waiter came and asked if they wanted anything else; he would call last orders in ten minutes. Kaja said no, and the waiter responded by putting the bill in front of Aslak.

'Why does Utmo carry a gun?' Kaja asked. 'As far as I'm aware, it isn't the hunting season now.'

'He says it's because of beasts of prey. Self-defence.'

'Are there any here? Wolves?'

'He never tells me exactly what kind of animal he means. By the way, there's a rumour going round that at night the boy's ghost walks the plains. And that if you see him, you have to be careful, because it means there's a sheer drop or an avalanche nearby.'

Kaja finished her drink.

'I can have drinking hours extended for a bit if you like.'

'Thanks, Aslak, but I have to be up early tomorrow.'

'Ooh,' he said, laughing with his eyes and scratching his locks, 'now that sounds like I . . .' He paused.

'What?' Kaja said.

'Nothing. I suppose you have a husband or boyfriend down south.'

Kaja smiled, though didn't answer.

Aslak stared at the table, and said quietly, 'Well, there you go: provincial policeman couldn't take his drink and started wittering.'

'That's alright,' she said. 'I haven't got a boyfriend. And I like you. You remind me of my brother.'

'But?'

'But what?'

'Don't forget I'm a real detective, too. I can see you're no hermit. There is someone, isn't there?'

Kaja laughed. Normally she would have left it at that. Maybe it was the wine. Maybe it was because she liked Aslak Krongli. Maybe it was because she didn't have anyone to talk to about that sort of thing, not since Even died, and Aslak was a stranger, a long way from Oslo, someone who didn't talk to her circle of acquaintances.

'I'm in love,' she heard herself say. 'With a police officer.' She put the glass of water to her mouth to hide a flurry of confusion. The strange thing was that it hadn't struck her as true until she heard the words said aloud.

Aslak raised his glass to hers. '*Skål* to the lucky guy. And the lucky girl, I hope.'

Kaja shook her head. 'There's nothing to *skål* about. Not yet. Maybe ever. My God, listen to me . . .'

'We don't have anything else to do, do we? Tell me more.'

'It's complicated. *He's* complicated. And I don't know if he wants me. In fact, that bit is fairly straightforward.'

'Let me guess. He's got someone, and he can't let go.'

Kaja sighed. 'Perhaps. I honestly don't know. Aslak, thank you for all your help, but I—'

'—have to go to bed now.' The police officer rose. 'I hope it all goes sour with your friend, you want to escape from your broken heart and the city and that you could envisage giving this a chance.' He passed her an A4 piece of paper with a Hol Police Station letterhead.

Kaja read it and laughed out loud. 'A post in the sticks?'

'Roy Stille is retiring in the autumn and good officers are hard to find,' Aslak said. 'It's our advertisement for the post. We put it out last week. Our office is in Geilo city centre. Time off every alternate weekend and free dentistry.'

As Kaja went to bed she could hear the distant rumbles. Thunder and snow rarely came as a joint package.

She rang Harry and got his voicemail. Left a little ghost story about the local guide Odd Utmo with the rotten teeth and brace, and about his son who had to be even uglier since he had been haunting the district for eighteen years. She laughed. Realised she was drunk. Said goodnight.

She dreamed about avalanches.

It was eleven o'clock in the morning. Harry and Joe had left Goma at seven, crossed the border to Rwanda without any problems and Harry was standing in an office on the first floor of the terminal building at Kigali Airport. Two uniformed officers were giving him the once-over. Not in an unfriendly way, but to check that he really was who he claimed to be: a Norwegian policeman. Harry put his ID card back in his jacket pocket and felt the smooth paper of the coffee-brown envelope he had there. The problem was that there were two of them. How do you bribe two public servants at once? Ask them to share the contents of the envelope and politely request them not to snitch on one another?

One officer, the same one who had inspected Harry's passport two days before, pulled his beret back on his head. 'So you want a copy of whose landing card? Could you repeat the date and the name?'

'Adele Vetlesen. We know she arrived at this airport on the 25th of November. And I'll pay a finder's fee.'

The two officers exchanged glances, and one left the room on the other's cue. The remaining officer walked over to the window and surveyed the runway, the little DH8 that had landed and which in fifty-five minutes would be transporting Harry on the first phase of his journey home.

'Finder's fee,' the officer repeated quietly. 'I assume you know it is illegal to try to bribe a public servant, Mr Hole. But you probably thought: Shiit, this is Africa.'

It struck Harry that the man's skin was so black it seemed like gloss paint.

He felt his shirt sticking to his back. The same shirt. Perhaps they sold shirts at Nairobi airport. If he got that far.

'That's right,' Harry said.

The officer laughed and turned. 'Tough guy, eh! Are you a hard man, Hole? I saw you were a policeman when you arrived.'

'Oh?'

'You examined me with the same circumspection that I examined you.'

Harry shrugged.

The door opened. The other officer was back accompanied by a woman dressed like a secretary with clickety-clack heels and glasses on the tip of her nose.

'I'm sorry,' she said in impeccable English, clocking Harry. 'I've checked the date. There was no Adele Vetlesen on that flight.'

'Mm. Could there be a mistake?'

'Unlikely. Landing cards are filed by date. The flight you're talking about is a thirty-seven-seater DH8 from Entebbe. It didn't take long to check.'

'Mm. If that's the case, may I ask you to check something else for me?'

'You may ask of course. What is it?'

'Could you see if any other foreign women arrived on that flight?'

'And why should I do that?'

'Because Adele Vetlesen was booked onto that flight. So either she used a false passport here—'

'I doubt that very much,' the passport officer said. 'We check all the passport photos very carefully before they are scanned by a machine that matches the passport number against the international ICAO register.'

'—or someone else was travelling in Adele Vetlesen's name and then used their own, genuine passport to pass through here. Which is more than possible, as passport numbers are not checked before passengers board the aircraft.'

'True,' the chief passport official said, pulling at his beret. 'Airline staff only make sure the name and photo match more or less. For that purpose you can have a false passport made for fifty dollars anywhere in the world. It's only when you get off the plane at your final destination and have to go through checks that your passport number is matched and false passports are revealed. But the question is the same: why should we help you, Mr Hole? Are you on an official mission here and have you got the papers to support that?'

'My official mission was in the Congo,' Harry lied. 'But I found nothing there. Adele Vetlesen is missing, and we fear she may have been murdered by a serial killer who has already murdered at least three other women, among them a government MP. Her name is Marit Olsen – you can verify that on the Net. I'm conscious that the procedure now is for me to return home and go through formal channels, as a result of which we will lose several days and give the killer a further head start. And time to kill again.'

Harry saw that his words had made some impression on them. The woman and the chief official conferred, and the woman marched off again.

They waited in silence.

Harry looked at his watch. He hadn't checked in on the flight yet.

Six minutes had passed when they heard the click-clack heels coming closer.

'Eva Rosenberg, Juliana Verni, Veronica Raul Gueno and Claire Hobbes.' She spat out the names, straightened her glasses and put four landing cards on the table in front of Harry before the door slammed behind her. 'Not many European women come here,' she said.

Harry's eyes ran down the cards. All of them had given Kigali hotels as their address, but not the Gorilla Hotel. He looked at their home addresses. Eva Rosenberg had given an address in Stockholm.

'Thank you,' Harry said, noting down the names, addresses and passport numbers on the back of a taxi receipt he found in his jacket pocket.

'I regret that we can't be of any more assistance,' the woman said, pushing her glasses up again.

'Not at all,' Harry said. 'You've been a great help. Really.'

'And now, Mr Policeman,' said the tall, thin officer, with a smile that lit up his black-as-night face.

'Yes?' Harry said in anticipation, ready to take out the coffee-brown envelope.

'Now it's time we got you checked in on the flight to Nairobi.'

'Mm,' Harry said, looking at his watch. 'I may have to catch the next one.'

'Next one?'

'I have to go back to the Gorilla Hotel.'

Kaja was sitting in the Norwegian railway's so-called 'comfort coach' which – apart from free newspapers, two cups of free coffee and a socket for your laptop – meant that you sat like sardines in a can instead of in the almost empty economy areas. So when her phone rang and she saw it was Harry, that was where she hurried.

'Where are you?' Harry asked.

'On the train. Passing Kongsberg right this minute. And you?'

'Gorilla Hotel in Kigali. I've had a look at Adele Vetlesen's hotel registration card. I won't get away now before the afternoon flight, but I'll be home early tomorrow. Could you ring your friend, pumpkin head, at Drammen police station, and see if we can borrow the postcard Adele wrote? You can ask him to come to the station with it. The train stops at Drammen, doesn't it?'

'You're pushing your luck. I'll try anyway. What are we going to do with it?'

'Compare the handwriting. There's a handwriting expert called Jean Hue who worked at Kripos before he retired. Get him to the office for seven tomorrow.'

'So early? D'you think he'll—'

'You're right. I'll scan Adele's registration card and email it to you so you can go to Jean's place with both this evening.'

'This evening?'

'He'll be happy to see you. If you had any other plans, they are hereby cancelled.'

'Great. By the way, sorry about the late call last night.'

'No worries. Entertaining story.'

'I was a bit tipsy.'

'Thought so.'

Harry rang off.

'Thanks for all your help,' he said.

The receptionist responded with a smile.

The coffee-brown envelope had finally found a new owner.

Kjersti Rødsmoen went into the common room and over to the woman looking out of the window at the rain falling on Sandviken's timber houses. In front of her was an untouched slice of cake with a little candle on.

'This phone was found in your room, Katrine,' she said softly. 'The ward sister brought it to me. You know they're forbidden, don't you?'

Katrine nodded.

'Anyway,' Rødsmoen said, passing it over, 'it's ringing.'

Katrine Bratt took the vibrating mobile phone and pressed answer.

'It's me,' said the voice at the other end. 'I've got four women's names here. I'd like to know which of them was not booked on flight RA101 to Kigali on the 25th of November. And to receive confirmation that this person was not in any booking system for a Rwandan hotel that same night.'

'I'm fine, thanks, Auntie.'

Silence for a second.

'I see. Ring when you can.'

Katrine passed the phone back to Rødsmoen. 'My auntie wishing me many happy returns.'

Kjersti Rødsmoen shook her head. 'Rules say the use of phones is forbidden. So there's no reason why you shouldn't have a phone, so long as you don't use it. Just make sure the ward sister doesn't see it, OK?'

Katrine nodded, and Rødsmoen left.

Katrine sat looking out of the window for a while, then got up and went towards the Hobbies Room. The ward sister's voice reached her as she was about to cross the threshold.

'What are you going to do, Katrine?'

Katrine answered without turning. 'Play solitaire.'

33

Leipzig

GUNNAR HAGEN TOOK THE LIFT DOWN TO THE BASEMENT. Down. Downer. Downtrodden. Downsized.

He got out and set off through the culvert.

But Bellman had kept his promise, he hadn't blabbed. And he had thrown him a line, a top-management post in the new, expanded Kripos. Harry's report had been short and to the point. No results. Any idiot would have realised it was time to start swimming towards the lifebuoy.

Hagen opened the door at the end of the culvert without knocking.

Kaja Solness smiled sweetly while Harry Hole – sitting in front of the computer screen with a telephone to his ear – didn't even turn round, just sang out 'siddown-boss-want-some-crap-coffee?' as though the unit head's doppelgänger had announced his forthcoming arrival.

Hagen stood in the doorway. 'I received the message that you were unable to find Adele Vetlesen. Time to pack up. Time was up ages ago, and you're needed for other cases. At least you are, Kaja Solness.'

'*Dankeschön*, Günther,' Harry said on the telephone, put it down and swivelled round.

'*Dankeschön*?' Hagen repeated.

'Leipzig Police,' Harry said. 'By the way, Katrine Bratt sends her regards, boss. Remember her?'

Hagen eyed his inspector with suspicion. 'I thought Bratt was in a mental institution.'

'No doubt about that,' Harry said, getting up and making for the coffee machine. 'But the woman's a genius at searching the Net. Speaking of searches, boss . . .'

'Searches?'

'Could you see your way to giving us unlimited funds to mount a search?'

Hagen's eyes almost popped out. Then he burst out laughing. 'You're bloody incredible, Harry, you are. You've just wasted half the travel budget on a fiasco in the Congo and now you want a police search operation? This investigation comes to a halt right now. Do you understand?'

'I understand . . .' Harry said, pouring coffee into two cups and passing one to Hagen, '. . . so much more. And soon you will too, boss. Grab my chair and listen to this.'

Hagen looked from Harry to Kaja. Stared sceptically at the coffee. Then he sat down. 'You've got two minutes.'

'It's quite simple.' Harry said. 'According to Brussels Airlines passenger lists Adele Vetlesen travelled to Kigali on the 25th of November. But according to passport control no one of that name entered the country. What happened is that a woman with a false passport made out in Adele's name travelled from Oslo. The false passport would have worked without a hitch until she reached her final destination in Kigali, because that's where it's computer-checked and the number's matched, isn't it? So this mysterious woman must have used her own passport, which was genuine. Passport control officials don't ask to see the name on your ticket, so any mismatch between passport and ticket is not discovered. So long as no one looks, of course.'

'But you did?'

'Yup.'

'Couldn't it just be an administrative oversight? They forgot to register Adele's arrival?'

'Indeed. But then there's the postcard . . .'

Harry nodded to Kaja, who held up a card. Hagen saw a picture of something akin to a smoking volcano.

'This was posted in Kigali the same day she was supposed to have arrived,' Harry said. 'But first of all, this is a picture of Nyiragongo, a volcano situated in the Congo, not Rwanda. Secondly, we got Jean Hue to compare the handwriting on this card with the check-in card the alleged Adele Vetlesen filled in at the Gorilla Hotel.'

'He established beyond doubt what even I can see,' Kaja said. 'It's not the same person.'

'Alright, alright,' Hagen said. 'But where are you going with all of this?'

'Someone has gone to great effort to make it seem as if Adele Vetlesen went to Africa,' Harry said. 'My guess is that Adele was in Norway and was forced to write the card. Then it was taken to Africa by a second person who sent it back. All to give the impression that Adele had travelled there and written home about her dream guy and that she wouldn't be back before March.'

'Any idea who the impersonator might be?'

'Yes.'

'Yes?'

'The immigration authorities at Kigali Airport found a card made out in the name of Juliana Verni. But our friendly fruitcake in Bergen says this name was not registered on any airline passenger lists to Rwanda or at any hotels with modern, electronic booking equipment on the date in question. But she is on the Rwandan passenger list from Kigali three days later.'

'Would I like to know how you acquired this information?'

'No, boss. But you would like to know who and where Juliana Verni is.'

'And that is?'

Harry looked at his watch. 'According to the information on the landing card, she lives in Leipzig, Germany. Ever been to Leipzig, boss?'

'No.'

'Nor me. But I know it's famous for being the home town of Goethe, Bach plus one of the waltz kings. What's his name again?'

'What has this got to do with . . . ?'

'Well, you see, Leipzig is also famous for holding the main archives of the Stasi, the security police. The town was in the old GDR. Did you know that over the forty years the GDR existed the German spoken in the East developed in such a way that a sensitive ear can hear the difference between East and West Germans?'

'Harry . . .'

'Sorry, boss. The point is that in late November a woman with an East German accent was in the town of Goma in the Congo, which is just a three-hour drive from Kigali. And I'm positive that, while there, she bought the murder weapon that took the lives of Borgny Stem-Myhre and Charlotte Lolles.'

'We've been sent a copy of the form the police keep when passports are issued,' Kaja said, passing Hagen a sheet of paper.

'Matches Van Boorst's description of the buyer,' Harry said. 'Juliana Verni had big rust-red curls.'

'Brick red,' Kaja said.

'I beg your pardon?' Hagen said.

Kaja pointed to the sheet. 'She's got one of the old-fashioned passports with hair colour listed. They called it "brick red". German thoroughness, you know.'

'I've also asked the police in Leipzig to confiscate her passport and check it has a stamp from Kigali on the date in question.'

Gunnar Hagen stared blankly at the printout. He appeared to be trying to absorb what Harry and Kaja had said. At length he looked up with one raised bushy eyebrow. 'Are you telling me . . . are you telling me that you may have the person who . . .' The POB swallowed, struggled to find an indirect way of saying it, terrified that this miracle, this mirage might vanish if he said it aloud. But he gave up the attempt. '. . . is our serial killer?'

'I'm not saying any more than what I'm saying,' Harry said. 'For the moment. My colleague in Leipzig is going through her personal data and criminal records now, so we'll soon know a bit more about Fräulein Verni.'

'But this is fantastic news,' Hagen said, sending a gleam from Harry to Kaja, who gave him a nod of encouragement.

'Not . . .' Harry said, with a swig from his cup of coffee, '. . . for Adele Vetlesen's family.'

Hagen's smile faded. 'True. Do you think there's any hope for . . . ?'

Harry shook his head. 'She's dead, boss.'

'But . . .'

At that moment the telephone rang.

Harry took it. '*Ja*, Günther!' And repeated with a strained smile: '*Ja*, Dirty Harry. *Genau*.'

Gunnar Hagen and Kaja observed Harry as he listened in silence. Harry rounded off the conversation with a '*Danke*' and cradled the receiver. Cleared his throat.

'She's dead.'

'Yes, you said that,' Hagen said.

'No, Juliana Verni is. She was found in the River Elster on the 2nd of December.'

Hagen cursed under his breath.

'Cause of death?' Kaja asked.

Harry stared into the distance. 'Drowning.'

'Might have been an accident.'

Harry shook his head slowly. 'She didn't drown in water.'

In the ensuing silence they heard the rumble of the boiler in the adjacent room.

'Wounds in the mouth?' Kaja asked.

Harry nodded. 'Twenty-four to be precise. She was sent to Africa to bring back the instrument that would kill her.'

34

Medium

'So Juliana Verni was found dead in Leipzig three days after she flew home from Kigali,' Kaja said. 'Where she'd travelled as Adele Vetlesen, booked in at the Gorilla Hotel as Adele Vetlesen and sent a postcard written by the real Adele Vetlesen, probably dictated.'

'That's about the size of it,' said Harry, who was in the process of brewing some more coffee.

'And you think that Verni must have done that in collusion with someone,' Hagen said. 'And this second person killed her to cover the traces.'

'Yes,' Harry said.

'So it's just a question of finding the link between her and this second person. That shouldn't be too difficult. They must have been very close if they committed this kind of crime together.'

'Well in that case I'd have thought it would be pretty difficult.'

'Why's that?'

'Because,' Harry said, smacking down the lid of the machine and flicking the switch, 'Juliana Verni had a record. Drugs. Prostitution. Vagrancy. In short, she was the type it would have been easy to hire for a job like this, if the money was right. And everything so far suggests that the person behind it won't have left any clues for us, that he has considered most angles. Katrine discovered that Verni travelled from Leipzig to Oslo. From there she continued to Kigali using Adele's name. Nevertheless, Katrine did not find so much as a phone conversation between Verni's mobile and Norway. This person has been scrupulous.'

Hagen shook his head dejectedly. 'So close . . .'

Harry sat on the desk. 'There is another dilemma we have to resolve. The overnight guests at Håvass cabin that night.'

'What about them?'

'We cannot exclude the possibility that the page torn out of the guest book is a hit list. They have to be warned.'

'How? We don't know who they are.'

'Through the media. Even if it means we would be letting the killer know we've picked up his trail.'

Hagen slowly shook his head. 'Hit list. And you've only reached this conclusion *now*?'

'I know, boss.' Harry met Hagen's eyes. 'If I'd gone to the media with a warning as soon as we stumbled on the Håvass cabin, it might have saved Elias Skog's life.'

The room went quiet.

'*We* can't go to the media,' Hagen said.

'Why not?'

'If someone responds to the media alert, perhaps we can find out who else was in the cabin and what really happened,' Kaja said.

'We can't go to the media,' Hagen said, getting to his feet. 'We've been investigating a missing persons case and uncovered links with a murder case, which is in the Kripos hands. We have to pass the information on and let them take it further. I'll ring Bellman.'

'Wait!' Harry said. 'Should he take all the credit for what we've done?'

'I'm not sure there will be any credit to share, will there?' Hagen said, heading for the door. 'And you can start moving out now.'

'Isn't that a trifle hasty?' Kaja said.

The other two looked at her.

'I mean, we've still got a missing person here. Shouldn't we try to locate her before we tidy up?'

'And how were you going to go about that?' Hagen asked.

'As Harry said before. A search.'

'You don't even know where you should bloody search.'

'Harry knows.'

They looked at the man who had just grabbed the jug from the coffee machine with one hand and was holding his cup under the mud-brown stream with the other.

'Do you?' Hagen said at length.

'Yes, I do,' Harry said.

'Where?'

'You'll get into hot water,' Harry said.

'Shut up, and out with it,' Hagen said, without noticing the contradiction. Because he was thinking, here I am, doing it again. What was it about this tall, fair-haired policeman who always managed to drag others along when he took headlong plunges?

Olav Hole looked up at Harry and the woman beside him.

She had curtsied when she introduced herself, and Harry had noticed that his father had liked that; he was always complaining that women had stopped curtsying.

'So you're Harry's colleague,' Olav said. 'Does he behave himself?'

'We're off to organise an operation,' Harry said. 'Just dropped by to see how you were.'

His father smiled wanly, shrugged and beckoned Harry to come closer. Harry leaned forward, listened. And flinched.

'You'll be alright,' Harry said in a sudden hoarse voice and stood up. 'I'll be back this evening, OK?'

In the corridor Harry stopped Altman and motioned for Kaja to go on ahead.

'Listen, I was wondering if you could do me a big favour,' he said when Kaja was out of range. 'My father's just told me that he's in pain. He would never admit that to you because he's afraid you'll give him more painkillers, and, well, he has a pathological fear of becoming dependent on . . . drugs. There's a bit of family history here, you see.'

'Thee,' the nurse lisped and there was a moment of confusion until Harry realised that Altman had repeated 'see'. 'The problem is that I'm being shifted between wards at the moment.'

'I'm asking this as a personal favour.'

Altman screwed up one eye behind his glasses, staring thoughtfully at a point between himself and Harry. 'I'll see what I can do.'

'Thank you.'

Kaja drove while Harry was on the phone to the chief of operations at Briskeby Fire Station.

'Your father seems like a nice man,' Kaja said as Harry rang off.

Harry took that in. 'Mum made him good,' he said. 'When she was alive he was good. She brought out the best in him.'

'Sounds like something you've been through yourself,' she said.

'What?'

'Someone made you good.'

Harry looked out of the window. Nodded.

'Rakel?'

'Rakel and Oleg,' Harry said.

'Sorry, I didn't mean to . . .'

'It's alright.'

'It's just that when I came to Crime Squad everyone was talking about the Snowman case. About him trying to kill them. And you. But it was already over before the case began, wasn't it?'

'In a way,' Harry said.

'Have you had any contact with them?'

Harry shook his head. 'We had to try to put it behind us. Help Oleg to forget. When they're that young they still can.'

'Not always,' Kaja said with a sardonic smile.

Harry glanced at her. 'And who made you good?'

'Even,' she answered without any hesitation.

'No great romantic passions?'

She shook her head. 'No XLs. Just a few smalls. And one medium.'

'Got your cap set at someone?'

She chuckled. 'Cap set at someone?'

Harry smiled. 'My vocabulary is somewhat old-fashioned in that area.'

She hesitated. 'I suppose I'm a bit hung up on a guy.'

'And the prospects are?'

'Poor.'

'Let me guess,' Harry said, winding down the window and lighting a cigarette. 'He's married and says he'll leave his wife and kids for you, but never does?'

She laughed. 'Let me guess. You're the type who thinks he's so damned good at reading other people's minds because he only remembers the times he got it right?'

'He said you've just got to give him some time?'

'Wrong again,' she said. 'He doesn't say anything.'

Harry nodded. He was about to ask more questions when it struck him: he didn't want to know.

35

The Dive

THE MIST DRIFTED ACROSS THE SHINY, BLACK SURFACE OF Lake Lyseren. Along the banks the trees stood with bowed shoulders like sombre, silent witnesses. The tranquillity was broken by shouted commands, radio communication and splashes as divers toppled backwards off rubber dinghies. They had started on the shore closest to the ropery. The heads of the search-and-recovery teams had sent their divers out in a fan formation, and now they were standing on land, crossing off the squares on the defined search grid they had covered, and signalling with a pull on the lifelines when they wanted the divers to stop or come back. The professional divers, such as Jarle Andreassen, also had wires in the lines which went up to full-face masks, allowing them to stay in verbal contact.

It was only six months since Jarle had taken his rescue course, and his pulse was still up during these dives. And a high pulse meant higher oxygen consumption. The more experienced men at Briskeby Fire Station called him 'The Float' as he had to rise to the surface and exchange oxygen cylinders so often.

Jarle knew that there was still good daylight at the top, but down here it was as black as night. He tried to swim at the regulation one and a half metres above the lakebed, yet he still stirred up mud, which reflected the light from his torch and partially blinded him. Even though he knew there were other divers a few metres away on either side, he felt alone. Alone and frozen to the marrow. And there were probably still hours of diving ahead of them. He knew he had less air left than the others and cursed to himself. Being the first fire station diver to change cylinders was fine by him, but he feared he would have to surface before the voluntary club divers as well. He refocused in front of him and stopped breathing. Not as a conscious action to reduce consumption. But because in the middle of his torch beam, inside the swaying forest of stalks that grew in the muddy bed closer to land, he could see a form floating free. A form that did not belong down here, that would be unable to live here. An alien feature. That was what made it so fascinating and at the same time so frightening. Or perhaps it was the light from his torch shining on the dark eyes that made it look as if it were alive.

'Everything OK, Jarle?'

It was the team head. One of his tasks was to listen to his divers' breathing. Not just to be sure they were breathing, but to hear if there were signs of anxiety. Or excessive calm. At twenty metres the brain began to store so much nitrogen that the so-called rapture of the deep could emerge, the nitrogen narcosis that meant you began to forget things, that simple jobs became more difficult and could, at greater depths, produce dizziness, tunnel vision and downright irrational behaviour. Jarle didn't know if they were just yarns that did the rounds, but he had heard of divers who had pulled off their masks with a smile at fifty metres below. So far the only narcosis he had experienced was the cosy red-wine-induced serenity that he enjoyed with his partner late on Saturday nights.

'Everything's fine,' Jarle Andreassen said and started breathing again. He sucked in the mixture of oxygen and nitrogen and heard it rumble past his ears as he released clusters of bubbles that fought their way desperately to the surface.

It was a large red stag. It was hanging upside down, its huge antlers apparently caught on the rock face. It must have been feeding on the bank and fallen. Or perhaps something or someone had chased it into the water. What else would it have been doing there? It had probably got tangled up in the rushes and the long stems of the water lilies, tried to struggle free, with the result that it had only got even more enmeshed in the tough, green tentacles. And then it must have gone under and wrestled on until it drowned. Sunk to the bottom and lain there until the bacteria and the body's chemistry had filled it with gas and it had risen towards the top again, but the antlers had snagged on the lattice of green plants growing down here. In a few days the gas would have drained from the cadaver and it would have sunk again. Just like a drowned human body. The same thing was as likely to have happened to the person they were looking for, and that was why the body had not been found: it had never floated to the surface. If so, it would be lying down here somewhere, probably covered with a layer of mud. Mud which inevitably swirled upwards as they approached, which meant that even small defined search areas such as this could keep their secrets concealed for all eternity.

Jarle Andreassen took out his large diver's knife, swam over to the stag and cut the stems obstructing the antlers. He had an inkling his boss would not appreciate that, but he couldn't bear the thought of this handsome beast being held under water. The cadaver rose half a metre, but then there were more stems holding it back. Jarle was careful not to let his lifeline get snarled in the reeds and made some hurried slashes. Then he felt a pull on the line. Hard enough for him to feel irritation. Hard enough for him to lose concentration for a moment. The knife slipped out of his hand. He shone his torch downwards and caught a glimpse of the blade before it was lost from view in the mud. Cautiously he swam after it. Thrust his hand into the mud drifting up towards him like ash. Groped along the bottom. Felt stones, branches, slippery, rotten and green. And something hard. Chain. Probably from a boat. More chain. Something else. Solid. The contours of something. A hole, an opening. He heard the sudden hiss of bubbles before his brain could formulate the thought. That he was afraid.

'Everything OK, Jarle? Jarle?'

No, everything was not OK. For even through thick gloves, even with a brain that seemed unable to absorb enough air, he had no doubts about where his hand had strayed. Into the open mouth of a human body.

PART FOUR

36

Helicopter

MIKAEL BELLMAN ARRIVED AT THE LAKE IN A HELICOPTER. The rotor blades whisked the mist into candyfloss as he dashed, bent double, from the passenger seat across the field to the ropery. Kolkka and Beavis followed at a half-run. From the opposite direction came four men carrying a stretcher. Bellman stopped them and lifted the blanket. The stretcher-bearers averted their faces as Bellman leaned over and studiously examined the naked, white bloated body.

'Thank you,' he said and let them continue towards the helicopter.

Bellman stopped at the top of the slope and looked down on the people standing between the building and the water. Among the divers divesting themselves of their equipment and dry suits he could see Beate Lønn and Kaja Solness. Further away was Harry Hole, talking to a man Bellman guessed was Skai, the local County Officer.

The POB signalled to Beavis and Kolkka that they should wait, and with lithe, nimble steps, he glided down the slope.

'Hello, Skai,' Bellman said, brushing twigs off his long coat. 'Mikael Bellman, Kripos, we've spoken on the phone.'

'Correct,' Skai said. 'The night his people found some rope here.' He jerked his thumb back towards Harry.

'And now it seems he's here again,' Bellman said. 'The question is, of course, what he's doing at my crime scene.'

'Well,' Harry said, clearing his throat, 'firstly, this is hardly a crime scene. Secondly, I'm looking for a missing person. And it does seem as if we've found what we were looking for. How's the triple murder going? Found anything? You got our information about the Håvass cabin, did you?'

The County Officer acknowledged a glance from Bellman and absented himself in discreet haste.

Bellman surveyed the lake while running a forefinger along his lower lip as if to rub in some ointment. 'Alright, Hole, you are aware, are you, that you have just ensured that both you and your superior officer, Gunnar Hagen, have not only lost your jobs but will also be charged with dereliction of duty?'

'Mm, because we do the job we've been entrusted with?'

'I think the Minister of Justice will be demanding a pretty detailed explanation as to why you initiated a search for a missing person right outside the ropery which supplied the rope that was used to kill Marit Olsen. I gave you Crime Squad people a chance. You won't get another. Game over, Hole.'

'Then we'll have to give the Minister of Justice a pretty detailed explanation, Bellman. Naturally, it will include information about how we found out where the rope came from, how we got onto the trail of Elias Skog and the Håvass cabin, how we found out that there was a fourth victim called Adele Vetlesen and how we found her here today. A job Kripos, with all its manpower and resources, failed to carry out over two months. Eh, Bellman?'

Bellman didn't answer.

'Frightened it might affect the Minister of Justice's decision on who is best suited to investigate murders in this country, are you?'

'Don't overplay your hand, Hole. I'll crush you just like that.' Bellman flicked his fingers.

'OK,' Harry said. 'Neither of us has a winning hand, so what if I pass over the kitty?'

'What the hell do you mean?'

'You get everything. Everything we have. We don't take credit for anything.'

Bellman looked askance at Harry. 'And why should you help us?'

'Simple,' Harry said, plucking the last smoke from the pack. 'I get paid for helping to catch the killer. That's my job.'

Bellman grimaced and his head and shoulders moved as if he were laughing, but not a sound issued forth. 'Come on, Hole, what do you want?'

Harry lit his cigarette. 'I don't want Gunnar Hagen, Kaja Solness or Bjørn Holm to take the rap for this. Your prospects in the force won't be affected.'

Bellman squeezed his full lower lip between thumb and first finger. 'I'll see what I can do.'

'And I want to be part of this. I want access to all the material you have and to resources for the investigation.'

'That's enough!' Bellman said, raising a hand. 'Are you hard of hearing, Hole? I told you to stay away from this case.'

'We can catch this killer, Bellman. Right now that should be more bloody important than who's in charge afterwards, shouldn't it?'

'Don't you . . . !' Bellman shouted, but held back when he saw a couple of heads turn in their direction. He took a step closer to Harry and lowered his voice. 'Don't you talk to me as if I were an idiot, Hole.'

The wind blew the smoke from Harry's cigarette into Bellman's face, but he didn't blink. Harry shrugged.

'Do you know what, Bellman? I don't think this has much to do with power or politics. You're a little boy who wants to be the hero who saves the day. Simple as that. And you're scared I'll ruin the epic. But there's an easy way of resolving this. What about unzipping and seeing who can piss as far as the divers' dinghy?'

When Mikael Bellman laughed this time, it was for real, with volume and everything. 'You should read the warning signs, Harry.'

His right hand shot out, so quickly that Harry didn't manage to react, struck the cigarette between his lips and knocked it away. It hit the water with a hiss.

'Smoking kills. Have a good day.'

Harry heard the helicopter take off as he watched his last cigarette floating in the water. The grey, wet paper, the black, dead tip.

Night had started to fall as the diving team's boat dropped Harry, Kaja and Beate ashore by the car park. There was sudden movement amid the trees followed by camera flashes. Harry instinctively held up an arm, and he heard Roger Gjendem's voice from out of the darkness.

'Harry Hole, there are rumours flying around that you've found a young woman's body. What's her name and how sure are you that this is connected with the other murders?'

'No comment,' Harry said, ploughing his way through, half blinded. 'For the moment this is a missing persons case, and the only thing we can say is that a woman has been found who might be the missing person. As far as the murder cases I assume you're referring to are concerned, talk to Kripos.'

'Woman's name?'

'She has to be identified first and relatives informed.'

'But you're not ruling out—'

'As usual, I'm not ruling out anything, Gjendem. Press conference to follow.'

Harry got into the car; Kaja had already started the engine and Beate Lønn was sitting on the back seat. They trundled onto the main road to the flashes of cameras behind them.

'Now,' Beate Lønn said, leaning forward between the seats, 'I still haven't been given an explanation as to how your search for Adele Vetlesen led here.'

'Deductive logic, pure and simple,' Harry said.

'Goes without saying,' Beate sighed.

'In fact, I'm embarrassed I didn't twig before,' Harry said. 'I went round wondering why the killer had made the effort to go all the way out to a disused ropery just for a piece of rope. Especially since that rope – unlike what he could have bought in a shop – could be traced back here. The answer was, of course, obvious. Nevertheless, it was only when I sat looking into a deep African lake that I realised. He didn't come here for the rope. He must have used the rope for something here – because it happened to be lying around – and then taken it home where he later used it to kill Marit Olsen. The reason he came here was that he already had a body he needed to dispose of. Adele Vetlesen. The local man, Skai, spelt it out for us the first time we came here. This is the deep end of the lake. The killer filled her trousers with rocks, tied up the waist and legs with rope, then dropped her overboard.'

'How do you know she was dead before she came here? He might have drowned her.'

'There was a large cut around her neck. It's my bet the post-mortem will show that there wasn't any water in her lungs.'

'And that ketanome is in her bloodstream, the same as with Charlotte and Borgny,' Beate said.

'I'm told ketanome is a fast-working anaesthetic,' Harry said. 'Strange I'd never heard of it before.'

'Not so strange,' Beate said. 'It's an old cheapo version of ketalar, which is used to anaesthetise patients with the advantage that they can still breathe by themselves,' Beate said. 'Ketanome was banned in the EU and Norway in the nineties because of side effects, so now you generally see it in underdeveloped countries. Kripos considered it a major clue for a while, but got nowhere with it.'

As they dropped Beate off at Krimteknisk in Bryn forty minutes later, Harry asked Kaja to hang on and got out of the car.

'There was one thing I wanted to ask you,' Harry said.

'Oh yes?' Beate said, shivering and rubbing her hands together.

'What were you doing at a potential crime scene? Why wasn't Bjørn there?'

'Because Bellman assigned Bjørn to special duties.'

'And what does that mean? Cleaning the latrines?'

'No. Coordination of Krimteknisk and strategic planning.'

'What?' Harry raised his eyebrows. 'That's a bloody promotion.'

Beate shrugged. 'Bjørn's good. It wasn't before time. Anything else?'

'No.'

'Bye.'

'Bye. Oh, by the way, just a moment. I asked you to tell Bellman where we'd found the rope. When did you pass the message on?'

'You rang me at night, remember, so I waited until the following morning. Why's that?'

'No reason,' Harry said. 'No reason.'

When he got back into the car, Kaja quickly slipped her phone into her pocket.

'News of the body's already on the *Aftenposten* website,' she said.

'Oh yes?'

'They say there's a big pic of you with your full name and that you're referred to as "heading the investigation". And of course they're linking this case with the other murders.'

'So, that's what they're doing. Mm. Are you hungry?'

'Quite.'

'Have you got any plans? If not I'll treat you to a meal.'

'Great. Where?'

'Ekeberg restaurant.'

'Ooh. Exclusive. Any particular reason you chose that one?'

'Well, it came to mind when a pal of mine was recounting an old story.'

'Tell me.'

'There's nothing to tell, it's just the usual adolescence thi—'

'Adolescence! Come on!'

Harry chuckled. And as they approached the city centre and it started snowing at the top of Ekeberg Ridge, Harry told her about Killer Queen, the darling of Ekeberg restaurant, once the most attractive functionalist building in Oslo. Which today – post renovation – it is again.

'But in the eighties it was so run-down that people had actually given up on the place. It had become a boozy dance restaurant where you went to tables and asked for the pleasure, trying not to knock over the glasses. And then shuffled round the floor propping each other up.'

'I see.'

'Øystein, Tresko and I used to go to the top of the German bunkers on Nordstrand beach, drink beer and wait for puberty to pass. When we were seventeen we ventured over to the restaurant, lied about our ages and went in. You didn't have to lie much – the place needed all the cash it could get. The dance band stank, but at least they played "Nights in White Satin". And they had a star attraction who guested almost every night. We called her Killer Queen. A female man-o'-war, she was.'

'A *man-o'-war*?' Kaja laughed. 'Set your cap at?'

'Yup,' Harry said. 'Bore down on you like a galleon in full rig, mean, sexy and dead scary. Equipped like a fairground. Curves on her like a roller coaster.'

Kaja laughed even louder. 'The local fun-fair, no less?'

'In a way,' Harry said. 'But she went to Ekeberg restaurant primarily to be seen and adored, I think. And for the free drinks from faded dance-floor kings, of course. No one ever saw Killer Queen go home with any of them. Perhaps that was what fascinated us. A woman who'd had to go down a league or two for admirers, but in a way still had style.'

'And then what?'

'Øystein and Tresko said they would each buy me a whiskey if I dared ask her to dance.'

They crossed the tramlines and drove up the steep hill to the restaurant.

'And?' Kaja said.

'I dared.'

'And then?'

'We danced. Until she said she was sick of having her feet trodden on and it would be better if we went for a walk. She left first. It was August, hot, and, as you can see, there's only forest round here. Thick foliage and loads of paths to hidden places. I was drunk, but still so excited that I knew she would be able to hear the tremor in my voice if I said anything. So I kept my trap shut. And that was fine, she did all the talking. And the rest, too. Afterwards she asked me if I wanted to go home with her.'

Kaja sniggered. 'Oooh. And what happened there?'

'We can talk about that during the meal. We're here.'

They came to a halt in the car park, got out and walked up the steps to the restaurant. The head waiter welcomed them at the entrance to the dining area and asked for the name. Harry answered that they hadn't reserved a table.

The waiter could barely restrain himself from rolling his eyes.

'Full for the next two months,' Harry snorted as they left, after buying cigarettes at the bar. 'I think I liked the place better when water was leaking into the restaurant and rats squealed at you from behind the toilets. At least we could get in.'

'Let's have a smoke,' Kaja suggested.

They walked over to the low brick wall from where the forest sloped downwards into Oslo. The clouds in the west were tinged with orange and red, and the queues of traffic on the motorway glittered like phosphorescence against the blackness of the town. It seemed to be lying there in wait, keeping watch, Harry thought. A camouflaged beast of prey. He tapped out two cigarettes, lit them and passed one to Kaja.

'The rest of the story,' Kaja said, inhaling.

'Where were we?'

'Killer Queen took you home.'

'No, she asked if I wanted to go. And I politely declined.'

'Declined? You're lying. Why?'

'Øystein and Tresko asked me that when I got back. I told them I couldn't just leave when I had two pals and free whiskey waiting for me.'

Kaja laughed and blew smoke over the view.

'But of course that was a lie,' Harry said. 'Loyalty had nothing to do with it. Friendship means nothing to a man if he has a tempting enough offer. Nothing. The truth is that I didn't dare. Killer Queen was simply in the scariest league of all for me.'

They sat silent for a while. Listening to the hum of the town and watching the smoke curl upwards.

'You're thinking,' Kaja said.

'Mm. I'm thinking about Bellman. How well informed he is. He not only knew I was coming to Norway, he even knew which flight I was on.'

'Perhaps he has contacts at Police HQ.'

'Mm. And at Lake Lyseren today Skai said that Bellman had rung him about the rope the same evening that we'd been at the ropery.'

'Really?'

'But Beate says she didn't tell Bellman about the rope until the morning after we'd been there.' Harry followed the glow of tobacco on its flight over the slope. 'And Bjørn has been promoted to coordinator for forensics and strategic planning.'

Kaja stared at him in surprise. 'That's not possible, Harry.'

He didn't answer.

'Bjørn Holm! Would he have kept Bellman informed about what we were doing? You two have worked together for so long, you're . . . friends!'

Harry shrugged. 'As I said, I think . . .' He dropped his cigarette onto the ground and crushed it with a swivel of his heel. '. . . friendship means nothing to a man if he has a tempting enough offer. Do you dare join me for today's special at Schrøder's?'

I dream all the time now. It was summer and I loved her. I was so young and thought that if you wanted something enough it was yours to have.

Adele, you had her smile, her hair and her faithless heart. And now Aftenposten *says they have found you. I hope you were as foul on the outside as you were on the inside.*

It also says they've put Inspector Harry Hole on the case. He was the one who caught the Snowman. Perhaps there's hope, perhaps the police can save lives after all?

I've printed out a photo of Adele from the Verdens Gang *website and pinned it on the wall, next to the torn page from the Håvass cabin guest book. Including mine, there are only three more names now.*

37

Profile

THE SPECIAL AT SCHRØDER'S WAS BUBBLE AND SQUEAK SERVED with fried eggs and raw onions.

'Nice,' said Kaja.

'The cook must be sober today,' Harry agreed. Then he pointed. 'Look.'

Kaja turned and looked up at the TV Harry was indicating.

'Well, hello!' she said.

Mikael Bellman's face filled the screen, and Harry signalled to Rita that they wanted the volume up. Harry studied the movements of Bellman's mouth. The soft, quasi-feminine features. The gleam in the intense brown eyes beneath the elegantly formed eyebrows. The white patches, like sleet on his skin, didn't disfigure him, quite the contrary, they made him more interesting to look at, like an exotic animal. If his number were not ex-directory, as was the case with most detectives, his phone would be full of lusting and love-lorn texters afterwards. Then the sound came on.

'. . . at Håvass cabin on the night of the 7th of November. So we are appealing to those of you who were there to come forward to the police as quickly as possible.'

Then the newsreader returned and there was a new item.

Harry pushed his plate away and waved for coffee. 'Let me hear your thoughts about this killer now that we've found Adele. Give me a profile.'

'Why?' Kaja asked, sipping water from her glass. 'From tomorrow we'll be working on other cases.'

'Just for fun.'

'Does profiling of serial killers come under your definition of fun?'

Harry sucked on a toothpick. 'I know there's a good answer to that, but I can't think of it.'

'You're sick.'

'So who is he?'

'It's still a he, first off. And still a serial killer. I don't necessarily think Adele was number one.'

'Why not?'

'Because it was so flawless that he must have kept a clear head. The first time you kill you're not so clear-headed. Besides, he hid her so well that we definitely were not intended to find her. That suggests he may be behind many of the present missing persons statistics.'

'Good. More.'

'Erm . . .'

'Come on. You just said that he made a good job of hiding Adele Vetlesen. The first of the murder victims we know anything about. How do the other murders develop?'

'He becomes bolder, more self-assured. He stops hiding them. Charlotte is found behind a car in the forest and Borgny in a cellar beneath a city centre office block.'

'And Marit Olsen?'

Kaja mulled this over. 'It's too overblown. He's lost control, his grip is going.'

'Or . . .' Harry said, '. . . he's gone up to the next level. He wants to show everyone how clever he is, so he starts exhibiting his victims. The murder of Marit Olsen in Frogner Lido is a huge scream for attention, but there are few indications of failing control in the execution. The rope he used was at worst careless, but otherwise he left no clues. Disagree?'

She deliberated and shook her head.

'Then there's Elias Skog,' Harry said. 'Anything different there?'

'He tortures the victim with a slow death,' Kaja said. 'The sadist in him reveals itself.'

'A Leopold's apple is also an instrument of torture,' Harry said. 'But I agree with you that this is the first time we've seen sadism. At the same time, it's a conscious choice; he reveals himself, he doesn't let others do it. He is still directing the show, he's in charge.'

The coffee pot and cups were dumped down in front of them.

'But . . .' Kaja said.

'Yes?'

'Doesn't it jar a bit that a sadistic killer would leave the crime scene before he can witness the victim's sufferings and final death? According to the landlady, she could hear banging noises from the bathroom after the guest had gone. He ran off . . . funny, eh?'

'Good point. So what have we got? A fake sadist. And why does he fake it?'

'Because he knows we'll try to profile him, the way we're doing now,' Kaja said eagerly. 'And then we'll go looking for him in the wrong places.'

'Mm. Maybe. A sophisticated killer, if so.'

'What do you think, oh, venerable wise one?'

Harry poured the coffee. 'If this is really a serial killer, I think the murders are well spread out.'

Kaja leaned across the table, and her pointed teeth glistened as she whispered: 'You think it might *not* be a serial killer?'

'Well, there's a signature missing. Usually, there are special aspects of the murder that trigger a serial killer, and thus certain things that recur throughout. Here we have no indications that the killer did anything sexual during the killing. And there's no similarity in the methods used, apart from Borgny and Charlotte both being murdered with a Leopold's apple. The crime scenes are quite different, and so are the victims. Both sexes, different ages, different backgrounds, different physiques.'

'But they have not been selected at random; they spent the same night in the same cabin.'

'Precisely. And that's why I'm not absolutely convinced we're up against a classic serial killer. Or, rather, not one with a classic motive to kill. For serial killers, the killing itself is generally enough of a motive. If, for example, the victims are prostitutes. It doesn't really matter whether they are sinners, just that they are easy prey. I know of only one serial killer who had criteria for the selection of individual victims.'

'The Snowman.'

'I don't think a serial killer chooses his victims from a random page of a cabin guest book. And if anything happened at Håvass to give the killer a motive, we're not talking about classic serial murders. Besides, the move to show himself was too quick for the usual serial killer.'

'What do you mean?'

'He sent a woman to Rwanda and the Congo to cover up a murder and at the same time to buy the murder weapon for the next. Afterwards he killed her. In other words, he went to extremes to hide one murder, yet for the next one, a few weeks later, he did absolutely nothing. And for the next murder again, he's like a matador shoving his bollocks in our faces with a flourish of his cloak. This is a personality change at fast-forward speed. It doesn't make sense.'

'Do you think there could be several killers? Each with a different method?'

Harry shook his head. 'There is one similarity. The killer doesn't leave any clues. If serial killers are rare, one that kills without leaving any clues is a white whale. There is only one of them in this case.'

'Right, so what are we talking here?' Kaja threw up her arms. 'A serial killer with multiple-personality disorder?'

'A white whale with wings,' Harry said. 'No, I don't know. And anyway, it doesn't matter. We're only doing this for fun. It's a Kripos case now.' He drained his coffee. 'I'm going to take a taxi to the hospital.'

'I can drive you.'

'Thank you but no. Go home and prepare for new and interesting cases.'

Kaja heaved a weary sigh. 'The business with Bjørn . . .'

'Must not be mentioned to a soul,' Harry completed. 'Have a good sleep.'

Altman was leaving Harry's father's room at Rikshospital when he arrived.

'He's asleep,' the nurse said. 'I gave him ten milligrams of morphine. You can sit here, no problem, but he's unlikely to stir for several hours.'

227

'Thank you,' Harry said.

'That's OK. I had a mother who . . . well, who had to put up with more pain than was necessary.'

'Mm. Do you smoke, Altman?'

Harry saw from the guilt-ridden reaction that Altman did, and invited him to join him outside. The two men smoked while Altman, first name Sigurd, explained that it had been because of his mother that he had specialised in anaesthesia.

'So when you gave my father an injection just now . . .'

'Let's say it was a favour from one son to another,' Altman smiled. 'But I cleared it with the doctor, naturally. I would like to keep my job.'

'Wise,' Harry said. 'Wish I were as wise.'

They finished their cigarettes, and Altman was about to go when Harry asked: 'Since you're an anaesthetics expert, could you tell me how a person might get hold of ketanome?'

'Oh dear,' Altman said. 'I probably shouldn't answer that.'

'It's OK,' Harry said with a wry smile. 'It's about the murder case I'm working on.'

'Aha. Well, unless you work with anaesthetics, ketanome is very hard to get hold of in Norway. It works like a bullet, almost literally – the patient is knocked flat. But the side effects – ulcers – are nasty. In addition, the risk of a cardiac arrest with an overdose is high. It's been used for suicide. But not any more. Ketanome was banned in the EU and Norway some years ago.'

'I know that, but where would you go to get ketanome?'

'Well, ex-Soviet states. Or Africa.'

'The Congo, for example?'

'Definitely. The producer sells it at dumping prices since the European ban, so it ends up in poor countries. It's always like that.'

Harry sat by his father's bedside watching his frail pyjama-clad chest rise and fall. After an hour he got up and left.

Harry decided he would postpone making a call until he had unlocked the house, put on 'Don't Get Around Much Any More' – one of his father's Duke Ellington records – and taken out the brown clump. He saw that Gunnar Hagen had left a message, but he had no intention of listening to it as he knew roughly what it was about. Bellman would have been nagging him again: from now on they were not allowed to touch the murder case however compelling their excuses. And Harry was to report for normal duties if he still wanted a job with the police. Well, perhaps not the last part. It was time to head off on his travels. And the travels should start here, now, tonight. He took out the lighter with one hand while the other brought up the two texts he had received. The first was from Øystein. He suggested 'a gentlemen's night out' in the not too distant future, with an invitation to Tresko, who was probably the most well-to-do of the three. The second was a number Harry didn't recognise. Harry opened the message.

I see from the *Aftenposten* website that you're in charge of the case. I can help. Elias Skog talked before he was glued to the bath. C.

Harry dropped the lighter, which hit the glass table with a loud bang, and he felt his heart race. During murder cases they always got loads of people ringing in with tip-offs, advice and hypotheses. People who were willing to swear they had seen, heard or been told all sorts, and couldn't the police spare them a moment to listen? Often it was the same old voices again and again, but there were always some new, mixed-up windbags. Harry was quite certain that this was not one of them. The press had written a lot about the case; readers possessed a considerable amount of information. The general public had not been told that Elias Skog had been glued to the bath, however. Or been given Harry's ex-directory mobile number.

38

Permanent Scarring

HARRY HAD TURNED DOWN DUKE ELLINGTON AND SAT WITH the phone in his hand. This person knew about the superglue. And had his number. Should he check the name and address of the caller, perhaps even have the person arrested because there was a chance he might frighten him off? On the other hand, whoever it was expected an answer.

Harry pressed 'return call'.

It buzzed twice, then he heard a deep voice. 'Yes?'

'This is Harry Hole.'

'Nice to talk to you again, Hole.'

'Mm. When have we spoken before?'

'Don't you remember? Elias Skog's flat. Superglue.'

Harry felt the carotid artery in his neck throb, cramp the space in his throat.

'I was there. Who am I speaking to, and what were you doing there?'

The other end went quiet for a second and Harry immediately concluded the person had rung off. But then the voice was back with a drawn-out 'Oh, sorry, I may have signed off the message with just C. Did I?'

'Yes, you did.'

'I generally do. This is Inspector Colbjørnsen. From Stavanger. You gave me your number, remember?'

Harry cursed himself, realised he was still holding his breath and let it out in a long hiss.

'Are you there?'

'Uh-huh,' Harry said, grabbing the teaspoon on the table and scraping off a bit of the opium. 'You said you had something for me?'

'Yes, I have. But on one condition.'

'Which is?'

'It stays between us.'

'Why's that?'

'Because I don't want that prick Bellman coming over here thinking he's God's gift to criminal investigations. He and fucking Kripos are trying to get a monopoly over the whole country. Far as I'm concerned he can go to hell. The problem is my bosses. I'm not allowed to touch the bloody Skog case.'

'So why come to me?'

'I'm a simple lad from the provinces, Hole. But when I see in *Aftenposten* that you've been given the case I know what's going to happen. I know you're like me, you won't just lie down and die, will you.'

'Well . . .' Harry said, looking at the opium in front of him.

'So if you can use this to outsmart the smart-arse and it leads to Bellman's plans for the evil empire being shelved, accept it with my blessing. I'll wait until the day after tomorrow before sending Bellman my report. That gives you a day.'

'What've you got?'

'I've spoken to folk in Skog's circle, which was small, as he was an oddball, unusually intense and travelled around the world on his ownsome. Two persons in all. The landlady. And a girl we traced via the phone numbers he had rung in the days leading up to his death. Her name is Stine Ølberg, and she said she spoke to Elias the night he was killed. They were on the bus leaving town, and he said he'd been to the Håvass cabin at the same time as the murdered girls in the newspapers. He thought it was strange no one had discovered they'd all been to the same cabin and he'd been wondering about whether to go to the police. But he was reluctant because he had no desire to get involved. And I can understand that. Skog had been in trouble with the police before. He'd been reported for stalking on two occasions. He hadn't done anything illegal, to be fair to him. He was, as I said, just the intense type. Stine said she had been frightened of him, but that evening it was the opposite: he was the one who had seemed frightened.'

'Interesting.'

'Stine had pretended not to know who the three murder victims were, and then Elias had said that he would tell her about someone else who had been there, someone he was sure she did know. And this is the really interesting bit. The man is well known. At least a B-list celebrity.'

'Oh yes?'

'According to Elias Skog, Tony Leike was there.'

'Tony Leike. Should I know who that is?'

'He lives with the daughter of Anders Galtung, the shipping magnate.'

A couple of newspaper headlines flashed in front of Harry's inner eye.

'Tony Leike is a so-called investor, which means he has become rich and no one quite understands how, just that it certainly wasn't by dint of hard work. Not only that, he's a real pretty boy. Hardly Mr Nice Guy, though. And this is the crunch. The guy's got a sheet.'

'Sheet?' Harry asked, affecting incomprehension to imply what he thought of Colbjørnsen's Americanisms.

'A record. Tony Leike has a conviction for violent assault.'

'Mm. Checked the charge?'

'Years ago Tony Leike beat up and maimed one Ole S. Hansen on the 7th of August between 11.20 and 11.45 p.m. It happened outside a dance venue where Tony was living with his grandfather. Tony was eighteen, Ole seventeen and of course it was over a piece of skirt.'

'Mm. Jealous kids fighting after drinking is not exactly unusual. Did you say violent assault?'

'Yes; in fact, there was more. After Leike had knocked down the other boy, he sat on him and carved up the poor lad's face with a knife. He was permanently scarred, though the report said it could have been much worse if people hadn't dragged Leike off.'

'But no more than the one conviction?'

'Tony Leike was known for his temper and was regularly involved in brawls. At the trial a witness said that at school Leike had tried to strangle him with a belt because he had said something less than flattering about Tony's father.'

232

'Sounds like someone should have a long chat with Leike. Do you know where he lives?'

'On your patch. Holmenveien . . . wait . . . 172.'

'Right. West End. Hm. Thanks, Colbjørnsen.'

'Not at all. Erm, there was one other thing. A man got on the bus after Elias. He alighted at the same stop as Elias, and Stine says she saw the man following him. But she couldn't give a description because his face was hidden by a hat. Might be of some significance, or not.'

'Right.'

'So I'm counting on you, Hole.'

'Counting on what?'

'You doing the right thing.'

'Mm.'

'Goodnight.'

Harry sat listening to the Duke. Then he grabbed the phone and looked up Kaja's number. He was about to press the call button but hesitated. He was doing it again. Dragging people down with him. Harry tossed the phone aside. There were two options. The smart one, which was to ring Bellman. Or the stupid one, which was to go it alone.

Harry sighed. Who was he kidding? He had no choice. So he stuffed the lighter in his pocket, wrapped up the ball in silver foil, put it in the drinks cabinet, undressed, set the alarm for six and went to bed. No choice. A prisoner of his own behaviour patterns whereby in reality every action was a compulsive action. In that sense, he was neither better nor worse than those he pursued.

And with this thought he fell asleep with a smile on his lips.

The night is so blessedly still, it heals your sight, clears your mind. The new, old policeman. Hole. I'll have to tell him that. I won't show him everything, just enough for him to understand. Then he can stop it. So that I don't have to do what I do. I spit and spit, but blood fills my mouth, over and over again.

39

Relational Search

HARRY ARRIVED AT POLICE HQ AT A QUARTER TO SEVEN IN the morning. Apart from the security guard on reception there was no one around in the large atrium inside the heavy front doors.

He nodded to the guard, swiped his card in the reader by the gate and took the lift down to the cellar. From there he loped through the culvert and unlocked the room. He lit the day's first cigarette and rang the mobile number while the computer booted up. Katrine Bratt sounded sleepy.

'I want you to run those relational searches of yours,' Harry said. 'Between a Tony Leike and each of the murder victims. Including Juliana Verni from Leipzig.'

'The Hobbies Room's free until half past eight,' she said. 'I'll get going this minute. Anything else?'

Harry hesitated. 'Could you check on a Jussi Kolkka for me? Policeman.'

'What's he about?'

'That's the point,' Harry said. 'I don't know what he's about.'

Harry put down the phone and set to work on the computer.

Tony Leike had one conviction, that was correct. And according to the register he had been in trouble with the police on two other occasions as well. As Colbjørnsen had indicated, both were for physical violence. In the first instance the charge had been withdrawn, in the other the case had been dropped.

Harry googled Tony Leike and got a number of hits: minor newspaper mentions – most of which were connected with his fiancée Lene Galtung – but there were also some in the financial press where he was referred to alternately as an investor, a speculator and an ignorant sheep. This last, in *Kapital*, was a reference to Leike belonging to the flock that mimicked a lead sheep, the psychologist Einar Kringlen, in everything he did: from buying shares, mountain cabins and cars to his choice of the right restaurant, drink, woman, office, house and holiday destination.

Harry searched through the links until he stopped at an article in a financial newspaper.

'Bingo,' he mumbled.

Tony Leike was clearly able to stand on his own two feet. Or in his own two mining boots. At any rate the *Finansavisen* wrote about a mining project with Leike as the entrepreneur and enthusiast. He was photographed alongside with his colleagues, two young men with side partings. They were not wearing the standard designer suits, but overalls and work clothes, sitting on a pile of wood in front of a helicopter and smiling. Tony Leike wore the biggest smile of them all. He was broad-shouldered, long-limbed, dark, both his skin and his hair, and he had an impressive aquiline nose that in conjunction with his colouring made Harry think that he must have at least a dash of Arab blood in his veins. But the reason for Harry's restrained outburst was the headline: KING OF THE CONGO?

Harry continued to follow the links.

The yellow press were more interested in the imminent wedding with Lene Galtung and the guest list.

Harry glanced at his watch. Five past seven. He rang the duty officer.

'I need assistance for an arrest in Holmenveien.'

'Detention?'

Harry knew very well that he didn't have enough to ask the police solicitor for an arrest warrant.

'To be brought in for questioning,' Harry said.

'I thought you said arrest? And why do you need assistance if it's only—?'

'Could you have two men and a car ready outside the garage in five minutes?'

Harry received a snort by way of response, which he interpreted as a yes. He took two puffs of his cigarette, stubbed it out, got up, locked the door and left. He was ten metres down the culvert when he heard a faint noise behind him which he knew was the landline ringing.

He had come out of the lift and was on his way to the door when he heard someone shout his name. He turned and saw the security guard waving to him. By the counter Harry saw the back of a mustard-yellow woollen coat.

'This man was asking for you,' the receptionist said.

The woollen coat turned. It was the type that is supposed to look as if it is cashmere, and on occasion it is. In this case, Harry assumed it was. Because it was filled out by a broad-shouldered, long-limbed man with dark eyes, dark hair and possibly a dash of Arab blood in his veins.

'You're taller than you appear in the photos,' said Tony Leike, exhibiting a row of porcelain dental high-rises and an outstretched hand.

'Good coffee,' said Tony Leike, looking as if he meant it. Harry studied Leike's long, distorted fingers wrapped around the coffee cup. It wasn't contagious Leike had explained as he had proffered his hand to Harry, just good old-fashioned arthritis, an inherited affliction that – if nothing else – made him a reliable meteorologist. 'But, to be frank, I thought they gave inspectors slightly better offices. Trifle warm?'

'The prison boiler,' Harry said, sipping his coffee. 'So you read about the case in *Aftenposten* this morning?'

'Yes, I was having breakfast. Almost choked on it, to be honest.'

'Why's that?'

Leike rocked in his chair, like a Formula One driver in a bucket seat before the start. 'I trust what I say can remain between us.'

'Who is *us*?'

'The police and me. Preferably you and me.'

Harry hoped his voice was neutral and did not reveal his excitement. 'The reason being?'

Leike took a deep breath. 'I don't want it to come out that I was in the Håvass cabin at the same time as the MP, Marit Olsen. For the moment I have a very high media profile because of my impending wedding. It would be unfortunate if I were to be linked with a murder investigation right now. The press would be on to it and that might . . . things would emerge from my past that I would prefer to be dead and buried.'

'I see,' Harry said innocently. 'Of course, I will have to weigh up a number of factors and for that reason cannot promise anything. But this is not an interview, just a conversation, and I don't usually leak this kind of thing to the press.'

'Nor to my . . . er, nearest and dearest?'

'Not unless there is a reason for it. If you're afraid it will be made public that you were here, why did you come?'

'You asked people who were at the cabin to come forward, so it's my civic duty, isn't it?' He sent Harry a questioning look. And then pulled a face. 'Christ, I was frightened, wasn't I. I knew that those who were there that night were next for the chop. Jumped in my car and drove straight here.'

'Has anything happened recently to make you concerned?'

'No.' Tony Leike scented the air thoughtfully. 'Apart from a break-in through the cellar door a few days ago. Christ, I should get an alarm, shouldn't I.'

'Did you report it to the police?'

'No, they only took a bike.'

'And you think serial killers do a spot of cycle-nicking on the side?'

Leike shook his head with a smile. Not the sheepish smile of someone who is ashamed of having said something stupid, Harry thought. But the disarming, winning smile that says 'you got me there, pal', the gallant congratulation from someone used to their own victories.

'Why did you ask for me?'

'The papers said you were in charge, so I thought it only natural. Anyway, as I said, I was hoping it would be possible to keep this between as few people as possible, so I came straight to the top.'

'I'm not the top, Leike.'

'Aren't you? *Aftenposten* gave the impression you were.'

Harry stroked his jutting jaw. He hadn't made up his mind about Tony

Leike. He was a man with a groomed exterior and bad-boy charm that reminded Harry of an ice-hockey player he had seen in an underwear ad. He seemed to want to present an air of unruffled, worldly-wise smoothness but also to come across as a sincere human being with feelings which could not be hidden. Or perhaps it was the other way round; perhaps the smoothness was sincere and the feelings were pretence.

'What were you doing at Håvass, Leike?'

'Skiing of course.'

'On your own?'

'Yes. I'd had a few stressful days at work and needed some time off. I go to Ustaoset and Hallingskarvet a lot. Sleep in cabins. That's my terrain, you could say.'

'So why haven't you got your own cabin there?'

'Where I would like to have a cabin you can't get planning permission any more. National park regulations.'

'Why wasn't your fiancée with you? Doesn't she ski?'

'Lene? She . . .' Leike took a sip of coffee. The kind of sip you take in mid-sentence when you need a bit of thinking time, it struck Harry. 'She was at home. I . . . we . . .' He looked at Harry with an expression of mild desperation, as though pleading for help. Harry gave him none.

'Shit. No pressure then, eh?'

Harry didn't answer.

'OK,' Leike said as though Harry had given a response in the affirmative. 'I needed a breather, to get away. To think. Engagement, marriage . . . these are grown-up issues. And I think best on my own. Especially up there on the snowy plains.'

'And thinking helped?'

Leike flashed the enamel wall again. 'Yes.'

'Do you remember any of the others in the cabin?'

'I remember Marit Olsen, as I said. She and I had a glass of red wine together. I didn't know she was an MP until she said.'

'Anyone else?'

'There were a few others sitting around I barely greeted. But I arrived quite late, so some must have gone to bed.'

'Oh?'

'There were six pairs of skis in the snow outside. I remember that clearly because I put them in the hall in case of an avalanche. I remember thinking the others were perhaps not very experienced mountain skiers. If the cabin is half buried under three metres of snow you're in a bit of a fix without any skis. I was first up in the morning – I usually am – and was off before the others had stirred.'

'You say you arrived late. You were skiing alone in the dark, were you?'

'Head torch, map and compass. The trip was a spontaneous decision, so I didn't catch the train to Ustaoset until the evening. But, as I said, they are familiar surroundings, I'm used to finding my way across the frozen wastes in the dark. And the weather was good, moonlight reflecting off the snow, I didn't need a map or a light.'

'Can you tell me anything about what happened in the cabin while you were there?'

'Nothing happened. Marit Olsen and I talked about red wine and then about the problems of keeping a modern relationship going. That is, I think her relationship was more modern than mine.'

'And she didn't say anything had happened in the cabin?'

'No.'

'What about the others?'

'They sat by the fire talking about skiing trips, and drinking. Beer perhaps. Or some kind of sports drink. Two women and a man, between twenty and thirty-five, I would guess.'

'Names?'

'We just nodded and said hello. As I said, I had gone up there to be alone, not to make new friends.'

'Appearance?'

'It's quite dark in these cabins at night, and if I say one was blonde, the other dark, that might be way off the mark. As I said, I don't even remember how many people were there.'

'Dialects?'

'One of the women had a kind of west coast dialect, I think.'

'Stavanger? Bergen? Sunnmøre?'

'Sorry, I'm not much good at this sort of thing. It might have been west coast, could have been south.'

'OK. You wanted to be alone, but you talked to Marit Olsen about relationships.'

'It just happened. She came over and sat down next to me. Not exactly a wallflower. Talkative. Fat and cheery.' He said that as if the two words were a natural collocation. And it struck Harry that the photo of Lene Galtung he had seen was of an extremely thin woman – to judge by the latest average weight for Norwegians.

'So, aside from Marit Olsen, you can't tell us anything about any of the others? Not even if I showed you photos of those we know to have been there?'

'Oh,' Leike said with a smile, 'I think I can do that.'

'Uh-huh?'

'When I was in one room looking for a bunk to crash out on, I had to switch on the light to see which was free. And I saw two people asleep. A man and a woman.'

'And you think you can describe them?'

'Not in great detail, but I'm pretty sure I would recognise them.'

'Oh?'

'You sort of remember faces when you see them again.'

Harry knew that what Leike said was right. Witnesses' descriptions were way out as a rule, but give them a line-up and they rarely made a mistake.

Harry walked over to the filing cabinet they had dragged back to the office, opened the respective victims' files and removed the photographs. He gave the five photos to Leike, who flipped through them.

'This is Marit Olsen, of course,' he said, passing it back to Harry. 'And these are the two women who were sitting by the fire, I think, but I'm not sure.' He passed Harry the pictures of Borgny and Charlotte. 'This may have been the boy.' Elias Skog. 'But none of these were asleep in the bedroom. I'm sure about that. And I don't recognise this one either, he said, passing back the photo of Adele.

'So you're unsure about the ones you were in the same room with for a good while, but you're sure about those you saw for a couple of seconds?'

Leike nodded. 'They were asleep, weren't they.'

'Is it easier to recognise people asleep?'

240

'No, but they don't look back at you, do they. So you can stare unobserved.'

'Mm. For a couple of seconds.'

'Maybe a bit longer.'

Harry put the photos back in the files.

'Have you got any names?' Leike asked.

'Names?'

'Yes. As I said, I was the first up and I had a couple of slices of bread in the kitchen. The guest book was in there and I hadn't signed in. While I was eating I opened it and studied the names that had been entered the night before.'

'Why?'

'Why?' Tony rolled his shoulders. 'It's often the same people on these mountain skiing trips. I wanted to see if there was anyone I knew.'

'Was there?'

'No. But if you give me the names of people you know or think were there, maybe I can remember if I saw them in the guest book.'

'Sounds reasonable, but I'm afraid we don't have any names. Or addresses.'

'Well then,' Leike said, buttoning up his woollen coat. 'I'm afraid I can't be of much help, can I. Except that you can cross my name off.'

'Mm,' Harry said. 'Since you're here, I've got a couple more questions. So long as you have time?'

'I'm my own boss,' Leike said. 'For the time being, anyway.'

'OK. You say you have a murky past. Could you give me a rough idea of what you mean?'

'I tried to kill a guy,' Leike said without embellishment.

'I see,' Harry said, leaning back in his chair. 'Why was that?'

'Because he attacked me. He maintained I'd stolen his girl. The truth was that she was neither his girl nor wanted to be, and I don't steal girls. I don't have to.'

'Mm. He caught you two in the act and hit her, did he?'

'What do you mean?'

'I'm trying to understand what sort of situation may have led to you trying to kill him. If you mean it literally, that is.'

'He hit *me*. And that was why I did my best to kill him. With a knife. And I was well on the way to succeeding when a couple of my pals dragged me off him. I was convicted for aggravated assault. Which is pretty cheap for attempted murder.'

'You realise that what you're saying now could make you a prime suspect?'

'In *this* case?' Leike looked askance at Harry. 'You kidding me? You lot have a bit more nous than that, don't you?'

'If you've wanted to kill once . . .'

'I've wanted to kill several times. I assume I've done it, too.'

'Assume?'

'It's not so easy to see black men in the jungle at night. For the most part you shoot indiscriminately.'

'And you did that?'

'In my depraved youth, yes. After paying for my crime, I went into the army and from there straight to South Africa and got a job as a mercenary.'

'Mm. So you were a mercenary in South Africa?'

'Three years. And South Africa is just the place where I enlisted; the fighting took place in the surrounding countries. There was always war, always a market for pros, especially for whites. The blacks still think we're smarter, you know. They trust white officers more than their own.'

'Perhaps you've been to the Congo, too?'

Tony Leike's right eyebrow formed a black chevron. 'How so?'

'Went there a while back, so I wondered.'

'It was called Zaire then. But most of the time we weren't sure which bloody country we were in. It was just green, green, green and then black, black, black until the sun rose again. I worked for a so-called security firm at some diamond mines. That was where I learned to read a map and compass from a head torch. The compass is a waste of time there, too much metal in the mountains.'

Tony Leika leaned back in his chair. Relaxed and unafraid, Harry noted.

'Talking of metal,' Harry said, 'think I read somewhere that you've got a mining business down there.'

'That's right.'

'What sort of metal?'

'Heard of coltan?'

Harry nodded slowly. 'Used in mobile phones.'

'Exactly. And in games consoles. When world mobile phone production took off in the nineties my troops and I were on a mission in the north-east of the Congo. Some Frenchmen and some natives ran a mine there, employing kids with pickaxes and spades to dig out the coltan. It looks like any old stone but you use it to produce tantalum, which is the element that's really valuable. And I knew that if I could just get someone to finance me I could run a proper, modern mining business and make my partners and myself wealthy men.'

'And that was what happened?'

Tony Leike laughed. 'Not quite. I managed to borrow money, was screwed by slippery partners and lost everything. Borrowed more money, was screwed again, borrowed even more and earned a bit.'

'A bit?'

'A few million to pay off debts. But I had a network of contacts and some headlines, as of course I was counting chickens before they hatched, which was enough to be adopted into the circle where the big money was. To become a member, it's the number of digits in your fortune that counts, not whether there's a plus or minus in front.' Leike laughed again, a hearty ringing laugh, and it was all Harry could do to restrain a smile.

'And now?'

'Now we're waiting for the big coup because it's time for coltan to be harvested. Yes indeed, I've said it for long enough, but this time it's true. I've had to sell my shares in the project in exchange for call options so that I could pay my debts. Now things are set fair, and all I have to do is get hold of money to redeem my shares so that I can become a full partner again.'

'Mm. And the money?'

'Someone will see the sense in lending me the money against a small share. The return is enormous, the risk minimal. And all the big investments have been made, including local bribes. We have even cleared a runway into the jungle so that we can load directly on to freight planes and get the stuff out via Uganda. Are you wealthy,

Harry? I can see if there's any chance for you to have a slice of the action.'

Harry shook his head. 'Been to Stavanger recently, Leike?'

'Hm. In the summer.'

'Not since then?'

Leike gave the question some thought, then shook his head.

'You're not absolutely sure?' Harry asked.

'I'm presenting my project to potential investors, and that means a lot of travelling. Must have been to Stavanger three or four times this year, but not since the summer, I don't think.'

'What about Leipzig?'

'Is this the point where I have to ask whether I need a solicitor, Harry?'

'I just want you eliminated from the case as soon as possible, so that we can concentrate on more relevant issues.' Harry ran his forefinger across the bridge of his nose. 'If you don't want the media to catch wind of this, I assume you won't want to involve a solicitor, or to be summoned to formal interviews, etc?'

Leike nodded slowly. 'You're right, of course. Thank you for your advice, Harry.'

'Leipzig?'

'Sorry,' Leike said, with genuine regret in his voice and face. 'Never been there. Should I have been?'

'Mm. I also have to ask you where you were on certain days and what you were doing.'

'Carry on.'

Harry dictated the four dates in question while Leike wrote them into a Moleskine notebook.

'I'll check as soon as I'm in my office,' he said. 'Here's my number by the way.' He passed Harry a business card with the inscription *Tony C. Leike, Entrepreneur*.

'What does the C stand for?'

'You tell me,' Leike said, getting to his feet. 'Tony's only short for Anthony of course, so I thought I needed an initial. Gives a bit more gravitas, don't you think? Think foreigners like it.'

Instead of taking the culvert, Harry accompanied Leike up the stairs to the prison, knocked on the glass window and a guard came and let them in.

'Feels like I'm taking part in an episode with the Olsen Gang,' Leike said when they were standing on the gravel path outside old Botsen Prison's fairly imposing walls.

'It's a little more discreet like this,' Harry said. 'You're beginning to become a recognisable face, and staff are arriving for work now at Police HQ.'

'Talking of faces, I see someone has broken your jaw.'

'Must have fallen and hit myself.'

Leike shook his head and smiled. 'I know something about broken jaws. That one's from a fight. You've just let it grow together again, I can see. You should go and have it seen to, it's not a big job.'

'Thanks for the tip.'

'Did you owe them a lot of money?'

'Do you know something about that, too?'

'Yes!' Leike exclaimed, his eyes widening. 'Unfortunately.'

'Mm. One last thing, Leike—'

'Tony. Or Tony C.' Leike flashed his shiny masticatory apparatus. Like someone without a care in the world, Harry thought.

'Tony. Have you ever been to Lake Lyseren? The one in Øst—?'

'Yes, of course. Are you crazy!' Tony laughed. 'The Leike farm is in Rustad. I went to my grandfather's there every summer. Lived there for a couple of years, too. Fantastic place, isn't it? Why d'you want to know?' His smile vanished at once. 'Oh, shit, that's where you found the woman! Bit of a coincidence, eh?'

'Well,' Harry said, 'it's not so unlikely. Lyseren is a big lake.'

'True enough. Thanks again, Harry.' Leike proffered his hand. 'And if any names crop up to do with the Håvass cabin, or someone comes forward, just ring me and I'll see if I can remember them. Full cooperation, Harry.'

Harry watched himself shake hands with the man he had just decided had killed six people in the last three months.

*　*　*

245

Fifteen minutes had passed since Leike left when Katrine Bratt rang.

'Yes?'

'Negative on four of them,' she said.

'And the fifth?'

'One hit. Deep in digital information's innermost intestinal tract.'

'Poetic.'

'You'll like it. On the 16th of February Elias Skog was called by a number that is not registered in anyone's name. A secret number, in other words. And that could be the reason that Oslo—'

'Stavanger.'

'—Police haven't seen the link before. But inside the innermost intestines—'

'By which you mean on Telenor's internal, highly protected register?'

'Something like that. The name of one Tony Leike, Holmenveien 172, turned up as the invoiced subscriber for this secret number.'

'Yess!' Harry shouted. 'You're an angel.'

'Poorly chosen metaphor, I believe. Since you sound as if I've just sentenced a man to life imprisonment.'

'Talk to you later.'

'Wait! Don't you want to hear about Jussi Kolkka?'

'I'd almost forgotten about that. Shoot.'

She shot.

40

The Offer

Harry found Kaja in Crime Squad, in the red zone on the sixth floor. She perked up when she noticed Harry standing in the doorway.

'Always got an open door?' he asked.

'Always. And you?'

'Closed. Always. But I can see you've thrown out the guest's chair. Smart move. People like to chew the fat.'

She laughed. 'Doing anything exciting?'

'In a way,' he said, entering and leaning against the wall.

She placed both hands against the edge of her desk, pushed, and she and the chair sailed across the floor to the filing cabinet. There, she opened a drawer, pulled out a letter and presented it to Harry. 'Thought you'd like to see this.'

'What is it?'

'The Snowman. His solicitor has applied for him to be transferred from Ullersmo to a normal hospital for health reasons.'

He perched on the edge of the desk and read. 'Mm. Scleroderma. It's progressing fast. Not too fast, I hope. He doesn't deserve that.'

He looked up and saw that she was shocked.

'My great-aunt died of scleroderma,' she said. 'A terrible disease.'

'And a terrible man,' Harry said. 'Incidentally, I quite agree with those who say that the capacity to forgive says something about the essential quality of a person. I'm the lowest grade.'

'I didn't mean to criticise you.'

'I promise to be better in my next life,' Harry said, looking down and rubbing his neck. 'Which, if the Hindus are right, will probably be as a bark beetle. But I'll be a *nice* bark beetle.'

He looked up and saw that what Rakel called his 'damned boyish charm' was having an effect. 'Listen, Kaja, I've come here to make you an offer.'

'Oh?'

'Yes.' Harry heard the solemnity in his voice. The voice of a man with no capacity to forgive, no consideration, no thoughts for anything except his own objectives. And plied the inverted persuasion technique that had worked for him far too often. 'Which I would recommend you decline. I have, you see, a tendency to destroy the lives of those I become involved with.'

To his astonishment, he saw that her face had flushed scarlet.

'But I don't think it would be right to do this without you,' he continued. 'Not now that we're so close.'

'Close . . . to what?' The blushes had gone.

'Close to apprehending the guilty party. I'm on my way to the police solicitor now to request a warrant for his arrest.'

'Oh . . . of course.'

'Of course?'

'I mean, arrest whom?' She heaved herself back to the desk. 'For what?'

'Our killer, Kaja.'

'Really?' He watched her pupils grow, slowly, pulsating. And knew what was going on inside her. The blood rush before bringing down, felling the wild animal. The arrest. Which would be on her CV. How could she resist?

Harry nodded. 'His name is Tony Leike.'

The colour returned to her cheeks. 'Sounds familiar.'

'He's about to marry the daughter of—'

'Oh yes, he's engaged to the Galtung girl.' She frowned. 'Do you mean to say you have evidence?'

'Circumstantial. And coincidences.'

He saw her pupils contract again.

'I'm sure this is our man, Kaja.'

'Convince me,' she said, and he could hear the hunger. The desire to swallow everything raw, to have a pretext for taking the craziest decision of her life so far. And he had no intention of protecting her against herself. For he needed her. She was media-perfect: young, intelligent, a woman, ambitious. With an appealing face and record. In short, she had everything he did not have. She was a Jeanne d'Arc the Justice Ministry would not want to burn at the stake.

Harry breathed in. Then he repeated the conversation he had had with Tony Leike. In detail. Without wondering at how he was able to reproduce what had been said word for word. His colleagues had always considered this ability remarkable.

'Håvass cabin, Congo and Lake Lyseren,' Kaja said after he had finished. 'He's been to all the places.'

'Yes, and he's been convicted for violence. And he admits his intention was to kill.'

'Great. But—'

'The really great bit comes now. He rang Elias Skog. Two days before he was found murdered.'

Her pupils were black suns.

'We've got him,' she said softly.

'Does the *we* mean what I think it does?'

'Yes.'

Harry sighed. 'You realise the risks of joining me in this? Even if I'm right about Leike, there's no guarantee that this arrest and a successful prosecution of the case are enough to tip the balance of power in Hagen's favour. And then you'll be in the doghouse.'

'What about you?' She leaned across the desk. Her tiny piranha teeth glistened. 'Why do *you* think it's worth the risk?'

'I'm a washed-up cop with little to lose, Kaja. For me, it's this or nothing. I can't do Narc or Sexual Offences, and Kripos will never make me an offer. But for you personally this is probably a poor decision.'

'My decisions usually are,' she said, serious now.

'Good,' Harry said, standing up. 'I'll go and get the solicitor. Don't run away.'

'I'll be here, Harry.'

Harry pivoted straight into the face of a man who had clearly been standing in the doorway for some time.

'Sorry,' the man said with a broad smile. 'I'd just like to borrow the lady for a while.'

He nodded towards Kaja, laughter dancing in his eyes.

'Be my guest,' Harry said, giving the man his abbreviated form of a smile, and strode off down the corridor.

'Aslak Krongli,' Kaja said. 'What brings a country boy to the big bad city?'

'The usual, I suppose,' said the officer from Ustaoset.

'Excitement, neon lights and the buzz of the crowd?'

Aslak smiled. 'Work. And a woman. Can I buy you a cup of coffee?'

'Not right now,' Kaja said. 'Things are happening, so I have to hold the fort. But I'd be happy to buy you a cup in the canteen. It's on the top floor. If you go ahead, that'll give me time to make a phone call.'

He gave her a thumbs up and was gone.

Kaja closed her eyes and drew in a long, quivering breath.

The police solicitor's office was on the sixth floor, so Harry didn't have far to walk. The solicitor, a young woman who had obviously been taken on since Harry last visited the office, peered over her glasses as he stepped in.

'Need a blue chit,' Harry said.

'And you would be?'

'Harry Hole, Inspector.'

He presented his ID card even though he could see from her some-what frenetic reaction that she had heard of him. He could just imagine what, and decided not to go there. For her part, she noted down his name on the search and arrest warrant and scrutinised his card with exaggerated squints, as though the spelling were extremely complicated.

'Two crosses?' she asked.

'Fine,' Harry said.

She put a cross against 'arrest' and 'search' and leaned back in her chair in a way that Harry bet was a copy of the you've-got-thirty-seconds-to-persuade-me pose she had seen more seasoned solicitors adopt.

Harry knew from experience that the first argument was the weighty one – that was when solicitors made up their minds – so he started with the call Leike made to Elias Skog two days before the murder. This despite Leike's assertions when talking to Harry that he didn't know Skog and hadn't spoken to him at the cabin. Argument number two was the assault conviction which Leike admitted was attempted murder, and Harry could already see that the blue chit was in the bag. So he spiced up proceedings with the coincidences of the Congo and Lake Lyseren, without entering into too much detail.

She removed her glasses.

'Basically, I'm sympathetic,' she said. 'However, I need to give the matter a little more thought.'

Harry cursed inwardly. A more experienced solicitor would have given him the warrant there and then, but she was so green she didn't dare without consulting one of the others. There should have been an 'in training' sign on her door, so that he could have gone to one of the others. Now it was too late.

'It's urgent,' Harry said.

'Why's that?'

She had him there. Harry made an airy gesture with his hand, the kind that is supposed to say everything, but says nothing.

'I'll make a decision straight after lunch . . .' She pointedly peered down at the form. '. . . Hole. I'll put the blue chit in your pigeon hole, if it gets clearance.'

Harry clenched his teeth to make sure he didn't say anything hasty. Because he knew she was behaving in a proper manner. Naturally, she was overcompensating for the fact that she was young, inexperienced and a woman in a male-dominated world. But she showed a determination to be respected; from the outset she demonstrated that the steamroller technique would not work on her. Well done. He felt like grabbing her glasses and smashing them.

'Could you ring my internal number when you've made up your

mind?' he said. 'For the moment my office is quite a distance from the pigeon holes.'

'Fine,' she said graciously.

Harry was in the culvert, about fifty metres from the office, when he heard the door open. A figure came out, hastily locked up after himself, turned and began to hurry towards Harry. And stiffened when he caught sight of him.

'Did I startle you, Bjørn?' Harry asked gently.

The distance between them was still over twenty metres, but the walls cast the sound towards Bjørn Holm.

'Bit,' said the man from Toten, straightening the multicoloured Rasta hat covering his red hair. 'You creep up on folk.'

'Mm. And you?'

'What about me?'

'What are you doing here? I thought you had enough to do in Kripos. You've been given a wonderful new job, I hear.' Harry stopped two metres from Holm, who was obviously taken aback.

'Not sure about wonderful,' Holm said. 'I'm not allowed to work on what I like best.'

'Which is?'

'Forensics. You know me.'

'Do I?'

'Eh?' Holm frowned. 'Coordination of forensics and strategic planning, what's that s'posed to be when it's at home? Passing on messages, calling meetings, sending out reports.'

'It's a promotion,' Harry said. 'The start of something good, don't you think?'

Holm snorted. 'Know what I think? I think Bellman's put me there to keep me out of the loop, to make sure I don't get any first-hand info. Because he suspects that if I do, he's not sure he'll get it before you.'

'But he's mistaken there,' Harry said, standing face to face with the forensics officer.

Bjørn Holm blinked twice. 'What the fuck is this, Harry?'

'Yes, what the fuck is it?' Harry heard the anger making his voice tight, metallic. 'What the fuck were you doing in the office, Bjørn? All your crap has gone now.'

'Doing?' Bjørn said. 'Fetching this, wasn't I.' He held up his right hand. It was clutching a book. 'You said you'd leave it in reception, remember?'

Hank Williams: The Biography.

Harry felt the shame flood into his cheeks.

'Mm.'

'Mm,' Bjørn mimicked.

'I had it with me when we moved out,' Harry said. 'But we did a U-turn halfway down the culvert and came back. Then I forgot all about it.'

'OK. Can I go now?'

Harry stepped aside, and listened to Bjørn stomping down the culvert between curses.

He unlocked the office.

Flopped into the chair.

Looked around.

The notebook. He flicked through. He hadn't taken any notes from the conversation, nothing that would pinpoint Tony Leike as a suspect. Harry opened the drawers in the desk to see if there were any signs of someone having rifled them. It all looked untouched. Could Harry have been wrong after all? Could he hope that Holm was not leaking information to Mikael Bellman?

Harry glanced at his watch. Praying the new police solicitor ate quickly. He struck an arbitrary key on the computer and the screen came to life. It was still showing the page with his last Google search. In the search box the name shone out at him: Tony Leike.

41

The Blue Chit

'SO,' SAID ASLAK KRONGLI, TWIRLING HIS COFFEE CUP. Kaja thought it looked like an egg cup in his large hand. She had taken a seat opposite him at the table closest to the window. The police canteen was situated on the top floor and was of standard Norwegian design, that is, light and clean, but not so cosy that people would be tempted to sit for longer than necessary. The great advantage of the room was its view of the town, but that didn't seem to interest Krongli much.

'I checked the guest books at the other self-service cabins in the area,' he went on. 'The only people who had written in the book that they were planning to spend the next night at Håvass cabin were Charlotte Lolles and Iska Peller, who were in Tunvegg the night before.'

'And we already know about them,' Kaja said.

'Yes. So in fact I have only two things that might be of interest to you.'

'And they are?'

'I was speaking on the phone to an elderly couple who were at the Tunvegg cabin the same night as Lolles and Peller. They said that a man had turned up in the evening, had a bite to eat, changed his shirt, then went on his way heading south-west. Even though it was dark. And the only cabin in that direction is Håvass.'

'And this person . . .'

'They barely saw him. Seemed as if he didn't want to be seen, either; he didn't take off his balaclava or his old-fashioned slalom goggles, not even when changing his shirt. The wife said she thought he might have had a serious injury at one time.'

'Why was that?'

'She could only remember thinking this, couldn't say why. Nevertheless, he might have changed direction when he was out of sight, and skied to another cabin.'

'Suppose so,' Kaja said, checking her watch.

'Anyone come forward in response to your crime alert, by the way?'

'No,' Kaja said.

'You look as though you mean yes.'

Kaja's eyes shot up at Aslak Krongli, who reacted by holding up his palms. 'Country clod in town! Sorry, I didn't mean anything by that.'

'Alright,' Kaja said.

They both inspected their coffee cups.

'You said there were two things I might be interested in,' Kaja said. 'What's the second?'

'I know I'm going to regret saying this,' Krongli said. The quiet laughter was back in his eyes.

Kaja guessed immediately which direction the conversation was going to take and knew he was right: he would regret it.

'I'm staying at the Plaza and wondered if you would like to have dinner with me there tonight.'

She could see by his expression that her own was not difficult to read.

'I don't know anyone else in town,' he said, contorting his mouth into a grimace that might have been intended as a disarming smile. 'Apart from my ex, that is, and I daren't ring her.'

'Would've been nice . . .' Kaja began, and paused. Conditional past. She saw that Aslak Krongli was already regretting his approach. '. . . but I'm afraid I'm otherwise engaged.'

'Fine, this was short notice.' Krongli smiled, threaded his fingers through his unruly, curly hair. 'What about tomorrow?'

'I . . . er, I'm pretty busy these days, Aslak.'

Krongli nodded, apparently to himself. 'Of course. Of course you're busy. The man who was in your room when I arrived is perhaps the reason?'

'No, I've got new bosses now.'

'It wasn't bosses I had in mind.'

'Oh?'

'You said you were in love with a policeman. And it seemed to me he didn't have much difficulty persuading you. Less than me anyway.'

'No, no, that wasn't him! Are you out of your mind? I . . . erm, must have had too much to drink that night.' Kaja could hear her own inane laughter and felt the blood rising up her neck.

'Oh well,' Krongli said, finishing his coffee, 'I'll have to go out into the big, cold city. I suppose there are museums to visit and bars to patronise.'

'Yes, you have to make the most of the opportunity.'

He arched an eyebrow and his eyes shed tears and laughed out loud. The way Even's had at the end.

Kaja accompanied him out. As he shook her hand, she couldn't help herself. 'Ring me if it gets too lonely and I'll see if I can slip away.'

She interpreted his smile as gratitude for allowing him the chance to decline an offer or at least to decide not to take her up on it.

Standing in the lift to the sixth floor, Kaja was reminded of what he had said, '. . . *didn't have much difficulty persuading you.*' How long had he actually been standing there by the door eavesdropping?

At one o'clock the telephone in front of Kaja rang.

It was Harry. 'I've finally got the blue chit. Ready?'

She could feel her heart beating faster. 'Yes.'

'Vest?'

'Vest and a weapon.'

'Delta will take care of weapons. They're ready in a vehicle outside the garage, just have to go down. And bring the blue chit from my pigeon hole, would you?'

'OK.'

Ten minutes later they were in one of Delta's blue twelve-seaters heading west through the city centre. Kaja listened to Harry explaining that he had rung Leike half an hour earlier at the building where he rented an office and they had said he was working off-site today. Harry had called his home number in Holmenveien, Tony Leike had answered and Harry had rung off. To lead the operation, Harry had specifically requested Milano, a dark, squat man with massive eyebrows, who did not have a drop of Italian blood in his veins, despite his surname.

They passed through Ibsen Tunnel, and rectangles of reflected light slid over the helmets and visors of the eight elite officers who appeared to be in deep meditation.

Kaja and Harry sat on the rear seat. Harry was wearing a black jacket with POLITI written in large yellow letters at the front and back, and had taken out his service revolver to check that there were bullets in all the chambers.

'Eight men from Delta and a blender,' Kaja said, referring to the blue light rotating on the roof of the MPV. 'Sure this isn't a bit over the top?'

'It *has* to be over the top,' Harry said. 'If we want to attract attention to the person who initiated this arrest, then we need a bigger party factor than usual.'

'Leaked it to the press?'

Harry clocked her.

'If you want attention, I mean,' she said. 'Imagine it, Leike, the celebrity, being arrested for the murder of Marit Olsen. They would pass up on the birth of a princess for that.'

'And what about if his fiancée is there?' Harry said. 'Or the mother? Are they going to be in the papers and on live TV, too?' He jerked the revolver and the cylinder clicked into place.

'What are we going to do with the big party factor then?'

'The press come later,' Harry said. 'They question the neighbours, passers-by, us. They find out what a magnificent show it was. That'll do me. No innocents involved, and we get our front page.'

She sent him a sideways glance as the shadows of the next tunnel passed over them. They crossed Majorstuen and went up Slemdalsveien, past Vinderen, and she saw him staring out of the window, at the tram stop, a naked expression of torment on his face. She felt an urge to place a hand over his, to say something, anything, that could remove that expression. She looked at his hand. It was holding the revolver, squeezing it, as though it was all he had. This could not go on, something was going to burst. Had already burst.

They climbed higher and higher; the town lay beneath them. They crossed the tramlines and then the lights began to flash behind them and the barrier was lowered.

They were in Holmenveien.

'Who's coming with me to the door, Milano?' Harry shouted to the passenger seat at the front.

'Delta 3 and Delta 4,' Milano shouted back, turning and pointing to a man with a large figure 3 chalked onto the chest and back of his combat suit.

'OK,' Harry said. 'And the rest?'

'Two men on each side of the house. Procedure Dyke 1-4-5.'

Kaja knew this was code for the formation. It had been borrowed from American football, and the aim was to communicate quickly without anyone else understanding, in case they had managed to tune into the radio frequencies that Delta used. They came to a halt a couple of houses down from Leike's. Six of the men checked their MP5s and jumped out. Kaja saw them move up through the neighbours' large gardens of brown, withered grass, bare apple trees and the tall hedges they had a proclivity for in west Oslo. Kaja checked her watch. Forty seconds had gone when Milano's radio crackled. 'Everyone in position.'

The driver released the clutch, and they drove slowly towards the house. Tony Leike's recently acquired home was yellow, single storey, impressively large, but the address was more resplendent than the architecture, which lay somewhere between functionalist and a wooden box, as far as Kaja could judge.

They stopped outside two garage doors at the end of a shingle drive leading to the front door. Several years back, during a hostage crisis in Vestfold where Delta had surrounded a house, the hostage-takers had escaped by strolling down a path from the house into the garage, starting up the house owner's car and simply driving off, to the open-mouthed amazement of the heavily armed police bystanders.

'Stay back and follow me,' Harry said to Kaja. 'Next time it's your turn.'

They got out and Harry immediately made for the house with the two other policemen one step behind and to the side, in a triangle formation. Kaja could hear from his voice that his pulse was accelerated. Now she could see it in his body language too, from the tenseness of the neck, from the exaggeratedly supple way he was moving.

They went up the steps. Harry rang the bell. The other two had positioned themselves at each side of the door, backs against the wall.

Kaja counted. Harry had told her in the car that in the FBI manual it said you had to ring or knock, shout 'Police!' and 'Please open up!', repeat and then wait ten seconds before you entered. The Norwegian police had no such precise instructions, but that didn't mean there weren't guidelines.

On this afternoon in Holmenveien, however, none of them were in evidence.

The door burst open. Kaja automatically recoiled a step when she saw the Rasta hat in the doorway, then saw Harry's shoulders swivel and heard the sound of fist on flesh.

42

Beavis

THE REACTION HAD BEEN INSTINCTIVE; HARRY HAD SIMPLY not been able to prevent it.

When Forensics Officer Bjørn Holm's moonlike face had appeared in Tony Leike's doorway and Harry had seen the other officers in full swing behind him, he realised in a flash what had happened and everything went black.

He just felt the punch register along his arm into his shoulder and then the pain in his knuckles. Opening his eyes again, he saw Bjørn Holm on his knees in the hall with blood streaming from his nose into his mouth and dripping from his chin.

The two Delta officers had leapt forward and pointed their weapons at Holm, but were obviously in a state of bewilderment. They had probably seen his familiar Rasta hat before and were aware the other men in white were crime scene officers.

'Report back that the situation is under control,' Harry said to the man with the figure 3 on his chest. 'And that the suspect has been arrested. By Mikael Bellman.'

Harry sat slumped in the chair with his legs stretched out as far as Gunnar Hagen's desk.

'It's very simple, boss. Bellman found out we were about to arrest Tony Leike. For Christ's sake, they've got the public prosecutor's office right across the street, in the same building as Krimteknisk. All he had to do was amble over and pick up a blue chit from one of the solicitors. He was probably done in two minutes, while I waited for two fucking hours!'

'You don't need to shout,' Hagen said.

'*You* don't need to, but *I* do!' Harry shouted, banging the armrest. 'Shit, shit, shit!'

'You should be happy Holm's not going to report you. Why did you hit *him* anyway? Is he the leak?'

'Anything else you wanted, boss?'

Hagen looked at his inspector. Then he shook his head. 'Take a couple of days off, Harry.'

Truls Berntsen had been called a lot of things in his childhood. Most of the nicknames were forgotten now. But he had been given a name soon after he finished school in the early nineties that had stuck: Beavis. The cartoon idiot on MTV. Blond hair, underbite and grunted laugh. OK, maybe he did laugh like that. Had done ever since primary school, especially when someone was given a beating. Especially when he was given a beating. He had read in a comic that the guy who made Beavis and Butt-Head was called Judge; he couldn't recall the first name. But at any rate, this Judge guy said he imagined that Beavis's father was a drunkard who beat his son. Truls Berntsen remembered he had just thrown the comic on the floor and left the shop, laughing this grunt laughter.

He had two uncles who were in the police force, and he had managed to satisfy the entrance requirements by the skin of his arse and with two letters of recommendation. And scraped through the exam with at least one helping hand from the guy at the next desk. It was the least he could do; they had been pals since they were small. Sort of pals. To be honest, Mikael Bellman had been his boss since they were twelve years old when they met on the large building site that was being blown up in Manglerud. Bellman had caught him trying to set fire to a dead rat. And had shown him how much more fun it was to stuff a stick of dynamite down a rat's throat. Truls had even been allowed to light it. And since that day he had followed Mikael Bellman wherever he went. When he was given permission. Mikael knew how to do all the things Truls did not. School, gym lessons, talk so that no one would give you any shit. He even had girls; one of them was older and had tits Mikael was allowed to stroke as much as he liked. There was only one thing Truls was better at: taking a beating. Mikael always backed down when any of the bigger boys found it hard to accept that the show-off had outdone them in the art of bad-mouthing and went for him with clenched fists. Then Mikael shoved Truls in front of him. For Truls could take a beating. He had plenty of training from home. They could knock him about until blood was drawn, but he still stood there with his grunted laugh, which just made them even wilder. But he couldn't stop himself, he simply had to laugh. He knew that afterwards he would receive a pat on the shoulder from Mikael, and if it was a Sunday, Mikael might say that Julle and TV were having another race. So they would stand on the bridge below the Ryen inter-section, smell the sun-baked tarmac and listen to the Kawasaki 1000cc engines revving up as the cheerleaders screamed and shouted. And then Julle's and TV's bikes would tear down Sunday's traffic-free motorways, pass beneath them and on to the tunnel and Bryn, and they might – if Mikael was in a good mood and Truls's mother was working a shift at Aker Hospital – go and eat Sunday lunch with fru Bellman.

Once Mikael had rung the bell at Truls's house and his father had shouted that Jesus had come to collect his disciple.

They had never argued. That is, Truls had never retaliated if Mikael was in a stinking mood and took the piss out of him. Not even at the party when Mikael had called him Beavis and everyone had laughed, and Truls had instinctively known that the name would stick. He had retaliated only once. The time Mikael had called his father one of the drunks from the Kadok factory. Then Truls had gone for Mikael with a raised fist. Mikael had curled up with an arm over his head, told him to take it easy, laughed and said he was just joking, he was sorry. But after-wards it was Truls who had been sorry and apologised.

One day Mikael and Truls had gone into one of the petrol stations where they knew Julle and TV stole fuel. Julle and TV filled the Kawasaki tanks from the self-service pumps while their girls sat at the back with their denim jackets casually tied around their waists covering the number plates. Then the boys jumped on their bikes and rode off full throttle.

Mikael gave them the full names and addresses of Julle and TV, but of just one of the girls, TV's girlfriend. The owner had looked sceptical, wondering whether he hadn't seen Truls's face before on a CCTV camera; at any rate he resembled the lad who had stolen a jerrycan of petrol not long before the empty workmen's shed at Manglerud went up in flames. Mikael had said he didn't want any reward for the information, he just wanted the guilty parties held responsible for their actions. He assumed the owner was aware of his social duty. The grown-up man had nodded, somewhat surprised. Mikael had that effect on people. As they left, Mikael said he was going to apply to Police College after school and Beavis should consider doing the same – there were even policemen in his family.

Later, Mikael had got together with Ulla, and they hadn't seen so much of each other. But after school and Police College they had been employed by the same police station in Stovner, a real east Oslo suburb with gang crimes, burglaries and even the odd murder. After a year Mikael had married Ulla and been promoted. Truls, or Beavis, as he had been called from day three, roughly, reported to him and the future had looked good for Truls and radiant for Mikael. Until some knucklehead, a civilian temp in the salaries office, had accused Bellman of smashing his jaw after the Christmas dinner. He had no proof, and Truls knew for certain that Mikael had not done it. But in all the hubbub Mikael had applied for a move anyway, been accepted at Europol, moved to the head office in The Hague where he soon became a star, too.

When Mikael returned to Norway and Kripos, the second thing he did was to ring Truls and ask: 'Beavis, are you ready to blow up rats again?'

The first was to employ Jussi.

Jussi Kolkka was a an expert in half a dozen martial arts whose names you forget before they have been fully articulated. He had worked at Europol for four years, and before that he had been a policeman in Helsinki. Jussi Kolkka had been forced to resign from Europol because he had crossed the line during an investigation into a series of rapes targeting teenage girls in southern Europe. Kolkka had, it was said, beaten up a sex offender so badly that even his brief had had trouble recognising him. But he had no trouble threatening Europol with a lawsuit. Truls had tried to get Jussi to tell him the gory detail, but he had just stared into the distance without speaking. Fair enough, Truls wasn't the talkative type, either. And he had noticed that the less you speak, the greater the chance people will underrate you. Which was not always a bad thing. Nevertheless. Tonight they had reason to celebrate. Mikael, himself, Jussi and Kripos had won. And in Mikael's absence they would have to call the shots themselves.

'Shut up!' shouted Truls, pointing to the TV attached to the wall above the bar at Kafé Justisen. And heard his own nervous grunted laugh when his colleagues actually did what he said. There was silence around the tables and the bar. Everyone was staring at the newsreader, who looked straight into the camera and announced what they had been waiting for.

'Today Kripos arrested a man suspected of killing six people, including Marit Olsen.'

Cheers broke out, mugs of beer were swung, silencing the newsreader until a deep voice with a Finnish-Swedish accent boomed 'Shut up!'

The Kripos officers obeyed and focused their attention on Mikael Bellman who was standing outside their building in Bryn with a furry microphone thrust into his face.

'This person is a suspect, will be interviewed by Kripos and thereafter appear in court for a preliminary hearing,' Mikael Bellman said.

'Does that mean you believe the police have solved this case?'

'Finding the perpetrator and getting him convicted are two different things,' Bellman said with a tiny smile at the corners of his mouth. 'However, our investigation at Kripos has uncovered so much circumstantial evidence and so many coincidences that we considered it appropriate to make an immediate arrest as there was a risk of further crimes and a tampering of evidence.'

'The man you have arrested is in his thirties. Can you tell us any more about him?'

'He has a previous conviction for violence; that is all I can say.'

'On the Internet there are rumours circulating about the man's identity. Suggesting he's a well-known investor who among other things is engaged to the daughter of a famous shipowner. Can you confirm these rumours, Bellman?'

'I don't think I have to confirm or deny anything except that we at Kripos are fairly confident that we will soon have this case solved.'

The reporter turned to the camera for an outro, but was drowned out by the round of applause at Justisen.

Truls ordered another beer as one of the detectives got up onto a chair and proclaimed that Crime Squad could suck his dick, at least the tip, if they said pretty please. Laughter resounded around the packed, sweaty, fetid room.

At that moment the door opened and in the mirror Truls saw a figure fill the entrance.

He felt a strange excitement at the sight, a tremulous certainty that something was going to happen, that someone would be hurt.

It was Harry Hole.

Tall, broad-shouldered, lean-faced with deep-set bloodshot eyes. He just stood there. And although no one shouted for the crowd to shut up the silence spread from the front to the back of Justisen, until a last shh was heard to quieten two garrulous forensics officers. When the silence was total, Hole spoke.

'So you're celebrating the job you succeeded in stealing from us, are you?'

The words were low, almost a whisper, and yet every syllable reverberated around the room.

'You're celebrating having a boss who's prepared to step over dead bodies – those that have piled up outside and those that will soon be carried from the sixth floor at Police HQ – just so that he can be the Sun King of fucking Bryn. Well, here's a hundred-krone note.'

Truls could see Hole waving a note.

'You don't have to steal this. Here, buy yourselves beer, forgiveness, a dildo for Bellman's threesome . . .' He screwed up the note and tossed it onto the floor. From the corner of his eye he could see Jussi was already moving. '. . . or another snitch.'

Hole lurched to the side to gain balance, and it was then that Truls realised that the guy – despite enunciating with the diction of a priest – was as stewed as a prune.

The next moment Hole performed a half-pirouette as Jussi Kolkka's right hook hit him on the chin, and then a deep, almost gallant bow, as the Finn's left buried itself in his solar plexus. Truls guessed that in a few seconds Hole – when he had got some air back in his lungs – was going to spew. In here. And Jussi was obviously thinking the same, that he would be better outside. It was a wonder to see how the tubby, almost log-shaped Finn lifted his foot high with the suppleness of a ballerina, placed it against Harry's shoulder and gently pushed so that the crumpled detective rocked backwards and through the door whence he had come.

The drunkest and youngest of them howled with laughter, but Truls grunted. A couple of the older ones yelled, and one screamed that Kolkka should bloody well behave himself. But no one did anything. Truls knew why. Everyone here remembered the story. Harry had dragged the uniform through the dirt, shat in the nest, taken the life of one of their best men.

Jussi marched towards the bar, po-faced, as if he had carried out the rubbish. Truls whinnied and grunted. He would never understand Finns or Samis or Eskimos or whatever the hell they were.

From further back in the room a man had stood up and made his way to the door. Truls hadn't seen him at Kripos before, but he had the circumspect eye of a policeman under all that dark, curly hair.

'Tell me if you need any help with him, sheriff,' someone shouted from his table.

Three minutes later, when Celine Dion had been turned back up and the chatting had resumed its previous levels, Truls ventured forth, put his foot on the hundred-krone note and took it to the bar.

Harry had his breath back. And he spewed. Once, twice. Then he collapsed again. The tarmac was so cold it stung his ribs through his shirt and so heavy he seemed to be supporting it and not vice versa. Blood-red spots and wriggling black worms danced in front of his eyes.

'Hole?'

Harry heard the voice, but knew that if he showed he was conscious it would be open season for a kicking. So he kept his eyes closed.

'Hole?' The voice had come closer and he felt a hand on his shoulder.

Harry also knew that the alcohol would have reduced his speed, accuracy and ability to judge distances, but he did it anyway. He opened his eyes, twisted over and aimed for the larynx. Then he collapsed again.

He had missed by half a metre.

'I'll get you a taxi,' the voice said.

'Will you fuck,' Harry groaned. 'Piss off, you bloody bastard.'

'I'm not Kripos,' the voice said. 'My name's Krongli. The County Officer from Ustaoset.'

Harry turned and squinted up at him.

'I'm just a bit pissed,' Harry said hoarsely and tried to breathe calmly so that the pain wouldn't force the contents of his stomach up again. 'No big deal.'

'I'm a bit pissed, too,' Krongli smiled, putting an arm around Harry's shoulders. 'And, to be frank, I have no idea where to get a taxi. Can you stand upright?'

Harry got one and then two legs beneath him, blinked a couple of times and established that at least he was vertical again. Semi-embracing an officer from Ustaoset.

'Where are you sleeping tonight?' Krongli asked.

Harry looked askance at the officer. 'At home. And preferably on my own, if that's alright with you.'

At that moment a police car pulled up in front of them, and the window slid down. Harry heard the tail end of some laughter and then a composed voice.

'Harry Hole, Crime Squad?'

'Sme,' Harry sighed.

'We've just received a phone call from one of the Kripos detectives requesting that we drive you home safe and sound.'

'Open the door then!'

Harry got onto the back seat, lolled against the headrest, closed his eyes, started to feel everything rotating, but preferred that to watching the two in the front ogling him. Krongli asked them to ring him at a number when 'Harry' was safely home. What the hell gave him the idea he was his pal? Harry heard the hum of the window and then the pleasant voice from the front seat again.

'Where do you live, Hole?'

'Keep going straight ahead,' Harry said. 'We're going to pay someone a visit.'

When Harry felt the car set off, he opened his eyes, turned and saw Aslak Krongli still standing on the pavement in Møllergata.

43

House Call

KAJA LAY ON HER SIDE STARING INTO THE DARKNESS OF her bedroom. She had heard the gate open and now there were footsteps on the gravel outside. She held her breath and waited. Then the doorbell rang. She slipped out of bed, into her dressing gown and over to the window. Another ring. She opened the curtains a fraction. And sighed.

'Drunken police officer,' she said out loud in the room.

She put her feet into slippers and shuffled into the hall towards the door. Opened it and stood in the doorway with crossed arms.

'Hello there, schweedie,' the policeman slurred. Kaja wondered if he was trying to perform the drunkard sketch. Or if it was the pitiful original version.

'What brings you here so late?' Kaja asked.

'You. Can I come in?'

'No.'

'But you said I could get in touch if I was too lonely. And I *was*.'

'Aslak Krongli,' she said. 'I'm in bed. Go to your hotel now. We can have a coffee tomorrow morning.'

'I need a coffee now, I reckon. Ten minutes and we'll ring for a taxi, eh? We can talk about murders and serial killers to pass the time. What do you say?'

'Sorry,' she said. 'I'm not on my own.'

Krongli straightened up at once, with a movement that made Kaja suspect he was not as drunk as he had seemed at first. 'Really? Is he here, that policeman you said you were so hung up on?'

'Maybe.'

'Are they his?' the officer drawled, kicking the enormous shoes beside the doormat.

Kaja didn't answer. There was something in Krongli's voice, no, behind it, something she hadn't heard there before. Like a low-frequency, barely audible growl.

'Or have you just put the shoes there to frighten off unwanted visitors?' Laughter in his eyes. 'There's no one here, is there, Kaja?'

'Listen, Aslak—'

'The policeman you're talking about, Harry Hole, came a cropper earlier this evening. Turned up at Justisen as drunk as a skunk, picked a fight and got one. A patrol car passed by to give him a lift home. So you must be free tonight after all, eh?'

Her heart beat faster; she was no longer cold under the dressing gown.

'Perhaps they drove him here instead,' she said and could hear her voice was different now.

'No, they rang me and said they had driven him way up the hill to visit someone. When they found out he wanted to go to Rikshospital and they strongly advised against it, he just jumped out at the traffic lights. I like my coffee strong, OK?'

An intense gleam had come into his eyes, the same Even used to get when he wasn't well.

'Aslak, go now. There are taxis in Kirkeveien.'

His hand shot out and before she could react he had grabbed her arm and pushed her inside. She tried to free herself, but he put an arm around her and held her tight.

'Do you want to be just like her?' his voice hissed in her ear. 'To cut and run, to scram? To be like all you bloody lot . . .'

She groaned and twisted, but he was strong.

'Kaja!'

The voice came from the bedroom where the door stood open. A firm, imperious man's voice that, under different circumstances, Krongli might have recognised. As he had heard it only an hour earlier at Justisen.

'What's going on, Kaja?'

Krongli had already let go and was staring at her, with eyes wide and jaw agape.

'Nothing,' Kaja said, not letting Krongli out of her sight. 'Just a drunken bumpkin from Ustaoset who's on his way home.'

Krongli backed towards the front entrance without a word. Slipped out and slammed the door. Kaja went over, locked it and rested her forehead against the cold wood. She felt like crying. Not out of fear or shock. But despair. Everything around her was collapsing. Everything she had thought was clean and right had finally begun to appear in its real light. It had been happening for some time, but she hadn't *wanted* to see. Because what Even had said was true: no one is as they seem, and most of life, apart from honest betrayal, is lies and deceit. And the day we discover we are no different is the day we no longer want to live.

'Are you coming, Kaja?'

'Yes.'

Kaja pushed off from the door through which she would so much have liked to flee. Went into the bedroom. The moonlight fell between the curtains and onto the bed, onto the bottle of champagne he had brought with him to celebrate, onto his naked, athletic torso, onto the face she had once thought the most handsome on this earth. The white patches on his face shimmered like luminous paint. As if he were aglow inside.

44

The Anchor

KAJA STOOD IN THE DOORWAY LOOKING AT HIM. MIKAEL Bellman. To outsiders: a competent, ambitious POB, a happily married father of three and soon-to-be head of the new Kripos leviathan that would lead all murder investigations in Norway. To her, Kaja Solness: a man she had fallen in love with from the moment they'd met, who had seduced her with all the arts at his disposal, plus a few others. She had been easy game, but that wasn't his fault, it was hers. By and large. What was it Harry had said? 'He's married and says he'll leave his wife and kids for you, but never does?'

He had hit the nail on the head. Of course. That's how banal we are. We believe because we want to believe. In gods, because that dulls the fear of death. In love, because it enhances the notion of life. In what married men say, because that is what married men say.

She knew what Mikael would say. And then he said it.

'I have to be off. She'll start wondering.'

'I know,' Kaja sighed and, as usual, did not ask the questions that always popped up when he said that: Why not stop her wondering? Why not do what you've said for so long? And now a new question emerged: Why am I no longer sure I *want* him to do this?

Harry clung to the banisters on his way up to the Haematology Department at Rikshospital. He was soaked in sweat, frozen, and his teeth were chattering like a two-stroke engine. And he was drunk. Drunk on Jim Beam, drunk and full of devilry, full of himself, full of shit. He staggered along the corridor; he could already make out the door to his father's room at the end.

A nurse's head poked out from a duty room, looked at him and was gone again. Harry had fifty metres to go to the door when the nurse, plus a skinhead male nurse, skidded into the corridor and cut him off.

'We don't keep medicines on this ward,' the skinhead said.

'What you are saying is not only a gross lie,' Harry said, trying to control his balance and the chattering of his teeth, 'but a gross insult. I'm not a junkie, but a son here to visit his father. So please, move out of my way.'

'I apologise,' said the female nurse who seemed quite reassured by Harry's immaculate pronunciation. 'But you smell like a brewery, and we cannot allow—'

'A brewery is beer,' Harry said. 'Jim Beam is bourbon. Which would require you to say I smell like a distillery, frøken. It's . . .'

'Nevertheless,' the male nurse said, grabbing Harry by the elbow. And let it go just as quickly when his own hand was twisted round. The nurse groaned and grimaced with pain before Harry released him. Harry rose to his full height and eyeballed him.

'Ring the police, Gerd,' the nurse said softly without letting Harry out of his sight.

'If you don't mind, I'll deal with this,' said a voice with a suggestion of a lisp. It was Sigurd Altman. He was walking with a file under his arm and a friendly smile on his face. 'Have you got time to come with me to where we keep drugs, Harry?'

Harry swayed back and forth twice. Focused on the small, thin man with the round glasses. Then he nodded.

'This way,' said Altman, who had already continued walking.

Altman's office was, strictly speaking, a storeroom. There were no windows, there was no noticeable ventilation, but there was a desk and computer, a camp bed, which he explained was for night shifts, so that he could sleep or be roused whenever needed. And a lockable cabinet Harry assumed contained a range of chemical uppers and downers.

'Altman,' Harry said, sitting on the edge of the bed, smacking his lips loudly as though they were coated with glue. 'Unusual name. Only know one person called that.'

'Robert,' said Sigurd, sitting on the only chair in the room. 'I didn't like who I was in the little village where I grew up. As soon as I got away I applied to change my surname from a much too common -sen. I justified my application by saying, as was the truth, that Robert Altman was my favourite director. And the case officer must have had a hangover that day because it was passed. We can all do with being reborn once in a while.'

'*The Player*,' Harry said.

'*Gosford Park*,' Altman said.

'*Short Cuts*.'

'Ah, a masterpiece.'

'Good, but overrated. Too many themes. The direction and editing make the plot unnecessarily complicated.'

'Life is complicated. People are complicated. Watch it again, Harry.'

'Mm.'

'How's it going? Any progress on the Marit Olsen case?'

'Progress,' Harry said. 'The guy who did it was arrested today.'

'Jeez, well, I can understand you celebrating.' Altman pressed his chin to his chest and peered over his glasses. 'I have to confess I'm hoping I can tell my grandchildren that it was my information about ketanome that cracked the case.'

'By all means, but it was a phone call to one of the victims that gave him away.'

'Poor things.'

'Poor who?'

'Poor all of them, I assume. So why the haste to see your father right now, tonight?'

Harry put his hand in front of his mouth and produced a noiseless belch.

'There is a reason,' Altman said. 'However drunk you are, there's always a reason. On the other hand, that reason is none of my business, so perhaps I should keep my mou—'

'Have you ever been asked to carry out euthanasia?'

Altman shrugged. 'A few times, yes. As an anaesthetic nurse, I'm an obvious choice. Why?'

'My father asked me.'

Altman nodded slowly. 'It's a heavy burden to place on someone. Is that why you came here now? To get it over with?'

Harry's gaze had already wandered around the room to see if there was anything alcoholic to drink. Now it did another round. 'I came to ask for forgiveness. For not being able to do it for him.'

'You hardly need forgiveness for that. Taking a life is not something you can demand of anyone, let alone of your own son.'

Harry rested his head in his hands. It felt hard and heavy, like a bowling ball.

'I've done it once before,' he said.

Altman's voice sounded more surprised than actually shocked. 'Carried out euthanasia?'

'No,' Harry said. 'Refused to carry it out. To my worst enemy. He has an incurable, fatal and very painful disease. He is slowly being suffocated by his own shrinking skin.'

'Scleroderma,' Altman said.

'When I arrested him, he tried to make me shoot him. We were alone at the top of a tower, just him and me. He had killed an unknown number of people and hurt me and people I love. Permanent damage. My gun was pointing at him. Just us. Self-defence. I didn't risk a thing by shooting him.'

'But you preferred him to suffer,' Altman said. 'Death was too easy for him.'

'Yes.'

'And now you feel you're doing the same with your father, you're making him suffer rather than allowing him release.'

Harry rubbed his neck. 'It's not because I hold with the principles of the sanctity of life or any of that bullshit. It's weakness, pure and simple. It's cowardice. Christ, you haven't got anything to drink here, have you, Altman?'

Sigurd Altman shook his head. Harry wasn't sure if it was in answer to his last question or the other things he had said. Perhaps both.

'You can't just disregard your own feelings like that, Harry. You, like everyone else, are trying to leapfrog the fact that we are governed by notions of what's right and wrong. Your intellect may not have all the arguments for these notions, but nonetheless they are rooted deep, deep inside you. Right and wrong. Perhaps it's things you were told by your parents when you were a child, a fairy tale with a moral your grandmother read, or something unfair you experienced at school and you spent time thinking through. The sum of all these half-forgotten things.' Altman leaned forward. '*Anchored deep within* is in fact a pretty apposite expression. Because it tells you that you may not be able to see the anchor in the depths, but you damn well can't move from the spot, that's what you float around and that's where your home is. Try and accept that, Harry. Accept the anchor.'

Harry stared down at his folded hands. 'The pain he has . . .'

'Physical pain is not the worst thing a human has to deal with,' Altman said. 'Believe me, I see it every day. Not death, either. Nor even fear of death.'

'What is the worst then?'

'Humiliation. To be deprived of honour and dignity. To be disrobed, to be cast out by the flock. That's the worst punishment, it's akin to burying a person alive. And the only consolation is that the person will perish fairly quickly.'

'Mm.' Harry kept eye contact with Altman. 'You don't have anything in that cupboard to lighten the atmosphere, do you?'

45

Questioning

MIKAEL BELLMAN HAD BEEN DREAMING ABOUT FREE FALL again. Climbing solo in El Chorro, the fingerhold that isn't, the mountain wall racing past your eyes, the ground accelerating towards you. The alarm clock ringing at the last moment. He wiped the egg yolk from his mouth and looked up at Ulla standing right behind him and filling his cup with coffee from the cafetière. She had learned to recognise the precise moment when he was ready to eat, and it was then and not a second before that he wanted his coffee, boiling hot, poured into the blue cup. And that was only one of the reasons he appreciated her. Another was that she kept herself in such good shape that she still attracted admiring glances at the parties they were invited to more and more often. Ulla had, after all, been Manglerud's undisputed beauty queen when they got together, he had been eighteen, she nineteen. A third reason was that Ulla, without making any great fuss about it, had set aside her dreams of further education so that he could prioritise his job. But the three most important reasons sat around the table arguing about who should have the plastic figure in the cornflakes box and who should sit in front today when she drove them to school. Two girls, one boy. Three perfect reasons to appreciate the woman and her genes' compatibility with his.

'Will you be late again tonight?' she asked, furtively stroking his hair. He knew she loved his hair.

'It might be a long session,' he said. 'We're starting with the suspect today.' He knew that over the course of the day the papers would publish what they already knew: that the arrestee was Tony Leike. But he had made it a principle never to reveal confidentialities even at home. That also enabled him to explain overtime regularly with 'I can't talk about that, darling'.

'Why didn't you question him yesterday?' she asked while buttering the children's bread for their packed lunches.

'We had to gather more facts. And finish searching his house.'

'Did you find anything?'

'Afraid I can't be that specific, darling,' he said and gave her the regretful confidentiality look so as not to reveal the fact that she had actually put her finger on a sensitive point. Bjørn Holm and the crime scene officers hadn't found anything during the search that could have linked Leike to any of the murders. Fortunately, for the moment, however, that was of minor importance.

'Softening him up in a cell overnight won't hurt,' Bellman said. 'It'll just make him more receptive when we start. And the first part of the questioning is always the crunch.'

'Is it?' she asked, and he could tell she was trying to sound interested.

'I have to be off.' He got up and kissed her on the cheek. Yes, he certainly did appreciate her. The thought of forgoing her and the children, the framework and infrastructure that had enabled him to rise through the ranks, through the classes, was of course absurd. To follow the impulses of his heart, to throw up everything for love or whatever it was, was utopian, a dream he could think and talk about, with Kaja as a listener. But if you were going to dream, Mikael Bellman preferred dreams that were grander than that.

He inspected his front teeth in the hall mirror and checked his silk tie was straight. The press were bound to be out in force.

How long would he be able to keep Kaja? He thought he had detected some doubts in her last night. And a lack of enthusiasm in their love-making. But he also knew that as long as he was heading for the top, as he had been doing so far, he would be able to control her. It wasn't that Kaja was a gold-digger with clear objectives of what he, as overall boss, could do for her own career. It wasn't about intellect; it was pure biology. Women could be as modern as they liked, but when it came to submitting to the alpha male they were still at primate level. However, if she was beginning to entertain doubts because she thought that he would never renounce his wife for her sake, perhaps it was time to give her some encouragement. After all, he needed her to feed him with inside info about Crime Squad for a while yet, until all the loose ends were tied, until this battle was over. And the war won.

He went over to the window while buttoning up his coat. The house they had taken over from his parents was in Manglerud, not the best area of town, if you asked the West Enders. But those who had grown up here had a tendency to stay; it was a quarter with soul. And it was his quarter. With a view over the rest of Oslo. Which would also soon be his.

'They're coming now,' the uniformed officer said. He stood in the doorway of one of the new interview rooms at Kripos.

'OK,' Mikael Bellman said.

Some interrogators liked to have the interviewee led to the room first, to keep him or her waiting, to make it clear who was in charge. So that they could enjoy the great entrance and go in hard straight away while they had them at their most defensive and vulnerable. Bellman preferred to be seated and ready when the suspect was ushered in. To mark his territory, to announce who owned the room. He was still able to keep the suspect waiting while he skimmed through his papers, able to feel the nervousness mounting in the room and then – when the time was ripe – raise his eyes and shoot. But these were the fine details of interview techniques. Which, naturally, he was happy to discuss with other competent chief interrogators. Again, he checked that the red recording light was switched on. Fiddling with technical equipment after the suspect had arrived could spoil the preliminary establishing of status.

Through the window he saw Beavis and Kolkka enter the adjacent office. Between them walked Tony Leike, whom they had brought from the custody block at Police HQ.

Bellman took a deep breath. Yes, his pulse was a bit higher now. A mixture of aggression and nerves. Tony Leike had declined the opportunity to have a solicitor present. In essence, of course, that was an advantage for Kripos, it gave them greater latitude. But at the same time it was a signal that Leike considered he had little to fear. Poor sucker. He can't have known that Bellman had proof that Leike had rung Elias Skog immediately before he was murdered. Someone whose name Leike had claimed he didn't even know.

Bellman looked down at the papers and heard Leike entering the room. Beavis closed the door behind him as he had been instructed.

'Take a seat,' Bellman said without looking up.

He heard Leike do what he was told.

Bellman stopped at an arbitrary piece of paper and stroked his lower lip with a forefinger while slowly counting to himself, from one upwards. The silence quivered in the small enclosed room. One, two, three. He and his colleagues had been sent on a course in the new interrogation methods they were being instructed to use – so-called investigative viewing – the point of which, according to these ungrounded academic types, was openness, dialogue and trust. Four, five, six. Bellman had listened quietly – after all, the model had been chosen at the highest level – but what sort of characters did these people actually think Kripos inter-viewed? Sensitive but obliging souls who tell you everything you want to know in exchange for a shoulder to cry on? They insisted the methods the police had used hitherto, the traditional nine-step American FBI model, was inhuman, manipulative, and it made innocent people confess to crimes they hadn't committed and was therefore counterproductive. Seven, eight, nine. OK, so say it put the odd suggestible chicken in the coop, but what was that compared with the grinning scum who strolled away, killing themselves with laughter at 'openness, dialogue and trust'?

Ten.

Bellman pressed his fingertips together and raised his eyes.

'We know you rang Elias Skog from Oslo, and that two days later you were in Stavanger. And that you killed him. These are the facts we have, but what I am wondering is why. Or didn't you have a motive, Leike?'

That was step one of the nine-step model drawn up by the FBI agents Inbau, Reid and Buckley: the confrontation, the attempt to use the shock effect to land a knockout punch straight away, the declaration that they knew everything already, there was no point denying guilt. This had one sole aim: confession. Here Bellman combined step one with another interviewing technique: linking one fact with one or several non-facts. In this case he linked the incontestable date of the phone call with the contention that Leike had been to Stavanger and he was a killer. Hearing the proof for the first claim, Leike would automatically conclude that they also had concrete proof for the others. And that these facts were so simple and irrefutable that they could jump straight to the only thing left to answer: why?

Bellman saw Leike swallow, saw him bare his white milestone-sized teeth in an attempted smile, saw the confusion in his eyes and knew that they had already won.

'I didn't ring any Elias Skog,' Leike said.

Bellman sighed. 'Do you want me to show you the listed calls from Telenor?'

Leike shrugged. 'I didn't ring. I lost a mobile phone a while back. Maybe someone rang him using that?'

'Don't try to be smart, Leike. We're talking about your *landline*.'

'I didn't ring him, I'm telling you.'

'I heard. According to official records, you live alone.'

'Yes, I do. That is—'

'Your fiancée sleeps over now and then. And sometimes you get up earlier than her and go to work while she's still in your apartment?'

'That happens. But I'm at hers more often than not.'

'Well, now. Has Galtung's heiress daughter got a more luxurious pad than you, Leike?'

'Maybe. Cosier, at any rate.'

Bellman crossed his arms and smiled. 'Nonetheless, if you didn't call Skog from your house, she must have done. I'm giving you five seconds to start talking sense to us, Leike. In five seconds, a patrol car on the streets of Oslo will receive orders to drive with sirens blaring to that cosy little pad of hers, cuff her, bring her here and allow her to phone her father to tell him you're accusing her of ringing Skog. So that Anders Galtung can gather the meanest pack of hardbitten solicitors in Norway for his daughter, and you have got yourself a real adversary. Four seconds, three seconds.'

Leike shrugged again. 'If you reckon that's enough to issue an arrest warrant on a young woman with a perfect, unblemished record, go ahead. But I somehow doubt it would be me who gained an adversary.'

Bellman observed Leike. Had he underrated him after all? He was more difficult to read now. Anyway, that was step one over. Without a confession. Fine, there were eight left. Step two in the nine-step model was to sympathise with the suspect by normalising actions. But that presupposed he knew the motive or he was working with something he could normalise. A motive for killing all the guests who had happened to stay over at a skiing cabin was not self-evident, over and above the obvious truism that most serial killers' motives are hidden in the psyche where the majority of us never go. In his preparations Bellman had therefore decided to tread lightly on the sympathy step before jumping straight into the motivation step: giving the suspect a reason to confess.

'My point, Leike, is that I'm not your adversary. I'm just someone who wants to understand why you do what you do. What makes you tick. You're clearly an able, intelligent person; you only have to look at what you've achieved in business. I'm fascinated by how people set themselves objectives and pursue them regardless of what others think. People who set themselves apart from the madding crowd of mediocrity. I may even say that I can recognise myself in that bracket. Maybe I understand you better than you think, Tony.'

Bellman had asked a detective to ring one of Leike's stock exchange buddies to find out whether Leike preferred his first name pronounced as 'Toeuny', 'Tony' or 'Tonny'. The answer was 'Tony'. Bellman hit the right pronunciation, caught his eye and attempted to hold it.

'Now I'm going to say something perhaps I shouldn't, Tony. Because of a number of internal issues we can't devote a lot of time to this case, and that is why I would like a confession. Normally we wouldn't offer a deal to a suspect with such overwhelming evidence against him, but it would expedite procedures. And for a confession – which, in fact, we do not even need to obtain a conviction – I will offer you a reduced sentence, which will be considerable. I am afraid I'm restricted by the legal framework with regards to offering a specific figure, but let's just say between you and me that it will be *con-sid-er-able*. Alright, Tony? It's a promise.

And now it's on tape.' He pointed to the red light on the table between them.

Leike subjected Bellman to a long, reflective look. Then he opened his mouth. 'The two who brought me in told me your name was Bellman.'

'Call me Mikael, Tony.'

'They also said you were a very intelligent man. Tough, but trustworthy.'

'I think you will discover that to be borne out, yes.'

'You said considerable, didn't you?'

'You have my word.' Bellman felt his pulse rising.

'Alright,' Leike said.

'Good,' said Mikael Bellman lightly, touching his lower lip with thumb and forefinger. 'Shall we start at the beginning?'

'Fine,' Leike said, taking from his back pocket a piece of paper that Truls and Jussi must have let him keep. 'I was given the dates and times by Harry Hole so this should be quick. Borgny Stem-Myhre died somewhere between 10 and 11 p.m. on the 16th of December in Oslo.'

'Correct,' Bellman said, sensing an incipient exultation in his heart.

'I checked the calendar. At that time I was in Skien, in the Peer Gynt Room, Ibsen House, where I was talking about my coltan project. This can be confirmed by the person who hired the room and roughly one hundred and twenty potential investors who were present. I assume you know it takes about two hours to drive there. The next was Charlotte Lolles between . . . let's see . . . it says between eleven o'clock and midnight on the 3rd of January. At that time I was having dinner with a few minor investors in Hamar. Two hours by car from Oslo. By the way, I took the train, and I tried to find the ticket, but sadly without any luck.'

He smiled in apology to Bellman, who had stopped breathing. And for a second Leike's milestone teeth appeared between his lips as he concluded: 'But I hope that at least *some* of the twelve witnesses present during the dinner may be regarded as reliable.'

'Then he said there was a possibility he could be charged with the murder of Marit Olsen, because even though he had been at home with his

283

fiancée he had, in fact, also been alone for two hours skiing on the floodlit course in Sørkedalen that evening.'

Mikael Bellman shook his head and stuffed his hands even deeper into his coat pockets as he examined *The Sick Child*.

'At the time when Marit Olsen died?' Kaja asked, inclining her head and looking at the mouth of the pale, presumably dying girl. She generally concentrated on one thing whenever they met at the Munch Museum. Sometimes it could be the eyes, another time the landscape in the background, the sun or simply Edvard Munch's signature.

'He said that neither he nor the Galtung woman—'

'Lene,' Kaja corrected.

'—could remember exactly when, but it could have been quite late, it usually was because he liked to have the course to himself.'

'So Tony Leike could have been in Frogner Park instead. If he was in Sørkedalen he would have passed through the toll stations twice, on the way out and back in. If he's got an electronic pass on his windscreen the time is automatically recorded. And then—'

She had turned and stopped abruptly when she met his frigid eyes.

'. . . But of course you've already checked that,' she said.

'We didn't need to,' Mikael said. 'He hasn't got an AutoPASS, he stops and pays cash. And so there is no record of the journey.'

She nodded. They strolled on to the next picture, stood behind a few Japanese tourists who were noisily pointing and gesticulating. The advantage of meeting at the Munch Museum in the week – apart from the fact that it lay between Kripos in Bryn and Police HQ in Grønland – was that it was one of those tourist destinations where you were guaranteed never to meet colleagues, neighbours or acquaintances.

'What did Leike say about Elias Skog and Stavanger?' Kaja asked.

Mikael shook his head again. 'He said he could probably be charged with that one, too. Since he had slept alone that night, and thus had no alibi. So I asked him if he had gone to work the next day and he answered that he couldn't remember, but he assumed he had turned up at seven as usual. And that I could check with the receptionist at the shared office block if I considered it important. I did, and it transpired that Leike had booked one of the meeting rooms for a quarter past nine. And talking with a few of the investor types in the office, I found out that two of them had been to the meeting with Leike. If he had left Elias Skog's place at three in the morning he would have needed a plane to make it. And his name is not on any passenger lists.'

'That doesn't mean much. He may have been travelling under a false name and ID. And anyway, we still have his phone call to Skog. How did he explain that away?'

'He didn't even try, he just denied it,' Bellman snorted. 'What is it that people reckon is so good about *The Dance of Life*? They haven't even got proper faces. Look like zombies, if you ask me.'

Kaja studied the dancers in the painting. 'Perhaps they are,' she said.

'Zombies?' Bellman chuckled. 'Do you mean that?'

'People who go around like dancers, but feel dead inside, buried, decomposing. No question.'

'Interesting theory, Solness.'

She hated it when he used her surname, which he did as a rule when he was angry or simply found it appropriate to remind her of his intellectual superiority. Which she let him do because it was obviously important for him. And perhaps he was intellectually superior. Wasn't it part of what had made her fall for him, his conspicuous intelligence? She didn't have a clear recollection any more.

'I have to go back to work,' she said.

'And do what?' Mikael asked, looking at the security guard standing behind the rope at the back of the room and yawning. 'Count files and wait for Crime Squad to be wound up? You know you've given me a massive problem with this Leike, don't you?'

'*I* have?' she burst out, incredulous.

'Keep it down, dear. You were the one who tipped me off about what Harry had dug up on Leike. Told me he was going to arrest him. I trusted you. I trusted you so much that I arrested Leike on the basis of your tip-off and subsequently as good as told the press the case was in the bag. And now this shit has exploded in our bloody faces. The guy has a watertight alibi for at least two of the murders. We're going to have to let him go at some point today. Daddy-in-law Galtung is no doubt already considering the lawyers from hell to sue us, and the Minister of Justice will want to know how the fuck we could have committed such a blunder. And now the head on the block won't be yours, Hole's or Hagen's, but mine, Solness. Do you understand? Mine alone. And we're going to have to do something about that. *You're* going to have to do something about it.'

'And what would that be?'

'Not much, a trifle, and we'll sort out the rest. I want you to take Harry out. Tonight.'

'Out? Me?'

'He likes you.'

'What makes you think that?'

'Didn't I tell you I saw you two sitting and smoking on the veranda?'

Kaja went pale. 'You arrived late, but you didn't say anything about having seen us.'

'You were so preoccupied with each other you didn't hear the car, so I parked and watched. He likes you, my love. Now I want you to take him somewhere. For a couple of hours, no more.'

'Why?'

Mikael Bellman smiled. 'He's spending too much time sitting at home. Or lying. Hagen should never have given him time off; people like Hole can't deal with it. And we don't want him to drink himself to death up in Oppsal, do we now. Take him to eat somewhere. Cinema. A beer. Just make sure he isn't at home between eight and ten. And be careful. I don't know if he's sharp or just paranoid, but he examined my car very closely the night he left yours. Alright?'

Kaja didn't answer. Mikael's smile was the one she could dream about in the long periods when he wasn't there, when job and family obligations prevented him from meeting her. So how come the same smile now made her feel as if her stomach was being turned inside out?

'You . . . you weren't thinking of . . .'

'I'm thinking of doing whatever I have to,' Mikael said, looking at his watch.

'Which is?'

He shrugged. 'What do you think? Swapping the head on the block, I reckon.'

'Don't ask me to do this, Mikael.'

'But I'm not asking you, dear. I'm ordering you.'

Her voice was barely audible. 'And if . . . if I were to refuse?'

'Then I'll not only crush Hole, I'll crush you, too.'

The light from the ceiling fell on the tiny white patches on his face. So handsome, she thought. Someone should paint him.

The marionettes are dancing as they should now. Harry Hole found out I rang Elias Skog. I like him. I think perhaps we could have been friends if we had met when we were children or in our teens. We have a couple of things in common. Like intelligence. He is the only detective who seems to have the ability to see behind the veil. That also means, of course, I will have to be careful with him. I am looking forward to seeing how this develops. With childlike glee.

PART FIVE

46

Red Beetle

Harry opened his eyes and stared up at a large, square red beetle crawling towards him between the two empty bottles while purring like a cat. It stopped, then purred again, tapped its way a further five centimetres towards him along the glass coffee table leaving a tiny trail in the ash. He stretched out his hand, grabbed it and put it to his ear. Heard his own voice sound like a rock being crushed. 'Stop ringing me, Øystein.'

'Harry . . .'

'Who the hell is this?'

'It's Kaja. What are you doing?'

He looked at the display to make sure the voice was telling the truth. 'Resting.' He felt his stomach preparing to evacuate its contents. Again.

'Where?'

'On the sofa. I'll ring off now unless it's important.'

'Would that mean you're at home in Oppsal?'

'Well, let me see. The wallpaper's right anyway. Kaja, I have to go.'

Harry threw the phone to the end of the sofa, lurched to his feet, stooped to find his centre of gravity and staggered forwards using his head as a navigation aid and battering ram. It led him into the kitchen without any collisions of consequence, and he placed his hands on both sides of the sink before the fountain of vomit gushed from his mouth.

Opening his eyes again, he saw that the plate rack was still in the sink. The thin, yellowish green vomit was running down a single upright plate.

Harry turned on the tap. One of the advantages of being an alcoholic back off the wagon was that by day two your sick stops blocking the drain.

Harry drank a little water from the tap. Not much. Another advantage the experienced alcoholic possesses is a knowledge of what his stomach can tolerate.

He went back to the living room, legs akimbo, as if he had just filled his pants. Which, as a matter of fact, he had not yet checked. He lay down on the sofa and heard a low croak coming from the far end. A small voice from a miniature person was calling his name. He groped between his feet and put the red mobile to his ear again.

'What's up?'

He wondered what he should do with the gall that was burning his throat like lava, cough it up or swallow it. Or let it burn, as he deserved.

He listened as she explained she wanted to see him. Would he meet her at Ekeberg restaurant? Like now. Or in an hour's time.

Harry looked at the two empty bottles of Jim Beam on the coffee table and then at his watch. Seven. The Vinmonopol was closed. Restaurant bar.

'Now,' he said.

He clicked off, and the phone rang again. He looked at the display and pressed answer. 'Hi, Øystein.'

'*Now* you're answering! Shit, Harry, I was beginning to wonder if you'd done a Hendrix.'

'Can you drive me to Ekeberg restaurant?'

'What the hell d'you think I am? A sodding taxi driver?'

Eighteen minutes later Øystein's car stood outside the steps to Olav Hole's house and he called through the opened window with a grin. 'Need any help locking the bloody door, you drunken sot?'

'Dinner?' Øystein exclaimed as they drove by Nordstrand. 'To *fuck* her or because you *have* fucked?'

'Calm down. We work together.'

'Exactly. As my ex-wife used to say: "You want what you see every day." She must have read it in a glossy mag. Only she didn't mean me, but that bastard at the office.'

'You haven't been married, Øystein.'

'Could have been. The guy wore a Norwegian sweater and a tie and spoke nynorsk. Not dialect, but fucking national-romantic Nynorsk, Ivar Aasen style, I kid you not. Can you imagine what it's like to sleep alone thinking that right now your could-have-been-wife is busy shagging on a desk. You visualise a coloured sweater and a bare white arse going hammer and tongs, until it stops and seems to suck in its cheeks and the clod howls: EG KJEM! I've come! In Nynorsk.'

Øystein glanced at Harry, but there was no reaction.

'Christ, Harry, this is great humour. Are you *that* pissed?'

Kaja sat by the window, deep in thought, taking stock of the town, when a low cough made her turn. It was the head waiter; he had that apologetic it's-on-the-menu-but-the-kitchen-says-we-don't-have-it look, and had stooped very low over her, but spoke in such muffled tones that she could still hardly hear him.

'I regret to say that your company has arrived.' Then he amended his statement with a blush. 'I mean, I regret to say we could not admit him. He's a tad . . . animated, I'm afraid. And our policy in such—'

'Fine,' Kaja said, getting up. 'Where is he?'

'He's outside waiting. I'm afraid he bought a drink from the bar on the way in, and he's got it with him. Perhaps you might be so kind as to bring the glass back in. We could lose our licence for that sort of thing, you know.'

'Of course, just get me my coat, would you, please?' said Kaja, hurrying through the restaurant with the waiter nervously tripping along after her.

On emerging, she saw Harry. He was standing, swaying, next to the low wall by the slope where they had stood last time.

She joined him. There was an empty glass on the wall.

'Doesn't look like we're meant to eat at this restaurant,' she said. 'Any suggestions?'

He shrugged and took a sip from his hip flask. 'Bar at the Savoy. If you're not too hungry.'

She pulled her coat around her more tightly. 'I'm not that hungry, actually. What about showing me around a bit? This is your stamping ground, and I've got a car. You could show me the bunkers where you used to spend your time.'

'Cold and ugly,' Harry said. 'Stink of piss and wet ash.'

'We could smoke,' she said. 'And admire the view. Have you got anything better to do?'

A cruise ship, lit up like a Christmas tree, glided slowly and soundlessly through the dark to the town on the fjord beneath them. They were sitting on wet concrete on top of a bunker, but neither Harry nor Kaja felt the cold creeping into their bodies. Kaja sipped at the hip flask Harry had passed her.

'Red wine in a hip flask?' she said.

'That was all that was left in Dad's cabinet. Just emergency supplies anyway. Favourite male actor?'

'Your turn to start,' she said, taking a longer swig.

'Robert De Niro.'

She pulled a face. '*Analyze This? Meet the Fockers?*'

'I swore eternal allegiance after *Taxi Driver* and *The Deer Hunter*. But, yes, it has been at some cost. What about you?'

'John Malkovich.'

'Mm. Good. Why?'

She deliberated. 'I think it's the cultivated evil. Not something I like as a human quality, but I love the way he reveals it.'

'And then he has a feminine mouth.'

'Is that good?'

'Yep. All the best actors have feminine mouths. And/or a high-pitched feminine voice. Kevin Spacey, Philip Seymour Hoffman.' Harry took a cigarette from the pack and offered her one.

'Only if you light it for me,' she said. 'Those boys are not exactly over-masculine.'

'Mickey Rourke. Woman's voice. Woman's mouth. James Woods. Kissable mouth like an obscene rose.'

'But not a high-pitched voice.'

'Bleating voice. Sheep. Ewe.'

Kaja laughed and took the lit cigarette. 'Come on. Macho men in films have deep, hoarse voices. Take Bruce Willis for example.'

'Yes, take Bruce Willis. Hoarse fits. But deep? Hardly.' Harry scrunched up his eyes and whispered in falsetto, facing the town: 'From up here it doesn't look like you're in charge of jack shit.'

Kaja burst out laughing; the cigarette shot from her mouth and bounced down the wall and into the thick shrubs sending off sparks.

'Bad?'

'Sensationally bad,' she gasped. 'Damn, now you've made me forget the macho actor with the feminine voice *I* was going to say.'

Harry rolled his shoulders. 'You'll think of it.'

'Even and I also used to have a place like this,' Kaja said, taking another cigarette and holding it between thumb and forefinger as if it were a nail she was going to hammer in. 'Somewhere for ourselves we thought no one else knew, where we could hide and tell each other secrets.'

'Feel like telling me about it?'

'About what?'

'Your brother. What happened?'

'He died.'

'I know. I thought you would tell me the rest.'

'And what is the rest?'

'Well, why have you canonised him for example?'

'Have I?'

'Haven't you?'

Her searching gaze lingered on him. 'Wine,' she said.

Harry passed her the hip flask and she took a greedy swig.

'He left a note,' she said. 'Even was so sensitive and vulnerable. At times he could be all smiles and laughter, it was like he brought the sunshine when he arrived. If you had any problems, they seemed to evaporate when he appeared, like . . . erm, like dew in the sun. And in the black periods it was the opposite. Everything went quiet around him, a brooding tragedy seemed to hang in the air and you could hear it in his silence. Music in a minor key. Beautiful and terrible at once, do you understand? And yet, some of the sunshine seemed to have been stored in his eyes, because they continued to laugh. It was eerie.'

She shivered.

'It was during the summer holidays, a sunny day, the kind only Even could make. We were at our summer house in Tjøme, and I had got up and gone straight to the shop to buy strawberries. When I returned breakfast was ready, and Mummy called up to the first floor for Even to come down. But he didn't answer. We assumed he was sleeping – now and then he had long lie-ins. I went up to fetch something from my room and tapped on his door and called out "strawberries" as I passed. I was still listening for a response when I opened the door to my room. When you go into your own room, you don't look around, you just look for whatever it is you want, the bedside table where you know your book is, the windowsill or the box of fishing lures. I didn't see him straight away, only noticed that something about the light was not as it should have been. Then I glanced to the side and at first saw only his bare feet. I knew every centimetre of his feet – he used to pay me a krone to tickle them, he loved that. My first thought was that he was flying, at last he had learned to fly. My gaze continued upwards; he was wearing the pale blue jumper I had knitted for him. He had hung himself from the lamp with an extension cord. He must have waited until I'd gone out, and then come into my room. I wanted to run, but I couldn't move, my legs were rooted to the floor. So I stood there staring at him, and he was so close, and I called my mother, I did all the things that should have produced a shout, but not a sound would come out of my mouth.'

Kaja bent her head and flicked her cigarette. Took a tremulous breath.

'I can only remember fragments of the rest. They gave me medicine, to calm me down. When I recovered, three days later, they had already buried him. They said it was just as well I wasn't there, that the strain might have been too great. I fell ill straight afterwards and was in bed with a fever for long periods over the summer. I've always thought it was a bit too hurried, the funeral, as if there were something shameful about the way he had died, don't you think?'

'Mm. You said he had written a note?'

Kaja gazed across the fjord. 'It was on my bedside table. He wrote that he had fallen in love with a girl he could never have, he didn't want to live any more and asked for forgiveness for all the pain he was inflicting on us, and that he knew we loved him.'

'Mm.'

'That came as quite a surprise. Even had never told me there was a girl, and he used to tell me most things. Had it not been for Roar—'

'Roar?'

'Yes. I had my first boyfriend that summer. He was so nice and patient, visited me almost every day when I was ill and listened to me talking about Even.'

'About what an immeasurably wonderful person he had been.'

'You've got it.'

Harry shrugged. 'I did the same when my mother died. Øystein wasn't as patient as Roar. He asked me straight out if I was founding a new religion.'

Kaja giggled and sucked on her cigarette. 'I think Roar eventually felt that the memory of Even was smothering all life as he knew it, including himself. It was a brief relationship.'

'Mm. But Even was still there.'

She nodded. 'Behind every single door I opened.'

'That's why, isn't it?'

She nodded again. 'When I came home from the hospital that summer and had to go to my bedroom, I couldn't open the door. I simply couldn't. Because I knew that if I did, he would be hanging there again. And it would be my fault.'

'It's always our fault, isn't it?'

'Always.'

'And no one can persuade us that it isn't – not even *we* can do that.' Harry stubbed out his cigarette in the dark. Lit another.

The cruise ship beneath them had slid into the quay.

A gust of wind whistled through the gun slits, making a hollow, gloomy sound.

'Why are you crying?' he asked softly.

'Because it *is* my fault,' she whispered with tears rolling down her cheeks. 'Everything is my fault. You've known all along, haven't you?'

Harry inhaled. Took out the cigarette and blew on the glow. 'Not all along.'

'Since when?'

'Since I saw Bjørn Holm's face in the doorway in Holmenveien. Bjørn Holm is a good forensics officer, but no De Niro. And he was genuinely surprised.'

'Was that all?'

'It was enough. I knew from his expression that he had no idea I was on to Leike. Therefore he had not seen anything on my computer, and he had not passed it on to Bellman. And if Holm wasn't the mole, there was only one other person it could have been.'

She nodded and dried her tears. 'Why didn't you say anything? Why didn't you do anything? Why didn't you behead me?'

'What would have been the point? I assumed you had a good reason.'

She shook her head and let the tears flow.

'I don't know what he promised you,' Harry said. 'I would guess a leading position in the new, all-powerful Kripos. And I was right when I said that the guy you were hung up on was married and told you he would leave his wife and kids for your sake, but he never would.'

She sobbed quietly, her neck bent as though it had become too heavy. Like a rain-burdened flower, Harry thought.

'What I don't understand is why you wanted to meet me this evening,' he said, giving his cigarette a disapproving look. Perhaps he should change brand. 'I thought at first it was because you wanted to tell me you were the mole, but I soon realised it wasn't. Are we waiting for someone? Is something going to happen? I mean, I've been sidelined, what harm can I do to them now?'

She looked at her watch. Sniffled. 'Can we go back to yours, Harry?'

'Why? Is someone waiting for us there?'

She nodded.

Harry drained his hip flask.

The door had been broken down. The splinters of wood on the floor suggested it had been levered open with a crowbar. Nothing refined, no attempt to be discreet. Police break-in.

Harry turned on the steps and looked at Kaja who had got out of the car and stood with crossed arms. Then he went inside.

The living room was dark; the only light came from the drinks cabinet, which was open. But it was enough for him to recognise the person sitting in shadow by the window.

'Bellman,' Harry said. 'You're sitting in my father's armchair.'

'I took the liberty,' Bellman said. 'Since the sofa had a particular smell. Even the dog shied away.'

'May I offer you something?' Harry nodded towards the cabinet and sat down on the sofa. 'Or did you find something for yourself?'

Harry could discern Bellman shaking his head. 'Not me. But the dog did.'

'Mm. I take it as read that you have a search warrant, but I am curious about the grounds given.'

'An anonymous tip-off about you having smuggled drugs into the country via an innocent third party and the possibility that it was here.'

'And it was?'

'The sniffer dogs found something, a ball of some yellowish-brown substance wrapped in silver foil. Doesn't look like the usual sort of thing we confiscate in this country, so for the moment it's not clear what we're dealing with. But we're considering having it analysed.'

'Considering?'

'It *might* be opium, or it *might* be a lump of plasticine or clay. It depends.'

'Depends on what?'

'On you, Harry. And me.'

'Really?'

'If you agree to do us a favour, I might tend to the view that it is plasticine and overlook any tests. A boss has to prioritise his resources, isn't that so?'

'You're the boss. What sort of favour?'

'You're a man who doesn't like beating around the bush, Hole, so let me give it to you straight. I want you to take on the role of scapegoat.'

Harry saw a brown ring of Jim Beam at the bottom of the bottle on the table but resisted the temptation to put it to his lips.

'We've just had to release Tony Leike as he has watertight alibis for at least two of the murders. All we have on him is a phone call to one of the victims. We've been a bit forceful with the press. Together with Leike and his future father-in-law they could make things uncomfortable for us. We'll have to issue a press statement tonight. And it will say that the arrest was undertaken on the basis of the blue chit you, the controversial Harry Hole, wheedled out of the poor sylphlike solicitor at Police HQ. And that this was a solo operation that you, and you alone, organised, and you shoulder all of the responsibility. Kripos smelt a rat after the arrest, intervened and in conversation with Leike clarified the facts. And immediately released him. You will have to join us and sign the press statement, and you will never make a statement about the investigation again, not a word. Understood?'

Harry contemplated the dregs in the bottle a second time. 'Mm. A tough order. Do you think the press will swallow the story after you were standing with your hands raised, taking the honour for the arrest?'

'I assumed responsibility, the press statement will say. I saw fronting the arrest as a management responsibility, even though we had misgivings that a policeman might have committed a blunder. But when Harry Hole later insisted on being allowed to take his place at the front, I didn't stand in his way because he was an experienced inspector and didn't even work for Kripos.'

'And my motivation is that if I don't sign I will be charged with drug smuggling and possession?'

Bellman pressed his fingertips together and rocked back in the chair.

'Correct. But more important for your motivation is perhaps the fact that I can see to it that you're held on remand with immediate effect. Shame since I know you would have liked to be at the hospital with your father who, I understand, has little time left. Very sad business.'

Harry leaned back against the sofa. He knew he ought to have been angry. The old – the younger – Harry would have been. But what this Harry wanted most was to bury himself in the sweat- and vomit-stained sofa, close his eyes and hope they would go, sling their hooks, Bellman, Kaja, the shadows by the window. But his brain continued its automatic acquired reasoning.

'Quite apart from me,' he heard himself say, 'why would Leike bear out this version? He knows it was Kripos who arrested him, who questioned him.'

Harry knew the answer before Bellman spelt it out.

'Because Leike knows that there will always be an unpleasant shadow hanging over someone who has been arrested. Especially unpleasant for someone such as Leike, who at this moment is trying to win the trust of investors, of course. The best way to rid himself of this shadow is to endorse a version that maintains the arrest was down to a loose cannon, an isolated unprofessional element in the police force who ran amok. Agreed?'

Harry nodded.

'Anyway, as far as the force is concerned . . .'

'I am protecting the name of the entire force by assuming all the guilt,' Harry said.

Bellman smiled. 'I've always held you to be a relatively intelligent man, Hole. Does that mean that we have reached an understanding?'

Harry considered. If Bellman went now he could see whether there really were a few drops of whiskey left in the bottle. He nodded.

'Here's the press statement. I want your name there.' Bellman pushed pen and paper across the coffee table. It was too dark to read. That didn't matter. Harry signed.

'Good,' said Bellman, taking the piece of paper and getting up. The light from a street lamp outside fell onto his face, causing the warpaint to shine. 'This is best for all of us. Think about it, Harry. And get some rest.'

The victor's merciful attentions, Harry thought, closing his eyes and feeling Morpheus welcome him into his arms. Then he opened his eyes again, struggled to his feet and followed Bellman down the steps. Kaja was still standing with arms crossed beside her car.

Harry saw Bellman send a nod of acknowledgement to Kaja, who responded with a shrug of the shoulders. Watched him cross the street, get into a car, the same one he had seen in Lyder Sagens gate that evening, watched him start the engine and drive off. Kaja had come to the foot of the steps. Her voice was still thick with tears.

'Why did you hit Bjørn Holm?'

Harry turned to go in, but she was faster, taking two steps at a time. She came between him and the door and blocked the way. Her breathing was accelerated and hot against his face.

'You hit him when you knew he was innocent. Why?'

'Go now, Kaja.'

'I'm not going!'

Harry looked at her. Knowing it was something he could not explain. How much it had hurt and surprised him when he realised the ramifications. Hurt him enough to make him lash out, punch the astonished, innocent moon-shaped face, the very reflection of his own gullible naivety.

'What do you want to know?' he asked and heard the metallic tone, the fury creeping into his voice. 'I really believed in you, Kaja. So I should congratulate you. Congratulate you on a job well done. Can you go away now?'

He saw the tears well up in her eyes again. Then she stepped aside, and he staggered in and slammed the door behind him. Remained in the hall in the soundless vacuum after the bang, in the good silence, the void, the wonderful nothingness.

47

Fear of the Dark

OLAV HOLE BLINKED INTO THE DARKNESS.

'Is that you, Harry?'

'Yes, it's me.'

'It's night, isn't it?'

'Yes, it's night.'

'How are you?'

'I'm alive.'

'Let me put on the light.'

'No need. I'm going to tell you something.'

'I recognise the tone. I'm not sure I want to hear.'

'You'll read about it in the papers tomorrow anyway.'

'And you have a different version you want to tell me?'

'No, I just want to be first.'

'Have you been drinking, Harry?'

'Do you want to hear?'

'Your grandfather drank. I loved him. Drunk or sober. There are not many people who can say that about a drunken father. No, I don't want to hear.'

'Mm.'

'And I can say that to you, too. I have loved you. Always. Drunk or sober. You weren't even difficult. Although you were always argumentative. You were at war with most people, not least with yourself. But loving you, Harry, is the easiest thing I have done.'

'Dad . . .'

'There's no time to talk about trivia, Harry. I don't know if I've ever told you this, Harry, I feel as if I have, but sometimes we think things so often that we simply believe they have been said aloud. I've always been proud of you, Harry. Have I told you that often enough?'

'I . . .'

'Yes?' Olav Hole listened in the dark. 'Are you crying, son? That's fine. Do you know what made me proudest? I've never told you this, but when you were in your teens one of your teachers rang us. He said you'd been fighting in the playground again. With two of the boys from the class above, but this time it hadn't turned out so well – they'd had to send you to hospital to have your lip sewn and a tooth taken out. I stopped your pocket money, remember? Anyway, Øystein told me about the fight later. You flew at them because they'd filled Tresko's rucksack with water from the school fountain. If I remember correctly you didn't even like Tresko much. Øystein said the reason you'd been hurt so badly was because you didn't give in. You got up time after time and in the end you were bleeding so much that the big boys became alarmed and went on their way.'

Olav Hole laughed quietly. 'I didn't think I could tell you at the time, it would only have been asking for more fights, but I was so proud I could have wept. You were brave, Harry. You were scared of the dark, but that didn't stop you going there. And I was the world's proudest dad. Did I ever say that, Harry? Harry? Are you there?'

Free. The champagne bottle smashed against the wall, and the bubbles ran down the wallpaper like boiling cerebral matter, over the pictures, the newspaper cuttings, the printout off the Net showing Harry Hole accepting the blame. Free. Free of blame, free to send the world into hell again. I tread on the broken glass, tread it into the floor, hear it crunch. And I'm barefoot. I skid on my own blood. Laughing until I howl. Free. Free!

48

Hypothesis

THE HEAD OF CRIME SQUAD, SYDNEY SOUTH, NEIL McCormack, ran a hand through his thinning mop of hair while studying the bespectacled woman across the table in the interview room. She had come straight from the publishing house where she worked. Her suit was plain and creased, but there was nevertheless something about Iska Peller that made him presume it was expensive, it wasn't just meant to impress simple souls like himself. But her address suggested that she was not particularly well off. Bristol was not the most fashionable area of Sydney. She seemed adult and sensible. Definitely not the type to dramatise, exaggerate, attract attention for attention's sake. Besides, they were the ones who had called her in; she hadn't come to Sydney Police of her own accord. He looked at his watch. McCormack had arranged to go sailing with his son this afternoon; they were due to meet in Watson Bay where the boat was moored. That's why he hoped this wouldn't take long. And everything had been fine until the last snippet of information.

'Miss Peller,' McCormack said, leaning back and folding his hands over his impressive pot belly, 'why didn't you tell anyone about this before?'

She hunched her shoulders. 'Why should I? No one asked, and I can't see it has any relevance to Charlotte's murder. I'm telling you now because you've asked me in such detail. I thought what happened in the cabin was what you were interested in, not the kind of . . . incident that took place afterwards. And that was what it was. A tiny incident, soon over, soon forgotten. You find idiots like him everywhere. As an individual you can't take on the task of reporting every single creep.'

McCormack growled. Of course she was right. And he didn't feel like following up the matter, either. There was always so much more trouble, unpleasantness and, not least, work when the person in question had a professional handle that either started or finished with the word *police*. He gazed out of the window. The sun was glittering on the sea by Port Jackson and on the Manly side where smoke was still rising despite it being a week since the season's last bush fire had been extinguished. The smoke was drifting south. A fine, warm northerly. Perfect for sailing. McCormack had liked Hole. Or Holy as he called the Norwegian. He had done a brilliant job when he'd helped them with the clown murder. But the lofty, fair-haired Norwegian had sounded weary on the phone. McCormack genuinely hoped that Holy wasn't going to keel over again.

'Let's take it from the start, shall we, Miss Peller?'

Mikael Bellman entered the Odin conference room and heard the conversations stop at once. He strode over to the speaker's chair, put down his notes, connected his laptop to the USB port and stood in the middle of the floor with his legs anchored. The investigation unit numbered thirty-six officers, three times what was normal for murder cases. They had been working for so long without results that he had had to boost morale a couple of times, but generally speaking they had stuck to it like heroes. That was why Bellman had allowed not only himself but his staff to enjoy what had seemed like their great triumph: the arrest of Tony Leike.

'You will have read the papers today,' he opened, surveying the assembly.

He had saved their hides. The front pages of two of the three biggest newspapers bore the same photograph: Tony Leike getting into a car outside Police HQ. The third had a picture of Harry Hole, an archive photo from a talk show where he had been discussing the Snowman.

'As you can see, Inspector Hole has assumed responsibility. Which is only right and proper.'

His words bounced back to him off the walls, and he met the silent officers' morning-weary gazes. Or was it a different kind of tiredness? In which case, it would have to be opposed. Because things were coming to a head now. The Kripos boss had dropped by to say that the Ministry of Justice had rung and was asking questions. The sands of time were running out.

'We don't have a prime suspect any more,' he said. 'But the good news is we have fresh leads. And they all take us from the Håvass cabin to Ustaoset.'

He went to the laptop, tapped a key and the first page of a PowerPoint presentation he had prepared came to life.

Half an hour later he had been through all the facts they possessed, with names, times and assumed routes.

'The question', he said, switching off the computer, 'is what kind of murders we are dealing with here. I think we can exclude the typical serial killer. The victims have not been chosen at random inside a demographic group; they are tied to a specific place and a specific time. Accordingly, there is reason to believe that we are also talking about a specific motive which may even be perceived as rational. If so, that makes the task considerably easier for us: find the motive and we have the killer.'

Bellman saw several detectives nod.

'The problem is that there are no witnesses to tell us anything. The only one we know to be alive, Iska Peller, was ill in bed, alone. The others are either dead or have not come forward. We know, for example, that Adele Vetlesen was with a man she had met recently, but no one in her circle of acquaintances seems to know anything about him, so we have to assume it was a short-lived relationship. We're looking at the men she contacted by phone or on the Net, but it will take time to work our way through them. And in the absence of witnesses we will have to find our own starting point. We need hypotheses for the motive. What is the motive for killing at least four people?'

'Jealousy or hearing voices,' someone from the back replied.

'All our experience tells us that.'

'Agreed. Who might hear voices commanding them to kill?'

'Anyone with a psychiatric record,' came a sing-song response from Finnmark.

'And anyone without one,' said someone else.

'Good. Who might be jealous?'

'Partner or spouse of someone there.'

'And who might that be?'

'But we've checked the victims' partners' alibis and potential motives,' another said. 'That's the first thing we do. And either they didn't have partners or we eliminated them from our inquiries.'

Mikael Bellman knew all too well they were just putting their foot on the accelerator while the wheels spun round in the same rut they had been in for a while, but the important point now was that they were ready to do exactly that: to put their foot down. For he was in no doubt that the Håvass cabin was a plank that could be levered under the wheel to get them out of the rut.

'We didn't eliminate *all* the partners and spouses,' Bellman said, rocking on his heels. 'We just didn't think every one was a suspect. Who didn't have an alibi for the time his wife was killed?'

'Rasmus Olsen!'

'Correct. And when I went to Stortinget and spoke to Rasmus Olsen he admitted that there had been what he called a little "jealous patch" some months ago. A woman Rasmus had been flirting with. And Marit Olsen went to the Håvass cabin for a couple of days to think things over. The days may match. Perhaps she did more than think. Perhaps she got her own back. And here's a thought. On the night in question, when the victims were at the Håvass cabin, Rasmus Olsen was not in Oslo; he was booked into a hotel in Ustaoset. What was Rasmus doing in the area if his wife was in Håvass? And did he spend the night in the hotel or did he go for a longish skiing trip?'

The eyes in front of him were no longer heavy-lidded or tired, quite the opposite, he was igniting a spark in them. He waited for an answer. Such a large investigative group was not normally the most efficient way to organise this kind of improvised brainstorming, but they had worked on the case for so long that everyone in the room had had their slants, their sure-fire hunches and fanciful hypotheses rejected and their egos flattened.

A young detective took a punt. 'He may have arrived at the cabin in the evening unannounced and caught her in the act. The guy saw and sneaked off again. Then planned the whole thing at his leisure.'

'Maybe,' Bellman said, going over to the speaker's chair and holding up a note. 'Argument one in favour of such a theory: I've just been given this by Telenor. It shows that Rasmus Olsen spoke to his wife on the phone some time that morning. So let's assume he knew which cabin she was going to. Argument two in favour of this hypothesis is the weather report, which shows there was a moon and clear visibility all evening and night, so he could easily have skied there, as Tony Leike did. Argument one against the hypothesis: why kill anyone apart from his wife and her alleged partner?'

'Maybe she had more than one,' shouted one of the female detectives, a short, buxom number Bellman reckoned was sufficiently lesbian for him to have toyed with the idea of inviting her to Kaja's one night. No more than a passing thought of course. 'Perhaps there was a whole fucking orgy going on up there.'

Laughter all round. Good, that lightened the atmosphere.

'He may not have seen who she was having sex with, didn't even know if it was a woman or a man, just that someone was under the covers with her,' another voice said. 'And so he hedged his bets.'

More laughter.

'Come on, we can't waste time on this rubbish,' said Eskildsen, a veteran, though no one knew exactly how long he had been a detective. The room fell silent. 'Any of you young 'uns remember the case they solved at Crime Squad a few years back when everyone thought there was a serial killer on the loose?' Eskildsen continued. 'When they got the killer it turned out he only had a motive for murdering number three. But because he knew he would come under suspicion if she was the only victim, he killed the others to camouflage it as an insane rampage.'

'Jesus Christ,' shouted a young officer. 'Did the Crime Squad actually manage to solve a case? Must have been a fluke.'

The young man looked around with a grin and his face slowly coloured as no response was forthcoming. Everyone with any investigative experience at all remembered the case. It was on the syllabus of all police colleges throughout Scandinavia. It was a legend. As indeed was the man who cracked it.

*   *   *

'Harry Hole.'

'G'day, Holy, mate. Neil McCormack here. How are you? And where are you?'

McCormack thought he heard Harry answer 'in a coma', but assumed he must have been saying the name of some Norwegian town.

'I talked to Iska Peller. She didn't have a lot to say about the night at the cabin. However, the following evening . . .'

'Yes?'

'She and her friend Charlotte were picked up from the cabin by a cop from the outback and taken to his place. Turned out that while Miss Peller was trying to sleep off her flu, the policeman and her friend were having a glass of grog in the sitting room and he tried to seduce Charlotte. Got pretty physical, so physical that she shouted for help, Miss Peller woke up, and rushed into the room where the policeman had already pulled her friend's ski pants down to her knees. He stopped, and Miss Peller and her friend decided to go to the station and stay at a hotel somewhere I'm afraid I can't . . .'

'Geilo.'

'Thank you.'

'You say "tried to seduce", Neil, but you mean *rape*, I suppose?'

'No, I had to do the rounds with Miss Peller before we landed on a precise formulation. She said her friend's description was that the policeman had pulled down her trousers against her will, but he hadn't touched her intimate parts.'

'But . . .'

'We can perhaps assume it was his intention, but we don't know. The point is that nothing punishable by law had happened yet. Miss Peller accepted that. After all, they hadn't bothered to report the matter, they just skedaddled. The cop had even found a village wacko to run all three of them to the station and he had helped them board the train. According to Miss Peller, the man seemed relatively unfazed by the whole business; he was more interested in getting the girlfriend's phone number than apologising. As if it were just perfectly normal bloke-meets-sheila stuff.'

'Mm. Anything else?'

'No, Harry. Except that we've given her police protection as you suggested. Twenty-four-hour service, tucker and necessities brought to the door. She can just enjoy the sun. If the sun shines in Bristol, that is.'

'Thanks, Neil. If anything—'

'—should crop up, I'll ring. And vice versa.'

'Of course. Take care.'

Says you, McCormack thought, ringing off and peering out at the blue afternoon sky. The days were a bit longer now in the summer, he could still get in an hour and a half's sailing before it was dark.

Harry got out of bed and went for a shower. Stood motionless, letting the boiling hot water run down his body for twenty minutes. Then he came out, dried his sensitive, red-flecked skin and dressed. Saw from his mobile phone that he had received eighteen calls while he had been asleep. So they had managed to get hold of his number. He recognised the first numbers as those of Norway's three biggest newspapers and the two most important TV channels since they all had switchboard numbers beginning with the same prefixes. The remainder were more arbitrary and probably belonged to comment-hungry journalists. But his gaze paused at one of the numbers, although he couldn't say why. Because there were some bytes up in his brain that had fun memorising numbers perhaps. Or because the dialling code told him it was Stavanger. He flicked back through his call log and found the number from two days earlier. Colbjørnsen.

Harry rang back and squeezed the phone between cheek and shoulder as he tied his boots and noted that it was time he bought some new ones. The iron plate in the sole, so that you could tread on nails without worrying, was hanging off.

'Bloody hell, Harry. They really hung you out to dry in the papers today. They butchered you. What does your boss say?'

Colbjørnsen sounded ill from overindulgence. Or just ill.

'I don't know,' Harry said. 'I haven't spoken to him.'

'Crime Squad comes out OK. It's you personally carrying the entire can. Did your boss make you take one for the team?'

'No.'

The question came after a long silence. 'It wasn't . . . it wasn't Bellman, was it?'

'What do you want, Colbjørnsen?'

'Shit, Harry. I've been running a somewhat illegal solo investigation, just like you. So first of all I have to know whether we're still on the same team or not.'

'I haven't got a team, Colbjørnsen.'

'Great, I can hear you're still on our team. The losers.'

'I'm on my way out.'

'Right. I had another chat with Stine Ølberg, the girl Elias Skog was so taken by.'

'Yes?'

'It transpires that Skog told her more about what went on in the cabin that night than I had understood at the first interview.'

'I've started to believe in second interviews,' Harry said.

'Eh?'

'Nothing. Come on, out with it.'

49

Bombay Garden

BOMBAY GARDEN WAS THE KIND OF RESTAURANT THAT DID not appear to have the right to keep going, but unlike its trendier competitors it had managed to survive year after year. Its location at the centre of east Oslo was dire, down a side street between a timber warehouse and a disused factory that was now a theatre. The alcohol licence had come and gone after countless breaches of the rules; the same was also true for its licence to serve food. The health inspectors had on one occasion found a species of rodent in the kitchen they had not been able to identify, beyond declaring it had a certain similarity to *Rattus norvegicus*. In the comments box of the report the inspector had let rip and described the kitchen as a 'crime scene' where 'murders of the foulest kind had unquestionably taken place'. The slot machines along the walls brought in quite a bit of money, but were regularly vandalised and robbed. The Vietnamese owners did not use the place to launder drugs money, as some suspected, though. The reason Bombay Garden could keep its head above water was to be found at the back, behind two closed doors. Concealed there was a so-called private club, and to be allowed in you had to apply for membership. In practice, that meant you signed an application form at the bar of the restaurant, membership was granted on the spot and you paid a hundred kroner as an annual fee. Afterwards you were escorted in and the door was locked behind you.

Then you stood in a smoke-filled room – as smoking laws do not pertain to private clubs – and in front of you there was a miniature oval racecourse, four metres by two. The course itself was covered with green felt and had seven tracks. Seven flat metal horses, each attached to a pin, moved forward in spasmodic jerks. The speed of each horse was determined by a computer that hummed and buzzed under the table, and was – as far as anyone had ascertained – completely arbitrary and legitimate. That is, the computer program gave some of the horses a greater chance of a higher speed, which was reflected in the odds and thus any eventual payout. Around the racecourse sat the club members – some were regulars, others were new faces – in comfortable leather swivel chairs, smoking, drinking the restaurant's beer at membership prices, cheering on their horse or the combination they had backed.

Since the club operated in a legal grey area with respect to gambling laws, the rules were that if twelve or more members were present, the stake was restricted to a hundred kroner per member, per race. If there were fewer than twelve, the club's regulations stipulated it was regarded as a limited gathering, and at small private gatherings you could not prevent adults from making private wagers. How much they chose to bet was up to the participants. For this reason, it was conspicuous how often precisely eleven people could be counted in the back room of the Bombay Garden. And where the garden came into the picture, no one knew.

At ten past two in the afternoon a man with the club's most recent membership, forty seconds old to be precise, was admitted into the room where he soon established that the only people there, apart from himself, were one member sitting in a swivel chair with his back to him and a man of presumably Vietnamese origin who was clearly administrating the races and stakes; at any rate he was wearing the kind of waistcoat croupiers do.

The back in the swivel chair was broad and filled out the flannel shirt. Black curls hung down onto the collar.

'Are you winning, Krongli?' Harry asked, sitting in the chair beside him.

The man's head of curls twisted round. 'Harry!' he shouted, with genuine pleasure in his voice and on his face. 'How did you find me?'

'Why do you think I'm looking for you? Perhaps I'm a regular here.'

314

Krongli laughed as he watched the horses jerking down the long straight, each with a tin jockey on its back. 'No, you aren't. I come here whenever I'm in Oslo, and I've never seen you.'

'OK. Someone told me I'd probably find you here.'

'Hell, have I got a reputation? Perhaps it's not quite appropriate for a policeman to come here, even though it's on the right side of the law.'

'Regarding right side of the law,' Harry said, shaking his head to the croupier who pointed to the beer tap with a raised eyebrow. 'There was something I wanted to talk to you about.'

'Fire away,' Krongli said, concentrating on the racecourse, where the blue horse on the far track was in the lead, but heading towards a wide outside bend.

'Iska Peller, the Australian woman you gave a lift to from the Håvass cabin, says you groped her friend, Charlotte Lolles.'

Harry didn't detect any change in Krongli's concentrated expression. He waited. At length, Krongli looked up.

'Do you want me to react?'

'Only if you want to,' Harry said.

'I interpret that as *you* would like me to. *Groped* is the wrong word. We flirted a bit. Kissed. I wanted to go further. She thought it was enough. I maintained a bit of constructive persuasion, the way women often expect of a man – after all, that's part of the role play between the sexes. But nothing more than that.'

'That doesn't match what Iska Peller says Charlotte told her. Do you think Peller's lying?'

'No.'

'No?'

'But I do think Charlotte wanted to give a slightly different version to her friend. Catholic girls like to appear more virtuous than they are, don't they?'

'They decided to spend the night in Geilo rather than at your house. Even though Peller was ill.'

'She was the one who insisted on leaving. I don't know what was going on between those two, friendship between girls is often a complicated business, isn't it. And it's my bet the Peller girl hasn't got a boyfriend.'

He lifted the half-empty glass in front of him. 'Where are you going with this, Harry?'

'It's a bit strange you didn't say anything to Kaja Solness about meeting Charlotte Lolles when Kaja was in Ustaoset.'

'And it's a bit strange you're still working on this case. Thought it was a Kripos matter, especially after the newspaper headlines today.' Krongli's mind was back on the horses. Out of the bend came the yellow horse in the third track, leading by a tin horse's length.

'Yes,' Harry said. 'But rape cases are still a Crime Squad matter.'

'Rape? Haven't you sobered up yet, Harry?'

'Well.' Harry pulled a pack of cigarettes from his trouser pocket. 'I'm more sober than I hope you were, Krongli.' He stuffed a crumpled cigarette between his lips. 'All the times you beat up and raped your ex up there in Ustaoset.'

Krongli turned slowly to Harry, knocking over his beer glass with his elbow. The beer was soaked up by the green felt; the stain advanced like the Wehrmacht over a map of Europe.

'I've just come from the school where she works,' Harry continued, lighting the cigarette. 'She was the one who told me I'd probably find you here. She also told me that when she left you and Ustaoset, she was escaping rather than moving out. You—'

Harry got no further. Krongli was fast, spun his chair round with his foot and was on Harry before he could react. Harry felt the grip around his hand, knew what was coming, knew because this was what they practised from the first year at college: the police power half nelson. And yet he was a second too late, two days' drinking too sluggish, forty years too stupid. Krongli twisted his wrist and arm behind his back and pushed his temple forward into the felt. The side of his damaged jaw. Harry screamed with pain and blacked out for a second. Then he was back with the pain and made a frenetic attempt to free himself. Harry was strong, always had been, but immediately knew he had no hope against Krongli. The powerfully built officer's breath was hot and moist against his face.

'You shouldn't have done that, Harry. You shouldn't have spoken to the whore. She says whatever comes into her head. Does whatever comes into her head. Did she show you her cunt? Did she, Harry?'

There was a crunch inside Harry's head as Krongli increased the pressure. A yellow and then a green horse banged against Harry's forehead and nose respectively as he brought up his right foot and stamped. Hard. He heard Krongli scream, twisted out of the half nelson, turned and struck. Not with his fist – he had destroyed enough bones with that nonsense – but with his elbow. It hit Krongli where Harry had learned the effect was greatest – not on the point of the chin, but slightly to the side. Krongli staggered backwards, fell over a low swivel chair and landed on the floor with his feet pointing north. Harry noticed that the material of Krongli's Converse shoe on his right foot was torn and bloodstained after its meeting with an iron plate under a boot that definitely should have been thrown away. He also noticed that his cigarette was still hanging from his lips. And – out of the corner of his eye – that the red horse in the first track rode in as the clear winner.

Harry bent down, grabbed Krongli's collar, pulled him up and dumped him in the chair. Took a deep drag, felt it burn and warm his lungs.

'I agree this rape case of mine doesn't have a lot going for it,' he said. 'At least since neither Charlotte Lolles nor your wife reported you. That's why, as a detective, I have to try and dig a bit deeper, isn't it. And that's why I come back to the Håvass cabin.'

'What the hell are you talking about?' Krongli sounded as if he had caught a bad chill.

'There's this girl in Stavanger who Elias Skog confided in the same evening he was murdered. They were on a bus and Elias told her about the night at Håvass when he'd witnessed what he subsequently thought might have been a rape.'

'Elias?'

'Elias, yes. I suppose he must have been a light sleeper. He was woken in the night by sounds outside the bedroom window and looked out. The moon was up and he saw two people in the shadow under the ridge of the outside toilet roof. The woman was facing him with the man behind her, hiding his face. Elias's impression was that they were screwing, the woman seemed to be performing a belly dance and the man had his hand over her mouth, obviously so that they wouldn't disturb anyone. And when the man had dragged her into the toilet, Elias – disappointed not to see a full live show – had gone back to bed. It was only when he read about the murders that he'd started to wonder. Perhaps the woman had been wriggling to get away. The hand over her mouth might have been to suffocate calls for help.' Harry took another drag. 'Was it you, Krongli? Were you there?'

Krongli rubbed his chin.

'Alibi?' Harry asked airily.

'I was at home, in bed, alone. Did Elias Skog say who the woman was?'

'No. Nor the man, as I said.'

'It wasn't me. And you're living dangerously, Hole.'

'Shall I take that as a threat or a compliment?'

Krongli didn't answer. But there was a gleam in his eyes, yellow and cold.

Harry stubbed out his cigarette and got up. 'By the way, your ex didn't show me anything. We were in the staffroom. Something tells me she's afraid of being alone in the same room as a man. So you achieved something, didn't you, Krongli.'

'Don't forget to look over your shoulder, Hole.'

Harry turned. The croupier appeared completely unruffled by the scene and had already set up the horses for another race.

'Wan' a bet?' he asked in pidgin Norwegian with a smile.

Harry shook his head. 'Sorry, got nothing to bet with.'

'All the more to win,' the croupier said.

Harry allowed that to sink in and concluded that either it was a linguistic error or his logic didn't carry that far. Or it was just another terrible Oriental proverb.

50

Corruption

MIKAEL BELLMAN WAITED.

This was the best. The seconds waiting for her to open up. Wondering with excitement whether – and yet at the same time sure – she would again exceed his expectations. For every time he saw her he realised that he had forgotten how beautiful she was. Every time the door opened, it was as if he needed a moment to assimilate all her beauty. To let the confirmation sink in. Confirmation that from the selection of men who wanted her – in practice, any heterosexual man with good eyesight – she had chosen him. Confirmation that he was the leader of the pack, the alpha male, the male with the first claim to mate with the females. Yes, it could be articulated in such banal and vulgar terms. Being an alpha male was not something you aspired to, you were born to it. Not necessarily the easiest or the most comfortable life for a man, but if you were called, you could not resist.

The door opened.

She was wearing the white high-necked jumper and had put her hair up. She looked tired, her eyes had less sparkle than usual. And still she had the elegance, the class, of which even his wife could only dream. She said 'Hi', told him she was sitting on the veranda, turned her back on him and walked through the house. He followed, collecting a beer from the fridge, and sat down in one of the ridiculously large, heavy chairs on the veranda.

'Why do you sit outside?' he sniffed. 'You'll catch pneumonia.'

'Or lung cancer,' she said, hoisting the half-smoked cigarette from the edge of the ashtray and picking up the book she was reading. He skimmed the cover. *Ham on Rye*. Charles . . . he squinted . . . Bukowski? As in the Swedish auction rooms?

'I've got good news,' he said. 'We've not only averted a minor catastrophe, we've turned the whole Leike incident to our advantage. The Ministry of Justice phoned today.' Bellman put his feet on the table and studied the label on the beer bottle. 'They wanted to thank me for intervening with such resolution and ensuring Leike was released. They were very worried about what Galtung and his pack of lawyers might have got up to if Kripos hadn't acted so quickly. And they wanted a personal assurance that I would have my hands on the wheel and no one outside Kripos would have the opportunity to foul things up.'

He put the bottle to his mouth and drank. Banged it down hard on the table. 'What do you think, Bukowski?'

She lowered her book and met his eyes.

'You should show a little interest,' he said. 'This concerns you as well, you know. What do you think about the case, my love? Come on. You're a murder investigator.'

'Mikael . . .'

'Tony Leike is a violent criminal, and we allowed ourselves to be duped by that. Because we know you can't rehabilitate violent criminals. The ability and the desire to kill are not granted to all, it's innate or acquired. But when the killer is in you, it's damned difficult to get it out again. Perhaps the killer in this case knows we know that? Knows that if he served us up Tony Leike, we would go into a frenzy and all cheer in unison "Hey, the case is cracked, it's the guy with the violent streak!" And that was why he broke into Tony Leike's apartment and rang Elias Skog. To stop us searching for any of the others who were in Håvass.'

'The call from Leike's house was before anyone outside the police knew that we had found the link with the Håvass cabin.'

'So what? He must have reckoned that it was only a matter of time before we stumbled on it. Damn, we should have found it long before!' Bellman grabbed the bottle again.

'So who is the killer?'

'The eighth guest in the cabin,' Mikael Bellman said. 'The boyfriend Adele Vetlesen took along, but whom no one knows.'

'No one?'

'I've had more than thirty officers on the job. We've combed Adele's flat. Nothing in writing. No diaries, no cards, no letters, barely any emails or texts. Those male acquaintances that we have identified have been questioned and eliminated. Also the female ones. And none of them thinks it strange that she changed partners as frequently as panties and did it without telling anyone. The only thing we have found out is that Adele was supposed to have said to a girlfriend that this cabin escort had a couple of what she termed "turn-ons" and "turn-offs". The turn-on was that he had asked her to go to a nocturnal rendezvous at an empty factory dressed as a nurse.'

'If that was the turn-on, I dread to think what the turn-off was.'

'The turn-off was apparently that when he spoke he reminded Adele of her flatmate. The girlfriend didn't have a clue what Adele meant by that.'

'The flatmate isn't a mate in the biological sense,' Kaja yawned. 'Geir Bruun is gay. If this eighth guest tried to shift the murders on to Tony Leike he must have known Leike had a criminal record.'

'The assault conviction is information that's open to the public. Also the location, i.e. in Ytre Enebakk municipality. Leike was on the way to becoming a murderer while living with his grandfather by Lake Lyseren. If you wanted to direct police suspicions towards Leike, where would you dump Adele Vetlesen's body? In a place where the police could find a link to him and a conviction on his record, of course. That was why he chose Lake Lyseren.' Mikael Bellman paused. 'Tell me, am I boring you?'

'No.'

'You look so bored.'

'I . . . I have a lot to think about.'

'When did you start smoking? So, I have a plan for how to find the eighth guest.'

Kaja stared at him.

Bellman sighed. 'Aren't you going to ask me how, darling?'

'How?'

'By using the same strategy as he does.'

'Which is?'

'Focusing on an innocent person.'

'Isn't that the strategy you always use?'

Mikael Bellman looked up sharply. Something was beginning to dawn on him. Something about being an alpha male.

He explained the plan to her. Told her how he would entice the man out.

Afterwards, he was shaking from cold and anger. He didn't know what made him angrier. The fact that she didn't respond with either a negative or a positive comment. Or that she sat there smoking, to all outward signs completely untouched by the case. Didn't she understand that his career, his moves, in these very critical days would be decisive for her future as well? If she couldn't count on being the next fru Bellman, she could at least rise through the ranks under his auspices, provided that she was loyal and continued to deliver. Or perhaps his anger was a result of the question she had asked. It had been about *him*. The other one. The old, doddery alpha male.

She had asked about opium. Asked if he really would have used it, if Hole had not ceded to his demand that he should accept the responsibility for Leike's arrest.

'Of course,' Bellman said, trying to see her face, but it was too dark. 'Why shouldn't I have? He had smuggled drugs.'

'I'm not thinking of him. I'm thinking of whether you would have brought discredit on the police force.'

He shook his head. 'We can't let ourselves be corrupted by that sort of consideration.'

Her laughter sounded dry as it met the dense night cold. 'You indisputably corrupted him.'

'He's corruptible,' Bellman said, draining the bottle in one swig. 'That's the difference between him and me. Now, Kaja, are you trying to tell me something?'

She opened her mouth. Wanted to say it. Should have said it. But at that moment his mobile rang. She saw him clutch his pocket as he did what he usually did, formed his lips into a pout. Which did not signify a kiss, but that she should shut up. In case it was his wife, his boss or anyone else he didn't want to know that he came here to fuck a Crime Squad officer who gave him all the information he needed to outmanoeuvre the unit competing for murder investigations. To hell with Mikael Bellman. To hell with Kaja Solness. And above all to hell with . . .

'He's gone,' Mikael Bellman said, putting the phone back in his pocket.

'Who?'

'Tony Leike.'

51

Letter

Hi Tony,

You've been wondering who I could be for a long time now. So long that I think it may be time I revealed my hand. I was at the cabin in Håvass that night, but you didn't see me. No one saw me, I was as invisible as a ghost. But you know me. Know me all too well. And now I'm coming to get you. The only person who can stop me now is you. Everyone else is dead. There's just you and me left, Tony. Is your heart beating a bit faster now? Does your hand grope for a knife? Do you slash blindly through the dark, dizzy with terror that your life will be taken from you?

52

Visit

Something had woken him. A sound. There were hardly any sounds out here, none he didn't know anyway, and those didn't wake him. He got up, placed the soles of his feet on the cold floor and peered through the window. His terrain. Some called it a deserted wasteland, whatever that meant. Because it was never deserted here, there was always something. Like now. An animal? Or could it be him? The ghost? There was something outside, that was for certain. He looked at the door. It was locked and bolted on the inside. The rifle was in the storehouse. He shivered in the thick, red flannel shirt he wore both day and night up here. The sitting room was so empty. It was so empty out there. So empty in the world. But it wasn't deserted. There were the two of them, the two of them who were left.

Harry was dreaming. About a lift with teeth, about a woman with a cocktail stick between cochineal-red lips, a clown with his smiling head under his arm, a bride dressed in white at the altar with a snowman, a star drawn in the dust of a TV screen, a one-armed girl on a diving board in Bangkok, the sweet smell of urinal blocks, the outline of a human body on the inside of a blue plastic waterbed, a compressor drill and blood spurting into his face, hot and death-bringing. Alcohol had acted as a cross, garlic and holy water against ghosts, but tonight there had been a full moon and a virgin's blood, and now they came swarming from the darkest corners and deepest graves and tossed him between them in their dance, fiercer and wilder than ever, to the cardiac rhythms of mortal fear and the incessant shrill fire alarm here in hell. Then there was sudden silence. Complete silence. It was here again. It filled his mouth. He couldn't breathe. It was cold and pitch black and he was unable to move, he . . .

Harry twitched and blinked in the darkness, dazed. An echo reverberated between the walls. An echo of what? He grabbed his revolver from the bedside table, placed the soles of his feet on the cold floor and went downstairs, into the living room. Empty. The empty drinks cabinet was still lit. There had been a solitary bottle of Martell cognac. His dad had always been careful with alcohol – he knew what genes he was carrying – and the cognac was to offer guests. There had not been many guests. The dusty, half-full bottle had disappeared in the tidal wave with Captain Jim Beam and Able Seaman Harry Hole. Harry sat down in the armchair, stuck his finger through the tear on the armrest. He closed his eyes and visualised himself filling a glass half full. The deep gurgles from the bottle, the sparkling golden-brown liquid. The smell, the quiver as he put the glass to his mouth and he felt his body fighting it, panic-stricken. Then he emptied the contents down his throat.

It was like a blow to the temple.

Harry opened his eyes wide. It had gone all quiet again.

And just as suddenly it was there again.

It bored its way along his auditory canals. The fire alarm in hell. The same one that had woken him. The doorbell. Harry looked at his watch. Half past twelve.

He went into the hall, switched on the outside light, saw an outline through the wavy glass, held the revolver in his right hand while grabbing the lock with his left thumb and forefinger and tore the door wide open.

In the moonlight he could see ski tracks crossing the drive. They were not his. And ghosts didn't leave trails, did they?

They went round the house, to the back.

At that moment it struck him that the bedroom window was open, he should have . . . He held his breath. Someone seemed to be breathing with him. Not someone, something. An animal.

He turned. Opened his mouth. His heart had stopped beating. How could it have moved so quickly, without making a sound, how could it have got so . . . close?

Kaja stared at him.

'May I come in?' she asked.

She was wearing an oversized raincoat, her hair was sticking up in all directions, her face was pale and drawn. He blinked hard a couple of times to check he wasn't still dreaming. She had never been more beautiful.

Harry tried to spew as quietly as he could. He hadn't tasted booze for more than a day, and his stomach was a sensitive creature of habits that rebelled against sudden bouts of drinking and sudden abstinence. He flushed, carefully drank a glass of water and returned to the kitchen. The kettle was making rumbling sounds on the stove and Kaja was sitting on one of the kitchen chairs looking up at him.

'So Tony Leike's gone,' he said.

She nodded. 'Mikael had given instructions that he was to be contacted. But no one could find him; he wasn't at home, in his office, and he hadn't left any messages. No Leike on any airline or ferry passenger lists for the last twenty-four hours. Eventually a detective managed to contact Lene Galtung. She believes he may have gone into the mountains. To think. Apparently he does that. If so, he must have caught the train because the car's still in the garage.'

'Ustaoset,' Harry said. 'He said that was his terrain.'

'Anyway, he's definitely not gone to a hotel.'

'Mm.'

'They think he's in danger.'

'They?'

'Bellman. Kripos.'

'I thought that was *we*. And why would Bellman want to contact Tony Leike anyway?'

She closed her eyes. 'Mikael has concocted a plan. To lure the killer out.'

'Uh-uh?'

'The killer's trying to remove everyone who was at the Håvass cabin that night. So he wanted to try to persuade Leike to be the decoy in a set-up. Get Leike to go for an interview with a newspaper, talk about the tough time he's been through and how he was going to relax on his own at a particular place to be revealed in the paper.'

'Where Kripos would set a trap.'

'Yes.'

'But now the plan's up the creek, and that's why you're here?'

She gazed at him without blinking. 'We have one person left we can use as a decoy.'

'Iska Peller? She's in Australia.'

'And Bellman knows she's under police protection, and you've been in contact with her and someone called McCormack. Bellman wants you to persuade her to come here.'

'Why should I agree?'

She looked down at her hands. 'You know. Same coercion tactics as last time.'

'Mm. When did you discover there was opium in the cigarette carton?'

'When I was putting the carton on the shelf in my bedroom. You're right, it has a strong smell. And I remembered the smell from your hostel. I opened the carton and saw the seal on the bottom packet had been broken. And found the clump inside. I told Mikael. He told me to hand over the carton whenever you asked.'

'Perhaps that made it easier for you to betray me. Knowing I had used you.'

She slowly shook her head. 'No, Harry. It didn't make it easier. Perhaps it should have done, but . . .'

'But?'

She shrugged. 'Passing on this message is the last favour I do for Mikael.'

'Oh?'

'Then I'm going to tell him I won't see him any more.'

The kettle's rumbling noises stopped.

'I should have done this a long time ago,' she said. 'I have no intention of asking you to forgive me for what I've done, Harry, that's too much to ask. But I thought I would tell you face to face so that you can understand. That's actually why I've come to see you now. To tell you that I did it out of stupid, stupid love. Love corrupted me. And I didn't think I was corruptible.' She put her head in her hands. 'I deceived you, Harry. I don't know what to say. Except that deceiving myself feels even worse.'

'We're all corruptible,' Harry said. 'We just demand different prices. And different currencies. Yours is love. Mine is anaesthetisation. And do you know what . . . ?'

The kettle sang again, this time an octave higher.

'. . . I think it makes you a better person than me. Coffee?'

He spun right round and stared at the figure. It was standing straight in front of him, unmoving, as if it had been there a long time, as if it were his shadow. It was so quiet; all he could hear was his own breathing. Then he sensed a movement, something being lifted in the dark, heard a low whistle through the air, and at that moment a strange thought struck him. The figure was just that, his very own shadow. He . . .

The thought appeared to falter, time was dislocated, the visual connection was broken for a second.

He stared before him in amazement and felt a hot bead of sweat run down his forehead. He spoke, but the words were meaningless, there was a fault in the connection between brain and mouth. Again he heard a low whistle. Then the sound was gone. All sound – he couldn't even hear his own breathing. And he discovered that he was kneeling and that the telephone was on the floor beside him. Ahead, a white stripe of moonlight ran across the coarse floorboards, but it vanished when the sweat reached the bridge of his nose, ran into his eyes and blinded him. And he understood it was not sweat.

The third blow felt like an icicle being driven through his head, throat and into his body. Everything froze.

I don't want to die, he thought, and tried to raise a protective arm over his head, but he was unable to move a single limb, and realised he was paralysed.

He didn't register the fourth blow, but from the wood smell he concluded he was lying face down on the floor. He blinked several times and sight returned to one eye. Directly in front of him he saw a pair of ski boots. And slowly sounds returned; his heaving gasps, the other's calm breathing, the blood dripping from his nose onto the floorboards. The other's voice was a mere whisper, but the words seemed to be screamed into his ear. 'Now there's only one of us.'

As the clock struck two they were still sitting in the kitchen talking.

'The eighth guest,' Harry said, pouring more coffee. 'Close your eyes. How does he appear to you? Quick, don't think.'

'He's full of hatred,' Kaja said. 'Angry. Out of balance, nasty. The kind of guy women like Adele run into, check out and reject. He's got piles of pornographic magazines and films at home.'

'What makes you think that?'

'I don't know. His asking Adele to go to an empty factory dressed in a nurse's uniform.'

'Go on.'

'He's effeminate.'

'In what way?'

'Well, high-pitched voice. Adele said he reminded her of her gay flatmate when he spoke.' She drew her cup to her mouth and smiled. 'Or perhaps he's a film actor. With a squeaky voice and a pout. I still can't remember the name of the macho actor with the feminine voice.'

Harry held up his cup in a toast. 'And the things I told you about Elias Skog and the late-night incident outside the cabin. Who were they? Had he witnessed a rape?'

'It wasn't Marit Olsen, anyway,' Kaja said.

'Mm. Why not?'

'Because she was the only fat woman there, so Elias Skog would have recognised her and used her name when describing the scene.'

'Same conclusion I came to. But was it rape, do you think?'

'Sounds like it. He put his hand over her mouth, stifled her cries, pulled her inside the toilet, what else could it have been?'

'But why didn't Elias Skog think it was rape straight off?'

'I don't know. Because there was something about the way . . . the way they were standing, their body language.'

'Exactly. The subconscious understands much more than the conscious mind. He was so sure it was consensual sex that he simply went back to bed. It wasn't until long after, reading about the murders and being reminded of a half-forgotten scene, that he had formed the idea it might have been rape.'

'A game,' Kaja said. 'That might smack of rape. Who does that? Not a man and a woman who have just met at a cabin and sneak out to become a little better acquainted. You have to be a bit more comfortable with each other.'

'So it's two people who've been together before,' Harry said. 'Which to our knowledge can only be . . .'

'Adele and the mystery man. The eighth guest.'

'Either that or someone else turned up that night.' Harry flicked ash off the cigarette.

'Where's the loo?' Kaja asked.

'Through the hall to the left.'

He watched the cigarette smoke curl upwards into the lampshade over the table. Waited. He hadn't heard the door open. He got up and went after her.

She was standing in the hall staring at the door. In the dim light he could see her taking gulps of air, could see a moist pointed tooth glistening. He placed a hand on her back and even there, through her clothes, he could feel her heart beating. 'Do you mind if I open it?'

'You must think I'm mental,' she said.

'We all are. I'm opening it now, OK?'

331

She nodded, and he opened the door.

Harry was sitting at the kitchen table when she returned. She had put on her raincoat.

'Think I'll have to go home now.'

Harry nodded and accompanied her to the front door. Watched as she stooped to pull on her boots.

'It only happens when I'm tired,' she said. 'The door stuff.'

'I know,' Harry said. 'I'm the same with lifts.'

'Oh?'

'Yes.'

'Tell me more.'

'Another time maybe. Who knows, perhaps we'll see each other again.'

She fell quiet. Took a long time to zip up her boots. Then, all of a sudden, she stood up, so close to him that he was aware of her scent following her, like an echo.

'Tell me now,' she said with a wild expression in her eyes he was unable to interpret.

'Well,' he said, his fingertips tingling, as if he had been cold and was warming up again. 'When we were young my little sister had very long hair. We had been visiting my mother in hospital and were about to get into the lift. Dad was waiting downstairs, he couldn't stand hospitals. Sis stood too near to the brick wall and her hair got caught between the lift and the wall. And I was so horror-stricken that I couldn't move. I watched Sis being dragged up by her hair.'

'What happened?' she asked.

They were standing a bit too close, he thought. They were standing at the limits of their personal space. And they knew. He took a breath.

'She lost a lot of hair. It grew back. I . . . lost something else. Which didn't grow back.'

'You think you failed her.'

'It's a fact that I failed her.'

'How old were you?'

'Old enough to fail her.' He smiled. 'Think that's almost enough self-pity for one night, don't you? My father liked you curtsying.'

Kaja chuckled. 'Goodnight.' She curtsied.

He opened the front door for her. 'Goodnight.'

She moved onto the steps and turned.

'Harry?'

'Yes?'

'Weren't you lonely in Hong Kong?'

'Lonely?'

'I watched you while you were asleep. You looked so . . . alone.'

'Yes,' he said. 'I was lonely. Goodnight.'

They stood there half a second too long. Five-tenths of a second before and she would have been down the steps and he would have been on his way back to the kitchen.

Her fingers closed around his neck and pulled his head down as she hoisted herself up on tiptoes. Her eyes lost focus, became a glittering sea and then she shut them. Her lips were half open as they met his. She held him and he didn't move, just felt the sweet dagger in his stomach, like a rush of morphine.

She let go of him.

'Sleep well, Harry.'

He nodded.

She turned and walked away. He closed the door quietly behind him.

He cleared away the cups, rinsed the kettle and had just put it away when the doorbell rang.

He went to answer it.

'I forgot something,' she said.

'What was that?' he asked.

She lifted her hand and stroked his brow. 'What you look like.'

He pulled her close. Her skin. The scent. He fell, a wonderful dizzying spiral downwards.

'I want you,' she whispered. 'I want to make love to you.'

'And I want you, too.'

They let go. Looked at each other. A sudden formality seemed to come between them, and for a moment it appeared to him that she had regrets. That he also had regrets. It was too much, too quickly. There were too many other things, there was too much clinker, too much baggage, too many good reasons. Nonetheless she took his hand, timid almost, whispered 'Come on' and led him up the stairs.

The bedroom was cold and smelt of parents. He switched on the light.

The spacious double bed was made with two duvets and pillows.

Harry helped her to change the bedlinen.

'Which side is his?' she asked.

'This one,' Harry pointed.

'And he continued to sleep there after she was gone,' she said, as if to herself. 'Just in case.'

They undressed without peeking. Crept under the duvets and met there.

At first they lay close to each other, kissing, exploring, careful not to ruin anything before they knew how it would be. Listened to each other's breathing and the odd isolated car rushing by. Then their kisses became greedier, their touching bolder, and he heard the excited hiss of her breath against his ear.

'Are you frightened?' he asked.

'No,' she groaned, grabbing hold of his erection, adjusting her hips and guiding him in, but he moved her hand and did it himself.

There was barely a sound, only a gasp as he penetrated her. He closed his eyes, lay still, enjoying the sensations. Then he began to move slowly, carefully. Opened his eyes, met hers. She seemed on the verge of tears.

'Kiss me,' she whispered.

Her tongue coiled around his, smooth underneath, rough on top. Faster and deeper, slower and deeper. She rolled him over without letting go of his tongue and sat astride him. She pressed against his stomach every time she came down on him. Then her tongue released his, and she leaned back and let out a moan. Twice, a deep animal noise that rose, and became high-pitched as she gasped for air and went quiet again. Her throat was thick with the scream that didn't come. He raised his hand, placed his fingers against the quivering blue artery under the skin on her neck.

And then she screamed, as if in pain, in anger, in liberation. Harry felt his scrotum tighten and came. It was perfect, so unbearably perfect that he threw his hand in the air and banged the wall behind him with his fist. And, as though she had been given a lethal injection, she collapsed on top of him.

They lay like this, limbs strewn randomly, like the dead. Harry felt the blood rush in his ears and well-being surge through his body. That and something he could have sworn was happiness.

He slept and was woken by her getting back into bed and snuggling up close to him. She was wearing one of Olav's vests. She kissed him, mumbled something and was gone, her breathing light and serene. Harry stared at the ceiling. Letting his thoughts churn, knowing there was no point resisting.

It had been so good. It hadn't been so good since . . . since . . .

The blind wasn't pulled down and at half past five cones of light from passing cars began to travel across the ceiling as Oslo woke and dragged itself off to work. He looked at her again. And then he was gone, too.

53

Heel Hook

WHEN HARRY WOKE IT WAS NINE O'CLOCK, THE ROOM WAS bathed in daylight and there was no one lying beside him. There were four messages on his phone.

The first was from Kaja, saying she was on her way home to get changed for work. And thanking him for . . . he couldn't hear what, just a shriek of laughter before she rang off.

The second was from Gunnar Hagen, who was wondering why Harry had not answered any of his calls and saying the press were on his back because of Tony Leike's unjustified arrest.

The third was from Günther, who repeated the Dirty Harry witticism and said the Leipzig police had not found Juliana Verni's passport and therefore could not confirm whether it had been stamped in Kigali or not.

The fourth was from Mikael Bellman, who simply told Harry to be at Kripos for two. He assumed Solness had passed on his instructions.

Harry got up. He felt good. Better than good. Fantastic maybe. He listened to his body. OK, fantastic was an exaggeration.

Harry went downstairs, took out a packet of crispbreads and made the important phone call first.

'You're talking to Søs Hole.' It was Søs, or Sis, as Harry called her. Her voice sounded so formal he had to smile.

'And you're talking to Harry Hole,' he said.

'Harry!' She screamed his name two more times.

'Hi, Sis.'

'Dad said you were home! Why haven't you rung before?'

'I wasn't ready, Sis. Now I am. Are you?'

'I'm always ready, Harry. You know that.'

'Yes, I do. Lunch in town before visiting Dad some time soon? My treat.'

'Yes! You sound happy, Harry. Is it Rakel? Have you been speaking to her? I spoke to her yesterday. What was that sound? Harry?'

'Just the crispbreads falling out of the packet onto the floor. What did she want?'

'To ask about Dad. She'd heard he's ill.'

'Was that all?'

'Yes. No. She said Oleg was fine.'

Harry swallowed. 'Good. Let's talk soon then.'

'Don't forget. I'm so happy you're home, Harry! I have so much to tell you!'

Harry put the phone on the worktop and was bending down to pick up the crispbreads when the phone hummed again. Sis was like that, remembering things she should have said after they had rung off. He straightened up.

'What is it?'

Sonorous clearing of throat. Then a voice introduced itself as Abel. The name was familiar, and Harry instantly ransacked his memory. There were the files of old murder cases, neatly organised with data that never seemed to be deleted: names, faces, house numbers, dates, sound of a voice, colour and year of a car. But he could suddenly forget the name of neighbours who had lived in his block for three years or when Oleg's birthday was. They called that the detective memory.

Harry listened without interrupting.

'I see,' he said at length. 'Thank you for ringing.'

He hung up and tapped in a new number.

'Kripos,' answered a weary receptionist. 'You are trying to get through to Mikael Bellman.'

'Yes. Hole from Crime Squad. Where's Bellman?'

The receptionist informed him of the POB's whereabouts.

'Logical,' Harry said.

'I beg your pardon,' she yawned.

'That's what he's doing, isn't it?'

Harry slipped the phone into his pocket. Stared out of the kitchen window. Crispbread crunched under his feet as he walked.

'Skøyen Climbing Club' it said on the glass door facing the car park. Harry pushed the door and entered. On his way in, he had to wait for a class of excited schoolchildren on their way out. He flipped off his boots by a shoe rack at the bottom of the stairs. In the large hall, there were half a dozen people climbing up the ten-metre-high walls, although they looked more like the artificial papier mâché mountainsides of Tarzan films Harry and Øystein had seen at Symra cinema when they were kids. Except that these were peppered with multicoloured holds and pegs with loops and carabiner hooks. A discreet smell of soap and sweaty feet emanated from the blue mats on the floor that Harry walked across. He stopped beside a bow-legged, squat man staring intently up at the over-hang above them. A rope went from his climbing harness to a man who at that moment was swinging like a pendulum from one arm eight metres above them. At the end of one arc he swung up a foot, threaded the heel under a pink, pear-shaped hold, put the other foot on a piece of the structure and clipped the climbing rope into the top anchor in one elegant sweeping movement.

'Gotcha!' he shouted, leaned back on the rope and placed his legs against the wall.

'Great heel hook,' Harry said. 'Your boss is a bit of a poseur, isn't he?'

Jussi Kolkka neither answered nor graced Harry with a glance, just pulled the lever on the rope brake.

'Your receptionist told me you'd be here,' Harry said to the man being lowered towards them.

'Regular slot every week,' Bellman said. 'One of the perks of being a policeman is being able to train during working hours. How are you, Harry? Muscles look defined at any rate. Lots of muscle per kilo, I reckon. Ideal for climbing, you know.'

338

'For limited ambitions,' Harry said.

Bellman landed with legs shoulder-width apart and pulled down some rope so that he could slacken the figure-of-eight knot.

'I didn't understand that.'

'I can't see the point of climbing so high. I clamber around a few crags now and then.'

'Clambering,' Bellman snorted, loosening the harness and stepping out of it. 'You know, it hurts more to fall from two metres without a rope than it does from thirty metres with one?'

'Yes,' Harry said, a smile tugging at his mouth. 'I know.'

Bellman sat down on one of the wooden benches, pulled off the ballet-shoe-like climbing slippers and rubbed his feet while Kolkka brought down the rope and started to gather it in a coil. 'You got my message?'

'Yes.'

'So what's the hurry? I'm seeing you at two.'

'That was what I wanted to clarify with you, Bellman.'

'Clarify?'

'Before we meet the others. Agreeing on the conditions for me to join the team.'

'*The team?*' Bellman laughed. 'What are you talking about, Harry?'

'Do you want me to spell it out for you? You don't need me to ring Australia and persuade a woman to come here to act as a decoy, you can do that yourself without any bother. What you're asking for is *help*.'

'Harry! Really now . . .'

'You look knackered, Bellman. You've started to feel it, haven't you. You've felt the pressure escalate since Marit Olsen.' Harry sat down on the bench beside him. Even then, he was almost ten centimetres taller. 'Feeding frenzy in the press every sodding day. Impossible to walk past a newspaper stand or switch on the TV without being reminded of the Case. The Case you haven't solved. The Case your bosses are nagging you about all the time. The Case that requires a press conference a day where the vultures scream questions into each other's beaks. And now the man you yourself released has vanished into the blue beyond. The vultures swarm in, some of them cackling in Swedish, Danish and even English. I've been where you are now, Bellman. Soon they'll be talking

339

fucking French. For this is the Case you *have* to solve, Bellman. And the Case has gone stale.'

Bellman didn't answer, but his jaw muscles were grinding. Kolkka had packed the rope in the sack and came towards them, but Bellman waved him away. The Finn turned and waddled towards the exit like an obedient terrier.

'What do you want, Harry?'

'I'm offering you the chance to get this sorted out one on one, instead of at a meeting.'

'You want me to *ask* you for help?'

Harry saw Bellman's complexion redden.

'What sort of bargaining position do you imagine you're in, Harry?'

'Well, I imagine it's better than it has been for a while.'

'You're mistaken there.'

'Kaja Solness doesn't want to work for you. Bjørn Holm you've already promoted, and if you send him back to being a crime scene officer he'll be only too pleased. The only person you can hurt now is me, Bellman.'

'Have you forgotten I can lock you up so that you can't visit your father before he dies?'

Harry shook his head. 'There's no one to visit any more, Bellman.'

Mikael Bellman arched an eyebrow in surprise.

'They rang from the hospital this morning,' Harry said. 'My father went into a coma last night. Dr Abel says he won't come out of it. Whatever was left unsaid between my father and me will remain unsaid.'

54

Tulip

BELLMAN LOOKED AT HARRY IN SILENCE. THAT IS, THE BROWN deer-like eyes were directed towards Harry, but his gaze was inverted. Harry knew that a committee meeting was in progress there, a meeting with a lot of dissenting opinions, it seemed. Bellman slowly loosened the strings of the chalk bag hanging around his waist, as if to gain time. Time to think. Then he angrily stuffed the chalk bag in his rucksack.

'If – and only *if* – I asked you for help without having anything to pressurise you with,' he said, 'why on earth would you do it?'

'I don't know.'

Bellman stopped packing and looked up. 'You don't know?'

'Well, it definitely wouldn't be out of love for you, Bellman.' Harry breathed in. Fidgeted with a pack of cigarettes. 'Let's say that even those who believe themselves to be homeless occasionally discover that they have a home. A place where you could imagine being buried one day. And do you know where I want to be buried, Bellman? In the park in front of Police HQ. Not because I love the police or have been a fan of what is known as *esprit de corps*. Quite the opposite – I spit on the police officer's craven loyalty to the force, that incestuous camaraderie that exists only because people think they may need a favour one rainy day. A colleague who can exact vengeance, make a testimony or, if necessary, turn a blind eye for you, I hate all that.'

Harry faced Bellman.

'But the police is all I have. It's my tribe. And my job is to clear up

341

murders. Whether it is for Kripos or Crime Squad. Can you grasp something like that, Bellman?'

Mikael Bellman squeezed his lower lip between thumb and first finger.

Harry motioned to the wall. 'What grade was the climb, Bellman? Seven plus?'

'Eight minimum. On sight.'

'That's tough. And I guess you think this is even tougher. But that's how it has to be.'

Bellman cleared his throat. 'Fine. Fine, Harry.' He pulled the strings of his rucksack tight again. 'Will you help us?'

Harry put his cigarettes back in his pocket and lowered his head. 'Of course.'

'I'll have to check with your boss to see if it's alright first.'

'Save yourself the effort,' Harry said, getting up. 'I've already informed him I'm working with you lot from now on. See you at two.'

Iska Peller peered out of the window of the two-storey brick building, at the row of identical houses on the other side of the street. It could have been any street in any town in England, but it was the tiny district of Bristol in Sydney, Australia. A cool southerly had picked up. The afternoon heat would release its grip as soon as the sun went down.

She heard a dog bark and the heavy traffic on the motorway two blocks away.

The man and woman in the car opposite had just been relieved; now there were two men. They drank slowly from their paper cups with lids. In their own good time, because there is no reason in the world to hurry when you have an eight-hour shift ahead of you and nothing at all is going to happen. Ratchet down a gear, slow the metabolism, do what the Aborigines do: go into that torpid, dormant state which is their diapause and where they can be for hours on end, days on end if need be. She tried to visualise how these slow coffee drinkers could be of any help if anything *really* happened.

'I'm sorry,' she said, trying to repress the tremble in her voice caused by suppressed fury. 'I would have liked to help you find who killed Charlotte, but what you're suggesting is utterly out of the question.' Then her anger gained the upper hand after all. 'I can't believe you're even asking! I'm enough of a decoy here. Ten wild horses couldn't drag me back to Norway. You're the police, you get paid to catch that monster, why can't *you* be the bait?'

She hung up and threw down the phone. It hit the cushion on the armchair and one of her cats jumped up and darted into the kitchen. She hid her face in her hands and let the tears flow again. Dear Charlotte. Her dear, dear, beloved Charlotte.

She had never been afraid of the dark before, now she thought of nothing else; soon the sun would go down, night would come, it was relentless, returning again and again.

The phone played the opening bars of an Antony and the Johnsons song, and the display lit up on the cushion. She walked over and eyed it. Felt the hairs on her neck rising. The caller's number started with 47. From Norway again.

She put the phone to her ear.

'Yeah?'

'Me again.'

She sighed with relief. Just the policeman.

'I was wondering, if you don't want to come here in person, whether we might at least have the use of your name?'

Kaja studied the man held in the red-haired woman's embrace, her head bowed over his bared neck.

'What can you see?' Mikael asked. His voice echoed around the walls of the museum.

'She's kissing him,' Kaja said, stepping back from the painting. 'Or comforting him.'

'She's biting him and sucking his blood,' Mikael said.

'Why do you think that?'

'It's one of the reasons Munch called this *The Vampire*. Everything ready?'

'Yes, I'm taking the train to Ustaoset soon.'

'Why did you want to meet here now?'

Kaja took a deep breath. 'I wanted to tell you that we can't go on meeting.'

Mikael Bellman rocked on his heels. '*Love and Pain*.'

'What?'

'That's what Munch originally called this painting. Did Harry go over the details of our plan with you?'

'Yes. Did you hear what I said?'

'Thank you, Solness, my hearing is excellent. Unless my memory is at fault, you've said that a couple of times before. I suggest you give it some thought.'

'I've finished giving it some thought, Mikael.'

He stroked the knot of his tie. 'Have you slept with him?'

She gave a start. 'Who?'

Bellman chuckled.

Kaja didn't turn round; she kept her eyes firmly fixed on the woman's face as his steps receded into the distance.

The light seeped through the grey steel blinds, and Harry warmed his hands around a white coffee cup with 'Kripos' inscribed in blue letters. The conference room was identical to the one in which he had spent so many hours of his life at Crime Squad. Light, expensive and yet spartan in that cool modern way that is not intentionally minimalist, just somewhat soulless. A room that demands efficiency so that you can get the hell out of it.

The eight people there constituted what Bellman declared the inner core of the investigative unit. Harry knew only two of them: Bjørn Holm and a robust, down-to-earth but not very imaginative female detective known as the Pelican who had once worked at Crime Squad. Bellman had introduced Harry to everyone, including Ærdal, a man in horn-rimmed glasses and a brown suit of the ready-made variety that led one's thoughts to the German Democratic Republic. He sat at the far end of the table cleaning his nails with a Swiss army knife. Harry conjectured a background in the military police. They had given their reports. Which all supported Harry's contention: that the case was in a rut. He noted the defensive attitude, particularly in the report on the search for Tony Leike. The officer responsible went through which passenger lists had been checked with which companies, to no avail, and which authorities in which telephone company had told them that none of their base stations had picked up signals from Leike's phone. He informed them that no hotels in town had anyone on their books under the name of Leike, but naturally the Captain (even Harry knew the self-appointed and overenthusiastic police informant-cum-receptionist at Hotel Bristol) rang to say he had seen a person answering Tony Leike's description. The officer gave a report that went into an impressive level of detail, but failed to notice that what emerged was a defence of the result. *Zilch. Nada.*

Bellman sat at the head of the table with crossed legs and trouser creases that were still as sharp as a knife. He thanked the officers for their reports and made a more formal introduction of Harry by reading quickly from a kind of CV: graduation from Police College, FBI course on serial killers in Chicago, the clown murder case in Sydney, promotion to Inspector and of course the Snowman investigation.

'So Harry is a part of this team with effect from today,' Bellman said. 'He reports to me.'

'And is subject to only your orders as well?' the Pelican boomed. Harry recalled that what she was doing now was precisely what had given her the nickname, the way she pushed her chin forward, the long, beak-like nose and the protracted, thin neck as she peered over her glasses. Sceptical and voracious at the same time, considering whether she wanted you on the menu or not.

'He is not subject to anyone's orders,' Bellman said. 'He has a free role in the team. We may consider Inspector Hole a consultant. Isn't that right, Harry?'

'Why not?' Harry said. 'An overpaid, overrated guy who thinks he knows something you don't.'

Cautious titters around the table. Harry exchanged glances with Bjørn Holm, who sent him a nod of encouragement.

'Except that in this instance he does,' Mikael Bellman said. 'You've been talking to Iska Peller, Harry.'

'Yes,' Harry said. 'But first I'd like to hear more about your plan to use her as a decoy.'

The Pelican cleared her throat. 'It hasn't been formulated in detail. For the time being, our plan is to bring her to Norway, make it public that she's staying at a place where it's obvious to the killer that she would be easy prey. And then sit back and hope he swallows the bait.'

'Mm,' Harry said. 'Simple.'

'Experience tells us simplicity works,' said the Swiss army knife man in the GDR suit concentrating on the nail of his index finger.

'Agreed,' Harry said. 'But in this instance the decoy won't play ball.'

Groans and sighs of despair.

'So I suggest we make it even simpler,' Harry said. 'Iska Peller asked why, if we were paid to catch the monster, we couldn't be the bait ourselves.'

He looked around the table. At least he had their attention. Convincing them would be harder.

'You see, we have an advantage over the killer. We assume he has the page torn from the Håvass guest book, so he has Iska Peller's name. But he doesn't know what she looks like. We're working on the assumption he was at the cabin that night but Iska and Charlotte Lolles got there first. And Iska was ill and spent the evening alone in a bedroom she shared solely with Charlotte. She stayed there until all the others had left. In other words, we can set up a little role play with one of our own number acting the part of Iska, without the killer being any the wiser.'

Another sweeping scan of the table. The scepticism on their faces was layers thick.

'And how had you envisaged getting someone to come to this perform-ance?' Ærdal asked, snapping the knife shut.

'By Kripos doing what they do best,' Harry said.

Silence.

'Which is?' asked the Pelican at length.

'Press conferences,' Harry said.

The silence in the room was tangible. Until the laughter shattered it. Mikael Bellman's. They looked at their boss in astonishment. And realised that Harry Hole's plan had already been given the go-ahead.

'So . . .' Harry began.

After the meeting Harry took Bjørn Holm aside.

'Nose still sore?' Harry asked.

'That you trying to apologise?'

'No.'

'I . . . well, you were lucky my nose didn't break, Harry.'

'Could have been an improvement, you know.'

'Are you apologising or not?'

'Sorry, Bjørn.'

'Great. And I suppose that means you want a favour?'

'Yes.'

'And that is?'

'I was wondering if you've been to Drammen to check Adele's clothes for DNA. She did meet this guy she was at the cabin with a few times.'

'We've been through her wardrobe, but the problem is that the clothes have been washed, worn and probably been in contact with lots of other people afterwards.'

'Mm. She wasn't a skier as far as I know. Checked her skiing gear, have you?'

'She didn't have any.'

'What about the nurse's uniform? Perhaps it was only used once and may still have sperm stains on.'

'She didn't have that, either.'

'No cheeky miniskirt and bonnet with a red cross?'

'Nope. There was a pair of light blue hospital trousers and top there, but nothing to get you going exactly.'

'Mm. Perhaps she couldn't get hold of the miniskirt variety. Or couldn't be bothered. Could you examine the hospital stuff for me?'

Holm sighed. 'As I said, we went through all the clothes there, and whatever could be washed had been washed. Not so much as a stain or a hair.'

'Could you take it to the lab? Give it a thorough going-over?'

'Harry . . .'

'Thanks, Bjørn. And I was only kidding, you've got a terrific conk. Really.'

It was four o'clock when Harry fetched Sis in the Kripos car Bellman had placed at his disposal until further notice. They drove to Rikshospital and talked to Dr Abel. Harry translated the bits Sis didn't understand, and she shed some tears. Then they went to see their father who had been moved to another room. Sis squeezed Olav's hand and whispered his name again and again as if to rouse him gently from sleep.

Sigurd Altman popped by, put a hand on Harry's shoulder, not too long, and said a few words, not too many.

After dropping off Sis at her little flat by Lake Sognsvann, Harry drove to the city centre where he kept going, twisting this way and that through one-way streets, roadworks and dead ends. He drove through the red-light district, the shopping area, the drugs zone and it wasn't until he had emerged and the town lay beneath him that he was aware he had been on his way to the German bunkers. He rang Øystein, who appeared ten minutes later, parked his taxi beside Harry's car, opened the door, turned up the music, came over and sat on the brick wall next to Harry.

'Coma,' Harry said. 'Not the worst thing that could happen, I suppose. Got a smoke?'

They sat listening to Joy Division. 'Transmission'. Ian Curtis. Øystein had always liked singers who died young.

'Shame I never got to talk to him after he fell ill,' Øystein said, taking a deep drag.

'You wouldn't have done, however long it had taken,' Harry said.

'No, that'll have to be my consolation.'

348

Harry laughed. Øystein sent him a sideways glance, smiled, unsure whether you were allowed to laugh when fathers lay on their deathbeds.

'What are you going to do now?' Øystein asked. 'Go on a bit of a binge? I can ring Tresko and—'

'No,' Harry said, stubbing out his cigarette. 'I have to work.'

'You'd prefer death and depravity to a glass or two?'

'You can drop by and say goodbye while he's still breathing, you know.'

Øystein shivered. 'Hospitals give me the creeps. Anyway, he can't hear jackshit, can he?'

'It wasn't him I was thinking about, Øystein.'

Øystein screwed up his eyes against the smoke. 'The little upbringing I had, Harry, I got from your father. D'you know that? My own dad wasn't worth a bloody fly's droppings. Go there tomorrow, I will.'

'Good for you.'

He stared up at the man above him. Saw his mouth move, heard the words issuing forth, but something must have been damaged, he couldn't assemble them into anything sensible. All he understood was that the time had come. The revenge. That he would have to pay. And in a way it was a relief.

He was sitting on the floor with his back to the large, round wood burner. His arms were forced backwards around the stove, his hands tied with two ski belts. He threw up from time to time, probably due to concussion. The bleeding had stopped and sensation had returned to his body, but there was a mist over his vision that came and went. Nonetheless, he was not beset by doubt. The voice. It was a ghost's voice.

'You're going to die quite soon,' it whispered. 'As she did. But there is still something to gain. You see, you still have to choose how. Unfortunately, there are only two options. Leopold's apple . . .'

The man held up a metal ball perforated with holes and a small loop of wire hanging from one of them.

'Three of the girls have tasted it. None of them liked it much. But it's pain-free and swift. And you only need to answer this: How? And who else knows? Who have you been working with? Believe me, the apple is preferable to the alternative. Which you, as an intelligent man, have probably worked out is . . .'

The man stood up, flailed his arms in an exaggerated manner, to keep warm, and put on a broad smile. The whisper was all there was to break the silence.

'It's a bit cold in here, don't you think?'

Then he heard a scraping sound followed by a low hiss. He stared at the match. At the unwavering, yellow, tulip-shaped flame.

55

Turquoise

EVENING CAME, A STARRY SKY AND BITINGLY COLD.

Harry parked the car on the hill outside the Voksenkollen address he had been given. In a street consisting of large expensive houses this one stood out. The building was like something out of a fairy tale, a royal palace with black timbers, immense wooden pillars at the entrance and turf on the roof. In the garden there were two other buildings plus a Disney version of a Norwegian storehouse supported on pillars. Harry thought it unlikely that the shipowner Anders Galtung did not possess a big enough fridge.

Harry rang the doorbell, noticed a camera high up the wall and said his name when requested by a female voice. He walked up a floodlit gravel drive that sounded as if it was eating what was left of his boot soles.

A middle-aged woman with turquoise eyes, wearing an apron, received him at the door and led him into an unoccupied living room. She did it with such an elegant mixture of dignity, superiority and professional friendliness that even after she had left Harry with a 'Coffee or tea?' he was unsure whether this was fru Galtung, a servant or both.

When foreign fairy tales came to Norway, kings and nobility did not exist, so in Norwegian versions the king was represented by a well-to-do farmer in ermine. And that was exactly what Harry saw when Anders Galtung came into the living room: a fat, smiling, gentle and some-what sweaty farmer in a traditional Norwegian sweater. However, after a handshake, the smile was replaced by a concerned expression, more fitting for the occasion. His question – 'Anything new?' – was followed by heavy breathing.

'Nothing, I'm afraid.'

'Tony has a habit of disappearing, I understand from my daughter.'

Harry thought he detected a certain reluctance to articulate the first name of his future son-in-law. The shipowner fell heavily into a rose-painted chair opposite Harry.

'Have you . . . any personal theories, *herr* Galtung?'

'Theories?' Anders Galtung shook his head, making his jowls quiver. 'I don't know him well enough to form theories. Gone to the mountains, gone to Africa, what do I know?'

'Mm. In fact, I came here to speak to your daughter—'

'Lene'll be right here,' Galtung interrupted. 'I just wanted to enquire first.'

'Enquire about what?'

'About what I said, whether there was anything new. And . . . and whether the police are sure the man has a clear conscience.'

Harry noticed that 'Tony' had been exchanged for 'the man' and knew his first instinct had not deceived him: the father-in-law was not enamoured of his daughter's choice.

'Do you think he has, Galtung?'

'Me? I would have thought I was showing trust. After all, I am in the process of investing a considerable sum in this Congo project of his. A *very* considerable sum.'

'So a lad in rags knocks on the door and gets a princess *plus* half a kingdom, like in a fairy tale, does he?'

Within two seconds flat the living room was quiet, as Galtung eyed Harry.

'Maybe,' he said.

'And maybe your daughter is exerting some pressure on you to invest. The venture is pretty dependent on finance, isn't it?'

Galtung opened his arms. 'I'm a shipowner. Risk is what I live off.'

'And could die of.'

'Two sides of the same coin. In risk markets one man's loss is another man's gain. So far the others have lost, and I hope this trend will continue.'

'Other people losing?'

'Shipowning is a family business, and if Leike is going to be family we have to ensure ...' He paused as the door opened. She was a tall, blonde girl with her father's coarse features and her mother's turquoise eyes, but without her father's bluff farmer-made-good air or her mother's dignified superiority. She walked with a hunched bearing, as if to reduce her height, so as not to stand out, and she observed her shoes rather than Harry when she shook hands and introduced herself as Lene Gabrielle Galtung.

She didn't have a lot to say. And even less to ask. She seemed to cower under her father's gaze every time she answered Harry's questions, and Harry wondered whether his assumption that she had forced her father to invest might be wrong.

Twenty minutes later Harry expressed his gratitude, stood up and, right on invisible cue, there she was again, the woman with the turquoise eyes.

When she opened the front door for him, the cold surged in and Harry stopped to button up his coat. He looked at her.

'Where do you believe Tony Leike is, fru Galtung?'

'I don't believe anything,' she said.

Perhaps she answered too quickly, perhaps there was a twitch at the corner of her eye, perhaps it was just Harry's intense desire to find something, anything, but he was convinced she was telling the truth. The second thing she said did not allow any room for doubt.

'And I am not fru Galtung. She is upstairs.'

Mikael Bellman adjusted the microphone in front of him and surveyed the audience. There was a hushed whisper, but all eyes were directed towards the podium, fearful of missing anything. In the packed room he recognised the journalist from *Stavanger Aftenblad* and Roger Gjendem from *Aftenposten*. He could hear Ninni, who was wearing a freshly ironed uniform, as usual. Someone counted down the seconds to the start, which was normal for live broadcasts of press conferences.

'Welcome, ladies and gentlemen. We have called this press conference to give you an update on what we are doing. Any questions . . .'

Chuckles all round.

'. . . will be answered at the end. I will pass over now to the officer leading the investigation, POB Mikael Bellman.'

Bellman cleared his throat. Full turnout. The TV channels had been given permission to place their microphones on the podium table.

'Thank you. Let me start by being a party-pooper. I can see from the attendance and your faces that we may have ratcheted up your expectations a little too high in calling you here. There will be no announcement of a final breakthrough in the investigation.' Bellman saw the disappointment on their faces and heard scattered groans. 'We are here in order to fulfil the desire you expressed to be kept informed. I apologise if you had more important things planned for today.'

Bellman gave a wry smile, heard a few journalists laugh and knew that he had already been forgiven.

Mikael Bellman gave them the gist of where the investigation stood. That is, he repeated their success stories, such as the rope being traced to a building by Lake Lyseren, finding another victim, Adele Vetlesen, and identifying the murder weapon used in two of the murders: a so-called Leopold's apple. Old news. He saw one of the journalists stifle a yawn. Mikael Bellman looked down at the papers in front of him. At the script. Because that was what it was, a script for a bit of theatre, each and every word written down, weighed carefully, gone over. Not too much, not too little; the bait should smell, but it shouldn't stink.

'Finally, something about the witnesses,' he began and the press corps sat up in their chairs. 'As you know, we have asked anyone who was at the Håvass cabin on the same night as the murder victims to come forward. And one person by the name of Iska Peller has come forward. She is arriving by plane from Sydney tonight, and she will proceed to the cabin with one of our detectives tomorrow. We will try to reconstruct the crime scene as faithfully as possible.'

Normally, they would never have mentioned the name of the witness, but it was important here that the man they were addressing – the murderer – would understand that they had indeed found someone from the guest book. Bellman had not laid special emphasis on the word 'one' when he mentioned the detective, but that was the message. There would be just two people, the witness and an ordinary detective. In a cabin. Far from habitation.

'We hope of course that Miss Peller will be able to give us a description of the other guests present that night.'

They had had a long discussion about the wording. They wanted to sow the seed that the witness could bring down the murderer. At the same time Harry thought it important that they didn't arouse too much suspicion with the witness being accompanied by only one detective, and that the pithy introduction 'Finally, something about the witnesses' and the downplayed 'we hope of course' signalled that the police did not consider this an important witness who would therefore require high-level protection. They hoped the killer would be of a different opinion.

'What do you think she may have seen? And can you spell the witness's name?'

This was the Rogaland journalist. Ninni leaned forward to remind them that questions would be at the end, but Mikael shook his head.

'We'll have to see what she remembers when she gets to the cabin,' Bellman said, stretching towards the microphone labelled NRK. The state channel. Nationwide. 'She will be going up there with one of our most experienced detectives and will be there for twenty-four hours.'

He looked at Harry Hole standing at the back, saw him give a slow nod. He had driven the point home. Twenty-four hours. The bait was prepared and the trap set. Bellman let his gaze wander further. It found the Pelican. She had been the only one to protest, to consider it scandalous that they were deliberately setting out to mislead the press. He had asked the group to take five and had talked to her privately. Afterwards she had concurred with the majority view. Ninni opened the floor for questions. The assembly came to life, but Mikael Bellman relaxed and made ready to give vague answers, glib formulations and the ever-useful 'I'm afraid we can't go into that at this phase of the investigation'.

* * *

355

His legs were freezing, so frozen that they were completely numb. How could that be? When the rest of his body was burning? He had screamed so loud he had no voice left; his throat was dry, dried out, riven asunder, an open wound with blood singed to red dust. There was a smell of burnt hair and flesh. The stove had seared through his flannel shirt into his back and as he screamed and screamed they fused. He melted as if he were a tin soldier. Feeling that the pain and the heat had begun to eat into his consciousness and that he was finally slipping into oblivion, he awoke with a start. The man had poured a bucket of cold water over him. The sudden relief had caused him to cry again. Then he heard the hiss of boiling water between his back and the stove and the pain returned with renewed vigour.

'More water?'

He looked up. The man stood over him with another bucket. The mist before his eyes cleared, and for a couple of seconds he saw him with total clarity. The light from the flames through the holes in the stove flickered on his face, making the beads of sweat on his forehead glisten.

'It's very simple. All I need to know is who. Is it someone in the police? Is it one of those who were at Håvass that night?'

'Which night?' he sobbed.

'You know which night. They're almost all dead now. Come on.'

'I don't know. I haven't got anything to do with this, you have to believe me. Water. Please. Plea . . .'

'. . . se? Please as in . . . please?'

The smell. The smell of his body burning. The words he stuttered were no more than a hoarse whisper. 'It w-was . . . just m-me.'

Gentle laughter. 'Smart. You're trying to make it sound like you would do anything to avoid the pain. So that I believe you when you can't cough up the name of your collaborator. But I know you can stand more. You're made of tougher stock.'

'Charlotte—'

The man swung the poker. He didn't even feel the blow. Everything went black for one wonderfully long second. Then he was back in hell.

'She's dead!' the man yelled. 'Come up with something better.'

'I meant the other one,' he said, trying to get his brain to work. He remembered now, he had a good memory, why was it failing him? Was he really in such bad shape? 'She's Australian—'

'You're lying!'

He felt his eyes wander again. Another shower of water. A moment of clarity.

The voice. 'Who? How?'

'Kill me! Mercy! I . . . you know I'm not protecting anyone. Lord Jesus, why should I?'

'I know nothing of the sort.'

'So why not kill me? I killed her. Do you hear me? Do it. Revenge is thine.'

The man put down the bucket, flopped into a chair, leaned forward with his elbows on the armrests and chin resting on his fists, and answered slowly as though he hadn't heard what had been said, but was thinking about something else. 'You know, I've dreamed about this for so many years. And now, now we're here . . . I had been hoping it would taste sweeter.'

The man struck him with the poker one more time. Tilted his head and studied him. With a sour expression, probingly, he stabbed the poker into his ribs.

'Perhaps I lack imagination. Perhaps this justice lacks the appropriate spice?'

Something made the man turn. To the radio. It was on low. The man went over to it, turned up the volume. News. Voices in a large room. Something about the cabin in Håvass. A witness. Reconstruction. He froze, his legs were no longer there. He closed his eyes and again prayed to his God. Not to be liberated from the pain, as he had been doing until now. He prayed for forgiveness, for all his sins to be cleansed by the blood of Jesus, for someone else to bear all that he had done. He had taken a life. Yes, he had. He prayed that he would be bathed in the blood of forgiveness. And then be allowed to die.

PART SIX

56

Decoy

A HELL OF LIGHTS. EVEN WITH SUNGLASSES HARRY'S EYES smarted. The sun was shining on the snow, which was shining back at the sun; it was like looking into an ocean of diamonds, of frantically glittering lights. Harry retreated from the window, although he was aware that, seen from the outside, the panes were black, impenetrable mirrors. He checked his watch. They had arrived at Håvass the previous night. Jussi Kolkka had installed himself in the cabin with Harry and Kaja, the others had dug themselves into the snow in two groups of four at opposite ends of the valley, separated by about thirty kilometres.

There were three reasons for choosing Håvass to lay the bait. First of all, because their being there made sense. Secondly, the killer would, they hoped, think he knew the area well enough to feel comfortable about an attack. Thirdly, because it was a perfect trap. The dip where the cabin lay allowed entry from only the north-east and the south. In the east the mountain was too steep and in the west there were so many precipices and crevices that you had to know the terrain very well to make any progress at all.

Harry grabbed the binoculars and tried to spot the others, but all he could see was white. And lights. He had spoken to Mikael Bellman, who was south of him, and Milano, who was in the north. Usually they would have used their mobile phones, but up here in the uninhabited mountains the only network that had coverage was Telenor. The former state-owned telephone monopoly had had the capital to build base stations on every wind-blown crag, but as several of the policemen, including Harry, subscribed to other companies, they were using walkie-talkies. So that they could get hold of him in case anything happened at Rikshospital, Harry had left a message on his voicemail before he left, saying that he would have no network coverage and had given Milano's Telenor number.

Bellman claimed they hadn't been cold during the night, that the combination of sleeping bags, heat-reflecting ground pads and paraffin stoves was so efficient that they'd had to take off clothing. And that now melted water was dripping from the ceiling of the snow caves they had scraped out from the side of the mountain.

The press conference had been so well covered on TV, radio and in the newspapers that you would have had to be absolutely indifferent to the case not to know that Iska Peller and a police officer had gone to Håvass. Every now and then Kolkka and Kaja went out and pointed to the cabin, the way they had come and the outside toilet. Kaja in her role as Iska; Kolkka as the lone detective helping her to reconstruct the events of the fateful night. Harry hid in the sitting room, where he kept his skis and ski poles, so that only the other two had their skis embedded in the snow outside where they could be seen.

Harry followed a gust of wind blowing a furrow across the bare wastes, swirling up the light fresh snow that had fallen in the hollow overnight. The snow was driven towards mountain peaks, precipices, slopes, irregularities in the terrain where it formed frozen waves and great drifts, similar to the one that protruded like a hat brim from the top of the mountain behind the cabin.

Harry knew of course that there was no guarantee that the man they were hunting would even show up. For some reason or other Iska Peller may not have been on the hit list, he may not consider this opportunity appropriate, he may have other plans for Iska. Or he may have smelt a rat. And there might be more banal reasons. Ill, on a trip . . .

Nonetheless. If Harry had counted up all the times his intuition had misled him, the number would have told him to give up intuition as a method and guide. But he didn't count them. Instead, he counted all the times intuition had told him something he didn't know he already knew. And now it was telling him the killer was on his way to Håvass.

Harry glanced at his watch again. The killer had twenty hours. In the huge fireplace the spruce crackled and spat behind the fine-mesh fireguard. Kaja had gone for a nap in one of the bedrooms while Kolkka sat by the coffee table oiling a disassembled Weilert P11. Harry recognised the German weapon by the fact that it had no gun sights. The Weilert pistol was made especially for close combat, when you had to remove it from a holster, belt or pocket at speed and with minimal risk of it snagging. In such situations sights were superfluous anyway; you pointed it at the target and shot, you didn't take aim. The spare pistol, a SIG Sauer, lay next to it, assembled and loaded. Harry felt the shoulder holster of his Smith & Wesson .38 chafe against his ribs.

They had landed by helicopter during the night by Lake Neddalvann, a few kilometres away, and had covered the rest of the way on skis. Under different circumstances Harry might have taken in the beauty of a snow-clad expanse bathed in moonlight, of the Northern Lights playing on the sky, or Kaja's almost euphoric expression as they glided through the white silence as if in a fairy tale, the lack of sound so complete that he had the feeling the scraping noises of their skis would carry for kilometres across the mountain plateau. But there was too much at stake, too little he could afford to lose for him to have his eyes on anything except the job, the hunt.

It was Harry who had cast Kolkka in the role of 'one detective'. Not because Harry had forgotten Kafé Justisen, but if things didn't go to plan, they could use the Finn's close combat skills. Ideally, the killer would make a move during the day and be seen by one of the two groups hidden in the snow. But if he came by night, without being noticed before he reached the cabin, the three of them would have to tackle the situation on their own.

Kaja and Kolkka took a bedroom each; Harry slept in the sitting room. The morning had passed without unnecessary chit-chat; even Kaja had been quiet. Concentrated.

From the reflection in the window Harry watched Kolkka assemble the gun, aim at the back of his head and fire a practice shot. Twenty hours left. Harry hoped the killer would waste no time.

* * *

While Bjørn Holm was taking the light blue hospital clothes from Adele's wardrobe he felt Geir Bruun's eyes on his back from the doorway.

'Why don't you just take everything?' Bruun said. 'Then I won't have the bother of throwing it out. Where's your colleague, Harry, by the way?'

'He's gone skiing in the mountains,' Holm said patiently, putting the garments individually in the plastic bags he had brought along.

'Really? Interesting. He didn't strike me as the skiing type. Where?'

'Can't say. Talking of skis, what was Adele wearing when she went to Håvass? There's no ski gear here.'

'She borrowed it from me, of course.'

'She borrowed ski stuff from *you*?'

'You sound so surprised.'

'You didn't strike me as ... the skiing type.' Holm noticed that his words projected an innuendo that had not been intentional and felt his neck glow.

Bruun chuckled and twirled round in the doorway. 'Right, I'm more ... the clothes type.'

Holm cleared his throat and – without knowing why – made his voice go deeper. 'May I have a look?'

'Ooh, goodness me,' Bruun lisped, seeming to revel in Holm's discomfort. 'Come on, let's go and see what I've got.'

'Half past four,' Kaja said, passing the pot of stew to Harry for the second time. Their hands didn't touch. Nor did their eyes. Nor their words. The night they had shared in Oppsal was as distant as a two-day-old dream. 'According to the script, I'm supposed to be standing on the south side now, smoking a cigarette.'

Harry nodded and passed the pot to Kolkka who scraped it out before shovelling down the contents.

'OK,' Harry said. 'Kolkka, will you take the west-facing window? The sun's low now, so check for any glinting of binoculars.'

'Not until I've eaten,' he answered slowly in Swedish and with emphasis, shoving yet another fully loaded fork into his mouth.

Harry cocked an eyebrow. Glanced at Kaja and motioned for her to go.

When she was outside Harry sat by the window and combed the plateau and the ridges. 'So Bellman employed you when no one else would, did he?' He said it softly, but the silence in the room was so complete he could have whispered it.

A few seconds passed with no response. Harry assumed Kolkka was processing the fact that Harry had engaged him on a personal matter.

'I know about the rumour that was spread after you were given the boot by Europol. You had beaten up an ex-con during questioning. That's right, isn't it?'

'That's my business,' Kolkka said, lifting the fork to his mouth. 'But he might not have shown me sufficient respect.'

'Mm. The interesting thing was that Europol spread the rumour themselves. So that the rumour would make things easier for them. And for you, I suppose. And of course for the parents and solicitors of the girl you were questioning.'

Harry heard the chewing behind him stop.

'So that they got their compensation on the quiet without having to drag you and Europol into a courtroom. The girl avoided having to sit in the witness box and say that when you were in her room asking her about the friend who had been raped, you got so excited by the answers that you started to touch her up. Fifteen years old, it says in Europol's internal files.'

Harry could hear Kolkka breathing heavily.

'Let's assume that Bellman also read the files,' Harry continued. 'Was given access via contacts and roundabout methods. Like me. He waited a bit before contacting you. Waited until the anger was out of you, until all the air was gone, until you were on the wheel rim, punctured. And then he picked you up. Gave you a job and gave you back some of the pride you had lost. And knew you would repay him with loyalty. He buys when the market is at the bottom, Kolkka. That's how he gets his bodyguards.'

Harry turned to Jussi Kolkka. The Finn's face was white.

'You're bought, but you're hardly paid, Jussi. Slaves like you don't gain respect, not from *Massa* Bellman and not from me. Christ, you don't even have any self-respect, man.'

Kolkka's fork fell to his plate with an almost deafening clatter. He got up, slipped his hand inside his jacket and pulled out a gun. He strode towards Harry and leaned over him. Harry didn't budge, just calmly looked up.

'So how are you going to find your respect again, Jussi? By shooting me?'

The Finn's pupils were quivering with rage.

'Or by working yourself to hell?' Harry looked out at the snowy expanse again.

Heard Kolkka's heavy breathing. Waited. Heard him turn. Heard him move away. Heard him sit down by the west-facing window.

The radio crackled. Harry grabbed the microphone.

'Yes?'

'Soon be dark.' It was Bellman's voice. 'He's not coming.'

'Still keep a lookout.'

'What for? It's clouded over and without moonlight we can't see a—'

'If we can't see, neither can he,' Harry said. 'So keep a lookout for a head torch.'

The man had switched off the head torch. He didn't need any light, he knew where the ski trail he was following led. To the Tourist Association cabin. And his eyes would get used to the dark, he would have large, light-sensitive pupils before he arrived. There it was, the log wall with black windows. As though no one were at home. The new snow creaked as the man kicked off and slid down the last few metres. He stopped and listened to the silence for a couple of seconds before soundlessly unclipping his skis. He took out the large, heavy Sami knife with the intimidating boat-shaped blade and the smooth, varnished yellow wooden hilt. It was as good at cutting down branches for a fire as carving up a reindeer. Or slitting throats.

The man opened the door as quietly as he could and entered the hall.

366

Stood listening at the sitting-room door. Silence. Too silent? He pressed the handle and threw open the door while standing back against the wall next to the doorway. Then – to make the target as elusive and small as possible – he crouched down and rushed into the darkness with the knife to the fore.

He glimpsed the figure of the dead man sitting on the floor with his head hanging and arms still embracing the stove.

He returned the knife to its sheath and switched on the light by the sofa. It hadn't struck him until now that the sofa was identical to the one at the Håvass cabin. The Tourist Association must have got a discount on a job lot. But the sofa cover was old, the cabin had been closed for several years, and it was in much too dangerous an area: there had been accidents with people plunging down cliff faces while trying to find the cabin.

Next to the wood burner, the dead man's head rose slowly.

'Sorry to burst in on you like this.' He checked that the chains holding the dead man's hands shackled around the stove were as they should be.

Then he began to unpack his rucksack. He had pulled his hat down and had been in and out of the shop in Ustaoset in a flash. Biscuits. Bread. Papers. Which had more about the press conference. And this witness at the Håvass cabin.

'Iska Peller,' he said aloud. 'Australian. She's at the Håvass cabin. What do you think? Could she have seen anything?'

The other man's vocal cords could hardly move enough air for them to make a sound. 'Police. Police at cabin.'

'I know. It's in the papers. One detective.'

'They're there. The police have rented the cabin.'

'Oh?' He looked at the other man. Had the police set a trap? And was this bastard in front of him trying to *help* him, to save him from falling into it? The very idea angered him. But this woman must have seen something anyway, otherwise they wouldn't have brought her all this way from Australia. He grabbed the poker.

'Fuck, you stink. Have you shat your pants?'

The dead man's head slumped onto his chest. The dead man had obviously moved in here. There were a few personal possessions in the drawers. A letter. Some tools. Some old family photographs. Passport. As if the dead man were planning an escape, thinking he could recover some-where else. Other than down there, down to the flames where he would be tortured for his sins. Even though he had begun to think that the dead man might not have been behind all the devilry after all. There are limits to how much pain a man can stand before he talks.

He checked the phone again. No coverage, shit!

And what a stench. The storehouse. He would have to hang him out to dry there. That was what you did with smoked meat.

Kaja had gone to her bedroom, and he hoped she would catch some shut-eye before it was her watch.

Kolkka poured the percolated coffee into his own and then Harry's cup.

'Thanks,' Harry said, staring into the darkness.

'Wooden skis,' Kolkka said, standing by the fireplace and inspecting Harry's skis.

'My father's,' Harry said. He had found the ski equipment in the cellar at Oppsal. The poles were new and made of some metal alloy that seemed to weigh less than air. Harry had for a moment wondered whether the hollow pole might have been filled with helium. But the skis were the same old broad mountain ones.

'When I was small we went to my grandfather's cabin in Lesja every Easter. There was this peak my dad always wanted to climb. So he told my sister and me that there was a kiosk at the top where they sold Pepsi, which was my sister's favourite drink. So if we could manage the last slope, then we . . .'

Kolkka nodded and ran a hand over the back of the white skis. Harry took a swig of the fresh coffee.

'Sis always managed to forget from Easter to Easter that it was the same old bluff. And I always wished I could have done the same. But I was lumbered with remembering everything that Dad instilled in me. The mountain code, how to use nature as a compass and how to survive avalanches. Norwegian kings and queens, the Chinese dynasties and American presidents.'

'They're good skis,' Kolkka said.

'Bit too short.'

Kolkka sat by the window at the other end of the room. 'Yes, you think it will never happen. Your father's skis being too short for you.'

Harry waited. Waited. Then it came.

'I thought she was so wonderful,' Kolkka said. 'And I thought she liked me. Strange. I only touched her breasts. She didn't put up any resistance. I suppose she must have been scared.'

Harry succeeded in curbing his urge to leave the room.

'You're right,' Kolkka said. 'You're loyal to those who raise you from the rubbish heap. Even though you can see they're using you. What else can you do? You have to choose sides.'

When Harry realised the conversational tap had been turned off, he got up and went to the kitchen. He went through all the cupboards in a vain attempt to find what he knew was not here, a kind of desperate diversion from the shouting inside his head. 'A drink, just one.'

He had been given a chance. One. The ghost had undone his chains, lifted him up, sworn because of the stench of shit and helped him into the bathroom, where he had dropped him on the shower floor and turned on the water. The ghost had stood there for a moment watching him while trying to make a mobile phone call, cursed the lack of coverage and then gone back into the sitting room where he heard him trying again.

He wanted to cry. He had moved up here, hidden himself away so that no one would be able to find him. Installed himself in the moth-balled Tourist Association cabin, taken with him what he needed. Thought he was safe among the precipices. Safe from the ghost. He didn't cry. For as the water seeped through his clothes, soaking the remains of the red flannel shirt stuck to his back, it dawned on him that this was his chance. His mobile phone was in the pocket of his trousers, folded on the chair beside the sink.

He tried to get to his feet, but his legs wouldn't respond. Didn't matter, it was only a few metres to the chair. He put his scorched black arms on the floor, defied the pain and dragged himself forward, heard the blisters pop, noticed the smell, but in two lunges he was there, searching his pockets, grabbing his phone. He had saved that policeman's number, mostly so that he would recognise it on the display if he called.

He pressed the call button. The phone seemed to be drawing breath in the tiny eternity between each ring. One chance. The shower was making too much noise for the man to hear him speak. There! He heard the policeman's voice. He interrupted him with his hoarse whisper, but the voice continued regardless. And he realised he was talking to voicemail. He waited for the voice to finish, squeezed the phone, felt the skin on his hand tear, but didn't let go. Couldn't let go. Had to leave a message about . . . finish for Christ's sake, come on, beeps!

He hadn't heard him come in, the shower had drowned his light steps. The phone was seized from his hand, and he had time to see the ski boot coming.

When he regained consciousness, the man was standing over him and studying his phone with interest.

'So you've got coverage?'

The man left the bathroom dialling a number, then the noise of the shower drowned everything. But not long after he was back.

'We're going on a journey. You and I.' The man seemed to be in a good mood all of a sudden. The man was holding a passport in one hand. His passport. In the other hand he was holding the pliers from the toolbox.

'Open wide.'

He swallowed. Lord Jesus, have mercy.

'Open wide, I said!'

'Mercy. I swear I've told you everything I—' He didn't say any more because a hand had grabbed him around the throat and stopped the supply of air. He fought for a while. Then at last came the tears. And then he opened wide.

57

Thunder

UNDER THE GLARE OF THE LAMP, BJØRN HOLM AND BEATE Lønn were standing by the steel table in the laboratory staring at the navy blue ski pants before them.

'That is definitely a semen stain,' Beate said.

'Or a line of semen,' Bjørn Holm said. 'Look at the shape.'

'Too little for an ejaculation. Looks like an erect, wet penis has been shoved up the bottom of the person wearing the ski pants. You said Bruun was homosexual, didn't you?'

'Yes, but he says he hasn't worn them since he lent them to Adele.'

'Then I would say we have semen stains typical of a rape. We'll just have to send them for DNA testing, Bjørn.'

'Agreed. What do you think about that?' Holm pointed to the light blue hospital trousers, to two friction marks under both back pockets.

'What is it?'

'Something that won't go away in the wash at any rate. It's a nonylphenol-based material called PSG. It's used in car cleaning products, among other things.'

'She's obviously been sitting somewhere.'

'Not just sitting, it's deep in the fibre. She's been rubbing. Hard. Like this.' He thrust his hips backwards and forwards.

'I see. Any theories as to why?'

She put on her glasses and looked at Holm as his mouth distorted into a variety of shapes to articulate expressions his brain generated and immediately rejected.

'Dry humping?' Beate asked.

'Yes,' Holm said, with relief.

'I see. And where and when does a woman who doesn't work at a hospital wear hospital gear and dry hump on PSG?'

'Simple,' said Bjørn Holm. 'At a nocturnal rendezvous in a disused PSG factory.'

The clouds parted, and again they were bathed in the magic blue light in which everything, even the shadows, became phosphorised, frozen as if for a still life.

Kolkka had gone to bed, but Harry presumed the Finn was lying in the bedroom with his eyes open and his other senses on maximum alert.

Kaja sat by the window with her chin resting on her hand looking out. She was wearing her white jumper as they only had electric radiators. They had agreed it might look suspicious if smoke was coming from the chimney all the time when apparently there were just two people there.

'If you ever miss the starry sky over Hong Kong, look outside now,' Kaja said.

'I can't remember any starry sky,' Harry said, lighting a cigarette.

'Isn't there anything about Hong Kong you miss?'

'Li Yuan's glass noodles,' Harry said. 'Every day.'

'Are you in love with me?' She had lowered her voice only a fraction and was looking at him attentively while tying an elastic band around her hair.

Harry examined his feelings. 'Not right now.'

She laughed, her face expressing surprise. 'Not right now? What does that mean?'

'That that part of me is tuned out as long as we're here.'

She shook her head. 'You're damaged goods, Hole.'

'About that,' Harry said with a crooked smile, 'there is little doubt.'

'And what about when this job is over in –' she looked at her watch – 'ten hours?'

'Then I may be in love with you again,' Harry said, placing his hand next to hers on the table. 'If not before.'

She looked at their hands. Saw how much bigger his were. How much more delicately shaped hers were. How much paler and how gnarled his were, with thick blood vessels twisting and turning all over the back of his hand.

'So you could be in love before the job is over after all, eh?' She placed her hand on his.

'I meant the job could be over before—'

She withdrew her hand.

Harry looked at her in surprise. 'I just meant—'

'Listen!'

Harry held his breath and listened. But heard nothing.

'What was it?'

'Sounded like a car,' Kaja said, peering out. 'What do you reckon?'

'Unlikely, in my opinion,' Harry said. 'It's more than ten kilometres to the nearest road open in winter. What about a helicopter? Or a snow-mobile?'

'Or what about my overactive imagination?' Kaja sighed. 'The sound's gone. And, on reflection, perhaps it was never there. Sorry, but you can easily become a bit oversensitive when you're afraid and—'

'No,' Harry said, getting up. 'Suitably afraid. Suitably sensitive. Describe what you heard.' Harry took his revolver from his shoulder holster and went to the second window.

'Nothing, I keep telling you!'

Harry opened the window a fraction. 'Your hearing's better than mine. Listen for both of us.'

They sat listening to the silence. Minutes passed.

'Harry . . .'

'Shhh.'

'Come and sit down again, Harry.'

'He's here,' Harry said, half aloud as though talking to himself. 'He's here now.'

'Harry, now it's you who's being oversensi—'

There was a muffled boom. The sound was low, deep, sort of slow, no forward thrust, like distant thunder. But Harry knew that thunder seldom occurred with a clear sky at seven degrees below zero.

He held his breath.

And then he heard it. Another roar, different from the boom, but this too was a low frequency, like the sound waves from a bass speaker, sound waves that move air, that are felt in the stomach. Harry had heard this sound only once before, but he knew he would remember it for the rest of his life.

'Avalanche!' Harry yelled and ran towards Kolkka's bedroom, which faced the mountainside. 'Avalanche!'

The bedroom door opened and there was Kolkka, wide awake. They could feel the ground shaking. It was a big avalanche. Whether the cabin had a cellar or not, Harry knew they would never have been able to make it there. For behind Kolkka fragments of glass from what had once been a window flew past, forced in by the air that avalanches push ahead of them.

'Take my hand!' Harry shouted above the roar and stretched out his hands, one to Kaja and one to Kolkka. He saw them race towards him as the air was sucked out of the cabin, as if the avalanche had breathed out first and then in. He felt Kolkka's hand squeeze his hard and waited for Kaja's. Then the wall of snow hit the cabin.

58

Snow

IT WAS DEAFENINGLY QUIET AND PITCH BLACK. HARRY TRIED to move. Impossible. His body seemed to be cast in plaster, he couldn't move one single limb. Indeed, he had actually done what his father had told him: held a hand in front of his face to make room for an air pocket. But he didn't know if there was any air in it. Because Harry couldn't breathe. And he knew the reason why. Constrictive pericarditis. What Olav Hole had explained happened when the chest and diaphragm were packed together so tight by snow that the lungs were unable to function. Which meant you had only the oxygen that was already in your blood, about a litre, and with normal consumption, at around 0.25 litres a minute, you would die within four minutes. Panic struck: he had to have air, had to breathe! Harry tensed his body, but the snow was like a boa constrictor that responded by tightening its grip. He knew he had to fight the panic, had to be able to think. And think now. The world outside had ceased to exist; time, gravity, temperature didn't exist. Harry had no idea what was up or down or how long he had been in the snow. Another of his father's wisdoms whirled through his brain. To find your bearings and determine which way you are lying, dribble saliva from your mouth and feel which way it runs down your face. He ran his tongue around his palate. Knew it was fear, the adrenalin that had dried out his mouth. He opened wide and used the fingers in front of his face to scrabble some snow into his mouth. Chewed, opened again and let the melted ice dribble out. He panicked instantly and jerked as his nostrils filled with water. Closed his mouth and snorted the water out again. Snorted out what was left of the air in his lungs. He was going to die soon.

The water had told him he was upside down, the jerk had told him it was possible to move after all. He tried another jerk, tautened his whole body in a spasm, felt the snow give a little. A little. Enough to escape from the stranglehold of constrictive pericarditis? He breathed in. Got some air. Not enough. The brain must already have been suffering from a lack of oxygen, nevertheless he clearly recalled his father's words from the Easters up in Lesja. In an avalanche where you can hardly breathe you don't die from a lack of air but from too much CO_2 in your blood. His other hand had met something, something hard, something that felt like wire mesh. Olav Hole: 'In snow you're like a shark, you'll die if you don't move. Even though the snow is loose enough for some air to come in, the heat of your breath and body soon forms a layer of ice around you, which means air won't come in and the poisonous carbon dioxide in your breath can't get out. You are simply making your own ice coffin. Do you understand?'

'Yes, Dad, but take it easy, will you? This is Lesja, not the Himalayas.'

Mum's laughter from the kitchen.

Harry knew the cabin was filled with snow. And that above him was a roof. And above that probably more snow again. There was no way out. Time was ticking. It would end here.

He had prayed that he wouldn't wake up again. That next time he slipped into unconsciousness would be the last. He was hanging upside down. His head was throbbing as if it would explode. It must have been all the blood filling it.

It was the sound of the snowmobile that had woken him.

He tried not to move. He had done at first, jerked, tensed his body, tried to free himself. But he had given up his attempts fairly quickly. Not because of the meat hooks in his calves – he had lost feeling in his legs long ago. It was the sound. The sound of tearing flesh and sinews, and muscles that snapped and burst when he jerked and twisted, making the chains attached to the storehouse roof sing.

376

He stared into the glazed eyes of a stag hanging by its rear legs and looking as if it was in mid-dive, antlers first. He had shot it while poaching. With the same rifle that he had used to kill her.

He heard the plaintive creak of footsteps in the snow. The door opened, the moonlight plunged inside. Then he was there again. The ghost. And the strange thing was that it was only now, looking at him from upside down, that he was sure.

'It really is you,' he whispered. It was so strange speaking without any front teeth. 'It really is you. Isn't it?'

The man walked behind him, untied his hands.

'C-can you forgive me, my boy?'

'Are you ready to travel?'

'You killed them all, didn't you.'

'Yes,' he said. 'Let's go.'

Harry dug with his right hand. Towards his left hand, the one which was squeezed up against some wire mesh he couldn't identify. Part of his brain told him he was trapped, that it was a hopeless race against time, seconds, that for every breath he took he was one step nearer death. That all he was doing was prolonging his suffering, postponing the inevitable. The other voice said he would rather die in desperation than in apathy.

He had managed to dig his way through to the other hand and put the right hand over the wire mesh. Pressed both hands against it and tried to push, but the mesh wouldn't budge. He sensed that his breathing was already heavier, the snow was becoming smoother and his grave coated with ice. Dizziness came and went, just for a second, but he knew it was the first warning that he was inhaling poisoned air. Soon the drowsiness would come, and the brain would shut down, room by room, like a hotel approaching the low season. And that was when Harry felt it, something he had never experienced before, not even during his worst nights at Chungking Mansion: an overwhelming loneliness. It wasn't the certainty that he would die that suddenly drained him of all will to live, but that he would die here, without anyone, without those he loved, without his father, Sis, Oleg, Rakel . . .

The drowsiness came. Harry stopped digging. Even though he knew this spelt death. A seductive, alluring death taking him into its arms. Why protest, why fight, why choose pain when he could succumb? Why choose anything other than what he had always done? Harry closed his eyes.

Wait.

The mesh.

It had to be the fireguard. The fire. The chimney. Rock. If anything had withstood the avalanche, if there was one place where the mass of snow had not penetrated, it would have to be the chimney.

Harry pushed against the wire again. It wouldn't budge a millimetre. His fingers clawed the mesh. Powerless, resigned.

It was predestined. This was how it would end. His CO_2-infected brain sensed a logic to it, but was unsure quite what it was. He accepted it though. He let the sweet, warm sleep envelop him. The sedation. The freedom.

His fingers slid along the wire. Found something hard, solid. Tips of skis. Dad's skis. He offered no resistance to the thought. It was less lonely like this, with his hand on Dad's skis. Together, in step, they would enter the kingdom of death. Take the last steep slope.

Mikael Bellman stared at what lay before them. Or to be more precise what *no longer* lay before them. Because it wasn't there any more. The cabin was gone. From the snow cave it had looked like a little drawing on a large white sheet of paper. That was before the boom and the faraway crash that had woken him. By the time he had finally pulled out his binoculars it was quiet again, there was just a distant, delayed echo reverberating from the Hallingskarvet mountain range. He had stared himself blind through the binoculars, scanned the mountainside beyond. It was as if someone had erased everything from the paper. No drawing, just peaceful and innocently white. It was incomprehensible. A whole cabin buried? They had snapped on their skis and taken eight minutes to arrive at the avalanche scene. Or eight minutes and eighteen seconds. He had noted the time. He was a police officer.

'Christ, the avalanche area is *a square kilometre*,' he heard a voice shout behind him and watched the frail yellow beams from their torches sweep across the snow.

The walkie-talkie crackled. 'Rescue Ops says the helicopter will be here in thirty minutes. Over.'

Too long, Bellman thought. What was it he had read: after half an hour the chance of surviving under snow was one in three? And when the helicopter got here, what the hell were they supposed to do? Stick their sonar probes in the snow to detect the remains of a cabin? 'Thanks, over and out.'

Ærdal came alongside. 'Spot of luck! There are two sniffer dogs in Ål. They're bringing them up to Ustaoset now. The County Officer in Ustaoset, Krongli, isn't at home – at least he's not answering the phone – but there was a man at the hotel with a snowmobile, and he can bring them here.' He was flapping his arms to keep warm.

Bellman looked at the snow beneath them. Kaja was down there some-where. 'How often did they say there were avalanches here?'

'Every ten years,' Ærdal said.

Bellman rocked on his heels. Milano was directing the others, who were trudging around prodding the snow with skis and poles.

'Sniffer dogs?' he said.

'Forty minutes.'

Bellman nodded. Knowing the dogs would make no difference one way or the other. By the time they arrived almost an hour would have passed since the avalanche.

The chances of survival would be less than ten per cent even before they started work. After an hour and a half they would be, to all intents and purposes, zero.

The journey had begun. He was driving a snowmobile. Both light and dark seemed to be coming towards him, as if the diamond-strewn sky was opening itself and welcoming him. He knew that behind him in the snow stood the man, the ghost, aiming at his burned, charred and blis-tered back through the sights of a gun. But no bullet could reach him

379

now, he was free, he was going where he intended, taking the path he had always been following. To the place where she had gone, along the same route. He was no longer tied up, and if he had been able to move his arms or legs he would have just stood up on the seat, twisted the accelerator and rushed forward even faster. He was cheering as he took off towards the starry sky.

59

The Burial

HARRY SANK THROUGH LAYERS OF DREAMS, MEMORIES AND half-chewed thoughts. Everything was fine. Apart from one voice intoning the same sentence, again and again. Dad's voice.

'... and in the end you were bleeding so much that the big boys became alarmed and went on their way.'

He tried to hold it at arm's length, to listen to one of the other voices. But even that one belonged to Olav Hole.

'You were scared of the dark, but that didn't stop you going there.'

Fuck, fuck, fuck.

Harry opened his eyes to the dark. Wriggled and twisted in the icy snow's iron grip. Tried to kick. Started digging in front of the wire. Made himself a bit more room. His fingers found the edge of the fireguard. He wasn't going to die. Olav Hole would have to go on ahead; he would have to be that much of a bloody father! His hands were paddling like shovels now that they had some room to move. He got both hands on the inside of the fireguard and pulled it towards him. There! It shifted. He pulled again. And felt it. Air. Stinking of ash, heavy. But air nonetheless. For as long as it lasted. He pushed the snow away. Stuffed his hands in; his fingers found something that felt like polystyrene. He realised it was half-burned logs. The fireguard had stood up to the avalanche, the fireplace was free of snow. He continued to dig.

A few minutes – or perhaps it was seconds – later and he lay curled up in the large fireplace gulping in air and coughing ash.

And he realised that so far he had been thinking about only one thing: himself.

He moved his arm around the corner of the fireplace, to where Dad's skis had been. Rummaged in the snow until he found what he was searching for. One of the ski poles. He grabbed the basket on the end and pulled. The smooth, light, rigid metal pole slipped through the snow. He brought the pole into the fireplace, placed it between his legs, jammed his boots together and ripped off the basket. Now he had a spear measuring a little more than a metre and a half.

Kaja and Kolkka couldn't be far away from where he had been lying. He conjured up an imaginary grid system, the way they did at crime scenes to examine for clues, and started poking. He worked quickly, poking as hard as he could; it was a calculated risk. The worst-case scenario was he connected with an eye or stabbed a throat, but the best-case scenario was only that they were still breathing. He poked to the left of where he reckoned he must have been lying and felt the point meet some resistance. He retracted the pole, prodded with care and felt it bounce off again. As he tried to retract it again he felt the pole jam. He released his grip and saw the pole pulled from him. Someone was holding the point and pulling it to and fro to show signs of life! Harry pulled the pole again, harder this time, but the other person was holding on with amazing strength. Harry needed the pole – it would be in the way when he started digging – so he put his hand in the wrist strap and even then had to use all his might to release the pole.

Harry lay wondering why he hadn't already put down the pole and started digging. Then he knew why. Hesitated for another second. Then he began to poke the snow again, this time to the right of where he had been. At the fourth prod he made contact. The same springy sensation. Stomach? He held the pole with his fingertips to see if he could detect any rising or falling, breathing, but there was no movement.

The decision ought to have been easy. The shortest way was to the first opening where there had been signs of life. To save whatever could be saved. Harry was already on his knees and digging like a madman. Towards the second.

His fingers were numb when they reached the body, and he had to use the back of his hand to feel if there was a woollen jumper. The jumper. The white one. He grabbed a shoulder, pushed more snow to the side, freed an arm and pulled the lifeless body through the passage in the snow. Her hair fell across his face; it still had Kaja's aroma. He managed to haul her head and half her upper body onto the hearth and felt for a pulse in her neck, but his fingertips were like cement. He placed his face against hers, but couldn't feel any breath. He opened her mouth, made sure her tongue wasn't in the way, inhaled and breathed into her mouth. Came up for fresh air, suppressed his cough reflex as he inhaled particles of ash and breathed into her mouth again. A third time. He counted: four, five, six, seven. His head was beginning to whirl; he imagined he was back by the fire in the cabin in Lesja, the little boy trying to blow the dying embers into life and his dad laughing as the boy staggered off, dizzy and close to fainting. But he had to go on, he knew the chances of resuscitating her were diminishing by the second.

Leaning over her to blow for the twelfth time, he felt it: a warm current against his face. He held his breath, waited, hardly daring to believe it could be true. The warm current faded. But then it was back. She was breathing! At that moment her body went into a convulsion and she began to cough. Then he heard her voice, faint.

'Is that you, Harry?'

'Yes.'

'Where . . . I can't see.'

'It's alright. We're in the fireplace.'

Pause.

'What are you doing?'

'Digging for Jussi.'

When Harry got Kolkka's head into the fireplace, he had no idea how much time had passed. Only that, as far as Jussi was concerned, there was none left. He lit a match and glimpsed the Finn's large, staring eyes before the flame went out.

'He's dead,' Harry said.

'Couldn't you try mouth-to-mouth . . . ?'

'No,' Harry said.

'What now?' Kaja asked in a faint, debilitated whisper.

383

'We have to get out,' Harry said, finding her hand. Squeezing it.

'Couldn't we just wait here until they find us?'

'No,' he said.

'The match,' she said.

Harry didn't answer.

'It went out immediately,' Kaja said. 'There's no air here, either. The whole cabin is buried under snow. That's why you didn't want to try to revive him. There's not even enough air for us two. Harry . . .'

Harry was on his feet, trying to force his way up the chimney, but it was too narrow, his shoulders got stuck. He crouched down again, broke both ends off the ski pole to make it into a hollow metal tube, put it up the chimney and got to his feet again, this time with his arms stretched above his head. It just reached. Claustrophobia cut in, but vanished at once, as though the body had decided irrational phobias were a luxury it couldn't afford right now. He pressed his back against one side of the chimney and used his legs to lever himself upwards. His thigh muscles ached, he was panting and the dizziness had returned. But he continued, one foot up, press, next foot up, . . . The higher he went, the hotter it was, and he knew that meant that the rising hot air couldn't escape. And he realised that if the fire had been lit when the avalanche crashed down on them they would have died long ago of carbon monoxide poisoning. That could have been called good luck in bad. Except that the avalanche was not bad luck. The boom they had heard . . .

The tube hit something above him. He clambered up. Groped with his free hand. It was an iron grille. The kind they put on the tops of chimneys to keep squirrels and other animals out. He ran his finger along the edge. It had been set in concrete. Fuck!

Kaja's faint voice reached him. 'I'm dizzy, Harry.'

'Breathe in deep.'

He pushed the tube through the fine-mesh grille.

There was no snow on the other side!

He hardly noticed the lactic acid burning in his thighs, as he excitedly pushed the tube further up. Only to experience disappointment when it hit something hard. The chimney cowl. He should have remembered that the cabin had such an attractive black metal cowl at the top of the chimney to protect it against snow and rain. He fumbled around until he angled the tube under the edge of the cowl and felt the hard-packed mass of snow, harder than in the cabin. But that could have been because the snow was now being forced down the opening of the hollow pole. He prayed that for every centimetre of ski pole he pushed into the snow he might feel it, the sudden absence of resistance, which would mean he had broken out of the snow hell. Which meant he could blow the snow out of this suction pipe and suck in air, fresh, life-giving air. Push Kaja up and give her the same injection of anti-death. But the breakthrough never came. He had the tube pressed right through the grille and nothing had happened. He tried anyway, sucked as hard as he could, getting cold, dry snow in his mouth and it was still blocked. He couldn't stand the pressure on his sides any longer and fell. Shouted, stuck out his arms and legs, felt the skin on his hands being scraped off, but slid further down. He hit the body beneath with both legs.

'Alright?' Harry asked, climbing up into the chimney again.

'Fine,' Kaja said with a deep groan. 'And you? Bad news?'

'Yes,' Harry said, scrambling down beside her.

'What? You aren't in love with me now, either?'

Harry chuckled and drew her to him. 'Oh, I am now.'

He felt hot tears on her cheeks as she whispered, 'Shall we get married then?'

'Yes, let's,' Harry said, aware that it was the poison in his brain talking now.

She laughed. 'Till death do us part.'

He felt the warmth of her body. And something hard. Her holster with the service revolver. He released her and groped his way to Kolkka. Already he thought he could see how Kolkka's cold face had started to turn to marble. Through the snow by the dead man's neck he bored his hand down to his chest.

'What are you doing?' she mumbled weakly.

'I'm getting Jussi's gun.'

He heard her stop breathing for a second. Felt her hand on his back, fumbling, like a small animal that has lost its orientation. 'No,' she whispered. 'Don't do it . . . not like that . . . let's just fall asleep . . . Even.'

It was as Harry surmised. Jussi Kolkka had gone to bed wearing his shoulder holster. He undid the button holding the gun in position, gripped the handle and dragged the gun from the snow. Ran a finger down the barrel. No sights, this was a Weilert. He stood up, too quickly, felt giddy, looked for support. Then everything went black.

Bellman was standing looking down at the almost four-metre-deep pit when he heard the intermittent whump-whump-whump of the rescue helicopter approaching, like a carpet beater on speed. His men were using rucksacks to transport snow, lifting it up with interlocking trouser belts.

'The window!' he heard the man in the pit yell.

'Smash it!' Milano shouted back.

The glass tinkled.

'Oh my God . . .' he heard. And knew the invocation boded bad news.

'Chuck down a ski pole . . .'

Bellman heard dogs barking. And tried to work out how many hours it would take to clear the snow from the cabin. Correction: days.

Harry came to with a terrible pain in his jaw and something warm running down his forehead between his eyes. He guessed he must have hit his head and jaw fracture against the rock when he fell. That was what must have woken him. The strange thing was he was still standing and still holding the pistol in his hand. He tried to inhale air that wasn't there. He didn't know if he had enough for a last attempt, but so what? It was simple: there was nothing else he could do. So he stuffed the pistol in his pocket and between gasps climbed up the chimney. Forced his legs against the sides when he was at the top, fumbled with the grille until he found the end of the metal pole that was still stuck in the snow. The pole was vaguely conical with the larger aperture at Harry's end where he inserted the gun barrel. It jammed two-thirds of the way along its length. Which also meant that it was perfectly aligned with the ski pole. It was like a silencer but one and a half metres long. A bullet would not penetrate one and a half metres of snow, but what if the pole was only a *short* distance from the end?

He leaned on the pistol so that the recoil wouldn't cause it to come free and fire at an angle. Then he fired. And fired. And fired. It felt as if their eardrums would explode in the hermetically sealed space. After four shots he stopped, put his lips around the pole and sucked.

He sucked in . . . air.

For a second he was so astonished that he almost fell back down. He sucked again, careful not to destroy the tunnel in the snow that the bullet would have made. The odd grain of snow fell and settled under his tongue. Air. It tasted like a mild, well-rounded whiskey with ice.

60

Pixies and Dwarfs

Roger Gjendem ran across Karl Johans gate where the shops were beginning to open. In Egertorget he peered up at the red Freia clock and saw that the hands were showing three minutes to ten. He increased his speed.

He had been summoned as a matter of urgency by Bent Nordbø, their retired and, in all ways, legendary editor-in-chief, now board member and temple guardian.

He bore right, up Akersgata where all the newspapers had bunched together in those days when the paper edition was the king of the journalistic heap. He turned left towards the law courts, right up Apotekergata and stepped, out of breath, into Stopp Pressen. It didn't seem quite to have been able to make up its mind whether it was going to be a sports bar or a traditional English pub. Perhaps both, as their aim was for all types of journalist to feel at home here. On the walls hung press photographs showing what had engaged, shaken, gladdened and horrified the nation over the last twenty years. They were mostly of sporting events, celebrities and natural disasters. Plus a number of politicians who fell into the latter two categories.

Since this establishment was within walking distance of the two remaining newspaper offices in Akersgata – *Verdens Gang* and *Dagbladet* – Stopp Pressen was almost considered an extended canteen for these two, but for the moment there were only two people visible inside. The barman behind the counter and a man sitting at the table furthest back, beneath a shelf of classic books published by Gyldendal and an old radio, which were obviously meant to give the place a certain cachet.

The man beneath the shelf was Bent Nordbø. He had John Gielgud's superior appearance, John Major's panoramic glasses and Larry King's braces. And he was reading a genuine newspaper's newspaper. Roger had heard that Nordbø read only the *New York Times*, *Financial Times*, *Guardian*, *China Daily*, *Süddeutsche Zeitung*, *El País* and *Le Monde*, although he did read them every day. He might take it into his head to flick through *Pravda* and the *Slovenian Dnevnik*, but he insisted that 'East European languages are so heavy on the eye'.

Gjendem stopped in front of his table with a cough. Bent Nordbø finished reading the last lines of an article about the Mexican immigrants' revitalisation of former condemned areas of the Bronx, glanced down at the page to make sure there was nothing else of interest. Then he removed his enormous glasses, snatched the handkerchief from the breast pocket of his tweed jacket and looked up at the nervous, and still breathless, man standing by his table.

'Roger Gjendem, I presume.'

'Yes.'

Nordbø folded the newspaper. Gjendem had also been told that when the man opened it again you could take it that the conversation was over. Nordbø tilted his head and started the not inconsiderable task of cleaning his glasses.

'You've worked on criminal cases for many years and you know many of the people at Kripos and Crime Squad, don't you?'

'Er . . . yes.'

'Mikael Bellman. What do you know about him?'

Harry scrunched up his eyes at the sun flooding into his room. He had just woken up and spent the first seconds shaking off dreams and reconstructing reality.

They had heard his shots.

And uncovered the ski pole at the first thrust of the spade.

Afterwards they had told him that what had frightened them most was being shot at while they were digging down to the chimney.

His head ached as if he had been off the booze for a week. Harry swung his legs out of bed and looked around the room he had been given at the Ustaoset mountain hotel.

Kaja and Kolkka had been taken by helicopter to Oslo and Rikshospital. Harry had refused to join them. Only after he had lied and said he'd had loads of air the whole time and was absolutely fine did they let him stay.

Harry put his head under the tap in the bathroom and drank. 'Water's never that bad and is sometimes quite nice.' Who used to say that? Rakel when she wanted Oleg to drink up at the table. He switched on his mobile phone, which had been off since he left for Håvass. There was coverage here in Ustaoset, the display said. It also showed there was a message waiting. Harry played it, but there was only a second of coughing and laughing before the connection was broken. Harry checked the caller's number. A mobile number, could be anyone's. There was something vaguely familiar about it, but it definitely wasn't from Rikshospital. Whoever it was would probably ring again if it was important.

In the breakfast room Mikael Bellman sat in solitary majesty with a cup of coffee in front of him. Papers folded and read. Harry didn't need to look at them to know it was more of the same. More about the Case, more about the police's helplessness, more pressure. But today's edition would hardly have been quick enough off the mark to include the death of Jussi Kolkka.

'Kaja's fine,' Bellman said.

'Mm. Where are the others?'

'They caught the morning train to Oslo.'

'But you didn't?'

'Thought I would wait for you. What do you think?'

'About what?'

'About the avalanche. Just something that can happen?'

'No idea.'

'No? Did you hear the boom before it came?'

390

'Might have been the snowdrift on top falling and hitting the side of the mountain. Which in turn triggered the avalanche.'

'Do you think it sounded like that?'

'I don't know what it's supposed to sound like. Noises do definitely trigger avalanches though.'

Bellman shook his head. 'Even experienced mountain folk believe that myth about sound waves triggering them. I climbed the Alps with an avalanche expert and he told me that people there still believe that the avalanches during the Second World War were caused by cannonfire. The truth is that for a shell to start an avalanche there has to be a direct hit.'

'Mm. So?'

'Do you know what this is?' Bellman held up a bit of shiny metal between his thumb and first finger.

'No,' Harry said, signalling to the waiter clearing away the breakfast buffet that he wanted a cup of coffee.

Bellman hummed the verse of Wergeland's 'Pixies and Dwarfs' about building in the mountains and blowing the rock to pieces.

'Pass.'

'You disappoint me, Harry. Well, OK, I may have a head start on you. I grew up in Manglerud in the seventies in an expanding satellite town. They dug plots around us on all sides. The soundtrack of my childhood was dynamite charges going off. After the builders had left I went around finding bits of red plastic cable and tiny fragments of paper off the dynamite sticks. Kaja told me that they have a special way of fishing up here. Sticks of dynamite are more common than moonshine. Don't say the thought didn't cross your mind.'

'OK,' Harry said. 'That's a bit of a blasting cap. When and where did you find it?'

'After you were transported out last night. A couple of the guys and I had a little recce around where the avalanche started.'

'Any tracks?' Harry took the coffee from the waiter and thanked him.

'No. It's so exposed up there that the wind had swept away any ski tracks there might have been. But Kaja said she thought she had heard a snowmobile.'

'Barely. And there was quite a time between her hearing it and the avalanche. He might have parked the snowmobile well before he got there so that we wouldn't hear it.'

'I had the same idea.'

'And what now?' Harry took a tentative sip.

'Look for snowmobile tracks.'

'The local officer . . .'

'No one knows where he is. But I've got us a snowmobile, map, climbing rope, ice axe, provisions. So don't get too comfortable with that coffee, there's snow forecast for this afternoon.'

To reach the top of the avalanche zone, the Danish hotel manager had explained that they would have to drive in a wide arc west of the Håvass cabin, but not too far north-west, where they would come into the area known as Kjeften. It had been given this name, 'jaws', on account of the fang-shaped rocks scattered about. Sudden crevices and precipices were carved into the plateau, making it an extremely dangerous place to roam in poor weather if you weren't familiar with the surroundings.

It was around twelve o'clock when Harry and Bellman looked down the mountainside, where they could make out the excavation of the chimney at the bottom of the valley.

Clouds had already moved in from the west. Harry squinted to the north-west. Shadows and contours were erased without the sun.

'It must have come from there,' Harry said. 'Otherwise we would have heard it whatever.'

'Kjeften,' Bellman said.

Two hours later, after crossing the snowscape from south to north in crab-like manner without finding any snowmobile tracks, they had a break. Sat next to each other on the seat, drinking from the Thermos Bellman had brought with them. A light covering of snow fell.

'I once found an unused stick of dynamite on the estate in Manglerud,' Bellman said. 'I was fifteen years old. In Manglerud there were three things kids could do. Sport, Bible or dope. I wasn't interested in any of them. And certainly not in sitting on the post office window ledge waiting for life to take me from hash and heroin, via glue-sniffing, to the grave. As happened to four boys in my class.'

Harry noticed how the old Manglerud patois had crept back into his Norwegian.

'I hated all that,' Bellman said. 'So my first step towards policing was to take the stick of dynamite behind Manglerud church where the dopeheads had their earth bong.'

'Earth bong?'

'They had dug a pit in which they placed, upside down, a decapitated beer bottle with a grille inside, where the hash smoked and stank. They had laid plastic tubes under the ground, running from the pit to various points half a metre away. Then they lay on the grass around the bong each sucking on their tube. I don't know why . . .'

'To cool the smoke,' Harry chortled. 'You get more of a buzz from less dope. Not bad coming from dopeheads, that one. I've obviously under-estimated Manglerud.'

'Nevertheless, I pulled out one of the tubes and replaced it with dyna-mite.'

'You blew up the earth bong?'

Bellman nodded, and Harry laughed.

'Soil hailed down for thirty seconds,' Bellman smiled.

Silence. The wind rushed, low and rasping.

'Actually, I wanted to say thank you,' Bellman said, looking down at his cup. 'For getting Kaja out in the nick of time.'

Harry shrugged. Kaja. Bellman knew that Harry knew about the two of them. How? And did that mean Bellman knew about Kaja and himself, as well?

'I had nothing else to do down there,' Harry said.

'Yes, you did. I looked at Jussi's body before the helicopter took him away.'

Harry didn't answer, just squinted through the thickening snowflakes that had begun to fall.

'The body had a wound at the side of the neck. And there were more on both palms. From the pointed end of a ski pole perhaps. You found him first, didn't you.'

'Maybe,' Harry said.

'The neck wound had fresh blood. His heart must have been beating when he received that wound, Harry. Beating pretty strongly, too. It should have been possible to dig out a living man in time. But you prioritised Kaja, didn't you.'

'Well,' Harry said, 'I think Kolkka was right.' He emptied the rest of his coffee in the snow. 'You have to choose sides,' he quoted in Swedish.

They found the snowmobile tracks at three o'clock, a kilometre from the avalanche, between two large fang-shaped rocks, a refuge from the wind.

'Looks like he paused here,' Harry said, pointing along the edge of the track left by the tread of the rubber belt. 'The vehicle has had time to sink in the snow.' He ran his finger along the middle of the left ski runner while Bellman swept away the light, dry, drifting snow.

'Yep,' he said, pointing. 'He turned here and then drove on north-west.'

'We're approaching the cliffs and the snow's getting thicker,' Harry said, looking up at the sky and taking out his phone. 'We'll have to ring the hotel and ask them to send a guide on a snowmobile. Shit!'

'What?'

'No coverage. We'll have to make our own way back to the hotel.'

Harry studied the display. There was still the missed call from the vaguely familiar number of someone who had left those sounds on his voicemail. The last three digits, where the hell had he seen them? And then it kicked in. The detective memory. The number was in the 'Former Suspects' file, and was embossed on a business card.

Along with 'Tony C. Leike, Entrepreneur'. Harry slowly raised his gaze and looked at Bellman.

'Leike's alive.'

'What?'

'At least his phone is. He tried to ring me while we were in Håvass.'

Bellman returned Harry's gaze without blinking. Snowflakes settled on his long eyelashes and the white stains seemed to be glowing. His voice was low, almost a whisper. 'Visibility's good, don't you think, Harry? And there's no snow in the air.'

'Exceptional visibility,' Harry said. 'Not a bloody flake to be seen.'

He quickly jumped back on.

They stuttered through the snowscape, a hundred metres at a time. Located the snowmobile's probable route, swept the tracks with a broom, took bearings, surged forward. The gouge in the left runner, probably caused by an accident, meant they could be sure they were following the right scooter tracks. In a few places, in tiny hollows or on wind-blown hillcrests, the trail was clear and they could make fast progress. But not too fast. Harry had already shouted warnings about precipices twice and they had had some very close shaves. It was getting on for four now. Bellman flicked the headlights on and off, depending on how much snow was drifting in their faces. Harry studied the map. He had no clear idea of where they were, just that they were straying further and further from Ustaoset. And that daylight was dwindling. A third of Harry was slowly beginning to worry about the trip back. Which just meant that the two-third majority couldn't care less.

At half past four they lost the trail.

The drifting snow was so thick now they could hardly see.

'This is madness,' Harry shouted above the roar of the motor. 'Why don't we wait until tomorrow?'

Bellman turned to him and answered with a smile.

At five they picked up the trail again.

They stopped and dismounted.

'Leads that way,' Bellman said, trudging back to the snowmobile. 'Come on!'

'Wait,' Harry said.

'Why? Come on, it'll soon be dark.'

'When you shouted just now, didn't you hear the echo?'

'Now you mention it.' Bellman stopped. 'Rock face?'

'There are no rock faces on the map,' Harry said, turning in the direction the tracks indicated.

'Ravine!' he yelled. And received an answer. A very swift answer. He turned back to Bellman.

'I think the snowmobile making these tracks is in serious trouble.'

'What do I know about Bellman?' Roger Gjendem repeated to gain some time. 'He's reputed to be very competent and extremely professional.' What was Nordbø, the legendary editor, really after? 'He does all the right things,' Gjendem went on. 'Learns quickly, can handle us press types now. Sort of a *whizz-kid*. Er, that is if you know . . .'

'I am somewhat conversant with the term, yes,' said Bent Nordbø with an acidic smile, his right thumb and forefinger furiously rubbing the handkerchief on his glasses. 'However, basically, I am more interested in if there any rumours doing the rounds.'

'Rumours?' Gjendem said, failing to notice a relapse into his old habit of leaving his mouth open after speaking.

'I am truly hopeful you understand the concept, Gjendem. Since that is what you and your employer live off. Well?'

Gjendem hesitated. 'There are all sorts of rumours.'

Nordbø rolled his eyes. 'Speculation. Fabrication. Direct lies. I'm not bothered with the niceties here, Gjendem. Turn the sack of gossip inside out, reveal the malevolence.'

'N-negative things then?'

Nordbø released a pondorous sigh. 'Gjendem, my dear man, do you often hear rumours about people's sobriety, financial generosity, fidelity to partners and non-psychopathic leadership styles? Could that be because the function of rumours is to please the rest of us by putting us in a better light?' Nordbø was finished with one lens and engaged on the cleansing operation of the second.

'It's a very, very idle rumour,' Gjendem said and added with alacrity: 'And I know for certain of others with the selfsame reputation who categorically are not.'

'As an ex-editor I would recommend you delete either *for certain* or *categorically*, it's a tautology,' Nordbø said. 'Categorically are not *what*?'

'Erm. Jealous.'

'Aren't we all jealous?'

'Violently jealous.'

'Has he beaten up his wife?'

'No, I don't think he's laid a hand on her. Or had reason to. However, those who have given her a second look . . .'

61

The Drop

HARRY AND BELLMAN LAY ON THEIR STOMACHS AT THE EDGE where the snowmobile tracks stopped. They stared down. Steep, black rock faces sliced inwards to the ground and disappeared in the thickening swirl of snow.

'Can you see anything?' Bellman asked.

'Snow,' Harry answered, passing him the binoculars.

'The snowmobile's there.' Bellman got up and walked back to their vehicle. 'We're climbing down.'

'We?'

'You.'

'Me? Thought you were the mountaineer here, Bellman.'

'Correct,' said Bellman who had already started strapping on the harness. 'That's why it's logical for me to operate the ropes and rope brake. The rope's seventy metres long. I'll lower it as far as it can go. Alright?'

Six minutes later Harry stood on the edge with his back to the chasm, binoculars around his neck and a cigarette smoking from his mouth.

'Nervous?' Bellman smiled.

'Nope,' Harry said. 'Scared shitless.'

Bellman checked the rope ran through the brake without a hitch, round the narrow tree trunk behind them and to Harry's harness.

Harry closed his eyes, breathed in and concentrated on leaning backwards, overriding the body's evolution-conditioned protest, formed from millions of years of experience that the species cannot survive if it steps off cliffs.

The brain won over the body by the smallest possible margin.

For the first few metres he could support his legs against the rock face, but as it jutted in he was left hanging in the air. The rope was released in fits and starts, but its elasticity softened the tightening of the harness against his back and thighs. Then the rope came more evenly, and after a while he had lost sight of the top and was alone, hovering between the white snowflakes and the black cliff faces.

He leaned to the side and peered down. And there, twenty metres below, he glimpsed sharp black rocks protruding from the snow. Steep scree. And in the midst of all the black and white, something yellow.

'I can see the snowmobile!' Harry shouted and the echo ricocheted between the rock walls. It was upside down with the skis in the air. Since he and the rope were unaffected by the wind, he could judge that the vehicle lay about three metres further along. More than seventy metres down. The snowmobile must therefore have been travelling at an unusually slow speed before it took off.

The rope went taut.

'More!' Harry shouted.

The resonant answer from above sounded as if it had come from a pulpit. 'There is no more rope.'

Harry stared down at the snowmobile. Something was sticking out from under it to the left. A bare arm. Black, bloated, like a sausage that had been on the grill for too long. A white hand against a black rock. He tried to focus, to force his eyes to see better. Open palm, the right hand. Fingers. Distorted, crooked. Harry's brain rewound. What had Tony Leike said about his illness? Not contagious, just hereditary. Arthritis.

Harry glanced at his watch. Detective's reflex. The dead man was found at 17.54. Darkness covered the walls down in the scree.

'Up!' Harry shouted.

Nothing happened.

'Bellman?'

No answer.

A gust of wind twirled Harry round on the rope. Black rocks. Twenty metres. And all of a sudden, without warning, he felt his heart pound and he automatically grabbed the rope with both hands to make sure it was still there. Kaja. Bellman knew.

Harry breathed in deep, three times, before shouting again.

'It's getting dark, the wind's picking up and I'm freezing my balls off, Bellman. Time to find shelter.'

Still no answer. Harry closed his eyes. Was he frightened? Frightened that an apparently rational colleague would kill him on a whim because circumstances happened to be propitious? Course he was bloody frightened. For this was no whim. It wasn't chance that he stayed behind to go into the frozen wastes with Harry. Or was it? He took a deep breath. Bellman could easily arrange for this to look like an accident. Climb down afterwards and remove the harness and rope, say that Harry had missed his footing in the snow. His throat had gone dry. This was not happening. He hadn't dug his way out of a sodding avalanche just to be dropped down a ravine twelve hours later. By a policeman. This didn't bloody happen, this . . .

The pressure from the harness was gone. He was falling. Free fall. Fast.

'The rumour is that Bellman is supposed to have manhandled a colleague,' Gjendem said. 'Just because the guy had danced a couple of times too many with her at the police Christmas party. The guy wanted to report a broken jaw and a cracked skull, but had no evidence – the attacker had been wearing a balaclava. But everyone knew it was Bellman. Trouble was brewing so he applied for a move to Europol to get away.'

'Do you believe there is anything to these rumours, Gjendem?'

Roger shrugged. 'It certainly looks as if Bellman has a certain . . . um, predilection for that kind of transgression. We've looked into Jussi Kolkka's background following the avalanche at Håvass. He beat up a rapist under interrogation. And Truls Berntsen, Bellman's sidekick, is not exactly a mummy's boy, either.'

'Good. I want you to cover this duel between Kripos and Crime Squad. I want you to let off a few bombshells. Preferably about a psychopathic management style. That's all. Then let's see how the Minister of Justice reacts.'

Without any gestures, or parting salutations, Bent Nordbø put on his newly polished spectacles, unfolded the newspaper and started to read.

Harry didn't have time to think. Not one thought. Nor did he see his life passing before him, faces of people he should have said he loved, or feel impelled to walk towards any light. Possibly because you don't get that far when you fall five metres. The harness tightened against his groin and back, but the elasticity in the rope allowed him a gentle slackening of speed.

Then he felt himself being hoisted up again. The wind was blowing snow in his face.

'What the fuck happened?' Harry asked when, fifteen minutes later, he was standing on the edge of the ravine swaying in the wind as he untied the rope from the harness.

'Scared then, were you?' Bellman smiled.

Instead of putting the rope down, Harry wound it round his right hand. Checked that he had enough slack in the rope to have a swing. A short uppercut to the chin. The rope meant he would be able to use his hand again tomorrow, not like when he hit Bjørn Holm and suffered two days of painful knuckles.

He took a step towards Bellman. Saw the POB's surprised expression when he noticed the rope around Harry's fist, saw him retreat, stagger and fall backwards in the snow.

'Don't! I . . . I just had to tie a knot at the end of the rope so that it wouldn't slide through the brake . . .'

Harry continued towards him, and Bellman – who was cowering in the snow – automatically raised his arm in front of his face.

'Harry! There . . . there was a gust of wind and I slipped . . .'

Harry stopped, eyed Bellman in surprise. Then he continued past the trembling POB and lumbered through the snow.

*   *   *

The icy wind blew through outer clothing, underclothes, skin, flesh, muscles and into the bones. Harry grabbed a ski pole strapped to the snowmobile, cast around for some other material he could tie to the top, but found nothing, and sacrificing anything he was wearing was out of the question. Then he speared the pole into the snow to mark the site. God knows how long it would take them to find it again. He pressed the button on the electric starter. Found the lights, turned them on. And Harry knew at once. Saw it in the snow blowing horizontally into the cones of light and forming an impenetrable white wall: they would never get out of this labyrinth and back to Ustaoset.

62

Transit

KIM ERIK LOKKER WAS THE YOUNGEST FORENSICS OFFICER at Krimteknisk. Accordingly, he was often given jobs of a less forensic nature. Such as driving to Drammen. Bjørn Holm had mentioned that Bruun was a homosexual of the flirtier kind, but that Kim Erik only had to hand over the clothes and then leave.

When the satnav woman in the car declared 'You have arrived at your destination', he found himself outside an old block of flats. He parked and wandered through open doors up to the second floor, to the door marked with the names GEIR BRUUN/ADELE VETLESEN on a sheet of paper stuck down with two bits of tape.

Kim Erik pressed the doorbell once, twice, and at last heard the sounds of someone stomping through the hall.

The door swung open. The man was wearing no more than a towel around his waist. He was unusually pale, and his smooth crown was wet and shiny with sweat.

'Geir Bruun? H-hope I'm not interrupting,' said Kim Erik Lokker, holding the plastic bag with outstretched arm.

'Not at all, I'm only screwing,' he said in the affected voice Bjørn Holm had imitated. 'What is this?'

'The clothes we borrowed. We've had to keep the ski pants until further notice, I'm afraid.'

'Really?'

Kim Erik heard the door behind Geir Bruun open. And an extremely feminine voice chirp: 'What is it, darling?'

'Just someone delivering something.'

A figure nestled up behind Geir Bruun. She hadn't even bothered with a towel, and Kim Erik was able to establish that the tiny creature was one hundred per cent woman.

'Hello there,' she twittered over Geir Bruun's shoulder. 'If there's nothing else, I'd like him back.' She raised a small, graceful foot and kicked. The glass in the door was shaking and rattling long after the door had slammed shut.

Harry had stopped the snowmobile and was staring into the drifting snow.

Something had been there.

Bellman had put his arms around Harry's waist and his head behind his back to shelter from the wind.

Harry waited. Stared.

There it was again.

A cabin. Notched logs. And a storehouse.

Then it was gone again, erased by the snow, as though it had never existed. But Harry had the direction.

So why didn't he just accelerate and head towards it, save their skins, why did he hesitate? He didn't know. But there was something about the cabin, something he had sensed in the few seconds it became visible. Something about the black windows, the feeling that he was looking at a building that was infinitely abandoned and yet inhabited. Something that was not right. And which made him press the accelerator gently so as not to be heard above the wind.

63

The Storehouse

Harry put a log in the wood burner.

Bellman sat by the table, his teeth chattering. The white stains had taken on a bluish sheen. They had hammered on the door and shouted in the howling wind for a while before smashing a window to an empty bedroom. A bedroom with an unmade bed and a smell that caused Harry to wonder whether someone had slept there very recently. He almost placed a hand on the bed to see if it was still warm. And even though the sitting room would have felt warm anyway – they were so cold – Harry put a hand inside the wood burner to feel if there might be any warm embers under the black ash. But there were not.

Bellman moved closer to the stove. 'Did you see anything apart from the snowmobile down in the ravine?'

They were the first words he had uttered since running after Harry, begging not to be left behind and throwing himself on the back of the snowmobile.

'An arm,' Harry said.

'Whose arm?'

'How should I know?'

Harry stood up and went to the bathroom. Checked the toiletries. The few there were. Soap and a razor. No toothbrush. One person, one man. Who either didn't clean his teeth or had gone away on a trip. The floor was damp, even along the skirting boards, as if someone had hosed it down. Something caught his attention. He crouched down. Half hidden by the skirting board there was something dark. Pebble? Harry picked it up, studied it. It wasn't lava anyway. He put it in his pocket.

In the kitchen drawers he found coffee and bread. He pressed the bread. Relatively fresh. In the fridge there were two jars of jam, some butter and two beers. Harry was so hungry he imagined he could smell roast pork. He rummaged through the cupboards. Nothing. Shit, did the guy live off bread and jam? He found a packet of biscuits on a pile of plates. Same type of plates they had at the Håvass cabin. Same furniture, too. Could this be a Tourist Association cabin? Harry stopped. He wasn't just imagining it, he *could* smell roast – correction: burnt pork.

He went back into the sitting room.

'Can you smell it?'

'What?'

'The smell,' Harry said, squatting down by the wood burner. Beside the door, on an embossed stag, there were three unidentifiable black bits burned to the cast iron and they were smoking.

'Did you find any food?' Bellman asked.

'Depends what you mean by food,' Harry said pensively.

'There's a storehouse on the other side of the yard. Maybe . . .'

'Instead of "maybe" perhaps you should go and check.'

Bellman nodded, got up and went out.

Harry walked over to the desk to see if there was anything he could use to scrape off the burned bits. He pulled out the top drawer. Empty. Harry pulled out the others, all empty. Apart from a sheet of paper in the bottom one. He picked it up. It wasn't paper but a photograph, face down. The first thing that struck Harry was that it was strange to have a family portrait in a Tourist Association cabin. The photo had been taken in the summer, in front of a farmhouse. A woman and a man sitting on a step with a boy between them. The woman in a blue dress and headscarf, no make-up, a tired smile. The man, with a pinched mouth, stern expression and the serious, closed face you find on embarrassed men who look as though they're hiding a dark secret. But it was the boy in the middle who caught Harry's attention. He resembled the mother; he had her open smile and gentle eyes. But he looked like someone else, too. Those large, white teeth . . .

406

Harry went back to the wood burner, he was suddenly cold again. The stench of smoking pork ... He closed his eyes and concentrated on breathing deeply and calmly through his nose a couple of times, but felt the nausea coming nonetheless.

At that moment Bellman stomped in with a broad smile on his face. 'Hope you like venison.'

Harry woke wondering what had roused him. Was it a sound? Or the absence of sound? For he realised the room was utterly still; the wind had stopped blowing outside. He threw off the blanket and stood up from the sofa.

Walked over to the window and peered outside. It was as if someone had waved a magic wand over the countryside. What, six hours previously, had been hard, merciless wilderness was now gentle, maternal, almost beautiful in the bewitching moonlight. Harry realised he was looking for prints in the snow. He *had* heard a sound. It could have been anything. A bird. An animal. He listened and heard light snoring from behind one bedroom door. So it wasn't Bellman who had got up. His gaze followed the footprints leading from the cabin to the storehouse. Or from the storehouse to the cabin? Or both, there were many. Could they be Bellman's from six hours ago? When had it stopped snowing?

Harry pulled on his boots, went out and looked towards the toilet. No tracks there. He turned his back on the storehouse and pissed against the cabin wall. Why did men do that, why did they have to piss *on* something? The remnants of a territory-marking instinct? Or ... Harry became aware that it wasn't what he was pissing on, it was what he had his back to that was important. The storehouse. He suspected he was being observed from there. He buttoned up, turned and looked at it. Then he moved towards it. Grabbed the spade as he passed the snowmobile. The plan had been to walk straight in, but instead he stood in front of the plain stone steps to the low door. Listened. Nothing. What the hell was he doing? There was no one here. He went up the steps, tried to raise his hand and grasp the handle, but it wouldn't move. What the hell was going on? His heart was beating so hard in his chest that it hurt, as if it wanted to burst out. He was sweating and his body refused to obey orders. And it slowly dawned on Harry that this was exactly how he had heard it described. A panic attack. It was the anger that saved him. He kicked open the door with immense force and crashed into the dark. The door swung shut. There was a strong smell of fat, smoked meat and dried blood. Something moved in the stripe of moonlight and a pair of eyes flashed. Harry swung the spade. And he hit something. Heard the dead sound of meat, felt it give. The door behind him fell open again and the moonlight streamed in. Harry stared at the dead deer hanging in front of him. At the other animal carcasses. He dropped the spade and sank to his knees. Then it came, all at once. The wall cracking, the snow consuming him alive, panicking that he couldn't breathe, the long gasp of pure white fear as he fell towards the black rocks. So lonely. For they had all gone. His father was in a coma, in transit. And Rakel and Oleg were silhouettes against the light at an airport, also in transit. Harry wanted to go back. Back to the dripping room. The solid, damp walls. The sweaty mattress and the sweet smoke that transported him to where they were. Transit. Harry bowed his head and felt hot tears streaming down his face.

I have printed a photo of Jussi Kolkka from Dagbladet's *web page and pinned it up on the wall next to the others. There wasn't a word in the news about Harry Hole and the other police officers who were there. Or Iska Peller, for that matter. Was it a bluff? They're trying anyway. And now there is a dead policeman. They're going to try harder. They HAVE to try harder. Do you hear me, Hole? No? You should do. I'm so close I could whisper it in your ear.*

PART SEVEN

64

State of Health

OLAV HOLE'S CONDITION WAS UNCHANGED, DR ABEL HAD said.

Harry sat by the hospital bed looking at his unchanged father while a heart monitor played its beep-beep song interspersed with skipped beats. Sigurd Altman came in, greeted Harry and noted down the figures from the screen onto a pad.

'Actually, I'm here to visit a Kaja Solness,' Harry said, getting up. 'But I don't know which ward she's in. Could you . . . ?'

'Your colleague who was brought in by helicopter the other night? She's in intensive care. Only until they've got all the test results. She'd been buried in the snow for quite a while. When they said Håvass I assumed she must have been this witness from Sydney the police were talking about on the radio.'

'Don't believe everything you hear, Altman. While Kaja was lying in the snow the Australian lady was safe and warm in Bristol, with her own guards and full room service.'

'Hang on.' Altman scrutinised Harry. 'Were you buried in the snow as well?'

'What makes you say that?'

'The unsteady step you just took. Dizzy?'

Harry shrugged.

'Confused?'

'Constantly,' Harry said.

Altman smiled. 'You've got a bit too much CO_2 in you. The body disposes of it quickly when you breathe in oxygen, but you ought to have a blood test so that we can check your carbon dioxide levels.'

'No, thank you,' Harry said. 'How's he getting on?' He nodded towards the bed.

'What did the doctor say?'

'Unchanged. I'm asking you.'

'I'm not a doctor, Harry.'

'So you don't need to answer like one. Give me an estimate.'

'I can't . . .'

'It'll remain between us.'

Sigurd Altman eyed Harry. Was on the point of saying something. Changed his mind. Chewed his lower lip. 'Days,' he said.

'Not even weeks?'

Altman didn't answer.

'Thanks, Sigurd,' Harry said and went to the door.

Kaja's face was pale and beautiful against the pillowslip. Like a flower in a herbarium, Harry thought. Her hand was small and cold in his. On the bedside table was today's *Aftenposten* with the AVALANCHE BURIES CABIN IN HÅVASS headline. It described the tragic event and quoted Mikael Bellman, who said it was a great loss that Officer Kolkka had died protecting Iska Peller. He was thankful, however, that the witness had been saved and she was now safe.

'So the avalanche was started with dynamite?' Kaja said.

'Yes, it's beyond doubt,' Harry replied.

'So you and Bellman worked well together up there, did you?'

'Yes, indeed.' Harry turned to shield his coughing fit.

'Heard you found a snowmobile at the bottom of a ravine. With a possible body underneath.'

'Yes. Bellman stayed in Ustaoset to go back to the site with the local County Officer.'

'Krongli?'

'No, he couldn't be located. But his deputy, Roy Stille, seemed solid.

They've quite a job on their hands, though. We weren't sure where we were, more snow has fallen and it's drifting, and in that terrain . . .' Harry shook his head.

'Any idea who the body might be?'

Harry shrugged. 'I would be very surprised if it wasn't Tony Leike.'

Kaja's head spun round. 'Oh?'

'I haven't told anyone yet, but I saw the corpse's fingers.'

'What about them?'

'They were twisted. Tony Leike had arthritis.'

'Do you think he started the avalanche? And then drove over the precipice in the dark?'

Harry shook his head. 'Tony told me he knew the area well, it was his terrain. It was a clear day and the snowmobile wasn't going fast – it landed only three metres from the point where it took off. And he had a burned arm, which was not caused by dynamite. And the snowmobile was not burned.'

'Wha—?'

'I think Tony Leike was tortured, killed and then dumped with the snowmobile so that we wouldn't find the body.'

Kaja pulled a face.

Harry rubbed his little finger. He wondered whether it could have frostbite. 'What do you think about this Krongli?'

'Krongli?' Kaja chewed on that one. 'If it's true he tried to rape Charlotte Lolles, he should never have become a policeman, should he.'

'He beat his wife up, too.'

'Doesn't surprise me.'

'It doesn't?'

'No.'

He looked at her. 'Is there something you haven't told me?'

Kaja shrugged. 'He's a colleague, and I thought he was just drunk, nothing I would spread around , but, yes, I've had a glimpse of that side of him. He came to my place and reckoned in a pretty persistent way we should get cosy.'

'But?'

'Mikael was there.'

Harry felt himself twitch.

Kaja pushed herself up into a sitting position. 'You don't seriously think Krongli might have . . .'

'I don't know. I only know that whoever started the avalanche must have known the area well. Krongli has a connection with some of those girls at Håvass. In addition, Elias Skog said before he was killed that he had seen something which might have been a rape at Håvass. Aslak Krongli sounds like he can be violent.

'And then there's this avalanche. If you wanted to kill a woman you thought was alone with a detective in a remote mountain cabin, how would you do it? Starting an avalanche doesn't exactly give you a guaranteed result. So why not make it simple and effective, take along your favourite murder weapon and go straight to the cabin? Because he knew that Iska Peller and the detective were not on their own. He *knew* we were waiting for him. So he sneaked in and attacked in the only way that would allow him to escape afterwards. We're talking about an insider. Someone who knew about our Håvass theories and understood what was going on when he heard us naming a witness at a press conference. The local County Officer at Ustaoset—'

'Geilo,' Kaja corrected.

'Krongli definitely received the urgent call from Kripos requesting permission to land the police helicopter in the national park that night. He must have known the circumstances.'

'Then he should also have known that Iska Peller wasn't there, that we wouldn't have endangered the life of a witness,' Kaja said. 'So it's odd he didn't keep well away.'

Harry nodded. 'Good point, Kaja. I agree. I don't think Krongli thought for a second that Peller was in the cabin. I think the avalanche was a continuation of what he's been doing for some time.'

'Which is?'

'Playing with us.'

'Playing?'

'I received a call from Tony Leike's phone while we were at the cabin. Tony saved my number, and I'm pretty certain it wasn't him who phoned me. The thing is the caller didn't ring off quickly enough, voicemail

414

started recording and you can hear something for a second before the connection is cut. I'm not sure, but to me it sounded like laughter.'

'Laughter?'

'The laughter of someone who is amused. Because he'd just heard my message saying that I would have no network coverage for a couple of days. Let's imagine it was Aslak Krongli who had just had his suspicions confirmed that I was at the cabin in Håvass waiting for the killer.'

Harry paused and stared into the air, deep in thought.

'Well?' Kaja said after a while.

'I just wanted to hear how the theory sounded when I said it aloud,' Harry said.

'And?'

He got to his feet. 'Sounded half-arsed, in fact. But I'll check Krongli's alibis for the dates of the murders. See you.'

'Truls Berntsen?'

'Speaking.'

'Roger Gjendem, *Aftenposten*. Have you got time to answer a few questions?'

'Depends. If you're going to pester me about Jussi, you'd better talk to—'

'This is not about Jussi Kolkka, but my condolences by the way.'

'OK.'

Roger was sitting with his feet up on his office desk in the Post Office tower gazing at the low buildings that constituted Oslo Central Station and down to the Opera House which would soon be finished. After the conversation with Bent Nordbø at Stopp Pressen he had spent the whole day – and parts of the night – poring over Mikael Bellman in greater detail. Apart from the rumour that the temp at Stovner police station had been beaten up, there were not a lot of tangible facts. But, as a crime journalist, over the years Roger Gjendem had gathered a number of regular and reliable sources who would gladly inform on their grandmothers for the price of a bottle of booze or a pouch of tobacco. And three of them lived in Manglerud. After a few calls it turned out all three of them had grown up there, too. Perhaps it was true what he had heard someone say, that no one moves from Manglerud. Or to Manglerud.

There were obviously very few secrets in this milieu, because all three remembered Mikael Bellman. Partly because he had been a bastard of a policeman at Stovner. But mostly because he had made a beeline for Julle's woman while Julle was serving a twelve-month sentence for an earlier drugs conviction, which had been suspended but became custodial after someone had shopped him for pinching petrol from Mortensrud. The woman was Ulla Swart, Manglerud's finest, and a year older than Bellman. When Julle's sentence was up and he strolled out of prison having vowed to all and sundry that he was going to take care of Bellman, there had been two guys waiting in the garage when Julle went home to pick up his Kawasaki. They had been wearing balaclavas and beat him black and blue with iron bars and promised there would be more where that came from if he touched either Bellman or Ulla. Rumour had it that neither of the two had been Bellman. But one of them had been someone they called Beavis, Bellman's eternal lackey. It was the only card Roger Gjendem had when he rang Truls 'Beavis' Berntsen. All the more reason to pretend he had four aces.

'I just wanted to ask if there was any truth in the assertion that on instructions from Mikael Bellman you once beat up Stanislav Hesse, who was depping at the wages and personnel office of Stovner police station.'

Thunderous silence at the other end.

Roger cleared his throat. 'Well?'

'That's a damned lie.'

'Which part?'

'I was never given any instructions by Mikael to do that. Everyone could see the bloody Pole was trying it on with his wife. Could have been anyone taking matters into their own hands.'

Roger Gjendem tended to believe the former, the bit about the instructions. But not the latter, the bit about 'anyone'. None of Bellman's other colleagues at Stovner that Roger had spoken to had anything directly bad to say about Bellman; however, it was evident that Bellman was not beloved, not a man for whom they would have answered a call to arms. Apart from one.

'Thank you, that was all,' Roger Gjendem said.

As Roger Gjendem put his mobile away, Harry rummaged in his jacket pocket and put his phone to his ear.

'Yes?'

'Bjørn Holm here.'

'I can see that.'

'Christ. Didn't think you would have bothered to set up a phone book.'

'I have indeed. You should feel honoured. You're one of the four names in it.'

'What's the racket in the background? Where are you actually?'

'Punters cheering because they think they're going to win. I'm at a horse race.'

'What?'

'Bombay Garden.'

'Isn't that a . . . did they let *you* in?'

'I'm a member. What do you want?'

'Jesus, Harry, are you gambling on horses? Didn't you learn *anything* in Hong Kong?'

'Relax, I'm here checking up on Aslak Krongli. According to his office he was on police business in Oslo when both Charlotte and Borgny were killed. Not that unusual actually, because it turns out he's quite often in Oslo. And I've just discovered the reason.'

'Bombay Garden?'

'Yup. Aslak Krongli has a not insubstantial gambling problem. Thing is, I've checked his credit card payments on the computer here. Time of payment and everything. Krongli has used his card a lot, and the times give him an alibi. Unfortunately.'

'I see. And they've got the computer in the same room as the race course?'

'Eh? They're in the final straight now, you'll have to talk louder!'

'They've . . . Forget it. I'm ringing to say we've got semen off the ski pants that Adele Vetlesen was wearing at Håvass.'

'What? You're kidding? That means . . .'

'We may soon have the DNA of the eighth guest. If it's his semen. And the only way we can be sure is by excluding the other men at Håvass.'

'We need their DNA.'

'Yes,' said Bjørn Holm. 'Elias Skog's fine, of course, we've got his DNA. Not so good with Tony Leike. We'd have found it at his house, no problem, but for that we need a warrant. And after what happened last time it's gonna be really tough.'

'Leave it to me,' Harry said. 'We should also have Krongli's DNA profile. Even though he didn't kill either Charlotte or Borgny, he may have raped Adele.'

'OK. How do we get it?'

'As a policeman he must have been at a crime scene at some point or other,' Harry said. It was unnecessary to conclude his reasoning. Bjørn Holm was already nodding. To avoid confusion and identity mistakes, fingerprints and DNA were routinely taken from all officers who had been present at a crime scene and had potentially contaminated it.

'I'll check the database.'

'Well done, Bjørn.'

'Wait, there's more. You asked us to look harder for a nurse's uniform and we did. We found one with PSG on it. And I've checked. There's a disused PSG factory in Oslo, up in Nydalen. If it's empty and the eighth guest had sex with Adele there, we may still be able to find semen there.'

'Mm. Knobbed in Nydalen and humped in Håvass. The eighth guest may just have fucked his bolt-hole. PSG, you said. Is that the Kadok factory?'

'Yes, how . . . ?'

'Pal's father worked there.'

'Repeat, there's a helluva racket now.'

'They're crossing the finishing line. See you.'

Harry put the phone in his jacket pocket, swivelled round in his chair, so he didn't see the gloomy faces of the losers around the felt course, nor the croupier's smile. 'Conglatulations again, Hally!'

Harry got up, donned his jacket and looked at the note the Vietnamese man was holding out for him. With the portrait of Edvard Munch. A thousand kroner.

'Mm, velly lucky,' Harry said. 'Put it on the green horse in the next race. I'll pick up the cash another day, Duc.'

Lene Galtung was sitting in the living room staring at the double-glazed window, at the double-exposed reflection. Her iPod was playing Tracy Chapman. 'Fast Car'. She could listen to the song again and again, never got tired of it. It was about a poor girl wanting to flee from everything, just get in her lover's fast car and leave the life she had, working on the till at the supermarket, being responsible for her drunken father, burn all the bridges. This could not have been further from Lene's own life, nevertheless the song was about her. The Lene she could have been. The Lene she actually was. One of the two she saw in the double reflection. The ordinary one, the grey one. In all her years at school she had been scared stiff that the classroom door would open, someone would come in, point a finger at her and say, we're on to you now, take off those fine clothes. Then they would toss her a few rags and say, now everyone can see who you really are, the illegitimate child. She had been sitting there, year in, year out, hiding, as quiet as a mouse, glancing at the door, just waiting. Listening to friends, listening for the telltale signs that would give her away. The embarrassment, the fear, the defence she put up seemed like arrogance to others. And she knew she overplayed her role as rich, successful, spoilt and carefree. She was not at all good-looking and radiant, like the other girls in her circle, the ones who could chirrup with a self-assured smile 'I don't have a clue', in the charming knowledge that whatever they didn't know couldn't possibly be important and that the world would never require any more from them than their beauty. So she had to pretend. That she was beautiful. Radiant. Superior to everything. But she was so tired of it. Had just wanted to sit in Tony's car and ask him to leave everything behind. Drive to a place where she could be the real Lene and not these two false personae who hated each other. As the song said, together, she and Tony could find that place.

The reflection in the glass moved. Lene recoiled when she realised it was not her face after all. She hadn't heard her come in. Lene straightened up and pulled out the earphones.

'Put the coffee tray there, Nanna.'

The woman hesitated. 'You should forget him, Lene.'

'Stop it!'

'I'm just saying. He won't be a good man for you.'

'Stop it, I told you!'

'Shh!' The woman smacked down the tray with a clatter on the table, and her turquoise eyes flashed. 'You have to see common sense, Lene. We've all had to do that in this house when the situation demanded it. I'm just saying this as your—'

'As my what?' Lene snorted. 'Look at you. What could you be to me?'

The woman ran her hands down the white apron, went to put one on Lene's cheek, but Lene waved it away. The woman sighed, and it sounded like a drop of water falling in a well. Then she turned and left. As the door closed behind her, the black phone next to Lene rang. She felt her heart leap. Since Tony had disappeared, her phone had been constantly switched on and always within arm's length. She grabbed it. 'Lene Galtung.'

'Harry Hole, Crime Squ— I mean, Kripos. I'm sorry to intrude, but I need to ask you for some help with a case. It's about Tony.'

Lene could feel her voice careering out of control as she replied: 'Has . . . has something happened?'

'We're looking for someone we suspect died from a fall in the mountains around Ustaoset.'

She felt herself going dizzy; the floor was rising and the ceiling falling.

'We haven't located the body yet. It's been snowing and the search area is vast and extremely rugged. Can you hear me?'

'Y–yes, I can.'

The policeman's voice, a touch hoarse, continued. 'When the body has been recovered, we'll try to get it identified as soon as possible. But there may be extensive burns. Therefore we require DNA now from anyone who might conceivably be the deceased person. And while Tony is a missing person . . .'

Lene's heart felt as if it was coming up her throat, ready to leap out of her mouth. The voice at the other end droned on.

420

'That is why I was wondering if you could help one of our forensics officers to find DNA material in Tony's home.'

'S-such as what?'

'A hair from a brush, saliva on a toothbrush, they know what they need. The important thing is that you, as his fiancée, give us permission and come to his house with a key.'

'Of c-course.'

'Thank you very much indeed. I'll send an officer to Holmenveien right away.'

Lene rang off. Felt the tears coming. Put her iPod earphones back in.

Caught Tracy Chapman singing about taking a fast car and keeping on driving. Then the song finished. She pressed repeat.

65

Kadok

NYDALEN EMBODIED THE DEINDUSTRIALISATION OF OSLO. The factory buildings that had not been demolished – and had not given way to gleaming, elegant designer office blocks in glass and steel – had been converted into TV studios, restaurants and large, open-plan red-brick affairs with exposed ventilation and plumbing.

The latter were often rented by advertising firms who wanted to flag up that they thought in untraditional ways, that creativity flourished just as well in cheap industrial rooms as in the expensive and centrally located head offices of their well-established competitors. But the premises in Nydalen now cost at least as much because all advertising agencies basically think in traditional patterns. That is: they follow the fashion and drive the prices upwards for whatever is the fashion.

The owners of the disused Kadok factory site had, however, not participated in this bonanza. When the factory had finally closed fourteen years ago, after several annual deficits and the dumping of PSG in China, the founder's heirs went for each other's throats. And while they were arguing about who should have what, the factory fell into decay, isolated behind the fences to the west of the River Akerselva. Shrubs and deciduous trees were allowed to grow wild and eventually masked the factory from its surroundings. Bearing all this in mind, Harry thought the large padlock on the gate seemed strangely new.

'Cut it,' Harry told the officer beside him.

The jaws of the enormous bolt cutter went through the metal as if it were butter, and the lock was snapped as quickly as it had taken Harry to get a blue chit. The solicitor at Kripos had sounded as if he had more important things to do than issue search warrants, and Harry had barely finished talking before he had the chit filled and signed in his hand. And he had thought to himself that they could do with a couple of stressed-out, negligent solicitors at Crime Squad as well.

The low afternoon sun flashed on the jagged glass of smashed windows high in the brick walls. The atmosphere was marked by the desolation you find only in disused factories where everything you see has been constructed for hectic, efficient activity, yet there is no one around. Where the echo of iron on iron, of workers shouting, cursing and laughing over the drone of the machines still reverberates silently between the walls, and the wind blows through the soot-darkened, broken windows, making the spiders' webs and the dead shells of insects quiver.

There was no lock on the door into the factory hall. The five men walked through a rectangular area with church-like acoustics, which gave the impression of an evacuation rather than closure; work tools were still laid out, a pallet loaded with white buckets labelled PSG TYPE 3 stood ready to be driven away, a blue coat hung over the back of a chair.

They stopped when they reached the centre of the hall. In one corner there was a kind of kiosk, shaped like a lighthouse and raised a metre off the ground. Foreman's office, Harry thought. Around the walls ran a gallery, which at one end led into a mezzanine floor with its own rooms. Harry guessed they were the lunch room and admin offices.

'Where shall we begin?' Harry asked.

'The same place as always,' Bjørn Holm said, casting round. 'Top left-hand corner.'

'What are we looking for?'

'A table, a bench with blue PSG on it. The stains on the trousers were rubbed in slightly below the back pockets, so she must have been sitting on something – in other words, she wasn't lying flat.'

'If you begin down here, this officer and I will go upstairs with the bolt cutters,' Harry said.

'Oh?'

'To open doors for you forensics boys. We promise not to spray semen anywhere.'

'Very droll. Don't—'

'—touch anything.'

Harry and the officer, whom he called 'officer' for the simple reason that he had forgotten his name two seconds after hearing it, stomped up a winding staircase, making the iron steps sing. The doors they met were open, and inside, as Harry had envisaged, there were offices from which the furniture had been removed. A cloakroom with rows of iron lockers. A large communal shower. But no blue stains.

'What do you think that is?' Harry asked, standing in the lunch room. He pointed to a narrow padlocked door at the back.

'Pantry,' the officer said, already on his way out.

'Wait!'

Harry went to the door. Scratched a nail on the apparently rusty lock. It was genuine rust. He turned it round, looked at the cylinder. No rust.

'Cut it,' Harry said.

The officer did as he was bidden. Then Harry opened the door.

The officer smacked his lips.

'Just a secret door,' Harry said.

Behind it was neither a pantry nor a room, but another door. Fitted with what looked like a solid lock.

The officer dropped the bolt cutter.

Harry scanned the area and found what he was looking for. A large red fire extinguisher, fairly conspicuous, hanging from the middle of the wall in the lunch room. Hadn't Øystein mentioned something about that once? The materials they made where his father worked were so inflammable that they were instructed to smoke by the river. In to which the cigarette ends were to be thrown afterwards.

He lifted the extinguisher off the wall and carried it to the door. Took a run-up of two strides, aimed and smashed the metal cylinder into the door like a battering ram.

The door split around the lock, but still clung to the frame.

Harry repeated the attack. Splinters flew all around.

'What the hell's going on?' he heard Bjørn call from the factory floor.

At the third attempt the door gave with a despairing scream and swung open. They stared into a pitch-black void.

'Can I borrow your torch?' Harry asked the officer, putting down the fire extinguisher and wiping off the sweat. 'Thanks. Wait here.'

Harry stepped into the room. There was a smell of ammonia. He shone the torch along the walls. The room – which he estimated was three metres square – had no windows. The beam swept across a black folding chair, a desk with a lamp and a Dell computer screen. The keyboard was relatively unworn. The desk was tidy and made of bare wood, no blue stains. In the litter bin there were strips of paper, as though someone had been cutting out pictures. And, sure enough, a *Dagbladet* with the front page cut up. Harry read the headline over the missing picture and knew they had come to the right place. They had arrived. This was it.

– DIED IN AVALANCHE –

Harry instinctively shone the torch upwards, on the wall above the desk, past some blue stains. And there they were.

All of them.

Marit Olsen, Charlotte Lolles, Borgny Stem-Myhre, Adele Vetlesen, Elias Skog, Jussi Kolkka. And Tony Leike.

Harry concentrated on breathing from his diaphragm. On absorbing the information piecemeal. The pictures had been cut out of newspapers or were printouts, probably from news pages on the Internet. Apart from the picture of Adele. His heart felt like a bass drum, dull thuds as it tried to send more blood to his brain. The picture was on photographic paper and so grainy that Harry assumed it must have been taken with a tele-photo lens and then blown up. It showed a car window, Adele's profile in the front seat from which the plastic cover did not seem to have been removed, and there was something protruding from her neck. A large knife with a shiny, yellow handle. Harry forced his eyes to look further. Underneath the pictures hung a line of letters, also printed off a computer. Harry skimmed the introduction to one of them.

IT IS SO SIMPLE. I KNOW WHO YOU KILLED.

YOU DON'T KNOW WHO I AM, BUT YOU KNOW WHAT I WANT.

MONEY. IF YOU DON'T PAY UP, THE COPS WILL BE ROUND. SIMPLE, EH?

The text continued, but his eye was caught by the end of the letter. No name, no sign off. The police officer was standing in the doorway. Harry heard his hand fumbling along the wall as he muttered: 'Must be a light switch here somewhere.'

Harry shone the torch at the blue ceiling, on four large neon tubes.

'There must be,' Harry said, illuminating the wall above several blue stains, before the cone of light found a sheet pinned to the right of the pictures. A tiny alarm bell had begun to go off in his brain. The sheet was torn at the side and covered in hand-drawn lines and columns. But there were different handwriting styles.

'Here it is,' the officer said.

For some reason, Harry suddenly thought about the work lamp. And the blue ceiling. And the smell of ammonia. And realised at that instant that the alarm in his head had nothing to do with the paper.

'Don't . . .' Harry started.

But too late.

The explosion was not technically an explosion but – as it would appear in the report the fire chief would sign the following day – an explosion-like fire triggered by an electric spark from cables connected to a canister of ammonia gas that in its turn ignited the PSG painted over the whole ceiling and splattered on the walls.

Harry gasped as the oxygen in the room was drawn into the flames and he felt an immense heat bear down on his head. He automatically fell to his knees and ran his hands through his hair to see if it was alight. When he looked up again, flames were coming off the walls. He wanted to breathe in, but managed to stop the reflex. Got to his feet. The door was only two metres away, but he had to have . . . he stretched for the sheet of paper. For the missing page from the Håvass guest book.

'Move away!' The officer appeared in the doorway with the fire extin-

426

guisher under his arm and the hose in his hand. As though in slow motion, Harry saw it squirt out. Saw the golden-brown jet released from the hose splash against the wall. Brown that should have been white; liquid that should have been powder. And already, before he looked into the jaws of the flames that rose on two legs and roared at him from where the liquid landed, before he smelt the sweet sting of petrol in his nostrils, before he saw the flames follow the jet of petrol towards the officer standing in the doorway, with the handle still depressed, in shock, Harry knew why the extinguisher had been hanging from the middle of the lunch-room wall, on display, impossible to miss, red and new, screaming out to be used.

Harry's shoulder hit the policeman at waist height, folding him over the rampaging inspector and knocking him backwards into the room with Harry on top.

They sent a couple of chairs flying as they skidded under the table. The officer, gasping for air, gesticulated and pointed while opening and closing his mouth like a fish. Harry turned. Wrapped in flames, the red extinguisher rumbled and rolled towards them. The hose was spitting melted rubber. Harry shot up, dragging the officer after him, pulled him to the door as a stopwatch ticked timelessly in his head. He shoved the swaying officer out of the room, onto the gallery, thrust him down to the floor alongside him as it came, what the fire chief in his report would describe as an explosion, and which blew out all the windows and set fire to the entire lunch room.

The cutting room is burning. It's on the news. You have to serve and protect, Harry Hole, not demolish and destroy. You will have to pay compensation. If not, I will take something from you that you hold dear. In a matter of seconds. You have no idea how easy it will be.

66

After the Fire

THE EVENING DARKNESS HAD DESCENDED OVER NYDALEN. Harry stood with a blanket over his shoulders and a large paper cup in his hand as he and Bjørn Holm watched the smoke divers running in and out with the last PSG buckets that would ever leave the Kadok factory.

'So he'd pinned up the pictures of the murder victims, had he?' Bjørn Holm said.

'Yep,' Harry said. 'Except for the prostitute in Leipzig, Juliana Verni.'

'What about the page? Are you sure it was from the Håvass guest book?'

'Yes. I saw the guest book when I was in the cabin and the pages were identical.'

'And so you were standing half a metre from the name of the eighth guest, but you didn't see it?'

Harry shrugged. 'Perhaps I need reading glasses. Things happened bloody quickly in there, Bjørn. And my interest in the page waned rather when the officer started spraying petrol.'

'Course, I didn't mean—'

'There were some letters on the wall. From what I could see they were blackmail letters. Maybe someone had already rumbled him.'

A fireman came towards them. His clothes creaked and groaned as he walked.

'Kripos, aren't you?' The man's voice resonated in a way that matched the helmet and boots. And he had body language that said boss.

Harry hesitated, but confirmed with a nod; no reason to complicate matters.

'What actually happened in there?'

'That's what I'm hoping you boys will eventually be able to tell *us*,' Harry said. 'But in general terms I think we can say that whoever found himself a rent-free office in there had a clear plan for dealing with uninvited guests.'

'Oh?'

'I should have known as soon as I saw the neon tubes on the ceiling. If they'd been working, the tenant wouldn't have needed a desk lamp. The switch was connected to something else, some kind of ignition device.'

'You think so, do you? Well, right, we'll get some experts in tomorrow morning.'

'What does it look like inside?' Holm asked. 'The room where it started.'

The fireman scrutinised Holm. 'PSG on the walls and ceiling, son. What do you *think* it looks like?'

Harry was tired. Tired of being on the receiving end, tired of being afraid, tired of always being too late. But right now most tired of grown men who never tire of playing cock of the walk. Harry spoke in a low voice, so low that the fireman had to lean in to hear.

'Unless you're seriously interested in what my forensics officer thinks about the room you've just sent umpteen smoke divers into, I suggest you spit out what you know in concise but exhaustive terms. You know there was a guy sitting there planning six or seven murders. Which he carried out. And we're *very* interested to know if we can expect to find clues which might help us to stop this very, very bad man. Can you be concise like that?'

The fireman straightened. Coughed. 'PSG is extremely—'

'Listen. We're asking you for the consequences, not the cause.'

The fireman's face had gone a colour that was not solely due to the heat from the burning PSG. 'Burned out. Totally burned out. Papers, furniture, computer, the lot.'

'Thank you, boss,' Harry said.

The two policemen watched the fireman's back as he left.

'*My* forensics officer?' Holm repeated, pulling a face as if he had swallowed something nasty.

'Had to sound like a bit of a boss, too.'

'Good to outsmart someone when you've just been outsmarted yourself, isn't it?'

Harry nodded and pulled the blanket around him more tightly. 'He said burned out, didn't he?'

'Burned out. How does that feel?'

Harry stared miserably at the smoke still seeping out of the factory windows into the fire service's searchlights.

'Like being knobbed in Nydalen,' he answered, draining the rest of the cold coffee.

Harry drove away from Nydalen, but got no further than the red lights in Uelandsgate before Bjørn Holm rang again.

'Forensics have done tests on the semen on Adele's ski pants, and we've got a DNA profile.'

'Already?' Harry exclaimed.

'Partial profile. But enough for them to state with 93 per cent certainty that we have a match.'

Harry sat up straight in the seat.

Match. What a wonderful word. Perhaps the day wasn't a waste after all.

'Out with it then!' Harry said.

'You've got to learn to savour dramatic pauses,' Holm said.

Harry groaned.

'OK, OK. They found the matching DNA profile with hair from Tony Leike's hairbrush.'

Harry stared into the distance.

Tony Leike had raped Adele Vetlesen at the cabin.

Harry hadn't seen it coming. Tony Leike? He couldn't make it tally. Violent criminal, yes, but to rape a woman who's come to a cabin with another man? Elias Skog said he'd seen him holding her mouth and pulling her into the toilet. Perhaps it wasn't a rape when it came to the crunch?

And then – all of a sudden – it did come to the crunch.
Harry saw it, crystal clear.
It wasn't a rape. And there it was: the motive.
The cars behind hooted. The lights had turned green.

67

Prince Charming

IT WAS A QUARTER TO EIGHT, AND THE DAY HADN'T YET adjusted colour and contrast. The grey morning light showed the countryside in a grainy black-and-white version as Harry parked beside the only other car by Lake Vøyentangen and ambled down to the jetty. County Officer Skai was standing at the edge with a fishing rod in his hand and a cigarette in the corner of his mouth. Wisps of mist hung in the air like cotton wool around the reeds poking up from the black, oil-smooth water.

'Hole,' said Skai without turning. 'Up early.'

'Your wife said you were here.'

'Every morning from seven to eight. Only chance I have to think before the hustle and bustle starts.'

'What have you caught?'

'Nothing. But there are pike in the reeds.'

'Sounds familiar. 'Fraid the hustle and bustle starts a bit earlier today. I've come about Tony Leike.'

'Tony, yes. His grandad's farm was in Rustad, east of Lake Lyseren.'

'So you remember him well?'

'This is a small place, Hole. My father and old Leike were friends, and Tony was here every summer.'

'What memories do you have of him?'

'Erm, funny guy. Lots of people liked him. Especially the women. He was pally with the girls, a sort of Elvis type. And managed to surround himself with a lot of mystery. Rumour was he had grown up alone with his unhappy, alcoholic mother until one day she sent him packing because the man she was with didn't like the boy. But women round here liked him a lot. And he them. That occasionally got him into some trouble.'

'Like when he cosied up to your daughter?'

Skai flinched as if he had got a bite.

'Your wife,' Harry said. 'I asked her about Tony, and she told me. It was your daughter Tony and a local boy were fighting over that time.'

The policeman shook his head. 'They weren't fighting, it was butchery pure and simple. Poor Ole, he'd got it into his head that he and Mia were a couple because he'd fallen in love with her and was allowed to drive Mia and her friend to a dance. He wasn't a fighter, Ole, he was more the bookish kind. But he went for Tony. Who laid him out flat, drew a knife and . . . it was pretty nasty, we're not used to that sort of thing here.'

'What did he do?'

'He cut off half his tongue. Put it in his pocket and left. We arrested Tony half an hour later at his grandfather's, told him the tongue was needed at the operating theatre. Tony said he'd fed it to the crows.'

'What I wanted to ask was whether you had ever suspected Tony of rape. Then or at any other time.'

Skai spun round.

'Let me put it this way, Hole. Mia was never the same happy-go-lucky girl again. She still wanted the headcase, of course, but that's the way girls are at that age. And Ole moved away. Every time the poor kid opened his mouth round here it was a reminder for him and others of the dreadful humiliation. So, yes, I would say that Tony Leike is the violent type. But, no, I don't think he raped anyone. If so, he would have raped Mia, if I can put it like that.'

'She . . . ?'

'They were in the woods behind the dance hall. She didn't let Tony have his way. And he accepted that.'

'You're sure? Sorry I have to ask, but it's—'

The hook leapt out of the water towards them. It glinted in the first horizontal rays of the sun.

'That's fine, Hole. I'm police too, and I know what you're working on.

433

Mia's a decent girl and doesn't lie. Not even in a witness box. You can have the report if you want the details. I would just prefer it if Mia didn't have to go through all of this again.'

'That won't be necessary,' Harry said. 'Thank you.'

Harry had informed the detectives assembled in the Odin conference room that the person he had seen under the snowmobile – who had still not been found despite the increased police presence – had Tony Leike's arthritic fingers. And then recounted his theory. He leaned back and waited for reactions.

The Pelican peered over her glasses at Harry, but seemed to be addressing the whole morning gathering.

'What do you mean you think Adele was willing? She was screaming for help, for goodness' sake!'

'That was what Elias Skog thought at a later point,' Harry said. 'His first impression was that he was watching two people having consensual sex.'

'But a woman who takes a man with her to a cabin doesn't have sex with a casual interloper in the middle of the night! Do you really have to be a woman to understand that!' she hissed, and with her new, sensationally unbecoming dreadlocks she reminded Harry of a furious Medusa.

The response came from Harry's neighbour. 'Do you really think gender automatically affords you superior knowledge of the sexual preferences of half of the earth's population?' Ærdal paused and studied the freshly cleaned nail on his little finger. 'Hasn't it already been made clear that Adele Vetlesen changed partners at the drop of a hat and frequently? She agreed to have sex with a man she hardly knew at a disused factory in the middle of the night, didn't she?'

Ærdal lowered his hand, started work on the ring finger and mumbled so low that only Harry heard it. 'Anyway, I've fucked more women than you, you scrawny wader bird.'

'Women fell easily for Tony and vice versa,' Harry said. 'Tony arrived at the cabin late, Adele's boyfriend was annoyed about something and had gone to bed. He and Adele were able to flirt undisturbed. He was having trouble on the home front, and she had started to lose interest in the man she was there with. Adele and Tony fancied each other, but there were people everywhere in the cabin. So later that night they sneaked out and met by the toilet. They kissed, groped, he stood behind her, pulled down his pants and was now so excited that there was what they call in the Sexual Offences Unit "pre-ejaculatory fluid" on the tip of his penis, which went over her ski pants before he could pull them down, and they had intercourse. She was so loud in her ecstasies that she awoke Elias Skog who watched them from the window. And I believe they woke her boyfriend up as well and that he saw them from his room. I don't think she could have cared less. Tony, on the other hand, tried to stifle her cries.'

'If *she* couldn't have cared less, why would *he*?' the Pelican burst out. 'After all, it's women who are stigmatised by this kind of looseness while men's status is only enhanced. Among other men, mind you!'

'Tony Leike had at least two good motives for stifling her cries,' Harry said. 'First of all, you would hardly wish to broadcast extra-curricular bonking if you're a fiancé plastered across the tabloids, and especially not if your future father-in-law's money is about to rescue your investments in the Congo. Secondly, Tony Leike is an experienced mountaineer who knows the area well.'

'What the heck does that have to do with the case?'

A chuckle was heard, and everyone turned to the head of the table where Mikael Bellman was sitting.

'Avalanche,' he laughed. 'Tony Leike was frightened Adele's howls would set off an avalanche.'

'Tony must have known that more than three-quarters of all avalanches provoking fatalities are triggered by humans,' Harry said.

Guffaws of laughter spread around the table. Even the Pelican had to allow herself a smile.

'But what makes you think Adele's boyfriend saw them?' she asked. 'And that Adele didn't care? Perhaps she was so enthralled that she forgot herself.'

'Because,' said Harry, leaning back in the chair, 'Adele has done this before. She texted her boyfriend a picture of herself being screwed by

435

another man. A heartless message that would leave no one in any doubt. Her friends said she didn't meet the boyfriend again after the trip to Håvass.'

'Interesting,' Bellman said. 'But where does it take us?'

'To the motive,' Harry said. 'For the first time in this case we have a possible "why".'

'So we're moving away from the theory of a crazy serial killer?' Ærdal asked.

'The Snowman also had a motive,' said Beate Lønn, who had just walked in and taken a seat at the end of the table. 'Insane, but definitely a motive.'

'This is simpler,' Harry said. 'Good old-fashioned jealousy. Motive for two out of three murders in this country. And in most other countries. In this sense, we humans are quite predictable.'

'It may explain the murder of Adele Vetlesen and Tony Leike,' said the Pelican, 'but what about the others?'

'They had to be eliminated,' Harry said. 'They were all potential witnesses of the events at the cabin and could have told the police, and provided us with the motive we lacked. And maybe even worse: they had been witness to his total humiliation – he had been cheated on in public. For an unstable person that would be motive enough on its own.'

Bellman clapped his hands. 'I hope we have some answers soon. I've spoken to Krongli on the phone and he says the weather in the search area has improved, so now they can send in the dogs and use helicopters. Any reason you didn't mention why you suspected the body of being Tony Leike before, Harry?'

Harry shrugged. 'I had assumed we would reach the body much more quickly, so I saw no reason to speculate aloud. After all, arthritis is not that unusual.'

Bellman rested his gaze on Harry for a second before addressing the rest. 'We have a suspect, folks. Anyone want to christen him?'

'The Eighth Guest,' said Ærdal.

'Prince Charming,' declared the Pelican.

For a few moments there was total silence, as though something had come up that required time to digest before they went on.

'Now I'm no strategist,' Beate Lønn began, in the secure knowledge that everyone in the room knew that Beate Lønn never commented on anything she hadn't researched thoroughly first, 'but isn't there something here that makes you sit up and wonder? Leike had an alibi for the times of the murders, but what about all these leads pointing to him? What about the call from his home phone to Elias Skog? What about the murder weapon that was acquired in the Congo? Furthermore from an area where Leike had financial interests. Chance?'

'No,' Harry said. 'From day one Prince Charming has guided us towards Tony Leike. It was Prince Charming who paid Juliana Verni to go to the Congo because he knew that any clue pointing to the Congo would point to Tony Leike. And as far as his phone call to Elias Skog is concerned, today I checked something we should have checked long ago, but which we typically let go when we were getting close to a result. Because we resist any weakening of our evidence. Around the time the call went out from Leike's house to Skog there were three calls made from Leike's direct line in the Aker Brygge office block. Leike can't have been in two places at the same time. I'd bet two hundred kroner he was in Aker Brygge. Any takers?'

Silent but wide-eyed faces.

'Do you mean that Prince Charming rang Elias Skog from Leike's house?' said the Pelican. 'How . . . ?'

'When Leike came to Police HQ he told me there had been a break-in through the cellar door a few days earlier. That matches the time of the phone call to Skog. Prince Charming took a bike to disguise it as a standard burglary, innocent enough for us to make a note of it, but no more than that. Leike knows we don't do anything about that kind of break-in, so he didn't even report it. And with that Prince Charming had planted some irrefutable evidence against Leike.'

'What a snake!' the Pelican erupted.

'I buy the explanation of how,' Beate Lønn said. 'But why? Why finger Tony Leike?'

'Because he knew that sooner or later we would link the murders with the Håvass cabin,' Harry said. 'And that would limit the number of suspects in such a way that everyone who had been there that night

437

would have the spotlight on them. There were two reasons he tore out the page from the guest book. Number one, he had the names of those who were there, so that he could find them and kill them at his leisure, while we didn't and were therefore unable to stop him. Number two, and more important, he could keep his own name hidden.'

'Logical,' Ærdal said. 'And to make quite sure we didn't go after him he had to supply us with an apparent guilty party. Tony Leike.'

'And that's why he had to wait until the end to kill Tony Leike,' said one of the detectives, a man with a fertile Fridtjof Nansen moustache whose surname was all Harry could recall.

His neighbour, a young man with bright, shiny skin and eyes, none of whose names Harry could remember, interjected: 'But unfortunately for him Tony had an alibi for the times of the deaths. And since Tony's role as a scapegoat was redundant now, it was finally time to kill enemy numero uno.'

The temperature in the room had risen, and the pale tentative winter sun seemed to be brightening the proceedings. They were making progress, the knot had finally loosened. Harry could see that Bellman was sitting further forward in his chair.

'That's all well and good,' Beate Lønn said, and while Harry was waiting for the but, he clicked what she was going to ask, knew she was going to play the devil's advocate because she knew he had the answers, 'but why has Prince Charming made this so unnecessarily complicated?'

'Because humans *are* complicated,' Harry said and could hear an echo of something he had heard and forgotten. 'We want to do things that are complex, that mesh, where we control our fates and can feel like rulers of our own universes. The room that burned down at the Kadok factory – do you know what it reminded me of most? A control room. The headquarters. And it's not certain he even planned to take Leike's life. Perhaps he just wanted him arrested and convicted.'

The silence was so pervasive that they could hear a bird twittering outside.

'Why?' asked the Pelican. 'If he could have killed him? Or tortured him?'

'Because pain and death are not the worst that can befall mankind,'

Harry said, again hearing the echo. 'Humiliation is. That was what he wanted for Leike. The humiliation of having everything you possess taken from you. The fall, the shame.'

He saw a tiny smile playing on Beate Lønn's lips, saw her give a nod of acknowledgement.

'But,' he continued, 'as has been indicated, Tony had – unluckily for our killer – an alibi. And so Tony got away with the subsidiary punishment. Which was a slow and decidedly brutal death.'

In the ensuing silence Harry sensed something flutter past. The smell of roasted meat. Then the room seemed to draw breath all at once.

'So what do we do now?' asked the Pelican.

Harry looked up. The twittering bird on the branch outside the window was a chaffinch. A migratory bird which had arrived too soon. Which gave people hopes of spring, but which froze to death on the first frosty night.

Buggered if I know, Harry thought. Buggered if I know.

68

Pike

It was a long Kripos meeting that morning.

Bjørn Holm reported back on the forensic investigations at Kadok. No semen was found, nor any other physical evidence of the perpetrator. The room he had used was indeed completely burned out, and the computer had been reduced to a lump of metal, leaving no chance of recovering any data.

'He's probably been online using those unsecured networks in the area. Nydalen's full of them.'

'He must have left some electronic trails,' Ærdal said, but it sounded more like a refrain he had heard than something he could expatiate on beyond 'must have' speculation.

'Of course, we could apply to access some of the hundreds of networks up there and search for whatever it is we don't know,' Holm said. 'But I have no idea how many weeks it could take. Or whether we would find anything.'

'Leave it to me,' Harry said. He had already got up and was on his way to the door while keying in a number. 'I know someone.'

He left the door ajar, and while he was waiting for an answer he heard one of the detectives say that no one they had spoken to had seen anyone come or go at Kadok, but that was not so surprising since it was hidden behind trees and bushes and, anyway, it was so dark now, in the winter months.

Harry got an answer. 'Katrine Bratt's secretary.'

'Hello?'

'Frøken Bratt is at lunch right now.'

'Sorry, Katrine, but eating will have to wait. Listen . . .'

Katrine listened as Harry explained what he wanted.

'Prince Charming had pictures on the wall that had probably been printed off Internet news sites. With the search engine you could get onto the networks in the area, check the server logs and find out who has been on the news pages which covered the murders. Loads of people must have been—'

'Not as much as he was,' Katrine said. 'I'll just ask for a list sorted according the number of downloads.'

'Mm. You've learned this quickly.'

'It's in the name. Katrine Bratt. Bratt, steep. Steep learning curve. Get it?'

Harry went back to the others.

They were playing the message that Harry had received from Leike's mobile phone. It had been sent to NTNU, the technical university in Trondheim, for voice analysis. They had achieved useful results with sound recordings of bank robberies, in fact better than with CCTV, as the voice – even if you try to distort it – is very difficult to disguise. But Bjørn Holm had been told that a bad recording of an indeterminate sound, coughing or laughter, was worthless and could not be used to make a voice profile.

'Damn,' said Bellman, banging the table with his hand. 'With a voice profile, a foothold, we could have started eliminating possible suspects from the case.'

'Which possible suspects?' mumbled Ærdal.

'The base station signal tells us that whoever used Leike's phone was near the centre of Ustaoset when he rang,' Holm said. 'The signal faded straight afterwards – the operators' network only has coverage around the centre of Ustaoset. But the fact that the signal faded strengthens the theory that it was Prince Charming who had the phone.'

'Why's that?'

'Even when the phone's not being used the base station will pick up signals every other hour. The fact that it didn't receive any signals shows that the phone, before or after the call, was in the deserted mountain region around Ustaoset. Where perhaps it was carried during the avalanche and torture and so on.'

No reaction. Harry knew that the euphoria from earlier had evaporated. He went to his chair.

'There's one possible way we could get a foothold as Bellman suggested,' he said softly, knowing that he no longer had to work to gain attention. 'Cast your minds back to Leike's house and the break-in. Let's assume our killer broke into Leike's place to ring Elias Skog from there. And let's assume that our white-clad crime scene officers were doing such a thorough job, as it appeared when I arrived and inadvertently . . . bumped into Holm . . .' Bjørn Holm tilted his head and sent Harry a spare-me-the-jokes look. '. . . Shouldn't we already have fingerprints from Holmenveien that might well be . . . Prince Charming's?'

The sun lit up the room again. The others exchanged glances. Ashamed almost. So simple. So obvious. And none of them had thought of it . . .

'It's been a long meeting with lots of new information,' Bellman said. 'Our brains are clearly beginning to get a bit sluggish. But what do you think about this, Holm?'

Bjørn Holm slapped his forehead. 'Course we've got all the fingerprints. We did the investigation thinking Leike was the killer and his house a possible crime scene. We were hoping to find fingerprints that would match some of the victims.'

'Have you got many that were not identified?' Bellman asked.

'That's the point,' said Bjørn Holm, smiling. 'Leike had two Polish women who did the cleaning once a week. They'd been there six days before and done a thorough job. So we only found prints for Leike himself, Lene Galtung, the two Polish women and an unknown person whose prints definitely did not match those of the victims. We stopped looking for matches after Leike came up with his alibi and was released. But I don't remember off the top of my head where we found the unknown prints.'

'But *I* do,' Beate Lønn said. 'I was given the report with sketches and photographs. The prints from X1's left hand were found on top of the pompous and very ugly desk. Like so.' She stood up and leaned on her left hand. 'If I'm not much mistaken, it's where the landline is. Like so.' She used her right hand to make the international sign for a telephone, thumb to her ear and little finger to her mouth.

'Ladies and gentlemen,' Bellman said with a broad smile and a sweeping arm gesture, 'I'll be damned if we don't have a genuine lead. Carry on searching for a match to X1, Holm. But *promise* me it isn't the husband of one of the Polish women who joined them to make a few free calls home, alright?'

On the way out, the Pelican sidled up to Harry. She tossed one of her new dreads. 'You might be better than I thought, Harry. But when you advance your theories, it wouldn't hurt to intersperse the occasional "I think" here and there.' She smiled and nudged him in the hip.

Harry appreciated the smile; the nudge in the hip on the other hand . . . His phone vibrated in his pocket. He took it out. Not Rikshospital.

'He calls himself Nashville,' said Katrine Bratt.

'Like the American town?'

'Yep. He's been on the websites of all the big newspapers, read the whole caboodle about the murders. The bad news is that's all I've got for you. Nashville's only been active on the Net for a couple of months, you see, and he's searched exclusively for things related to the murders. It almost seems as if Nashville has been waiting to be investigated.'

'Sounds like our man, alright,' Harry said.

'Well,' Katrine said, 'you'll have to search for men with cowboy hats.'

'What?'

'Nashville. Mecca of country music and all that.'

Pause.

'Hello? Harry?'

'I'm here. Right. Thanks, Katrine.'

'Kisses?'

'All over.'

'No, thank you.'

They rang off.

Harry had been allocated an office with a view of Bryn and was observing some of the more unlovely details of the area when there was a knock at the door.

Beate Lønn was standing in the doorway.

'Hm, how does it feel to be in bed with the enemy?'

Harry shrugged. 'The enemy's name is Prince Charming.'

'Good. Just wanted to say we've run the fingerprints on the desk against the database and he's not on it.'

'I didn't expect him to be.'

'How's your dad?'

'Days away.'

'Sorry to hear that.'

'Thank you.'

They looked at each other. And suddenly it struck Harry that this was a face he would see at the funeral. A small pale face he had seen at other funerals, tear-stained, with large tragic eyes. A face as if made for funerals.

'What are you thinking about?' she asked.

'I know only one killer who has murdered in this way,' Harry said, turning back to the view.

'He reminds you of the Snowman, does he?'

Harry nodded slowly.

She sighed. 'I promised I wouldn't say, but Rakel rang.'

Harry stared at the blocks of flats in Helsfyr.

'She asked about you. I said you were fine. Did I do the right thing, Harry?'

Harry took a deep breath. 'Sure.'

Beate remained in the doorway for a while. Then she left.

How is she? How is Oleg? Where are they? What do they do when night falls, who looks after them, who keeps watch? Harry rested his head on his arms and covered his ears with his hands.

Only one person knows how Prince Charming thinks.

The afternoon gloom descended without warning. The Captain, the over-enthusiastic receptionist, rang to say someone had called to ask if Iska Peller, the Australian lady in *Aftenposten*, was staying there. Harry said it was probably a journalist, but the Captain thought even the lowest press vermin knew the rules of the game; they had to introduce themselves by name and state where they worked. Harry thanked him and was on the point of asking him to call back if he heard any more. Until he considered what this invitation would involve. Bellman rang to say there was a press conference; if Harry felt like taking part, then . . .

Harry declined and could hear Bellman's relief.

Harry drummed on the desk. Lifted the receiver to phone Kaja, but cradled it again.

Raised it again and rang some city centre hotels. None of them could recall being asked questions about anyone called Iska Peller.

Harry looked at his watch. He felt like a drink. He felt like going into Bellman's office, asking what the hell he had done with his opium, raising his fist and watching him cower . . .

Only one person knows.

Harry got up, kicked the chair, grabbed his woollen coat and strode out.

He drove to town and parked in a glaringly illegal spot outside the Norwegian Theatre. Crossed the street and went to the hotel reception desk.

The Captain had acquired his nickname while he was working as a doorman at the same hotel. The reason was probably a combination of the gaudy red uniform and the fact that he was continually commenting on, and issuing commands to, everyone and everything around. Furthermore, he saw himself as an intersection for anything of importance that happened in the city centre, the man with his finger on the city's pulse, the man who *knew*. The Informant with a capital I, an inestimable part of the police force's machinery keeping Oslo safe.

'Right at the very back of my brain, I can hear a rather special voice,' the Captain said, tasting his own words with an appreciative smack. Harry caught the rolling eyes of his colleague standing next to the Captain behind the reception desk.

'Sort of gay,' the Captain concluded.

'Do you mean high-pitched?' Harry asked, thinking of something Adele's friends had mentioned. Adele had said it was a turn-off the way her boyfriend spoke, like her gay flatmate.

'No, more like this.' The Captain crooked his hands, fluttered his eyelashes and peformed a parody of a loud-mouthed queen. 'I'm just sooo cross with you, Søren!'

His colleague, who, sure enough, was wearing a name tag inscribed with SØREN, giggled.

Harry thanked him and again it was on the tip of his tongue to ask the Captain to call him should anything else occur to him. He went outside. Lit a cigarette and looked up at the hotel sign. There was something . . . At that moment he spotted the Traffic Department car parked behind his and the overalled warden jotting down his registration number.

Harry crossed the street and held up his ID card. 'I'm on police business.'

'Makes no difference. No parking is no parking,' Overalls said without pausing his writing. 'Send in a complaint.'

'Well,' Harry said, 'you know we also have the authority to dish out parking fines if we want to?'

The man poked up his head and grinned. 'If you think I'm going to let you write your own fine, you're wrong, pal.'

'I was thinking more of *that* car.' Harry pointed.

'That's mine and the Traffic—'

'No parking is no parking.'

Overalls sent him a grouchy look.

Harry shrugged. 'Send in a complaint. Pal.'

Overalls slammed his notepad shut, spun on his heel and walked back to his car.

As Harry drove up Universitetsgata, his phone rang. It was Gunnar Hagen. Harry could hear the quiver of excitement in the usually controlled voice of the Crime Squad boss.

'Come here right away, Harry.'

'What's happened?'

'Just come. The culvert.'

Harry heard the voices and saw the flashes going off long before he had reached the end of the concrete corridor. Gunnar Hagen and Bjørn Holm

446

were standing by the door to his old office. A woman from Krimteknisk was brushing the door and door handle for fingerprints while a Holm lookalike was taking pictures of half a boot print in the corner.

'The print's old,' Harry said. 'It was here before we moved in. What's going on?'

The lookalike questioned Holm, who nodded that would be enough.

'One of the prison wardens discovered this on the floor by the door,' Hagen said, holding up an evidence bag containing a brown envelope. Through the transparent bag Harry read his name. Printed on an address label stuck to the envelope.

'The prison warden reckoned it had been lying here for a couple of days max. People don't go through this culvert every day, of course.'

'We're measuring the moisture in the paper,' Bjørn said. 'We've put a similar envelope here and are waiting to see how long it takes to reach the same level of moisture. Then we work backwards.'

'There you go. Shades of *CSI*,' Harry said.

'Not that the timing will help us,' Hagen said. 'There are no surveillance cameras where I assume he must have been. Which, of course, is fairly straightforward. Into a busy reception area, in the lift, down here, no locked doors before you go up into the prison.'

'No, why should we lock up here?' Harry said. 'Anyone object to me having a smoke?'

No one answered, but looks were eloquent enough. Harry shrugged.

'I suppose at some point someone is going to tell me what was in the envelope,' he said.

Bjørn Holm held up another evidence bag.

It was difficult to see the contents in the poor lighting, so Harry stepped closer.

'Oh shit,' he said and recoiled half a step.

'The middle finger,' Hagen said.

'The finger looks as if it might have been broken first,' Bjørn said. 'Clean, smooth cut, no ragged skin. Chop. An axe. Or a large knife.'

From the culvert came the resonant sound of rapid strides approaching.

Harry stared. The finger was white, drained of blood, but the tip was a bluish-black.

'What's that? Have you taken fingerprints already?'

'Yes,' Bjørn said. 'And if we're lucky the answer is on its way.'

'My guess is right hand,' Harry said.

'You're correct. 'Well observed,' Hagen said.

'Did the envelope contain anything else?'

'No. Now you know as much as we do.'

'Maybe,' Harry said, fidgeting with the cigarette packet. 'But I know something else about the finger.'

'We thought about that, too,' Hagen said, exchanging glances with Bjørn Holm. The sound of clomping steps rose. 'The middle finger of the right hand. It's the same finger the Snowman took off you.'

'I've got something here,' the female forensics officer interrupted.

The others turned to her.

She was squatting down holding an object between her thumb and first finger. It was greyish black. 'Doesn't it look like the tiny stones we found at the Borgny crime scene?'

Harry went closer. 'Yup. Lava.'

The runner was a young man with a police ID card hanging from the breast pocket of his shirt. He stopped in front of Bjørn Holm, placed his hands on his knees and gasped for breath.

'Well, Kim Erik?' Holm said.

'We found a match,' the young man panted.

'Let me guess,' Harry said, poking a cigarette between his lips.

The others turned their attention to him.

'Tony Leike.'

Kim Erik looked genuinely disappointed: 'H-how . . . ?'

'I thought I saw his right hand protruding from under the scooter, and it wasn't missing any fingers. So it must have been the left.' Harry nodded towards the evidence bag. 'The finger isn't broken, it's just distorted. Good old-fashioned arthritis. Hereditary but not contagious.'

69

Looped Writing

THE WOMAN WHO OPENED THE DOOR OF THE TERRACED HOUSE in Hovseter was as broad-shouldered as a wrestler and as tall as Harry. She gazed at him and waited patiently, as if in the habit of giving people the necessary seconds to state their business.

'Yes?'

Harry recognised Frida Larsen's voice from the telephone. Which had made him visualise a slender, petite woman.

'Harry Hole,' he said. 'I found your address through the phone number. Is Felix in?'

'Out playing chess,' she intoned flatly; a standard response, it seemed. 'Email him.'

'I would like to talk to him.'

'What about?' She filled the doorway in a manner that prevented prying. And not only through the size of her.

'We found a fragment of lava down at the police station. I was wondering if it was from the same volcano as the previous sample we sent him.'

Harry stood two steps below her, holding the little stone. But she didn't budge from the threshold.

'Impossible to see,' she said. 'Email Felix.' She made a move to close the door.

'I suppose lava is lava, is it?' Harry said.

She hesitated. Harry waited. He knew from experience that experts can never resist correcting laymen.

'Each volcano has its own unique lava composition,' she said. 'But it also varies from eruption to eruption. You have to analyse the stone. The iron ore content can tell you a lot.' Her face was expressionless, her eyes uninterested.

'What I would really like,' Harry said, 'is to enquire about these people who travel round the world studying volcanoes. There can't be that many of them, so I was wondering if Felix had an overview of the Norwegian contingent.'

'There are more of us than you imagine,' she said.

'So you're one of them?'

She shrugged.

'What's the last volcano you two were on?'

'Ol Doinyo Lengai in Tanzania. And we weren't on it, but nearby. It was erupting. Magmatic natrocarbonites. The lava that emerges is black, but it reacts with air and after a few hours it's completely white. Like snow.'

Her voice and face were suddenly alive.

'Why doesn't he want to speak?' Harry asked. 'Is your brother mute?'

Her face went rigid again. The voice was flat and dead. 'Email.'

The door was slammed so hard Harry got dust in his eyes.

Kaja parked in Maridalsveien, jumped over the crash barrier and trod carefully down the steep slope to the wood where the Kadok factory was situated. She switched on her torch and tramped through the shrubs, brushed away bare branches that wanted to thrust themselves into her face. The growth was dense, shadows leapt around like silent wolves and even when she stopped, listened and watched, shadows of trees fell upon trees, so that you didn't know what was what, like in a labyrinth of mirrors. But she wasn't frightened. It was an oddity that she who was so frightened of closed doors was not frightened of the dark. She listened to the roar of the river. Had she heard anything? A sound that ought not to be there? She went on. Ducked under a wind-blown tree trunk and stopped again. But the other sounds stopped the second she stopped. Kaja took a deep breath and finished her line of thought: as if someone who didn't want to be seen was following her.

She turned and shone the light behind her. Was no longer so sure about not being scared of the dark. Some branches swayed in the light, but they must be the ones she had disturbed, mustn't they?

She faced forward again.

And screamed when her torch lit up a deathly pale face with enlarged eyes. She dropped the torch and backed away, but the figure followed her with a grunting noise reminiscent of laughter. In the dark she could make out the figure bending down, standing up, then the next moment the blinding light from her torch was shining in her face.

She held her breath.

The grunted laughter stopped.

'Here,' rasped a man's voice and the light jumped.

'Here?'

'Your torch,' the voice said.

Kaja took it and shone the torch to the side of him. So that she could see him without blinding him. He had blond hair and a prognathous jaw.

'Who are you?' she asked.

'Truls Berntsen. I work with Mikael.'

She had heard of Truls Berntsen, of course. The shadow. Beavis – wasn't that what Mikael called him?'

'I'm—'

'Kaja Solness.'

'Right, how do you . . . ?' She swallowed, reformulated the question. 'What are you doing here?'

'Same as you,' he answered with a single-toned rasp.

'Right. And what am I doing here?'

He laughed his grunt-laugh. But didn't reply. Stood right in front of her with his arms hanging down and away from his sides. One eyelid twitched as if an insect were trapped beneath it.

Kaja sighed. 'If you're doing the same as me, you're here to keep an eye on the factory,' she said. 'In case he might reappear.'

'Yes, in case he might reappear,' said the Beavis type without taking his eyes off her.

'It's not so unlikely, is it?' she said. 'He may not know it's burned down.'

'My father worked there,' Beavis said. 'He used to say he made PSG, coughed PSG and became PSG.'

'Are there a lot of Kripos people in the area? Did Mikael give you orders to come here?'

'You don't meet him any more, do you? You meet Harry Hole.'

Kaja felt a chill in her stomach. How on earth did this man know that? Had Mikael really told people about them?

'You weren't at Håvass,' she said to change the topic.

'Wasn't I?' Grunted laughter. 'I suppose I was free. Time off. Jussi was there.'

'Yes,' she said quietly. 'He was there.'

A gust of wind swept in, and she twisted her head to prevent a branch scratching her face. Had he been following her or had he been here before she arrived?

When she turned to ask him, he wasn't there. She shone her torch between the trees. He was gone.

It was two in the morning when she parked in the street, went through the gate and up the steps to the yellow house. She pressed the button over the painted ceramic tile bearing the words 'fam. Hole' in ornate looped writing.

After ringing for the third time she heard a low cough and turned to see Harry returning a service revolver to the lining of his trousers. He must have crept around the corner of the house without making any noise.

'What's up?' she asked, terrified.

'Just being extra careful. You should have phoned and said you were coming.'

'Sh-shouldn't I have come?'

Harry went up the steps past her and unlocked the door. She followed him in, put her arms around him from behind, clung to his back and kicked the door shut with her heel. He freed himself, turned, was about to say something, but she stopped him with a kiss. A greedy kiss that demanded reciprocity. She put her cold hands up his shirt, felt from the glowing hot skin that he had come straight from bed, removed the revolver from his trousers and banged it down on the hall table.

'I want you,' she whispered, bit his ear and pushed her hand down his trousers. His dick was warm and soft.

'Kaja . . .'

'Can I have you?'

She thought she could discern a slight hesitation, a certain reluctance. She wrapped her other hand around his neck, looked into his eyes. 'Please . . .'

He smiled. Then his muscles relaxed. And he kissed her. Cautiously. More cautiously than she wanted. She groaned with frustration, undid his trouser buttons. Held his dick firmly without moving her hand, felt it grow.

'Fuck you,' he sighed and lifted her. Carried her up the stairs. Kicked open the bedroom door and laid her on the bed. On his mother's side. She tilted back her head, closed her eyes, felt her clothes being removed, quickly, efficiently. Felt the heat radiating from his skin the moment he lowered himself onto her and forced her legs apart. Yes, she thought. Fuck me.

She lay with her cheek and ear against his chest, listening to his heart-beat.

'What were you thinking,' she whispered, 'when you were lying there knowing you were going to die?'

'That I was going to live,' Harry said.

'Just that?'

'Just that.'

'Not that you were going to . . . meet those you loved?'

'No.'

'I did. It was strange. I was so frightened that something special was going to pieces. And then the horror passed and instead I was filled with peace. I just slept. And then you came. And woke me up. Rescued me.'

Harry passed her his cigarette and she took a drag, then sniggered.

'You're a hero, Harry. The type they give medals. Who would have thought that of you, eh?'

Harry shook his head. 'Believe me, sweetheart, I was thinking only of myself. I didn't spare you a thought until I reached the fireplace.'

'Maybe not, but when you got there you still had very little air. By digging me out you knew we would use up the air twice as quickly.'

'What can I say? I'm a generous guy.'

She slapped his chest with a laugh. 'A hero!'

Harry inhaled hard. 'Or perhaps it was survival instinct outmanoeuvring conscience.'

'What do you mean?'

'The person I found first was so strong he almost managed to keep the pole. So I guessed it had to be Kolkka and that he was alive. I knew it was a question of seconds and minutes, but instead of digging him out I prodded the snow to find you. You were quite still. I thought you were dead.'

'So?'

'So maybe I was thinking deep down that if I dug out the dead one first the one who was alive might die in the meantime. In that way I could have all the air to myself. It's hard to know what governs your actions.'

She went quiet. Outside, the snarl of a motorbike rose and fell. A motorbike in March. And today she had seen a migratory bird. Everything was out of balance.

'Do you always brood so much?' she asked.

'No. Maybe. I don't know.'

She wriggled closer to him. 'What are you brooding about now?'

'How he can know what he knows.'

She sighed. 'Our killer?'

'And why he's playing with me. Why he sends me a bit of Tony Leike. How he thinks.'

'And how are you going to find out?'

454

He stubbed out the cigarette on the bedside table. Took a deep breath and released it in a long hiss. 'That's the point. I can only think of one way. I have to talk to him.'

'Him? Prince Charming?'

'Someone *like* him.'

The dream came on the threshold of sleep. He was staring up at a nail. It was sticking out of a man's head. But there was something familiar about the face tonight. A familiar portrait, one he had seen so many times. Seen recently. The foreign object in Harry's mouth exploded and he twitched. He was asleep.

70

Blind Spot

HARRY WALKED ALONG THE HOSPITAL CORRIDOR WITH A prison warder dressed in civilian clothing. Two strides in front was the doctor. She had informed Harry of his condition, prepared him for what he should expect.

They came to a door and the warder unlocked it. Inside, the corridor continued for a few metres. There were three doors in the wall to the left. A uniformed prison warder stood in front of one of them.

'Is he awake?' asked the doctor while the warder searched Harry. The officer nodded, put all the contents of Harry's pockets on the table, unlocked the door and stepped aside.

The doctor signalled that Harry should wait a moment and entered with the warder. She came back out immediately.

'Fifteen minutes maximum,' she said. 'He's doing better, but he's weak.'

Harry nodded. Took a deep breath. And stepped inside.

He stopped by the door and heard it close behind him. The curtains were drawn, and the room was dark apart from a lamp by the bed. The light fell on a figure sitting semi-upright against a pillow, head bowed and long hair hanging down on each side.

'Come closer, Harry.' The voice had changed; it sounded like the lament of unoiled door hinges. But Harry recognised it, and his blood ran cold.

He approached the bed and sat on the chair that had been provided. The man raised his head. And Harry stopped breathing.

He looked as if someone had poured hot wax over his face. Which had stiffened into a mask that was too tight, pulling the forehead and the chin back and turning the mouth into a small, lipless gap in a lumpy landscape of bony tissue. The laughter was two short blasts of air.

'Don't you recognise me, Harry?'

'I recognise the eyes,' Harry said. 'That'll do. It's you.'

'Anything new from . . .' The small carp-like mouth seemed to be forming a smile. '. . . our Rakel?'

Harry had prepared himself for this, braced himself the way a boxer braces himself for pain. Nonetheless, the sound of her name in his mouth made him clench his fists.

'You agreed to talk to me about a man. A man we think is like you.'

'Like me? Better-looking, I trust.' Again two short blasts. 'It's bizarre, Harry. I've never been a vain man; I thought the pain would be the worst aspect of this illness. But do you know what? It's the deterioration. It's seeing yourself in the mirror, seeing the monster emerge. They still let me go to the toilet alone, but I avoid the mirrors. I was a good-looking man, you know.'

'Have you read the things I sent you?'

'I had a quick skim. Dr Dyregod's of the opinion I shouldn't wear myself out. Infections. Inflammations. Fever. She's genuinely concerned about my health, Harry. Quite astonishing when you consider what I've done, eh? Personally I'm more interested in dying. That's precisely where I envy those I . . . but you put a stop to that, didn't you, Harry?'

'Death would have been too kind a punishment.'

Something seemed to ignite in the sick man's eyes and appeared as a cold white light from the slits in his face.

'At least I have a name and a place in the annals of history. People will read about the Snowman. Someone will inherit the mantle and act out my ideas in life. What have you got, Harry? Nothing. Quite the contrary, you've lost the little you had.'

'True,' Harry said. 'You won.'

'Do you miss your middle finger?'

'Well, I'm missing it right now.' Harry raised his head and met the other's gaze. Held it. Then the small carp mouth opened. The laughter sounded like a gun with a silencer.

'At least you haven't lost your sense of humour, Harry. You know I'm going to demand something in return, don't you?'

'No cure, no pay. But go ahead.'

The man twisted with some difficulty to the bedside table, lifted the glass of water standing there and put it to his mouth. Harry stared at the hand holding the glass. It resembled a white bird's claw. After finishing, the man carefully put the glass back and spoke. The lament was fainter now, like a radio on low batteries.

'I believe there is something in the prison manual about high suicide risks. At any rate, they watch me like hawks. They searched you before you came in, didn't they? Afraid you would bring me a knife or something similar. But I don't want to see any further deterioration, Harry. It's enough now, don't you think?'

'No,' Harry said. 'I don't think so. Talk about something else.'

'You could have lied and said yes.'

'Would you prefer that?'

The man waved a hand dismissively. 'I'd like to see Rakel.'

Harry raised an eyebrow. 'Why's that?'

'I'd just like to say something to her.'

'What?'

'That is a matter between her and me.'

The chair scraped as Harry stood up. 'It won't happen.'

'Wait. Take a seat.'

Harry took a seat.

The man looked down and tugged at the bedcover. 'Don't misunderstand me. I have no regrets about the others. They were whores. But Rakel was different. She was . . . different. I just wanted to say that.'

Harry studied him, dumbfounded.

'So what do you think?' the Snowman said. 'Say yes. Lie if you have to.'

'Yes,' Harry lied.

'You're a bad liar, Harry. I want to talk to her before I help you.'

'Out of the question.'

'Why should I trust you?'

'Because you have no choice. Because thieves trust thieves when they have to.'

'Do they?'

Harry forced a thin smile. 'When I bought opium in Hong Kong, for a while we used a disabled toilet in The Landmark shopping complex, Des Voeux Road. I went in first, put a baby's bottle under the cistern lid in the cubicle on the far right. Went for a walk, looked at fake watches, returned and my bottle was still there. Always with the right quantity of opium in. Blind faith.'

'You said you used the toilet "for a while".'

Harry shrugged. 'One day the bottle went missing. Perhaps the dealer cheated me, perhaps someone had seen us and made off with the money or the goods. There are no guarantees.'

The Snowman eyed Harry thoughtfully.

Harry walked down the corridor with the doctor. The warder went first.

'That didn't take long,' she said.

'He kept it brief,' Harry said.

Harry strolled through the reception area, out to the car park, unlocked his car. Watched his hand tremble as he put the key in the ignition. The back of his shirt was drenched with sweat as he leaned against the seat.

He had kept it brief.

'Let's assume he's like me, Harry. After all, that assumption is vital if I am to be able to help you. Motive first. Hatred. A red-hot, burning hatred. This is the stuff of survival, it's the magma inside that keeps him warm. And, just like magma, hatred is a precondition of life, so that everything doesn't freeze to ice. At the same time the pressure from the internal heat will inevitably lead to an eruption, the destructive element will be released. And the longer it goes without an eruption, the more violent it will be. Now the eruption is in full flow, and it is violent. Which tells me you will have to search way back in time for the cause. Because it is not the actions committed out of hatred, but the cause of the hatred that will solve this riddle for you. The actions will make no sense without the cause. Hatred takes time to build up, but the cause is simple. Something happened. It's all about this one thing that happened. Find out what it is and you've got him.'

459

Of all the metaphors, what had made him use a volcano? Harry drove down the steep, winding road from Bærum Hospital.

'Eight murders. He's the king now, at the top. He's built a universe in which everything appears to obey him. He's the puppet master, and he's playing with you all. And especially with you, Harry. It's hard to see why you should have been appointed – perhaps it's a matter of chance. Gradually, though, as he controls his puppets, he will look for more thrills. He will talk to the puppets, be close to them, enjoy his triumphs where he can enjoy them most, together with those over whom he triumphs. But he's well disguised. He doesn't stand out like a puppet master, he may even seem subservient, someone who is easily led, someone who is underrated, someone you would never imagine could direct such a complex drama.'

Harry was heading for the city centre on the E18. There was a jam. He shifted into the public transport lane. He was a policeman, for Christ's sake. And this was urgent, urgent, urgent. His mouth was dry, the dogs were in full cry.

'He's close to you, Harry, of that I'm pretty certain, he simply can't let go. But he's closed in on you from a blind spot. Stolen into your life in some way and inspired trust at a time when you had your attention focused elsewhere. Or when you were weak. He's at home where he is. A neighbour, a friend, a colleague. Or someone who's simply there, right behind another person who is clearer to you, a shadow you don't even think about, other than as an appendix to this first person. Think about those who have crossed your field of vision. Because he has been there. You know his face already. He may not have exchanged many words with you, but if he's like me, he hasn't been able to restrain himself, Harry. He's *cosied up to you*.'

Harry parked outside the Savoy and went to the bar.

'What can I get you?'

Harry let his eyes wander along the bottles on the glass shelves behind the barman.

Beefeater, Johnnie Walker, Bristol Cream, Absolut, Jim Beam.

He was searching for a man with a burning hatred. Someone who didn't let his emotions stray. Someone with an armoured heart.

His wandering eyes came to a halt. And jumped back. His mouth fell open. It was like a divine flash. And *everything*, everything was in that flash.

The voice came from a distance.

'Sir? Excuse me, sir?'

'Yes.'

'Made a decision?'

Harry nodded slowly.

'Yes,' he said. 'Yes, I've made a decision.'

71

Bliss

Gunnar Hagen was rolling a pencil between his forefingers and observing Harry, who for once was sitting – and not lying – in the chair in front of his desk.

'Technically, for the time being, you are employed by Kripos and thereby part of Bellman's team,' the Crime Squad boss said. 'Ergo, an arrest by you would be a home win for Bellman.'

'And if I – all this is still perfectly hypothetical – informed you and left the arrest to someone at Crime Squad, say, Kaja Solness or Magnus Skarre?'

'I would be forced to refuse such a generous offer even from you, Harry. As I said, I am bound by agreements.'

'Mm. Bellman's still got a hold on you?'

Hagen sighed. 'If I were to work a dodge like taking an arrest off Bellman in Norway's biggest murder case, the Ministry of Justice would want to know everything straight away. If I were to defy them and bring you back here to investigate this case, that would be regarded as disobeying orders. And it would hit the whole unit. Sorry, Harry, but I can't.'

Harry mused, staring into middle distance. 'OK, boss.' He jumped up from the chair and strode to the door.

'Wait!'

Harry waited.

'Why are you asking me about this now, Harry? Has something happened that I ought to know about?'

Harry shook his head. 'Just testing a few hypotheses, boss. That's our job, isn't it?'

Harry spent the hours until three o'clock making phone calls. The last one was to Bjørn Holm, who agreed to drive without a second thought.

'I haven't told you where or why,' Harry said.

'No need,' said Bjørn and continued, stressing every word. 'I-trust-you.'

A pause arose.

'Guess I deserved that,' Harry said.

'Yes,' said Bjørn.

'I have a feeling I apologised, but did I?'

'No.'

'I didn't? OK. Mm . . . Mm . . . Mm. Christ, this is hard. Mm . . . Mm . . .'

'Sounds like you've got a slow starter there, buddy boy,' Bjørn said, but Harry could hear he was smiling.

'Sorry,' Harry said. 'I hope I have some fingerprints for you to check before we leave. If they don't match, you won't have to drive, if you get my drift.'

'Why so secretive?'

'Because you trust me.'

It was half past three when Harry knocked on the door to the small duty room at Rikshospital.

Sigurd Altman opened.

'Hi, could you take a look at these?'

He passed the nurse a small pile of photographs.

'They're sticky,' Altman said.

'They've come straight from the darkroom.'

'Hm. A severed finger. What's that about?'

'I suspect the owner has been given a hefty dose of ketanome. I was wondering if you as an anaesthetics expert can say whether we will be able to find any traces of the drug in the finger.'

'Yes, no doubt, it circulates through the whole body with the blood.'

463

Altman flicked through the photographs. 'The finger looks pretty drained of blood, but in theory one drop is enough.'

'Then the next question is whether you can assist us with an arrest tonight?'

'Me? Haven't you got pathologists who—?'

'You know more than they do about this. And I need someone I can trust.'

Altman shrugged, looked at his watch and passed the photographs back. 'I'm off duty in two hours, so . . .'

'Great. We'll pick you up. You're going to be part of Norwegian crime history, Altman.'

The nurse gave a wan smile.

Mikael Bellman rang as Harry was on his way to Krimteknisk.

'Where've you been, Harry? Missed you at the morning meeting.'

'Round and about.'

'Round what?'

'Our wonderful city,' Harry said, dropping an A4 envelope on the bench in front of Kim Erik Lokker and pointing to his own fingertips to show him he wanted the contents checked for prints.

'I get nervous when you're not even on the radar for a whole day, Harry.'

'Don't you trust me, Mi-ka-el? Afraid I'll end up on the booze?'

The other end went quiet.

'You report to me, and I would like to be kept informed, that's all.'

'Reporting in to say there's nothing to report, boss.'

Harry rang off and went in to see Bjørn. Beate was already sitting in his office waiting.

'What did you want to tell us?' she asked.

'A real cops and robbers story,' Harry said, taking a seat.

He was halfway through his narrative when Lokker stuck his head round the door.

'I've found these,' he said, holding up a fingerprint transparency.

'Thanks,' said Bjørn, sitting by the computer and taking the transparency. He put it on his scanner, brought up the file of the prints they had found in Holmenveien and started the matching program.

Harry was aware it would take only a couple of seconds, but he closed his eyes, felt his heart throbbing even though he knew – he knew. The Snowman knew. And had told Harry the little he had needed, formulated the words, made the sound wave that would trigger the avalanche.

This was how it had to be.

It should only take a couple of seconds.

His heart was thumping.

Bjørn Holm cleared his throat. But said nothing.

'Bjørn,' Harry said, still with his eyes pinched shut.

'Yes, Harry.'

'Is this one of those dramatic pauses you want me to savour?'

'Yes.'

'Is it over now, you bloody sod?'

'Yes. And we have a match.'

Harry opened his eyes. Sunlight. Flooding into the room, filling it so that they could veritably swim out on it. Bliss. Fucking bliss.

The three of them stood up at the same time. Staring at each other with open mouths forming mute roars of delight. Then they embraced each other in a clumsy group hug with Bjørn on the outside and little Beate squashed flat. They continued with muffled shouts, cautious high fives, and Bjørn Holm concluded with what Harry considered above and beyond any normal demands of a Hank Williams fan, a flawless moonwalk.

72

Boy

THE TWO MEN STOOD ON A LITTLE GRASSY KNOLL – EXCEPT that there was no grass – between Manglerud church and the motorway.

'We used to call it an earth hookah or an earth bong,' said the man in the leather biker jacket, tossing the long, thin strands of hair to the side. 'In the summer we lay here smoking all the stuff we had. Fifty metres from Manglerud police station.' He smirked. 'There was me, Ulla, TV, his woman, plus a few others. Those were the days.'

The man's eyes glazed over as Roger Gjendem made notes.

It had not been easy to find Julle, but in the end Roger had tracked him down to a bikers' club in Alnabru where it turned out he ate, slept and lived his life as a free man; he moved no further afield than the supermarket to buy snus and bread. Gjendem had seen it before, how prison made people dependent on familiar surroundings, routine, security. Though, strangely enough, Julle had agreed quite willingly to talk about the past. The operative word had been Bellman.

'Ulla was my woman and it was so bloody good because everyone round Manglerud was in love with Ulla.' Julle nodded as if agreeing with himself. 'But no one was so insanely jealous as him.'

'Mikael Bellman?'

Julle shook his head. 'The other one. The shadow. Beavis.'

'What happened?'

Julle opened his palms. Roger had noticed the scabs. A jailbird migrating between dope in prison and dope outside. 'Mikael Bellman grassed me up over nicking some petrol; I already had a suspended sentence for hash, and so had to do time. I heard rumours that Bellman and Ulla had been seen together. Anyhow, when I got out and went to pick her up, the Beavis guy was waiting for me. Almost killed me. Said Ulla belonged to him. And Mikael. Not to me, at any rate. And if I ever showed my face near . . .' Julle ran his forefinger across a lean neck with grey stubble. 'Pretty insane. And bloody scary. No one in the sodding gang believed me when I told them the Beavis guy had been *so* close to doing me in. The slavering idiot just trotted after Bellman.'

'You mentioned something about quantities of heroin,' Roger said. When he interviewed people in drugs cases he always made sure he used precise terminology that could not be misunderstood, as the slang expressions changed quickly and meant different things in different places. For example, smack might mean cocaine in Hovseter, heroin in Hellerud and anything that got you high in Abildsø.

'Me, Ulla, TV and his woman were on a bike tour in Europe the summer I went to the slammer. We took half a kilo of boy with us from Copenhagen. Bikers like me and TV were checked at every single border crossing, but we sent the girls over separately. Jesus, they looked good, wearing summer dresses, with blue eyes and a quarter of a kilo up their cunts. We sold most to a dealer down in Tveita.'

'You're very open,' Roger said while taking notes, putting brackets round 'cunts' for later rewording and adding 'boy' to a long list of synonyms for heroin.

'Time's lapsed, so they can't arrest anyone for it now. The point is that the dealer in Tveita was arrested. And was offered a reduced sentence if he grassed on the suppliers. Which, of course, he did, the scumbag.'

'How do you know?'

'Hah! The guy told me a few years later when we were doing time together in Ullersmo. He'd given the names and addresses of all fucking four of us, including Ulla. All that was missing was our national identity numbers. We were so bloody lucky that the case was shelved.'

Roger made feverish notes.

'And guess who had the case at the Stovner cop shop? Guess who questioned the guy? Who in all probability recommended the case should be dropped, thrown out, shelved? Who saved Ulla's skin?'

'I'd like you to say, Julle.'

'Very happy to. It was the cunt thief himself. Mikael Bellman.'

'One last question,' Roger said, knowing he had arrived at a critical point. Could the story be proved? Could the source be checked? 'Have you got the name of the dealer? I mean, he's not risking anything and his name won't be mentioned anyway.'

'Would I grass him up, you mean?' Julle laughed out loud. 'You bet your ass I will.'

He spelt the name, and Roger turned a page and wrote it in capital letters while noticing that his jaw was broadening. Into a smile. He controlled himself and put on a straight face. But he knew the taste was going to be there for a long time: the sweet taste of a scoop.

'Thank you for your help,' Roger said.

'Thank *you*,' said Julle. 'Just make sure you crush that Bellman, then we're even.'

'Er, by the way, out of curiosity, why do you think the dealer told you he had informed on you?'

'Because he was frightened.'

'Frightened? Why?'

'Because he knew too much. He wanted others to know the story in case the cop carried out his threat.'

'Bellman *threatened* the informer?'

'Not Bellman. His shadow. He said if the guy so much as mentioned Ulla's name again he would put something in him that would shut him up. For ever.'

73

Arrest

Bjørn Holm's Volvo Amazon turned into Rikshospital, opposite the tram stop. Sigurd Altman stood waiting with his hands in his duffel coat pockets. Harry beckoned him from the back seat. Sigurd and Bjørn said hello, and they drove onto Ringveien where they continued eastwards towards the Sinsen intersection.

Harry leaned forward between the seats.

'It was like one of the chemistry experiments we did at school. In fact, you have all the ingredients you need to get a reaction, but you don't have the catalyst, the external component, the spark that's necessary to trigger it. I had the information, all I needed was something to help me assemble it in the correct fashion. My catalyst was a sick man, a murderer known as the Snowman. And a bottle on a bar shelf. Alright if I have a smoke?'

Silence.

'I see. Well . . .'

They drove through the tunnel at Bryn, up towards the Ryen intersection and Manglerud.

Truls Berntsen stood on the old undeveloped site, looking up the slope, up to Bellman's house.

How peculiar it was that he who had so often eaten dinner, played and slept there when they were growing up had not been there a single time since Mikael and Ulla took over the house.

The reason was obvious: he had not been invited.

He sometimes stood where he was now, in the afternoon dusk, looking up at the house to catch a glimpse of her. Her, the unattainable one no one could have. No one except him, the prince, Mikael. Now and then he wondered whether Mikael knew. Knew and that was why they didn't invite him. Or was she the one who knew? And made it clear to Mikael, without saying as much, that this Beavis he had grown up with was not someone they needed to associate with privately. At least not now his career had finally taken off, and it was more important to move in the right circles, meet the right people, send out the right signals. It wasn't tactically astute to surround yourself with ghosts from a past that contained things best forgotten.

Oh, he knew that. He just didn't know why she couldn't understand it: that he would never hurt her. The opposite. Had he not protected her and Mikael all these years? Yes, he had. He kept watch, was there for them, cleared up. Ministered to their happiness. Such was his love.

The windows up there this evening were lit. Were they having a party? Were they eating and laughing, drinking wines the Manglerud Vinmonopol had never stocked and speaking in the new way? Was she smiling and were her eyes sparkling, eyes that were so beautiful it hurt when they looked at you? Would she see more in him if he acquired money, became rich? Was that a possibility? So simple?

He stood for a while at the bottom of the explosion-riddled building site. Then he lumbered home.

Bjørn Holm's Amazon tilted majestically around the Ryen roundabout.

A sign showed the exit for Manglerud.

'Where are we going?' Sigurd Altman asked, leaning against the door.

'We're going where the Snowman said we should go,' Harry said. 'Way back in time.'

They passed the exit.

'Here,' Harry said, and Bjørn bore right.

'The E6?'

'Yep, we're going east. To Lyseren. Know these parts, Sigurd?'

'Well enough, but—'

'This is where the story starts,' Harry said. 'Many years ago, outside a dance hall. Tony Leike, the man who owned the finger I showed you photos of before, is standing at the edge of the wood, kissing Mia, County Officer Skai's daughter. Ole, who's in love with Mia, goes out to look for Mia and bumps into them. Ole, devastated and angry, throws himself on the interloper, the charmer Tony. But now another side of Tony reveals itself. Gone is the smiling, charming flirt everyone likes. To be replaced by a beast. And like all animals that feel threatened he attacks, with a fury and brutality that numb Ole, Mia and subsequent onlookers. The blood mist has descended, he takes out a knife and cuts off half of Ole's tongue before he is dragged away. And even though Ole is innocent in this matter, he is the one who is afflicted by shame. The shame of his unrequited love exhibited in front of others, humiliation in rural Norway's ritual mating duel and his stunted speech as eternal evidence of his defeat. So he flees. Flees. Are you with me so far?'

Altman nodded.

'Many years pass. Ole has established himself somewhere new, has a job where he is well liked and respected for his abilities. He has friends, not many, but enough; all that counts is that they don't know his past. What's missing in his life is a woman. He has met some, via dating websites, personal ads, on the odd occasion at a restaurant. But they soon evaporate. Not because of his tongue, but because he carries the defeat with him like a rucksack full of shit. Because of ingrained self-denigrating modes of speech, anticipations of rejection and suspicion of women who behave as if they actually *do* want him. The usual stuff. The stench of defeat that everyone flees. Then one day something happens. He meets a woman who has done the rounds. She even lets him live out his sexual fantasies; they have sex in a disused factory. He invites her on a skiing trip in the mountains, as a first sign he means business. Her name is Adele Vetlesen, and she joins him with some reluctance.'

Bjørn Holm turned off by Grønmo where the smoke from incinerated refuse rose into the air.

'They have a great skiing trip in the mountains. Maybe. Or maybe Adele is bored, she's a restless soul. They go to a cabin in Håvass where

471

there are already five people. Marit Olsen, Elias Skog, Borgny Stem-Myhre, Charlotte Lolles and a sick Iska Peller who is sleeping off her fever in a room alone. After dinner they light the fire and someone opens a bottle of red wine while others go to bed. Like Charlotte Lolles. And Ole who is lying in a sleeping bag in the bedroom waiting for his Adele. But Adele would rather be up. Perhaps at last she has begun to notice the stench. Then something happens. One last person arrives late at night. The walls are thin and Ole hears a new man's voice from the sitting room. He stiffens. It's the voice from his worst nightmare, from his sweetest dreams of revenge. But it can't be him, it *can't* be. Ole listens. The voice talks to Marit Olsen. For a while. Then it talks to Adele. He hears her laughing. But gradually they lower their voices. He hears the others go to bed in adjoining rooms. But not Adele. And not this man with the familiar voice. Then he hears nothing. Until the sounds outside reach his ears. He creeps over to the window, looks out, sees them, sees her eager face, recognises her moans of pleasure. And he knows the impossible is happening; history is repeating itself. For he recognises the man standing behind Adele, who is taking her. It's him. It's Tony Leike.'

Bjørn Holm turned up the heating. Harry pushed himself back in the seat.

'When the others get up the following morning, Tony has left. Ole acts as if nothing has happened. Because he is stronger now; many years of hatred have hardened him. He knows the others have seen Adele and Tony, they have seen his humiliation, just like before. But he is calm. He knows what he is going to do. He might have been longing for it, this last nudge, the free fall. A couple of days later he has a plan ready. He returns to the Håvass cabin, maybe gets a lift there on a snowmobile, and tears out the page in the guest book detailing their names. For this time it won't be him who flees the witnesses in shame; they are the ones who are going to suffer. And Adele. But the person who will suffer most is Tony. He will have to carry all the shame Ole has carried; his name will be dragged through the mud; his life will be destroyed; he will be smitten by the same unjust God who allows tongues of the lovelorn to be severed.'

Sigurd Altman rolled down the window and a soft whistling sound filled the car.

'The first thing Ole has to do is find himself a room, a headquarters where he can work undisturbed and without fear of being discovered. And what could be more natural than the disused factory where he experienced the happiest night of his life? There he starts gathering information about his victims and planning in detail. Of course, he has to kill Adele Vetlesen first as she was the only person at Håvass to know his full identity. Names that may have been exchanged up there would have been forgotten soon enough and no copy of the guest book page existed. Sure about the cigarette, boys?'

No answer. Harry sighed.

'So he arranges to meet her again. He picks her up in a car. Which he has covered internally with plastic. They drive to an undisturbed spot, probably the Kadok factory. There he takes out a large knife with a yellow handle. He forces her to write a postcard he dictates and to address it to her flatmate in Drammen. Afterwards he kills her. Bjørn?'

Bjørn Holm coughed and changed down a gear. 'The autopsy shows he punctured her carotid artery.'

'He gets out of the car. Takes a picture of her sitting in the passenger seat with a knife in the neck. The photograph. Confirmation of revenge, of triumph. It's the first photo that goes on his office wall in the Kadok factory.'

An oncoming car swerved out of its lane, but went back in and hooted its horn as it passed.

'Perhaps it was easy to kill her. Perhaps not. Nevertheless, he knows she is the most critical victim. They hadn't met very often, but he can't know for sure how much she has told her friends about him. He only knows that if she is found dead and her death can be linked to him, a dumped lover will be the police's main suspect. *If* she is found. If, on the other hand, she apparently disappears, for example during a trip to Africa, he is safe.

'So Ole sinks her body in a place he knows well, where the water is deep and what's more where people keep well away. The place with the jilted bride in the window. The ropery by Lake Lyseren. Then he travels to Leipzig and pays the prostitute, Juliana Verni, to take the postcard Adele wrote with her to Rwanda, to stay at a hotel under Adele's name and send the card to Norway. Furthermore, she has to bring Ole something back from the Congo. A murder weapon. A Leopold's apple. The special weapon is not plucked out of the air, of course, it has to have some connection with the Congo and prompt the police to become suspicious about the Congo traveller, Tony Leike. Ole pays Juliana on her return to Leipzig. And perhaps it is there, standing over the trembling Juliana, in tears as she opens her mouth to receive the apple, that he begins to experience the joy, the ecstasy of sadism, an almost sexual pleasure he has developed and nourished for years with his lonely daydreams of revenge. Afterwards he dumps her in the river, but the body surfaces and is found.'

Harry took a deep breath. The road had become narrower, and the forest had slunk in, was dense on both sides now.

'In the course of the next weeks he kills Borgny Stem-Myhre and Charlotte Lolles. Unlike with Adele and Juliana he doesn't try to hide their bodies, quite the contrary. Nevertheless, the police investigation does not lead them to Tony Leike, as Ole has hoped. So he has to continue killing, continue to leave a trail, to push them. He kills Marit Olsen, the MP, exhibits her in Frogner Lido. Now the police have to see the connection between the women, have to find the man with the Leopold's apple. But it doesn't happen. And he knows he will have to intervene, give a helping hand, take a risk. He watches Tony's house in Holmenveien until he sees him leave. Then he breaks in through the cellar, goes up to the living room and calls the next victim, Elias Skog, from Tony's phone on the desk. On the way out he steals a bike to make the break-in appear normal. Leaving fingerprints upstairs in the living room doesn't bother Ole; everyone knows the police don't investigate run-of-the-mill burglaries. Then he goes to Stavanger. At this point his sadism is in full bloom. He kills Elias by glueing him to the bathtub and leaving the tap running. Hey, petrol station! Anyone hungry?'

Bjørn Holm didn't even slow down.

'OK. Then something does happen. Ole receives a letter. It's from a blackmailer. He writes that he knows Ole has killed and he wants money.

Otherwise the police will be round. Ole's first thought is that it must be someone who knows he was at Håvass, so it must be one of the two survivors. Iska Peller. Or Tony Leike. He excludes Iska Peller right away. She's Australian, went back and, anyway, is hardly likely to write in Norwegian. Tony Leike, what irony! They never met at the cabin, but Adele may of course have mentioned Ole's name while they were flirting. Or Tony may have seen Ole's name in the guest book. At any rate, Tony must have guessed the connection as the murders appeared in the newspapers. The blackmail attempt squares pretty well with what the financial press is writing about Tony being desperately in need of funds for his Congo project. Ole takes a decision. Even though he would have preferred Tony to live with the shame, he has to turn to the second option before things spiral out of control. Tony has to die. He tails Tony. Follows him onto the train which goes where Tony always goes – Ustaoset. Follows his snowmobile tracks which lead to a locked Tourist Association cabin situated among cliffs and crevices. And that's where Ole finds him. And Tony recognises the ghost, the boy from the dance hall, the boy whose tongue he cut off. And realises what's in store for him. Ole takes his revenge. He tortures Tony. Burns him. Maybe to make him reveal possible partners in the blackmail venture. Maybe for his own enjoyment.'

Altman rolled the window back up, hard.

'Cold,' he said.

'While this is going on, he hears on the news that Iska Peller is in the cabin at Håvass. Ole senses that the final solution may be at hand, but smells a trap. He remembers the snowdrift above the cabin that locals said was dangerous. He reaches a decision. Perhaps he takes Tony with him as a guide, heads for the Håvass cabin, starts the avalanche with dynamite. Then he drives the snowmobile back, unloads Tony – dead or alive – off the precipice and sends the snowmobile after him. If, contrary to expectation, the body should ever be found, it will look like an accident. A man who has burned himself and is on his way to find help perhaps.'

The countryside opened up. They passed a lake with the moon reflected in it.

'Ole triumphs, he's won. He's tricked everyone, pulled the wool over their eyes. And he's started to enjoy the game, the feeling of being in power, of having everyone follow his directions. So the master, who has bound eight individual fates into one big drama, decides to leave us with a parting gesture. To leave me with a parting gesture.'

A cluster of houses, a petrol station and a shopping centre. They took the left exit off a roundabout.

'Ole cuts off the middle finger of Tony's right hand. And he has Leike's phone. It's the one he used when he called me from the centre of Ustaoset. My number is ex-directory, but Tony Leike has my number on his mobile phone. Ole doesn't leave a message. Perhaps it was just playful whimsy.'

'Or to confuse us,' Bjørn Holm said.

'Or to show us his superiority,' Harry said. 'Like when he quite literally gives us the finger by leaving Tony's middle finger outside my door, inside Police HQ, right under our very noses. Because he can do that. He's Prince Charming, he's recovered from the shame, he's retaliated, avenged himself on all those who mocked him and on their understudies. The witnesses. The whore. And the lech. Then something unforeseen happens. The headquarters at Kadok are found. In fact, the police still don't have any evidence to lead them straight to Ole, but they're beginning to get dangerously close. So Ole goes to his boss and says that finally he'll take his holiday and accumulated time in lieu. He'll be away for a good while. His plane goes the day after tomorrow by the way.'

'Twenty-one fifteen to Bangkok via Stockholm,' Bjørn Holm said.

'OK, lots of the details in this story are assumptions, but we're getting close. Here we are.'

Bjørn turned off the road and onto the gravel in front of the large, red timber building. Stopped and switched off the ignition.

There was no light in any of the windows, but advertisements hung on the ground-floor walls, showing that a corner of the building had once been a grocery shop. At the other end of the square, fifty metres in front of them and beneath a street light, stood a green Jeep Cherokee.

It was still. Sound-still, time-still, wind-still. From the top of the window on the driver's side of the Cherokee cigarette smoke rose into the light.

'This is the place where it all began,' Harry said. 'The dance hall.'

'Who's that?' Altman asked, nodding towards the Cherokee.

'Don't you recognise him?' Harry took out a packet of cigarettes, placed one between his lips, unlit, and stared hungrily at the tobacco smoke. 'You might be deceived by the street lamp, of course. Most of the older street lamps cast a yellow light, making a blue car seem green.'

'I've seen the film,' Altman said. '*In the Valley of Elah.*'

'Mm. Good film. Almost Altman class.'

'Almost.'

'Sigurd Altman class.'

Sigurd didn't answer.

'So,' Harry said. 'Are you happy? Was it the masterpiece you had envisaged, Sigurd? Or can I call you Ole Sigurd?'

74

Bristol Cream

'I PREFER SIGURD.'

'Pity it's not as easy to change first names as surnames,' Harry said, leaning forward between the seats again. 'When you told me you'd changed the usual -sen surname, I didn't think that the S in Ole S. Hansen might stand for Sigurd. But did it help, Sigurd? Did the new name make you into someone different from the person who lost everything in the gravel on this very spot?'

Sigurd shrugged. 'We flee as far as we can. I suppose the new name took me part of the way.'

'Mm. I've checked out a number of things today. When you moved to Oslo you started nursing studies. Why not medicine? After all, you had top grades from school.'

'I wanted to avoid having to speak in public,' Sigurd said with an ironic smile. 'I assumed as a nurse I would be exempt.'

'I rang a speech therapist today, and he told me it depends which muscles are damaged. In theory, even with half a tongue you can train yourself to speak almost perfectly again.'

'The "s"s are tricky without the tip of a tongue. Was that what gave me away?'

Harry rolled down the window and lit his cigarette. Inhaled so hard the paper crackled and rustled.

'That was one of the things. But we went off on the wrong track for a while. The speech therapist told me that people have a tendency to associate lisping with male homosexuality. In English it's called a "gay lisp" and does not constitute lisping in a speech-therapy sense, it's just a different way of articulating the letter "s". Gay men can switch lisping on and off, they use it as a sort of code. And the code works. The speech therapist told me an American university had done some linguistic research to see whether it was possible to deduce sexual tendencies in people by listening only to recorded speech. The results were fairly accurate; however, it transpired that the perception of a gay lisp was so strong that it overrode other language signals that were characteristic of heteros. When the receptionist at Hotel Bristol said that the man asking after Iska Peller spoke in an effeminate way he was a victim of stereotypical thinking. It was only when he acted out how the person had spoken that I realised he had allowed himself to be duped by the lisp.'

'There must have been a bit more than that.'

'Yes indeed. Bristol. It's a suburb in Sydney, Australia. I can see you've twigged the connection now.'

'Hang on,' Bjørn said. '*I* haven't.'

Harry blew smoke out of the window. 'The Snowman told me. The killer wanted to be close. He had crossed my field of vision, he had cosied up to me. So when a bottle of Bristol Cream crossed my field of vision, I clicked at long last. I remembered seeing the same name, and telling someone something. Someone who had cosied up to me. And then I realised that what I had said had been misunderstood. I gave Iska Peller's place of residence as Bristol. By which the person inferred I meant Hotel Bristol in Oslo. I said that to you, Sigurd. At the hospital right after the avalanche.'

'You have a good memory.'

'For some things. When suspicion first fell on you, other things became quite obvious. Like you saying that you have to work in anaesthestics to get hold of ketanome in Norway. Like a friend of mine saying that we often desire those things we see every day, which would suggest that whoever has sexual fantasies about women dressed in a nurse's outfit may work at a hospital. Like the the computer at the Kadok factory being called Nashville, the name of a film directed by . . .'

'Robert Altman in 1975,' Sigurd said. 'A much underrated masterpiece.'

'And the chair at the headquarters being, it goes without saying, a director's chair. For the master director, Sigurd Altman.'

Sigurd didn't react.

'But still I didn't know what your motive was,' Harry continued. 'The Snowman told me that the killer was driven by hatred. And the hatred was engendered by one single event, one that lay back in the mists of time. Perhaps I already had a hunch. The tongue. The lisping. I got a friend from Bergen to do a bit of digging on Sigurd Altman. It took her about thirty seconds to discover your change of name on the national register and to connect it with the old name mentioned in Tony Leike's conviction for assault.'

A cigarette was flicked out of the Cherokee window leaving a trail of sparks.

'So there was just the question of the timeline left,' Harry said. 'We checked the duty roster at Rikshospital. That seems to give you an alibi for two of the murders. You were working when Marit Olsen and Borgny Stem-Myhre were killed. But both murders were committed in Oslo, and no one at the hospital can remember with certainty having seen you at the times in question. And since you travel between departments no one would have missed you if they hadn't seen you for a couple of hours. Correct me if I'm wrong, but I think you'll tell me you spend most of your free time alone. And indoors.'

Sigurd Altman shrugged. 'Probably.'

'So there we are,' Harry said with a clap of his hands.

'Just a minute,' Altman said. 'The story you've told is pure fiction. You don't have a scrap of evidence.'

'Oh, I forgot to say. You remember the snaps I showed you earlier today? The ones I asked you to flick through and you said were sticky?'

'What about them?'

'You get great fingerprints from them. Yours matched the ones we found on the desk at Leike's place.'

Sigurd Altman's expression changed slowly as the realisation sank in. 'You only showed them to me . . . so that I would hold them?' Altman stared at Harry for a few seconds, as if turned to stone. Then he put his face in his hands. And a sound emerged from behind his fingers. Laughter.

'You considered almost every angle,' Harry said. 'Why didn't you think it prudent to find yourself a respectable alibi?'

'It didn't occur to me that I needed one.' Altman took his hand away. 'You would have seen through everything anyway, Harry, wouldn't you.'

The eyes behind the glasses were moist, but not devastated. Resigned. Harry had experienced this before. The relief at being caught. Being able to unburden yourself at last.

'Probably,' Harry said. 'I mean, officially, I didn't see through any of this. The man sitting in the vehicle over there did. He's the one who will arrest you.'

Sigurd removed his glasses and dried his tears of laughter. 'So you were lying when you said you needed me to tell you about ketanome?'

'Yes, but I wasn't lying when I said your name would go down in Norwegian crime history.'

Harry nodded to Bjørn, who flashed his lights.

A man jumped out of the Cherokee in front of them.

'An old acquaintance of yours,' Harry said. 'At least his daughter was.'

The man ambled over, slightly bow-legged, hitched up his trousers by the belt. Like an old policeman.

'One last thing I was wondering,' Harry said. 'The Snowman said you would steal up on me, unnoticed, while I was vulnerable maybe. How did that come about?'

Sigurd put his glasses back on. 'All patients admitted have to give the name of their next of kin. Your father must have given your name because in the canteen one of the nurses mentioned that the father of the man who had caught the Snowman, Harry Hole himself, was on her ward. I took it for granted that someone with your reputation would be given the case. At that time I was actually working on other wards, but I asked the ward manager if I could use your father in an anaesthesia paper I was writing, said he fitted my test group exactly. I thought that if I could get to know you via your father then I would find out of how the case was going.'

'You could be *close*, you mean. Feel the pulse of the case and have your superiority confirmed.'

'When you finally made an appearance, I had to take care not to ask you direct questions about the investigation.' Sigurd Altman took a deep breath. 'I didn't want to arouse suspicion. I had to be patient, wait until I had built up trust.'

'And you succeeded.'

Sigurd nodded slowly. 'Thank you, I like to believe I inspire trust. By the way, I called my office at the Kadok factory the cutting room. When you broke in I lost my mind. It was my home. I was so furious I was on the point of disconnecting your father from the respirator, Harry. But I didn't. I would like you to know that.'

Harry didn't respond.

'One more thing.' Sigurd said. 'How did you find out about the locked Tourist Association cabin?'

Harry shrugged. 'By chance. A colleague and I had to stay the night. It seemed as if someone had just been there. And something was stuck to the wood burner. Bits of flesh, I guessed. It was a while before I connected it with the arm sticking out from under the snowmobile. It looked like an overdone sausage. The County Officer went to the cabin, poked at the flesh and sent the bits for DNA testing. We'll have the results in a few days. Tony kept personal possessions there. I found a family photo in a drawer, for instance. Tony as a lad. You didn't clear up after yourself properly, Sigurd.'

The policeman had stopped by the driver's window, and Bjørn rolled it down. He stooped, looked past Bjørn and at Sigurd Altman.

'Hi, Ole,' Skai said. 'I am hereby arresting you for the murder of a whole load of people whose names I should have swotted up on, but we'll take things one step at a time. Before I come round and open the door, I would like you to place both hands on the dashboard so that I can see them. I'm going to handcuff you, and you will have to accompany me to a nice, freshly spruced-up cell. The wife has made meatballs with mashed swede. Seem to remember you like that. That sound alright, Ole?'

PART EIGHT

75

Perspiration

'WHAT THE FUCK'S THIS SUPPOSED TO MEAN?'

It was seven o'clock, the Kripos building was stirring into life and in the doorway to Harry's office stood a fuming Mikael Bellman with a briefcase in one hand and a copy of *Aftenposten* in the other.

'If you're thinking about *Aftenposten*—'

'I'm thinking about this, yes!' Bellman smacked the newspaper down on the desk in front of him.

The headlines covered half the front page. PRINCE CHARMING ARRESTED LAST NIGHT. The press had got hold of the sobriquet Prince Charming the same day they had christened him in the Odin conference room. ARRESTED LAST NIGHT was not quite accurate, of course, it was more early evening, but Skai had not had time to send out the press report until midnight, after the TV stations' last news programmes and before the newspapers' deadlines. It had been brief and did not specify the time or circumstances, only that Prince Charming, after intense investigation by local police, had been arrested outside the old dance hall in Ytre Enebakk.

'What's this supposed to mean?' Bellman repeated.

'I presume it means the police have one of Norway's most notorious killers under lock and key,' Harry said, trying to release the high-backed chair.

'The police?' hissed Bellman. 'The local police in –' he had to consult the newspaper – 'Ytre Enebakk?'

'I don't suppose it matters who clears up the case so long as it's cleared up, does it?' said Harry, groping for the lever beside the seat. 'How do these things work?'

Bellman shut the door. 'Listen here, Hole.'

'No Harry any more?'

'Shut your mouth and listen carefully. I know what's gone on here. You've been talking to Hagen and were told you couldn't hand over the arrest to him and Crime Squad, it was too risky. So, as you couldn't go for a home win, you went for a draw. You bequeathed the honour and the points to a police bumpkin who couldn't tell you one end of a murder investigation from the other.'

'Me, boss?' Harry said, giving him a blue-eyed, aggrieved look. 'One of the bodies was found in his district, so it's natural enough that he followed up on a local level. Then he picked up on this background story about Tony Leike. Cracking police work, if you ask me.'

The white patches on Bellman's forehead seemed to be turning all the colours of the rainbow.

'Do you know how this will be construed by the Ministry of Justice? They have put the investigation in my hands, I keep at it week after week, no result. Then along comes this bloody inbred and after a couple of days cuts us up on the inside lane.'

'Mm.' Harry yanked at the lever and the seat tipped back violently. 'Doesn't sound too good when you put it like that, boss.'

Bellman placed his palms on the desk, leaned forward and snarled, sending small, white spit balls in Harry's direction. 'I hope it doesn't sound too good, Hole. This afternoon a lump of opium found in your house is going to the lab to be identified. Your goose is cooked, Hole!'

'And afterwards, boss?' Harry bobbed up and down as he wrestled with the lever.

Bellman frowned. 'What the hell do you mean?'

'What are you going to say to the press and the Ministry of Justice? When they see the date of the search warrant you used, issued in your name? And ask how it can be that the day after you find opium at a policeman's house, you give the selfsame officer a prominent position in your own investigative unit? Some might claim that if Kripos is governed like that, it's no wonder a country copper with one cell and a wife who cooks is better at finding killers.'

Bellman's jaw dropped and he kept blinking.

'There!' Harry leaned against the seat back, now locked into position, with a contented smile on his face. And screwed up his eyes to meet the rush of air after the door was slammed.

The sun had slipped over the edge of the mountain as Krongli stopped the snowmobile, got off and went over to Roy Stille, who was standing beside a ski pole stuck deep in the snow.

'Well?'

'I think we've found it,' Stille said. 'This has to be the stick that Hole fellow marked the site with.'

The soon-to-be-retired policeman had never had any ambitions to rise up the career ladder, but the thick white hair, the intent gaze and the calm voice were such that when he spoke people concluded he was the superior officer and not Krongli.

'Oh?' Krongli said.

He accompanied Stille to the edge of the precipice. Stille pointed. And there, down in the scree, he saw the snowmobile. He adjusted the binoculars. Focused on the bare, burned arm sticking out. Mumbled half aloud: 'Oh shit. At last. Or both.'

The breakfast customers had begun to leave Stopp Pressen when Bent Nordbø heard a cough, looked up from the *New York Times*, removed his glasses, squinted and mustered the closest he would ever get to a smile.

'Gunnar.'

'Bent.'

The greeting, saying each other's name, was something they had from the lodge and always reminded Gunnar Hagen of ants meeting and exchanging smells. The Crime Squad boss sat down, but did not remove his coat. 'You said on the phone you'd found something.'

'One of my journalists has dug this up.' Nordbø pushed a brown envelope across the table. 'Looks like Mikael Bellman protected his wife in a drugs case. It's old, so from a legal point of view they're untouchable, but in the press ...'

'... they're always touchable,' Hagen said, taking the envelope.

'I believe you may safely regard Mikael Bellman as neutralised.'

'At least a balance of terror can be achieved. He has things on me, too. Besides, I may not even need this – he's just been humiliated by an officer from Ytre Enebakk.'

'I read that. And the Ministry of Justice has read it too, isn't that so?'

'Up there, they read papers and keep their ears to the ground. But thank you, anyway.'

'My pleasure, we help each other.'

'Who knows, I may need this one day.' Gunnar Hagen put the envelope inside his coat.

He didn't receive a response as Bent Nordbø had already resumed his reading of an article about a young black American senator by the name of Barack Obama who, the writer maintained in all seriousness, could one day become the President of the United States.

When Krongli was down, he called up to the others that he had arrived, and he untied the rope.

The snowmobile was an Arctic Cat and lay with its runners in the air. He dragged himself the three metres to the wreck and instinctively became conscious of where he was placing his feet and hands. As if he were at a crime scene. He crouched down. An arm was protruding from under the snowmobile. He touched the vehicle. It was swaying on two rocks. He took a deep breath and tipped the snowmobile on its side.

The dead body lay on its back. Krongli's first thought was that *presumably* it was a man. The head and face had been crushed between the vehicle and the rocks, and the result looked like the remains of a crab party. He didn't need to feel the smashed body to know it was like jelly, like a piece of tender meat with the bones removed or that the torso had been squashed flat, hips and knees pulverised. Krongli would hardly have been able to identify the body, had it not been for the red flannel shirt. And the single rotten, brown-stained tooth left in the lower jaw.

76

Redefinition

'What did you say?' Harry exclaimed, pressing the phone harder to his ear as if the mistake were there.

'I said the body under the snowmobile is not Tony Leike,' Krongli said.

'Who then?'

'Odd Utmo. A local recluse and local guide. He always wears the same red flannel shirt. And it's his snowmobile. But it was the teeth that decided it. One single rotten stump of a tooth. God knows what happened to the rest of his teeth and the orthodontic brace.'

Utmo. Orthodontic brace. Harry remembered Kaja telling him about the guide who had driven her to Håvass.

'His fingers though,' Harry said. 'Aren't they distorted?'

'Sure. Utmo had terrible problems with arthritis, poor fella. It was Bellman who asked me to inform you directly. Wasn't quite what you hoped for, eh, Hole?'

Harry pushed the chair from the desk. 'At least not quite what I was expecting. Could it have been an accident, Krongli?'

But he knew the answer before it came. There had been moonlight the whole evening and night; even without headlamps the ravine would have been impossible to miss. Especially for a local guide. Especially when he was driving so slowly that he landed only three metres from a perpendicular drop of over seventy metres.

'Forget it, Krongli. Tell me about the burns.'

The other end went silent for a bit before the answer came.

'Arms and back. The skin on the arms was cracked and you can see the red flesh beneath. Parts of the back are charred. And a motif has been scorched in between the shoulder blades . . .'

Harry closed his eyes. Saw the pattern on the wood burner in the cabin. The smoking fragments of flesh.

'. . . looks like a stag. Anything else, Hole? We have to start moving—'

'No, that's it, Krongli. Thanks.'

Harry rang off. Sat for a while deliberating. Not Tony Leike. Of course that changed the details, but not the bigger picture. Utmo was probably a victim of Altman's avenging crusade, someone who had found himself in the way of something or other. They had Tony Leike's finger, but where was the rest of his body? A thought struck Harry. If he was dead. In theory, Tony could be locked up somewhere. A place only Sigurd Altman knew.

Harry tapped in Skai's number.

'He refuses to say a single word to anyone,' Skai said, masticating something or other. 'Apart from his solicitor.'

'Who is?'

'Johan Krohn. Do you know him? Looks like a boy and—'

'I know Johan Krohn very well.'

Harry rang Krohn's office, was transferred and Krohn sounded half welcoming and half dismissive, the way a professional defence counsel should when a prosecuting authority calls. He listened to Harry. Then he answered.

'I'm afraid not. Unless you have concrete evidence that can establish beyond doubt that my client is keeping someone locked up or otherwise exposing someone to danger by not revealing their whereabouts, I cannot allow you to speak to Altman at this juncture, Hole. These are serious allegations you're making against him, and I don't need to tell you that it is my job to protect his interests as far as I am able.'

'Agreed,' Harry said. 'You didn't need to tell me.'

They rang off.

Harry looked out of the window onto the city centre. The chair was good, no doubt about that. But his eyes found the familiar glass building in Grønland.

Then he dialled another number.

Katrine Bratt was as happy as a lark, and twittered like one, too.

'I'm going to be discharged in a couple of days,' she said.

'I thought you were there of your own free will.'

'Yes I am, but I have to be formally discharged. I'm looking forward to it. They've offered me a desk job at the station when my sick leave runs out.'

'Good.'

'Anything special you want?'

Harry explained.

'So you'll have to find Tony Leike without Altman's help?'

'Yup.'

'Any ideas where I can start?'

'Just one. Right after Tony went missing we checked he hadn't stayed anywhere around Ustaoset. Thing is, I've checked recent years a bit more closely, and he's almost never registered at accommodation anywhere in Ustaoset, a couple of Tourist Association cabins, that's all. And that's weird because he's been up there a lot.'

'Perhaps he was freeloading at the cabins, not registering or paying.'

'He's not the type,' Harry said. 'I wonder if Tony has a cabin or such-like up there no one knows anything about.'

'OK. Anything else?'

'No. Yes – see what you can find out about Odd Utmo's activities over the last few days.'

'Are you still single, Harry?'

'What sort of a bloody question's that?'

'You sound less single.'

'Do I?'

'You do. But it suits you.'

'Does it?'

'Since you ask, no.'

*   *   *

Aslak Krongli straightened his stiff back and looked up the scree.

It was one of the men in the search party who had called, and he was shouting again now, obviously excited. 'Over here!'

Aslak uttered a low curse. The crime scene officers had finished, and the snowmobile and Odd Utmo had been hoisted to the top. It was complicated and time-consuming work as the only possible access to the scree was by rope, and even that was hard enough.

In the lunch break one man had told them something a maid at the hotel had whispered into his ear in confidence: there were bloodstains on the sheets in the room occupied by Rasmus Olsen, the husband of the dead woman MP, when he checked out. At first, she had thought it was menstrual blood, but then she had heard that Rasmus Olsen had been on his own and his wife had been at the Håvass cabin.

Krongli had answered that he must have had a local girl in his room or met his wife the morning she arrived in Ustaoset and they had made up in bed. The man had mumbled it was not certain it was menstrual blood.

'Over here!'

What a lot of hassle. Aslak Krongli wanted to go home. Dinner, coffee, sleep. Put this whole shitty case behind him. The money he had owed in Oslo was paid, and he would never go there again. Never go back down into the quagmire. It was a promise he would keep this time.

They had used a dog to be sure they found all the bits of Utmo in the snow, and it was the dog that had leapt up the scree and stood barking a hundred metres further along. A hundred steep metres. Aslak assessed the climb.

'Is it important?' he shouted and set off a symphony of echoes.

He received an answer, and ten minutes later he was staring at what the dog had dug up from the snow. It was wedged in between the rocks so tightly that it must have been impossible to spot from the top.

'Jesus,' Aslak said. 'Who could that be?'

'Not that Tony Leike anyway,' said the dog handler. 'Here in the cold scree it would be a long time before the skeleton was picked that clean. Several years.'

'Eighteen years.' It was Roy Stille. The officer had followed them and was panting.

'She's been here eighteen years,' Roy said, crouching down.

'She?' Aslak queried.

The officer pointed to the hips on the skeleton. 'Women have a larger pelvis. We never did find her when she went missing. That's Karen Utmo.'

Krongli heard something he had never heard before in Roy Stille's voice. A quiver. The quiver of a man emotionally upset. Grief-stricken. But his granite face was as smooth as always, closed.

'Well, I never, so it was true then,' said the dog handler. 'She topped herself out of anguish for her boy.'

'Hardly,' Krongli said. The other two looked at him. He had stuck his little finger in a delicate round aperture in the forehead of the skull.

'Is that a bullet hole?' the dog handler asked.

'Yep,' said Stille, feeling the back of the skull. 'And there's no exit wound, so I reckon we'll find the bullet in the skull.'

'And should we bet that the bullet will match Utmo's rifle?' said Krongli.

'Well, I never,' the dog handler repeated. 'Do you mean he shot his wife? How is that possible? To kill a person you've loved? Because you think she and your son . . . it's like entering hell.'

'Eighteen years,' Stille said, getting up with a groan. 'Seven years left before the murder was deemed too old. That must be what they call irony. You wait and wait, afraid of being found out. The years pass and then, when you're approaching freedom – bang! – you're killed yourself and end up in the same scree.'

Krongli closed his eyes and thought, yes, it is possible to kill a person you have loved. Easily possible. But, no, you're never free. Never. He would never come here again.

Johan Krohn enjoyed the limelight. You don't become the country's most popular defence counsel without enjoying it. And when he had agreed to defend Sigurd Altman, Prince Charming, without a second's hesitation, he knew there was going to be more limelight than he had hitherto experienced in his remarkable career. He had already reached his goal of beating his father as the youngest lawyer ever entitled to attend the Supreme Court. As a defence counsel in his twenties he was already being proclaimed the new star, the wonder boy. But that might have gone to his head a bit; he had not been used to so much attention at school. Then he had been the irritating top pupil who always waved his hand too eagerly in the classroom, who always tried a bit too hard socially and yet was always the last to know where the Saturday-night party was – if he knew about it at all. But now young female assistants and clerks might giggle and blush when he complimented them or suggested a dinner after work. And invitations rained down, to give talks, participate in debates on radio or TV and even to the odd premiere his wife valued so highly. Such events may have occupied too much of his attention over recent years. At any rate, he had detected a downward trend in the number of legal triumphs, big media cases and new clients. Not so many that it had begun to affect his reputation, but enough for him to be aware that he needed the Sigurd Altman case. Needed something high profile to put him back where he belonged: at the top.

That was why Johan Krohan sat listening quietly to the lean man with the round glasses. Listening while Sigurd Altman told a story that was not only the least likely story Krohn had ever heard but also a story he *believed*. Johan Krohn could already see himself in the courtroom, the sparkling rhetorician, the agitator, the manipulator, who nonetheless never lost sight of legal justice, a delight for both layman and judge. He was therefore disappointed at first when Sigurd Altman revealed the plans he had made. However, after reminding himself of his father's repeated admonition that the lawyer was there for the client, and not vice versa, he accepted the brief. For Johan Krohn was not really a bad person.

And when Krohn left Oslo District Prison where Sigurd Altman had been transferred during the day, he saw new potential in the assignment, which in its way, despite everything, was extraordinary. The first thing he did when he got back to his office was contact Mikael Bellman. They had met only once before, at a murder trial of course, but Johan Krohn had immediately known where he was with Bellman. A hawk recognises a hawk. So he appreciated how Bellman was feeling after the day's headlines about the County Officer's arrest.

495

'Bellman.'

'Johan Krohn. Nice to talk to you again.'

'Good afternoon, Krohn.' The voice sounded formal, but not unfriendly.

'Is it? I imagine you feel you've been overtaken down the final straight, don't you?'

Short pause. 'What's this about, Krohn?' Teeth clenched. Angry.

Johan Krohn knew he was on to a winner.

Harry and Sis sat by their father's bed at Rikshospital. On the bedside table and on two other tables in the room there were vases of flowers that had appeared from nowhere in the last few days. Harry had done the rounds and read the cards. One of them had been addressed to 'My dear, dear Olav', and was signed 'Your Lise'. Harry had never heard of any Lise, even less considered the notion that there may have been any women in his father's life other than his mother. The remaining cards were from colleagues and neighbours. It must have reached their ears that the end was nigh. And despite knowing that Olav would not be able to read the cards, they had sent these sweet-smelling flowers to compensate for the fact that they had not taken the time to visit him. Harry saw the flowers surrounding the bed as vultures hovering around a dying man. Heavy, hanging heads on thin stalk necks. Red and yellow beaks.

'You're not allowed to have your mobile on here, Harry!' Sis whispered severely.

Harry took out his phone and read the display. 'Sorry, Sis. Important.'

Katrine Bratt got straight to the point. 'Leike has undoubtedly been in Ustaoset and the surrounding district a fair bit,' she said. 'In recent years he's bought the odd train ticket on the Net, paid for fuel with a credit card at the petrol station in Geilo. The same with provisions, mostly in Ustaoset. The only thing to stand out is a bill for building materials, also in Geilo.'

'Building materials?'

'Yep. I went onto the lists of invoices. Boards, nails, tools, steel cables, leca blocks, cement. Over thirty thousand kroner's worth. But it's four years old.'

'Are you thinking what I'm thinking?'

'He's been building himself a little annexe or something up there?'

'He didn't have a registered cabin to build an annexe on to, we've checked. But you don't stock up with provisions if you're going to live in a hotel or Tourist Association cabins. I reckon Tony built himself an illegal bolt-hole in the national park, just as he told me he dreamed about. Well hidden from view, of course. A place where he could be very, very undisturbed. But where?' Harry realised he had got up and was pacing to and fro in the room.

'Well, you tell me,' said Katrine Bratt.

'Wait! What time of the year did he buy this?'

'Let me see . . . The 6th of July it says on the printout.'

'If the cabin has to be hidden it must be somewhere off the beaten track. A desolate area without roads. Did you say steel cables?'

'Yes. And I can guess why. When Bergensians built cabins in the most wind-blown parts of Ustaoset in the sixties, they generally used steel cables to anchor the cabins.'

'So Leike's cabin would be somewhere wind-blown, desolate, and he has to transport thirty thousand kroner's worth of building materials there. Weighing at least a couple of tons. How do you do that in the summer when there's no snow, so you can't use a snowmobile?'

'Horse? Jeep?'

'Over rivers, marshland, up mountains? Keep going.'

'I have no idea.'

'But I do. I've seen a picture of it. OK, bye.'

'Wait.'

'Yes?'

'You asked me to look into Utmo's activities during the final days of his life. There's not very much on him in the electronic world, but he did make some calls. One of the last ones he made was to Aslak Krongli. Just got voicemail, looks like. The very last conversation on his phone was with SAS. I went through their booking system. He booked a plane ticket to Copenhagen.'

'Mm. He doesn't seem the type to travel much.'

'That's for sure. A passport was issued to him, but he isn't registered in a single booking system. And we're talking many years here.'

'So a man who has barely left his home district suddenly wants to go to Copenhagen. When would he have travelled by the way?'

'Yesterday.'

'OK. Thanks.'

Harry rang off, grabbed his coat, turned in the doorway. Looked at her. The attractive woman who was his sister. Was about to ask if she was coping on her own, without him. But managed to stop himself asking such an idiotic question. When had she not coped without him?

'Take care,' he said.

Jens Rath was in the reception area of the shared office block. Inside his jacket and shirt, his back was drenched with perspiration. Because he had just received a call from the office that the police were paying him a visit. He had had a skirmish with the Fraud Squad a few years ago, but the case had been dropped. Nevertheless, he still broke out into a sweat whenever he saw a police car. And now Jens Rath could feel his pores opening big time. He was a small man and looked up at the officer who had just risen to his feet. And continued to rise. Until he towered half a metre above Jens and gave him a cursory, firm handshake.

'Harry Hole, Crime Sq— Kripos. We've come about Tony Leike.'

'Anything new?'

'Shall we sit down, Rath?'

They took a seat in a pair of Le Corbusier chairs, and Rath signalled discreetly to Wenche in reception that she *shouldn't* serve them coffee, which was standard policy when investors came visiting.

'I want you to show us where his cabin is,' the policeman said.

'Cabin?'

'I saw you cancel the coffee, Rath, and that's fine – like you I don't have much time. I also know that your Fraud Squad case has been dropped, but it would take me one phone call to reopen it. They may not find anything this time, either, but I promise you that the documentation they will demand you make available . . .'

Rath closed his eyes. 'Oh my God . . .'

'. . . will keep you busy for longer than it took to build a cabin for your colleague, pal and bedfellow, Tony Leike. OK?'

Jens Rath's sole talent was that he could calculate worthwhile risks faster and more efficiently than anyone else. Accordingly, it took him approximately one second to respond to the calculation with which he had just been presented.

'Fine.'

'We're leaving at nine tomorrow morning.'

'How . . . ?'

'The same way you transported the materials. Helicopter.' The policeman stood up.

'Just one question. Tony's always been terribly concerned that no one should know about this cabin – I don't even think Lene, his fiancée, knows about it – so how . . . ?'

'An invoice for building materials from Geilo, plus the photo of you three in work gear sitting on a pile of timber in front of a helicopter.'

Quick nod of the head from Jens Rath. 'Course. *The* photo.'

'Who took it by the way?'

'The pilot. Before we left from Geilo. And it was Andreas's idea to send it with the press report when we opened the offices. He thought dressing in work clothes was cooler than in suits and ties. And Tony agreed because he reckoned it looked as if we *owned* the helicopter. Anyway, the financial papers use the photo all the time.'

'Why didn't you and Andreas mention the cabin when Tony was reported missing?'

Jens Rath shrugged. 'Don't get me wrong, we're just as keen as you for Tony to return pronto. We've got a project in the Congo which will go belly up unless he can find ten million readies. But whenever Tony goes walkabout it's always because he wants to. He can look after himself. Don't forget he was a mercenary. I would guess that right now Tony is sitting somewhere with a shot of the hard stuff, some exotic wildcat of a woman on his arm and grinning because he's come up with a solution.'

'Mm,' Harry said. 'I assume the feline chomped off his middle finger then. Fornebu Airport nine tomorrow.'

Jens Rath stood watching the policeman. The sweat was pouring off him, he was being washed away.

When Harry returned to Rikshospital Sis was still sitting there. She was leafing through a magazine and eating an apple. He surveyed the kettle of vultures. There were more flowers.

'You look worn out, Harry,' she said. 'You should go home.'

Harry chuckled. 'You can go. You've been sitting here on your own for long enough.'

'I haven't been on my own,' she said with a mischievous smile. 'Guess who was here.'

Harry sighed. 'I'm sorry, Sis, I do enough guessing as it is in my job.'

'Øystein!'

'Øystein Eikeland?'

'Yes! He brought a bar of milk chocolate with him. Not for Daddy, but for me. Sorry, there's none left.' She laughed so much her eyes shrank into her cheeks.

When she got up to go for a walk, Harry checked his phone. Two missed calls from Kaja. He pushed the chair into the wall and leaned back.

77

Fingerprint

AT TEN MINUTES PAST TEN THE HELICOPTER LANDED ON A ridge west of the Hallingskarvet mountains. By eleven they had located the cabin.

It was so well hidden from view that even if they had known more or less where it was, they would have struggled to find it without Jens Rath's help. The cabin was built on rock high up to the east, the leeward side of the mountain, too high to be affected by avalanches. The stones had been carried there from surrounding areas and cemented in against two enormous rocks forming the side and rear walls. There were no conspicuous right angles. The windows resembled gun slits and were set so deep into the wall that the sun did not reflect off them.

'That's what I call a decent cabin,' Bjørn Holm said, unstrapping skis and immediately sinking up to his knees in the snow.

Harry told Jens that they no longer needed his services, and that he should go back to the helicopter and wait there with the pilot.

The snow was not so deep by the front door.

'Someone's been digging here not that long ago,' Harry said.

The door was fitted with a plate and a simple padlock which ceded to Bjørn's crowbar without much protest.

Before opening the door, they removed their mittens, put on latex gloves and blue plastic bags over their ski boots. Then they entered.

'Wow,' Bjørn said under his breath.

The whole cabin consisted of one single room of around five by three metres and was reminiscent of an old-fashioned captain's berth with porthole-like windows and compact, space-saving solutions. The floor, walls and ceiling were clad with coarse, untreated boards that had been given a couple of coats of white paint to exploit the little light that was let in. The short wall to the right was taken up by a plain worktop with a sink and a cupboard underneath. Plus a divan obviously doubling up as a bed. In the middle of the room there was a table with a single spindleback chair spattered with paint. In front of one window stood a well-used writing desk with initials and snatches of songs carved into the wood. To the left, on the long wall where the rear rock was revealed, there was a black wood burner. To make maximum use of the heat, the flue was diverted around the rock to the right, then rose vertically. The wood basket was filled with birch and newspapers to get the fire started. On the walls hung maps of the local area, but there was also one of Africa.

Bjørn looked out of the window above the desk.

'And that's what I call a decent view. Jeez, you can see half of Norway from here.'

'Let's get cracking,' Harry said. 'The pilot's given us two hours. There's cloud coming in from the coast.'

As usual Mikael Bellman had got up at six and jogged himself into consciousness on the treadmill in the cellar. He had been dreaming about Kaja again. She had been riding pillion on a motorbike with her arms around a man who was all helmet and visor. She had smiled so happily, showing her pointed teeth, and waved as they rode away. But hadn't they stolen the bike? Wasn't it his? He didn't know for sure as her hair, which was fluttering in the wind, was so long it covered the number plate.

After running, Mikael had taken a shower and gone upstairs for breakfast.

He had steeled himself before opening the morning paper that Ulla – also as usual – had placed next to his plate.

Lacking a photograph of Sigurd Altman, alias Prince Charming, they had printed one of County Officer Skai. He was standing outside the police station with his arms crossed, wearing a green cap with a long peak, like a bloody bear-hunter. The headline: PRINCE CHARMING ARRESTED? And beside it, above the photograph of a smashed yellow snowmobile: ANOTHER BODY FOUND IN USTAOSET.

Bellman had scanned the text for the word Kripos or – worst of all – his name. Nothing on the front page. Good.

He had opened the pages referred to, and there it was, photo and all:

The head of Kripos, Mikael Bellman, has said in a brief comment that he does not wish to make a statement until Prince Charming has been questioned. Nor has he anything in particular to say about the arrest of the suspect by Ytre Enebakk police.

'In general, I can say that all police work is teamwork. In Kripos we do not attach too much importance to individuals who receive the hero's garlands.'

He shouldn't have said the last bit. It was lies, would be perceived as lies and stank from some distance of a bad loser.

But it didn't matter. For if what Johan Krohn, the defence counsel, had told him on the phone was true, Bellman had a golden opportunity to fix everything. Well, more than that. To receive the garlands himself. He acknowledged that the price Krohn would demand was high, but also that it wouldn't be him who had to pay. But the sodding bear-hunter. And Harry Hole and Crime Squad.

A prison warder held the door to the visitors' room open and Mikael Bellman let Johan Krohn go first. Krohn had insisted that as this was a conversation, not a formal interview, it should take place, as far as was possible, on neutral ground. Since it was inconceivable that Prince Charming would be allowed out of Oslo District Prison, where he was in custody, Krohn and Bellman agreed on a visitors' room, one of the ones used for private meetings between inmates and family. No cameras, no microphones, just an ordinary windowless room where half-hearted attempts had been made to jolly the place up with a crocheted cloth on the table and a Norwegian tapestry, a bell-pull, on the wall. Sweethearts and spouses were granted permission to meet here, and the springs on the semen-stained sofa were so worn that Bellman was able to observe Krohn sink into the material as he took a seat.

Sigurd Altman was sitting on a chair at one end of the table. Bellman sat at the other end so that he and Altman were at almost exactly the same height. Altman's face was lean, his eyes deep-set, the mouth pronounced with protruding teeth, all of which reminded Bellman of photos of emaciated Jews in Auschwitz. And the monster in *Alien*.

'Conversations like this don't proceed by the book,' Bellman said. 'I therefore have to insist that no one takes notes and anything we say does not go beyond these walls.'

'At the same time we have to have a guarantee that the conditions for a confession are fulfilled on the prosecuting authority's side,' Krohn said.

'You have my word,' Bellman said.

'For which I humbly thank you. What else have you got?'

'What else?' Bellman gave a thin smile. 'What else would you like? A signed written agreement?' Arrogant bloody prick of a counsel.

'Preferably,' Krohn said, passing a sheet of paper across the table.

Bellman stared at the paper. He skimmed over it, his eyes jumping from sentence to sentence.

'Won't be shown to anyone, of course, if it doesn't have to be,' Krohn said. 'And the document will be returned when the conditions have been fulfilled. And this –' he passed a pen to Bellman – 'is an S.T. Dupont, the best fountain pen you can find.'

Bellman took the pen and placed it on the table beside him.

'If the story's good enough, I'll sign,' he said.

'If this is supposed to be a crime scene, the person concerned tidied up after themselves pretty well.'

Bjørn Holm put his hands on his hips and surveyed the room. They had searched high and low, in drawers and cupboards, shone a torch everywhere for blood and taken fingerprints. He had put his laptop on the desk, connected it to a fingerprint scanner the size of a matchbox, similar to those used at some airports now for passenger identification. So far all the prints had matched one person in the case: Tony Leike.

'Keep going,' Harry said, on his knees under the sink, dismantling the plastic pipes. 'It's here somewhere.'

'What is?'

'I don't know. Something or other.'

'If we keep going, we'll certainly need a bit of heating.'

'Fire her up then.'

Bjørn Holm crouched down by the wood burner, opened the door and began to tear up and twist the newspaper from the wood basket.

'What did you offer Skai to get him to join your little game? He risks all sorts if the truth comes out.'

'He's not risking anything,' Harry said. 'He hasn't said an untrue word. Look at his statements. It's the media that have jumped to the wrong conclusions. And there are no police instructions stipulating who can and who cannot arrest a suspect. I didn't need to offer anything for his help. He said he disliked me less than he disliked Bellman, and that was justification enough.'

'That was all?'

'Hm. He told me about his daughter, Mia. Things haven't gone so well for her. In such cases parents always look for a cause, something concrete they can point to. And Skai reckons it was the night outside the dance hall that marked Mia for life. Local gossip is that Mia and Ole had been going out and it wasn't just innocent kissing in the woods when Ole found Mia and Tony. In Skai's eyes Ole and Tony carry the blame for the daughter's problems.'

Bjørn shook his head. 'Victims, victims, wherever you turn.'

Harry had come over to Bjørn, holding out his hand. In the palm lay bits of what looked like wire cut from a fence. 'This was under the drainpipe. Any idea what it is?'

Bjørn took the pieces of wire and studied them.

'Hey,' Harry burst out. 'What's that?'

'What's what?'

'The newspaper. Look, that's the press conference where we launched the Iska Peller ruse.'

Bjørn Holm looked at the photo of Bellman which had been uncovered when he had torn off the page in front. 'Well, I'll be . . .'

'The newspaper's only a few days old. Someone's been here recently.'

'Well, I'll be.'

'There might be prints on the front pa—' Harry looked in the woodburner where the first pages were just going up in flames.

'Sorry,' said Bjørn. 'But I can check the other pages.'

'OK. Actually, I was wondering about the wood.'

'Oh?'

'There isn't a tree for a three-mile radius. You check the papers and I'll have a walk around.'

Mikael Bellman studied Sigurd Altman. He didn't like his cold eyes. Didn't like the bony body, the teeth pressing against the inside of his lips, the staccato movements or the clumsy lisp. But he didn't need to like Sigurd Altman to see him as his redeemer and benefactor. For every word Altman said, Bellman was a step nearer his triumph.

'I assume you've read Harry Hole's report presenting the course of events,' Altman said.

'You mean Skai's report?' Bellman said. 'Skai's presentation?'

Altman let slip a wry smile. 'As you prefer. The story Harry told was astonishingly accurate, anyway. The problem with it is that it contains only one concrete piece of evidence. My fingerprints at Leike's. Well, let's say I was there. I was paying him a visit. And we talked about the good old days.'

Bellman shrugged. 'And you think a jury will fall for that?'

'I like to think I can inspire trust. But . . .' Altman's lips stretched and revealed his gums, '. . . now I won't ever have to face a jury, will I.'

Harry found the woodpile under a green tarpaulin beneath a rock jutting out from the mountainside. An axe stood bowed in a chopping block, beside it a knife. Harry looked around and kicked the snow. Not much of interest here. His boot brushed something. An empty white plastic bag. He bent down. On it was a contents label. Ten metres of gauze. What was that doing here?

Harry angled his head and examined the chopping block for a few moments. Looked at the black blade in the wood. At the knife. At the handle. Yellow, smooth. What was a knife doing on a chopping block? Could be several reasons, of course, yet . . .

He laid his right hand on the block in such a way that the remaining stump of his middle finger pointed upwards and the other fingers pressed down beside it.

Harry freed the knife cautiously with two fingers at the top of the handle. The blade was as sharp as a razor. With traces of the material he was always seeing in his profession. Then he ran like an elk on long legs through the deep snow.

Bjørn looked up from the computer as Harry burst in. 'Just more Tony Leike,' he sighed.

'There's blood on the blade,' Harry said, out of breath. 'Check the handle for prints.'

Bjørn held the knife with care. Sprinkled black powder on the smooth, varnished yellow wood and blew gently.

'There's only one set of prints here; however, they are tasty,' he said. 'Maybe there are epithel cells here, too.'

'Yess!' Harry said.

'What's the deal?'

'Whoever left the fingerprint cut off Leike's finger.'

'Oh? What makes you—'

'There's blood on the chopping block. And he had gauze ready to bandage the wound. And I have an inkling I've seen that knife before. On a grainy photo of Adele Vetlesen.'

Bjørn Holm whistled softly, pressed the transparency against the handle so that the powder stuck. Then he put the transparency on the scanner.

'Sigurd Altman, you might have got a good lawyer to explain away the prints on Leike's desk,' Harry whispered while Bjørn pressed the search button and they both followed the blue line that moved in fits and starts towards the right of the bar. 'But not the print on this knife.'

Ready . . .

Found 1 match.

Bjørn Holm pressed 'show'.

Harry stared at the name that came up.

'Still think the print belongs to the person who cut off Tony's finger?' Bjørn Holm asked.

78

The Deal

'After I saw Adele and Tony banging away like dogs by the toilet, everything came back to me. Everything I had succeeded in burying. Everything the psychologist said I had put behind me. It was like an animal that had been chained up, but it had been fed, it had grown and was stronger than ever. And now it was free. Harry was quite right. I planned to avenge myself on Tony by humiliating him just as he had done to me.'

Sigurd Altman looked down at his hands and smiled.

'However, from thereon Harry was wrong. I didn't plan Adele's murder. I just wanted to humiliate Tony in public. Particularly in front of those he hoped would become his in-laws, the milch cow Galtung who was to finance that Congo adventure of his. Why would someone like Tony bother to marry a field mouse like Lene Galtung otherwise?'

'True enough,' smiled Mikael Bellman, to show he was on his side.

'So I wrote a letter to Tony pretending to be Adele. I wrote that he had made me pregnant and I wanted the child. However, as a future single mother I would have to provide for it, and therefore I wanted silence money. Four hundred thousand first time round. He was to show up at midnight in the car park behind Lefdal electrical appliances in Sandvika with the money two days later. Then I sent Adele a letter, pretending to be Tony, and asked if we could meet at the same time and place for a date. I knew the setting would be to Adele's taste, and I assumed they hadn't exchanged names and phone numbers, if you know what I mean. The deception wouldn't be discovered until it was too late, until I had what I wanted. At eleven I was in position, sitting in my car with a camera ready. The plan was to take photos of the rendezvous however it ended up, a row or bonking, and to send the whole lot to Anders Galtung with the revelatory story. That was all.'

Sigurd looked at Bellman and repeated: 'That was all.'

Bellman nodded, and Sigurd Altman continued. 'Tony arrived early. He parked, got out and did a recce. Then he disappeared into the shadows under the trees by the river. I hid behind the steering wheel. Adele came. I rolled down the window to catch what happened. She stood there waiting, looking around, checking her watch. I saw Tony right behind her, so close it was unbelievable she couldn't hear him. I saw him pull out a large Sami knife and close his arm around her neck. She wriggled and kicked as he carried her to his car. When the door fell open I saw that he had plastic over the seats. I didn't hear what Tony said to her, but I picked up my camera and zoomed in. Saw him pressing a pen into her hand, obviously dictating what she was to write on a postcard.'

'The postcard from Kigali,' Bellman said. 'He had planned everything in advance. She was going to disappear.'

'I took pictures, not thinking about anything else. Until I saw him suddenly raise his hand and drive the knife into her neck. I couldn't believe my own eyes. Blood spurted out spraying the windscreen.'

The two men were unaware that Krohn was gasping for air.

'He waited a while, leaving the knife in her neck, as though he wanted to drain her of blood first. Then he lifted her up, carried her to the rear of his car and dumped her in the boot. As he was about to get back in the car, he stopped and seemed to sniff the air. He was standing under the light of a street lamp, and that was when I saw it: the same widened eyes, the same grin on his lips that he'd had when he pinned me down outside the dance hall and forced the knife in my mouth. Long after Tony had driven off with Adele, I was still in my car, numb with horror, unable to move. I knew I couldn't send a letter telling all to Anders Galtung now. Or to anyone else. Because I had just become an accessory to murder.'

Sigurd took a tiny, restrained sip of water from the glass in front of him and glanced at Johan Krohn, who nodded in return.

Bellman cleared his throat. 'Technically speaking, you were not an accessory to murder. The worst charge would have been blackmail or deception. You could have stopped there. It would have been very unpleasant for you, but you could have gone to the police. You even had photographs proving your story.'

'Nevertheless, I would have been charged and found guilty. They would have maintained that I, better than anyone else, knew Tony reacted with violence when put under pressure and that I had started the whole business, it was premeditated.'

'Hadn't you considered that this might happen?' Bellman asked, ignoring the admonitory glare from Krohn.

Sigurd Altman smiled. 'Isn't it odd how often our own deliberations are the hardest to interpret? Or remember? I honestly don't recall what I anticipated would happen.'

Because you don't want to, Bellman thought, nodding and mmm-ing as if in gratitude to Altman for giving him new insights into the human soul.

'I deliberated for several days,' Altman said. 'Then I went back to the Håvass cabin and tore out the page in the guest book with all the names and addresses. Then I wrote another letter to Tony. In which I said that I knew what he had done, and I knew why. I had seen him screw Adele at the cabin in Håvass. And I wanted money. Signed it Borgny Stem-Myhre. Five days later I read in the papers that she had been killed in a cellar. It should have stopped there. The police should have investigated the case and found Tony. That's what they should have done. Arrested him.'

Sigurd Altman had raised his voice and Bellman could have sworn he saw tears welling up in the eyes behind the round glasses.

'But you didn't even have a lead, you were completely befogged. So I had to keep feeding him with more victims, threatening him with new names from the Håvass list. I cut out pictures of the victims from the papers and hung them on the wall of the cutting room in the Kadok factory with copies of letters I had sent in the victims' names. As soon as Tony killed one person, another letter arrived insisting *they* had sent the previous ones and now they knew he had two, three and four lives on his conscience. And that the price for their silence had risen accordingly.' Altman leaned forward; his voice sounded anguished. 'I did it to give you a chance to catch him. A killer makes mistakes, doesn't he. The more murders there are, the greater the chance he will be arrested.'

'And the better he becomes at what he's doing,' Bellman said. 'Remember that Tony Leike was no novice at violence. You aren't a mercenary in Africa for as long as he was without having blood on your hands. As you yourself have.'

'Blood on my hands?' Altman shrieked, in a sudden burst of anger. 'I broke into Tony's house and rang Elias Skog so you would find the trail at Telenor. It's you who have blood on your hands! Whores like Adele and Mia, murderers like Tony. If not—'

'Stop now, Sigurd.' Johan Krohn had got to his feet. 'Let's have a break, shall we?'

Altman closed his eyes, raised his hands and shook his head. 'I'm OK, I'm OK. Let's get this over and done with.'

Johan Krohn eyed his client, glanced at Bellman and sat down.

Altman took a deep, tremulous breath. Then he continued. 'After the third murder or so, Tony knew, of course, that the next letter was not necessarily from the person it purported to be from. Nonetheless, he went on killing them, in increasingly violent ways. It was as if he wanted to frighten me, make me pull back, to show that he could kill everyone and everything and in the end would kill me, too.'

'Or he wanted to get rid of potential witnesses who had seen him and Adele,' Bellman said. 'He knew there had been seven other people at Håvass, he just didn't have the means to establish who they were.'

Altman laughed. 'Imagine! I swear he went up to the cabin to look at the guest book. Only to find the stub of a torn-out sheet. Tony Pony!'

'What about your motive for continuing?'

'What do you mean?' Altman asked, on the alert now.

'You could have given the police an anonymous tip-off much earlier in the case. Perhaps you wanted to get rid of all the witnesses as well?'

Altman tilted his head, so that his ear almost touched his shoulder.

'As I said, it's difficult to keep tabs on all the reasons for doing what you do. Your subconscious is controlled by your survival instinct and is therefore often more rational than conscious thought. Perhaps my subconscious realised it would also be safer for me if Tony eliminated all the witnesses. Then no one would be able to say I was there, or suddenly recognise me one day in the street. But we will never get an answer to that, will we.'

The wood burner crackled and spat.

'But why on earth would Tony Leike chop off his own finger?' Bjørn Holm asked.

He had settled down on the sofa while Harry went through the first-aid kit he had found at the back of a kitchen drawer. It contained several rolls of bandages. And an astringent ointment that made blood coagulate faster. The date on the tube showed it was only two months old.

'Altman forced him,' Harry said, revolving a tiny unlabelled brown bottle. 'Leike had to be humiliated.'

'You don't sound as if you believe that yourself.'

'I damn well do believe it,' Harry said, unscrewing the lid and sniffing the contents.

'Oh? There's not a single fingerprint here that isn't Leike's, not a hair that isn't Leike's raven-black hair, not a shoe print that isn't size forty-five, Leike's. Sigurd Altman is ash blond and takes size forty-two, Harry.'

'He made a good job of clearing up afterwards. Remind me to have this analysed.' Harry slipped the brown bottle into his jacket pocket.

'A good job of clearing up? In what probably isn't even a crime scene? The same man who didn't care about leaving big fat fingerprints on Leike's desk in Holmenveien? Who you said yourself didn't clear up very well at the cabin where he killed Utmo? I don't think so, Harry. And you don't, either.'

'Fuck!' Harry shouted. 'Fuck, fuck, fuck.' He rested his forehead on his hands and stared at the table.

Bjørn Holm held one of the small bits of wire from under the drainpipe in the air and scraped off the gold coating with his fingernail. 'By the way, I think I know what this is.'

'Oh?' Harry said, without lifting his head.

'Iron, chrome, nickel and titanium.'

'What?'

'I had a dental brace when I was a kid. The wires had to be bent and clipped on.'

Harry suddenly looked up and stared at the map of Africa. He studied the countries that slotted into each other like jigsaw pieces. Except Madagascar, which was separate, like a bit that didn't fit.

'At the dentist's—'

'Shh!' Harry said, holding up a hand. Now he had it. Something had just clicked into place. All that could be heard was the wood burner and the gusting wind that was closer outside now. Two jigsaw pieces that had been far apart, each on their own side of the puzzle. A maternal grand-father by Lake Lyseren. Father of his mother. And the photograph in the drawer at the cabin. The family photograph. The picture didn't belong to Tony Leike, but to Odd Utmo. Arthritis. What was it that Tony had told him? Not contagious, but hereditary. The boy with the large, bared teeth. And the man with the hard, pinched mouth, as if he were hiding a dark secret. Hiding his rotten teeth and a brace.

The stone. The dark stone he had found on the bathroom floor in the cabin. He put his hand in his pocket. It was still there. He tossed it over to Bjørn.

'Tell me,' he said with a gulp. 'I came across this. Think it could be a tooth?'

Bjørn held it up to the light. Scraped it with his nail. 'Could be.'

'Let's get back,' Harry said, feeling the hairs on his neck prickle. 'Now. It wasn't bloody Altman who killed them.'

'Oh?'

'It was Tony Leike.'

'You must have read in the papers that Tony Leike was released after being arrested,' Bellman said. 'He had a wonderful little thing called an alibi. He could prove he was somewhere else when Borgny and Charlotte died.'

'I know nothing about that,' Sigurd Altman said, crossing his arms. 'I know only that I saw him stick a knife into Adele's neck. And that the letters I sent caused the ostensible senders to be murdered straight afterwards.'

'You're aware that at least makes you an accessory to murder, aren't you?'

Johan Krohn coughed. 'And you're aware, aren't you, that you made a deal that will serve up the real killer on a silver platter, for you and Kripos? All your internal problems will be solved, Bellman. You'll get all the credit, and you have a witness who will say in court that he saw Tony Leike kill Adele Vetlesen. What happened beyond that remains between you and me.'

'And your client goes free?'

'That's the deal.'

'What about if Leike kept the letters and they turn up at the trial?' Bellman said. 'Then we have a problem.'

'That's precisely why I have a feeling they won't turn up,' Krohn smiled. 'Or, will they?'

'What about the photographs you took of Adele and Tony?'

'Went up in the blaze at Kadok,' Altman said. 'That bastard Hole.'

Mikael Bellman nodded slowly. Then he lifted his pen. S.T. Dupont. Lead and steel. It was heavy. Once he had set it to paper, though, it was as if the signature wrote itself.

'Thanks,' Harry said. 'Over and out.'

He received a rasping sound by way of answer and then it was still, there was only the helicopter engine's monotonous noise outside his headset. Harry bent the microphone and looked out.

Too late.

He had just finished talking over the radio to the tower at Gardemoen Airport. For security reasons they had access to most information, including passenger lists. And could confirm that Odd Utmo had travelled on his pre-booked ticket to Copenhagen two days ago.

The countryside moved slowly beneath them.

Harry visualised him standing there with the passport of the man he had tortured and killed. The man or the woman behind the counter routinely reading to see if the passport matched the name on the list and thinking – if they looked at the photo at all – that was one hell of a brace. Looked up and registered the same dental work on the probably artifically browned teeth in front of him, a brace which Tony Leike must have had to bend and cut to fit on top of his own porcelain high-rises.

They flew into a rainstorm that exploded on the plexiglas bubble, ran to the sides in quivering streaks of water and disappeared. Seconds later it was as if they had never been there.

The finger.

Tony Leike had cut off his finger and sent it to Harry as a final red herring, to demonstrate that Tony Leike had to be considered dead. He could be forgotten, written off, put aside. Was it chance that Leike had chosen the same finger as Harry's missing digit, that he had made himself like him?

But what about the alibi, his water-tight alibi?

Harry had entertained the thought before, but had rejected it because cold-blooded murderers are rarities, deviants, perverted souls in the true sense of the word. But could there have been someone else? Could the answer be as simple as Tony Leike working together with a sidekick?

'Fuck!' said Harry, loud enough for the sound-sensitive microphone to transmit the last part of the syllable to the other three headsets in the helicopter. He caught Jens Rath's sidelong glance. Maybe Rath had been right after all. Maybe Tony Leike was indeed sitting with a shot of the hard stuff, some exotic wildcat of a woman on his arm and grinning because he had come up with a solution.

79

Missed Calls

AT A QUARTER PAST TWO THE HELICOPTER LANDED AT Fornebu, the disused aerodrome twelve minutes' drive from the city centre. When Harry and Bjørn went through the door of the Kripos building and Harry asked the receptionist why neither Bellman nor any of the senior detectives were answering their phones, he was told they were all in a meeting.

'Why the hell weren't we called?' mumbled Harry as he strode down the corridor with Bjørn jogging after him.

He pushed open the door without knocking. Seven heads turned towards them. The eighth, Mikael Bellman's, didn't need to turn as he was sitting at the end of the long table facing the door, and he was the one on whom all the others had been focused.

'Stan and Ollie,' Bellman chortled, and Harry gathered from the chuckling that they had been a subject of conversation in their absence. 'Where have you been?'

'Well, while you were sitting here and playing Snow White and the seven dwarfs we've been to Tony Leike's cabin,' Harry said, throwing himself down on a free chair at the opposite end of the table. 'And we have some news. It isn't Altman. We've arrested the wrong man. It *was* Tony Leike.'

Harry didn't know what reaction he had expected, but at any rate it hadn't been this: none at all.

The POB leaned back in his chair with a friendly quizzical smile.

'*We*'ve arrested the wrong man? To my recollection, Skai was the officer who took it upon himself to arrest Sigurd Altman. And, regarding news value, this is pretty scant. As for Tony Leike, perhaps we should be saying "Welcome back".'

Harry's gaze jumped from Ærdal to the Pelican and back to Bellman as his brain churned. And drew the only possible conclusion.

'Altman,' Harry said. 'Altman said it was Leike. He knew all the time.'

'He not only knew,' Bellman said. 'Just as Leike triggered the avalanche in Håvass, Altman set this whole murder case in motion, without even realising. Skai arrested an innocent man, Harry.'

'Innocent?' Harry shook his head. 'I saw the pictures in the Kadok factory, Bellman. Altman is involved here, I just don't know how as yet.'

'But we do,' Bellman said. 'So if you wouldn't mind leaving this to us . . .' Harry heard the word 'adults' forming in Bellman's mouth, but it came out as: '. . . enlightened ones, you can join in when you're up to speed, Harry. Alright? Bjørn, too? So let's move on. I was saying that we cannot exclude the possibility that Leike had a partner, someone who committed at least two of the murders, the two for which Leike has an alibi. We know that when both Borgny and Charlotte died Leike was at business meetings with several witnesses present.'

'A clever bastard,' said Ærdal. 'Leike knew, of course, that the police would find a link between all the murders. So if he found himself a cast-iron alibi for one or two of them, he would automatically be cleared of the others.'

'Yes,' said Bellman. 'But who is the accomplice?'

Harry heard suggestions, comments and queries fluttering past him in the room.

'Tony Leike's motive for killing Adele Vetlesen was hardly the demand for four hundred thousand,' the Pelican said. 'But rather the fear that if it came out that he had got some woman pregnant, Lene Galtung would end the relationship and he could kiss goodbye to the Galtung millions for the Congo project. So the question we should be asking ourselves is who had identical interests.'

'The other investors in the Congo,' said the smooth-faced detective. 'What about his financial friends at the office block?'

'It's make or break for Tony Leike with the Congo project,' Bellman said. 'But none of the other finance squirts would have killed two people to secure their ten per cent share in a project. Those boys are used to winning and losing money. Besides, Leike had to collaborate with someone he could trust at both a personal and a professional level. Bear in mind that the murder weapon was the same for Borgny and Charlotte. What did you call it, Harry?'

'A Leopold's apple,' Harry intoned, still befuddled.

'Louder, please.'

'A Leopold's apple.'

'Thank you. From Africa. Same place Leike had been a mercenary. It is therefore fair to assume that Leike used one of his former comrades, and I think we should start there.'

'If he used a mercenary for murders number two and three, why not for all of them?' the Pelican asked. 'Then he would have had an alibi right the way through.'

'He would have got a per capita discount, too,' the Nansen moustache said. 'The mercenary can't get any more than life imprisonment anyway.'

'There may be angles of which we are unaware,' Bellman said. 'Banal reasons like not having enough time or Leike not having the money. Or the most usual reason in crime cases: it just happened like that.'

Nods of agreement round the table; even the Pelican seemed content with the answer.

'Any other questions? No? Then I would like to use this opportunity to thank Harry Hole who has been with us thus far. As we no longer have any use for his expertise, he will return to Crime Squad with immediate effect. It was stimulating to experience another view of how to work on murders, Harry. You might not have solved this case but who knows. There may be some interesting Crime Squad cases waiting for you down there in Grønland, if not murders. So thank you again. I have a press conference now, folks.'

Harry looked at Bellman. He could not help but admire him. The way you admire a cockroach you flush down the toilet, that comes creeping back. Again and again. And in the end it inherits the world.

* * *

At Olav's bedside in Rikshospital, seconds, minutes and hours passed in a slow, undulating swell of monotony. A nurse came and went, Sis came and went. Flowers moved imperceptibly closer.

Harry had seen how many relatives could not bear to wait for the last breath of their loved ones, how in the end they prayed, begged for death to come and liberate them. Them, meaning themselves. But for Harry it was the opposite. He had never felt closer to his father than now, here, in this wordless room where all was breathing and the next heartbeat. For seeing Olav Hole there was like seeing himself, in the peace-filled existence between life and nothingness.

The detectives at Kripos had seen and understood a lot. But not the evident link. Which made the entirety so much clearer. The link between the Leike farm and Ustaoset. Between the rumours and the ghost of a missing boy from the Utmo farm and a man who called the wasteland 'his terrain'. Between Tony Leike and the boy in the photograph with his ugly father and beautiful mother.

Now and then Harry glanced at his mobile phone and saw a missed call. Hagen. Øystein. Kaja. Kaja again. He would have to answer her calls soon. He rang her.

'Can I come to yours tonight?' she asked.

80

The Rhythm

THE RAIN BEAT DOWN ON THE BOARDS OF THE JETTY. Harry walked up behind the man standing at the edge, facing the other way.

'Morning, Skai.'

'Morning, Hole,' the officer said without turning. The tip of the fishing rod was bent towards the line that disappeared in the reeds on the opposite bank.

'Caught something?'

'Nope,' Skai said. 'Snarled up on the bloody reeds.'

'Sorry to hear that. Read the papers today?'

'They don't arrive before late morning in the sticks.'

Harry knew that was not true, but nodded anyway.

'But I suppose they've written that I'm a village idiot,' Skai said. 'They had to get townsfolk in from Kripos to sort out the muddle.'

'As I said: I'm sorry.'

Skai shrugged. 'I've got no complaints. You gave it to me straight, I knew what I was doing. And it was a bit of fun, too. Not much happens out here, you know.'

'Mm. They don't write much about you, they're mostly interested in Tony Leike being the killer, after all. Bellman is much-quoted.'

'He is that.'

'Soon they'll work out who Tony's father is as well.'

Skai turned and looked at Harry.

'I should have thought of it before, and especially after we talked about the changing of names.'

'Now I don't follow you, Hole.'

'You were even the person who told me, Skai. Tony lived with his grandfather at the Leike farm. Mother's father. Tony had taken his mother's name.'

'Nothing unusual in that.'

'Maybe not. But in this case there was a good reason for it. Tony was hiding at his grandfather's. His mother sent him there.'

'What makes you think that?'

'A colleague,' Harry said, and for a second he seemed to have the night's scent of her in his nostrils again. 'She told me something the Ustaoset officer had told her. About the Utmo family. About a father and a son who hated each other so intensely that it threatened to culminate in murder.'

'Murder?'

'I've checked Odd Utmo's record. He was, like his son, known for his rages. As a young man he went to prison for eight years for committing a murder out of jealousy. After that, he moved into the wastelands. He married Karen Leike, and they had a son. The son reached his teens and was already good-looking, tall and a charmer. Two men and a woman in almost total isolation. A man who had a conviction for killing in a jealous rage. It looks like Karen tried to prevent a tragedy unfolding by sending her son away in secret and leaving one of his shoes in an area where there had just been a big avalanche.'

'News to me, Hole.'

Harry nodded slowly. 'I'm afraid she managed only to postpone the tragedy. Her body has just been found at the bottom of a precipice with a bullet through the head. A few metres away her husband and murderer was crushed beneath a snowmobile. He'd been tortured, had most of the skin on his back and arms burned off and his teeth ripped out. Guess who did it?'

'Oh, my God . . .'

Harry put a cigarette between his lips.

'How did you trace the link?' Skai asked.

'The similarity, the genes.' He lit the cigarette. 'Father and son. You can try to run, but it will always be there, like a curse. I think Odd Utmo realised the Håvass murders meant he would be hunted, too, and that it was the ghost of his own deceased son who was after him. So he fled from the farm up to this Tourist Association cabin safely hidden between precipices. He took a family photo with him, the family he had himself destroyed. Imagine, a frightened, maybe remorseful killer alone with his thoughts.'

'He had already been given his punishment.'

'I found the photo. Tony was lucky, he took after his mother in looks. It was hard to see anything of the adult Tony in the photograph of the boy. But he already had the big white teeth. While his father hid his. That's where they were different.'

'I thought you said it was the similarity that gave them away?'

Harry nodded. 'They had the same disease.'

'They were killers.'

Harry shook his head. 'Disease, as in physical ailment, Skai. I meant they both had arthritis. The family relationship was confirmed this morning. The DNA analysis of the flesh on the wood burner and Tony Leike's hair prove they are father and son.'

Skai nodded.

'Well,' Harry said. 'I came by to thank you for your help and to bemoan the outcome. Bjørn Holm sends his regards to your wife and says she makes the best meatballs and mashed swede he's ever tasted.'

Flicker of a smile from Skai. 'Most people think that. Even Tony liked them.'

'Oh?'

Skai shrugged and pulled a knife from the sheath on his belt.

'I told you Mia was stuck on the boy, didn't I? It was soon after he had knifed Ole. She brought him home for lunch one day when she knew I wouldn't be there. The wife said nothing when they showed up, though there was a humdinger when I got to hear about it, of course. But you know what girls are like at that age and in love. I tried to explain that Tony was violent, fool that I was. I should have known the worse I made her boyfriend out to be, the more determined she would become to hang on to him. Then it's two together against the rest of the world, kind of. Well, you've seen it yourself with women who start writing letters to convicted murderers.'

Harry nodded.

'Mia would have left home, followed him to the end of the world, there was no moderation in anything,' Skai said, cutting the fishing line and reeling in.

Harry followed the retreat of the slack line. 'Mm. End of the world.'

'Yep.'

'I see.'

Skai stopped winding and looked at Harry. 'No,' he said with conviction.

'No what?'

'No to what you're thinking.'

'Which is?'

'That Mia and Tony met again later. He broke up with her; since then they have never met. Her life has continued without him. She has nothing to do with this case, got it? You have my word. She is putting her life together again, so please don't . . .'

Harry nodded and took the cigarette, which had been extinguished by the rain, from his mouth.

'I'm not on the case any more,' he said. 'But your word would have been good enough, anyway.'

As Harry drove from the car park he looked in the mirror and watched Skai packing up his fishing gear.

Rikshospital. He was in the rhythm now. Time was not chopped up by events; it flowed in an even stream. He had thought of asking for a mattress. That would be a bit like Chungking Mansion.

81

The Cones of Light

THREE DAYS PASSED. HE WAS ALIVE. EVERYONE WAS ALIVE.

No one knew where Tony Leike was, the trail of the fake Odd Utmo ended in Copenhagen. A photograph of Lene Galtung with a shawl over her head and large sunglasses in the best Greta Garbo style was splashed across one newspaper. The headline was: NO COMMENT. And now no one had seen her for two days after she had gone into hiding, apparently at her father's house in London. The photograph of Tony in work clothes in front of the helicopter had been in several newspapers. It was captioned PRINCE CHARMING'S VANISHING ACT in one. He had been dubbed Prince Charming now, people had taken to it, and anyway, it suited Leike better than Altman. Strangely enough, no one in the press had managed to link Tony Leike with the Utmo farm yet. The mother and later Tony had obviously covered their tracks well.

Mikael Bellman had daily press conferences. In a TV talk show he demonstrated his pedagogic skills and flashed his winsome smile explaining how the case had been cracked. His version of the story, that went without saying. And made it seem like an oversight that the killer had not been arrested; the important thing first off was that Tony 'Prince Charming' Leike had been unmasked, rendered ineffective, sidelined.

The dark descended a few minutes later every evening. Everyone was waiting for spring or frost, one of the two, but neither came.

The cones of light swept across the ceiling.

525

Harry lay on his side, staring at the smoke from his cigarette curling up towards the ceiling in intricate and ever-unpredictable patterns.

'You're so quiet,' Kaja said, snuggling up to his back.

'I'll be here until the funeral,' he said. 'Then I'm off.'

He took another drag. She didn't answer. Then, to his surprise, he felt something warm and wet on his shoulder blade. He put the cigarette on the edge of the ashtray and turned to her. 'Are you crying?'

'Trying not to,' she laughed with a sniffle. 'I don't know what's got into me.'

'Do you want a cigarette?'

She shook her head and dried the tears. 'Mikael rang today, wanting to meet.'

'Mm.'

She laid her head against his chest. 'Don't you want to know what I answered?'

'Only if you want to tell me.'

'I said no. Then he said I would regret that. He said you would drag me down. That it wasn't the first time you had done that to someone.'

'Well, he's right.'

She lifted her head. 'But that doesn't matter, don't you understand? I want to be wherever you are.' Tears began to roll again. 'And if it's down, I want to be there, too.'

'But there'll be nothing,' Harry said. 'Not even me. I'll have gone. You saw me in Chungking. It would be like right after the avalanche. The same cabin, but alone and abandoned.'

'But you found me and got me out. I can do the same for you.'

'What about if I don't want to get out? You haven't got any more dying fathers to entice me with.'

'But you love me, Harry. I know you love me. That's a good enough reason, isn't it? *I'm* a good enough reason.'

Harry caressed her hair, her cheeks, caught her tears with his fingers, carried them to his mouth and kissed them.

'Yes,' he said with a sad smile. 'You are reason enough.'

She took his hand, kissed it where he had kissed it.

'No,' she whispered. 'Don't say it. Don't say that's why you're going.

So that you don't drag me down. I'll follow you to the end of the world, you see?'

He pulled her into him. And at once felt something slacken, like a muscle that had been held in quivering tension for a long time without his realising. He let go, gave up, let himself fall. And the pain that had been there melted away, became something warm following the bloodstream around his body, softening it, giving it peace. The feeling of free fall was so liberating that he felt his throat thicken. And knew part of him had wanted it, this, also up there in the snowy mist above the scree.

'To the end of the world,' she whispered, already breathing faster.

The cones of light swept across the ceiling, again and again.

82

Red

HARRY WAS SITTING BY HIS FATHER'S BEDSIDE. IT WAS STILL dark when a nurse came in with a cup of coffee, asked him whether he had had any breakfast and dropped a glossy mag in his lap.

'You have to think about something else, you know,' she said, angling her head and giving the impression she was about to stroke his cheek.

Harry dutifully flicked through the magazine while she tended to his father. But he couldn't distract himself in the celebrity press, either. Photographs of Lene Galtung leaving premieres, gala lunches in her new Porsche. MISSING TONY was the headline, and the assertion was underpinned by comments not from Lene herself, but from celebrity friends. There were pictures outside the gates of a house in London, but no one had seen Lene there, either. At least no one had recognised her. There was a grainy photograph taken from a distance of a red-haired woman in front of Crédit Suisse in Zurich, which the magazine claimed was Lene Galtung, because they were able to quote Lene's hairstylist who Harry assumed had been paid a sizeable sum to say: 'She asked me to curl her hair and dye it brick red.' Tony was referred to as a 'suspect' in what was portrayed as an average society scandal rather than one of the country's worst ever murder cases.

Harry got up, went into the corridor and rang Katrine Bratt. It still wasn't even seven o'clock, but she was up. She was leaving today. Beginning at Bergen Police Station over the weekend.

He hoped she would take it easy at the start. Although it was difficult to imagine Katrine Bratt taking anything easy.

'Last job,' he said.

'And after that?' she asked.

'Then I'm off.'

'No one will miss you.'

'. . . more than I will.'

'There was a full stop at the end, dear.'

'It's about Crédit Suisse in Zurich. I'd like to know if Lene Galtung has an account there. She's supposed to have been given a whopping pre-inheritance. Swiss banks are tricky. Probably take a bit of time.'

'Fine, I'm getting the hang of this now.'

'Good. And there's a woman whose movements I want you to check.'

'Lene Galtung?'

'No.'

'No? What's the name of the beast?'

Harry spelt it for her.

At a quarter past eight Harry pulled up outside the fairy-tale homestead in Voksenkollen. There were a couple of cars parked, and through the raindrops Harry could make out the tired faces and the long telephoto lenses of paparazzi. They seemed to have been camping there the whole night. Harry rang the bell by the gate and went in.

The woman with the turquoise eyes was standing by the door, waiting.

'Lene's not here,' she said.

'Where is she?'

'Somewhere they won't find her,' she said, motioning to the cars outside the gate. 'And you lot promised me you would leave her alone after the last interview. Three hours it lasted.'

'I know,' Harry lied. 'But it was you I wanted to talk to.'

'Me?'

'May I come in?'

He followed her into the kitchen. She gestured to a chair, turned her back on him and filled a cup from a coffee machine on the worktop.

'What's the story?'

'Which story?'

'The one about you being Lene's mother.'

The coffee cup hit the floor and smashed into a thousand pieces. She clutched the worktop, and he could see her back heaving. Harry hesitated for a moment, but then took a deep breath and said what he'd made up his mind to say.

'We've done a DNA test.'

She whirled around, furious. 'How? You haven't . . .' She came to an abrupt halt.

Harry's gaze met her turquoise eyes. She had fallen for the bluff. He was aware of a vague sense of discomfort. Which could have been caused by shame. It melted away, nonetheless.

'Get out!' she hissed.

'Out to them?' Harry asked, nodding towards the paparazzi. 'I'm finishing my police career, going to travel. I could do with a bit of capital. If a hairstylist can be paid twenty thousand kroner for saying which hair colour Lene requested, how much do you think I'd get for telling them who her real mother is?'

The woman took a step forward, raising a hand in anger, but then her tears flowed, the burning light in her eyes extinguished and she sank into a kitchen chair, impotent. Harry cursed himself, knowing he had been unnecessarily brutal. But time was not on his side for any finely attuned stratagems.

'I apologise,' he said. 'But I'm trying to save your daughter. And to do that I require assistance. Do you understand?'

He placed a hand upon hers, but she pulled it away.

'He's a killer,' Harry said. 'But she couldn't care less, could she. She'll do it anyway.'

'Do what?' the woman sniffled.

'Follow him to the end of the world.'

She didn't answer, just shook her head weeping silent tears.

Harry waited. Stood up, poured himself a cup of coffee, tore a sheet off the kitchen roll, put it on the table in front of her, sat down and waited. Took a sip. Waited.

'I said she shouldn't do what I did,' she sniffled. 'She shouldn't love a man because he . . . because he made her feel *beautiful*. More beautiful than she is. You think it's a blessing when it happens, but it's a curse.'

Harry waited.

'When you've seen yourself become beautiful in his eyes once it's like . . . like being bewitched. And so you are. Again and again, because you think you'll be allowed to see it one more time.'

Harry waited.

'I spent my early years in a caravan. We travelled around, I wasn't able to go to school. When I was eight the child welfare people came for me. At sixteen I began to clean at the shipping company owned by Galtung. Anders was engaged when he got me pregnant. He wasn't the one with the money, she was. He had gambled in the stock market, but the prices for tankers fell and he had no choice. He sent me packing. But she found out. And it was she who decided I would keep the child, that I would be retained as a house cleaner, that my little girl would be raised as the daughter of the house. She couldn't have any children herself, so they took Lene from me. They asked what kind of upbringing I could offer her. Me, a single mother, uneducated, no family around me, did I really wish to deprive my daughter of the chance of a good life? I was so young and afraid, I thought they were right, this was for the best.'

'No one knew about it?'

She took the kitchen paper and wiped her nose. 'It's strange how easy it is to deceive people when they want to be deceived. And if they are not deceived, they don't let it show. That didn't matter much to me. I had only been a womb to produce an heir for the Galtungs, so what?'

'Was that it?'

She shrugged. 'No. After all, I had Lene. Nursed her, fed her, changed her nappies, slept by her. Taught her to speak, brought her up. But we all knew it was short-term. One day I would have to let go.'

'Did you?'

She gave a bitter laugh. '*Can* a mother ever let go? A daughter can let go. Lene despises me for what I've done. For what I am. But look at her. Now she's doing the same.'

'Following the wrong man to the end of the world?'

She shrugged again.

'Do you know where she is?'

'No. Only that she's left to be with him.'

Harry took another swig of coffee. 'I know where the end of the world is,' he said.

She didn't answer.

'I can go and try to bring her back for you.'

'She doesn't want to be brought back.'

'I can try. With your help.' Harry pulled out a piece of paper and placed it in front of her. 'What do you say?'

She read. Then she looked up. The make-up had run from her turquoise eyes down her hollow cheeks.

'Swear to me that you'll bring my girl back safe and sound, Hole. Swear. Do that and I'll agree.'

Harry studied her.

'I swear,' he said.

Outside again, with a cigarette lit, he thought about what she had said. *Can a mother ever let go?* About Odd Utmo who had taken a photograph of his son with him. *But a daughter can let go.* Can she? He blew out the cigarette smoke. Could *he* let go?

Gunnar Hagen was standing beside the vegetable counter of his favourite Pakistani grocer's shop. He ogled his inspector with utter disbelief. 'You want to go back to the Congo? To find Lene Galtung? And that has nothing to do with the murder investigation?'

'Same as last time,' Harry said, lifting a vegetable he didn't recognise. 'We're after a missing person.'

'Lene Galtung has not been reported missing by anyone except the gutter press, as far as I know.'

'She has now.' Harry took a sheet from his coat pocket and showed Hagen the signature. 'By her biological mother.'

'I see. And how am I going to explain to the Ministry of Justice that we should launch this search in the Congo?'

'We have a lead.'

'Which is?'

'I read in *Se og Hør* that Lene Galtung asked to have her hair dyed brick red. I don't even know if that's a colour we use in Norway, that's probably why I remembered it.'

'Remembered what?'

'That it was the hair colour given in the passport belonging to Juliana Verni from Leipzig. At the time I asked Günther to check if there was a stamp from Kigali in her passport. But the police didn't find it, the passport was gone, and I'm convinced Tony Leike took it.'

'The passport? And?'

'Now Lene Galtung has got it.'

Hagen put some pak choi in his shopping basket while slowly shaking his head. 'You're basing a trip to the Congo on something you read in a gossip rag?'

'I'm basing it on what I – or I should say Katrine Bratt – found out about what Juliana Verni has been doing recently.'

Hagen started to make a move towards the man at the cash desk on a podium by the right-hand wall. 'Verni's dead, Harry.'

'Do dead people catch flights? Turns out Juliana Verni – or let's say a woman with curly brick-red hair – has bought a plane ticket from Zurich to the end of the world.'

'The end of the world?'

'Goma, the Congo. Early tomorrow.'

'Then they will arrest her when they discover she has a passport belonging to a person who has been dead for more than two months.'

'I checked with ICAO. They say it can take up to a year before the passport number of a deceased person is crossed off the books. Which means someone may have travelled to the Congo on Odd Utmo's passport, too. However, we have no cooperation agreement with the Congo. And it's hardly an insurmountable problem buying your way out of prison.'

Hagen let the cashier tot up his goods while he massaged his temples in an attempt to pre-empt the inevitable headache. 'So go and find her in Zurich. Send the Swiss police to the airport.'

'We've got her under surveillance. Lene Galtung will lead us to Tony Leike, boss.'

'She'll lead us to perdition, Harry.' Hagen paid, took his items and marched out of the shop into rainy, wind-blown Grønlandsleiret where people rushed past with upturned collars and downcast faces.

'You don't understand. Bratt managed to find out that two days ago Lene Galtung emptied her account in Zurich. Two million euros. Not a staggering sum and definitely not enough to finance a whole mining project. But enough to bridge a critical phase.'

'Idle speculation.'

'What the hell else is she going to do with two million euros in cash? Come on, boss, this is the only chance we'll get.' Harry stepped up the pace to stay level with Hagen. 'In the Congo you don't find people who don't want to be found. The fucking country is as big as Western Europe and consists largely of forest no white man has ever seen. Go for it now. Leike will haunt your dreams, boss.'

'I don't have nightmares like you do, Harry.'

'Have you told the next of kin how well you sleep at night, boss?'

Gunnar Hagen came to an abrupt halt.

'Sorry, boss,' Harry said. 'That was below the belt.'

'It was. And actually I don't know why you're hassling me for my permission. You've never considered it important before.'

'Thought it would be nice for you to have the feeling you're the man in charge, boss.'

Hagen fired a warning shot across Harry's bows. Harry shrugged. 'Let me do this, boss. Afterwards you can give me the boot for refusing to obey orders. I'll take all the flak, it's OK by me.'

'Is it OK?'

'I'm going to resign after this anyway.'

Hagen eyed Harry. 'Fine,' he said. 'Go.' Then he set off again.

Harry caught up with him. 'Fine?'

'Yes. Actually it was fine from the very beginning.'

'Oh? Why didn't you say so before then?'

'Thought it would be nice to have the feeling I was the man in charge.'

PART NINE

83

The End of the World

SHE DREAMED SHE WAS STANDING BEFORE A CLOSED DOOR and heard a cold, lone bird's cry from the forest, and it sounded so peculiar because the sun was shining and it was hot. She opened the door . . .

She woke up with her head on Harry's shoulder and dried saliva in the corners of her mouth. The captain's voice announced they were about to land in Goma.

She looked out of the window. A grey stripe in the east presaged the arrival of a new day. It was twelve hours since they had left Oslo. In a few hours the Zurich flight with Juliana Verni on the passenger list would land.

'I'm wondering why Hagen thought it was alright to shadow Lene like this,' Harry said.

'He probably valued your cogent arguments,' Kaja yawned.

'Mm. He seemed a bit too relaxed. I reckon he's got something up his sleeve. There's some guarantee he's got they won't bollock him for this.'

'He might have something on someone in the Ministry of Justice,' Kaja said.

'Mm. Or on Bellman. Perhaps he knows you and Bellman were having a relationship?'

'Doubt it,' Kaja said, peering into the dark. 'There are hardly any lights here.'

'Looks like a power cut,' Harry said. 'The airport must have its own generator.'

'Light over there,' she said, pointing to a red shimmer north of the town. 'What's that?'

'Nyiragongo,' Harry said. 'It's the lava lighting up the sky.'

'Is that right?' she said, pressing her nose against the window.

Harry drank his glass of water. 'Shall we go through the plan one more time?'

She nodded and straightened her seat back.

'You stay in the arrivals hall and keep an eye on the landing times. Make sure everything is going to plan. In the meantime I'll go shopping. It's only fifteen minutes to the centre, so I'll be back in plenty of time before Lene's plane lands. You watch, see if anyone is there to collect her, and stay on her tail. As Lene knows my face I'll be outside in a taxi waiting for you. And should anything untoward happen, you ring me at once. OK?'

'OK. And you're sure she'll stop over in Goma?'

'I'm not sure of anything at all. There are only two hotels in Goma that are still functional, and according to Katrine there's nothing booked, neither in Verni's name, nor in Galtung's. But the guerrillas control the road to the west and north, and the closest town south is an eight-mile drive.'

'Do you really believe the only reason Tony has brought Lene here is to milk her for money?'

'According to Jens Rath, the project is at a critical stage. Can you see any other reason?'

Kaja shrugged. 'What if even a killer is capable of loving someone so much that he simply wants to be with her? Is that so inconceivable?'

Harry nodded. As if to say 'yes, you have a point', or 'yes, it is inconceivable'.

There was a humming and a clicking, like a camera in slow motion, as the wheels were lowered.

Kaja stared out of the window.

'And I don't like the shopping, Harry. Why the weapons?'

'Leike is violent.'

'And I don't like travelling as an undercover cop. I know we can't smuggle our own weapons into the Congo, but couldn't we have asked the Congolese police for assistance with the arrest?'

'As I said, we have no extradition agreement. And it's not improbable that a financier like Leike has local police in his pay who would have warned him.'

'Conspiracy theory.'

'Yep. And simple mathematics. A policeman's wage in the Congo is not enough to feed a family. Relax, Van Boorst has a wonderful little ironmongery and he's professional enough to keep his mouth shut.'

The wheels emitted a scream as they hit the landing strip.

Kaja squinted out of the window. 'Why are there so many soldiers here?'

'UN flying in reinforcements. The guerrillas have advanced in the last few days.'

'What guerrillas?'

'Hutu guerrillas, Tutsi guerrillas, Mai Mai guerrillas. Who knows?'

'Harry?'

'Yes.'

'Let's get this job done quickly and go home.'

He nodded.

It had already grown lighter when Harry walked along the line of taxi drivers outside. He exchanged a few words with each and every one until he found someone who could speak good English. Excellent English, in fact. He was a small man with alert eyes, grey hair and thick blood vessels above the temples and sides of his high, shiny forehead. His English was definitely original, a kind of stilted Oxford variant with a broad Congolese accent. Harry explained to him that he would hire him for the whole day, they quickly agreed a price and exchanged hand-shakes, a third of the agreed sum in dollars, and names, Harry and Dr Duigame.

'In English literature,' the man elucidated, openly counting the money. 'But as we're going to be together the whole day you can call me Saul.'

He opened the rear door of a dented Hyundai. Harry indicated where Saul was to drive, to the road by the burnt-down church.

'Sounds like you've been here before,' Saul said, steering the car along a regular stretch of tarmac which, as soon as it met the main traffic artery, became a moonscape of craters and cracks.

'Once.'

'Then you should be careful,' he smiled. 'Hemingway wrote that once you have opened your soul to Africa you won't want to be anywhere else.'

'Hemingway wrote that?' Harry queried with some scepticism.

'Yes, he did, but Hemingway wrote that sort of romantic shit all the time. Shot lions when he was drunk and pissed that sweet whiskey urine on their corpses. The truth is that no one comes back to the Congo if they don't have to.'

'I had to,' Harry said. 'Listen, I tried to get hold of the driver I had last time when I was here, Joe from Refugee Aid. But there's no response from his number.'

'Joe's gone,' Saul said.

'Gone?'

'He took his family with him, stole a car and drove to Uganda. Goma's under siege. They'll kill everyone. I'm going soon, too. Joe had a good car, maybe he'll make it.'

Harry recognised the church spire towering over the ruins of what Nyiragongo had eaten. He held on tight as the Hyundai rolled past the potholes. There were nasty scrapes and bumps to the chassis a couple of times.

'Wait here,' Harry said. 'I'll walk the rest of the way. Back soon.'

Harry stepped out and inhaled grey dust and the smell of spices and rotten fish.

Then he started walking. An obviously drunk man tried to ram Harry with his shoulder, but missed and staggered into the road. Harry had a couple of choice words hurled after him and walked on. Not too fast, not too slow. Arriving at the only brick house in the square of shops, he went up to the door, banged hard and waited. Heard quick footsteps inside. Too quick to be Van Boorst's. The door was opened a fraction and half a black face and one eye appeared.

'Van Boorst at home?' Harry asked.

'No.' The large gold teeth in the upper set glinted.

'I want to buy some handguns, Miss. Can you help me?'

She shook her head. 'Sorry. Goodbye.'

Harry shoved his foot in the gap. 'I pay well.'

'No guns. Van Boorst not here.'

'When will he be back, Miss?'

'I not know. I not have time now.'

'I'm looking for a man from Norway. Tony. Tall. Handsome. Have you seen him around?'

The girl shook her head.

'Will Van Boorst be coming home this evening? This is important, Miss.'

She looked at him. Weighed him up. Lingered, from top to toe. And back. Her soft lips slid apart over her teeth. 'You a rich man?'

Harry didn't answer. She blinked sleepily, and her matt-black eyes glistened. Then she smirked. 'Thirty minutes. Come back then.'

Harry returned to the taxi, sat in the front seat, told Saul to drive to the bank and rang Kaja.

'I'm still sitting in the arrivals hall,' she said. 'No announcements to say anything except that the Zurich flight is on time.'

'I'll check us into the hotel before I go back to Van Boorst and buy what we need.'

The hotel lay to the east of the centre towards the Rwandan border. In front of reception was a car park coated with lava and wreathed with trees.

'They were planted after the last eruption,' Saul said, as though reading Harry's thoughts. There were almost no trees in Goma. The double room was on the first floor of a low building by the lake and had a balcony overlooking the water. Harry smoked a cigarette, watching the morning sun glitter on the surface and glint off the oil rig far out. He checked his watch and went back to the car park.

Saul's state of mind seemed to have adapted to the sluggish traffic he was in: he drove slowly, talked slowly, moved his hands slowly. He parked outside the church walls, a good distance from Van Boorst's house. Switched off the engine, turned to Harry and asked politely but firmly for the second third of the sum.

'Don't you trust me?' Harry asked with a raised eyebrow.

'I trust your sincere desire to pay,' Saul said. 'But in Goma money is safer with me than with you, Mr Harry. Shame but true.'

Harry acknowledged the reasoning with a nod, flipped through the rest of the money and asked if Saul had something heavy and compact in the car, the size of a pistol, such as a torch. Saul pursed his lips and opened the glove compartment. Harry took out the torch, stuffed it in his inside pocket and looked at his watch. Twenty-five minutes had gone.

He strode down the street, his eyes fixed straight ahead. But sidelong glances registered men turning after him with appraising eyes. Appraising height and weight. The elasticity of his strides. The jacket hanging slightly askew and the bulky shape in the inside pocket. And dismissing the opportunity.

He went up to the door and knocked.

The same light steps.

The door opened. She glanced at him, then her gaze wandered past him, to the street.

'Quick, come in,' she said, grabbing his arm and pulling him inside.

Harry stepped over the threshold and stood in the semi-gloom. All the curtains were drawn, apart from by the window over the bed where he had seen her lying half naked the first time he was here.

'He not arrive yet,' she said in her simple but effective English. 'Soon come.'

Harry nodded and looked at the bed. Tried to imagine her there, with the blanket over her hips. The light falling on her skin. But he couldn't. For there was something trying to catch his attention, something was not right, missing, or was there and shouldn't have been.

'You come alone?' she asked, walking around him and sitting on the bed. Placing one hand on the mattress, allowing the shoulder strap of her dress to slip down.

Harry shifted his gaze to locate what was wrong. And found it. The colonial master and exploiter King Leopold.

'Yes,' he said automatically, without quite knowing why yet. 'Alone.'

The picture of King Leopold which had been hanging on the wall was gone. The next thought followed hard on its heels. Van Boorst wasn't coming. He was gone, too.

Harry took half a step towards her. She tilted her head slightly, moistening her full, red-black lips. And he was close enough to see now, to see what had replaced the painting of the Belgian king. The nail the picture had been hanging from impaled a banknote. The face that made the note distinctive was sensitive and sported a well-tended moustache. Edvard Munch.

Harry realised what was going to happen, was about to turn, but something also told him it was far too late, he was positioned exactly as planned in the stage directions.

He sensed more than saw the movement behind him and didn't feel the precise jab in his neck, only the breath against his temple. His neck froze to ice, the paralysis spread down his back and up to his scalp, his legs buckled beneath him as the drug reached his brain and consciousness faded. His last thought before darkness enveloped him was how amazingly fast ketanome worked.

84

Reunion

KAJA BIT HER LOWER LIP. SOMETHING WAS WRONG.

She called Harry's number again.

And got his voicemail yet again.

For several hours, she had been sitting in the arrivals hall – which, as far as that went, was also the departures hall – and the plastic chair rubbed against all the parts of the body with which it came into contact.

She heard the whoosh of a plane. Immediately afterwards the only monitor present, a bulky box hanging from two rusty wires in the ceiling, showed that flight number KJ337 from Zurich had landed.

She scanned the gathering of people every second minute and established that none of them was Tony Leike.

She phoned again, but cut the connection when she realised she was doing this for the sake of doing something, but it wasn't action, it was apathy.

The sliding doors to baggage reclaim opened and the first passengers with hand luggage came through. Kaja stood up and went to the wall beside the sliding doors so that she could see the names on the plastic signs and the scraps of paper the taxi drivers were holding up for the arriving travellers. No Juliana Verni and no Lene Galtung.

She went back to her lookout post by the chair. Sat on her palms, could feel they were damp with sweat. What should she do? She pulled down her sunglasses and stared at the sliding doors.

Seconds passed. Nothing happened.

Lene Galtung was almost concealed behind a pair of violet sunglasses and a large black man walking in front of her. Her hair was red, curly, and she was wearing a denim jacket, khaki trousers and solid hiking boots. She was dragging a wheeled bag tailor-made to the maximum measurements allowed for hand luggage. She had no handbag, but a small, shiny metal case.

Nothing happened. Everything happened. In parallel and at the same time, the past and the present, and in a strange way Kaja knew the opportunity was finally there. The opportunity for which she had been waiting. The chance to do the right thing.

Kaja didn't look straight at Lene Galtung, just made sure she was to the left of her field of vision. Stood up calmly after she had passed, took her bag and began to follow her. Into the blinding sunlight. Still no one had addressed her, and judging from her quick, determined steps, Kaja assumed she had been schooled down to the last detail about what she was to do. She walked past taxis, crossed the road and got into the back seat of a dark blue Range Rover. The door was held open for her by a black man in a suit. Slamming it after her, he then walked round to the driver's seat. Kaja slipped onto the back seat of the first taxi in the queue, leaned forward between the seats, reflected quickly, but concluded that basically there was no other way of formulating it. 'Follow that car.'

She met the driver's eyes and arched eyebrows in the rear-view mirror. Pointed to the car in front of them, and the driver gave a nod of comprehension, but still kept the car in neutral.

'Double pay,' Kaja said.

The driver jerked his head and let go of the clutch.

Kaja rang Harry. Still no answer.

They crawled their way west along the main thoroughfare. The streets were full of lorries, carts and cars with suitcases tied to the roofs. On each side, people were walking with huge piles of clothes and possessions balanced on their heads. In some places the traffic had come to a complete standstill. The driver had obviously got the point, and he was keeping at least one car between them and Lene Galtung's Range Rover.

'Where are they all going?' Kaja asked.

The driver smiled and shook his head to signify that he didn't under-stand. Kaja repeated the question in French with no luck. In the end she pointed to the people shuffling past their car with an interrogative grimace.

'Re-fu-gee,' the driver said. 'Go away. Bad people come.'

Kaja mouthed an 'Aha'.

Kaja texted Harry again. Trying to stave off panic.

In the middle of Goma the road forked. The Range Rover swung left. Further on it took another left and rolled down towards the lake. They had come to a very different part of town with large detached houses behind high fences and surrounded by well-tended gardens with trees to offer shade and keep out prying eyes.

'Old,' the driver said. 'The Bel-gium. Co-lo-nist.'

There was no traffic in the residential area and Kaja signalled that they should hang back further, even though she doubted Lene Galtung had any schooling in detecting tails. When the Range Rover stopped a hundred metres ahead, Kaja motioned to the driver to stop, too.

An iron gate was opened by a man in a grey uniform, the car drove in and the gate was closed again.

Lene Galtung could hear her heart pounding. It hadn't beaten like this since the telephone had rung and she had heard his voice. He had told her he was in Africa. And said she should come. That he needed her. That only she could help him. Save the fine project that was not only his, but would become hers, too. So that he could have work. Men needed work. A future. A secure life, somewhere children could grow up.

The chauffeur opened the door for her, and Lene Galtung stepped out. The sun was not as strong as she had feared. The house that stood before her was magnificent. Solid, built at leisure. Brick by brick. Old money. The way they would do it themselves. When she and Tony had met he had been so intrigued by her family tree. Galtung was a Norwegian aristocratic family, one of the very few that had not been imported, a fact Tony repeated again and again. Perhaps that was why she had decided to postpone telling him that she was like him: of normal, modest origins, a grey rock in the scree, a social climber.

But now they would create their own nobility, they would shine in the scree. They would build.

The driver went ahead of her, up the brick steps to the door, where an armed man in camouflage opened it for them. A genuine crystal chandelier hung from the ceiling in the entrance hall. Lene's hand squeezed the sweaty handle of the metal case containing the money. Her heart felt as if it would explode in her chest. Was her hair alright? Could you see the effects of the lack of sleep and the long journey? Someone was coming down the broad staircase from the first floor. No, it was a black woman, probably one of the servants. Lene gave her a friendly but not an exaggeratedly welcoming smile. Saw the glint of gold teeth when the woman acknowledged her with a cool, almost impudent smile and left through the door behind her.

There he was.

He stood by the banisters on the first floor and looked down at them.

He was tall, dark and draped in a dressing gown. She could see the attractive thick scar gleam white against his tanned chest. Then he smiled. She heard her breathing quicken. The smile. It illuminated his face, her heart, held more light than any crystal chandelier could.

He strolled down the stairs.

She put her case on the floor and flew towards him. He opened his arms and received her. And then she was with him. She recognised his smell, stronger than ever. Mixed with another strong, spicy aroma. It had to come from the dressing gown, for now she saw that the elegant silk garment was too short in the arms and not at all new. It wasn't until she felt him freeing himself that she realised she had been clinging to him, and she let go abruptly.

'Darling, you're crying,' he laughed, stroking her cheek with a finger.

'Am I?' She laughed too, drying under her eyes and hoping her makeup hadn't run.

'I have a surprise for you,' he said, taking her hand. 'Come with me.'

'But . . .' she said, turning to see that the metal case had already been removed.

They went upstairs and in through a door to a large, bright bedroom. Long, gossamer curtains swayed gently in the breeze from the terrace door.

547

'Were you asleep?' she asked, gesturing to the unmade four-poster bed.

'No,' he smiled. 'Sit here and close your eyes.'

'But . . .'

'Just do as I say, Lene'.

She thought she could hear a suggestion of annoyance in his voice and hastened to do what he said.

'They'll soon be arriving with champagne, and then I want to ask you something. But first I'm going to tell you a story. Are you ready?'

'Yes,' she said, and knew. Knew this was the moment. The one she had been waiting for. The moment she would remember for the rest of her life.

'The story I am going to tell you is about me. You see, there are a few things you ought to know about me before you answer my question.'

'I understand.' It was as if the champagne bubbles were already coursing through her veins, and she had to concentrate in order not to giggle.

'I've told you I grew up with my grandfather, that my parents were dead. What I omitted to say was that I lived with them until I was fifteen.'

'I knew it!' she exclaimed.

Tony cocked an eyebrow. A delicately shaped, oh-so-beautiful eyebrow, she thought.

'I've always known you had a secret, Tony,' she laughed. 'But I also have a secret. I want us to know everything about each other, everything!'

Tony assumed a lopsided smile. 'So let me continue without any more interruptions, my sweet Lene. My mother was deeply religious and met my father in a chapel. He had just been released after serving time for murder in a fit of jealous rage, and while in prison had found Jesus. For my mother this was something straight out of the Bible, a repentant sinner, a man she could help to find redemption and eternal life while she did penance for her own sins. That was how she explained to me why she had married the bastard.'

'What—?'

'Shh! My father repented for the murder by labelling everything that was not in praise of God a sin. I was not allowed to do any of the things other children did. If I contradicted him I got a taste of the belt. He tried to provoke me, say that the sun went round the earth, as it said in the Bible. If I protested he beat me. When I was twelve I was in the outside toilet with my mother. We used to do that. When I came out he hit me with a spade because he thought it was a sin, that I was too old to go to the toilet with my mother. He marked me for life.'

Lene gulped as Tony lifted a distorted, arthritic finger and ran it along the top part of the scar on his chest. And then she noticed his missing finger.

'Tony! What happ—?'

'Shh! The last time my father beat me I was fifteen, and he used the belt for twenty-three minutes without a break. One thousand three hundred and ninety-two seconds. I counted them. He hit me every four seconds like a machine. Kept hitting me, his rage steadily increasing because I refused to cry. In the end his arm was so tired that he had to give up. Three hundred and forty-eight lashes. That night I waited until I heard his snoring, sneaked into their bedroom and poured a drop of acid into his eye. He screamed and screamed while I held him and whispered in his ear that if he touched me again I would kill him. And I felt him stiffen in my arms, I knew he knew I was stronger than him. And he knew I had it in me.'

'Had what in you, Tony?'

'Him. The killer.'

Lene's heart stopped pumping. It was not true. Couldn't be true. He had told her it wasn't him, they were mistaken.

'After that day we watched each other like hawks. And Mum knew it was either him or me. One day she came to me and said he had been to Geilo to buy ammunition for the rifle. I had to get away, she had decided with my grandfather what had to be done. He was a widower and lived by Lake Lyseren. He knew he would have to keep me hidden, otherwise the old man would come after me. So I left. Mum made it look as if I had been killed in an avalanche. My father shunned society so it was always Mum who did anything that required contact with people. He thought she had reported me missing, but in reality she had informed only one person what she had done and why. She and Officer Roy Stille, they . . . well, they knew each other very well. Stille was wise

549

enough to know that the police could do little to protect me against Dad and vice versa, so he helped to cover our traces. I was fine at Grandad's. Until the message came that Mum had gone missing in the mountains.'

Lene put out her hand. 'Poor, poor Tony.'

'I said: close your eyes!'

She winced at the snarl in his voice, retracted her hand and squeezed her eyes shut.

'I couldn't go to the service, my grandfather said. Nobody should find out I was alive. When he returned he told me word for word what the priest had said about her in his speech. Three sentences. Three sentences about the world's strongest, most beautiful woman. The last was "Karen trod lightly on this earth". The rest was about Jesus and forgiveness of sins. Three sentences and forgiveness of sins she had never committed.' Lene could hear Tony breathing heavily now.

'Trod lightly. The bastard priest stood there in the pulpit and said she had left no prints. Vanished as she had lived, without leaving a trace. On to the next verse in the Bible. Grandad told me this straight, no beating about the bush, and do you know what, Lene? It was the most important day in my life. Do you understand?'

'Er . . . no, Tony.'

'I knew he was sitting there, the bastard who had killed her. And I swore I would take my revenge. I would show him. I would show them all. That was the day I decided that whatever happened I would not end up like him. Or her. Three lines. And neither I nor the bastard sitting there needed forgiveness for their sins. We would both burn. Rather that than share paradise with a God like this.' He lowered his voice. 'No one, no one was going to stand in my way. Do you understand me now?'

'Yes,' Lene smiled. 'And you've deserved it, Tony. Everything. You've worked so hard!'

'I'm glad you're so understanding, my sweet. Here comes the rest. Are you ready?'

'Yes,' Lene said, clapping her hands. She would see, her too, sitting at home, envious, lonely and bitter, begrudging her own daughter the chance to experience love.

'I had it all in the palm of my hand,' Tony said, and Lene felt his hand on her knee. 'You, your father's money, the project here in Africa. I thought nothing could go wrong. Until I fucked that randy bitch at the cabin in Håvass. I couldn't even remember her name when I received a letter from her saying she was pregnant and wanted money. She was in the way, Lene. I was meticulous in my planning. Covered the car in plastic. Took a blank postcard of the Congo I had lying around, forced her to write a few lines explaining her disappearance. Then I plunged the knife into her neck. The sound of blood on plastic, Lene . . . it's something quite unique.'

85

Edvard Munch

It was like someone had banged an icicle into Lene's skull. Nevertheless she forced her eyes open again. 'You . . . you . . . killed her? A woman you . . . slept with in the mountains?'

'My libido is stronger than yours, Lene. If you don't do what I ask I get others to do it.'

'But you . . . you wanted me to . . .' Tears strangled her vocal cords. '. . . That's not natural!'

Tony chuckled. 'She didn't mind, Lene. Juliana didn't, either. She was well paid for it, though.'

'Juliana? What are you talking about, Tony? Tony?' Lene was groping in the dark like a blind person.

'A German whore from Leipzig I met regularly. She does anything for money. Did.'

Lene felt the tears running down her cheeks. His voice was so calm; that was what made it all seem so unreal.

'Say . . . say it isn't true, Tony. Please stop now.'

'Shh. I was sent another letter. With a photo. You can perhaps imagine my shock when I saw it contained a photo of Adele in my car with a knife in her neck. The letter was signed by someone called Borgny Stem-Myhre. She wrote that she wanted money, otherwise she would report me for the murder of Adele Vetlesen. Of course, I knew I would have to get rid of her. But I needed an alibi for the time of death in case the police started to link me with Borgny and the blackmail attempt. In fact,

I had been thinking of sending Adele's little postcard from Africa the next time I was here, but then I happened on an even better idea. I contacted Juliana and sent her here to Goma. She travelled around using Adele's name, sent the card from Kigali, went to Van Boorst and bought an apple I had been thinking of serving up to Borgny. Juliana came back and we met in Leipzig. Where I let her have the first taste of the apple.' Tony chuckled. 'She thought it was a new sex toy, poor thing.'

'You . . . you killed her too?'

'Yes. And then Borgny. I followed her. She was unlocking the door to the block of flats where she lived when I went up to her with the knife. I took her down to the cellar in Nydalen where I had everything prepared. Padlock. Apple. I gave her a shot of ketanome in the neck. Then I went to Skien, to an investors' meeting where all my witnesses were waiting. The alibi. I knew that while we were raising a toast, Borgny would be doing the job herself. They all do in the end. Then I went back, went through the cellar, picked up my padlock, took the apple out of her mouth and went home. To you. We made love. You pretended to come. Do you remember?'

Lene shook her head, unable to speak.

'Close your eyes, I said.'

She felt his fingers glide over her forehead and close her eyelids, like an undertaker. Heard his voice drone on as if to himself.

'He liked to hit me. I can understand that now. The feeling of power that lies in inflicting pain, seeing another person succumb to you, having thy will being done on earth as it is in heaven.'

She could smell the scent on him, the scent of sex. Of a woman's sex. Then his voice was there again, close to her ear now. 'As I killed them something began to happen. It was like their blood was watering a seed that had been there the whole time. I began to grasp what I had seen in my father's eyes that time. The recognition. For just as he saw himself in me, I began to see him when I looked at myself in the mirror. I liked the power. *And* the impotence. I liked the game, the risk, the simultaneous highs and lows. When you stand on top of the mountain with your head in a cloud and hear the choir of angels in paradise you also have to hear the hissing fires of hell beneath you for it to mean anything. That was what my father knew. And now I know it, too.'

Lene saw red stains dancing on the insides of her eyelids.

'I didn't realise the extent of my hatred until a few years later when I was standing with a girl on the edge of the wood outside a dance hall. A boy attacked me. I saw jealousy burning in his eyes. I saw my father coming at me and my mother with the spade. I cut the boy's tongue out. They arrested me, and I was given a prison sentence. And there I discovered what it does to you. And why Dad never mentioned his spell in the clink. Not a word. I received a short sentence. Nevertheless I almost went mad inside. And while I was doing time I realised what I had to do. I had to have him put in prison for murdering my mother. Not kill him, but have him incarcerated, buried alive. First, though, I had to find the proof, the remains of my mother. So I built a cabin up in the mountains, far from habitation, to ensure there was no chance of anyone recognising the boy who went missing when he was fifteen. Every year I searched the plateau, square kilometre by square kilometre, began as soon as most of the snow had gone, preferably at night when no one else was out and about, trawling precipices and avalanche areas. If I had to, I would stay the night in a Tourist Association cabin where people were only passing through. But some of the locals must have seen me anyway; at any rate, rumours began to circulate about the ghost of the Utmo boy.' Tony chuckled. Lene opened her eyes, but Tony didn't notice, he was studying a cigarette holder he had just taken out of the pocket of the dressing gown. Lene hurriedly closed her eyes again.

'After Borgny's murder a letter came signed "Charlotte", who wrote that she had been behind the previous letter. I saw that I was caught in a game. It could have been another bluff or it could have been anyone who was in the Håvass cabin that night. So I went up to have a look at the guest book, but the page for that night had been torn out. So I killed Charlotte. And waited for the next letter. It came. I killed Marit. And then Elias. After that things went quiet. Then I read in the paper that they were asking people who had been to the Håvass cabin the same night as the murder victims to come forward. I knew, of course, that no one would guess I had been there, but also that if I came forward I might find out from the police who had been there. Find out who was after me. Who was left to kill. So I went straight to the person I assumed would know most. This detective, Harry Hole. I tried to pump him about the other guests. Fat lot of good that did. Instead, this Mikael Bellman came along and arrested me. Someone had used my phone to call Elias Skog, he told me. And then I saw the light. This wasn't about money; someone was trying to get me arrested. Imprisoned. Who could stand by and cold-bloodedly watch people being murdered and still persist . . . with this crusade against me? Who could hate me so much? Then the final letter arrived. This time he didn't reveal his identity, just wrote he had been to the Håvass cabin that night, as invisible as a ghost. Said I knew him all too well. And he was coming to get me. And then it clicked. At last he had found me. Dad.'

Tony paused for breath.

'He had planned the same for me as I had planned for him. To be buried alive, incarcerated for life. But how had he managed it? I wondered if he had kept the Håvass cabin under surveillance. Is that how he knew I was alive? Had he been following me from a distance? After I got engaged to you, the celeb gossip press started printing pictures of me, and perhaps even Dad occasionally flicked through those magazines. But he had to be working with someone. For example, he couldn't have gone to Oslo and broken in, he couldn't have taken the photo of Adele with the knife in her neck. Or could he? I found out that he had fled the farm, the slippery bastard. What he didn't know was that I was now much more familiar with the area than him after searching for my mother for all those years. I found him at the Tourist Association cabin in Kjeften. I was as happy as a child. But it was an anticlimax.'

Rustling of silk.

'I derived less pleasure from torturing him than I had hoped. He didn't even recognise me, the blind idiot. But it didn't matter. I wanted him to see me as he himself had never managed to be. A success. I wanted to humiliate him. Instead he saw me as himself. A killer.' He sighed. 'And I began to realise he hadn't been working with anyone. And he didn't have the ability to do all this alone, he was too fragile, too frightened and too cowardly. I started the avalanche at Håvass, almost in a panic. Because

I knew now: there was someone else. An invisible, inaudible hunter standing in the dark somewhere with his breathing attuned to mine. I had to get away. Out of the country. Somewhere I couldn't be found. So here we are, my love. On the edge of a jungle the size of Western Europe.'

Lene was trembling uncontrollably. 'Why are you doing this, Tony? Why are you telling me . . . this?'

She felt his hand on her cheek. 'Because you deserve it, my love. Because your name is Galtung and you will have a long commemorative speech when you die. Because I think it's right you should hear all about me before you give me your answer.'

'Answer to what?'

'Whether you want to marry me.'

Her brain was in a spin now. 'Whether I want . . . want . . .'

'Open your eyes, Lene.'

'But I . . .'

'Open them, I said.'

She did as she was told.

'This is for you,' he said.

Lene Galtung gasped.

'It's made of gold,' Tony said. The sunlight gleamed on the matt golden-brown metal as it lay on a sheet of paper on the coffee table between them. 'I want you to wear it.'

'Wear it?'

'After you've signed our marriage contract, of course.'

Lene blinked repeatedly. Tried to rouse herself from the nightmare. The hand with the distorted fingers moved across the table, covering hers. She looked down, looked at the pattern on the burgundy silk of his dressing gown.

'I know what you're thinking,' he said. 'That the money you've brought with you will only last a while, but marriage will give me certain inheritance rights when you die. You're wondering if I intend to take your life. Aren't you?'

'Are you?'

Tony chuckled and squeezed her hand. 'Do you intend to stand in my way, Lene?'

She shook her head. All she wanted was to be there for someone. For him. As though in a trance she took the pen he passed her. Guided it down to the paper. Her tears fell on her signature causing the ink to blotch. He seized the document.

'That'll do nicely,' he said, blowing on it and motioning towards the coffee table. 'Let's see you wearing it then.'

'What do you mean, Tony? It's not a ring.'

'I mean I want you to open wide, Lene.'

Harry blinked. A single lit bulb hung from the ceiling. He was supine on a mattress. He was naked. It was the same dream, except that he wasn't dreaming. Above him a nail stuck out of the wall, and on the nail was impaled the head of Edvard Munch. A Norwegian banknote. He yawned so hard it seemed his shattered jaw would tear, and yet the pressure continued, almost exploding his head. He wasn't dreaming. The ketanome had worn off and the pain allowed no further dreams. How long had he been lying here? How long till the pain drove him mad? He carefully twisted his head and scanned the room. He was still in Van Boorst's house and he was alone. He wasn't shackled, he could stand up if he wanted.

His gaze followed the wire attached to the handle of the front door and running through the room to the wall behind him. He carefully twisted his head the other way. The wire ran through the U bolt in the wall right behind his head. And from there to his mouth. Leopold's apple. He was tethered firmly in position. The door opened outwards so that the first person to pull would release the needles that would pierce his head from inside. And if he moved too much that would also release the needles.

Harry put his thumb and first finger either side of his mouth. Felt the circular ridges. Tried in vain to get a finger underneath one of them. He had a coughing fit and everything went black as he struggled to breathe. He realised the ridges had caused the flesh around his pharynx to swell and he risked suffocation. The wire to the door handle. The severed finger. Was this chance or did Tony Leike know about the Snowman? And was he intending to outdo him?

Harry kicked the wall and tensed his vocal cords, but the metal ball stifled the scream. He gave up. Leaned against the wall, braced himself for the pain and forced his mouth shut. He had read somewhere that the human bite is not much weaker than that of the white shark. Yet the jaw muscles only just managed to press the ridges down before the mouth was forced back open. There seemed to be a pulse, a living iron heart in his mouth. He touched the wire hanging from the apple. His every instinct shrieked for him to pull it, to pull the apple out. But he had seen a demonstration of what would happen, he had seen photos of crime scenes. If he had not seen . . .

And at that second Harry knew. Knew not only how he himself would die but also how the others had died. And why it had been done like that. He experienced an absurd desire to laugh. It was so devilishly simple. So devilishly simple that only a devil could have devised it.

Tony Leike's alibi. He hadn't had an accomplice. That is to say, the victims themselves had been his accomplices. When Borgny and Charlotte had come to after being drugged they hadn't a clue what it was they had in their mouths. Borgny had been locked in a cellar. Charlotte had been outside, but the wire from her mouth had led to the boot of the wrecked car in front of her, and however much she struggled, scraped and pulled at the boot lid it was, and remained, locked. Neither of them had a chance in hell of escaping from where they were, and when the pain was too great they had taken the predictable route. They had pulled the wire. Had they anticipated what would happen? Had the pain made them give way to hope, the hope that pulling the wire would retract the circular ridges in the mysterious object? And while the girls had slowly but surely gone through the agonies of doubt and conjecture before the inevitable act, Tony Leike was many kilometres away at a dinner or a lecture, secure in the knowledge that the girls would perform the final part of the job themselves. Giving him the best possible alibi for the time of the death. In the strictest sense, he hadn't even murdered them.

Harry twisted his head to see what radius of movement he had without tightening the steel wire.

He had to do something. Anything. He groaned, thought the wire seemed to tighten; he stopped breathing, stared at the door. Waited for it to open, for . . .

Nothing happened.

He tried to remember Van Boorst's demo of the apple, how long the ridges remained out if there was no resistance. If only he could open his mouth even wider, if only his jaws . . .

Harry closed his eyes. It struck him how strangely normal and obvious the idea seemed, how little resistance he felt. Quite the opposite, he felt relief. Relief at inflicting even more pain on himself, if necessary risking his own life in an attempt to survive. It was logical, simple, the black void of doubt repressed by a bright, clear, insane idea. Harry turned round on his stomach with his head against the U bolt so that there was some slack in the wire. Then he cautiously got up onto his knees. Touched his jaw. Found the point. The point where everything centred: the pain, the jaw joint, the knot, the jumble of nerves and muscles that only just held his jaw together after the incident in Hong Kong. He wouldn't be able to hit himself hard enough, there had to be body weight behind it. His first finger tested the nail. It protruded about four centimetres from the wall. A standard nail with a large, broad head. It would smash through everything that came in its path if there was enough force. Harry took aim, rested his jaw against the nail in rehearsal, stood up to calculate at what angle he would have to fall. How deep the nail would have to penetrate. And how deep it *must* not penetrate. Neck, nerves, paralysis. Did calculations. Not coldly and calmly. But he calculated anyway. Forced himself. The nail head was not like the top of a T, it sloped down towards the shank so that it would not necessarily tear everything with it on its way out. Finally, he tried to identify anything he hadn't considered. Until he realised this was his brain trying to delay events.

Harry took a deep breath.

His body would not obey. It protested, resisted. Wouldn't lower his head.

'Idiot!' Harry strove to shout, but it turned into a whistle. He felt a hot tear trickle down his cheek.

Enough crying, he thought. Time to die a little now.

Then he brought his head down.

The nail received him with a deep sigh.

Kaja was fumbling for her mobile phone. The Carpenters had just shouted a three-part 'Stop!' And Karen Carpenter answered 'Oh, yes, wait a minute.' The SMS alert.

Outside the car, night had fallen with sudden brutality. She had sent three messages to Harry. Told him what had happened and that she was parked up the road from the house Lene Galtung had entered, awaiting further instructions and a sign of life.

> Well done. Come and pick me up from the street to the south of the church. Easy to find, it's the only brick house. Come straight in, it's open. Harry.

It was in Norwegian. She passed on the address to the taxi driver who nodded, yawned and switched on the engine.

Kaja texted back in Norwegian *On my way* as they drove north along the illuminated streets. The volcano lit up the night sky like an incandescent lamp, obliterating the stars and lending everything a faint blood-red shimmer.

A quarter of an hour later they found themsleves in a darkened bomb crater of a street. A couple of paraffin lamps hung outside a shop. Either there was another power cut or this neighbourhood didn't have electricity.

The driver stopped and pointed. Van Boorst. Sure enough, there it was, a brick house. Kaja looked around. Further up the street she saw two Range Rovers. Two bleating mopeds passed with wobbly lights. Heavy African disco came belting out of one door. Here and there she could see the glow of cigarettes and white eyes.

'Wait here,' Kaja said, pushing her hair up into the peaked cap and ignoring the driver's warning cries when she opened the door and slipped out.

She walked quickly up to the house. She had no naive preconceptions about the chances a white woman had in a town like Goma after night-fall, but right now darkness was her best friend.

She could make out the door with black lava boulders on either side, knew she had to hurry, she felt it coming, she would have to pre-empt it. She almost stumbled, rushed onwards, breathing through an open mouth. Then she was there. She placed her fingers on the door handle. Although the temperature had sunk surprisingly fast after the sun had set, sweat was streaming down between her shoulder blades and her breasts. She forced herself to press the handle down. Listened. It was so eerily quiet. As quiet as the time when . . .

Tears thickened like a viscous cement mix in her throat.

'Come on,' she whispered. 'Not now.'

She closed her eyes. Concentrated on breathing. Emptied her brain of any thoughts. She would manage this now. Her thoughts slowed. Delete, delete. That's the way. Just one tiny thought left, then she could open the door.

Harry woke with something yanking at the corner of his mouth. He opened his eyes. It was dark. He must have fainted. Then he became aware of the wire pulling at the ball that was still in his mouth. His heart started, accelerated, hammered away. He pushed his mouth up against the bolt, absolutely clear that none of this would help if someone opened the door.

A strip of light from outside struck the wall above him. The blood glistened. He guided his fingers into his mouth, placed them over the teeth in his lower jaw and pressed. The pain made everything go black for a second, but he felt his jaw give. It was dislocated! As he pressed his jaw down with one hand, he took the apple with the other and pulled.

He heard sounds outside the door. Fuck, fuck, fuck! He still couldn't get the apple past his teeth. He pressed his jaw down further. The sound of bone and tissue crunching and tearing resonated as if it came from his ears. He might just be able to pull his jaw down so far on one side that he could get the apple out sideways, but there was a cheek in the way. He could see the door handle moving. There wasn't time. No time. Time stopped here.

That last tiny thought. The Norwegian SMS. *Gaten. Kirken.* The street. The church. Harry didn't use those endings. *Gata. Kirka.* That's what he said. Kaja opened her eyes. What was it he had said on her veranda when they were talking about the title of the Fante book? He never texted. Because he didn't want to lose his soul, because he preferred not to leave any traces when he disappeared. She had never received a single text from him. Not until now. He would have rung. This didn't stack up; this was not her brain finding excuses not to open the door. This was a trap.

Kaja gently let go of the door handle. She felt a warm current of air on her neck. As though someone was breathing on her. She cancelled the 'as though' and turned.

There were two of them. Their faces melded into the darkness.

'Looking for someone, lady?'

The feeling of déjà vu struck her before she had answered. 'Wrong door, that's all.'

At that moment she heard a car start up; she turned and saw the rear lights of her taxi swaying along the street.

'Don't worry, lady,' the voice said. 'We paid him.'

She turned back and looked down. At the pistol pointing at her.

'Let's go.'

Kaja considered the alternatives. Didn't take long. There weren't any.

She walked ahead of them towards the two Range Rovers. The rear door of one swung open as they approached. She got in. It smelt of spiced aftershave and new leather. The door slammed behind her. He smiled. His teeth were large and white, the voice gentle, cheerful.

'Hi, Kaja.'

Tony Leike was wearing a yellow-and-grey combat uniform. Holding a red mobile in his hand. Harry's.

'You were told to go straight in. What stopped you?'

She shrugged.

'Fascinating,' he said, angling his head.

'What is?'

'You don't seem the slightest bit afraid.'

'Why should I be?'

'Because you're going to die soon. Have you really not understood?'

Kaja's throat constricted. Even though part of her brain was screaming this was an idle threat, that she was a police officer, he would never take the risk, it was unable to drown the other part, the one that said Tony Leike was sitting in front of her and knew exactly what the situation was. She and Harry were two kamikaze clods a long way from home, without authorisation, without backup, without a plan B. Without a hope.

Leike pressed a button and the window slid down.

'Go and finish him off, then take him up there,' he said to the two men, and the window slid back up.

'I think it would have added a touch of class if you had opened the door,' Leike said. 'I sort of think we owe Harry a poetic death. Now, though, we'll have to opt for a poetic farewell.' He leaned forward and peered up at the sky. 'Beautiful red colour, isn't it?' She could see it in his face now. Heard it. And her voice – the one that told the truth – told her. She really was going to die.

86

Calibre

KINZONZI POINTED TO VAN BOORST'S BRICK HOUSE AND told Oudry to drive the Range Rover right to the door. He could see the light behind the curtains and remembered that Mister Tony had determined it was to be left on when they were not there. So that the white man could see what awaited him. Kinzonzi got out and waited for Oudry to pocket the car key and follow. The order was simple: kill him and take him there. It aroused no emotion. No fear, no pleasure, not even tension. It was a job.

Kinzonzi was nineteen years old. He had been a soldier since he was eleven. The PDLA, the People's Democratic Liberation Army, had stormed his village. They had smashed his brother's head with the stock of a Kalashnikov and raped his two sisters while forcing his father to watch. Afterwards the commander had said that if his father didn't perform intercourse with his younger sister in front of them, they would kill Kinzonzi and his elder sister. But before the commander had finished his sentence, Kinzonzi's father had impaled himself on one of their machetes. Their laughter had filled the air.

Before leaving, Kinzonzi had eaten the first decent meal he'd had for several months and was given a beret which the commander said was his uniform. Two months later he had a Kalashnikov and had shot his first human, a mother in a village who refused to hand over her blankets to the PDLA. He had been twelve when he queued with other soldiers to rape a young girl not far from where he had been recruited. When it was his turn it suddenly struck him that the girl could have been his sister, the age would have been right. But when he studied her face he saw that he could no longer remember their faces: Mum, Dad, his sisters. They were gone, erased from his memory.

Four months later, he and two comrades chopped the arms off the commander and watched him bleed to death, not out of revenge or hatred but because the CFF, the Congo Freedom Front, had promised to pay them better. For five years he had lived off what the CFF raids in the northern Kivu jungle brought in, but all the time they had had to watch out for other guerrillas, and the villages they came to had been so plundered by others over time that they could barely feed themselves. For a while the CFF had negotiated with the government army: disarmament for an amnesty and employment. But discussions broke down over wages.

Hungry and desperate, the CFF attacked a mining company extracting coltan, even though they were aware that mining companies had better weapons and soldiers than they did. Kinzonzi had never had any illusions that he would live a long life or that he would die any other way than fighting. So he hadn't even blinked when he came round and found himself staring up the gun barrel of a white man speaking to him in a foreign language. Kinzonzi had just nodded for him to get it over with. Two months later the wounds were healed, and the mining company was his new employer.

The white man was Mister Tony. Mister Tony paid well but showed no mercy if he saw the slightest sign of disloyalty. Yes, he spoke to them and was the best boss Kinzonzi had ever had. And yet Kinzonzi would not have hesitated for a second to shoot him if it had been worth his while. But it wasn't.

'Hurry up,' Kinzonzi said to Oudry, loading his pistol. He knew it could take time for the white policeman to die from the metal apple that would be activated in his mouth when they opened the door, so he would shoot him at once in order to get going to Nyiragongo, where Mister Tony and the women were waiting.

A man who had been seated on a chair smoking outside the adjacent shop got up and was lost in the darkness, mumbling angrily.

Kinzonzi regarded the door handle. The first time he had been here was to pick up Van Boorst. It was also the first time he had seen the legendary Alma. At that time Van Boorst had been spending all his money on Singapore sling, protection and Alma, who was not exactly cheap to maintain. Then Van Boorst, in his desperation, committed the final mistake of his life: blackmailing Mister Tony with threats of going to the police. The Belgian had seemed more resigned than surprised when they came, and had finished his drink. They had carved him up into suitably large pieces to feed to the paradoxically fat pigs outside the refugee camp. Mister Tony had taken over Alma. Alma of the hips, gold tooth and the sleepy fuck-me look that could have given Kinzonzi another reason to put a bullet in Mister Tony's head. If it had been worth his while.

Kinzonzi pressed the handle. And pulled the door hard. It swung open but was stopped halfway by a thin steel wire fastened to the inside of the door. The moment it tightened, there was a loud, clear click and the sound of metal on metal, like the sound of a bayonet thrust into an iron sheath. The door opened with a creak.

Kinzonzi stepped in, dragged Oudry after him and slammed the door. The bitter smell of vomit stung their nostrils.

'Switch on the light.'

Oudry did as he was ordered.

Kinzonzi stared at the end of the room. On the wall, drenched in blood, a banknote hung from a bare nail, from which a red stream led down to the floor. On the bed, in a pool of yellow sick, lay a blood-covered metal ball with long needles sticking out, like rays of a sun. But no white policeman.

The door. Kinzonzi whirled around with his gun at the ready.

No one there.

He dropped to his knees and looked under the bed. No one.

Oudry opened the door to the only cupboard in the room. Empty.

'He's fled,' Oudry said to Kinzonzi, who was standing by the bed pressing a finger into the mattress.

'What is it?' Oudry asked, going closer.

'Blood.' He took the torch from Oudry. Shone it on the floor. Followed the trail of blood to where it stopped in the middle. A trapdoor with an iron ring. He advanced on the hatchway, ripped open the door and shone the torch down into the darkness beneath. 'Get your gun, Oudry.'

His comrade went outside and returned with his AK-47.

'Cover me,' said Kinzonzi, descending the ladder.

He reached the bottom and held the pistol and torch in a double grip as he swivelled round. The torchlight swept over cupboards and shelves along the wall. Continued over a free-standing unit in the middle of the floor with grotesque white masks on the shelves. One with rivets for eyebrows, a lifelike one with a red asymmetrical mouth going right up to the ear on one side, one with empty eyes and a spear tattooed on both cheeks. He shone the light on the shelves on the facing wall. And stopped suddenly. Kinzonzi went rigid. Weapons. Guns. Ammunition. The brain is a fantastic computer. In a fraction of a second it can register tons of data, crunch them and reason its way to the correct answer. So when Kinzonzi swung the torch back on the masks, it already had the right answer. The light fell on the white mask with the asymmetrical mouth. Displaying the molars. Glistening red. The same way the blood on the wall under the nail had glistened.

Kinzonzi had never had any illusions that he would live a long life. Or that he would die any other way than fighting.

His brain told his fingers to squeeze the trigger of his pistol. The brain is a fantastic computer.

In one microsecond the finger squeezed. At the same time as his brain had already finished its reasoning. It had the answer. Knew what the outcome would be.

Harry had known there was only one solution. And there wasn't any time to waste. So he had smacked his head against the nail, a little higher this time. He had hardly felt it when the nail perforated his cheek or when it struck the metal ball inside. Then he had lowered himself on the bed, forced his head against the wall and pulled back with his full weight while trying to tense the muscles in his cheek. At first nothing happened, then the nausea came. And the panic. If he threw up now, with the Leopold's apple in his mouth, he would suffocate. But it was

567

unstoppable, he could already feel his stomach contracting to send up the first load through the oesophagus. In desperation, Harry raised his head and hips. Then let himself fall hard. And felt the flesh of his cheek give, tear, rip open. Felt the blood stream into his mouth, down the trachea, activating the coughing reflex, felt the nail bang against his front teeth. Harry put his hand in his mouth, but the apple was slippery from all the blood, his fingers slithered on the metal. He inserted one hand behind the ball, pushed while pressing his jaw down with the other. Heard it scrape against his teeth. Then – in a huge surge – the vomit came.

Maybe that was what had forced the metal apple out. Harry lay with his head against the wall looking at the shiny death-bringing invention bathed in his sick on the mattress beneath the U bolt.

Then he got up, naked and on shaky legs. He was free.

He staggered towards the front door, then remembered why he had gone to the house. At the third attempt he managed to open the trap-door. He skidded in his own blood on the way down the steps and fell into the pitch black. Lying on the concrete floor gasping for breath, he heard a vehicle pull up. He heard voices and doors slamming. Harry struggled to his feet, groped in the dark, took the steps in two strides, got a hand on the hatch and closed it as he heard the front door open and the savage click of the apple.

Harry moved back down the ladder with care until he sensed the cold concrete floor beneath his soles. Then he closed his eyes and strained his memory. Conjured up the image of his previous visit here. The shelves to the left. Kalashnikov. Glock. Smith & Wesson. The case with the Märklin rifle. Ammunition. In that order. He fumbled his way forward. Fingers strayed over a gun barrel. The smooth steel of a Glock. And, there, they recognised the shape of a Smith & Wesson .38 calibre, the same as his service revolver. He took it with him and fumbled on towards the ammo boxes. Felt the wood on his fingertips. He heard angry voices and footsteps above. Just had to open the lid. Needed a bit of luck now. He stuffed his hand in and grabbed one of the cardboard packets. Ran his fingers over the contours of the cartridge. Fuck, too big! As he raised the lid of the next wooden box, the trapdoor opened. He grabbed at a packet, had to take a chance on it being the right calibre. At that moment light penetrated the cellar darkness, a circle, as from a spotlight, lit up the floor around the steps. It gave Harry enough light to read the label on the packet. 7.62 millimetres. Fuck! Harry looked on the shelf. There. The box next to it. .38 calibre. The light went from the floor and juddered across the ceiling. Harry saw the silhouette of a Kalashnikov in the opening and a man on his way down the steps.

The brain is a fantastic computer.

As Harry pulled open the lid of the box and took a cardboard packet, it had already done its calculations. It was too late.

87

Kalashnikov

'THERE WOULDN'T BE A ROAD HERE IF WE HADN'T BEEN running a mining business,' Tony Leike said as the car bounced along the narrow cart track. 'Entrepreneurs like me are the only hope for people in countries like the Congo to get to their feet, to follow us, to become civilised. The alternative is to leave them to their own devices so that they can continue doing what they have always done: kill each other. Everyone on this continent is both a hunter and a victim. Don't forget that as you look into the imploring eyes of a starving African child. Give them a bit of food and those eyes will soon be looking at you again, from behind an automatic weapon. And then there is no mercy.'

Kaja didn't answer. She stared at the red hair of the woman in the passenger seat. Lene Galtung had neither moved nor said anything, merely sat there with an erect back and retracted shoulders.

'Everything in Africa goes in cycles,' Tony continued. 'Rain and drought, night and day, eating and being eaten, living and dying. The course of nature is everything, nothing can be changed, swim with the flow, survive for as long as you can, take what's offered, that's all you can do. Because your forefathers' lives are your life, you cannot make a change, development is not possible. That's not African philosophy, just the experience of generations. And it is the *experience* that has to change. It is experience that changes mindsets, not the other way round.'

'And if it's your experience that white people exploit you?' Kaja said.

'The idea of exploitation has been sown by white men,' Tony said. 'But the term has proved to be a useful tool for African leaders who need to point to a common enemy to get their people behind them. Right from the dismantling of colonialist governments in the sixties, they have used white people's feelings of guilt to acquire power, so that the real exploitation of the population could begin. The whites' guilt about colonising Africa is pathetic. The real crime was to leave the African to its own butchering and destructive ways. Believe me, Kaja, the Congolese never had it better than under the Belgians. The revolts had no foundation in popular will, but in individuals' greed for power. Tiny factions stormed the Belgians' houses here by Lake Kivu because the houses were so elegant they assumed they would find something there they desired. That was how it was, and that is how it is. That's why properties always have at least two gates, one at each end. One through which robbers can charge in and one through which inhabitants can flee.'

'So that was how you left the house without me seeing you?'

Tony laughed. 'Did you really think it was you tailing us? I've been keeping an eye on you ever since you both arrived. Goma is a small town with little money and a clear power structure. It was very naive of you and Harry to come alone.'

'Who's naive?' Kaja said. 'What do you think will happen when it comes out that two Norwegian police officers have gone missing in Goma?'

Tony hunched his shoulders. 'Kidnapping is a relatively common occurrence in Goma. It wouldn't surprise me if the local police soon receive a letter from a freedom fighter demanding an exorbitant sum of money for you two. Plus the release of named prisoners who are known opponents of President Kabila's regime. Negotiations will continue for a few days, but lead nowhere, as of course the demands will be impossible to fulfil. And then you won't be seen again. Daily fare, Kaja.'

Kaja tried to catch Lene Galtung's eye in the mirror, but she kept her gaze averted.

'What about her?' Kaja said. 'Does she know you've killed all these people, Tony?'

'She does now,' Tony said. 'And she understands me. That's real love for you, Kaja. And that's why Lene and I are getting married this evening.

You're invited.' He laughed. 'We're on our way to the church. I think it will be a very atmospheric ceremony when we swear eternal fidelity to each other, don't you, Lene?'

At that moment Lene bent forward in her seat, and Kaja saw the reason for her retracted shoulders: her hands were held behind her back by a pair of pink handcuffs. Tony leaned over, grabbed Lene's shoulder and roughly pushed her back. Just then Lene twisted round to face them, and Kaja recoiled in horror. Lene Galtung was nigh on unrecognisable. Her face was smeared with tears, one eye was swollen, and her mouth was forced open in such a way that her lips formed an O. Inside the O she glimpsed matt metal. From the golden sphere hung a short red wire.

And the words Tony uttered were for Kaja an echo of another marriage proposal on the threshold of death, a burial in snow: Till death do us part.

Harry slipped behind the shelf of masks as the figure stepped down from the ladder, turned and flashed his torch. There was nowhere to hide, just a countdown to when he would be seen. Harry closed his eyes so as not to be blinded, while opening the packet of cartridges with his left hand. Took four bullets; his fingers knew exactly what four bullets felt like. He swung the cylinder to the left with his right hand, let the by now reflex movements take place, the way they had done when he was sitting alone in Cabrini Green and, out of sheer boredom, practising quick-loading. But here he was not alone enough. Nor bored enough. His fingers trembled. He saw the red insides of his eyelids as the light fell on his face. He braced himself. But the shots did not materialise. The light moved. He wasn't dead, not yet. His fingers obeyed. They pushed bullets into four of the six empty chambers, relaxed, fast, one-handed. The cylinder fell into place. Harry opened his eyes as the light hit his face. Blinded, he fired into the sun.

The light swung upwards, over the ceiling and was gone. The echo of the shots hung in the air while the torch rolled on its own axis, making a loud rumbling noise and shining a low beam around the walls like a lighthouse.

'Kinzonzi! Kinzonzi!'

The torch came to rest, against the shelf. Harry rushed forward, grabbed it, rolled onto his back, holding the torch at arm's length, as far from his body as possible, concertinaed his legs against the shelving unit and pushed off towards the ladder until he had the trapdoor directly above him. Then the bullets came, sounding like whiplashes, and he felt the spray of concrete dust against his arm and chest as they bored into the floor by the torch. Harry took aim and shot at the illuminated figure standing astride the hatchway. Three quick squeezes.

The Kalashnikov came first. It hit the floor beside Harry's head with a loud bang. Then came the man. Harry just managed to wriggle away before the body landed. No resistance. Meat. Dead weight.

It was quiet for a couple of seconds. Then Harry heard Kinzonzi – if that was his name – give a low groan. Harry got up, still with the torch at his side, saw a Glock lying on the floor near Kinzonzi and kicked it away. He grabbed the Kalashnikov.

Then he dragged the other man to the wall, as far from Kinzonzi as possible, and shone the light on him. Predictably enough, he had reacted as Harry had; blinded, he had shot into the sun. Harry's detective eyes automatically registered that the man's groin was soaked in blood; the bullet must have continued up into his stomach but was hardly likely to have killed him. A bleeding shoulder, therefore one bullet had probably entered his armpit. That explained why the Kalashnikov had come first. Harry crouched down. But that didn't explain why the man wasn't breathing.

He shone the light on his face. Why the *boy* wasn't breathing.

The bullet had gone in under his chin. From the angle he had fired the lead must have passed into his mouth, through his palate and up into the brain. Harry inhaled. The boy couldn't have been much more than sixteen or seventeen. An altogether good-looking lad. Wasted beauty. Harry stood up, put the gun barrel to the dead man's head and shouted: 'Where are they? Mr Leike. Tony. Where?'

He waited a bit.

'What? Louder. I can't hear you. Where? Three seconds. One. Two . . .'

Harry pressed the trigger. The weapon must have been on full auto because it fired at least four times before he managed to release his finger. Harry closed his eyes when the salvo hit his face, and when he opened them again he saw that the boy's attractive features had disintegrated. Harry noticed hot, wet blood was running down his naked body.

Harry stepped over to Kinzonzi. Stood astride him, shone the torch on his face, pointed the gun to his forehead and repeated the question word for word.

'Where are they? Mr Leike. Tony. Where? Three seconds . . .'

Kinzonzi opened his eyes. Harry saw the whites quiver. The terror of dying is a prerequisite for wanting to live. It had to be, at least here in Goma.

Kinzonzi answered, slowly and clearly.

88

The Church

KINZONZI LAY QUITE STILL. THE TALL, WHITE MAN HAD placed the torch on the floor so that it lit up the ceiling. Kinzonzi watched him put on Oudry's clothes. Watched him tear his T-shirt into strips and tie them round his chin and head so that the gaping jaw, the wound running from his mouth to his ear, was covered. Tightened it to stop the mandible from hanging on one side. Blood soaked through the cotton material as Kinzonzi looked on.

He had answered the few questions the man had asked. Where. How many. What weapons they had.

Now the white man went to the shelf, pulled out a black case, opened it and examined the contents.

Kinzonzi knew he was going to die. A young, violent death. But perhaps not now, not tonight. His stomach stung as though someone had poured acid on him. But it was OK.

The white man was holding Oudry's Kalashnikov. He moved towards Kinzonzi, stood over him with the light behind his back. A towering figure with his head wrapped in white cloth, the way they used to bind the chin for death before the deceased was buried. If Kinzonzi was going to be shot, it would happen now. The man dropped the torn strips of T-shirt he hadn't used on Kinzonzi.

'Help yourself.'

Kinzonzi heard him groaning as he went up the ladder.

Kinzonzi closed his eyes. If he didn't wait too long, he could stop the worst bleeding before he fainted from blood loss. Get to his feet, crawl across the road, find people. And he might be lucky, they *might* not belong to the species: Goma vulture. He might find Alma. He could make her his. Because she had no man now. And Kinzonzi no longer had an employer. He had seen what was in the case the tall white man had taken with him.

Harry stopped the Range Rover in front of the low church walls, radiator-to-radiator with the chunky Hyundai that was still standing there.

A cigarette glowed in the car.

Harry switched off the headlamps, rolled down the window and stuck his head out.

'Saul!'

Harry saw the cigarette glow move. The taxi driver came out.

'Harry. What happened? Your face . . .'

'Things didn't quite go to plan. I didn't imagine you'd still be here.'

'Why not? You paid me for the whole day.' Saul ran his hand over the bonnet of the Range Rover. 'Nice car. Stolen?'

'Borrowed.'

'Borrowed car. Borrowed clothes, too?'

'Yes.'

'Red with blood. The previous owner's?'

'Let's leave your car here, Saul.'

'Will I want this trip, Harry?'

'Probably not. Does it help if I say I'm one of the good guys?'

'Sorry, but in Goma we've forgotten what that means, Harry.'

'Mm. Would a hundred dollars help, Saul?'

'Two hundred,' Saul said.

Harry nodded.

'. . . and fifty.'

Harry got out and let Saul take the wheel.

'Are you sure that's where they are?' Saul asked, as the car purred onto the road.

'Yes,' Harry said from the back seat. 'Someone once told me that it's the only place where people in Goma can get to heaven.'

'I don't like the place,' Saul said.

'Oh?' Harry said, opening the case beside him. The Märklin. The instructions for how to assemble the rifle were glued to the inside of the lid. Harry set about the job.

'Evil spirits. Ba-Toye.'

'You studied in Oxford, didn't you say?' Matt, greased parts readily clicked into place.

'You don't know anything about the fire demon, I suppose.'

'No, but I know these ones,' Harry said, holding up one of the cartridges from its own compartment in the Märklin case. 'And I would back them against Ba-Toye.'

The feeble yellow interior light made the gold-coloured cartridge casing gleam. The lead bullet inside had a diameter of sixteen millimetres. The world's largest calibre. When he had been working on the report after the Redbreast investigation, a ballistics expert had told him the calibre of a Märklin was way beyond all sensible limits. Even for shooting elephants. It was better suited to felling trees.

Harry clicked the telescopic sights into place. 'Put your foot down, Saul.'

He laid the barrel over the top of the empty passenger seat and tested the trigger while keeping his eye some distance from the sights because of the bumpy ride. The sights needed adjusting, calibrating, fine-tuning. But there would be no chance to do that.

They had arrived. Kaja looked out of the car window. The scattered lights beneath them, that was Goma. Further away, she saw the illuminated oil rig on Lake Kivu. The moon glittered in the greenish-black water. The last part of the road was no more than a dirt track winding round the top, and the car headlamps swept across the bare black moonscape. When they had reached the highest plateau, a flat disc of rock with a diameter of around a hundred metres, the driver had headed for the far end, through clouds of drifting white smoke tinted red beside the Nyiragongo crater.

The driver switched off the ignition.

'May I ask you something?' Tony said. 'Something I have given a lot of thought to over the last few weeks. How does it feel to know you're going to die? I don't mean how it feels to be afraid because you're in danger. I've experienced that several times myself. But to be absolutely certain that, here and now, your life will cease to exist. Are you capable . . . of communicating that?' Tony leaned forward a fraction to catch her eye. 'Just take your time to find the right words.'

Kaja held his gaze. She had expected to panic. But it just didn't come. Emotionally, she was like the stone in the terrain around them.

'I don't feel anything,' she said.

'Come on,' he said. 'The others were so frightened that they couldn't even answer, could only babble. Charlotte Lolles was transfixed, as if in shock. Elias Skog couldn't keep his language clean. My father cried. Is it mere chaos or is there some reflection? Do you feel sorrow? Remorse? Or relief that you don't have to put up a fight any more? Look at Lene, for example. She's given up and is going to her death like the meek lamb she is. How is it with you, Kaja? How much do you long to relinquish control?'

Kaja could see there was genuine curiosity in his eyes.

'Let me ask you instead how much you longed to *gain* control, Tony,' she said, scouring her mouth for moisture. 'When you killed one person after the other, under the guidance of an invisible person who turned out to be a boy whose tongue you had cut off. Can you tell me that?'

Tony looked into the middle distance and slowly shook his head, as if answering another question.

'I had no idea until reading on the Net that good old Skai had arrested someone from my village. Ole, no less. Who would have thought he had the guts?'

'The hatred, don't you mean?'

Tony took a pistol from his pocket. Checked his watch.

'Harry's late.'

'He'll come.'

Tony laughed. 'But unfortunately for you minus a pulse. I liked Harry, by the way. Really. Fun to play with. I called him from Ustaoset – he had given me his number. Heard the voicemail say he would have no network coverage for a couple of days. That made me laugh. He was at the cabin in Håvass, of course, the old sly boots.' Tony rested the pistol in one palm while stroking the black steel with the other. 'I could see it in him when we met at the police station. That he was like me.'

'I doubt that.'

'Oh yes, he is. A driven man. A junkie. A man who does what he must to have what he wants, who walks over dead bodies if need be. Isn't that right?'

Kaja didn't answer.

Tony checked his watch again. 'I reckon we'll have to start without him.'

He'll come, Kaja thought. I'll have to play for time.

'So you did a runner, did you?' she said. 'With your father's passport and teeth?'

Tony looked at her.

She knew that he knew what she was doing. And also that he liked it. Telling her. How he had tricked them. They all did.

'Do you know what, Kaja? I wish my father were here to see me now. Here, on the top of my mountain. To see me and understand me. Before I killed him. The way that Lene understands that she must die. The way I hope you understand too, Kaja.'

She felt it now. The fear. More as a physical pain than a fit of panic that would cause her rational brain to implode. She saw clearly, heard clearly, reasoned clearly. Yes, clearer than ever before, she thought.

'You started killing to hide that you had been unfaithful,' she said, her voice hoarser now. 'To safeguard the Galtung millions. But what about the millions you have tricked Lene out of here, are they enough to save your project?'

'I don't know,' Tony smiled, grasping the butt of the pistol. 'We'll have to see. Out.'

'Is it worth it, Tony? Is this really worth all these lives?'

Kaja gasped as the gun barrel was jabbed into her ribs. Tony's voice hissed in her ear.

'Look around you, Kaja. This is the cradle of humanity. See what a human life is worth. Some die and even more are born in one unending feverish race, round and round, and one life gives no more sense than any other. But the game makes sense. The passion, the fervour. The gambling addiction, as some idiots call it. It's everything. It's like Nyiragongo. It's all-consuming, all-destroying, but it is a prerequisite of all life. No passion, no meaning, no boiling lava within and everything out here would be stone dead, frozen stiff. Passion, Kaja – have you got any? Or are you a dead volcano, a speck of human dust, summed up in three sentences in a funeral speech?'

Kaja jerked away from the barrel, and Tony cackled with amusement.

'Are you ready for the wedding, Kaja? Ready to thaw?'

She smelt the stench of sulphur. The driver had opened the door, watched Kaja with indifference, pointed a short-barrelled gun at her. Even here in the car, ten metres from the edge of the crater, she could feel the overwhelming heat. She didn't move. The black man leaned in and grasped her arm. She let him pull her without offering any resistance, just made sure she was heavy enough for him to be off balance, so that when she suddenly bounded out he would be caught by surprise. The man was amazingly slight and probably a bit shorter than she was. She struck with her elbow. Knowing it was much more powerful than a fist. Knowing that the neck, the temple, the nose were good targets. The elbow hit something with a crunch, the man fell and dropped his weapon. Kaja lifted her foot. She had learned that the most effective way to neutralise a person on the ground was to trample on the thigh. The combination of a full-bodied stamp from the top and the pressure from the ground underneath will immediately cause such widespread bleeding to the thigh muscles that the person will be rendered incapable of pursuit. The alternative is to stamp on the chest and neck with potentially fatal consequences. She had her eyes fixed on the exposed neck when the moonlight fell on the man's face. She hesitated for a fraction of a second. He couldn't have been older than Even.

Then she felt arms enclosing her from behind, her own arms forced into her sides and the air from her lungs expelled as she was lifted off the ground with her legs kicking helplessly. Tony's voice close to her ear sounded cheerful. 'Good, Kaja. Passion. You want to live. I'll make sure his wages are docked, I promise you.'

The boy on the ground in front of her got to his feet and grabbed his weapon. The indifference was gone now; a white fury shone in his eyes.

Tony pressed her hands together behind her back and she felt thin plastic ties being tightened around her wrists.

'So,' said Tony. 'May I ask you to be Lene's maid of honour, frøken Solness?'

And now – at last – it came. The panic. It emptied her brain of all else, rendered everything blank, clean, cruel. Easy. She screamed.

89

The Wedding

KAJA STOOD AT THE EDGE LOOKING DOWN. THE SCORCHING air rose, hit her face like a hot breeze. The poisonous smoke had already made her dizzy, but perhaps that was just the tremulous air blurring her vision, making the lava quiver, down there in the abyss where it shone with tinges of yellow and red. A strand of hair fell into her face, but her hands were bound behind her back with the plastic ties. She stood shoulder to shoulder with Lene Galtung who, Kaja assumed, must have been drugged from the way she stood staring in front of her like a sleep-walker. A white-clad, living corpse with only frost and wasteland within. A shop dummy dressed as a bride in the window of a ropery.

Tony was right behind them. She felt his hand on the small of her back.

'Do you take the man at your side and promise to love, honour and respect him for better, for worse, for richer, for poorer, in sickness or in health . . .' he whispered.

This wasn't out of cruelty, he had explained. It was just so practical. There wouldn't be a trace left of them. Barely a question. People in the Congo go missing every day.

'I hereby declare you married.'

Kaja mumbled a prayer. She imagined it was a prayer. Until she heard the words: '. . . because it is impossible for me and the person I want to have to be together.'

The words from Even's farewell note.

A car engine roared in a low gear with headlamps scanning the skies. The Range Rover appeared on the other side of the crater.

'And there are the others,' Tony said. 'Wave goodbye, there's good girls.'

Harry didn't know what sight would greet him when they turned onto the plateau by the crater. Kinzonzi had said that, apart from the girls, Mister Tony had only his chauffeur with him. But that he and Mister Tony were armed with automatic weapons.

Before they reached the top Harry had offered Saul the chance to be dropped off, but he had declined. 'I have no family left, Harry. Maybe it is true that you are on the side of the angels. Anyway, you paid for the whole day.'

They skidded to a halt.

The headlights pointed across the crater, to the clutch of three standing on the edge. Then they disappeared in a cloud, but Harry had seen them and already summed up the situation: one man with a short-barrelled gun behind the three of them. One parked Range Rover. And no time. Then the cloud wafted past and Harry saw that Tony and the other man were shielding their eyes as they watched the car, as though expecting something.

'Switch off the engine,' Harry said from the back seat, resting the Märklin on the front seat. 'But leave the lights on.'

Saul did as instructed.

The man in camouflage knelt down with the gun to his shoulder and took aim.

'Flash the lights a couple of times,' Harry said, putting his eye to the sights. 'They're waiting for some signal or other.'

Harry squeezed his left eye shut. Closed out half the world. Closed out the wan faces, the fact that Kaja was there, that Lene was there with bulging cheeks and shock-blackened eyes, that these seconds counted. Closed out the turquoise eyes examining him as he said the words: 'I swear.' Closed out the popping sound of a shot that told him they had sent the wrong signal, closed out the clunk as the bullet hit the car body, followed by another thud. Closed out everything that did not concern the light refraction on the windscreen, the light refraction in the quivering heat above the crater, the bullet's probable deviation to the right, the same way the clouds of steam were drifting. He knew that now he was being sustained by one thing: adrenalin. Knew the effect of the natural stimulant would be short. It could wear off at any second. But as long as his heart was still supplying blood to the brain, it was the second he needed. For the brain is a fantastic computer. Tony Leike's head was half hidden by Lene's, but it was a little higher.

Harry aimed at Kaja's pointed teeth. Moved to the gleaming ball between Lene's lips. Moved the sights up higher. No fine-tuning. Chance. Place your bets, last race.

A cloud of steam was coming from the left.

Soon they would be enshrouded in it, and as if he had been granted a second of visual clarity, Harry saw it: that when the cloud had passed no one would be standing there any longer. Harry pressed the trigger. Saw Kaja blink above the cross on the sights.

I swear.

He was doomed. At last.

The inside of the car felt as if it would explode with the sound; his shoulder as if it would be knocked out of joint. There was a small, frost-white perforation in the windscreen. The blood-red cloud covered everything on the other side of the crater. Harry took a deep, tremulous breath and waited.

90

Marlon Brando

HARRY WAS LYING ON HIS BACK, FLOATING. FLOATING AWAY. Sinking into Lake Kivu while the blood, his and that of others, mingled with the lake's, became one, disappeared in the universe's great sleep, and the stars above him were extinguished in the cold, black water. Peace in the depths, silence, nothingness. Until he resurfaced in a bubble of methane gas, a night-blue corpse with Guinea worm-infected flesh that seethed and churned beneath the skin. And he had to get out of Lake Kivu to live. To wait.

Harry opened his eyes. He could see the hotel balcony above him. He rolled onto his side and swam the few metres to the shore. Rose from the water.

Soon dawn would break. Soon he would be sitting on the plane back to Oslo. Soon he would be in Gunnar Hagen's office telling him it was over. That they were gone, gone for ever. That they had failed. So he, too, would try to be gone.

Trembling, Harry wrapped himself in the large white towel and walked towards the stairs up to his hotel room.

When the cloud passed, no one was standing by the edge of the crater.

Harry's sights had automatically sought the marksman. Found him and he had been on the point of firing. But discovered he was looking at the man's back, heading for the car. Then the Range Rover had started up, passed them and gone.

He had moved the sights back to where he had seen Kaja, Tony and Lene. Adjusted the optics. Seen the footprints. Three sets.

Then he had thrown down the rifle, jumped out of the car and run around the crater with his revolver held in front of him. Had run and prayed. Skidded onto his knees beside them. Already knowing he had lost before he focused.

Harry unlocked his hotel-room door. Went to the bathroom, removed the wet bandage around his head and applied a new one he had been given in reception. The temporary stitches held his cheek together; it was a different matter with his jaw. His bag was packed and ready by the bed. The clothes he would travel in hung over the chair. He took the cigarette pack out of his trouser pocket, went onto the balcony and sat down on one of the plastic chairs. The cold dulled the pain in his jaw and cheek. He looked out over the shimmering silver lake he would never see again as long as he lived.

She was dead. The lead bullet with a diameter of one and a half centimetres had pierced her right eye, taking with it the right half of her head, taking Tony Leike's large white front teeth through his skull, opening a crater at the back and spreading everything over an area of a hundred square metres of volcanic rock.

Harry had spewed up. Spat green mucus on them and staggered backwards.

He flipped two cigarettes out of the packet. Put them between his lips and felt them bobbing up and down against his chattering teeth. The plane left in four hours. He had arranged to go to the airport with Saul. Harry was so exhausted he could hardly keep his eyes open, yet neither could nor wanted to sleep. The ghosts were refused admission for the first night.

'Marlon Brando,' she said.

'What?' Harry replied, lighting the cigarettes and passing her one.

'The macho actor whose name I couldn't remember. He has the most feminine voice of them all. Woman's mouth, too. Have you noticed, by the way, that he lisps? It's not that audible, but it's there, like a kind of overtone the ear doesn't perceive as a sound, but the brain registers anyway.'

'I know what you mean,' Harry said, inhaling and observing her.

She had been sprayed with blood, tissue, bone fragments and brain matter. It had taken a long time to cut the plastic ties binding her wrists; his fingers had simply not obeyed him. When she was finally free she had got to her feet, while he lay on all fours.

And he had done nothing to stop her grabbing Tony's jacket collar and belt, and rolling the body off the edge into the crater. Harry had not heard a sound, only the whisper of the wind. He had watched her looking down into the volcano until she turned to him.

He nodded. She didn't need to explain. That was how it had to be done.

She had cast an enquiring glance at the body of Lene Galtung. But Harry had shaken his head. He had weighed up the practical versus the moral considerations. The diplomatic consequences versus a mother having a grave to visit. The truth versus a lie that might have made life more liveable. Then he had got to his feet. Lifted Lene Galtung, almost collapsing under the weight of the slight, young woman. Stood on the edge of the abyss, closed his eyes, felt the longing, swayed for a second. And then let her go. Opened his eyes and watched her descent. She was already a dot. Then it was swallowed by the smoke.

'People go missing in the Congo every single day,' Kaja had said on the drive back from the volcano with Saul, and Harry had sat on the back seat holding her.

He knew it would be a short report. No traces. Vanished. They could be anywhere. And the answer to all the questions they would be asked would be this: people go missing in the Congo every single day. Even when she asked, the woman with the turquoise eyes. Because it would be simplest for them. No body, no internal inquiry, which was routine when officers had fired a shot. No embarrassing international incident. No dropping of the case, at least not at an official level, but the continued search for Leike would just be for appearances' sake. Lene Galtung would be reported missing. She hadn't had a plane ticket and the immigration authorities in the Congo hadn't registered her entry into the country. It was for the best, Hagen would say. For all parties. At any rate, those parties which counted.

And the woman with the turquoise eyes would nod. Accept what she was told. But she might know anyway, if she listened to what he didn't say. She could choose. Choose to hear him say her daughter was dead. That he had aimed between Lene's eyes instead of what he assumed would be accurate, a bit further to the right. But he had wanted to be sure the bullet didn't deviate so far to the right that he might shoot his colleague, the woman with whom he was working on this job. She could choose that or the lie that pushed sound waves up ahead, the ones that gave hope instead of a grave.

They changed planes in Kampala.

Sat in hard plastic chairs by the gate watching planes coming and going until Kaja fell asleep and her head slid down onto Harry's shoulder.

She was woken by something happening. She didn't know what, but something had changed. The room temperature. The rhythm of Harry's heartbeat. Or the lines in his drained, pale face. She saw his hand putting the phone back in his jacket pocket.

'Who was it?' she asked.

'Rikshospital,' Harry said, his eyes going absent to her, slipping past her, disappearing out of the panoramic windows, to the horizon of the concrete runway and the dazzling, light blue sky.

'He's dead.'

PART TEN

91

Parting

It rained at Olav Hole's funeral. The turnout was as Harry had expected: not as good as at Mum's funeral, but not embarrassingly sparse.

Afterwards Harry and Sis stood outside the church receiving condolences from old relatives whose names they had never heard, old teaching colleagues they had never seen and old neighbours whose names they recognised, but not their faces. The only people whose turn to face the Grim Reaper was not imminent were Harry's police colleagues: Gunnar Hagen, Beate Lønn, Kaja Solness and Bjørn Holm. Øystein Eikeland definitely looked as if he was on the point of checking out, but excused himself by saying he had been on a real bender the night before. And that Tresko, who couldn't come, sent his regards and condolences. Harry scanned the church for the two he had seen on the bench at the very back, but they had obviously left before the coffin was borne out.

Harry invited everyone for meatballs and beer at Schrøder's. The small gathering had a lot to say about the weather, but little about Olav Hole. Harry finished up his apple juice, explained he had a prior arrangement, thanked everyone for coming and left.

He hailed a taxi and gave the driver an address in Holmenkollen.

There were still some snowflakes in the gardens at these heights.

As they drove up to the black timber house, Harry's heart was beating hard. And, even harder, standing in front of the familiar door, after ringing and hearing the approach of footsteps. Familiar steps, too.

She looked as she always had. As she always would. The dark hair, the gentleness in her brown eyes, the slim neck. Sod her. She was so beautiful it hurt.

'Harry,' she said.

'Rakel.'

'Your face. I saw it in church. What happened?'

'Nothing. They say it will heal fine,' he lied.

'Come in and I'll make some coffee.'

Harry shook his head. 'I have a taxi waiting down on the road. Is Oleg here?'

'In his room. Do you want to see him?'

'Another day. How long are you staying?'

'Three days. Maybe four. Or five. We'll see.'

'Can I see you both soon? Would that be OK?'

She nodded. 'I don't know if I did the right thing.'

Harry smiled. 'Well, who knows what that is?'

'In church, I mean. We left before we . . . got in the way. You had other things to think about. Anyway, we went for Olav's sake. You know that he and Oleg . . . well, they got on. Two reserved personalities. You can take nothing for granted.'

Harry nodded.

'Oleg talks about you a lot, Harry. You mean more to him than you ever realised.' She looked down. 'More than I ever realised, too, perhaps.'

Harry cleared his throat. 'So everything here is unchanged since . . . ?'

Rakel nodded quickly so he was spared from having to complete the impossible sentence. Since the Snowman had tried to kill them in this very house.

Harry gazed at her. He had only wanted to see her, hear her voice. Feel her eyes on him. He hadn't wanted to ask her. He cleared his throat again. 'There's something I have to ask you.'

'What's that?'

'Can we go into the kitchen for a minute?'

They went in. He sat at the table opposite her. Explained slowly and at some length. She listened without interrupting.

'He wants you to visit him at the hospital. He wants to ask you for forgiveness.'

'Why should I agree?'

'You have to answer that one for yourself, Rakel. But he hasn't got much time left.'

'I've read you can live for a long time with that disease.'

'He hasn't got much time left,' Harry repeated. 'Think about it. You don't need to answer now.'

He waited. Saw her blink. Saw her eyes fill, heard the almost noiseless crying. She gasped for breath.

'What would you do, Harry?'

'I would say no. But then I'm a pretty bad human being.'

Her laughter mixed with the tears. And Harry wondered at how much it was possible to miss a sound, a certain oscillation of the air. How long you can yearn for a certain laugh.

'I need to be off now,' he said.

'Why?'

'I have three meetings left.'

'Left? Before what?'

'I'll ring you tomorrow.'

Harry got up. He had heard music from the first floor. Slayer. Slipknot.

After getting into the taxi and giving the next address, he thought about her question. Before what? Before he wanted to have everything finished. To be free. Maybe.

It was a short drive.

'This one might take a bit longer,' he said.

He breathed in, opened the gate and went to the door of the fairy-tale house.

He thought he could see the turquoise eyes following him from the kitchen window.

92

Free Fall

Mikael Bellman stood inside the entrance door of Oslo District Prison watching Sigurd Altman and a prison officer sauntering towards the counter.

'Checking out?' the officer behind the counter asked.

'Yes,' said Altman, handing over a form.

'Anything from the minibar?'

The second officer chuckled at what was undoubtedly a stock-in-trade at releases.

Personal effects were unlocked from a cupboard and returned with a broad smile. 'Hope your stay met expectations, herr Altman, and that we see you again soon.'

Bellman held the door open for Altman. They walked down the stairs together.

'The press are outside,' Bellman said. 'So let's go through the culvert. Krohn's waiting for you in a car at the rear of Police HQ.'

'Master of bluffs,' Altman said with a barbed smile.

Bellman didn't ask which he was alluding to. He had other questions. The final ones. And three hundred metres within which to have them answered. The lock buzzed, and he pushed open the door to the culvert. 'Now the deal is done I thought you might be able to tell me a couple of things.'

'Shoot, Bellman.'

'Like why you didn't correct Harry as soon as you realised he was going to arrest you?'

Altman shrugged. 'I considered the misunderstanding a priceless treat. I understood entirely, of course. What was not understandable was that the arrest would take place in Ytre Enebakk. Why there? And when there's something you don't understand, it's best to keep your trap shut. So I did, until the blinding light, until I saw the whole picture.'

'And what did the whole picture tell you?'

'That I was in a see-saw situation.'

'What do you mean by that?'

'I knew about the conflict between Kripos and Crime Squad. And I saw it gave me an option. Being in a see-saw situation means that you're in a position to apply weight to one side or the other.'

'But why didn't you try the same deal with Harry that you did with me?'

'In a see-saw situation you always turn to the losing party. That's the party which is more desperate, more willing to pay for what you have to offer. It's a simple gambling theory.'

'Why were you so sure that Harry wasn't on the losing side?'

'I wasn't sure, but there was another factor. I had begun to get to know Harry. He's not like you, Bellman, a man of compromises. He couldn't care less about personal prestige, he only wants to catch the bad boys. All the bad boys. He would have seen things in the following way: if Tony was the main actor, I was the director. And therefore I should not get off lightly. I reckoned that a career man like you would see things differently. And Johan Krohn agreed with me. You would see the personal gain in being the person who caught the murderer. You knew that people were keen to know who *did* it, who physically performed the killing, not who did the *thinking*. If a film flops, it's great for a director to have Tom Cruise in the main role because he's the one people will slaughter. Audiences and the press like to have things simple, and my crime is indirect, complicated. A court of law would undoubt-edly have handed down a life sentence, but this case isn't about courts of law, but about politics. If the press and the people are happy, the

Ministry of Justice is happy, so everyone can go home more or less happy. Getting away with a slap on the wrist, maybe a suspended sentence, is a cheap price to pay.'

'Not for everyone,' Bellman said.

Altman laughed. The echo drowned his footsteps. 'Take some advice from someone who knows. Let it go. Don't let it eat you up. Injustice is like the weather. If you can't live with it, move. Injustice is not part of the system's machinery. It *is* the machinery.'

'I'm not talking about me, Altman. I can live with it.'

'And I'm not talking about you, either, Bellman. I'm talking about the person who can't live with it.'

Bellman nodded. For his part, he certainly could live with the situation. There had been telephone calls from the Ministry. Not from the minister himself, of course, but the feedback could be interpreted in only one way. That they were happy. That this would have positive consequences, both for Kripos and for him personally.

They went up the stairs and into the daylight.

Johan Krohn stepped out of his blue Audi and extended a hand to Sigurd Altman as they crossed the road.

Bellman stood watching the released man and his counsel until the Audi disappeared round the bend to Tøyen.

'Don't you say hi when you come to see us, Bellman?'

Bellman turned. It was Gunnar Hagen. He was on the pavement across the road, no jacket, arms folded.

Bellman went over, and they shook hands.

'Anyone spreading gossip about me?' Bellman asked.

'Here at Crime Squad everything is brought to light,' Hagen said with a broad smile, shivering and rubbing his hands for warmth. 'By the way, I have a meeting with the Ministry of Justice at the back end of next month.'

'Oh, yes,' Bellman said, unconcerned. He knew very well what the meeting would be about. Restructuring. Downsizing. Transfer of responsibility for murder cases. What he didn't know was what Hagen meant with his allusion to everything coming to light.

'But you know all about the meeting, don't you.' Hagen said. 'We've both been requested to forward a recommendation for the future organ-isation of murder investigations. The deadline's approaching.'

'I hardly think they'll lay much weight on our one-sided presenta-tions,' Bellman said, looking at Hagen and trying to interpret where he was going. 'I suppose we just have to give our opinions, in the name of tolerance.'

'Unless we both believe that the present structure is preferable to all the investigations being placed under one roof,' Hagen said through chat-tering teeth.

Bellman chortled. 'You're not wearing enough clothes, Hagen.'

'You could be right. But I also know what I would think about a new murder unit being led by a policeman who had used his position to let his future wife go free after she had been smuggling drugs. Even though witnesses had pointed her out.'

Bellman stopped breathing. Felt his grip slacken. Felt gravity taking hold of him, his hair rising, his stomach falling. This was the nightmare he had been having. Nerve-jangling in sleep, brutal in reality; the fall without any rope. The solo climber's fall.

'Looks like you're feeling the cold, too, Bellman.'

'Fuck you, Hagen.'

'Me?'

'What do you want?'

'Want? Long term, I want the force to be spared yet another public scandal calling into doubt the integrity of the regular policeman. As far as restructuring is concerned . . .' Hagen's head receded between his shoulders and he stamped his feet on the ground. 'Now, the Ministry of Justice might want murder investigation resources all in the same pot, quite irrespective of the leadership question. If I were to be asked to lead such a unit I would, of course, consider the offer. But, in general, I think things are functioning well as they are. By and large, murderers receive their punishment, don't they. So if my counterpart in this matter shares that view, I will be prepared to continue with investigations both in Bryn and here at Police HQ. What do you think, Bellman?'

Mikael Bellman felt the jerk as the rope caught him after all. Felt the harness tighten, felt himself being torn into two, felt his back unable to cope with the strain and it broke, the mixture of pain and paralysis. He dangled, helpless and dizzy, somewhere between heaven and earth. But he was alive.

'Let me think about it, Hagen.'

'Think away. But don't take too much time. Deadline, you know. We have to coordinate.'

Bellman stood watching Hagen's back as he loped to the entrance of Police HQ. Then turned and stared over the rooftops of Grønland. Studied the town. His town.

93

The Answer

HARRY WAS STANDING IN THE MIDDLE OF THE LIVING-ROOM floor, looking around, when the phone rang.

'Rakel here. What are you doing?'

'Examining what's left,' he said. 'After a person dies.'

'And?'

'There's a lot. And yet not much. Sis has said what she wants, and tomorrow some guy's coming to buy up the goods and chattels. He intimated he would pay fifty thousand to buy the lot, lock, stock and barrel. And he'll clean up after him. That's . . . er . . .' Harry couldn't find the word.

'I know,' she said. 'It was like that for me when my father died. His things, which had been so important, so irreplaceable, seemed to lose their meaning. It was as if he alone was the one who had given them value.'

'Or perhaps it's those of us left realising we have to clear up. To burn. To start afresh.' Harry went into the kitchen. Looked at the photograph hanging under the kitchen cupboard. A photo from Sofies gate. Oleg and Rakel.

'I hope you said goodbye properly,' Rakel said. 'Saying goodbye is important. Especially for those left behind.'

'I don't know,' Harry said. 'We never properly said hello, he and I. I let him down.'

'How was that?'

'He asked me to dispatch him. I refused.'

The line went quiet. Harry listened to the background noise. Airport noises.

Then her voice was back. 'Do you think you should have helped him on his way?'

'Yes,' Harry said. 'I do. I think so now.'

'Don't think about it. It's too late.'

'Is it?'

'Yes, Harry. It's too late.'

The line went quiet again. Harry could hear a nasal voice announcing boarding for a flight to Amsterdam.

'So you didn't want to meet him?'

'I can't do it, Harry. I suppose I'm a bad human being, too.'

'We'll have to try to do better next time then.'

He could hear her smiling. 'Can we do that?'

'It's never too late to try. Say hello to Oleg from me.'

'Harry . . .'

'Yes?'

'Nothing.'

Harry stood looking out of the kitchen window after she had rung off.

Then he went upstairs and started to pack.

The doctor was waiting for Harry when he came out of the toilet. They continued down the last stretch of the corridor towards the prison officer.

'His condition is stable,' she said. 'We might transfer him back to prison. What's the purpose of this visit?'

'I want to thank him for helping us to clear up a case. And to get back to him about a wish he had expressed.'

Harry took off his jacket, gave it to the officer and held out his arms while he was searched.

'Five minutes. No more. OK?'

Harry nodded.

'I'll come in with you,' said the prison guard who was unable to take his eyes off Harry's disfigured cheek.

Harry arched an eyebrow.

'Rules for civilian visits,' the officer said. 'It has come to our ears that you've resigned from the force.'

Harry shrugged.

The man had got out of bed and was sitting on a chair by the window.

'We found him,' Harry said, pulling a chair close. The prison guard stood by the door, but was within hearing distance. 'Thanks for your help.'

'I kept my part of the bargain,' the man said. 'What about yours?'

'Rakel didn't want to come.'

The man's face didn't move a muscle, he just shrank as if hit by an ice-cold gust of wind.

'We found a bottle of medicine in the chest at Prince Charming's cabin. I had a drop of the contents analysed yesterday. Ketanome. Same as he used on his victims. Do you know the drug? Fatal in large doses.'

'Why are you telling me this?'

'I was given some of it myself recently. In a way, I liked it. But then I like all kinds of drugs. Only you know that, don't you? I told you what I did in the toilet at The Landmark in Hong Kong.'

The Snowman eyed Harry. Glanced cautiously at the prison officer and then back at Harry.

'Oh yes,' he said in a monotone. 'In the cubicle at the end on . . .'

'. . . the right,' Harry said. 'Well, as I said, thanks. Don't look in the mirror.'

'Same applies to you,' the man said and offered him a bony, white hand.

When Harry was shown out at the end of the corridor, he turned and caught a glimpse of the Snowman tottering towards them with the guard. Before going into the toilet.

94

Glass Noodles

'Hi, Hole.' Kaja smiled up at him.

She was sitting in the bar, on a low stool, on her hands. Her gaze was intense, her lips blood red, her cheeks glowing. It struck him that he had not seen her wearing make-up before. And it was not true what he had once believed, in his naivety, that a woman cannot be made more beautiful with cosmetics. She was wearing a plain black dress. A short necklace of gold and white pearls rested against her collarbone and when she breathed they reflected soft light.

'Been waiting long?' Harry asked.

'No,' she said, getting up before he had a chance to sit down, pulling him over, laying her head on his shoulder and holding him like that. 'I'm just a bit cold.'

She didn't care about other people in the bar watching her, she didn't let go, instead she stuffed both hands under his suit jacket, stroking his shirted back up and down to get them warm. Harry heard a discreet cough, looked up and received a friendly nod from a man with body language that said head waiter.

'Our table is ready,' she said.

'Table? I thought we were only having a drink.'

'We have to celebrate the end of the case, don't we? I ordered the food beforehand. Something very special.'

They were shown to a table by the window in the fully occupied restaurant. A waiter lit the candles, poured apple cider into the glasses, put the bottle back in the ice bucket and left.

She raised her glass. '*Skål.*'

'To what?'

'To Crime Squad continuing as before. To you and me catching bad men. To being here now. Together.'

They drank. Harry set his glass down on the cloth. Moved it. The base had left a wet mark. 'Kaja . . .'

'I've got something for you, Harry. Tell me what your greatest wish is right now.'

'Listen, Kaja . . .'

'What?' she said, breathless, and leaned forward, eager to hear.

'I told you I would be on my travels again. I'm leaving tomorrow.'

'Tomorrow?' she laughed, and the smile faded as the waiter unfolded their serviettes and spread them, heavy and white, over their laps. 'Where to?'

'Away.'

Kaja stared down at the table without saying a word. Harry wanted to put his hand on hers. But refrained.

'So I wasn't enough?' she whispered. 'We weren't enough?'

Harry waited until he could catch her eye. 'No,' he said. 'We weren't enough. Not enough for you, not enough for me.'

'What do you know about what's enough?' Her voice was thick with tears.

'Quite a lot,' Harry said.

Kaja breathed heavily, tried to control her voice. 'Is it Rakel?'

'Yes. It was always Rakel.'

'But you said yourself she didn't want you.'

'She doesn't want me the way I am now. So I have to repair myself. I have to be well again. Do you understand?'

'No, I don't understand.' Two tiny tears clung to the lashes under her eyes, wavering. 'You *are* well. The scars are just—'

'You know very well it's not *those* scars I'm talking about.'

'Will I ever see you again?' she asked, trapping one of the tears with a fingernail.

She grasped his hand, squeezed it so tight the knuckles went white. Harry looked at her. Then she let go.

'I won't go and bring you back another time,' she said.

'I know.'

'You won't cope.'

'Probably not,' he smiled. 'But then who does?'

She tilted her head. Then she smiled with those small pointed teeth of hers.

'I do,' she said.

Harry remained in his chair until he heard the soft slam of a car door in the darkness and the diesel engine starting up. He looked down at the cloth and was about to get up when a soup plate came into his eyeline and he heard the head waiter's voice announce: 'Special order at the lady's instructions flown over from Hong Kong. Li Yuan's glass noodles.'

Harry stared down at the plate. She is still sitting in her chair, he thought. The restaurant is a soap bubble and now it is taking off, hovering over the town and is gone. The kitchen never runs out and we never land.

He got up and made a move to leave. But changed his mind. Sat down again. Lifted the chopsticks.

95

The Allies

HARRY LEFT THE DANCE RESTAURANT THAT WAS NO LONGER a dance restaurant, drove down the hill to the Seamen's School that was no longer a seamen's school. Continued to the bunkers that had defended the country's invaders. Beneath him were the fjord and the town, hidden by mist. Cars crept forward carefully with yellow cat's eyes. A tram emerged from the mist like a ghost gnashing its teeth.

A car stopped in front of him, and Harry jumped into the front seat. Katie Melua oozed through the speakers with her honey-dripping agony, and Harry desperately searched for the 'off' switch on the radio.

'Jesus Christ, what do you look like!' Øystein said, horrified. 'The surgeon must have definitely failed the sewing course. But at least you'll save a few kroner on the Halloween mask. Don't laugh or your mug'll tear again.'

'I promise.'

'By the way,' Øystein said, 'it's my birthday today.'

'Oh, fuck. Here's a smoke, from me to you. Free.'

'That's exactly what I wanted.'

'Mm. Any bigger presents you'd like?'

'Like what?'

'World peace.'

'The day you wake up to world peace, you don't wake up, Harry. Because they've dropped the big one.'

'OK. No private wishes?'

'Not a lot. New conscience maybe.'

'*New* conscience?'

'The old one's not so good. Smart suit you've got. Thought you had only the one.'

'It's Dad's.'

'Jesus, you must have shrunk.'

'Yes,' Harry said, straightening his tie. 'I have shrunk.'

'How's Ekeberg restaurant?'

Harry closed his eyes. 'Fine.'

'Do you remember the leaky shack we sneaked into that time. How old were we? Sixteen?'

'Seventeen.'

'Didn't you dance with the Killer Queen there once?'

'Possibly.'

'Frightening to think that the MILF of your youth has ended up in an old people's home.'

'MILF?'

Øystein sighed. 'Look it up.'

'Mm. Øystein?'

'Yes.'

'Why did you and I become pals?'

'Because we grew up together, I suppose.'

'Is that all? A demographic coincidence? No spiritual fellowship?'

'Not that I've noticed. As far as I know, we've only ever had one thing in common.'

What's that?'

'No one else wanted to be pals with us.'

They wound their way through the next bends in silence.

'Apart from Tresko,' Harry said.

Øystein snorted. 'Who stank so much of toe-fart no one else could bear sitting next to him.'

'Yes,' Harry said. 'We were good at that.'

'We nailed that one,' Øystein said. 'But, Christ, how he stank.'

They laughed together. Gentle, light-hearted. Sad.

∗   ∗   ∗

Øystein had parked the car on the brown grass with the doors open. Harry clambered up onto the top of the bunker and sat on the edge with his legs dangling. From the speakers inside the car doors Springsteen sang about blood brothers one stormy night and the vow that had to be kept.

Øystein passed Harry the bottle of Jim Beam. A lone siren from the town rose and fell until it lost power and died. The poison stung Harry's throat and stomach, and he threw up. The second swig went better. The third was fine.

Max Weinberg sounded as if he was trying to destroy the drumhead.

'It often strikes me how I *ought* to wish I had more regrets,' Øystein said. 'But I don't give a shite. I think I just accepted from my first waking second that I was a bloody slob. What about you?'

Harry ruminated. 'I have loads of regrets. But perhaps that's because I carry around such high notions of myself. In fact, I imagine I could have chosen differently.'

'But you bloody couldn't.'

'Not at that time. But next time, Øystein. Next time.'

'Has it ever happened, Harry? Ever in the fucking history of mankind?'

'Just because nothing has happened doesn't mean that it can't happen. I don't know that this bottle is going to fall if I drop it. Fuck, which philosopher was it again? Hobbes? Hume? Heidegger? One of the head-cases beginning with H.'

'Answer me.'

Harry shrugged. 'I think it's possible to learn. The problem is that we learn so damned *slowly*, so that by the time you've realised, it's too late. For example, someone you love might ask you for a favour, an act of love. Like helping him to die. Which you say no to because you haven't learned, you haven't had the insight. When you do finally see the light, it's too late.' Harry took another swig. 'So instead you perform the act of love for someone else. Perhaps for someone you hate, even.'

Øystein accepted the bottle. 'Got no idea what you're chuntering on about, but it sounds fucked up.'

'Not necessarily. It's never too late for good actions, is it.'

'It's *always* too late, don't you mean?'

'No! I always thought we hate too much for it to be possible for us to obey other impulses. But my father had a different opinion. He said hatred and love are the same currency. Everything starts with love, hatred is the reverse side of the coin.'

'Amen.'

'But that must mean you can go the other way, from hatred to love. Hatred must be a good starting point for learning, for changing, for doing things differently next time.'

'Now you're so optimistic I'm considering puking, Harry.'

The organ came in the refrain, a whine, cutting through like a circular saw.

Øystein leaned his head to the side while flicking ash. And Harry was almost moved to tears. Simply because he saw the years that had become their lives, that had become them, in the way his friend flicked ash as he had always done, leaning to the side as if the cigarette were too heavy, his head angled as if he liked the world better from a slanted perspective, the ash on the floor of the smokers' shed at school, down an empty beer bottle at a party they had gatecrashed, on the cold, rough concrete of a bunker.

'Anyway, you're beginning to get old, Harry.'

'Why do you say that?'

'When men start quoting their fathers, they're old. The race has been run.'

And then Harry found it. The answer to her question about what he most wanted right now. He wanted an armoured heart.

Epilogue

BLUISH-BLACK CLOUDS SWEPT OVER HONG KONG'S HIGHEST point, Victoria Peak, but it had finally stopped raining after dripping constantly since the beginning of September. The sun poked through, and a huge rainbow formed a bridge between Kong Island and Kowloon. Harry closed his eyes and let the sun warm his face. The spell of good weather had come just in time for the horse-racing season due to open in Happy Valley later that evening.

Harry heard the buzz of Japanese voices approach and then pass the bench on which he was sitting. They were coming from the funicular railway, which since 1888 had attracted tourists and locals up here to the fresh air above the town. Harry opened his eyes again and flicked through the racing programme.

He had contacted Herman Kluit as soon as he'd arrived in Hong Kong. Kluit had offered Harry a job as a debt collector, that is, he had to trace people who were trying to flee from their debts. In this way, Kluit would not have to sell the debt with a substantial discount to the Triad, or think about the brutal recovery methods they employed.

It would have been stretching things to say Harry enjoyed the job, but it was well paid and simple. He didn't have to recover the money, just locate the debtors. However, it turned out that his appearance – one metre ninety-two and a grinning scar from mouth to ear – was often enough for them to settle their accounts on the spot. And he very rarely had to resort to using a search engine on a server in Germany.

The trick, nevertheless, was to keep off dope and alcohol, which he had succeeded in doing thus far. There were two letters waiting for him in reception today. How they had found him he had no idea. Only that Kaja must have been involved. One letter bore the logo of Oslo Police District on the envelope, and Harry guessed Gunnar Hagen. With the other he didn't need to guess, he immediately recognised Oleg's upright and still childish handwriting. Harry had put both letters in his jacket pocket without taking a decision on when or indeed whether he would read them.

Harry folded the racing programme and put it down beside him on the bench. He peered across to the Chinese mainland where the yellow smog was becoming thicker by the year. But up here at the top of the mountain the air still felt almost fresh. He looked down on Happy Valley. On the cemeteries, west of the Wong Nai Chong road, where there were separate sections for Protestants, Catholics, Muslims and Hindus. He could see the racecourse where he knew jockeys and horses were already on the turf being tested before the evening's races. Soon the spectators would be pouring in: those with hope, those without, the lucky and the unlucky. Those who went to have their dreams fulfilled and those who went purely to dream. The losers who took uncalculated risks and those who took calculated risks, but lost anyway. They had been here before, and they all came back, even the ghosts from the cemeteries down there, the several hundred who died in the great fire at Happy Valley Racecourse in 1918. For tonight it was definitely their turn to beat the odds, to conquer chance, to stuff their pockets full of crisp Hong Kong dollars, to get away with murder. In a couple of hours from now they would have entered the gates, read the racing programme, filled the coupons with the day's doubles, quinellas, exactas, triples, superfectas, whatever their gambling god is called. They would have queued by the bookies' hatches, holding their stakes at the ready. Most of them would have died a bit every time the tape was crossed, but redemption is only fifteen minutes away, when the staring gates open for the next race. Unless you're a bridge jumper, of course, someone who risks all their assets on one horse in a race. But no one complains. Everyone knows the odds.

But you have those who know the odds, and then you have those who know the outcome. At a racecourse in South Africa they recently found underground pipes in the starting gates. The pipes contained compressed air and mini-darts with tranquillisers that could be fired into the horses' stomachs by pressing a remote control.

Katrine Bratt had informed him that Sigurd Altman was booked into a hotel in Shanghai. It was barely an hour's flight away.

Harry cast a final glance at the front page of the programme.

Those who know the outcome.

'It's just a game.' Herman Kluit used to say that. Perhaps because he used to win.

Harry looked at his watch, got to his feet and started to walk to the tram. He had been tipped off about a promising horse in the third race.

Jo Nesbo is a musician, songwriter, economist and author. His first crime novel featuring Harry Hole was published in Norway in 1997 and was an instant hit, winning the Glass Key Award for best Nordic crime novel (an accolade shared with Peter Høeg, Henning Mankell and Stieg Larsson). *The Leopard* is the sixth of Nesbo's novels to be translated into English.

Don Bartlett lives in Norfolk and works as a freelance translator of Scandinavian literature. He has translated, or co-translated, Norwegian novels by Lars Saabye Christensen, Roy Jacobsen, Ingvar Ambjørnsen, Kjell Ola Dahl, Gunnar Staalesen and Pernille Rygg.

SECOND LOVE

JUDITH GOULD

SECOND LOVE

LITTLE, BROWN AND COMPANY

A *Little, Brown* Book

First published in the United States of America by Dutton 1997
First published in Great Britain by Little, Brown and Company 1998

Copyright © Judith Gould 1997

The moral right of the author has been asserted.

All characters in this publication other than those clearly in the public domain are fictitious and any resemblance to real persons, living or dead, is purely coincidental.

All rights reserved. No part of this publication may be reproduced, stored in a retrieval system, or transmitted, in any form or by any means, without the prior permission in writing of the publisher, nor be otherwise circulated in any form of binding or cover other than that in which it is published and without a similar condition including this condition being imposed on the subsequent purchaser.

A CIP catalogue record for this book is available from the British Library.

ISBN 0 316 88153 8

Printed and bound in Great Britain by Clays Ltd, St Ives plc

Little, Brown and Company (UK)
Brettenham House
Lancaster Place
London WC2E 7EN

To
Nancy K. Austin and Bill Cawley
and the entire Menagerie

Love to faults is always blind,
Always is to joy inclin'd,
Lawless, wing'd, and unconfin'd,
And breaks all chains from every mind.
— WILLIAM BLAKE

There is no animal more invincible
than a woman, nor fire either, nor
any wildcat so ruthless.
— ARISTOPHANES, *Lysistrata*

PREFACE

This is the third and final novel of a trilogy that began with *The Texas Years*, and continued with *The Love Makers*.

Although I had all intentions of covering the time period from 1986 to 1990, there occurred one of those serendipitous cases where magic and reality conspired otherwise. The characters and plot literally took on a life of their own, and *Second Love* subsequently is set in 1996 and 1997.

To the faithful readers who wrote me, exhorting me to get on with this book, I offer grateful thanks. As for those newer readers who are, as yet, unfamiliar with either *The Texas Years* or *The Love Makers*—take heart. Both novels are still in print; if your bookstore is out of them, they can easily order you paperback editions.

If this sounds like a sales pitch, it is and it isn't: *Second Love* has what I like to call "legs." That is, it stands on its own, and is a complete work in and of itself.

Granted, the main character, Dorothy-Anne Hale Cantwell, is reprised from *The Love Makers*, as is the hotel empire founded by her great-grandmother, Elizabeth-Anne Hale.

But here, as elsewhere, art imitates life.

The business world has changed dramatically since I first wrote *The Texas Years* and *The Love Makers*. Back then, who could have predicted the extent of multinational conglomerates, hostile takeovers, and mega-mergers —which have become the stuff and substance of every business day?

However, people—bless 'em—never seem to change. There were villains and heroes yesterday. There are villains and heroes today. And there will surely be villains and heroes tomorrow.

And where villains and heroes dare to tread, their shadow, the novelist, tiptoes right behind. Observing. Soaking up inspiration. And invariably owing debts of thanks.

So, very special *danke schöns* to Peter Bevacqua, Stephen King (the one of New York and Claverack, *not* Maine), and Robert and Dawn Gallaher.

Sometimes, songs hit the nail right on the head. You gotta have friends. . . .

JUDITH GOULD
26 June 1997

PROLOGUE

I t could have been any of the thousands of uninhabited green islets that rose like dragon's teeth from the depths of the emerald-green South China Sea. Anchored in its lee, the junk was like countless others that still plied these waters, and the islet provided it privacy and refuge—as well as convenience. By helicopter it was a mere forty-minute hop from Hong Kong, yet it might have been worlds away.

The six elders had arrived separately. Two had come by helicopter and four by small powerboats capable of attaining speeds of up to fifty knots per hour. In order to draw as little attention to themselves as possible, they had arrived at twenty-minute intervals, and their boats and helicopters had immediately been covered with camouflage netting.

Each elder was permitted one armed bodyguard to accompany him out to the junk. Once aboard, the bodyguards remained up on deck to perform guard duty.

Below, in the luxurious rosewood-paneled main cabin, the six elders sat around a circular cinnabar table, which symbolized that here each was of equal stature and importance. Uneasy partners and suspicious of one another though they were, they had secretly united to hatch this one plan, which was in their mutual best interests.

They did not address each other by name. At their first meeting a bowl had been passed and they had reached inside and chosen a folded scrap of paper at random. On each was written the animal name for a different Chinese year.

Those became the code names that they now used.

After several hours of intense discussion, they had winnowed down their choices.

The eldest, Honorable Ox, a Chiuchow with a wispy goatee who was

1

the *lung tao* of Hong Kong's most notorious crime syndicate, bowed graciously. He spoke in halting English as had been prearranged, due to their various languages and dialects.

"The time has come," he said, "to cast our votes. As agreed, we will mark our choices and vote by secret ballot in the barbarian fashion. The bird, since it soars like the human soul, signifies yes. The fish, since man cannot breathe underwater, means no. Are there any questions?"

There were none.

Each of the six men opened an identical teak box and extracted two short ivory chops, each pair of which had been identically carved with one of two delicate symbols—a bird or a fish.

Selecting the appropriate chop, the men pressed it into the solid ink in the imperial jade pot and stamped a chop mark on a sliver of rice paper. These ballots they then folded in half, and waited for their code names to be called before dropping them into the blue and white Ming "dice" bowl in the center of the table.

"I hereby cast the first vote," said Honorable Ox, dropping his folded slip into the bowl. "Honorable Tiger?"

The Laotian general who protected the rich upland poppy fields of Laos added his vote.

"Honorable Rooster?"

The Thai chemist whose countless makeshift laboratories processed raw opium into heroin cast his.

"Honorable Dragon?"

The head of the Golden Triangle's largest underground banking system added his ballot.

"Honorable Snake?"

The government minister from Beijing, under whose aegis the refined drug was shipped overland to Hong Kong, added his slip of rice paper.

"And I," said the man named after the year of the Horse, who controlled the major poppy-producing highlands of Burma, "add mine." He held out his hand and let the ballot flutter into the bowl.

"It is done," said Honorable Snake.

"The die is cast," added Honorable Ox. "Honorable Dragon, would you be so gracious as to empty the bowl?"

Honorable Dragon upended it, six tiny folded slips of paper fell out, and he unfolded them.

"Ah!" Honorable Dragon nodded in approval. "It is unanimous. You see? The gods are already smiling upon our endeavor. We shall enjoy very good joss."

"I believe we have voted most wisely," added Honorable Tiger. "This shall give us unprecedented money-laundering facilities in over a hundred countries and a thousand cities around the world. Forty-four million dollars per day. Illustrious Dragon can see to it that the funds necessary to finance the first"—Honorable Tiger searched his mind for an appropriately delicate euphemism—"*phase* toward our legitimacy will be taken out of our special account. I believe Honorable Ox is in the best position to recruit the necessary talent."

They all looked at the leader of the Hong Kong crime syndicate.

"We must use no one of Asian descent," Honorable Ox decided thoughtfully. "Not even some Korean or Japanese devil. I shall send one of my men to recruit a Western barbarian." He looked at the others. "By using a Westerner, we will be yet another step removed, and Oriental involvement will not be suspected."

Honorable Rooster nodded. "This is most wise. We cannot be careful enough."

"Good," Honorable Ox said. "It is decided." He paused. "We shall depart separately, just as we arrived. As host, I shall be the last to leave."

He and the others placed their chops back in the boxes and pocketed them. Then he stood up and bowed.

He said: "Until the next time, Illustrious Elders. May the gods of fortune attend you."

Honorable Ox waited until the others were long gone before he had his bodyguard row him ashore. Five minutes later they were airborne, skimming above the sea in the black Jet Ranger helicopter. As they flew past the anchored junk, he counted to ten before pressing the remote control in his hand.

Behind the helicopter, the junk exploded in a blossoming fireball, tossing lengths of timber, as if they were toothpicks, hundreds of feet into the air.

Within minutes all signs of the clandestine meeting were obliterated. It might never have taken place.

BOOK ONE

THE COLDEST WINTER

I t should have been an uneventful flight.

At Aspen's smart little airport, the departing Learjet was unremarkable on all counts. At an airport where private birds had to be double-parked, everyone had long become inured to the comings and goings of the rich and famous in their luxurious aircraft: the rock star and his entourage stumbling out of a Challenger 600 in a pharmaceutically induced Rocky Mountain high, the European royals swooping down without fanfare in a Citation III, the multibillionaires zipping in and out on their big Gulfstream IVs and Falcon 900Bs, the planeload of elegant hookers flown in from Vegas on a Falcon 200 for a visiting Arab, and the film stars commuting from Hollywood and Palm Springs in a veritable private air force—Hawker 700s, Falcon 50s, Learjet 31s, Citation Is, and Gulfstream IIs.

Freddie Cantwell—who was not a movie star, and who cultivated a low profile—had not rated a single glance as he'd boarded the small Lear 35, a stepchild among the impressive array of flying heavy metal. Even the flight plan his pilot had filed—Aspen to San Francisco—was unworthy of meriting attention.

In fact, the only notable distinction about this flight was that the predicted snowstorm had already begun, all incoming flights had been rerouted, and the Learjet was the last aircraft to take off before the runway was closed down. Thick swirls of powdery snow had reduced visibility to a hundred feet, obscuring the usual spectacular view. The weather reports had predicted ten to twelve inches, and airport employees were battening down the hatches.

Undaunted, the Learjet hurtled down the runway and climbed steeply through snow and clouds and then burst through the woolpack into a cerulean sky where the sun shone brightly and the world below was one endless mass of fluffy white cotton.

A normal takeoff in all respects.

Freddie Cantwell unbuckled his seat belt, placed his IBM Thinkpad on the walnut fold-down table in front of him, flipped up the screen, and switched it on. Changing floppy disks, he hit a few keys and brought up the massive file devoted entirely to the Hale Eden Isle Resort, currently under construction on an island off Puerto Rico.

He'd left there yesterday morning, after spending two grueling days on the site . . . two exhausting days of cracking the whip, inspecting the construction, attempting to ferret out ways to slash costs.

Costs.

Somehow it always came down to costs. Finding ways of cutting corners without compromising either safety, comfort, or the overall plan.

He sighed to himself, mentally inventorying what he'd accomplished—precious little, considering it was a billion-dollar project financed privately, and without shareholders.

A billion dollars.

Madness!

No wonder he'd stopped overnight in Aspen. He'd craved resuscitation from the oppressively humid tropical heat of the Caribbean, the pressures of a billion dollars' worth of responsibilities. His business in Aspen had helped.

And everything behind schedule and way, way over budget . . . Christ! What had he and Dorothy-Anne been *thinking*? he wondered. Why hadn't they been satisfied? They should be *downsizing*!

Meanwhile, the Eden Isle Resort loomed in the future like a curse. Too far along to stop, yet too far behind to see a light at the end of the tunnel.

He rubbed the weariness from his eyes, shook his head as if to clear it. Then gazed abstractedly out the porthole at the field of clouds.

The jet was heading directly into the sun, and dusk was fast approaching; soon the clouds would do their disappearing act. He glanced around the compact cabin made posh by portholes with walnut tambour shades, six seats in fragrant butterscotch glove leather, generously sized folddown tables, custom carpeting, and recessed lights.

Nothing had been overlooked. The jet was equipped with all the latest safeguards and state-of-the-art navigational aids.

Convenience, comfort, luxury, *safety*.

Freddie glanced at his watch. It was three p.m. Rocky Mountain Time. The 900-mile flight would take approximately two hours, perhaps longer, depending upon the jet stream. Time enough to stall the inevitable for an hour and a half before shaving for a second time that day and changing into his formal wear. Then, the moment he landed at SFO, he'd transfer to a waiting helicopter. With the rooftop landing, he'd make the grand opening in time.

Freddie knew how important his punctual arrival was. *This is one occasion for which I can't be late,* he told himself. *Dorothy-Anne's counting on me. We're supposed to perform the ribbon-cutting ceremony together.*

The inauguration of the newest and brightest jewel in the Hale Hotel empire had been planned to achieve maximum publicity. The guests included the governor of California, both senators, assorted congressmen, the mayor, celebrities from Marin County, and four hundred of the Bay Area's richest and most influential people. Plus, the press would be out in full force to cover the event.

And an event it would be.

The San Francisco Palace, located in the heart of the financial district, took up an entire square block, and no expense had been spared. It boasted four identical, architecturally pure Palladian facades of limestone, with two stories of arched shopping colonnades interspersed with Ionic pilasters. From the core of this immodest landmark rose the all-suite hotel—forty-two stories of earthquake-proof high-rise topped by a recessed penthouse with private rooftop pool, wraparound terraces, and helipad.

There was a lot riding on the San Francisco Palace. It had been conceived as the standard by which all future hotels would be judged, combining Pacific Rim luxury with European hospitality and the best of American conveniences.

Per sqare foot, it was the most expensive hotel ever built.

A splashy grand opening was essential for its success. *And it* will *be a success,* Freddie thought, *especially since Dorothy-Anne has everything to say about it.*

He thought of her again and sighed. Chairman and chief executive of the Hale Companies, Inc., whose core business was Hale Hotels—the largest privately held hotel empire in the world—Dorothy-Anne was nothing if not a shrewd businesswoman.

She's never come up with a turkey yet, he thought. *Nor will she ever.*

And he should know; he was president and chief operating officer of the Hale Companies as well as Dorothy-Anne's husband, and father of their three children.

I can't spoil the grand opening party. Too much is riding on it.

Outside the porthole, the winter afternoon was rapidly dwindling. Twilight was at hand, the sun into which they were headed sinking into the sea of fleece. Far back, the first stars were beginning to prick the purpling eastern sky.

The jet engines droned healthily; up here, miles above the blizzard-lashed Rockies, he couldn't have asked for a smoother flight.

Meanwhile, time was fleeting.

Better use it to advantage.

But first things first. Dorothy-Anne was expecting his call.

He reached for one of the satellite-linked telephones and called San Francisco.

Dorothy-Anne sounded overjoyed. "Oh, darling! I was so afraid you wouldn't make it. I was told the Aspen airport's been closed."

"You know me," he said. "I've got the luck of the devil. Made it out just in the nick of time."

"I'm so glad, darling," she said softly. "This evening's meant to be shared."

"And it will be, honey. I just called to let you know I'm on my way."

"Where are you now?"

"Somewhere over Colorado."

"Darling," she said, "I can't wait to see you. I must confess, I still don't understand why you had to stop in Aspen," she was saying. "You made it sound so mysterious! I'm simply dying to know what it is."

Deciding it was time to deflect the subject away from Aspen, he said, "How's everything going at your end?"

"Oh, you know. Frantic, as expected . . . all your typical last-minute problems. Just minor ones, thank God. I'm so keyed up, I don't know how I'd handle a major crisis if one popped up."

"And the monsters?" he asked. "Have you spoken to them?"

Dorothy-Anne laughed. "Actually, I just got off the phone with them. Talk about getting an earful about being left home alone! Liz is especially consummate at making me feel guilty. Nanny said what they need is a drill sergeant."

He laughed. "When you speak to Nanny again, tell her that as soon as we're back I'll give the troops a severe dressing-down."

"*You!*" Dorothy-Anne hooted. "You, who shamelessly spoils them rotten? *That'll* be the day!"

"If I spoil them, it's because I love them," he said thickly, overcome by a rush of emotion. "And I love you, too, honey."

Suddenly it seemed imperative that he emphasize this, as if he might never have the chance to tell her these words again.

"I love you no matter what, and more than life itself. You do believe me when I say that, don't you?"

"D-dar . . . *ling?*" Her voice rose slightly in pitch. "What's *wrong*? Is . . . is it something with the plane?"

"No, no, no," he assured her. "There's nothing wrong with the plane. Why should there be?"

"I-I don't *know*. . . . It's just . . . there was something in your tone. . . ."

"Relax." He tipped his head back. "I'm fine and the plane's fine. There's not even the slightest turbulence."

"Freddie . . . ?"

"I'm still here."

"I love you, too." She paused. "Arrive safely, darling, will you?"

"Don't I always?"

"Yes. Of course you do."

Freddie hung up, turned his head sideways, and sat there, staring out the porthole.

Arrive safely. . . .

Dorothy-Anne had sounded uncharacteristically uneasy—and worried.

Suddenly he was filled with a powerful sense of foreboding, a prescience of menace he was unable to shake. It was the kind of feeling he got when a storm was brewing and the air was full of electricity, or he awoke in the middle of the night, wondering what it was that had disturbed his sleep.

He stared out at the star-spattered night. The jet was hurtling through a darkness as clear as crystal and deeper than death, its wings calcimined by platinum moonlight. The thick sea of clouds below was silvery, and he could make out the aircraft's tiny, distorted faint shadow racing across them. The engines hummed confidently.

How silly of me, he chided himself. *Everything's fine. Nothing's going to happen to me.*

Gradually, he began to feel calmer. His heart slowed, and the sense of foreboding seemed to lessen its grip on him.

Suddenly there was a loud *ca-rack!* and the little jet pitched to starboard.

Freddie grabbed the armrests of his seat. The IBM Thinkpad crashed to the carpet, and loose objects went flying around the cabin.

What the hell—?

The jet slowly straightened.

Freddie's hands trembled as he depressed the intercom button. "What happened?" he demanded hoarsely.

"Sorry, Mr. Cantwell," the pilot said calmly over the speaker, so calmly he might have been parking a car in a garage. "We had it on autopilot. We're on manual now. Wouldn't hurt if you fastened your seat belt, though."

"But—"

"Just turbulence, sir. Nothing to worry about."

Freddie buckled up. *Just turbulence,* he told himself. *Nothing to worry about—*

And then it happened again. Another *CA-RACK!* but a lot louder than the first. The plane lurched again, this time pitching to port. But instead of straightening, it continued to spin around, whirling sickeningly around and around like some carnival ride from Hell.

Freddie's heart was in his throat. He couldn't understand what had gone wrong. The plane was always kept in tiptop condition. Mechanics swarmed over it regularly. No expense was spared.

Then suddenly he became aware of the silence . . . the sudden, horrible silence.

The engines had died, and without their thrust the jet was no longer propelled forward but cartwheeling straight down in a freefall, whistling as it plunged silently through the night like a whirling bomb, down, down, down through the clouds, and Freddie knew this was the last flight he'd ever take, and suddenly he could no longer hold his screams inside.

Dorothy-Anne stood alone on the rooftop. Up here, forty-three floors above street level, the wind whipped and cleaved, and despite the cashmere throw she'd wrapped around herself, the chill cut through to the bone.

It was hours since the fog, driven by a Pacific wind, had rolled in through the Golden Gate. Night had fallen. Alcatraz, Tiburon, Sausalito—even the great swagged bridge spanning the bay—all their lights were obscured by that impenetrable blanket of gray from which foghorns resounded mournfully, like drowned sailors calling up from the haunted deep.

Beyond the railing of the terrace, the bright windows of the financial district's towers came and went, as though viewed through layers of slow-moving scrims. In this setting, it was easy to imagine herself in a ghostly gondola, floating in midair through an eerily lit, unpopulated metropolis. It was an image both beautiful and menacing, like an opera set remembered from some lost and half-forgotten dream, but it didn't disturb her; this was her building—*hers.* With it she had left her mark on yet another city's skyline, had expanded her globe-girdling empire by another notch.

Like a spirit, she glided southward along the terrace, past the lighted sliding glass doors of the penthouse, tendrils of fog swirling around her, ethereal ribbons of vapor reaching out, only to vanish into nothingness when touched.

For a while she stood there and gazed south, in the direction of the airport, as if through will alone she could conjure Freddie's helicopter from out of the mist and set it safely down atop the penthouse roof.

Odd, the fanciful spells such an evening can weave, even upon a realist unused to daydreaming. Standing there, buffeted by the icy damp scalpel of the wind, Dorothy-Anne could have sworn that this enchantment had been specially concocted for her own pleasure.

A silly notion, but in such unearthly surroundings nothing seemed impossible, no whim too far-fetched. Not even to a woman with both feet rooted firmly in the ground. And Dorothy-Anne's were, as her many acquaintances and few intimates could attest; she was practical and killer sharp.

She was also a provocative beauty.

Dorothy-Anne Cantwell was thirty-one years old. She had wheat gold hair, which she was wearing pulled back in a French twist for the formality of the grand opening. Brilliant aquamarines for eyes, truly beautiful lips, a stubborn chin, and a profile lifted straight from a cameo. She was five feet ten inches tall, slight of build—no one would call her voluptuous—and had a long-waisted body and legs that went forever.

But she was more than just a pretty face.

Dorothy-Anne Cantwell had inherited an empire and had built it into something even bigger. In fact, according to *Forbes,* Dorothy-Anne Cantwell was *the* richest woman in America. Some said the world.

All that talk about money never fazed her. Like Mount Everest, the fortune was simply *there.* To her, it was a business like any other, and she worked her fanny off to steer it through treacherous financial waters. The fact that the Hale Companies consisted of hotels, resorts, a cruise line, apartment complexes, service industries, and investments in one hundred foreign countries, and that she was worth an estimated $7.8 billion had not gone to her head.

On the contrary. She saw herself as a businesswoman responsible for the livelihoods of tens of thousands of employees and as the temporary custodian of her children's birthright. For Dorothy-Anne had inherited her great-grandmother's shining sense of values and was, above all, a devoted wife and mother.

In a toss-up, family always came first.

Which was why she moved heaven and earth to keep out of the public eye, and why, to date, she'd never granted a single interview.

It wasn't that she was shy. In guarding her privacy, she was motivated solely by a deep maternal instinct and the firm belief that families thrive best outside the glare of publicity.

Protecting her children from the great unwashed public had always been her primary concern. That she achieved this at the expense of her own social life seemed a small enough price to pay.

She had never regretted it.

But tonight, all that was going to change. She sighed to herself. Tonight, tonight. She was making her first exception tonight. And only because of Freddie's powers of persuasion.

"We've got to have a splashy opening," he'd argued. "This hotel cost three hundred and fifty mil—a twentieth of our total assets. If we don't start packin' 'em in, we'll be in deep shit. We need publicity, and unless we pull out all the stops . . ."

She had tried to dissuade him.

"You know we're overleveraged, honey," he'd told her gently. "Right now, our worldwide revenues barely cover our debts."

Naturally, he'd refrained from verbalizing the reasons. There'd been no need to. Nor was it Freddie's style to point fingers. There'd been no need to do that, either.

She knew who was to blame.

Me, she thought. *I overrode his objections on this project, just as I turned a deaf ear to his advice against expansion. The decisions were mine to make, and I made them.*

And so . . . she'd gone out on a limb with rapid—*too* rapid, as it turned out—expansion into emerging markets, mainly in Eastern Europe and the former Soviet Union. It had been a costly but, in her view, justified gamble. There was a new world order. Getting a jump on the competition only made sense.

However, she hadn't anticipated the political turmoil that would break out in various hot spots around the world, and that was now jeopardizing the company's financial well-being.

We're overleveraged. . . .

God, but she hated that term! If only she'd heeded Freddie's counsel!

But I didn't, so it's no use crying over spilt milk. What's done is done . . . and cannot be undone.

She was not used to being cornered. It was an entirely new experience, and she didn't like it one damn bit.

Dorothy-Anne's features abruptly tightened. The aquamarine eyes in the smooth unlined face had hardened, were flinty, determined, stubborn with resolve, and distinctly at odds with her innate femininity. Her beauty had been accidental, the result of an exceptional gene pool; her head for business could be traced back to her great-grandmother; but her toughness in the face of adversity came from an inner resource all her own.

She drew a deep breath, her nostrils flaring.

Overleveraged!

A few weeks ago, another hot spot had ignited, this one in Latin America. Freddie had flown down to reconnoiter the situation, and she'd been sick with worry for his safety, the fate of the beautiful beachfront hotel, and the well-being of its staff. The Gulf War was still fresh in her mind—always would be, ever since she'd toured the fire-blackened shell of the once proud Kuwait City Hale, a total write-off, thanks to Mr. Saddam Hussein. But even worse were the people out of work, the em-

ployees who had been slaughtered, the wives of slain breadwinners beseeching her for help.

It was then that she'd established the Hale Foundation, whose aim
was specifically targeted to help the employees and their families in times
of crises.

When Freddie returned from Latin America, they'd sat down and had
their talk. "We're overleveraged, honey."

Overleveraged. It was the first time he'd ever used that word in regard
to Hale Companies.

"All right," she said quietly, raising her head. "So what do you suggest we do?"

"The only things we can do, which is what every major corporation's
doing. Downsizing. Slashing costs. Running a tighter ship. Pruning un-
profitable operations. Laying off several thousand—"

"Layoffs!" She was aghast.

"That's right," he said reasonably. "If we do all those things, there's
no reason why we shouldn't weather this crisis."

"And if we don't take such drastic actions?" she half whispered.

"Then our only alternative is to raise cash through a public stock
offering."

"You must be joking!" She was shocked.

"If only I were."

"Freddie! You know I can never let that happen!" She swept her
hands through the air, as if wiping an invisible window. "This is a *private*
company. It always has been, and always *will* be—at least so long as *I*
have anything to say about it!"

"There's one more thing," he said softly.

More?

She slumped back in her chair and rubbed her forehead wearily with
her thumb and forefinger. "All right. Hit me with it."

He tightened his lips grimly. "On the flight back, I stopped off at the
Eden Isle Resort. Just to see how things were progressing."

She lowered her hand to her lap and looked at him warily. "And?"

He sighed heavily. "It doesn't look good. The project's way behind
schedule. Worse, it's sucking us dry."

She nodded. "We knew from the start it was going to cost big bucks."

"I know that. But we've sustained a lot of heavy losses that insurance
won't cover."

She stared at him. "Freddie? Just what are you trying to say?"

He was silent for a moment. "In my opinion, we should put a mora-
torium on Eden Isle. At least for the time being."

She gasped. "Are you mad? Freddie! We can't stop now! Not after
pouring two hundred and fifty million dollars into it!"

"You're forgetting something," he said tightly. "To finish it, it's going to cost another three quarters of a billion. Minimum."

She looked down at her hands. They were trembling as she clutched them in her lap.

"I can't imagine stopping in midstream," she said quietly. "Besides, Eden Isle's always been your pet project!"

"Tell me about it." He bared his teeth. " 'Freddie's Folly.' That's what it *should* be called!"

"Aren't you being a little harsh on yourself? Or have you forgotten? We're in this *together*."

He laughed bitterly. "Yeah, thanks to *me*! If I hadn't been so hepped up on it—"

"Stop it," she said firmly. "I was just as hepped up on it as you were. As a matter of fact, I still am."

"I say we cut our losses, get out, and write it off."

She raised her chin. "No. I won't give up that easily."

"And what do we use for money, pray tell?"

"Really, Freddie!" She laughed with genuine amusement. "When will you ever learn? I've got more than I know what to do with!"

"No, you don't." He shook his head soberly. "You need it as a cushion. What if some other tragedy pops up, and the company's cash flow's interrupted?" He stared into her eyes. "What then?"

"If you'd rather, we'll borrow what we need. From the bank."

"Are you saying we should borrow *seven hundred and fifty million*?"

She shrugged. "Why not? What other choice do we have?"

He sighed and shrugged. "It's your call."

"And I've called it. Is there anything else?"

"As a matter of fact, yes. But you won't like this, either."

"So? Just spit it out. At least this way we can get it out of the way."

He looked uncomfortable. "It concerns the grand opening of the San Francisco Palace."

"And?"

He drew a deep breath. "Due to the losses we've suffered," he said, tight-lipped, "it's time to start pulling out all the stops."

She frowned. "I'm not sure I quite follow you. Darling, you'll have to be a little more specific."

"Okay." He hesitated. "It would help a lot if you became more visible."

"More visible?" she repeated, the corners of her lips turning down even further. "What the devil's that supposed to mean?"

"Simply that beginning with the grand opening of the San Francisco Palace, it would help enormously if you'd do some publicity. You know . . . put a face to this company? Show its human side?"

Dorothy-Anne stared at him. "Publicity?" Her whisper was raw. "You want *me* to do publicity?"

He nodded.

"I've spent years working to stay out of the public view." Her aquamarine eyes seemed to turn into the color of blue-gray steel. "Now I'm suddenly supposed to throw myself out there?"

"It would help," he said simply. "Yes."

For the first time in her adult life she felt helpless and adrift, as though her destiny had been taken out of her hands and she was being guided by unseen forces. Her voice was a tremolo. "Oh, Christ, Freddie!"

He sighed. "I knew you wouldn't like it," he said gently. "But it's no longer a matter of choice, honey. It's a matter of survival."

So much for my rules of never appearing in public or granting interviews, Dorothy-Anne thought sardonically.

What it boiled down to was throwing open the sluicegates she had so carefully erected . . . and inviting the sharks in to feed.

She sighed to herself. It was either that, going public, or imperiling Great-Granny's legacy and permitting the children's inheritance to shrink.

What would Great-Granny have done? she asked herself, but she already knew the answer to that. *She'd have chosen the lesser of three evils and done whatever it takes. Just as I will.*

She sighed deeply. "All right, Freddie. If I have to dance with the devil," she said with resignation, "so be it."

Now, on the rooftop of the San Francisco Palace, Dorothy-Anne stood resolute as a rock, her eyes searching the foggy skies, her ears straining, in vain, to hear the clamor of a helicopter. The wind tugged at her, kept rearranging the scrims of fog so that they were constantly in motion, the eerie yellow lights in the buildings all around brightening and dulling in undulating waves, like never-ending brownouts and power surges on the set of some cosmic theater.

What's keeping Freddie? The fog? Is it too thick for the helicopter? Is he being driven in from the airport by limousine?

God, but this waiting was unbearable! How she longed for Freddie's comforting embrace and his strength! And never had she needed it more. Plus, there was the surprise she had in store for him.

She couldn't wait to see his expression when she told him: "I'm pregnant, darling. I'm carrying our fourth child."

Oh, she wished he would hurry! Why wasn't he here already? It was getting late. If he didn't arrive soon, she'd have to go downstairs and face the feeding frenzy on her own.

Beside her, one of the large glass doors slid open and floor-length white sheers billowed out into the night like ghosts.

"Girl!" scolded a husky contralto, and Venetia Flood parted the sheers and stepped out onto the terrace. "You're going to catch your death if you don't get back inside!"

Dorothy-Anne smiled at her. "Why do you think I wrapped this around myself?"

"That!" Venetia scoffed, with a despairing shake of her head. "You know what Mark Twain supposedly said, don't you?"

Dorothy-Anne laughed. "Who doesn't? 'The coldest winter I ever spent was summer in San Francisco.'"

"You ask me, he was right," Venetia said. "But not just summer. The same goes for winter, spring, *and* fall. It's this *damp*. The chill penetrates right to your bones."

Venetia Flood was vice president of public relations for Hale Companies. She was black and beautiful—her accent was pure Alabama.

She was six feet tall and had skin the color of pure honey. Slanted feline eyes, brutally slashing cheekbones, and a thick mane of long, combed-out black hair. Plus that proud, regal kind of bearing you only saw in certain Africans or on fashion runways.

Venetia was thirty-eight years old and Dorothy-Anne's best girlfriend and confidante. A former top model, she had quit while she was still ahead, wisely deciding that the business world held a longer future than a glamour industry that worshiped youth.

Now a top executive, Venetia still possessed a passion for clothes—clothes with an attitude, which were the only kind she wore, and the creations of Issey Miyake, her favorite designer, in particular. His oyster silk tunic dress, which she had on this evening, was masterfully cut, architecturally pure, and almost monastic in its deceptive simplicity.

"I suppose I don't need to guess what you're doing out here." Venetia slid Dorothy-Anne an oblique look. "Didn't anyone ever tell you? The watched pot never boils."

"That's easy for you to say." Dorothy-Anne's anxious eyes were still searching the shifting fog.

"Stop worrying," Venetia advised. "Freddie will get here when he gets here. But it's up to me to hustle you downstairs. It's all Derek can do to keep the carnivores at bay."

Derek Fleetwood, chairman of the Hale Hotels, was Hale Companies' number three executive, after Dorothy-Anne and Freddie.

"Not only are the natives becoming restless, but the press is beginning to get verrrrry antsy," Venetia added ominously. "And that makes for verrrrry bad publicity."

"But I can't go down without Freddie!" Dorothy-Anne protested.

"You can, you must, and you will," Venetia said firmly, placing one hand atop each of Dorothy-Anne's shoulders and steering her inside. "With this fog, Lord only knows when he'll arrive."

Venetia slid the door shut, gave a theatrical shudder, relieved Dorothy-Anne of the throw, and tossed it on the nearest chair.

"Now then, let me see how you look."

Venetia gave Dorothy-Anne a swift, professional once-over. Then, red-taloned fingers flying, she pinched a little here and tugged a little there on Dorothy-Anne's black boiled mohair gown with its curved neckline, snug three-quarter sleeves, and pool of excess fabric fanning out on the floor.

Finally she stepped back and eyed her critically some more.

"Wearing your hair that way lends you a kind of early Grace Kelly quality," she said, nodding with approval. "And, I just looooove what this gown does for you. Girl! Didn't I tell you Comme des Garçons is right up your alley?"

"I'm just afraid I'll trip on the hem," Dorothy-Anne fretted. She pinched each side of the skirt, lifted it, and looked down at herself. "Or worse, that someone else might!"

"Bah!" Venetia flapped a jangling, lavishly bangled limp wrist. "Trust me. It looks fabulosa—*especially* the way it spills fluidly out all around you. And, I'm glad you took my advice and wore all black onyx with diamonds." She paused. "Well? Ready to go down and show them what dressed to kill *really* means?"

"But my speech! Freddie was supposed to bring it."

Venetia waved a hand dismissively. "All taken care of. He faxed it to me from Aspen. I put one copy on the lectern downstairs, and an extra copy in your clutch purse. That's just in case. All you have to do when we get downstairs is wait to be introduced and read it." She smiled encouragingly. "That doesn't sound so difficult, now, does it?"

"And the ribbon cutting?"

"Derek will hand you a giant pair of gold-leaf scissors. I know you and Freddie were going to cut the ribbon together, but since he's not here, catch the governor's eye. Ask him to help you do the honors. That'll make page one for sure!"

Dorothy-Anne made a fluttery little gesture. "I . . . I'm not sure I'm ready for all this."

"Sure you are. Now grab that exorbitantly expensive Judith Leiber clutch or else I will—and then you'll never see it again! Oh, before I forget. One last thing."

Venetia grabbed her own purse and pulled out a pair of glasses with thin black frames. She held them out.

Dorothy-Anne frowned at them. "What are those?"

"What are these? You are trying this girl's patience. Yes, indeed. What do you think they look like?"

"Venetia! You know I don't need glasses."

Venetia smiled. "You know that, and I know that, but *they* don't know that." She unfolded the earpieces and popped them expertly on Dorothy-Anne.

Dorothy-Anne looked around and frowned. Held a hand up in front of her face and frowned some more. "They don't do a thing!"

"Oh yes, child, they *do*. They may just be plain clear glass *but . . .*"

Venetia took her by the arms and turned her around to face the full-length mirror.

"See?"

Dorothy-Anne stared at her reflection. Turned her head this way and that. "I . . . I don't believe it!" There was a note of surprise in her voice.

Venetia grinned. "They add just the right touch, don't you think? You don't look a day older or any less beautiful, but they lend you a kind of . . . authority. Give you that serious air. Believe me, the men will respect you more, and the women will feel less threatened. Now, let's go and get this ceremony over with, shall we? You know me. I can't wait to get down and *boogie!*"

3

It was more than a grand opening, it was an event. The towering marble and gilt lobby was all decked out with pinkish white Pristine roses. The flawless blooms were everywhere. Lushly crammed into giant garden urns. Spiraling in thick garlands down the fluted *brèche d'Alep* marble columns. Tucked in clusters among the crystals of the massive four-tier chandeliers. And swagged like huge floral bunting along the walls, around the doorways, up the balustrades of the grand staircase, and along the mezzanine railings.

Every square inch was packed with formally dressed men and women. Nothing like it had ever been seen in San Francisco. It was a hothouse of roses, gowns, and rare jewels.

The staircase had been roped off, and a lectern with a microphone had been set up on the third step from the bottom.

At the foot of the stairs, the Fourth Estate was out in full force—television reporters, video crews, and still photographers. Up in the mezzanine, the print journalists were proceeding to get smashed.

Derek Fleetwood was waiting at the top of the staircase when Dorothy-Anne and Venetia stepped out of the private elevator. If he was surprised by Dorothy-Anne's glasses, he didn't show it. He gestured down at the jammed lobby. "What do you think of the turnout?"

For a moment all Dorothy-Anne could do was stare. Turnout was putting it lightly.

Venetia was right. If we don't have the ribbon cutting soon, they'll be storming the ballroom.

"Shall we?" Derek hooked his arm through hers and together they descended the low broad steps to the lectern. He was six feet tall, had thick black hair graying at the temples, and cobalt blue eyes set in a strong, handsome tanned face.

The hivelike noise of the guests became a slowly diminishing drone; Dorothy-Anne was suddenly aware of faces looking up in expectation, of dark glassy camera lenses aimed and whirring. Her hand tightened on Derek's arm, and she was conscious of moving stiffly.

He glanced sideways at her and smiled. "Relax."

"Believe me," she said out of the side of her mouth, "I'm trying."

"Just remember. They can kill you, but they can't eat you. Right?"

She laughed. He was right. What was the worst that could happen? She looked up at him. "Thank you, Derek."

He smiled. "What for?"

"Helping me get through this without Freddie. Giving me confidence."

"I'm always glad to accommodate a beautiful lady." He let go of her arm. "Wait here until I've introduced you. Okay?"

She nodded.

"You'll be fine," he said. "Trust me."

And with that, he bounded down the last few stairs, where he rested his arms comfortably on the lectern and looked around, as though searching for someone.

He had their full attention now. Everyone had fallen quiet, and the lack of sound was such that the silence seemed somehow more tangible than even the noise had been.

He let the suspense build, then flashed his 250-watt Jumbocharger smile.

"Gee," he said into the microphone, "thanks for the applause. Who'd you expect? Frank Sinatra?"

That earned him laughs, and the ice was broken.

"Seriously now. Ladies and gentlemen, first of all let me thank you on behalf of all of us at Hale Hotels for attending this opening. Unfortunately, the speaker who was supposed to introduce Ms. Dorothy-Anne Hale Cantwell has yet to arrive. Between the snowstorm in the Rockies, and the fog enveloping this city, he's been delayed—or maybe he popped in, took one look around, and decided San Francisco society was just a little *too* formidable!"

There was more appreciative laughter, this time accompanied by scattered applause.

My God! Derek's a natural. He makes it look so easy. He's already got them eating out of his hand!

"... And now, I have the privilege of introducing the person entirely responsible for erecting this beautiful world-class building. Ladies and gentlemen, please help me welcome Ms. Dorothy-Anne Hale Cantwell!"

There was a flurry of applause as he stepped aside and gestured up to Dorothy-Anne.

She took her cue and came slowly down the steps. Only when she stood behind the lectern and looked out at the assembled guests did the applause die down.

Her voice was strong and steady as she gestured around. "What is this? The Rose Bowl parade?"

There was a resounding roar of spontaneous applause, and she smiled until it grew silent.

"Ladies and gentlemen. I'll keep this short and sweet, since if I were in your shoes, I'd wish the speaker would hurry the hell up so I can get down and *party*."

Laughter and more applause greeted her.

"First of all, let me thank each and every one of you for coming and helping make this a memorable evening. As you are probably aware, for years now, hotels in the Far East—forgive me if I don't name the competition—have been crowing about setting the standard by which all other hotels are judged. Well, that made me so mad that I rectified the situation by erecting this, the San Francisco Palace, to show those Far Easterners a thing or two. Especially that *American* hotels—and one in *San Francisco* in particular—*are* and *always will be* NUMBER ONE!"

"Hear, hear!" someone called out.

"Thank you." She smiled in the direction of the voice.

"This sounds like a campaign rally," a journalist shouted. "Does this mean you're running for office?" .

Dorothy-Anne held up both hands, palms facing outward. "Please. I have my hands full putting the American hotel industry back where it belongs—in the leadership position. What you *are* hearing is the shot heard 'round the Pacific!"

Again, she had to wait until the waves of exuberant applause died down.

"So *willkommen, bienvenue,* welcome. Tonight you are the guests of the San Francisco Palace. Please, just remember that drinking and driving don't mix. There's a suite upstairs reserved for *every* one of you. Just show your invitation to the concierge and you'll be given a key card to spend the night as my guest. Room service is included. As for entertainment, there's formal dancing in the ballroom for the conservative. For the young—and that goes for the young at heart, too—rock bands will be performing in the basement level Cave Club. And nostalgia buffs can twist the night away to live nineteen fifties rock and roll in the Cadillac Bar. You'll find buffet tables everywhere. So please. Eat, drink, be merry, and enjoy yourselves. Thank you, ladies and gentlemen."

Derek had come up beside her holding a huge pair of gold-leaf shears.

Dorothy-Anne leaned into the microphone once more. "Now then, if Governor Randle would please be so kind as to help me cut the ribbon . . ."

The governor was happy for the photo opportunity. He was a large, heavy man, beefy rather than fat, with a shock of white hair and a ruddy complexion.

In short order, the doors to the Regency-style ballroom were thrown open. It wasn't until then that Dorothy-Anne realized she hadn't bothered to consult the prepared speech. She'd ignored it altogether, and had ad-libbed her own.

Good golly, Miss Molly. Will wonders never cease?

The governor led her into the ballroom, and a swarm of couples followed them inside, lining the peacock blue and gilt–boiseried walls, careful to leave the dance floor empty. On the dais, one of Peter Duchin's society orchestras launched into "Sentimental Journey."

"I don't know how to thank you, Governor Randle," Dorothy-Anne told him softly.

"Oh, I can think of a way." He smiled.

Her eyes sparkled mischievously. "You mean . . . through a campaign contribution?"

He laughed heartily—the deep kind of belly laugh that comes from way down inside. "Actually, I was thinking about something a little less costly," he said.

"And what might that be?"

"Giving me the first dance."

She smiled brilliantly. "It'll be my pleasure."

He was still chuckling as he led her out onto the dance floor—shaking his head, murmuring, "Campaign contribution!" to himself, and chuckling.

Then, while the cameras whirred, he took her in his arms and they moved, smoothly as well-oiled machines, in time to the music. Gradually, the dance floor around them began to fill, until it became a sea awash with glamorous couples floating beneath the crystal chandeliers.

She had to hand it to him. Big man or no, he was light as air on his feet. Obviously he'd gotten plenty of practice during a lifetime of fundraisers.

The song ended and they stopped dancing. A man's voice came from behind them. "Well, Governor? Are you going to share the wealth, or are you going to be selfish and keep this beautiful young lady all to yourself?"

They turned and Dorothy-Anne found herself face-to-face with the most extraordinarily handsome man. He had charm, sex appeal, and charisma—plus the kind of self-assurance that came from the world being your oyster.

Everything about him was California-perfect. His height—six foot two. His physique—the spare fitness that is the sign of the true athlete. His screen-star good looks—the hungry youthful face with its lapis blue eyes, sun-bleached hair, strong jaw, and terrific teeth.

Hunt Winslow had it all. In spades.

The governor sighed. "Winslow," he growled, "don't you have any respect for your elders? You made it clear you want my job. Now you want my dance partner, too."

Dorothy-Anne and the man exchanged smiles.

"Well, far be it from me to be ungracious. Ms. Cantwell, may I present my political rival and bête noir, Mr. Huntington Netherland Winslow the Third."

Dorothy-Anne held out her hand, and Winslow took it.

"Hunt," he said, flashing a blinding smile. "I go by plain old Hunt."

"Plain, my foot!" harrumphed Governor Randle. "Careful about Hunt here, Ms. Cantwell. He's our ladykiller-about-state."

Dorothy-Anne laughed. "You don't have to worry about me, Governor. I'm a happily married woman."

"Glad to hear it. Which reminds me. I'd better be getting back to the lady I came with." He made a courtly bow. "Ms. Cantwell, it was a pleasure."

"The pleasure was all mine," she said.

Dorothy-Anne watched the governor leave. Then she turned to Hunt. "Well? Are you really the ladykiller he claims?"

He laughed. "You mustn't believe everything you hear, Ms. Cantwell."

"My friends call me Dorothy-Anne."

"Then I'd be delighted to join their ranks, Dorothy-Anne."

"Are you his rival?" she asked.

"You mean, Old 'Randy Randle's'?"

"Is *that* what they call him? Really?"

Before he could reply, the orchestra began to play "I Left My Heart in San Francisco."

"Shall we dance?" he said, putting his arm around her, and she could feel an involuntary ripple go through her, could sense the strength that lay hidden beneath his clothes.

The governor was right. Hunt's a dangerous man. Too sexy for his own good . . . or mine.

"So will you?" he asked as they danced cheek to cheek.

She looked up at him. "Will I what, Mr. Winslow?" she said softly.

"Hunt," he corrected her.

She smiled. "Hunt, then."

"Leave your heart in this city?"

She laughed. "Oh, a tiny bit of it, I'm sure. It seems to me I leave little bits and pieces of it everywhere I open a hotel."

"Sort of like Hansel and Gretel scattering crumbs?"

She laughed and they danced smoothly on. When the music stopped, they drew apart and clapped politely. Dorothy-Anne caught Venetia signaling her and motioned her over.

"Venetia, this is Huntington Winslow III. Hunt, this is Venetia Flood, my publicist."

Venetia shook hands with him. "Senator," she said softly.

"Senator!" Dorothy-Anne stared at him. "You didn't tell me *that.*"

"State senator," he said, giving a dismissive shrug. "Can I get you ladies a drink?"

"That would be lovely," Dorothy-Anne said, and she and Venetia moved to the edge of the dance floor. "Any word from Freddie?" she asked anxiously.

Venetia shook her head. "Not yet."

"Damn."

"Derek's calling the airports. He's left instructions all over the place that you're to be notified the instant Freddie touches base."

"I just hope he's all right," Dorothy-Anne fretted.

"Of course he is. *And,* if he knows what's good for him, he'd better hurry—because here comes your ravishing young senator."

"Venetia!" Dorothy-Anne protested. "He's not mine!"

"Girl? You sure about that?"

"Of course I am," Dorothy-Anne whispered. "Now off with you!"

"*Ciao,*" Venetia sang. "Just remember"—she held out a limp hand and waggled her fingers, multiple gold rings flashing—"he's wearing a wedding band!" she stage-whispered. "I checked."

And off she sailed in a swirl of Issey Miyake, smiling and plucking a glass of champagne out of Hunt's hand without even slowing.

The party was in full swing. Drinks and champagne had loosened tongues and inhibitions. The noise level had risen markedly, and the sumptuous spreads on the buffet tables were being ravaged.

Waiters stood behind the guests, helping to serve beluga caviar, gravlax, truffled pâté in port aspic, and smoked trout salad. The toqued chefs were busy carving paper-thin slices from racks of lamb, baked hams, turkeys, and smoked salmon. Busboys were constantly replenishing the chafing dishes with escargot stew, grilled duck livers, and beef bourgignon.

The seats in the lobby were occupied by guests eating from their laps when Venetia saw Dorothy-Anne coming up the spiral stairs from the Cave Club. Venetia caught her eye, then nodded toward one of the thick marble columns.

Dorothy-Anne followed her gaze.

A woman was slumped against the marble, highball glass in hand.

She should have been beautiful. She was high-fashion thin and groomed to the nines. With just the right amount of makeup, subdued and expertly applied. Very tasteful. Her hair was straight and dark and shoulder-length, and she had a fortune on her back: a full-skirted Oscar de la Renta ballgown of sapphire blue silk taffeta, which matched the real sapphires at her neck, wrists, and ears. But for all her efforts, nothing could hide the dissipation of a hard boozer.

Dorothy-Anne looked back at Venetia, nodded that she would take care of it, and approached the woman. "Hello," she greeted in a friendly voice. "I don't believe we've met."

The woman's face came up slowly. She peered suspiciously at Dorothy-Anne through glassy, startlingly sapphire eyes. "Wha' *you* want?" came the loud, slurred reply.

Uh-oh. Should have left well enough alone.

"Can I get you anything?"

"Why'd you wanna do that?" The woman lifted her glass to her lips, but it was empty. She held it up in front of her eyes. "Shit," she mumbled. "Need 'nother one." Her look turned sly. "Why'nt you get it for me?"

"Perhaps you'd like something to eat?" Dorothy-Anne suggested tactfully.

"Fuck eatin'!" the woman snarled insolently. Her eyes were suddenly wild, and her lips sneered ferociously, like a rabid dog's. "What I need's 'nother vodka!" She started to walk away, swaying slightly and moving with the careful, exaggerated steps of a drunk. Before she'd gone two steps, she stumbled.

"Whoa, there." Dorothy-Anne held out a hand to steady her.

The woman recovered her balance and shook Dorothy-Anne's hand off. "Don' wan' your help!" she shouted belligerently, causing heads to turn and conversations in the vicinity to halt in midsentence. "Don' need it. 'Specially not from some bitch tryin' to steal my husban'!"

More than a little shaken, Dorothy-Anne stood there, staring after her with revulsion as she weaved off in the direction of the nearest bar.

"I'm awfully sorry," a familiar voice said from beside her.

She turned to him. It was Hunt Winslow, and his face was wearing a fixed expression that was a peculiar mixture of weariness and embarrassment.

Dorothy-Anne laughed. "You don't have to be sorry," she said with genuine amusement. "Really, Hunt. You're not responsible for your entire constituency, you know."

His lips tightened. "Oh, but I am," he said quietly. There was a catch in his voice. "At least for that particular constituent. That's my wife. Gloria."

Dorothy-Anne stared at him. "Oh, God, Hunt. I didn't know. Otherwise I'd never have put my foot in my—"

"How were you to know? You're new here." He smiled sadly. "Not that it's any secret in this town. 'Poor Gloria.' " His voice was soft, and a pained look came into his eyes. "That's how everyone refers to her: 'Poor Gloria.' It wouldn't surprise me if they started calling me 'Poor Hunt'—or worse yet, 'Poor long-suffering Hunt'!—behind my back!"

Dorothy-Anne was surprised by his attitude of patience, considering the situation. She wished she knew how to respond. *What can one say in these circumstances?* She really had no clue.

He shook his head wearily. "Well, I'd better go and exercise damage control," he said, giving a little smile. "Have to baby-sit. Perhaps we can talk later?"

"Yes, perhaps," Dorothy-Anne said. Her heart went out to him as she watched him follow his wife. She couldn't begin to imagine the hell he was going through.

Venetia came up to her. "Sugar?" she said solemnly. "Can we go somewhere quiet and talk?"

Dorothy-Anne stared at her. She had a terrible premonition of what was coming. "Freddie!" she gasped, the color draining from her face. She felt suddenly dizzy and she clutched Venetia's arm with a fierce, clawlike grip. "Something's happened to him!"

"Why don't we use one of the offices?" Venetia suggested compassionately.

"No." Dorothy-Anne shook her head. "Tell me *now*!"

Venetia took a deep breath. She wished there was some gentler way to break the news. She said, "It is about Freddie."

Dorothy-Anne's pupils dilated wildly. "There's been an accident. Is he—?"

"We don't know, sugar."

"But . . ." Dorothy-Anne let go of her and stood there, frozen, her hand scrabbling at her breast like a pet crab. "What happened?" she whispered.

"No one's sure. His plane disappeared off the radar screens."

Dorothy-Anne shut her eyes, and she could feel herself spinning down, down, down into the bottomless whirlpool of despair. She tried to breathe, but steel bands seemed to encircle her chest. After a moment she opened her eyes.

"They lost radio contact," Venetia said.

"Where did it happen?"

"Somewhere over the Rockies."

"But they're not sure the plane"—Dorothy-Anne couldn't verbalize the word *crashed*—"went down?"

"No, they're not. But every indica—"

"Search parties. They've sent them out already?"

Venetia held her by both arms. "They can't, sugar. Not until day-break. And even then . . ." Her voice trailed off and she sighed. "A two-day blizzard's just begun," she explained. "It'll be impossible to mount a search until the snow stops. I'm so sorry, sugar."

Dorothy-Anne suddenly smiled, and her eyes shone with unnatural brightness. "Don't worry so much, Venetia. Let's go have something to eat. Freddie's fine. He's just delayed, that's all. Perhaps you could use a drink? A shot of brandy, maybe?"

"Sugar . . ."

"That's right. I forgot. You don't drink alcohol. How thoughtless of me."

Venetia stared at her, thinking, *Oh, God. She's in shock. I'd better go get help.* She looked around in desperation. *Where's Derek when I need him?*

Then Dorothy-Anne's eyelids fluttered and her body went limp. Venetia caught her just as she fainted.

Dorothy-Anne came to in the penthouse suite. She was lying under the covers, and Venetia was sitting on the edge of the bed, holding her hand. *That's funny,* she thought. *I don't remember getting undressed.*

"How did I get up here?" she asked in a strained whisper.

"We carried you into the elevator. You'd passed out."

Dorothy-Anne frowned, and then it all came rushing back to her. Freddie. *His plane disappeared off the radar screens.*

She stared at Venetia's concerned face. "He's only missing!" she said vehemently. "Freddie's only missing."

Venetia tried to smile. "I know that, sugar," she soothed, wiping a cool washrag across Dorothy-Anne's forehead. "I know that." Venetia turned and nodded to the man standing at the foot of the bed, who drew closer.

Dorothy-Anne frowned up at him. *I've never seen him before.*

"Who's . . . he?"

"That's Dr. Nouri. He's our house doctor and he's going to give you a sedative. You need to conserve your strength and try to sleep."

Dorothy-Anne turned her head away. *I'm not the one who needs a doctor,* she thought bleakly, visualizing Freddie's battered, broken body lying in some ravine in the blizzard.

She barely felt the prick of the hypodermic needle puncturing her arm. She turned to Venetia. "The party—"

"Shhhhh," Venetia lulled softly, dabbing the washrag on Dorothy-Anne's face. "Everything's fine. Derek's downstairs filling in for you."

"I've ruined the grand opening."

"Girl! Will you *stop?*"

Dorothy-Anne could feel the sedative beginning to work. Her eyelids suddenly felt like lead weights, and it was all she could do to hold them open.

"The children," she mumbled sleepily, slurring her words. "Have to call Nanny Florrie . . . mustn't learn about this from TV . . . or the papers . . ."

"I'll take care of it."

Reality was slipping away. "Have to tell them . . . come out here . . . first flight . . ."

"Consider it done," Venetia said, but it didn't register. The voice was muffled and seemed to be coming from underwater, and the lead weights were pressing Dorothy-Anne's eyelids shut.

And as the sedative brought sleep, sleep brought her Freddie.

Maybe it was a memory. Or just a dream. She had no idea. But they were writhing and bopping alone to a distant and steady rhythm, and then, as is the way of dreams, they were suddenly in the midst of a jam-packed dance floor, and the nonstop music blasted a torturous, mind-numbing beat.

It was so densely packed the crowd seemed to hold them up. Overhead, a mirrored ball spun slowly, sending reflections floating all around, then colored gels blinked, and blinding strobe lights freeze-framed everyone like a stop-motion camera.

It was a serious dance club, and she recognized the music as late seventies, early eighties. The DJ had his finger on the pulse of the crowd, and one catchy disco tune thundered seamlessly into the next.

Everyone was lost to the beat, waving raised arms like orgiastic worshipers. The heat and sweat mingled with the overpowering stench of amyl nitrate and ethyl chloride, and from time to time she caught fleeting glimpses of a slender, bare-chested young man in a world all his own, dancing an enchanted solo with two giant Japanese paper fans.

Dreams can blend the most fantastic sublimities with the oddest touches of the mundane. As she danced, Dorothy-Anne realized she was wearing the same prim navy business suit, white silk blouse, and lightweight wool coat she'd worn when she and Freddie had first met, on the windswept roof atop a construction site in Chicago. And he, absurdly, had on the same soiled T-shirt and 501s, which showed off his thick arms and tapered waist to perfection.

Hardly club attire.

No matter.

The tempo sped up and the dancers all around pushed and pressed closer, squeezing them against each other. Freddie grinned at her, the laugh lines around his eyes crinkling, and he was mouthing something, but the din swallowed his words and made it impossible to hear.

On they danced, and she could feel the growing erection in his jeans with each thrust of his pelvis. At first she glanced around in embarrassment, but everyone was too involved in their own business to notice.

And so the eroticism of their moves increased. No longer was this a mere dance. This was sexuality incarnate. Their every motion suggested a carnal act, a frenzied, pornographic rite played out as choreography.

She could feel the wetness flooding into her loins. They were all but making it right there, in the middle of the dance floor.

Suddenly no one else seemed to exist. It was as if they were alone, and the others were indifferent witnesses.

He pulled her close and held her there. Took her hand and guided it down to his groin.

They continued their sexually charged dance even as she felt his rocklike shaft with her fingers. Her mouth was suddenly dry, and she could barely breathe.

"Take it out!" he mouthed, and although his words were lost in the concussive bass beat, she could read his lips.

She stared at him, her eyes wide, and glanced around in protest.

He shook his head. "Forget them!" he mouthed fiercely. "They won't notice!"

For a moment she hesitated; then her fingers undid the metal buttons and she slipped her hand inside his fly.

He was hot and ready, as evidenced by the thick length of his beautifully hard penis. She grasped it by the base and struggled to free it from its snug denim prison.

It sprang out, into her hand.

And again this dream dance did the impossible, for suddenly her skirt and slip were no longer a hindrance, and his phallus leaped at her like a striking snake. She gave a startled cry as as he entered and impaled her.

At first she felt paralyzed, numbed. And then her insides blazed like a furnace.

Now their dance turned truly frenetic. She was lost in abandon, a heathen worshiping Priapus, connected to him by his mighty thrusting phallus.

Never before had she experienced a consummation such as this. It was dizzying. It was bliss—at once exhilarating and agonizing, and her sexual hunger knew no bounds. No longer was she aware of the music, only of the rhythm of their bodies moving in perfect syncopation.

When it came, the first orgasm sent her reeling into the outer limits. Somehow she jackknifed her legs around his waist; clung to him for dear life as she arched herself backward until her hair brushed the floor, their writhing pelvises joined as one.

The force of his driving thrusts quickened and jolted and sent tremors throughout her body. She shut her eyes and cried out at each powerful impact. Already she could feel another tidal wave cresting toward her, swallowing her completely, and she thought she must surely die.

Life, death, eternity! In the throes of passion, the wonders and secrets of the universe were revealed in all their splendor. The answers were right there, in the seeds of life he would sow inside her!

This, she thought rapturously, this glorious timeless act could go on forever, without end.

Please God, she prayed. *Don't ever let him stop.*

But before the bellow could rise from Freddie's throat, he withdrew his phallus, gently but firmly unclamped her legs from around him, lifted her up, and set her carefully on her feet.

She stared up at him with a mixture of hurt and confusion. She couldn't understand it. Why would he want to stop? And why so *soon*?

"I have to go now," he mouthed, gently pushing her away.

She was stunned. She couldn't believe it. They'd barely begun!

"Don't go," she begged. Now that he was no longer inside her, a terrible, lacerating pain tore through her groin. "Please, Freddie. Stay with me!"

"I can't." He was steadily receding backward, gliding into the crowd as though pulled by a force beyond his control.

She stretched out both arms beseechingly. "Freddie!" she cried desperately. "Don't leave me!"

As if in slow motion, he smiled, placed a hand to his lips, and threw her a kiss. Then the fan dancer, hitherto unnoticed, rose fluidly up directly in front of her. His face was a hideous Kabuki mask, and the colorful, mesmeric fans he wielded wove hypnotically, hiding Freddie from sight. When they parted again, she could see that Freddie was much farther away.

Back and forth those fans waved, embroidering the air with kaleidoscopes of color and pattern.

They parted once more.

Freddie was gone.

"Freddie!" she screamed. "Freddie! *Freddie!*"

She felt someone shaking her, and a voice reached deep down through thick, cottonlike layers of sleep: "Wake up. Come on, sugar. You're having a bad dream."

"*Freddie!*" Dorothy-Anne sat bolt upright in bed. Her heart was pounding and she could feel the blood racing madly through her veins. She glanced around wildly. "Where'd he go? He was *here*!"

"It's all right," Venetia said softly from the chair she'd pulled up to the bed, where she'd spent the night, her Issey Miyake none the worse for having slept in it. "It was only a dream."

Dorothy-Anne shook her head as if to clear it. "But . . . it seemed so *real*."

Venetia laughed. "It must have, from the way you were thrashing around. Girl! This is the first I ever heard of a woman having a wet dream!"

Dorothy-Anne frowned at her. "What . . . do you mean?"

"The way you were tossing, it looked as if you were having sex. Oh, for God's sake. Will you stop looking so embarrassed? It's the sedative. Dr. Nouri warned me to expect strange behavior."

Suddenly an agonizing pain ripped through Dorothy-Anne's abdomen. Her face twisted in anguish. "Oh, God!" she gasped.

"Sugar?" Venetia was suddenly alarmed. "What's wrong?"

"I . . . I don't . . ."

Dorothy-Anne's abdomen convulsed again, and she clasped her arms around herself, biting down hard on a scream.

Swiftly Venetia jumped up and pulled back the covers. She lifted Dorothy-Anne's nightgown.

One look was enough.

Dorothy-Anne was bleeding badly.

Venetia snatched up the bedside telephone and punched Dr. Nouri's home number, which he'd scribbled on his business card. Then she paced impatiently as far as the cord would permit as it rang at the other end.

Come on, she willed. *Answer it, somebody . . .*

It was picked up on the sixth ring. " 'Lo?" a voice mumbled sleepily.

"Dr. Nouri? Venetia Flood here." She glanced at Dorothy-Anne, then turned away and cupped her hand around the receiver. "You'd better get over here on the double. I think Ms. Cantwell is having a miscarriage."

Venetia stalked the waiting room like a tigress. She hated hospitals, even spacious modern ones like California Pacific Medical Center. By the time the surgeon came out she'd made dozens of calls on her cellular phone—all to no avail.

Still no word about Freddie.

And now this.

Dr. Chalfin, the surgeon, hadn't changed from his OR greens, and she pounced on him before he was all the way through the swinging doors. "How is she, Doctor?"

"She's in post-op recovery. You can relax now. She'll be all right."

"Thank God." Venetia let out a dizzying breath of relief. "That's the first good news I've had in forever. Any problems?"

"Some." He seemed to hesitate. "How close are you to her?"

She looked at him directly. "Very. We're like sisters. Why?"

"Because I'd like somebody to be there when I tell her."

Venetia's voice was hushed. "What? That she lost the baby?"

"That, too." He nodded. "But mainly that we've had to perform an emergency hysterectomy. That's what took us so long."

Venetia stared at him in shock. "Oh, Jesus."

Shakily she lowered herself into one of the molded orange plastic chairs. She'd guessed about the miscarriage—but a hysterectomy? That came from way out in left field.

"Hasn't she been through enough?" she said quietly.

The doctor did not speak.

"First, her husband's plane is missing; presumably it went down in the Rockies. Then the miscarriage. And now *this*! How much more can she take?"

His voice was soft. "If it's any consolation, it could have been a lot worse."

She looked up at him sharply. "What do you mean?"

"We found an ovarian mass, which we removed at once."

Venetia frowned. "I don't understand." She looked confused. "An ovarian mass?"

"We're talking cancer," the doctor explained. "Ovarian cancer."

Venetia was shaken. *Ovarian cancer!* For a moment she just sat there, dumbfounded.

"The good news," he said, "is that we got it all. Of course, she'll have to get regular checkups. But all in all, I'd say she's one lucky lady. If we hadn't discovered it now . . ." He shrugged, adding softly: "Who knows what might have happened?"

Venetia was filled with dread. "And the . . . hysterectomy?" she asked haltingly. "How radical was it?"

"In medical terminology, what we performed was an abdominal hysterectomy with bilateral salgimpingo oopherectomy."

"I'm afraid you've lost me, doctor. In simple English, *please*."

"Yes. Of course. I'm sorry. In layman's terms, we had to remove the entire uterus, both ovaries, and both tubes."

Venetia momentarily shut her eyes. "In other words . . ." She could not voice it.

"She can never have another baby," he finished for her.

Oh, Christ! Venetia sighed deeply and rubbed her face with both hands. She could not begin to imagine how Dorothy-Anne was going to take this. *She wanted the baby so badly. Now she can never have another. . . .*

"I'd appreciate your not mentioning anything to her just yet," the surgeon was saying. "As I said, I want you to be there to give her moral support, but it's important that I'm the one who breaks the news. That way I can clear up any misunderstandings and misconceptions she might have."

Venetia nodded. "When will you tell her?"

"As soon as she's strong enough. Tomorrow afternoon . . . perhaps the day after." He paused. "I'm awfully sorry about this."

"So am I." Venetia sighed. Her hands fluttered helplessly in her lap, like a trapped bird with a broken wing. "When can I see her?"

"As soon as they move her from recovery down to her room. It shouldn't be more than a few hours." He flagged down an approaching nurse. "In what room are they putting Ms. Cantwell?"

"I'll go check right now, Doctor," the nurse said.

Venetia got up and grabbed her bag. She shook the surgeon's hand. "Thank you, Doctor," she said warmly. "I appreciate everything you're doing."

"Just don't tire her out," he warned. "She needs her rest."

"Don't worry," Venetia assured him. "I'll make sure she gets it." And she hurried off, catching up with the nurse in a few gazelle-like strides.

The room turned out to be small but private, and it had a wall-mounted television and a tiny adjoining bathroom with a shower stall. The curtains were drawn across the large picture window, and Venetia twitched them aside.

All she could see was her own reflection in the sheet of glass.

As far as hospitals went, she knew it wasn't bad. Not bad at all.

Her investigation over, she settled down in the visitor's chair and promptly fell asleep.

She snapped awake when they wheeled Dorothy-Anne in, and she quickly got up, moved the chair into the corner, and stood back out of the way. Two orderlies transferred Dorothy-Anne so gently from the gurney into the bed that she slept right through it. An efficient nurse bustled about, checking the IVs and hooking up various monitors.

When the orderlies had gone, Venetia approached the bedside and stood there, looking down. Dorothy-Anne seemed to be sleeping. Her wheat-gold hair fanned out across the white pillow, and she looked small and fragile and pale. Almost childlike in her helplessness.

Suddenly her eyes blinked open. They were unfocused and frightened, the aquamarine emphasizing her pallor. Slowly she turned her head on the pillow. Her hand crept toward Venetia. "Worst dream," she slurred hoarsely.

"Hi, sugar," Venetia whispered. She took Dorothy-Anne's hand and held it. It felt hot and clammy and frail. "How do you feel?"

Dorothy-Anne stared at her. "I dreamed Freddie came and took my baby away! He said I'd never see either of them ever again!"

"Shhhhh," Venetia soothed. "It was only a bad dream."

"A bad dream," Dorothy-Anne repeated slowly. "Only a bad dream?"

"That's right, sugar. That's all it was."

Dorothy-Anne's eyes began to close. "Only a bad dream," she murmured, and as she went back to sleep, she found herself drifting back through the years, to another time, another place, and the extraordinary woman to whom she owed everything. . . .

5

Dorothy-Anne's great-grandmother entered the world with all strikes against her.

She was a woman.

She was born poor.

She was orphaned at age six.

And she grew up in the harsh, opportunity-less climes of southwestern Texas.

But she dared to dream.

And from a single rooming house and the crucible of the Great Depression, she forged an empire.

She was Elizabeth-Anne Hale, and everything about her was bigger than life.

Her empire, which spanned six continents. Her self-made fortune, which made her the richest woman in the world. And her power, which was incalculable. Add a dollop of longevity, a New York *Social Register* husband, and four children, and you had yourself a dynasty. With a clean slate, a foot in society, and the world as her chess set. Plus that seemingly effortless, magical knack for multiplying her fortune. By the time her great-granddaughter was born, Elizabeth-Anne was absolute ruler of an empire richer than many countries. Her power was legendary, and her name synonymous with luxury. She rubbed shoulders with presidents, prime ministers, dictators, movie stars, artists, ballet dancers, and royalty. Such was her influence that bankers, politicians, ambassadors, and high-ranking members of the clergy regularly curried her favors.

She lived like a queen. Her New York penthouse and various far-flung houses were filled with museum-quality furnishings and she had one of the finest art collections in existence.

Elizabeth-Anne was not beautiful, but she was a handsome woman, with a regal bearing and strong features. She had a thin, straight nose, direct aquamarine eyes, and striking wheat-gold hair. There was about her an air of no-nonsense efficiency, and yet she was decidedly feminine. People who met her for the first time were enchanted by her genteel manner, warmth, and lack of airs, and it was said she could charm the rattlers off a snake.

She was also a formidable enemy. Those who crossed her soon discovered they were dealing with a shark, and in the treacherous shoals of business, she proved the female of the species to be deadlier than the male.

As she told one reporter: "I'm a woman in a man's world. To become successful, I've had to trade in my white gloves for boxing mitts. To stay successful, I don't dare take them off."

But success carried a price of its own. For all the glamorous trappings—the private planes, couture wardrobes, fine jewels, and friends in high places—Elizabeth-Anne had suffered more than her share of tragedies.

There were so many:

Her first husband, the father of her children, wrongly convicted of murder and hanged . . .

The deaths of three of her four children . . .

The loss of her second husband . . .

The granddaughter who disappeared into the chaos of World War II, and who, as fate would have it, resurfaced years later—married to none other than Elizabeth-Anne's own grandson, Henry. That husband and wife were too closely related was a fact known only to Elizabeth-Anne. Unwilling to spoil the couple's happiness, she had kept her silence, and taken her secret to the grave.

And finally, there was the tragedy of Dorothy-Anne's birth. When her mother died in the delivery room, Henry—grieving, heartbroken, unforgiving Henry—unjustly blamed his daughter for his wife's death.

"To see the baby, just tap on the nursery window," the doctor told him and Elizabeth-Anne. "A nurse will show you the child. It's a beautiful baby girl."

Elizabeth-Anne immediately started down the hall. Then, realizing that Henry wasn't beside her, she turned around. "Henry!" she called impatiently.

"Go ahead," he said grimly. "I want nothing to do with that kid."

His words went through Elizabeth-Anne's heart like a dagger. She couldn't believe his reaction. This wasn't the way it was supposed to go. Daddies and their little girls were supposed to be special.

The doctor couldn't help overhearing the exchange. "Don't worry," he told Elizabeth-Anne gently. "He's grief-stricken. You wait and see. He'll come around in no time."

Several days later, after the graveside service, Elizabeth-Anne took her grandson aside. She said, "Henry, it's time you fetched your daughter from the hospital."

He stared at her. "I don't have a daughter!" he snapped, and then stalked off to drown his sorrows in booze.

Elizabeth-Anne attributed his outburst to the shock of burying his wife. *It won't be long before he gets over it,* she thought.

In the meantime, she had Max, her chauffeur, drive her to the hospital, where she collected the infant herself. After holding Dorothy-Anne and marveling at her exquisite features, flawless pink skin, golden hair, and aquamarine eyes, she declared her a true Hale and took her up to Henry's magnificent estate in Tarrytown, New York, with its forty-room colonial mansion set amid fifty acres of manicured grounds. There she turned Dorothy-Anne over to the British nanny she'd personally selected and hired. "Now take good care of her," she cautioned.

Nanny, whose body in profile looked remarkably like a map of Africa, cradled the baby in her arms and smiled. "Don't you worry, madam. I'm not going to let this wee lass out of my sight."

A few days later, Elizabeth-Anne once again had Max drive her up to Tarrytown. She had timed her visit to coincide with a business trip of Henry's.

After pushing the perambulator around the vast parkland, she and Nanny had tea on the terrace overlooking the Hudson. "You're doing a fine job," she assured Nanny.

"Thank you, madam, but it's easy with such a lovely child. She's like a fairy creature, isn't she?"

"Yes, she is," Elizabeth-Anne agreed. She set down her cup and held Nanny's gaze. "I believe I made it clear from the beginning who's paying your salary?"

"Oh, yes, madam. That you did."

"And do you also remember what we agreed upon when I hired you?"

Nanny glanced around to make sure there were no servants within earshot. "Yes, madam. That I was to keep nothing from you as far as the little one's concerned."

"That's right." Elizabeth-Anne folded her hands in her lap. "Then perhaps you can tell me how her father is treating her?"

Nanny hesitated, and when she spoke, she chose her words carefully. "Well . . . he's not *mis*treating her, if that's what you're wondering."

"Oh?" Elizabeth-Anne arched her eyebrows. "Then what is he doing?"

Nanny sighed. "That's just it, madam. Nothing! He hasn't come to the nursery once to see the poor thing. Not a once! It's as if he's decided she doesn't exist."

Elizabeth-Anne nodded. She had been afraid of that.

"Also . . ."

"Yes, Nanny?"

"He gave me specific orders to keep her out of his sight."

Her grandson's cruelty made Elizabeth-Anne want to weep. However, she wasn't one to show emotions in front of the help. Thanking Nanny for being so forthcoming, she smoothly changed the subject, pointing out the vivid scarlet plumage of a cardinal as it alighted on the branch of a nearby tree.

But she was deeply disturbed by Henry's blaming Dorothy-Anne for his wife's death.

It's just a passing phase, she told herself on the ride home. *Henry's still in mourning. He'll snap out of it. He has to. For Christ's sake, he's Dorothy-Anne's father!*

During the next five years, Dorothy-Anne did not want for anything. She was the princess—the heiress to the Hale empire—and she grew up with every conceivable luxury. Elizabeth-Anne dropped by regularly, and from the beginning, a special bond developed between them. Dorothy-Anne couldn't wait for her great-grandmother's visits, and she charmed everyone with that way she had of pronouncing Great-Granny—"Gweat-Gwanny."

And then there were the servants. From Cook and the maids down to the gardeners and the chauffeur, she had them all enchanted. They vied for her attention and spoiled her shamelessly, but the one person's love she sought so desperately—her father's—continued to elude her.

Henry was a stranger, a mysterious presence who lived under the same roof, but whose path rarely crossed hers. The few times it did, he rebuffed her coldly, ordering a servant to whisk her out of his sight.

Thus, as far as her father was concerned, the rule that children were neither to be seen nor heard was drummed into her; understandably, this only strengthened the bond between her and "Gweat-Gwanny."

Then came Dorothy-Anne's fifth birthday. It was a cats-and-dogs kind of day, with thunderstorms raging as she and Nanny climbed into the long black limousine for the drive downriver to Manhattan, that magical wonderland that looked like a massive storybook castle with its thousands of towers.

Dorothy-Anne thought it the most exciting place she had ever seen.

At Park Avenue and Fifty-first Street, they got out of the car, went into one of the brightly lit towers, and took the elevator up, up, to her great-grandmother's office high in the clouds.

But what should have been a celebration turned into a tragedy.

Elizabeth-Anne, realizing that Henry's rejection of Dorothy-Anne could not go on indefinitely, had taken matters into her own hands. On the agenda was lunch, although Henry was under the mistaken impression that it was a business lunch, not a birthday celebration at Serendipity for his daughter. He only discovered that when Elizabeth-Anne summoned him to her office.

Before Henry could get started, Elizabeth-Anne asked Dorothy-Anne and Nanny to wait outside her office. Not that it did much good: they could hear the shouting match clearly, even through the closed doors.

Henry finally stomped off—and Elizabeth-Anne suffered a massive stroke. She lay in a coma for four months and three days. When she came out of it, she was paralyzed from the waist down, condemned to spend the remainder of her life in a wheelchair.

A lesser woman might have modified her activities, but Elizabeth-Anne was not your ordinary woman. She refused to let her paralysis put a dent in her life. Her first order of business was to recuperate, which she did with a therapist, two nurses, and Dorothy-Anne—in Europe.

And it was there, in the mimosa, jasmine, and oleander-scented hills of Provence, that the idea of starting yet another chain of hotels—converting country villas, French castles, and Tuscan farmhouses into ultraluxurious, intimate lodgings called Les Petits Palais—was born.

For Dorothy-Anne, it was the lesson of a lifetime. Great-Granny was unsinkable, unstoppable, and undefeatable: the perfect role model for a wounded spirit.

Likewise, in Dorothy-Anne, the old lady relived her own youth, rediscovering the long-vanished innocence and sense of wonder she'd thought forever lost; the excitement of seeing things with a fresh eye, as if noticing them for the very first time, be it a particularly splendid sunset, the scent of wild herbs, the beauty of a valiant flower growing from between the cracks of a cobble-paved courtyard.

It was truly a magical time. The love they shared worked wonders, healed the scarred spirit, and forged an already strong relationship into unbreakable links.

For Dorothy-Anne, it was as if she'd died and gone to heaven. This, being showered with abundant daily doses of love such as she had never before known, made every waking hour a joy. And when Elizabeth-Anne shared her recollections of the past, Dorothy-Anne came to realize, for the first time in her life, that she was part of something bigger than the loveless confines of the Tarrytown estate: a heritage that belonged to her, and that no one, not even her father, could ever take away.

Nor could she hear enough about how her great-grandmother had built the mighty Hale hotel chain, and it was there, in those fragrant, breezy hills high above Cannes, that the impressionable child became the passionate pupil, that Dorothy-Anne took the first leap toward eventually assuming leadership of Hale Hotels. For even if she herself did not yet recognize the burning passion within her, Elizabeth-Anne did.

But honeymoons have a tendency to end, and so too did those blissful, magical months. The time came to pack up, leave Provence, and return to the States.

Dorothy-Anne wished they didn't have to go. She had tasted the fruit of love and nurturing, and like a lovingly tended plant, had just begun to blossom. Never before had she known such peace of mind and self-confidence, such feelings of being connected, of *belonging*. . . . Why couldn't life be like this all the time? However, she was careful not to voice these opinions aloud. She knew Elizabeth-Anne had to get back. Still wheelchair bound, she had recuperated all she could, and had an empire to run.

During the last night of their stay, Dorothy-Anne had trouble sleeping. All she could do was lie in the dark and think about how happy and carefree she'd been here. If only there were a way to avoid returning to Tarrytown. She wished she could unload her heart and beg her great-grandmother to take her in, but she knew that was impossible. Ever since the stroke, Elizabeth-Anne had required the services of a full-time nurse. The last thing she needed was to be saddled with a child as well.

The following day, Dorothy-Anne was silent during the long flight home. She spent most of it with her eyes shut, pretending to sleep while reliving those wonderful past months in her head.

And it was then, somewhere over the North Atlantic, that she stumbled on a great truth. She was leaving Provence, but Provence would never leave her. It would always be there. The memories were part of her now, and she had only to summon them at will. Each marvelous day was there, ready to sustain her.

Dorothy-Anne heard the pilot announce their imminent arrival at JFK International, and she shelved her mental diary. Before long, the Pan American 747 made a perfect landing and soon, too soon, she was in a limousine speeding to Tarrytown—and back to harsh reality.

6

"Ma—?"

"*Mommy!*"

Dorothy-Anne was sitting up in the hospital bed, wearing one of her own short-sleeved, Empire-waisted cotton nightgowns, the bodice femininely adorned with delicate needlework, tuck pleats, and lace edges, and wondering where all the flower arrangements, silver balloons, and teddy bears atop the air-conditioning–heating unit had come from, when the voices—clear, pure trebles—preceded three small bodies, which hurtled into the room.

"Och!" scolded a flustered, out-of-breath Nanny Florrie from close behind, her uplands Scots accent as thick as the day she had left Galashiels. "I'll nae have all this noise. I tauld you, 'tis a 'ospital!"

Dorothy-Anne smiled indulgently. They were as lively as Mexican jumping beans: her Liz, Fred, and Zack. Tornadoes of energy that whirled here, there, everywhere. Fueled by urgency and excitement, charging furiously through life, as yet unaware that time would eventually overtake them, that someday they'd wonder where all the years had gone.

The mere sight of them gave her heart a kick and flooded it with love; made her blink back tears of pride and joy.

God, how she loved them: the Three Cantwelleers.

At eleven, Liz was the oldest. She was aquamarine-eyed, and her blond hair was gathered in a fountain on top of her head and tied with a red ribbon. With her black turtleneck, Black Watch plaid skirt, and Mary Janes, she was determinedly—deceptively—preppie. Ralph Lauren on the outside, cyberpunk on the inside. A modem-toting Miss American Pie whose mind was sharp as a razor, and who had one foot poised in this world, and the other planted firmly way out in cyberspace.

45

Then there was ten-year-old Fred. The spitting image of his father, but with longish raven hair parted in the center and falling down either side of his face. Very hip-hop and current, in super-baggy jeans, shirttails out, thin gold loops in each pierced earlobe. A wire ran from his pants pocket up into a set of headphones and into his brain. Watchful, introspective, and a child of few words, he munched from an open bag of Doritos. Bopped his head to the beat of music only he could hear.

And finally the youngest. Zack, her nine-year-old wonder. Auburn-banged, blue-eyed, and with energy to burn. Trying to look with-it like his brother, but too darling to pull it off. Baseball cap worn fashionably backward, electronic game in hand.

They all stared at her, the hospital bed and IV and monitors giving them pause. Then Zack broke the silence.

"M-M-Mommy?" he gulped, close to tears. "Y-you're not going to d-d-d-die, are you?"

"Y'know, you are like really, *really* totally a dope," sniffed Liz, with the superior air of an elder. "Mom's like stressed to the max, is all." She hesitated, tipped her head to one side, and eyed her mother anxiously. "I mean, that *is* all it is . . . isn't it, Mom?"

"Yes, sweetheart." Dorothy-Anne dredged up a voice of maternal assurance. "That's all it is."

"Is it true 'bout Dad?" Fred blurted, then guiltily ducked his head and eyed his sneakers, his hair falling down over his face.

Zack dropped his computer game and pummeled Fred with his little fists. "Daddy's *not* dead!" he cried, his voice plaintive with denial. "He's *not*! He's *not!*"

"For Gude's sake, lad!" Nanny hissed at Fred, grabbing Zack's flailing arms. "Dinna you listen to a word I saed? I've told ye nae to upset yer mum!"

Rebuked, Fred sighed and shrugged and shifted his weight from one foot to the other.

"Niver ye mind yer brother, laddie," Nanny said to Zack. "He dinna mean it."

"It's okay, Nanny," Dorothy-Anne said quietly. "They have a right to know."

"It was in all the papers," Fred mumbled sullenly. Tossing his head to get the hair out of his face, he looked up and met his mother's gaze directly.

Dorothy-Anne sighed to herself. *I should have guessed. They're too old not to have found out by themselves.* Still, she wished she could have been the one to tell them. *I wanted to break it to them gently.*

But it was too late now, and the children were waiting. Silent. Watching her warily. Despite the armor of pierced ears and hip togs, they seemed suddenly young, abandoned, *vulnerable.*

They're counting on me, Dorothy-Anne told herself. *I've got to be strong. For their sake.*

It was all she could do to hold out a leaden arm and gesture. "Come closer, sweethearts," she said quietly. "Family powwow."

Zack was the first to tumble forward. Dorothy-Anne rested her arm on his shoulder and stroked the back of his head. Then Fred and Liz stepped spontaneously to either side of him, the three of them erecting a protective barricade.

Dorothy-Anne took a deep breath. "I don't know what you've read or heard," she said carefully. "It's true your father's plane is missing, yes. But we don't know he's dead. I'm praying he's alive and they find him in time. For all we know, they could have crash-landed safely in some valley, and the radio equipment got smashed. . . ." Even to herself, it sounded implausible and thin, hopelessly unrealistic.

In every family, each member has his or her assigned role, and Fred, though the middle child, was physically the strongest, and had thus become the protector and spokesman for all three. "You mean there's a chance, Ma?" He held her gaze. "A real chance?"

Dorothy-Anne hesitated. She had always taken pains never to be condescending toward her children, or to paint glossy veneers on ugly truths. She had earned their trust and respect the hard way—through honesty, fairness, and treating them like the little adults they were. However, they'd never had to face a crisis of this magnitude before. Now she found herself in a quandary, torn between honesty and compassion.

Which was better for them? The pablum of reassurance? Or making them face the worst scenario?

It was a difficult decision, but she made it. "We have to keep praying for the best," she said, a slight tremor to her voice. "We cannot lose hope. But remember: no matter how things turn out, so long as we're strong, we'll get through it. We're together, and that's all that counts."

But we aren't together. Freddie's missing. How can we ever be together without him?

"We must be brave," she continued. "Your daddy wouldn't want us to fall apart, now would he?"

All three of them shook their heads, but their faces were pinched and their eyes reflected fear.

"I'm scared, Mommy," Zack whimpered.

"You know something? So am I, sweetheart." She rubbed the back of his head. "So am I. But you're a big, strong young man now. Aren't you?"

He nodded solemnly. "I-I guess so," he said, sounding unsure.

"Well, I *know* so," she said warmly, still stroking the back of his head. "And do you want to hear why?"

He nodded.

"Because we're a *family*. Because we've got *each other*. Just as you can count on me, I'll be counting on each of you. Together we can face anything . . . even the worst, though I'm praying it won't come to that." She looked at each of them in turn, then locked eyes with Fred. She was silent for a moment. "I can count on you, can't I?"

"You bet, Ma," Fred said, the catch in his voice belying his aw-shucks bravado. "Don't worry about me. I'll be okay."

Said like a real man. She had to fight back her tears.

"I'll be fine, too," Liz spoke up softly. "Like no matter what happens."

Dorothy-Anne looked at her gratefully. *How brave they are, the Three Cantwelleers!*

Just then the nurse popped her head in the door. The big-bosomed Jamaican ran a tight ship. "Five minutes is up. Come on, mon. You gonna tire her."

Suddenly Dorothy-Anne felt worn out. The nurse was right. The visit had taken its toll. "You heard the boss," she urged in a whisper. "Go on, now."

Fred hung back while Nanny shepherded the others into the hall. "What about you, Ma?" he asked. "You gonna be okay?"

Dorothy-Anne dredged up a smile. "Don't worry, sweetheart. Now run along. I'm fine."

But I'm not fine.

I may never be fine again.

It was early afternoon when Venetia returned to the hospital. She swivel-hipped into the room, stopped short, and lowered her head, the better to peer over the tops of her tinted, photochromatic shades with bubinga wood frames. "Formal arrangements, silver balloons, *and* teddy bears?" She let out a throaty guffaw and rolled her eyes. "Girl! When *are* these honkies going to acquire some *taste*?"

Dorothy-Anne had the motorized bed in the upright position, and was sipping ice water through an angled straw from a big paper cup. She looked at Venetia hopefully.

"Sorry to let you down, sugar," Venetia said gently. "Still no word."

Dorothy-Anne set the paper cup on the swing-arm hospital tray. "It's going on two days now," she said quietly.

Venetia nodded. "Blizzard's not over yet."

"Damn." Dorothy-Anne leaned back on the pillow and sighed.

Venetia took off her glasses and stuck them into her chocolate suede shoulder bag. Then she unslung it and let it drop to the floor. "The good news is," she said, "the blizzard's finally abating. The search parties are all geared up and ready to roll. They should be able to move out first thing in the morning."

"Thank God."

Venetia slid out of her taupe suede duster and tossed it over the chair. Then she plopped herself down and scooted the chair closer to the bed.

She was wearing brown leather pants and chocolate-colored cowboy boots with intricate taupe swirls stitched into the leather. She had on an espresso-colored sweater, a chunky Armani necklace of color-fused resin and bronze, and matching earrings.

"So, child. Other than being sick with worry over Freddie, and feeling like shit, how're you *really* doing?"

"I still feel weak," Dorothy-Anne admitted. "I don't know what they did to me, but it feels like they turned me inside out."

Venetia winced. "How about the pain? Is it bad?"

"Not really. I can regulate the painkillers myself. Want to see?" With her IV hand, Dorothy-Anne held up the release button, which let her self-administer intravenous doses as needed.

"What are they giving you?"

"Demerol."

"Girl! Do you have any idea how lucky you are? No, you do not. Believe me, word of this gets out, druggies'll be lining up around the block."

"Well, they can gladly take my place. I can't wait to get out of here." Dorothy-Anne tightened her lips. "The surgeon's coming by soon. The nurse told me he wants to talk to me."

Venetia kept her face carefully neutral. She wondered how much Dorothy-Anne already guessed. Not the true extent of damage she'd suffered, of that she was certain.

She decided to steer the conversation to safer waters. "I thought you'd like to read about the party and get the press's reaction to the hotel. I brought you some clippings."

She reached down, heaved the shoulder bag to her lap, and took out a manila envelope. She laid it on the bed.

"Also, I brought you some fashion slicks."

Out came current issues of American and French *Vogues* and *Bazaars*.

"And, in case the food in here gets to you—*voilà!*"

The plastic air-sealed container was filled with a variety of pastries: slices of various tortes, a Napoleon, cranberry bread, and a small kiwi tart.

"Venetia! If I eat all these I'll gain ten pounds!"

"Well, dig in. You've got to keep up your strength. Oh, I nearly forgot. I brought some hotel forks."

They were individually wrapped inside heavily starched, rolled linen napkins.

Dorothy-Anne laughed. "At least now I know what you tote around in those shoulder bags of yours."

"Yeah, survival kits." Venetia looked suddenly stricken. "Oh, damn! I'm sorry, sugar. Bad choice of words."

"Forget it. Anyway, I'll have the tart. But only if you eat something, too."

"Well, maybe just a teensy little bite." Venetia's red-taloned fingers hovered indecisively, then swooped and broke off a tiny corner of cranberry bread. She nibbled maybe a crumb. "Mmm. Not bad."

Dorothy-Anne forked up a bite of tart. "Yummy," she said. "By the way, the kids were here."

"I saw them. Nanny Florrie looks like she's got her hands full." Venetia paused and looked at Dorothy-Anne questioningly. "What did you tell them?"

"The truth."

"And how did they take it?" Venetia nibbled another crumblet.

"They're frightened, but brave."

Venetia nodded. "They're good kids."

Knuckles tapped lightly on the open door. Dorothy-Anne looked over at it and Venetia twisted around in her chair.

"Anybody home?" a man's voice inquired.

Whoever it was, he couldn't be seen for the giant arrangement of all-white flowers he carried: calla lilies, huge branches of bloom-laden orchids, tulips, big fat open roses, lilies, narcissus, tuberoses, iris, amaryllus, hyacinths, scilla, fritillaria, and peonies.

"Ms. Harlow, she gone," said Venetia, in blackese. And in a stage whisper to Dorothy-Anne: "Not a balloon or teddy bear in sight. Quick! Better grab 'em while you can."

The man came in and set the vase down on the swing-arm table. It turned out to be Hunt Winslow.

"Seems I'm bringing coals to Newcastle," he said wryly, eyeing all the arrangements squeezed along the window.

"You did not bring coals to Newcastle," Venetia laughed. "Not, that is, unless you've got a teddy bear on you."

"No bears," he promised, raising his right hand. "No balloons, either."

"Thank God." Venetia got up and made room in the center of the wide ledge and had him hand her the monster arrangement. "Listen," she said. "I'm going to run downstairs and get a cup of coffee. Either of you want anything?"

Dorothy-Anne and Hunt both shook their heads.

"You can keep my seat warm," Venetia told him, grabbing her shoulder bag and sailing out.

"I must say." Hunt pinched his pant creases as he sat down. "Ms. Flood is the very soul of discretion."

"That she is," Dorothy-Anne agreed.

"She looks like a model," he said.

The light pouring in through the window and beating down from the fluorescents was unflattering to the extreme, but it made her do a new take on him. Hunt Winslow was much better looking than Dorothy-Anne remembered; the lighting at the party had robbed him of his naturally healthy glow and fresh-faced vitality.

It was in full force now. And how.

He looked younger than his mid-thirties, his skin smooth and full of high color. His lapis eyes and lopsided grin hinted at humor and mischief, and his clean-cut sex appeal made you think of oranges and surfboards; the kind of guy you'd take barefoot walks on the beach with, trousers rolled up, shoes tied together and hanging from around his neck. His sun-bleached hair would smell of freshness. His lips would taste of passion.

"Venetia was one of Eileen Ford's biggest discoveries," Dorothy-Anne said. "Ten years ago, she was on every other cover of *Vogue*."

She frowned, realizing he had yet to take his eyes off hers. Other than Freddie, she couldn't remember the last time anyone had met her gaze so uncompromisingly. She let a thoughtful silence pass, and said, "How did you know where to find me?"

"Easy. This is a small town. Between the hotel opening and your husband's missing plane, the papers are full of you. Your condition's even reported on every day in the society pages."

She tilted her head to one side. "Somehow you don't strike me as the type who reads gossip columns."

He chuckled. "I don't. But my assistant does. Just in case my name pops up and the record needs to be set straight."

Her voice was dry. "And there I was, popping right off the page."

A faint smile touched his lips. "And there you were," he nodded. "How are you?"

She made a face. "How do I look?"

"Not bad, actually."

"Liar! I look like shit and you know it."

He laughed—a blaze of white teeth. "So what? Nobody looks their best in hospitals."

Then he fell silent and regarded her with solemnity. Gone now was the easy familiarity and jocular smile. It was replaced by a gentle serious-ness, a *studious* seriousness, his gaze intent as he appeared to study her, the whole of her, his expression thoughtful.

She felt suddenly uncomfortable. *Why is he staring at me like that? I wish he wouldn't. I know I look like something the cat dragged in.*

Then she realized the covers were down around her waist, and that he was eyeing her nightgown. It was one of the romantic smocked ones.

Surely he wasn't admiring the Belgian openwork embroidery? No, he obviously wasn't interested in that. His attention was riveted on the swell of her breasts, which was accentuated by the high Empire waistline, and at the heat that rose from the modest neckline to suffuse her face with color.

Suddenly she wished he'd stayed away. His presence was altogether too disturbing. For one thing, he was not merely endowed with good looks: he was, bar none, the best-looking man she had ever laid eyes on. For another, his testosterone level was too high for comfort.

And then there was the clincher: his unhappy marriage.

Everything about Hunt spelled T-R-O-U-B-L-E. She'd have to be nuts to get involved with him. Life was complicated enough as it was.

Freddie, she reminded herself. *My Freddie, who's missing . . .*

She felt a stab of guilt and instantly broke eye contact with Hunt. Quickly she scooped up another morsel of tart just to have something to do. Her hand was shaking, and she didn't notice the pastry falling off the fork until her lips tasted tines.

"Damn!" she swore, looking down around her. "I couldn't be klutz-ier if I tried!"

"So you dropped it. Big deal." Hunt half rose and retrieved it from the covers. "Here." He held it out to her.

She stared at it and started to reach out, then hesitated. There was something too intimate about this simple action. Quickly she withdrew her hand and shook her head emphatically. "No." Her voice was low, almost trembling.

They both understood what that *no* encompassed: an out-and-out declaration of noninvolvement. It put to rest any chances whatsoever of a relationship, no matter how innocent, between them; it put her off limits to his touch.

Hunt acted as if that were of no consequence. He sat back, popped the piece of tart in his mouth, and chewed. "Very tasty." He nodded in approval.

She put the fork down on the tray and met his gaze head-on. "Hunt, why did you come?"

He seemed surprised by the question. "To offer my services, see if there was anything you needed. After my wife's behavior at the party, I thought it was the very least I could do."

Dorothy-Anne's expression did not change. "Does she know you're here?"

"Gloria?" He shook his head. "No."

"Where does she think you are?"

He laughed bitterly. "That depends upon what condition she's in. If she's drunk, she's almost certainly convinced I'm shacked up with some-one. If not, that I'm out pressing the flesh or mingling with constituents."

"But I'm not a constituent," Dorothy-Anne said quietly. "I'm not even a registered voter in this state."

"In my experience, everyone's a potential voter." He grinned easily. "And if they aren't, they have friends or relatives who are."

She drew a deep breath. "I . . ." she began, and shook her head. She clasped her hands in her lap. "I'm sorry. You'll have to excuse me, Hunt. I'm afraid I tire out awfully fast. The painkillers and all . . . "

He smiled and rose to his feet. "I understand. Anyway, in case you change your mind, here's my card." He did a nifty little sleight-of-hand trick and seemingly snatched one out of thin air. He placed it on the swing-arm tray. "If there's anything you need—*anything*"—he tapped the card—"don't hesitate to call. I'm not without influence, you know."

"I'll remember that," she said.

"No strings attached," he added.

She smiled. "Thanks for coming by, Hunt. The flowers are lovely."

"No balloons or teddy bears." He winked. "See that you get well soon."

"I will."

As soon as he was gone, her smile faded. She let her head sink back on the pillow and shut her eyes.

Here's my card . . . if there's anything you need . . . I'm not without influence. . . .

She sighed deeply. Hunt could have saved himself a card. Strings or no strings, she wasn't about to court trouble by getting in touch with him. She'd observe etiquette and send him a thank-you note for the flowers—period. Anything else might be misconstrued, and she didn't want to lead him on.

I'm happily married. I have three beautiful children. What more could I want?

Freddie safe and sound.

That isn't too much to ask for. Is it?

She heard footsteps and then Venetia said softly: "Sugar? You awake?"

Dorothy-Anne opened her eyes and nodded.

"Good. Dr. Chalfin's here."

Dorothy-Anne glanced past Venetia. The surgeon was standing there, just inside the door, his white lab coat so starched it could have stood there on its own.

"Good afternoon, Mrs. Cantwell," he said. "How do you feel?"

"That all depends, Doctor. Why don't you tell me?"

Burt Chalfin didn't so much as smile.

Cheerful soul, Dorothy-Anne thought sardonically. *He can probably sit through a Marx Brothers movie without cracking up.*

She watched him shut the door, step forward, and lift her chart off the foot of the bed. Every movement he made was done with precision and forethought. Even the way he flipped through her chart, nodding to himself from time to time; the deliberation with which he reached for his gold ballpoint pen and twisted it to write, making a neat notation; the compulsive manner in which he hung the chart back at the foot of the bed, making sure it was perfectly aligned.

"Well? Am I going to live?" Dorothy-Anne quipped.

"Oh, definitely," he said in all seriousness. "You're recovering nicely. In fact, we'll have you out of here in no time."

"Now, that's the first good news I've heard in ages."

He untwisted his pen and clipped it just so to the inside of his breast pocket. Then he frowned and eyed Dorothy-Anne thoughtfully. "Ms. Flood tells me she's a close friend of yours."

Dorothy-Anne glanced fondly at Venetia and smiled. "Yes, she is."

"Then you won't mind if she sits in on this? If she's party to what I have to say?"

Dorothy-Anne's eyes snapped back to him. "Why?" she asked, suddenly wary. "Is it necessary?"

"Not at all. But I've found that certain situations are easier when a patient has a member of the family or a close friend at hand."

Dorothy-Anne felt a sick, churning feeling rise up inside her. The cloying scent from the flowers nauseated her and the room seemed stiflingly hot. Her heart began speeding, pounding out a percussive beat.

She stared at Burt Chaflin. "What's the matter, Doctor?" she whispered. "What's wrong with me?"

Dr. Chalfin glanced at Venetia.

Venetia glanced back at him.

Then they both looked at Dorothy-Anne.

"For God's sake!" Dorothy-Anne blurted. "Will somebody please let *me* in on whatever the hell is going on? This *is* my body, you know!"

Saturday afternoon, Jimmy Vilinsky called Joel, his bookie, from a pay phone at Grand Central saying he wanted to put five grand on the Rodriguez kid for tonight's fight at the Garden. "The Kid" was the underdog, and the odds were twenty to one—against. But *if* he came up the winner, Jimmy stood to rake in a cool hundred grand. Just like that.

Joel, growling around a cigar at the other end of the line, rasped, "Jimmy, Jimmy. You'd lay bets if ya saw two roaches crawlin' across a kitchen counter." Pausing to see how Jimmy reacted to *that*.

He didn't, just kept breathing into the phone.

Joel laying it on a little thicker now, saying: "And you know somethin', Jimmy? Outta them two roaches? You'd sure as shit pick the loser!"

Jimmy rolled his eyes, held the phone away from his ear, and made yak-yak motions with his hand. Like he needed this shit! Just because he and Joel went way back, growing up in Hell's Kitchen together, didn't mean he had to listen to him flapping his lip.

Jimmy heard Joel say, "Whyn't ya take some friendly advice, huh, Jimmy? Your markers are startin' to add up again. Do yourself a favor and lay off the bettin'."

After the squawking stopped, Jimmy said, "Joel? Blow it out yer ass. Five grand on 'The Kid.' "

Telling it like it is and hanging up.

That taken care of, Jimmy strode through the terminal. He was a skinny guy, late thirties, with black hair slicked back with gel. He had a pointy ferret kind of nose and blackcurrant eyes that kept darting about, like jumpy little raisins, and he liked to act cool.

At the moment, Jimmy Vilinsky was flying high. Had been, ever since that phone call out of the blue had changed his life.

Now, putting a little extra swagger in his step, he permitted his thoughts to drift back to that night. . . .

Back to when the phone had rung . . .

Coming when it did, at four-something in the morning, the jangling was enough to raise the dead. Jimmy, asleep one minute and sitting up too suddenly the next, felt the shock of pain splitting his skull in two. Groaning, he looked around in confusion, trying to get his bearings.

From the light left burning in the bathroom, he ascertained that the bed was his own.

So far, so good.

He could also make out the quart of Four Roses, what was left of it, two smudged glasses, and overflowing ashtrays. The familiar stench—stale cigarette smoke, sweaty sheets, semen, and cheap bourbon—all rang a bell, only he couldn't remember why.

Meanwhile, the phone on the far nightstand kept up its jangling. He was tempted to hurl it across the room, the noise too much after tying one on.

Wishing he'd switched the damn thing off before crashing, Jimmy muttered, "Shit!" Started to reach for it, then felt the smooth, naked warm body sleeping next to him.

That stopped him short.

Blinking, he stared down in surprise.

A girl Jimmy had never seen before was lying there on her belly. Tight little rear end up, face turned sideways on the pillow. Cute as a button, with a trim little figure and loose dark hair, not too long.

He couldn't for the life of him remember where she'd come from, or what, if anything, they'd done—definitely a bad trip in this day and time. With dread disease stalking the streets, all it took was the wrong casual screw and—whammo! Sex equaled death.

Deciding he'd better answer the phone before his skull shattered, he crawled over the girl, whoever she was, unable to help brushing against her. It didn't wake her; she merely rolled over on her side and curled up and went right on sleeping.

Grabbing the receiver, Jimmy was about to lift it when he had second thoughts.

Uh-oh.

The muzziness starting to clear now, his mental gears going clickety-click. One thing for sure, the call couldn't be friendly. Not at this hour, the way it was ringing off the hook—what? Fifteen, twenty times already?

Something like that.

Now he started thinking along that track, the jangling did have that certain sound, like the call had to be about all the money he owed.

What happened, these past few months had been a real bitch. A losing streak had wiped him out completely, and he'd relied on markers to try and recoup. But Lady Luck, that two-faced whore, had turned her back on him, and the markers only got him deeper and deeper in the hole.

Soon he owed everybody and his brother. Not just Joel, but a dozen syndicate and Chinatown bookies as well.

Next thing he knew, they'd cut off his running tab, and the bookies' collectors were dropping by, making nasty noises.

Then they'd started threatening him outright, spelling out exactly how they could affect his personal health and well-being.

And most recently, they'd stepped up their campaign to the point where he was seriously contemplating the merits of vamoosing. Maybe heading out to the Coast and lying low.

Still the damn phone kept on ringing. Like that Energizer bunny that wouldn't stop. As if the caller *knew* he was home and listening.

How the girl slept through it, he'd never know.

Exasperated, Jimmy finally grabbed the receiver and snarled, "Yeah!" Expecting the shoe to drop.

Some smooth-talking guy said, "Mr. Vilinsky?" and waited.

"Who's callin'?"

"A friend. How you doing?"

Jimmy said, "Look, cut to the chase, willya? I ain't got no friends."

"You sure about that, Mr. Vilinsky?" The voice sounded like velvet.

"Course I'm sure!" Jimmy making out like he was getting ready to hang up. "You fuckin' realize what time it is?"

The voice said, "Of course, Mr. Vilinsky. It's forty minutes and twenty-four seconds past four."

Jimmy wanted to say, *Hey, smartass? Fuck you and the donkey you rode in on. I'm goin' to bed and switchin' the phone off.*

The thing was, his curiosity was getting the better of him. Long as he stayed on the line, maybe he could figure out the guy's angle . . . see what he was up to. You never knew. Could be this guy might prove useful somewhere down the road. . . .

"Mr. Vilinsky? You there?"

"Yeah. Lemme guess."

Idly Jimmy scratched his crotch, which for some reason or other had started to itch.

"Next thing I know, you'll be all buddy-buddy. Telling me, 'Lookit, I'm yer friend. I don't wanna see ya get hurt.' Somethin' like that. Am I right?"

The guy surprised him.

"No, Mr. Vilinsky, you're reading it all wrong. See, I didn't call to twist your arm. And another thing?"

Jimmy waited.

"Nobody's going to call up or drop by to pester you. The dogs have been called off."

"Is that so?"

"You have my word on it."

"Yeah, but who're *you*?"

"I'm the man bought up your markers. You understand what I'm saying?"

Jimmy wide awake now, drawing in his breath, thinking, *The fuck—?* He felt a knot of alarm twisting his bowels as the wind outside gusted and howled. The windows shook, making him think of that story, the one about the Three Little Pigs. The wind not the wind anymore, but the guy on the phone; the Big Bad Wolf breathing down his neck.

"Mr. Vilinsky . . ." That smooth, cold voice again.

"Yeah, yeah."

Jimmy rubbed his face, working on keeping his voice cool. Acting like he was surprised, yeah, but not scared shitless.

He said, "Why'd ya buy 'em up?" Taking the guy for some hard-ass collector who went around, buying up markers at a discount.

But the guy was full of surprises.

"Because I wanted to hire you, Mr. Vilinsky. Only instead of getting paychecks? You work off what you owe."

Jimmy said, "Work it off *how*?" Trying to show some spunk.

"Why, same as you'd work your way out of any mess, Mr. Vilinsky. You get into a bind? Do whatever it takes."

"Who *are* ya?"

"I don't believe you really want to be privy to that, Mr. Vilinsky."

Jimmy rubbed his face some more. "This one of them offers I can't refuse?"

The laugh was as soft as it was mirthless. "Well, I suppose you *could* refuse. But I were in your shoes? I'd think it over real carefully first."

Jimmy sighed. "Okay. What you want me to do?"

So much for his spunk.

"Good. I was hoping you'd be reasonable. Now, what the job entails? You act as a go-between. All you do, you make contact with a certain person. From then on, you simply relay information between myself and him."

"And that's all?" Jimmy asked suspiciously.

"That's all, I assure you."

Jimmy didn't believe it. "There's gotta be a catch."

"But there isn't. What I explained is all there is to it. And each time you relay a message, I tear up one of your markers, mail it to you."

"Yeah?" Jimmy turning it over in his head, scratching his itching nuts and wondering if maybe, just maybe, the girl wasn't a walking flea circus.

"I'll be in touch, Mr. Vilinsky. You'll receive detailed instructions later this afternoon."

"Hey! Wait a sec. Before you hang up? You never mentioned yer name."

"I already told you, Mr. Vilinsky. You really don't want to know."

"Yeah, but how about a first name? That way, when ya get in touch? I'll know it's you."

"I'm sure you'll recognize my voice. Good *night*, Mr. Vilinsky."

And the phone went click.

The first thing Jimmy did, once it was daylight, he gave the girl a resounding slap on her bare ass.

"Ow!" she yowled, jerking upright. "What are you? Some kinda perv?"

"I got business to take care of. Whyn't ya take a hike, huh?"

"Gladly!" she huffed, giving him an eyeful of major bazoombas as she bounded out of bed.

Jimmy sprang an instant hard. He had a thing for big lungs, and on a scale of one to ten, this broad's were definitely an eleven.

How could he not remember them? Still, all was not lost, he decided with a knowing leer, especially since he gave good sweet talk and wasn't too proud to apologize.

"Oh, honey," he began, in hopes of getting something memorable going. "I'm sorr—"

She whirled on him, all blazing hair and teeth and boobs and—

Holy shit!

He stared, looked away, and did a classic double take. Then flinched as before an assailant.

His one-eyed snake shriveled.

He liked his women well endowed, yeah, but not with cock and balls! *Shit!*

Shock brought his universe to a standstill. His perception narrowed to the offending anatomy. There was a taunting sense of mockery about the same body sharing voluptuous female breasts with male genitalia, a macabre, surreal kind of travesty that he found aggressively repellent.

He'd picked up a . . . what *did* they call transsexuals who'd had silicone implants but had yet to undergo the knife? He searched his memory. There was some phrase . . .

Chicks with dicks. That was it.

Not a man—or a girl.

Both, and yet neither.

"And what," demanded the woman with a penis—or was it a man with breasts, "are *you* staring at?"

Jimmy recoiled, too dumbstruck to speak. He watched in horrified fascination as the creature stalked around, plucking pieces of female clothing off the floor and donning them.

Once dressed, she flounced out, head held high, threw him a birdie, and slammed the door so hard that a framed blow-up of Jimmy's favorite horse, Sunday Silence, went crashing to the floor.

He put his head in his hands and shut his eyes. Oh, the indignity. The disgrace. The *shame.*

His self-esteem had been dealt a severe blow—not least by the fact that "her" prick had been bigger than his.

In the meantime, fact-finding calls to his various bookies provided a much needed diversion. Besides which, he was curious about the guy who'd phoned. Wanted to see if he was full of shit, or what.

His first call was to his old pal Joel, who ran his business out of the back booth of a seedy bar over on Tenth Avenue. The bookie had been giving him the cold shoulder lately.

"Hey, Jimmy!" Joel's greeting was genuinely enthusiastic. "Long time no see. How you doin'?"

It was the warmest reception Jimmy had gotten out of him since his credit had been cut off.

"Pretty good," Jimmy told him. "How's business?"

"Sluggish." Joel laughed. "I feel the pinch without yer bets."

Jimmy's ears perked up. "That right?" he said.

"Yeah. Listen, pal. Anytime you wanna run up a tab again? It's fine by me."

"Swell. You'll be hearin' from me real soon, Joel."

As Jimmy hung up, his head was spinning. Would wonders never cease?

Hot damn! he thought. *I'm cookin'!*

That had been—what? Six, eight weeks ago now? Something like that, Jimmy thought as he bopped through Grand Central Station.

And so far all he'd been required to do was write down a name he'd been given, seal it in an envelope, and give it to the mother of some Eye-talian named Carmine. Getting an offshore bank account number in return, which he then passed along to the guy that called.

Sure enough. Two days later, one of his markers, torn in half, came in the mail.

Whoo-ee! Talk about gettin' something for next to nothin'! Only thing he wished, this guy would hurry up, have some more jobs lined up. Get those markers outta the way, since he'd incurred new debts on account of some football games.

Passing a newsstand, Jimmy Vilinsky stopped and bought both the *Post* and the *Daily News*.

Usually he didn't bother reading anything but the sports pages. Even the lurid headlines never piqued his interest. Yet something about these did. Which was *weird* . . .

But what *was* it had grabbed his eye?

Frowning, he stared at the screaming four-inch-high letters:

BILLIONAIRE'S PLANE STILL MISSING
SEARCH AND RESCUE ATTEMPTS
HAMPERED BY BLIZZARD

A grainy blow-up of a man's face accompanied the headlines.

Jimmy squinted at the photo, but it didn't ring any bells. And then the name in the caption popped off the page: Freddie T. Cantwell.

Jimmy drew a sharp breath. Could feel his skin start to tingle.

"Holy shit!" he whispered.

Taking his time, he studied the picture carefully now. Held the paper at arm's length, then brought it in real close, right up in front of his eyes, before moving it slowly back again.

Staring at the guy's mug. Feeling a strange kind of kinship, this being the guy whose name he'd passed along to Carmine—the guy now missing and feared dead.

"Now, ain't that a coincidence," he muttered to himself.

Only thing was, Jimmy Vilinsky did not believe in coincidences. Something was going on . . . had to be. Something . . . fishy. Yeah. Come to think of it, something *real* fishy.

So he wasn't exactly a rocket scientist. So what? Neither was he a fool.

Next time I get a call from Mr. Smooth, Jimmy decided, *I'm gonna lay it on the line. Tell him I don't mind passin' along contract hits, long as they up the ante—tear up* all *my markers each time!*

L ife slowed to a crawl. A lethargic, laggardly snail's pace in which seconds stretched into long minutes, and minutes into interminable infinity.

The very texture of reality had undergone a change. The air surrounding Dorothy-Anne seemed to have thickened and grown heavy, miring her in molasseslike sluggishness, while a coarse-grained gauze descended over her vision, robbing everything of clarity, contrast, and color—as if her eyes had been substituted with poor-quality, out-of-focus 16mm lenses.

She felt numb and dazed. Punched, battered, pummeled, beaten; finally KO'd by one uppercut too many. That she still sat upright was by virtue of her hospital bed's having been in that position when Dr. Burt Chalfin, chief of surgery, came by—he of the smooth, well-rehearsed bedside manner—to explain why, despite what he had to tell her, she was one very lucky lady.

Whoever said that trouble always comes in threes is wrong. Trouble doesn't come in threes. It comes in fours. Freddie missing . . . then losing the baby . . . being told I had cancer—

And, as if that hadn't been enough, she'd now sustained yet another cataclysmic upheaval.

Her reproductive organs were gone.

Gone!

I've been spayed.

The thought burst in her mind like an artillery shell.

I no longer have a womb.

How can I be a woman when I've been neutered?

62

Somehow, Burt Chalfin's voice breached the sludgelike pressure that threatened to crush her from all sides. "Mrs. Cantwell? Mrs. Cantwell!"

Dorothy-Anne's eyes slowly focused. "Life is a game of chance," she whispered desolately, "and I keep throwing snake eyes."

"Aw, sugar," Venetia, perched on the edge of the bed and holding Dorothy-Anne's hand, said commiseratingly. "Honey, we're with you all the way. We'll help you get through this."

Dorothy-Anne looked at her through pain-racked eyes. "No," she said dully. "No one can help me. Not with this."

Burt Chalfin cleared his throat behind a cupped hand. He said, "Under the circumstances, Mrs. Cantwell, it's only normal that you'll be feeling depressed—"

A sharp pain shot through Dorothy-Anne's heart. For a moment the world stretched elastically out of shape, then suddenly snapped back into place.

"Depressed!"

She stared at him.

"Jesus and Mary on a bicycle!" she said thickly, blinking back tears. "I lost my baby, dammit, and you just got through telling me I can't have another! This isn't depression! This is dying and going to fucking hell!"

He looked at her gently. "But don't you see, Mrs. Cantwell? The child would never have stood a chance. At least this way we discovered the ovarian mass in time. Also, if you hadn't been brought in when you were, you'd have hemorrhaged to death. All in all, you might want to count your blessings."

"My blessings," she said sardonically.

"Dr. Chalfin's right," Venetia said huskily. "You're alive, sugar. Alive!"

Alive. "My baby died, and for all I know, Freddie's dead, too! What the hell's the use of being alive?"

"Oh, sugar."

Venetia glanced worriedly up at Dr. Chalfin and then back at Dorothy-Anne.

"Honey, you've got plenty of reasons to go on living. For starters, there're the kids. . . ."

But Dorothy-Anne wasn't listening. She turned her head sideways on the pillow and looked away, past the irritating silver balloons, teddy bears, and floral arrangements worthy of a Mafia don's funeral, and stared dully out the window at the brick wall beyond.

Venetia fell silent and once again glanced up at Dr. Chalfin.

He nodded and said, "The good news, Mrs. Cantwell, is so long as you take it easy, we'll have the catheter out of you by tomorrow. And discharge you in a few days."

"Thank you," Dorothy-Anne said listlessly.

And still keeping her face averted, she thought: *Must I lose everything I hold precious?* She wondered at the injustices of fate. *Is this what life has in store for me?*

"Mrs. Cantwell," the doctor said.

Dorothy-Anne soughed a deep sigh.

Dr. Chalfin's voice was soft. "It's not the end of the world, you know."

But Dorothy-Anne knew better.

For me it is.

"Och! Now wha' the divil's come into the three o' ye?" demanded Nanny Florrie despairingly in her broad central uplands accent.

Fedora-ed, loden caped, and sensibly shod, she had her hands full, trying in vain to shoo the three obstinate little bodies, their feet planted in unyielding, wide-legged stances, out of the hospital room.

Apprehensively Zack blurted, as the firm Scottish hands came to rest on his, the littlest shoulders: "*Mom*my! But we just *got* here! Why do we have to leave already?"

Liz, precociously attuned to the subtleties of mood shifts, however slight, cocked her head to one side, the corners of her lips turning down in a frown.

"Mom," she said. "Like this is really, *really* weird. I mean, there's something negative you aren't telling us. Y'know?"

And Fred, with a casual toss of his head to flip his longish, centrally parted hair out of his eyes, gazed at his mother through slitted lashes, his slim, model-perfect face, raven eyebrows, and sulky expression conveying suspicion.

"It's bad news, isn't it?" he asked gently. " 'Bout Dad?"

Hearing the fear in their young, pure voices brought an ache to Dorothy-Anne's heart. Clearly, their alarm was a matter of transference, a direct result of her own numb listlessness rubbing off on them.

They're looking to me for strength and succor. They need me now as they've never needed me before.

But the fact of the matter remained that she *wasn't* here for them. Not this time. Too many disasters had piled up too fast, had taken too massive a toll. All her emotional reservoirs had been drained and squeezed dry; all her reserves had been used up.

They need me. But how can I help them when I can't even help myself?

"No, sweethearts," she managed in a strained whisper, "it's not about your father. There's still been no word of him."

"Then what's *wrong*, Ma?" Fred persisted.

"D-d-don't you love us anymore?" blubbered Zack, on the verge of tears.

Dorothy-Anne felt her insides contract. *Oh, God. What kind of mother am I? How can I let them down at a time like this?*

"Oh, sweetheart."

Dorothy-Anne held out a weak hand.

"Come here to Mommy."

But Zack didn't rush into her arms. Instead, he remained where he was, intractably wedged between the protective flanks of his older siblings. And how solemn, how uncharacteristically subdued they were, these usual bundles of high-octane energy!

"Sweetie?"

Dorothy-Anne kept her arm extended. Finally, when it became clear that he was determined to defy her, she wearily let her arm drop.

She glanced to either side of him. At Liz, chewing thoughtfully on her lower lip. Fred, impatiently shifting his weight from one foot to the other. And all three of them pinning her with their intense gazes. Waiting for the explanation they deserved, but which refused to come.

Burning guilt flooded through her. She just didn't have the strength to provide the necessary balm that would magically dissolve their fears. And saddling them with the cruel, additional freight of the truth was unthinkable.

Bad enough their father was missing and their mother hospitalized. That was enough to weigh on the strongest young shoulders.

Now if only I could weave some plausible white lie . . . some harmless explanation. But what? What . . . ?

She struggled to think, but her brain refused to cooperate. She could almost feel her mental cogs and gears mired in that grainy-textured, thick and heavy sludge that made it seem she was inhabiting a monochromatic world with a different, deeper atmospheric pressure.

It was Venetia who saved the day. Venetia who came around from the other side of the bed and to the rescue. Venetia crouched down in front of the trio and embraced them in her extraordinarily long, amazingly graceful slender arms.

"Hey guys," she told them huskily, "now listen up. Your mama's had a tough time. She's just as desperate for news of your dad as you are. And being sick on top of it doesn't make it any easier." She held their gazes solemnly. "Catch my drift?"

"Y'mean Mom's really sick?" Liz said, aquamarine eyes widening. "Not just stressed to the max, but, like, *sick* sick?"

Venetia looked at Liz sternly. "Child? You going around putting words in this girl's mouth?" she demanded, striking just the right balance between adult authority and one-on-one equality.

Liz shook her head.

"Good. 'Cause if I were you, I wouldn't. Just remember, you're being kept informed. Soon as we know something, we'll let you know. You can bank on it. You with me so far?"

She waited for their nods.

"Good. Meanwhile, your mama's exhausted. You can see that for yourself. And, as far as what's wrong with her, you know how medicine can make you feel kinda dopey or woozy? Like you're really out of it?"

Zack's head bobbed up and down almost immediately. But Fred and Liz weren't easily conned. Smelling a rat, their eyes probed Venetia's for signs of deception while their minds speed-searched instant replays of her words for implausibility. They had the ring of truth, but . . .

"Now, the doctor told your mama she can go home in a few days," Venetia said. "That is, *if* she gets enough rest."

"Really?" The clear treble voice was Zack's.

"Really." Venetia nodded. "So you see? It's up to the three of you to see that she gets it." She looked at each of them in turn. "You do want her out of here pronto, don't you?"

Again they nodded solemnly, their heads bobbing out of sync.

"But Mommy will be okay?" Zack asked. "You promise?"

"Your mama will be just fine, sugar." Venetia removed her arms from around them, smiled, and held up a long-nailed, red-taloned hand. "Scout's honor."

They all stared at her.

"So. We on the same wavelength?" she asked.

"I guess so," Fred said, speaking for them all.

"Great." Venetia gave the threesome another hug and then stood up. She grinned at Nanny Florrie. "Nanny? They're all yours."

"Thank Gude. I dinna ken how ye dae it."

Nanny proceeded to shepherd her charges around the bed and toward the door, clucking and scolding like a disapproving hen.

"Ah, come on now, laddies. An' ye too, lassie! I willna have nae more o' this nonsense. 'Tis no way to behave, yer poor mother needin' 'er rest an' all. Ye have to be braw. Now, what havena we seen? How aboot Alcatraz?"

Both Liz and Fred groaned.

"I want to go back to the Ripley's Believe It or Not Museum!" Zack piped up, tugging on Nanny's cape.

"Dae ye, wee laddie? Weel . . ."

"Oh, puh-leeze," sniffed Liz, rolling her eyes heavenward. "It's, like, yuck! Beyond grody and soooo immature. *I'll* go back to the hotel and my computer."

"And I wanna pick up a new video game," Fred mumbled.

Venetia stood by the bedside, her arms folded in front of her as she and Dorothy-Anne watched them troop out.

"They're good kids," Venetia observed softly.

"Yes. And I've let them down," Dorothy-Anne whispered thickly, tears trailing a rivulet down each cheek.

Venetia heaved an exasperated sigh. "Girl!" she exclaimed, placing her hands on her hips and spiking Dorothy-Anne with her eyes. "You are one fiiiiine piece of work! Have you taken a good look around you lately?"

"Have I . . . ?" Dorothy-Anne blinked.

"Where are you?" Venetia grilled.

"In the hospital."

"My point exactly. And you're in here for a reason. Right?"

"But I'm their *mother*! It's up to me to—"

"It's up to you to get better," Venetia interrupted with no-nonsense finality. "And there's no way you can help them without doing that. Now get some rest. You look like you sure do need it."

Dorothy-Anne sighed and nodded and turned her head sideways on the pillow.

A major mistake. Floral arrangements, teddy bears, and balloons filled her vision and grated.

"Venetia," she sighed. "See all that stuff?"

Venetia looked toward the window and nodded. "What about it, sugar?"

Suddenly Dorothy-Anne felt bone-weary. Venetia was right. She needed to rest. She turned her head in the opposite direction and shut her eyes. "Get rid of it," she said.

High atop Pacific Heights in the Beaux Arts mansion overlooking the bay, Gloria Anne Watters Winslow anointed herself with dabs of Jaïpur. Slowly, she touched the cool wet glass stopper to the backs of her ears, the hollow of her throat, both the fronts and backs of her wrists and, finally, to the cleft of her bosom. As she buttoned her scoop-necked, flesh-tone silk blouse, she inhaled deeply, her nostrils flaring appreciatively. She loved smelling expensive, just as she loved dressing expensively and living expensively. She almost loved it as much as drinking. But not quite.

Gloria reached for the flute of champagne on her lace-skirted vanity, lifted it, and then, frowning, put it shakily back down. She eyed it balefully.

Enough was enough. It was not even half past noon, and she'd nearly demolished a bottle of Cristal '79—on an empty stomach yet. Any more, and the cloud of well-being she moved around in would start playing havoc with her equilibrium.

That decided, she headed for her room-sized walk-in closet. She was halfway there when the telephone began to chirrup. Gloria gnashed her teeth and decided to ignore it. It was still chirruping when she entered her boutiquelike closet. At least from in here the insistent sound was distant, muted.

Gazing around, she wondered what she was going to wear. Lunch at Act IV. With the Queen of Toad Hall. Definitely not an occasion she looked forward to.

At last the telephone fell silent and the house was once again blessedly quiet. Thank God. Now she could select her outfit in peace. What to wear, what to wear . . .

She started a slow circumference of the closet, rippling the expensively laden, silk-padded hangers with outstretched fingers. The overstuffed, built-in racks of brilliant patterns and colors soon hurt her eyes. Damn. She should have lit a cigarette before coming in here. She should have finished the champagne, too. A maintenance drink never hurt.

Out in the bedroom, the intercom clicked on and she could hear the butler's voice. "Mrs. Winslow? Mrs. Winslow?"

Oh, damn! Now what?

Gloria stalked back out into the bedroom and hit the intercom button. "What is it, Roddy?" she snapped.

"Your mother-in-law is holding on line three."

Mother-in-law. The elder Mrs. Winslow. The Queen of Toad Hall.

Gloria sighed mightily. "Oh, all *right*," she grumbled truculently. "I'll take it."

Gloria clicked off, downed the rest of the champagne in one swallow, pressed extension three, and picked up the phone. She hoped the old bitch was calling to cancel. Now that would be welcome news.

"Hello? Mother Winslow?"

"I'm just leaving the house, Gloria." As always, her mother-in-law's voice was full of starch, vigor, and disapproval. "Are you dressed yet?"

"Of course I'm dressed," Gloria lied.

"Well, I hope you're wearing an American designer. You know the press will pick you to pieces if you don't."

"You didn't tell me this was going to be a press conference."

Althea Winslow's voice turned hard and cold. "It isn't. But you never know who we'll run into. It's important always to give the right impression. Must I continuously remind you that Hunt's political future is at stake?"

Gloria rolled her eyes. "No, Mother Winslow."

"You haven't begun drinking yet," the old lady asked suspiciously, "have you?"

Gloria felt the familiar surge of resentment. The old coot just couldn't leave it alone. She had to keep needling her.

"No, Mother Winslow. I skipped breakfast, and I can't take alcohol on an empty stomach."

"Good. Then we'll be able to enjoy a nice cocktail each."

Jesus H. Christ! Gloria stifled the urge to burst into peals of wild laughter. *A nice cocktail each!*

Would the old bitch never get it? Just *seeing* her was reason enough to get smashed beforehand. In fact, it was essential—like getting inoculated before traveling to Africa or the Amazon.

No way was she going to face that old dragon sober. It was bad enough doing it wrecked.

"I'll see you at the restaurant, Gloria. We'll have a nice lunch," her mother-in-law said crisply in parting, and rang off.

Gloria blinked. A nice lunch? Who was the old bat kidding?

Slamming down the phone, she decided to inaugurate her new Chanel suit just for spite. The lavender one with the baby blue trim and micro-mini. No blouse.

That'll teach her to tell me what to wear!

Suddenly Gloria felt the overpowering craving for a drink. And not champagne, either. A real drink. Something with a bite. Something, say . . . eighty proof.

Yes. Eighty proof would do nicely.

Why was it that talking to Althea always had that effect on her? No matter how high she might be, the Queen of Toad Hall inevitably brought her crashing back down.

Well, no matter. Mrs. Gloria Winslow was nothing if not prepared.

Vodka. She had pint bottles stashed in the pockets of all her fur coats—as well as in a dozen other hidey holes.

Vodka. It was just what the doctor ordered to see her through the ordeal ahead.

Humming to herself, Gloria went back into the walk-in closet, grabbed the Chanel suit by the hanger, and tossed it onto the big center island, under which Lucite-fronted drawers were filled with no end of accessories; scarves, gloves, belts, hair bows, sunglasses. All carefully folded or rolled and systematically lined in neat rows by category, color, and designer.

But orderliness was not on Gloria's mind as she made a beeline for the ranks of fur coats and her objective, the first flask-shaped bottle of Smirnoff she came across. With shaking fingers, she unscrewed the cap and hoisted the bottle in a sardonic toast.

"Here's to you, Althea, you old bitch!" she mumbled. Then she put the bottle to her lips, threw back her head, and drained a third of it in a single long swig.

It burned its way down her throat and exploded in her stomach. She screwed up her face in revulsion and nearly gagged; involuntary shudders racked her body and she doubled over, hugging herself tightly. Then the sick, queasy feeling passed. A radiant warmth rushed through her bloodstream and the sun came out and shone brightly.

All her cares had evaporated.

Suddenly everything was right with the world.

Ahhh! She set the bottle down with a bang and beamed. *There. That's a helluva lot better, isn't it? Goddamn right!*

She'd be able to face Althea without difficulty. Hell, she'd be able to endure an atomic blast and feel absolutely no pain.

As she unbuttoned her blouse, she caught sight of her reflection in one of the six-foot-tall mirrors. Still fiddling with the tiny gold buttons, she found herself drawn toward it.

She shrugged herself out of the blouse and let it drop to the carpet. Ditto her brassiere.

Clad only in panties, she studied her body.

All things considered, not bad for a thirty-five-year-old, she decided, luxuriating in the pleasure of her reflection. *No, not bad at all . . .*

Gloria Winslow had the long-waisted, bone-thin figure of a model. Gravity had yet to take its toll. There wasn't an ounce of excess fat on her lean hips or smallish but well-shaped breasts. Her belly was concave, her buttocks firm.

She leaned in close to peruse her face. She was strikingly beautiful, with shiny shoulder-length hair the color of moon-licked mink, and eyes the precise shade of Ceylonese sapphires. Her skin was still smooth, without a crow's foot in sight.

Little things like that made all the difference.

Gloria nodded to herself. Turned her head this way and that. Said aloud, "Hey, beautiful."

Unfortunately, Gloria also noticed that she'd have to start taking better care of herself. Her eyes were beginning to look just the teensiest bit puffy from drinking. But Visine had cleared up the rheumy redness, while ten uninterrupted hours of sleep had gotten rid of the hollows beneath.

Overall, she knew she still had the stuff that made heads swivel. And as long as they swiveled, she was far from over the hill.

Yup. She not only looked good—she looked *damn good.* And, if men's eyes were any indication, the opposite sex found her exceedingly attractive—even if Hunt didn't.

The bastard.

She thought of him now as she got dressed. Huntington Netherland Winslow III. Mr. Charisma. Mr. Shit. The hottest new star in the political firmament, if you believed the news media.

How the public loved him.

And God, how she loathed him! She was sick and tired of playing the part of the adoring wife. She was sick and tired of his do-gooder attitude. She was sick and tired of his trying to get her to some alcohol rehab place. Sick and tired of his going to AlAnon and trying to get her to go to A.A. She wanted out of the marriage so badly she could taste it.

Sad to say, divorce was not in the cards. When she'd first broached the subject, all hell had broken loose.

Gloria tried to ward off the memory, but she was already spinning two years backward through time, to Althea's formal French drawing room in the greystone mansion at the top of Nob Hill . . . to the day she discovered her marriage to be little more than a gilded prison . . .

* * *

"Mrs. Althea is waiting for you, madam," the butler told Gloria as he held open the door of Althea's drawing room.

"Thank you, Colin," she said, and stepped inside.

Northern light and undiluted sunshine, intensified by being refracted from San Francisco Bay, streamed through the tall windows, conspiring to give the richly paneled room a crisp-edged, Scandinavian kind of clarity. The eggshell blue of the elaborately carved paneling glowed, and the parquet floor shone like the surface of a frozen lake. Anchored in the middle of it, the big Savonnerie was like an island of color, and centered directly above it, the great thirty-light crystal chandelier sparkled like a stalactite of pure clear ice.

It was cold perfection, that twenty-foot-tall double cube of a room, an intimidating, grandiose museum of the very, very fine and the exceedingly rare. Everything—the Gobelins tapestries, the gilt bronze cartel clock over the marble mantel, the Louis XV bergères by Georges Jacob, upholstered in almond cut velvet; the marble-topped, giltwood console tables; the gargantuan pair of intricately carved, Dieppe ivory mirrors; the inlaid amaranth and satinwood tables and Riesener commodes; the priceless Renoir, Gauguins, and Van Goghs—all had been collected to create a setting worthy of Althea Magdalena Netherland Winslow.

She seemed so right seated there, enthroned like an empress on a Louis XV canapé, one hand stroking Violetta, her favorite Pekingese, which had pride of place on her lap. Two other ginger-colored, silken-haired Pekes, curled on the seat cushion on either side of her, raised their flat-faced heads and sniffed the air disdainfully before settling their chins back down onto their paws, ignoring Gloria as not worthy of a tail-wagging welcome.

"My dear child," Althea greeted smoothly, with barely subdued sarcasm. "I'm so glad you could come." She paused and inspected Gloria with an unsmiling, unblinking gaze. "Especially at such short notice."

Gloria dutifully bent down to kiss the proffered cheek. "Hello, Mother Winslow."

The unpleasant scrutiny continued a few seconds longer, then Althea gestured to the nearest fauteuil. "Do have a seat, my dear."

Gloria did as she as told. Whether she liked her mother-in-law or not, one couldn't help but admire her. Althea had to be in her sixties, but didn't look a day over fifty. Unlike her daughter-in-law, she had never been a beautiful woman.

Not that it mattered. Althea was regal and patrician and elegant, with good, clean bone structure, willful, intelligent eyes, and a presence that made her stand out in a crowd. Gloria had never seen her when she hadn't been groomed to perfection. From her sardine-silver helmet of a

meringue hairdo to the polished soles of her shoes, Althea May
Netherland Winslow was prepared for any eventuality.

"Would you like a cup of tea, dear?"

On the low table between them was a silver tray with all the accoutre-
ments: a flowered Meissen teapot with a cut-lemon finial and branch
handle, matching creamer, sugar bowl, a plate with lemon wedges individually wrapped in cheesecloth, and two cups and saucers. Plus the requisite monogrammed napkins and heirloom spoons.

Gloria shook her head. "No, but thanks all the same."

Althea nodded and poured herself a cup, used silver tongs to add a
lump of sugar, and squeezed a few drops from a cheesecloth-wrapped
wedge of lemon. She stirred it briskly, then lifted the cup delicately to her
lips and sipped. She put the cup down. "Hunt came by for lunch," she
began. Her voice was distinctly crisp, cultured, and disapproving.

"H-He said he would. . . ." Gloria murmured, unable to control her
stammer. Althea could do it every time. Reduce her to the nervous fiancée
again. All tensed and flustered and tongue-tied.

Althea continued to stroke Violetta, her eyes fixed on Gloria.

"Now, just what seems to be the problem, *dear*—"

Oh, but how those sarcastic "dears" and "my dears," and "my dear
childs" grated!

"—and don't tell me there aren't any. If there weren't, you wouldn't
have approached my son for a divorce."

My son. Not Hunt. Not your husband. *My* son.

"It's just . . ." Gloria started.

Althea cut in softly. "Let me guess. You've grown apart. Is that it?"

Gloria looked at her in surprise. "Why, yes! How did you . . ." Then
her surprise faded. "Oh. Hunt must have told you."

Althea snorted. "He did nothing of the sort. But then, he didn't have
to, my dear." She sat ramrod straight and tall—boarding school posture—and everything about her brought to mind a polished, razor-edged
sword.

"I realize that divorce has become epidemic these days," Althea went
on, "but when I was young, marriage vows stood for something. And you
know what? To me, they still do. Marriage is a sacred sacrament, forever
binding." She raised a hand, anticipating a response from Gloria, and
adroitly headed it off. "I know, I know. Call me terribly old-fashioned if
you will. Or incurably dated. However, that should come as no surprise.
You are well aware that divorce is unheard of in this family. Neither the
Netherlands nor the Winslows have ever stooped to marital breakups.
Oh, there has been discord here and there, true. But those problems have
always been settled within the family. We never aired our laundry in
public." *Nor, I assure you, my dear child, do I intend to permit it to happen
now!*

Gloria bit her lip and shifted uneasily in her chair.

"In fact, I distinctly recall discussing this very subject with you before I reluctantly gave you and Hunt my blessing. Remember? We sat right here . . . in this very room." Althea's cobalt eyes were cold and penetrating. "Surely you haven't forgotten that little talk?"

How could I? Gloria thought bitterly, but said: "No, Mother Winslow," and gave a weary sigh. "But don't you see? I was so young and naive then!" Suddenly impassioned, she sat forward, gripping the arms of her chair. "I couldn't possibly realize what I was getting myself into—"

"Which is precisely why we had that discussion—so you'd fully understand *beforehand* what to expect. Surely you don't think I talked just to hear myself speak?"

"No, but—" Gloria pleaded.

"And did I not tell you then that divorce would forever be out of the question?"

Gloria was silent.

"And did you not assure me that you were marrying for life? For richer and for poorer? For better and for worse?" Althea's cobalt eyes became piercing drillbits.

"But that was *then*, Mother Winslow! And this is *now*. . . ."

It was the tone that Althea seemed to have been waiting for, and she snapped: "Stop sniveling, and pull yourself together, child! You are exhausting my patience!"

So saying, she lifted Violetta from her lap and rose, setting the fluffy creature gently on the canapé before drifting toward the windows, where, outlined against the shimmering blue sky, she stopped briefly to admire the view framed by the bobble-fringed, blue brocade curtains. It was a favorite device of hers, this calculated habit of putting a conversation on hold, a way to flex the muscles of her authority by letting it be known that the panorama deserved at least as much attention as the subject at hand.

Granted, it was a spectacular view, what with the city rolling like great white swells over the dramatically shaded, plunging hills, the immense blue bay below daubed with tufts of whitecaps and regattas of triangular sails tacking into the wind.

With a sigh Althea turned away from the view, retraced her steps, and sat back down. "Now then," she began, pausing as Violetta hopped back onto her lap and made herself comfortable.

"Yes?" Gloria's eyes shone with fervent hope—hope that died the instant Althea resumed speaking.

"What you're asking, my dear, is out of the question. For better or for worse, Hunt is your husband." Anticipating an objection, she again waved a hand to forestall it. "I am not a prude, you know. Nor am I a fool who believes that any marriage is perfect. In short, I don't care what you do, or do not do . . . or with whom . . . behind closed doors. All I demand is that you and Hunt observe discretion and, whatever your arrangements, keep up appearances. If that means having affairs, fine. But in public, I expect you both to be the perfect couple. The very picture of propriety."

Arrangements . . . discretion . . . appearances . . . affairs . . .

Gloria stared at her mother-in-law. Her head was spinning with the implications of what had been said, and even more, with what had been left unsaid.

"I . . . I can't cheat on Hunt," she managed to say.

"How charming." Althea gave a brittle laugh. "My dear, you can do anything you like—so long as you and Hunt remain married. However, what I will *not* tolerate is so much as a whiff of scandal. Hunt has a brilliant career ahead of him, and anyone who tries to derail it will have to answer to me." She paused, drilling Gloria with eyes that would have cracked marble. "Do I make myself clear?"

"Perfectly. But wouldn't divorce be simpler and . . . well, *cleaner?*"

"It certainly would not! Voters put much stock in marital stability."

"But other politicians have gotten divorces," Gloria pointed out. "Look at Ronald Reagan and Jane Wyman! And Reagan made it to the White House."

Althea's expression was glacial. "I don't *care* if Reagan was divorced. That was long before he entered politics. Must I remind you, *dear*—"

There she went again, twisting the dagger deeper in the wound!

"—of the promise you made to me twelve years ago? That if you could marry Hunt you would always stick by him publicly . . . no . . . matter . . . what? Even if it meant keeping up appearances *for a lifetime?*"

Gloria sighed. "Yes, of course I remember," she said testily.

I should have known, she brooded. *Pleading for my freedom was hopeless, as I'd feared it would be. Althea wouldn't be swayed so long as she has one breath left. For her, the sun rises and sets on her son's political career; no doubt she believes all the planets in the solar system revolve around it, too.*

Hunt and his damn political future! Christ. If she heard about it one more time, she'd really let go and start screaming. She was sick and tired of hearing nothing but endless talk of Hunt and politics.

Althea reached for her teacup and lifted it to her lips. Then, glancing over the rim at Gloria, she feigned a look of surprise. "I said, that will be *all,* my dear," she emphasized, dismissing Gloria as coldly as she would a servant.

Gloria rose to her feet. For a moment she just stood there, girding her strength. Then, surprising even herself, she clenched her fists at her sides and blurted: "I have the right to sue for a divorce. You can't stop me, Mother Winslow! Nobody can! I have every right!"

"Why, of course you do, *dear*," Althea said, laying on the honey. She smiled, but her eyes were frighteningly icy. "But do bear in mind the prenuptial agreement you signed. I suggest you read it thoroughly. Or better yet, seek legal counsel before you come to any hasty decisions."

The air between them hummed and thrummed with bad vibrations.

After a moment Althea set down her teacup and rang for the butler. The door opened shortly.

"You rang, madam?"

"Yes, Colin," Althea said. "The other Mrs. Winslow was just leaving. Could you kindly show her out?"

"Of course, madam."

Gloria pulled herself together. "That won't be necessary," she said stiffly. "God knows, I've been here often enough."

She glanced at the butler and then back to Althea. Her eyes were bright and challenging.

"I'll find a way out," she said quietly, her voice heavy with menace.

Althea held her gaze. "You do that, dear."

But of course, Gloria never did. What chance did she have? That prenuptial agreement was almost as thick as the telephone directory, and as precise as a law volume.

The Winslow attorneys had been nothing if not thorough. They'd anticipated every eventuality. Even Raoul Mankiewicz, the big-gun L.A. divorce lawyer Gloria retained, couldn't find a single loophole.

What it boiled down to was that a divorce would buy Gloria her freedom—period.

Unfortunately, it wouldn't buy much else. Both the controlling interest in Winslow Communications, Inc., and the entire Winslow fortune, were owned outright by Althea.

As was everything else.

Nothing was in Hunt's name, not even the mansion in Pacific Heights. It too was Althea's—along with the furnishings, the paintings, and the cars.

Hunt's only real asset was his state senator's salary.

"I'm sorry," Raoul Mankiewicz informed her solemnly. "I call it as I see it."

The short, bald lawyer, all liver spots and big, black-rimmed spectacles and bespoke tailoring, was a sharp, stringy old bird.

She heaved a deep sigh, grateful that at least he didn't try to beat around the bush. "And there's no way around it?" she asked.

He shook his head. "Absolutely none. So long as your mother-in-law is alive, you'll get zilch."

"And when she dies?"

"Now you're talking a whole new ballgame. As an only child, your husband stands to inherit the entire kit and caboodle. You ask me, *that's* the time for you to sue; then your chances of breaking the prenup in a court of law and getting a handsome settlement are anywhere from fair to good."

Gloria brooded in silence. Hoping for Althea to drop dead was a lost cause. She thought, *That old dragon will outlive us all. Just for spite.*

"However," he said, "I did find two rather . . . ah . . . most illuminating points in the prenuptial agreement. Both of which are, happily, very much in your favor."

"Oh?" Gloria's ears perked up and she sat a little straighter. "And what might those be, Mr. Mankiewicz?"

"First, should your husband demand a divorce, you're entitled to an unspecified financial settlement. One mutually agreed upon by the Winslow attorneys *and* counsel of your own choosing."

"In other words . . ."

He half smiled. "That's right. If your husband instigates the proceedings, and his mother wants him to get the divorce badly enough, you've got them by the *beytzim*."

"Mmm . . ." Gloria murmured, "that does put a different spin on things . . ."

She stared unseeingly past him, out the wall of windows, at the smoggy world beyond. After a moment, she drew her eyes back in.

"You said there were two things, Mr. Mankiewicz," she said softly.

"That I did." He folded his liver-spotted hands on the mirrorlike surface of the *bureau plat* and leaned forward. "As you know, your husband is an only child; thus, your mother-in-law has only one direct heir. Apparently, she seems obsessed on keeping Winslow Communications intact after her death. So obsessed, in fact, that should your husband predecease you, the sole beneficiary changes."

"Of course it would," she said irritably. "Dead men can't inherit. Even I know that." Then she frowned. "But who would she choose?"

He answered her question with a question: "Who do you think, Mrs. Winslow?"

She shrugged. "Beats me."

His voice was hushed. "Would you believe—*you?*"

She stared at him. *Me?* she mouthed silently, pointing at herself in disbelief.

He chuckled. "And your mother-in-law is worth in excess of two billion dollars."

"Two *billion!*" Gloria stared at him. "So much!"

He was silent.

"I knew she was wealthy, but . . . *that* wealthy? I had no idea."

He held her gaze. "Well? Do you still wish to file for divorce?"

Gloria rose from her seat. "I'll have to think this over very carefully; I see that now," she said. "Good-bye, Mr. Mankiewicz. I can't thank you enough. You've put a whole new perspective on things."

As the elevator door slid shut, Gloria's gray cells were spinning. Not that any thinking was called for.

Her mind was already made up. She'd decided to stick it out with Hunt—no matter what.

Why try for a mere settlement when she could have the whole she-bang? The two-billion-dollar jackpot that was Winslow Communications?

Why indeed.

So she would have to contend with Hunt and Althea on a daily basis. So what? All it meant was finding a means of escape.

Thus it began. The magic combo of vodka, Percodan, and Xanax. They provided just what she needed.

Booze and pills. She'd been on them for two years now.

They made life bearable. They fuzzed the hard edges and killed the pain.

As she finished dressing, Gloria heard the intercom in the bedroom click back on. "Mrs. Winslow," her butler's disembodied voice announced, "your car is waiting."

Quickly Gloria popped some Percodan and Xanax and washed them down with a last slug of vodka. Then she stuck an emergency flask in her purse, popped a breath mint in her mouth, and sallied forth.

Lunch with Althea. She wondered what the old buzzard wanted this time.

Not that it mattered. She'd simply do what she'd done for the past two years. Tune her out.

10

Around the world, times and dates vary. Noon in California is four a.m. in southeastern China. But due to the international date line, in China it is also a day later; December 8 in San Francisco is December 9 in Shenzhen.

And it was on this date, and at that ungodly hour, that the six elders met again. They sat on folding chairs around a circular folding table, sipping tea in the dining room of an otherwise empty, newly completed house.

By Western standards, it was a modest suburban split-level. But here, in the booming, sky's-the-limit, free economic zone of Shenzhen—gateway to the world's fastest-growing economy and single largest consumer market, where millionaires made their fortunes overnight—such a house carried much "face," as well as a hefty price tag.

Half a million dollars.

No matter. Demand far outstripped supply, and the entire development had been snapped up by eager buyers before it was even off the drawing board.

Such is the boomtown mentality and buying frenzy that is Shenzhen.

Now, each elder's armed bodyguard kept vigil in the nighttime shadows outside. To avoid arousing the suspicion of security patrols, the various Mercedeses in which the elders had arrived were parked in the garages of neighboring houses.

They had chosen to meet here expressly because the development was still uninhabited. No prying eyes could observe their furtive arrivals and departures. No alert ears could overhear their discussion.

Honorable Horse spoke English. "Your tea has the fragrance of a most delicate garden, Honorable Snake," he said graciously as he put down his tiny china cup.

The government minister from Beijing gestured negligibly. "A mere hasty effort undeserving of praise," he replied humbly, also in English. "A thousand pardons that I could not tempt the palates of such illustrious company more worthily."

Honorable Horse nodded approvingly. "And I beg a thousand pardons for the temerity of calling this meeting so hastily." Now that they had refreshed themselves, it was time for serious business to commence. "Honorable Ox brings news of our endeavor. We must decide upon how to proceed."

The five of them looked at the wispy-bearded *lung tao* from Hong Kong, who inclined his head courteously. "The gods of fortune attend us," he said softly. "The woman's husband was on board an airplane that has crashed."

"Bad joss," Honorable Dragon said automatically.

The others clucked their tongues and nodded in agreement, carefully hiding their smiles.

Honorable Ox continued. "It is believed that he is dead."

"Believed? Ayeeeeyah!" Honorable Tiger could not contain his shock. "Many pardons, but how in the name of the Heavenly Whore is 'believed' supposed to help us?"

"There was a blizzard at the time," Honorable Ox explained calmly. "The aircraft crashed high in the mountains of the state called Colorado. Search parties have been unable to go in quest of possible survivors. Until they find the crash site"—he shrugged—"it will be impossible to verify his death."

"Ah." Honorable Tiger felt himself relax. "And the motherless whore who arranged the poor fornicator's inauspicious flight?"

"He is a man known only as the Sicilian, but his talents appear to be formidable."

"No one has an inkling as to the Sicilian's identity?"

"None whatsoever." Honorable Ox hawked deeply, turned his head, and spat on the floor. "No pictures, nor even descriptions, of him exist. It is said his given name is Carmine, but that could easily be explained by his calling card."

"Eeeeeh!" Honorable Tiger was beside himself with excitement. "He leaves behind *clues?*"

The old *lung tao* nodded. "He drops a carmine-colored necktie at the scene of each assassination. Sometimes it was used to strangle his victim; more often he deliberately leaves it to taunt the authorities."

"Ayyeeyah!" Honorable Snake exclaimed breathlessly. "By all gods great and small! He truly farts in those turds' faces this way?"

Honorable Ox nodded. "He signs his work as proudly as any artist signs a masterpiece."

"Carmine . . . the Sicilian . . ." murmured Honorable Rooster. "I beg for your indulgence, Illustrious Elder, but if he is so formidable, why is it we have never heard of him, *heya*?"

The old *lung tao* grunted. "Do you not see? That is his greatest strength! It gives him the ability to move about like a specter. Besides, you know the authorities. I'll bet those eaters of turtle shit are afraid to lend him credence, for fear of appearing outwitted. Also, they must be keeping the matter of the neckties from the public as a means to ferret out false informers."

"Then he does have credentials?" asked Honorable Dragon.

"Indeed he does." Honorable Ox permitted himself a modest little smile. "If what is whispered is only half true, his assassinations are legion. The head of the Bundesbank in Germany, the closest advisers of Yassir Arafat, the heads of international corporations on behalf of business rivals. All these can be laid at his door. So long as he is paid in advance, there is no one he will not eliminate."

"His services must be expensive," mused Honorable Snake.

"Three million dollars U.S. per contract. However, for guaranteed results I do not find that unreasonable."

The barrage of questions continued.

Honorable Rooster: "But there is no way the barbarian's handiwork can be traced back to us?"

"Absolutely none. Sonny Fong, my wife's fifth cousin twice removed, lives in New York. It is he who recruited the third party, through whom we contacted the Sicilian this last time."

Honorable Dragon: "Then now is the time to strike? While this airplane crash is fresh, and the woman is at her most vulnerable?"

"No," Honorable Ox said softly.

The others turned to him. As the eldest, he was deemed the wisest, and was thus the most worthy of their respect.

"From where comes this need for such haste?" He lifted a hand, the pinkie and forefinger raised in caution. "Think of the master carver who has in his possession a piece of the rarest, finest white jade. If he is a wise man, does he rush to fetch his tools and begin to carve?"

He shook his head.

"No. He understands that a priceless stone demands exacting study and forethought. Undue haste has turned many a masterpiece into worthless trinkets peddled to the devil-borne tourists."

"Illustrious Ox speaks most wisely," Honorable Dragon agreed. "Men of wisdom put thought before action."

The old Chiuchow inclined his head graciously, adding, "We must never forget what Confucius once said: 'The cautious seldom err.' So too must we wait for the most auspicious moment. Before we put forth an offer, the fornicating whore must first sample a taste of our thunder."

"But how, Esteemed Elder?" Honorable Snake inquired. "Hers is a private corporation. There is no public stock that can be manipulated."

The old *lung tao* sipped his jasmine tea delicately. "Ah, but think of a duck and its many uses, Honorable Snake."

"*Ayeeyah!* What do you mean, think of a duck, *heya*? What use does it have other than to be cooked and eaten?"

"True. But in the hands of a skilled cook it may be prepared a multitude of ways, can it not? Imagine the hundreds of succulent dishes that can be made from a mere lowly duck."

"Of course! There is no single way to cook it!" Honorable Snake clapped his hands, then bowed his head humbly. "A thousand pardons for my ignorance, Illustrious Ox. Your mind truly has the cunning of a fox."

"I am honored by your graciousness, but unworthy of such praise. A mighty tree relies upon an abundance of strong roots."

They all knew what he meant. United, their strength had multiplied geometrically; divided, each individual's power would diminish accordingly.

The old *lung tao* looked around the table. "Is there one amongst us who could have purchased the Pan Pacific Commonwealth Bank on his own?"

"Your words have the brightness of a thousand suns," said Honorable Snake, the government minister from Beijing. "There is strength to be found in numbers."

The old Chiuchow stroked his wispy beard. "As one of Asia's most respected and venerable institutions," he continued, "Pan Pacific is our greatest asset as well as our most potent weapon. It alone made it possible for us to acquire eight percent of the voting stock in AmeriBank."

"The gods of fortune have indeed attended us," murmured Honorable Rooster, the Thai chemist who processed raw opium into heroin.

Honorable Ox nodded. "And may they continue to do so." Again, he took a delicate sip of tea. "As you know, the woman who stands in our way has suffered much bad joss. Her efforts at rapid expansion in the late eighties have led to what the Westerners call being overleveraged."

"A fancy euphemism for incurring debts!" snorted Honorable Dragon, whose underground banking system was the largest in the Golden Triangle. "Fornicate all euphemisms! Why the round eyes cannot call a debt a debt surely baffles the most patient of the gods!"

The old *lung tao* permitted himself a rare smile. "Aside from the mealy-mouthed whore's debts, she has yet to recover from the so-called

Black Friday in the Year of the Ox. Twice already AmeriBank has had to reschedule her loans."

"*Ayeeyah!*" Honorable Snake reached for the pot and poured more tea for his guests. "Then she is like a tree full of fruit, ripe and ready to be plucked!"

"Riper and readier than you think!"

"Eh?" Honorable Snake stopped pouring and blinked.

"I am pleased to announce that as of yesterday, Pan Pacific's negotiations to purchase her outstanding loans from AmeriBank have been finalized. The notes and their collateral now belong to us. Although she has yet to realize it, the foreign devil is already in our power."

"Eeee, then the Golden Country dogmeat is already trapped!" exclaimed Honorable Tiger.

"Like a fish in a floating basket," Honorable Ox cackled, "still in its water, swimming happily, and unaware of the fire heating the wok, *heya!*"

"Best of all," the old *lung tao* announced quietly, "only recently she added two hundred and fifty million dollars to her debt. Incurred by trying to turn a pile of dung in the sea into a resort."

"Interesting," Honorable Dragon observed. "When are her next notes due?"

"In less than five cycles of the moon. Fifty million dollars on the fifteenth of May." The old *lung tao* smiled coldly. "This time her request for an extension shall be turned down."

"And we shall seize her collateral!" marveled Honorable Snake. "*Ayeeyah*, the gods have bestowed a thousand summers upon us!" He bowed respectfully to the old *lung tao*. "I was wrong, Esteemed Elder. You not only have the cunning of a fox, but the accumulated wisdom of your honorable ancestors."

The old *lung tao* made a casual gesture. "If so, it is only because when I move among the foreign devils, I keep my eyes and ears open and my mouth firmly shut."

"Is it true," asked Honorable Tiger, the Laotian general who protected the rich poppy fields of his country, "that the men of the wide eyes are worse chatterboxes than a brothel full of harlots?"

"Yes, far worse. Which reminds me; I have been as stupid as a water buffalo treading in its own dung. . . ." Honorable Ox's voice trailed off. Then he was silent, staring past the men seated directly across from him. It was a far-seeing stare, and the others knew he was not looking at the wall or the covered windows, but past them, into some distant realm only he could see.

"What is it, Illustrious Elder?" inquired Honorable Rooster with agitation.

"Yes, honor us with your esteemed wisdom," urged Honorable Dragon, sitting stiffly immobile and attentive.

The old *lung tao* sighed and drew his eyes back in. He took a sip of tea from his refilled, lotus-shaped cup and set it carefully back down. His deceptively gentle, dried-apple face was knit with unease.

"My gravest concern," he said slowly, "is the involvement of the third party, for which I am to blame, may all gods protect me from my own stupidity!"

"How so?" asked Honorable Rooster, ever the alarmist.

"If the Sicilian deserves the esteem in which he is held, then he is a strong link in the chain that stretches between him and ourselves, *heya?*"

The others listened intently and glanced uneasily at one another.

"But this third party through whom my wife's fifth cousin twice removed passes along all communication. I asked myself, Who *is* this barbarian intermediary? More to the point, what do we *know* of him?"

Honorable Tiger said, "You told us he is nothing. A mere greedy, expendable barbarian with a weakness for games of chance. That Sonny Fong recruited him specifically to exploit this weakness, since he could not settle his debts."

Honorable Ox grunted. "The barbarian owed large sums to the long-nosed Sicilians, as well as to our own people in Chinatown. Since Sonny Fong paid those debts, and therefore holds the man's markers, I was certain he could easily be controlled."

He looked around at the inscrutable faces, expecting reproval, but none was forthcoming.

The old *lung tao* sipped some more tea. "According to Sonny Fong, the *kwai lo* has not only made the connection between Carmine and the airplane crash, but is actually demanding an increase in pay!"

"Ayeeyah!" Honorable Horse stared at him. "May the blackmailing thief's secret sack rot and shrivel and fall off!"

"And mine also!" the *lung tao* spat angrily. "I believed he was as clay in our hands, forgetting the intrinsic properties of that substance!"

"But how so?" inquired Honorable Snake. "Clay can, after all, be molded and shaped and formed by one's own hand—"

"*Fang-pi!*" the old man swore, his flinty eyes narrowing. "You see? You have fallen into the self-same dung-filled trap! By all gods great and small, clay *breaks!*"

To demonstrate, he turned sideways in his chair, held out the lotus cup from which he had been sipping, and deliberately let it drop.

It hit the floor with a thud and shattered into pieces.

A pallor spread across Honorable Snake's face. "A thousand pardons," he said softly, bowing his head and casting his eyes downward in shame. "I was speaking of raw clay. Before it is glazed and fired."

The *lung tao* nodded. "And so did I think, forgetting that eventually all clay must be fired—and that many pieces survive not even the furnace!"

His voice was soft, but his eyes were steely and unforgiving as he looked around the table at the others.

"Then which path do you suggest we take?" inquired Honorable Snake.

The old *lung tao* steepled fingers as gnarled as ginseng roots. "The only possible path," he said.

"Prune the deadwood, clear the creepers, and watch our tree bloom!" Honorable Snake chortled, his narrowed eyes gleaming. "Bury the *kwai lo* like stinking manure! Then use your wife's fifth cousin twice removed to contact the Sicilian, *heya*?"

"Exactly." Honorable Ox bowed his head, then looked up, his face proud. "Sonny Fong is a most ambitious, clever, and enterprising young man. Unbeknownst to the gambler, he has doggedly followed his every step like a shadow."

"Eh? Then he could easily pass a message directly to the Sicilian!"

"Not directly . . . nor indirectly either." Seeing their perplexed frowns, the old *lung tao* explained: "Arranging it seems to require the intercession of a woman known as Mama Rosa. She is said to be the Sicilian's mother, although that might well be speculation."

"But contacting her. That should not prove difficult?"

"No, not so long as she is willing. She owns a restaurant named after her in Little Italy. I will tell my wife's fifth cousin twice removed to accomplish this most speedily."

"Thereby bypassing the diseased *kwai lo*, making him redundant, and severing the fornicating dog's head and silencing him for eternity!" Honorable Snake nodded with satisfaction.

"I agree," the old *lung tao* said. "Only by so doing can we achieve harmony, not look over our shoulders, and ensure continued good fortune."

He glanced around. "The time is come. Let us cast our votes. Those in favor of eliminating the *kwai lo*, use the chop depicting the bird. Those opposed, use the fish."

As at their previous meeting, all six of them opened their small teak boxes, selected the appropriate chop, and marked their choices on tiny squares of rice paper. After folding them in half, they ceremoniously dropped them, one by one, into the famille rose bowl in the center of the table.

"It is done," said Honorable Snake.

"The die is cast," added the old *lung tao*. "Honorable Horse, would you graciously do the honors?"

"With pleasure." The Burmese, who controlled the major poppy fields of his country, carefully picked up the bowl and upended it, then slowly unfolded the six tiny slips of paper.

The others leaned across the table and eyed them with curiosity.

"Six birds denoting yes," said Honorable Ox dryly. "The majority has spoken," he announced. "Sonny Fong shall receive his instructions, and through him, hopefully, so shall the Sicilian. Meanwhile, we will wait to deal with the woman until her husband's death is confirmed. Are there any other questions?"

There were none.

"Good. As in the past, we shall depart at intervals of ten minutes. Honorable Snake, as our gracious host you shall be the last to leave. Please ensure that all evidence of our meeting is destroyed."

"Consider it done."

Honorable Ox rose painfully to his feet, and the others followed suit. They all bowed formally to one another.

"May the gods of fortune attend you," each told the others in parting.

The meeting was over.

Twenty minutes after Honorable Snake departed, an explosion rocked the empty house. The flash fire that followed gutted it completely.

That it was due to an explosive device, and not a faulty gas line, was never established. The traditional payoff forestalled any investigation.

11

" ❝ *hild!* I am *excited.* This girl brings you *good* news! Things are *happening.*"

Thus spoke Venetia as she strode, all six feet of her, into the hospital room like a commanding general. Her open, floor-length, rubberized khaki duster swirled about her like Rommel's greatcoat, though no commanding general in military history—not Ike, Pershing, Patton, nor the previously mentioned Rommel—had ever worn a coat with quite such authoritative élan or inimitable, fashion-runway flair.

At Venetia's entrance, Dorothy-Anne instantly sat up straight—too straight and too quickly, judging from the grimace of pain that shot across her face—and that Dr. Burt Chalfin, standing at the foot of her bed, chart in hand, eyed with more than a little concern.

Not that Dorothy-Anne noticed. Her attention was riveted on Venetia. Had she heard correctly? Or were her ears playing tricks on her?

Venetia gyrated out of her duster. "The search parties left at the crack of dawn. Did you hear me, child?" Her husky contralto filled the room. "*Honey!* This is what we have been *waiting* for. This is serious keep-our-fingers-*crossed* time!"

Search parties?

Dorothy-Anne stared at her blankly for a moment. Then the news registered.

Heaving a sigh of relief, she let her head sink back on the pillows. "Thank God!" she whispered. "Let's just pray that it's—not too late. . . ."

"No, no, no!" Venetia scolded, wagging an admonishing finger, her multiple bracelets clunking softly. "Sugar, I will *not* have you thinking negative thoughts. No. Just remember what *this* girl always says. . . ."

She draped her duster over the back of the visitor's chair and took a seat, clad this morning in loose, free-flowing pineapple-fiber trousers, and worn with a sand-colored, crinkle-pleated blouse and a brown leather, alligator-embossed corset belt.

" 'It's not over until it's over.' You *know* that's always been *my* motto, honey. And right now it had better be yours, too. Don't you go jumping to any conclusions. I will not tolerate that kind of thinking, child. It is counterproductive."

Ashamed of her pessimistic thoughts, Dorothy-Anne dropped her gaze. From out in the hall, she could hear sounds: a gurney rolling rapidly past, followed by the hurried squeaks of rubber-soled shoes; the murmur of hushed voices; a distant cry of pain. Finally she looked back up.

"You're right," she said quietly. "I've been wallowing in self-pity."

"Well, now's the time to stop. Because, *child,* we have got to keep the *faith.* We have got to think *positive.*"

"I've been trying," Dorothy-Anne sighed. "God knows, I really have—"

"Course you have, sugar. And you've been hit with three major whammies. I know that, too."

Venetia rose and bent over the bed and hugged Dorothy-Anne, who instinctively moved into the embrace.

"There, there," Venetia said softly. She patted Dorothy-Anne's back, kissed her forehead, made maternal little noises.

"I'm just . . . so *scared,*" Dorothy-Anne whispered into Venetia's shoulder. "I-I'm afraid to get my hopes up! It's such an enormous search area . . . and with all the snow that's fallen—feet of it, Venetia, *feet!*"

"Girl! *Will* you stop?" Venetia gave her an affectionate little shake. "Obviously, you don't realize the scope of the rescue mission that's been mounted."

Dorothy-Anne shook her head. "Nooooo . . ."

"Which means you haven't been following the news." Venetia nodded in the direction of the wall-mounted television.

"God, no!" Dorothy-Anne shuddered. "I-I can't bring myself to watch in case—" Aghast at her own words, she raised a hand to her mouth.

"Forget that for now." Venetia pulled away, took her seat, and crossed one leg over the other. "Because girl, didn't I tell you things are in the *works?* Yes, child. They have pulled out all the stops. They have gone that extra mile *and then some.*" She sat there, swinging her leg back and forth, smiling like the Cheshire cat.

"What do you mean?"

Venetia grinned. "I gather you remember State Senator Hunt Winslow?"

Dorothy-Anne smiled. "How can I forget?"

"Well, you owe him," Venetia said. "Big. He's apparently called in a debt from his counterpart in Colorado, who in turn called a senator who owed *him* a favor, who—anyway, to cut a long story short, it is like D-Day in the Rockies. Girl, I am *serious.* They have squadrons of planes—a veritable air force—flying grid-pattern searches *right as we speak*! Plus, there are armies of searchers—mountaineers, paratroopers, volunteers, specially trained dogs, you name it. That's right, sugar. They've even called out the National Guard."

"Good Lord." Dorothy-Anne could feel her pulse quickening. "I-I had no idea!"

Venetia grinned. "Believe it. Girl, when I say you've got friends in high places, I mean they're in *mighty* high places!"

Dorothy-Anne's pale, lackluster features underwent a rapid transformation. One moment, she was lethargic and dispirited; the next, her face literally came alive. She positively glowed with color and vitality, and the sharp, determinedly mischievous glint was back in her eyes.

She forced herself to draw several deep, sobering breaths to calm herself. In the light of Venetia's revelations, it was easy to get carried away, difficult to remain cool, collected, and level-headed.

Confronting adversity, she would—*must!*—show strength and backbone. Become a shining example—for herself, yes. But especially for the children.

Above all, for them.

Slowly, stiffly, she drew herself up in bed. Armed with the lantern of hope, she was ready to take on whatever the future held in store. Come what may, she would confront it boldly.

But she needed to *be* there. Not to participate in the search itself; that was medically out of the question. But so long as she could wait in the general vicinity, she would feel a lot better. . . .

She must sign herself out. Gather up the brood—fly to Colorado.

The piano tinkles from the lounge filtered into the dining room of the Act IV restaurant of the Inn at the Opera, rippling a delicate étude through the civilized lunchtime hush.

Gloria and Althea had a corner table, where they sat at right angles, looking out at the intimate dining room with its white-clothed tables, Belgian-tapestried walls, gleaming woodwork, and mirrors in ornately carved wood frames. Gloria watched her mother-in-law spear a ladylike morsel of tuna with her fork.

Althea ate in the European manner, fork in her left hand, knife in the right. She used the blade to push a tiny dab of fried leeks with pink peppercorns and capers atop the tuna.

"My dear child," she observed crisply, gesturing with her knife. "You are not eating."

"I'm suddenly not hungry." Gloria placed her knife and fork in an *X* across her untouched plate, signifying that she was finished.

The waiter instantly hurried over. "Something is not to madame's satisfaction?" he inquired, with much wringing of hands. "Madame would perhaps like to change her order?"

"Madame certainly would not!" Gloria retorted snappishly.

"My daughter-in-law has digestive problems," Althea said smoothly. "As for the food, it's superb as always. My compliments to the chef."

"Madame is too kind."

Relieved, the waiter scurried off with Gloria's plate.

"Now, why did you have to tell him that?" Gloria groused belligerently.

Althea swallowed her morsel of tuna. When she spoke, her voice was

90

frosty. "Must you be so contrary, my dear? Really, such behavior does get to be a trifle boring."

"And here I was, trying to liven up the joint. See if I could maybe wake up some of these stiffs. Oh, well."

Gloria opened her purse just far enough to reach inside for her cigarette case and lighter without her mother-in-law catching sight of her flask. Putting the purse down, she unsnapped the brushed gold case and selected a cigarette.

"Put that away," Althea said quietly. "You know very well that this is a no-smoking area."

Gloria clicked the case shut but kept the cigarette out and tapped it against the brushed gold.

"So?" She shrugged. "Why should I care?"

She started to stick the cigarette between her lips, but she wasn't quite fast enough.

Quick as a flash, Althea laid down her cutlery and caught Gloria around the wrist. Old lady or no, she had the grip of a smithy. She pulled Gloria's hand down off the table and out of sight.

Gloria twisted her wrist to free it, but Althea's hold was like a vise.

Gloria's eyes widened with a kind of surprise. To all outward appearances, Althea seemed remarkably composed. She sat erect and tall, nothing in her carriage or expression hinting at the struggle taking place. But then, she'd had a lifetime's experience having the upper hand, this mother-in-law of hers.

"Now I suggest you listen, and listen well." Althea turned her voice up a setting colder, a setting clearer. "I'm finding these drunken episodes of yours increasingly tiresome."

Gloria gave a theatrical sigh. "Here comes the lecture."

"I'm afraid so, my dear. My only regret is that I've obviously waited too long."

"So that's what this lunch is all about. I should have guessed."

Althea's fingers tightened. "Now are you, or are you not, going to put that cigarette away?"

Gloria glared at her.

Althea's thumb found the sensitive nerve on the inside of Gloria's wrist and applied pressure.

Gloria clenched her teeth. It was all she could do not to yelp aloud in pain.

The old lady waited.

Gloria stared at her with hate-filled eyes.

"Well?"

"Oh, all *right*," Gloria said truculently.

Althea waited a few beats, then let go.

Gloria massaged her wrist and scowled. Once she got the circulation going, she moodily stuck the cigarette back in the case and put it away.

Althea raised her chin. "That's better. Thank you, my dear." A curious kind of triumph shone in her eyes.

Gloria was seething. She restrained herself by taking deep breaths and mentally chanting the three-word mantra that had kept her going for the last couple of years. *Two billion dollars*, she reminded herself. *Two billion dollars.*

All she had to do was be patient and wait and it would be hers.

Two billion dollars . . .

Althea lifted her crystal wineglass and took a sip of Pinot Noir.

How like the old bitch, Gloria thought bitterly, eyeing her own glass of Calistoga water with disgust. *She would limit me to one drink. And then what does she go ahead and do? Guzzles away right in front of me!*

Althea put down the wineglass and resumed eating, fork in her left hand, knife in her right.

"Now then, my dear. It pains me to have to say this, but you've become the subject of quite a bit of gossip over the past several days."

"Only the past several days?" Gloria asked, unable to keep the sarcasm from surfacing.

Althea took her time chewing and swallowing. "Everywhere I go, I hear mention of it." Her eyes were like cobalt drill bits. "I am, to say the least, quite perturbed."

"I think you'll have to be a little more specific, Mother Winslow. I really have no idea what you're talking about!"

"Then let me refresh your memory. The grand-opening party of the San Francisco Palace." Althea paused. "It seems you made quite a spectacle of yourself that night."

Again Gloria could feel the outrage boiling up inside her. "You know what would be nice?" she said tightly.

Althea raised her eyebrows. "What, dear?"

"If people stopped trashing *me*."

"It's your behavior that's caused all this talk, my dear," Althea said calmly. "Not Hunt's."

"Hunt, Hunt, Hunt!" Gloria gloomed resentfully. "Christ. He's all you ever think about. Isn't that right, Mother Winslow? Nothing ever matters, except for the way it might affect Hunt?"

Althea was never one to beat around the bush. "That's right."

"And you'd forgive your precious son anything, wouldn't you?"

The old lady seemed surprised the question was even posed. "Why, yes," she said, "of course I would. I'm his mother. He's my son."

"And me? What does that make me, Mother Winslow? Or shouldn't I ask?"

"Of course you may ask." Althea's eyes were bright and steady. "You're my daughter-in-law. As Hunt's wife, it's up to you to complement your husband."

"Complement his image, you mean," Gloria said bitterly. "In other words, I'm window dressing. Let me guess where I stand. Somewhere below campaign buttons but above bunting?"

"Now you're being silly, dear," Althea said, taking another sip of wine.

When she put her glass down, the waiter materialized with the chilled, open bottle. With a practiced twist of his wrist, he topped off Althea's glass without spilling a drop.

Gloria eyed the bottle longingly. "I wouldn't mind trying a glass of that," she said.

The waiter glanced inquiringly at Althea, who dismissed him with: "Thank you. That will be all."

He left with the bottle.

Gloria could feel her face burning with humiliation and resentment.

No ice bucket for this table! she thought peevishly. *No ma'am! The old bat's got the staff trained to dive through flaming hoops—waiting to be thrown a fish for not serving the young Mrs. Winslow an alcoholic beverage, no doubt. ("She's a lush, you know. It's for her own good, the poor dear." Tsk, tsk.)*

Christ, how it galled! If the Queen of Toad Hall *really* cared, she'd have chosen a restaurant without a liquor license. But that would have been too easy.

Besides which, Gloria suspected, *the old biddy doesn't want me totally sober. Not really. She probably thinks I'm easier to control if she can dole out a drink every now and then—so long as it suits her purpose!*

Well, there was more than one way to skin *that* cat!

"If you'll excuse me, Mother Winslow," Gloria said, taking her purse and starting to get up, "I have to visit the powder room."

Althea's smile was frozen. "I really wouldn't go if I were you, my dear."

Gloria stared at her. "What are you talking about?"

"I am talking about—cleverness, guile, deceit." Althea made circular motions with her knife, as if casting a spell to make Gloria sit.

Gloria remained half standing. "I really don't know what you mean." She sniffed belligerently.

The old lady glanced up at her. "My dear child," she said calmly. "We both know exactly what I mean. You're pickled as it is—partly due to your previous two visits to the ladies' room, no doubt. You do realize that those breath mints of yours don't fool me for an instant?"

"Right." Gloria laughed humorlessly. "As if anyone in this restaurant would dare serve me a drink without your permission!"

Althea sighed. "I do wish you'd stop insulting my intelligence. Honestly, dear. You think I don't know about the spares you carry around with you?"

"Spares?" Gloria repeated defensively. "What kind of spares? I wish I knew what you're referring to."

"I am referring to hidden stashes. I am referring to a flask or a bottle or whatever it is you've got tucked in your purse or wherever."

Shit! Gloria thought. *The old bird would be on to me!*

She took a deep breath. Then slowly she sank back down in her chair, mentally reciting her mantra: *Two billion dollars.* Inhale. *Two billions dollars.* Exhale.

Althea was giving her a long, hard look. "You know, Gloria, I do so hate ultimatums. They can be so counterproductive. However, if you don't start toeing the line, well . . . you're not going to leave us much choice."

Gloria leaned across the table. "Yes, Mother Winslow?" she asked quietly. "What if I decide not to toe the line? What happens then? No, don't tell me. Let me guess. You'll call in Torquemada, and out come the thumb screws and electrodes. Isn't that right?"

"Really, my dear! You don't know what you are saying!"

"Ah, but I know what *you're* saying, Mother Winslow. You're threatening to have me committed again. And don't tell me I'm wrong."

Althea gave her narrow shoulders a delicate, ladylike shrug. "Let's just hope it doesn't have to come to that, shall we? It really is so unpleasant all around."

Unpleasant? Gloria could only blink in open-mouthed disbelief. *Jesus H. Christ!* she thought. *That's like calling the Great Pyramid of Giza a garden ornament!*

She was sure some piece of work, this mother-in-law of hers. Sitting there like a harmless, meringue-haired old lady in her good apricot wool suit and priceless real pearls, daintily picking at her lunch and taking little sips of wine while quietly dropping bombshells. Anyone looking at her could have sworn she was discussing the latest opera or ballet.

"For you information, Mother Winslow," Gloria said tightly, struggling to keep her anger in check and her voice calm, "last time they broke two of my ribs *and* my hip!"

The old lady's eyes never flinched. "Don't be absurd," she replied. "We both know what happened, my dear."

Gloria stared at her. "One of us certainly does!" she whispered hoarsely, her eyes beginning to fill with tears. "And pardon me for saying so, Mother Winslow, but I was fucking *there.*"

Althea ignored the blunt expletive. "Then surely you realize that despite your being strapped down, your injuries were a direct result of your going into convulsions during withdrawal."

She paused and flicked a hand, relegating the subject to ancient history.

"But let's do drop this dreary subject, shall we? Now that we each know where we stand, what do you say we order some coffee and dessert? They bake the most wonderful warm chocolate truffle torte to order."

"You go ahead," Gloria said dully. "I think I'll pass."

"But you haven't touched a bite!"

Gloria thought: *I'd sooner break bread with the devil.* She said, "If you'll excuse me, Mother Winslow, I've really got to be going. There are some things I have to think over."

"Yes, dear. I quite understand. Well, run along and think about what I've said." Althea held up her cheek for a kiss.

Gloria dutifully kissed it, thinking: *I wonder what a Judas kiss feels like?*

As she left the dining room, she was still taking deep, calming breaths. Trying to imagine how big a cube two billion dollars in hundred-dollar bills would make.

Two billion dollars, she kept telling herself, *two billion dollars . . .*

It was her mantra, her goal, her raison d'être.

And she wondered, as she so often did, whether it was worth the wait.

13

In Aspen, the winter season was already in full swing. Duvets of snow cloaked the ski slopes, the hotels were jam-packed, and the movie stars, the rich and famous, and the anonymous rich were in residence in their secluded log mansions. Nestled at the base of Aspen Mountain nearly eight thousand feet above sea level, and surrounded by four snow-clad peaks, the silver mining town turned Hollywood nirvana was a world-class winter resort, with chic boutiques, trendy restaurants, pedestrian malls, and a jumping, casual nightlife.

The chartered Gulfstream IV approached from the north, and its descent into the Roaring Fork valley was smooth. From the port side of the jet, Venetia, an avid skier who for the past ten years had spent at least one week each year on Aspen's slopes, pointed out the sights to the kids.

"That's the town of Aspen, and right behind it is Aspen Mountain. The locals call it Ajax, after an old miner's claim. Those are the Aspen Highlands . . . that's Buttermilk Mountain, which is the best place to learn to ski—"

"—and there's the airport where we're going to land!" Zack piped up excitedly.

"That's right, sugar. It's called Pitkin County Airport, but it's also known as Sardy Field. Oh, and over there, past it?" She tapped glossy apricot nails on the perspex. "That's Snowmass Village."

Zack exclaimed over the ant-sized skiers dotting the hundreds of trails far below, the chair lifts, which seemed to angle up every possible slope, and the snowmobiles, horse-drawn sleighs, and teams of dogsleds, all rendered minuscule by distance.

Dorothy-Anne, reclining on the starboard side, slid her window shade shut. The last thing she wanted to see was another mountain. *I need that like a hole in the head.*

The flight over Colorado's Northern Rockies had been a sobering experience. The thousands of square miles of snow-capped peaks, sawtooth ridges, vertical ravines, and precipitous canyons had hammered home the reality of just how treacherous a wilderness Freddie had disappeared into, how hostile an environment he faced.

Her brief burst of hope, rekindled earlier that morning, had waned. She wished now that she had remained in San Francisco, or that a sea of clouds could at least have masked the sheer vastness, the seeming endlessness of that wild chaos of range after range of jagged pikes, plunging drop-offs, corrugated slopes, and bottomless gorges.

I was foolish to think that his plane could have made a safe emergency landing. She knew now that even if it had, there were so many other variables to consider. The elements, for one. The days-long blizzard. The freezing cold. And that didn't take into account possible injuries, or lack of medical care. *How can anyone possibly have survived?*

Then the jet touched down, and the flurry of arrival provided a blessed distraction. Thanks to Venetia's gift for last-minute sorcery, everything proceeded like clockwork. Ground transportation awaited, as did a secluded log house situated on thirty-five acres high on a knoll west of the town.

Actually, "house" didn't begin to describe it. It was a lodge, a giant, modern, post-and-beam basilica built on several levels, with soaring cathedral ceilings, huge cedar beams continuing inside, and massive granite fireplaces. Entry was through an airlock to conserve energy, and the Great Hall had a thirty-foot-high wall of fenestration with commanding views of the entire Roaring Fork valley, from the spot where it began as a narrow ravine near Rifle, all the way over to its broad base below the 12,095-foot-high summit of Independence Pass.

"Cool," Fred commented, once they were inside. "Far out."

Zack yanked on Nanny Florrie's hand and let out a whoop. "Wow!" he cried excitedly, eyes wide and aglow with wonder. "This is *neat!*"

Nanny Florrie took one look around the Great Hall with its various granite levels, conversation pits, and banisterless wood staircases at either end—one leading up to a balcony where the master loft floated like a bridge, the other to five guest bedrooms—and saw skinned knees, scraped elbows, and fractured bones.

She tightened her grip on Zack's hand. "For Gude's sake!" she gasped in horror. " 'Tis nae hoose! 'Tis daft!"

"Is not!" Zack said indignantly. "It's like a fort! Or a treehouse!"

"Is it now? Weel, there's gang be nae climbin' or runnin' wild in 'ere, laddie, or ye'll hear frae me. Aye."

And scowling, Nanny Florrie lowered her brow at what she considered an architectural monstrosity.

" 'Tis nae place fer bairns," she added darkly. " 'Tis an accident waitin' to haepin. Aye. Ye mark my words."

Liz, standing with her head tipped back, was staring up at the underside of the mammoth chandelier hanging directly above her, one of three contrived of countless caribou antlers, each fixture some ten feet in height. After a moment she glanced at Venetia.

"We're in like a really weird house, y'know? Take those lights up there—those *lights*. I mean, I ask you? They're like totally yuckoid. How'd you ever find *this* place?"

Venetia, sunglasses perched atop her head like a tiara, paused in the midst of unbuttoning the frog closures of her Afghan kilim coat. "In case you're unaware of it, there's no Hale Hotel in this town. The ones there are—and believe me, there are plenty—are booked solid. That's right, child. There's no room at the inn. None. And you want to know why? Let me give you a clue."

Venetia pointed at the towering glass wall and the amazing snowscape beyond.

"You recognize all that white stuff out there?"

Liz rolled her eyes. "Gimme a break, Venetia, would ya? Like, this isn't the *first* time I've ever seen snow. *Okay?*"

"The point I'm simply making is this: the winter season's already begun. Try finding a house—any available rental—within twenty miles of here. Believe me, you can't. But try coming up with one with only a couple of hours' notice."

All right, all right! Liz thought feistily, impatiently shifting her weight from one foot to the other.

"The only reason we lucked into this place," Venetia explained, "is because the owner's a close friend who's in Jamaica shooting a music video. Which reminds me . . ."

She turned to include Fred and Zack in the conversation.

"Okay, listen up, gang. I'm going to have to establish a few ground rules."

Liz and Fred groaned and Zack made vomiting noises, but Venetia ignored them.

"First, your mama just got out of the hospital. She needs peace and quiet to recuperate. Also, I don't need to remind you that your daddy's still missing. Out of respect for him, try to keep it toned down. Okay?"

Sobered, their three small heads bobbed in earnest unison.

"Second, this is a private home, and since I arranged to borrow it, I'm the one who's responsible for any damages it sustains. So . . . there's to be no horseplay inside this house. In fact, there's to be no rowdiness, *period*. If you want to do that, go outside and play in the snow."

The kids fidgeted, impatient for her to finish.

"Third, try not to break anything. And fourth, whatever you do, for heaven's sake do *not*—I repeat, *not*—touch any of the Pueblo pottery or American Indian art. Better yet, don't even *look* at it. I am serious. That pertains to the feather headdresses displayed on the stands, the beaded ceremonial tunics hanging on the walls, as well as the various decorative items. They are all authentic antiques and are not, under any circumstances, to be used as toys."

One by one, she looked each of them straight in the eye.

"Do I make myself clear?"

All three youngsters nodded their heads.

"Good. Then why don't you go upstairs and select your bedrooms? I've got to go help your mama settle into the master suite."

And with that, Venetia hurried off.

"Jeez!" Fred muttered to Liz. "I wonder what's eating *her*?"

"Are the monsters settling in okay?" Dorothy-Anne asked as Venetia came up the stairs.

"Don't worry about them." Venetia smiled. "You know kids. Everything's one big adventure."

"I heard you talking to them, but I couldn't make out the words."

Venetia looked at her; Dorothy-Anne was sitting up in the huge log bed, which looked out over the balcony of the loft and at the three-story wall of windows beyond. To give a measure of privacy, a Navajo rug had been draped over the log railing.

"I was spelling out the dos and don'ts," Venetia said, "and they were doing the listening."

She pulled up a Mexican Cuerno chair and sat down on the black-and-white cowskin cushion. She gestured at the wall of windows.

"Hey, did you notice? Girl, you have been upgraded. Yes, child. In this place you rate a view. Nice, huh?"

"Yeah." Dorothy-Anne's voice was grim. "Just what I need. Lest I forget"— she gestured toward the windows, her lips twisting into a bitter smile—"the beautiful majestic Rockies!"

Venetia felt like kicking herself. *Damn,* she thought. *How stupid can I be? I should have realized the view would be a constant reminder of Freddie. Why the hell didn't it occur to me before?*

She said, "Sugar, I tell you what. Why don't we move you into one of the smaller, walled-in rooms? That way you'll at least have some curtains to draw."

Dorothy-Anne shook her head. "No," she said thickly, staring at the jagged, snow-covered peaks in the distance. "Those are the mountains into which Freddie disappeared. Who knows? Perhaps I'm going mad, but I can't shake the feeling that if I stare at them long enough, they'll give him back to me."

Venetia leaned forward and gripped Dorothy-Anne's shoulder.

"*Stop* it!" she whispered harshly. "Honey, *listen* to me! Haven't you been through enough these past few days? Torturing yourself further is not going to help anybody. Not you, not Freddie, not the child you lost."

It was the last thing Dorothy-Anne wanted to hear. All the pent-up rage and fear, potent and blinding and explosive, came to a savage boil. Without warning, she turned on Venetia.

"How the hell would *you* know?" she shouted, a sudden wildness blazing in her eyes. "It's not *your* husband who's missing! Not *your* baby that miscarried! *You* weren't the one who woke up to find her womb missing!"

Venetia sat very still, each verbal arrow slamming into her like a physical wound. It was all she could do to keep from flinching as the volleys hit home, piercing her heart.

"Down, girl," she said softly. "I'm on your side—or have you forgotten?"

For a moment Dorothy-Anne seemed elsewhere, somewhere remote and unreachable. Her eyes still burned feverishly. Then suddenly the fire in them dimmed, and the rage inside her died. Physically she seemed to shrink, deflating like a punctured balloon. Turning her head into the pillows, she began to weep.

Swiftly Venetia got up, sat on the edge of the bed, and gently but firmly took hold of Dorothy-Anne. She pulled her up, pressing her face to her breast. She could feel her trembling.

"There, there," she comforted, one hand stroking the back of Dorothy-Anne's head, the other patting the convulsing back. "It's okay, honey."

"No, it's not!" Dorothy-Anne's voice was muffled. "It's just that I'm so . . . *scared*! I-I've never been so scared in my entire life!"

"Girl, if you weren't, you wouldn't be human. Or would you rather be a robot?"

Slowly Dorothy-Anne pulled away and raised her tear-streaked face. She stared at Venetia. "I'm sorry," she whispered miserably. She sniffled and wiped her eyes. "I don't know what got into me."

"Shush, child," Venetia soothed. "I know you didn't mean it."

"But I had no right—"

"Hey." Venetia placed her hands on Dorothy-Anne's shoulders and smiled. "Haven't you heard? Everyone's entitled to vent their emotions once in a while."

"No." Dorothy-Anne frowned deeply and shook her head. "Venting emotions is one thing. But taking it out on *you* . . ."

"Girl? Now *will* you forget it? What do you think best friends are for?"

Dorothy-Anne's eyes were wet with tears. "Then I'm . . . forgiven?" she asked in a small voice.

"Hell, no!" Venetia chuckled. She fingered aside the tracks of tears on Dorothy-Anne's cheeks. "And girl? You want to know *why*?" She looked deep into Dorothy-Anne's eyes. "Because there isn't anything *to* forgive."

The cellular phone in Venetia's pocket warbled, startling them both. Dorothy-Anne drew in a sharp breath and jerked away, scrabbling backward on the bed, as if to distance herself from something lethal. The telephone warbled a second time. She looked at Venetia through huge, frightened eyes. On the third ring, Venetia had the phone out and unfolded. "Yes?" she spoke into it, and then listened.

Not daring to breathe, Dorothy-Anne lifted a hand to her mouth and held it there. She could catch the faint crackling of static, and distorted squawk of the voice at the other end, but couldn't make out any of the individual words.

Her gaze shifted past Venetia and out to the mountains, where snow as white as fresh laundry shimmered blindingly and the vast blue of the big sky vibrated with an eye-aching intensity.

"They're sure?" Venetia was saying quietly. "Absolutely positive?" She listened some more. "Okay, hold on. I'll check and see if she's available."

She held her hand over the mouthpiece and turned to Dorothy-Anne. "Sugar?"

Dorothy-Anne's gaze snapped back inside. She looked at Venetia searchingly.

"It's the coordinator of the search parties. They've located the plane."

"Freddie?" Dorothy-Anne whispered from behind her fingers. "Is he—?"

"It's still too early to tell. But he asked to talk to you. You up to it?" Venetia held out the receiver.

Dorothy-Anne stared at it, as if at a poisonous reptile. With an effort, she slowly reached out and took it and raised it clumsily to her ear. "Hello?" she said tentatively.

A man's voice came over the airwaves. It had a sort of outdoorsy, unhurried Midwestern inflection. "Mrs. Dorothy-Anne Cantwell?"

"This . . . this is she."

"I'm Captain William Friendly, coordinator of the Mountain Rescue Teams." His delivery was flat and unemotional, level in the way law enforcement officers all over the country learn to speak. "I'm sorry to have to bother you at a time like this, ma'am."

Dorothy-Anne swallowed hard. "Ms. Flood said you found my husband's plane."

"Not found, ma'am. But we've located it."

She was confused. "Aren't they one and the same?"

"I'm afraid not, ma'am. Not in this day and age. You see, we located it through its electronic emergency transmitter, which sends out automatic distress signals over a special frequency. Luckily, it wasn't damaged upon impact."

Impact, she thought queasily. *How can such a simple little word adequately describe a major catastrophe?*

She clenched her left hand and pressed it against her throbbing temple. "Then what's the problem?" she asked shakily.

"The problem, ma'am, is that we can't get to it. The aircraft is precariously lodged on the western slope of a tremendously steep mountain, right at the edge of a ravine. Normally, we'd lower a search team by helicopter. In this case, however, we're afraid the noise and winds whipped up by the rotor could start an avalanche, sending the plane plunging down a thousand-foot drop. It's in a real bitch of a location, if you'll pardon my French."

"But *will* somebody be able to reach it?" she asked anxiously.

"Yes, ma'am. But by the slow, old-fashioned method. As we speak, two teams of experienced climbers are climbing the mountain. One is tackling the north face, and the other the south. If all goes according to plan, they should reach the site by this afternoon."

Dorothy-Anne shut her eyes.

The edge of a ravine.

A thousand-foot drop.

Just thinking about it was enough to give her vertigo. "Were there"—she took a deep breath and rubbed her knuckles against her forehead—"any signs of survivors?"

"No, ma'am. But that doesn't mean there aren't any. By the same token, I don't want to give rise to false hopes. The aircraft's buried under snow. There's no way we'll know anything until later."

Later. "I appreciate your calling, Captain."

"I'm just doing my job, ma'am. I'll contact you the instant we learn anything. You have my word on that."

"Thank you, Captain."

Dorothy-Anne lowered the receiver and punched the End button. For a long time she sat there, staring out the three-story wall of plasticized, urethaned Disneyesque cedar and glass, her mind on a single word.

Later.

14

Breathing hard and concentrating fiercely, Gloria fought to retain her composure. Her eyes glistened brightly, but the tears that threatened were blinked back. Cloaking herself in dignity, she walked purposefully from the dining room, through the clublike lounge, and down the short hall lined with etchings of ballet dancers. Head held high, she made it across the foyer of the Inn at the Opera, and only once she hit the sidewalk out on Fulton Street did her composure crack.

That bitch! Gloria railed inwardly, her blood boiling furiously. *How dare Althea threaten to have me committed again! HOW DARE SHE!*

Gloria was impervious to the buffeting, bone-chilling wind. All she was aware of were the furies howling and shrieking inside her, the demons that clawed and lashed and generated the hatred from which she fed—the kind of pure, undiluted rage that, perversely, sustained and empowered her—and stoked her resolve to deny Hunt and Althea the satisfaction of ever seeing her bend to their will.

She looked up and down the block, but her limo was nowhere in sight.

Raising her wrist, she held her tiny diamond wristwatch at a distance and squinted at the dial to bring it into focus. Eyeglasses would have helped, but vanity came first.

She blinked. Was it possible? Was she *really* thirty-eight minutes early? Could it be she had thirty-eight *more* minutes to kill before her car arrived?

Balls! And all because she'd told that numbskull driver that she'd be tied up for an hour and a half! He would have to take her seriously. Why the hell couldn't he have figured out that something could go wrong with her luncheon, or that she might change her mind?

Now what was she supposed to do? She was stuck here, behind the Center for the Performing Arts, of all places, and if she wanted a cab she'd have to go back inside the Inn at the Opera and have someone call one.

No. She wasn't about to set foot in *that* place again, even if it killed her. Hell would have to freeze over first!

So.

So now what?

Hoofing it held little appeal. And she certainly wasn't just going to stand here, hoping for a taxi to venture by.

Gloria stood there indecisively, considering her options. Behind her, she heard playful giggles.

Scowling, she turned around. An attractive young couple—tourists, no doubt—came gamboling out of the Inn at the Opera with leggy grace and headed bouncily east, toward the starkly modern opera house, multiple lanes of Van Ness, and gold-domed City Hall beyond. There was something about the way the young brunette clung adoringly to the man's arm, about the staged, picture-perfect quality of their carefree spontaneity and obvious intimacy, that rasped on Gloria's nerves.

Lovers? Newlyweds? *Honeymooners?* Which were they? she wondered, watching them stop and grope each other in a Cinemascope kiss. Well, *she* could tell them a thing or two about the days of wine and roses! she thought acidly. And as for leaving their hearts in this town—ha! Tony Bennett didn't live here, did he?

Her disgust at the couple and the city was, Gloria realized, merely a reflection of her own gnawing disgruntlement. As if she needed reminding of what was missing in her life, dammit!

Was that what she resented? The handsome couple's unquestioning faith that love conquered all . . . or was it the naïveté of youth, their belief that any obstacle was surmountable and that unhappiness was the exclusive province of their wretched elders? A Mustang convertible with the top down sped by, Des'ree blaring, the two couples inside it laughing, bopping to the beat; then, tires squealing, it careened around the corner and was gone, the music fading. And, like the couple on foot, the car's occupants seemed to inhabit some brighter, livelier world than her own. Did she resent not their happiness, but the arrogant confidence of their youth, the uncomplicated, clean slates of their futures? Could that be it?

Gloria turned, lips twisting in bitterness, and abruptly started walking west—expressly heading in the direction opposite from the one the young couple had taken. She wasn't about to follow in their wake and have to witness any more of their lovey-dovey, smoochy little antics. Christ. Enough was enough!

On she rushed—not so much walking as fleeing, low heels clacking an ever-quickening staccato as she zigzagged among unfamiliar blocks, crossing whichever pedestrian lights happened to be green at the moment.

She lost all track of time, all sense of direction. The day's chill and dreariness went unnoticed. So too did the respectability of the city's civic hub as it gave way to grimier businesses, buildings converted into flats, mom-and-pop corner markets.

Nothing registered. Not even the thrum and vibration of traffic rushing along the raised airport freeway high above her, or the sudden increased stench of exhaust fumes.

Gloria was impervious to it all: the wolf whistles of construction workers, the stares from drab housewives who eyed her Chanel suit with envy, the scolding tongue clucks of the elderly, who were appalled at her folly: *How could anyone wearing such ostentatious jewelry venture into a neighborhood like this? And on foot yet!*

But it never occurred to Gloria that her heavy, 18-karat gold Cartier necklace and bracelet, designed to resemble bamboo, her diamond-encrusted wristwatch, and her assorted rings were an open invitation for muggers. Personal safety was not on her mind as she tore, with the desperation of hunted prey, in whichever direction her legs happened to carry her.

Nor did she stop to consider the futility of her flight. It was no mere mortal enemy but the personal demons of her loveless marriage she was fleeing, and that was one wolf pack from which there was no escape.

She could run, but she could not hide.

Two and a half years.

Two and a half *interminable* years.

That was how long it had been since their marriage had hit rock bottom, since she and Hunt had been man and wife in the biblical sense. And even then, that last physical act hadn't been very good.

On she hurried now, her footsteps quickening as memories snapped and snarled and she tried, for what must have been the thousandth time, to pinpoint exactly where in her life she had made the wrong turn. She was still in her prime . . . wasn't she? Certainly men still found her attractive.

So why, *why* was she doomed to be married in name only? Leading, for all practical purposes, the celibate life of a spinster? Would she never again feel the strength and warmth of a man inside her?

Was her sex life as doomed as her sham of a marriage?

Oh, *Christ!*

Gasping, she abruptly lurched to a halt, then slumped back against a dirty stuccoed wall to catch her breath. Her lungs were burning, and a stitch pierced her side. And God, were her feet ever killing her.

These shoes, she thought wryly, lifting one Manolo Blahnik–shod foot and massaging the ankle, *were not made for pounding the pavement.*

She clenched her teeth. *Might as well face it, Glo. You can run as fast and as far as you like, but you'll never outdistance your demons. There's only one thing that can keep them quiet and at bay.*

And she knew what that was.

A drink.

Yes! That was exactly what she needed! A nice little swig to fill the perpetual pain of emptiness, soothe her multitude of sorrows.

Turning around and facing the wall, she unsnapped her handbag and furtively took out her flask. It felt alarmingly light, and when she shook it, no liquid sloshed around inside.

Damn! She must have finished it off in the ladies' room in the restaurant.

Fingers shaking, she stuffed it back inside her purse.

Now what?

A bar, what else?

Yes. She needed to find herself a nice, cozy little bar where she could nurse a guilt-free little comfort drink or two.

Only now that she turned back around to look for one, her head swiveling slowly, almost mechanically, like some searching, preprogrammed radar dish, did she notice how seedy and unfamiliar her surroundings looked.

Good Lord, why, there were derelicts—*derelicts!*—passed out in doorways and along the sidewalk! And a long shuffling row of them lined up in front of a soup kitchen across the street.

The homeless! Where the hell . . .

Her eyes sought out the nearest street sign in panicky, intense bewilderment. Howard Street! Now she was totally confused. When the hell had she crossed Market, that wide, diagonal thoroughfare that cut a swath and separated South of Market from the rest of San Francisco? Surely she hadn't crossed all those lanes with their planted medians without noticing?

But she must have.

Shit! Once again, tears stung in her eyes. Silently she cursed Althea. If the old bitch hadn't made lunch so miserable, then she wouldn't have felt the necessity to flee and end up here, *South* of Market—on Skid Row, of all places!

Good heavens, she thought with contempt, *I wouldn't be found dead in any of these dives!*

She stepped forward on the cracked sidewalk, her molars grinding as she looked up and down the street, searching the dense, exhaust exhaling traffic for an unoccupied taxi.

An exercise in futility.

Then her heart skipped a beat as she spied the rusty sign, its crippled neon and optimistically winking martini glass dangling out over the sidewalk: WHITE ROSE SALOON. *Cocktails.*

Well, well, well, she thought. *What do you know? And only two doors down . . .*

Then she made a face and sniffed disdainfully.

A Skid Row hangout, no doubt.

She hesitated, almost able to taste the wonderfully soothing balm of drowning her sorrows.

Oh, what the hell? A drink is a drink, she decided.

And before she could change her mind, she squared her shoulders, marched purposefully to the White Rose, and yanked open the door.

Once inside, she instantly recoiled, her nostrils twitching in disgust. It was cavelike. Very warm. Very dim. And very, very shabby. The reek of spilled beer and stale smoke all but overwhelmed.

Momentarily undecided, she stood just inside the door, blinking her eyes and waiting for her sight to adjust to the darkness.

Slowly things came into focus. Undulating waves of warped linoleum confettied with cigarette butts. Figures hunched corpselike over the bar, as if glued to their stools in front of the fly-speckled mirror. A potbellied bartender poring over a racing form. And, mounted on the wall above him, a soundless TV set spasming with bad reception.

Nobody occupied any of the tables. No one was speaking to one another. Even the jukebox was silent, the only sound provided by one of the patrons, who emitted long, grinding snores.

Well, so what? I didn't pop in for scintillating conversation. Nor did I expect the Ritz. All I want is a drink and anonymity.

She made her way to a little table at the far end of the room, where she pulled out a rickety bentwood chair. She sat down primly, put her purse on the table, and started to place her elbows on it, too. Then, spying a sticky spot, she thought better of it, and folded her hands in her lap.

After a while the bartender shuffled over. "What'll it be, lady?" he wheezed, sounding put out.

"A double vodka, please," Gloria ordered. "Straight."

A major mistake. It was Skid Row hooch and tasted it: the tiny exploratory sip scorched her throat. It was like drinking burning napalm. Pulling a face, she shuddered involuntarily, cursing herself for not having specified a decent brand.

Still, it's better than nothing, she told herself, powerless to resist it, to do anything but toss it down.

She raised the glass mockingly.

"To absent bitches," she toasted bitterly, hatred flashing from her eyes. "Here's to your ill health, Althea!"

And bracing herself, Gloria tipped back her head, lifted the glass to her lips, and bolted the contents in one long chugalug, her throat muscles flexing and contracting, working overtime to swallow gulp after gulp. Finally she slammed the empty glass down on the table.

And not a moment too soon. The rotgut didn't punch her in the gut; it detonated. Instantly she felt her eyes water, her face turn ashen, and her stomach convulse. Her features distorted in disgust as she hunched over the table, pressing the heel of one hand against her stomach and clapping the other over her mouth.

Oh, God! She stifled a groan. *I'm going to be sick!*

She clenched her teeth, fighting the urge to heave it back up—

—when *snap!* The wave of nausea diminished and was gone.

Ahhh, sweet surcease . . .

She felt a rosy inner glow spreading throughout her system.

Gone were her troubles, gone were her cares.

Another round, and she'd be *cooking!*

Twisting her head to get the bartender's attention, she became aware of an unmistakably masculine presence. Then she saw from whom it emanated.

One of the men at the bar had swung around on his stool and was lounging casually back, both elbows resting on the bar rail. Swiveling slowly, deliberately, from side to side on the stool.

The better to showcase his Levi's-sheathed pelvis.

Something about him gave her pause.

He was young to be a patron here; somewhere in his mid-twenties. Tall and dark, with virile good looks. Liquid bedroom eyes—either smoky black or dark brown; in this light, she couldn't be sure which, but they held a challenging glint that she imagined could turn very hard indeed.

Certainly not a man to trifle with.

And yet . . .

Yet he was the best-looking male animal she had come across in . . . well, in forever. *And,* he was giving her the kind of leisurely, brazen examination that caused her skin to tingle and a flush to rise to her face.

Her first cognizant thought was: *Good Lord. He's coming on to me!*

From across the room, he flashed her a very white, lopsided grin.

He wants me, she thought.

And then, surprising herself: *I want him, too!*

Nor was he a bum. Down, maybe, but certainly not out. Besides, what did that matter, when she was luxuriously aware of the strong body, both muscular and lean, that lurked, barely concealed, under his brown leather windbreaker, plaid workshirt, and snug, faded Levi's?

What indeed.

He had all the right stuff. And in all the right places.

This was the high dive. The jump-off point. Now or never.

Instantly she felt a wave of guilt. Breaking eye contact, she quickly looked away. She knew she was acting prudishly: brows pinched into a frown, lips compressed in uptight disapproval, fingers clenching her glass.

Her *empty* glass.

Immediate problem: how to get the bartender's attention without giving that sexy, macho stud any ideas.

The dilemma resolved itself. She felt more than heard the bartender approach.

"What's the best vodka you serve—" she began, turning to him. And then the cat got her tongue.

Because it wasn't the bartender. It was him—*him!* The guy who'd been eyeballing her.

The breath caught in her throat.

Amazingly, he was even better looking up close. His eyes weren't brown or black after all, but a shadowy cobalt, and his long, hard body seemed barely able to contain its raw power.

He was six feet tall and exuded testosterone. Had a face sunned to an even tan, a certain air of danger, and what looked like a designer stubble. Plus attitude out the wazoo.

She thought, *My God, he's a knockout!* And from his cockiness, she knew that he knew it.

He flashed her a lupine grin; his teeth were whiter than brand new bathroom tiles. "One vodka comin' up," he said.

Gloria started to protest, but he silenced her with a look. Fascinated, she watched him turn on the heel of his Westerns and return to the bar.

He should have been in pictures. Where else did one see such a horny, hip-swaying, groin thrust of a strut?

Dear Lord, she thought weakly, *this isn't a man; this is an honest-to-goodness, living and breathing sex machine!*

And she knew something else now, too. She wanted him. God, did she ever! She wanted him so badly she could taste him!

When he came back, he was carrying a drink in each hand, one clear and one golden.

"Gordon's. Best this joint's got," he said. He brushed his arm deliberately against her breast as he set the clear drink in front of her.

Quickly she looked up at him. There was something about his rough-edged, no-nonsense come-on, and subdued air of menace that she found exceedingly sexy.

And all the while he stood there staring down at her she felt her body temperature growing warmer and warmer.

After a moment, he sauntered to the other side of the table, swung the wobbly chair around so he could lean forward across its back, and swung a leg over the seat as though it were a saddle.

He held his glass aloft. "Here's to beauty," he said.

She picked up her vodka and raised it. "Cheers." She threw back her head and gulped a third of it.

After the previous glass, it slid down smooth as velvet. She smiled. "Major improvement over the house brand."

He grinned. "What wouldn't be?"

She felt his eyes zero in on her cleavage. Suddenly she no longer felt the least bit awkward, guilty, or repressed. That last slug of Gordon's had done it. Now she was glad she hadn't worn a blouse under her suit. Real glad.

She thought: *Take that, Mother Winslow, and blow it out your ass!*

"Y'know, the view from over here's miiiiighty nice," he said appreciatively.

Gloria liked his directness. Here was one guy who didn't waste time beating around the bush.

Slowly he raised his eyes and met hers. "Christos Zzzyanopoulos," he said.

"Say again?"

"Christos Zzzyonopoulos. That's my name. Zzzyanopoulos. With three Zs."

She burst out laughing. "You've got to be pulling my leg!"

"Hey, I'm serious. If I were in the phone book? Mine'd be the last listing in the white pages."

She curled the fingers of both hands around her glass. It was glazed and warm and begging to be drunk.

"Do you have a name?" he asked.

"Everyone's got a name," she murmured.

Then, lifting the glass with both hands, she emptied it in one king-size swallow, and set it back down. She let out a deep, contented sigh.

He was still staring at her.

"Glo," she said.

He tipped his head sideways.

"I said," she repeated, "*Glo*. It's short for Gloria."

"I hear ya."

"That's my name. It's for real, too." She couldn't take her eyes off him. "Just like your Zs."

He leaned across the table, his hands reaching for hers.

His touch was like fire—a flamethrower reaching deep inside her.

"Tell me something, Glo," he said softly. "You believe in love at first sight?"

"Sure," she laughed derisively. "Along with Santa Claus, the Tooth Fairy, and the Easter Bunny!"

His cobalt gaze was locked onto hers. "Bet you believe in lust at first sight, though."

This time she didn't reply.

"Tell you what, Glo," he suggested quietly. "What do you say we blow this joint, buy us a bottle of something decent, and go someplace?"

"Go someplace?" she repeated.

"Yeah. You know." His callused fingers stroked her hands gently. "To make love."

She drew a deep breath. "I-I have to be getting back home soon," she stuttered weakly.

"So?" He grinned again. "I'm sure you can squeeze me in." He gave her his most appealing look. "It's what you want to do, Glo. Isn't it?"

She made a flustered gesture. "This is all so . . . so sudden!"

"Aren't all the best things in life?"

She stared at him.

He stared at her.

Testosterone and estrogen ricocheted between them.

"I-I'd better have another drink first," she said huskily.

"And after?" he asked.

Her voice was a whisper. "We'll get us a bottle of something decent and go someplace."

"Aw*right!*" He lost no time getting to his feet. "Another round comin' right up!"

"One thing first, though." She wiggled a finger, signaling him to come closer.

"Yeah?"

"Kissy," she demanded, raising her face and puckering warm, inviting lips.

Always happy to accommodate a lady, he leaned down and chivalrously gave it his all.

15

Midblock on Mulberry Street.

Sonny Fong brought his black Lexus to a screeching halt, and with a blithe disregard for traffic laws, backed it directly next to the hydrant in front of Mama Rosa's.

Climbing out unhurriedly, he cased the neighborhood while brushing his lapels with his fingers—a John Gotti touch. Then, playing to the kids on the sidewalk, he leaned into the side mirror, smoothed his hair, and grinned at his reflection.

He was Mr. Cool. Looked sharp and knew it.

No Hong Kong tailoring for him. No, sir. Armani all the way: suit, black T-shirt, tinted shades. Plus Gucci loafers in black crocodile and a big gold Rolex.

Hey—if you've got it, flaunt it. And if you haven't, move over.

Sonny Fong was in the fast lane. Zooming to "Big Time" at turbo-charged speed.

He was slim as a blade and moved with the grace of a kickboxer. Raven hair snipped by a scissored Rodin, cold almond-shaped eyes, and the wiry, muscle-packed body of Bruce Lee. He was twenty-three years old and pissed ice-cold ambition.

Once on the sidewalk, he aimed his remote at the car. Locked it and set the alarm with the punch of a button. Then, scanning the kids, he selected the oldest and gestured him over.

"Yeah, mister?" Dark streetwise eyes stared up suspiciously.

In reply, Sonny fished out a twenty-dollar bill, tore it in half, and held out one of the pieces.

The urchin made a grab for it, but Sonny wasn't ready to relinquish it quite yet.

"You watch my wheels, you get the other half once I leave. If they ticket me, forget it. If they try to tow, I'll be in there." He pointed with his forehead in the direction of Mama Rosa's. "Got that?"

"Sure, mister."

Sonny still didn't let go of the kid's half of the twenty.

"Anybody *thinks* of fuckin' with that car, they're dead meat. You read me?"

The kid grinned. "Loud 'n' clear!"

Sonny loosened his grip on the money and pinched the kid's cheek. "You'll go far, kid," he said.

And whistling confidently, he jauntily approached the five-story tenement, pausing under the canopy that angled sharply down to the garden level in order to peruse the mounted chalkboard:

TODAY'S SPECIALS

24 oz. USDA prime shell steak w/baked potato & green salad
$12.95

tonno in padella—tuna & fennel seeds w/garlic-sauteed
escarole   7.95

pesce spada alla siciliana—stuffed swordfish sicilian style
w/asparagus   7.95

salsiccia alla siciliana—homemade sicilian sausage w/spicy
vegetables & sliced tomatoes w/ basil   6.95

calamari fritti—fried squid w/ stuffed artichoke   6.95

Sonny couldn't believe his eyes. For Manhattan, the prices were cheap—ridiculously cheap. Hell, twenty-four ounces of USDA prime *cost* more than this place was charging for an entire meal!

Guess it all fell off a truck, he thought, with a knowing smirk. *Mama Rosa's obviously well connected.*

Which didn't exactly come as a surprise. After all, this was Little Italy. A world within a world. Much like Chinatown, the way it was shut to outsiders, its secretive workings shrouded by layer upon layer of mystery.

And with those thoughts, he descended the eight steep steps, pulled on the oaken door, and entered the ristorante.

After the cacophonous madness of rush-hour Manhattan, the transition into this hushed, cavelike serenity seemed positively eerie, and Sonny stopped to remove his shades. He did an immediate double take.

"Whoa," he exclaimed under his breath, staring about in amazement.

Before him stretched a warren of cozy, low-ceilinged rooms interconnected by open brick arches. Mahogany booths, upholstered in scarlet velvet luxury, lined the right wall; an old, carved mahogany bar reposed splendidly along the left. And everywhere, a sea of tables dressed in crisp white linens stood at the ready, surrounded by lacquered black chairs with upholstered seats.

As though attending to dining ghosts, waiters in red jackets were circulating, realigning a chair here and straightening a fork there, while busboys in white shirts were making the rounds, silently lighting each table's candle, which was sheltered inside a net-covered red jar.

But that hadn't drawn Sonny's attention. What had were the paintings.

There were hundreds of them, in all sizes and shapes—squares, rectangles, ovals, octagons, circles; some elaborately gilt framed, others unframed—and they covered every available bit of wall surface like strange murals of murky, grisly splendor.

Without fail, they represented religious subjects.

There were pietàs and entombments galore; grotesque Saint Jeromes with skulls, gory crucifixions, about-to-be-sacrificed Isaacs, bleeding martyrs in torment, countless saints enduring gruesome tortures, emaciated Christs with bloody wounds, various descents from the Cross, slaughters of the Innocents, and more decapitations than you could shake a knife at—Salomes with heads of John the Baptist, Davids with heads of Goliath, Judiths with heads of Holoferneses—the majority of which rested, appropriately enough, since this was a restaurant, on a variety of platters.

Sonny had never seen any place like this.

Bon appétit, he thought sardonically, wondering who would want to eat surrounded by all these gruesome depictions.

"Yes?" a voice inquired coldly.

Sonny turned around. An arthritic, white-haired waiter with startling, bristly black eyebrows had approached, and was staring at him with open hostility.

Sonny wasn't fazed. As an Asian-American—Chinese father, Chinese mother, but Chinatown-born and thus a U.S. citizen—he'd encountered attitude and prejudice from day one. No matter. Between school and the streets he'd proven himself capable in any situation. It took a lot more than one old geezer to scare him off.

"Tell me something," Sonny said. "People really eat here? Surrounded by all this shit?" He indicated the walls with a thrust of his chin.

The hostility grew, then the waiter snapped. "We don't open until six, and require reservations. Now if you'll please—"

"Step aside, Gramps." With the flat of his hand, Sonny gently but firmly pushed the old man out of his way. Then, sauntering casually along the bar, he stopped, clasped his hands in the small of his back, and rocked back and forth on his heels as he gazed around some more.

He shook his head with incredulity. *Grisly. Truly an awesomely gruesome spectacle.*

The waiter had limped after him. "I must ask you to leave." His voice was high-pitched with affront.

Sonny was aware of all activity in the room having ceased. He could feel menacing stares emanating from the busboys and other waiters. Obviously, they took care of their own.

Unconcerned, he stuck his hands in his trouser pockets. "I'm here on business," he said calmly. "Now, why don't you go tell Mama Rosa she's got a visitor?"

"It's almost dinnertime. She's very busy."

"So? Tell her anyway."

Slitted rheumy eyes regarded him with suspicion. "She expecting you?"

Sonny cracked an insolent grin. "Maybe she is, and maybe she isn't."

The old man clicked his dentures in worried indecision and stared at him some more. It took a few moments, but his face finally wrestled itself into submission. With a reedy sigh, he said, "Wait here."

Leaving Sonny, he hobbled arthritically to the back of the dining room. After what seemed an eternity, female voices and the clanging of pots and pans rose and fell as a door was opened and shut.

The waiters and busboys continued about their business, but kept a wary eye peeled. Sonny ignored them and paced slowly, peering at another batch of paintings.

More of the same.

He shook his head and clucked his tongue softly. *If I told anyone about this place, they wouldn't believe me.*

Eventually, the waiter returned and cleared his throat. "Mama Rosa will see you," he said, "but you'll have to go to her. She can't come out."

"Just lead the way."

Sonny followed him from one arched room into another before the old man gestured at a swinging door. It had a round glass porthole set into it, and through it filtered the sounds of cooking, rapid-fire gossip, and laughter.

Sonny marched directly to the door, pushed his way through, and entered the kitchen. The blast of heat hit him like a solid wall.

Recoiling, he looked around, his spiffy threads out of place in this steamy, stifling atmosphere of bubbling pots, sizzling pans, and shrill jabber. It was all the noisy ventilation fans could do to keep up, and he found himself raising his voice to make himself heard. "Which of you ladies is Mama Rosa?"

The voices instantly fell silent as the dozen or so women turned to appraise the stranger.

At a big marble work surface, a huge, red-faced woman stopped cutting out sheets of stuffed dough. Putting down her ravioli cutter, she clapped flour off her pudgy hands and rubbed them on her apron. She used her wrist to wipe aside strands of graying black hair that had sprung loose from her bun and hung down into her face.

Then she slowly waddled forward. She was wearing a washed-out blue housedress, the bottom half of her apron—the top was folded over and hung down over it—and baby blue vinyl slippers.

She stopped in front of Sonny, hands resting on ample hips. He could see beads of sweat glistening on her forehead and moist upper lip, where a large brown mole and the shadow of a mustache were all too evident.

"Who wants to know?" she demanded harshly, beady black eyes drilling right through him.

Sonny stared right back at her. "I do."

"Well, you're talking to her." She drew herself up with dignity. "I," she said proudly, thrusting out her massive double-prowed bosom, "am Mama Rosa. Now, what do you want?"

He lowered his voice. "I've got to get in touch with Carmine," he said softly.

The big woman's face closed. If the name registered, she wasn't letting on.

"Carmine?" she repeated, with a theatrical frown. Then, one eye squinting shrewdly: "*Which* Carmine? Down here, everybody and his brother is named either Anthony or Carmine."

Sonny held her gaze. "I'm looking for the Carmine who's also known as the Sicilian."

Pendulous breasts jiggled as Mama Rosa heaved rich, deep peals of laughter. "Take a look around you." A wave of a fat hand encompassed the entire kitchen and the women who were watching. "Everyone you see in here's a Siciliana."

He frowned slightly. "You mean . . . they're all Italian. Right?"

"Wrong! We are *not* Italian!" she spat, her eyes narrowing in magnificent fury. "The Neapolitans, the Venetians, the Romans, the Milanese"—she gestured deprecatingly—"bah! They are nothing!" Then her voice took on a note of pride. "We are *Sicilianos*. And we only socialize with other Sicilianos, so the only Carmines we know are Sicilianos, too. Not Milanese or Neopolitans. *Sicilianos! Capite?*"

He nodded slowly. "Yeah, I do see. It's like us. People think we're Chinese, but we're not. I am Chiuchow, since my parents came from Swatow. That makes us neither Chinese nor Mandarin nor Cantonese nor Szechwan. We're *Chiuchow*. It is a matter of ethnic pride."

She nodded approvingly. "Good." She patted his arm warmly. "Then you understand."

"The Carmine I have to find," he confided very quietly, "is said to be your son."

"*My* Carmine?" Her eyes widened and she raised both plump arms. "*In nome di Dio!*" She squinted suspiciously at him. "What would you want with *my* Carmine? Eh?"

"I . . ." Sonny looked around furtively. "I've come to offer him a job," he whispered.

Mama Rosa turned around. "*Giovinettas!*" she called out loudly to the other women. "You have to hear this! He says he has a job—for my Carmine!"

The women burst into high-spirited gales of laughter.

Sonny Fong flushed, and was momentarily flummoxed. *Here I am trying to be discreet, and meanwhile she's all but shouting from the rooftops. Shit! This is one crazy mama!*

"What's so funny?" he wanted to know.

Mama Rosa let out another bray and slapped her thigh. "Madonna! Hey—*giovinettas!* Now he wants to know why you're laughing!" She joined in the hilarity. "Maybe one of you should tell him, eh? Maybe that way, it won't sound so much like a mama's boasting."

"Carmine's already got a job," one of the women chortled.

"And I bet it's a better job than any *you* can offer!" added a young one, with a saucy flounce. "You should see the way Carmine takes care of his poor mama!"

"Such a good boy," spoke up a third, her voice wistful. "All our sons should be like her Carmine!"

Mama Rosa sniffled and wiped a tearing eye and beamed. "You see?" she told Sonny. "You're wasting your time. Carmine doesn't need any job."

"Look, it's important." Sonny dropped his voice for emphasis. "*Real* important." He paused, and asked: "Does the name Jimmy Vilinsky mean anything to you?"

Mama Rosa frowned. "Jimmy . . . who?"

"Vilinsky."

She screwed up her face and looked thoughtful. Finally she shook her head. "Nope. The name doesn't ring a bell." She glanced over at the white marble work surface. "Look, I got to get back to my *minni di Sant'-Agatha.*"

"Just give me a minute to explain!" Sonny pleaded. "*Please?*"

She shrugged. "So explain. But you better do it while I work."

He followed her to the worktable and stood back as she yanked open an oven door. Using her apron as a potholder, she expertly slid out one cookie sheet after another, slipping each into a big stainless steel baking rack to cool. Then she slammed the oven door shut, and with a sigh turned back to the dough awaiting her.

"Smells good," he said, inhaling appreciatively.

Mama Rosa rolled her eyes. "Now I suppose you want to taste Mama's baking," she said with mock gruffness. "Is that it? Like I'm not busy enough?" Then she relented. "Oh, go ahead. Taste one. But first, bring it here."

He went to the rack, squatted down, and from one of the cool trays on the bottom selected a puffy, golden round cookie topped with a maraschino cherry. Swiftly Mama Rosa sprinkled it with confectioner's sugar.

"Now *mange*," she urged. "*Mange!* Eat!"

He bit into it. It was deliciously crunchy, with a sweet, creamy chocolate filling. "Hey—these are great!"

Mama Rosa looked indignant. "Of course they are," she sniffed. "I make only the best!"

"What're these called?"

"*Minni di Sant'Agatha.*" The Italian rolled smoothly off her tongue.

"*Minni* . . . what?"

"In English, the translation is Saint Agatha's nipples."

He nearly choked on a mouthful. "You're joking—right?"

Mama Rosa glowered. "We never joke about our saints!" she warned darkly, and swiftly crossed herself.

Then he watched as, fingers flying, she stuck maraschino cherry halves atop a tray of unbaked cookies. He looked at the half-eaten one in his hand.

Now that he thought of it, it did resemble a breast with a nipple. It really did.

"It's a measure of devotion, not blasphemy," Mama Rosa explained as she worked. "Saint Agatha is the patron saint of Palermo and Catania. You see, the prefect of Catania wanted to sleep with her, but she refused. For revenge, he tortured her by cutting off her *minnas*—her nipples. So we Sicilians honor her chastity by naming the cookies after her. *Capite?*"

"Er . . . yes," Sonny agreed quickly. "Perfectly."

In truth, he didn't understand; the reasoning behind it was entirely beyond him.

But it wouldn't do to disagree. He wasn't about to get on Mama Rosa's bad side—he needed her help in contacting the Sicilian.

Sonny's distant cousin, the *lung tao* in Hong Kong, had stressed urgency. And Sonny wasn't about to let him down. Especially since he was Sonny's nonstop ticket to the top.

The old man practically owns half of Chinatown, he reminded himself. *If I succeed with this, I've got it made.*

"About this Jimmy Vilinsky," he said.

Mama Rosa rolled her eyes. "I already *told* you," she said wearily. "I don't know any Jimmy Whatever."

Sonny masked his growing sense of frustration. "Look, all I'm asking is that you pass a message along to Carmine. That's all. Will you do that?"

"Oh, all right," she grumbled. "What do you want me to tell him?"

Sonny came up with a business card. "Give him this. Tell him I'm the new contact. That I've replaced Jimmy Vilinsky."

"I'll try to remember."

Shit! Sonny Fong thought. *The way she's acting, you'd think I asked her to memorize the Gettysburg Address.*

"He can reach me at this number."

Mama Rosa shook her head. "He's not going to call you."

"Why not?"

"Carmine never talks to nobody."

"So what do I do?"

"Come back tomorrow night . . . say at eleven? Maybe by then I'll have a message for you. Then again, maybe I won't." She shrugged disinterestedly. "With Carmine you never can tell. Sometimes he calls his mama, and sometimes he forgets. But right now I've got to finish cooking. This place is going to fill up soon."

She made shooing motions with her hands.

"Now *avanti. Avanti!* Go!"

And with that, he was summarily dismissed.

Glad to get out of that stifling kitchen, he waved at the other women, who threw him kisses, struck lewd poses, and laughed uproariously.

Goddamn dagos! he thought, striding through the warren of cool dining rooms. Well, at least he'd made contact. That was the first step.

Sonny was home at six-thirty. He berthed his wheels in the underground garage of the East Seventy-fourth Street high-rise and took the elevator up to the thirty-sixth floor.

First things first. He headed straight to the desk in front of the panoramic living room window and sat down at his Packard Bell 1.2 gigabyte Pentium computer. An aquarium of electronically generated tropical fish swam lazily across his monitor.

Getting busy, he tapped out a message and converted it into code.

Decoded, it would read:

Greetings, most honorable fifth cousin twice removed. I am to contact our business partner 11:00 P.M. my time tomorrow night. Please advise me regarding the severance package for our middleman. If I may humbly suggest, I would be honored to take care of it capably at this end. That would result in an immense savings to the company. However, I shall do nothing without your consent. May the gods of fortune attend you. Your dutiful fifth cousin twice removed.

Sonny accessed the Internet, then routed and rerouted the message through such a complicated maze of educational institutions, government agencies, and various corporations, that it made it all but impossible to trace it back to him.

Once he sent it to Hong Kong via its convoluted detour, he erased the message from both his floppy and hard disks.

Then he waited.

Thirteen times zones away, the coded message arrived at its destination, a terraced, 1920s Italianate villa built on the hillside near the top of Victoria Peak. As one of the fewer than sixty freestanding houses in all of Hong Kong, and located on the only street zoned exclusively for one-family estates, the residence was a testament to the owner's incalculable wealth and power.

The E-mail, in indecipherable code, was received by a young Chinese computer operator. He printed one copy, deleted the message from the computer, and brought the printout to the *lung tao*'s secretary in the paneled office next door.

Spring Blossom Wu had worked for Kuo Fong for more than three decades. A slim woman of fifty-five, she still retained the delicacy of her once youthful beauty, and looked to be in her mid-forties.

Her oval face was smooth and unlined, and her skin was the color of rose ivory. She had on well-applied makeup, and her black hair was pinned up. She was wearing a yellow silk *chong sam* with a mandarin collar and black high heels.

Swiftly decoding the message by hand, she fed the coded copy into the shredder, picked up her steno pad and pen, and went out onto the wide terrace.

As always, she stood there a moment, deriving pleasure from the surroundings.

The acre of beautifully planted garden was fragrant with jasmine and gardenias, white ginger, and year-round roses. The grass around the lap pool was billiard-table perfect. And the unrivaled view encompassed forested mountains, the high-rises of Aberdeen, and the island-dotted South China Sea.

There was the *lung tao*. Standing on the lawn at the far end of the aqua pool. A thin and commanding figure dressed in an exquisite, gold-embroidered ceremonial robe fit for an emperor.

He was indulging his great-grandchildren. There were eight of them, the youngest of whom was attempting to launch a kite, and the children's laughter and singsong voices embroidered the air.

Moving gracefully, Spring Blossom Wu descended the three flights of stone steps and made her way to the far end of the pool.

She bowed respectfully. "A thousand pardons, most venerated Kuo," she apologized, speaking Chiuchow.

Like the *lung tao,* she too had come from Swatow many decades earlier, and had proudly retained the culture, customs, and language of her native province.

Kuo Fong looked at her. "Yes, Spring Blossom?"

"A message has come for you from New York."

A look of regret crossed the ancient man's face. Glancing at his great-grandchildren, he sighed and then clapped his hands sharply. "That is enough for now," he said.

The children's amah got up from the bench in the gazebo and waddled forward. Taking the two youngest by the hands, she led the way to the house, the older six following in their wake.

Spring Blossom Wu waited, her eyes modestly downcast.

Once the amah and his great-grandchildren were out of earshot, Kuo Fong said: "I would be honored if you read the message to me."

When Spring Blossom was through, he nodded sagely and walked, deep in thought, along the plantings at the edge of the property.

Spring Blossom followed him at a discreet distance. Finally he turned to her and dictated a reply, which she jotted down.

"Encode it, destroy your copy, and send the coded message to New York through the usual channels," he told her.

"At once, honorable Kuo."

In New York, Sonny Fong received his reply within half an hour of sending his message. Quickly he decoded it:

> Greetings, Sonny Fong, fifth cousin twice removed. Remember the Confucian analect: To go beyond is as wrong as to fall short. Be filial and respect your elders. You did well to consult me. Contact our business partner but be wise! Let him take care of his specialty. You are to do nothing in this matter. There are other plans for you. Visit our immigration facilitator in Chinatown tomorrow. He has information for you. Remember, cousin, be as the tortoise which would rather be alive and wagging its tail in the mud than have its remains venerated. Observe caution and obey.

Sonny's face clouded in disappointment. He wasn't in the least bit surprised. He had expected his suggestion about Jimmy Vilinsky to be overruled. Still, he couldn't help but feel let down.

More than anything, he felt consumed by the need to prove himself to Kuo Fong. Unfortunately, that would have to wait a little longer. Perhaps his visit to the smuggler of illegal aliens would provide the opportunity. He hoped so.

But that was tomorrow.

In the meantime, Sonny deleted the message and exited the program, leaving the monitor to the electronic fish while he went out to get himself something to eat.

16

Christos handed Gloria inside the telephone-summoned taxi and firmly shut the door from the outside. For once, nothing could put a damper on her spirits, not even the torn vinyl upholstery and cheap, overpowering air freshener. Quickly ducking down, she clutched the back of the driver's seat with one hand and felt thrilled to the tips of her toes when Christos touched his fingertips to his lips.

As if on its own accord, her own hand rose to her lips to mirror his.

"Where to, lady?" the cabby asked.

"Broadway and Baker." Despite the dirty glass barrier, Gloria's eyes never left Christos. As the taxi lurched off and accelerated, she swiftly turned around and stared out the spotted rear window at his receding figure, her fingertips still poised against her lips.

Only once the cab careened around the corner and he disappeared from sight did she finally face frontward and let her hand drop, ever so reluctantly, into her lap.

Settling back in her seat, she heaved a deep, contented sigh of pleasure. She was in seventh heaven, bleary with postcoital bliss.

And ah, what bliss!

The three hours—*three entire hours;* good Lord, could it possibly have been *that* long?—they'd spent in that seedy room-by-the-hour had flown by and disappeared—*poof!*—just like that, as though envious gods had snapped their fingers.

Now, oblivious of the cab's defective shock absorbers, she permitted herself the luxury of reliving the events that had transpired.

She'd barely been aware of the whore's dormitory to which Christos had taken her.

Nor had she noticed the garish denizens and furtive customers or, for that matter, the scabrous, peeling walls and squalor of that fleabag hotel.

Even the cigarette-scorched furnishings and sagging bed with its pilly sheets had escaped her notice.

Sex, not decor, had been foremost on her mind.

Christos had washed out the single bathroom tumbler, which they shared, drinking the Absolut they'd picked up along the way.

Hormones took care of the rest.

Before she knew what was happening, they were bouncing energetically on the narrow twin mattress, the rusty springs squeaking and groaning.

Christos, in bed, proved himself an admirably inventive lover. He had reawakened feelings in her that she had almost forgotten could exist. And had done things to her that she had never dared try—let alone imagined herself doing.

But do them she did.

Never, never had her carnal appetite been so ferocious. So it wasn't love. Who cared, when lust felt this good?

Gloria couldn't believe her ravenousness. After having done without for so long, she was like a child let loose in a candy store. Suddenly she couldn't get enough.

At least, not as far as Christos was concerned.

For starters, there was his body. Tight, sinewy, and hairless, with sculpted abs, steely thighs, and the cutest, firmest little buns this side of the Rockies. He didn't carry a spare ounce of fat, and the way the muscles rippled beneath his skin made watching his every movement a study in anatomy.

But most impressive of all was his equipment. He was a walking tool box—with balls like succulent ripe fruits and a penis to die for. Larger, thicker, harder, and more superb than anything Gloria had ever dreamed of, its veins standing out in chiseled, bold relief.

She had been right. Christos Zzzyonopoulos was sex personified.

He was also unburdened by societal hang-ups.

"Hey—if it feels good, do it," he murmured, and his mouth came down on hers in a frenzy of crushing possession while his middle finger authoritatively reached between her slender thighs and slid up her already engorged clitoris.

She nearly went out of her mind. Through instinct or experience, he instantly, unerringly found the precise location from which all her heat and desires stemmed, and fingered the lubricated warm flesh accordingly.

She shuddered with the excruciating need to yield completely.

"Oh . . . my God . . . Christos!" she cried, clenching her pelvic muscles and tightening her arms around him. "I want *you* inside me. . . ."

"Don't be in such a damned rush," he whispered, nibbling gently on her earlobe. "I want to enjoy you . . . *all* of you. And I want *you* to enjoy me . . . *all* of me. . . ."

And thus began that afternoon of revelations, the embarkment on her voyage to sexual rediscovery.

Layer by layer, as though shedding her of cumbersome, unnecessary clothes, he stripped away her prudish inhibitions and soon had her eating out of his hand.

But first, he ate *her*.

His probing tongue was paralyzing. She lay there, a pliant vessel, legs splayed and eyes closed, luxuriating in the delectable sensations he aroused with each feathery flick and whorl of his tongue.

The thrumming and the sweetness and the world light-years away . . . no one else inhabited this garden of earthly delights; no one witnessed the two of them merging into a single entity whose sole aim it was to derive the most exquisite pleasures life could offer. This—*this*—was heaven as she'd never known it.

Nothing else mattered.

Nothing else existed.

She was aware only of gratification and ravenous impulses, and she knew with a certainty that from here on there was no turning back, that she had reached a crossroads and was forever and completely, irrevocably lost.

Forgotten now was her thirst for vodka. It had been replaced by a craving infinitely more unquenchable—the need to explore and familiarize herself with every contour, every nook, every curvature and last square inch of his sublime male body.

Like an acrobat, he balanced himself on one arm and executed a 180-degree turn in midair. Then, bending his body in a great lengthwise arc over her, he supported himself on his elbows and toes.

She could feel the warm puffs of his breath grazing her groin, could see his raised pelvis poised high above her face, her entire field of vision filled with that rose quartz hardness that protruded so assertively, so tauntingly, from the dark curly thicket of his hair.

And suddenly she realized what it was he wanted of her.

"No, please . . ." Her voice was faint. She pulled a face and shook her head.

Anything but this, she projected, *just not this. I cannot do it. I will not. I don't want to.*

"Please, I . . . I've never tried . . ."

He laughed softly. "Then how do you know you won't like it?" he said. "Bet you ten to one you will."

Her eyes were wide, as though she were hypnotized by the monster phallus. She could see it strain and twitch, jerking and leaping in anticipation.

"Just go with the flow," he advised gently. "Let it come naturally."

Gloria drew a deep breath. The idea of going down on a man had always repelled her. She had never been able to understand women who enjoyed performing such debasing, abominable acts. And now here she was. Not only considering it, but becoming fascinated with it. Why this should be she couldn't have begun to explain, but a part of her—a stronger, baser, more primitive personality emerging from some dark recess of her being—actually *wanted* to do it!

For a fraction of a second he was statue still, seemingly suspended in the air above her. Then he thrust ever so slowly downward—and her lips parted, as though of their own volition.

Gone suddenly were her qualms. No longer was her sexuality pliant and yielding. Now it was overpowering and voracious, as if it had a force of its own—a force even she could not control.

Her lips opened, as though in protestation, but widened in welcome.

Smoothly he slid into her moist oral cavity.

She needed no prompting. Her mouth immediately locked itself around the pulsating thickness, as if it were something alive, something she felt the need to nurture and give succor to.

Her sudden ravenousness enslaved her. Caused the wetness to flood from her loins as he gently thrust himself further down her throat.

For one long, terrible moment, she was afraid she was going to gag. Then it passed, and a great dizzying whirlpool of abandon caught hold of her and swept her away.

Flesh, flesh, flesh! Inside her mouth, where he belonged to no one but her. Where she possessed the very essence of man in its entirety and there was no one, no one under the sun, to steal it away!

Then, like a bee in search of nectar, she felt his head once again dip between her splayed thighs and seek out the very epicenter of her feminine being.

Together now, they feasted—he on the moist pink succulence of her petaled blossom, she on the hard sword of his flesh, nuzzling his testicles and inhaling his delicious maleness and wondering how she could ever have shied away from something so utterly, so depravedly, so sinfully delicious.

Then the first tide crested and crashed over her, and she gripped his buttocks, pulling him closer and sucking with renewed vigor.

But he was not yet ready. She knew what he was doing. Holding back and saving himself.

Words—endearments, thanks, flatteries, praises, gratitude—all so hopelessly inadequate, sprang to her mind.

I love you! she wanted to cry out. *Oh, Christos, you beautiful, beautiful man! God help me, how I love you and need you! I was slowly dying inside until our paths crossed. Now here you are, lighting up my darkest hour of wretchedness. Giving me the greatest gift imaginable . . .*

Then he withdrew from her mouth.

A soft mewl of distress escaped her, and tears sprang into her eyes. Not having him inside her was a little like death, like losing her hold on reality and discovering a vast emptiness.

"Don't stop!" she pleaded in a whisper.

He smiled, caressing her body with gentle, loving hands. "Who said I was through?" he mocked, scooting around and straddling her. He knelt there for a moment, cupping her breasts in his hands, his thumbs brushing a vibrato across the erect, tender buds of her nipples.

She looked up at him. A vision he was, with his tightly muscled torso sleeked with perspiration, and his phallus rigid, prepared for assault.

Then, worshipfully, he bent his head to one willing breast and rolled the rosy nipple gently between his sharp white teeth.

Little beaks of pleasure pecked and stung, shot erogenous pulses throughout her body.

"Oh, God!" She writhed wildly, whipping her head back and forth as he increased the pressure of his teeth and fingers. "Oh God, oh God—"

"Oh *God!*" Now it was he who bellowed, and he threw himself across her and slammed himself savagely up into her.

The impact of penetration, like a completed electrical circuit, jolted with a galvanic burst of initial energy, diminished slightly, wavered until the voltage stabilized and then, as Christos began to thrust, jolted again and again with carefully calibrated, steadily increasing amperage.

Gloria clung to him in a jailer's grip.

It was agony. It was ecstasy. It was heaven and hell all rolled into one.

"Oh, yes—" she panted, every second word cut short by the tooth-jarring impacts of their bodies. "God, yes! Say you—love me! *Love me!* LOVE ME—"

"Love you," he gasped obligingly, his magnificent body pounding her tender flesh. His every muscle rippled and strained in glorious sculptural relief, and his face was a contorted mask of determination.

Gloria reveled wantonly. She lifted her hips to meet his every thrust, so that their pelvic bones struck glancing blows as his shaft buried itself in to the hilt.

And still he hammered. Faster and faster. Harder and harder.

Faster—

—harder—

—faster—

—harder—

—until his buttocks blurred and in perfect unison they both tensed, arched their backs, and cried out.

It was as if the earth itself trembled. Darkness brightened, trumpets blared, and the four winds whipped up tempests of sound and fury. This—this precisely synchronized climax—this was the beginning and the end, the Creation and the Apocalypse.

And still the orgasm seemed to continue, forever and without end as, together, they careened out over the edge of the universe and into the void beyond.

Finally they collapsed, lying atop each other in an inert tangle of limbs, lungs burning, hearts pounding, pulses racing.

If the afternoon had ended there, Gloria would have been grateful for all eternity. But it didn't end there. As it turned out, this was merely the beginning.

After a while, when their breathing had returned to normal, they sipped vodka—*sipped* it, not guzzled—and cautiously tested the conversational waters. Not prying, just volunteering this and that.

Gloria telling Christos she was married, but not happily.

Christos mentioning that he was between jobs at the moment, but hey—it was a temporary setback; no big deal.

Whereupon Gloria offered to "loan" him a couple of hundred bucks.

Which he emphatically refused to accept. "Thanks, but no thanks. I can scrape by."

She urged him to go ahead and take it anyway.

And this time he didn't object.

As far as Gloria was concerned, they were the best two hundred dollars she had ever spent. Christos was a bargain. Nothing, not even charging up twenty thousand an hour at Saks, had ever given her such a thrill.

Myriads of thoughts flitted through her head:

How could I have been celibate for so long?

What is it about this beautiful man that he alone should be able to awaken me, like some fairy-tale princess, from a hundred-year-long slumber?

And irony of ironies: To think I have Althea, of all people, to thank for meeting him!

Now, seated in the rear of the taxi, Gloria smiled, complacent and appeased, out at the passing traffic on Van Ness. Briefly she wondered whether her expression of satiated overindulgence was a dead giveaway.

Could strangers tell, merely by looking at her, that she'd just gorged herself on the most splendidly prodigal and gloriously masculine of all male flesh?

Well, what did she care if they could?

Humming to herself, Gloria thought of him during the entire ride home. Christos Zzzyonopoulos. So he wasn't rich. So what? His hidden assets more than made up for any financial shortcomings.

But best of all, they'd made a date to meet again tomorrow.

Would wonders never cease?

Gloria certainly hoped not!

She was crashing. He could tell from the way she paced the room, rubbing her thin, crossed arms and drawing deep, rapid puffs on her cigarette. Eyeing his progress each time she passed by.

"For chrissake, will ya sit *down*," he said harshly, without looking up. "Stop bein' so damned jumpy. You're actin' like you're gonna jump outta your skin."

"Okay . . . *okay*." The naked girl with the waist-length black hair parked herself on the edge of the sagging mattress. "But she's a live one?" Her eyes glittered greedily. "Which means she's rich, right?"

"You'd better believe it, babe." The naked man didn't look up from the dinette table, where he was cutting thin lines of cocaine on a square of mirror with a single-edged blade.

"Money!" the girl breathed dreamily.

She dropped backward on the rumpled bed, both arms extended, and stared ecstatically up at the peeling ceiling.

"Soon's we get some dough, first thing *I* wanna do's move outta this dump! You know, into one o' them nice new high-rises with views like you only see in pi'tures?" She rolled over onto an elbow. "What about you, hon' bunch? What do *you* want?"

He humored her with one of his stretched grins. "I just want you, Amber."

"Yeah?"

"Yeah." He bent over, stuck a short straw up his nose, and snorted a line. Sniffed and swallowed and changed the straw to his other nostril. Horned another line.

From the bed, Amber was watching avidly, her eyes bright.

"Hey, babe." He held out the straw. "Want a toot?"

Did she *want* one? She launched herself across the room in a flash.

"Unh-unh." He held the straw out of her reach and grinned. "Didn't your momma teach you any manners?"

Amber giggled. "Uh-*huh*."

"Well, lemme see 'em."

Dropping to her knees, she reached for his penis and gently peeled back the foreskin. Then, cupping his heavy testicles in one hand, she flicked her tongue across the swollen head of the glans.

"Please?" she asked softly, glancing up at him.

"That's better, babe. I'd say that's a *lot* better." Grinning down at her, he let her have the straw.

She seized it, popped to her feet, and tossed her hair back out of the way. Hunching over the table, she snorted a line expertly.

The coke flew up inside her nostrils and burned. Flinging her head back, she shut her eyes for a moment. Then she repeated the maneuver with the other nostril.

The kick of the drug made the nipples of her small, hard breasts rise from the dusky pink areolae. "Wow!" she breathed. "That's good shit."

"Only the best for us, babe. Got us two whole grams. Best Bolivian on the street."

Her eyes opened wide. "Then you already got hold of some money?"

"Yeah." He laughed softly. "Cash. Good old Ben Franklins."

"So you weren't shittin' me? You really *did* find a live one!"

"Hey . . . " He reached out and pulled her close. "Does your old man ever shit you?" His white teeth blazed like flashing neons.

Amber shook her head, her left arm sliding languorously around his neck, her right hand trailing slowly along his tightly muscled body and down to his crotch. Gently her fingers curled around the base of his penis. She could feel it throb and rear under her touch.

"Tell me about her," she said softly. "Everything you know."

He laughed. "Don't know much yet, 'cept she's got moolah comin' outta her ears."

Amber frowned. "How're we gonna play it? The usual con?"

"Hell no! This time we're in it for the long haul. If we play our cards right, we can milk her for years to come." He tightened his grip on her. "We'll be set for *life*."

Amber rubbed a nipple across his face. "You know this mark's name?"

"Yeah. Snuck a look in her wallet while she used the john."

"So what's she called?"

"Gloria Winslow," said Christos Zzzyonopoulos.

17

From the twelve-thousand-foot summit, as rescue team leader Chuck Renfrew first laid eyes on the steep slope where, far below, the Learjet lay buried beneath a yard or more of snow, the location had looked deceptively benign—hardly more dangerous than the expert slopes of the Cirque at Snowmass, which he skied regularly.

Now, glancing up at the two- and three-hundred-foot vertical drops that divided the slope like some giant's looming rocky steps, from which his team's rappelling lines hung like threads, he had a healthy respect for the diciness of the location. Besides the sudden drop-offs, a good seventy inches or more of powder blanketed the 130-degree slopes—thousands of tons of potential avalanche just waiting to come rushing down, annihilating everything in its path.

And mere feet from where the aircraft was precariously lodged, a precipice plunged another thousand feet straight down.

A perilous spot under the best of circumstances.

And then there were the winds.

Thirty- and forty-mile-an-hour gusts shrieked and howled, battered his orange-clad rescue team as the men stared at their accomplishment. Racing against the clock, they had succeeded in digging the snow from around the wreckage before nightfall.

What they had uncovered was not a pretty sight.

The fuselage of the Learjet was lying on its side, a wounded black bird with a broken wing thrust beseechingly into the sky.

The nose and flight deck had been accordioned by the impact. The passenger section, still round as a scorched tin can, lay drunkenly on its side, its charred, blistered shape giving rise to images of campfire provisions cooked directly in the can—an image Chuck Renfrew tried desperately, unsuccessfully to quash.

He breathed deeply several times. Faced with the pried–open cabin door on what was now the roof, he quailed at the odiousness of the task ahead. He knew only too well what lay in store.

He looked around. The looming mountains were darkening and pressed closer. The snow was tinted faint pink as the sun began to disappear behind the peaks.

He leaned his head way back and gazed up at the shimmering sky and its vivid blue eternity.

Fire. No explosion. Curious, that . . .

"Sir?"

Renfrew started and drew his eyes back in.

It was Kligfeld—the newest and youngest addition to his team, eager to prove himself and win acceptance from the others—as if this appalling tragedy were some perverse rite of passage.

"We got it open, sir."

"Yeah, yeah," Renfrew said testily, and thought: *Well, enough procrastination. Here goes . . .*

He tramped to the plane, leaned forward, and shaped his body to the curvature of the fuselage. Reached overhead. Grasped the bottom edge of the horizontal doorway with both gloved hands and hoisted himself up. Then, swinging his legs up and around, and feeling his way carefully with his feet, he lowered himself down into the cabin as if through a trapdoor.

He let himself drop, absorbing the impact with bent legs.

Darkness here; soot covering everything. The portholes above blackened by smoke and flames, the door a skylight barely able to penetrate the gloom. Air acrid with smoke and jet fuel burned his lungs. His eyes began watering.

After the howling wind outside, the silence was unearthly. Tomblike.

He found himself shivering. From experience, he knew that disasters always held unknown terrors. The only question was: What specific horrors awaited him here?

"We'll soon see," he muttered grimly, unclipping the flashlight from his web belt. He switched it on, played the powerful beam around—and recoiled.

"Aw, *Christ!*" he whispered, shutting his eyes. "Oh, sweet baby Jesus . . ."

He pressed his hands to the sides of his head and shook it in denial.

To no avail. He had seen what he had seen.

All the eye shutting in the world was futile against that; nothing could banish the horror from his mind's camera. Even now the terrible afterimage swam on his closed eyelids, provided fodder for a lifetime of nightmares.

The passenger—rather, what had once been the passenger—was fused to a seat frame bolted to the floor, now an upright wall. Frozen sideways in a seated position. Hairless, fleshless, sexless. Skeletal and charred. Destroyed by fire and then ice. No longer human but . . . a creature. Something Hollywood had concocted for a horror flick.

And the face! Oh, Christ Jesus, the *face!* Frost sheathed and grotesque.

Eyeless sockets leering . . . mouth stretched in a rictus.

I've seen hell, Renfrew thought. *This is hell . . . hell . . . hell . . .*

His stomach churned, the odors of jet fuel and smoke slowly nauseating him.

Have to get moving, he told himself. *The sooner this is over with, the better.*

Renfrew calmed himself by concentrating on the minutiae of things that had to be done:

Getting dark soon . . . need to have the men set up camp here on the ledge . . . start recovering the bodies at first light . . . search for the black box. But first . . .

The flight plan had listed one passenger and two crew.

First, he had to account for the pilot and copilot.

And then radio in his findings . . .

The sun had fallen from the sky and the night was purple as the rising and dipping headlights probed the dark, snow-laden incline leading up to the house. Dorothy-Anne stared out the wall of windows at the approaching vehicle, thinking: *If it were good news, they would have telephoned. They only come in person when it's bad.*

She sat there with prim dignity, hands clasped in her lap. Incredibly, her breathing was normal. Now that the moment was at hand she felt curiously calm. There was something strangely anticlimactic about the predictability of what was to come.

The others sensed it also.

Venetia rose from the sofa to stand beside her. Fred, Liz, and Zack quietly gathered behind her in a protective semicircle of linked hands. Even Nanny Florrie, who'd nodded off, came to with a start, looked momentarily bumfuzzled, then pushed herself to her feet and took up a position behind the children like a hen guarding her brood.

No one spoke. There was no need for words.

It seemed to take the car forever to crawl uphill. To Dorothy-Anne, it was like watching a film in slow motion. She was aware of seeing and hearing everything with an acute, brutal clarity. The leaping fire in the grate roaring and crackling and snapping up a storm, tinting everything with a flickering red and yellow glow. The gusts of wind buffeting the Thermopane wall, causing the grids of glass to quiver. The headlights finally disappearing around the back . . .

Soon now . . .

Slam of a car door.

Very soon.

The doorbell did not sound like a chime; to Dorothy-Anne, it seemed to toll.

She could hear the housekeeper's heels clack briskly on granite and fade; the hissing sighs of the airlock as the two sets of front doors out in the entry, one after the other, slid open and shut. The murmur of low voices drifting, like a conspiracy, on currents of warm air. And, after what seemed an interminable time, two sets of footsteps approaching the Great Hall—Mrs. Plunkett ushering in someone with a quieter, longer-legged stride.

Slowly Dorothy-Anne raised her eyes. She saw a lean, farmerish-looking man with a long thin face, weathered skin, and pallid blue eyes. He wore what looked like a uniform of sorts and held the inevitable Stetson, this one light gray, which he kept turning this way and that in front of him like a steering wheel.

His glance took in the phalanx of six anxious faces, then settled upon hers. "Ma'am," he said.

Mrs. Plunkett introduced him, agitatedly twisting her apron between plump-fingered hands. "This is Captain Friendly," she said.

Dorothy-Anne felt her world contract and then expand.

"Yes, I remember. We spoke on the phone. You're the coordinator of the mountain rescue teams."

He nodded. "That's right, ma'am." His Midwestern twang sounded more pronounced in person than on the phone. "You must be Mrs. Cantwell."

She met his gaze directly. "I am."

He heaved a sigh, glanced down at his feet, then looked back up and held her gaze once more. "I wish I could say it's a pleasure, ma'am, but under the circumstances . . ."

Dorothy-Anne sat there and nodded. *The poor man. He looks like he'd rather be anywhere but here.* Not that she could blame him. *I'd rather be someplace else, too.*

"I'm awfully sorry, ma'am. When we reached the plane, there was nothing we could do. Everyone on board was long dead."

Dorothy-Anne's expression did not alter, but her face went chalky. *It's strange. Even if you know what's coming, you're still never prepared to actually hear it verbalized.*

When she finally spoke, her voice was hushed. "How . . . how did it happen?"

"That can't be determined yet. First we have to find the flight recorder, the so-called black box. Also, the NTSB is flying in a team to mount an investigation."

"When will they recover the—"

She couldn't go on, and shut her eyes in pain.

"With luck," he said, "as soon as tomorrow."

She opened her eyes. "You'll let me know? So I can see him?"

He tightened his thin lips. "I . . . I really don't think that's . . . er . . . advisable, ma'am."

Dorothy-Anne stared at him. "What are you *saying*?"

He stood there awkwardly, uncomfortably twisting his hat left and right and left, as though steering along a zigzagging road.

"I see," she whispered faintly.

So it was that bad. We can't even see him one last time. We can't even say our last good-byes.

Captain Friendly tried to comfort her. "If it's any consolation, ma'am, death was instantaneous."

But was *it instantaneous?* Dorothy-Anne could only wonder. *What about* before *the actual crash itself? Were Freddie and the crew alive as the plane dove down, down . . . who knows how many miles, and for how long, down . . . ?*

"*Daddy!*" blurted Zack with a bursting, convulsive sob. "D-Did . . . did . . ."

Dorothy-Anne felt an unbearable stab of agony shoot through her. What was it about a child's piercing cry that shatters a mother's heart?

"Did Daddy *scream*?"

"Oh, sweetie," Dorothy-Anne said thickly. Turning around, she looked at his quivering lips and huge, hurt eyes and wished, too late, that she had seen Captain Friendly in private. That way she could at least have spared the children the worst of the shock. She might even have managed to find a way to break the news more gently.

As if there was such a way.

"*Did* he?" Zack demanded in defiant outrage. "*Did* he scream?"

Dorothy-Anne reached out, wrapped her arms around him, and pressed his anxious, hyperventilating face against her breast. She rocked him back and forth.

"I'm sure Daddy didn't have a chance to scream," she soothed. "Did he, Captain?"

She turned her head and looked beseechingly at Captain Friendly.

"N-no," he said hoarsely. "It happened so fast he couldn't have screamed . . . or even known what was happening."

She nodded gratefully, her eyes bright with held-back tears.

Quickly he looked away, unable to hold her gaze any longer.

He knows. He knows they must have been alive as the plane plummeted down.

The terror inside that cabin was beyond comprehension.

A mile is 5,280 feet. If an object falls at the rate of twenty feet per second, that makes two minutes and two seconds of unadulterated horror.

An unimaginable lifetime.

Her flesh had gone icy. She kept wanting to break down and howl, yet she fought it, not wanting to share her grief with a stranger.

Pulling herself together, she said, "I realize how difficult and thankless this errand must be, Captain. I'm sorry to have caused you so much bother."

"It's no bother at all, ma'am."

"And I've been very lax," she said. "Can I offer you some refreshment? Coffee or tea? Perhaps something a little more bracing?"

He shook his head. "No, ma'am. But thanks all the same. If there's anything—"

"We'll be fine, Captain."

"Well . . . if you're positive . . ." he said hesitantly.

"I am."

"Well, then, I guess I'll be on my way, ma'am. You have my most sincere condolences."

"Thank you, Captain. And thank you for coming."

He stood there awkwardly, trying to think of something else to say, but came up empty. "Good-bye, Mrs. Cantwell," he said.

"Good-bye, Captain Friendly. You're a very nice man."

Still holding Zack's face against her breast, Dorothy-Anne watched Mrs. Plunkett escort him out. Only once he was gone did she, the children, and Venetia instinctively seek the warmth of each other's arms, hugging each other fiercely in a joint embrace.

And it was then that the floodgates opened and their grief poured forth.

It was official. Freddie was dead.

18

Gray skies. Chill wind. Rain in the air.

Christos Zzzyonopoulos hopped off the bus at Jackson, crossed Van Ness, and proceeded to hike uphill, purposely leaving two blocks between himself and Broadway—a precaution in case Gloria Winslow happened to drive by. This was her neck of the woods, and he'd rather she didn't see him and get the idea he was there to case her real estate. Which he was. But why take unnecessary risks?

Why indeed.

Nonetheless, it was necessity, not curiosity, that prompted this trek. Matching a mark with her domicile was essential in ascertaining that she was the real McCoy. He'd learned that the hard way in Miami, where he'd zeroed in on Marifé, a Spanish lady with big bazooms and a blue Rolls Corniche.

Their relationship ended when he woke up one morning and found she'd taken a powder—along with his gold Rolex and his ten-thousand-dollar stash.

Guess who'd been conning whom.

A subsequent trace of the Rolls's license plate led to Marifé's employer, a Palm Beach divorcée who'd returned from Europe to find her silver missing, her Corniche dented, and her maid gone.

Talk about adding insult to injury. He'd targeted an heiress and ended up romancing a freakin' maid!

Worse, she'd cleaned him out. Completely. Christos had yet to recover from his loss. It was as if Marifé had put a hex on him. Maybe that explained why his life had gone downhill ever since.

Because it took money to make money, dammit! Without some cash to flash, his overtures were instantly suspect.

The ladies he hit upon were not impressed. They could smell desperation from a mile away.

Then came the last straw—a midnight visit from the repo man.

Deciding a change of scenery was in order, Christos hitchhiked west, meeting and hooking up with Amber along the way. Their destination: sunny southern California. However, a ride headed for the Bay Area— and a severe shortage of cash—necessitated an unplanned stopover.

So here they were. In foggy, chilly northern California. Barely scraping by.

Meanwhile, the unplanned stopover had stretched into six months.

And then yesterday, clear out of the blue—*whammo!* He'd found a live one—or rather, she'd stumbled across him. More amazing yet, all his instincts told him he'd struck paydirt.

Maybe his luck was finally changing. It was about time!

But once burned, twice shy. After Marifé, Christos had stopped taking anyone at face value. Which was why he'd just come from City Hall, where he'd done a property title search.

The address had presented no problem. He'd gotten that, along with Gloria's name, off her driver's license while she'd been using the john.

Discovering that the property wasn't owned by Gloria, but by one Althea Magdalena Netherland Winslow, didn't deter. At least it was in the Winslow family.

Still, it behooved him to check out Gloria's digs for himself.

On he walked. Franklin, Gough, Octavia . . . Webster, Fillmore, Steiner.

Holy shit! he thought. He knew Pacific Heights was swanky, but the farther west he walked, the freakin' bigger the houses got! He couldn't believe the size of those places!

Divisadero, Broderick, *Baker.* He made a right, wishing he could do his recon by drive-by. It was a lot easier to remain anonymous in a car than it was on foot.

Fine time to be without wheels, he thought sardonically.

He reminded himself that it was merely a temporary inconvenience. So long as he played his cards right—and he held a winning hand, he could *smell* it—he'd soon be sitting behind the wheel of a brand-new Mercedes. A sporty silver 500SL. Or, at the very least, a nifty red Mustang convertible. A GT, with mag wheels and tan leather bucket seats.

Until then he'd have to bus it and walk. Hey, a little exercise never hurt anybody. It helped keep him trim and fit. His body was his fortune, right?

Damn right. It behooved him to stay in prime shape.

Pacific. Broadway. And there it was—

"Hot *damn!* " he breathed aloud, coming to a dead halt.

One mother of a mansion set on half a city block of manicured sloping lawn. A great white palace with a sweet tooth's architectural predilic-
tions: all turn-of-the-century pilasters and cornices and two stories of
pedimented French windows. A freakin' Versailles!

So this is what Gloria Winslow calls home, he thought. *This is where,
right this very minute, she could be taking a bath or counting her money
and getting waited on hand and foot. Hopefully remembering her date with
yours truly later in the afternoon . . .*

Quickly, before he attracted undue attention to himself, he turned
around and strode back the way he had come. His mind was spinning
out of orbit.

One thing was for sure. The Winslows had greenbacks coming out
their ears.

And another thing. Gloria Winslow was one lady he wasn't about to
let slip through his fingers. No, sirree, Bob. She was his *future.* His one-
way ticket to *Paradise.*

And it would be first class all the way!

Christos! In the gilded prison of her half of the mansion, Gloria repeated
his name silently to herself throughout the morning and early afternoon.
She obsessed on him; he was all she could think of.

Was it really possible that they'd met only yesterday, that they'd
shared but a few stolen hours? And yet that brief encounter had swollen
to monumental importance in her life.

Christos, Christos. His name, chanted mentally like a mantra, was a
sunbeam bringing warmth and light into the joyless mausoleum of luxury
she inhabited, to the icy, lifeless luxury to which she was shackled: the
Winslow billions, that inexorably insensate and pitiless pile of cold, hard
cash.

Christos. Somehow, his presence in her life changed her perception
of that fortune, reduced it from some awesome, unimaginably powerful
but unseen abstract force into something far less mighty and manageable.

And with that realization came a multitude of others. It was as if her
eyes had suddenly been opened and she could see, really *see.*

For the first time in years, she noticed—truly noticed—the fine view
through the living room's tall French doors. She stood in front of one
and lingered, her admiring gaze traveling downhill, past the enviable expanse of sharply sloped manicured lawn, the staggered rooftops of the
mansions clinging to the side of the hill below, the whiteness of the
houses down in the flatlands of the marina, where the small craft harbor
sailboats and cabin cruisers, buffeted by the winds of the approaching
storm, heaved in agitation.

It was a magical moment, a moment to be cherished, to be *shared* with somebody—but not just anybody; no. With that somebody special; yes, with *Christos*! A moment so achingly beautiful that seeing it alone made her want to weep.

There was a discreet knock; a polite cough.

"Mrs. Winslow?" The butler's voice intruded on Gloria's aura of well-being, sent her thoughts scattering like so many sparks.

Gloria turned around in annoyance. "Oh, what is it now, Roddy?" she asked in a vexed tone.

The butler crossed the huge room, his face impassive.

"Mr. Winslow's publicist telephoned, madam." If Roddy found it embarrassing to act as go-between for husband and wife, he was careful never to let on.

Gloria sighed. "Do tell," she said archly, "what message did the estimable Ms. Beckett ask you to pass along?"

"That Mr. Winslow would be flying back from Sacramento late this afternoon, madam. His estimated time of arrival is five o'clock. Ms. Beckett said to remind you that the visit to the Senior Citizens' Center in Burlingame is at six-thirty."

Damn, Gloria thought. *I forgot about that one.*

"Also, the political fund-raising dinner at the Legion of Honor is at nine. Due to the tight scheduling, I was specifically asked to convey that Mr. Winslow would . . . er . . . appreciate leaving here at five-thirty sharp."

How typical! thought Gloria sourly. *Not only does it take* two *intermediaries to pass along a command—for that's what it amounts to—but naturally, I'm expected to twitch and jerk like a marionette, jumping whenever Hunt pulls a string.*

"Is there anything else?" she asked coldly.

"No, madam." Roddy's face was an impenetrable mask.

"No call from the other Mrs. Winslow?" she asked in surprise. *Telling me how I should look. What I should say.*

"No, madam."

Well, what do you know? Miracle of miracles.

"If she does call, you're to tell her I'm out. Is that understood?"

"Quite, madam."

"Also, have the car waiting out front at three. I have some last-minute shopping to do."

"Very well, madam."

"Thank you, Roddy," Gloria said dismissively, in an unconscious imitation of her mother-in-law. "That will be all."

"Thank you, madam," he said, leaving the room and shutting the double doors behind him.

Gloria sighed to herself. Reality. It would have to intrude. Now it had taken the shine off her day.

Or had it?

There was no law that said she had to cut short her rendezvous with Christos, was there? And anyway, it would do Hunt some good to keep him waiting, letting him stew.

Besides, she thought with contempt, *why should I rush? Those dreary senior citizens aren't going anywhere. Make them wait. What else do they have to do, except mark time?*

That decided, Gloria instantly felt her spirits lift.

Christos! She wanted him so badly she could taste it, just as, yesterday, she had tasted him. Sucking and licking; consuming his burning flesh as he had consumed hers.

In a few hours they would be tearing their clothes off each other, and she would be drowning in pleasures, swept away on tidal waves of magnificent release.

Forgotten now was Hunt's third-hand message; her so-called duties that everyone took for granted she'd docilely perform.

Well, were they in for a big surprise!

Visions of Christos dancing in her head, Gloria hummed softly to herself and waltzed around the room, heedless of her alcohol-induced stumbles. Now more things, little things previously taken for granted, captured her notice. The lavish arrangement of pink parrot tulips and full-blown white roses, for one.

Pausing, she did something she hadn't done in years. Bent her face into a rose and drew a deep breath, shutting her eyes as she inhaled the sweet, heady fragrance, understanding, once and for all, what it was that bees sought inside those precious petals.

The same thing Christos seeks in the blossom between my legs, she thought pleasurably. *I am his stamen. He is my pistil. Together we are as one.*

She and Christos. They had arranged to meet at three-thirty.

Gloria could hardly wait.

Amber flew to the door and had it open before Christos could turn his key in the lock. He was soaked to the skin; water dripped off him in puddles.

"Aw, *man!*" she exclaimed, backing away from him in disgust. "You're all wet!"

He thought: *This is the way I get welcomed back to this dump?*

"No shit, Sherlock." He yanked his key out of the lock and tossed it on the dinette table, where it landed with a clatter. "Case ya haven't noticed, *babe,* it's rainin' cats an' dogs."

He kicked the door shut with his heel. Reached behind him and slammed the bolt home. Then shook his head like a wet dog, sending droplets of water flying in all directions.

Amber squealed, slapping at the cold drops landing on her arms as if they were live bugs.

Christos grabbed a dish towel from the one-unit kitchenette and proceeded to rub his hair furiously.

"Hon' bunch?" Amber's voice took on a reproachful, childish whine. "You was s'posed to be back hours ago. Where've you been all this time? I was startin' to think you took a powder."

Head cocked to one side, Christos stopped drying his hair and contemplated her with one baleful eye. Jeez! Just what he needed—the freakin' Inquisition!

"Amb? Where'd I say I was goin'?" He tried for patience, but it came out sounding testy. Too bad: how many times had he told her to stifle the wifely noises?

Amber scratched her bare belly—a fidgety, nervous reaction. She was wearing skin-tight Guess? jeans and a sleeveless, faded pink T-shirt cut off at midriff, which exposed her navel and accentuated her flat, boyish breasts, prominent shoulder blades, and fragile thinness. "To check out the woman?" she replied hesitantly, as if unsure of supplying the right answer.

Einstein she wasn't, but her exotic dancing kept them from starvation. Just.

"If you knew that, then why're ya bustin' my balls?" he groused.

She sulked, waiflike eyes huge with hurt. It made her look like one of those cheap, mass-produced paintings sold in malls. "And?" she asked tentatively.

He tossed the drenched towel on the floor, shed his wet jacket, added it to the growing pile, and started unbuttoning his soaked shirt. "And what?" he asked.

She fidgeted and shrugged. Popped a wad of gum. Drew aside her curtain of long, limp black hair with her index fingers and looped it carefully behind her ears. "You know . . ." she prompted.

"I do?"

"Yeah." Her hesitant smile quivered on and off.

He stripped off his shirt, then his T-shirt, and after kicking off his Westerns, began to divest himself of his trousers. "What do I look like? Jeanne fuckin' Dixon?"

"*Christos!*" Her tone became wheedling. "You're holdin' out on me!"

He looked at her, his lips drawing back over his lupine teeth in a smile. "Now why would I wanna do that?" he asked. "Huh, babe?"

"I dunno." Amber gave a sullen shrug, fished a mangled pack of cigarettes out of her rear pocket, and stuck one in her mouth. She flicked her Bic, dipped the cigarette into it, and dragged deeply. "So whatcha find out?" She exhaled the smoke from her mouth and drew it right back up through her nostrils. "About the woman. She loaded, or what?"

The crazy hold that greed exerts on you. The sudden reluctance to share, fifty-fifty, what you promised and shook on. Christos no longer wanted to part with half the loot. Shit, no. Not on a jackpot *this* size.

"Oh, she's got plenty," he said vaguely, deciding there was no need for a full disclosure. With luck, he'd be able to fob Amber off with a couple of grand. That would get her out of his hair. And, more importantly, out of his life.

The sooner she was history, the better. Especially now that small-time hustles and penny-ante rip-offs were a thing of the past.

Christos was amazed at the way his view of the future had changed. For the first time in his life he had plans. Major plans. And they didn't include two women.

No, ma'am. Where he was headed, there was room for only one.

He thought of her now. Gloria Winslow. Mrs. Hunt Netherland Winslow.

He'd suspected from the start that she was wealthy, true. And after checking out the property deed and the house, it became clear that the Winslows were more than merely wealthy—they were rich.

However, it was after his spur-of-the-moment inspiration—his visit to the public library where he'd leafed through the last issue of the *Forbes* Four Hundred—that it became clear just how filthy dirty rich the Netherland Winslows of San Francisco really were.

The discovery had blown his mind.

Two billion smackeroos and counting. He wouldn't have believed it if anyone had told him. But there it had been, in black and white.

And Gloria . . . *Glo* . . . the lush he had honored with the pleasure of his cock, was married to the sole heir, the crown prince, the golden boy of California politics.

Christos, whose mama hadn't raised a fool, recognized the chance of a lifetime when he saw it. He also knew better than to fuck it up. But he'd have to proceed slowly, carefully. Feel his way inch by cautious inch and play his cards just right.

This wasn't the kind of score where you got a second chance.

But Amber was a definite liability. Trouble was, for the time being he needed the extra cash her topless dancing brought in.

"Babe?" He tossed his trousers on the wet heap and stood there, naked as a jaybird. Looking good and knowing it. "We got a dry towel anywhere?"

His nudity had the desired effect. She took one last puff off her cigarette, squashed it in the foil ashtray, and hurried to fetch one.

When she returned, he reached out to take it, but Amber shook her head. "No," she said. "Lemme dry you off."

She began by toweling off his moist broad back, then working her way around to the front. Her fingers were light and quick, and she found the male scent of him intoxicating; it rose pungently from his glistening wet skin.

"Oh, hon' bunch!" she sighed, wrapping towel and arms tightly around him. She rested her face sideways against his chest. Beneath the layer of densely packed muscle she could feel and hear the healthy beat of his heart. "You don't know how worried you had me," she whispered. "Sometimes I get so scared!"

"Scared!" He laughed soundlessly. "For chrissake, why?"

Amber gazed up at him, her seaweed green eyes wide with fear. "What if . . . if something were to happen to you?" He could feel her shivering. "I don't know what I'd do then!"

"Shit, babe. You're not exactly helpless. Y'always got your dancin' to fall back on. Besides, what could happen to me?" He flashed her a cocky grin. "I know how to take care of myself."

"Yeah, but what if—"

He silenced her by kissing her lips in midsentence.

Amber purred and wriggled closer, her bony hips grinding against his.

Whammo! The reaction from the old flagpole was immediate, but sex was out of the question. He had to save his energies for Gloria Winslow.

He attempted to disengage himself from Amber, but she kept clinging to him.

"Hon' bunch, please?" she pleaded. "Pretty please?"

"Unh-unh, babe," he said. "Not now." He flashed her his best smile. "Magic Man's got to get movin', go work some of his magic."

Amber tightened her grip on him and plastered herself even closer.

"Why don't you work some of that magic on me?" she crooned softly, running the tip of her tongue across his nipple. "I'll prime your pump for ya. That way you won't have any trouble gettin' it up for that ugly ole hag."

He took exception to that. He never had trouble getting it up— although there were times he wished he did. It would certainly simplify his life.

"Later," he told her. "After I'm back."

"Please?" Clever fingers walked spiderlike down his chest to his flat washboard and then gripped hold of his hard-on. Slowly she peeled back his foreskin. "Just a quickie?"

He stood very still, then gently pushed her away. "First work," he said softly. "*Then* play."

She sighed. "It's not 'cause you're still angry with me, is it?" She looked up and held his gaze.

"Angry?" He forced a laugh. "Why should I be angry?"

"I dunno." She shrugged. "But you weren't exactly in the best mood when you walked in."

"That's only 'cause I got caught in the downpour," he lied.

"That's all it was?"

"Wouldn't I tell you if it weren't?"

She was suddenly all smiles. "I'm so glad!" She hugged him again. "Oh, God, hon' bunch!" she whispered. "If you only knew how much I love you!"

He looked out over her head, to the dirty window at the far end of the room, and some invisible point beyond. "Yeah, babe," he replied absentmindedly. "Me too."

Then he slapped her playfully on the rump.

"Now why don't you scare up some dry clothes for me, huh? I gotta make a good impression. An' hurry. I'm runnin' late."

Convinced that all was well, she gave his lips a quick peck and happily went about assembling his wardrobe.

Watching her, her wondered what Amber would think if he told her that Gloria was neither ugly, old, nor a hag.

Better she doesn't find out, he thought pleasurably. *For a slightly mature woman, that Gloria Winslow is one fine piece of ass.*

He and Gloria. It wouldn't be long before they'd be tumbling into bed.

Christos could hardly wait.

19

I n front of Mama Rosa's, a double-parked black stretch Caddie with blacked-out windows blocked the No Parking zone by the fire hydrant.

Problema? Not for Sonny Fong. He welcomed the opportunity to flex his automotive muscle.

Shifting into reverse, he jammed the accelerator to the floor and twisted the heel.

With a squeal of burning rubber, the Lexus swung behind the Caddie in a single, artfully executed maneuver. Then, accurately gauging the distance between his front bumper and the limo's rear, Sonny shifted into drive, shot forward, and slammed on the brakes.

The Lexus screeched to a halt with a fraction of an inch to spare.

Both front doors of the limo burst open. A beefy driver jumped out one side, a just-as-beefy bodyguard out the other. Both were armed and rushed the Lexus, rapping on the side windows with the barrels of their Uzis.

Sonny Fong was unfazed. He was Mr. Cool. Uzis or no, he wasn't about to be hurried.

He switched on the interior lights. He squirted Binaca in his mouth. He craned his neck to check out his tie in the rearview mirror, eyed his hair critically, and glanced at his gold Rolex.

His breath was minty fresh, his Windsor knot perfectly tied, his blow-dried hair required just a run-through with his fingers, and he was fifteen minutes early. Only then did he open his door and get out.

"Whatcha got, a death wish?" yelled the limo driver, poking the barrel of his Uzi into Sonny Fong's chest.

"Yeah, ya got any idea *whose* limo this here is?" growled the body-

146

guard, coming around the back of the Lexus and taking up a threatening stance beside the driver.

Sonny yawned and gave them a bored look—letting them see just how unimpressed Mr. Cool was. "You may put the hardware away, gentlemen," he said politely. "That way, no one will get hurt."

"Get 'em up, ya fuckin' gook!" snarled the bodyguard.

Wearily Sonny raised both hands in surrender. Then, as if something had caught his attention, he flicked his eyes in the direction of the restaurant's awning.

Both goons fell for it and shifted their gaze.

A major mistake. Sonny's hands chopped down straight and true.

Both men's shoulder blades cracked noisily under the impact and they fell grunting to their knees. They were still struggling to lift their weapons when Sonny jabbed the nerves inside their elbows.

Their gun arms went dead.

Relieving them of the Uzis was like taking candy from a baby. Sonny grasped each weapon by the barrel and swung the stock ends, swiping each man across the side of the head.

They fell face-flat in tandem, lights out.

Sonny tossed the weapons on top of them, unfolded a perfectly pressed handkerchief, and wiped his hands as he headed for the restaurant.

A small shadow detached itself from a nearby doorway. "Cool!" a young voice said admiringly. "You're one bad dude, mister!"

Sonny glanced at him. It was the same urchin who had guarded his car yesterday.

"Watch my wheels," he said, a folded twenty appearing magically between his index and middle fingers.

"Sure, mister." The kid eyed it warily, then stepped forward and quickly fished it from Sonny's fingers. He said, "Ain't ya gonna tear it in half?"

Sonny glanced pointedly over his shoulder, then looked at the kid without expression. "I don't think there's any need for that," he said softly. "Do you?"

"No, *sir*!"

"I didn't think so."

And with that, Sonny descended the steps and entered the bizarre, semi-churchly atmosphere of Mama Rosa's.

First thing he did, he cased the joint.

Except for a single booth near the front, the rabbit warren of low-ceilinged, interconnected arches was empty of diners. Sonny glanced at the men occupying the nearby booth. There were four of them, and all wore custom-tailored suits and had "mob" written all over them.

Two hulks, also in suits, hovered close by. It didn't take a rocket scientist to make them for bodyguards, especially with their too-tight jackets showing the outlines of their shoulder holsters.

"Hey," the bartender growled. "The restaurant's—"

Sonny turned and silenced him with a look. "I've got an appointment to see Mama Roma," he said quietly. "So why don't you let her know I'm here?"

"Oh. *You're* the guy."

Appeased, the bartender looked around and snapped his fingers. Presently the ancient waiter Sonny remembered from the previous day came shuffling over.

The bartender said: "Tell Mama she's got a visitor. *Pronto.*"

Wordlessly the waiter limped off toward the back.

Sonny sauntered to the booth where the four men were seated.

"Excuse me," he said quietly.

Four well-fed faces whiplashed in his direction. Sonny felt more than saw a movement from behind, but a mobster lifted a finger, stilling the bodyguards in their tracks.

Another mobster said, "Shit. What we got here? A wise ass?"

"Well, least he ain't yellow," wheezed the fattest, "though he sure looks it. Must be dim and then some!" He shook with silent laughter.

Sonny struggled to keep his facial muscles from tightening. It was all he could do to swallow the heat of his rage. He stared down at he man, his expression carefully bland. This was neither the time nor the place to show his anger. Besides, he recognized the racist's face, recalled its grainy monochrome from dozens of tabloid photographs: Marco "the Clam" Capozzi, so nicknamed for his refusal to talk to the authorities—Marco on the federal courthouse steps, Marco in cuffs headed for a country club prison, Marco ducking into his limousine, into the social club that was said to be his "family's" headquarters.

He said, "That limo outside. It wouldn't happen to belong to one of you?"

"What if it does?" wheezed the fat mobster. "You ram it?"

"No, but there were two men inside it."

The fleshy eyes squinted meanly. "Whatcha mean, 'were'?"

"Unfortunately, they have a tendency to poke their weapons at people." Sonny shrugged. "It made me nervous, so I . . . ah . . . neutralized them."

The fat mobster signaled to one of the bodyguards, who hurried out to investigate.

"You kill 'em?" inquired the youngest, a sleek, baby-faced killer in his forties.

Sonny shook his head. "No. Just knocked them unconscious, that's all."

"Yeah? Whatcha use?"

"Just these." Sonny lifted his hands.

"You're full o' shit!" Marco huffed, grabbing his Sambuca and taking a slug. He banged the glass down on the table. "My guys're tough as they come!"

From the back of the dining room came the cacophony of kitchen noises and women's chatter as a door opened and shut, then opened and shut again a minute later.

The bodyguard came running back inside. "Hey, boss!" he called out.

Marco swiveled his head. "What?" He glared angrily.

"You ain't gonna believe this, but Tony and Sal? They was both out cold."

"What! Damn incompetent fools! I'll deal with them later!"

"They're startin' to come to, an' I asked 'em what happened? They said they don't know what hit 'em."

Marco's ruddy face grew even redder. The veins on his forehead bulged like worms trying to pop out from under the skin. He stabbed a sausage-link finger at Sonny. "As for this fuckin' clown, take him away. He's fish food!"

From behind him, Sonny heard the slides on guns being pulled back and released; the unmistakable metallic clicks of pistols being cocked.

"*Who's* fish food?" The strong female voice carried from the back.

They all turned and watched Mama Rosa, huge and imposing, come waddling forward. She was wearing the same washed-out blue housedress and baby blue vinyl slippers as yesterday. Even her apron looked identical.

"Put the guns away," she commanded, scowling at the bodyguards, who in turn looked searchingly at Marco. Her dark eyes flashed. "You know the rules. You pull a piece in my place, you're eighty-sixed. And since they're your guys," she told Marco in no uncertain terms, "that includes you."

"But this slope—"

"Unh-unh. I don't want to hear no excuses!"

Mama Rosa rested her hands on her hips. Her massive bosom rose and fell, and on her forehead and upper lip, droplets of sweat gleamed moistly.

"Well?" She scowled at Marco.

Marco sighed and gestured to his bodyguards, who put their weapons away.

"That's better." Mama nodded approvingly. "You want my advice, Marco, I wouldn't mess with this guy. He's a friend of my Carmine's."

She put a fleshy arm around Sonny's shoulder.

"Now, I'm taking this gentlemen upstairs to my place. He has business with Carmine."

She took Sonny's arm.

"Now let's go upstairs so you can take care of business," she said, guiding him through the sea of tables to a door marked PRIVATE.

It didn't lead to an office, as Sonny expected, but into a shabby, dim hallway and the tenement's staircase.

Mama Rosa grabbed hold of the banister."Now," she sighed, "we climb. I live five flights up."

"Is Carmine waiting upstairs?" Sonny asked hopefully.

"We talk in private," Mama admonished. Then, huffing and puffing, she slowly labored up the steep stairs.

The front door opened directly into the eat-in kitchen, which still retained its original cast-iron bathtub.

Sonny looked around.

The layout was your typical Little Italy railroad—four narrow rooms, like a series of nearly windowless boxcars, one leading into the next.

In the kitchen, every available wall space was hung with decoratively carved and painted shrines.

"Reliquaries," Mama Rosa, wheezy and breathless from the climb, explained proudly. "I collect saints' relics. Carmine, he brings them back from his travels. See this one here?"

Sonny nodded.

"It contains genuine remains of Saint Catherine of Siena. And the one up there? It's got some relics of Saint Mark. And that one, it's got a piece of bone of Saint Anthony of Padua. . . ."

No piece of Noah's Ark or the True Cross? Sonny was tempted to crack, but curbed the impulse.

"My Carmine, he treats his mama like a queen," she said, her voice bursting with pride. "He bought me this entire building. Imagine! How many sons would do that for their mama, eh?"

"Speaking of Carmine," Sonny said, anxious to be on his way, "where is he?"

"All in good time," she said, making a beeline for the big deep double sink. "First, Mama Rosa needs your help."

My what? "I'm not sure I understand," he said cautiously.

"This place?" She gestured around. "It's gettin' filthy."

Sonny watched her bend over and pull a galvanized bucket filled with cleaning supplies out from under the sink. She carried it over and set it down in front of him.

What in hell? He stared down at the containers of Mr. Clean, Fantastik, and Windex; rags, sponges, and paper towels.

"The living room needs a good cleaning," Mama Rosa said. "So does Carmine's room, but that can wait. He hardly ever spends the night here anymore." She tapped the closet door. "The vacuum cleaner's in here. So are the mops and dustcloths."

Jesus H. Christ! Sonny thought, with rising alarm. *She can't be serious! Me—clean?*

He said, "Look, I'm in kind of a hurry. . . ."

She waved away his protests. "That's the trouble with all you young people," she said. "Always in a hurry."

"Yes, but—"

"I gotta go back downstairs," she said.

"But—"

"I'll be back before you know it. Meanwhile, you clean." Her eyes glinted shrewdly. "Mama saved you from Marco. Right?"

"Well, yeah . . ."

"Now you can repay the favor."

"But what about Carmine?"

She said, "When I come back."

And she was gone.

Sonny stood there glowering. "Shit!" he shouted, giving the bucket a violent kick and sending it flying across the linoleum. "How the hell did I get myself into this? I'm not the fuckin' maid!"

He stomped into the living room, its furniture, cheap and garish in the too-bright glare of the table lamps, an eyesore of overly ornate, cast resin "carving." The upholstered pieces were zippered in thick, protective clear vinyl covers. And, unlike the paintings in the restaurant, the pictures up here were ghastly. A machine-made tapestry of the Kennedy brothers, John and Robert, on one wall. A tapestry portrait of the pope on another. A New York skyline executed on black velvet studded with twinkle lights.

The only decent piece in the entire room was the television—a giant, forty-inch picture tube Mitsubishi.

Probably fell off a truck, Sonny thought sardonically. *Either that, or Carmine bought it for her.*

Carmine!

What was it she'd said? Something about Carmine's room . . .

Christ, Carmine!

His heart began knocking excitedly against his rib cage. Talk about a golden opportunity. *I might even discover the assassin's identity!* he thought euphorically.

He crossed to what must be a bedroom door, and opened it. Maybe this was Carmine's room.

The first thing he noticed was the acrid, lingering odor of recent cigarette smoke. A day or two old, no more.

Sonny carefully lowered the blinds before switching on the lights.

Nothing ornate or frilly in here. Oak and mahogany, an old brass bed kept lovingly polished, a bookcase groaning with titles. Atop a dresser rested a portable Sony television, a VCR, and a stereo set with a record changer.

The bed was freshly made, and one nightstand held a reading lamp, a clean ashtray, an open pack of Camels, a well-worn missal bound in black leatherette, and a copy of *The Plague* by Albert Camus. On the other was a matching lamp, a telephone, an answering machine, and a silver-framed, eight-by-ten photograph of Mama Rosa.

Sonny felt a wave of euphoria. *Carmine's room!* he thought, barely able to contain himself. *It's got to be!*

Aware that a person's taste in reading is one of the best reflections of his personality, Sonny made a beeline for the bookcase.

The first thing that struck him was the almost pathological sense of order. Carmine had categorized the nonfiction books by content, and had shelved the biographies alphabetically by subject and the works of fiction alphabetically by author.

He scanned the titles.

The histories included *The Civilization of the Middle Ages* by Norman Cantor, and Winston Churchill's four-volume *The World Crisis* series; the biographies, on the other hand, consisted entirely of grandiose warped minds: Attila the Hun, Caligula, Adolf Hitler, Genghis Khan, and Joseph Stalin.

Lovely, Sonny thought sardonically. *Birds of a feather flock together.*

But most surprising were the works of literature. They ranged from the likes of James Agee and Vladimir Nabokov to Marcel Proust, Leo Tolstoy, and Émile Zola.

The bottom shelf was devoted exclusively to LPs. There were boxed sets of Italian operas. Caruso and Mario Lanza on 78s. Count Basie, Ella Fitzgerald, and Billie Holiday on 33s. Plus Tony Bennett, Vic Damone, and Sinatra.

Sonny smiled to himself. Slowly but surely, a picture of Carmine was emerging.

If the photographs were any indication, the assassin was dark-haired and would be approximately thirty years of age. Judging by the books on his shelves, he was an intellectual and a history buff, and harbored a morbid bent for real-life monsters. The missal indicated he probably attended Mass sporadically, if not regularly.

He was also highly organized, smoked unfiltered Camels, and liked listening to opera, jazz, and Italian crooners.

It's a beginning, Sonny thought. *Now to flesh him out even further . . .*

Sonny checked out Carmine's closet next.

Strong smell of cedar. Wooden hangers all facing in the same direction. Clothes sorted according to season—spring wardrobe on the left, summer and fall in the middle, winter on the right.

A cursory examination of the labels showed they ran the gamut. Armani and Cerutti overcoats. Custom-tailored suits by Huntsman and Son of Savile Row. Sportswear from the Gap, Banana Republic, and Calvin Klein. Knockaround gear from J. Crew, Tommy Hilfiger, and Champion.

The jackets were 41 long, the pants 30 in the waist and 34 in length.

So he's probably six foot one, Sonny thought, *and in top physical condition.*

Hardly surprising, considering Carmine's profession.

Neckties on the rotating rack ranged from Fendi and Hermès to Jerry Garcia, and a slant-fronted, three-tier rack on the floor contained Italian custom-made lace-ups and Gucci loafers, size $10^1/_2$. Each pair was polished, fitted with shoe trees, and lined up with military precision. Sneakers were Mephistos and Nikes.

Sonny shut the closet door. Next on the agenda was Carmine's dresser.

The first two drawers he tried contained freshly laundered Turnbull and Asser shirts in poplin, linen, and cotton. The middle ones were devoted exclusively to immaculately folded underwear and perfectly aligned rows of expensive, rolled-up socks.

But it was in the bottom drawers that he hit pay dirt.

Squatting on his haunches, Sonny stared, unable to believe his eyes. He hadn't known what he might find—but this—*this!*

His head spun with the magnitude of the evidence before him and its implications.

Both deep drawers contained a veritable arsenal of disguises. *Grist for the mill for a slippery chameleon.* Hair dye, toupees, self-adhering moustaches and beards. *Grist for the mill for a slippery chameleon.* Tinted contacts, foam pads to fill out cheeks and jaw, various styles of eyeglasses fitted with plain glass lenses. *Grist for the mill for a slippery chameleon.*

Sonny's mental picture of Carmine fragmented, dematerialized back into shadow. The assassin would be impossible to recognize. Hair, eyes, age—*chameleon.* Like an actor switching roles, Carmine would simply shed one skin and slip into another, morphing himself into characters and personalities too numerous to follow.

Sonny felt a grudging admiration for the assassin. Clearly no fool, Carmine was not a man to be underestimated.

Or trifled with.

Closing the left-hand drawer, he was about to push the right one shut when a flash of vivid red in the back left corner captured his notice.

Red, the color of blood.

It's impossible! he thought, his pulse quickening. *It can't be!*

He took a deep breath, hesitated only briefly, and pulled the drawer further open.

But it was. Right there in front of him. A neatly folded stack of Carmine's silk neckties—the calling cards the assassin left behind at the scene of each job.

"By all gods great and small!" Sonny whispered in the Chiuchow dialect.

Unable to help himself, he reached a hand inside, his fingers trembling as they made contact with the silk. It felt soft and smooth and almost obscenely luxurious, the red, bright as the blood it symbolized, linking killer and victim as participants in that most unholy communion of all, sharing life's final and most intimate moment—death.

Death . . . Carmine . . . silk . . . death . . .

Sonny snatched his hand back as if the silk burned. Quickly he pushed the drawer shut and stood up. Fear pounded against his rib cage—no, not fear, he told himself; a kind of adrenaline-induced excitement.

Turning away, the telephone answering machine attracted his notice.

God only knows what that tape contains, he thought.

The temptation to hit the Playback button and listen to its possible trove of unerased messages was overwhelming. But consulting his gold Rolex, he ascertained that he'd pushed his luck far enough.

The last thing I need is for Mama Rosa to catch me red-handed.

Prudently Sonny Fong switched off the lights, raised the blinds, and left the room, shutting the door behind him.

It was time to clean the living room—lest Mama Rosa suspect he'd been up to no good.

And shedding his jacket, Sonny rolled up his sleeves and got to work.

More than two hours passed before Mama Rosa trudged heavily up the stairs.

Finally! Sonny thought sourly as she lowered her bulk into a recliner. He glanced around. The living room sparkled, and there wasn't a speck of dust in sight.

"Well?" he asked. "What do you think? Looks pretty good, huh?"

"It'll do," she said wearily, not bothering to look around.

It'll do? Sonny was incensed. After working his ass off and all but ruining his Armani, *this* was the thanks he got?

"About Carmine," he said.

"Oh, yeah," she said. "I'm glad you reminded me. He dropped by the restaurant and told me to give you something."

She groped around in her apron pocket and handed him a wrinkled, unsealed envelope.

Sonny opened it. Inside it were two folded sheets of paper. Laser-printed on the first was the name of a bank on Grand Cayman Island, instructions for bank wire transfers, and an eight-digit account number. The second sheet was blank.

Sonny gnashed his teeth in frustration. *For this I waited around for over two hours and played maid?* Concealing his disgust, he thrust the paper into his suit pocket.

"No." Mama Rosa shook her head. "Carmine said you're to memorize it."

I'm to what? He appraised her closely to see whether or not she was joking. From her answering stare, it was clear she wasn't.

"All right." He sighed.

"And I'm to burn it before you leave," she added, digging around in her apron pocket for a Mama Rosa's Ristorante matchbook. When he handed the sheet of paper back to her, she held it by the top, scratched a match, and lit the bottom corner.

Greedily the flames consumed it, the charred end curling and flaking. Before it burned her fingers, she dropped it into the ashtray on the table next to the recliner.

"Carmine said to write down the job you want done on the blank sheet. Then put it in the envelope and seal it. As soon as the money's in the account, he'll get started."

Sonny produced a gold Meisterstück fountain pen, wrote down the name, folded the paper, and slid it back inside the envelope. Inwardly he grimaced as he licked the dirty gummed flap and sealed it.

"Here," he said, holding it out.

But Mama Rosa didn't take it. Nor was she even listening. Her head was tilted sideways.

She had nodded off.

20

Same hotel, different room.

Was it a sign of her perverseness that the squalor actually added to her excitement? That everything in the room reeked deliciously of sex, of thousands upon thousands of sordid, illicit acts?

If walls could only talk, Gloria thought dreamily, *I wonder what tales these could tell.*

She wondered, too, at the molten ease with which lies flowed smoothly, silkily, off the tip of her tongue. Getting into the Lincoln, she had instructed Laszlo to take her to the St. Francis.

"I'm having tea with a friend, and then I may do some shopping," she told him as he pulled up outside the Union Square entrance. "I don't know how long I'll be. I'll phone you when I want to be picked up. I'll be right up front here."

Before Laszlo could respond, Gloria jumped out of the car, went up the front steps, and through the heavy revolving door. Unerringly she cut across the hotel lobby as quickly as dignity would permit, heedless of the golden gloom, the flower-patterned carpet, the soaring granite columns capped with gilded Corinthian capitals.

She strode rapidly down the long corridor to the right, not noticing the well-dressed guests raising their eyebrows at her single-minded determination to cleave through the crowd. The fresh bouquets at the flower stand, the latest fashions on display in the mall-like boutique windows— nothing caught her eye as she bore down on her objective, the Post Street exit through which she sailed back outside.

She hopped into the back of a waiting cab. "Mission between Seventh and Eighth," she said breathlessly.

The driver, surprised at the destination of his exceedingly well-dressed passenger, flicked a glance in his rearview mirror. "You're sure that's the address you want, lady?"

"Am I sure? Of course I'm sure! Damn this weather—you'd think people would be used to it by now! Instead, it slows everything down." Gloria, for once more intoxicated on rampant anticipation than on booze, was only the slightest bit tipsy. "Now step on it. I haven't got all day, you know."

"It's your neck," the cabbie grumbled, switching on the meter.

The distance between the two hotels was ten short blocks and about a hundred million dollars. No gilt-topped columns here, no great modern towers with glass elevators supplementing the old-fashioned facade. Just grimy brick and broken neon and—there! Christos, *her* Christos!—waiting just inside the iron-barred front door, the cracked glass of which was held together with strips of masking tape.

Gloria didn't bother putting up her umbrella. Her Burberry raincoat and Hermès scarf were sufficient for darting from cab to hotel to Christos's warm, inviting arms.

"Am I glad to see you!" she sighed, happily yielding to his embrace.

"Hey!" he said. "That was supposed to be my line."

She laughed with utter sweetness. Then he kissed her deeply and she was drowning in sensations, in the yin and yang of him: the raspy designer stubble and the smooth moist hungry mouth and the callused but gentle hands and his eyes like shadowy cobalt. And his touch—dear sweet Jesus, like a blast furnace it was, igniting her insides!

"Enough!" she whispered suddenly, extricating herself from his clinch. Her eyes were shiny. "I purposely didn't wear panties, and I'm already all wet! If I don't watch it, my skirt'll get soaked!"

He laughed. "In that case, we'd better go see about a room."

She discreetly slipped him a thick envelope. "Take it out of this."

And then they were upstairs, frantically tearing at each other's clothes. Giving the walls one more tale they could have told.

Ah, how she basked in this sordidness! How she reveled in the vileness of these grim, sex-consecrated surroundings!

Was it indicative of degeneracy that she should find slumming so thrilling a luxury—and paying for sex more arousing and titillating than any she had ever experienced?

Legally it was a crime to pay for sexual services.

Legally it was a crime for room-by-the-hour whores' dormitories like this one to exist, let alone flourish. And yet flourish it did: weren't the moans and groans filtering in from neighboring rooms proof positive?

So she was the wife of a prominent politician. So *what?* Gloria couldn't care less. Let Hunt, followed by a veritable army of politicians, campaign on platforms of law and order and cleaning up the streets;

she, Gloria Winslow, had discovered the most exciting, gratifying, and dangerous liaison of them all.

As for the fact that any scandal on her part could ruin her husband's career neither goaded Gloria on nor gave her pause, quite simply because sex with Christos was the most exciting thing to have happened to her in years. He was at once her passion and her boy toy, a living, breathing sex object of incomparable physical perfection, a male she could procure whenever the mood possessed her, who could awaken in her all the urges for which her body had been starved.

Now, gazing at him in the nude, she was once again amazed at the sheer reality of him, for she hadn't painted him nearly as scrumptuous in her memory as he was in the flesh.

She wondered how that could be possible. Surely it should be the other way around, shouldn't it? After all, one's mind was wont to embellish one's heartthrob with characteristics he didn't possess—airbrushing a physical flaw here, adding a soupçon of flesh there, perhaps rendering his small firm buns as, well, smaller and firmer than they actually were.

But no. Astonishingly, she had retained an *under*imbued memory of him, and especially in the department where it counted the most, right there between his legs.

Well, goodness me, Gloria thought as she regarded the already hard member protruding proudly from its curly dark nest. It was prodigiously long, stupendously thick, and so preeminently well shaped it could have served as the model for the ideal dildo.

How *could* she have remembered it as something less when it was the very quintessence, the absolute idealization of the perfect penis?

He turned up the megawatts of his blinding whites. "Well?" he said, with obvious amusement. "You just gonna stand there and stare? Or what?"

Holding his gaze, she reached out slowly and placed the tips of her fingers in his mouth. She watched him close his lips around them, felt the surge of suction, then the ever-so-gentle nibbles of lupine teeth.

"Hmmm, what big healthy teeth you have!" she observed.

He let go of her fingers in a flash. "The better to eat you with, my dear!"

And with a playful growl, he grabbed hold of her buttocks, slid to his knees, and buried his face in the wetness of her mound.

"Christos!" she gasped, thrusting her hips forward and clutching his shoulders for support. "Oh, God! Oh, God! Oh, sweet—"

Suddenly words no longer sufficed in this sexually charged atmosphere of pure vibrating energy. Words held no meaning for bodies hurtling into the very vortex of a great cosmic collision. Only sounds existed: the incoherent cries, bestial grunts, and drawn-out screams of pure, undiluted pleasure.

Gloria cried out the instant his mouth sealed itself over her secret lips like an airlock.

She cried out again as his hands, cupping her buttocks, brutally pulled her deeper into his face.

And she cried out again and again as his tongue, that craftiest of all pleasure-seeking appendages, flicked and probed her innermost sanctum.

It was more than she could bear—and less than she desired.

More, more, more! Down there where her cavern guarded the treasure of her womanhood. Where his tongue was an oral cock sending wild electrical pulses zipping and zinging, and nothing, not life or even death, could sunder them!

Never, never in her wildest fantasies had she imagined being this completely crazed, this totally and erotically possessed! Even yesterday had been a mere prelude, a foretaste, a preview of coming attractions.

But this! *This* carnal abandon was more than just sex. It was something deeper and headier, infinitely stronger. The chemistry that bound her to his gravitational pull, the thrill of liberation that filled her to bursting—as if she had sprouted enormous white wings and were on the verge of taking flight—nothing had prepared her for passions so fierce, needs so fiery, joys so uncontainable.

This was the power and the glory. The beginning and the end. Death and resurrection.

Her appetite was whetted, and there was no turning back.

A sense of corruption such as she had never known came up in her. Gladly now she surrendered to her basest animal urges. .

Forward she rocked on the balls of her feet.

Wildly, shamelessly, *obscenely* she twisted her hips, rubbing and thrusting her opening in his face.

And still he grasped tightly to her smooth solid buttocks, still he gulped mouthfuls of nectar from her bottomless well.

Again she cried out, digging her nails into the granitic, plaited muscles of his shoulders. So intense was the spasm, so overwhelming the sensation of being swept away and flung out of the cosmos, that she clung to him for dear life.

Then, her entire body weak and racked with tremors, she sank unsteadily to her knees. Her firm breasts and flat belly rose and fell, and still she kept clutching him, drawing one deep, ragged breath after another.

It was her first orgasm of the afternoon, but not the last.

Barely had she recovered when Christos laid her, faceup, on the abrasive, dirty ochre carpet as though upon a flower-strewn altar of devotion.

Never had cushions of silk felt finer than these chafing nylon fibers! Never had the ministrations of priest or lover raised her to such transcendental consciousness.

With bated breath she waited. With eyes wide and luminous, she gazed at him raptly, following his every move.

No detail escaped her heightened senses. Not the rain squiggling down the closed window above them, which cast pale, wormlike shadows to crawl and wiggle down his face and gleaming nude body; not the reflection of herself she saw in his eyes, two miniature Glorias captured within those exceptional rings of dark cobalt; not the musky scent of her climax that lingered on his breath.

"And now," he whispered, "we begin. Really begin."

"*Yes!*" she breathed eagerly. "Oh, Christos! *Yes!*"

He knelt over her, took her by the wrists, and gently spread-eagled her arms and pinioned them to the floor. Then, dipping his head, he gave his undivided attention first to one plumply nippled breast and then the other.

His lips were paralyzing. She lay there, eyes closed, the better to concentrate on every exquisite sensation. She felt his velvet tongue trace a snail's trail of leisurely concentric circles, explore the soft, warm valley between her bosom, brush the tender, swollen buds of her nipples.

Like a newborn he suckled, inflaming her aching need and drawing out the inevitable, deliberately prolonging the sweet, maddening torture by thwarting her urgency.

Then she felt his delicious weight atop her, and her pulse quickened. Tears sprang to her eyes—tears of joy and exhilaration. "Yes!" she gasped. "Oh, Christos, now! *Now!*"

"Easy . . ." he breathed, the word a cool exhalation against her feverish skin. "Easy does it. There's no rush."

She groaned, unable to bear her deferred desires a moment longer— no, not a *moment!*—but still he continued to tease, merely letting her feel the straining length of his phallus trapped between their bellies.

She lifted her head, her expression accusing. "Christos!"

But he wasn't about to be hurried, and took obvious delight in her frustrated hands clenching and unclenching, her arms and thighs tensing, her torso thrusting upward, demanding to be filled.

"Inside me!" she gasped. "For the love of God, Christos! Put it *inside* me!"

Now he suckled her teats with the passion of a grown man: nipping harder, more urgently. Rolling a plum-tipped nipple gently between his teeth.

Her eyes were once again shut and she moaned and writhed, whipping her head from side to side. Carefully his teeth applied more pressure, and she thrashed wildly, her mouth gaping wide, as if she sought intoxicated ecstasy from the very air itself.

Now he felt his blood racing through his veins, the sense of power, as though mainlined, gathering strength and centering in his penis. Cruelly, he bit down hard.

This time her screams echoed off the walls as the pain shot through her. Her eyes flew open and she stared at him wildly.

"Open your legs," he whispered. "Part your thighs."

She needed no prompting. Greedily her legs parted and she bent her knees pliantly, drawing them toward her shoulders and bracing herself with her forearms.

His hands gripped her hips and then he straddled her.

She closed her eyes, welcoming the blackness. Purposely banishing all visual distractions so that she might relish every last, delicious morsel of sensation.

Slowly he entered her.

Pain and pleasure. She gasped aloud as the two merged and became one.

And suddenly the veil of blackness lifted and she saw scenes of infinite wonder: ever-shifting pictures transforming themselves like fleeting dreams—a swan taking wing, only to morph into a pale pink rosebud that opened as though filmed with time-lapse photography.

Everything she felt became visions of inordinate beauty. His gentle thrusts were fleecy clouds wafting, feather-light, against the bluest of blue skies. His full deep penetration became a herd of leaping white stallions. And when she contracted her muscles around him and met his every thrust, she saw a vivid cloud of violet-and-pink butterflies take flight.

Dear God in heaven: impossible, this consuming ecstasy, this wild, impassioned rapture of flesh merged with flesh! Sizzling embers hissed and burst, sent white-hot sparks shooting from her fiery core out through her extremities.

And still the mental images kept coming: thousands upon thousands of flickering candles. A burning prairie. The tide receding from a sandy-bottomed ocean, the water building into a far-off wall, and the top cresting into a single giant tidal wave.

Then the entire ocean suddenly raced toward her, lifting her high into its concave curl and thrashing her about—

—and with her entire body and soul she climaxed.

It was as if the floor gave way beneath her and the heavens exploded. Screaming, she convulsed and raked Christos's bare back with her nails.

Now that he'd brought her to orgasm, he abandoned all attempts at self-control. With renewed urgency he plunged furiously in and out, in and out, faster, faster! In and out, in and out, in and out and in and—

Then the dark, primal bellow rose from the depths of his throat as he, too, climaxed in a storm of magnificent, earth-shaking release.

Together now, they slumped, gasping and shuddering, into each other's sweat-sleeked, trembling arms.

If the afternoon had ended there, Gloria would have been more than satisfied.

But it didn't end there. Christos wasn't done yet. And he soon proved that he was, in fact, only just beginning . . .

"Well, I see you're finally home," Hunt said.

Gloria, heels clicking on the foyer's checkerboard marble, stopped cold in front of the baroque giltwood mirror, drew a deep breath, and then turned swiftly around.

Hunt, leaning in a doorway, held a drink in his hand.

Gloria said, "Look, I lost all track of—"

"You don't need to explain, Gloria. Spare me the lies and excuses." Hunt downed a slug of bourbon.

"But the Burlingame—"

"—Senior Citizens visit? Has been rescheduled due to unforeseen events," Hunt said. "I waited around too long, hoping you'd appear." His smile was mirthless.

Gloria looked at him questioningly. "And the fund-raising dinner?"

"Can't be rescheduled," he said, with a shrug. "*I'm* going, at any rate. Have to, even if you won't."

With an angry glare, Gloria crossed the foyer and stood in front of him. "You bastard!" she expelled softly. "You think I'm drunk, don't you?"

He didn't reply.

"For your information," she said icily, "I'm *not* drunk. Oh, granted I've had a *few,* just like you're having one right now." She glanced derisively at the tumbler in his hand. A frenzy of rage, all-consuming, sudden, and frightening in its fury, detonated inside her.

He saw the blur of her open palm, but neither ducked nor tried to block it. With a crack, her hand caught him across the face, causing his head to swivel sideways, stamping the scarlet imprint of her fingers upon his cheek.

Still leaning casually in the doorway, he stared at her. He didn't appear to be the least bit surprised.

Somehow, his lack of reaction and defense enraged her all the more. Again she slapped him, harder. Then again. Harder yet. And again and again.

But he merely continued to lean casually against the doorway, his head swiveling with every slap, his cheek and jaw steadily reddening.

Her eyes shone with a wild kind of triumph. "I don't suppose you want to *hear* why I'm late, do you, Hunt?" she panted tauntingly, and he could glimpse something sharp and lethal glinting through the anger. "I guess you'd rather not *know* every gory little detail?"

"As a matter of fact," he said calmly, "yes. I would. Believe it or not, I'm concerned about you, Gloria."

She looked away for a moment and when she looked back up at him, her eyes were blazing and filled with a wildness such as he had never seen.

"Well, then I'll *tell* you where I was!" she spat triumphantly. "I was out *fucking*, Hunt! I was out *screwing my little brains out! That's* what your wife was doing!" Gloria trilled brittle, bitter laughter. "But *you* needn't worry, darling. I was discreet . . . just as discreet as your mother— yes, *your mother,* Hunt! Your very own *mother!*—told me to be!"

He stared at her, his face chalk white.

"What's the matter?" she inquired, laying on the syrup. "I haven't *disappointed* you, now have I?"

"Please, Gloria. Stop now," he whispered.

But she wasn't finished. Not by a long shot. All the poisons that had been bottled up inside her for years suddenly came spewing forth in a torrent.

"That's right, Hunt. Imagine! I found myself a man! A *man,* Hunt! A *real* man! And my neglected, shriveled-up privates are *alive!* They're more *alive* than they've ever been! If you listen closely, why, you can practically hear them *sing!*"

He shut his eyes, his face clouded with pain. "Stop it!" he said hoarsely.

But she was ranting and raving, and there was no stopping her.

"Isn't it *hilarious,* Hunt? Can't you just *hear* it already? All those tongues wagging?"

Gloria tilted her head, made a production of cupping a hand behind her ear, and pretended astonishment.

"Why, just *listen* to them! They're saying Mrs. Hunt Winslow, wife of the Desert Storm hero and rising political star, is a *whore!* Why, she's nothing but walking white trash, is what they're saying! And . . . what's that? 'What can he expect, his wife coming from the wrong side of the tracks, and all?' "

"For the love of Christ, Gloria!" Hunt said thickly. "Stop it!"

But she threw back her head and blurted hysterical laughter.

Closing his eyes in anguish, Hunt took a steadying breath and exhaled slowly. He could feel the sweat running in rivulets down his tensed arms, the tingling itch of his trembling, clenched knuckles.

"Oh, you should have seen it, Hunt!" she taunted. "Really, you should! I wish you'd *been* there!"

He opened his eyes to see her dancing back and forth in front of him. Shimmying her hips here. Striking a Marilyn pose there.

"Because I *debased* myself, Hunt!" she trumpeted proudly, the triumph rich in her voice. "Yes! I *degraded* myself! I *defiled* myself! I wallowed in filth like a *pig!*"

The light shone in her huge round eyes as she leaned into him, her face inches from his. Despite her expensive perfume he could smell the sour, underlying stench of stale sex and spent passions.

"And you know what?" Her face blazed with an unholy feverishness. "I *loved* it! That's right, Hunt! *I . . . loved . . . every . . . fucking . . . minute* of it!"

"Stop it!" he said. "Stop it now!"

But she was too far gone.

"Don't you *see?*" she goaded. "*Someone's* got to give it to me, Hunt! I've got to get fucked *somewhere* if I can't get it at home! And it's not like I fucked any of your *friends*—"

"Goddamn it!" he roared. And flinging his arm back, he hurled the tumbler at the gilt-framed antique mirror.

One moment, the crystal glass seemed suspended in midair. The next, it smashed into the sheet of glass.

Ca-*rack!* The mirror exploded into a jagged cobweb that blew outward, the shards crashing down to the marble and fragmenting yet further.

Her gaze flickered feebly, then her footsteps echoing like a reproof, she turned and ran swiftly across the foyer and up the sweeping marble stairs.

And then there was silence: sudden, utter, and unearthly.

"Oh, God," Hunt whispered, staring at the silvery rubble in horror.

The damage seemed a reflection of his marriage, of lives doomed to explode into a thousand infinities. As his had.

But what was that compared to the sheer hatred Gloria had vented? Her revelations still reverberated in his head like seismic aftershocks jolting whatever ruins were left standing.

Slowly, wearily, he sought refuge in the antique hall porter's chair. As he sank down into it, he felt something hard and unyielding beneath him.

Frowning, he lifted his buttocks and reached underneath.

The box was small and crisply wrapped in glossy white paper and red ribbon. Frowning, he kept turning it over and over, wondering how it had gotten there.

And then he remembered.

He himself had placed it there only an hour and a half earlier.

The gift from Cartier.

The agony in his gut flared ulcerously, almost causing him to double over. He had bought it for Gloria at the branch shop on Post Street, positive she didn't think he would remember.

But he had. It was she who had forgotten.

His lips twisted into a bleak rictus. Today was their anniversary. Their Silk Anniversary.

Letting the box drop, he covered his face with his hands.

They'd been married for twelve years . . . twelve interminable years of a life sentence without parole.

And he'd bought her a gift—a gift! As though it were an occasion to celebrate.

How stupid could he be?

21

The rituals of death follow prescribed rules of etiquette. Like christenings or marriages. In fact, weddings and funerals have more in common than people like to think. Both can be ruinously expensive. Both usually call for masses of floral arrangements. The ceremonies often involve members of the clergy, and afterward, whether it be a wedding reception or a wake, food and alcohol are consumed in great quantities.

The cynical observer notices something else: for the celebrants (or mourners), both occasions are often the only chance they get to ride in limousines.

Dorothy-Anne, who had ridden in limousines since birth, and who attended church services only sporadically, found no solace in these carefully structured traditions. How could she? Freddie had been her other half, her anchor and her bulwark, her soul mate and lover and business partner.

Without him, she was . . . incomplete. A mere shadow of herself adrift in a strange, lonely void.

The funeral only slammed home the enormity of her loss.

The service was held in Chatham, a drive of two hours and fifteen minutes up the Taconic from Manhattan. Dorothy-Anne had insisted he be laid to rest here, far from the madding crowd.

It's what Freddie would have wanted, she thought. And it was what she wanted, too. As a family, she and Freddie and the kids had spent the happiest times of their lives in nearby Old Chatham, where Meadowlake Farm, the 732-acre estate they'd acquired after Liz was born, served as a bolt-hole from the pressure cooker of Manhattan and the unrelenting demands of running an international empire.

The turnout at the local funeral home was small; Dorothy-Anne had insisted on a quiet private service. Freddie's brother, Rob, had flown in from Chicago with his wife, Ellen. Derek Fleetood, chairman of the Hale Corporation's hotel division, was there, as were Maud Ehmer, Freddie's prim, devoted secretary of eleven years, and Venetia.

No other executives, colleagues, friends, or acquaintances had been invited. The only exception was the staff of Meadowlake Farms: the caretaker couple, the horse trainer, grooms, stable lads, cook, and gardeners.

Dorothy-Anne sat through the service with a taut-faced, quiet dignity. To either side of her, the children were red-eyed and uncharacteristically subdued. Nanny Florrie kept sniffling and dabbing her eyes with a handkerchief.

The closed mahogany coffin spoke volumes, a persistent reminder of the terrible way in which Freddie had died.

The Episcopal priest was saying: " 'The first man is from earth, made of dust. The second man is from heaven. And when this perishable body has been clothed with the imperishable, and our mortality has been clothed with immortality, then is Death defeated.' "

And the service was over. It was time to go outside and get into the long black limousines and follow the hearse to the cemetery.

It was a joyless ride—all the more so because the houses along the way were festooned for the holiday season.

Dorothy-Anne shut her eyes against the multicolored lights outlining windows, the red-ribboned wreaths on doors, the life-size plaster crèches and one-dimensional Santas in reindeer-pulled sleighs propped up on front lawns.

Santa won't be coming to us, she thought. *The angel of death came instead.*

The cemetery was bleak and cold. With a wind-chill factor of ten below, the graveside ceremony was mercifully short and to the point.

" 'In the midst of life we are in death . . . earth to earth, ashes to ashes, dust to dust . . .' "

Then the ropes were paid out, the coffin was lowered into the maw of the grave, and someone placed a little shovel in Dorothy-Anne's hand.

Dry-eyed, her face and posture rigid with held-back emotions, she scooped up some soil and cast it down upon the coffin. The frozen clumps rattled on the lid like hailstones.

She winced against the sound.

"Good-bye, Freddie," she whispered. "Good-bye, my love."

Then she felt a firm grip on her elbow.

"Come on, girl," Venetia said gently. "Best we get out of the cold before we catch pneumonia."

I wish I would catch it. Then I could die and join Freddie.

Reluctantly, she allowed herself to be steered to the limousine, all the while glancing back over her shoulder at the grave.

Is this all there is? Can this be what life is ultimately all about?

For Dorothy-Ann, Meadowlake Farm had always been a refuge, a magical green fortress to which she could escape from the world and slam a door on its troubles, the one place where reality was never permitted to intrude.

She and Freddie had spent six years lovingly restoring the three-hundred-year-old eyebrow colonial and its ramshackle outbuildings with their own hands, coming here to unwind and recuperate, to spend weekends and holidays, to lead a normal family life.

As the limousine turned into the lane leading to the farmhouse, Dorothy-Anne remembered what John Donne had written: "No man is an island, entire of itself; every man is a piece of the continent, a part of the main."

She stared out at the leafless orchards, at rows of apple trees contorted like charred skeletons against the milky gray of the winter sky.

She couldn't imagine Meadowlake Farm without Freddie.

It's become a mere shell. Like Freddie himself, a lifeless body without a soul.

Yet to be anywhere else right now was unthinkable. Deep in her subconscious, she knew that the farm was the only place where she could come to terms with his death.

As if such a thing were possible.

It has to be, she told herself grimly. *What choice do I have? I'm a mother, and my children have lost their father. They need me now as they've never needed me before.*

She had to be there for them.

Had to.

Yes, she thought wearily, *but who's going to be there for me?*

Despite its arcadian serenity, Meadowlake Farm had turned into one vast torture chamber. Every room and nook and cranny was haunted by memories. There was no escaping them. Reminders of Freddie were everywhere.

There were times she swore she heard his tread on the steps, or saw him out of the corner of her eye. But when she looked, there was nobody there.

Sometimes she forgot herself. Unthinkingly she would set an extra place for him at the table. Or she found herself telling one of the grooms to saddle up his horse. She even called out to him from the bathroom: "Freddie? Could you bring me an extra towel?"

And then she would catch herself and remember that he was gone, that the earth had swallowed him up and he would never walk through the door again.

I'm a widow, she kept reminding herself.

Widow. What an ominous word. It made her feel strangely self-conscious and tainted, as though she were the carrier of some highly communicable disease.

Widows are supposed to be old. I'm only thirty-one. How can I be a widow when I'm so young?

Venetia stayed on in a guest room, running her office by fax and phone. Offering what little consolation she could. Suspecting that Dorothy-Anne would have preferred mourning in seclusion, but wanting to be there for her, just in case.

One morning, passing the open door of the master bedroom, she saw Dorothy-Anne pressing clothes of Freddie's against her face, inhaling his lingering scent.

Venetia's heart went out to her. *The poor thing,* she thought, quietly moving on before Dorothy-Anne could notice her. *If only there were something I could do.*

There was.

Later that day, Venetia sat down with her. "Christmas is just around the corner, honey," she said. "The children will expect a tree."

"Freddie will put one up—" Dorothy-Anne began, then caught herself, put her face in her hands, and wept.

Venetia put an arm around her. "Honey," she said gently, "Freddie's gone. You've got to let go."

Dorothy-Anne gave a little nod but continued to weep.

"Life goes on," Venetia said.

But Dorothy-Anne knew better. *No. Life doesn't go on. It comes to a screeching halt. The only thing that goes on is the pain.*

Venetia sat with her for a while, and then sought out the housekeeper. "What kind of Christmas tree does the family usually have?"

"An eight-foot Douglas fir."

"Right."

Venetia got her coat, borrowed a Jeep Cherokee from the garage, and went to see a man about a tree.

"Tell me if it's straight."

It was the following day, and Venetia had conscripted the children into helping trim the tree.

Three sets of eyes looked up. She was on the ladder, crowning the treetop with the exquisite baroque angel. It was a South German antique, of papier-mâché and gold lace over gray silk, with great gilt wings and a wire halo, so beautifully crafted that it looked as if it belonged in some rococo church.

"Looks okay to me," Fred said disinterestedly, shrugging and tossing his head to flip the hair out of his eyes in that way of his.

"Does *not!*" Zack blurted. "It's *crooked!*"

"You dweeb," sniffed Liz. "It is *not.*"

"Is *too!* Ask *Mommy*. M-M-M-Mommy? It *is*, isn't it?"

Zack turned imploringly to Dorothy-Anne, who was carefully lifting a fragile glass ornament out of its nest of tissue paper. It was the Victorian bird of paradise with feather plumes that she and Freddie had unearthed in a London flea market.

During our first trip abroad together, she remembered, with a pang.

"*Mommy!*" Zack cried plaintively, stamping an impatient foot.

"Hey. Guys." Venetia clapped her hands to get their attention. "Turn down the volume, huh? Tell you what. This girl says the angel's straight, so it's straight."

She started down the ladder.

"Is *not!*" Zack bawled.

Nanny Florrie, bustling in from the adjacent room, scolded, "For Gude's sake, laddie! Will ye quiet doon?"

But Zack wasn't about to. Though at first the family's mounting tragedies hadn't seemed to affect the children as much as their mother, the cumulative buildup of loss and grief and anger had taken their toll. Now their suppressed rage was surfacing, bursting like pus from some fetid, festering wound.

"It's *crooked!* It's *crooked! Dad*dy never put it up crooked! If Daddy were here—"

"Stop it!" Dorothy-Anne whispered hoarsely.

Her face had gone ashen and her hands were shaking. The glass bird slipped from her fingers, hit the floorboards, and shattered.

"No!" she gasped. "Not the bird . . ."

She backed away from the fragments, the shattered ornament both a symbol of her sundered family and a brutal, mocking reminder of joyous Christmases past.

"See what you did?" Liz hissed, elbowing Zack. "You upset Mom. God. Like you are sooooo immature."

"Am *not!* Am *not!*"

"Are too!"

"Am *not!*"

"Och!" Nanny Florrie exclaimed. "'Tis nae time to fight." She wagged an admonishing finger at them. "Ye both best behave and mind yer Nanny, else Santa will nae hae presents for you!" she said darkly.

"Santa!" Fred scoffed sullenly. "Even Zack's too old to believe that crap. Dad and Ma bought the presents."

"Did *not!*" Zack yelled, his huge blue eyes gushing tears, his short small arms windmilling—ineffectually slapping and pummeling his big brother. "*Liar! San*ta brought them! *You'll* see. *San*ta'll bring them again this yea—"

The telephone rang, silencing him like a school bell.

"I'll answer it," Venetia said, offering up a prayer of thanks for its quieting effect. Stepping barefoot off the ladder, she hurried to the phone and picked up on the fourth ring. "Hello?"

It was Derek Fleetwood. He was calling from White Plains.

"Hold on," Venetia told him.

She took the phone into the dining room, hearing little smears of interference crackling in the ether as she moved about. She shut the door, pulled out a side chair, and sat down wearily, one elbow resting on the table.

"Okay, Derek. What's up?"

"What isn't, you mean." He paused. "Venetia, things are getting pretty hairy here in the office," he said gravely.

"Want to trade places? Try this end for a change?"

He laughed mirthlessly. "No, thanks. I've got my hands full."

She waited.

"Look," he said awkwardly. "I know this is bad timing, but I don't have any choice. We're sitting on a backlog of decisions only Dorothy-Anne can make, and things have really gotten down to the wire. When do you think we can expect her in?"

In . . . ?

Venetia felt a surge of outrage at the call, of business being conducted as usual. For crying out loud! What was he *thinking*?

"Derek, for God's sake, it's too soon! She's not ready. She just buried her husband four days ago. You saw her, you were *there*!"

"I know, I *know*," he commiserated. "Christ, if I could I'd make the damn decisions and sign for her! But I *can't*. That's the trouble—nobody can. We're not authorized. You know that. Freddie was the only—"

"All right, all *right*!" she snapped, raking her fingers through her mane, clutching the remote phone tighter in her hand. "Let me *think*."

"You know I wouldn't be calling if it wasn't imperative."

It was true. She'd never known Derek to be a worrywart; he was, in fact, the last person on earth to cry wolf, or make much ado about nothing.

"Derek," she said gently, "I can't make any promises, but I'll see what I can do."

"Great!" There was no mistaking the relief in his voice. "Thanks, Venetia. I knew I could count on you!"

"I wouldn't if—" she began, but he had already hung up.

"—I were you," she completed in a murmur.

She pressed the Off button, pushed the aerial down, and put the receiver on the mirrorlike surface of the mahogany table. For a while, she just sat there.

From a professional standpoint, she could appreciate Derek's position. In the Hale Companies, only two people were authorized to approve any major decisions.

One of them is dead, and the other might as well be.

"Shit," she enunciated quietly.

Later that evening, Dorothy-Anne heard a knock at her door. "Come in," she said.

"Hi, Mom." It was Liz.

"Hi, sweetie," Dorothy-Anne said. "Come over here and sit beside me. Now what is it?"

"Mom," Liz said. "I just want you to know that Fred and Zack and I talked it over, and we'll do everything we can to make things easier for you."

Tears welled up in Dorothy-Anne's eyes, and she didn't trust herself to speak.

"We know that this is harder on you than anybody," Liz said. "We just want you to know that we're here for you."

Dorothy-Anne hugged her daughter to her. "I'll be here for you all too, sweetie," she said through her tears. *They're being so brave. I've got to be here for them, too. I've got to go on living for them.*

22

The distance between Little Italy and Chinatown is an alphabet and a cuisine. Otherwise, the seemingly disparate neighborhoods have much in common.

Both are composed largely of tenements. Each maintains strong cultural ties to the Old Country. And behind the facades offered to the casual tourist exist societies that are exceptionally insular, secretive, and impossible for outsiders to breach.

Another similarity is ethnic pride. Just as a Sicilian makes the distinction of *not* being a Neapolitan, so too does a Swatow of not being a Cantonese.

Appropriately, restaurants flourish in both neighborhoods. As does crime.

In Little Italy the mob runs things, whereas in Chinatown it is the tongs.

Sonny Fong—who gave a good impression, and whose trappings placed him in the sleek, well-heeled cosmos of the Upper East Side—felt the gravitational pull of his ancient culture as he goosed his Lexus through Chinatown's maze of one-way streets and teeming back alleys.

He instantly fell into the rhythm of familiarity. Sloughed off now was his tony uptown skin, his polished Western veneer. Even the cleaved flat planes of his face seemed more pronounced, glinted with a sharper, unmistakably lethal edge.

He cruised slowly, surely, his X-ray eyes seeing through the lies sold to tourists. This was one place where nothing ever changed, where nothing was what it appeared to be. Chinatown was a netherworld of mysterious layers, of boxes within boxes, a painted whore of shadows and corruption decked out in gaudy native costume.

Parking the Lexus in an unlighted alley, he killed the headlights, unscrewed the overhead dome light, and slipped out of the car. Melting into the shadows, he felt for the unmarked steel door. Rap-tap-tapped a soft code with his knuckles. Then waited, not bothering to look around.

Even if there had been any light, which there wasn't, he knew exactly what he'd see. Grimy blank walls on both sides, with bricked-up windows violating every city ordinance and fire code. Bricked up for dual purposes—locking sweat shop crews in and keeping strangers and authorities out.

Soundlessly, the steel door opened an inch. The lights inside were off, a precaution to avoid anyone from being silhouetted against it. And for good reason. Triad rivalry was fierce, with bloodshed the norm rather than the exception.

Sonny's voice was quiet. "I come on behalf of an esteemed elder," he said in the Chiuchow dialect. "He hears your tea is renowned for curing a faltering love life."

"You arrived at a most fortuitous time," a voice whispered out of the darkness. "I believe the fabled remedy is in stock."

"My esteemed elder would be most grateful if you could check."

Now that the passwords were exchanged, the door opened wider. Sonny crossed the threshold and slipped off to the side. Something hard prodded his belly. Then the door snapped shut again. A low-wattage bulb clicked on overhead.

Sonny stared down at his midsection, where the muzzle of a Colt .45 pressed into his stomach. He raised his eyes slowly, without fear.

A hard-faced youth in jeans, futuristic Nikes, and a yellow satin baseball jacket was eyeing him coldly. Sonny recognized him at once. Itchy Finger Sung was a triggerman for the Shadow Dragons, the Chiuchow tong, said to be Chinatown's most vicious. Lean and wiry, Itchy Finger had a pockmarked face and a propensity to shoot first and never ask questions—hence his nickname.

"You look more like a barbarian all the time, Sonny Fong." Itchy Finger's smile was spiteful. "Soon you will be as unrecognizable as the round-eyed devils you cavort with!"

Sonny returned the smile, teeth glistening. "And that fornicating tongue of yours," he said softly, "will soon rot with the rest of you on a fly-ridden dung heap."

Itchy Finger spat on the worn linoleum. Then he stared at Sonny a while longer, reluctantly withdrew the revolver, and tucked it into his waistband. "You're expected," he said harshly. He jerked his chin down the dim, narrow corridor and grunted, "Come with me."

Sonny followed him—an olfactory experience. From the front of the building—actually three interconnected tenements—came the overpowering stink of a fish store, and the rancid odors of grease from the restaurant next door. From the basement below, where bean sprouts were cultivated on a vast scale, rose the graveyard stench of chlorophyll.

But even without these smells the building would have reeked to high heaven. For beneath these individual odors lurked one other—the rankness of too many people crammed into too small a space. Sweat, vomit, urine, garbage, filth. They made an olfactory brew that was the same the world over.

Sonny closed his nose to it.

The stink of poverty.

The effluvia of survival.

He kept his sharp-eyed gaze on alert. Caught liquid shadows sliding along the edges of the walls in near invisibility—enforcers on constant patrol. Nipping problems in the bud *before* they could become problems.

Breathing through his mouth, he followed Itchy Finger up a rickety wooden staircase, on up past the second floor, where an herbalist's cures and an opium den added to the general miasma. And where cell-like rooms were crammed from floor to ceiling with crude two-by-four-and-plywood bunks.

Chinatown housing for sweatshop labor.

On they climbed, Sonny and Itchy Finger, up to the third-floor landing, where the stairs abruptly ended and a formidable steel door barred the way.

Itchy Finger pushed a buzzer and spoke rapidly into an intercom. The door opened and two toughs in black tie gestured for Sonny to assume the position. He raised his hands and they expertly patted him down. Finding him clean, they nodded at Itchy Finger to take him on in.

Sonny played the wise guy, making a production of straightening his tie and shooting his cuffs and giving the hem of his jacket little tugs. Only then did he flash a smile and, adopting a little extra swagger, follow Itchy Finger through the door.

It led into a duplex of astounding sumptuousness. No warped or worn linoleum here; no sign of cracked plaster walls or cheap bare bulbs, either. The carpeting was deep and lush, the lighting recessed and muted, and the walls covered in squares of real gold leaf. On them hung large unfurled scrolls, delicate ink paintings depicting erotic scenes.

Sonny Fong knew them to be priceless antiques, but Itchy Finger Sung didn't spare them a glance. He led the way straight into a sprawling space where lamps with fu dog bases and silk shades cast a golden glow, and spiral stairs of icy Lucite curved elegantly up to the floor above.

Instead of the stench of poverty, the air was fragrant with the scents of hyacinth, jasmine, and expensive perfumes.

Sonny, who'd been here on more than one occasion, nevertheless looked around in approval. There were polished rosewood tables with vases of cut flowers, their petals as palely pink as the heavenly gate between a woman's legs. Off in one corner, an old black man in formal wear was caressing the keys of a grand piano, crooning "You're the Tops."

And all around, displayed on silken banquettes, was the merchandise. Flesh.

Undeniably, the choicest female flesh Chinatown had to offer.

The dozen girls, mostly Chinese, were all in various stages of undress, and eyed Sonny's arrival with cash-register eyes. The experienced ones instantly dismissed him. They had only to look into his face to know that here was a man who took, rather than purchased, his pleasures.

The proprietor of this establishment, a woman in a green silk *chong sam,* was at the far end of the room, spitting whispers into a cellular phone—a digital model on which her conversation was secure.

Itchy Finger pointed at an empty banquette. "Sit there," he told Sonny, and left.

But Sonny had other ideas. He decided to mosey around. Check out the merchandise up close.

The girls were pros. Even though he wasn't buying, they automatically struck seductive poses. Some glanced demurely over a bare shoulder, others extended a perfect haunch and smiled saucily, or leaned back on both arms, letting their breasts ride high for his appraisal.

Sonny Fong nodded in appreciation. He considered himself a connoisseur of the female form, and what he saw met with his approval—and then some. These girls weren't only beautiful. They were the cream of the crème de la crème.

Across the room, the woman on the phone caught his eye. She leveled an index finger at him, then stabbed it in the direction of the banquette. The empty one Itchy Finger had indicated.

Sonny sighed to himself. He knew better than to test Madame Chang's patience. She carried a lot of weight with the old *lung tao.* Speculation had it that, once upon a time, she'd been the old man's favorite mistress. Whether this was the case or not, one thing was clear: she operated under Kuo Fong's personal protection.

To insult her was to insult the Esteemed Elder himself.

Pinching his knife-creased trousers, Sonny sank down on the low banquette, leaning back and watching Madame Chang from a distance as he waited.

When she put down the phone, she lit a long, thin black cigar and stood with her back turned, smoking in silence. Finally she turned around, took a seat in a rosewood chair, and crossed her legs. She gestured for Sonny to approach.

He sprang to his feet and hurried forward. "Greetings, Honored Sister," he said, with a polite bow.

She took his deference as her due and nodded, then sat there, legs crossed, puffing clouds of blue smoke, her hawklike gaze regarding Sonny thoughtfully. She did not invite him to sit.

While she studied him openly, he did the same—surreptitiously.

Emerald Chang was somewhere between fifty-five and eighty—through the alchemy of lighting, surgery, and makeup, it was impossible to tell. Only one thing was for certain. Though petite and delicately formed, underneath she was all wire and tough steel.

Hers was a formidable presence.

She had classic Asian features and pitch black hair worn in a high, old-fashioned Chinese topknot. Her *chong sam* was nearly floor-length, but the short sleeves and the slits up the sides exposed still shapely limbs that were firm and graceful. Her legs, like a dancer's, were surprisingly muscular and slender in form, and ended in three-inch spike heels.

She had fingernails that were long and square-cut and painted cinnabar. Her lips were bow-shaped and also cinnabar. She wore false eyelashes and a lot of expertly applied makeup and dangle earrings of priceless carved jade.

Leaning forward, she placed her cigar in an ashtray and clapped her hands sharply.

At the signal, the girls on the banquettes rose as one and filed out of the room; simultaneously, the piano player began pounding deafening ragtime.

This was a conversation not intended for prying ears.

"Our Illustrious Elder"—Emerald Chang spoke softly in the Chiuchow dialect, careful not to use names—"sent an emissary with a verbal message." She nodded gravely. "He deems it of such importance that he did not trust to put it on paper, even in code."

Sonny bowed his head. "I am honored to be the recipient of such a momentous communication," he said humbly.

"Yes, and so you should be!" She leaned farther forward, her narrowed eyes flashing within the furry caterpillar lashes. "But listen closely, heed my words, be like a sponge, and absorb—he says the decision of whether or not to entrust this message to you is mine!"

Sonny jerked as though struck. "He knows I can be trusted!" he snapped bitterly. "How often must I be tested? My lips are sealed, I am like a clam—"

"Ah, but clams need only to be steamed and their shells gape wide, their meat ready to be plucked and eaten!"

Sonny felt his temperature skyrocket and his face prickle with heat. "By all gods great and small, I have always—"

"Silence!" Her voice cleaved his in mid-sentence.

Rebuked, he bit down on his words and inclined his head, waiting for her to proceed.

For a while she was silent. Her legs were uncrossed now, and her hands cupped the arms of her chair. Regal she was. Like an imperial empress on her throne, chin raised, staring at him intently, her eyes studying, gauging, probing, deciding . . .

She said: "You know the esteem in which our Illustrious Elder holds me."

"Of course." Sonny bowed graciously.

"Then you are also aware that I have served him faithfully for more years than you have lived."

He bowed again. "Your voice is his voice," he said softly. "I am told you have greater standing at his side than any man, even the oldest and wisest."

The words he spoke were not empty ones. Unknown to everyone but Sonny and two or three of the *lung tao*'s closest, most trusted and highly placed lieutenants, was the fact that Emerald Chang's establishment was a front, a profitable sideline.

Her actual function and true vocation was managing a far more lucrative and dangerous business—the smuggling of illegal aliens from the Far East to these shores. That she had done it successfully for so long, while remaining unknown to both the authorities and those who worked for her, was a testament to her strength, courage, and cunning.

She had earned the old *lung tao*'s respect and trust a hundred times over.

Sonny, on the other hand, had yet to prove himself. *They still don't trust me completely,* he realized bitterly. *What more must I do to prove my allegiance?* He had no idea.

"The task at hand is crucial," Emerald Chang now said. "It demands the utmost secrecy, as well as delicacy. There is no room for error! The slightest miscalculation and—" her hand blurred and whipped a horizontal karate chop through the air—"*disaster!*"

She leaned forward, her eyes keen and shiny as jet beads, her dangle earrings swaying.

"Search deep within yourself," she advised. "Then ask: are you prepared to accept so great a responsibility?"

Sonny didn't hesitate. "I am prepared and ready," he said with quiet conviction. His eyes glowed with a strange inner light. "I am willing to stake my life on it!"

She smiled coldly. "Only the young and foolish gamble so recklessly with their lives! Tell me: which are you? Young? Or foolish?"

"Neither," he said, his voice gaining strength. "I'm confident."

"Good." She nodded her head and sat back. "Then accept my wisdom: watch your tongue and be frugal with your words, lest you tempt the gods of misfortune and live to regret it!"

He bowed his head. "I shall heed your wisdom, Elder Sister," he replied softly.

She studied him a moment longer, her face thoughtful. Then she made up her mind.

"You will travel to Atlanta," she said. "There, you are to make the acquaintance of a highly respected and important man. It is within his power to procure something which is vital to us."

Sonny stared at her. "Who is this man?"

She said: "He is a Chinese immigrant. A researcher. His name is Dr. Wo Sheng Yi."

23

'Twas the night before Christmas.

Through habit, rather than conscious decision, the family had gathered in the living room.

Outwardly, all was calm. All was bright. The Christmas tree was lit. The Yule log blazed. Boughs of holly and fragrant pine festooned the mantel and the staircase in the center hall. Sprigs of mistletoe hung in doorways, and Bing Crosby alternated with Luciano Pavarotti on the sound system. Venetia's SOS calls to F.A.O. Schwarz, Bergdorf Goodman, and half a dozen other emporiums had resulted in the overnight delivery of a closetful of beautifully wrapped, extravagant gifts.

A festive Christmas by all appearances.

Except . . .

Except for Freddie's absence, which loomed oppressively. This, the first Christmas without him, coming as it did on the heels of his funeral, made it an especially painful event.

Not surprisingly, Dorothy-Anne was grim faced and silent, the children were strangely subdued, and Nanny Florrie's knitting needles flew furiously, as though she feared the devil's workshop.

Venetia spent the time agonizing over her procrastination. Four days had already passed since Derek's call, and she had yet to broach the subject of Dorothy-Anne's return to work.

Pavarotti held his last note and the CD player went silent. Venetia started to get up and change discs when they all heard it. The unmistakable thunder of approaching hoofbeats coming from outside.

"Santa!" Zack cried.

Letting out a whoop, he charged to the nearest window, scrambled atop a sofa, and pressed his nose flat against the glass. When he turned around, his eyes shone with wide-eyed wonder.

"It *is!*" he shouted ecstatically. "It's *San*ta! *See?* He *did* come! He *did!*"

Dorothy-Anne looked baffled, as though she hadn't heard right. Fred and Liz exchanged skeptical glances. Nanny Florrie put aside her knitting. And Venetia, already on her feet, strode to one of the other windows, shielded her reflection by cupping both hands, and peered out into the darkness. Her breathing clouded the glass, but not before she saw the most amazing sight.

"Well, I'll be!" she exclaimed softly.

When she turned around, she caught Dorothy-Anne's inquiring gaze.

"What is it?" Dorothy-Anne asked.

Venetia laughed. "You're not going to believe this, but honey? Unless this girl's eyes are deceiving her, and they're not, Zack is right. It really *is* Mr. Claus."

"Yeah, right," Liz interjected sarcastically. "An' I'm the Easter Bunny!"

"Then baby, maybe you just are," Venetia told her. "Better take a look outside."

Curiosity got the better of them. One by one, they found themselves getting up and approaching the windows. Even Dorothy-Anne couldn't help herself.

Sure enough. In the glow of the front door's twin coach lamps, they watched Santa hop down off his conveyance, grab a huge sack, and sling it over his shoulder.

Dorothy-Anne was nonplussed. So it wasn't a sleigh, but a mere farm wagon. So they weren't really reindeer, but horses with branches tucked behind their bridles. So whoever it was in the padded Santa suit wasn't really Mr. Claus.

So what. What mattered was the unexpected surprise.

"Venetia," she said, with fond exasperation. "What are we going to do with you?"

"With *me!*" Venetia shook her head. "Unh-unh, baby. Don't go putting this on *my* doorstep. This isn't any of this girl's doing." She peered out some more. "Who on earth do you think it could be? Not Derek, that's for sure. He's too much of a stuffed shirt."

"It's *San*ta," Zack cried, "that's who!" Bouncing off the sofa, he charged energetically across the room and out into the center hall.

From the window, the others watched the bright parallelogram of light spill from the front door and widen as it crossed the porch and rippled down the steps. They laughed as Santa quickly adjusted his beard and adopted a jolly mien.

"Well?" Venetia said. "I don't know about you three, but I'm itching to find out who's wearing that fake beard!"

So saying, she cut a swath across the living room and out into the center hall, leaving Dorothy-Anne, Fred, and Liz trailing in her wake.

"Ho, ho, ho!" greeted a falsely deep, rich cheerful voice. "Merry Christmas! Happy New Year!"

Venetia squinted at him suspiciously.

Santa Claus was six foot two, not counting the boots and flossy wig and dangling red cap. He had a terrific tan, lapis blue eyes—the penetrating, not twinkly, kind—and the type of lithe, hard-bodied physique no amount of padded red felt and faux fur could completely disguise.

To any observant female—and when it came to men, Venetia Flood was the most observant of all—the potbellied Santa suit and jolly sexlessness simultaneously gave off a comforting, teddy bear–like cuddliness and sense of safety, while the lean, youthful face behind the cotton-candy beard, coupled with the splendid body she sensed underneath, made for one rampantly sexy Santa.

Santa unslung his bag, bent down in front of Zack, and pinched his cheek. "Ho, ho, ho! And were *you* a good little boy this year?"

Zack was momentarily tongue-tied, and Venetia, standing there with her arms folded, suddenly began to laugh. "Well, I'll be damned!" she said in amazement.

Santa wagged a cautionary finger at her. "Now, we'll have none of that language in front of the children," he admonished, pretending to scowl. "*You* are a very, very naughty girl! Yes, indeed."

At which Venetia laughed all the harder.

Dorothy-Anne tugged on her sleeve. "Who is it?" she hissed.

"Who do you think? Girl, I've seen a lot of strange things in my day, but believe me—this sure beats all!"

Dorothy-Anne was flummoxed. Shock, mourning, depression, loss, anxiety, pain, fear—of late, those had become the staple of her emotions, everyday grist for the mill of despair. But *pleasant* surprises? Happiness? Cheer? *Joy?* Her emotional reservoir no longer had room for such frivolous luxuries.

Abruptly Santa leaned right into her face. "Ho, ho, ho!" He leered. "Tell me, little girl. Were *you* naughty, or were you nice?"

Startled, Dorothy-Anne flinched like a child encountering its first circus clown, and she shrank back, prepared to flee.

Venetia caught her by the wrist. "Girl, *will* you chill out?" she whispered. "My God, when you think of how far he came—"

"All the way from the North Pole!" Santa interjected, with a jolly wink. "Ho, ho, ho!"

He rubbed his raw pink hands briskly together and blew on them.

"Seeing as it's freezing out," he said, "and Mrs. Claus forgot to remind me to bring my gloves, won't somebody offer poor Saint Nick a toasty seat by the fire? And perhaps bring him a bracing shot of something or other?"

And it was then that memory clicked and everything suddenly fell into place. Dorothy-Anne matched Santa's voice with his peerless blue eyes, those perfect specimens of the world's finest lapis lazuli—if semiprecious stones could convey both lively good humor and an acerbic, fascinating touch of mockery.

Her hands flew to her lips and two perfect orbs of embarrassment glowed brightly on her cheeks. *Good Lord,* she thought, experiencing a growing charge of electricity, *can it be? Is my mind playing tricks on me? No—it is him!*

"Oh . . . my . . . God!" she exclaimed in utter astonishment. "I don't believe it! Hunt? Hunt *Winslow?*"

Santa doffed his pompom-tailed cap and sketched an elaborate bow. "At your service, madam. Now and always and forever."

For the first time in weeks, Dorothy-Anne felt her spirits sustain a galvanic boost. "You crazy, loony, unpredictably dizzy—"

"Don't forget daffy," he added.

"Marvelously daffy, maniacally zany nutcase! I can't *believe* it's really you!"

"Believe it."

He yanked down his beard and flashed a gigawatt grin.

"See? The one and only. Me, myself, and I."

He let the beard pop back with an elastic snap.

"But . . . I mean . . . what on earth possessed you to come here?" she sputtered. "And how did you ever find me? And above all, what *are* you doing in that ridiculously padded, absolutely wonderful outfit?"

"Why, I'm doing what Santa does every year," he replied, hooking his thumbs in his wide vinyl belt. "Spreading holiday cheer. What does it look like I'm doing?"

"You *are* certifiable!" she said fondly. "You know that?"

"You may well have a point," he admitted cheerfully, staring deep into her eyes.

Dorothy-Anne's femininity thrilled to the open admiration of his gaze and his undeniable, easygoing masculine charm, even as the newly bereaved widow in her pierced the moment's pleasure. She stood there awkwardly, aware of the children's interrogative scrutiny, dreading the cross-examination she knew would sooner or later be forthcoming.

He's just a friend, darlings, that's all. . . . She would stick to the truth. And if they asked why he'd traveled three thousand miles, pursuing her cross-country: *I can't answer that, he's a nice man. . . .*

Inwardly she cringed at how feeble, how utterly, inexcusably false it sounded! And yet it was the truth.

Or was it?

Either way, the inevitable, remorseless fangs of guilt were already feasting at her expense, savaging her insides while her conscience ceaselessly reprimanded and scolded, its incessant cries of "Shame! Shame! Shame!" reverberating in her mind with ever-increasing volume. . . .

The moment stretched and tension twitched in her arms. Finally, she lifted her hands in exasperation. "Really, Hunt. This is all so . . . so . . . unexpected." She let her hands drop. "You caught me completely by surprise."

"Which was my intention," he smiled.

"But it's . . . it's *Christmas!*"

"My point exactly."

"Yes, but . . . what about your wife? Aren't you planning to spend the holidays with her?"

He heaved a deep sigh and turned away, but not before she saw the flicker of pain cross his face. Wearily he dragged the hat, wig, and beard from his head, disheveling his sun-bleached hair in the process.

"Gloria," he explained in a tight, strained voice, "has made her own plans for the holidays. Clearly, they didn't include me."

"Oh, God."

Dorothy-Anne silently cursed herself. *How insensitive can I be? And how could I not have guessed? He wouldn't be here at Christmas if he had anywhere else to go.*

"I'm sorry," she said miserably. Her hands clutched and clenched each other like insects performing an intricate mating dance. "If I had known . . ."

"How could you have?" He turned to her with a sad smile.

"But surely you must have some family?" Her voice trailed off.

"Family? Well, there is my mother."

"And? You're not estranged from her, are you?"

"From Mother?" He laughed. "I can tell you two haven't met!"

"Oh? And why is that?"

"Because then you'd know that Althea Winslow doesn't *permit* estrangements. Petty squabbles, quiet feuds, social terrorism, backstabbings—everything short of bloodshed, yes. But estrangements? Never.

"Mother," he added sardonically, "is a firm believer in remaining on speaking terms with everyone—friend *and* foe. That way she can keep an eye on her enemies."

"Such as . . . your wife?" Dorothy-Anne guessed waspishly.

"Especially my wife. Believe it or not, they lunch together regularly—not that Gloria likes it."

"Then why doesn't she just say no?"

"To Mother?" He laughed. "Even Gloria wouldn't dare! Fact is, no one would."

"She sounds like quite a lady."

"A regular field marshal, you mean."

A shadow that Dorothy-Anne would have identified as encumbrance in anyone else crossed his face for a moment, then was replaced by a look of admiration, the accordance of respect. Althea had obviously earned his, and Dorothy-Anne surmised he didn't grant it lightly.

"So what about her?" Dorothy-Anne asked quietly, steering the conversation back on track. "Your mother certainly doesn't strike me as the type who would spend Christmas alone."

"Althea? Alone? God forbid!"

His laughter was both mockingly chiding and infinitely forgiving.

"She's in Barbados. She has friends she stays with every Christmas through New Year's. It's become a tradition of sorts."

"And you weren't invited?" Dorothy-Anne couldn't imagine such a thing.

"Oh, I was," Hunt pulled a face. "Always am, in fact. And, as always, I politely RSVP'd, regretfully citing prior, unspecified commitments."

She tilted her head. "But not because of your mother, I take it."

"No." He shook his head. "Nor because of the hosts, either. It's the Others who scare me off."

"The Others?" Dorothy-Anne repeated blankly. "What Others?"

The way he'd said it conjured up images of low-budget 1950s sci-fi movies, of flying saucers invading planet Earth and decanting dome-headed aliens who brainwashed the inhabitants and turned them into zombies known as the Others.

He said, "Well, start by imagining a house party of eight 'ultra-amusing' couples. A tart-tongued fashion designer, for instance. And a television talk show hostess. A senator . . . that recording tycoon with his decorator wife . . . the usual assortment of bony socialites with their fat husbands . . ." He shuddered theatrically. "Thanks, but no thanks. Barbados isn't big enough to contain that many puffed-up egos."

Dorothy-Anne wasn't quite sure how to respond.

"Ergo," he pronounced, looking appealingly forlorn, "one little Winslow found himself home all alone. With nowhere to go. And only this"— he gestured at himself—"to wear."

"Oh, Hunt." Dorothy-Anne's voice was husky with feeling. "I am sorry."

"Don't be." He flashed her a lopsided grin. "Right now, I can honestly say there isn't another place I'd rather be."

The air fairly hummed with silent vibrations. Again, she was overly conscious of his luminous eyes reaching deep inside her, as if he could see into her very soul.

She sighed inwardly. *I don't need this complication,* she told herself. *I just want to be left alone.*

No. That wasn't entirely true.

I prefer company. I want him to stay!

Jesus, Mary, and Joseph! She was so turned around she didn't know *what* she wanted anymore!

"I realize there's nothing as rude as gate crashers," he said softly, "so whether or not you chase me away is up to you. Either way, there won't be any hard feelings on my part."

"*Please* stay!" Zack chimed up.

Dorothy-Anne gave a start as her youngest dashed forward, threw himself at Hunt, and yanked desperately on his sleeves.

"*Don't* go!" Zack implored, looking up at Hunt with huge beseeching eyes. Then, twisting his head around, his gaze shifted desperately to his mother. "Mommy! *Make* Santa stay! Mommy, *please!*"

Dorothy-Anne was at an utter loss. Damn and blast it! Now she couldn't very well *not* extend Hunt an invitation! She turned to Liz and Fred, her eyes appealing for their help.

Typically, they both pretended bored indifference: Fred projecting listless tedium; Liz adopting the jaded, incurious attitude of the tolerantly superior.

Great. Now what? I'm damned if I do and damned if I don't.

Sensing Dorothy-Anne's quandary, Venetia unerringly came to the rescue. Prepared to shoulder all blame, she squatted down in front of Zack.

"Of course Santa can stay, honey," she said throatily, holding his apprehensive gaze. "It's Christmas. And we can't very well chase Santa away, now, can we?"

He shook his little head solemnly.

Smiling, she affectionately tousled his thick auburn bangs.

"Especially," she added, with a conspiratorial wink, "not before we see what he's brought you!"

Zack's delicately lashed, big blue eyes lit up, then dimmed a hair as he looked searchingly over at his mother.

"Mommy, *can* he stay?"

Dorothy-Anne sighed, then smiled at Zack. "Of course Santa is welcome to stay, sweetie," she said hoarsely. "That goes without saying. We'll get the best guest room ready for him."

The radiance on Zack's face could have lit up an entire city—reward enough for any mother's aching heart, whatever the cost.

Venetia gave Zack a hug and grinned. "You see? Child, what did I tell you? Huh?"

And rising to her full height, Venetia hooked her arm through Hunt's. Behaving as though the two of them were buddies who went way back and Dorothy-Anne was the bit player in *their* little drama.

"Come on, Santa," she said, a hint of laughter in her voice. "Let's go see about that drink . . . and then I'll get someone to look after your . . . er . . . reindeer, are they?"

"There's no need," Hunt replied blithely. "One of the elves is taking them back to the stables as we speak."

What!

Dorothy-Anne stared at him through slitted eyes.

Why, the louse! Of all the low-down rotten tricks! So he had *been counting on staying, the dirty devil!*

She didn't know whether to feel angry or pleased. Perhaps equal measures of both.

It was later.

The fire was burning low. Torn shreds of festive wrapping paper were strewn here, there, everywhere.

Zack, fighting sleep and wearing Hunt's Santa cap, which kept sliding down over his face, was blearily happy.

So were they all.

For the past few hours, reality had been suspended, the all-too-recent tragedies held at bay. They'd sung carols, drunk eggnog (in the adults' case, spiked with booze), and the children had attacked their presents.

Fred couldn't decide which he liked better—the vintage electric guitar, the new portable CD player, the piratical pair of gold earrings, or the yet-to-be-released Hootie and the Blowfish and Pearl Jam CDs. "Coo-ool. But how'd you *get* these recordings?" he asked Hunt in astonishment. "They're not due out for another three, four months yet!"

"Oh, never underestimate Santa," was the vague reply.

Zack hit the jackpot with tons of video games, hip-hop clothes only a mother could hate, a mountain bike, vintage baseball cards, and the gift he prized most of all—two autographed baseballs, one signed by Joe DiMaggio and the other by Ted Williams.

Liz was deluged with clothes from Ralph Lauren, a virtual reality system, a pair of RollerBlades, an antique sterling vanity set, and, from Venetia, the latest state-of-the-art color scanner.

"You haven't been spending any time at your computers," Venetia told her. "Hopefully the scanner will get you back on track."

Dorothy-Anne couldn't believe it. All things considered, it was turning out to be a memorable Christmas.

When Venetia's cellular phone chirruped, Dorothy-Anne said, "Oh, just let it ring. Why spoil a wonderful evening?"

Venetia went to answer it all the same.

"It's got to be important," she said. "Very few people have this number."

She picked up the phone and activated it.

"Hello? Oh, Derek. Merry . . ." Then she listened. "*What*! Oh, *shit*!"

She glanced across the room to where Dorothy-Anne, recognizing the shock in her voice, stood rigidly behind a chair, her hands digging into its upholstered back.

"No, we aren't wired for cable!" Venetia snapped into the phone. "Wait. There's a satellite dish. CNN? Okay. Call you right back."

She quickly pressed the End button.

"What is it?" Dorothy-Anne felt a terrible sense of foreboding.

"Trouble," Venetia said succinctly.

Phone in hand, she lost no time striding rapidly across the room, out through the center hall, and into the study beyond. She grabbed the remote off the coffee table, aimed it at the big-screen TV, and clicked it on. By the time Dorothy-Anne, and then Hunt and the children hurried in, Venetia already had the channel set to CNN.

The picture on the Trinitron fluttered on, and the female anchor was saying, "This story just breaking. In Singapore, health authorities have confirmed an outbreak of Legionnaires' disease at the luxurious Hale Dynasty Hotel. . . ."

"No!" Dorothy-Anne heard herself gasp. "No, no, no, no, *no*!"

She snatched the remote out of Venetia's hand and squeezed the volume button until the anchor's voice reverberated with distortion.

". . . more from our Singapore correspondent, May Lee Chen."

The picture switched to a pretty Asian woman in her twenties, fine black hair ruffled by a sunny breeze, microphone in hand, waiting intently for her cue. From the staggeringly lush tropical plantings behind her rose the opulent marble and glass high-rise with its distinctive, pagoda-roofed top—a silhouette as unmistakable as the former AT&T Building in New York, the Transamerica Pyramid in San Francisco, or the Sydney Opera House in Australia.

"Less than a year after its opening," the reporter said earnestly into her microphone, "medical disaster has struck one of the Pacific Rim's newest and most luxurious hotels. In what is Singapore's first known outbreak of Legionnaires' disease, local health authorities have announced the deaths of two guests, one of them an American, and the hospitalization of twenty-two confirmed, and at least sixty-eight suspected cases . . ."

Dorothy-Anne was too shocked to speak. Slowly, as though physically injured, she lowered herself carefully into an armchair and stared numbly at the screen, listening in mounting horror as the news was trumpeted via satellite to every corner of the globe:

"The sick guests, among six hundred staying at the hotel, were not the only casualties. Several of the two hundred employees have also reported symptoms."

"Good God!" Dorothy-Anne whispered. "Those are *our* guests and employees she's talking about! How on *earth*—?"

She glanced searchingly at Venetia, but her friend's attention was riveted to the screen, her face expressionless except for the intelligent dark eyes, which betrayed a calculating glint: the cool professional already weighing the best possible options for minimizing what was surely any public relations expert's worst nightmare.

The excoriating report continued, the camera panning to the hotel entrance, where medics were carrying the ill on stretchers while the healthy, loaded down with luggage, milled around the waiting buses and taxis.

"The hotel is being evacuated as health workers are trying to trace the source of the *Legionella* bacteria. Meanwhile, this once-proud building"—the screen showed a distant shot—"one of the world's most distinguished architectural landmarks, has become a symbol of just another of the twentieth century's perplexing medical mysteries. Reporting from Singapore, this is May Lee Chen."

"Damn, damn, *damn!*" Dorothy-Anne said explosively. She hit the Off button, then slumped back in the chair and brooded. In the sudden silence, the television emitted a faint ticking, like that of a warm car engine.

Or a bomb about to detonate.

Memory's vulture beat its mocking wings.

Nothing generic.

How well—how too damn well!—Dorothy-Anne remembered her brief to the architects.

I want this building to announce *itself—to* declare *itself! I want it so identifiable that the instant people see a picture of it in Cairo or Rio, they'll think, That's the Hale Hotel in Singapore!*

And now that brief had returned to haunt her.

The visual impact of her architectural showstopper with its pagoda-like top, the symbol of Hale Hotels' presence in the Pacific Rim, had instead become a symbol of—she shut her eyes—*disease, suffering, and death.*

"God . . ." she breathed slowly. "Oh, God . . ."

"Honey," Venetia said softly. "I'm sorry. Looks like I'm off to Singapore. Damage control time."

Dorothy-Anne nodded. She looked small, vulnerable, defeated. As though the chair was growing, and she, like Alice, was shrinking.

Wearily, she wiped at her face. "I just don't get it!" she said intensely. "How did this *happen*? How *could* it?"

Venetia sighed. "Honey, that's what the health authorities are trying to determine."

"*No.*" Dorothy-Anne shook her head adamantly. "They're barking up the wrong tree."

"But honey, their findings—"

Dorothy-Anne looked up sharply. "I don't give a damn about their findings!" she said fiercely. "Venetia! Don't you see? This can't *all* be coincidence! My medical problems, yes. But Freddie's crash? And this outbreak on *top* of it? I'm telling you, it's too *much!*"

"And it is," Venetia soothed. "But you know the old adage. Sometimes it's true that trouble comes in threes."

But Dorothy-Anne wasn't buying it.

Venetia's wrong, she thought. *Freddie's plane crash, my miscarriage, and the cervical cancer made three. The hysterectomy made four. And now this makes five.*

Trouble didn't come in fives.

And something else about it—she couldn't quite put her finger on what, exactly . . . the timing, perhaps?—didn't sit right.

Didn't *feel* right.

Venetia perched herself on the arm of Dorothy-Anne's chair. "Listen, honey," she said softly. "I realize what a blow this must be. Especially considering everything else you've—"

"That's just it! There are too *many* tragedies piling up! Since when does lightning strike the same spot so often?"

From experience, Venetia had learned to trust in Dorothy-Anne's intuitions, no matter how bizarre or far-fetched they might at first appear.

"And if you're right?" she asked softly. "If this wasn't an accident and really *was* intentional? Why would anyone—?"

"Why?"

Dorothy-Anne held up her hands.

"Who knows why? For the same reason someone would set off poison gas canisters in the Tokyo subways. Or plant bombs on the streets of Paris. Or engage in drive-by shootings in California. Or set homeless people on fire in New York City."

"To strike terror," Venetia whispered. "To cause confusion and fear."

"That's right."

Venetia rubbed the bridge of her nose, as if to clear her sinuses.

"So what do we do?"

"The only thing we can," Dorothy-Anne replied. "We try to get to the bottom of this . . . and hope we can do it in time. *Before* more lives are lost. Before . . ." Her voice trailed off.

"Before what?"

Dorothy-Anne did not mince words. "Before we're ruined," she said grimly.

24

"The husband is dead," announced Honorable Horse. He looked around the table. The others were sitting quietly, sipping their tea.

"A tragedy," murmured Honorable Ox, a veil dropping across his small dark eyes. He put down his delicate cup. "Buddha has not watched over him, but one man's tragedy is many another man's blessing."

The six elders were inside the central room of a derelict mansion on what, forty years earlier, had been one of French Indochina's proudest plantations near Hanoi. Outside, their armed, shirtsleeved guards patrolled the two-tiered veranda that completely encircled the crumbling, once elegant house.

It was midafternoon, and the tropical heat was oppressive. But that wasn't what kept the guards on the shady veranda. What did was the unchecked progress of nature.

The surrounding garden of palms, frangipani, flame trees, and hibiscus had long since been reclaimed by the jungle, and was virtually impassable. Monstrous undergrowth had shot fifty feet high, and parasitic vines had strangled the once famous cultivated grounds, encroaching on the ruined outbuildings and creating a nearly impenetrable wall of rain forest.

Upon arrival, it had been all their vehicles could do to negotiate the green tunnel that had once been the drive, and then only because it was paved with stone, an obscene reminder of embarrassing colonial riches.

The old *lung tao* from Hong Kong was saying, "Now that the gods have seen fit to take the husband, the woman is in mourning. She is vulnerable. The time has come for us to strike."

"Praise all gods great and small!" exclaimed Honorable Dragon. "We have waited long enough!"

191

"And have much product to move," murmured the Laotian general. "The crops in our highlands have enjoyed a most auspicious year. Never before have the pods of the poppy yielded such abundance."

"My lands have also been thus blessed," added Honorable Horse. "This is by far the most fortuitous harvest since the Year of the Hare."

"Yes, and it is all our refineries can do to process so much product," sighed Honorable Rooster. "Our workers toil in shifts from sunrise to sunrise."

The old *lung tao* stroked his wispy beard. "Indeed, the gods of fortune have been most beneficent . . . despite the pressure exerted on our governments by the pallid pink toads."

"Only because our own fat authorities have pockets without bottoms and hands covered with fragrant grease!" grumbled Honorable Dragon. "Ayeeyah, the greed of those thieves! Each year they multiply like mice and extort more and more of the squeeze."

"A small enough price to pay," said the old *lung tao* calmly, with a casual gesture. "The less product that is confiscated or destroyed, the more bountiful are our profits."

"Perhaps," sniffed the ever worried Honorable Rooster. "However, so abundant a crop demands most careful distribution. An oversupply can easily bring down the price, devour our profits, and erode our power as surely as the sea reclaims the land."

The old *lung tao* sipped his tea fastidiously. "A thousand pardons," he said politely, "but I must disagree."

Honorable Rooster's eyes flickered, but he bottled his anger and bowed graciously.

"Kindly permit me to explain," continued Honorable Ox. "The barbarians' tastes have recently undergone a change for the better."

"Yes?" Still seething at his suggestion being dismissed so out of hand, Honorable Rooster nevertheless managed to feign respectful interest. "How so, Honored Elder?"

"For two decades we have watched the South American coca plant seduce our customers, while the demand for our poppy has continuously dropped off."

"Honorable Ox speaks the truth," interjected Honorable Dragon. "Only by raising our prices have we managed to prosper, while those motherless lumps of Colombian dogmeat have amassed mountains of gold by merely sitting around lazily and scratching their piles!"

The old *lung tao* nodded. "Now, however, the wheel of fortune has once again turned in our favor. The consumption of the coca powder has dropped markedly, while our poppy has once again regained popularity. The abundant harvest with which the gods have seen to bless us is in much demand. Thus we need not worry about regulating the market."

"Perhaps not the market," grumbled Honorable Dragon, "but moving the vast amounts of additional currency is a most vexing problem. My secret banking system has branches all over civilized Asia and is much respected. But in the West? *Ayeeyah!* There, banking is a minefield! Ten thousand laws, controls enough to confuse all the gods, and government interference at every turn! You would think they would welcome enormous transactions, *heya*?"

"One would assume so," said Honorable Rooster. "Don't they?"

"No, they do not!"

Honorable Dragon turned his head, hawked loudly, and spat the evil god spirit on the floor lest it choke him.

"Those duck-fornicating bankers quiver before the authorities like virgins in a waterfront brothel! Imagine, being so choosy! It is a wonder they make any profit at all!"

Honorable Rooster could only shake his head in bemusement. More often than not, the folly of the barbarian devils was beyond his grasp.

Honorable Dragon summed up the situation: "Perhaps now you can appreciate why we need the woman's hotels so urgently," he said. "How else are we to launder, transfer, and legitimize the immense sums such a heaven-blessed harvest will bring?"

"Honorable Dragon is right." The old *lung tao* nodded sagely, then looked at the government minister from Beijing. "Honorable Snake?"

"Yes, Esteemed Elder?"

"Has everything been done?"

"Yes. My sources contacted certain elements in the former Soviet Union. Art treasures, grenade launchers, uranium, nuclear warheads"—he cackled—"those foul, apelike pieces of dung will sell anything as casually as a dog farts—even their own mothers as whore-strumpets if the price is right!"

"Then I take it you offered the right price for something useful?"

"Something highly useful. A tiny phial of a most ingenious substance."

"Indeed!" The old *lung tao* leaned forward. "Do tell."

Honorable Snake smiled his thin smile. "Lowly bacteria."

"Ah!" Honorable Ox steepled his rootlike fingers and tapped them against his lips. Tilting his head, he said, "Hopefully one which cannot be traced back to us?"

"Neither to us nor to anyone else!" chortled Honorable Snake. "It shall truly confound the experts and have them chasing their own tails!"

"How so?"

"Its beauty lies in its simplicity. They are bacteria unknown to germ warfare, but much feared in occasional outbreaks. They were procured through the hairy apes' disease control center, where samples are kept for research and study."

The old *lung tao* nodded with satisfaction. "As all gods bear witness, you have done well, Honorable Snake. Were these bacteria unleashed according to plan?"

"The plan was blessed by the gods of fortune," Honorable Snake answered. "It was completely successful."

There were nods and murmurs of congratulations around the table.

The old *lung tao* nodded with satisfaction. "Good. Now that the woman has tasted of our power, we shall extend her an offer she dare not refuse."

"And if she does?" asked Honorable Rooster. "What then?"

The old *lung tao* blinked. "How can she? She is deeply in debt, and the notes for seven hundred and fifty million dollars come due on the twenty-first day of August. More immediately, she also has a rescheduled interest payment of fifty million dollars coming due on the Ides of May. Clearly, her back is to the wall."

"Yes, but is not a cornered tigress more dangerous than one in the wild?"

"Under ordinary circumstances, yes. However. With our acquisition of Pan Pacific Commonwealth Bank, have we not purchased eight percent of the voting stock in AmeriBank?"

Honorable Rooster nodded.

"And has Pan Pacific not bought up the woman's notes?"

Honorable Rooster nodded again.

"There you have it. The hotels are her collateral, we hold the paper, and come May, we twist the faucet, cut off her cash flow, and in August we call in her notes and reach heaven with one step!"

There was an awed silence.

He half smiled. "I believe by Western standards the woman is considered a most fair flower, although everyone knows barbarians are stupid about such things. But wait and see. She will soon learn that so delicate a flower belongs in a garden, not on the battlefield with men!"

Honorable Rooster bowed. "Ten thousand apologies for questioning your superior wisdom."

The old *lung tao* nodded. Then he turned to the Burmese. "Honorable Horse, you have been most wise in selecting this site for our meeting. As our host, you will see to it that the usual precautions are observed?"

"Have no fear, Illustrious Elder. My bodyguard is a man of many talents. The explosives are already in place. The moment we are gone, this spot will be but a memory."

"I am honored to have such gifted brethren."

The old man pushed back his chair and slowly rose to his feet. The others rose also.

"We shall depart at the usual intervals," Honorable Ox said, with a deep bow.

The others bowed even more deeply to show their respect.

"May the gods of fortune attend each and every one of you," he said. "And may you enjoy ten thousand summers."

"*Doh jeh,*" said the old man in thanks.

The meeting was over.

25

Same old song, different tune.

"Jimmy, Jimmy," Joel rasped over the phone. "Youse killin' me with yer losses. You know that?"

Some things never changed.

"Yeah, yeah." Jimmy Vilinsky had trouble standing still. He bopped up and down, the pay phone wedged between his shoulder and his ear. "I know. Your fuckin' heart's bleedin' for me."

"Lemme ask you one." Joel sounding like a big brother.

Jimmy wanted to say, *Hey, Joel? Cut the crap. You mind? Like you really give a shit . . . unless bookies are suddenly in the business of hoping their marks will win and fleece 'em?*

Right. That *would* be the day.

"It's been what now," Joel was saying, "since your markers was paid. Six days? Seven?"

Jeez! Jimmy thought, hopping in place with agitation. *Like I need this crap!*

"Somethin' like that," he said pugnaciously. "Why?"

All the while standing with his back to the wall, twitchy little raisin eyes darting here, there, everywhere. Watching the bustle and the hustle.

Port Authority.

As usual, the bus terminal was teeming—only more so today, the cold having driven all the riffraff in off the streets.

Port Authority.

Happy hunting grounds for pimps in search of new beaver—plus all the other low-lifes and fuckups. Hungry-eyed jail bait on the make; nervous junkies looking to score; pickpockets working the cash-carrying crowd—these travelers too poor to afford cars or plane tickets or credit

196

cards or checking accounts. Forced to leave the driving to Greyhound and Trailways—and running the gauntlet of circling sharks. And, here and there, he could see pairs of big-hipped uniforms on foot patrol, acting like they were keeping law and order, except that they didn't really give a shit, either.

Just like Joel . . . who was turning up the rasp now, saying, "Hey? Jimmy? You still there?"

"No. I took a whatchamacallit. You know. One o' them astral voyages?"

"Huh?"

"Course I'm here! Christ! Now, you gonna put my six grand on the Dolphins, or what?"

"*Your* six grand?" Joel sputtered, sounding like he'd swallowed his cigar. "You know how much you're already in the hole for? Just since this past week?"

"Yeah, sure."

"Twenty-seven fuckin' grand, that's how much!"

"Joel? Since when did you start freakin' over chickenshit amounts like that? Huh?"

Jimmy playing with him. Giving Joel's balls a good squeeze.

Sure, he'd suffered big losses. Big fuckin' deal.

"Lemme get this straight," Joel said. "You calling twenty-seven grand *chickenshit*? Whatcha do, Vilinsky? Win the lottery?"

"Lottery, shit, I got me a job."

"That right?"

"Yeah." Jimmy's eyes kept hopscotching, caught two purse snatchers choosing their victims. "Real high-payin', too."

"Mind tellin' me what this, ah . . . job entails?"

"Wish I could, Joel. Really do, buddy. But it's confidential, see."

That got a chuckle.

"Hey, go ahead!" Jimmy huffed. "Laugh your fuckin' head off. See if I care. They don't call me 'KO' for nuthin'!"

Joel guffawed. "You the one's gettin' KO'd! Lookit what happened. One week an' *whammo*! Wipe-out! You and the Rodriguez kid. Both o' you down for the count."

"Hey, Joel?" Setting him up.

"What?" Joel walking right into it, eyes wide open.

"Shove it up your ass. Six grand on the Dolphins!" Jimmy having the last word and quickly hanging up.

Goddamn, he wished he could have told Joel how he was going to divvy up! That would've impressed him, all right. Especially after that crack about being down for the count. It would have felt real good, making him eat his words. The bastard.

The trouble with that was, Jimmy really did have to keep his lips zipped. Shooting his mouth off was one surefire way of nuking a good thing.

Well, fuck Joel! he growled to himself. *Fuck him and the horse he rode into town on! For that matter, fuck the whole bunch o' them!*

Feeling a little better, Jimmy decided he might as well go take a stroll. Maybe check out a peep show or porn flick.

Whatever. He had nothing better to do.

Cutting across the bus terminal, he exited through the Eighth Avenue doors.

Whoa!

He couldn't remember it being this freakin' cold. The way the wind was blasting down from up north, it was like hitting a wall of ice. Almost instantly, the snot in his nose crystallized.

But Jimmy Vilinsky wasn't about to be put off. It took more than a little windchill factor to slow *him* down.

Wrapping his scarf around the lower half of his face, he hunched forward into the wind and headed uptown on foot. Managing, despite the cold, to put a strut in his step, a cocksure bounce that declared these mean streets to be *his.*

Which, if truth be told, they were.

Hadn't he been born and raised just a few blocks north of here, over toward Ninth Avenue? And wasn't Hell's Kitchen still home sweet home?

Fuckin' A, it was!

To hear Jimmy tell it, the City That Never Sleeps was *it,* man. Day or night, rain or shine. "The only place worth livin' or dyin' in," the way he liked to put it.

Never having a clue how prophetic those words would be . . .

Death was stalking Jimmy Vilinsky.

Carmine was just another well-bundled pedestrian on the opposite sidewalk, across multiple lanes of noisy, belching traffic.

Despite the weather, it was commerce as usual on Eighth Avenue's gaudy midway of peep shows and porn parlors. Whores in miniskirts huddled in doorways, pandhandlers rattled their paper cups, and shills stamped their feet in an effort to keep warm while halfheartedly trying to lure suckers into their establishments. And, wherever a building's hot air exhausts happened to vent, there were the homeless, those pitiable human bundles of rags who fought a minute-to-minute battle for mere survival.

Carmine, watch cap pulled low and scarf wound protectively around neck, mouth, and nose, scowled with disgust. Wondering, as always, what this city had come to.

Everywhere you looked, you saw the dregs of humanity. And every year, the refuse of society just kept on multiplying.

Like rabbits, Carmine thought, with a shudder. *Heaven help us. Some-body ought to do them a favor and put them out of their misery.*

Across the street, Jimmy Vilinsky had stopped outside a dive where flashing neons advertised LIVE SHOWS! BURLESK! GIRLS! GIRLS! GIRLS!

Carmine slowed, watching Jimmy ignore the shill and study some photos on display before moving on again. Obviously unaware that his time on earth was running out.

Not that Carmine was in a hurry.

Take your time, the hired killer projected across the busy lanes of traffic. *It's no skin off my back. Unlike you, Jimmy, I've got plenty of time. All the time in the world.*

The place Jimmy chose, a dump that ran porno flicks, wasn't because he was anxious to get in out of the cold, or because the movie they were running, a flick called *Wet Dreams,* was one he was particularly dying to see. What decided him was a simple matter of economics.

Jimmy had priorities. The way he figured it, why stand in an upright coffin and keep feeding money into a mechanism that raised a window-shade—and for what? Just to see some stoned bimbo jiggling her knock-ers? Or fork over cold hard cash in order to watch a "live" stage show that was obviously faked? Or, worse yet, be served overpriced, watered-down rotgut just to watch a broad clinging to a chrome pole like a fuckin' monkey?

Why indeed?

At least with movies you got your money's worth. Sometimes you even got to see real semen squirting all over the place, and if you were lucky, you could whack off and squirt some of your own.

An appealing bargain.

He paid the entrance fee at the ticket window, said, "How you doin'?" to a guy who couldn't care less, and pushed his way through the turnstile.

The small theater was dark and nearly empty, and the action on-screen involved two well-endowed young women making out, licking each other's titties and bumping pussy.

He took a seat near the back, unbuttoned his coat, and settled down to enjoy himself.

Now this is more like it! he thought, feeling the stirrings of a generous erection.

Unzipping his fly, he dug out his penis and started to masturbate. The girls on-screen getting it on—Look at that. Not the least bit inhibited.

Feeling his juices starting to rise, Jimmy ascertained that he'd better stop and give it a rest. *Don't want to shoot my wad too soon. Hell, no. Want this to* last . . .

The celluloid events continued to hold him in thrall—so much so that he never noticed someone slipping quietly into the seat behind his.

Now one of the girls in the film was lying back and parting her legs, the better to be eaten—and for the camera to zoom in real nice and close. Talking dirty as her partner dove, tongue flicking, between her splayed thighs:

"Oh, yeah. Oooooh, baby. That's right. Eat me . . . eat me *good*. . . ."

Behind Jimmy, Carmine sketched a swift sign of the cross and murmured, "Forgive me Father, for I have sinned by entering this den of foul iniquity. . . ."

Carmine knew all about the pitfalls of pornography and the evil to which it inevitably led.

If people only remembered that God created sex for procreation, not recreation, how much better off we would all be. Instead, we've permitted the world to become one big Sodom. Is it any wonder that disease, abortion, and birth control are epidemic?

As for self-abuse, what was masturbation if not birth control by another name?

The slaughter of the unborn, that's what it is, Carmine thought grimly, reaching into a pocket and slipping out a length of piano wire attached to two wooden handles. *For this alone, Jimmy Vilinsky deserves to die.*

Carmine was quick as a flash.

The instant Jimmy continued to masturbate, the garrotte was around his neck and Carmine was twisting the wooden handles with practiced flicks of a wrist—choking him to death.

What the fuck?

It took Jimmy several seconds to realize what was happening, and by then it was too late. The wire was already digging into his neck, cutting off the flow of oxygen to his brain.

He gasped for air, his mouth gaping wide, his fingers scrabbling desperately at his throat. But it was futile. No matter how hard he struggled, he was unable to loosen the ever-tightening wire or even whisper for help.

Tears trickled from his bulging eyes. And all the while, he was getting weaker and weaker even as his head seemed to expand, feeling as if it were getting bigger, bigger, as though someone was pumping it full of air.

Then, just when he thought his skull would surely burst, a pleasant light-headedness came over him, and his erection was fiercer than any he had ever experienced.

But perhaps strangest of all was the sudden euphoria: the lack of oxygen to his brain brought on a languid muzziness, and the borders between fantasy and reality merged.

The girl on-screen had ceased to be a mere projection. For Jimmy, she had become his very own living, breathing sex goddess. Her parted thighs embraced his face, and he could feel the moist dark patch of her pubis writhing against his mouth, hear her crying out to him, her distant voice echoing in his head: "I'm coming! Oh, God! Jimmy! *Jimmmmmy . . .*"

And Jimmy realized that the reason he couldn't breathe was that her legs were locked so fiercely around his head. Then he tasted her nectar— all sweet honey and myrrh, and he no longer cared about breathing. A rushing, surflike noise crescendoed and deafened his ears, and he could feel the torrent rise in his loins.

Jimmy was unable to contain himself. His testes seemed to explode and he screamed soundlessly in exquisite agony, and then the veil dropped down and the world went dark.

Jimmy Vilinsky died as he had lived. Owing a bundle.

26

Two days later. Ten-thirty in the morning.

Dorothy-Anne's chauffeur-driven Infiniti Q45, sleek and black as a Stealth bomber, bore her in silent luxury down the Sawmill River Parkway to the Henry Hudson Parkway, where it joined the coagulation of traffic at the toll booths.

The traffic backup normally wouldn't have bothered her, but today it did. She realized her annoyance was a direct result of the summons—couched in the polite language of a request, but an unmistakable summons nonetheless—which her bankers had sprung on her the previous afternoon.

It did not bode well, Dorothy-Anne suspected, and she wondered what their major concern would be. The effect of the Legionnaire's disease on the bottom line? Freddie's death and the lack of a strong male executive at her side? Or did they simply want to reassure themselves that she was still of sound mind and body?

Not that it mattered. Whatever the reason, she'd had no choice but to agree to the meeting.

Because she owed.

Seven hundred and fifty million. *Plus* a $50-million payment due in May.

All of which, she told herself reasonably, gave AmeriBank the right to be worried. They were, after all, holding a hell of a lot of paper.

Yes, but they have the Hale Company as collateral, she reminded herself.

Forbes's last estimate of her worth was $8.3 billion.

And that's not exactly chopped liver.

Rennie pulled up in front of One AmeriBank Plaza, a soulless steel and glass tower down near Wall Street. She watched Rennie as he came around and held open the rear door. A sudden blast of icy wind, cold as bankers' blood, hit Dorothy-Anne squarely, made her recoil.

Well, here goes, she thought, grimacing as she pulled together the front of her brown shearling wrap, cut wide and long, with chocolate embroidery and shearling fringes, an elegant concoction by Fendi that softened the severity of what she thought of as her "banker's suit." Then she got out, leaned into the oncoming wind, and averted her face as she climbed the three shallow steps up to the granite-paved plaza.

It was an engineering disaster, a vertical wind tunnel where invisible cyclones whirled around a red abstract sculpture. Keeping her eyes narrowed against airborne grit, she fought her way to the building's entrance and pushed her way through the revolving door.

After the plaza outside, the heated, high, white marble lobby felt especially welcoming.

Dorothy-Anne went straight to the long black lozenge of a marble reception desk, where she had to sign in and wait to be cleared by security before getting on an elevator.

The elevator stopped smoothly and the doors sighed open. As she stepped out into the reception area, she felt the usual sense of disorientation.

The building's lobby and elevator might have been ultramodern, but the fifty-seventh floor reeked of an earlier era, with the kind of staid, traditional decor bankers and lawyers go for in a big way. Mahogany paneling. Chesterfield sofas. Groups of leather wing chairs. All intended to convey an air of financial solidity, no doubt.

But the low ceilings and lack of windows spoiled the effect, interjected a disturbing false note. To pull it off successfully, the interior needed height, windows, proportions.

There was no need for Dorothy-Anne to announce herself to the receptionist: a young executive in a Brooks Brothers suit was coming toward her, hand extended in welcome. "Mrs. Cantwell?" he said pleasantly.

Dorothy-Anne looked at him. "That's right."

"I'm Mike Mellow." He smiled. "One of Mr. Priddy's assistants."

They shook hands, their grips equally firm and cool. Not friendly but courteous.

Dorothy-Anne knew his type. A gofer with an MBA, itching to go places. The business world was full of Mike Mellows.

"Mr. Priddy didn't want to keep you waiting," he said. "If you'll come this way, please?"

He led the way down a mahogany-paneled corridor. Both walls were lined with gloomy, gilt-framed portraits. These, Dorothy-Anne knew from previous visits, were the long-dead founding fathers of the various banking institutions that, over the past two hundred years, had coalesced into this one immense entity. To a man, they were all somberly dressed and emanated stern disapproval and thin-lipped thrift.

A far cry from her own inviting, people-friendly headquarters.

She followed Mike Mellow through a waiting room, where several men were biding their time to see Julian Priddy, then an outer office where two secretaries were busy at computer terminals and a third was on the telephone, and straight to the Big Man's door.

Mellow knocked, and without waiting for a response, opened it and stepped inside, letting Dorothy-Anne enter first.

Julian Tyler Priddy always reminded her of the hood ornament on a classic car: tall, slim, patrician, buffed, and beautifully turned out, with a sleek, aerodynamic face and swept-back silver hair. His custom-made pinstripes were Savile Row, and his conservative silk tie was fashioned in a perfect Windsor knot. He had cold eyes and the disconcerting habit of blinking rapidly.

"Mrs. Cantwell."

His voice was sonorous and his accent Bostonian; he had grown up on Beacon Hill. He rose from the high-backed red leather swivel behind his desk and came around it to shake hands.

"First of all, on behalf of myself and this bank, I would like to express my most sincere condolences." His eyelids blinked rapidly. "Your husband was a fine man."

Dorothy-Anne nodded. "Yes, he"— she almost said "is," but caught herself in time—"he was."

Mike Mellow hovered on the periphery of her awareness; closer in, her attention was drawn to the stranger who had risen from a heavy club chair. She glanced at him, then raised questioning eyebrows at Julian Priddy.

If Priddy was the least bit uneasy, he didn't let it show. "Mrs. Cantwell, may I introduce Sir Ian Connery," he said, launching smoothly into the introduction. "Sir Ian, Mrs. Cantwell."

Sir Ian shook hands with her. "Mrs. Cantwell."

"Sir Ian."

Dorothy-Anne appraised him warily. She hadn't been forewarned that a third party would be present at the meeting, and the fact that a surprise had been sprung on her made her deeply suspicious. From experience, she had learned to be distrustful of surprises. Nine times out of ten, they boded no good.

For this reason she gave Sir Ian a longer and more thorough once-over than was her habit.

Sir Ian Connery was chubby: too well fed to let her accurately guess his age. His face was pink and his skin was baby smooth and he wore large black-framed glasses. His hair was white and receding, and his eyebrows were black and gray barbed wire. He had on a double-breasted black wool suit with a fine gray pinstripe in it, and a tie of regimental stripes. A yellow silk handkerchief with a tiny paisley pattern showed in his breast pocket. His hands were small and pudgy and as pink and smooth as his face.

"Mr. Priddy informed me of your recent loss," he told Dorothy-Anne. The voice he projected was rich and plummy. "Most regrettable." He shook his head gravely and murmured: "Bad joss. Bad. Bereavement's no time to conduct business. Wish it weren't necessary."

Dorothy-Anne's gaze flickered coldly with suspicion. "And what business might that be?" she asked sharply.

"Why don't we sit down?" Priddy broke in, clasping his hands and rubbing them together. "Mike!" This to the distantly hovering Mellow.

"Sir!"

"Why don't you take Mrs. Cantwell's coat, then scare up two coffees and another tea?"

The Caucasian, Yale-educated Step-'n-Fetchit jumped to. Eagerly helped Dorothy-Anne out of her coat and rushed off again.

Priddy, with the air of a mother hen, shepherded Dorothy-Anne and Sir Ian to the red leather club chairs arranged around a Chippendale silver table with elaborate fretwork. Leather upholstery sighed under their weight. Sir Ian interjected sadness in a neutral smile, and noticed the tension in Dorothy-Anne's posture. She sat a little too erect, her eyes bright and alert, like those of a cat caught in a sudden light.

Clearing his throat, Priddy said: "Sir Ian is from Hong Kong. He is chief executive of the Pan Pacific Bank."

Dorothy-Anne waited.

"Doubt it rings a bell," Sir Ian added, smiling forgiveness at Dorothy-Anne. "Small bank. Strictly private until recently. Still small, in fact. Not even a vest pocket compared to this." He indicated AmeriBank with a sweeping glance around the spacious corner office. "Not even a blip on the financial radar screen."

"Sir Ian is being modest," Priddy told Dorothy-Anne. "We all know Asia and the Pacific Rim are exploding. These days it's where the action is. Everywhere you look there's double-digit growth."

"Yes, but we're not telling Mrs. Cantwell anything she doesn't already know." Sir Ian smiled pleasantly at her. "The Hale Companies have been a major player in the Far East for . . . what? Nearly two decades, is it?"

Dorothy-Anne nodded but did not speak. She knew a tag team in action when she saw one.

I've been set up, she realized.

The only thing she couldn't figure out was why.

I have to be careful, she cautioned herself. *I'm squared off against two cunning opponents. One will try to distract me while the other goes in for the kill.*

If only she knew what in God's name was going on!

I'm *AmeriBank's customer!* she wanted to remind Priddy. *You're supposed to be on* my *side!*

Julian Priddy continued, "If Pan Pacific grows at just half the rate as the rest of the region, it will soon be a power to be reckoned with."

Sir Ian chuckled. "Don't listen to him, Mrs. Cantwell. Mr. Priddy accused me of being modest. Well, now I can accuse him of being too kind."

They fell silent as Mike returned with a pewter tray and set it down on the fretwork table. The coffee and tea were already poured, served in gilt-rimmed white Wedgwood cups and saucers. A matching creamer, sugar bowl, and saucer filled with packets of Equal were on the side.

"Thank you, Mike. That will be all." Priddy dismissed him without a glance and handed the cups around.

"Sugar?" he asked Dorothy-Anne. "Cream?"

She shook her head. "No, thank you. Black's fine." She took a polite sip, then set the cup and saucer down.

Coffee, not lunch. I obviously no longer rate lunch.

"Unfortunate, this Singapore thing," Sir Ian said casually, while sipping his tea. He looked over the cup at Dorothy-Anne. "Can't be good for business. Hear you had a spate of cancellations."

Dorothy-Anne felt an icy chill. "And what, may I ask, is your interest in all this?" she inquired coldly.

But it was Priddy who took the ball and ran with it. "Sir Ian," he announced quietly, "has a vested interest in the Hale Companies."

"Oh?" Dorothy-Anne spiked Priddy with a glare. "And just what might this vested interest be?"

Impervious to her visual daggers, Priddy continued to speak in calm, measured tones.

"As you are doubtless well aware, it is common practice among insurance companies to diversify their liabilities. That way, when a catastrophe strikes they don't have all their eggs in one basket."

"But you're not an insurance company," Dorothy-Anne pointed out inexorably.

"Granted, we're not. But when it comes to loans, banks also like to spread the risk around. And for the exact same reason: in case of default, no one institution takes a mortal beating—"

"Whoa! Back up there just a minute!" Dorothy-Anne interrupted heatedly, her voice, hard and serrated, slicing through Priddy's calm, emotionless delivery like a knife. "Let me get this straight. . . ."

She trembled in outrage, and every atom of her body, thrumming with indignation, emanated mutinous affront.

"Are you suggesting that the *Hale* Companies are such a risk? That we're in danger of *defaulting*? That we're going *under*?"

"I'm suggesting no such thing," he replied in burnished tones, without answering her question. "I'm simply stating facts. At your request, we have already rescheduled your loans twice."

"A not uncommon practice, which, I might point out, has nothing to do with altruism," Dorothy-Anne reminded him stingingly. "This bank profits quite nicely on the interest."

"I'm not suggesting otherwise," he said, slippery as an eel. "However, unlike the Hale Companies, this bank is a publicly held corporation. As such, we have a duty, a sacred obligation, as it were, to our shareholders—"

"Let's cut the crap, Mr. Priddy. Just put the cards on the table. What I assume you're trying to say, but have been beating around the bush about, is that you wish to sell the Hale Companies' notes to this . . . this small bank, which is supposedly"—she mimicked Sir Ian bitingly—" 'hardly a blip on the financial radar screen.' That *is* what this meeting is about, isn't it?"

"It's what I planned to discuss, yes." He nodded. "Except for one, er, major detail."

She stared at him. "And what, may I ask, might that be?"

Julian Priddy was looking exceedingly uncomfortable. This wasn't going at all as he had planned. Due to her bereavement, he had fully expected Dorothy-Anne to take the news sitting down—a presumption that, he now realized, had been a serious miscalculation on his part. He had failed to take into account her fighting spirit, and it was reasserting itself sooner than he had anticipated. Now what should have been a piece of cake suddenly wasn't.

"Mr. Priddy?" Dorothy-Anne was waiting.

Sir Ian came to his aid. "Mrs. Cantwell, you're a businesswoman and I'm a banker, and we shall be working closely together. Please allow me. . . . What Mr. Priddy wishes to convey is that his bank no longer holds your notes. Pan Pacific's already purchased them. *Fait accompli*, I'm afraid. Done deal."

Done . . . ?

Dorothy-Anne sat there in stunned disbelief, too shocked to put her emotions into words. She stared at Julian Priddy, who refused to meet her eye.

The son of a bitch!

The bile of betrayal burned raw in her throat.

He sold me out!

He didn't even have the decency to tell me beforehand!

"Doesn't really change things," Sir Ian went on easily. "Simple matter of sending interest payments to Hong Kong. Terms're the same. Notes aren't due till June thirtieth. Time comes, we'll work on rescheduling. . . ."

But Dorothy-Anne wasn't listening. Her head spun with the concussion of the bombshell. She had a vision of structural weaknesses, of essential underpinnings giving way and the whole elaborate, interconnected entities of her empire collapsing, piece by piece, like giant dominoes racing around the world, knocking each other down, one after another, and another, and another . . .

Death . . . miscarriage . . . outbreak . . .

And now betrayal. That on top of everything else. . . .

Death . . . miscarriage . . . outbreak . . . betrayal.

As if she hadn't suffered enough direct hits already!

Priddy moved importantly in his chair, raised his sleek head, and cleared his throat. Initially, Dorothy-Anne's verbal onslaught had caught him unprepared, but he'd quickly snapped back into his role, his self-confidence fully restored. Once again he was the banker, clothed in the vestments of power, authority, control.

"Mrs. Cantwell," he purred, "surely you realize that it was strictly a business decision. You mustn't take it personally."

His voice breached the ramparts of her shock, switched some mental circuit breaker back on.

Not take it personally!

She glared at him, her contempt blazing. "Mr. Priddy." She rose shakily to her feet. "I cannot help but take this personally. *Extremely* personally! But what is truly beyond me, what I find intolerable and *most* unforgivable, is that I wasn't even *told*! Why, common courtesy—"

"I didn't"—Priddy cleared his throat and started over—"that is, the bank didn't . . . wish to intrude upon your grief."

"My grief!" she exclaimed softly. "As an excuse, you dare bring up my *grief*?" She shook her head in wide-eyed amazement. "My God! You really are one fine piece of work!"

He smiled sourly, his lips edged in condescension. "It seems no time is better than another to break this kind of news, doesn't it?"

She did not deign to reply.

"Naturally, it's understandable that you're upset. I'm truly sorry, Mrs. Cantwell, but"—he shrugged and raised his hands, palm sides up—"business is business."

"Yes," Dorothy-Anne said dryly, "it certainly is—and ethics be damned!"

"It's perfectly legal," Priddy sniffed, with affront.

"No doubt it is. However, you're no longer my banker, and I've wasted enough precious time. I hope you'll excuse me."

Hands clenched at her sides, she turned to Sir Ian. "I'll be in touch," she told him, "as soon as my office receives the requisite paperwork. I wish I could say it's been a pleasure."

Both men placed their hands on the arms of their chairs and started to get up, but Dorothy-Anne stilled them with a shake of her head.

"Please, gentlemen," she said, "remain seated. I can see myself out."

Then, head raised, and armored in dignity, she stiffly crossed the carpet to the door and pulled it open. Hand on the knob, she paused momentarily and looked back at them.

"Happy New Year," she said quietly.

Before they could answer, she was gone.

Rennie put the Infiniti in gear. "Upstate, Mrs. C.?"

"What? Oh." Dorothy-Anne shook her head. "No, Rennie. I've changed my mind. Just drop me off uptown."

"At the townhouse, ma'am?"

"That's right."

The double-width townhouse on East Sixty-ninth Street between Fifth and Madison was the Cantwells' primary residence and, as such, was kept fully staffed and prepared.

On the drive there, Dorothy-Anne called Meadowlake Farm on the car phone and spoke to Nanny Florrie. "Pack up the brood, Nanny, would you please? One of the staff can drive you down."

"Och! You maun we're cooting the holidays oop here short?"

"That's exactly what I mean." Dorothy-Anne pressed her End button, replaced the phone, and sat back, nervously clenching and unclenching her hands.

The drive uptown seemed to take forever.

When she arrived, she left instructions that she was not to be disturbed and went directly upstairs to the second-floor study overlooking the wintry garden out back. Locking herself in, she kicked off her shoes, lit the stacked logs in the fireplace, and absorbedly poured herself a splash of brandy. Not to drink; the glass was a mere prop. Somehow, simply cupping the snifter in her hands seemed oddly reassuring, an end in itself. Gave her something to do with her hands besides fidget.

She sank into an easy chair by the fire, lost in deep thought.

"Doesn't really change things."

Sir Ian's words replayed themselves in her head like an ominous recording.

The hell it doesn't! she thought angrily, exhaling a long, shuddering growl. *What do they take me for? It changes everything!*

She stared into the cheerfully crackling flames. Despite the heat, she couldn't seem to get warm, and kept shivering. It was impossible to shake the sense of chill dread and foreboding that engulfed her.

"Terms're the same. . . . Time comes, we'll work on rescheduling."

She desperately wanted to believe that, but some sixth sense, an intuition she'd long learned to trust, told her to beware. Pan Pacific was an unknown element; she'd never dealt with them before. Hell, before today she'd never even *heard* of them!

Know Thine Enemy. It was the first rule of business.

Dorothy-Anne made a mental note to learn what she could about Pan Pacific. She'd get Derek Fleetwood on it right away.

Meanwhile . . .

She sighed heavily. Meanwhile, a fifty-million-dollar payment was due in May. And the whopper—the notes for $750 million—came due on the twenty-first of August.

In exactly two hundred and fifty-two days.

What if, at that time, Pan Pacific *didn't* reschedule the loans? What if, despite Sir Ian's vague assurance, they exercised their right and demanded the $750 million in full? What then?

But Dorothy-Anne knew the answer to that. *I'd be up shit's creek.* The Hale Company was her collateral. *I'd lose everything.*

Suddenly a steely resolve came into her eyes.

No. She *wouldn't* lose everything—for the simple reason that she could not, would not, *must* not stand by and let that happen! The Hale Company was more than just a corporation. It was her great-grandmother's legacy.

Through sheer determination and strength, Elizabeth-Anne Hale had built the company from a single motel into a globe-girdling giant. No war nor family calamity nor outside enemies had ever been allowed to breach its defenses.

Elizabeth-Anne hadn't permitted it. She had been a strong leader.

I have to be just as strong, Dorothy-Anne told herself. *Only strength will see me through this crisis. I've got to fight!*

She squared her shoulders.

And I shall fight—and fight to win! No one was going to take her great-grandmother's legacy—nor her own children's—away from them! No one!

August twenty-first . . .

Two hundred and fifty-two days . . .

She was aware of a soft but constant internal ticking, as though the timer on a bomb had been activated.

And it had been.

The countdown had begun.

BOOK TWO

THE HOUNDS OF SPRING

27

D r. Wo Sheng Yi, Director of Bacteriology, was in his cinder block laboratory burning the midnight oil. As a department head who preferred lab work over paper pushing and budget scrounging, this was especially precious time, and he always tried to make the most of it.

But try as he might, he was for once unable to concentrate on the microorganisms to which he had devoted his life's work.

Finally, resigning himself to the fact that his personal demons were hampering his thought processes, he switched off his electronic microscope, took off the black-framed glasses that made him look like I. M. Pei, and massaged the red impressions they had left on the bridge of his nose.

Then he just sat there, gazing around abstractedly, as if he had suddenly been transported from the familiarity of his lab to some utterly alien environment.

Which, in a way, he had.

It was astonishing, he thought, truly astonishing and awesomely frightening how quickly—how obscenely *suddenly*!—the carpet of one's life could be yanked out from under one's feet.

Dr. Wo Sheng Yi was no stranger to upheaval. Indeed, since his birth in Shanghai, forty-eight years earlier, he had suffered more than his fair share of turmoil.

But now Dr. Wo Sheng Yi was living the American Dream, or had thought he was, until a short time ago when a request—no, a *demand*— had come.

Whatever the reason, his nephew, "Little" Wo, could not go through official channels to leave China, nor could he wait for the requisite paperwork. The message had been quite clear on that point. It had stressed urgency; had emphasized that it was a matter of life—Wo hugged himself with his arms—and death.

He quailed at the undertaking demanded of him, felt outrage at the very idea. But what choice did he have? Like it or not, he *had* to do it, consequences be damned.

And the smugglers of human cargo, with whom the underground banker in New York had put him in contact, were determined to turn him into no less than a sneak and a thief and a traitor to his noble profession. They refused to accept money for Little Wo's passage, had demanded bacteria from the CDC's vast stock of frozen specimens instead.

Bacteria!

Common bacteria, Dr. Wo, nothing contagious . . . The smuggler's words. A calm voice on the telephone, nobody he'd ever met—*just salmonella, nothing exotic or ordinarily life-threatening . . .*

And they wanted it tonight. *Tonight!* Little Wo's safe passage in exchange for a disease.

Wo slumped in his government-issue chair. *God help me,* he thought queasily, hugging his stomach even tighter. *God have mercy on my soul. . . .*

"Hey, Doc? *Doc!*"

With a start, Wo snapped back to the blurry present. He looked up and blinked owlishly, then slipped his thick glasses back on.

The fog focused, and he seemed surprised to find himself in the familiar confines of his office, and startled to see Dottie Stoller standing in the open doorway.

Dottie was the tropical disease whiz of his department, a petite, gamine woman with an Audrey Hepburn neck and silver hair snipped in a youthful pageboy. You had to get up close before you realized she was in her sixties.

"What's the matter, Doc?" she cracked. "Clarice finally come to her senses and throw you out? Or don't you realize what time it is?"

"Time?" Wo looked bewildered.

He was aware of himself as all clumsiness and guilt. What was it with him? Surely she couldn't miss his nervousness, his uncharacteristic furtiveness and the smell of his fear?

Consciously avoiding her eyes, he quickly consulted the Swatch watch on his wrist. A Christmas gift from his youngest daughter. It was vervy and with-it—and made him feel each of his forty-eight years, but he wore it daily. 10:26.

"Goodness!" he murmured. "How did it get so late?"

He decided he'd better get moving if he was to do what he must do.

"See you tomorrow." Dottie waved, disappeared, then poked her head back around the door frame. "And don't forget to go home!"

He nodded, then sat there a moment and listened. The building was quiet. He could hear its sounds—the creaks of its joints, the hum of the overhead fluorescents, the bell of the elevator Dottie had summoned.

Sighing to himself, he rolled back his chair and pushed himself reluctantly to his feet. It was now or never.

Now . . .

And sighing out misery, Dr. Wo Sheng Yi, world-renowned researcher and director of the CDC's Bacteriology Department, left his office and trudged down the worn linoleum hallway, his destination the maximum containment lab.

It's only a bacterium, he told himself, locking a mental door on all but the immediate present. *It's merely salmonella, which is rarely fatal.*

He nodded to himself. He was reaching, yes. But he needed the balm of a placebo.

It's not as if they'd demanded something truly lethal, a virus, for instance.

He'd never have gone for that. God, no!

"Hey, Doc," Sonny Fong said amiably. "Thanks for the present."

Dr. Wo Sheng Yi stood silent and motionless on the dark country road.

Sonny placed the container in his car, then drew his gun. "Now, Doc," he said, "get back in your car. You're going for a little ride."

Three hours later, an encrypted E-mail message streaked its way to the other side of the world. Decoded in Kuo Fong's Italianate villa high above Hong Kong, it read:

> Greetings, most honorable fifth cousin twice removed. I am honored to report that I am in possession of the product we required. My business here is completed and our local employee has received his severance package. Due to airline security baggage checks, I am driving to my destination by car. I estimate my travel time shall take four to five days. I will confirm the success of my humble endeavor upon completion. May the gods of fortune attend you. Your dutiful fifth cousin twice removed.

28

T he calendar said spring. The weather said winter.

Flurries of snowflakes swirled in the air as the smartly uniformed guard waved the chauffeured black Infiniti through the gates.

With a burst of speed the car swept smoothly along the landscaped drive, its destination the red brick building set atop a slight incline so that it dominated the surrounding acres and appeared to lord it over the vast parking lot.

Built a mere eight years earlier of weathered antique bricks, the imposing, three-story facade with its octagonal, weathervaned cupola looked as if it had been uprooted from colonial Williamsburg and set down here, intact, a half hour's commute from midtown Manhattan, in White Plains.

In reality, it was the world headquarters of the Hale Companies, the parent corporation of Hale Hotels, and the brain center of a polyglot empire whose various subsidiaries had tentacles in every conceivable service industry.

Each red brick building had its own particular function. One was devoted exclusively to managing the hotel chain; another housed the offices of Hale Lines, the corporation's seventeen-ship luxury cruise line; yet a third contained the administrative staff of the worldwide Vacation Village resorts. Others functioned as the headquarters of the Hale Companies' vacation time shares program, or marketed specific services such as catered in-flight meals for airlines, or cleaning crews for independently owned hotels. There was even a hotel, motel, and restaurant management school.

And then there was the nerve center for FLASH, the Hale Companies' airline, hotel, and rental car reservations system—the most extensively used hookup of its kind in the world.

All told, each subsidiary was a billion-dollar-a-year industry in and of itself. And each was accountable to one person: the passenger in the Infiniti.

A spread like this had never been necessary in Great-Granny's day, Dorothy-Anne was thinking. Seated in the plush rear seat of the car, she stared out at the beautiful complex. *Back then two floors of a high-rise office building at Park Avenue and Fifty-first Street had sufficed.* But that was back then, and this was now. Times had changed, and the Hale Companies had had to change with them.

And will keep on changing, Dorothy-Anne thought, recognizing flexibility and swift adaptation as her greatest assets. *If only they could help me now. . . .*

The main building's reception area was like the lobby of a cozy hotel, with comfortable sofas and club chairs, a fire in the grate, and a receptionist behind the desk. Security guards in well-cut suits frowned at clusters of reporters who had disregarded their suggestions and had decided to camp out on the sofas, hoping to catch Dorothy-Anne upon arrival.

They could have saved themselves the bother. Dorothy-Anne wasn't using the lobby. Her Infiniti drove around the back of the building, then dipped down into an underground parking garage, where a uniformed guard was waiting.

Here a smaller, private elevator required the use of a special key. It was to this that Dorothy-Anne, briefcase in hand and wearing a long, black, open cashmere coat, made a rapid beeline. Slowing but not stopping, she greeted the guard by name, then swept into the elevator, the door to which he had unlocked and was holding open.

He pushed it smartly shut, and the press of a button whisked her up, past the lobby, to the second floor and the privacy of her inner office, the elevator having been designed expressly for this purpose, to bypass her staff and impatient visitors in general, and members of the press in particular.

The atmosphere of Dorothy-Anne's spacious inner office was welcomingly warm and deliberately cozy, as unofficelike and antitechnoid as a workplace could possibly be, so that upon entering she would usually feel immediately and comfortably at home. In here it was perpetually, unseasonably summery, as if to give lie to the dervishes of snow swirling on the other side of the windows.

"Morning," Venetia, sipping from a demitasse, called crisply from a sofa across the room.

Dorothy-Anne looked over at her. "I notice you left off the 'Good,'" she observed wryly, tugging at the fingers of her black kid gloves.

"Yes, child. That is because there's nothing good about it. This girl is drowning in a public relations trauma. Yes. I am seriously distressed."

Dorothy-Anne whirled a finger at one of a pair of Karelian birch armchairs in front of her rosewood desk. Then, while Venetia, demitasse and saucer in hand, moved forward to take the indicated chair, Dorothy-Anne prowled restlessly, like an agitated, fault-finding hostess inspecting her premises before a party.

Normally she would have drawn delight from this sprawling room, been cheered by its eclectic exuberance.

Not for her the icy perfection of the sleek executive suite. On the contrary. Floral chintz from Lee Jofa covered walls and sofas and framed the windows in lush folds. Underfoot, the wall-to-wall sisal was scattered with a profusion of nineteenth-century needlepoint rugs. A convivial fire fluttered in the marble fireplace, morocco-bound volumes filled the built-in bookcases to bursting, and lamps shaded in green silk cast soft pools of light.

Silver-framed photographs abounded. They were tucked among the shelves and scattered atop beautifully veneered tables piled with books and bibelots—photographs of herself with presidents, prime ministers, and celebrities; of the children at various ages; the children with Freddie; and most painful of all, the snapshots of herself with him.

As if to counteract the painful memories, the air was hypnotically fragrant: terra-cotta pots of blooming paperwhites had been placed here, massive vases with branches of flowering quince there, little beakers of tightly bunched roses everywhere.

Neoclassical chairs, casually flung cashmere shawls, framed floral still-lifes, the odd Moroccan table inlaid with bone—everything had been arranged with a wizard's studied haphazardness, lending the office that often emulated but rarely successful English country house air, so easy and reassuring that all it lacked was the requisite brace of dogs napping in front of the fire.

Indeed, the only concessions to this last decade of the twentieth century were the laptop computer and the multiline telephone on the graceful Regency desk; the fax machine tucked discreetly out of sight; and an executive's best friend—an ergonomic monstrosity of a high-backed, leather-upholstered swiveling chairman of the universe armchair.

It was to this that Dorothy-Anne gravitated after her circumference of the room. "So," she murmured, standing there, hands clutching the chair back while she stared off into space. "I take it this outbreak's genuine."

"Just like the outbreak of Legionnaires' disease back in December, the only differences being the bacteria and the location." Venetia, seated on the Russian armchair, put down her cup and saucer and nodded. "The Federal Centers for Disease Control and Prevention calls it, and I quote, 'symptoms of salmonella poisoning.' The four private, independent labs we've consulted concur—except *they* left off the 'symptoms of.' " Her voice gentled. "Baby, it's the real McCoy, all right. Two hundred and forty-nine cases, all guests at the Hale Hotel and Beach Resort in Hua-tulco, Mexico."

"Damn!" Dorothy-Anne shoved the chair aside and slammed a hand down on her desk. "How could someth—" She broke off and looked up as the door to the outer office opened.

Cecilia Rosen came marching in with a silver tray of freshly brewed cappuccino, grapefruit juice, and a plate of tiny, fat-free Danish. She nudged the door shut with a practiced cock of her hips. "Don't let me spoil the fun," she said dryly.

Rail thin, unflappable, and severely chic without trying, Cecilia Rosen was on the other side of fifty, and had spent a third of her adult life as Dorothy-Anne's personal secretary. "A secretary of the *old* school," she'd sniff proudly, head held high, whenever confronted by the lesser executives' legions of "administrative assistants" or self-proclaimed "associates."

"Better dig in," she advised now, setting the tray on the desk. "You'll need that energy boost." She shot Dorothy-Anne a significant look. "But I wouldn't tarry over breakfast too long. The conference room is packed, and let me tell you, those poison pens are *poised.*"

"And a good morning to you, too," Dorothy-Anne said sourly.

"What's good about it?" Cecilia retorted. "This office is the only oasis of calm in this entire complex."

"Is it now?"

"Try being Out There." Cecilia pointed her chin at the door. "From the way everyone's reacting, you'd think World War Three had been declared. The phones are ringing off the hook. If it's not the CDC, it's reporters. And if it's not them, it's attorneys, or relatives of the sick, or travel agents or tour operators canceling in droves—and that's not taking the crank callers into account. Everybody and his brother is flooding the switchboard."

"Just like back in December," Venetia muttered quietly.

"Why, yes!" Cecilia's eyes widened perceptibly. "Come to think of it, it *is* almost an identical replay of Singapore!"

Dorothy-Anne stared at her. "Too identical, perhaps?" she voiced aloud, tapping her lips thoughtfully with an index finger. "I wonder . . ."

"Honey, we've already been *over* that," Venetia reminded her gently. "Those two hundred and forty-nine guests are not faking it. Believe me. They really *do* have salmonella poisoning."

"I'm not saying they don't. And for Christ's sake, stop giving me that look."

Dorothy-Anne paused to accept the cup of cappuccino from Cecilia.

She took a quick sip and it scalded her tongue. She was so worked up she'd forgotten how hot Cecilia served it. She put the cup down carefully.

Venetia looked at her obliquely. "I'm not saying you're obsessed. But accidents happen, baby. They happen all the time."

Feeling herself deflate, she slumped wearily down into her chair and rubbed her face. "Sorry. I didn't mean to overreact."

"I know that, baby."

"It's just that I've been desperately grasping at straws."

"You're not alone, honey. We've all been doing that. The thing to do now is finish your coffee, eat a Danish—"

As if on Cue, Cecilia, having hung the coat in the closet, now passed the plate of pastries under Dorothy-Anne's nose.

Dorothy-Anne waved it away. "No, thanks. I don't have any appetite."

"You really ought to put something in your stomach," Venetia urged. "Especially before a press conference."

Dorothy-Anne smiled grimly. "In that case, how about some hemlock?"

"Verrrry funny."

Switching into her business mode, Venetia tapped some papers on the desk with glossy, cabernet-tipped fingers.

"Now, this is your prepared press statement. The legal department's been over it with a fine-tooth comb. So long as you stick to the text, neither accepting nor denying responsibility—"

"Whoa." Dorothy-Anne held up a hand, palm facing outward. "Hold it right there."

"Sure." Venetia shrugged, as if it were of no consequence, but eyed her warily. "You're the boss."

"Right. So why don't you brief me on how the *victims* are doing?"

Venetia flinched at the word. "Please. Do *not* refer to them as victims during the press conference," she advised.

"Oh?" Dorothy-Anne raised her eyebrows. "And pray tell why not?"

"Because it could be interpreted as an admission of negligence. And that could make us legally culpable."

"*What!*" Dorothy-Anne's mouth dropped open in stunned disbelief. "My God! These people are our *guests*! We're responsible for their safety and well-being and . . . And you're worrying about *legal culpability*?"

Venetia looked at her levelly. "I'm just telling you our attorneys' position."

"Attorneys!" Dorothy-Anne snorted and made a dismissive gesture. "The hell with attorneys! Venetia." Her voice dropped to a whisper. "We . . . made . . . people *sick*!"

"And we're doing what we can to rectify this unfortunate inci—"

Dorothy-Anne waved a hand irritably. "Let's save the public relations jargon for the press, shall we?"

Venetia felt her cheeks sting at the rebuke. It wasn't like Dorothy-Anne to rake anyone over the coals; rarer yet for Venetia to be at the receiving end when she did.

"Now, then." Dorothy-Anne folded her hands on the desk and leaned forward, eyes fervent with genuine concern. "Tell me what we're doing for the victims. And yes, you heard correctly: I said *victims*. I want to know specifics."

"Very well." Venetia sat back down. "Two hundred and forty-nine guests came down with diarrhea, stomach cramps, and fever. Of these, twenty were taken to the emergency room at Santa Cruz Bay, treated, and then released. No one required hospitalization."

"Go on."

"The other two hundred and twenty-nine cases were milder, but just to be on the safe side, we hired private, round-the-clock nurses. Treatment basically consists of making sure the patient gets plenty of fluids."

"And there've been no fatalities?"

Venetia shook her head. "If there had been, we'd have told you right away. Apparently, fatalities occur only in extreme cases. Even then, it's mostly the chronically ill, people with suppressed immune systems, or the very young and the very old."

In other words, the helpless and the harmless, Dorothy-Anne thought sadly, *the weak and the innocent . . .*

"Everything considered," Venetia was saying, "we're getting off lightly."

"Lightly!" Dorothy-Anne looked at her sharply.

"Yes. It was a mild outbreak."

"Thank God for small favors, you mean?" Dorothy-Anne said tartly.

"That's right." Venetia ignored the blunt sarcasm. "Believe me, honey, it could have been worse. A whole *lot* worse."

An updraft stirred up the snowflakes outside, sent them spiraling skyward in great swirls. Gusts of wind buffeted the windows like a barrage of accusations. The glass panes quivered against the onslaught.

She swiveled her chair back around. Leather creaked as she leaned forward. "Any idea as to how these . . . these appalling bacteria were spread?"

"Yes." Venetia nodded. "The usual way, through food. The most likely culprit is eggs, meat, fish, or poultry. They're zeroing in on the *camarones en escabeche rojo*—shrimp in red chili sauce, but that's only a guess. We'll know for sure sometime tomorrow."

Tomorrow, Dorothy-Anne thought grimly. *God alone knows what other crises tomorrow will bring.*

"How about the stricken?" she asked, steepling her hands and raising one eyebrow. "Other than medically, what are we doing for them?"

"We've provided flights home for the dozen or so who've requested it. Also, we're refunding the cost of the entire hotel stay *and* round-trip airfare for any ill guests"—she eyed Dorothy-Anne severely, as if to emphasize the largesse of the corporate coffers—"in addition to which, they're getting vouchers for another vacation, all expenses paid, at the Hale resort of their choice."

"Something I'd think twice about redeeming," Dorothy-Anne murmured sourly.

"I take exception to that"—Venetia sat forward and locked eyes with Dorothy-Anne—"especially since we're doing everything we possibly can. Honey, we're bending over *backward*. You *know* that!"

"Yes, yes," Dorothy-Anne said irritably, swiveling the chair.

The snow was coming down heavier now, and the entire campuslike complex, even the cars in the parking lot below, were obscured by the trillions of whirling white daubs. From where she was sitting, the monochromatic sky seemed alive. As if a plague of white locusts . . .

She tried to quash the menace of the mental image.

Steady on, old girl, she told herself. *It's just snow. An unseasonably late snowfall. That's all it is.*

Tightening her lips with resolve, she squeezed the hallucinogenic image from her mind. Leather creaked as she propelled her chair back and reluctantly stood up. "Well. Might as well go and face the music, eh?" Her voice and facial expression left no doubt as to the distaste with which she regarded the task. "The sooner I get this over and done with, the better."

Venetia rose to her feet also. With a rustle of papers, she quickly retrieved the prepared press statement from the desk. "Don't forget this." She held the papers out. "You'll be needing it."

Dorothy-Anne eyed them with apparent disapproval. "No." She shook her head firmly.

"No? What do you mean, no?" Venetia stared at her. "Girl?" She poised one elegant hand on a slender hip. "Have you gone bonkers?"

"No to that, too. It's just"—Dorothy-Anne raised both hands in the air—"prepared statements are too heartless . . . too . . . *cold.*"

"But that's the point!"

Dorothy-Anne shook her head. Golden hair swayed like diagonally cut curtains framing her face. "The point is," she said, fingering one sheaf of hair behind her ear, "if I've got to do this unpleasant chore, I want it to . . . come from the heart."

Still clutching the papers, Venetia leaned her knuckles on the desk and heaved a massive sigh. "Why," she deplored despairingly of her reflection in the mute polished desktop, "am I not surprised?"

29

Gloria said to Christos, as the two of them were lying naked on the rumpled sheets of the tiny Russian Hill house she had rented for their trysts, the blinds closing off Alcatraz, the Golden Gate, and the entire world beyond, "Darling, must you smoke that dreadful weed? Really, marijuana gives off the most sickeningly sweet odor."

Unperturbed, Christos flicked his Bic and relit the joint. He sucked on it noisily, then held it out to her.

She pulled a face. "No, thanks. That's one thing I'd rather not get into."

"Best shit there is." His voice sounded constipated from holding in the smoke. "It's Hawaiian."

She shook her head. "I already told you. I don't want to."

He shrugged as he exhaled. "Your loss is my gain. 'Sides, it isn't like you're Mary Poppins." He grinned and winked knowingly. "Right?"

"I never pretended to be Mary Poppins," she said stiffly. "It's just that I prefer my drinkie-pie-poos."

He lay there and took another toke, feeling a pleasant buzz to his high. "Well, you know what I say. To each his own."

Gloria rolled over on her side and propped herself up on an elbow, the better to admire the chiseled naked perfection and . . . well, the intense *maleness* of him. They'd been seeing each other regularly for . . . what? Three months now?

Her alcohol-impaired brain counted backward.

No. *Over* three months. Which was remarkable—especially in light of the fact that the novelty still hadn't worn off.

If anything, she was crazier about him than ever.

But what is *it that makes him such a turn-on?* she wondered, not for

223

the first time. *And why am I so attracted to this lean, mean, blue-collar sex machine? What's he got that other men don't?*

Wisely, she decided these were questions best left unanalyzed. Everyone knew it was dangerous to probe the Freudian minefields of passion and arousal—you never knew what you might come up with.

Keeping the magic going was her reason for leasing this house. And it had made all the difference. No more furtive comings and goings from sleazy flophouses. No more smirking front desk clerks or flea-ridden mattresses to contend with. Tiny though it was, this bougainvillea-shrouded hideaway gave her a sense of privacy and protection. More important, it imparted a stamp of respectability and legitimacy to their liaisons.

She watched as he carefully pinched out the joint and put it on the bedside ashtray. Then she felt him hook his warm muscled leg across hers.

Her reaction was instinctive. She gasped as a thrill hummed through her body.

"Gettin' enough of an eyeful?" he teased cockily.

"Christos, you're awful! Really, sometimes I wonder why I put up with you."

She pretended to pout.

He laughed. "Wanna know why? 'Cause I'm always ready, willing, and able. 'Cause I'm hot to trot and a hunk and a half. 'Cause I'm one righteous dude who knows how to dive between a lady's legs and eat her sweet pussy—"

"Ugh!" she said in disgust. "*Must* you use that term? You know how I hate it."

"Yeah, yeah." He flashed her a Chiclet grin. "So you *say*. But ya ask me?"

She was silent.

"Deep down inside, you're turned on by my dirty talk. Why else would ya"—he winked slyly—"how'd ya put it? Put up with me?"

How well he knew her.

Sighing, she let her fingers do the walking across his firmly muscled chest and down his gleaming abs. Reaching his nest of pubic hair, she stroked his penis with her fingertips. Lo and behold. It rose to the occasion. Again.

Would wonders never cease?

Gazing steadily into his eyes, Gloria gently pulled back his foreskin. "Just so you know," she said huskily, "the reason I put up with you is because I . . . I . . ."

Realizing what she was about to say, she swiftly bit down on her lip.

"Yes?" His dilated pupils glowed raptly. "*Say* it! *Tell* me!"

She swallowed, aware of her fluttering pulse. "I love you," she whispered hoarsely, a flicker of anguish crossing her face, as though her own words had shocked her.

Quickly she looked away.

"Hey, babe. Don't turn away." He took her by the chin and forced her to look at him, his thumb stroking her jaw.

Her breasts rose and fell; spots of bright red prickled on her cheeks. Was he torturing her deliberately? Or merely playing some perverse kind of game? Leading her on so she would make a total fool of herself?

She wished she knew. At times she believed *she* was in charge. That she was the one putting *him* through his paces. And other times, like now, she wasn't quite so sure if he wasn't pulling *her* strings.

His voice was unexpectedly soft as he said, "Come here." And taking her in his arms, he pulled her atop him.

She could feel herself melt. Moist was his skin; warm and redolent with the musk from their previous bouts of lovemaking. And all the while she was aware of his penis, trapped between her belly and his, twitching and straining with renewed urgency.

"Say it again, Glo," he whispered, his hands gliding smoothly, expertly, down her silky back and soft buttocks. "Open up your heart. Share your secrets."

Eyes widening, she stared at him, her dark shoulder-length hair swaying like a curtain. Looking into his luminous eyes was like losing touch with reality, like diving into a swirling vortex despite being aware of its hazards.

Oh, how easily, she thought, *how willingly and gladly I would drown in those heavy-lashed, cobalt pools. . . .*

Her fingers dug into his shoulders.

"I love you, Christos!" she whispered fiercely. "God, if you only knew how *much*!"

Without warning, she began to tremble all over. Tears leaked from the corners of her eyes.

"Hey!" He was all kindness and concern. "Babe? You okay?"

She was silent.

He raised his head, his tongue, swift and snakelike, darting from between his lips. Catching each salty tear before it dropped.

"I love you, too," he said softly.

Her tears stopped as abruptly as they'd started.

"You . . . do?" she said tentatively. She looked at him in childlike surprise, as though suspecting a trick.

"Sure I do. And I'd prove it, except—" He sighed and shrugged eloquently.

Except . . . ? Gloria felt her stomach contract. *What does he mean by except?*

And then it dawned on her.

"N . . . *nooooo!*" With a great howl of anguish, she yanked herself loose and backed away.

"Glo?" Christos shot up into a sitting position. "What the fuck?"

"There's someone else!" she accused bitterly, her face flashing poison. "That *is* what you're trying to tell me. Well? Isn't it?"

"Yeah, but—"

She didn't let him finish. "Why, you . . . you prick!" she hissed. "You piece of *shit!*"

Christos was taken aback. This was a new Gloria, an entirely different one from the Gloria he knew. Something ugly and monstrous, hideous as bone stripped of its flesh, seemed to have pushed through the surface of her face.

He stared at her. "What the hell's gotten into you?"

"Into *me?*" She glared at him. "My, God! Why didn't I see it coming? How could I have been so fucking blind?"

He tried to be reasonable. "Look, Glo—" he began.

But she was too far gone. "Don't you Glo me!" she screeched. And swinging her arm back, she brought it flashing forward in a blur.

Christos saw it coming, but didn't try to block it. The loud *ca-rack!* sounded like a pistol shot as her palm connected with his cheek. His head snapped sideways, her handprint glowing whitely on his skin.

"Son of a *bitch!*" she panted, slapping him again, this time with her other hand.

His head pivoted in the opposite direction, but he refused to protect himself. "For chrissake, Glo," he said calmly. "Will ya get hold o' yourself?"

But her eyes were glazed from her liquid breakfast, and there was no stopping her. Again and again she slapped him, alternating sides so that his head swiveled left, then right, then left and right, left and right.

"Two-timing bastard!" she hissed. "Goddamn prick!"

"I said stop it," he warned softly.

The quiet threat in his voice made absolutely no impression. Liquor-fueled rage, blinding and all-consuming, pumped madly through her veins, pounded wildly in her heart.

Hurt, dammit, hurt! Returning pain in kind was all she could think of. *Two eyes for an eye! Two teeth for a tooth!*

The furies that drove her were too volcanic to be contained, too chaotic and elemental to do anything except let them run their course. Her slaps were increasing in speed even as they began to lose their sting.

But Christos had had enough. Quick as lightning, his hand darted out, intercepted hers, and caught her by the wrist. She swung with her other hand, but he seized hold of that wrist, too.

Her breasts heaved as she struggled to pull free. When it proved futile, she raised her head. "Motherfucker!" she panted. And hawking deeply, she drew her lips back across her teeth and spat in his face.

He didn't so much as flinch.

Her eyes flashed fire and ice. "Now let go of me."

"Unh-unh." He shook his head. "Not till you get yourself under control."

"What bloody nerve!" Her eyes raked him up and down. "Really! Just *who* do you think you are, telling *me* what to do?"

"Wanna know somethin' funny, babe?" he retorted. "I've been askin' myself the same thing. Only with me it's, 'What the *fuck* am I doin' around this crazy-ass bitch!' "

A mask seemed to descend over her face. Her eyes went dark, then narrowed into slits. "Aren't you forgetting something?" she said coldly.

"Lemme guess. If I am, you're gonna tell me. Right?"

She stared daggers, then lowered her head, took a moment to compose herself, and raised her chin.

He was so taken aback, he almost let go of her wrists. The transformation was that sudden and startling.

The woman who'd attacked him was a foul-mouthed fishwife. The woman who now spiked him with a haughty glare was every inch the Pacific Heights socialite.

"What you are forgetting," she pointed out icily, "is that ours is a capitalist arrangement. In other words, *I* pay *you* to get what *I* want." She smiled sweetly, but her eyes were like whirring drill bits. "And what *I* want right this very moment is for you to take your filthy paws off me."

"Jee-zus!" he exclaimed softly. "You know somethin'? You really are one helluva bitch!"

"It's all a matter of interpretation. *I* view it as being assertive. But if *you* take it to mean I'm being a bitch, well"—Gloria shrugged—"who cares what *you* think, anyway. Now. The choice is yours: either you let go of me, or you'll never see another red cent. Which'll it be?"

"Is that all you think I'm after? Your freakin' dough?"

"Well, aren't you?" Her smile sharpened into a taunting scimitar. "Correct me if I'm *wrong*, but I don't *recall* your ever turning my money *down*."

"You know somethin', lady? Fuck *you*!"

"My, my!" she said, heaping on the sarcasm. "*Such* a gentleman!"

He heaved a massive breath, held it in to steady himself, and let it out slowly.

"You just might be wrong," he said tightly.

"Oh?" She arched perfectly tweezered eyebrows. "And why is that?"

"It ever occur to you that maybe, just maybe, I really care about you?"

She began to laugh. "Oh, give me a break! If that isn't the second oldest line in the world! Face it, *babe*"— her face contorted with malice as she flung his own endearment back at him—"maybe *you* think you're a stud. But you want to know something?"

He didn't, but he figured she was going to tell him anyway.

"You," she trumpeted, "are no better than a Polk Street runaway!"

His face hardened. "Is that so? Well, then why don'tcha go to Polk Street and find yerself one? An' good riddance!"

He let go of her wrists and shoved her away from him. She flopped over backward, bounced on the mattress, then scrambled to her knees and watched as he grabbed his 501s and yanked them on.

"And where," she inquired, "do you think you're going?"

"Someplace sane."

He paused as he did up his fly, buttoning it from the bottom up. Then he plucked his gray T-shirt off the floor, gave it a good shake, and pulled it on over his head. Hurriedly tucking it into his jeans, he cinched his belt and glanced over at her.

"Someplace where it ain't always Looney Toons time."

Gloria laughed again. "Let me guess." She tapped her lips playfully with a forefinger. "You're exercising your macho prerogative by walking out on me. Is that it?"

"You said it, lady."

Gloria didn't seem the least bit fazed. "You'll come back," she said knowingly. "Your type always does."

Christos gave her a look, no game playing in his eyes. "I were you?" he said. "I wouldn't hold my breath."

She pretended a loud yawn. "Believe me, darling, I'm not."

Her anger had dissipated, and she was deriving a perverse satisfaction from toying with him. And why shouldn't she? She was, after all, the injured party. Hadn't Christos all but confessed about there being someone else?

He had. And, true to male form, wasn't he behaving exactly like you'd expect a guilty man to act? Huffing and puffing and making a big show of ruffled feathers as though *he* were the victim?

Yes. He deserved to squirm. And she would take great pleasure out of seeing him wheedle, cajole, and beg his way back into her good graces.

Whoever came up with the old adage was wrong, Gloria thought, watching in amusement as Christos stomped around collecting his socks and boots. *Revenge is not a dish best served cold.* Quite the contrary. *To truly savor it, revenge is best served hot—scalding, steaming, bubbling hot!*

Christos, boots in one hand and socks in the other, was standing there, scowling at her. "You still think this is some kind o' game," he said tightly. "Don't you?"

"Oh, darling." Gloria rolled her eyes to heaven. "You don't really expect me to take you seriously. Do you?"

He glared pugnaciously. "Matter o' fact, yeah," he said. "I do. I'm out that door?" He cocked a finger and pointed, pistollike, toward it. "It's *adios* for good."

"Oooooh!" She shuddered theatrically. "Famous last words, I presume?"

He shrugged. "Believe what you want. See if I care."

With the grace of a dancer, he bent over, balanced himself balletically on one leg, pulled a sock and Western on the other foot, then reversed the process. Carefully, he pulled his jeans down over his boots, stretched to his full height, and looked around for his Levi's jacket.

"Musta left it downstairs," he muttered to himself. Then he looked over at Gloria. "I'll see myself out. Oh, before I forget." He dug out the set of keys she had given him from his jeans pocket. "Here." He tossed them on the bed. "I won't be needin' 'em anymore."

With that, he turned and strode to the door.

When his keys landed beside her, warning bells had gone off in Gloria's head. *My God!* she thought in a sudden explosion of understanding. *He really is serious!*

He was already at the door, his hand turning the knob.

"Christos!" she cried.

Shutting his eyes, he stood very still and said, "Shit!" under his breath. But he didn't turn around. *Now what?* he wondered wearily.

Her voice trembled with fear. "About your . . . your not coming back. You really meant what you said, didn't you?"

For crying out loud! What did she think? That he talked just to hear himself jaw?

"That's right." He opened the door wide.

"Wait!"

In a panic she flew off the bed and launched herself naked across the room. His face was expressionless as her hands clutched him fiercely and her lips peppered him with urgent little kisses: they landed here, there, everywhere.

But Christos did not respond. He wanted out. So badly, in fact, that he no longer cared how big the Winslow fortune might be. All the gold at Fort Knox wasn't worth putting up with this kind of shit.

"Please, don't leave me!" Gloria begged in a torrent of words. "Darling, *don't!* I'm sorry! I'm so sorry!"

He turned his red-cheeked face away from her desperate kisses. He'd had it with her. *Why,* he implored silently, *can't she just shut up and let me go?*

Her body was heaving with sobs. "I didn't mean any of those ugly

things I said," she moaned miserably. "Not one of them! It's just that"—
Gloria dropped to her knees and wrapped her arms tightly around his
legs, her shuddering, tear-streaked face pressing against the pale blue
denim of his thighs—"when you admitted there was someone else in
your life, I . . . I could see my entire world crumbling! It hurt so much
that I went berserk!"

"Shit," he scoffed.

"It's *true!*" she insisted. "Why won't you believe me?"

Christos shook his head hopelessly. "You still don't fuckin' get it, do
ya?"

She lifted her tear-streaked face and stared up at him.

"Get *what?*" she cried. "Christos, what the hell are you talking
about?"

"I'm talking about, you know—engagements, weddin's, vows?"
Seeing her deepening frown, his voice took on the exasperated tone of a
tutor dealing with a particularly backward pupil. "I'm talkin' about—*the
obstacle between us?* The one that'll always be there, keepin' us apart?"

"Darling," she pleaded, *"please!* Will you stop torturing me with riddles?"

Christos inhaled, exhaled sharply. Glaring at her, he prised one of her
arms loose from around his legs. Taking it by the wrist, he held her hand
up to her face for inspection.

Her big diamond engagement ring and baguette-studded wedding
band flashed brilliantly as he passed the bejeweled finger back and forth
in front of her eyes.

So? she thought. *Big fucking deal.* She wore them all the time.

"*Now* do you get it?" he asked.

"No." She shook her head. "I can't honestly say that I do."

"Y'know, for one smart lady you can be pretty dense." His voice
turned ice cold. "Course I was talkin' about you! Just take a look at your
ring finger! Then tell me there isn't another man in your life!"

She stared at him. "Surely you can't mean my husband!" she said
incredulously.

"And why the fuck not?"

She all but burst out laughing. And to think she'd been afraid there
was another woman! She felt light-headed—dizzy, euphoric, and deliri-
ous with relief.

She said: "Surely you can't consider Hunt a threat. Darling, if I told
you once, I told you a thousand times: we're married in name only."

"So?" he said harshly. "You think I wanna share you forever?"

She stared at him.

"But *you*"—he let go of her wrist and gestured—"right away *you*
wanted to believe the worst! That the someone else was in *my* life!"

He turned away and kicked the door jamb. "Shit! That the thanks I get for lovin' you?"

She lowered her head, silently staring down at the rings on her finger. A sick feeling came up inside her. What a fool he must think her to be! For all her sophistication, for all her intelligence, for all her resourcefulness, she had thrown a tantrum worthy of a spoiled, jealous child. And over what? Nothing!

Was it any wonder she was on shaky ground with everyone she knew? Even Christos?

"Oh, darling," she whispered sorrowfully. "If only I'd known!"

"How could ya?" His voice was derisive and he still had his back turned to her. "You're always so wrapped up in yourself you can't see, hear, or think straight!"

She flinched at the stinging truth behind his rebuke. "But why did you have to beat around the bush?" she asked. "Couldn't you have come right out and said what was on your mind?"

"Hell, lady. I tried." He twirled around. "Before I could finish? You'd already taken it the wrong way."

A pained look crossed her face. *He's right,* she thought. *I never gave him a chance.*

Holding onto him, she climbed unsteadily to her feet. The tears were rolling down her cheeks.

"Please don't leave," she said softly. "We can work this out!"

His face was expressionless. "Yeah," he said cynically. "Sure."

"We *can!*" she insisted. Her face was stubborn, childlike, desperate.

"And what about next week?" he said savagely. "And next month? And next year? We gonna sneak around for the rest of our freakin' lives?"

A strange look came into her eyes. "We wouldn't be arguing about this if I weren't married."

"Maybe." Christos shrugged. "Then again, maybe not. But the thing is, you're hitched, Glo. Face it. There's no gettin' around that."

She kissed his cheek, barely touching it lest she cause him more pain. *How could I have slapped him like that?* she wondered guiltily. *What in God's name came over me?*

Her voice dropped to a hushed whisper. "And if I were single? Would you walk out on me then?"

"Get real, Glo. That's . . . what's the word? Hypothetical? Yeah. Hypothetical."

"Perhaps," she whispered. "But don't you see? We can do something about that. We can make it into reality!"

He squinted at her. "You sayin' you're gonna file for divorce?"

She sighed deeply. "Well, not exactly."

He stared at her. "Then just what *are* ya tryin' to say? Huh?"

"A divorce isn't that simple."

"Why is it," he inquired, "that things with you never are?"

"Because," she said bitterly, "before I got married I signed a prenuptial agreement."

"Uh-huh," Christos said, seeing it coming.

"So if I divorce him, it'll leave us high and dry."

Christos almost smiled. *Listen to her,* he thought. *Saying "us." It'll leave* "us . . ."

"So?" he said. Deliberately playing it cool. "Say you don't get jack shit. So what? Y'got me, babe. What more d'you want?"

Toying with her. Throwing out bait just to get a reaction.

Gloria zeroed in on it like a shark after blood.

"Listen!" she hissed. "I've *earned* my share of the pie! Do you have any idea what it's like, always playing the kissy-kissy couple in public and then, once we get home—bam! It's like a curtain comes down and I don't exist?"

Christos said, "Okay, so you're unhappy. I can dig that. And if you walk out on him, you get screwed. Big fuckin' deal." He shrugged. "Who needs his dough?"

"Who in hell do you think? *We* do!"

"Glo . . ."

"I mean it! Haven't you realized it costs money just to breathe?"

"Yeah, but if gettin' unhitched means you get zilch, and you ain't willin' to settle for that, what's the point of even discussin' it?"

"Because there's another way!" she said softly. "A way to have our cake and eat it, too!"

He kept his expression guarded. "And what way's that?"

Gloria pressed her nakedness against his clothed body. She tilted her head way back and stared up at him.

He could see a peculiar light dancing in the depths of her eyes, the booziness giving her an unfocused look. But he noticed something else, too, something hard and inflexible and disturbing lurking just beneath the woozy surface.

"Who knows what might happen from one day to the next?" she whispered. "Maybe Hunt could have an accident!"

Her bright eagerness jolted Christos. For a moment, he could only stare at her in disbelief. When he finally found his voice, it was as shocked as his expression.

"*What* did you say?" he whispered hoarsely.

A hurt look crossed her face. "Why are you giving me that evil look? Darling, what *is* it?"

"What *is* it?" he whispered in horrified awe. "Y'got to *ask*? My God!"

He pressed his hands to the sides of his temples and shook his head slowly, as if to reorient himself back to reality.

"Just listen to yourself, will ya? Don't you realize what you're *sayin'*?"

"Of course I do," she said serenely. "Believe me, I've given it a great deal of thought. If there were any other way—"

"I can't believe I'm hearing this!" He looked and sounded amazed, as if he were witnessing a truly spectacular and immensely gruesome accident unfolding before his eyes.

"Darling," she said softly, "you do see, don't you? It's the only choice we have. . . ."

His temper reached the snapping point. "God*dammit*, Glo!" he exploded. "What kind of shit you feedin' me? It *ain't* the only choice!"

She drew back and flinched against his outburst.

"But you want to ice him?" he continued. "Fine! Go right ahead and do it. Me? I don't ice *nobody*. Got that?"

"But . . . but accidents happen all the time," she cajoled. "The only thing we have to do is to help one along—"

He grabbed her by the arms and shook her roughly. "Accidents like that don't just happen!" he snarled. "At least, not around me, they don't!"

She sulked prettily. "I only want what's best for us."

"I don't give jack shit why you want it!" His voice abruptly quieted. "I already told you. Murder's where I draw the line."

Again she pressed herself up against him, and he could feel the quick, wild beating of her heart. "He's rich, Christos!" she whispered.

He could see his tiny reflection mirrored on each of her pupils, his twin faces shining like newly minted coins—gold ducats just waiting to be plucked, he thought, then shut his eyes to quash the greediness of the image.

But it was no use. The shiny coins imprinted with his visage were superimposed on his retina; danced a gilded waltz across his closed lids.

Gold! The standard of wealth and power. The universal symbol of all that money could buy, all that desire could fulfill—and for which men, over the millennia, had murdered one another to possess.

Murdered . . . ?

With a start, he opened his eyes. Gloria was still staring up at him, a calculating cast to her face.

"My husband's not just rich," she whispered, her voice that of the seductress—Eve and Delilah and Salome all rolled into one. "He's not even rich-rich. He's filthy, dirty, super rich! Darling, do you have any idea what that means? Can you possibly imagine the magnitude of such a fortune?"

As a matter of fact he could, but Christos wisely held his tongue. He wasn't about to let on that he'd checked out the Winslows in *Forbes*—or knew it was Old Lady Althea who controlled the purse strings. The less Gloria thought he knew, the better off he'd be.

"He's worth billions!" she breathed. Her eyes glittered feverishly. "That's right, darling. *Billions!* With a capital *B*!"

"I already told you," he said tightly. "I ain't into murder!"

She clutched him by the arms. "What's the matter with you? Don't tell me you're afraid of becoming a billionnaire?"

"Hell, no. Why should I?"

"Then what's holding you back?"

He gazed coldly into her upturned face. "Just a little matter of not wantin' to end up on Death Row," he said grimly.

"Death Row!" She gave a little laugh. "For crying out loud, darling! We're not idiots! We'll plan it real carefully." Her voice took on a dreamy timbre. "Just think of all those billions and billions of dollars. . . ."

For a moment, he opened the floodgates and allowed his imagination to soar. It was wild, thinking you could have anything in the world you ever dreamed of—and a lot you never even knew existed. Rolls-Royces, Ferraris. Lamborghinis. Private jets and yachts and limos. Helicopters. Closets full of custom-tailored shirts and suits. Mansions, penthouses, beachfront estates. Servants waiting on you hand and foot.

Money to spend.

Hell, money to *burn*!

Feeling himself poised on the edge, he reeled his imagination back in.

Gloria's eyes glowed vividly, as though she'd journeyed alongside him in his flight of fancy.

"Can you imagine it?" she whispered. "Just you and me, darling! You and me and all those beautiful, beautiful billions! If that isn't happily ever after, what is?"

He didn't reply.

But he didn't have to. She hid her smile, knowing that the seed had been sown. And for now, that was enough.

30

The reporters smelled blood.

The instant Dorothy-Anne stepped into the conference room, pandemonium broke loose. Flashbulbs popped, blinding her and leaving a succession of afterimages burning on her retinas. Dark-lensed video-cams whirred and microphones were thrust in her face.

"S'cuse us! S'cuse us . . ." Cecilia Rosen marched briskly forward, clearing a path through the throng.

She was closely followed by Derek Fleetwood, six feet tall and sleekly handsome, and Venetia, equally tall and fashion-runway perfect, who formed a protective barrier on either side of Dorothy-Anne as they hustled her forward to the lectern. Sandwiched between them, Dorothy-Anne appeared small, pale, and extremely fragile.

That did not stop the journalists from hurling a barrage of questions:

The financial reporter from *The Wall Street Journal:* "Ms. Hale! This is only your second press conference ever. Does your appearance imply your company's in financial difficulties? Rumors to that effect have been circula—"

The photographer from one of the wire services: "Ms. Hale! Could you look over this way—"

The cockney-voiced scandalmonger from *The Enquirer:* Ms. Hile! Any more news on what caused your husband's pline crash—"

The sleazy Australian from a competing tabloid: "Is it true you're suing the maker of your late husband's aircraft—"

Dorothy-Anne's face was a carefully composed mask. She stared straight ahead, adroitly avoiding direct eye contact by gazing at a point above everyone's heads. It was a trick practiced by celebrities, movie stars, and members of royal families the world over, and it served Dorothy-

Anne equally well. Even the sharp-eyed observer would have been hard pressed to guess at the storms raging inside her.

And rage they did.

How dare *they!* she cried to herself, each verbal arrow piercing the armor of her dignity. *What gives them the* right *to breach the precious walls of my privacy? Is nothing sacred?*

It was all she could do to contain her outrage. The personal nature of these questions was—beneath contempt. This . . . this free-for-all! . . . was *not* why this press conference had been called!

Venetia felt her tension. "Don't lose it, honey," she murmured out of the side of her mouth. "That's why they're baiting you."

Dorothy-Anne drew a deep breath. Then, head held high, she walked over to the fruitwood lectern and stood behind it. Emblazoned on the front was the logo of the Hale Companies, a large stylized *H,* and on the wall above her, brushed bronze letters spelled out THE HALE COMPANIES, INC.

The moment she took up her position, camera shutters clicked and flashbulbs exploded; videocams zoomed in on her. She cleared her throat and glanced around.

The journalists had fallen silent.

Too late, she wished she had heeded Venetia's advice. *Right now I could use a prepared speech,* she realized in a panic. *I've got no idea what I'm expected to say!*

And offering up a silent prayer, she leaned forward into the cluster of microphones bearing the symbols of CBS, NBC, ABC, CNN, and Fox 5.

"Ladies and gentlemen of the press," she began, "thank you for braving the weather and being here today. I'll get right to the point, but before I start, I'd like to clear up a couple of minor misunderstandings. Please bear with me.

"I've heard some of you call me Ms. Hale. For the record, I'm Mrs. Cantwell. Unlike my great-grandmother, who founded this corporation and kept her maiden name throughout her married life, I chose to take my late husband's.

"Which brings me to the second subject."

She paused, wishing she could have bypassed this topic completely. But she had to bring it up, if only to spare herself additional pain later on.

She said: "Undoubtedly, you are aware that four months ago, my husband died in a tragic airplane crash that claimed three lives."

She heard a few murmurs, and here and there saw some sympathetic nods. The rest of the journalists were spellbound. Camcorders whirred; pens flew across the pages of steno pads.

"I don't need to tell you that grief is a highly private matter," she said softly, a catch in her voice. "As such, I hope you'll respect my privacy and understand my refusal to respond to any questions regarding my late husband and/or the crash. I shall, however, make one exception so that I might address a specific comment regarding this matter.

"I am not now pursuing, nor am I considering, a lawsuit against the manufacturer of the aircraft. Where these rumors come from, God alone knows. I assure you, there are absolutely no facts to substantiate them.

"Furthermore, if inquiring tabloids report that I was abducted by aliens, and am starting a chain of intergalactic hotels, I hope you will disregard those stories as well."

A wave of appreciative laughter reduced the tension in the room.

Atta girl! Venetia applauded mentally from where she stood off to the side, arms crossed in front of her.

"Now that we've cleared that up," Dorothy-Anne said, "let's get down to the issue at hand—the tragic outbreak of salmonella poisoning at the Hale Hotel and Resort in Huatulco, that's in Oaxaca, Mexico."

Drawing on her memory's stores, she proceeded to fill them in on everything she knew, making it clear she was not glossing over the facts, withholding any information, or playing spin doctor by downplaying a dreadful situation.

"No matter what the culprit turns out to be," she went on, "this is an unforgivable occurrence. There is no excuse for it."

Venetia braced herself, fearing she knew what was coming. *Girl,* she thought, *will you shut up while you're ahead?*

Dorothy-Anne said, "While it's true that accidents do happen, neither the Hale Companies nor I myself intend to diminish the seriousness of this tragedy. It's appalling, and quite frankly, should never have occurred.

"In short, I personally take full responsibility for it. The buck has to stop somewhere, and it stops here."

Venetia shut her eyes. *Shit,* she thought in despair. *She's gone and done it! Thrown open the doors to a class-action lawsuit—not to mention a slew of individual cases!*

Dorothy-Anne concluded by saying, "Ladies and gentlemen, I've shared all the information available to me thus far. We will keep you posted on any new developments as they unfold. In the meantime, if you have any questions . . ."

A forest of hands shot up.

Now's the time to ask, Dorothy-Anne completed sardonically to herself. She pointed to a well-coiffed brunette from ABC.

"Ms. Hale—sorry." The reporter grimaced at her gaffe. "I meant, Mrs. Cantwell—"

"That's quite all right," Dorothy-Anne said graciously. "Please, do continue."

Mrs. Cantwell, you've always made it a point to stay out of the public eye. Could you comment on what caused you to shun publicity in the first place? And what, specifically, made you change your mind?"

"I can," Dorothy-Anne responded. "Above everything, I've always treasured my family and my privacy—and in that order. Does it not stand to reason that the mother in me should want to shield my children from the public eye? Well, that has not changed.

"However, there comes a time when a corporation grows so large that it's in danger of becoming a faceless, anonymous entity. This, I felt, was happening to Hale Hotels.

"And our guests deserve better. Much better.

"So, in order to put a human face to the organization, I decided to step forward. This way, our guests can be assured that a real and caring individual actually *is* in charge."

A kind of respect showed in the reporter's face. Dozens of hands flew back up.

Dorothy-Anne picked a journalist from the *Washington Post.*

"Mrs. Cantwell." He made a production of frowning. "You mentioned that there've been no fatalities as a result of the salmonella poisoning."

"That is correct." Dorothy-Anne nodded.

"But given the outbreak of Legionnaire's disease in Singapore last December, where there *were* fatalities—"

"Seven deaths at the Hale Dynasty Hotel," Dorothy-Anne confirmed grimly, with a sigh. "How well I remember."

Venetia winced and thought: *For God's sake! Did she have to put a specific number on past fatalities? And worse—identify the hotel by its full travel-brochure name?*

The reporter from the *Washington Post* was saying: "Legionnaire's disease and salmonella are both bacterial infections. Don't these outbreaks indicate that health problems are more prevalent in your hotels than, say, in another chain's?"

"Not necessarily. No."

Instead of raising her voice, Dorothy-Anne lowered the pitch.

"Around the world, our levels of service, safety, sanitation, and luxury far exceed the industry standard. In fact, a little research on your part will reveal that, from Antigua to Zimbabwe, Hale Hotels are without peers in all these categories."

"That still doesn't answer my question, Mrs. Cantwell. Perhaps I should rephrase it."

The reporter paused and tapped his lips, as if deep in thought.

"Mrs. Cantwell. Your hotels have had two outbreaks of infectious bacterial diseases within a space of three months. Don't you find this an extraordinary coincidence?"

"As a matter of fact, yes," Dorothy-Anne replied truthfully, "I do. And because of that, we have hired several independent research laboratories to conduct their own investigations."

Venetia nearly groaned aloud. *Girl,* she thought, *now you've truly left yourself wide, wide open.* She wondered how much more of this she could watch. *Really, there ought to be a law for well-intentioned people. They need protection, if only from themselves.*

"I beg your pardon, Mrs. Cantwell, but I'm not sure I heard right. Correct me if I'm wrong. *You* are mounting your own investigation? In *addition* to those of the CDC and the local authorities?"

"That's right." Dorothy-Anne stared at him challengingly. "I would be remiss in my duties if I did otherwise."

"Why? Do you have reason to suspect something might be amiss?"

"I did not say that. However, being responsible for hundreds of thousands of guests each and every—"

"Thank you, Mrs. Cantwell." The reporter was smiling.

The room erupted in a show of hands. Dorothy-Anne pointed to a woman from the Associated Press.

"Mrs. Cantwell, I am a mother myself. As such, from one mother to another, would you want *your* children to stay in a Hale Hotel? Or would you have qualms?"

"I would have no qualms whatsoever," Dorothy-Anne said staunchly. "Moreover, we often do stay in our hotels."

"Then despite these two outbreaks, you wouldn't fear for your children's safety?" the reporter pressed.

"Why should I? So long as they're adequately supervised, they couldn't be in a safer place than a Hale Hotel. I firmly believe that. The mother in me would never, ever, knowingly permit me to expose my children to any health or safety risk."

The hands lunged back up. She selected an Englishman from the London *Times.*

"Mrs. Cantwell. Financial centers the world over are awash with rumors concerning your company's liquidity."

They're *what?*

Dorothy-Anne stifled a gasp. She felt her stomach contract, as if slammed by an invisible fist, and her heart seemed to stop. Yet somehow, despite the icy grip of fear shriveling her insides, she managed to keep her face expressionless.

How did this get out? she wondered. *Only a handful of people even know!* It occurred to her that someone must have leaked the information. *But who? And, if these rumors are circulating, why wasn't I forewarned?*

But of course she knew why. Freddie had always overseen the day-to-day operations of the empire. It was he who'd kept his ear close to the ground; who'd met with bankers and power brokers; who'd stage-managed the deals; all so she could concern herself with the Big Picture.

But Freddie was gone, both from her life and the business they'd shared, and the position he'd held in the company had yet to be filled. Trouble was, she'd been unable to bring herself to find a replacement—as if by doing so she'd be severing the very last, and final, earthly tie between them.

But now, sobered by the consequences, she realized just how danger-ously close to the brink her procrastination had brought her. She'd been operating in a vacuum, juggling his duties along with her own.

Yes. It was high time she faced it. Like it or not, Freddie's position had to be filled. And fast—*before* the Hale Companies suffered irreparable harm.

The Englishman was saying: "According to our sources, the Hale Companies borrowed heavily in the late eighties in order to finance rapid—some say too rapid—expansion. Also, rumors have it that the Hale Eden Isle Resort is not only far behind schedule, but alarmingly over budget. Could you elaborate on any of this, and possibly shed some light on the actual severity of the company's debt load?"

"I can try," Dorothy-Anne said, "though quite frankly, as a privately held corporation it's our prerogative—and company policy—not to dis-close financial data to the public.

"But to address your question about expansion. First, you must bear in mind that we've become a highly diversified company. The hotels are but one entity of what is essentially a conglomerate. In fact, of all our subsidiaries, the hotel division's profits to earnings ratio is a frac—"

She was interrupted by the bleating of a cellular telephone. It be-longed to the reporter from the *Washington Post.*

Wouldn't it just, Dorothy-Anne thought, spiking him with a glare.

He answered with a sibilant "Yes!" that was amplified in the silence, and which showed a cruel disregard for her and everyone else. As he listened, he seemed to grow as richly satisfied as a Roman emperor after an orgy of a meal.

She bridled. *Arrogant bastard,* she thought in disgust, impatiently tap-ping her fingernails on the polished lectern. She waited until he'd switched the phone off.

"An urgent call?" she inquired stingingly.

"As a matter of fact, ma'am," he replied, "yes, It was."

"Good." She smiled frostily. "I wouldn't have wanted you to miss it."

"Actually," he said, luxuriating in confidence and playing cat to her mouse, "you might wish I had."

"Oh?" She raised her eyebrows.

Yawning, he pretended abject boredom, but his eyes gleamed as he dropped the bombshell. "That," he said, sitting back casually and sounding contented. "was our correspondent in Huatulco."

Oh, no, she thought, clutching the edge of the lectern with white-knuckled fingers. *Dear God, please . . .*

"Seems one of your salmonella patients has just died. Wouldn't have a comment, would you?"

For a moment Dorothy-Anne felt the floor drop out from under her. Tension squeezed her forehead and temples until it seemed her skull must surely fracture. The floodlights aimed on her glared like searchlights trapping a fugitive.

She had to force herself to lean forward into the microphones, and when she spoke, her voice was weary and uneven.

"My comment," she said shakily, "is that this press conference is over."

Her announcement was met with a chorus of groans.

She said, "I'm truly sorry, ladies and gentlemen. But I must leave for Huatulco at once."

It was the last place she wanted to go.

"Thank you," she said.

And Cecilia Rosen, Derek Fleetwood, and Venetia quickly hustled her back out.

"Jesus H. *Christ!* I have never, but *never,* been so humiliated in my entire life!"

The explosion occurred the moment Cecilia pushed shut the sound-proofed door of Dorothy-Anne's office, and only a fraction of a second after Dorothy-Anne irritably shook her arms free of Derek's and Venetia's well-meaning hands.

Both of them instantly backed off and exchanged raised eyebrows.

"But do you know what I find *truly* amazing? Do you know what *really* gets my goat?"

Dorothy-Anne's voice was sharp as a scalpel, and slashed the fragrant conviviality of the country house atmosphere. It plunged the room temperature to the wind-chill-driven snow outside and rendered Derek, Venetia, and even Cecilia speechless—all the more since each of them had fully expected her to be drained after the ordeal of the press conference, and had been convinced she would require their soothing ministrations.

Instead, what they had on their hands was a chief on the warpath—as infrequent an occurrence as a giant meteor hurtling toward earth, and equally as unwelcome.

Now, barely daring to breathe, this triumvirate eyed Dorothy-Anne warily as she stalked the overlapping needlepoint rugs, hands clenched at her sides, cheeks flaming as though with warpaint, her stride swift, dangerous, *angry;* a jungle beast undecided as to which prey to rip into first.

"How *is* it," she was demanding icily, "that members of the press—yes, *reporters*!—should be better informed about the state of this company's affairs than *I* am?"

She whirled around in fury.

"Can any of you possibly explain that?"

Her eyes pierced each of them in turn.

Venetia and Derek flinched, but remained prudently silent; Cecilia, over her initial shock, looked on with an expression of mild boredom. It took more than her boss letting off steam to ruin *her* day.

"Granted," Dorothy-Anne continued bitingly, "these last several months have hardly been my idea of a *dream,* and *granted,* after Freddie's death I needed a period of adjustment. However, I am not *now,* nor was I *ever,* as fragile and helpless as to need protection from this . . . this utterly *sorry* . . . this . . . this hideously appalling and inexcusable state of affairs!"

Unable to stand still, Dorothy-Anne resumed her agitated pacing; nervous energy, anger, determination, and displeasure bounced off her like visible sonar.

"My God!"

She pressed the fingertips of one hand against her forehead.

"What has this place *deteriorated* to when the *chief executive*"—her head snapped up, as if to catch her captive audience in some indiscretion—"yes, I am speaking about *myself*!—needs to learn things from"—she drew a deep breath and expelled it verbally—"members of the press!"

There was utter silence.

"So, what we are going to *do*"—Dorothy-Anne glared at Derek, Venetia, and Cecilia—"what I deem it *necessary* to do, is to call an emergency meeting." She was silent for a moment, then said briskly: "Cecilia."

"Boss?"

"Get hold of the heads of each of our divisions. Posthaste. Tell them I'm calling an impromptu conference."

"Yes, but I thought you were flying off to Huatul—"

"I am." Dorothy-Anne cut her off and smiled fiercely. "But I didn't say I was going to fly there alone, now, did I?"

Three sets of eyes stared at her.

"Stop looking at me like I've lost my mind. Why should I waste time when I can turn the flight into a briefing?"

"Ah!" Cecilia nodded, and from her pocket produced the little pad and pen she carried on her person at all times. Flipping the pad open, she clicked the ballpoint, poised it over a page, and waited.

"I want the executive in charge of each division to be present,"

Dorothy-Anne continued. "By that, I mean *everyone.*" She rolled the word on her tongue. "If anyone has appointments—too bad. They'll have to cancel or reschedule them. And I don't care if they're expected at the White House. You may quote me on that!"

"Oh . . . kaaaaay," Cecilia said.

"The only acceptable excuses are being out sick, or being away on a business trip. In either of those instances, the next senior-most executive shall take his superior's place. Also, everyone is to bring their floppy disks, and all their latest reports and sets of figures. Passports won't be necessary; we'll stop at Dallas/Fort Worth so they can get off. Oh. Arrange to have one of our Gulfstreams waiting there to fly them back, will you?"

"Got it."

Now that she had determined a course of action, Dorothy-Anne turned toward the windows and looked out at the snow blowing in spectral whirlwinds. Gusts of wind battered the panes of glass, shook the branches of skeletal trees half obscured by the milky wall of flurries.

She felt the dead weight of responsibility press heavily on her shoulders. She had no wish to fly through snow, absolutely no desire to be reminded so vividly of Freddie's accident. But she had no choice. Duty required it.

Now if only the airport isn't shut down . . .

Turning back around, she said: "Besides Derek and Venetia here, who'll represent their respective departments, I want Bernie Appledorf and Arne Mankoff along." The comptroller and house attorney, respectively.

Cecilia made swift shorthand notes. "Anybody else?"

"Let me see . . . Heather Solis from Vacation Villages, Paul Weekley from the Hale Line, Mark Levy from Service Industries . . ."

Dorothy-Anne resumed pacing, but slowly, tapping her lips thoughtfully with a forefinger.

"Kevin Armour from Real Estate . . . Lana Valentine from Time Shares . . . Truman Weaver from FLASH . . . Owen Beard from Sky Hi Catering . . . Kurt Ackerman from Special Projects, and Yoshi Yamada from Investments. Oh, and Wilson Cattani from the Hotel and Motel Management School. Got that?"

"Yep." Cecilia glanced at her. "Which plane are you planning to take?"

Dorothy-Anne stopped strolling, her unlined oval face taking on an expression of wry humor. "The one," she said dryly, "certain office wags have taken to calling 'Hale One.' "

Cecilia looked surprised. "You do keep an ear to the ground, don't you?"

"Obviously not close enough," Dorothy-Anne said, "which is why

I'm calling this meeting. Now, get on the horn. Have the plane prepared for takeoff. And make sure every division is represented."

She glanced at her watch.

"We'll be taking off in exactly an hour and a half. Make it clear that anyone who doesn't get their keister onboard can start perusing the want ads. Do I make myself clear?"

The way Cecilia hurried out was answer enough.

"One more thing," Dorothy-Anne said.

Cecilia turned around, her hand on the door knob. "Yes, boss?"

"I want a copy of every division's printout covering the last twenty-four hours. That's in hand. *Before* we leave."

"You got it." Cecilia hurried out.

Venetia nudged Derek with an elbow. "Hey, kemo sabe. We'd better get a move on, too," she said. "Unless we want to miss the flight."

They headed to the door.

"Derek," Dorothy-Anne called out.

He stayed behind. "Yes?"

Dorothy-Anne moved back to the windows, staring out at the swirling snow.

"Anything new on Pan Pacific?" she asked. "Who owns them? What their assets are? *Anything?*"

He shook his head. "Not yet," he sighed. "Private banks are a bitch. And private *foreign* banks are the worst. I'm still trying."

She continued to stare out at the snow. "Try harder," she said.

A lot harder, she thought.

31

F ew cities are as defined by their geographical parameters as San
Francisco. Occupying the very tip of a peninsula, and surrounded
by water on three sides, the city is locked in place, unable to expand
beyond its limits.

It is only natural in such a situation that real estate is at a premium,
and priced accordingly. It is also only natural that since its inhabitants
prize single-family dwellings, every precious square inch of property
counts.

The result is a city of plunging hills with sugar cubes adhering to
every steep surface.

Nowhere is this more prevalent than on Russian Hill. Here, the nearly
vertical streets of a Wayne Thiebaut painting are lined with apartment
blocks, but between them, alleys and stairs cut to a hodgepodge of picturesque private houses in back. Reachable only by a network of single-file
walkways and steps, such is this rabbit warren of exquisite dwellings that,
often as not, one must pass several properties before reaching one's destination.

Invariably, the miniature gardens are terraced and well tended, the
roofs below falling away to provide an unimpeded panorama beginning
with the cinnabar swags of the Golden Gate Bridge and Mount Tamalpais
to the left, then on past the rocky whale's hump of Alcatraz, all the way
to the great curve of the Bay Bridge and mountainous Berkeley in the
distant haze beyond.

Amber—whose suspicions that Christos was holding out on her had
led her to tail him here—felt like a fish out of water as she tried to make
herself inconspicuous, not the easiest task in an intimate neighborhood

where houses are jammed, with seeming haphazardness, side by side and virtually one on top of the other.

There were no recesses she could melt into, no shadows where loitering would go unnoticed. The windows all around made her feel exposed, as if the entire neighborhood was on alert, watching her every move.

Remaining near the bottom of the steps, she'd peered over the top riser. Watched while Christos, whistling a tune and tossing and catching a bunch of keys, made his way jauntily to the fourth house over. A creamy, freshly painted two-story cottage with drawn window shades and an upper deck jutting, like a porch, out over the little front garden.

She waited until he disappeared underneath it.

Quick.

Thankful for her rubber-soled Nikes, she took the stairs two at a time and darted forward along the white gravel path—just in time to see Christos letting himself in. With his own key!

Amber's sallow-complexioned face froze, her mouth gasping at the treachery. *Well, well, well,* she thought darkly. *What do you know . . .*

Yet another bit of information he'd been withholding.

"Same old hag, same sleazy hotel." His exact words when she'd asked, earlier, where he was headed.

Sleazy hotel indeed! What a prick!

Tears threatened as she slowly retreated, wondering what other deceits lay in store. Well, she'd find out soon enough. She wasn't quite as dumb and helpless as Christos liked to believe.

Meanwhile, she had more immediate concerns. Specifically, how to conduct her surveillance in such an open space. Lighting a cigarette, she glanced around. Except downhill, everywhere she looked there were windows and more windows. Windows up above. Windows on both sides. No doubt windows with curious eyes trained down on her.

And she out here in the open . . .

She shuddered at her vulnerability. She couldn't remember when she'd felt so uncomfortable—or so aware of not fitting in. This was a neighborhood where sprayed-on jeans, red tube top, and a Levi's jacket were not the clothes of choice. She tossed her head, whipping around her waist-length black hair, retreating farther from the cottage. She quick-puffed on her cigarette, eyes darting—searching.

Where to position herself . . . *where?*

Snap! The unmistakable sound of a closing door.

With a start, Amber peered over the shoulder-high retaining wall of the garden next door to the cottage. A bougainvillea-smothered jewel box of a house: small tiled patio with wrought-iron outdoor furniture, junipers in big terra-cotta planters. And a briefcase-toting female executive type, consulting her wristwatch and cursing in aggravation. Obviously late for an appointment.

Amber felt her heartbeat quicken. She must move on. Now, *before* she aroused suspicion.

Nevertheless, she was fascinated by the fastidiousness of the woman. The way she carefully locked her front door, tested it, then zipped her keys in her purse while click-clacking across the patio and down several stone steps to the walkway.

Too late.

Face-to-face meeting for the woman and Amber.

"Oh!" Halting abruptly on the last step, the woman looked down at her, a frown of distaste registering disapproval of Amber's outfit. "Are *you* from around here?"

At a loss, Amber pointed shyly at the cottage next door.

"Oh. One of *those* neighbors."

The woman sighed, then made a face as Amber drew nervously on her cigarette.

"If you must smoke," she sniffed primly, "kindly don't litter. Around here, we don't appreciate cigarette butts."

Smiling pallidly, Amber nodded and turned and pretended to mosey toward the cottage. *Now if only Christos isn't looking out a window . . .*

Hearing the crunch of gravel, she glanced back over her shoulder. Saw the woman hurry along the path, then heard the click-clack of heels as she descended the flight of steps down to the shadowy alley and the street beyond.

Gone.

Amber leaned back against the retaining wall, soughed a deep breath of relief, and continued to scan her environs.

Where to hide, where to hide . . .

And then it hit her. Of course! What better place was there? And best of all, any busybodies watching from their windows would have seen her and the woman talking! Would have assumed them to be on friendly terms . . .

Quickly now, Amber retraced her steps and climbed the stone stairs to the woman's house. On the tiled patio, a furled sun umbrella protruded from the middle of a round glass table.

She eyed it appraisingly. If she raised the umbrella, tilted it at just the right angle, she would be shielded from the cottage but able to keep it under surveillance.

Perfect.

In a jiffy, she cranked it open and had it tilted, then sat down and chain-smoked. Felt a perverse sense of satisfaction in dropping ashes on the spotless tiles. Ditto her cigarette, which she ground out under her heel.

The bitch with the briefcase would throw a fit.

Big fucking deal. Amber had no intention of sticking around that long.

As she waited, she suddenly became aware of the view. It had been there all along, of course, but it hadn't made any impression on her. Until, sneaking up on her like bits and pieces of an unfinished jigsaw puzzle, it now exploded in front of her in all its breathtaking, completed glory.

People really live like this.

The thought burst inside her mind like a revelation.

It's like something out of a dream or a movie, only it's for real.

It's how I want to live!

The last thought stunned her, all the more, since she'd never seriously contemplated such a thing—at least not as a real possibility.

But such was the inspiring nature of the view that, at this moment at least, nothing seemed truly impossible.

It was that incredible, this sun-drenched panorama with the roofs and gardens dropping away from one terraced level to the next, a whole different galaxy from the grimy streets, garish strip joints, Greyhound stations, and flophouses of her own—could it be?—was it really true?— yes—it was time to admit it—*her squalid little existence!*

Funny; she'd never considered it squalid. But that was before she'd had something to hold up and compare it with. Now the contrast was obvious, would always be so.

She watched bees buzzing indolently; a hummingbird as it hovered within arm's reach before darting off. Overhead, crying gulls wheeled in the sunny skies. She could feel the universe broadening, expanding, stretching elastically—only to snap back as the sharp click-clack of a woman's heels pierced her consciousness.

Holy shit! The bitch! Amber thought. *She's back!* Scrambling to her feet, she glanced around, desperately searching for a hiding place—

Not the bitch.

Amber's relief was like a physical pain. Slowly, stiffly, she lowered herself numbly back down into her chair.

The woman who passed by was strikingly beautiful, with prominent cheekbones and shoulder-length, mink-colored hair. She was high-fashion thin and wore well-applied makeup, an expensive turquoise coat, matching high heels, and carried a turquoise lizard purse. Gold and diamonds shone on wrist, ears, and fingers, and she seemed to move inside an invisible cloud of fragrance.

Amber's immediate thought was: *So that's what's meant by "smelling expensive."*

Sitting forward, she lifted aside the fringes of the umbrella and watched the woman pause, slide a loose stone out of the wall, and fish out a set of keys. Then, replacing the stone, the woman disappeared under the jutting deck of the cottage next door.

Next door—

The realization of who this woman was lancinated Amber's heart.

"Same old hag": Christos's words.

Amber felt suddenly deprived of oxygen, as if the air itself had mysteriously evaporated. She began to hyperventilate, took great heaving gulps of breaths that refused to fill her lungs. Her breasts, held captive within the red stretch tube top, rose and fell with a convulsive shudder. Equal proportions of pain and fury narrowed her world, condensed it to agony.

She flinched as she heard the cottage door open, the familiar voice saying: "Heyyyyy!" She jerked and doubled over, as though fatally wounded by the verbal knife thrust. "Babe, you're late. . . . Jeez, hon, you had me kinda worried—"

"You? Worried? Oh, darling!" Laughter rippled from next door, cut off by an obvious kiss.

Darling . . . ?

Tears blurred Amber's vision as she gasped asthmatically. *No,* she cried silently to herself. *No, no, no, no, no!*

Sleazy hotel . . . old hag . . . babe . . . hon . . . Her hands gripped the arms of the chair. *Lying bastard! Some hag!*

The cottage door slammed shut. Amber could no longer contain her anguish. It filled her like an insidious poison gas. Racked by soundless sobs, she rested her arms on the table and buried her face in rough denim sleeves. That her weeping was silent did not lessen its potency.

Deceived.

The pain burned ulcerously.

Sleazy hotel . . . old hag.

Lies! *All* lies!

How many more untruths were there, just waiting to be discovered? How much else had he purposely withheld? Was he perhaps plotting this very instant, intent on keeping it a secret?

"We're a pair, babe. A dynamic duo."

How often had he repeated those words, when what he intended all along was a solo act?

Christ, but he must think her a twit! A real pushover.

Is that all I am? A doormat?

She shuddered in quaking spasms, as if the fault-lined earth itself were undergoing a tectonic upheaval. And in the midst of it all, she could picture what was going on next door. Tearing off each other's clothes, grappling nakedly—!

She felt a stifling wave of nausea, followed by a blinding rage that threatened to consume her.

Christ, they were doing it right now—and next door, yet! And when payday rolled around, Christos wasn't going to divvy up fifty-fifty as they'd agreed.

No, sirree, Bob. He was planning to split, cutting Amber out completely.

It didn't take a rocket scientist to figure that out.

Christos. He was a shit, all right.

A true shit of the highest order!

When Amber's tears were finally spent, she still continued to sob, and when her sobs at last subsided, and her hyperventilating ceased, she raised her head. Her eyes looked bruised, red, *hurt;* her face was puffy and splotched, and her tear-blurred vision reduced everything to a watery, blue-and-white smear.

Christos.

Amber's face hardened and she flicked a hand through her long hair, looping its silken blackness carelessly behind her ears.

Just thinking about him was enough to get up her dander.

Well, she was through with him. Suckering a mark was one thing. But when the mark turns out to be a knockout zillionnairess, and the con tries to con his fellow con and partner, then—Amber's eyes narrowed into slits—it's good-bye, Charlie!

She fished a crooked cigarette out of the squashed pack and lit it with trembling fingers. Drew the acrid smoke deep into her lungs and watched it drift off in the breeze when she exhaled.

Puffing rapidly, she contemplated how she should proceed.

Go next door and barge in on them? Maybe expose Christos for the fraud he was? Or wait and confront him alone?

Or, better still . . .

Hmmmmm.

Should she play it cool? Pretend she didn't suspect a thing, but tail him some more? See what else she might discover?

She smiled bitterly.

Yes, why *not* keep her lips zipped and her eyes open? Following him wouldn't be difficult, especially since he was convinced she was lacking in the brains department. Besides, chances were he already had a bundle of cash stashed somewhere.

In that case, it only behooved her to spy on him for a while. Then, as long as she played her cards right, she'd be able to get him to hand over her share.

Her *fair* share.

Bending forward, she moved aside the fringes of the umbrella and looked at the cottage. "You want to play dirty pool?" she whispered in its direction. "Well, two can play *this* game!"

Letting the fringes fall back in place, she wondered whether she should stick around a while longer. Wait for Christos to appear, then follow him to . . . wherever.

No, she decided. She'd learned quite enough for one day. She really couldn't stomach much more treachery right now.

Much as she hated to, it was time to leave this heavenly spot and head back to their rat trap in the Tenderloin. Maybe pretend she'd stayed in the entire time.

Whatever. She'd see what transpired and play it accordingly.

But before she left, Amber did something entirely alien to her. She got down on all fours and collected her mashed cigarette butts, used her cuff to wipe away the telltale lengths of ash and shredded bits of tobacco.

After all, she told herself, *what's the use of having something nice if you don't take care of it?*

Just as homemakers compute the inherent savings in turning down the thermostat and clipping cents-off coupons, so top-level executives can calculate the worth of their most precious commodity: time. If, for instance, a manager is responsible for a department with $10 million in gross annual revenues, his or her time is worth a hefty $5,000 per hour. And if that same executive spends a total of a thousand hours per year on air travel, the delays and layovers common with commercially scheduled airlines can be staggeringly costly.

Enter the corporate air force. ·

Thanks to company planes, a busy executive can board an aircraft when and where he desires, take wing immediately, arrive at his destination none the worse for wear, take care of business, and fly right off again—without enduring time-, and therefore money-consuming, waits or delays.

Even more important, the entire flight can be spent working, without distractions of any kind.

Like other major corporations, the Hale Companies maintained their own private fleet of birds. Consisting of eleven aircraft (down from twelve since Freddie's crash), they ranged from nonjets (twin-engine King Air turboprops and a pair of Bell JetRanger helicopters), to small jets (Lear 35s), midsize jets (Citation IIIs), and true heavy metal (two Gulfstream Vs, both capable of flying nonstop from New York to Tokyo with fuel to spare).

But the pride of the fleet, as befitted a chief executive, belonged to Dorothy-Anne. Upon retiring her great-grandmother's aging 727-100, she'd traded up to a brand new Boeing 757-200. Though snidely referred to as "Hale One," this, the flagship of the Hale fleet, was extremely economical for its size. With only two engines, its fuel consumption was relatively frugal, while its state-of-the-art electronics required a crew of merely two in the cockpit. Yet it had a range of 3,200 miles, enough to fly nonstop across the Atlantic, and then some.

Custom built and outfitted like a yacht, it was part business command center and part flying palace. Measuring a hair over 155 feet from nose to tail, its fuselage was divided into thirds.

The front third contained the cockpit, a toilet, and a small passenger section with four rows of reclining, first-class seats—twenty-four in all. Here, too, began the narrow corridor that led back along the port side, much like on a railway car, with sliding doors opening into two small offices and several compact guest cabins.

In the midsection, there was a satellite communications center, a gourmet galley, a large conference room that also served as a sit-down dining room, and Dorothy-Anne's private office.

And here the corridor ended, for the rear third was devoted exclusively to Dorothy-Anne's private suite. Comprising a spacious salon and separate bedroom, both of which extended the full width of the jet, it was sumptuously appointed in earthy tones of beige, brown, fawn, russet, and black, a palette Coco Chanel had originated but Dorothy-Anne had unabashedly borrowed and updated.

The salon was rich with custom-designed sofas and chairs of suede and velvet mohair, all cunningly fitted with tucked-away seat belts. The flick of a button folded or unfolded the armorial Coromandel panels that lined the entire fuselage, and hid both rows of portholes.

Other buttons activated the intrajet intercom, the concealed television screens, the latest in sound systems, and the rheostats on the bolted-down, crystal-balustered lamps, whose shades cast subtle pools of light. And there were polychromed wood deer, permanently secured to the floor, grazing on the carpet in perpetual bliss, seemingly unaware of the king's ransom mounted on the bulkheads at either end of the salon: rare gilt-embossed Art Deco panels by Jean Duhamel, depicting Diana, the huntress, bow in hand amid a jungle of stylized foliage.

No expense had been spared, no creature comfort overlooked.

The beige carpet was of the plushest luxury, and every tabletop had recessed insets to hold drinks during midair turbulence. Extra sound-proofing muffled the roar of the engines, reduced it to a muted whisper, and an overabundance of air jets provided unprecedented ventilation of fresh, instead of recycled, in-flight air.

The bedroom, done in the same earth tones as the salon, would have done an apartment proud. There was a queen-size bed covered in oyster silk satin and flanked by little gilt tables, more walls of coromandel, and built-ins—vanity, large-screen TV, and VCR. Generous closets were

254 J U D I T H   G O U L D

stocked for any eventuality, from landing in a tropical paradise to attending a ball at the Ritz to putting down in subzero Greenland.

The adjoining washroom was replete with gilt-and-rock crystal fixtures, a bidet, and a shower that doubled as a steam sauna.

All in all, something special in the air.

During takeoff, Dorothy-Anne remained in her suite and kept the coromandel screens shut, as if cocooning herself from the snowy world outside, and concentrated on the printout of Hale Hotels' computerized, twenty-four-hour worldwide occupancy report.

She felt dizzy, almost physically ill and panicked, as the jet hurtled down the runway and ascended steeply into the air. The sensation of leaving the ground and suddenly being airborne felt unnatural, heightened her awareness that fragile metal wings and jet propulsion were all that stood between streaking forward and—

No! she told herself firmly. *I mustn't dwell on that.*

Squeezing her eyes shut, Dorothy-Anne gripped the arm of the couch with one hand, and crushed a chamois cushion with the other. She broke out in a cold sweat, gasping for breath.

Ever since Freddie's crash, a feeling of doom seized her during every takeoff and landing. The only exceptions had been the flight from San Francisco to Aspen, followed by the flight to New York with Freddie's casket.

On both occasions a doctor had given her tranquilizers.

Now, as had become her habit, she reiterated Franklin D. Roosevelt's famous words: "The only thing we have to fear is fear itself. . . . The only thing *I* have to fear is fear itself. . . ."

She wondered if anyone had an inkling how terrified she had become of flying. Or, for that matter, of going on living.

There's nothing that doesn't scare me anymore. Everything else is just an act.

What she found amazing was that nobody saw through it.

But then, how could they? She never gave them a chance.

Like now. Citing a desire for privacy, she had locked herself in her suite, where she'd remain until the worst of the bile and fear had passed, until her breathing stabilized.

While Dorothy-Anne battled her fears at the rear of the jet, Venetia and Derek, occupying one guest cabin apiece, were reviewing their departments' reports on their laptops.

Ditto the rest of the passengers, who were ensconced in the leather seats in the forward section, where they flipped through reports or studied the screens of their laptops, like students cramming for exams.

Except Cecilia.

As the 757-200 climbed diagonally through the snow and thick banks of clouds, she hit the buckle of her seat belt, got up, and hurried midship to inspect the conference room, where two stewards were busy arranging the table.

Cecilia's perfectionist's gaze did a swift visual inventory. Laptop computers, calculators, pens, notepads. Blind Earl cups and saucers. Sparkling cut-crystal tumblers, bottles of Evian spring water. All were neatly aligned at the fourteen places set at the glossy, zebrawood extension table.

Oberto, the white-gloved chief steward, appeared at her elbow. "Is everything to your satisfaction, Ms. Rosen?" he inquired politely.

Though the jet was officially his domain, he bowed to her superior judgment when it came to the conference room and on-board offices.

Cecilia looked around once more and gave a single brisk nod. "Yes, Oberto. Thank you."

"Should I escort our passengers in now?"

"Yes, thank you," Cecilia said. "But I'll inform Ms. Flood and Mr. Fleetwood personally. As soon as everyone's seated, you may call Mrs. Cantwell and tell her we're ready whenever she is."

"Yes, ma'am." He left and walked to the front of the plane.

At that moment, the jet burst through the clouds and sunlight—bright, dazzling, delectable—streamed in through the portholes. Momentarily distracted, Cecilia approached the nearest porthole and peered out. The sky was the precise shade of Wedgwood blue, and the blanket of cotton below was not only impossibly white and airy but immaculately, irreproachably, bleached and fluffed.

Then, losing no more time, Cecilia went to summon Derek and Venetia. When she returned, she stood aside as the briefcase- and report-toting passengers filed aft.

Cecilia watched them take the same places around the table as they would have in the Hale Companies' conference room. Bernie Appledorf and Arne Mankoff the seats nearest the head of the table. Derek and Venetia the next ones down. Then Yoshi Yamada, Kurt Ackerman, and Kevin Armour. Heather Solis and Owen Beard. Mark Levy, Truman Weaver, and Lana Valentine.

Plus the two new faces. A handsome young black executive named Marvin Short, who was filling in for Paul Weekley, and Karen Yee, an exceedingly petite and exceedingly pretty Amerasian sitting in for Wilson Cattani.

Cecilia pointed out which of the two empty places their superiors would have occupied. Meanwhile, briefcases were being unsnapped, printout and reports produced, floppy disks fed into laptops.

Pen and steno pad at the ready, Cecilia took a seat on the sidelines.

Oberto reappeared at the door. "I just spoke with Mrs. Cantwell," he said. "She said to tell you she would be detained a few minutes."

There was a communal sigh of relief. This hastily called meeting was ominous enough, but Dorothy-Anne's delay permitted additional precious cramming, praise God!

Ten minutes later, Dorothy-Anne came in carrying a thick pile of computer printout under one arm. She looked so supremely poised and in command, so utterly calm, cool, and collected, that no one would have guessed this very same woman had, during takeoff, locked herself in her suite and been a hopeless nervous wreck.

There was a rustle at the table as the men and women quickly rose to their feet.

"Sorry to have kept you waiting," Dorothy-Anne apologized, depositing the pile of printout on the table. "Please, be seated."

She took her own presiding place at the head of the table and waited for a steward to fill the coffee cups from a silver pot. Only once he was gone, and had shut the door behind him, did she open the meeting.

"First, I want to thank you all for accompanying me on such short notice," she said, looking around, "and I apologize for any inconvenience I might have caused you. However, I believe you will appreciate the importance of this meeting."

She paused, took a sip of black coffee, and put the cup back down. She was frowning slightly.

"I notice there are two faces I'm only vaguely familiar with," she said.

The young black man spoke up first. "Marvin Short from Hale Lines, Mrs. Cantwell."

Dorothy-Anne held his gaze. "And Mr. Weekley is . . . ?"

"Inspecting one of the ships, ma'am."

"Oh? And which one might that be?"

"The *Hale Holiday*."

Dorothy-Anne looked thoughtful. "The *Holiday* . . . the *Holiday* . . . Correct me if I'm wrong," she said slowly, "but isn't the *Holiday* currently cruising the eastern Caribbean?"

"Yes, ma'am."

"On ten-day cruises out of Fort Lauderdale, if I'm not mistaken," she murmured. "And how long is Mr. Weekley gone for?"

He shifted uncomfortably. "Ten days, ma'am."

"Ah. You mean he's on vacation."

"No, ma'am. He said—"

"Never mind what he said." Dorothy-Anne's voice came a little colder. "I think I get the idea. He's enjoying a ten-day cruise on company time. That *is* what it amounts to, isn't it?"

Marvin, enduring Dorothy-Anne's pinpoint gaze, wished he were anywhere else—even Timbuktu was preferable—just so long as he wasn't right here, right now.

Sensing his discomfort, Dorothy-Anne took pity on him. *The poor kid,* she thought. *It's not his fault.*

Nor, she reminded herself, was he a kid. Youthfully handsome, yes, but he had to be in his mid-thirties.

"Well, that should be easy enough to check," she said.

She leaned forward and switched on the laptop in front of her.

Almost instantly, crisp graphics in all spectrums of the rainbow jumped onto the screen. Fingers flying, she nimbly daubed the keys, expertly accessing Menu, Submenu, Division, Category.

"Here's the Hale Line," she murmured, bringing it up on her screen. "Now for the *Holiday . . .*"

She tapped some more keys.

"And there she is. Sixty-seven thousand tons, et cetera, et cetera . . . scheduled to put into Barbados a.m. tomorrow. Now to take a gander at the passenger manifest . . ."

She scrolled through it, the two thousand alphabetized names flying upward in an incandescent burst of a blur. Then she slowed.

U's, *V*'s, *W*'s.

"Ah," she said. "Here we are. Weekley, Paul, Mr."

Taking her finger off the key, Dorothy-Anne sat back and eyed the information that glowed accusingly.

"Cross-indexed with a Ms. Tracie Himmel," she read aloud, "price code C4631, which translates into official comps . . . Sun Deck suite with private verandah . . ."

She shook her head chidingly.

"He does like his luxuries, our naughty Mr. Weekley."

Marvin Short merely sat there, wishing himself invisible.

"Tracie Himmel . . . Tracie Himmel," Dorothy-Anne mused aloud. She drummed her fingernails on the glossy tabletop. "Now *where* have I heard that name before?"

She shot a questioning look at Marvin, who shifted uncomfortably in his chair.

"Is she an employee?"

He inflated his cheeks, held the air in, and exhaled slowly.

"You needn't worry about disloyalty, Mr. Short. You're not ratting on your boss. He made his own bed. All I'm asking is a straightforward question, and all I expect is an honest answer."

Swallowing, he said miserably, "She's his secretary."

Dorothy-Anne, no gourmand of unpleasant situations, made a face of distaste. "Oh. I see," she said. "Yes. I do see."

She felt repulsed by the trivial sordidness, the embarrassing *ordinariness* of a boss faking a business trip in order to have a fling with his secretary. How unoriginal could one get? Yet why should she be surprised? Intraoffice affairs, however frowned upon, were as old as the hills.

But to flaunt *such behavior!* Dorothy-Anne thought. *To take advantage of the company and, in effect, flip* me *the birdie!*

Yet she quailed against the action required of her—the fallout he himself had provoked. Like a dedicated surgeon, she drew no satisfaction from discovering a malignant tumor. On the contrary. If it hadn't been there in the first place, it wouldn't require surgical excision, dammit!

But what choice did she have?

He's given me no choice, Dorothy-Anne thought grimly. *I have to make an example of him. If I don't, I'll be considered a pushover, and others will try to get away with—whatever.*

Yes. She had to nip it in the bud. *Now,* while it was still fresh.

"Cecilia," she said wearily, "prepare a letter of termination. Mr. Weekley is fired, effective immediately. Both he and Ms. Himmel are to disembark at Barbados. As soon as I've signed it, fax it to the *Holiday.*"

Cecilia made a note of it. "Will do."

"Also, prepare a separate fax for the *Holiday*'s purser. It should clearly state that Mr. Weekley is no longer permitted to sign for *anything* on board. That includes the bar and the casino." She tightened her lips. "He's enjoyed all the freebies he's going to get."

"I'll take care of it." Cecilia nodded.

"Oh, and check and see if Ms. Himmel is on vacation time. If she isn't . . . well, let's hope for her sake that she is."

"What about Mr. Weekley's corporate credit cards."

"I'm glad you reminded me. Cancel them. At once."

"Right."

With that unpleasant business out of the way, Dorothy-Anne focused her attention on the Amerasian woman.

"And you are . . . ?"

"Karen Yee. From the Hotel and Motel Management School."

"I take it Mr. Cattani couldn't make it?"

"No, ma'am. He's at Sloan-Kettering."

"Sloan-Kettering! Good lord. I had no idea he's ill!"

"He isn't. It's his wife. She's undergoing treatment for stomach cancer."

Dorothy-Anne winced, her own recent bout of cervical cancer all too fresh in her mind. "How is she doing?"

Karen Yee sighed. "Not very well, I'm afraid. They're doing what they can, but . . ." She shrugged expressively.

Dorothy-Anne nodded. *In other words, it's terminal.*

"I understand," she said softly. "Cecilia, see to it that two floral arrangements are sent. One from the company, the other from me personally." Then, turning back to Karen Yee: "Is our medical coverage adequate for her treatment?"

"I . . . I'm really not sure . . ."

"Find out. Then let me know at once."

"Yes, ma'am. I'm certain Mr. Cattani will appreci—"

Dorothy-Anne cut her off by clearing her throat. "We've wasted enough time." She placed her hands flat on the table and looked around. "Let's get started, shall we?"

33

Rain drummed on the roof of his cruiser as Sheriff Otis Mosbey stared out past the streaky arcs cleared by his windshield wipers. Flashing red lights from a variety of emergency vehicles reflected off the wet pavement of this usually quiet stretch of Route 18, some thirty-five miles south of Atlanta near Zebulon, Georgia. It was already getting dark, and they turned the twilight a hellish pulsating red, like the strobe lights of some demonic dance club.

The crackle of disembodied voices and bursts of static from the various radios added to the surreal atmosphere.

Besides his own cruiser, Sheriff Mosbey could see his deputy's patrol car, an ambulance, a fire truck, a tow truck, and two cars belonging to the divers. They had converged on this side of the bridge spanning the Flint River after two kids reported glimpsing a submerged car while fishing.

With the exception of the tow truck, all the vehicles had been parked facing the river, their high beams aimed, like makeshift floodlights, at the dark, rain-dimpled water.

Sheriff Mosbey waited in his cruiser while the medics and firemen milled around outside, everyone biding their time until the divers signaled the tow truck operator to begin hauling the submerged car up the steep bank. The kids who had reported it kept trying to sneak in for a closer look, only to be shooed away, and Deputy Scruggs was stationed in the middle of the road, using his flashlight to wave on what traffic came along.

Word had already spread, and a small crowd of locals had gathered, parking their cars along both shoulders of the road.

Hoping to see something gruesome, Sheriff Mosbey thought grimly. It never ceased to amaze him how tragedies and accidents fascinated the populace at large.

Otis Mosbey was not in the best of moods. He was cold, crabby, hungry, drenched, and tired. *Gettin' too old for this kind of shit,* he thought, chewing a wad of tobacco.

Weatherwise, it was the kind of evening he'd have liked to spend indoors. Someplace snug and warm and dry—preferably Lurleen's mobile home out in the boonies, with an X-rated video in the VCR, an ice cold beer in one hand, and Lurleen, the exotic dancer from the Crazy Kitty, exchanging professional courtesies. They had an understanding, he and Lurleen. The cops didn't roust the club so long as she serviced him regularly.

A sudden flurry of activity drew the medics and firemen to the edge of the riverbank.

"She-it," Sheriff Mosbey muttered. "Here goes."

He chucked open his door, scooted his big-bellied bulk out of the cruiser, grabbed his Stetson, and shoved it down on his head.

"Comin' through," he growled, clearing himself a path to the prime vantage point.

Down in the water, the divers, shiny as seals in black neoprene, signaled the tow truck operator. The winch started up and began pulling in the cable, and the divers expertly flippered themselves out of the way.

Slowly the trunk of a dark 1996 Chevy Lumina broke the surface, silty water sluicing off the rounded curves.

"What d'ya make of it, Sheriff?" one of the firemen drawled.

Mosbey grunted. "Too soon to tell," he muttered, wishing Lurleen wasn't going on duty right now. Shit. After this drenching, he could use some TLC—which, in Lurleen's case, inevitably amounted to LLC—Lots of Lovin' Care.

Just his bad luck to have this car found in his jurisdiction.

The Lumina was half out of the river now, water pouring out its open windows.

"Sheriff? Looks like we got ourselves a stiff," one of the firemen called out.

"Son of a bitch." Sheriff Mosbey spat out his wad of tobacco, hiked up his pistol belt, and strolled leisurely around the tow truck to the driver's side of the Lumina.

Taking his time now, not about to rush things.

He stood there, big meaty red hands resting on big wide hips, staring expressionlessly in through the open window.

Sure enough. A pale, bloated corpse was slumped over the steering wheel. The air bag, he noted, had inflated but been punctured.

Purposely? he wondered. *To make sure the vehicle sank quickly? That would explain why all the windows had been rolled down.*

An investigation would tell.

But he had a gut instinct for accident scenes because he'd seen plenty of them, more than he would have liked. And the feeling he got from this one was that something wasn't quite right. He couldn't have explained why. But that was the hunch he had.

"Don't nobody touch this here vehicle," he said.

Using that soft authoritative drawl. Looking around at everybody through squinty eyes, making sure they knew he was serious.

Then, unclipping his flashlight from his belt, he took a few steps back and played the light around the Lumina's rear license plate, returned to his cruiser, and squeezed in behind the wheel.

He picked up the mike from the console and got on the radio.

"Sally, hon?" he told the dispatcher. "Run the following Georgia plates through DMV while I wait, will ya?"

He proceeded to reel off the letters and numbers.

A minute passed. Through his squeaky windshield and thumping wipers, he could see the hood of the floodlit Lumina slowly coming up out of the water, the metal body pulsating blood red from the flashing emergency lights.

"Sheriff?" Sally came back on amid squawks and static. "Those plates're registered to a Dr. Wo Sheng Yi."

Otis Mosbey frowned. "That supposed to ring a bell?"

"Uh-huh. 'Member that Chinese doc from the CDC? One whose wife made a stink about the police waitin' seventy-two hours before listin' him as missin'?"

"Vaguely," Sheriff Mosbey said. The unsettling notion that things were about to become a lot more complicated was getting stronger by the second.

"I was you, Sheriff?" Sally said. "I'd try to look a li'l spiffy. Y'know?"

"Yeah? An' why's that?"

" 'Cause I got me a feelin' the newspaper and TV people're gonna show up for this one."

Sheriff Mosbey caught sight of approaching headlights. A familiar van with a satellite dish on top was coming over the bridge. He didn't need to see the logo on the sides to recognize it.

"Sally, hon?" he said wearily.

"Sheriff?"

"You're wrong," Otis Mosbey grumped.

"How's that, Sheriff?"

"The vultures are already here," he growled, getting ready to replace the mike. "Over 'n' out."

34

"I'm not going to mince words. The reason I summoned you is because this company is in the midst of a crisis. Probably the biggest crisis we've ever faced."

Dorothy-Anne looked around the airborne conference room. Her words had hit the department heads like a shock wave. That was clear from the jumpy glances they exchanged, the moist furrows that suddenly contoured usually smooth, dry brows, the worry clouding eyes that were unused to anticipating anything but the sunniest, most certain of all futures.

Now, the realization that they, the corporate Chosen, might face the same uncertain job security that haunted their counterparts in other companies filled them with dread.

It's true, Dorothy-Anne realized. *You really can smell fear.*

"I shouldn't have to mention that everything we discuss here is strictly confidential," she continued. "However, just so that we understand each other, I'll say it again. You are not—repeat *not*—to discuss this with anyone. That includes your spouses. Leaks of any kind, be they intentional or unintentional, shall not be tolerated."

Pausing, she added: "That's a surefire way to join Mr. Weekley."

Her eyes held no mercy as she looked around the table. "Do I make myself clear?"

"Yes, ma'am." The hushed chorus came from everyone present.

"Good," she said. "Now, as you're probably aware, Hale Hotels has suffered its second bacterial outbreak in four months. How or why this has occurred, I do not know, though I intend to find out. What I *do* know is that the result is nothing short of . . . catastrophic.

"That's right. *Cat-a-stroph-ic!*" She pronounced each syllable separately. "We've been flooded with cancellations, not only in the hotel division, which has been the hardest hit, but"—she lifted a hand and brought it down hard on the pile of printout she'd carried in, so hard that the resulting thunderclap caused everyone to jerk like marionettes whose strings had been twitched—"across . . . the board!"

Dorothy-Anne's cheeks were suffused with an angry flush. After a moment she withdrew her hand and sat back, nostrils flaring.

No one spoke. It was obvious she hadn't finished, just as it was obvious that speaking out of turn was like taunting a grizzly cub in the presence of its mother, only more dangerous.

"Ladies and gentlemen," she said softly, "if an occasion ever called for radical measures, this is it. During the ride to the airport I spent a highly unpleasant forty-five minutes scanning the overnight updates of your various departments. The overall picture does not look good. It looks, in a word, dismal."

"How dismal, exactly?"

The question came from Yoshi Yamada, who handled the Hale Companies' investments, the one division impervious to the trials and tribulations of everything except the stock and bond markets.

Dorothy-Anne's voice was hushed. "So dismal that we may be forced to liquidate our investments, Mr. Yamada. So dismal that we could well be facing disaster. Yes, disaster: even filing for bankruptcy protection is not entirely out of the question."

Bankruptcy!

There was a communal gasp of disbelief, bewildered utterances of shock.

A midair collision couldn't have stunned them more completely. That things were temporarily shaky they could understand; after all, what company didn't experience occasional crises, or have its ups and downs?

That was the price of doing business.

But that the foundation—the very bedrock—that had solidly supported this multibillion-dollar behemoth should suddenly have turned to sand, and that this could happen to the Hale Companies, long known as a bastion of security, was inconceivable.

Her senior executives' numb stupefaction reminded Dorothy-Anne of news footage, of a camera intruding upon the survivors of a disaster.

Only they're sitting down instead of wandering around in a daze.

"Believe me," she resumed, the irony evident in her tone, "if anyone can understand your shock, it's me. Admittedly, I described the worst-case scenario. The trouble is, there's no such thing as a *good* one, not in this case. The threat we're facing is real—all *too* real."

Hands gripping the armrests of her seat, she sat slightly forward, her sharp-eyed gaze scanning her audience.

"The trouble," she went on, "seems to be that despite our efforts at diversification, in spite of making sure each department is a separate entity, we haven't diversified *enough*. In our clients' minds, our divisions remain psychologically linked, which is why the ripple effect is being felt throughout the company.

"Take Hale Lines, for instance. It's been horrendously affected. And why not? After all, what *is* a cruise ship but a floating hotel with multiple restaurants?"

She stopped strolling and looked across the table.

"Mr. Short."

"Ma'am?" Marvin replied, coming to attention in his seat.

"As the acting head of your department, you're more knowledgeable about Hale Lines' day-to-day operations than anyone present, myself included. Could you give us your assessment of the current situation?"

"In one word? Bad."

"I'd rather you were a little more specific. Why don't you tell us exactly *how* bad."

Taking a deep breath, he said: "Several major tour operators in Germany and Japan have canceled block bookings on our ships. A lot of travel agencies, including the big chains, are sitting on the fence and taking a wait-and-see attitude."

"In short," Dorothy-Anne said quietly, for the benefit of the others, "while not canceling any reservations, they're not booking anyone on our boats, either."

"That's right." Marvin nodded. "They're steering their customers to Carnival, Royal Caribbean, Princess, and Crystal."

Dorothy-Anne smiled sourly, her mouth expressing the aftertaste of the bitter pill she was being forced to swallow.

"Mr. Short. Could you tell us how much revenue we've lost through cancellations?"

"You mean, since yesterday?"

"Yes."

"If you'll give me a moment, sure. I can make this baby"—he patted his laptop—"give up all its secrets and then some."

"Take all the time you need," she said in a kind voice.

Marvin lifted his hands, shot back his cuffs, and wiggled his fingers dramatically, then attacked the keyboard like a concert pianist. After a minute, he let out a soft whistle, shook his head in stunned disbelief, and slumped back in his seat.

"Holy shit!" he exclaimed under his breath, and stared up at Dorothy-Anne in horrified awe.

"And what number did you come up with, Mr. Short?" she asked.

"One point . . ." His voice cracked.

"Yes?" Dorothy-Anne asked inexorably.

He swallowed and tried again: "One point eight six nine mil!" he whispered hoarsely. "*Plus* loose change. That's . . . that's nearly two million dollars!"

"That's right."

Dorothy-Anne nodded briskly, and continued to prowl around the cabin.

"And bear in mind, ladies and gentlemen, that's just the Hale Lines, and just since *yesterday*. God only knows what tomorrow will bring."

She added grimly: "Not that it matters. Even if our ships are half empty, they still have to keep their scheduled departures and sail."

"Wait a minute," rasped Bernie Appledorf. "Back up there, will ya?"

"Yes, Bernie?" Dorothy-Anne looked over at him.

He was a tall, ill-formed dybbuk of a man, all sharp angles and gaunt, twisted branches for limbs. He had a balding head with a few long, thin strands of hair trained across it. A narrow face half hidden by thick-lensed, black-framed glasses, eyes lugubrious and bloodhoundish. But his mind was abacus sharp, and his knowledge of corporate finances and tax law was such that he could send an army of senior IRS agents chasing their tails for years.

"Ya ask me," he growled, "ya better start canceling some o' them cruises."

"Spoken like a true comptroller," Dorothy-Anne observed, with a thin smile. "You're a numbers cruncher and bean counter, Bernie, and admittedly the best there is. But permit me, when it comes to the hospitality business, *I* know best."

He blinked at her from behind Coke bottle lenses. "So what's that got to do with the price o' oranges?"

"Everything, Bernie," she sighed, "absolutely, positively everything. If we cancel so much as a single cruise, we'll be perceived as an unreliable carrier, and then we'd really be up the creek."

"Sounds like we're up it as it is," he pointed out gloomily.

"Yes, but at least we still have part of a paddle. But if we stopped honoring our commitments, we'd lose it—and fast. Travel agents and tour operators are notoriously fickle about carriers that don't deliver. Our reputation's on the line here, Bernie, our reputation. Once you've lost that . . . well, in this business, it's good night, nurse!"

"Yeah, but sailin' half-empty ships? You'd have to be crazy!" He shook his head. "Even you can't afford to do that."

"Bernie, we can't afford *not* to," she retorted. "Among other things, we'd be in danger of losing our berthing slots. Every port has a limited number, and the other lines would grab ours in a minute." She shook her head vehemently. "We fought long and hard to get those slots, and by God, I'll be *damned* if I'm going to relinquish them!"

"Seems to me you'll be damned if ya don't," Bernie rasped.

"Anyway, enough about Hale Lines," Dorothy-Anne decided. "Let's move on to another division that's been affected by the hotel's outbreak of salmonella: Sky Hi Catering.

"Owen? Why don't you fill us in on the fallout you've been receiving."

Owen Beard, the president of the airline catering division, drew himself up in his seat. A golf enthusiast, he had boyish good looks, with a face like an apple at the tail end of its blushing freshness, a ready smile, lively gray eyes, and an infinite repertoire of locker room jokes.

Like his colleague Bernie Appledorf, Owen Beard was a notorious corporate penny pincher. His proudest achievement—and there were many—had been to remove the single cherry tomato garnishing the salads Sky Hi Catering supplied its airline clients, an inspiration he'd had in the midst of swinging his club at the eighteenth hole of that toughest of all American golf courses, the Koolau Golf Course at the base of Oahu's Pali cliffs in Hawaii, an inspiration that had caused him to lose his concentration *and* the game, but which had resulted, in sheer volume, to a savings of nearly a quarter of a million dollars each year.

"I've been fielding calls all morning from our clients," he announced in his rich, plummy voice, then tossed his head. "From the head honchos, actually."

Dorothy-Anne nodded and sighed.

Owen said, "Naturally, they're very concerned—our largest client in particular—and although none of them would come out and say as much—golf buddies that we are—they all hinted at the health and safety clause in our contracts."

Dorothy-Anne stopped behind her seat, her fingers squeezing its glove leather back. "In other words," she said tightly, "they're threatening to use the escape clause and take their business to Skychefs. Is that it?"

"They didn't put it that bluntly," he said, "but in essence, that's what it boils down to. Yes." He nodded.

Dorothy-Anne thought: *If the situation were reversed, that's exactly what I would do.*

"I wish I could say I blame them," she said, "but I can't." Her eyes glittered with anger even as her voice reflected the weariness she felt. Steeling herself for the worst, she said, "Dare I ask the outcome of the calls?"

"Well, my next three weekends are shot." He smiled disarmingly. "I lined up four games of golf."

For the first time since boarding the jet, the tension eased and there was a round of chuckles. Even Dorothy-Anne had to smile.

"Phoenix, Ponte Vedra, and Rancho Mirage," he said. "We'll continue the discussions when we tee off."

"So they won't pull their accounts until after you've talked face-to-face?"

"That's right." His grin broadened.

Dorothy-Anne felt a few pounds of the crushing tonnage lift from her overburdened shoulders. "Good work, Owen." She shook her head admiringly. "I don't know how you do it. Is it your silver tongue or your golf swing?"

"I like to think it's both." His good-natured grin abruptly disappeared. "But we're not out of the woods just yet," he warned. "I'm ninety-nine percent certain I can talk them out of defecting to Skychefs. But that's contingent on no more of these damned outbreaks occurring! If one does . . ." He shrugged eloquently.

"Let's pray it doesn't." Dorothy-Anne's eyes swept around the conference table. "Better yet, let's all make sure it *can't!*"

"Amen to that," Venetia murmured.

Dorothy-Anne fixed her gaze on Heather Solis. A well-groomed, silver-haired woman in her mid-fifties, Heather Solis projected the air of a kindly, well-to-do maiden aunt. Actually, she was happily married, was the mother of three, and had six grandchildren to dote on, and was the president of Hale Vacation Villages, the Hale Companies' family-oriented theme resorts.

Located in such varied paradises as Hawaii, Mexico, Belize, the Aegean, Fiji, the U.S. Virgin Islands, and the Great Barrier Reef, the resorts offered all-inclusive family vacation packages at affordable prices.

Dorothy-Anne said, "I noticed the Vacation Villages were particularly hard hit with cancellations."

Heather winced. "Tell me about it," she said glumly. "We're in the same boat as Hale Lines, since our bookings are done entirely through tour operators and travel agents. Except we're feeling the heat even worse!"

Dorothy-Anne nodded and sat back down. "That stands to reason. After all, the Villages are family-oriented resorts. That puts things in an entirely different light."

"That's what I keep telling myself."

"Well? It's only natural that parents should be concerned about their children's health and well-being. If I were a travel agent, I'd want to err on the safe side, too."

"I suppose you're right," Heather gloomed. "Amazing, isn't it, the speed with which bad news travels?"

"What would amaze me more," Dorothy-Anne replied, "is if good news traveled even half that fast. Unfortunately, like no news being good news, good news amounts to being no news. Only tragedies make good copy."

"In that case," Heather said darkly, "at least we have one thing less to worry about. Tragedy won't be striking the Vacation Villages anytime soon."

"Oh?" Dorothy-Anne looked perplexed. "And why is that?"

"The way cancellations are piling up, there won't *be* anybody there, that's why. They'll be ghost towns." She sighed deeply. "With what you're spending on the Eden Isle Resort, you need this like a hole in the head!"

Dorothy-Anne made a painted face. "Which reminds me . . ."

She glanced at Kurt Ackerman, director of Special Projects, who was doodling on a piece of paper.

"Kurt?" When there was no reply, she repeated his name more sharply: "*Kurt!*"

Her raised voice did the trick. Kurt Ackerman, shoulder-length hair held back in a brown-and-gray ponytail, looked up with a startled expression in his usually dreamy, cinnamon-colored eyes. Tall, lean, and in his forties, he topped out at six-foot-three, and was the only man present not dressed in a business suit.

Which was fine with Dorothy-Anne. She hadn't lured him away from his job at Walt Disney World, where he'd created rides and fantasy worlds, just to turn him into another "suit." God knew, executives were a dime a dozen. What she needed was a creative genius, and after raiding Disney's talent pool for the best, she wasn't about to stifle him by sticking him in a Brooks Brothers, Hickey Freeman, or even Savile Row suit. That would have defeated the purpose.

In fact, she found Kurt's artfully casual manner of dressing both reassuring and inspiring. Today it was a tobacco-brown cashmere shirt, a lamb suede baseball jacket the precise shade of French's mustard, black Levi's 501s, striped pink and yellow socks, and white Mephistos.

He looked exactly what he was, this Steven Spielberg of amusement rides—a grown-up kid who'd never lost his sense of wide-eyed wonder, a man who preferred the innocent merriment of delighting children of all ages to using his technical talents to think up destructive playthings for the military, a man whose imagination created a kinder, gentler, and more laughter-filled world.

"Sorry," he said, with a sheepish little grin. "I just had this totally brilliant idea for improving the raft ride. You were saying . . . ?"

"I was saying there won't *be* a raft ride if we don't do something about this company's finances," Dorothy-Anne said severely. "The hotels and resorts are our bread and butter. Without their income, we can't even meet our interest payments, let alone decrease our debt load. What we've got to do is complete Eden Isle—while cutting out as much pork as possible."

"I'll see what I can do about scaling back the costs," Kurt promised, with a sigh. "Talk about creative thinking."

"I'd really appreciate it," Dorothy-Anne said. "I think we all would." She added: "On my way back from Huatulco, I'll stop off at Eden Isle and see how things are progressing. Maybe I'll get some ideas, too."

"Want me to be there?" Kurt asked.

"I'll call and let you know if I do," Dorothy-Anne answered.

Heather Solis was wringing her hands in agitation. "If only the Vacation Villages and Hale Hotels weren't so inextricably *linked* in consumers' minds!" she lamented. "That's what's killing us. If we could somehow separate the one from the other . . ."

"That's asking for the impossible," Dorothy-Anne said, "short of selling the Vacation Villages, or divorcing them entirely from the Hale Companies. As far as selling is concerned, it's out of the question. I won't *hear* of it. And separating it would be counterproductive in the long run."

"But—"

Dorothy-Anne waved her to silence. "You're forgetting the reason the Villages have been so wildly successful in the first place."

"The Hale name," Heather admitted, giving a pained sigh.

"Precisely." Dorothy-Anne nodded brusquely and sat back.

"But now we're paying the price," Heather reminded her edgily. "With these cancellations, our overhead's shot through the roof. I've calculated that before we left for the airport, our operation costs had already mushroomed to double our income . . . and are no doubt rising as we speak!"

Heather caught sight of Owen Beard as he sat as loftily remote and above it all as a weather satellite tracking a hurricane from the safety of its peaceful orbit in outer space.

"I must say I envy you, Owen," she said moodily. "Managing a subcontracting division sure looks good from where *I'm* sitting!"

Owen looked startled, taken aback by the sudden vehemence of Heather's usually mild tone.

"Admit it, Owen," Heather snapped, pursuing the subject as doggedly as a Rottweiler. "If your trucks didn't have 'Sky Hi Catering, A Division of the Hale Companies,' plastered all over them, the public at large would never even equate Sky Hi with the Hale Companies, now, would they?"

"*Heather* . . . ?" Dorothy-Anne said in a faint, uneven tone that barely managed to hide the jolt of excitement that had all but robbed her of the power of speech.

Heather turned to her. "Y-yes?"

"Could you . . . would you mind repeating what you just said?"

"What?" Heather frowned. "About Owen's being a subcontractor?"

"No, no, *no*," Dorothy-Anne responded impatiently, shifting in her chair so that she faced Heather directly. "About the *trucks*." Her eyes positively glowed. "The *trucks*, Heather!"

"Oh. You mean, if they didn't have 'A Division of the Hale Companies' emblazoned—"

"*Exactly!*" Dorothy-Anne blurted. "That's *it!*" Her voice trumpeted such blaring triumph, such combative spirit in the face of defeat, that it electrified the very air and galvanized the others, Owen included, into sitting up straighter and taking notice.

A tangible frisson rippled through the cabin. There was an exchange of knowing glances, looks of eminent relief. For the first time in ages, Dorothy-Anne was truly her old self—taking control, real control, and they could each pinpoint the last time she'd been this highly charged and inflamed—right before Freddie Cantwell's tragic, final flight.

Now, witnessing her old fighting spirit reasserting itself, they found it a wondrous thing to behold and felt giddily infected, like battle-worn troops rallied into action by a new, charismatic commander-in-chief.

"This company," Dorothy-Anne declared, "will not, I repeat *not*, go quietly into the night!"

Too excited to stay seated, she jumped to her feet and prowled restlessly, like a caged animal, gesticulating urgently as she spoke:

"I refuse to sit back and watch the decline and fall of this empire. *Yes!* Somehow we must—we *shall*—stem the tide. In the immortal words of John Paul Jones, 'I have not yet begun to fight!' Well, neither have *you*."

She whipped around and stood there, lighting up the cabin like a beacon, then pointed a quivering, all-encompassing finger from one end of the table to the other.

"Neither have *any* of you!" she completed, pausing just long enough to draw the quickest of breaths. "Venetia!"

"Boss?"

"We need to get that publicity mill churning—and I mean *churning!* I want to see a flood, an avalanche, a veritable *tidal wave* of positive articles about us in every major newspaper and magazine in the Western world. Also, we have to shore up our current advertising. By that, I mean a saturation bombing by radio, television, and print in the neighborhood of . . . hmmm . . . for starters, shall we say . . . double our usual volume?"

"Double *what!*" burst out Bernie, hoisting himself from his seat. "Th-that's not even meshuggah!" he sputtered. "That . . . that's certifiably—"

"You're right, Bernie," Dorothy-Anne soothed, bestowing upon him the most understanding and winsome smile in her vast repertoire. "We shouldn't double it. Venetia? Scratch that, will you?"

"*Whew!*" Bernie sat back down and wiped his glistening brow. "For a moment there, ya really had me worried."

As well you should be, Dorothy-Anne thought.

"We'll *triple* it," she decided, hearing Bernie choke. "And really, Bernie. Stop acting as if you're having a coronary. It's not your money. It's mine to spend, and I'll spend it as I wish."

Blazing circles, like red-hot burners, had ignited on her cheeks.

"And what I intend to spend it on is saving this company," she said forcefully. "Let there be no mistake. I'll do what I must to achieve it— even if it takes every last red cent!" she swore before her impassioned, saber-rattling battle cry ended as she realized she had made her point.

Pausing breathlessly, she looked around. Bernie, elbows on the table, was holding his head in his hands and shaking it while muttering under his breath, but everyone else stared at her with a kind of rapt, radiant respect.

"If you'll bear with me," she said in a deliberately soft, unthreatening voice, "I'd like to share a short anecdote with you. Many years ago, when my great-grandmother bought her very first hotel, the Madison Squire, she met with all her new employees. To start off on the right foot, do you know the first thing she did?"

Only Venetia, who was familiar with this tale, did not shake her head.

"She demanded a letter of resignation from each and every employee. That's right." Dorothy-Anne stared at each of them in turn. "*A letter of resignation,*" she emphasized quietly, so quietly and with such implacable solemnity and authority, that the inherent threat was more potent than any explosion. "From the manager right down to the scullery maids and the boiler stokers."

She could feel the rapt excitement turn to wary unease, could sense the tension and anxiety levels around the table ratcheting up, could catch the faint but unmistakable whiff of fear.

"And you know what?" she asked.

No one spoke; the only sound was the muted roar of the jet engines.

"She proved her point. Almost to a man and woman, her employees worked their keisters off and proved themselves worthy. The few who didn't were provided with references and severance packages. The rest had their letters of resignation torn up."

Again Dorothy-Anne paused. If anything, the silence in the cabin seemed to have deepened, as though some powerful alien life form had invaded it and taken up residence.

She said, "Before we stop over in Dallas, I expect each and every one of *you* to hand me your letters of resignation. No one is exempted . . . not you, Mr. Armour—"

Hearing his name, the heavy, ruddy-faced president of the Hale Real Estate division flinched, the thick flesh of his sagging cheeks puffing like a bellows.

"Nor you, Mr. Weaver . . . nor you, Ms. Valentine . . ."

They all sat there in thunderstruck shock, reeling as if they'd been punched by an upper cut from an invisible fist.

"Then, after a four-week probationary period, during which you'll have hopefully proven your worth, I shall review your performances and either tear up your letters or hold you to your resignations.

"But it's up to you—each and every one of you—to validate both your departments *and* your own positions. The best way to do that is through creative management and producing new sources of income. In short, I want you to show me just *why* I should continue to overpay you so extravagantly."

Dorothy-Anne's voice dropped an octave as she once again addressed everyone:

"You know, it's strange," she said. "While not exactly lackluster, our performance certainly hasn't been what it should be. Or, more importantly, what it *could be*. We've . . . well, let's be honest. We've been able to coast and rest on our laurels for far too long. Sadly, it took two tragedies to shake us out of our lethargy and take notice. But believe you me—I, for one, *am* taking notice!"

Her piercing gaze sought out Owen Beard.

"Owen!" she said.

He jerked upright as though he'd been goosed.

"About the catering trucks," Dorothy-Anne said, hitting her stride and moving about with the authoritative command of a conquering general, a chieftain, a czarina, so certain of her power to triumph that her clipped speech sped up to match her aggressive gait. "Heather was right. All you have to do is spray over the 'Hale Companies' on the side panels of the trucks."

Owen looked taken aback. "Just . . . spray over it?" he sputtered. "You don't mean . . . use *spray paint*?"

"That's exactly what I mean, Owen. And, in its place, reletter it to read, 'A Division of HCI,' or something like that."

"HCI?" he repeated, dumbfounded.

"HCI or whatever I decide on," she said. "And that's only until this blows over. When the Hale name regains its former glory."

She stopped walking, planted herself in a foursquare stance, and placed her hands on her hips, sweeping her audience with needle-like eyes.

"The clock's ticking, ladies and gentleman. I suggest you make every second count.

"This meeting is hereby adjourned. Now get to work."

35

Mexico's gold coasts have long been legendary for luring sun worshipers to their sandy shores and tropical seas. Each decade has seen the birth of a major new resort. In the 1950s it was Acapulco, and in the sixties Richard Burton and Liz Taylor put Puerto Vallarta on the map. The seventies heralded a monstrously overbuilt Cancún, and during the eighties Mazatlán, Manzanillo, and Ixtapa became all the rage.

Now, for the coming millennium, a new eighty-mile stretch of virgin beaches and jungle shores have been discovered: the unspoiled Pacific coast of Oaxaca. Encompassing the still untrammeled fishing villages of Puerto Escondido and Puerto Angel, the true jewel in Oaxaca's crown are the nine glorious, crescent-shaped bays of Huatulco.

Hale Hotels, which had gotten in on the ground floor, had been among the first big investors on the Oaxacan coast, an area that, according to projections, would be Mexico's largest resort by the year 2018. Having learned their lesson the hard way with Cancún and Acapulco, Mexico's tourism development agency had enforced strict building codes and pollution controls.

The Hale Hotel and Resort went one better. Even a height restriction of six-story buildings had been too high for Dorothy-Anne's taste. She had worked closely with the architects in planning the development.

"I want you to reach back," she had instructed the architects in the fall of 1986, as they followed a matchete-wielding guide who wandered ahead of them, clearing a swath for their walking tour of the near-vertical, junglelike site. "And by back, I mean way, *way* back. Think *pre*-Spanish colonial. I won't have acres and acres of glaring, blinding white stucco sugar cubes like at Las Hadas, so don't even *try* to sell me on that! Brrrrr!"

She pulled a face to go along with her dramatic shudder.

"God, no. I want something entirely . . . you know . . . indigenous. Sensuously organic and environmentally in tune with nature . . ."

Before she realized it, Dorothy-Anne was off and running, fervidly spinning concepts that blossomed with vivid details of the exacting shapes, styles, and tonalities she envisioned. Launching into a celebration of pueblo chic, she touched on the regional Mexican vernacular, before singing the praises of the simple rustic beauty found in the local roadside vegetable and fruit stands. Not once pausing for breath, she proceeded to paint glorious verbal color samples of the precise shades she had in mind—delicious pale ambers and evocative turquoises, ceruleans and pinks, and native sands, terra cottas, and clays. Carried away by the intensity of her vision, she went on to describe rooms that suspended the barrier between indoors and out, where strong saplings supported thatched roofs and each three-walled guest cottage had its own small private pool, going on to construct orally a hotel of individual huts with individual pools cascading down the steep hillside all the way to the golden beach far below.

"With just a touch, a soupçon of Mediterranean thrown in," she waxed poetically. "But everything has to fade into the hillside. *And,* I want no building higher than one story. That's your brief, gentlemen. Now use your imagination."

The architects first looked at one another, and then turned to her in unison, their faces reflecting undisguised horror.

"If it'll help inspire you," she said sweetly, "think hemp and straw and rattan. Woven Indian fabrics. Ceiling fans and mosquito netting. Clay sinks—"

"*Clay!*" One of the architects, who had been driven from the airport past shallow brown rivers where local Indians bathed and washed their clothes and did God only knows what else in plain sight, recoiled in genuine horror.

"That's right, *clay,*" Dorothy-Anne insisted, undeterred. "Good, old-fashioned, honest, plebeian *clay.* Earthenware, which, I needn't remind you, has been around and servicing mankind quite nicely for millennia. Now, taking that as your cue, I want everything distilled down to its basic, most simplistic, and primitive purity . . . its very essence, if you will. That, gentlemen, is what true luxury will mean here."

"Hmmm," one of the designers murmured thoughtfully, tapping his lips. "I can almost see it. Jacuzzis with vast ocean views—"

"*No* Jacuzzis," Dorothy-Anne decreed firmly.

"What! None?" The designer was scandalized.

"Absolutely not!" She withered him with a glare. "Who do I look like? Donald Trump? And need I remind you that whirlpools are noisy, vile pieces of machinery?"

That silenced him.

"Think natural," she extrapolated. "*Natural!*"

And so, in turns prodded, cajoled, pushed, bullied, worn down, and threatened, the team found itself stymied in attempting to impose its signature stamp of polished steel and towering glass and soaring atriums upon the project, and had ended up giving her what she had demanded—a bravura creation as breathtaking as it was architecturally daring.

Situated at the very tip of the promontory jutting out of the bay known locally as Bahía Cahue, the completed Huatulco Hale Hotel and Resort fit perfectly into the dramatic landscape of plunging emerald hills and verdant cliffs, fit in so naturally with its geographic habitat that it was virtually indistinguishable from the surrounding flora and looked, once one became aware of it, as if it had been there, gently guarded by the jungle, for untold centuries.

Which was exactly the way Dorothy-Anne had envisioned it. Small wonder that it instantly became her favorite among all the Hale Hotels.

On this fragrant morning the day after her arrival at Huatulco, she awakened from a deep sleep, the most satisfying sleep she had enjoyed in almost half a year. For a while she permitted herself the sheer pleasure of just lying there, luxuriating on the smooth cotton sheets inside her sumptuously veiled, mosquito-netted bed.

Had anyone ever slept so soundly, she wondered blissfully, or felt this surprisingly rejuvenated and not the least bit jet-lagged? It was truly a miracle, especially considering the daunting paces she'd been put through just yesterday.

First, there had been the swarm of reporters who'd been camped out at the Santa Cruz airport in anticipation of her arrival. When they descended on her en masse, she had been required to hold an impromptu press conference, if only to keep them at bay.

Naturally, it was almost identical in tone, content, and mood to the press conference she'd endured earlier in White Plains. These reporters, too, had been far more interested in her private life and the Hale Companies' state of finances than in the tragedy that had brought her here.

Then, after being whisked to the Huatulco Hale Hotel and Resort, she had spent countless hours making the rounds, visiting each of the 236 recovering salmonella patients.

It was a task she did not relish, and wished she could have postponed. But duty called. She felt a moral obligation to see this through.

Somebody has to be held accountable, she told herself grimly. *And somebody is. Me.*

And she reminded herself: *This is my company. The buck stops here.*

The first patients she visited, Jim and Moira Kelso, were retirees in their sixties. Dorothy-Anne pulled a chair up beside their beds.

"I'm ever so sorry," she said softly. "I'm afraid I've ruined your vacation."

"Only a few days of it," Moira, a chirpy Midwesterner, piped up cheerfully. "Other than that, this is still our favorite place on earth."

"And hopefully it will be again," Dorothy-Anne replied. "That's why I've come—to get to the bottom of this. I don't like it when things aren't up to snuff."

"Oh, but they are," Jim Kelso assured her. "These things happen. You should have seen how sick the little woman got in Egypt—"

Moira slapped his leg and hooted. "Oh, yeah? That was nothing compared to you in Kenya!" She turned to Dorothy-Anne: "Jim here was as green as a Martian! I wish you'd seen him. All he needed was a set of rabbit ears. . . ."

The next couple, the Bentons, were attractive young newlyweds from Raleigh, North Carolina. Despite still feeling under the weather, they couldn't stop touching and hugging each other.

"This place is sensational," the blushing bride told Dorothy-Anne. "You just wait and see. I don't care how sick we were, we're coming back!" She wrapped her arms around her husband and smiled. "Aren't we, hon?"

"We sure are, sug," he replied, nuzzling her affectionately.

Dorothy-Anne cleared her throat. "Well, if there's anything, anything at all that I can do, you'll let me know?"

The young husband winked. "We sure will."

Next were the Kitamuras, a Japanese family with two beautiful pre-teens. They graciously invited Dorothy-Anne to partake of tea.

"We would be much honored if you joined us," Mr. Kitamura told her. "It is no trouble. You see, my wife is making some now."

Mrs. Kitamura, kneeling on the floor, smiled up at Dorothy-Anne as she poured boiling water into an earthenware cup and then used a reed whisk to mix a pale green froth.

"I am highly honored by your kind invitation," Dorothy-Anne replied politely. "Unfortunately, my duties require I visit all who fell ill."

"Ah, duty. *Giri.*" Mr. Kitamura nodded. "I quite understand."

Dorothy-Anne told him to feel free to summon her personally, day or night, if necessary. "The concierge will put you through to me immediately." She paused and lowered her gaze. "I am truly sorry for this outbreak. I feel personally responsible."

"No, no," Mr. Kitamura assured her hastily. "There is a limit to *giri.* It is we who are sorry for inconveniencing you."

And so it went. The hours Dorothy-Anne spent visiting the stricken passed with remarkable speed. She was amazed at how good-humored the guests were about the outbreak. Almost without fail, they seemed genuinely pleased to see her. The fact that she had taken the trouble of showing up herself, rather than sending an emissary, was obviously appreciated.

What's more, the reception she received was so warm she felt humbled.

But what really threw her, what Dorothy-Anne found almost beyond all comprehension, was that most of the patients blamed neither her nor the hotel—some, like Mr. Kitamura, actually apologized for falling ill!

As if it had been *their* fault!

She couldn't believe it. After steeling herself to bear the brunt of highly justifiable anger and outrage, her guests had ended up comforting her—*and* singing the praises of the staff!

It was the last thing she had expected, and it renewed her faith in the human race. People, she realized, could be absolutely amazing. And incredibly decent.

But most surprising of all, she discovered that she enjoyed—yes, genuinely *enjoyed*—these face-to-face encounters with her guests, ill though they might be. There was something satisfying about taking a hands-on approach and dealing with real-life people instead of so many faceless statistics and sheer numbers.

For the first time, Dorothy-Anne understood exactly what it was that had driven her great-grandmother to build the hotel empire.

It's more than just about corporate expansion and the amassing of wealth and power, she realized. *It's the people business. It's making strangers feel at home* away *from home!*

This awakening made her wonder why she had always shied away from personal interaction with guests. Good heavens, they were nice people! What was there to be afraid of?

Why had she always left that to Freddie or various underlings?

Buoyant from her experience, she decided a nap before a late dinner was in order. Repairing to her own suite, she hung out the Do Not Disturb sign and stretched out in bed for a quick snooze.

The next thing she knew, it was morning. Such had been her exhaustion—or else so welcoming, cocooning, and soothing was this quiet paradise of adobe walls, thatched roofs, and rooms open to the sea.

Having awakened to the soothing sounds of water, a sound as ever present as the seductive breezes that rustled the tropical foliage and wafted, fragrant, invisible, and caressing, through the open-walled rooms and shady terraces, Dorothy-Anne couldn't think of a place she'd rather be.

Sitting up, she stretched languorously and yawned, then parted the mosquito netting.

She literally gasped at the spectacle of cascading water, overflowing pool, big sky, and endless ocean, an ocean that proved that blue was far from a single identifiable color, but rather covered a vast spectrum ranging from palest turquoise to darkest indigo.

Getting out of bed, she padded barefoot over cool, unglazed tiles to the shaded terrace, where teak chaises with canary yellow cushions were invitingly arranged facing the free-form pool.

She spread out on one, wondering whether she should ring for breakfast and coffee. Maybe just lounge here for a while, gorging her eyes on this unparalleled feast of a view, with the day's first windsurfers skimming the waves on the Pacific with sails like huge butterflies? Or, if she felt so inclined, she could always enjoy a lazy prebreakfast dip before taking the funicular either up to the clifftop restaurant or down to the beachfront terrace far below.

Well, there was no rush. Later, she would check up on the ill guests once more. In the meantime, she could do what she pleased—or nothing at all, even if it took her half the day to decide exactly which wonderful act of doing absolutely nothing it would be.

Hmmm, she thought blissfully, *no wonder people go on vacations. Just the idea of a total change of scenery and getting away from it all . . . of being somewhere and unwinding and leaving all one's troubles and cares behind . . . now, that was heaven. Oh, yes, pure unadulterated heaven . . .*

Before she was aware of it, Dorothy-Anne's eyelids fluttered shut, and she must have nodded off again, because the next thing she knew the sun was high in the sky and flooding her pool with rays.

Glancing at her watch, she realized it was a few minutes past noon.

Noon! Holy guacamole! She jumped to her feet. If she didn't get a move on, she would miss the best part of the day!

Now that she was wide awake she no longer had to agonize over her destination. The beach, she decided, instinctively and without conscious thought, her mind no longer encumbered by indecisiveness. She would head down to the only sensible spot at this hour of the day, the water's edge.

Getting her tush in gear, she changed into a black maillot with an open, black net shirtdress over it, and put on black sandals and sunglasses. She would enjoy a casual, leisurely lunch under one of the *palapas,* those thatched palm sunshades along the beach. After all, what good was being in paradise if you didn't avail yourself of its splendors, she rationalized with the laid-back, pleasurable guilt of a kid playing hooky from school.

"Criminal charges! Goddamn criminal charges!" Hunt Winslow roared, jumping angrily to his feet and brandishing the official letter in his hand.

Shaking his interpreter's hand off his arm, he glared down at the chief of police in outrage. Whoever still thought policemen south of the border were fat and slothful had obviously never crossed swords with Fernando Davalos Zuñiga. The man's imperviousness to pleas, threats, and bribes, combined with his impeccable, starched tan uniform, neatly trimmed little mustache, steel-rimmed glasses with round lenses, and a propensity for going by the book, only added to Hunt's anxiety and annoyance at all things Mexican.

Whatever had happened, he wondered nostalgically, to the good old days when you could at least count on the insufferably torpid, greasy-fingered local authorities with their attitudes of *mañana, mañana,* everything being able to wait until *mañana*—but who nevertheless snapped to whenever they heard the unmistakable rustle of *yanqui* greenbacks?

Gone the way of the Edsel, Hunt told himself, with an inner sigh. This new breed of dedicated young law enforcement professionals, a group to which Chief Zuñiga obviously belonged, not only proved that the *policia* could be above such schemes as petty racketeering and extortion but made it clear that any attempt at bribery would result in the appropriate judicial action.

Pox on all civil servants! Hunt cursed silently, the heat of his anger causing him to forget, momentarily, that as a state senator back in California, he fell into that very same category.

"As I have told you repeatedly," he enunciated icily, speaking slowly for the sake of the official interpreter, although why one should be necessary, since the chief of police could speak perfectly adequate English, was beyond him, "the boy has only turned fourteen."

"*Catorce,*" the interpreter concluded.

"*Fourteen!*" Hunt emphasized, with an accusatory stare.

"*Catorce!*"

Unperturbed, Fernando Davalos Zuñiga, slight, fastidious, and not about to let some well-dressed *gringo politico* stomp on his turf, sat back and politely offered Hunt a cigarette.

"Thanks, but no thanks," Hunt said, pulling a grimace of distaste.

Shrugging, Chief Zuñiga selected a cigarette in that delicate manner peculiar to many Latin Americans and lit it. He drew the smoke deep into his lungs and exhaled. "Please, *señor.*" He gestured. "Do continue."

Hunt smiled, but it was a mirthless smile. "It would seem obvious," he said coldly, "that just by *looking* at the child, anyone in his right mind would realize he is not your average teenager. My God"—he rested one hand flat on the desk and leaned forward—"surely even *you* have heard of Down's syndrome!"

Chief Zuñiga smoked in stony-faced silence.

"The poor child can barely communicate, let alone commit the crime of which he's accused! But all that aside, this document"—Hunt waved it and tossed it on the desk with a flourish—"signed by the governor of this state of Oaxaca, clearly states that Kevin Whitman is to be released. At once!"

"*Sí, señor.*" Chief Zuñiga puffed delicately on his cigarette. "That is what it says."

"Then what, for the love of God, is the holdup?"

The chief sighed out smoke and tapped a length of ash into a scallop shell. "As I, too, have repeatedly tried to explain, I have no choice, *señor.* Until I receive official notification, I am duty bound to keep the boy in prison—"

"Prison!" Hunt scoffed. "You call that stinking hellhole a prison?"

Chief Zuñiga smoked calmly, the very picture of serenity.

Hunt, realizing that his anger was getting the better of him, took a deep breath and counted to ten. The air-conditioning buzzed, but not loudly enough to drown out the drone of a large fly that hovered and scrabbled furiously, first at one shut window, then streaking across the room and flinging itself angrily at the other.

"Look," Hunt said quietly, "can't we clear this up reasonably? You have a copy of the governor's letter right in front of you. Surely you are empowered to act on it. What more notification could you possibly need?"

"If you will kindly forgive me, *señor,* but letters have been known to be forged." Before Hunt could get hot under the collar, Chief Zuñiga held up a pacifying hand. "Please, do not get me wrong, *señor.* I am not suggesting this document to be anything other than genuine. However, I have made it the policy of this office never to accept anything at face value, or from third parties."

"So what," Hunt asked wearily, "are we supposed to do in the meantime?"

"The only thing we can, *señor.*"

Chief Zuñiga stubbed out his cigarette in an ashtray. Then he glanced up at Hunt.

"We wait, *señor.* As soon as a copy of this letter is transmitted from the governor's office to mine, the child shall be released to the custody of his parents."

"In other words, the extenuating circumstances don't matter?"

"Extenuating circumstances?"

Zuñiga turned to look at the window where the fly was droning. Sunlight flashed off the round lenses of his glasses, making them opaque. He turned back to Hunt.

"Circumstances such as what, *señor?*"

"The age and mental incompetence of the child."

"I am sorry, *señor.* This is not your California. Contrary to popular belief, all Mexicans are not soft on drugs. Remember, the cocaine was found on the child's person."

"And what about the sworn statements of the three eyewitnesses?" Hunt asked tightly. "They all saw those two teenagers thrusting a package at him as they ran away from your men."

"Unfortunately, those witnesses were tourists. They have since returned to their own countries."

"In other words," Hunt said, "their sworn statements are meaningless . . . because they were foreigners and not Mexican nationals. Is that it?"

Zuñiga shrugged.

"Sounds like reverse discrimination to me."

"*Señor*, please," the chief said. "Try to understand. I am doing what I can."

Hunt nodded stiffly, the fly's droning sounding louder and more furious. "You know where to find me," he said thickly. Then, clearing his throat, he said, "I'll be at the hotel."

Zuñiga nodded politely. "I will keep you informed, *señor*. In the meantime, might I suggest you take advantage of our scenic wonders? Natural beauty is said to be therapeutic."

Hunt's cheeks smarted with anger. But most of all with failure, he thought, keeping his temper in check as he turned around and crossed to the door with all the dignity and military posture he could muster. As he opened the door, he heard more than saw the fly streak back across the room.

He glanced over his shoulder. Almost lazily, Zuñiga reached up, caught the insect in midair, and closed his fist around it.

That's right, Hunt thought grimly. *Get your cheap thrill and squash it to death.*

Actually, he wouldn't have put it past Zuñiga to play with it first, slowly pulling off one wing at a time.

Instead, Zuñiga rose from behind his desk, crossed to one of the windows, and opened it. He put his fist outside, released the fly, and then shut the window again.

That small act of mercy only enraged Hunt all the more.

What sort of man, he wondered, *gives freedom to a fly while incarcerating a helpless, hapless child?*

Zuñiga's gaze met Hunt's. The message in his eyes was as taunting and unmistakable as if he were speaking aloud.

It's one of ours, the look said. *Yes, one of ours*, this lowly fly, not some rich norte americano we're forced to put up with and pretend to welcome. Not one of those *louts* in their shameless string bikinis and thongs who invade like locusts and stay just long enough to litter and pollute.

Who think everything is *theirs*! That everything was put here solely for the benefit of their pleasure, like in some vast oceanic amusement park. Entertain us, wait on us, scramble for our tips!

Hunt broke the malevolent eye contact, stepped out into the hallway, and shut the door quietly. A couple was seated on the hard wooden bench by the opposite wall. The instant they saw him, they looked at him searchingly.

He shook his head in reply and went over to talk to them.

"I'm sorry," he said softly. "I did what I could."

The woman nodded. "I know you did," she said bravely.

She was thin and strong-boned, with direct brown eyes and an old-fashioned beauty parlor perm. If you looked past the celadon pantsuit, the white polyester blouse with the big bow at the neck, and the big, clear violet frames of her designer glasses, you could see remnants of her pioneer forebears. She had an American Gothic kind of strength, and pride and faith in abundance.

Hunt had to hand it to her. She really was the proverbial tower of strength.

Her husband was another story. He took the news hard, and made no attempt to hide the tears in his eyes. His cheerful resort garb—yellow golf slacks, riotous aloha shirt, and Forty-niners baseball cap—clashed with his lugubriousness, and underscored the tragedy of a family vacation gone wrong.

Terribly wrong.

The man's shattered, Hunt realized. *If his son isn't released soon, it won't be long before he falls to pieces.*

"Poor Kev." Joe Whitman rubbed his face wearily. "If only I hadn't insisted on bringing him along."

"Stop torturing yourself," Hunt said gently. "You can't think that way. You're not at fault."

But it was as if Joe Whitman hadn't heard. He shook his head and heaved a sigh and looked up at Hunt with haunted, baggy eyes.

"We've always taken Kev everywhere," he said huskily. "We never once had any trouble. Not ever. Just ask Midge."

Head raised, his wife looked at Hunt directly.

"Joe's right," she confirmed. "But Kev's a good kid. He'll be fine."

"How can you *say* that?" her husband blurted. He stared at her, his body quivering from fraught nerves. "*Midge!* He is *not* fine! In that—that stinking hellhole—he's about as far from fine as you can get!"

She shook her head. "The Bible says, 'Who ever perished being innocent?'" she quoted, with the calm sureness of the true believer. "Well, Kev's innocent. You mark my words, Joe. The Lord is looking after him as we speak."

Confronted with this simple declaration of faith, Hunt felt a renewed surge of anger. Damn and blast Chief Zuñiga to hell! He had the urge to march back into that office and tear the nitpicking bastard from limb to limb.

The Whitmans were innocent. Any idiot could see that. Good Lord, if ever there was a classic case of what you see is what you get—in this case decent, law-abiding, God-fearing tourists—you didn't have to look any further.

Instead of being hounded, the Whitmans should be lauded, Hunt thought.

He envied their basic goodness, their simplicity, their nonjudgmental love. Though their child had been born less than perfect, there'd been no question of feeling shame, or of loving him less, or, God forbid, of placing him in an institution.

No. Joe and Midge Whitman had showered Kevin with love. Had, in fact, gone out of their way to let him enjoy as normal a life as circumstances would permit.

If the Whitmans were guilty of anything, it was being in the wrong place at the wrong time. It was just one of those things. A classic instance of bad timing. While shopping for souvenirs in Santa Cruz Bay, the elder Whitmans had stepped into a boutique, leaving Kevin waiting outside.

Who could have predicted that two teens, chased by plainclothesmen, would give their pursuers the slip, but not before thrusting their booty at Kevin?

Literally leaving him holding the bag.

That had been two weeks earlier. Since then, neither the Whitmans' pleas, the statements of the witnesses, the intercession of the local consul, nor the American ambassador in Mexico City had managed to win the boy's release.

Increasingly frustrated, and growing ever more desperate, the Whitmans had appealed to everyone they could think of for help—including Hunt Winslow, their state senator back home.

They'd hoped that by casting a wide net, they'd find someone—anyone—who'd be able to effect Kevin's release. But what they *hadn't* expected, what had taken them totally by surprise, was that Hunt Winslow dropped everything and flew to their aid.

When he'd shown up in person, you could have knocked them over with a feather.

Kevin's plight had struck a deep, personal chord in Hunt. A chord so deep, and so intensely personal, that he'd had his aides clear his calendar.

Now, standing in the shiny tiled hallway outside Chief Zuñiga's office, Hunt shot back his cuff and checked his Breitling for the time. "It's past noon," he noted. "Tell you what. Why don't I take you both to lunch?"

Midge Whitman looked up at him. "Thank you," she declined with prim politeness, "but my husband and I'd much rather remain here. You know"—she gestured—"just in case."

Hunt nodded. "I understand completely," he said gently.

"But don't let that stop you from eating," she urged. "Please, go on and have some lunch. We'll be fine."

He nodded again. "I won't be more than an hour or so."

And shooting a contemptuous glance at Chief Zuñiga's door, he added: "Who knows? Perhaps by then, the local Gestapo chief'll have come to his senses!"

Midge Whitman attempted a smile, but it never quite reached her lips. Clearing her throat, she clasped her hands in her lap.

"May I asked you a question, Mr. Winslow?" she asked haltingly.

"Please, Mrs. Whitman." He smiled disarmingly and gestured. "Feel free to."

"I don't mean to sound ungrateful," she said slowly, obviously choosing her words with care, "because God knows, we *are* grateful!" She looked at him with clear-faced sincerity. "It's just . . ." Her hands fluttered uncertainly.

"Yes?" he prodded.

Her gaze was direct. "You're going through so much trouble for us. What I can't figure out is *why*. I mean, we're nobodies . . ."

Hunt shook his head. "You're wrong," he said quietly, with conviction. "Everyone on this planet is somebody. *Everyone.*"

"Yes, I suppose you're right." She bit her lip and sighed, as if torn between keeping silent and confessing something. Then, as if she could no longer contain her burden, she blurted: "But we . . . we didn't even vote for you!"

"So?" Hunt smiled easily. "That's your prerogative. Or have you forgotten? We live in a democracy."

His smile abruptly faded as he added, "At least, north of the border, we do!"

They both fell silent as two policemen, manhandling an old drunk, approached from down the hall. Hunt made room for them by flattening himself against the wall; Joe and Midge shifted position on the bench, turning their knees sideways in tandem.

Noisily, the trio jostled past, leaving boozy fumes and the cops' merciless taunting in their wake. As Hunt and the Whitmans watched, one of the officers purposely stuck out a foot. The drunk stumbled, and the cops swiftly set about pummeling him.

Midge flinched at the violence. "My God," she whispered. "That's police brutality!" Her face was white as she stared up at Hunt. "And the poor man's perfectly harmless."

Hunt nodded his head. "Yes, he is."

"Then why do they treat him so *roughly*? What's *wrong* with this place?"

"It's not the place," he replied tightly. "It's who's in charge."

"You mean . . ."

Hunt looked at her. "That's right. Chief Zuñiga."

She stared at him. "But something's got to be done about this!" Her voice was sharply outraged.

"Something should," Hunt concurred. "Unfortunately, there's nothing we can do—not without jeopardizing Kevin's release. God knows what other charges Zuñiga could trump up."

Midge lowered her eyes and sighed.

"Look, you've got worries of your own," Hunt said gently. "Your only concern right now must be for Kevin."

She looked down at her hands some more and then raised her eyes. "You're right," she said softly.

"Now, I'd better get a move on," Hunt said, "or I'm liable to miss lunch. If you like, I can have the hotel send over some sandwiches."

"Oh, no!" Midge protested. "Thank you for offering, but we're fine. I'll pop out in a while and get us a little something." She continued to hold his gaze. "You still haven't answered my question, you know."

Hunt nodded. "I know," he replied softly. And buttoning his suit jacket, he bowed slightly, then turned on his heel and took his leave.

36

Sonny Fong was back. In Manhattan and the swing of things.

So it was grimy, gloomy, and wet. So what? Even in the thrashing rain, the urban colossus had never looked better.

The streets thrummed. The drains were overflowing and the traffic was backed up. Buses and trucks belched exhaust, gridlocked cars and cabs honked an impatient symphony, and the crazies who hadn't taken shelter were ignored by the armies of pedestrians, the true Manhattanites distinguishing themselves by the offensive expertise with which they wielded their umbrellas.

By all gods great and small, but it was good to be home! After driving to Atlanta, and then all the way down to Mexico and back, returning to the Big Apple was like a breath of fresh air.

To really appreciate this city, Sonny thought, *you occasionally have to leave it. That will do it every time.*

He had additional reasons to feel good. He had successfully completed each of the tasks the old *lung tao* had set out for him.

All had gone without a hitch.

He had procured the salmonella samples in Atlanta and dispatched Dr. Wo Sheng Yi.

He had crossed the border checkpoints into Mexico unchallenged, the guards on both sides waving the Lexus and its cargo—the refrigerator flask filled with liquid nitrogen, which contained the CDC microbes— blithely through.

Nobody cared what went *into* Mexico; only what was being brought out.

Even posing as a busboy in the kitchens of the Hale Hotel and Beach

Resort in Huatulco had been a breeze—as had spiking the pots of freshly cooked shrimp with *Salmonella.*

He'd ditched the refrigerator flask on the long drive back to the border.

This time his car was assiduously searched. For drugs, of course. Which he'd fully expected, and of which there were none.

As if he was that stupid!

Feds! he'd thought in disgust. *The fools would help let you smuggle a nuclear bomb into Mexico! All they cared about was cocaine and illegal aliens coming north.*

In retrospect, his tasks had been simple, almost an insult to his talents. Still, there had been any number of times when things might have gone wrong.

The gods of fortune had indeed attended him.

Since they had, he decided a celebration was in order. Instead of heading to his luxury high-rise uptown, he changed direction and drove over to Chinatown. How better to celebrate than by paying Emerald Chang's establishment a visit?

The instant Sonny was shown into the sumptuous duplex, he saw the girl he wanted.

She was all of sixteen and delicate as porcelain. Her skin was smooth and still in its first flower of youth, her face was a perfect oval, and she had dark, almond-shaped eyes and lips formed like a tiny bow.

But it was not her looks that had decided him. There was a refreshing shy innocence about her that none of the other girls, however beautiful, could lay claim to.

However, before business could be transacted, there were certain formalities that had to be observed first.

Emerald Chang, resplendent in a gold *chong sam,* greeted him from her rosewood throne. Her ageless face was devoid of expression and she was smoking one of her long thin cigars, but her eyes, surrounded by the furry caterpillar lashes, sized up Sonny shrewdly.

She knew he was here of his own accord, otherwise the old *lung tao* in Hong Kong would have seen fit to inform her of his visit. She also knew what it was Sonny Fong was seeking.

She bade him to sit and clapped her hands sharply. A serving girl brought him tea.

Sonny sipped it politely, then put down his cup and spoke in the Chiuchow dialect. "Your tea has the fragrance of ten thousand flowers, Honored Sister."

Emerald Chang bowed graciously. "You are most kind, though it is not worthy of such an honorable guest."

Sonny hid the beginnings of a smile. During his previous visits Emerald Chang had demanded deference; now that he was the client, she subtly deferred to him.

"Your garden has a beautiful new flower," he observed.

Emerald Chang drew on her cigar and nodded. "Her name is Autumn Moon," she said. "She is the youngest and most precious of all the blooms in my garden."

"Then she is also the least experienced in the secrets of pleasure."

"Which makes her all the more valuable," Emerald Chang replied. "Youth is but a fleeting treasure. A gift such as hers can be savored but rarely."

"Perhaps so," Sonny said. "But the gift of which you speak is the gift which can be savored but once."

Emerald Chang inclined her head. What he said was true. Autumn Moon was no longer a virgin; a connoisseur had paid twenty-five thousand dollars for the privilege of deflowering her.

Keeping her face neutral, she tried to gauge how much Sonny might be willing to spend. "Autumn Moon's jade gate was unlocked only several days ago. So fresh a bud must not be forced into full bloom. She must be allowed to flower slowly, lest she wither on the vine."

"For that and other reasons, I am prepared to be generous," Sonny said formally. "For the youth and high regard in which you hold her, I am prepared to pay two thousand dollars."

He slipped a thick envelope from his breast pocket and counted out twenty one-hundred-dollar bills. Emerald Chang drew on her cigar and watched as he placed them in two neat stacks on the banquette beside him.

"And to compensate you for the loss of any innocence I might cause her, I offer a further two thousand dollars."

He counted out the bills and put down two more stacks.

Now a gasp rose from the girls seated at the far end of the room. Autumn Moon, however, sat silently in their midst, eyes cast down in seemly modesty. But Emerald Chang's eyes glittered like jet beads within the furry, caterpillar lashes.

"And, merely to show my appreciation for the beauty you cultivate in your garden, Honored Sister, I will give"—with a dramatist's instinct, Sonny paused and counted out yet two thousand dollars more, which he also placed on the banquette—"an additional two thousand dollars," he said, rising to his feet. "Six thousand dollars. For just two hours of her time."

The other girls sprang up and surrounded Autumn Moon in a circle. They were chattering excitedly. Not one among them could remember such largesse, at least not since the nights their jade gates had first been broached.

Emerald Chang pushed herself to her feet and clapped her hands. "Autumn Moon, take our honorable guest to the Dragon Suite."

They all knew that this particular suite was rarely used. It was reserved for very special occasions and only a handful of the most highly esteemed and select of clients.

Then, turning to Sonny, Emerald Chang bowed graciously. "You have brought great honor to my house. You will always be welcome here."

He bowed politely in return. "The honor is all mine, Esteemed Sister."

The other girls eyed Autumn Moon covetously as she escorted Sonny from the room.

Emerald Chang nodded to herself in approval. *The old* lung tao *would be pleased,* she thought. *His young cousin has shown himself to be a man of great standing.*

For through his generosity, Sonny Fong had gained immense face for them all:

For herself.

For her establishment.

For Autumn Moon.

For the old *lung tao.*

And above all, for Sonny himself.

All in all, it was six thousand dollars well spent—a small price to pay for so many dividends.

Emerald Chang sat back down and smoked her cigar thoughtfully. The young man was probably more clever than she had credited him with being. And more ambitious than the *lung tao* feared.

By the time Sonny got home, daylight was fading. The rain had stopped, and Manhattan, scrubbed and scoured, glittered like some vertical, earthbound constellation.

He parked in his usual slot in the underground garage, retrieved his suitcase and garment bag from the trunk, and boarded the elevator. He punched the button marked 36.

The doors sighed shut and the elevator rose swiftly.

Sonny was feeling good. He had left Madame Chang's six thousand dollars poorer, but the esteem it had purchased him was priceless.

He was also satiated. What Autumn Moon had lacked in skill, she more than made up for in compliance. Three times he had impaled her with his jade stick, and three times he had filled her with his torrent.

The recent activities lingered freshly on his memory's palate.

I chose well, he thought, the lean, ruthless planes of his face as merciless as the cruelty shining in his eyes. *I chose very well. Autumn Moon did things any experienced girl would have refused.*

For what excited Sonny Fong was not sex. His aphrodisiac was corruption. Specifically, the corruption of any vestige of innocence and illusions Autumn Moon might have harbored.

And these he had systematically set out to shatter.

And how easily he had accomplished that! All it had required were a few simple commands . . . whispered almost lovingly, as though they were endearments . . . and thus she had been forced to debase herself by performing the repellent, the disgusting, the unspeakable.

Yet she had obliged without complaint. Nor, he was certain, would she complain. Face would not permit. After the generosity he had shown, voicing a grievance would only bring shame on herself and the house of Madame Chang.

One thing's for sure, Sonny thought. *Autumn Moon's never going to forget me. Every time a customer looks at her, fear and disgust will flash through her head. And all because I put it there.*

He smiled to himself. Ah, corruption. In corruption was fear. And loathing. And power. Above all, power.

The next time I celebrate, he promised himself, *I'll treat myself to the gift that can be savored but once.*

Yes. To degrade a virgin prostitute, and sour her to sex from the very first, would be worth almost any price.

The elevator slowed and stopped on his floor. The doors slid open. Sonny stepped out and went down the corridor to his apartment.

Once inside, he flicked a wall switch in the foyer. Soft pools of light sprang on throughout the apartment. He parked his suitcase and garment bag by the front door.

Unpacking could wait.

Loosening his tie, he strode through the expensively furnished, agreeably sparse living room, past long, sleek black leather couches, to the wall of windows and its million-dollar view.

But the dazzling Manhattanscape did not register. City lights were not on Sonny's mind as he headed to the desk facing the windows, on which his Packard Bell computer hummed ever so quietly.

Remaining standing, he clicked on the monitor, and with one finger tapped in his password on the keyboard.

First, he checked his E-mail. Nothing noteworthy there.

Next, he took a look at the faxes. Two had come in, nothing of interest there either.

Then he pulled out his sleek chrome and leather desk chair, and sat down and quickly typed out an E-mail message:

Greetings, most honorable fifth cousin twice removed . . .

He summed up the success of his mission in Mexico. When he was finished, he concluded with the traditional closure:

May the gods of fortune attend you. Your dutiful fifth cousin twice removed.

Sonny converted the words into code, then accessed the Internet and sent it to Hong Kong via the usual convoluted, untraceable maze of routes and reroutes.

37

Gloria Winslow's limousine was so hushed and smooth it seemed to float on a cushion of air. Indeed, if she hadn't been looking out the windows she'd hardly have noticed that they were already on the off ramp at the Black Mountain–Hayne Road exit.

No, that was stretching it, she thought, the corners of her mouth mimicking her displeasure. In fact, it was stretching it a lot.

The truth was, she knew every mile, every curve, every bump of this loathsome drive; had it memorized to the point where she could have pinpointed her exact location blindfolded.

A familiar tightness suddenly swelled her throat. Damn. It never failed. This turnoff did it every time.

Slumping back into her seat, Gloria shut her eyes against the passing scenery as the limousine turned left and surged north along Skyline Boulevard. The familiarity of these surroundings grated, provoked memory's video to replay too many other such trips, none of them pleasant.

Lunching with Althea in town was punishing enough. But driving down here, to snooty Hillsborough and that monstrosity of an estate that, in the time-honored tradition of the ego-driven robber barons, the first Huntington Netherland Winslow had built to reflect his glory—and blatantly remind everyone else of their lower, more worthless stations in life—was sheer torture.

But what really rankled was the way the old lady managed to fill each of the hundred-odd rooms with her presence. As if the mansion and its surroundings somehow magnified the potent brew of wealth, power, and position that pumped through Althea's veins.

Eyes still shut, Gloria felt the big car slow, make a right turn, then roll to a brief stop.

293

The tightness inside her ratcheted up a notch. She didn't have to open her eyes to know where she was. She could see it even with her eyes closed. The big main gate with its piers surmounted by majestic stone lions.

And beyond it, another world.

Cascades. Rival of Biltmore, San Simeon, and Marble House. But with one notable exception. It was still in private hands. The great un-washed public had yet to tromp through its manicured gardens and trea-sure-filled halls. Nor would they, so long as Althea was alive.

There was a sour kind of smile on Gloria's lips as she thought about the name. Cascades. Fitting for the turn of the century, perhaps, when the quarter mile of cascading pools for which it had been named could spout and guzzle water with conspicuous impunity. But times had changed, and the cascades were dry. California's chronic water shortage had seen to that.

The limousine began to creep forward. The electronic eye of the vid-eocamera had granted access. Gloria could visualize the gate sweeping open left and right.

A quarter of a mile ahead, at the end of a shady, sun-dappled allée of copper beeches, was the House.

Only outsiders called it by its name. Within the family and its highly select orbit of the very rich and famous, it was always referred to as "the House." Never Cascades, or the Mansion, or the Big House, but simply "the House"—as if the use of that term brushed aside all other houses as beneath contempt.

The drive was white gravel, and popped gently beneath the tires. As one approached, the House grew steadily in size until the car finally surged out from under the tunnel of beeches and swerved neatly around the circular drive with the huge dry fountain in its center.

Gloria sighed and opened her eyes. As usual, the drive was empty of other vehicles. That was par for the course. Althea insisted that all cars be promptly garaged, as if their presence were an unforgivable blight, and might somehow taint the House.

Gloria's chauffeur got out, came around, and opened the rear door. She glanced up at his outstretched hand and ignored it. She didn't need his help getting out. Hell, no. For once, she was stone cold sober. Well, not Breathalyzer sober, but as sober as she'd been in years.

She had Christos to thank for that. Since meeting him, she hadn't needed to drink nearly as much. Just a maintenance shot every now and then . . .

Stepping out of the car, Gloria paused to take in the House. It was amazingly symmetrical. Like a drawing you could fold exactly in half.

The limestone walls were voluptuously carved, a blowzy riot of Second Empire quoins, pediments, and cartouches. All crowned by a hipped mansard roof and acres of verdigris copper, elaborate dormers, and fanciful chimneys. Grandiose stone steps curved up to the main entrance, and pedestaled urns overflowing with fuchsias lined the balustraded front terrace.

It was the kind of place only pre-income-tax dollars could have built. And only someone beyond ordinary wealth, like Althea Magdalena Netherland Winslow, could afford to maintain it.

Gloria squared her shoulders, then marched briskly up the wide, sweeping stone steps. To her, the House had never presented a blank facade. On the contrary. Even after all these years, she still couldn't throw the impression that its French doors and windows were like so many hooded eyes constantly on the alert for any transgressions she might commit.

Of course, she knew it was ridiculous. But she couldn't help it. It was just one of those things.

Before she could push the chimes, the great front door opened and a different butler from the one in town greeted her respectfully.

"Mrs. Winslow," he murmured, in appropriately sepulchral tones. Ushering her in, he shut the door soundlessly behind her. "Mrs. Althea is expecting you. She's in the rose garden."

Gloria employed a smile. "Thank you, Withams. I can find my own way."

"Very well, madam. I'm told lunch shall be al fresco . . ."

He cleared his throat in that discreet way that only the very best trained butlers seem to know exactly how to employ.

"If you'd like to freshen up a bit first . . . ?"

Gloria instantly warmed to his suggestion. "Why, what a marvelous idea! Yes, Withams. I believe I'll do just that!"

And changing directions, she sailed across the vast reception hall and made a beeline for the powder room door, set between a pair of monumental, ormolu-mounted commodes, not noticing the matched William Kent mirrors that had cost a king's ransom, blind to the two little Canalettos of Venice resting on tabletop easels. Althea's latest acquisitions made absolutely no impression on Gloria as she hurried into the powder room and swiftly locked the door. She had a far more pressing matter at hand.

Like getting out her flask. Unscrewing the lid. Throwing back her head and taking a long, thirsty swig.

The muscles of her long, thin neck worked overtime to swallow, so ferocious was her need. She could feel her trusty old friend, vodka, that magic elixir to oblivion, burn down the length of her throat. Greedily she drank, more and more—when suddenly it exploded in her stomach like a bomb.

The agony was indescribable. She was literally doubled over and gasping. Beads of sweat popped out on her forehead, and for one long, terrible moment she thought she was going to be sick.

Fighting it, she panted and clenched her teeth. Gripped the marble vanity so fiercely she might have been trying to reduce it to dust.

Oh, Christ! she thought, wrapping an arm around her middle. *Oh, sweet baby Jesus! I'm really going to have to start watching it.*

But that was easier said than done, and no one knew that better than Gloria. The trouble was, she had no way of gauging how much it was going to take to numb her against reality—the least little sip or the whole damn bottle.

With shaking fingers she struggled to screw the cap back on the flask. Now the very touch of the container was enough to bring on another wave of nausea. Swiftly she thrust it back in her purse, out of sight and—

Blink!

The sick feeling was gone and the edges of reality blurred.

Ah, surcease . . . sweet, sweet surcease, she thought, eyeing herself in the giltwood mirror as she dabbed moisture from her brow with a cotton ball.

What a difference a drink makes.

The narcotizing effect didn't make visiting Toad Hall a picnic, exactly. Nothing could do that. However, it did lessen the unpleasantness; made setting foot here infinitely less painful. Marginally bearable even. But most important, it imbued her with courage and lent her an aura of supreme confidence.

She thought: *At least now I can face the old dragon—without being eaten alive!*

Gloria waited until the color returned to her face. Then, popping a breath mint in her mouth, she swept grandly out of the powder room. Fortified, self-assured, and game: her heels clicked fearlessly on shiny parquet as she cut through pale, high-ceilinged rooms rich with auction room plunder. Salon, hallway, music room, library. She let herself out through a pair of imposing French doors.

The rear terrace was twice again as broad as the one up front. A formation of lemon standards, heavily laden with fruit, marched decoratively along the balustrade.

But Gloria did not notice the fragrant hybrids. As always, her eye was involuntarily drawn to the gentle incline beyond, where the uphill swath of lawn, plump specimen trees, and clipped topiaries was rent in half, as if through some violent tectonic upheaval, by a dry limestone channel.

But nature had no hand in forming this blight. It was entirely manmade—the erstwhile cascade down which water had once rushed, and for which the House had been so grandiosely named.

Now it was a quarrylike blight, a stony scar that stretched, like a graduated ramp, to the top of the grassy rise.

Closer in, and to either side of the channel, was a parterre as formal as any to be found at a French château. Each was an exacting geometric pattern, with radiating gravel paths and triangular beds planted with floral color, all within a border of perfectly manicured, foot-high hedges.

The one on the left was planted with annuals, the one on the right with roses.

There was Althea. Seated in the very epicenter of the rose parterre some sixty feet distant. As slender, relaxed, and elegantly posed as a portrait by Boldini. Dressed for outdoors in a wide-brimmed straw hat and layered, long, soft green silk.

Everything matched. The jacket with big bold buttons. The even longer silk organza tunic underneath. The very loose, pajamalike pants beneath that. Even her low-heeled shoes. Only Althea's Hermès scarf, loosely knotted, made a palette of color around her neck.

She was facing away from Gloria, seated on that most unusual of wingback armchairs, one of a pair of magnificent overscaled *fauteuils à oreilles*, museum pieces that had never been intended for outdoor use, but which had been carried outside all the same. If she was aware of Gloria's arrival, she didn't let on, but kept stroking Violetta, who was curled on her lap. The other two Pekingese sunned themselves on peach velvet tabourets, as languid and superior as cats. In one of the gravel beds a round, linen-draped table had been laid for two, with a pair of upholstered, beechwood *chaises à la reine.*

Althea was instructing two gardeners. Both wore gloves and wielded wicked-looking shears. As Althea would point, they would snip the selected rose, which had to be at the very peak of its bloom, not a single day more or a single day less. Then it was brought to her and held this way and that so that she might inspect it thoroughly, either approving it with a nod or relegating it to mulch with a flick of her wrist.

Well, here goes, Gloria thought. *Might as well greet the old dragon. See what complaints she's got now.*

Althea sensed Gloria's approach and dismissed the gardeners. One picked up the basket containing the choicest blooms and headed toward the House. The other took the larger basket, obviously throwaways, and lugged it off to the compost pile.

Gloria was still several steps away when Althea turned her head and studied her in one long, sharp-eyed gaze. Her face betrayed neither approval nor disapproval.

"My dear child." Althea turned a cheek to be kissed. "You are almost on time."

Gloria ignored the rebuke. *Thank God I popped into the powder room,* she thought. *Without fortification, I'd never be able to hold my tongue.*

"Hello, Mother Winslow," she said.

"You look different," the old lady observed keenly. "You must be taking better care of yourself."

Gloria let that one slide, too. She was wondering how long she could last before she needed another swig. *Trust a mother-in-law,* she thought wearily. *She'll drive you to drink every time.*

Althea indicated the facing *fauteuil.* "Do sit, my dear."

Gloria obediently sat down. She looked around. "The roses are lovely, Mother Winslow."

"Yes, some of them have turned out rather well," Althea allowed. "Take the pink *Königin von Dänemark* there, and that violet *Cardinal de Richelieu* over there." She gestured. "They are particularly splendid." Then her lips turned down in a frown. "But the *Maiden's Blush* and the white *Madame Hardy* are disappointing this year. And as for these new, repeat-blooming cultivars"—she threw up both hands—"never again! The blooms and fragrance have been sacrificed for sheer quantity. But then, isn't that the way with everything these days? Take apples, for example: so succulent and promising on the outside. So tasteless and mealy on the inside."

Gloria nodded, then frowned. "But isn't it a little early for roses? I thought they only bloomed in summer."

"That's because you're from back East," Althea reminded her crisply. "You forget: out here we have two growing seasons."

"Yes, but I thought that was just for vegetables. And annuals."

"Usually it is." The old lady smiled ever so slightly. "But that's why I have two hothouses—to keep one cold. It permits me to play with the seasons."

How like Althea, Gloria couldn't help thinking. *Fiddling with the climate as if she's God.*

A servant came to inquire if he could get them anything.

"Mineral water," Gloria said, knowing she'd be limited to a single glass of wine. *And I'd better save that for later, when I really need it.*

Just to be perverse, she added sweetly: "Could you make that Apollonaris, by any chance?"

"I'm sorry, ma'am. There's Perrier, San Pellegrino, Evian, Naya, Calistoga, and club soda."

"Pellegrino, then."

"And I'll have wine, Henry," Althea said. "Mondavi Cabernet. The '91 Reserve to go with lunch."

"Yes, ma'am."

Gloria opened her purse and took out her gold lighter and brushed gold cigarette case. Then she remembered herself.

"You don't mind, Mother Winslow, do you? Seeing as we're out of doors?"

Althea looked put upon. "Well, I'd really rather you *didn't.*" She sighed. "However, if you must . . ."

"Thanks."

Gloria snapped open the box, took out a cigarette, and clicked her lighter. She drew the smoke deeply into her lungs, tilted her head back, and exhaled an extravagant plume. She took another quick puff and then waved her cigarette hand in the air, as if casting an arcane spell with a swirl of smoke as she indicated the nearby cascades.

"Have you ever thought of having that dug out and filled in?"

Althea looked at her through hooded eyes, then followed her hand to the limestone channel. "As a matter of fact, I have considered it." She nodded. "Yes."

Gloria drew on her cigarette. "But you decided against it?"

The older woman shook her head. "Not at all. As a matter of fact, I didn't make up my mind either way. Neither for demolition, nor against it."

Gloria looked at her. "Now I think you've lost me."

Althea was silent for a moment. "My great-grandfather bought this land," she said, her voice echoing with pride.

Gloria nodded. "I know that."

"He built this house and constructed those cascades. Everything you see on these thousand acres is his legacy. He moved entire hills . . . some say mountains."

Gloria nodded again. "I know that too, Mother Winslow," she said.

The old lady sat erect and regal, a symbol of everything the House, its grounds, and the power of the Winslows stood for. Even Violetta, curled on her lap, took this moment to raise her head, seemingly to mirror her mistress's pride, the silken chin with the overbred underbite jutting out with superior disdain.

Damn dog! Gloria felt the overwhelming urge to strangle the furry bitch. God, but she hated those pekes!

"It's peculiar," Althea murmured, "how those cascades seem to sum up everything that is gone and passé and frivolous." She stared over at them. "Yet at the same time, demolition seems almost . . . well, sacrilegious."

She gave a dry little laugh and drew her eyes back in.

"I'm afraid it's rather difficult to explain," she said.

Gloria nodded silently. It sounded like a lot of hogwash, yet on a strange, subliminal level, she understood perfectly. That was one advantage of coming from a branchless tree. If you couldn't trace your own roots, you had an envious appreciation of those who could.

"It's all about continuity, you see," her mother-in-law continued. "Heritage. Family. History. Who knows?" She shrugged. "Maybe I'm just a sentimental old fool."

Gloria doubted that. Well, sentimental and old, maybe. But a fool? No one would ever mistake Althea for one of those.

The old lady looked at her directly. "I know what you're thinking. That no one would dare call me that." She smiled slightly. "At least, not to my face."

The servant returned carrying a big silver tray. The mineral water and Cabernet were in bottles, the glasses were cut crystal, and the ice was in a separate silver bucket. As the guest, Gloria was served first. Then came the wine-tasting ritual.

"Lovely," Althea pronounced, after savoring the bouquet and lingering, opulent taste. "An excellent vintage. Thank you, Henry."

He left and they sat silently for a few minutes.

"It really is a pity," Althea said wistfully. "When I was a child, the cascades were always flowing. You can't imagine how magical it was. Like something out of a dream."

The old lady took another sip of her wine.

"But that was before Silicon Valley. Before the Bay Area's population explosion. Before the curse of water conservation!"

"Which is not going to go away," Gloria pointed out. "If anything, the chronic water shortage will only get worse."

"As if the same water pumped over and over is such an extravagance! Really. Sometimes I wonder what the world has come to."

"If you miss the cascades so much, why don't you arrange for tankers to come and fill them? That's what they do with swimming pools."

Althea shook her head. "That's out of the question. It would send the wrong message, and could jeopardize Hunt's entire future. As it is, great wealth can be a terrible handicap politically."

Gloria begged to differ, but didn't. She really wasn't in the mood to argue. All she wanted was to get lunch over with, suffer through whatever Althea had summoned her here for, and get the hell back to the city.

Althea was looking at her directly. "Of course, I realize it's all a matter of impressions," she went on. "But then, one mustn't underestimate their importance. Impressions really do count for so much." She smiled brightly. "Don't you agree, my dear?"

Warning bells went off in Gloria's head. *Here comes,* she thought, sipping her water. *No more beating around the bush. We're finally getting to the nitty-gritty.*

Althea's talent for steering a conversation exactly where she wanted never ceased to amaze people. But not Gloria. Nothing her mother-in-law said or did could surprise her any longer. She'd seen it all.

The old lady came right to the point. "While we're on the subject of impressions, there's something important we need to discuss." Her voice was firm but smooth, and implied she would brook no argument. "It pertains to you and my son."

Gloria put a lid on her anger. She didn't know how Althea did it, but the old dragon always managed to put her down. Like referring to Hunt as *"my* son." Making it clear a daughter-in-law was exactly that: an in-law, not a blood relation.

As if I need constant reminding, Gloria thought bitterly.

"What about Hunt and me?" she asked warily.

"Well, it's hardly a secret that things have lately been . . . shall we say, unusually difficult between the two of you?"

Difficult! Gloria scowled at her. *If that wasn't the understatement of all time!*

"But those kinds of problems are only to be expected," Althea said, so indifferently they might have been discussing the weather in some remote part of the world. "What marriage doesn't have its ups and downs?"

"That's just it, Mother Winslow." Gloria's voice small and tight. "Our marriage doesn't *have* any ups! It's *all* downs."

Althea fixed her with those cold, cobalt blue eyes. "Please, dear. Hear me out before you get yourself all worked up. That's not asking for too much, is it?"

Gloria sighed and shifted sulkily in her chair. The opened bottle of wine was in her direct line of vision. She eyed it longingly, thinking: *I could sure use a drink right about now.*

"It's been months now since you and my son have last been seen together in public," Althea said. "It is generating talk. People are starting to speculate. It's time to stop the rumors before they get out of hand."

"I wasn't aware that anyone showed much interest in us."

"Poppycock! You know they do. Family values have become all the rage these days. A wife can be a politician's most valuable asset . . . or his worst liability. If you continue to stay out of the picture, I'll have to presume the worst."

The breeze died down and the sun was suddenly too hot. The scent of roses overwhelmed: too many sweet, intermingled fragrances were making Gloria nauseous. She pressed the cool sweating glass of water against her temple and rolled it slowly back and forth across her forehead.

Althea said: "As you know, Hunt has always run as an Independent candidate. However, that's likely to change in the very near future."

This was news to Gloria. Her husband had always taken great pride in being the gadfly in both the Democrats' and the Republicans' oint-ment. He ran successfully on his own platform and was answerable to no political machine, no business interests, and no lobbyists. He was the *people's* candidate—and proud of it.

"Are you certain?" she asked. Much as she loathed Hunt as a hus-band, she grudgingly admired his political integrity. "Did he tell you that?"

"He didn't have to," Althea said crisply. "I have my own sources. Suffice it to say he'll soon receive an offer he can't refuse."

"I'll believe that when I see it. Mother Winslow, I *know* Hunt. He can't be bought."

"He won't have to be. Both parties are willing to bend over backward. And well they should. All the polls indicate he's the most trusted politician in the state."

Gloria stared at her without speaking.

"Now that you know what's at stake, I'm sure you can understand why it's so imperative you toe the line," Althea continued. "It's essential . . . for my son's future *and* this country's."

Her gaze was so intense that her eyes seemed to bore, like whirring drill bits, straight into Gloria's, and her manner, speech, and expression were cool, powerful, competent, and direct.

She added: "Just so that we understand each other, I'm asking you to make a special effort."

Althea asking *for something?* Gloria very nearly laughed aloud. *That's rich,* she thought. *Althea never asks! She demands—even if her orders are couched in politesse!*

"Aren't you forgetting something, Mother Winslow?" she asked quietly.

"Not that I'm aware of."

Gloria chuckled humorlessly. "Well, the last *I* heard, it takes two to tango."

"Please get to the point, my dear."

Gloria stared sullenly back at her. *God,* she thought, *what I wouldn't give for a drink.*

"The point being, Mother Winslow, shouldn't you be having this conversation with Hunt?"

"I fully intend to. As soon as he returns from Mexico."

So that's where he is. "And you really think he'll listen?"

"Once he grasps the magnitude of the situation, yes," Althea said briskly, "I do. But what I'd like from you is your assurance that you'll at least try to meet him halfway."

Gloria let out a deep sigh. "Even if I do, it won't be of any use." Her voice was harsh. "Hunt can't stand the sight of me!"

"Well, don't you think that could have something to do with your having been . . . ah . . . under the weather for so long?"

"Under the weather!" Gloria chortled. "That's a good one!" She glared angrily. "You want to call me a *drunk,* but you can't bring yourself to say the word, can you?"

"Really, my dear—"

But Gloria wasn't finished. "I'm a *boozer,* Mother Winslow! Your daughter-in-law's a common al-co-*hol*-ic! Can't you *say* it?"

Althea waved off the outburst with an airy hand. "Call yourself what you will. The fact that you're much improved speaks for itself . . . as does this discussion."

"Oh?" Gloria eyed her narrowly. "And how's that?"

Althea looked at her coldly. "If I thought you were such a hopeless case, would I be wasting my time having this talk?"

"Gee, thanks for the vote of confidence!"

"You can take it whichever way you like," the old lady said dryly. "A pat on the back or a kick in the fanny. It's up to you."

A wild, unholy gleam suddenly danced in Gloria's eyes. "Would you care to know the *real* reason why I've been drinking less, Mother Winslow?"

Althea looked away; she really didn't want to hear it.

Gloria leaned forward. "Well, I'll tell you anyway, Mother Winslow! It's because, for the past several months, I *haven't* been pretending to be the adoring, photogenic wife! It's because I *haven't* been pretending to have a handsome, loving husband!" Her lips curled into a sneer. "Hell, I haven't even pretended to have a marriage—*period*!"

Althea's face remained impassive.

Gloria stared at her. "Don't you see, Mother Winslow? For the first time in years I've been totally honest with myself!"

"In my experience," Althea said, "honesty is a matter of . . . degrees. But rather than get into a philosophical debate, why don't we stick to the subject at hand?"

"Like pulling the wool over the public's eye, you mean."

"Call it what you will. However, if you agree to play ball, I can promise you one thing. You won't be sorry."

"In other words, you've already made up your mind that you've hooked me. Is that it?"

"I believe you'll do the sensible thing"—Althea nodded—"yes."

Gloria laughed bitterly. "Tell me something, Mother Winslow. Is there anything, or anyone, you think *can't* be bent to your will?"

Althea looked surprised. "Why, no," she said brightly. "I don't suppose there is!"

Gloria let it go. She should have known. Try as she might, she just couldn't get through. A mile-wide chasm separated her from her mother-in-law, and never the twain would meet.

"Ah!" announced Althea in her best hostess voice. "Here comes lunch."

Gloria turned toward the house. Sure enough. There was Withams, leading two servants carrying domed silver trays across the lawn.

"Why don't we move to the table," Althea suggested smoothly.

She picked up Violetta, rose to her feet, and put the dog back down on the *fauteuil.* Then, in a rare gesture of friendliness, she took Gloria by the arm.

"It should prove to be quite an interesting meal," she confided. "My chef is retiring, and I'm testing a replacement."

"What did you have him make? Boeuf Bourguignonne and baked Alaska?"

"Actually, I asked him to do a roast chicken."

Gloria stared at her. "And that's a *test*?" she snickered. "You can't be serious!"

"Oh, but I am. Did you know that roast chicken, done to just the proper turn, is one of the most difficult of all dishes to get right?"

Gloria didn't, nor could she care less. "I'll have wine with lunch," she said, testing the waters. "That is, if you don't mind?"

Althea patted her arm. "My dear child. So long as it's drunk in moderation, why would I?"

That was sure a turnaround.

She must want my help real badly.

It was an hour and a half later. Althea, in yet another uncharacteristic display of friendliness, walked Gloria to the car. The chauffeur was holding the rear door open, and the three Pekingese obediently stayed on the lawn, daintily sniffing at shrubs. One of them hiked its leg.

"Thanks for the lunch, Mother Winslow. I really enjoyed it," Gloria lied, air-kissing both of the old lady's cheeks.

Althea smiled. "I'm so glad, my dear. We'll do it again sometime soon."

Then the smile disappeared and Althea's face underwent a dramatic change. Gone now was any pretense at conviviality. This was the Althea with whom Gloria was used to dealing.

"You *will* think about what we discussed, won't you, my dear?"

"Of course, Mother Winslow," Gloria said, although her mind was already made up. *It'll be a cold day in hell before Hunt sees my help!*

The old lady seemed to read her mind. "I really would consider it carefully," she urged, dropping her voice so the chauffeur couldn't overhear.

She stared hard into Gloria's eyes.

"I don't ask for many favors. When I do, I tend to reward them generously."

Left unsaid was that the opposite also held true. But then, Althea didn't need to spell that out. Gloria was only too familiar with her mother-in-law's methods. It was stick and carrot all the way.

"Do think about it, my dear."

"Yes, Mother Winslow. I will."

"That's all I ask. Good-bye, my dear."

Gloria started to duck into the car. She was almost inside when she paused and looked back over her shoulder. "Oh, by the way, Mother Winslow. You never did say whether or not you're going to hire the new chef."

Althea frowned slightly. "I don't believe I will." She shook her head. "No."

"But the chicken was delicious!"

"Granted, it was golden brown and crisp on the outside," Althea allowed, "and juicy and buttery on the inside."

"Then what was wrong with it?"

"My dear child, didn't you notice?"

Gloria blinked. *Notice? Notice what?*

"It was slightly overcooked."

"Ah. Of course." Gloria climbed on into the car, thinking, *That's Althea for you. Talk about a chef lucking out!*

"I'll be in touch after I speak to Hunt," Althea said in parting. Then she stepped back so the chauffeur could shut the rear door.

Gloria raised a hand and waved from the other side of the glass. The instant the car was moving, she raided the built-in bar. She didn't bother with a glass, but drank the vodka straight from the heavy crystal decanter.

Some of it dribbled down her chin, but she couldn't care less. Lunch was over, thank God! For a while there, she'd been afraid it might never end.

She took another swig, replaced the decanter, and wiped her chin. Then, picking up the car phone, she punched the by now familiar number.

There was no answer, but the machine picked up on the fourth ring. "Talk to me," Christos's recorded voice said.

Gloria waited for the beep. She said, "It's me, Glo. I've been through the wringer and could use some TLC. I'll be at the usual place within the hour."

Althea remained in the drive and followed the limousine's progress as it crunched around the big dry water fountain. Only once the allèe of copper beeches swallowed it in its maw did she make her way back toward the House, her three Pekingese underfoot.

There, she thought. *Gloria's gotten the message loud and clear.* Hopefully her daughter-in-law would act accordingly. *If she doesn't, I'll just have to apply more pressure.*

Althea hoped it wouldn't come to that. But if it did, she was ready.

38

Lunchtime on the beach at Huatulco.

Dorothy-Anne had a table under the thatched-roofed *palapas* at water's edge, but she drew no enjoyment or satisfaction from the splendid view. Reality, in the form of the previous night's occupancy reports, which had been faxed to her from White Plains, had popped the insular bubble of her earlier sense of well-being.

She felt leaden, drained, *numb*. The bounce with which she'd awakened had deserted her. Even the beachfront table and the perfection of the cloudless sky could not lift her sagging spirits. Everywhere she looked, her experienced hotelier's gaze found reason to be depressed.

Like an evacuated vacation spot in the path of an approaching hurricane, the great crescent-shaped bay around the Hale Hotel and Resort was dishearteningly lifeless. There were only two windsurfers skimming the bright blue waves and a half dozen swimmers in the crystal clear water. The number of sun worshipers soaking up the rays could be counted on both hands. In the distance, a single speedboat pulled a lone water-skier across the vast bay.

The turnout wasn't much better at the beachfront dining area. Unoccupied tables outnumbered the occupied ones three to one.

A grim legacy of the bacterial outbreak.

This joint is definitely not jumping, Dorothy-Anne thought gloomily, dipping a finger in her glass of iced tea and stirring the cubes despondently. *If it gets any less lively, it'll become a ghost resort.*

"Mind if I join you?"

Dorothy-Anne looked up. Venetia was wearing a white tube top and white linen trousers. Plus big, white, plastic-rimmed Jackie O. sunglasses and heeled white sandals. She had a local straw tote slung over one bare shoulder.

"Make yourself comfortable," Dorothy-Anne invited. "I can use the diversion."

She licked iced tea off her finger and glanced around broodingly.

"You can amuse me . . . help take my mind off the lack of customers."

"Honey, that is one tall order. But you know me. If there's a challenge, this girl is up to it!"

Venetia pulled out a chair, flung her straw bag across the back, and folded her elongated body onto the seat. As usual, her every movement had a regal, unstudied, and wholly unself-conscious grace.

"So," she said cheerfully. "What's up?"

"You mean, what *isn't*," Dorothy-Anne growled. "And, since you're so damn chipper, I'd like to hear your spin on this turnout. Hmmmmm?"

She fell silent as an exceptionally handsome, exceptionally young, dark-haired waiter came to take Venetia's order.

"Hel-*lo*-oh! And who is *this*?" Venetia murmured, very slowly pulling down her shades and looking up over the tops of the frames at him. "Do you think he's of statutory age?"

"Oh, stop," Dorothy-Anne said, a trifle impatient. "Since when have you started robbing the cradle? Anyway, I thought you liked older men."

"Girl, what can I tell you? Tastes change."

"*Señorita?*" the waiter asked. "Would you like something?"

Venetia sighed. "Child, what I would *like* and what I can *get* are two entirely different things."

He looked puzzled. "*Señorita?*"

"I'll have a martini," Venetia said. Then, remembering she was in the land of tequila, she changed her mind. "On second thought, scratch that. Make it a margarita. With tons of salt."

"Salt!" Dorothy-Anne exclaimed. "I thought you'd cut down on your sodium intake!"

"Girl, will you hush? You're making me sound old! Besides, a margarita without salt is like"—Venetia grinned wickedly—"sex without orgasm," she whispered, with a giggle. "It just wouldn't be a margarita."

"No, I don't suppose it would."

Venetia pushed her glasses atop her head like a tiara, the better to eyeball the waiter as he left. She cocked her head to one side.

"Now, are those cute buns? Or are those cute buns?"

"Oh, Christ!" Dorothy-Anne muttered irritably, fighting the urge to grab Venetia and give her a good shake. "Just when I need a sympathetic ear, not to mention a professional colleague, what do I have to put up with? 'Buns'!"

"Heyyyyy! Don't lose your sense of humor. Baby, what's wrong?"

Dorothy-Anne stared at her in outrage. "What's wrong? You have to ask, what's *wrong!* Look around you! This place is what's wrong! It's usually so packed you have to make reservations the day before. *Now* look at it!"

"Salmonella will do it every time," Venetia said dryly.

"Tell me something I don't already know."

Venetia eyed her severely. "Honey, will you chill out? It is time you looked on the bright side."

"Th-the bright side!" Dorothy-Anne sputtered. She shook her head incredulously. "My God! You've got to be kidding."

"No, child. I am serious. The reason I popped by was to bring tidings of great joy."

"Yeah," Dorothy-Anne said morosely. "Sure. Go ahead. Make my day."

"I aim to. Girl, get this action. Right before coming down here, I just got off the phone with White Plains. And guess what?"

"The other shoe dropped?"

"It most certainly did not!" Venetia sniffed, pretending affront. Then she leaned forward across the table and grinned. "But what *has* happened is—are you ready? Cancellations have begun to slow. Baby, you heard correctly, but I shall repeat it anyway, just so you can read my lips. The cancellations are *slooooowing.* You wait and see. Another couple of days, and business will be booming."

"Here's hoping. Our cash flow wasn't all that great before this happened. But if things get any worse . . ."

Dorothy-Anne bit down on her lip. She didn't need to complete the sentence. The Hale Companies' debt load was a threatening, looming cloud shadowing even the most trivial of their daily triumphs.

"I hear you, honey," Venetia said gently. "But believe me"—she leaned forward and tapped a confident finger on the table—"by tomorrow, this outbreak will be yesterday's news."

"Not to the people who were stricken," Dorothy-Anne retorted grimly.

"No," Venetia sighed, "not to them."

"And certainly not to the guest who died—*or* his family."

"True. But the important thing to remember is that you have done everything you could—and more—to rectify a tragic situation. Ah. Here comes Cute Buns with my drink."

Dorothy-Anne, forced to endure Venetia's lapse into girlish adolescence, rolled her eyes heavenward. Was there anything, she wondered disgustedly, anything under the sun more ludicrous than a mature woman going all fluttery in the presence of a young man still in his teens? Really, there ought to be a law . . .

"*Señorita.*" The waiter flashed his pearly whites as he set the margarita down with a flourish.

"*Muchos gracias,*" Venetia said dreamily. "*Gracias, gracias, gracias.*"

"*De nada,*" he said. The black, innocent eyes shone in his lean, dark-complexioned face with rich and yet-unmined promises.

Venetia watched him leave. *He certainly has all the right things in all the right places,* she was thinking. *And he's treading time waiting on tables down here.*

Offhand, she could think of half a dozen men's fashion editors and stylists who would jump at the opportunity of signing him on.

Which isn't exactly a bad way to break the ice, she considered. *No, not bad at all . . .*

She picked up the glass, took a little sip, and put it back down.

"Yummy." She licked salt off her upper lip. "Nothing like a good margarita." Then, adjusting her facial muscles into an expression of appropriate solemnity, she said: "Anyway, before Cute Buns there gets me totally distracted, there is one other significant item of good news."

Dorothy-Anne looked at her askance. "And what might that be?"

Venetia seemed surprised that she had to ask. "Why, the response to your press conference. What else?"

Dorothy-Anne flicked a derisive wrist. "A highly unpleasant but necessary evil."

"Perhaps. But baby, let me tell *you.* The feedback has been nothing short of phenomenal. Yes." Venetia rapped her knuckles on the table. "Phe-nom-en-*al!*" She underscored each syllable with a rap.

"And how, might I ask, did you jump to that conclusion?"

"The usual way. We did an opinion poll."

"Polls! I should have guessed."

"Hey, don't knock them. The public perception is that you have bent over backward. Honey, no one is blaming *you* for the outbreak."

"Why, isn't that *nice!*" Dorothy-Anne said sharply. "It makes *all* the difference!" She shook her head in disbelief. "My God!" Her voice was so incredulous it descended a full octave. "As if I'm worried about blame! Venetia! I voluntarily shouldered responsibility!"

"I know, baby, but—"

"And that aside, there's still the unresolved matter of our reputation. It's been irreparably damaged—"

"Not irreparably." Venetia shook her head firmly. "There I beg to differ."

"Oh?" Clouds of suspicion, an obvious dimming of faceted aquamarines, shadowed Dorothy-Anne's eyes. "How so?"

"From the feedback I have gotten, you can forget worrying about our reputation. Don't get me wrong. I am not saying our reputation *hasn't* been . . . well, not compromised, exactly, but . . . let's say tarnished a little. Because it *has* been. But, girl, that is only temporary. A bit of spit here, and a touch of polish there, and we'll be right back where we were. On *top!*"

"Aren't you forgetting something?"

Venetia's smooth forehead furrowed. "Like what?"

"Like tour operators and travel agents. They have long memories."

"So?"

"So, in the future, they're going to think twice about booking people with us."

Venetia tossed her head, her dark eyes glinting. "Not necessarily," she said, the corners of her lips forming a Cheshire smile.

"Oh? And what makes you say that?" Dorothy-Anne sipped some iced tea. It was just the way she liked it. Refreshingly cool, not too sweet, and heavy on the mint.

"Because," Venetia said smugly. "I haven't lost sight of what drives them."

"Ah," Dorothy-Anne murmured, setting the tumbler back down. "Commissions."

"Uh-*huh!* And girl? Trust me. When it comes to chasing a buck, travel agents and tour operators are second only to used-car dealers!"

"In other words, you're suggesting we raise their commissions."

Venetia's smile broadened. "That's right, honey. It's the one sure-fire bet to bring on communal memory loss—*and* have them fighting to throw business our way!"

She paused to scrutinize Dorothy-Anne's reaction. "Well? What do you think?"

Dorothy-Anne was staring at her. "What do I think? Venetia darling, I'm thinking that you're either shrewd, devious, or eerily clairvoyant . . . I'm still not exactly sure which."

"My God!" Venetia shook her head admiringly. "You came up with the same idea! Now, why am I surprised?"

Dorothy-Anne smiled sourly. "A strategy I wish could be attributed to great minds and all that. However, in this instance, I'm afraid it's necessity—not to mention desperation—being the mother of invention. When you're cornered, there aren't a whole lot of options open to you."

"No, I don't suppose there are," Venetia murmured, the brightness fading from her face.

She gazed past Dorothy-Anne to the lush, nearly vertical hillside where the open-air rooms were tucked, hidden from view by thick tropical foliage. Only the silver sheets of water dropping from one cantilevered pool down to the next marked their locations. A breeze stirred the giant, Rousseau-like leaves and shifted the sun-dappled shadows; activity on one of the terraces startled a flock of parrots. Screeching, they took wing in a dazzling burst of color. She noticed the thatch-roofed funicular beginning its slow descent down the hillside. Electrically powered, and therefore silent, it didn't make a sound.

She pulled her gaze back in. "What about figures?" she asked. "Do you have a specific commission raise in mind?"

Dorothy-Anne shook her head. "Not yet. I wanted to get your input first. What about you?"

Venetia exhaled a deep sigh. "Child, let me tell you. This is one area where this girl is *stumped*. Raising the commissions will cost us, and the tour groups we handle are already steeply discounted. Our profit margin averages . . . what? Around eight percent?"

Dorothy-Anne nodded her head. "Somewhere in that vicinity. Obviously, it depends on various factors." She ticked them off on her fingers. "Volume. Availability. Locale. How early a tour is booked . . ." She held up her hands. "These all directly affect the bottom line. But I'm not telling you anything you don't already know."

"And eight percent severely restricts our generosity," Venetia pointed out in a murmur.

"I can't argue with that," Dorothy-Anne said, her voice almost emotionless. "Whether by hook or by crook, we have to jump-start our recovery, and fast. The only way to do that is to get our vacancy rate below twenty-two percent. That's our break-even point. Otherwise . . ."

"Don't tell me," Venetia said gloomily. "We're in deep shit."

"What it all boils down to is volume," Dorothy-Anne said. "And there's the catch-22. The more rooms we can fill, the more generous we can be with commissions. Likewise, the more generous we are with commissions, the more rooms we have to fill."

"A quarter of a percent?" asked Venetia, testing the waters. "Would that be enough?"

"For short-circuiting long memories?" Dorothy-Anne laughed. "My God! We can't afford to be cheapskates, not if we want customers in droves. I'd say the *minimum* would be a full percentage point. Ideally, it would be two."

"*That* much! Honey, aren't you going a bit overboard?"

"Am I?" Dorothy-Anne's voice was soft. "Venetia, we're fighting for our future. Our very existence is at stake! Or hasn't that sunk in yet?"

"Believe me, baby, it has. Like a ton of bricks." Venetia, in the process of lifting the margarita to her mouth, suddenly froze, the glass halfway to her lips. Behind Dorothy-Anne, the funicular had reached the bottom of the hill, and she'd caught sight of a single passenger stepping off.

Can it be? Venetia wondered. *Or are my eyes playing tricks on me?* For if they weren't, she could swear that the man who'd gotten off was— could it be?—was it her imagination?—no—*Hunt Winslow!*

"What's the matter?" Dorothy-Anne looked concerned. "Darling, you look as if you've seen a ghost."

Venetia didn't look at her. "Child," she murmured, "you haven't, by any chance, been holding out on me? Have you?"

"About what?"

But Venetia didn't reply. She raised a slender arm and waved until she caught the new arrival's attention.

Hunt's face registered his reaction, a reaction that, like Venetia's, began as stunned disbelief, changed to incredulous surprise, and finally radiated pure, unaffected pleasure.

"Venetia!" Dorothy-Anne cried, starting to turn around.

But Venetia reached out, caught her by the arm, and applied pressure. "Girl!" she spat out of the corner of her smiling mouth, "will you stop being so obvious? Just stay put and play it cool. I want to see the cheeriest, sunniest smile you can muster. C'mon, now," she cajoled. "Say 'Cheese.'"

Cheese?

Dorothy-Anne glared at her. "I will do no such thing!" she huffed, prickly with dignity. "I want to know what the hell is going on, or so help me God, I'm warning you, Venetia, I . . . I won't be responsible for my actions!"

"Then don't be," Venetia said with a shrug. "It's no skin off my back. Because baby, this girl is making herself *scarce.*"

With that, Venetia gulped her margarita, valiantly stifled a burp, and collected her tote. She pushed back her chair and popped to her feet.

"Arrivederci," she grinned. "Baby, I'm outta here."

That did it. Despite her irritation, Dorothy-Anne's curiosity got the better of her. She twisted around in her seat, scanned the dining area.

Empty tables, a smattering of diners, a man who vaguely resembled Hunt Winslow . . .

She dismissed the resemblance out of hand, started to turn back around, then did a classic double take.

Holy Moses.

No vague resemblance—the real McCoy!

Dear God in heaven. Hunt! In the flesh! Bearing down on her—him, that outrageously tall, beautiful male specimen.

A whimper surfaced from deep within Dorothy-Anne's chest. "Hunt?" she squeaked, her voice so disbelieving it trailed into thin air.

She glanced up at Venetia with suddenly panicked eyes.

"Hunt . . . *Winslow?*"

"Uh-huh, baby," Venetia confirmed. "The one and only!"

Dorothy-Anne watched, trembling, as he made a graceful beeline toward her with that easy familiarity, every step of that unmistakable, self-confident stride expressing urgency of purpose. And, while he might have been oblivious to the sensation he created, she was all too aware of the heads craning in his direction.

The closer he came, the bigger he seemed to get, until he filled her vision entirely. At least, that was the impression from where she was sitting.

"Venetia!" Dorothy-Anne wailed in distress. "You can't leave me alone with him!"

"Oh no?" Venetia's smile lengthened. "Just watch me."

"And where are you off to when I need you most?"

"I," Venetia said loftily, shouldering her straw bag and pulling her glasses down over her eyes, "am about to do my public service."

"Say that again?"

"Well, what else would you call broadening a sheltered young man's horizons?"

"Oh, Christ," Dorothy-Anne said in disgust. "I should have known. Go."

She flicked her hands.

"Go. Rob the cradle."

"I fully intend to." Venetia punctuated her smile with a slight lift of her eyebrows. "Just remember, honey. Be sure and do everything I would do!"

And with a waggle of her fingers, off she sailed, leaving Dorothy-Anne to fend for herself.

Dorothy-Anne threw a glare at Venetia's receding back. It glanced off harmlessly, and she sat there, resting her chin on her hand. Brooding.

Not fifteen feet away, Venetia slowed as she intercepted Hunt. "She's all yours, baby," she crooned, playfully goosing his arm. "But take care. She's still very fragile."

She tilted her head forward, the better to level serious eyes at him over the tops of her shades. Wordlessly warning him that if he hurt Dorothy-Anne he'd have her, Venetia, to contend with.

He read her loud and clear. "You don't have to worry," he assured her.

Venetia nodded. "You're a good man, Charlie Brown." Then, turning her head, she tossed Dorothy-Anne a blazing smile over her shoulder. *Enjoy!* she mouthed wordlessly.

And made herself scarce.

Enjoy! Dorothy-Anne grumped crossly to herself. She scowled. *What's to enjoy about being left in the lurch?*

Hunt swiftly closed the distance between them. He stopped when he reached the table, and stood there, staring down at her.

She had a curious sensation of shrinkage, of the rest of the world dwindling to nothing. As if the two of them were the only people on the planet.

She and Hunt.

Hunt Winslow.

Her heart was pounding wildly, knocking seismically against her rib cage. It seemed her sternum must surely crack under the repeated impacts.

And what of *him*? What about Hunt?

Could he be unaware of her sudden shortness of breath, her skyrocketing body temperature, the telltale flush that shot up her face as blatantly as the indicator on a thermometer?

How could he not be? His mere proximity did things to her, dammit! Made her feel things she wasn't ready to feel.

Guiltily she flashed back to the ballroom of the San Francisco Palace. Back to what she thought of as *Before*.

Even now, after all this time and after all that had happened, she could still remember Governor Randle's jovial words. Verbatim.

"*Careful about Hunt here, Ms. Cantwell. . . . He's our ladykiller-about-state.*"

Oh yes, she remembered it perfectly. Just as she remembered the orchestra launching into "I Left My Heart in San Francisco." To which she and Hunt had danced cheek-to-cheek—even as, unknown to her, Freddie's body had lain amid the wreckage on that blizzard-lashed mountainside in Colorado.

The mental image sent a shiver down her spine.

I didn't know! If I had, I'd never have flirted with Hunt. She wished she could shed the guilt. *Dear God, is it going to weigh on me forever? Is that what I deserve?* She really didn't know.

"Dorothy-Anne," Hunt said softly.

"Hunt," she whispered back, feeling at a disadvantage by remaining seated.

"Do you mind if I join you?" he asked, bowing his head ever so slightly.

She sighed inwardly. As if she could refuse.

"Please," she said politely. She indicated the chair Venetia had vacated, wishing she had the bad manners and, above all, the willpower, to send him away.

Unfortunately, she had neither.

She stared down into her iced tea. When she raised her eyes again he was seated across from her, his warm smile tempered by a shadow of pain. So he was slightly discomfited too, was he? She remembered his wife and the scene she had created.

What a pair we are! she thought. *He saddled with a drunk and I with a ghost.* Did he realize how irresistible and disarming that hint of tragedy made him? How it caused her to want to reach out and—

No. She mustn't think that way. She mustn't think that way at all.

"I was just about to order lunch," she said, using etiquette to cover her disconcerting sense of unease. "Which do you prefer? Fish, rabbit in adobe, or authentic hot and spicy?"

39

*L*ater.
  After the appetizer, which was mesquite-grilled shrimp, and during the main course, which the waiter served with much fuss, Dorothy-Anne told Hunt, "Everyone has an ego, and God knows, I'm no exception."

She moved forkfuls of spicy *huachinango a la Veracruzana* around on her plate. Other appetites, which had nothing to do with food, had relegated eating to the back burner of her priorities.

"However," she continued, "I won't flatter myself into thinking you're here because of me. I'm not that egocentric. So out with it, Hunt Winslow. Just what *are* you doing here?"

Hunt tested his *quesillo,* a uniquely Oaxacan specialty consisting of fiery local chiles stuffed with stringy cheese. "Very goo—" he began, and then the chiles hit.

His eyes bulged.

He dropped his fork with a clatter.

And swiftly washed the chiles down with a mouthful of beer.

"Hot, hot, hot!" he gasped, furiously fanning his mouth with one hand.

His throat was on fire and his vision was swimming.

"My *God!* What was that—napalm? I think it got rid of my sinuses for good!"

"And probably sprouted some more hair on your chest," Dorothy-Anne said unrepentantly. "But don't worry. Ask any woman: no man can have a furry enough chest. Besides, you asked for it."

"I asked for hot," he objected hoarsely, taking another quick swig of beer. "I didn't ask for lighter fluid."

He added, looking wounded: "You could have warned me, you know."

"What do you think I meant when I said, 'authentic hot and spicy'?" she demanded, watching him polish off a tall glass of ice water.

His eyes were still streaming tears, and he looked so comical and boyishly miserable that she had to laugh, a laugh that came from deep down inside, a laugh so spontaneous that it changed the serious, tragedy-mauled businesswoman into a sunny, fun-loving young Holly Golightly.

"What's so funny?" he growled, crunching an ice cube between his teeth. It was all he could do to hide the joy he felt at hearing her laugh.

"Oh, just you. There's nothing like seeing a grown man cry. Men can be such babies. Anyway," she said solemnly, taking pity on him and switching plates, "here. Try mine. I'm really not very hungry."

He eyed her plate with suspicion, sniffed it with little twitches of his nose, and then flicked a glance at her. "What is it?"

"Red snapper. And stop looking like that. It's spicy, but modified for the north of the border palate."

She paused, gazing at him from under half-lowered lashes. "Well?" she asked.

He was giving the fish little prods with his fork. "Well what?"

"You still haven't answered my question."

"Sorry. I didn't realize you'd asked one."

Her laughter was gone and she had reverted to her serious mode. "What brought you to these parts?" she asked softly.

"Why?" He looked at her. "Does my presence strike you as that unusual?"

"As a matter of fact," she nodded, "yes. It does. I mean, this isn't exactly Madison Avenue or the Georges Cinq."

"No," he agreed, "it isn't."

"Huatulco," she went on, "is not on the beaten track. It's definitely not the sort of place one accidentally bumps into friends or acquaintances. At least, it won't be for some years to come."

"Actually," he said, taking a very cautious, and very tiny nibble of red snapper, "I'm here on business."

"Ah. Don't tell me; let me guess. Courting future constituents . . . the illegal alien vote?"

But her dry humor went right over his head. Hunt was too preoccupied with enjoying the red snapper. His taste buds were singing. It was everything a freshly caught fish should be—and then some. Crisp on the outside and flaky and moist on the inside, with a sauteed topping concocted by a toqued Picasso.

"Now, this is more like it!" he enthused.

And Dorothy-Anne, forgetting that the way to a man's heart is through his stomach, rested her chin on her hand and watched him eat.

It's so easy, she thought. *So damn easy! Two minutes with him, and I feel as if I've known him a lifetime. Could it be we were meant for one another?*

It occurred to her it was time to rein in her emotions. Around him, they tended to shoot into the stratosphere.

I must not get carried away, she warned herself firmly. *I have to stop fantasizing. I've got to draw a line and not cross it.*

It was a vow, a goal, her very, very best of good intentions. But even as she resolved to back away, she found herself helpless in the tidal pull of his enchantment.

Why was it that everything about him—even the simplest and most mundane of everyday functions such as eating—took on a kind of sexual intimacy?

Without consciously realizing it, she said: "After lunch, why don't I show you around? Maybe once you've eaten, you'll be more forthcoming. Then you can tell me all about what brought you here."

A little later.

Getting off the thatch-roofed funicular at the top of the hill, Dorothy-Anne hooked an arm through Hunt's and said, "Let's walk off lunch, why don't we?"

"What's to walk off? You hardly ate," he pointed out.

She smiled gorgeously and gave his arm a squeeze. "Yes, but *you* pigged out. We'll both walk off your lunch!"

The gardens—there were two, actually, one the "tropical rain forest," which thrived in the hot dry coastal climate, thanks to hidden sprinklers delivering a twice-daily downpour, and the more arid, less water-dependent "Mexican" garden.

Consulting her watch, Dorothy-Anne steered Hunt to the former. "We'd better see this one first," she decided. "Otherwise we might get caught in the middle of a 'shower.' The watering system's computerized, and believe you me, when it 'rains' here, it *pours!*"

They passed a sign that specified that children under eighteen had to be accompanied by an adult. Other signs warned:

DANGER!

PLANTS CAN BE POISONOUS!

DO NOT TOUCH

Hunt raised an amused eyebrow. "Isn't that a bit melodramatic?"

Dorothy-Anne shook her head. "Not at all. Come, I'll show you."

The path, a carpet of mosslike selaginella, was soft and springy underfoot, and meandered, by means of switchbacks, through a tunnel of dense, lush tropical foliage. Coconut palms, giant-leafed banana trees, and towering tree ferns filtered out the bright sunlight and provided the backdrop for thousands of flowering plants. There were rare orchids of all sizes and enormous hibiscus and spiky birds of paradise. Each curve of the path revealed new delights and breathtaking riots of color.

"My God!" Hunt exclaimed. "You must need a full-time botanist!"

Dorothy-Anne smiled. "Actually, there is one on staff."

"He must be kept very busy."

"She," Dorothy-Anne corrected him gently, "and she is. Consider the orchids. We have over a thousand species of them alone. Many were specially gathered in Brazil and flown here."

He shook his head in amazement. "You must be very proud of this place."

Dorothy-Anne's expression turned wistful. "I was," she admitted quietly. "But for obvious reasons, I'm not so proud of it right now."

A little farther on, Hunt stopped to study a waxy, flowering cluster arcing down from a bromeliad. "Interesting, isn't it? One tends to forget how many plants are parasites."

"Ah, but *Vriesea simplex* isn't a true parasite," she said. "Granted, it clings to trees, but it's an air plant. It draws no sustenance from its host. Now, about those warning signs you saw back there . . ."

"Yes, what about them?"

Still arm in arm, she led him a little farther down the path, then stopped and pointed to a large, spectacular red and yellow bloom.

"Behold," she said. "*Gloriosa superba,* a climbing lily from Sri Lanka. Its root looks like a yam, but woe to anyone who ingests it. It contains a deadly poison."

Hunt stared at the flamelike lily. "Much like a woman I know," he murmured. "Beautiful to look at, but poisonous to the core."

Dorothy-Anne looked at him sharply. He was obviously referring to his wife. *His marriage really must be hell,* she thought, and her heart went out to him.

She said, "Perhaps now you can appreciate all those warning signs."

He smiled. "Not only that, but I'll never see flowers in the same light again. Remind me not to send you any."

She laughed. "Roses are always a safe bet."

"I shall stick to roses, then."

They continued on, and as they walked, Hunt filled her in on Kevin Whitman's plight.

Dorothy-Anne listened, appalled. "The poor kid!" she exclaimed softly. "As if suffering Down's syndrome is not enough! His parents must be going out of their minds!"

Hunt thought of Midge and Joe Whitman. "What's truly amazing," he said, "is that they're holding up as well as they are. Midge especially is a tower of strength."

"But it's . . . inhuman!"

"Tell me about it! You should see the inside of that jail. It's a hellhole. But do you know what really burns me up?"

Dorothy-Anne shook her head.

"Chief Zuñiga!" The name tore angrily from his lips. "*Despite* the letter I hand-carried from the governor, he still refuses to release Kevin! The son of a bitch is determined to hold him until he receives written instructions *direct* from Oaxaca—as if the copy I brought is suspect!"

Dorothy-Anne sighed deeply and looked at a cluster of green-lipped, insect-trapping plants from Malaysia. Her voice was very low. "This isn't the first run-in tourists have had with Zuñiga. One of these days he'll really go too far. What I can't understand . . ."

"What?"

She turned toward him. "Why no one informed me about the Whitmans."

"That's simple. They're not staying at this hotel. It's a little . . . ah . . . too rich for their wallets."

She nodded. "And you?" She held his gaze. "I didn't check the guest register. Are you staying here?"

A faint smile came to his lips. "Indeed I am."

"Hear, hear." Her tone was gently mocking. "Weren't you afraid of salmonella poisoning?"

"Actually, I tried to get a room at the Whitmans' hotel, but they were all booked. So then I tried here."

She pulled a face. "Where you could have rented half the hotel."

He didn't speak.

She stared off into the distance. "That damn outbreak! You try to anticipate everything, but . . ." She shrugged helplessly.

"Accidents will happen," he said softly.

She sighed heavily. "Don't they just. And especially to me. Sometimes I think . . ." Her voice trailed off.

"Yes? What do you think?"

She shook her head. "It can keep. Besides, I've detained you long enough. If we don't get a move on, the Whitmans will think you've deserted them. Tell you what. Why don't I grab one of the hotel cars and drop you off at the police station myself?"

Twenty minutes later:

Dorothy-Anne hit the brakes of the white Sebring convertible and pulled up in front of the soulless headquarters of the *Policia*. Hunt popped his seat belt and chucked open the passenger door and hopped out.

He slammed the door shut. "Thanks for the lift," he said, holding on to the side panel.

Dorothy-Anne smiled from behind her shades. "We try to please. After all, you're that rare commodity around here. A paying guest."

"We'll talk later?"

She nodded and watched him start toward the building. But before she could put the car in gear, the doors of the police station burst open and she heard a woman's excited cry: "Mr. Winslow! Oh, Mr. Winslow!"

The sound of happiness bubbled in the air.

Dorothy-Anne kept the car in park as the thin woman in the celadon pantsuit and large-framed glasses rushed to give Hunt a fierce hug. *Midge Whitman,* she guessed. *With good news.*

Then a man in an aloha shirt, yellow slacks, and a Forty-niners base-ball cap joined them. He had his arm around a pale, blank-faced youth who blinked in the glare of bright sunlight.

Joe and Kevin Whitman. Dorothy-Anne smiled to herself, then felt her eyes mist over as Hunt embraced the boy. Joe Whitman, obviously embarrassed by the displays of affection, stood by, looking at his feet.

Dorothy-Anne hit the horn lightly, and they all turned in her direction.

She stood up in the convertible. "Well?" There was laughter in her voice. "Are you folks just going to stand there? Or do you want to get out of here?"

Still later.

The little jet belonging to Winslow Communications reflected the blinding sunlight as it hurtled down the runway of the Santa Maria Hua-tulco airport. Dorothy-Anne and Hunt waved and watched the Falcon 50 climb steeply toward the Sierra Madre del Sur. Then they climbed back into the Sebring.

Dorothy-Anne put the car into gear and drove off the tarmac. "They're nice people," she said.

"Yes, they are. Real and unspoiled."

"It was sweet of you to put your jet at their disposal."

Hunt shrugged it off. "They've been through hell down here. I fig-ured the sooner they're back on U.S. soil, the better. Why should they have to wait for a commercial flight?"

She nodded and swung the car onto the road that would take them back to the coast. His reply was what she liked about him: the way he took charge, went beyond the call of duty, and then just shrugged it off, aw-shucks-like, as if it was nothing. In many ways, Freddie had been like that, but Hunt was even more so. He instinctively knew what needed to be done, and how to go about the right way of doing it.

"Besides," he said, "I'm not the only Good Samaritan in these parts. You chauffeured us around."

"Oh, balls! It was the least I could do."

"Maybe," he said. "The point is, you didn't *have* to do it."

"No one *has* to do anything," she growled, accelerating to pass a diesel-belching bus.

She drove like a man: neatly, confidently, and with no hesitation whatsoever. When she pulled over in front of the bus, her voice was suddenly husky.

"Anyway, it did me good," she said, tossing her mussed hair and glancing out the side of her dark shades at him. "Sometimes it takes other people's problems to put your own into perspective."

"Yes." Hunt nodded. "I know."

She switched conversational gears. "Want the top up and the air conditioning on?"

"Nah." He shook his head and flashed a boyish grin. "I like the wind blowing through my hair. It takes me back to my wild youth."

"Good." Her smile lit up her face, and she decided to test him further. "Radio?" she asked.

"And ruin the rushing of the wind? No way!"

He wins with flying colors, she thought happily, and for a while they drove in silence, elbows sticking out over the road. But it was a companionable silence. They were both at ease, and drew pleasure from simply basking in each other's company, from sitting back and enjoying the ride.

Enjoying their being *together.*

Dorothy-Anne imagined this was what it was like to be inside a big, shiny, clear glass bubble. A bubble in which painful pasts and pressing futures did not exist . . . only the wonderful here and now.

And there was something else too, she realized. She felt alive around Hunt—so truly and thoroughly alive it was as if she'd awakened from a hundred-year-long sleep. She could swear the sky was bluer and more flawless than she'd ever seen it, the trees greener and glossier, the clay earth richer and redder. Everything around her seemed to have taken on added clarity and texture and substance.

It's because of Hunt, she thought. *He does something to me. Oh yes, he does a* lot!

She kept sneaking quick little sideways peeks at him, and when he caught her at it, they both burst into peals of delighted laughter.

Words were unnecessary and speaking redundant.

Heaven help me. God, he was irresistible! I'm falling for him. I can't help it.

Just before reaching Highway 200, where a left turn would take them back to Huatulco, Dorothy-Anne had a sudden inspiration. She slowed down and glanced at Hunt.

"There's a place I'd like to show you. Mind if we take a detour?"

He smiled. "I'm game if you are."

So she took a right on 200 and stepped on the gas. "It's just a little ways up the coast."

The route cut through tropical ranch land. They saw horses grazing beneath coconut palms and banana trees, and Indian women washing clothes in the shallow, clay-colored streams on the sides of the road, doing their laundry the way their mothers and their mothers' mothers had done it before them, while the twentieth century sped past.

Some twenty miles later, at the town of Pochutla, Dorothy-Anne slowed and swung a left off the highway.

"Hold on," she warned. "Here's where the going gets tough. This road's a real bitch."

The words were barely out of her mouth when the Sebring dipped and began bouncing down the steep incline.

Hunt braced his feet and held onto the dashboard. On both sides, dark green foliage appeared to jump and twitch and whip by in a drunken blur, while intermittent flashes of sunlight flickered through the leafy canopy overhead.

Dorothy-Anne handled the car expertly, easing up on the accelerator instead of applying the brakes. Even so, it was a tooth-jarring experience. Like slaloming down a jungle chute.

"*Madre de Dios!*" Hunt exclaimed, shouting to make himself heard.

Dorothy-Anne laughed. "I didn't know you spoke Spanish," she shouted back.

He grinned and held on. "I don't. It's just one of the phrases I picked up from the household help. The others would curl your ears!"

And at last they were there.

"*Voilà*," Dorothy-Anne announced. "Welcome to Puerto Angel."

Hunt looked around with delight.

Puerto Angel was the real thing—a genuine, honest-to-goodness fishing village curled around a small, shimmering bay. The picturesque waterfront was lined with *palapas* offering freshly cooked seafood and exotic fruits. Lobster boats bobbed gently in the sheltered inlet, and a gray Mexican naval vessel was docked at the pier. From high atop a steep hill, an old red and white building presided over it all like a watchful dowager.

"What's that up there?" Hunt asked, pointing up at it.

"The Hotel Angel del Mar. It's gotten pretty seedy, but the view is out of this world."

Dorothy-Anne parked by the pier and switched off the ignition.

"This is where we get out," she said. "If it tells you anything, even the taxi drivers from Escondido and Huatulco refuse to go beyond this point."

Hunt looked up and down the rutted, unpaved road and laughed. "I can't imagine why!"

"Oh, this is nothing. You should see the cobbled street that spirals up to the Angel del Mar."

"You mean it's worse than *this*?"

"Believe you me. That drive puts new meaning into the phrase 'taking your life in your hands.'"

They spent the next couple of hours wandering around on foot. The waterfront was lively. There were young tourists from a dozen countries and weatherbeaten lobstermen relaxing after a busy morning and uniformed sailors from the naval ship checking out the pretty young *señoritas.*

"Don't ask me why, but for some reason the Mexican navy considers this to be one of their bases," Dorothy-Anne said, explaining the presence of the sailors.

"But it's a fishing village!"

"Try telling them that."

They browsed in the shops, where Dorothy-Anne bought gifts to take back to the kids, and Hunt insisted on buying her a big, ridiculous straw hat.

"Hunt!" she protested, laughing. "I'm not a hat person!"

He plopped it on her head before she could duck. "Oh, but you are. Now stand still." He shaped the brim to maximize its jauntiness. "There."

She rolled her eyes. "God, I must look goofy!"

"Charmingly goofy."

So to please him, she went ahead and wore it. *After* cocking it a little more for extra élan.

Naturally, at the next shop they passed *she* bought *him* an even more outrageous hat. A giant sombrero.

"Now we're even Steven," she giggled.

It was an afternoon Dorothy-Anne wished could last forever. She didn't know the last time she had enjoyed herself so thoroughly. For the moment, at least, she didn't have a care in the world.

They went to Suzy's, one of the two most popular establishments, where they drank margaritas and got into the salsa rhythm, and then Dorothy-Anne took him to see Zipolite, the town's famous nudist beach.

"You see those thatched huts?" She pointed to them.

He nodded.

"A lot of the nudists actually live in them."

"Ah." He tried for wistfulness. "The lifestyles of the young and daring."

She elbowed him in the ribs.

"All right," she laughed, "you've had your eyeful. On we go—before you get ideas. The next thing I know, you'll suggest *we* strip and join them!"

"No danger of that," he grinned. "I doubt I'd survive the fights."

"Fights?" She looked puzzled. "What fights?"

"The ones you'd get me into—what else? I've got jealous bones all over my body. Any guy ogles you—even the right way—I'd be forced to defend your honor."

"How marvelous!" She laughed beautifully and squeezed his arm. "You'd do that?"

His face became serious. "Till the end of time," he vowed softly.

Swiftly she let go of his arm and looked away. Somehow they'd stepped over the boundary from fun and games to territory that belonged to serious.

And she wasn't ready for serious. Not even jokingly.

Steady, old girl, she warned herself. *Don't read things into it that aren't there.*

She reminded herself that these few stolen hours were just a fluke.

You and Hunt were thrown together by chance. After today, he'll fly home to resume his life, and you'll fly back and pick up yours. You'll probably never see each other again.

Reality had an awful habit of asserting itself.

Hunt was looking at her strangely. "Is something wrong?"

"No." Dorothy-Anne glued on a smile. "Why, should there be?"

But of course, there was. Because now she knew what Cinderella felt like.

Sometime or other, we're all Cinderella. Only the hour is different. The stroke of midnight comes at different times for each of us.

And later yet:

The afternoon was drawing to a close. Hats in hand, they were walking barefoot at surf's edge, along a deserted stretch of shell-strewn beach.

Soon now the sun would set, and the two of them would be silhouetted against a painted sky. Then dusk would fall swiftly and they would be heading back to Huatulco.

Dorothy-Anne was painfully aware of every passing minute.

"With the Whitmans gone, I guess your business here is done," she said quietly.

"Yes," Hunt replied. "And yours?"

"I want to make one last round of our salmonella patients, but after that I'm done too."

"And off you fly? Into the wild blue yonder?"

"That's right." She nodded.

"So it's back to the rat race," he sighed. "San Francisco for me. New York for you."

"Actually, I've got to stop off in the Caribbean first. A resort we're developing is running way over budget and way over schedule. It's time I kicked some butt."

"The Caribbean," he murmured dreamily. "Powdery white beaches . . . whispering palms . . ."

"Bulldozers," she added, "backhoes . . . cement mixers . . ."

He wasn't fazed in the least. "How long will you be there?"

She shrugged. "Two days . . . three at the outside." She glanced at him. "Why?"

"I could always delay my return a couple of days. Maybe charter us a sailboat, keep it anchored offshore. What do you think?"

Her heart skipped a beat, then added velocity to what she had been feeling. Heavens above, what did he *think* she thought? It was only the most tempting proposition she'd had in eons.

Then caution intervened, and she stopped walking so she could examine his face to see if he was having her on.

He wasn't. His expression was sincere—and so unguardedly ardent, so wholeheartedly eager and enthusiastic, that seeing it brought a sudden blush to her face.

"You're crazy!" she laughed.

"Maybe," he admitted softly. "But I've never been more serious in my life."

A breeze sprang up and tugged at her hair. She fingered it back over her ears, then turned and stared out to sea. The setting sun had electroplated the ocean with molten gilt, and the lights of a big sportfisherman heading back to shore semaphored a victorious catch.

"Well?" Hunt prodded.

Dorothy-Anne drew a little breath and held it, then let it escape. One part of her was dying to jump at his offer. *Today doesn't have to be the end!* she thought exultantly.

But another part of her was coldly rational. *The sooner we part company, the easier it'll be on both of us. I'm not ready for a relationship, and neither is he. He's already got a wife.*

Dorothy-Anne had no intention of becoming the Other Woman. God, no. Her life was filled with enough complications. The last thing she needed was to add to them.

His voice was a whisper above the roar of the surf. "What's the matter? Can't you just say yes?"

She turned and looked up at him and started to say no. Instead, she could feel his eyes reaching out and pulling her in, and the word died on her tongue. Damn. She didn't *want* to turn him down! She *wanted* to say yes!

Hunt was the only man who had attracted her since Freddie had passed away. But that wasn't quite true. In fact, it wasn't true at all. *I might as well be honest with myself. Hunt attracted me from the very beginning—even* before *I learned of my beloved's tragedy. The moment I laid eyes on Hunt, and he on me, something between us clicked.*

Yes. She had been swept up in the blinding aura of his charisma from the start.

The freight of guilt pressed heavily on her shoulders. Surely by merely *being* with Hunt she was besmirching Freddie's memory—how could it be otherwise? And sharing yet *more* time with Hunt would be . . .

Her breath sighed out. "I'd *like* you to come along," she told Hunt carefully, her lips pursed in a puritanical frown. "I'd really like to . . ."

"Then why do I hear a 'but' coming on?"

"Because I'm not ready for a commitment. Oh, Hunt! Don't you see? It's too soon!"

He drew closer to her. "I'm not looking for a commitment," he said softly. "I don't intend to make any demands."

She made an agitated gesture.

"Can't we just enjoy each other's company?" he asked.

She stared at him. "Can we, Hunt? Can we really? Or would we only be fooling ourselves?"

He looked deep into her eyes. "Since when has friendship been a crime?"

Dorothy-Anne could feel her resistance crumbling. It wasn't as if she was going to kick up her heels and spread her legs.

Friendship, she silently told the hovering presence of Freddie. *Since when has that been such a crime?*

Friendship.

That's all it is.

The following morning, when she boarded her jet to fly to Eden Isle, Hunt went with her.

40

Unappreciated: the vast blue sky, the clouds like tiny white puff-balls from antiaircraft fire. Unappreciated too: the houses stacked like firewood on Russian Hill, presumptuously soaking up the sun as though it were their rightful due; the crisp diorama of bay and mountains and bridges; the flotillas of sailboats skimming across the blue sheet of water like tiny gulls.

Amber had no use for the view. She was conscious of herself as a sallow, conspicuous intruder whose worn denims, old Nikes, and waist-length black hair branded her as a trespasser. She was too different, too hardened for this genteel neighborhood of freshly painted houses and tiny, tended gardens. No one would ever mistake her for a homemaker or a professional woman. Her body language was too defiant, her eyes too furtive.

She was convinced she had trouble written all over her. Why else would the cabbie who'd dropped her off have regarded her with suspicion, demanding she flash her cash before accepting her as a fare?

His assumption that she'd stiff him stung at Amber's pride, left her with the bitter aftertaste of resentment.

"Fuckin' lowly cabbie!" she cursed to herself.

Under normal circumstances, she'd have told him where to shove it, but urgency would not permit. She didn't have time to wait for another cab. If she didn't hurry, Christos or the woman might beat her to the house—ruin her plans.

Like hell they will! she thought, anger propelling her forward. It was imperative that she get there first—unnoticed. Her entire future hinged upon it. Christos had become unusually secretive of late. *He's holding out on me.* Obviously something was afoot. *Something big, which doesn't include me.*

Hair flying, she darted along the narrow walkways that linked the rabbit warren of little houses. What she was up to was illegal, could easily land her in jail—reason enough to be jumpy. She tried to will the twitches in her muscles to cease, was unable to keep from rotating her head to scan the surroundings, casting guilty glances uphill and down and back over her shoulder.

She felt exposed out here in the open, could almost *feel* the local busybodies flattening their noses against their windows. Watching her every move. No doubt wondering what the stranger in their neighborhood was up to. No good, surely . . .

She reached the second house in, her elbow brushing the diseased hedge of thin waist-high boxwood, when a dog started barking furiously.

Amber froze with shock, like a rabbit caught in the glare of oncoming headlights. Heart lurching, she tensed herself for an imminent attack. Then the dog barked some more, and she realized it was several houses away.

Stupid, her panicked reaction! She should have realized how sound here carried.

The relief she breathed was tight in her chest. For a moment, she just stood there, wobbly kneed and cold. She heard a sharp male voice yell at the dog. The frenzied barking continued. Then came a yelp, a whine, and silence.

Amber hurried past the third house in, the bougainvillea-smothered cottage above the shoulder-high retaining wall. Home of the female executive she'd run into the last time, from whose terrace she'd kept Christos under surveillance, shielded from sight by the tilted sun umbrella.

The memory triggered a moment's pleasure, and Amber recalled the sweet yearning she had felt, the daydream she had allowed herself of living in a house such as this.

A few leisurely steps later, she arrived at her destination, the cream-painted little house with the second-floor deck projecting, porchlike, out over the tiny, terraced front yard.

The place to which she'd tailed Christos.

How well Amber remembered his song and dance about how he was going to a "sleazy hotel" to meet the "old hag."

Only there was no hotel. No old hag, either. However, Gloria Winslow existed.

Oh, did she ever!

Naturally, she wasn't a bit like Christos had described.

The remembered treachery detonated like shrapnel inside her, and Amber wondered how she could have been so dumb. She, of all people, should have known better than to swallow the crapola Christos handed out.

Letting her fingers do the walking, Amber felt along the retaining wall for the loose stone behind which Gloria Winslow hid the house keys. Despite the sunshine, the rough-hewn chunks of granite were cool to the touch. Cool and unyielding.

Which one, which one?

While she searched, Amber's head throbbed with the two messages she'd intercepted on the answering machine.

Yesterday afternoon's: *"It's me, Glo. I've been through the wringer and could use some TLC. I'll be at the usual place within the hour."*

A spur-of-the-moment impulse on Gloria Winslow's part. Amber knew Christos hadn't met up with her, because he'd been out all day.

Then today, not half an hour ago, another message. Christos was in the shower, and Amber, on her way out to the topless club where she worked, turned up the volume on the answering machine to listen.

Gloria Winslow again: *"Hell are you? Timbuktu? It's Glo. Guess you know that. I'm heading over to Russian Hill. Do try to make it, will you?"*

Amber turned the volume back down and hastily made tracks. *Screw work,* she decided. This was the opportunity she had been waiting for. Lord only knew when she'd get another.

So here she was, prodding at the retaining wall with her fingertips. Searching for the loose stone. Surely she hadn't been mistaken! It *had* to be right about—

A chunk of granite shifted slightly.

—here!

"Well, praise the Lord!" she offered up thankfully, jiggling the stone loose and pulling it out. It was barely an inch thick, and not very heavy. With an expression of distaste, she brushed aside a spider, then reached quickly into the hole with her free hand.

Her fingers groped crablike. *Please be there,* she prayed. *Please* . . .

They were.

With a cry of triumph, she snatched up the bunch of keys, withdrew her hand, and glanced down at her prize. Four keys on a chrome ring.

Way to go!

She closed her fingers tightly around them. But instead of getting her going, their reality unnerved her. She stared at her clenched, white-knuckled fist. What she intended wasn't exactly "breaking," but it *was* "entering."

Did that make it a felony? Or a misdemeanor? She wasn't sure. However, either one could land her in jail.

But only if I get caught, she told herself. *And I won't, not if I'm careful.*

Positive thinking got her moving. But first she glanced cautiously—furtively—to her right, checking the walk one last time.

The coast was still clear. No Gloria Winslow—yet.

Moving in a swift crouch, Amber loped up the stone steps to the front door, grateful for the protruding deck overhead. She felt less exposed in the sanctuary of its cool, dark shadows.

Now for the door.

She eyed it uneasily. It was white and looked solid. Steel, she strongly suspected.

Just don't let there be an alarm. That's all I ask.

Fingers trembling, Amber tried the first key, fumbling badly and scratching it across the lock, steadying her hand only to find the key didn't fit, then trying the second one, and the third—

She heard the soft click of the tumbler being thrown.

Here goes, she thought. She tensed against the shrill, accusatory shriek of an alarm as she turned the knob and inched the door open, unprepared for—silence?

Yes, silence.

No electronic wails. No deafening warbles. Only the distant skrieks of the seagulls, the tinkles of wind chimes, the peaceable sounds of a quiet neighborhood going about its normal business.

Slowly, shakily, Amber wiped her brow with her sleeve, then left the door cracked and hurried back down the steps. She thrust the keys into their hole, replaced the stone, and scuttled guiltily back to the house.

Once inside, she slammed the door and threw the latch, then leaned weakly back against it. For a moment, she breathed in the sweet, soothing balm of relief even as her subconscious reached out, testing the parameters of her surroundings.

Except for her rapid heartbeat and noisy breathing, her mind registered nothing; the house was pervaded by that stillness peculiar to buildings devoid of all human activity.

So far, so good.

Amber was nearly giddy with relief. She was alone and in. *In,* yes, but she wasn't *out* of the woods quite yet. Not by a long shot.

Pulling herself together, she glanced around and took a swift inventory.

She was in a small, low-ceilinged entrance hall with a highly polished wooden floor. In front of her, a flight of narrow, uncarpeted steps rose steeply up to the second floor. To her right, an open arch led into what she presumed was the living room, judging from her partial view of a brick fireplace, and to her left, an identical arch opened into what was obviously the kitchen.

Amber decided a brief reconnaisance of the premises was in order.

Without further ado, she proceeded to acquaint herself with the layout.

Downstairs were the entry hall, living room, dining area, powder room, and kitchen. Other than the kitchen cabinets and appliances, the rooms were empty. There wasn't a stick of furniture to be seen, or carpeting to absorb sound, or curtains to soften harsh acoustics. Amber was uncomfortably aware of a constant hollow echo as flat, hard surfaces amplified the squeaks of her rubber-soled Nikes on oak, the rasps of her agitated breathing.

Without fail, the blinds were pulled down over all the windows, with only thin slivers of light leaking in around the edges.

A cursory examination of the refrigerator revealed chilled bottles of champagne, tonic water, and club soda; the freezer contained frosted bottles of Stolichnaya.

Upstairs were a landing, three bedrooms, and a tiled bathroom. Just like downstairs, the two smaller bedrooms were entirely devoid of furnishings. As for the master bedroom . . .

The expanse of mirrors on the far wall visually doubled the room and everything in it, reduced in size the doorway in which she was framed, and from where she stared at her smaller, reflected self. Even from this twofold distance she couldn't help but recognize her expression of covetous longing, the envy shining in her eyes.

She ran her tongue across her lower lip. The bedroom was picture perfect, the kind of room you saw in glossy magazines.

For a moment she savored the scent of fresh linens, admired the bed, anchored like an island of white luxury: curvaceous white cane headboard and footboard; snowy sheets trimmed in lace; a cloudlike dream of a duvet; plump, lace-edged European squares. On either side of the bed, beautiful brass tables held silk-shaded lamps, cut crystal ashtrays, telephone, tissue box, small Cartier clock. And to her left, also reflected in the mirrors across the room, a wooden table patinaed with great age. Serving as a bar, it was laden with a silver tray of crystal tumblers and one bottle each of scotch and vodka.

But what truly took her breath away was the carpet, which took up most of the floor. A floral needlepoint, it depicted a riotous garden at the height of full bloom, with cabbage roses and all manner of detailed flowers, and was so skillfully stitched it seemed a crime to walk on.

But neither the needlepointer's art nor the exquisite room could distract Amber from her mission, or from the unsettling notion that Gloria Winslow might at this very instant be arriving, retrieving the keys from behind the loose stone, perhaps already unlocking the front door and getting ready to mount the stairs. Only to discover, like the three bears finding Goldilocks, a stranger in her house.

And then what?

Then I'm in deep shit, Amber thought, crossing the carpet to check out the wall of mirrors.

Each pair of panels, it turned out, opened into a closet; from the rods hung bare wooden hangers.

And that was it for the bedroom, with the exception of the sliding glass patio doors, also fitted with drawn shades, which faced the foot of the bed.

Where to hide?

There wasn't much choice.

None, actually—except for the obvious.

From experience, Amber knew that Christos never hung up his clothes. The big question was, did Gloria Winslow?

Amber sincerely hoped not.

Striding to the mirrored wall of closets, she chose the section nearest to the head of the bed, ducked inside, and pulled the doors shut.

They closed with a snap.

Darkness engulfed her.

Trying to get comfortable, she sat cross-legged on the floor and settled down.

She didn't have long to wait.

Gloria's first order of business was pouring herself a king-size dose of Stoli from the freezer in the kitchen and tossing it down the hatch in three breathtaking gulps; then, grabbing a chilled bottle of Cristal by the neck, she headed up the stairs.

In the bedroom, she kicked off her shoes, shrugged herself out of her coat (a lightweight pink cashmere from Chanel), and left it lying where it landed on the floor. Ditto the pink tweed jacket of her two-piece suit. Without thinking, she popped the champagne cork, topped off a glass, and parked herself on the bed, bottle within easy reach on the floor, glass even handier on the bedside table.

Firing up a cigarette, she lay back. Puffed angry bursts of smoke at the ceiling.

If only Christos would get a move on, she thought, with a scowl. The fucking prick.

Gloria didn't like being kept waiting. In fact, she strongly suspected Christos of playing with her head—not showing up (yesterday), and making her wait (today), being part of a macho attempt at puffing up his ego.

As if that would prove he was boss!

What a joke!

The absurdity almost made her laugh out loud.

Well, he can play all the games he wants, she thought, malevolently sipping some champagne. *He'll soon see how far it gets him. All I've got to do is tighten my purse strings and whammo!*

That would teach him.

Yes, indeedy. And for a start, she could give him an icy reception . . . a little foretaste of things to come.

Four cigarettes and two glasses of champagne later, she finally heard his footsteps on the stairs.

About time! she huffed, shooting a glare in the direction of the open door. Then, deciding to play it cool, she cleared her face of expression, lit another cigarette, and struck a sexy pose.

Strutting into the bedroom, Christos looked properly contrite. "Hey, babe. Ya caught me in the shower."

It never failed. The moment Gloria looked at him, she was gone. He always had that effect on her.

It was so difficult to remain angry with him.

She watched him saunter toward her and stand at the side of the bed, pelvis thrust forward, eyes sweeping across her curves.

"Soon as I listened to your message, I threw on my clothes and came runnin'," he said. "See?" He bent his head forward and gestured. "Didn't even wait to dry my hair."

But Gloria couldn't care less about his hair. All she had eyes for was his snug denims—or, more to the point, the impressive equipment contained therein.

Hooking a finger in his belt, she pulled him on top of her. "Why don't you throw those clothes right back off?" she suggested huskily, looking up at him from under half-lowered eyelids. "But first, a little kissy. Hmm?"

She parted her lips in anticipation and he obliged, tongue diving deep and tickling her tonsils.

So much for small talk.

Time for some action.

"I'm all wet already!" she whispered, shoving his head down her short pink skirt. "Eat me, baby! Eat me and fuck me good!"

Christos raised his head and looked at her. "Heyyyy, look who's talkin' dirty! An' last time you gave *me* a hard time about it!"

Her eyes were shiny, like little round dental mirrors. "A hard time's what I *want,* lover boy. So are you going to give it to me? Or are we just going to talk?"

His trouser rat rose to the challenge.

In due course, they burst across the finish line in a climax of seismic shudders.

"Was that an earthquake, or was that us?" he panted.

"That," she crooned, tightening her vaginal muscles and keeping him trapped inside her, "was us. I hope you're in top form, big boy. 'Cause for me, that was just the warm-up!"

*   *   *

Amber witnessed the Sexual Olympics in their entirety, courtesy of the crack between the closet doors. Belatedly, she wished she'd never had the bright idea of spying on Christos and Gloria. What she'd learned from Round One—and there were clearly more rounds to follow—pierced her with pain.

She had seen and heard more than she wanted—a *lot* more. Worse yet, several disturbing facts became apparent, the first and foremost being that it wasn't a case of Christos's having to grin and bear it. Or even work at getting it up.

No, sirree. He was in hog heaven, and enjoying every minute of it.

Amber's lips twitched, and silent tears blurred her vision.

He gets off on Gloria Winslow.

The realization was like a punch in the gut.

Matter of fact, they get off on each other.

I'm the one he has to work to get it up for—and that's only if he throws me a mercy fuck!

And even those occasions had become increasingly rare of late.

Bitterly Amber wondered: Who had seduced Christos? Gloria Winslow, the woman? Or Gloria Winslow, the walking, talking, and eminently fuckable bank account?

Not that it mattered much. Whichever Gloria it had been, Amber knew she could never hope to compete—especially if Christos and Ms. Rich Bitch were hooked on each other.

And from the look and sound of it, they most definitely were.

Suddenly a slew of inexplicable behaviors on Christos's part fell into place. Like the reason he'd chilled toward his old friend and partner, Amber Stich. And why he'd been treating her like shit. Always finding fault, picking on her, putting her down. Making her feel stupid. As if she couldn't do anything right.

And then there were those silences, those long, drawn-out silences. That windchill factor, his emotional temperature plunging, freezing her out.

He wants to get rid of me.

The knowledge surfaced before she had a chance to block it.

Shit!

Amber stifled a groan and hugged herself tightly. She had the urge to rub her arms to restore her circulation, but was afraid of making noise. Meanwhile, she suffered in silence: her muscles cramped from sitting immobile all this time, legs going to sleep, head spinning from what she'd discovered . . . or rather, what she'd suspected all along for the last couple of months, but hadn't been able to face—had put off facing.

There's no room for me in his life, now that he's got Gloria Winslow.

Now, listening to the postcoital murmurs leaking into the closet,

Amber couldn't help noticing the easy familiarity between Christos and Gloria, that comfortable intimacy of two people who got off on each other without the baggage of guilt or shame. They were tuned to a wavelength all their own.

And it doesn't include me.

"Well, babe?" Even muffled by the closet doors, Christos's voice came across low-down and dirty. "Ready for the fuck o' your life?"

Babe.

The word ricocheted wildly inside Amber's head, whizzed around in her skull like a bullet seeking escape.

He calls her babe!

She clapped her hands over her ears.

It's what he used to call me!

She didn't think she could stand any more of this. God, no. Her insides already felt like one vast wound, and everything she heard and saw ripped savagely into raw bleeding flesh. If only she could make tracks and flee . . .

Wishful thinking. There was only one way out, and while Amber couldn't care less about Gloria's reaction, she wasn't all that keen on Christos's finding out she was spying on him. No, not keen at all. Every instinct told her that if he did, it would all be over, *finito*—a mental hand snapped its fingers in her ears—like *that!*

And then what? She would have no one to cling to. She'd have lost him for good.

If she wanted to hang on to him—and she did; God, did she ever!— she had to ride this out. *Had* to!

Outside the closet, the dirty talk trailed off, became moist little kissing and sucking sounds, low, throaty moans. Amber could hear the rustle of bed linens, the creaks of bedsprings, the soft slap of flesh against flesh.

She wiped away her tears and leaned forward. Squinted through the crack between the doors with one eye.

And bit down a cry of pain.

Round Two had begun.

Later, quite a while later, they lay side by side, Gloria's head resting on his sleek, hard-muscled chest. "Christos," she whispered. "What am I going to do? I need you worse than an addict needs a fix. Much worse!"

He nuzzled her hair with his lips.

She shifted position and rolled on top of him. Raised herself on her elbows, her breasts dangling like firm, ripe fruit, her eyes staring down into his. "I'm serious. You're the only man who's ever been able to satisfy me!"

He smiled lazily. "Heyyyyy. That's what I'm here for, babe."

"Yes, but this is *today*."

"That's right."

"So what about tomorrow? And the day after?"

"What are you worried about? I'm your own Dial-a-Stud. Remember?"

Suddenly she began to tremble and tears sprang to her eyes. "Don't make jokes about it!" she said fiercely. "I told you I love you!"

"I know, babe," he soothed.

"And you said you loved me." Her smooth brow furrowed with fear. "You meant it, didn't you, Christos? You weren't just stringing me along?"

He laughed and pulled her down and pressed her head against his chest. "Jee-zus. Don't be so dense, Glo. What d'you think I do? Cruise the streets, tellin' every chick I run across that I love her?"

Gloria gave her head a little shake. "No," she said in a tiny voice. "Of course not."

"Ya got that right. An' you wanna know why?"

She was silent.

"'Cause I got *you*, babe," he said softly, touching her chin with his forefinger and tilting her head up to face him. "*You*," he repeated, looking into the depths of her eyes. "An' deep down inside, you know it, don'tcha?"

She gave another little nod. "I . . . I know I'm being silly, Christos, but I . . . I can't help it! Sometimes I'm so afraid."

"Afraid!" He laughed. "What've you got to be afraid of?"

She sighed and laid her head back down against his chest. "Losing you," she whispered.

"Aw, for chrissake, Glo! That's the last thing you need to worry about."

"No, it's not!" she said stubbornly. "We both know this can't go on forever. Not like this. Sooner or later, something's going to happen to spoil our happiness."

He didn't speak, but she felt his heartbeat speed up.

Her long, soft, dark lashes descended over her eyes. "Have you given any thought to what we discussed the last time?" Meaning getting rid of her husband, but not putting it in so many words.

Christos shrugged his shoulders and played dumb. "Shit, Glo. We talked about lots of stuff."

Gloria raised her head off his chest, her eyes going right into his. "For God's sake, Christos!" she said huskily. "You know very well what I'm referring to."

He drew a deep breath, held it to the count of ten, then slowly exhaled the pressure in his lungs. Very gently, as though she were exceedingly fragile and might break, he carefully rolled her off him.

With a sickening lurch of fear, Gloria watched him turn his back on her, swing his legs over the edge of the bed, and sit there, hunched forward. For a moment, she wondered whether she mightn't have pushed him too far.

Maybe he doesn't have it in him, she thought. *Maybe I should just forget about it.*

But she couldn't. She was too close to give up now. All she needed was to find the one final button to push, and Christos would do her bidding.

He has what it takes, she told herself. *I know it, even if he doesn't.*

Well, he would realize it soon enough. She was certain of it.

Rolling her head sideways, she looked at him appraisingly. He was still sitting there, elbows on his thighs, head in his hands, like his skull was about to come apart and split in two if he didn't hold both sides together.

Gloria scooted around. Her eyes were hard and calculating, but her body was soft and warm and inviting.

"Christos," she breathed, wrapping her arms around him. "Darling?"

He tried to shrug her off. "Back off, Glo," he growled. "I already told yuh! I'm not killin' anybody!"

Undeterred, she knelt behind him and pressed her creamy breasts against his back.

"I don't know why you're all worked up," she said, putting a little pout in her voice. "I only have our best interests at heart."

He laughed harshly. "That's a good one. Lemme guess. It's somethin' in the air?"

The air? Gloria frowned. *What on earth is he talking about?*

She said: "I'm afraid you've lost me."

"The *air,*" he said bitterly. "Up there in High Society. It sure must be different from what the rest of us folks breathe down here."

She stiffened. "And what makes you say that?"

" 'Cause if yuh had both feet on the ground, yuh wouldn't be talkin' such shit!"

"I am not talking shit," she enunciated quietly. "I'm dead serious."

"Okay," Christos said. "Let's say yuh are. Just for the sake of argument."

She shrugged. "Fine."

"Got any idea what you'd be gettin' us into?"

"You're the expert," she said. "Why don't you tell me."

"Aw right. Lemme see now. For starters, we're lookin' at murder one."

"Only if we get caught," Gloria pointed out.

"An', since it's premeditated, and this is California, it's a capital offense."

Her face was expressionless. "I can live with that."

"Yeah? You ever hear o' Death Row?"

She had to fight to keep from showing her anger. God, but he could be dense! Even after all these months, he *still* didn't get it. She was tempted to snap: *Oh, I know Death Row all right! I live on it. Every minute of my married life kills me a little bit at a time.*

But she'd voiced that opinion often enough; repeating it would only be a waste of time. Go straight in one ear and out the other.

"An'," he continued, "last but not least, since yer plan involves the two of us, we'd be facin' one more doozy of an offense. This federal statute known as conspiracy?"

Now Christos paused. Waiting to see what kind of reaction he'd provoked.

But Gloria still didn't speak.

"Well?" he demanded. "Now the cards are on the table, what d'you think?"

Gloria stared off into space. Her lack of expression hadn't changed. "Like I told you, I can live with it."

"Well, maybe *I can't*," he retorted. "Ever think o' that?"

She gazed at their reflection in the wall of mirrors opposite the bed. *We truly make a gorgeous couple,* she thought.

"It isn't the killing that's really bothering you, is it?" she asked softly.

Christos twisted around, his head snapping up. "Hell you talkin' about?"

Expertly Gloria began to knead the muscles in his shoulders. They felt tight and knotted from sudden tension.

"I am talking about—oh, you, me, us. I am talking about a long-term relationship, an utter, drastic change in your lifestyle."

"An' what's that got to do with anything?"

"It's got everything to do with it, darling. Big changes invariably cause stress. Quite simply, you're unprepared to deal with all that pressure. It's not an unheard of phenomenon, you know."

"*Huh?*" He gaped at her and blinked. "Speak English, will ya?"

"Having money," she explained patiently, "*real* money, can be an awesome responsibility. Add power and committing yourself to me . . . to *us* . . . and I don't blame you for getting cold feet. It's an awfully big step to take."

Suddenly he burst out laughing. "Aw, Christ, Glo! Ya just don't get it, do ya?"

Jerking his shoulders loose from her massaging hands, he jumped to his feet and looked down at her, clenched fists trembling at his sides.

"Ya know what yer problem is, Glo?"

She took a cigarette from the nightstand and lit it. "I'm sure you'll tell me," she said, exhaling a plume of smoke.

"Betcha ass I will! Ya think you're the sun, an' all the rest of us are expendable little planets circlin' around ya! Jumpin' when ya say 'jump.' Fuckin' when ya say 'fuck'!"

She looked amused. "Is *that* what you think?"

"That's what I *know*! Well, for yer information, I'm not one o' those planets!" he snapped. "An I ain't gonna ice *nobody*! Not for you. Not for anybody!"

Gloria was oddly calm. "Darling, I'm not naive. I don't expect you to do it for me. In fact, you'd be a fool to."

"Ya got that right!" he huffed, stomping around the room.

"But the reason you'll do it," she continued placidly, "is for yourself. For two billion dollars and counting."

She drew deeply on her cigarette and added: "Think of it as the biggest lottery jackpot on earth—because that's what it *is*! And you already have the winning ticket: me."

Christos shoved his fingers through his hair and began pacing agitatedly back and forth, his impressive credentials swinging.

"An' how do I know you ain't gonna screw me over?" he snarled cruelly. "For all I know, you're out to frame me. So you can waltz off with the dough while *I* take the fall!"

He stopped pacing and glared over at her.

"What guarantee do I have that I ain't just the patsy? Huh?"

"Because I love you," she said simply.

"Love! Shit." He rolled his eyes and paced some more.

"Darling," she said, "sometimes people have to trust one another. This happens to be one of those times. Neither of us can pull this off alone. We need each other to do it."

"Yeah." He clenched his hand and pounded it against his temple. "But *you* don't have to do the actual killin'!"

He slid her an accusing look.

"No," she admitted, "but it *was* my idea. I *am* the one who involved *you*. And, I'll still be a coconspirator. I can go to the gas chamber as easily as you."

Despite himself, Christos had to smile. Somehow it was difficult to imagine Gloria Winslow being strapped into Old Sparky. If she were, she'd most likely shoot the electric current right back at her would-be executioners; fry *them* instead of her.

"I don't know, Glo." He sighed deeply. "It's a big risk."

"It's a big prize," she reminded him quietly. "Two billion and counting. For a jackpot that size, I'd say the risk is negligible."

"Still, it means we gotta get away with murder," he said thoughtfully.

She raised her chin. "That is our intention, yes."

"Two billion," he mused in awe. "Two billion fuckin' dollars!" He squinted at her sharply. "Split how? Fifty-fifty?"

"Sure." Gloria stubbed her cigarette out in the crystal ashtray and shrugged. "Why not? You'll have earned it."

He paced silently some more, then went and sat down heavily on the bed. "It'll take careful plannin'," he said.

"*Very*," she agreed, scooting close and kissing the nape of his neck.

"An', we need to keep it simple."

"You'll get no argument from me there."

"The most obvious thing'd be to stage an accident," he thought aloud. "Trouble is, the police ain't dumb."

Her fingers went itsy-bitsy spider up his thigh. "So what do you suggest, lover boy?"

"Dunno. But your husband's a politician."

"Yesssss . . ."

"So why not try for an old-fashioned assassination? You know, someplace public? Where there'll be a crowd? That way, instead o' suspectin' a member o' the immediate family, the cops'll be searchin' for a nut case."

"You see?" Gloria purred. "I knew I could leave the details up to you!"

Then, lavishing her considerable talents upon his splendid penis, she added: "Now what do you say we seal our partnership with another fuck?"

Long after Christos and Gloria had gone, Amber remained in the house. *So Christos has a new partner,* she thought grimly.

Not that the news came as a big surprise. She had half-suspected as much, and had prepared herself for the worst. But what left her totally stunned was how astronomically the ante had been upped.

Two billion *dollars!*

The amount was so humongous, so outside the realm of her imagination, that Amber couldn't fully comprehend it—neither in numbers, nor in purchasing power. What she did understand, and very clearly, was that it required Christos to commit murder—premeditated, cold-blooded, first-degree murder.

He'll never get away with it, Amber thought bitterly. With shaking fingers she lit a cigarette. *How can he be so blind?* she wondered. *Can't he see the bitch is setting him up?*

Amber was at a complete loss. She had no idea how to proceed, or whom to turn to. If only she could talk to Christos and reason with him. If necessary, try to shake some sense into him.

Unfortunately, it was imperative that he never suspect her of knowing a thing.

I've got to stop him, Amber thought. *I've got to!*

If only she could think of a way . . .

41

The pilot brought Hale One down to twenty-five hundred feet and swung the jet into a wide, banking turn.

"I asked him to circle the island so you can get a three-hundred-sixty–degree view," Dorothy-Anne told Hunt.

He gazed out the porthole at the lozenge-shaped island below. At first all he could see were forested slopes of volcanic origin rimmed by the white sand beaches and aquamarine sea of the Greater Antilles. Then he began to discern all the activity. Eden Isle was one huge hive of a construction site, and it was jumping.

Big yellow earth-moving machines on steel tracks were leveling some slopes and creating new ones; others were ripping out dense jungle growth or scooping out trenches and canals and pools. Cranes hoisted burdens of steel struts and pallets. Just inland from a turquoise cove, workmen were swarming over a giant wooden skeleton of a building.

Everywhere he looked, it seemed construction was under way. Only the easternmost tip of the island, where a village of Quonset huts looked like half-buried tin cans, was temporarily immune.

He whistled softly and glanced at her. "What are you building? The Eighth Wonder of the World?"

Dorothy-Anne smiled. "Sometimes, that's exactly what it feels like."

"I'm impressed," Hunt said, meaning it.

"Don't be. You wouldn't be, if you could hear what you can see."

"You mean . . . one big sucking sound?"

She laughed. "You got it."

"I'm not surprised. This project's enormous! Small wonder you decided on that get-up."

During the flight, Dorothy-Anne had changed into a pair of loose, lightweight khaki slacks, tan guayabera, and steel-toed construction boots, the orangey lace-up kind.

She pointed north, to a land mass of mysterious, fog-wreathed mountain ranges. "That over there," she said, "is the southern coast of Puerto Rico. It may look like a hop and a skip, but between here and Phosphorescent Bay are twenty-two miles of open water. It can get pretty choppy at times—ah, that's the landing strip coming up."

Directly below them, a single runway cut a white swath from the sea inland. Parked by the terminal at the landlocked end were a small executive jet, two twin-engine prop jobs, and a Sikorsky chopper designed for hauling heavy loads. From the air, they all looked like toys.

"We'll have to swing out to sea and come in from over the water," Dorothy-Anne explained. "Oh, before I forget. A pilot is standing by with one of the Cessnas. As soon as we land, he'll fly you over to Guánica to pick up the boat."

"A Cessna?" Hunt pretended to be hurt. "After this flying palace, all I rate's a lowly puddle jumper?"

Dorothy-Anne laughed. "What can I tell you? Life is tough."

They buckled their seat belts as the pilot made the final approach. There was a faint whir and a shudder as the landing gear came down and locked into place. Then the jet descended rapidly until it seemed to skim the very tops of the waves.

"Here we go," Dorothy-Anne said.

Water flashed past in a blur, turning from deep aquamarine to light turquoise, and the wheels made contact with the runway.

"Perfect three-point landing," Hunt noted, with approval.

The engines whined shrilly as the pilot threw them in reverse, and the big plane began to slow. Like a bird to the skies born, the jet was graceless and gawky on the ground, shuddering as it taxied clumsily toward the end of the runway and its destination, the white, cast-iron terminal that looked like a garden gazebo on steroids.

"Who are they?" Hunt asked, motioning out the porthole at a group of men lined up in a row like soldiers. All were wearing yellow hard hats.

Dorothy-Anne sighed. "My welcoming committee."

A set of metal boarding stairs was driven to the plane, and Oberto, the chief steward, lifted the main cabin door aside, letting in a burst of hot sunlight and air laden with humidity.

Dorothy-Anne and Hunt released their seat belts and got up. "You go on ahead," Dorothy-Anne told him. "I've got to deal with the welcoming committee. Your pilot's waiting by the Cessnas. We'll meet on the boat, say, late this afternoon?"

Hunt smiled. "Late this afternoon sounds just fine," he said softly. Impulsively he gave her a chaste kiss on the cheek.

She drew in a sharp breath. The touch of his lips came as a shock, and she lifted a hand to her cheek, her face reflecting a mixture of confusion, astonishment, wonder, and surprise. It was the first time a man—any man—had kissed her since Freddie's death, and she felt a sharp stab of guilt.

Will I feel remorse every time a man kisses me? she wondered. *Has Freddie's death left me that emotionally crippled?*

She could only hope it was a phase she was going through; part of the mourning process.

Hunt doesn't merit a frigid woman. He deserves better. . . .

She waited a moment to clear her head of personal baggage, then went down the boarding stairs to greet the assembled contingent. Introductions were unnecessary; she was acquainted with all eight of the men.

Four were architects, three were engineers, and the eighth was Kurt Ackerman, director of Special Projects, who'd flown down in the little executive jet.

Starting at the left and working her way to the right, Dorothy-Anne shook hands all around. She was on familiar terms with everyone, and greeted each man warmly:

"Helmut." The reserved German engineer. "How is the new baby?"

"Very well, Mrs. Cantwell. I call my wife every evening."

"Jim." The Princeton genius with an alternative lifestyle. "Did you contact our Human Resources Department about domestic partner benefits?"

"Yes, Robbie and I can't thank you enough, Mrs. Cantwell."

"Ettore." The outgoing Italian architect. "Your mother's recipe for spaghetti Bolognese is making me gain weight!"

"She wrote that your chicken pot pie recipe is *bellissimo!*"

Dorothy-Anne had kind words for everyone.

Kurt Ackerman was the eighth and last man in the row. As usual, the pony-tailed wunderkind of amusement rides looked hip and with-it.

He had on blue-lensed rimless sunglasses and a short-sleeved, aqua airtex shirt he wore open, shirttail out, over a white T-shirt. The front of the T-shirt was printed with a contructivist, Soviet-era poster of a foreshortened steam locomotive in red and black, and had stylized Cyrillic lettering.

"I decided I'd better pop down to see you," he said, explaining his presence.

"Why?" Dorothy-Anne looked at him sharply. She was alerted as much by his reticence as by the somberness of his expression. "Don't tell me *more* problems have cropped up?"

"No, no," he said quickly. "I just need to discuss a personal matter. In private."

"You know I'm always available. We can talk in the car."

Kurt handed her an extra hard hat he was holding. She took it, but glanced at him questioningly.

"New regulations," he explained. "The insurance company insists. Unless hard hats are worn outdoors at all times, even in nonconstruction zones, the premiums will go up."

Nodding, she put it on and followed him into a green Range Rover. The other men followed in two mud-spattered black Jeep Wranglers. As they drove off the tarmac, she could hear the single engine of a Cessna cough, sputter, and start up. Then they left the terminal behind, taking an unpaved tunnellike road through high, overarching trees.

Kurt flicked a sideways glance at her as he negotiated the bumps and ruts. "I always wanted to know how you did that," he said.

Dorothy-Anne was puzzled. "How I did what?"

"You know, that trick of remembering everybody's names? Details of their personal lives? I guess you must keep notes and refer to them beforehand, huh?"

"Notes?" Dorothy-Anne frowned and shook her head. "No. I just remember things, that's all."

"It's amazing," he said.

"Not really. When people are my employees, they don't work *for* me, they work *with* me. I genuinely care about them."

He swung around a puddle and she glanced into the side mirror. Behind them, the two Wranglers bounced up and down, out of sync with the Rover and each other.

"You wanted to talk in private," she said.

Kurt nodded.

"This is private."

He kept his eyes on the road. "Do you remember how long it's been since you lured me away from Disney World?"

Dorothy-Anne smiled. "Of course. How could I forget? It's nearly three years now."

"That's right." He nodded slowly. "Sometimes it seems like yesterday. And at others . . ." His voice trailed off.

"It seems like forever," she completed. "I know the feeling."

They came to a fork in the road, and Kurt hung a left. The two Jeeps behind them made a right turn and disappeared from the mirror.

"I don't believe I ever told you this," Dorothy-Anne said. "When my husband originally came up with the concept for Eden Isle, he said it would take one of three technical wizards to make it click."

Kurt kept his face bland.

Her voice was soft. "Your name was at the top of his wish list. Did you know that?"

He shook his head. "No, I didn't. I'm very flattered."

"When you accepted our offer, so were we."

He was silent for a moment. "Do you know what clinched the deal for me?"

"Yes. At the time, you said it was because you would have complete creative control."

"Your memory really *is* something else," he said admiringly. "But there was another reason, too."

"And what was that?"

"The opportunity to be in on a project of this magnitude from the ground up. You know . . . creating an entire grand scheme from scratch? The challenge was irresistible."

"In other words, you liked the idea of playing God on a small scale?"

He looked thoughtful. "I wouldn't go so far as to say *that*. I suppose what fired my imagination the most was creating something that has never been done before. Think about it. How many people get the chance to make Fantasy Island a reality?"

She nodded to herself. "My husband chose well," she said. "He was right to put you at the top of his list."

Kurt allowed himself a modest smile. "I like to think I chose well also."

"I'm glad." Dorothy-Anne's voice was warm. Then it became brusque and businesslike. "But all that aside, a trip down memory lane isn't what you wished to speak about in private."

He glanced at her. "Well, it is and it isn't."

She gave him a strange look. "Now you're talking in riddles."

"What it is," he said, "is here we are, three years later. And I'll be damned if history isn't repeating itself."

"I'm afraid you've lost me."

"Well, when your husband first contacted me? I was at the tail end of planning a new park addition at Disney World."

"That I know," she said.

"Now it seems I'm at the same crossroads again."

Dorothy-Anne was watching him closely. "You'll have to be a little more specific."

"Look at it this way," he said quietly. "The plans for Eden Isle are finished. What was conceived on paper and computers and with scale models is becoming the real thing."

Her expression did not change.

"Oh, there'll be the usual problems that pop up during any construction project," he said. "That's par for the course. But basically, we've conquered it. Themes, engineering, refinements—you name it, we've done it. We even planned added attractions for years to come. The creative part's finished. Eden Isle is becoming a reality."

But not fast enough, Dorothy-Anne thought. *Not fast enough by halves.*

They drove in silence as the dirt road narrowed and became a series of switchbacks that took them higher and higher up the south face of the ridge that formed the spine of the island.

Dorothy-Anne stared down over the drop-off. The slopes were green and lush, punctuated at regular intervals with towering steel pylons where cable cars would ferry visitors to the top of the ridge, across the ancient, water-filled crater, and back down the other side.

Halfway to the top, Kurt pulled over and turned off the engine. "Let's stretch our legs," he said.

They got out of the Rover and walked to the edge of the road, looking out over the southern half of the island. A breeze stirred the air, the sky was stacked with layers of big fat cumulus clouds, and the sea looked like a sequined sheet stretching to the blue horizon. Closer in, long white rollers curled up onto snow white beaches.

Kurt thrust the tips of his hands into the back pockets of his jeans. He was nervous. She could tell from the way he had trouble standing still, constantly shifting his weight from one foot to the other. "Do you believe in déjà vu?"

Dorothy-Anne kept her eyes on the panorama. "That all depends."

"Try this on for size," he said. "Night before last, I worked real late. By the time I got home to Mount Kisco, the wife and kids were already tucked in, so I hit the sack, too. Sometime later, the phone woke me up. When I answered it, I was sure it was part of a dream." He shook his head. "It was weird, man. Far-out weird."

Dorothy-Anne felt a premonition, as though furry microscopic legs were dancing along her spine. Her voice was a near whisper. "What did the caller want?"

"That's just it," he said. "It was almost an exact replay of when your husband first called me three years ago."

Her eyes cut sideways at him. "It wasn't a dream, then?"

"Oh, no. It was real, all right. The caller had a British accent and identified himself as George Blackwell, an investment adviser based in Kuala Lumpur."

"Kuala Lumpur," she repeated thoughtfully.

"That's right. He told me he was in town for a couple of days and was familiar with my work and wanted to run a business proposal by me. So I thought, Sure, why not? There's no harm in listening."

Dorothy-Anne's throat felt constricted. "Go on," she said hoarsely.

Kurt shifted uncomfortably from foot to foot. "We met for lunch in the Grill Room of the Four Seasons. That was yesterday."

Dorothy-Anne nodded silently.

"Apparently Beijing gave his consortium the green light to build a Western-style theme park in southern China."

"In other words, he made you an offer you found difficult to refuse?"

"You could say that," Kurt said frankly. "I'd have full creative control and, as with Eden Isle, be in on it from the ground up. I can also write my own ticket, so long as it's within reason."

"They must want you pretty badly." Dorothy-Anne stared blankly off into space. She had the peculiar sensation of being aboard a doomed ship, with every blow she suffered causing the deck to list ever more precariously.

Kurt's right about one thing, she thought. *It really is a replay of when Freddie lured him away from Disney World.*

Now the big question remaining was whether George Blackwell's call was a coincidence or . . .

Or what?

Part of an ominous plot directed specifically at her?

Her mind was in overdrive. *Kuala Lumpur is in Malaysia,* she thought, mentally connecting the dots. *The Hale Dynasty Hotel, where the outbreak of Legionnaires' disease occurred, is in Singapore.*

And there was more.

Sir Ian Connery is based in Hong Kong, as is Pan Pacific Bank.

Dorothy-Anne wasn't sure what to make of it all. An awful lot of Asian connections were affecting the Hale Companies recently—and in the most detrimental way possible.

Surely too many to be coincidental?

Dorothy-Anne's memory dredged up a long-forgotten line from *Goldfinger:* "Once is happenstance, twice is coincidence, and the third time it's enemy action."

Is that what this is? she wondered. *Enemy action? Or am I trying to fit a conspiracy theory where none exists?*

She honestly didn't know.

Keeping her voice calm, she turned her attention back to Kurt. "May I ask where you and Mr. Blackwell left things?" she inquired.

"Up in the air," Kurt said, sighing, his features molded to an expression of apologetic but loyal candor. His eyes were pained, as though he found himself battling an internal war, unable to decide which option to pursue. "I told him I would have to think about it."

"And?"

Kurt pulled a face. "He said that I shouldn't wait too long."

Dorothy-Anne nodded. "In other words," she murmured, "the offer doesn't stand indefinitely."

"I'm afraid not." He smiled ruefully at her. "But the challenge of a new project aside, what really makes this so darn tempting is my wife. As you know, she's Amerasian. Her father was an American GI, and her mother was Vietnamese. She has relatives over there she's never seen."

Dorothy-Anne thought, *I wonder if George Blackwell isn't aware of that fact?* She knew Kurt well enough to realize he was incapable of deception. There was an almost childlike innocence about him. *If his family is being used as a bargaining tool, he's probably not even aware of it.*

Folding her arms, she stared reflectively into the distance. Her fingers fluttered at her elbows like trapped birds, then abruptly froze.

"Kurt?"

"Yes?"

"What—" Her voice carried an unsteady vibrato and she had to clear her throat and swallow before continuing. "What does this Mr. Blackwell look like?"

He thumbed the brim of his hardhat, tilting it back on his head. "You mean physically?"

"That's right." She nodded.

"Well, I can sketch him a lot faster and more accurately than I could describe him. I've got pen and paper in the car."

"Could you?" she said. "You don't mind?"

For the first time since she'd landed, his lips broke into a smile. "Why would I mind?" he said, his arm executing an exaggerated flourish. "Step into my atelier, madam. It's right this way."

He led her to the rear of the Range Rover, where she waited as he got a felt pen and the artist's pad off the backseat. Flipping it open to a blank page, he uncapped the pen and propped the pad against the rear window.

Dorothy-Anne watched the creative process in silence.

First Kurt became very still. He puckered his lips slightly, just enough to give the impression he was blowing a kiss, and then the eyes behind the rimless blue lenses seemed to go totally blank.

Then, nodding briskly to himself, he put pen to paper. His long, slender hand blurred. So swiftly and assertively did he sketch that the felt tip literally flew across the thick buff sheet.

It was amazing.

A few deft sketches, and a baby-faced gent of Dickensian proportions began to take shape. A few inspired lines more, and eyes resting in heavy hammocks of flesh appeared, and receding hair, and a certain smug, superior set to the chubby features.

As the drawing progressed, Dorothy-Anne felt her skin crawl.

Dear God, she prayed, her eyes veiled with premonition. *Don't let it be him! Please let me be wrong about this!*

Kurt's pen thatched a pair of prickly, barbed-wire eyebrows, then added a set of black-framed spectacles.

Dorothy-Anne gasped. With one hand, she clutched a fistful of her guayabera and wrung it.

Dear God! she thought. *It is him! Him!*

Unaware of her reaction, Kurt tore the sheet from the pad and proffered it. "Voilà!"

Dorothy-Anne drew back as if from a snake. A groan escaped her lips, and she felt her cheeks sinking inward.

There was no mistaking the man Kurt knew as George Blackwell. She knew him too.

It was Sir Ian Connery.

At least, that's what he went by in Julian Priddy's office. Dorothy-Anne wondered who he really was. *I damn well better find out. He's the man who's holding the bloody paper on my company's loans!*

The thought was enough to make her dizzy.

Kurt was looking at her strangely. "What's wrong?" he asked. "You look as if you've seen a ghost."

"No," she croaked, "not a ghost." *I'd gladly take a ghost over reality, any day.*

Kurt tossed the drawing into the Range Rover, then put a hand under her elbow, another around her waist, and steadied her. "Are you going to be all right?"

"Yes, Kurt." She nodded, but her breathing was ragged and uneven. "I—I'm fine."

"You sure don't look it."

She wished, devoutly, that she was stronger, or at the very least, *appeared* stronger. "Maybe it's the heat," she said weakly.

"Let's get you back in the car," he said. "I'll turn on the air conditioning and take you down to the visitors' quarters. You could probably use some rest."

"Rest. Yes." She allowed him to lead her to the passenger side of the Rover, hating the way it made her feel like an invalid.

"We'll reschedule your inspection of the site for later," Kurt said. "Maybe we should put it off until tomorrow."

But Dorothy-Anne wasn't listening to a word he was saying. She was still trying to assimilate this latest shock.

It was obvious what Sir Ian Connery—or whatever his name was!—was up to. *Pan Pacific wants me to default.*

Something else was obvious, too. *Sir Ian wants me to know I'm cornered. Otherwise he would never have contacted Kurt personally.*

He was sending her a message by raiding her talent.

She sat stiffly in the passenger seat, staring blankly out the windshield. She knew what Pan Pacific was up to.

They want my collateral, she thought. *The want the Hale Companies.*

Worst of all, they had a very good chance of succeeding.

42

The yacht was named *Quicksilver.* Sleek, rakish, and white, it seemed to float at anchor like an airborne balloon, high above the sun-dappled, mottled turquoise of the coral reefs.

From all appearances, the two people on desk basked in carefree, leisurely luxury.

Dorothy-Anne lay belly down in the shade of the blue bimini top, her elbows on the canvas cushions, her chin on her hands. She was wearing a cropped, navel-length polo shirt with horizontal black and white stripes and a matching bikini bottom. Her hair was pulled back and held in place by a black band, and her body gleamed with sunscreen and oils.

Staring toward shore, she had the peculiar sensation that the sloop's deck was stationary, and that it was Eden Isle that actually rose and dipped like an unmoored island, bobbing gently as it drifted wherever the currents took it.

Hunt was stretched out across the transom, at a right angle from her. He was shirtless, his muscular shoulders resting against the inverted U of a life preserver, his upper torso tapering down into his denim cutoffs. His arms were crossed behind his head and he had on the hat he'd bought Dorothy-Anne in Puerto Angel, which he wore jauntily, way down over his eyes.

But their poses were deceptively relaxed. Forgotten, for the moment, were the tall, sweating glasses of iced tea on the collapsible table in the center of the cockpit; untouched were the bowl of black olives, the platter of cold shrimp. Dorothy-Anne had just spent the better part of an hour detailing the troubles that plagued the Hale Companies. It hadn't been her intention to share her problems with him; in fact, she'd valiantly put her best face forward.

Which he'd seen through right away. Still, it had taken a lot of prying on his part to get her to open up.

Once started, she left nothing out, including her suspicions that the bacterial outbreaks had been no accident.

"In other words," he said softly, "you're talking sabotage."

"That's right."

She stared broodingly at the green island a hundred yards away. The volcanic ridge seemed to rise for the sole purpose of scraping the high white clouds before dipping back down and etching its profile against the china blue of the sky.

"But you're not sure," he said.

"Venetia thinks I'm imagining conspiracies where none exist." Dorothy-Anne turned her head and looked at him questioningly. "What's your take on it, Hunt? Do you think I'm whistling in the wind? Maybe just being paranoid?"

He frowned and took off the hat and stuck his index finger in the crown and slowly began twirling it around.

"No," he said quietly, "I don't think you're being paranoid. Granted, the evidence is circumstantial. But it's *there*."

She nodded. Hearing him say it didn't make her feel any better. On the contrary—it only reinforced her own worst fears.

"Look, why don't we break it down?" he suggested. "Take this incident by incident, see what we come up with?"

She rolled over on her back. If only she could empty her mind, however temporarily, and forget all her worries for a little while. What a nice change that would be.

She stared up at the tightly stretched blue canvas awning overhead. The sun's refraction off the water spangled it with dancing spots of bright light. She nodded. "Yes. I'm up to it," she said.

"Good. Let's start with the bank loans."

"Ouch." She pulled a face. "You really do cut to the chase, don't you?"

"That's because money's the motive behind most everything. People kill for it all the time. Just ask any cop."

Her face had paled. "I'm not sure I like the direction this is headed."

"You don't have to like it," Hunt said gently. "But you have to face it. You've got seven hundred and fifty million bucks in paper floating around out there, and your company's the collateral. That's an awfully big prize for somebody who wants to pick up an eight-billion-dollar corporation for twenty cents on the dollar. All they've got to do is see to it that you default."

"You sure know how to scare a girl," she said in a shaky voice.

"I'm only stating the obvious."

Dorothy-Anne sighed, her breasts heaving.

"Now let's do a logical jump and move on to the bacterial out-breaks," Hunt continued. "The way I see it, one incident like that's unfortunate. Not that I'd exactly condone it—but hey. Accidents happen. They happen all the time. But *two*?"

He shook his head. "You ask me, it seems like a surefire way to cut off your cash flow."

"Thereby causing me to default on my loans," Dorothy-Anne whispered.

"That's right. And it's not a far-fetched scenario, either. Not when you consider what's at stake."

Dorothy-Anne sighed. The yacht was rocking gently, and she could hear the soft slapping of the waves, the little creaks from the pressure of the water against the wooden hull.

"At least you've convinced me I'm not paranoid," she said at last. "I suppose I should be grateful for that."

"Sometimes a little paranoia can be healthy," he said.

"What's so amazing," Dorothy-Anne murmured, "is that until now, I never gave any of this so much as a thought."

"And why should you? Your industry is hospitality and leisure."

He reached for his glass of iced tea and picked it up. A paper napkin was affixed to the glass with a rubber band. He took a sip and then set it carefully back down.

The wind was starting to pick up and he looked beyond Dorothy-Anne. To the south, a squall was building, and the waves chucking rhythmically against the hull were already leaping higher, their tips frothing with foam. The rocking of the yacht became more noticeable.

"Squall's forming," he observed.

She glanced over her shoulder. "Oh, that," she said, with a shrug. "This is the tropics. You know how it is. One moment the sun's out, and the next it pours. Then *bing*! The sun's back out again."

He nodded. "If you're not worried, I'm not either. But just to be on the safe side, let me go and secure the hatches."

She nodded and he got up. Keeping his head down, he walked his fingers across the varnished table and then swung himself expertly out from under the awning. She watched as he made his way forward along the narrow side deck in bare feet, locking and testing each of the ventilation hatches, his coordination and balance perfect. Obviously, being on boats was second nature to him.

When he was done, he returned aft and disappeared down the companionway. She could hear him moving about belowdecks, snap-locking the sliding ports in the saloon and then in each of the two forward cabins. When he reappeared, he sat back down in the cockpit and sketched a goofy salute.

"Aye, aye, skipper," he reported. "Ship's dogged down."

Dorothy-Anne glanced up at the blue awning. "What about the top?"

"It can stay. If need be, I can have it down in seconds."

She smiled. "Nothing like a great crew, is there?"

He flashed her a thousand-watt grin. "We aim to please."

Then his demeanor was suddenly serious again. Frowning, he reached for his iced tea and scratched at the moist napkin around the glass with his fingernails, shredding off tiny crescents of paper that blew away in the wind.

"Getting back to the subject at hand," he said.

She waited.

"The way I see it, we've figured out motive. Who knows?" Hunt shrugged and looked at her. "Could be, we're way off base. Maybe the outbreaks *were* accidental."

"A wish I'd give my eyeteeth for," Dorothy-Anne murmured fervently.

"But in case they weren't, why don't we see how the other incidents fit in?"

"I suppose it can't hurt," Dorothy-Anne replied. "Besides, bacteria and viruses aren't exactly my favorite subjects." She made an expression of distaste and stared off into space. "But then, neither are my outstanding bank loans."

"Can't say I blame you. However, AmeriBank *did* sell your loans to Pan Pacific. And that's not speculation. It's fact."

"A highly unpleasant fact," she agreed, nodding.

"Also, as you yourself pointed out, Pan Pacific is an unknown quantity." He frowned thoughtfully. "That disturbs me. So does AmeriBank's selling them your loans without notifying you first. The whole thing stinks."

"Damn right, it does! And to high heaven!" Dorothy-Anne's nostrils flared angrily. "As far as Pan Pacific goes, I don't trust them an iota. I haven't from the start."

"With good reason, apparently."

She was silent.

The low, dark clouds were scudding directly overhead now, blotting out the sun and throwing the afternoon into semidarkness. The wind had increased markedly. It whipped the waves to a froth and tugged at the canvas awning. The twelve-meter sloop tossed and reared like a thoroughbred trying to slip its reins, but the anchor held fast.

Neither Hunt nor Dorothy-Anne seemed to be aware of the effects of the storm.

"And finally," Hunt said, "there's the suspicious timing of Kurt Ackerman's so-called job offer."

"*And* Kurt's sketch," Dorothy-Anne added.

"That's right. And his sketch. If Kurt is only half the artist you claim he is—and I trust your opinion—I'd say you have every right to be leery of Sir Ian or Mr. George Blackwell or whatever his real name is. If you hadn't made the connection that the two are one and the same, Pan Pacific could have walked off with the entire candy store."

"They still might," Dorothy-Anne reminded him.

Her pale eyes were filled with shadows and resembled the surrounding shoals with their dark blue patches like clouds of ink.

"I'm not out of the woods yet," she said.

"I realize that. But my money's on you." Hunt smiled confidently. "Something tells me Sir Ian and Pan Pacific will rue the day they decided to mess with you."

"Do you mean that, Hunt?" she whispered. "Do you really?"

He reached out and placed one hand on hers. His touch was like an electrical current. She felt the pulsating warmth emanate from his fingers, felt it spread swiftly throughout her body.

"You bet I mean it," he said staunchly.

Her voice was hesitant. "Then you don't think I'm . . . crazy?"

"Crazy!" His teeth gleamed and his laughter reached his eyes. "Of course not! If you were, then I'd have to be certifiable, too. And we can't both be afflicted with the same mental disorder at the same time, can we?"

Her brows knit together and she dropped her eyes, as if she'd become absorbed in the teak grain of the table.

"I wish that made me feel better," she said slowly, "but it doesn't."

"I'm not trying to make you feel better. I meant every word I said."

She lifted her eyes up to meet his. "That's just it!"

"What is?" He gave his head a shake. "Now you've got me thoroughly confused."

"Hunt, don't you see? Your believing me makes the whole thing that much more real and scary! It's no longer an abstraction!"

"Dorothy-Anne, listen to me!" Hunt still had his hand on hers, and he leaned toward her across the table and looked deep into her eyes. "There's no need to be frightened," he said softly. "You'll lick 'em. I know you will!"

But his words went in one ear and out the other. Dorothy-Anne was too distracted by Hunt's disturbing proximity—his hand on hers, his face so close she could smell the faint, lingering fragrance of soap from his shower, the spicy aroma of mint leaves on his breath from the iced tea. Masculine scents, the lot of them: clean and fresh and healthy, unsullied by cologne or aftershave or talcum. And underneath them all she caught a whiff—the merest suggestion, the barest hint, really—of that most powerful, provocative, and naturally intoxicating of any man's scent, testosterone.

She felt she was drowning in his eyes, being inhaled by his breath. A noise like the amplified rushing of surf filled her head.

If the table weren't separating us, she realized, *we would be kissing. . . .*

Then the first heavy raindrops fell, puckering the canvas above them, and suddenly the clouds burst. Eden Isle was swallowed up by a thick curtain of water, and the noise was such that they couldn't hear themselves think.

The downpour ended as abruptly as it had begun. One moment, the rain was coming down in sheets; the next, the sun shone gloriously and Eden Isle reappeared in even sharper focus than before.

The yacht had ridden out the squall like a champ. Dorothy-Anne and Hunt had remained on deck for the duration, only slightly the wetter for wear.

"Bracing," he pronounced.

"Exhilarating!" she agreed. Her eyes were clear and wide and bright. The cloudburst had been like an amusement ride, a welcome diversion, however brief, from the troubles at hand.

Hunt smiled at her.

She smiled back at him.

Then they got seriously back down to business, continuing where they'd left off.

"First thing you need to do," Hunt said, "is to find out who owns Pan Pacific."

"I know. Derek's been working on that."

"And?"

"And nothing. He's been on top of it since the end of December."

"Yes?"

Dorothy-Anne let out a sigh. "So far he hasn't gotten to square one. We still don't know any more than we did when he started."

"You're putting me on." Hunt's voice was incredulous. "And he's had three *months?*"

"That's right." She nodded. "He keeps running into obstacles. Private banks in Asia apparently bring new meaning to the word 'inscrutable.' They make the Swiss look like a bunch of gossips."

Hunt shook his head. "I don't buy that. There's always a weak link. You just have to know where to look."

He paused and gazed off at the horizon, where the hazy blue sea met the hazy blue sky.

"Maybe it's time you brought in a professional," he suggested.

Dorothy-Anne tossed him a frown. "What kind of a professional?"

He drew his eyes back in and folded his hands on the table.

"A private investigator."

"A P.I.!" she sputtered, unable to contain her mirth. "Like in the movies? Hunt, please tell me you're kidding!"

"A friend of mine from way back founded one of the top firms in the business," he added. "I highly recommend him. If anybody can get you results, it's him. We met in the navy."

"You were in the service?"

"Yep. I signed up for four years, right after I graduated from Yale."

"You went into the navy from *Yale*?"

"What can I say? It's a family tradition. Also, my mother was convinced it would ensure my political career. I decided to indulge her—for my sake. It was either that, or working for Winslow Communications and reporting directly to her."

He smiled wryly.

"When she found out I went behind her back and joined the SEALs, she nearly blew a gasket."

He chuckled at the memory.

"So you were a SEAL," Dorothy-Anne marveled, her eyes aglow. "An honest-to-goodness, daredevil SEAL." Somehow Hunt never failed to surprise. Perhaps it was this unpredictability that made him so attractive? She wasn't quite sure; most likely, it was the sum total of everything.

He reached out, chucked a finger under her chin, and raised it. "Just think about a P.I. Okay?"

"Your advice is duly noted," she said, folding her arms in front of her breasts. "But I don't think my staff could possibly sell me out."

Hunt changed the subject. "Aren't you supposed to be getting back to shore? Doing your queen bee act on the drones?"

Dorothy-Anne shook her head. "I thought I told you. I postponed the inspection tour until tomorrow morning."

She paused, cocked her head to one side, and eyed him speculatively. Ordinarily, she didn't believe in mixing business with pleasure, but it wouldn't hurt for Hunt to see just how unjustified and baseless his suspicions were. No, she decided, it certainly couldn't hurt, not this once.

"You wouldn't, by any chance, care to tag along?" she asked, her voice a curious mixture of cajolery, seduction, and challenge.

He didn't hesitate. "I'd like that," he said, a smile broadening his eminently kissable mouth, a smile she had to remind herself to fight and resist. "Hmmm. Yes, I think I'd like that a whole lot."

A steady light rain was falling, and Victoria Peak was wreathed in clouds. In his villa near the summit, the *lung tao* was at a potting table, grafting a hybrid tea rose with one of his prized pink weeping tree roses.

Instead of the ceremonial robes he usually favored, he was in his gardening pajamas. He had on a loose, black mandarin-collared top over baggy black peasant trousers. Though they made him seem smaller, he looked far from ordinary; his commanding presence was such that no one would ever mistake him for hired help.

Hearing the brisk click-clacks of high heels, Kuo Fong said: "That is you, Spring Blossom?" He spoke Chiuchow, and kept concentrating on his work.

"Yes, most venerated Kuo." Although he did not look up, she bowed graciously all the same. "You called for me?"

"Unfortunately, this rose requires my immediate attention. Just a moment."

"Of course, venerable Kuo," she said.

She waited while he fitted the rose branch into the surgical incision he'd made in the delicate trunk.

"I am most grateful," he said when he was done. "If you would be so kind, call Pan Pacific and tell Sir Ian the *lung tao* wishes to see him. At once, *heya?*"

"Yes, venerable Kuo."

"But when the motherless fornicator arrives, make him wait for an hour before you bring him in here."

Spring Blossom stifled a cackle. She despised the foreign devil for his condescending manner and rude pomposity, and looked forward to keeping him waiting—all the while mouthing meaningless strings of flowery apologies.

She bowed respectfully. "Consider it done."

Sir Ian Connery knew a summons when he received one. He had his chauffeur bring his car around, told his secretary to cancel the rest of the morning's appointments, and was off.

He stared uneasily out the window as his garnet Rolls-Royce conquered the curves of Victoria Peak. No matter where he looked, all he could see beyond the rain-streaked glass were thick shrouds of blanketing cloud. Their pewter opacity seemed especially fitting, since the purpose of this trip was as obscure as the world beyond the piercing beams of the yellow fog lights.

He tried to guess what the *lung tao* wanted this time, but came up empty. There was simply no telling. The only constant was the ride up Victoria Peak—it never failed to fill him with dark premonitions and dread.

Sir Ian's fear was palpable. It was like a physical force, a fluttering of muscular tics, a twitching of his extremities, an asthmatic wheeze as he tried to breathe. His hands dug into the edge of the garnet-piped leather seat, imprinting the soft, wildberry hide with the deep impressions of his fingers.

Fear: yes. The old man frightened him—and in a way no gang of switchblade-wielding street toughs ever could. For Kuo Fong possessed true power, a power so self-evident there was never any need to assert it, and that was so absolute that it brooked no argument, nor tolerated any mercy.

But Kuo Fong possessed much more.

He owned people.

Sir Ian, for one. In fact, the old *lung tao* owned everything except Sir Ian's impoverished title. All the rest—the props so indispensible to a well-turned-out aristocrat, were Kuo Fong's: Sir Ian's plum position at Pan Pacific; his elegant penthouse condominium; the expensive memberships in Hong Kong's most exclusive clubs; this very car, in fact, in which he was now riding. Even the beautifully tailored clothes on his back—all were conditional. His for as long as he played the *lung tao*'s British stooge.

Without these necessary appurtenances, without these costumes, these props, Sir Ian knew he'd be just another in a long row of threadbare aristocrats.

So he danced to whatever tune the old *lung tao* played.

Sir Ian danced. And danced. And the more he danced, the more impossible it was to stop. It was as if he'd foolhardily slipped his feet into the Red Shoes.

Painfully, heavily, he exhaled a sigh. *The red shoes demanded nonstop dancing.* Engraved invitations, dinners, cocktails, restaurants, yacht races, the track. *The red shoes demanded nonstop dancing.* Sir Ian. Banker. Committee chair. Well-fed man about town. *The red shoes demanded nonstop dancing.* Gossip, secrets, favors, loans, payoffs, bribes . . .

At first he had tried to fool himself, but by now he was reconciled. There were no other options open to him. You didn't just pack your bags and leave the *lung tao*'s employ. Not, that was, if you valued your health and well-being.

Once recruited, you belonged to the old man . . . either for life, or until death did you part.

The big car slowed, then swung a sharp left and stopped. Beyond the Rolls's silver lady, a pair of elaborate iron gates loomed tall, the combination of fog lights and drifting cloud making for a theatrical effect. Tall, dark privet hedges faded, as though through thickening scrims, into the mist on either side. There was a microphone mounted on a post outside the driver's window.

Before his chauffeur could speak into it, the electronic gates swung slowly inward, and Sir Ian was reminded of cyclopean lenses and hidden surveillance cameras.

Gravel crunched as the car rolled forward.

Sir Ian drew a deep breath. *When in doubt, bluster.*

Squaring his shoulders, he sat erect and tossed his freshly barbered head. Dressed himself in the raiments of pomposity. Adorned himself with ornaments of self-importance.

He willed himself larger, more imposing, *confident.*

The Rolls drew to a halt under the porte-cochere of the house, and the usual drill commenced.

It never varied. The chauffeur came around and held the rear door. The butler let him into the house and took his coat. A bodyguard expertly patted him down. Then a houseman led him to the familiar, marble-floored reception room where a fire fluttered in the grate.

There he was relegated—purposely, no doubt—to the same, uncomfortably low, too soft easy chair as always, the one from which he'd have difficulty rising. He waved away the customary offer of refreshment and settled down to wait.

The house was quiet. The fire crackled, spraying occasional sparks against the screen. On the mantel, the French clock ticked metronomically, as though mocking him for rushing to get here.

Five minutes passed. Then ten.

Impatiently he shot back his cuff and scowled at his gold Rolex. Testily drummed his fingertips on the upholstered arms of the chair.

This was not the first time he had been kept waiting in this house.

Far from it. It had become an epidemic of late. And Hong Kong had yet to be turned over to the Chinese! If the *lung tao* and his people saw fit to toy with *him*—a titled British subject!—this way already, what would it be like *after* the official takeover?

And, more important and to the point, could it be that his usefulness was drawing to a close? Was he to be discarded like an old shoe—no longer serviceable or of need?

Which sent other, even more disturbing questions rumbling, like approaching thunder, along the horizon of Sir Ian's mind.

If they decided to discard him, then *how* would they go about it? He had been privy to too many dirty secrets; had been the front man in too many underhanded deals. They couldn't just retire him and let him walk.

So. How will they go about it?

He shuddered to think.

Yet he knew better than to chalk up these fears as mere manifestations of paranoia. A little paranoia could be extremely healthy, as evidenced by the dozen or so people—*inconvenient* people—he'd known who had simply disappeared into thin air, so mysteriously and effectively they might never have existed in the first place.

Is that to be my fate, too? he wondered, his broad pink forehead breaking out in glistening beads of perspiration.

No, no, he reassured himself. *I must stop jumping to conclusions. I have to calm down. . . .*

He plucked a fresh white handkerchief out of a pocket and delicately blotted his forehead, struggling to even his breathing, to control the betrayals of muscular tics.

Calm is called for. Yes, calm . . .

Fifteen minutes. Twenty . . .

Presently the door opened and quick-stepping heels resounded on marble. He squinted owlishly through the lenses of his large, black-framed glasses. Spring Blossom Wu was crossing the room toward him, her purposeful but compact gait dictated by the narrow cut of her bright blue *chong sam.*

"Ah! Ms. Wu!" Sir Ian fell into the bumbling, avuncular character of the dotty Englishman abroad. He quickly brushed his thinning hair back with his fingers, then placed his hands on the chair's arms to push himself to his feet.

"No, no, Sir Ian. Please to remain seated." Spring Blossom's voice was pleasingly soft, even musical.

She bowed politely.

"Honorable Kuo begs a thousand pardons. He is momentarily detained. I must apologize for any inconvenience."

He blinked away a scowl, but not fast enough to hide his displeasure. The waiting game rankled, and outrage feasted on his ulcer.

"I have, of course, informed Honorable Kuo the moment you arrived." She smiled brightly. "Could I offer you some tea, Sir Ian?"

"A spot of tea?" he said, clearly disappointed.

He would have welcomed a gin or scotch, but to ask for something that wasn't offered was considered barbaric by these people. *When in Hong Kong . . .*

He shook his head lugubriously. "Lovely of you to offer, but no. Thanks all the same."

She nodded. "Your patience is much appreciated, Sir Ian. It will surely not be much longer."

"Sooner the better, eh?" He forced out a chuckle.

"Yes, yes. Soon." She nodded happily. "Very soon."

But it was another forty minutes, interspersed by two more apologetic visits from her, before she finally said, "Sir Ian? Honorable Kuo will see you now. Again, a thousand heartfelt apologies."

He nodded, his lips forming a chilly, formal smile. Each of her appearances had provoked a new level of insult within him, and he had become too angry to trust himself to speak. His clenched fists quivered at his sides.

"This way, please."

The long hall she led him down echoed their heels like a deserted museum. She took him not to the *lung tao*'s study, as he had expected, but past it to a nautiluslike staircase of marble with five landings. Although the street front of the villa was two-storied and deceptively modest, the back was built down the plunging hillside, so that the bulk of the structure was hidden from the road.

Descending the stairs, they passed niches in the wall, each devoted to a single priceless, spotlit artifact. The collection seemed to encompass the entire spectrum of Chinese dynasties.

None bought through the usual channels, Sir Ian was willing to bet. *Plundered from archeological digs on the mainland,* he was certain. *Before they could be inventoried.*

At the bottom of the staircase, he followed Spring Blossom down yet another luminously floored marble hall. Along both walls, pedestals displayed ancient Near Eastern texts. Sumerian pictographic script on stone tablets. An earthenware cylinder with rows of cuneiform, from Nebuchadnezzar II, King of Babylon. Cappadocian business letters in *Sammerlurkunde* text.

Sir Ian smirked. *These he had to pay for.*

At the end of the hall, Spring Blossom Wu opened a door and stepped aside. She gave a courteous bow.

"Please to go in, Sir Ian," she said.

He stepped across the threshold—"Jesus, *fuck!*"—and gagged, recoiling from the glutinous wall of heat, humidity, and nauseatingly rank manure that smacked him squarely in the face. Swiftly he whipped out his handkerchief and pressed it over his nose and mouth. His eyes, already watering behind his lenses, leaped about.

He was in a garden room, one of those Victorian-style conservatories with glass-paned walls and a glass ogee roof. The kind that had once again become all the rage, and was usually added onto a house as a winter garden or dining room.

Not this one. It was used for its originally intended purpose—hence the maze of five-tiered étagères lined with precise formations of potted roses.

Handkerchief to his face, and taking shallow breaths through his mouth, Sir Ian turned a full circle.

Roses. They were everywhere. Hundreds of them. All in various stages of growth.

Here, brutally pruned sticks, like ugly amputees grafted with donor limbs. There, slender prickly green stalks, some with leaves and buds. And everywhere, many—too, too many by far—in gloriously full, funeral-ready bloom.

He winced against the association, but it stuck. And how could it not?

For even the potent stench of manure, the very worst manure he'd ever had the displeasure to smell—and he hadn't known, not really (why should he?) that all manure did *not* smell unlike—was unable to overpower the organic, earthy odors of chlorophyll and potting soil, all underlaid by the richly sweet, cloying fetor of rot.

Sir Ian diverted his gaze. He glanced up through the churchlike arches of the glass ceiling, then longingly over toward the far wall where, he sensed, outside the glass panes a clear day would permit the *lung tao* to survey his dual domains—the immediate property, with the level backyard of pool and garden, and the greater realm beyond the panoramic drop-off, where all Hong Kong awaited—a vast carcass ripe for continued plucking.

But all that was visible today were the clouds. They pressed against the glass like a fog bank, as though they had been provided specifically to shroud this meeting in secrecy.

Meeting! What meeting? he thought, certain he was alone, brought here expressly to endure yet another round of humiliation.

But this was too much! Puffing himself up with dignity, he started back toward the door when—*Snick!*—a metallic, man-made sound carried from nearby.

Curious, he changed course, carefully threading his way forward through the maze of étagères, arms raised protectively against the thorny branches. He cursed under his breath as he pushed blooms out of his face, as thorns caught on the sleeves of his chalk-striped black suit . . . his beautiful, new, soon-to-be-ruined suit if he didn't get the hell out of this wretchedly hot atmosphere of stifling dampness and excrement and cloying sweetness!

Christ! Was a worse combination of smells possible?

He thought, *Surely not,* and hoped his suit would not absorb the odors, or that if it did, the cleaners could get it out.

He was feeling decidedly wilted. Runnels of sweat were trickling down his forehead, beads of sweat were popping out above his upper lip, a veritable flood of sweat was sluicing down his back. Already, his shirt was plastered to his shoulders.

And his eyes! They burned from the pungent stench and brimmed with tears, but all the same he became aware of the colors. Such a startling variety they were. Rose blossoms in sugar white, lemon yellow, sunny yellow, cognac, and brass. Roses in tangerine, coral, ruby-edged ivory, lavender, raspberry, scarlet, crimson, blood.

The spectrum seemed endless.

As did their shapes.

Eventually he came upon a wooden potting table where perfectly pruned rose standards, like colorful floral poodles, stood in a row. And there behind it, dwarfed by the shrubs, was the old *lung tao.* In black pajamas. Pruners in hand.

He was gardening—frigging gardening!

Sir Ian's chubby face turned scarlet with anger. He couldn't believe it.

All the time I've been kept waiting, he's been bleeding gardening!

The insult burned like a slap in the face.

Looking up, the old man affected a look of surprise. Then he bowed graciously.

"Sir Ian," he said in his accented, singsong English. "I am honored by your presence in my house."

Handkerchief still pressed to his face, Sir Ian returned the bow and rattled off the standard reply: "I thank the Honorable Kuo for his gracious hospitality."

As always, he was amazed that this tiny ancient, with his wispy white hair, scraggly goatee, and wizened skin the color of golden rum, should wield such enormous power.

The old man gestured with a liver-spotted hand. "I see you are unused to the smell. I beg a thousand pardons. I forget that not everyone is used to it."

"Never smelled anything like it," Sir Ian admitted, coming around the table. "What the devil is it?"

The *lung tao* smiled. "The best fertilizer in the world for roses, chicken dung."

Sir Ian grimaced. *No wonder it stinks to high heaven!*

"It is ironic, is it not, that cultivating beauty should depend upon something so vile?" The old man stroked his goatee and regarded Sir Ian with a knowing look. "But it is so throughout nature. The most exquisite delights and delicacies require rot and excrement. Consider shellfish. Do they not feed upon the very bottom of the sea?"

"Can't argue with that, can I?"

The old man turned to a bush of long-stemmed, big-blossomed roses. At first glance they appeared white, but were actually the very palest of pinks, with pale apricot centers. Selecting a bloom, he used his pruners to snip off a stem, then held it up to the light and rotated it to inspect its translucent quality. He looked at Sir Ian inquiringly.

"Tell me, Sir Ian. Are you fond of roses?"

"Don't know much about them, I'm afraid. 'Rose is a rose is a rose,' and all that."

The *lung tao* nodded. "This is my very own hybrid," he said, of the rose in his hand. "I named it Sun Cloud, after my eldest grandchild."

He snipped the stem to within two inches, and stripped off a thorn with a horned thumbnail the color of tortoiseshell. Then he proffered the rose to Sir Ian.

"For your buttonhole," he said humbly.

Sir Ian accepted it. "I thank you for so personal a gift." Etiquette demanded graciousness, and he had no choice but to wear the boutonniere. But to get it on his lapel required both hands. Reluctantly he pocketed his handkerchief.

Without it, the stench threatened to overwhelm. He nearly reeled, but managed to slip the rose through the buttonhole.

"How's it look? A bit formal, isn't it?"

"Not at all." Kuo Fong allowed himself a faint smile. "You are kind to humor an old man. Now come. Walk with me—I must inspect my hybrids. We have urgent business to discuss."

"As always, I am at the *lung tao*'s service."

As they moved among the roses, Kuo Fong deadheaded blooms by pinching them between his thumb and index finger. "You are to take the next available flight to New York. Make no appointment. Give no warning whatsoever. Simply show up."

The *lung tao* stopped beside a hybrid tea rose with pointy, pure white petals with vivid pink streaks and violet edges.

"This is Heavenly Flower. It is the most recent result of my hybridizing. I named it in honor of my youngest granddaughter, of whom I am most fond."

They moved on.

"This trip to New York," Sir Ian said. "What's it entail? Whom am I to see?"

The old man stopped walking and turned and looked up at him directly. "Mrs. Cantwell of the Hale Companies."

"And the purpose of this unexpected visit?"

Something crafty flashed in the depths of Kuo Fong's eyes. "You are to put a proposal before her. I will give you the details momentarily. But first, there is another rose I wish to show you. . . ."

Sir Ian followed the old man. *Now I get it,* he thought. *It's about the loans. I'm to be the hatchet man.*

He wasn't looking forward to it. At best, it would be a highly unpleasant experience. And at worst . . .

But he wouldn't think about that now. He had no choice in the matter. At any rate, it beat the alternative.

At least I'm not the one being axed. I'd rather be a hatchet man any day.

44

Dorothy-Anne was subdued. This was hardly her first visit to her husband's pet project, but in the past she had always been accompanied by him. Eden Isle had, after all, been Freddie's brainchild. As such, she had been careful to remain in the background, letting him call the shots.

And now it was up to her to see it through to completion.

She looked around his office in the air-conditioned Quonset hut. It was spare, masculine, utilitarian.

Everywhere, form followed function.

It was evident in the plain metal filing cabinets and the cork boards, pinned with blueprints, that were propped along both curved walls; in the L-shaped desk in front of the window at the end wall; in the gray metal swivel chair behind it and the semicircle of stackable resin chairs facing it.

The surface of the desk was free of clutter, the way Freddie liked it. The short end of the L held his computer, keyboard, and printer. On the longer surface were a blotter, an executive pen set, a desk lamp, and several telephones. The sole decorative touch was a framed photograph of Dorothy-Anne and the children.

The poignancy of it brought tears to Dorothy-Anne's eyes.

The wall opposite the windows was fitted with three identical doors. The one in the center, Dorothy-Anne knew, led out to a communal office packed with workstations. At the moment, it held no interest for her.

Instead, she opened the door on the right and walked into a compact bathroom. It contained a sink, a toilet, and a fiberglass shower stall. Clean white towels hung from a chrome bar, and the shelf above the sink still held Freddie's electric toothbrush, half a tube of toothpaste, a can of shaving cream, and his ivory-handled straight razor.

As if he was expected to return at any moment.

But Freddie is never coming back, Dorothy-Anne reminded herself soberly. *He's gone for good. It's time I packed up his personal belongings.*

She walked back out and closed the door quietly behind her. Hunt, she noticed, had his back turned. He was leaning forward, hands folded in the small of his spine, pretending keen interest in some tacked-up blueprints.

He doesn't want to intrude on my privacy.

Dorothy-Anne was grateful for his tact. He clearly sensed how difficult this was for her.

Suddenly she was glad he had come along. *I'm not alone,* she told herself. *That's the most important thing.*

The door on the left led to the bedroom where Freddie had slept whenever he'd spent the night here. Dorothy-Anne opened the door and went inside.

For a moment she stood there, trembling, as she looked around. The cot was neatly made, and on the narrow, gray metal hanging locker was Freddie's hard hat, the yellow one with his name stenciled across the front.

Seeing it triggered a series of split-second images, fleeting as the lighted windows of a train rushing in the opposite direction. She could see Freddie trying it on, adjusting it various ridiculous ways, his face grinning. What a handsome, playful devil he had been! Small wonder she had loved him so much, missed him so dreadfully . . .

As if watching herself on film, she relived her first trip to Eden Isle. Freddie was leading her by the hand, rushing her through the junglelike growth, pointing excitedly here, there, everywhere, weaving a dream world out of words and gestures.

And the memories kept coming, flashing at her with painful clarity.

She was fully clothed and Freddie was pulling her into the sparkling water of a hidden pool, the white ribbon of waterfall drowning out her squeals. Then they were kissing and ripping off each other's clothes and making urgent, passionate love.

The scene was so vivid that Dorothy-Anne cried out his name.

"Freddie!"

But his presence was ephemeral, and the mental film strips began to fade. Now all that was left was the knowledge that these were but memories.

Memories . . .

Dorothy-Anne quickly shut the locker, then left the room and closed the door. She was weeping soundlessly.

Hunt came over and put his arms around her. "If you'd rather be alone, I'll understand," he said gently.

She shook her head. "I don't want you to go," she said huskily.

He held her at arm's length. "Are you sure?"

She nodded. "Yes. I am."

She moved out of his arms and went behind the desk. She pulled out the swivel chair and sat down. It was a little high for her, but she didn't want it adjusted.

It's up to me now, she thought.

Earlier, she had been in contact with White Plains from aboard the *Quicksilver.* The news had been encouraging.

Now, seated behind Freddie's desk, she replayed the telephone conversations back in her head.

"Child!" Venetia crowed jubilantly, "I do not know how you did it! No, I do not. Were you ever right about tripling the ad budgets! And sweetening the travel agents' commissions? Girl, that was a stroke of genius. Mm-*hmm!* Some of our rooms are already overbooked! Did you hear me? O-ver-booked!"

"Then let's pray it stays that way," Dorothy-Anne replied fervently.

"Oh, but that is not all. Baby, get a load of this. I called in every outstanding favor anybody's ever owed me? *Plus,* I took the IOU deep dive for years to come? I'll probably live to regret it, *but*—are you ready?"

Venetia paused dramatically.

"Sunday *Parade* is doing a glowing feature on our vacation resorts!"

"They what?" Dorothy-Anne didn't quite trust her ears.

"Girlfriend, you heard me. In fact," Venetia added smugly "they had to pull a Dennis Rodman exclusive to fit us in!"

"Venetia! How in God's name did you ever pull that off?"

"Better," Venetia replied darkly, "that you shouldn't know."

"You truly are amazing," Dorothy-Anne marveled. "Now I owe you big."

"Wrong. You owe me huge, but don't you go worrying your pretty little head about it right now," Venetia said generously. "You'll have plenty of opportunities to repay me. And girl? Just in case you forget, I'll make sure I remind you."

Next, Dorothy-Anne spoke to Bernie Appledorf. He had been more reticent—not that she expected anything less from a bean counter.

"Your eggs ain't hatched yet," he grumped sourly, "so don't go around counting 'em. When you upped the commissions and ad costs at the front end, you took a beating at the back."

Good old Bernie, she thought. *Spoken like a true accountant.*

"Bernie, just this once, spare me the lecture. I only called to get our daily earnings figures."

"Okay," he said. "Somehow, miraculously, we actually broke even yesterday."

"We *did*?"

"That's what it says."

"Oh, Bernie!" Dorothy-Anne yelped in excitement. "If you were here, I'd kiss you!"

"Save yourself the kisses," he growled. "And here's some free advice. Consider yesterday a miracle, not a trend."

What is it with this guy? Dorothy-Anne wondered. *And what would it take to make him cheerful? Or is Bernie doomed to curmudgeondom forever?*

"Tell me something, Bernie," she said. "Is there anything, anything at all on God's earth, that could lift those sourpuss spirits of yours?"

"Strange that you should ask."

"Aha!" she cried. "I knew there had to be something. Well, what is it? Let me guess. A private chorus line of naked Rockettes? Breaking the bank in Vegas? Winning the Lotto jackpot? What?"

"My idea of bliss," Bernie confided yearningly, "is a nice, steady, undramatic balance sheet, for a change. You know, one that doesn't look like a psychotic's polygraph test? That would lower my blood pressure substantially, which in turn would make me feel absolutely ecstatic."

"I walked right into that one," Dorothy-Anne muttered gloomily.

"And there's something else that would make me even happier. Care to know what it is?"

"To tell you the truth, Bernie, no. But I can guess. And right now, I don't need you on my back."

"Well, as your comptroller and your friend, I'd be remiss if I didn't harp on it. Someone's got to get you to shut down that off-the-wall money pit you're calling from. If you'd heed that bit of advice, I'll have died and gone to heaven."

"Bernie, Bernie," said Dorothy-Anne, in order to forestall further discouraging words. "How often must I tell you? Eden Isle is the future."

"Wrong," he rasped. "Eden Isle's gonna be your *past*. Your very own Waterloo."

"And what's so bad about Waterloo?" she cracked smugly. "So it was the end of Napoleon. Admit it, Bernie: it was one hell of a triumph for Wellington. You see? It all depends from whose viewpoint you look at it."

But Bernie wasn't biting. "Nice rationalizing, but no dice. So far, you managed to slide by on the skin of your teeth. But believe you me, unless you cut your losses, you might not survive another catastrophe. On the other hand, without that white elephant you're dead set on building, you just might—and notice I said *might*—survive tough times ahead."

Dorothy-Anne knew further argument was useless. "All right," she said, "you've made your point. Your advice is noted, and I'll consider it."

"Well, I'm not gonna hold my breath," he mumbled, in parting.

Now, recalling the conversation, Dorothy-Anne had to admit that from a number cruncher's standpoint, Bernie's advice was sound. But accountants weren't visionaries.

She eyed the telephones on the desk and scanned the labels beside the automatically dialed numbers, noting that the first four were hers—the townhouse, her office in White Plains, her car phone, and the farm upstate. Then she saw it. On the left row, the fifth number down: Ackerman.

Without wasting another moment, she picked up the receiver and punched the button.

Dorothy-Anne introduced Kurt to Hunt, waved both men into the resin chairs facing the desk, and got right down to business.

"Kurt, Mr. Winslow is an old friend of the family," she said, stretching the truth a bit. "You may speak freely in front of him."

Kurt nodded, accepting the little fiction. He was wearing a red Coca-Cola T-shirt under a short-sleeved aloha shirt with a pattern of hula dancers, and white shorts printed to look as though they'd been spattered with paint. He had on lime green tennis shoes and rose-tinted glasses.

"Now, about your resignation," Dorothy-Anne said briskly. "That was quite a bombshell you dropped on me yesterday."

Kurt shifted uncomfortably in his chair. He looked embarrassed, and sucked his lower lip in over his lower teeth.

"I didn't mean to offend you," he said earnestly. "It's nothing personal."

Dorothy-Anne nodded, adding a smile to show that there were no hard feelings. "I realize that."

She folded her hands on the desk blotter.

"Also, I sympathize with your desire for new challenges. If anyone can relate to that, it's me. Because I'm the same way."

He nodded.

"So I won't try to talk you out of leaving. I know it would be futile. Free spirits can't be tied down. However, that doesn't mean I want to see you go, Kurt. I don't."

"I appreciate that," he said thickly.

She said, "I don't think I need to mention that your departure comes at a rather . . . well, inopportune time?"

"I realize that—"

She held up a hand to silence him. "Don't worry about it. There probably isn't such a thing as a good time for it, anyway. However, before you leave, I shall require your help."

"Sure." Kurt looked eager to oblige. "Just tell me what you want."

She sat back and cupped her hands over the arms of her chair.

"As you know," Dorothy-Anne said slowly, "my late husband was the driving force behind Eden Isle. All this"—she lifted a hand and waved it around—"is his doing. I'll need to be familiarized with every aspect of the operation."

"No problem." Kurt smiled. "I'll be happy to take you around. Give you a cram course."

"You'd better assume I'm a babe in the woods. Where Eden Isle is concerned, I really know next to nothing."

That wasn't entirely true, but it wasn't a total lie, either. Dorothy-Anne had been kept informed of progress along every step of the way as Eden Isle underwent its transformation from an unhabited island to the massive construction site it was today. However, what she needed was Kurt's singular take on the project. She wanted to see it through *his* eyes.

"The thing to remember," he said, "is that Eden Isle was conceived as your ultimate vacation destination, a completely self-contained resort in every way. Anything anyone could want will be here. Hotels for every budget. Shops. Amusement park. The world's largest natural aquarium."

Dorothy-Anne nodded. She knew all that, but Hunt didn't, so she let Kurt continue.

"Almost everything we're doing here has never been done before," Kurt was saying. "Well, at least not on this grand a scale, and certainly not on an uninhabited island this size. That's worked both for and against us."

From his voice, his pride in the project was unmistakable, and Dorothy-Anne couldn't help thinking of Freddie. *No wonder he and Kurt had gotten along so famously.*

"One of our biggest advantages," Kurt went on, "is that we won't have any of the problems normally associated with seaside resorts. Take pollution, for example. We're nipping it in the bud *before* it can happen.

"The same with crime. Since there's no native population, there's no existing crime rate. And we intend to keep it that way."

Kurt smiled and sat forward.

"Think about it! Where else can people walk the beach at four in the morning, without fear of getting mugged? Naturally, we want things to stay that way, so we're forming our own police force."

Kurt's enthusiasm was infectious, and Dorothy-Anne found herself getting caught up in the excitement. She glanced at Hunt. He, too, was following every impassioned word with interest.

"Of course, for every upside, there's a downside," Kurt admitted. "We've encountered no end of problems. Being on an island can complicate even the simplest things."

Dorothy-Anne nodded. She knew this, too. *It's why Eden Isle is way behind schedule. And why it's gone stratospherically overbudget.*

"Also, starting from scratch meant we first had to put the entire infrastructure in place," Kurt explained. "That can get pretty involved when you're talking the equivalent of a town of six thousand people."

Hunt whistled softly. "You're going to accommodate six thousand guests?"

Kurt shook his head. "Not just guests. That figure includes the staff."

"But won't that many people have a negative impact on the ecosystem?"

Kurt shook his head again. "It shouldn't. From the start, we've been determined to keep the 'Eden' in Eden Isle."

"And how did you go about doing that?" Hunt was genuinely fascinated.

Kurt allowed himself a modest smile. "During the preliminary planning stages, we had various scientists figure out the maximum number of people who could be on this island at any given time."

"And they came up with six thousand?"

"Actually, they didn't. We did." Kurt looked at Dorothy-Anne. "Mrs. Cantwell is the expert when it comes to hotel and resort occupancy. I believe she's in the best position to explain it."

Dorothy-Anne looked at Hunt. "What we did was hire five teams of scientists, all of which worked independently of each other. The figures they came up with ranged anywhere from seven to nine thousand people. Any more would almost certainly damage the environment . . . perhaps irreparably."

"I see." Hunt nodded. "So you decided to play it safe."

"That's right. It's better than being sorry." Dorothy-Anne smiled. "So after deciding on our self-imposed limit of six thousand, we broke that down further to four thousand guests and a permanent staff of a thousand, as well as a rotating staff of another thousand."

"That's still quite a crowd."

"Yes, it is," she agreed. "Of course, we're talking maximum capacity. In the hotel business, a hundred percent occupancy rate is almost unheard of. There's always a percentage of unoccupied units. We're banking on a year-round average of seventy-five percent."

"Sounds to me like you'll have to charge top dollar just to break even."

Dorothy-Anne shook her head. "On the contrary. We plan on being competitively priced, and intend to give steep tour operator discounts. But although we'll be a family resort with theme parks, we'll also have twenty-four-hour casinos, with roulette, baccarat, craps, poker, and eight hundred slot machines. For high rollers, there'll even be a salon privé. Most of our profits will come from gambling."

"Ah. The Vegas principle. Family fun and sin—all under one roof."

"Well, quite a few roofs, but yes. It's a combination family resort and theme part with select adult entertainment."

Hunt was impressed. "This project sure is a lot more ambitious than I first thought."

"Wait until I take you around," Kurt added, with an easy grin. "Then you'll really see what's involved. Speaking of which"—he cocked his arm to consult his Mickey Mouse watch—"why don't we head out into the field? Nothing beats seeing the real thing."

He glanced at Dorothy-Anne. "There's been a lot of progress since your last visit. I think you'll be quite pleased."

Dorothy-Anne rolled back the swivel chair and popped to her feet. "Well?" she demanded, positively trembling with excitement and sense of purpose. "What are we waiting for? Let's *go!*"

Kurt led them out to the parking lot, where he had one of the green Range Rovers waiting. When they were seated he shut the doors, walked around to the driver's side, climbed in, and started the ignition.

Kurt glanced over at Dorothy-Anne. "I thought we'd start by heading north and taking the sixteen-mile drive, doing the complete circumference. If that's all right with you, of course."

"It's fine," Dorothy-Anne assured him.

They drove slowly out of the veritable boomtown of Quonset huts, manufactured homes, prefabs, RVs, and big military surplus tents, all of which served as temporary quarters, offices, and recreational facilities for the construction crews.

They passed through a tropical forest of old-growth mahogany trees and dense vegetation. Then the road climbed the gentle slope at the very outer edge of the volcanic ridge that rose sharply to form the spine of the island.

Kurt stopped the Range Rover at the crest of the slope. He was saying, "Down there to the right is Sunrise Bay. This is one of the few spots from which the sea is visible from the road. The yacht you see anchored off-shore is yours."

He drove on, and they stopped at the water treatment plant and then he took them a little further up the coast, to the electricity generating facility, a huge, sloping concrete structure abutting the side of a rocky, hundred-foot-high cliff that jutted into the sea.

"From up here, it looks like a fortress," Hunt observed, leaning over the railing at the top and looking down. "Or the front of a dam."

"What it is," Kurt told him, "is the true heart of the island. Let me show you."

He led the way to a low, windowless structure, and used a touch-tone pad set into the wall to gain access. He punched 7476. "That's July 4,

1776," he told them. "The signing of the Declaration of Independence." Dorothy-Anne and Hunt followed him inside, and then down two flights of grated steel stairs.

"This," Kurt said, tapping the code on the electronic lock of a polished steel door, "is the Energy Control Center."

The door slid aside with a sigh and they went inside.

Hunt looked around in awe. "Wow!" he said softly. "Holy Moses!"

One entire wall was of cantilevered glass, and overlooked two massive, three-story-high gas turbines. On the other three walls were banks of switches and electronic schematic diagrams of transmission lines and transformers. These were overseen by four engineers in white lab coats who were seated at computer workstations.

Hunt stood at the cantilevered wall of glass and stared down at the gleaming turbines. He could hear and feel their muffled throbs, like a sleeping Goliath's reverberating heartbeat.

Hunt shook his head. "I'm sure glad it's not my checkbook," he said.

They went back to the Rover and continued onward, driving north through dense foliage and dappled shadows.

Kurt swung a right at the next turnoff, and the Rover once again left the ring road behind.

As the foliage petered out, Hunt lowered his head and leaned forward between the two front seats. He wished he had thought to bring a bathing suit. The palm-lined beach up ahead looked like confectioner's sugar, and the sea was inviting: emerald green inside the reef, and a deep dark blue beyond it.

"Today's a bit hazy," Kurt said, "but if you look closely, you can just make out the southern coast of Puerto Rico. It's twenty-two miles from here over to Phosphorescent Bay."

Now that he looked for it, Hunt could discern the silhouette of a bluish landmass poking up along the horizon.

Kurt pulled up and parked, and they got out.

"This is where the adults-only complex will be. Right on the beach will be the Planter's Mansion." Kurt used his finger to point to the spot. "Directly behind it will be the casino for high rollers. No slots here. It'll be strictly salon privé. There'll also be beach bungalows and a golf course."

Hunt walked over to a drop-off and looked down. It was an eight-foot-wide concrete trench with gutters running along each side of the bottom. He reckoned it was around seven feet deep. At regular intervals, he noticed ladders embedded in the walls, as well as electric utility lights in wire cages.

"Let me guess," he joked. "Booby traps for unwelcome visitors? Or preparations for trench warfare?"

Kurt came over to him. "That's one of the service trenches," he explained. "A concept we borrowed from Walt Disney World."

"Service trenches."

"That's right. They're so shift changes, routine maintenance, emergency repairs, or just litter collection—all the unglamorous, behind-the-scenes stuff—will be invisible to the guests. We dug forty miles of these. They're all part of one big interconnected network."

Hunt stared at him. "Did I hear you say forty *miles?*"

"You did."

Hunt whistled softly. Then, leaning forward some more, he scanned the length of the trench more closely. Now that he knew what to look for, he detected where another trench bisected this one a hundred feet away.

"It must be a maze! Won't the people who work here get lost?"

"Not at all," Kurt replied. "It's really very simple. Think of Manhattan above Fourteenth Street. Now. You see that solid yellow stripe painted down the middle?"

"Yes."

"That stripe indicates that this trench runs longitudinally. Like an avenue running uptown to downtown. Now see that big *G* stenciled on the wall every so often?"

Hunt nodded.

"Well, *G* is the seventh letter of the alphabet. Therefore, this is the seventh 'avenue' over. There are seven in all. *A* is the nearest to the western coast, *D* runs more or less down the middle of the island, and G here is closest to our eastern coast."

"You're right," Hunt said. "It is simple. I take it the cross trenches are numbered consecutively? Like city streets?"

"You got it. There are eighteen in all. One is at the top of the island, and eighteen is at the bottom."

"But what about the center of the island?" Hunt asked. "It's extremely mountainous. Do the trenches stop there?"

"No." Kurt shook his head. "In places, the trenches get deeper, and they become tunnels where necessary."

"And transportation?" Hunt asked. "Obviously these trenches are roadways of some sort."

"That's right, they are. We'll be using a fleet of narrow electrically powered carts specially built for us by Mitsubishi."

Kurt paused.

"So what do you think?" he asked.

Hunt thought it was ingenious.

The tour lasted most of the afternoon.

Next on the agenda was the amusement park for preteens. Its focal point, the shallow one-acre swimming pool, was empty but had already been poured and tiled. Permanently "anchored" at one end was the towering hull of Jolly Roger's treasure galleon. On the opposite "shore," the cinder block walls and towers of the *castillo* awaited its final coat of patinaed, stone-scored concrete, heraldic pennants, and pretend princesses.

Then they stopped at the family-oriented Grand Victoria Hotel. It was a sprawling behemoth, the timber framework near enough complete so that the towers, turrets, deep loggias, and steep roofs revealed the architectural fantasy it would shortly become.

The three of them headed toward the empty free-form pool. Situated between the front of the hotel and the beach, it was so huge it seemed like an ocean in its own right, with concrete islands and a rope suspension bridge.

"The islands are hollow for holding soil," Kurt shouted. "We're putting in grown palms. The pool itself is over nine hundred feet long."

As soon as they'd toured it, Dorothy-Anne was ready to move on. "Where to now?" she demanded of Kurt, her eyes positively shining.

"The Oceanographic Institute. It's close, so we might as well go on foot. And after that, there's the lagoon—"

"Well, come *on*!" Dorothy-Anne cried out over the din from all around. She led the way, grabbing Hunt by the hand and tugging him along.

The Oceanographic Institute was a few hundred yards down the beach, near the southern tip of the island. Built on a rocky spit of land created by a long-ago lava flow, it had an imposing presence, and although it was newly constructed, looked as if it had occupied the site for centuries—a direct result of being based on a seventeenth-century mansion in Old San Juan.

The details were in keeping with Spanish Colonial vernacular: mellowed, patinaed pink stucco walls, ground-floor arches, wrought-iron balconies, and wooden shutters. It was surrounded on three sides by a balustraded, limestone-paved terrace.

"Except for the exhibits," Kurt said, "it's finished."

"Well?" Dorothy-Anne said. "Why don't we see how the inside of this place turned out?"

Kurt led them across the terrace and under the arches. He held the front door open. "I think you'll be pleased," he told Dorothy-Anne.

She nodded wordlessly and went inside, gazing around the high-ceilinged lobby. Straight ahead, a wide limestone staircase rose up to the second floor. It was flanked by two tall, symmetrically placed doors. The one on the left had a sign that read Entrance; the one on the right was marked Exit.

Kurt made a beeline to the left and they followed him into a long, dark windowless hall. Then he flicked a switch.

Eerie greenish lights flickered on, illuminating the insides of enormous, empty aquariums. They lined both walls completely.

"These tanks are for endangered aquatic species," Kurt said. "We're committed to breeding them and setting the offspring free in their natural habitats. At least, that's the idea."

"You sound slightly skeptical," Hunt observed.

"That's because it's difficult to predict how animals will behave in captivity. Some adapt better than others. Still, we have to try. *Before* it's too late."

Next, Kurt took them upstairs to a room that had large-screen televisions recessed in the walls. Beneath them, earphones hung on hooks.

"Using animation, we're going to use these to illustrate the effects of global warming," Kurt explained. "People will get to see how much landmass will be under water with every degree of rising temperature. An independent studio is producing the videos for us."

He ushered them into another, larger room. "Here," he said, "exhibits will educate the public at large about the dangers of pollution, drift netting, and overfishing. We'll also teach people ways they can personally help—by cutting up plastic six-pack holders, for instance, so fish don't get caught in them."

Finally, he took them downstairs to a cavernous subbasement at sea level. The floor was metal grating, and underneath it was water.

Kurt said: "A natural underwater cave lets out directly into the lagoon from here. And these two babies"—he indicated a pair of small, two-person red submersibles with Plexiglas bubble tops, which bobbed gently at their slips—"are *Neptune I* and *Neptune II*."

Hunt eyed the vessels admiringly. They each had two cylindrical air tanks attached to each of their sides. "I gather these minisubs aren't for guests?" he said.

"You gather correctly. They cost far more to run than we could charge for the ride. They're for maintenance in the lagoon, and are battery powered so they won't cause any pollution."

"And those arms at the front . . . the ones with those wrenchlike ends? They're robotic hands?"

"Right again," Kurt said. "They can be manipulated from inside the vessels."

They went back upstairs and out into the sunshine. After the darkness of the subbasement, the bright light hurt their eyes.

"And now," Kurt announced, "comes the *pièce de résistance.* Predators' Lagoon."

Hunt flicked him a squinty glance. "Sounds ominous."

"Really, Kurt," Dorothy-Anne said, shielding her eyes from the sun with her hand. "Why don't we hold off on that until it's finished? Hunt will never imagine the full effect just by walking along the shore."

Kurt grinned. "Who said anything about walking along the shore?"

She let her arm drop and stared at him. "You don't mean . . ."

"Yep. Indeed I do. I checked while you were having lunch. The gerbil tube was finished early this afternoon."

"And you didn't tell me!" Dorothy-Anne cried accusingly.

"If I had, you'd have wanted to see it right away."

"And what's wrong with that, may I ask?"

"Nothing. Except that every great showman knows you have to save the best for last."

"Gerbil tube?" Hunt asked. "Will somebody," he implored, "please fill me in on what you're talking about?"

"You'll see. Come *on!*" Dorothy-Anne flung over her shoulder as she took flight, her destination the closer of what looked like two hexagonal bandstands with shell-encrusted roofs, which jutted out over the lagoon.

Hunt reached the open-air pavilion and looked around, but Dorothy-Anne was nowhere in sight.

Where in the name of God could she have disappeared to?

Perplexed, he stepped up into the pavilion. Then he noticed the ramp, surrounded on two sides by protective railing, which spiraled gently down from one side and curved out of sight somewhere in the darkness below.

So that's where she went, he thought, and headed down the ramp.

As the daylight receded behind him, he became aware of a faint, wavering green light emanating from somewhere ahead of him. It was the same iridescent green as the hands of an alarm clock. Radioactive green, he would have called it.

The ramp made a second spiral, and with every step he took, the green now gained incandescence. He was certain of one thing: the source of that light was natural; no degree of electrically generated light could create such subtle patterns of rhythmically shifting luminescence.

He went around another curve. And there it was.

The gerbil tube.

"Holy Moses!"

Hunt's gasp rang out in the hushed, unearthly silence and hung there like a shout.

The ramp ended in a tunnel—but not just any tunnel. This was an arched tunnel of clear glass that had been welded together in big sections. It was completely underwater, and stretched for several hundred feet along the floor of the lagoon.

At first he was gripped by such awe and wonder that he was too stunned to move.

So this was the source of that light, this green-tinted, watery universe where, instead of sky, the surface of the lagoon glimmered brightly far overhead, refracting the sun and dappling the coral reef with squirming reflections.

"Unbelievable!" he whispered.

He drew forward, reaching out and touching the curvaceous glass. He tapped it ever so lightly with the tips of his fingers. It was cool and smooth to the touch. Specially molded and tempered; thick and strong to withstand the pressure of the water.

His eyes darted everywhere at once.

No matter in which direction he looked—in front of him, in back, and overhead—marauding sharks cruised like silent torpedos and elongated barracudas shot past, arrow-thin soloists streaking this way and that. Schools of large, disc-shaped fish swam first in one direction, then abruptly turned tail and swam gracefully in another: dancers in a perfectly choreographed show. A piscine corps de ballet.

"So. What's your verdict?" Dorothy-Anne asked softly.

Hunt gave a start. He hadn't been aware of her proximity. Like him, she was a dark silhouette against the soft green world outside the tunnel.

He shook his head. "I'm floored," he began. "I'm . . ." Then he cried, "Look! There!"

He pointed at an ungainly, giant sea turtle as it paddled awkwardly past, like some bloated, dinosaurian bat.

"This really beats all!" he marveled.

"You think so?"

He could feel her eyes on his face. Outside, a pale eel, like a wavy ribbon, slithered gracefully by, just inches from the glass.

He tore his eyes away from the aquatic circus and looked at her.

"I don't think so," he said quietly. "I know so. You're going to make a killing."

45

"**Y**ap-yap-yap! I don't know what's gotten into ya lately, but ya sure as hell are startin' to nag like a goddamn wife!" Thus spake Christos to a pale, teary-eyed Amber.

He waved a hand in front of her pinched face and waggled his fingers. "Ya see a ring on this finger? I sure as hell don't!"

Flinching, she drew back and gnawed on her lower lip.

"And ya aren't gonna see one there, neither!" Christos steamed.

With that, he grabbed his Levi's jacket, stalked out, and slammed the door behind him.

For a moment he stood out on the landing, chest heaving as he struggled to get his breathing back to normal.

"Shit!" he muttered to himself, scratching his impressive abs through his T-shirt. He didn't know what Amber was on the rag about, but one thing was for sure. He wanted to wash that girl right outta his hair.

The dumb bitch. She never knew when to leave well enough alone. In fact, he had a good mind to dump her.

Yes, sirree. Dump her, blow this joint, and never return. He wouldn't exactly be homeless. He could always stay at the house on Russian Hill.

Talk about upward mobility!

It was tempting. Except . . .

Except you never knew what might happen. What if fate gave him the finger and something went wrong? Getting rid of Gloria's husband was light-years from the petty scams he was used to running. Should worse come to worst, Amber might come in very useful as an alibi.

Yeah. He'd better not tell her to take a hike quite yet. The last thing he needed was to be at the mercy of a woman scorned. And the female of the species, as Christos had learned the hard way—in more ways than one—was a highly fickle, unpredictable lot.

Maybe it's time to turn up the old charm, he thought. *Bring Amber some flowers. Take her out to eat.*

It couldn't hurt. Hell, in a worst-case scenario, it might even save his skin.

That decided, he shrugged himself into his jacket and popped a stick of Doublemint in his mouth. Then, Westerns pounding, he hurried down three flights of narrow, listing stairs.

At the bottom landing, he stood aside, making room for a voluptuous lady on her way up. Checked her out appreciatively as she passed, experienced eyes sweeping every knockout curve.

She smiled coyly and fluttered false eyelashes. Christos started to return the compliment, then noticed the telltale hint of blue shadow under heavily rouged cheeks.

Shit! Just his kinda luck—a freakin' drag queen!

He beat it, leaping down the last half flight in two single bounds.

"What's the matter, huh-ney?" The reverberating falsetto echoed in the narrow lobby, spilled out into the bright sunshine after him. "Am I too much girl for you?"

He slammed the front door. Jesus H. Christ! He certainly wouldn't rue the day he moved outta *this* dump!

Hitting the sidewalk, he slowed his pace. Pulled up his collar. Became Mr. Cool. Not that he had to work at it. Christos had the stud walk down pat, moving along with that rolling, lazy, hip-swaying thrust with unselfconscious ease.

It did have one drawback, though. In this town, it tended to attract more gays than chicks.

He wondered briefly how, of all the urban areas of the country, he'd ended up in San Francisco, the one city where women—at least biological women—were at a premium.

Tony Bennett can keep this place, he thought moodily. *I sure as hell ain't leavin' my heart here!*

A perusal of the oncoming traffic revealed a cruising cab. Talk about a minor miracle. He put two fingers to his lips and hailed it with an ear-splitting whistle.

The cab coasted over to the curb and stopped—another miracle. Hopping in, Christos gave the driver directions.

First stop: Russian Hill.

Christos had the cabbie wait on the near-vertical street while he dashed between the apartment blocks to the picturesque little house in back. Once inside, he headed straight for the kitchen and the dishwasher—an inspired if impromptu hidey-hole for his stash.

Grabbing a bundle of cash—about five grand, he judged—he divided it like a deck of cards, rolled up one half tightly, and stuffed it deep inside his right boot. The rest, an assortment of twenties, fifties, and hundreds, he distributed in the various pockets of his jeans, shirt, and jacket.

Without further ado, he dashed back out to the waiting cab.

Next stop: the Tenderloin.

Christos paid off the cabbie, added a generous tip, and pushed his way thorugh the swinging doors of a dive that catered to the liquid breakfast crowd. The stench of stale beer and acrid smoke hit him right way, but it took a few moments for his eyes to adjust to the gloom.

A mahogany-skinned man with a polished skull and something Indian in his cheekbones caught Christos's reflection in the fly-specked mirror behind the bar. He spun around on his barstool and grinned, a gold tooth glinting in the front of his mouth.

The man called out, "Yo, bro. 'Bout time you show."

Christos feigned surprise, saying, "Heyyyyy, Slick," as if he hadn't come expressly to see him, and then going over and slapping palms.

"Ain't seen you walk, ain't heard you talk." Slick squinched his eyes. "You bin layin' low. Any reason I should know?"

"Naw. I've been around." Christos slid onto the empty barstool beside Slick. "Long time no see. How you doin', buddy?"

Slick said, "Ain't got no beef."

"Good. That's real good, man."

Behind the bar, a Godzilla of a woman with makeup like putty tore herself way from the *National Enquirer*. She wore a wine red muumuu studded with rhinestones, and had a cigarette glued to her lower lip. She walked with a mincing, almost dainty limp, as if every step was painful.

"You gonna order something?" she rasped, squinting against the smoke. "This ain't no freebie social club."

Christos grinned. "Yeah, I missed you too, Shirl. Gimme a Coors. Draft."

Still looking at Christos, she muttered, "The last of the big spenders," but went and drew a glass from the tap. When she banged it down in front of him, foam slid down the sides. "That's a dollar fifty," she said, cigarette still dangling. "Cash."

"You know what, Shirl?" Christos said. "You're a laugh a minute."

She looked hard at him and started to take the glass back.

"Not so fast! Jesus, Shirl. Where's your sense of humor?"

He half stood and slid a twenty out of his right front pocket. He dropped it on the bar and she took it over to the cash register and rang it up, returning to slap eighteen bucks and two quarters down in front of him.

He shoved a buck and both quarters toward her.

"What you do?" she chortled, scooping up his tip. "Mug a tourist?"

Her massive breasts heaved in silent laughter, and the rhinestone sparkles on the velvet muumuu winked as she tippy-toed her inquiring mind back down to the other end of the bar.

"Think it's weight," Slick asked, "or hem'rrhoids?"

Christos was drinking a third of the beer in a single long swallow, his throat muscles working overtime. He banged the glass down and exhaled appreciatively, rubbed his foam mustache off with his sleeve.

"What are you talkin' about?" He looked at Slick blankly.

Slick said, "Shirl," keeing his voice down. "That way she walk."

"What about it?"

"I'm thinkin', maybe it's hem'rrhoids is makin' her take them funny li'l baby steps. You know? Like she needs to take a dump, but keeps holdin' it in?"

Christos, wanting to cut to the chase but without seeming too eager, moved his shoulders. "Personally, I never notice."

"Wish I didn't. Thing is, amount of time I spend in here? I can't *help* but noticin'."

"Maybe ya ought to switch bars. Find yourself another hangout."

"Shit. Most o' them places? They find out your bidness? Every single time, someone drop a dime."

"Yeah. It's tough out there." Christos decided he'd wasted enough time. Glancing up and down the bar, then back over both shoulders, he leaned toward Slick and said, "Speakin' of business," sounding real cool and quiet. "Ya got any blow?"

Slick gave him a look. "You know me. It depends who can see."

Slick playing it cool, not committing himself.

"Ain't anybody in here would give a rat's ass," Christos pointed out.

" 'Cept Shirl." Slick's eyes darted about. "How much you in the market for?"

Christos didn't answer right away. What he had the urge to say was, How about five grand worth? Think you can handle that kinda deal? Wanting to see Slick's eyes pop, but deciding against it. Right now, the lower his profile, the better off he'd be. What he said was, "A gram?"

Slick giving him another look: "You got the cash, I got the stash."

Christos nodded. He and Slick reached surreptitiously into pockets. Money and a tiny glassine bag changed hands.

The transaction complete, they sat there, making a show of looking innocent. Slick finished what he was drinking.

Christos watched him in the dirty mirror over the bar. He decided to wait a few minutes, then mosey on to the john, where he'd treat himself to a well-deserved toot.

But first, there were two more items of business on his agenda. He'd

come here to score coke, yeah, but he'd specifically sought out Slick because of his prodigious memory and underworld connections. Of all the
dealers Christos had become acquainted with, Slick was a veritable directory of lowlifes—extortionists, pimps, mobsters, gangs, you name it. To
hear him tell it, he was plugged right into the steamy underbelly of this
town.

Or, as Slick liked to put it: "Slick is the name and information's my
game."

Now Christos was about to put it to the test. "Whatcha drinkin'?" he
asked, just to keep the conversation going.

Slick heard something in Christos's voice, nothing he could put his
finger on, just a nuance in the undertone, that told him the guy wanted
more than just the dope he'd been sold.

He turned his way, scrutinized Christos from under hooded, cold
eyes. He said, "What I drink depends on who's pickin' up the tab."

"I'm buyin'."

Slick called out: "Yo, Shirl! My girl!"

"Yeah, yeah." Her disinterested voice let him know he was interrupting her reading.

Slick said to Christos, "You hear that? We got ourselves a definite
attitude problem." And louder: "Hey, Shirl? You runnin' a bar or a library? We could use some serious drinks down here."

"An' I could use one wise ass less," came the reply.

Christos leaned forward and looked past Slick down the length of the
bar. He saw Shirl place both hands flat on the counter, slide her fat ass
off her stool, and push herself to her feet.

Smirking as she came tippy-toeing their way, Slick said, "See what I
mean? 'Bout the constipated way she walk?" Then changing his expression, giving her a wide, gold-toothed smile.

Shirl didn't return it. "Okay," she said, one hand on a hip. "You got
my attention. You gonna order, or what?"

Slick said, "Why you always gotta be a hard-ass?" sounded wounded,
his voice rising to a high-pitched whine.

"'Cause of people like you. Now you want something or not?"

"Yeah. Pour me a Johnny black. Straight."

She acted surprised. "You're kidding, right?"

"Nope. My man here is buying, so make that a double." Slick paused
and said, "An' I want the real shit. None of that rotgut you funnel into
the bottles on the counter."

Shirl nailed him with her eyes. "You wanna get eighty-sixed, just keep
it up." But she reached under the counter for the bottle she kept there
and squirted scotch into a clean glass.

"An' don't skimp," Slick warned her. He grinned at Christos. "Ya
gotta watch Shirl, here. She'd screw her own mammy."

Shirl said, "Hey, Slick? Fuck you." And slammed the glass down in front of him.

She took a fiver from Christos's bar change and rang it up, bringing back a buck. Christos slid her two singles for a tip, which she took without so much as a thank-you.

"You know, Slick. Something tells me she doesn't like you."

Slick shrugged, picked up the glass, and held it delicately aloft, pinkie extended. He gestured a toast, then tossed down the contents in a single belt. He shut his eyes and belched.

"Mammy's milk, and smoother than silk."

He opened his eyes. For a minute or so he was quiet.

Finally he said to Christos, "Now, you didn't buy the Slick a drink 'cause you like his looks. We gonna sit here all day, chase each other by the tail, or what?"

"I need some information."

Slick nodded. "I got a reputation. Keep one ear to the ground, don't fuck around."

"Okay. Here's how it is."

Christos scooted his barstool closer to Slick's, leaned sideways toward him, lowered his voice confidentially.

"Say I got a wax impression of a key."

He was taking it slow, not wanting to say too much.

Slick said, "Yeah?"

"What I need to know is, where can I take it? You know, to get it cast, no questions asked?"

"What kind of key we talking here?"

Christos shook his head. "That's my business."

Acting like a tough dude.

Slick pointed in the air around him. "You see me hang out a shingle says 'Information Booth'?" He picked up his empty glass, held it up. "You see a sign says 'Questions Answered for a Free Drink?' "

Christos took the hint and worked a twenty out of his jeans pocket. He laid it on the bar.

Slick shook his head and pushed it away.

He said, "Want my advice, deal two twenties twice."

Christos frowned. He scratched his chin, pretending to have to think this over. Not that he had any choice. He didn't know who else to ask. Hell, he was still a newcomer, and to him, this town might as well be someplace in Siberia.

With a sigh, he pulled three more twenties out of his pocket.

Slick palmed the four bills expertly.

"There's this hardware store," he said. "On Mission, between Eighteenth and Nineteenth. They do locksmith work."

"This is a Spanish place?"

"Yeah. Guy you want's this pinto bean works there, short dude with black hair? Carlos? You'll know him by his shirt. Wears one of them gray ones, the kind with his name stitched across the pocket?"

"Like an auto mechanic?"

"Yeah. But don't be a fool, play it real cool. He ain't there, don't ask no questions. Just leave and go back till he there. Catch my drift?"

Christos nodded. "And this guy Carlos. He's good?"

Slick narrowed his eyes.

He said, "Yo. Whoever the Slick know, he a pro. Now *go*."

That said, Slick swiveled himself frontward on his barstool, a clear signal that the conversation was over.

But Christos didn't move. He was still leaning toward him.

Finally Slick looked at him and said, "What's with you, man? We an item I don't know about? We gonna go steady, maybe get married?"

Christos said, "There's one more thing. . . ."

"Then say it. No reason to shout, just spit it out."

Christos hesitated. He realized he was at the biggest crossroads of his entire life, and whether he committed himself and took the plunge, or chickened out and walked away, was totally up to him.

To him, and him alone.

Which will it be? he wondered. *The same old shit, day in, day out, for the rest of my life? Or will I take a chance, do Gloria's husband, and see what happens?*

Slick said, "Hey, I ain't got all day, so say what you got to say."

Suddenly Christos had the strangest sensation that he was outside his own body, floating high up in the air and looking down on his double—and that it wasn't him, it was his freakin' double who was asking, "Where can I buy me a rifle? You know, with no paperwork? No ID or waiting period? Strictly cash and carry?"

And Slick said, "Jesus Christ." He said, "Shit." He said, "Man, whatever you involved in, I don't want to know fuckin' nothing. We clear on that?"

46

S tarry, starry night.

The moon had been waiting in the wings, pale and round and visible, while the sunset had burned itself out in a brilliant burst of pyrotechnics. Now with the sky blue-black and velvety, it was the moon's turn to show off. It began journeying across the star-filled sky, distancing itself from its squirming white twin in the sea below.

In Sunrise Bay, the water was like a sheet of black glass. Lamplight glowed yellow in *Quicksilver's* portholes, giving the illusion that there were two yachts, one upside down, both joined at the waterline like Siamese twins.

The generator was silent, the lights battery powered. Except for the occasional fish bursting through the surface before splashing back under, the only other sounds were the occasional creaks of the hull and Hunt's voice coming softly from belowdecks.

Dorothy-Anne was seated on a cushion in the cockpit, legs tucked under her, a light shawl around her shoulders. When Hunt stopped talking, she glanced toward the open hatch.

She could see his shadow moving about below, then watched it precede him up the teak steps. For a moment, his body seemed to block out the light completely, then it seemed to stream up behind him. He hit a switch and the lamps went dark.

He felt his way along the cockpit and sat down next to her.

"Everything's arranged," he said. "The P.I. will be at your office the day after tomorrow. I told him eleven in the morning was okay. If it isn't, I can call him back and change it."

"Eleven's fine," she assured him. "I really appreciate your help."

"Help!" He laughed softly. "All I did was make a phone call."

She looked at him. The bright full moon bathed him in sterling. Only his face was in shadow.

Her voice turned husky. "Sometimes a phone call is enough. Poor Hunt. Always galloping to the rescue. First the Whitmans, now me . . ."

He smiled. "I'm hardly the knight errant you make me out to be."

"Aren't you?"

He laughed again and they sat there quietly, watching the moonlight on the water, neither of them speaking or touching, but feeling intimate all the same.

After a while she turned to him. "Hunt."

He looked at her.

"I have a question," she said softly, "but you don't have to answer it."

"Okay."

For a moment she looked away. When she turned back to him, her eyes searched his face. "I mean it," she said. "If I'm poking my nose where it doesn't belong, just tell me and I'll butt out."

"Why would I want to do that?"

Her expression didn't change. "I'm serious, Hunt. If I'm out of line, just say so."

He looked into her eyes. They were deep and pale and moonlit. "You could never be out of line," he said quietly.

Dorothy-Anne hesitated; not uncomfortable, merely choosing the right words. Then: "Being in public service . . ." she began. She pulled the shawl closer around her, one hand, like a decorative silver brooch, clasping the fringed ends together. "I gather you must get quite a few petitions. You know, from constituents needing help?"

"A few!" He chuckled. "That's putting it mildly. Inundated is more like it."

"Which brings me to the Whitmans."

"Yes? What about the Whitmans?"

"Well, you flew clear to Mexico to help them. And you made it plain you didn't want any publicity out of it. So with all the requests you receive, what made you drop everything and help *them*? There must have been *something* that gave their case priority over the others."

"Oh boy." He rubbed a hand down his face as thought to wash it. "You really know which questions to ask."

"It's like I said. You can always tell me to get lost."

"No." He shook his head and stared out to sea. "It's just as well that you asked. There comes a point when it's time to air out the family closet. To free those unseemly skeletons, those . . . inconvenient *embarrassments* only the best families can hide so well!"

Dorothy-Anne reached for his hand. "Hunt, if it's too personal—"

"No!" His voice was quiet but fierce, and he withdrew his hand from hers. "There are things you have a right to know. I don't want us to have any secrets. What are we, ultimately, if not the sum of our truths?"

Dorothy-Anne sighed. Hearing so much pain and anger in his voice lanced her heart.

If only I could help alleviate his suffering, she thought. Then she realized that she could. *By being a good listener. Sometimes that can make all the difference...*

"Now, about the Whitmans," Hunt said. "You asked me why they struck such a chord, so I shall tell you. I grew up an only child, in a mausoleum of a house. One of the so-called *Great Houses*"—he snorted with contempt—"one of what I *believe* are referred to as the 'Castles of America.'"

He paused, staring off into the star-spangled night.

"Naturally, it's got a *name*," he said acidly. "All great houses *have* to have a pretentious name. Did you ever notice?"

Dorothy-Anne shook her head. "Actually I never thought about it."

"Anyway, it's called Cascades. Apparently that evoked the appropriate images of grandeur. It's even been *said*'"—Hunt's tone was mocking—"to be the West Coast equivalent of the Breakers or Biltmore."

He laughed softly. "Not quite San Simeon, though. And not for want of trying, you understand, but only because old William Hearst wouldn't be outdone."

"Cascades," Dorothy-Anne murmured. "You sound as though you hate it."

"Let's just say I dislike it, and leave it at that."

"Because it was a mausoleum?"

"That, and what it stands for," he went on. "Oh, you couldn't begin to imagine it. One icy room of period perfection after another. Everything Louis This and Adam That... and peopled by servants as silent and invisible as ghosts. Don't get me wrong. I'm not making it into anything it isn't. Cascades is only a house. Perhaps even a *great* house. But what it *isn't*—what it never was, or ever could be—is a *home.*"

Dorothy-Anne looked at him. Anger and hurt were vivid in his celestially illuminated face. His hands, resting on his thighs, were clenched.

"But I am getting ahead of myself. To appreciate my sympathy for the Whitmans, you have to understand a little about the Winslows. Specifically, the things you won't read about in *Forbes* or *Fortune* or *Town and Country.*"

He paused, as if listening to great unseen schools of fish passing just beneath the water's surface.

"The Winslow fortune," he continued, "goes back to the Gold Rush of forty-nine. That's when my great-grandfather, a typesetter in Baltimore, headed West to seek his fortune. What he discovered was that there were more prospectors than gold, and that unfounded rumors and speculation were the norm. There simply were no reliable sources of information. And so, seeing that need, he filled it."

"By starting a newspaper."

He nodded. "A single-sheet daily, to be exact. Yes."

"And the rest, as they say, is history."

"That's right. My grandfather went on to expand the chain and branched out into magazines and radio stations, and my father helped pioneer network television. Today, of course, we're into every conceivable form of communications—from the printed page to satellite TV, cellular phones, cable, you name it."

"But how do the Whitmans fit into all this?"

"I'm coming to that."

He paused again, as if wrestling some internal demons before continuing. Then:

"The point I'm making is this. Since my family disseminated the news, they were in a position to exert a tremendous amount of power and influence. In the beginning, of course, this was limited to northern California."

"But not for long."

"No, not for long. Soon all the large cities in California had a Winslow newspaper, then all the Western states, and finally the entire country. Needless to say, our influence and power increased exponentially. And of course, the temptation to wield it was irresistible."

"But surely your family wasn't alone in that. Look at William Randolph Hearst. He wasn't exactly an angel."

"Perhaps not," Hunt agreed. "But that does not excuse us. Understand: I am not talking about mere editorial slants, or backing certain politicians while attempting, often successfully, to destroy others. Nor am I referring to exhortations for readers to vote for certain candidates or legislative propositions, all of which would benefit my family directly, though we were masters at that, too."

"Then what are you referring to?"

"The abuse of power," he whispered.

He sighed and tilted back his head and raised his eyes to the pock-marked moon, then looked at Dorothy-Anne and smiled bitterly.

"You cannot begin to imagine the power of the media. The great unwashed public wasn't always as savvy as it is today. There was a time when people were far more gullible . . . when the written and broadcast word was gospel—and went unquestioned. And naturally, we did not police ourselves. You don't, when you have the advantage."

"You keep saying 'we' and 'us' and 'ourselves,' " Dorothy-Anne noted. "Surely you can't hold yourself responsible for the misdeeds of your forebears!"

"No, but I can feel shame."

His breathing had become harsh, and Dorothy-Anne listened to it as attentively as a doctor.

"You wouldn't believe the things we Winslows were capable of! Bending the law *and* public opinion. Buying judges and entire police departments. Backing crooked politicians because we had them in our pockets. Pressuring crime victims to drop charges when it suited us, and arranging for trumped-up charges when that served our purposes. Oh, we thought we were a law unto ourselves."

He shook his head.

"The way we manipulated the public—the way we misused its trust— was *criminal!*"

Hunt's exhalation betrayed a heavy sense of weariness. He leaned back and rubbed his face once more. Then, his voice quiet, his words slow, he recited a damning litany:

"Take the congressman at the turn of the century who inconveniently raped children, but conveniently looked out for our best interests on Capitol Hill. Or the alcoholic friend of my grandfather's, who was involved in a fatal hit-and-run. Despite eyewitnesses to the crime, sworn statements by the *right people,* by *people like us,* placed him a hundred miles away. At a fund-raiser to which he was never invited!"

Dorothy-Anne sat absolutely still. She could understand the anger burning within him. *If only I could help ease it,* she thought, *or find the right words to say.*

But she knew it was impossible. And she perceived something else, too.

This is the first time Hunt has confided about this to anyone. Not that he'd said as much. *He doesn't have to. I can tell.*

"The crimes," he said disgustedly, "are endless. *Endless.* Bribes, slander, ruination . . . I could go on for hours. There was nothing we would not stoop to in our quest to amass ever more power. But, experts that we were at *fixing* things, at *hushing* things up, guess where we were most proficient?"

Dorothy-Anne was silent.

"Burnishing our own image—what else?" He shook his head. "Oh, but we glowed with righteousness! And how could we not? Consider the great pains we went to, always casting ourselves in the best possible light. Trumpeting our good deeds in voice and print as if they were *news!*"

Once again he gave a hollow laugh.

"And suddenly we were philanthropists. Patrons of museums and charities. Yes. We passed ourselves off as the self-proclaimed champions of the downtrodden, the voice of the common man—when, in reality, we were his greatest enemy!"

Dorothy-Anne winced against his burst of bitter mockery. She felt his pain as her own, a throbbing physical wound as if someone had stabbed her. She felt his anger and outrage.

"From my great-grandfather," he went on, "down to my grandfather and my late father . . . and now my mother . . . from the very *start*, we Winslows were pros when it came to self-preservation. But what we were most adept at is what is nowadays called 'spin.' Long before there was a term for it, *we* were the original spin doctors. But do you know what really takes the cake?"

Dorothy-Anne shook her head.

"It's that nothing was ever enough," he brooded. "Steering legislature in our favor, hoodwinking our readers and listeners, even glossing over the nasties so we smelled like roses to the public—*we* had to take it a step further. We had to rewrite our history within the family itself!"

"How do you mean?"

"Oh, you know," he said. "Lies. Twisted truths. Sins of omission. I'd only known the *sanitized* family history, the rewritten, edited version. I was never privy to the sordid secrets. I only learned the truth from my paternal grandmother. As she lay dying, she told me everything."

He shook his head. "Imagine! If not for her, I'd *still* be in the dark— the same as poor John Q. Public!"

Hunt fell silent then. A sorrowful look had come over his countenance. It was clear that his mind was neither here nor now, but in the past.

At his grandmother's deathbed, Dorothy-Anne realized.

"Grandmother Winslow told me these things in the hope that I might be different," he said thickly. "She said she couldn't rest in peace unless I swore an oath."

"And so you swore it."

"Yes. I was sixteen at the time."

"And that's the reason you went into politics? To fulfill the oath and make up for the sins of the fathers?"

"Actually, the political arena wasn't my idea," said Hunt. "It was my mother's." He smiled sourly. "After a family has achieved great wealth, social standing, and fame, I suppose there's only one game left."

"Politics," Dorothy-Anne said softly.

"The ultimate power trip." He nodded. "You should have seen Mother when I acquiesced—although she wouldn't have been so thrilled if she'd suspected my motive."

"By motive, I take it you mean your oath."

"Yes, Dorothy-Anne. My oath. From the beginning, I had my own agenda. Of course, I wasn't naive enough to think that a single apple could make up for an entire spoiled barrel. But I was determined to make a difference, however small."

"And when your mother found out you were your own man? That you were looking out for your constituents' interests rather than your family's? How did she react to that?"

He barked a short laugh.

"As you'd expect. I wish you could have seen her. She was furious! However, that only lasted about five seconds. True to form, she immediately seized upon my impartiality as an advantage. You must understand; Mother has an intuitive feel for these things. You could practically see visions of the White House dancing in her head."

He gave Dorothy-Anne a sad little smile.

"But to backtrack: there was one family secret my grandmother did not share with me. I had to discover it for myself. Afterward, I thought she'd been holding out on me. But in retrospect, I realize I was wrong. She may have *suspected* the truth, but she couldn't prove it. If she'd been able to, I'm sure she would have told me."

"Told what?"

Hunt stared out at the starry horizon, then slumped back and shook his head. For a moment he shut his eyes. His breath soughed like a moaning wind. Then he opened his eyes.

"Remember what I told you? About growing up an only child?"

"At Cascades. Of course."

"And do you recall my greatest wish?"

"Yes." Dorothy-Anne nodded. "You desperately longed for a brother. Or sister."

"And how. I would have given anything for a sibling—anything on earth! I hoped. I prayed. I made extravagant promises to God if he would only answer my prayers."

He shook his head once more.

"Of course, it was not to be. And eventually, I resigned myself to that fact. And my prayers stopped."

"I know how you must have felt," Dorothy-Anne said softly. "We have more in common than you think."

"Then you understand."

She nodded. "Far better than you can imagine. My childhood was much the same. But continue. Finish your story."

Taking a deep breath, he said, "Five years after my grandmother's death, my father passed on. It was in June, a week after I turned twenty-one. Stanford had let out for the summer. Usually I would travel, roaming Europe or Latin America or the Far East. But since my mother was alone, I spent that summer at Cascades."

"Where," Dorothy-Anne murmured knowingly, "you were lonelier than ever."

"Which is putting it mildly. Anyway, on the seventh of August—I shall never forget that date for as long as I live—I was in my father's study, sorting through papers. As fate would have it, the telephone rang. Not the regular phone, but my father's private line. It had no extensions, and no one else was ever allowed to touch it. Somehow, it had slipped our minds to have it disconnected."

His voice cracked and he fell silent. Dorothy-Anne noticed that his eyes glistened moistly in the moonlight. Then she saw it. A single tear trailing a snail's track down his cheek.

She sought his hand again. This time he didn't pull away, but closed his fingers around hers. They sat like that, in silence, for several minutes.

"I'm sorry," Hunt said thickly. "I don't usually get this choked up."

"It's not a crime to show your emotions." She gave his hand a gentle squeeze. "And you don't have to tell me this."

"No. I want you to hear it. It's . . . important to me."

She nodded, and waited for him to continue:

"Of course I answered the telephone. More out of habit than curiosity. A man was on the line. He asked for Mr. Winslow. I automatically said, 'Speaking.' You see, I'd momentarily forgotten that it was my father's private line.

"The caller then identified himself. 'This is Dr. Zahedi,' he said. The name meant nothing to me. Why should it? I didn't know Dr. Zahedi from Adam. When I didn't reply, he said, 'From Pacific Acres in Pebble Beach.'

"Since I wasn't sure how to respond, I said, 'Yes, Dr. Zahedi. What can I do for you?'

"He was very apologetic. 'I'm sorry to bother you with mundane matters, Mr. Winslow. But you specifically told me to deal with you personally on all matters concerning your son.'

"Naturally, I assumed he was talking about *me*! Also, it was obvious that he hadn't heard about my father's death, and believed he was speaking to him. My father's voice and mine, you see, sounded very much alike. People often mistook one of us for the other over the telephone.

"Admittedly, by now my curiosity was aroused. I longed to know what Dr. Zahedi, whom I did not know, had to say to my father about me. So I didn't correct him.

"He sounded embarrassed. 'We have not received your checks for July or August. It's not that we're pressing you for payment, Mr. Winslow. We know you're good for it.'

"I made some noncommittal noises.

" 'I only called to see if everything was satisfactory,' he said. 'Or, if it isn't, how we might improve things, or whether you were planning to move Woodrow to another institution.'

"And that was when it hit me! *He wasn't talking about me at all!* But he *was* talking about my father's son—a son named Woodrow! A son I never knew existed!

"I believe my heart stopped. At least, that was what I remember feeling.

"Somehow I found my voice and said, 'You're speaking about . . . my *son*, Woodrow?' For I had to know right away.

"Dr. Zahedi obviously thought I was distracted, for he said, 'If I'm calling at a bad time, Mr. Winslow—'

" 'No, no, Dr. Zahedi,' I assured him. 'You're not inconveniencing me at all. In fact, I'll drive down this afternoon, drop a check off personally, and pay Woodrow a visit.'

"Dr. Zahedi said that would be very nice and thanked me and hung up."

"But, how *awful!*" Dorothy-Anne whispered. A shiver went through her. "To have to find out like that! Oh, Hunt . . ."

"Needless to say, my emotions were in turmoil. I didn't know whether to jump for joy, or weep with sorrow, or scream from anger. But I couldn't wait. I immediately jumped into my car and drove down to Carmel.

"Once there, I asked for directions. Despite its name, Pacific Acres was not on the ocean, but slightly inland. Like many such places, it had once been a grand old mansion, and part of a much larger estate. High stone walls surrounded it completely. I think you get the picture."

"Oh, yes," Dorothy-Anne whispered. "I'm afraid I do."

"I had to show my driver's license to the guard at the gate, who checked my name against a list. It's ironic, isn't it? Had my name not been exactly the same as my father's, I might not have gained entry so easily.

"But I digress. Once inside, I parked in the visitors' parking lot. Mine was the only car there. Apparently, relatives are not big on visiting their kin at Pacific Acres.

"And of course, I knew at once what this place was—a dumping ground for the unfortunate relatives of the rich and famous. A place where one can stick the family embarrassment—the crazy aunt, the deformed child, the deranged brother, the incontinent grandparent, the vegetating accident victim. All *wonderfully* cared for! Not wanting for a *thing!* Very *conveniently* tucked out of sight, and therefore, presumably, out of mind!"

Dorothy-Anne shuddered. "It sounds so . . . cruel. So unnecessarily cruel."

"It *is* cruel," he said grimly. "Crueler and more depressing than you can surmise. My first instinct was to get back into my car and flee. Yet I could not. I had to go through with this visit. I knew I could not rest until I discovered the truth."

"And you learned it."

"Did I ever."

He shook his head and drew a deep breath and let it out slowly.

"Dr. Zahedi met me at the entrance. The instant he saw me, he was visibly shaken. I had no idea why, since he looks like one of those men who naturally exude confidence. I told him that my father had died, and that since I was of age, I was now the titular head of the family."

"Were you?'"

"No. My mother was, but Dr. Zahedi could not know that.

"But to continue: An orderly took me upstairs and down a corridor lined with small private rooms. The doors were all open, so that the staff could keep an eye on the . . . I keep wanting to say *inmates,* but that's not the correct word. Nor can I call them patients, because that suggests their conditions might improve. The staff refer to them as *residents,* but that makes it sound as if they're there by choice. And they're not. What they are is victims of circumstances—whether through accident, birth, disease, or genetics.

"The room I was shown to was number 211. And there I discovered . . . there I *found* . . . Woodrow. Yes. My younger brother. A year younger than me, almost to the day."

"Oh, Hunt!" Dorothy-Anne whispered.

Still holding onto his hand, she put her other arm around him and pressed him against her in an effort to share his terrible burden. The moon traveled higher. The night was cool.

Finally Hunt continued to bare his soul, his voice quavery and tortured:

"Dr. Zahedi had seen to it that Woodrow had been prepared for my visit. He was freshly bathed and neatly dressed and his hair was combed—as if cosmetic touches could have made any difference!"

Dorothy-Anne's voice was hushed. "And the visit? How did it go?"

"For me, horribly. For Woody"—he shrugged— "I might as well not have been there. When I came in, he was seated at his desk in front of the window, concentrating on a jigsaw puzzle. I sat down beside him on the bed, but he . . ." Hunt's voice faltered ". . . he took no notice of me. None whatsoever."

"Then he's . . ."

"Autistic," he sighed, and nodded. "Yes. But I saw at once what had shaken Dr. Zahedi. It was our physical resemblance. Woody and I . . ."

He turned to Dorothy-Anne and looked deep into her eyes.

"We might have been twins!" he whispered hoarsely. "We are almost mirror images of each other, except . . ."

"Except for his illness," Dorothy-Anne finished gently.

"Yes. There was absolutely no expression on his face. No emotion at all. His face was blank . . . but it was a peaceful blank. And when I spoke to him, he didn't respond. But when I touched him . . ."

Dorothy-Anne listened in silence, her heart stricken.

"He jerked and pulled away! I simply didn't register to him."

As a mother with three lively—sometimes almost *too* lively hand-fuls—Dorothy-Anne couldn't begin to imagine the bleak emotional land-scape Hunt painted. It made her leadenly aware of what an utter crap shoot every conception, pregnancy, and birth could be.

But a completely unresponsive child like Woodrow?

That was almost beyond her comprehension.

Kids can't be lively enough, Dorothy-Anne thought. *From now on, I'll treasure their every yell and shriek and laugh.* She silently blessed her own rambunctious brood. *The next time Liz and Fred and Zack get into a fight, I'll welcome it. Never again shall I take their normality for granted.*

Normality. It was such a simple little word.

And yet it's the greatest gift of all.

"You asked me why the Whitmans struck such a chord in me," Hunt said quietly. "Now you know."

"Because they didn't lock Kevin away," Dorothy-Anne said softly.

"Damn right, they didn't! They went out of their way to give him a normal life! To them, it doesn't matter if Kevin isn't *photogenic*! He doesn't *embarrass* them! They *love* him—even though he isn't anyone's ideal of perfection. Nor does it matter that he'll never be able to love them back!" His voice broke. "Their love is unconditional."

"As opposed to the love of your parents," she said.

He nodded. "That's right. They hid Woody . . . and edited him com-pletely out of our lives . . . as if he'd never existed. And for me, he *hadn't*. That's how thorough they were. If it weren't for my father's death, and my answering that phone . . ."

Hunt shook his head, flexing his fingers on his thighs. His breathing was thick, heavy, and rapid with anger.

"What they did—my parents—is the modern-day equivalent of the ancient Greeks. Only instead of leaving Woody on a hillside for the wolves, they locked him away for life."

"It sounds so . . . cold-blooded!"

"I suppose they rationalized it as doing the right thing. 'He's best off this way.' You know the old argument."

"Yes." Dorothy-Anne nodded. "But I don't necessarily agree with it."

"I guess the biggest surprise is that they *didn't* leave him on a hillside! I mean, wasn't that *humane* of them! Wasn't that exceedingly *kind*!"

Hunt stopped to glare out toward the open sea. His face was hard, etched with unforgivingness, and the moonwash delineated the clenched, defiant set to his jaw, the narrowly focused resentment burning within his eyes.

Dorothy-Anne waited, acutely attuned to his feelings. If he decided to continue, she would gladly listen, and if he wanted to drop the subject, that was okay with her too. She herself had endured enough tragedy of late to be an expert, however unwilling, on loss and suffering and pain—and she had a good idea how difficult this must be for Hunt.

Baring the pent-up frustrations of a lifetime could not be easy.

It's damn hard! Especially when we've been taught to keep our emotions private and our grief in check.

Clearing his throat, he said, "Sorry about that. I didn't intend to unload all this on you."

"You have nothing to be sorry about," she said. "And every reason to be angry." Then her voice softened. "Where is Woody now?"

"Still at Pacific Acres. That first day, I was determined to bring him home and welcome him into the fold. Which just goes to show how naive I was."

He sighed and shook his head at his folly.

Dorothy-Anne looked at him inquiringly. "What made you change your mind?"

"Dr. Zahedi. He sat down with me and gave me a crash course on autism. What I could expect, and what I couldn't. He convinced me that Woody would be better off staying there. At any rate, I wasn't in a position to provide a better home. I was just on the verge of leaving the nest myself."

"And your mother?" Dorothy-Anne asked. "She wouldn't have him?"

"Mother won't even *discuss* Woody, let alone have him around. As far as she's concerned, he was never born."

"How awful!"

"Yes, isn't it? Just goes to prove you don't have to be autistic to be emotionally impaired!"

"So she doesn't even visit him?"

"*Visit* him?" Hunt chuckled mirthlessly. "She hasn't been to see him once. Not *once!*" he emphasized. "So much for the old maternal instinct, eh?"

"But you visit Woody regularly, don't you?"

"I usually manage to get there about once a week."

He sucked in his cheeks, then tossed his head, his hair flopping aside as if to fling off some irritating insect.

"Isn't that saintly of me?" he said stingingly. "Why, if I'm not careful I might yet be canonized!"

Dorothy-Anne ignored his self-inflicted sarcasm. Her eyes cast about the tranquil, constellation-filled night. Mars shone brightly, and Porrima flickered amid Virgo's tail, the entire heavens twinkling like diamonds scattered upon a jeweler's cloth of midnight blue velvet.

"Has Woody shown any improvement?" she asked. "Any at all?"

Hunt shook his head. "I'm afraid not., After all these years he still isn't cognizant of me. That's the single worst thing about autism. Being shut out like that."

She nodded thoughtfully.

"In other words," she said, "he inhabits his own little world."

"And the rest of us don't exist," he said. "Period."

"So there's no way to reach him."

"None. But what's so curious is what he does respond to. Jigsaw puzzles."

She frowned. "Isn't that a little odd?"

"What's even odder is that he's such a whiz at them. I bring him several new ones each time I visit. You should see him. He can finish a thousand-piece puzzle in under an hour."

"An *hour*? Good Lord. He must be incredibly intelligent!"

"On that one level, yes." Hunt nodded. "But *only* on that level. On all others, including emotional development and response to his surroundings, it's hopeless."

"Is that the reason you don't have children of your own? Because you're afraid you might pass on a genetic defect?"

"No," he said. "I *wanted* kids, and the more the merrier. Only Gloria never seemed to get pregnant. And not for lack of trying on my part."

Had it been any less bitter, the sound he made might have been a laugh.

"Fool that I was," he said, "I tried. And tried. I was the goddamn Energizer bunny, the way I kept on trying."

"Are you saying," Dorothy-Anne asked carefully, "that your wife couldn't conceive?"

"Nope. It wasn't that she couldn't." He shook his head. "It's that she wouldn't."

Dorothy-Anne was silent. She could tell he was thinking back, his mind thousands of miles away in some intolerably hellish past.

"Then, as luck would have it," he said, "I stubbed my foot on the bedpost. This was a couple of years ago. Gloria's bathroom was closer than mine, so I went into hers for a Band-Aid. Guess what I found in her medicine cabinet?"

Dorothy-Anne sat very still. "I think I get the picture."

"Yeah," he said bitterly. "Birth control pills. All these years while I tried for children, she'd been on birth control!"

"You must have been devastated," she said quietly.

"I was," he admitted. "But you know what hurt the most?"

"Other than the fact that you felt betrayed."

"Other than that, yes."

He breathed in some air and exhaled it slowly through his nostrils.

"My own stupidity," he said. "You'd think I'd have caught on, right? But no. I was so gullible the truth had to hit me over the head. And even then I didn't want to believe it."

"Could it be you might have suspected it, but suppressed it?"

He frowned and thought about it a moment and then nodded.

"Could be," he said.

"Is she still on the pill?"

Hunt shrugged. "Hell if I know. Hell if I care, either."

"But you did care," Dorothy-Anne said. "Once upon a time."

"True," he acknowledged. "But not after I found the pills. That did it for me."

"But you tried to patch things up, didn't you?"

"No," he said. "I couldn't find it in my heart to forgive her—I still can't. Gloria *knew* how important children are to me."

He raised a clenched fist, then let it drop on his thigh.

"Dammit, she *knew!*" he whispered.

Dorothy-Anne looked at him quizzically. "Yet you remain married," she observed.

He flicked a hand dismissively. "A mordant joke. Our house is divided—like Korea."

He laughed softly.

"We even have a demilitarized zone!"

She flinched under the acid of words, then cocked her head like a bird, saying:

"But if things are that bad, there are remedies. Divorce, for instance."

Hunt turned his head slowly and inspected her as if she were a mutant curiosity the likes of which he had never before seen.

"Divorce?" His voice dripped sarcasm. "Haven't you heard? Winslows don't *get* divorced. We live with our miseries."

Dorothy-Anne shook her head. "Somehow I can't picture you in such an antagonistic union. Not for the rest of your life."

"Neither can I. Sooner or later, divorce is inevitable. I know that. The trouble is, the timing's never good."

"When it comes to divorce, timing never is."

He smiled sourly. "Good point."

They fell quiet, watching the moon float a little higher. It looked like a great wheel of gorgonzola. Somewhere in the darkness something broke the surface of the water. There was another little splash and it was gone.

After a while, Dorothy-Anne said: "Something evidently keeps you married."

He nodded. "Two things, actually. First, there's the prenuptial agreement. "If *I* sue for divorce, Gloria walks away rich. Very rich. But if *she* sues, she walks away with little. Relatively speaking."

"But doesn't California have community property laws?"

"Those won't help her much. My own assets are pretty modest. My mother owns or controls most everything. While Mother's alive, Gloria would have to fight *her*." His voice was soft, even amused. "Now that would be an interesting match."

"You said there were two reasons," Dorothy-Anne reminded him.

"What? Oh, right. My campaign managers. The word *divorce* isn't exactly music to their ears, as you can well imagine."

"You're speaking in the plural. How many campaign managers do you have?"

"Two, but only one who really counts. Althea Netherland Winslow."

"Your mother."

"That's right. Divorce doesn't figure into her political strategy."

His features clouded again, as if he were looking —at what? Not the moon and the whirling constellations splayed across the night. Nor the horizon where sea melted into sky . . . no, something far more distant; the corridors of power for which he had been groomed since birth. He made a face.

"Mother," he said, "is determined to see a Winslow occupying 1600 Pennsylvania Avenue."

"But what does divorce have to do with the presidency? I mean, look at Bob Dole. He was divorced. That didn't stop him from running for president."

"He didn't win, though, did he?" Hunt said with a slightly twisted smile.

"No. But Ronald Reagan was divorced from Jane Wyman before marrying Nancy. That didn't hurt him any."

"True," Hunt said. "But there's still reason number one."

"The money," Dorothy-Anne said.

He nodded. "No way is Mother going to sit back and watch Gloria waltz off with a chunk of the family fortune."

"I should think your mother would want what's best for you. Surely she must realize how bad your marriage is!"

"Mother's aware that things are bad," he said. "She just doesn't know how bad."

"I see. Then she's not aware of your wife's having been on the pill?"

Hunt shook his head. "I keep some parts of my life private. Mother knows what she's told . . . or learns on her own. Which"—he uttered a low, ironic laugh—"can be a lot. She's quite aware that Gloria and I have grown apart. That's hardly a secret. Nor is Gloria's drinking. Gloria sees to that. But Mother refuses to see how irreconcilable the situation really is."

He paused and looked at Dorothy-Anne as if he were far away. If he was, he returned to the here and now fast.

"From the way I sound," he went on, "you're probably getting the impression that I'm weak, cowardly, given to bouts of self-pity, and completely under my mother's thumb."

"Not at all," Dorothy-Anne said gently. "I understand."

She really did, too.

He's telling me the important things. Not his favorite color or the wines he prefers, but the nitty-gritty about himself. He's baring his soul and exposing his vulnerabilities.

She knew it took immense courage on his part and felt privileged for his trust.

He was saying, "What it is, I try to avoid confrontation whenever possible. Especially on the domestic front. I abhor unpleasant scenes."

Dorothy-Anne had to smile. *Don't we all.*

"You're hardly alone in that," she told him softly.

But it was as if he hadn't heard.

"It's strange, isn't it?" he murmured, half to himself. "Life never turns out the way we expect . . . or intend. Imagine! There was actually a time when I foolishly *believed* in happily ever afters!"

A shadow passed over his face.

"Well, my marriage put paid to that. Gloria turned me off women completely . . . I feared for good."

His eyes left Dorothy-Anne and he stared forward once more, as if looking into the past.

"Two years," he said, sounding slightly amazed himself. "That's how long it's been since Gloria and I have had intimate relations."

"Two years can be an awfully long time," Dorothy-Anne said.

He smiled a bitter scimitar. "Yes, it can be. But let me tell you what's really weird. *I . . . didn't . . . miss it!*"

His eyes went wide and round.

"Isn't that incredible? Until now, I haven't even given it any thought!"

"And in all that time, there's been no one else in your life?" Dorothy-Anne asked quietly. "No lady friend at all?"

He shook his head. "Not a one. And not for lack of opportunity. It was disinterest on my part. I suppose when love dies, it does not die alone. Why shouldn't sex die along with it?"

He was silent for a moment, then glanced over and gave her an inquiring look. His voice was soft:

"You do understand, don't you?"

"Yes," Dorothy-Anne nodded.

She slowly let go of his hand and let her arm drop from his shoulder, then scooted back a little ways, as though intent on studying his profile from a slight distance.

"So for two years," Hunt went on, "I've been as celibate as a monk. Can you believe it?" He made a short ironic sound. "Hell, I've probably been *more* celibate than a lot of monks!"

A small silvery fish leapt high out of the water, did an acrobatic flip, and dove back under. Hunt stared intently at the moon-flecked ripples, as though the spreading phosphorescent circles held the key to some elusive answer.

"Do you think," he asked slowly, "that I might have stayed married purposely? Because a wife, even a wife in name only, would keep others of the species at bay?"

"That sounds terribly cynical."

He laughed softly.

"Why shouldn't it? I *am* cynical. I am cynicism personified."

"And this is what she did to you, Hunt? Drained your life of all its joy and wonder?"

"No. The blame is *mine*."

He leaned heavily forward, his hands gripping his kneecaps.

"I permitted it to happen. Of course, I wouldn't have *remained* married if I'd imagined the future held any chance of happiness for me. But I had become jaded, you see. I was convinced that love—that the very *idea* of a loving relationship—was pure romantic bull."

"Oh, Hunt!" Dorothy-Anne whispered. "If you only knew! I can assure you: the love you dismiss so diffidently *does* exist. I know, because I'd found it. Yes. Freddie and I . . . oh, we were head over heels in love! And our love grew stronger with every passing day, with every child we conceived, with every passing year! It was indescribable in its pleasure, and sublime in its pain. And then . . . suddenly last winter . . ."

Her voice faltered and sputtered out. The night seemed to swallow the sound, and she pressed a splayed hand over her face. She could not go on. The agony was too excruciating, the loss too recent, the wounds still too raw.

"If only I had experienced a day of what you speak of," Hunt murmured yearningly. "How glorious that might have been!"

"Don't be insane!" Dorothy-Anne hissed. "Never wish for anything so powerful!"

"Why on earth not?"

She lowered her hand jerkily from her face, then wrapped both arms around her middle. For a moment, she rocked forward and back and forward again, doubled over in spasming pain.

"Because," she whispered hoarsely, "when a love is so great, and one or the other of you dies, your very soul withers and shrivels. You literally starve for lack of nourishment!"

She paused and added: "One can die of a broken heart. I am convinced of that now. I might have wasted away . . . but for my children."

"They say life goes on."

"They say many things. 'This too shall pass. . . . This is but a moment in time. . . .' But the fact of the matter is, the emptiness remains."

She sighed and sat up straighter and fluttered her hands in the air, as if attempting to scatter invisible ghosts.

"I'm sorry," she said. "I didn't mean to get maudlin on you."

"Hey," he said, "you're entitled."

"I'm tons of fun." Dorothy-Anne snorted. "A regular barrel of laughs, huh?"

Hunt's eyes were intent, his voice low and thick. "I'm not looking for a barrel of laughs. Hell, I wasn't looking for anything! I've already told you: I'd sworn off women. And then—there *you* were. First in San Francisco. Then in Huatulco."

She was frowning in disapproval, her expression guarded, and yet her pulse was racing madly.

"It makes me wonder," he said thoughtfully. "Is it fate? Were our lives destined to intersect? Coincidence seems far too trivial an explanation."

"Please, Hunt," Dorothy-Anne begged softly. "Don't talk like this!"

"But it's what I *feel!*" he insisted.

She reached out to silence his lips but her slender hands fluttered, as if of their own accord, back down into her lap, where they roosted uneasily. Her ears hummed. The air was charged and all but crackled, and she became aware of an intense heat growing between them.

"If only we'd met years ago!" he said. "Think of how different things might have turned out!"

They would have been different, all right, she thought. *Freddie would never have existed. Neither would the pearls of our relationship, Liz, Zack, and Fred.*

Life without the children was inconceivable. Unthinkable. Not worth living.

Hunt is wrong, she realized in an incisive flash. *Things couldn't have been any different. I wouldn't have wanted them to be.*

"Sometimes, whatever will be must be," she whispered. "Obviously, meeting sooner wasn't in the cards."

"Not then," Hunt agreed. "But now . . ."

His eyes were bright with excitement, and his words flowed forth in an impassioned rush:

"Don't you see, Dorothy-Anne? Fate is offering us *both* a second chance! We *can* be together! Yes—money be damned! I shall initiate divorce proceedings at once—"

He broke off and looked surprised at his own words. Then, in one fluid motion, he moved close to her. The next thing she knew she was engulfed by his warm, powerful arms, and he pressed her against him, but gently, as he might a fragile treasure.

She found she was trembling, and yet . . .

Yet she felt the most extraordinary sense of elation, of no longer being earthbound, and soaring higher and higher!

She clutched his arms to pull away, but gripped him firmly to her instead.

"Dorothy-Anne!" Hunt's whisper was a tingly breath in her ear. "My love. My salvation. My second chance."

"Hunt, don't!" she murmured.

"Shhhhh . . ." he said.

She turned her face up to his. Her eyes were large and luminous and moved around rapidly, like a dreamer who slept with open eyelids—or a fugitive searching for a place to hide.

She told herself that she must be strong. That she must resist him.

But it was impossible. Her arms had no strength, and she was paralyzed.

There was alchemy at work here, powers she was helpless to counter.

Then his lips fastened on hers. All thoughts of resistance scattered like sparks. Her fingers dug into his arms and pulled him even closer, and she returned his kiss passionately, as ravenously as a starving creature finding sustenance.

His voice was a whisper in the night. "What do you say we go down below?"

I'll regret this in the morning, she thought.

But morning was hours away. And in the meantime, the promise of night stretched to infinity.

"Yes!" she whispered, staring into his eyes. "Let's go below."

47

Body his, body hers.

The bed in the guest cabin was queen-size, but Hunt's cock, Dorothy-Anne reflected dreamily, was definitely king-size. Oh, my, oh my. Oh, most definitely. Hunt Winslow, she mused, was a perfect "ten" in every way. . . .

But these thoughts came after. In the meantime she savored every last moment of this, their maiden voyage of carnal discoveries. And what a voyage it was!

They began nice and easy. Taking their sweet time, acquainting themselves with each other's geography. Slats of golden light leaked dimly through the louvered door from the lamps in the saloon. It was just enough to see by, aiding the examination of fleshy hillock, ample valley, sumptuous mound, and perfumed curve; perfect for spelunking the hidden secrets of orifice, crevasse, protuberance, and cave.

"Yes. Oh, yesssss . . ." Dorothy-Anne sighed out pleasurably as Hunt prepared to undress her.

She lay supine, luxuriating in sinful leisure on the quilted blue satin spread, staring up at him with an expression of utter bliss. Her breasts, snug against her boatneck sweater, rose and fell with anticipation and she watched, with rapt intoxication, while he, still fully clothed, knelt astride her.

"You're so beautiful," he whispered.

Without hurry, he loosened the waist of her white pleated cotton shorts, his hands gliding across her firm silken flesh as he slid the sweater a few inches up her flat, softly muscled belly.

"So very, very beautiful . . ." he murmured.

Holding her gaze, he slowly lowered his head, kissed her navel, then probed it with delicate, snakelike flicks of his tongue.

Small electric shocks streaked through her, and the breath caught in her throat.

"Oh, Hunt!" she moaned, writhing under his tender ministrations.

Dorothy-Anne let her eyes drift shut, the better to savor every delicious sweet morsel of physical sensation. She trembled as Hunt inched the sweater farther up her rib cage, his languid tongue leaving a moist trail on her sternum. And finally, after what seemed forever, he drew the sweater up over her arms and head and cast it away.

Dorothy-Anne's breasts leaped free, full and strong and voluptuously tipped with dusky rose nipples.

She heard his sharp exhalation and half opened her eyes. He was staring down at her, transfixed by the perfection of her breasts, the concavity of her tiny waist, the marvelously rounded symmetry of her hips.

"Practically perfect," he said hoarsely, admiring the way her fine, firm rosebud nipples, free of the constraints of her sweater, became plumply erect and unmistakably aroused. "Yes. Practically perfect in every way."

Dorothy-Anne's thin nostrils flared.

"And what the hell," she inquired, raising herself forward on her elbows, "is with this 'practically' business?"

"That's just so you don't get a swollen head," he soothed, with a disarming grin. And rapidly closing the distance between them, he sought her mouth and captured it with his lips.

Now, this is more like it! she thought happily, lying back down and returning his kiss in kind.

What began as teasing little nips and sucks soon progressed to downright ardor. The sensation of his tongue had no beginning and no end. It reached everywhere, and her entire body thrummed like one vast tuning fork. Paradoxically, she felt on fire even as her skin shivered deliciously with the chill of gooseflesh.

Her senses were swimming.

Was it possible, she marveled, aware of a familiar moistness welling up between her legs, that a mere *kiss* could trigger such astonishingly deep and powerful currents of arousal?

Obviously, it was. And could. And did.

Finally their lips broke contact. Her breasts rose and fell sharply, and her diaphragm expanded and contracted as she inhaled deeply, in an effort to catch her breath.

"Wow!" she whispered. Her eyes were wide and glowed with wonder.

"You ain't seen nothing yet," Hunt smiled, moving to the foot of the bed to finish undressing her.

She lay there pliantly, lifting her buttocks up off the bed as he divested her of her shorts, then her tiny flesh-tone briefs. They crackled with static as he flung them aside.

Dorothy-Anne held her breath. She could scarcely believe where her desires had led her. Hunt was, admittedly, a hunk and a half, but who would have anticipated that she, of all people—she, who had only slept with one other man in her entire life, her late husband—could suddenly feel so violently excited, so utterly swept away by the promise of passion? Who would have thought she could just lie here, naked as Eve and shameless as Jezebel, offering herself to this beautiful man and finding it absolutely natural, gloriously sinful, and—yes—as necessary as oxygen?

Certainly not me, she thought dizzily, letting the questions waft out of sight, out of mind, and off into the night.

Now Hunt was undressing himself. She raised herself up, watching in rapt concentration as he crossed his arms, grabbed the bottom of his polo shirt, and whisked it up over his head.

Dorothy-Anne couldn't keep her eyes off him.

His body was perfection. Chest broad, like burnished bronze sprinkled with golden fleece. Stomach flat, hard, and etched with the merest suggestion of a washboard. And hips as narrow and tapered as an Olympic gymnast's.

With gleaming eyes, the Jezebel part of her continued to assess his physical attributes, and she watched intently while he unbuckled his belt, unzipped his white, trouser-length deck pants, and let them drop.

She gasped when she saw the monster phallus straining his briefs.

It simply cannot be, she thought, certain it was a trick of the light . . . or that she was imagining things . . . though why its size should surprise her, Dorothy-Anne couldn't quite say. Everything else about Hunt was, after all, intensely and devastatingly male.

Why *shouldn't* the penis match the man?

Why not, indeed . . .

Holding her breath, her eyes were locked on him as he bent forward, his arm and thigh muscles flexing as he raised first one leg, and then the other, and slipped out of his briefs.

Naked now, he turned to her, and her gaze was inexorably drawn to his phallus.

It seemed to leap from the gilt thicket of his pubic hair, darker than the surrounding flesh below his tan line, and proportionate in size to his family jewels.

No, her eyes had definitely not been playing tricks on her. It was unimaginably huge, prodigally excessive, and almost preposterously thick. Veins stood out on it in bold relief.

She felt a fresh torrent of wetness flooding into her loins, and her heart was pounding so violently the walls of the cabin seemed to pulsate with its deafening beat.

"Make love to me!" she whispered fiercely. Her eyes were wide and moist and pleading. "Put it all the way inside me! Show no mercy!"

"Don't be in such a hurry," he murmured, amusement glinting in his eyes. "Where's the fire?"

"*Inside* me!" she gasped.

"Well, in that case," he replied solemnly, "we'll just have to put it out, won't we?"

And he knelt inside her carelessly splayed legs, his splendidly engorged, imperial-sized tumescence resting heavily on her belly.

Words failed her as his hands cupped her breasts, his thumbs gently strumming her erect nipples.

Vibrations of pleasure radiated throughout her body. She let her head drop back down on the pillow and tossed it from side to side while moans, like feline growls, escaped her lips.

Then his mouth sought one of her breasts, and she cried aloud.

"Yes!" she panted, "yes—yes—" her words punctuating his every marvelous nibble.

He bit and squeezed a little harder, and beneath him, her entire body arched upward with longing, everything within her demanding more, *more*, MORE!—that one repeated word, "Yes!" an exhortation—that he plunge that magnificent Jeroboam of a cock that lay, rock hard on her belly, inside her to the hilt.

But Hunt was not one to be rushed.

"Patience," he murmured, still intent on savaging her luscious, long-nippled breasts. He moved his free arm behind and under him, his hand feeling along the smooth tender skin of her inner thighs. Unerringly, his fingers homed in on her pouting, engorged wet clitoris, the very nucleus from which the heat of all her pleasures sprang, and slowly he rubbed his middle finger across it.

"God!" she gasped explosively.

She was thrashing around on the bed now, hips grinding in rhythm with his finger, face screwed up in intense concentration. Her flesh shone bright with a sheen of sweat, and heavy shudders, foreshocks of an imminent orgasm, began to rack her entire body.

He fingered her some more.

"Oh, God!" she screamed. "Oh, God, oh God, oh—"

And only then did he finally thrust his own hips back until the blunt end of his phallus was lined up precisely with her opening.

"Yes!" she breathed.

A crazed kind of light seemed to glow from Dorothy-Anne's eyes and her hands clutched his shoulders, her fingers digging into the flesh.

"Yes! Oh, Hunt, *please!*"

For a moment he hesitated. Then, measuring his entry, and prolonging the exquisite agony, he very slowly pressed his way inside her until he had filled her entirely.

For a moment she thought she might scream. It felt as if he had inserted something other than his cock, something alien and inanimate. Surely this was too huge, too rigid, and altogether too painful and intrusive to be a mere penis. . . .

Then Hunt gripped her by the hips, pulled her closer, and thrust his pelvis forward a few millimeters more. Groin to groin they were now, joined like Siamese twins. And slowly, ever so slowly, he pulled back out, careful never to lose contact with her swollen clitoris.

Now there was no doubt in her mind. The pulsating giant inside her was neither alien nor inanimate, but alive—*alive!*

Oh, and how! And the sensations it aroused! They were truly beyond description, and ignited the heat that threatened to consume them both.

Dorothy-Anne's eyes took on a glazed, luminous look.

Is this pleasure or is it pain? She couldn't be sure. *Where does the one stop and the other begin? And is there really a difference?*

She didn't know.

What she *did* know, however, was that the farther he withdrew, the emptier she felt—and that she was desperate for him to fill her again.

Her fingers dug deeper into his shoulders. But how utterly maddening, these leisurely, restrained maneuvers of his!

Why can't he just get on with it?

"Faster, dammit!" she croaked, her teeth clenched with agonized frustration.

If he heard her, he didn't let on. With the precision of a brain surgeon, he slowly thrust forward again, sliding into her for what seemed an eternity. Again, the pain inside her blossomed in intensity until she thought she might faint.

Slowly in . . .

Slowly out . . .

Slowly . . . slowly . . .

She lost count of how many times he meted out those precise, patient measures, only that it was *too* slow. If he didn't speed it up, she would soon be climbing the walls!

"Faster!" she urged. "Please—*please*—"

Slowly, he penetrated her to the hilt one last time, then shoved his arms beneath her back and half lifted her off the bed. Instinctively she scissored her legs around his hips and cleaved to him, her mound impaled against the very stem of his trunk.

Now he began his assault in earnest, and a cry tore from her lips.

Faster, faster!

The physical momentum was like a furnace, and they were glued together, their sweat-sheened skin merging to create a single, mindless organism with but one intention, the fulfillment of ecstasy.

Nothing else existed, only the reality of the flesh.

Dorothy-Anne was in a delirium. Her mouth was agape as she panted and grunted in rhythmic time to Hunt's pummeling hips. The rushing of her blood roared in her ears, and her heart pounded like sledgehammers. He was her and she was him and they were one.

And then the first explosions detonated deep in her core and her body spasmed.

"Hunt!" she screamed. *"Oh, Hunt!"*

In her mind's eye she saw a vast plain of yellow daffodils, and then they shattered and became giant blooms of pink dahlias that erupted like fireworks, only to turn into blinding flashes of a thousands suns.

Her screams increased in volume. They bounced off the teak bulkheads and echoed inside the cabin and finally burst out of the screened portholes and across the sea.

And now her racking shudders triggered his own.

Feeling the urgency rising from his own testes, Hunt let go of her, grabbed her brutally by the hips, and held tight.

She fell backward, away from him, her shoulders, arms, and head hitting the mattress, her legs still fiercely locked around his waist. Pelvis to pelvis they were joined, seemingly in midair.

Cruelly now he plunged in and out, freed from all restraint, and went at it like a madman.

Harder, harder!

His face was contorted in agony and his hips pistoned like an engine, slamming himself in and out, in and out—

—in and out—

Picking up speed and tempo.

—in and out, in and out, in and—

Dorothy-Anne reached one hand beneath herself and felt for his testicles. She caught them, cupped them in her hand, and squeezed the heavy sacs gently.

"You've got such beautiful big balls!" she marveled. "Oh, Hunt! You've got the biggest balls I've ever seen!"

She squeezed them a little harder and an animal growl rose from his throat.

Below him, she screamed again as another wave of orgasm washed over her, and her hold on his scrotum tightened.

Now he was unable to hold back any longer. As the torrent rose, Hunt's growl became a roar and he rammed himself inside her to the hilt. Then he abruptly ceased moving and froze, his hands clutching her hips, his phallus motionless inside her.

And then she felt it. The huge live thing buried deep within her. It throbbed and contracted mightily as he filled her with his seed.

The ejaculation seemed to take forever.

For a long time neither of them moved. Then, still joined at the hip, they collapsed together, lying face-to-face and holding each other closely. Their hearts were pounding, and they gulped breath after ragged breath.

"Now, that," he said, between drawing deep mouthfuls of air, "certainly qualifies as an earthshaking event."

"How earthshaking?" she asked softly. "Seven point five?"

"On the Richter scale?"

She nodded. Her eyes were pale and bottomless and her nude body gleamed in the dim light.

"I'd say it was more like an eight," he said, smoothing her damp hair back from her face.

She stared at him. "In that case," she suggested thickly, "shall we try for a nine?"

Already, he could feel his slumbering giant stir inside her.

He laughed. "Well, maybe an eight and a half," he allowed.

Her voice was husky. "I'm up to it if you are."

"Isn't that supposed to be my line?"

"Whoever's," she said, and shrugged. "Want to go for it?"

He smiled. "Why not?"

Morning shed a different light on the events of the night before. Guilt, regrets, and the pain of departure weighed heavily.

Dorothy-Anne was up and dressed by the crack of dawn. Tiptoeing around, she opened the door of the main cabin, then stopped and turned around. She stared at the bed.

Hunt slept on. He was lying on his back in the tangle of sheets, one leg cocked, knee in the air, arms outspread. His mouth was slightly agape and he was snoring softly.

She debated waking him, but was spared making the decision, because, as if by some telepathic alarm that was activated by her merely looking at him and thinking about him, he awoke suddenly and looked straight at her.

"Hey," he said sleepily, his tousled hair giving him a boyish charm. He turned on the full wattage of his pearly whites. "You're up awfully early."

Dorothy-Anne stared at him. He was irresistible, even first thing in the morning, but this was one morning she was very definitely going to resist. "I've got to get back to Eden Isle," she said coolly. "Then head straight home, Hunt."

If he heard the detached and somewhat formal tone in her voice, he didn't act like it. He jumped out of the bed and padded over to her on bare feet, his magnificently lean and muscular body totally naked. He leaned his arms on the cabin wall, one to either side of her. "How about a good-morning kiss?" he said, nuzzling her with his day's growth of beard.

Dorothy-Anne's body suddenly went stiff and she looked away.

"Hunt," she finally said, "I've really got to hurry." Then she looked into his eyes. "Sorry."

When he felt the tenseness in her body and saw the look on her face, he drew back. He had noticed that she was curiously withdrawn and quiet. "Uh-oh," he said. "It's like that, huh?"

Dorothy-Anne didn't respond.

"A case of the morning-after guilts." He gently chucked her under the chin, then turned and headed for his clothes, obviously deciding not to pressure her.

"How about some breakfast?" he said, beginning to get dressed. "I scramble a mean egg."

She shook her head. "No, thanks."

"Coffee, then," he said, pulling on a shirt. "It won't take but a minute."

"Okay," Dorothy-Anne said, making an effort to appear more at ease than she felt. "A quick cup of coffee, then I really have to go."

"You got it," he said affably. "Why don't you make yourself comfortable, and I'll bring it to you."

He turned to her. "How do you like it?"

"Black is fine," she said, and turned and left the bedroom. She realized that they knew very little about their likes and dislikes, about the quotidian details that made up the daily business of living.

She sat in the saloon, thumbing through an old boating magazine, looking at the photographs but not seeing anything, her mind a maelstrom of conflicting thoughts and emotions. The night had been one of utter magic, but now all she wanted to do was run. It was so crazy, she thought. It made no sense. She wanted to be with Hunt, yet she felt she had to get out of here.

He came in from the galley, carrying two mugs of coffee. "Here you go," he said, handing her one of the mugs, a smile on his handsome, tanned face.

"Thanks, Hunt," Dorothy-Anne said, taking the mug and sipping the coffee. It was very strong, but tasted delicious.

Hunt sat down in a chair opposite her and sipped his coffee, looking over at her tentatively.

In the ensuing silence, she could swear that the sound of the waves slapping against the sides of the boat and the occasional cries of gulls were amplified, making the quiet all the more awkward.

Finally, Hunt put his mug down. "You want to talk about it?" he asked.

Dorothy-Anne took another sip of coffee, then shook her head. "I don't know what to say, Hunt. I just . . . I guess I'm just confused, and a little scared."

"Dorothy-Anne," he said, sensitive to her obvious discomfiture, "I'm not going to push you, but you know as well as I do that what we did last night was wonderful. It was beautiful, and there was nothing wrong with it."

Dorothy-Anne gazed into her mug thoughtfully. "I guess . . ." she began hesitantly, "I guess its all just moving a little too fast for me, Hunt." She looked up at him. "I need time. Time to sort out my feelings."

Hunt took another sip of coffee, then stared at her. "I'll be waiting for you," he said softly. "But I want you to remember what I said last night. I'm going to give it up with Gloria, and I hope that you'll allow yourself to give the two of us a chance."

Dorothy-Anne sighed. He was so responsive to her needs. So understanding and gentle. *Dammit!* But she still had the overwhelming urge to be alone to think things through, to get a grip on the maddening swirl of conflicting thoughts and feelings going around in her head.

"I better get going, Hunt," she finally said.

"Okay," he replied. He got to his feet immediately. "I'll get the Zodiac fired up. Ready?"

Dorothy-Anne nodded. She took a last sip of coffee, put her mug down, and stood up.

"After you," he said, an easy smile on his face, then he followed her out onto the deck.

On the short trip back to Eden Isle, they were both silent, the only sound the roar of the Zodiac's outboard engine. Once there, Hunt went with her straight to the landing strip.

"Do you mind if I call you?" he asked when she was ready to board the Hale Companies' 757–200.

Dorothy-Anne turned to him. "No," she said. "I don't mind at all. But I'm going to be awfully busy when I get back, Hunt."

"Okay," he said, and suddenly he leaned over and kissed her chastely on the cheek. "I love you," he whispered into her ear. "Just remember that."

Dorothy-Anne stood motionless, and when he pulled back and stared into her eyes, she merely nodded, not trusting herself to speak.

"See you," he said, and she turned and climbed the boarding stairs.

Once in the huge jet, she headed straight back to her private suite in the rear. She sank into one of the custom-designed sofas and strapped herself in.

Glancing out a porthole, she saw Hunt standing there, his hair ruffled by the wind, looking for her. She gazed at him for a moment, then depressed a button and coromandel screens slid over the portholes, completely blocking her view. It was too painful to see him standing there, knowing that he wanted her—knowing that she wanted him.

God, he is so perfect. So very much the man of any woman's dreams. So very much like . . . Freddie.

Tears, unbidden and unexpected, came into her eyes now. *Oh, Freddie, what have I done? Why have I betrayed your memory like this? Why have I acted as if you were never a part of me?*

Three short months. That's how long it had been since his death. Three short months, that's all. Three short months, and she had completely forgotten his ever having existed. Three short months, and she had completely forsaken him.

And for what? she asked herself. *One night of unbridled physical pleasure. One night of sex. Pure and simple.*

Guilt washed over her. Guilt that she hadn't given him a thought while she was with Hunt. Guilt that she hadn't even given their children a thought while she was so selfishly indulging herself. Guilt that she had allowed any of this to happen.

But Freddie's gone, she reminded herself. *Gone. Now and forever. There is no bringing him back.*

Oh, Freddie, she cried silently, *what am I to do? What would you have me do?* What?

But no voice to her, there was only the distant hum of the jet engines in the silence. There were no magical answers she could pull out of the air to assuage her guilt, to relieve her sorrow.

She thumbed the tears from her eyes, then closed them, resting her head back on the couch.

Then she suddenly realized with a shock that while she was racked with a guilt she didn't know how to cleanse herself of, she still, undeniably and irrevocably, wanted Hunt Winslow.

She craved him like a drug. Already she missed his lean, muscular arms around her, his lips on hers, his manhood in her. Already she needed the sense of peace and understanding that he gave her, the unconditional love that he felt for her. And that—yes!—she felt for him. There was no denying that.

Would Freddie deny me that? she wondered. *Would he want me to go on living without the same loving shelter he always provided for me?*

She didn't think so.

Was it possible that one could love a second time as completely, as purely, and as beautifully as the first time?

When a first love had been as perfect as hers and Freddie's, was it even conceivable that it could happen again in one lifetime? She wasn't sure she knew, but she was convinced that Hunt had been right about one thing: What they had done had been wonderful. It had been beautiful. And it had been anything but wrong.

Why, oh why, then, did she still feel guilty, ashamed, *unfaithful*?

Her mind so consumed with these thoughts, it wasn't until the jet was preparing to land that Dorothy-Anne suddenly realized that, for the first time since Freddie's death, she had not once felt a fear of flying.

49

Christos headed up Market Street on foot, checking out his reflection in the plate glass windows. Used to be, he'd get on Amber's case about it, she was always doing that. Course, she never looked any different from one day to the next. Same old hip-hugger jeans, short, itty-bitty little tops that left her navel exposed, shapeless Levi's jackets, long straight hair.

Same-o, same-o.

Thing was, he had something to look at, having stopped in a floozy men's store where he'd shelled out a wad on new threads. Which he wore out, no shopping bags, thanks, and could you dump this old shit?

So here he was, struttin' his stuff in a new band-collared black shirt and a three-button Calvin Klein sport coat. The kind with lapels and pocket flaps. Cut like a suit jacket, man, but cool, not being fabric, but icy blue glove leather. His 501s and beat-up Westerns made a nice contrast.

No doubt about it: clothes made the man. Got the chicks checking him out, too.

He was thinking, A gold Rolex Oyster would hit the spot. Maybe he'd mention it to Gloria in passing, see if she'd spring for it. Pretty sure she'd be happy to, the way she was constantly looking for things to give him. Sure, why not?

Strolling on, it wasn't long before he reached his destination, the stretch of used car lots with colorful little plastic pennants fluttering in the breeze, dealers trying to turn used cars into goddamn fiestas.

The new duds worked magic. The first lot he stopped at, a salesman with fifty extra pounds around his middle came rushing out. Practically rubbing his hands, booming, "You lookin' for a car, or just wheels?" and going, "Har-har-har!" All that excess flab jiggling like Jell-O.

Christos didn't say a word. Just took his time moseying around. Not seeing anything he wanted, and moving on up the street to the next lot.

It had the same little pennants strung all around, the cars sporting painted-on prices on the windshields. This time a smarmy little guy with a pencil-line moustache and a loud plaid sport coat came charging outside.

"Just lookin' for wheels?" he asked cheerfully. "Or a whole car?" Showing teeth like big white tiles.

Was he looking for a whole car. The fuck was it with these guys?

Christos stared him down. "You secondhand dealers all failed comedians? What d'you do, get together after hours? Shoot the shit, and share jokes?"

See if that didn't put a dent in the little guy's grin.

But Christos didn't wait for his reaction. He was already scanning the lot. And wouldn't you know it. Right away he saw a set of wheels he liked.

It was an '85 Coupe de Ville. A big mother. Black vinyl top. Tons of shiny chrome. And it was the exact same icy blue as his new jacket.

How about that.

He went over and walked circles around it, the little guy in tow. Kicked the Armor-Alled tires. Inspected the body for rust. Bent down and looked in through the windows at big black leather seats and a dashboard like a 747.

But what sold him on it was the color. That icy blue. Hell, it was like a sign. Matching car and coat.

Then and there, he decided to buy it—depending on how it ran.

The smarmy little guy said, "Wanna take her on a test drive?" Anxious to make a sale.

Christos decided to play it real cool. "Naw. Not yet."

Besides, the Caddy wasn't what he was really after. Oh, he'd buy it, yeah. But that was just a fringe benefit. The real reason was to throw off suspicion.

The way he had it figured, if he bought one car from a dealer, this de Ville for instance, no one would connect him with the car he was really after—the getaway car he was scouting around for. The one he'd have to come back for at night and steal.

It had to be a vehicle nobody would notice, like that silver Tercel over there, at the edge of the lot. Parked where you could drive right off with it.

But first he'd have to take the getaway out for a spin, make sure it wouldn't die on him. And, since grand theft auto wasn't exactly his specialty, it couldn't have any alarm systems that needed disconnecting, or freezing with liquid nitrogen. Also, he'd have to make a wax impression of the key, since he wasn't good at using a slim jim, either, and didn't have the tools or the know-how to punch out the ignition and yank the steering column locks.

Christos turned to the little guy. "Before I take any test drives, I wanna know one thing."

"Sure. Shoot it by me."

Christos winced inwardly at the choice of words. He didn't want to be reminded of any shooting. That was a bridge he'd have to cross soon enough.

But keeping his cool, he said, "What kinda discount do I get if I pay cash?"

50

ome sweet home!
The double-width townhouse on East Sixty-ninth Street had never looked so good to Dorothy-Anne. Inside, the house was very quiet, very still. The children were all in school, and the staff were all busy doing their jobs.

Now is as good a time to start as any.

She headed straight upstairs to her bedroom, kicked off her shoes, and stripped of her clothes. She padded into the bathroom on bare feet, splashed her face with cold water, then dried off vigorously. Finished, she walked back through the bedroom to her dressing room, where she grabbed clothes. Simple, comfortable gym sweats. *Just the thing for the job,* she thought. Finally, she slipped her feet into comfy old flat mules.

That done, she was ready. *I know what I have to do,* she thought. *What I must do.*

Even though she felt racked with guilt over her night with Hunt, strangely enough, their intimacy had somehow finally propelled her to face this onerous task. It had been three months since Freddie's death, and it was time she went through his clothes, and then down the hall to clean out his office.

Yes, she thought, *is is time now . . . time for a sense of closure.* She knew that it was a task she couldn't possibly leave to somebody else, but even so, she didn't know when she'd ever dreaded anything so much.

She squared her shoulders and strode purposefully over to Freddie's large dressing room and put a hand on the handle and turned. She took a deep breath and opened the door.

Tears, unexpected and sudden, sprang to her eyes.

She reached up with a finger and brushed at them, standing there peering into the darkness, breathing in her dead husband's scent, a scent still very much alive in here.

It's time, she thought again. *Time to put the past behind me.*

With a strengthened resolve, she quickly selected a few sweatshirts and baseball caps emblazoned with various team logos, and carried them out to the bedroom, where she laid them down on the bed.

They may be the least valuable things in his wardrobe, she thought, *but they will be the most treasured by the children.*

She went back to the dressing room and picked up some empty shoe boxes off the floor, then began emptying the drawers in the built-in chest of loose tie clasps, engraved belt buckles, money clips, wallets, and such.

Then she began to take out the extremely valuable dress sets—cuff links and studs, all in their individual leather boxes. She opened the first one. A Verdura eighteen-karat gold, enamel, and diamond "Night and Day" set. Day in turquoise enamel with gold maps, and night in midnight blue enamel with diamond stars. Verdura baroque pearl, diamond, and sapphire cuff links. On and on and on. All of these gifts from her. Freddie would never have gone out and bought them for himself.

She began shoveling these precious objects and many others into the empty shoe boxes. When she was finished, she carried them out to the bedroom and placed the boxes on a chest.

Looking at them, she thought, *Someday the children can pick and choose what they want, or the whole lot will go to Christie's to be auctioned.*

She returned to the dressing room and had a last look around inside, then switched off the light. Just as she was closing the door, she heard her name being called out.

"Dorothy-Anne!" Venetia called. "Girlfriend! Where are you?"

"I'm in here," Dorothy-Anne called back. "The bedroom."

Venetia swept in, a vision in a cloud of oyster silk. "Ohhhh! Welcome back!" She rushed toward Dorothy-Anne with her arms spread out, and grasped her in a tight hug.

Dorothy-Anne laughed and hugged her back. "Oh, Venetia, you are a sight for sore eyes." She stood back looking at her friend. "You look beautiful. As usual."

Venetia suddenly caught sight of the sweatshirts and baseball caps on the bed, then saw the shoe boxes on the chest. The smile instantly disappeared from her face and she stared at Dorothy-Anne.

"You're finally doing it?" she asked softly. "Clearing out his things?"

"Yes," Dorothy-Anne answered her.

"Good girl," Venetia said. She reached out and took one of Dorothy-Anne's hands in hers. "I think it will make you feel better. Maybe not today, but soon."

"It certainly isn't easy," Dorothy-Anne said.

Venetia squeezed her hand and smiled. "Is there anything I can do to help? I mean *any*thing."

"Oh . . . I don't know." Dorothy-Anne hesitated. "Not really. I—"

"Get real, girl," Venetia broke in. "This is Venetia, okay? Remember me? Your best friend? I'm in this with you. Now *what*? Tell me."

"Well, I got everything out of his dressing room that I want. The rest gets packed up for pickup."

"Done," Venetia said. "Where's it going? Goodwill? Salvation Army?"

"No," Dorothy-Anne replied. "I want it all to go to that thrift shop that benefits AIDS patients, whatever it's called."

"Housing Works," Venetia quickly responded. "I'll call them for a pickup. Meanwhile, I know there are eighty million boxes down in the basement in a storage room. So I'll go down and rustle up some help with those. I'll have that dressing room empty before you can bat those beautiful eyes of yours."

"Oh, Venetia, you're too much. Really." Tears welled up in Dorothy-Anne's eyes again. "I don't know what I'd do—"

"Shush," Venetia said, hugging her again. "Let's just get busy. Get the deal done."

"Okay," Dorothy-Anne said, extricating herself from Venetia's embrace. She wiped at her eyes. "You're right. I'm going to be down the hall clearing out Freddie's office. If you need anything, I'll be there."

She walked down the hall to Freddie's office, and had no sooner opened the door than she heard the shrieks of three boisterous children, then the thunder of their steps on the stairway. Nanny Florrie's admonishing voice followed them up the steps.

"Quiet with you now. Like a herd of elephants! And slow doon!"

Dorothy-Anne closed Freddie's office door again and quickly strode down the hall to the stairs. The moment she got there, Zack slammed straight into her.

"Mommie!" he yelped, throwing his arms around her tightly. "Mommie! Mommie! Mommie!"

Behind him, Fred and Liz, wide grins on their faces, called out, "Mom!" in unison.

Dorothy-Anne bent down and kissed Zack, then, one arm around his shoulder, she held the other out for Liz and Fred. Hugging and kissing them in turn, despite Zack's efforts to push them away.

Dorothy-Anne's heart swelled to bursting. Never had she heard such beautiful music as their squeals and bickering, their clamor for her attention.

Nanny Florrie finally arrived at the top of the stairs, huffing and puffing loudly, her face red with both exertion from the climb and exasperation with her charges.

"They'll be the death o' me," she complained. "Miss Venetia hae a nice surprise fer ye young'uns doonstairs in the basement. She says to tell ye that it involves a nice cash reward if ye get doon there in a hurry."

Three sets of ears perked up.

Zack squealed "Money, money, money!" and took off down the stairs, taking them three at a time.

Dorothy-Anne stood and watched them go, thinking that she must be the luckiest woman alive to have three such wonderful children. Then she turned and went back to Freddie's office.

She opened the door and switched on the light, then stood there for a few moments before closing the door behind her. Her eyes swept over Freddie's Jeffersonian hideaway, taking in its spare but luxurious appointments:

The highly polished oak floors and gleaming brass chandelier and wall sconces. The antique architect's table on which she saw plans spread out for Eden Isle. The old framed architectural drawings on the pistachio green walls. Louis XV chairs that may have belonged to Jefferson himself. The George II mahogany kneehole desk on which was perched his desktop computer. Surprisingly, it didn't look out of place in this timeless room.

She walked first to his desk and looked down. The breath caught in her throat when she saw his desk calendar: December 15, 1997, it read. *The day of his death.*

Bracing herself on the desk, Dorothy-Anne closed her eyes and took a deep breath. *I've got to go on,* she told herself. *It's time to finish what I've begun.*

Opening her eyes, she looked down at his appointments for that day and noticed that there was a note, scratched out in Freddie's unmistakable script: "Copy slush file to diskette. Take to Aspen!!! Call C. to confirm." Followed by a telephone number.

What's the slush file? she wondered. *Why take it to Aspen? And who is this C.?* All this on the day he died.

Well, there's one way to find out. She picked up the telephone and dialed the number. After a moment she heard the click of a machine and a female voice came on the line, simply stating that the caller should leave a message. Dorothy-Anne left her name and telephone number and hung up.

Now her curiosity was more aroused than ever. *A woman's voice on the machine. Was she "C."?* She made a mental note to call the number again later, if she hadn't received a call back.

She began rifling through the neat stack of mail stacked on the lower left-hand corner of the desk. Nearly all of it, she noted, was requests for charitable contributions. There was very little of a personal nature. A few invitations, to parties, to gallery openings, auction previews, and such. Dorothy-Anne picked up the stack and unceremoniously dumped it into the wastebasket.

Next, she went through a stack of papers perfectly aligned in a mahogany tray on the upper left-hand side of the desk. Mostly copies of faxes relating to Eden Isle. All of it, she was certain, with backup copies at Hale headquarters. She dumped them in the wastebasket as well.

Finally, she began opening desk drawers. Nearly everything else she found was business related, all information that she was certain, once again, would have copies at Hale headquarters. She starting dumping as she went, quickly eyeballing everything first.

That was how she almost failed to see an ordinary-looking manila envelope with no labels on it whatsoever. Its weight was suddenly what attracted her attention. She opened the envelope and saw that it contained a single computer diskette. On it a label read "Slush File."

Dorothy-Anne felt a shiver of anticipation rush through her, and the hair at the nape of her neck stood up. For some reason she felt that she was on the brink of a discovery, of solving some mystery she hadn't known existed in the first place.

She looked over at Freddie's desktop; its darkened, blank monitor sat there staring back at her. She knew very little about computers, but she knew someone who knew a great deal.

But what if there's something on the diskette that she shouldn't see?

She decided that she would just have to risk it. Freddie, after all, had been the most trustworthy person she'd ever known. She couldn't imagine that there would be anything his own wife and daughter shouldn't see on this mysterious diskette.

Dorothy-Anne picked up the house phone and punched out Nanny Florrie's number. When she answered, she told her to send Liz upstairs to her father's office immediately.

It was only moments before there was a knock at the door. "Mom?" Liz's voice was very soft and full of apprehension, as if she were worried about her mother on the other side of the door.

"Come on in, sweetie," Dorothy-Anne answered her.

Liz opened the door and came into the office. "What is it, Mom?" She looked relieved to see that Dorothy-Anne was okay.

Dorothy-Anne looked over at her. "Liz, you've got to help me with something." She held up the diskette. "I found this in your father's desk. I don't know what's on this diskette, but it was more or less hidden, and coded, and it's something I know nothing about."

Liz grinned widely. "No problem. It's a cinch!" She went over to the desk, pulled out the chair, and sat down. Then she reached over, booted up the computer, took the proffered diskette from Dorothy-Anne's hand, and slipped it in the drive.

"Uh-oh," Liz said after a moment. "You know Daddy's password?"

"No." Dorothy-Anne's heart sank. "I have no idea."

"Don't worry, Mom," Liz said encouragingly. "I know Daddy . . . *knew* Daddy," she corrected herself. "And I betcha I can crack it in minutes."

Liz tucked her head down and concentrated on the keyboard with grim determination.

Dorothy-Anne watched over Liz's shoulder as she hit keys, typing away quickly, expertly. Not for the first time, she marveled that this wondrous creature could be her daughter.

Occasionally Liz would stop, scratch her head, then continue, fingers flying.

It seemed mere seconds before Liz shouted: "Voilà!" She beamed triumphantly up at her mother. "Slush File," she said.

"How did you do it?" Dorothy-Anne asked excitedly.

"I told you," Liz replied. "I knew my dad. It *had* to be a password that had to do with *us*. *All* of us. So I tried all sort of things. Our names combined various ways, our initials. Finally, knowing how Dad thought, I tried F plus D equals five. Freddie plus Dorothy-Anne equals five, with the three of us children. It's a simple equation, streamlined, includes all of us. And that was it."

Dorothy-Anne was utterly amazed. She encircled Liz with her arms from behind and bent over and planted a kiss on the top of her head.

"You are one of the great wonders of the world," she said.

"No," Liz said matter-of-factly, "but I'm glad you think so." She grinned, then said, "Let's see what we've got."

Dorothy-Anne peered at the monitor closely. Under the file title, she immediately noticed the same telephone number she'd seen scratched out on Freddie's calendar. And next to it a name: Caroline Springer-Vos. She quickly checked his calendar to make certain she was correct. *Yes!* The phone number was the same. And this Caroline Springer-Vos *must* be "C." Yes.

Caroline Springer-Vos.

Who was she? Why did her name ring a faraway bell? Dorothy-Anne didn't know, but she was sure that she had heard the name before.

Looking back at the monitor, she saw the file name, "Slush," at the top of the page, followed by the name and telephone number. Immediately following this were columns with headings.

On the right were company names, abbreviated as they appeared on the various stock exchanges. She noticed DIS for Walt Disney, SRV for Service Corporation International, IBM for International Business Machines, of course. There was Intel, Microsoft, Netscape. And on and on and on, dozens of company names, primarily blue chip, but, she noticed, there was a smattering of names she'd never heard of before. To the right of these were columns of number of shares purchased and dollar figured paid.

Liz scrolled the file on the screen without her mother asking her to, and Dorothy-Anne looked at the monitor with a mixture of awe, astonishment, and growing excitement.

The list went on for page after page after page. Dorothy-Anne saw that there were year-end summaries going all the way back to the year she and Freddie were married. These included total amounts invested, percentage return, dividends paid, and she noted that all profits were reinvested.

"Look, Mom," Liz shrieked. "The most recent year-end summary." She looked up at her mother. "Get a load of this. Value of investments to date."

Dorothy-Anne peered at the monitor closely, and saw where Liz had the cursor pointed. And was stunned.

Seventy-three million dollars!

Could this be right? Could she be imagining this? Or was she completely wrong about what this entire file meant?

For she was *certain* she knew exactly what it was: Freddie had invested nearly every penny of his salary—*since they had first married.*

A million dollars a year.

As she stood there trying to digest this information, Dorothy-Anne thought back to conversations they'd had in the distant past about Freddie's salary. Despite his protests, they'd each drawn a million dollars a year in salary. But Freddie had always said that he could never spend it, that he had no use for it with all the company benefits: cars, planes, generous expense accounts, and staying in their own hotels when he traveled.

Now Dorothy-Anne remembered her reply. "Then bank it. It's yours. You've *earned* it."

"Mom?"

Dorothy-Anne was jerked out of her reverie by Liz's voice. She looked at her daughter questioningly.

"You didn't know about this investment fund, did you?" Liz had a serious look on her face.

"No, sweetie," Dorothy-Anne said shakily. "I knew absolutely nothing about it."

Liz got up and hugged her mother tightly. "Oh, Mom," Liz said, "this is just like Daddy. A big surprise gift . . . from . . . beyond."

There was a knock at the door, and Venetia called out. "Dorothy-Anne?"

"Come on in, Venetia," Dorothy-Anne answered.

Venetia came into the room slowly, warily, eyeing the two of them suspiciously. "Am I interrupting something?" she whispered.

Liz and Dorothy-Anne saw the expression on her face and laughed in unison.

"What . . . what's going on?" Venetia asked cautiously.

Dorothy-Anne gave Liz a squeeze and let her go. She turned to Venetia and said, "You're not going to believe it. Look at the monitor. See for yourself."

"Mom," Liz said, "if you don't need me anymore, is it all right if I go do some computer work of my own?"

"Sure," Dorothy-Anne said. "And Liz." She looked into her daughter's eyes. "Thank you."

"Any time!" Liz said, and left the room.

Venetia stood peering at the computer monitor, scrolling the document on the screen back and forth. She finally looked over at Dorothy-Anne with a gleam in her eyes and a wide smile on her lips.

"Child!" she said in a near-whisper. "This is, like, blowing your girlfriend away. I mean . . . this is one hell of a piece of news!" She looked at Dorothy-Anne seriously. "You didn't know anything about this?"

Dorothy-Anne shook her head. "No," she replied. "It came as a complete surprise. I saw a note on Freddie's calendar. It was about this file and getting in touch with somebody in Aspen. It turned out to be this woman . . . Caroline Springer-Vos." She looked at Venetia questioningly. "Did you ever hear of her?"

"Hear of her!" Venetia exclaimed. "You haven't? Where have you been, girl?"

"I know I've heard the name," Dorothy-Anne said, "but I can't for the life of me remember who she is."

"Dorothy-Anne," Venetia said, as if lecturing a child, "she is only the greatest financial investment adviser in the whole wide world. As in the planet. As in Earth?" She gave Dorothy-Anne a significant look.

"Only she's about a hundred and fifty years old and has been more or less retired for years," Venetia continued. "And from what I hear, she only works for two or three very special people. All very secretive."

"Of course," Dorothy-Anne said. "It's just been so long since I've heard anything about her, I couldn't place the name."

The telephone rang on Freddie's desk. It was his private line. "You want me to get it?" Venetia asked.

Dorothy-Anne considered for a moment, then said, "No, Venetia, thanks," she finally said. "I think I can handle it." She picked up the receiver. "Hello?"

Her eyes grew wide with excitement and she put her hand over the receiver. "It's Caroline Springer-Vos," she whispered to Venetia.

"You want me to leave?" Venetia whispered back.

Dorothy-Anne shook her head.

Venetia began pacing the room, trying to ignore Dorothy-Anne's voice in the background as she talked to the legendary financial wizard. At Freddie's antique architect's table, she stopped to look at the plans for Eden Isle spread out there, studying them for the umpteenth time, still fascinated by the imagination that created them.

Finally, Dorothy-Anne hung up the telephone and turned to Venetia. She was obviously still nervous with excitement, but trying to contain it. "Venetia," she said. "Caroline Springer-Vos just confirmed everything. There is seventy-three million dollars in the account—and it's in *my name, too*. It was a joint account, automatically transferable to either of us should something happen to the other. Without going through probate."

"But why didn't she let you know about this?" Venetia asked. "My God, it's been three months!"

"She tried to," Dorothy-Anne said. "She's been leaving E-mail messages ever since she found out about Freddie's death. She said that Freddie insisted that she was only to contact me via E-mail here at home, should something happen to him. He didn't want anyone else to know about this. I didn't have Liz check his E-mail. It hasn't been checked since his death!"

"Freddie knew if anything happened, his brilliant daughter would eventually be getting to his E-mail." Venetia laughed. "Only she got to this file first."

"The only reason Springer-Vos called me now," Dorothy-Anne said, "was because I left a message for her personally after I found her number."

"So she assumed it was cool," Venetia said.

"I can still hardly believe it," Dorothy-Anne said. She stared at Venetia. "Do you know what this *means*, Venetia?" she asked.

"I think I'm going to find out," came Venetia's retort.

"The fifty million dollars due on May fifteenth is in the bag," Dorothy-Anne said triumphantly. "It will be paid in full before Sir Ian or the bank can do anything." She shot an arm into the air. "*Yes*," she crowed. "It will be paid *in full*, straight from this account."

Dorothy-Anne smiled at her friend with mischievous glee in her eyes. "But we'll keep this to ourselves, won't we? I want to surprise these nasty bankers."

A conspiratorial smile spread across Venetia's face. "My lips are sealed," she said with impish delight.

"I can hardly wait to see the look on that smug face," Dorothy-Anne said gloatingly, "when Sir Ian sees the check."

And she thought: *Somewhere Freddie is smiling.*

51

So, no rest for the weary. Now Amber was on his case. Nag-nag-nag. Bitching about how he wasn't around enough lately so she could bitch at him! Something eating at her, only she wouldn't come right out and say what.

Not that Christos gave a rat's ass. He tuned her out and tried to get some shut-eye.

He needed rest. It had been a long day, and he had an even longer night ahead of him.

Instead of counting sheep, he decided to review the events of the day.

His accomplishments had been prodigious.

The silver Tercel had checked out. The model was old enough not to be equipped with car alarms, and a test drive had proved it to be in sound mechanical condition. The body was a little rusty, but hey. Big fuckin' deal. It wasn't like he was shelling out good money for it. And besides, a look under the hood ascertained that it came equipped with a new battery.

Moreover, Christos was now the proud owner of a certain icy blue '85 Coupe de Ville, for which he'd paid legal tender. It was registered to one Ivan P. Smirke, the name on an extra driver's license Christos happened to be carrying around.

For the time being, the Caddy was safely stashed in a parking garage off Van Ness—mainly so Amber would be none the wiser.

In the afternoon, Christos had gone looking for Carlos, the locksmith, at the hardware store on Mission, between Eighteenth and Nineteenth. It was the kind of place that catered to a Spanish clientele and sold tools, toasters, cheap boxed knife sets and plastic dishes, and was big on layaways.

He'd had to drop by twice before he found the guy with the name *Carlos* embroidered on his work shirt. A wiry little squirt, sleeves rolled up to display jailhouse tattoos.

Christos waited for him to finish laying away a set of nonstick cookware boxed in shrink wrap for a Spanish lady, five dollars down, two bucks a week for nine weeks.

As soon as she was gone, Christos sidled up to the counter and looked at Carlos, saying, "Slick sent me," by way of an introduction.

Carlos motioned him aside and looked him over. "Yeah?"

"Said you were the man to see about getting this made." Christos showing him the little slide-top contraption with the wax impression.

Carlos wasn't stupid. Recognizing the mold as a car key, he put two and two together. "Cost you four C-beels," he said. "Half een advance, half when you peek eet up."

Four hundred smackeroos?

"You got to be kidding." Christos looking to see if he was.

And Carlos, deadpan, shrugged his shoulders and said, "Take eet or leave eet. Ees no skin off my back, man."

Christos knew he was in no position to argue. Shit. He needed that key. Carlos was no doubt aware of that fact. So he went ahead and peeled off two hundred-dollar bills from the wad in his pocket. Crisp new ones, kind that looked like play money with the big engraving of Ben Franklin.

Carlos palmed the bills and the wax mold. "Come back before closing time."

When Christos returned at a quarter to six, Carlos had the key ready. But before handing over the final two hundred, Christos had a question. "What if it doesn't fit?"

Carlos giving him a look, quiet for a moment. "Eet feet," he said real softly.

"You sound sure of yourself."

"I am sure, man."

Then Carlos surprised him, saying, "Here. Thees ees on the house." Handing him a little brown paper bag.

Christos looked inside. It was a screwdriver.

"Eet so you don' forget to sweetch license plates. My advice, do eet right away. Eef you fock around, *you* be stampin' out license plates, man. Hear what I'm saying'?"

Christos, not sure how to take it—as well-intentioned advice or a put-down—just nodded and left.

Next, he'd driven the de Ville out to the airport, SFO. Parked it in the short-term garage, and headed to the long-term garage on foot. Keeping his eyes peeled for the oldest car around, one that probably wasn't equipped with an alarm.

Once again, fortune smiled on him. He found an old Celica, unscrewed its plates, stuck them inside his jacket, and returned to the de
Ville. Driving back into the city, he decided he'd wait until after the bars
closed, two in the morning, to boost the Tercel. Then switch plates at the
first opportunity.

Now, letting Amber's yakking go in one ear and right out the other,
something about their not communicating, Christos rolled over. The next
thing he knew he must have dozed off, because when he awoke, Amber's
plastic wall clock, one of those pink cats with bug eyes clicking left and
right, left and right, with a pendulum for a tail, indicated it was nearing
midnight.

Yawning, he sat up and rubbed his hair.

He was alone. Amber was gone, probably at the topless club, shaking
her boobs at tourists. He decided some strong coffee was in order. He
had a car to boost, and it behooved him to be fully awake.

52

Monday, Dorothy-Anne strode out of the private elevator that let out directly into her office. It was ten a.m. and she had a confident spring in her step and a glow on her face. Her cream Chanel suit was trimmed with aqua braid the precise shade of her sparkling eyes and had gilt buttons that complemented the gold of her hair.

She swung her Vuitton briefcase onto her Regency desk, unlatched it, popped it open, and withdrew a sheaf of papers.

Before she could sit down, Cecilia Rosen, severely chic as ever, elbowed her way through the door from the service area next door, sterling tray in hand. On it were the requisite cappuccino, grapefruit juice, and tiny, fat-free Danish.

"You've got an unexpected arrival in the outer office," she said without fanfare. "Ian Connery is chomping at the bit to see you. He doesn't have an appointment. Didn't call beforehand. Nothing. Just showed up." She looked at Dorothy-Anne with disgust.

Sir Ian Connery, Dorothy-Anne mused. *Well, well, well. Now I wonder what he could want?*

But, of course, she was certain that she knew. He was here to deliver the bad news. From Pan Pacific Bank. They were not going to extend the due date for the fifty million dollars due on May 15. This was one bearer of bad tidings she couldn't wait to see.

Cecilia was staring at her, with an expectant look on her face. She set her cup of cappuccino down. "So. Shall I send in Sir Ian now?"

Dorothy-Anne stared at her thoughtfully. "Why don't we finish our coffee at a leisurely pace, then you can show Sir Ian in. Okay?"

Cecilia grinned. "I *see.* Keep the snotty vulture waiting a little longer. *Great.*"

The service area door opened again and Venetia swept into the room. "My, my! Just in time for a kaffee klatsch, I see!" She went over to the tray and poured herself a cup of cappuccino, then took a seat in the chair next to Cecilia and crossed her long, elegant legs.

"Good morning!" Dorothy-Anne said with a smile. "Am I glad you're here."

"What's up?" Venetia asked, sipping her cappuccino.

"We have a very special visitor," Dorothy-Anne said. "And I think you'll enjoy seeing him today."

"Who?" Venetia asked.

"Sir Ian Connery," Dorothy-Anne replied with a mirthful tone of voice.

Venetia almost choked on her cappuccino. She put her cup down and clapped her hands together with glee. "Ah! This is rich! Really rich! I can hardly wait!"

Cecilia looked from Venetia to Dorothy-Anne and back again. Then she set her cup down, brushed off her hands, and stood.

"I think I'll make myself scarce," she said with a hint of self-righteousness. "*I've* got a lot to do today while you two talk in riddles." She looked at Dorothy-Anne. "Buzz me when you're ready for Sir Ian."

Dorothy-Anne looked up at her. "Don't be offended, Cecilia," she said. "We'll fill you in on the details later. In the meantime, why don't you send Sir Ian on in?"

"Right away," Cecilia responded and walked purposefully out of the office.

Venetia looked over at Dorothy-Anne and gave her a quick wink and a thumbs-up sign.

It was only moments before Cecilia opened the door to the outer office and announced Sir Ian Connery.

"Mrs. Cantwell," Sir Ian intoned in his rich, plummy voice. "How are you? Well, I trust?"

The well-fed aristocrat strode toward Dorothy-Anne with a small, pudgy hand extended. Dorothy-Anne rose from behind her desk and walked around to shake it, noting that he seemed puffed up with self-importance today.

"Fine, thank you, Sir Ian," Dorothy-Anne responded, shaking his hand. "And you?"

"Very well, thanks," he said, a smile planted on his chubby, pink face. *A greedy smile*, Dorothy-Anne thought. *A vulture's smile.*

"Venetia," Dorothy-Anne said, "I'd like you to meet Sir Ian Connery of Pan Pacific Bank. Sir Ian, Venetia Flood, our head of publicity."

Sir Ian turned to the beautiful African-American woman, who had risen from her chair, hand proffered. He merely gave a nod of his head. "How do you do?" he said in an offhand manner.

Venetia drew her hand back to her side, smiled widely, despite the slight, and said: "A pleasure, Sir Ian. One I've been waiting for."

"Why don't you have a seat, Sir Ian," Dorothy-Anne said, indicating the chair next to Venetia, "and tell us what this surprise visit is about." She returned to her seat, and Venetia sat down again.

Sir Ian Connery looked from Venetia to Dorothy-Anne. "I think, Mrs. Cantwell," he said, "you'll want to have this conversation in privacy. A bit personal." He chuckled. "No offense, of course."

"Of course," Dorothy-Anne said coolly. "However, anything you have to discuss with me, you can discuss in front of Ms. Flood. She is one of the powers that be behind the Hale Companies, and my best friend. I have no secrets from her."

"If you insist," Sir Ian said. He sat in the chair next to Venetia, and crossed the chalk-striped, black legs of his Savile Row suit. Then he shot his cuffs and eyed his gleaming gold Rolex.

"Why don't you get straight to the point, Sir Ian?" Dorothy-Anne said, staring at him levelly.

"Yes, yes," Sir Ian said. "You see, Mrs. Cantwell. Here as a representative of Pan Pacific. The bank, of course. Regrettably, they have sent me to inform you that they have decided *not* to extend the due date for the fifty million dollars." He paused, the benign smile on his face widening somewhat. "The hour is at hand, so to speak."

"I see," Dorothy-Anne said neutrally.

"However," Sir Ian continued, "we do have a proposal. One you can't refuse, I think." He chuckled lightly.

Dorothy-Anne stared at him wordlessly, and caught Venetia looking at him with an expression of barely contained amusement. "And what is this offer I can't refuse," she replied.

"What we're willing to do, Mrs. Cantwell," he went on, "is take a percentage. Of the Hale Companies. A small percentage of stock, you understand." He stared at her over the desk. "But control of the board-room." He raised his barbed-wire eyebrows at her. "Managerial control. One might say. Have to work out the details, of course."

"In other words, Sir Ian," Dorothy-Anne said in a frigid tone, "you want a percentage of the Hale Companies and you want to kick me out. So you can run it yourself. Right?"

"Bluntly put," he replied. "One might say that is essentially what we're offering. To salvage your company, of course." Sir Ian's smile never wavered. "Run it the way we see fit. We would be doing you a huge favor. Huge favor."

Dorothy-Anne exchanged glances with Venetia, whose eyes had grown wide with genuine amazement. Then she turned the full power of her beautiful, now blazing, aquamarine eyes on Sir Ian.

"I think, Sir Ian," she said quietly, "that we might as well end our little meeting."

"What? We're in agreement, then," he said. "Very good."

"I don't think so," Dorothy-Anne said, her voice dripping with ice.

Sir Ian looked at her, surprise registering on his baby-smooth face as he finally took in her meaning.

Dorothy-Anne picked up the stack of papers she had taken from her briefcase earlier, and extracted a letter with a check attached to it.

She handed the letter and check over the desk to Sir Ian, and sat back, a snow queen's smile on her face.

"If you'll notice, Sir Ian," she said, "that is a check drawn on me personally for the full fifty million dollars that is coming due."

She paused, and stared at the look of utter bewilderment that now crossed his features, then the—yes! there was no other way to describe it—mounting *horror,* which followed it. His eyes seemed to grow huge behind his large, black-framed glasses.

"You will also note," she continued, "that the check can be cashed on the loan's due date."

The check and accompanying letter jerked in one hand as Sir Ian reached for a handkerchief and dabbed at his forehead. "Well . . . yes . . . yes," he finally sputtered. "Indeed . . . indeed . . . I see . . ." *The bloody fucking bitch!* he thought. *She's bloody fucking ruined my fucking life!*

He looked over at her and, with a supreme and noticeable effort, smiled. "Everything in order, then. Yes, yes." He seemed to regain some of his lost composure. "I'll report to the bank. Straightaway, then." He folded the letter and check and tucked them into an inside jacket pocket.

"You do that, Sir Ian," Dorothy-Anne said. She rose from behind the desk, and extended one hand, buzzing Cecilia with the other. "It was a pleasure to see you. Cecilia will show you out." Then she added: "Ms. Flood and I have a very busy day."

Sir Ian pushed himself to his feet and took her hand in his. "Good day, Mrs. Cantwell," he said primly. He turned, and Cecilia, who had just entered the office, showed him out.

A wide smiled spread across Venetia's face as she got to her feet and leaned across the desk, the palm of her hand extended in the air. "Give me five," she said.

Dorothy-Anne slapped Venetia's palm with hers, and then they both burst into laughter.

53

H unt stepped out of the shower, toweled himself off vigorously, then began shaving in the bathroom mirror. All the while thinking of Dorothy-Anne, feeling a lonely ache deep inside him, and wishing she were here with him now.

He had returned the *Quicksilver* to Puerto Rico from Eden Isle, then flown straight back to California. During the flight, he had mentally prepared himself to tell Gloria that he wanted a divorce, various scripts of the scene running through his head. He had arrived at the house, anxious to tell her right away. But Gloria, as was more and more frequently the case nowadays, was not at home. When he'd asked Roddy, the butler had replied that he didn't know where Mrs. Winslow might be, nor did any of the staff.

Now he wished that the confrontation with her was over, and that the words he'd rehearsed in his mind to use had been heard and, hopefully, accepted. What's more, he wanted to tell his mother and be done with that. But he thought it was only fair to talk to Gloria first.

Althea, Hunt knew, was not going to take it lightly. In fact, she would not cotton to the idea at all. Obsessed with appearances as she was, and with his political career of tantamount importance to her, divorce was anathema. But he also knew that Althea would finally see reason. Once she was convinced his mind was absolutely made up and could not be changed, she would come to accept the inevitable and work with it.

He finished shaving and threw on some clothes, an old worn pair of chinos and a faded blue polo shirt. Then he slid into an ancient pair of Top-Siders and headed for the kitchen. Thought maybe he would pop a beer and make himself a real sandwich, not one of the petite "society" sandwiches the staff made.

But he never made it.

In the entrance foyer, Gloria, who'd apparently just come in, was starting for the stairs.

She looked up at him. "Well, you look nice and tan," she said in a taunting voice. "Been working out in the sun, I suppose?"

"You don't really care what I've been doing, Gloria," Hunt said.

"No," she replied. "You've got that right. I don't." Then suddenly her eyes flashed with rage. "But what I *do* care about is that while you've been working on your tan, *I've* had to go out to Cascades and have lunch with your goddamn mother!"

Hunt ignored her outburst. "We've got to talk," he said calmly.

"Oh, Hunt," Gloria sighed. "Not now. I'm going up to my room. I'm tired."

"This can't wait," he said. "Why don't we have a drink in the library?"

Gloria didn't hesitate. The idea of a drink appealed, and whatever he had to say would be tempered with a good stiff vodka. "Okay," she said. She turned on her heels and headed for the library with Hunt following behind.

In the library, she made a beeline for the drinks table, where she splashed vodka into a crystal highball glass, then, using her fingers instead of the tongs, put several cubes of ice into her drink.

Hunt watched her. "Don't you want some tonic or something in that?" he asked.

Gloria smirked. "Why ruin good vodka?" she said, then sat down on the leather-upholstered couch, kicked off her shoes, and drew her legs up onto the well-worn leather.

Hunt made himself a scotch and water and sat opposite her.

"Cheers," Gloria said, holding her glass up. And then drank down half of it in one swallow.

Hunt didn't respond but took a sip of his scotch, watching her. Then he set down his drink and cleared his throat. "I want to discuss something very serious," he said.

Gloria arched her eyebrows in a look of mock interest and concern. "And?" she said flippantly.

"This marriage is not working," Hunt began. "And—"

"What an acute observer you are," Gloria broke in with a sarcastic snarl. She took a sip of her drink.

"I think it's time we get a divorce," Hunt said.

Gloria stared at him. *Oh, Jesus,* she thought. *He would decide that now. Now that I've found somebody to get rid of him for me.*

When she spoke, her voice was devoid of any sign of flippancy. "Are you sure about this, Hunt?" she asked.

"Absolutely," he said.

"What's your mother going to think?" Gloria swirled the ice around in her drink with a finger, then licked it off. Trying to remain calm. Trying to appear to be casual.

"It doesn't matter what she thinks," he said. "It doesn't matter what anybody thinks, for that matter." He paused and took a sip of scotch. "This marriage is a farce. We both know that, and it's time we ended it."

Gloria felt a rising panic and got up and went back to the drinks table. She poured another splash of vodka into her glass and took a large swallow. Then she turned to him. "Why now?" she asked.

Hunt didn't respond for a moment. Finally he said, "Why not?"

Gloria walked back over and sat down again. "It just seems so sudden," she said. "I thought we could go on . . . you know . . ."

" 'Go on' what, Gloria?" he asked. "Torturing each other? Living like strangers in the same house? Being seen together for the sake of appearances?" He slammed his drink of the table. "I'm sick of it. I'm sick of the whole charade, and I want it over."

Oh, God, what am I going to do? Gloria wondered, her panic now in full gallop, threatening to overwhelm her. *Time. I have to buy time. Time for Christos to take care of this. To take care of* him. For she knew there wouldn't be nearly as much money if she and Hunt were divorced. And she also knew that, although they had talked about divorce before, this time Hunt was serious. Deadly serious.

"I'll make certain you're well taken care of, Gloria," he said gently but firmly. "I want this to be as painless as possible for both of us." He paused and sipped at his scotch again. "But I definitely want divorce proceedings to start."

Gloria was silent for a moment, her best effort at a look of utter sadness and desolation fixed on her face. She would have to talk to Christos soon. To convince him to take care of Hunt fast. In the meantime, she would play along with Hunt. Appear to be saddened but accepting. Willing to cooperate with him.

Well, she thought, *I will grit my teeth and do it. Whatever it takes. I want that money. I want that money and I want Christos.*

"So it's really over," she finally said in as defeated a little voice as she could manage.

"Yes, Gloria," Hunt answered softly. "It's over."

He looked over and saw the look of desolation on Gloria's face and wondered for a moment what his wife was really thinking and feeling. He hadn't expected quiet acquiescence. If anything, Gloria was a fighter, and a very nasty one at that. But, he told himself, it was finally time to quit wondering and worrying about her. It was time to let go.

"Like I said, I want this to be as painless as possible for both of us," he said. "I hope you do, too."

"Yes, Hunt," Gloria said, sighing, her sad and defeated act beginning to wear on her. *Jesus,* she thought. *I've got to get out of here. Got to get this over with and go call Christos.*

"I'm awfully tired now, Hunt," she said. "Regardless of what you might think, this has come as a blow."

"I'm sorry, Gloria," Hunt said. "Sorry for everything."

"Yes," she said. "Me, too." Gloria leaned down and picked up her shoes. "I'll do whatever you say," she said. "But I want to be by myself now." She got to her feet and, shoes in one hand and drink in the other, she left the room.

Hunt watched her go with a sense of relief that their talk was over, that he'd finally told her he wanted to get a divorce. At the same time, somewhere in the back of his mind, little alarm bells were going off. He was beset by niggling little doubts and worries he couldn't pinpoint, couldn't identify. This was not quite the Gloria he knew.

What was she up to?

54

O kay, he had the two cars, the de Ville in the garage off Van Ness, the Tercel with the Celica's plates in a multideck garage off Union Square, where he was now, needing the Tercel for the drive over to San Leandro, to see a man about a gun.

Boosting the Tercel had been ridiculously easy, like taking candy from a sleeping baby. In retrospect, Christos didn't begrudge Carlos the four hundred bucks he'd charged for the key. Hell, it had been money well spent. As it turned out, the hardest part had been scraping and Windexing the price, $2,499, off the windshield.

Christos still couldn't believe his luck. So far, everything had gone according to plan, without so much as a single hitch.

He hoped it was an omen of things to come.

Unlocking the Tercel, he got in, started it, and backed neatly out of the slot. Drove it down the tight turns of the spiral ramp, tires squealing, four floors to street level. Said, "How you doin'," to the attendant in the booth, handing the guy his check-in stub and a twenty-dollar bill. Didn't bother to count the change, just shoved it into the glove compartment, then drove out into the bright Saturday afternoon and slipped on his mirrored aviator shades. Kept the windows rolled down, his bent elbow sticking out as he drove.

Once he was across the bay, he found that San Leandro was not the kind of place they featured in the tourist brochures. In a way, it reminded Christos of Long Island City. It was flat and industrial, with the same preponderance of warehouses, factory buildings, and storage facilities.

But with one major difference. Parts of it were residential, the houses small, single-family dwellings, one right after another. Most were of beige- or turquoise-painted stucco. All showed their age, along with not-so-benign neglect.

Christos wasn't keen on the neighborhood. It was decidedly grim and down-at-the-heels. Enough so that he pulled over and took the precaution of stashing most of his loot down into his boots. He switched the radio off.

Then, following the directions he had been given, he drove around for a while. He realized it was a circuitous route, expressly designed so that anyone watching could tell if he was being tailed, or was part of a police sting.

Slick's contacts were obviously a cautious and suspicious lot.

Good. That cut both ways.

Presently Christos reached his destination, a potholed street empty of cars and trucks, lined on both sides with deserted, graffiti-covered warehouses. Not a human being in sight.

He pulled over, killed the engine, and waited. Time crawled by. He waited some more, starting to wonder if perhaps this wasn't somebody's idea of a bad joke. If it was . . .

Up ahead, at the next cross street, a cute black kid, maybe ten or eleven, wearing a towering knit red-and-white *Cat in the Hat* hat, streaked by on a mountain bike.

Christos sat up straighter, peered forward, looked in his rearview mirror, and saw nothing. He settled back again. Then, a few minutes later, he caught the same kid in his mirror, streaking behind him, a shadowed, high-hatted blur against the burst of sunlight, and then he was gone.

The kid whizzed a couple of snappy circles around the car, then skidded to a halt beside the driver's-side window, the friction of his giant-tread tires throwing up a rooster's tail of loose gravel.

"C'mon. You to follow me," the pint-size ordered, pushing off and peddling madly.

Christos waited a moment, undecided, then started the engine. He followed the kid, careful to keep his distance since the little squirt didn't bother using hand signals, just made these crazy, spur-of-the-moment lefts and rights, unexpected shortcuts through the doorless maws of deserted warehouses, then bursting out the other side into brilliant sunshine.

Block after block it went; light, shadow, darkness, until Christos lost his sense of direction entirely. He wondered at the desolation as they zigged and zagged this way and that, without so much as a single car, truck, or workman in sight.

And then he remembered. It was Saturday. During the week these same deserted streets would be a hive of noise and activity, jammed with container trucks and forklifts, the air throbbing with the noises of engines, machinery, and shouts.

The kid cut through a rubble-strewn lot and then another deserted warehouse . . . or were they backtracking? Going around in circles? It sure *looked* like the same warehouse.

But Christos didn't have time to ponder it. Back out in the sunlight, the kid abruptly braked, jumped the bike into midair, and turned it around on its own length, so when the tires hit the ground he was facing the oncoming Tercel.

"*Shit!*" Christos screamed.

He slammed on his brakes and screeched to a stop with only inches to spare.

"You nuts?" he yelled out the window at the kid. "Whaddya tryin' to do, get yourself killed?"

The kid pulled up nonchalantly to the driver's side, reached into a pocket, and tossed Christos something.

He caught it—a black, bunched-up knit rag, it seemed. He held it up. No. Not a rag. A ski mask.

"For your own protection," the kid said. He turned and pointed to an open loading dock door some twenty yards away. "Af'er you puts it on, you to drive in there."

Christos stared at the kid.

"They don't wanna know what *you* looks like," the kid explained. "An' they in masks, too. You don' wanna know what *they* looks like. Them dudes, they some *baaaaad* mothers."

When Christos didn't respond, the kid's voice rose to a falsetto. "Watch you waitin' for, man?" he scolded, making shooing motions. "Put it on! Don't want to drive in there wit'out it. Go on now!"

And with that, the Cat in the Hat hit the road, pedaling furiously away.

Christos looked at the ski mask in his hands. *Might as well get it over with,* he thought, and pulled it down over his head.

It felt hot and scratchy and cut down on his peripheral vision. But a glance in the mirror showed a black knit head with three paler circles. Okay, so it looked bizarre. But he found the precaution reassuring. At least these guys were pros.

He drove toward the open garage door and into the loading dock. As soon as he was inside and had the Tercel in park, someone pulled on the big overhead door.

It came down with a thundering crash.

The sudden darkness was total.

Someone else, up front and above him, shone a high-powered flashlight at his windshield. He shielded his eyes with his arm.

"After you out of the car, lean up against it," a deep baritone called. "Like we the cops and you assuming the position. Dig?"

Christos chucked his door open. The dome light clicked on briefly, then he was outside and snapped the door shut. The flashlight stayed on him as he leaned against the side of the car, arms and legs spread.

Someone else came up from behind him.

"Just checkin' to make sure you ain't wired," a bass voice said, so close he could feel the warm breath on the back of his neck.

Then he was being expertly patted down, no social niceties observed: arms, underarms, chest, back, belly, buttocks, crotch, legs, boots . . .

A large pair of hands felt through the stitched leather of his Westerns and squeezed. "Well, what you know. This where you keep your bankroll?"

"Hey!" Christos protested.

The guy who'd been patting him down got up and chuckled. "Man, we no thieves. We bidnessmen. We wanna *steal*? You be seein' stars and hearin' tweety birds by now."

Then, calling out to his accomplice holding the flashlight: "He clean."

A series of overhead fluorescents flickered on. Christos blinked and looked around. He was in a vast empty warehouse, all concrete and cinder block. Beside him, a big guy, the one who'd patted him down, was also in a ski mask. So was the skinny dude up on top of the loading dock who had a flashlight in one hand and a revolver in the other.

"C'mon." The big guy. "We got bidness to conduct. Don't got all day. Or ain't you heard? Time, it *money*."

The loading dock was chest deep, and they hoisted themselves up, swinging their legs sideways to the warehouse level.

"This way."

Christos fell in behind the big guy; the skinny one with the revolver made up the rear. They marched over a few bays, to where a bright blue tarp covered what looked like a minivan. A Plymouth Voyager maybe. Something like that. It was hard to tell.

The guy in the lead hopped down off the dock, landing neatly in the bay. Christos followed suit. Then the skinny guy, who slid aside the van's side doors.

Christos noticed that the passenger seats had been removed, and that another tarp covered the entire floor of the van.

The skinny guy reached in and pulled the tarp aside.

"Holy shit!" Christos whispered.

The van was an arsenal on wheels, the gray carpet covered with every kind of gun imaginable. All neatly arranged by type, like merchandise in a glass case. Revolvers and pistols on the left. Rifles and carbines in the middle. And semi-automatics and automatics on the right. Directly behind the front seats were cases of ammo.

"You a revolver guy?" the skinny one asked.

Christos shook his head. "Rifle."

"Take you pick."

The skinny guy stood there, one latex-gloved hand on his hip, the other pointing as he rattled off his wares.

"You prob'ly lookin' for a bolt gun. Basically, they customized Remington 700s. Civvie model. Some got night-vision scopes, got a couple mounted with lasers, this one here got a Leupold scope, what police marksmen use. . . . That one there got an Unertl 10X. Marine Corps like Unertls. Or, you want, we got semiautos."

Christos stared, bumfuzzled. His head was spinning. He was looking for a rifle, yeah. But shit! You needed to be a hard-core gun freak to figure out what most of this shit was for, and how to use it.

"I don't wanna know your bidness," the skinny guy went on. "But you give me some idea what you re-quire, maybe I can fix you up with the right weapon. Then I won't try to sell you on this M-16, e-quipped with an HELH4A Sionics suppressor, and sniperscope with high-voltage VDC nickel cadmium battery pack for a power supply source. Know what I mean?"

Christos swallowed. Actually, he didn't. This was all way over his head.

So what he said was, "I just wanna hit a target from, say, a hundred, hundred and fifty yards. I'm lookin' for somethin' accurate and simple. Easy to use. None of that high-tech shit."

"All right, now we communicating. This for daylight, nighttime, what?"

Christos shrugged. "I don't know yet. But I wanna keep it real simple."

"Then you want the Remington 700 with either the Leupold police marksman, or the Unertl 10X scope. I was you, I'd go for the 10X."

The skinny guy handed Christos a pair of latex gloves. "This so you prints ain't all over my merchandise," he added.

While Christos snapped the gloves on, the guy reached into the van and took out a rifle.

"This here the Remington 700. Simple scope. Easy focus. Accurate. Just load and pull the trigger—*bam!*"

He tossed the rifle, butt down and muzzle up, over to Christos.

Christos caught it neatly, hefted it, and turned away. Shouldered it and squinted through the scope. A little fiddling, and the far wall jumped into the magnified focus.

"Is it traceable?"

Behind the mask, the dark eyes with yellow-brown whites were steady. "This *my* merchandise you talking about, man. Serial numbers, they *gone.*"

Christos nodded, squinted through the scope some more. "How much?"

"Three grand."

He lowered the rifle and turned around. "Ain't that a little steep?"

"Maybe. But you looking at a sniper carbine. You paying premium for a clean weapon. You paying for no questions axed."

"What about a case? Somethin' to carry it around in?"

"Don't come with no case. See, a gun case *look* like a gun case. What you do, you go find a pawnbroker, buy yourself a cello. Throw the fiddle away, save the case. Carry you carbine around in it, like you a mu-sician."·

Christos laid the carbine on the loading dock, then dug in his pocket for his bankroll. He peeled off thirty Ben Franklins.

The big dude, the one who'd patted him down, took it, did a swift recount, and switched on a portable ultraviolet light. He passed each bill under it.

"Can't be too careful," the skinny guy said. "There a lot of funny money around."

And in a friendlier voice, he added: "You don't look like no deer hunter, so I'm going to give you some free advice. When you go for it, line up you target. Take you time. One shot, hit or miss, get outta there. Remember that. One shot."

"Money checks out," the big guy said.

Christos put his hands flat on top of the loading dock and hoisted himself up. "Nice doin' business with you," he said, picking up his purchase and starting toward the Tercel.

"Yo! Bro!"

Christos turned around and looked down. "Yeah?"

The skinny guy tossed several boxes up at him, one after another.

They were heavy, but Christos caught them, piling them against his chest.

"Ammo, man. Wit'out ammo, you fucked."

55

Sunday dinner at Cascades was a time-honored ritual. Unless Hunt
was out of town, and barring severe illness, Althea expected him and
Gloria to show up—even if, as today, they arrived in separate cars.

Hunt was driving a midnight blue Buick Park Avenue. Being a politician, a foreign car was anathema, and would have left him wide open to
attack. Still, he often wondered how voters would react if they knew the
other reason he drove a G.M. product: Althea's stock portfolio. It included some twelve million dollars worth of shares in General Motors.

Approaching the Black Mountain–Hayne Road exit, Hunt left the
freeway and headed north on Skyline Boulevard. Before long, he swung a
right and stopped in front of the main gate with its majestic stone piers
and carved stone lions.

Cascades. The House, in which he'd spent the loneliest, most impressionable years of his life, his childhood.

When he pulled up in front of the House, he couldn't tell if Gloria
had arrived yet. As usual, the white gravel drive was empty of cars; the
staff was swift to remove all offending vehicles from Althea's sight.

The massive, carved front door opened as he reached the top of the
sweeping stone steps. On the other side of the threshold stood a very tall,
very slim, and very dignified man with silver hair. "Welcome home, Mr.
Winslow," he intoned, stepping aside.

"Hello, Withams. Is my mother still mistreating you?"

The butler looked shocked. "Of course not, sir! Mrs. Winslow never
mistreats anyone! She is a lady." He shut the door quietly. "She asked me
to convey that she shall be down shortly. The other guests are already in
the salon."

"Other guests?" Hunt asked, arching an eyebrow in surprise.

Traditionally, Sunday dinner was just the three of them—Althea, Gloria, and himself.

"Yes, sir," Withams said. "The younger Mrs. Winslow is here, along with Governor Randle and Mr. Drucker."

"I see," Hunt said impassively, crossing the vast reception hall.

So Mother called out the big guns, he thought. Inwardly he had to smile. Sometimes Mother did know best. Especially when it came time to lay down the law.

For who knew the law better than the big-time lawyer himself?

Eli Drucker. Family friend. Confidant. And lawyer extraordinaire. He had attended to the family's legal affairs ever since Hunt could remember—and as the senior partner of Drucker, Mason, Stapleton, and Lovelace, P.C., San Francisco's most powerful and prestigious law firm, merely invoking his name was enough to make most people think twice.

Hunt chuckled to himself. *Poor Gloria,* he thought. Then he tightened his lips. *Poor Gloria indeed!* If anyone could take care of herself, it was his wife . . . his soon-to-be ex-wife.

He noticed her the moment he entered the salon. She was standing at one of the French doors, glass in one hand, cigarette in the other. Quick-puffing nervously and blowing smoke outdoors. She hadn't heard him come in.

Neither had Governor Randle and Eli Drucker. The two men were seated side by side on matching giltwood fauteuils by the fire, heads together and tumblers in hand while they conversed in low tones.

Hunt's arrival, however, did not go entirely unnoticed. Two of Althea's Pekingese had been curled on the canapé opposite the men. In unison, the dogs lifted their heads, sniffed the air suspiciously, and emitted soft growls. Then they leaped down and charged across the Savonnerie, yapping up a storm and nipping at his heels.

The men looked up. "Hunt, my boy!" the governor boomed heartily, getting heavily to his feet, his hand outstretched.

"Governor," Hunt acknowledged, shaking the big man's hand. Then he turned to the attorney. "Mr. Drucker," he said politely.

"Hunt." Eli Drucker's handshake was firm but dry. "It's good to see you again."

Behind Hunt, Withams cleared his throat. "May I get you a drink, Mr. Winslow?"

Hunt turned around. "Please, Withams. A splash of scotch. Lots of ice."

The three of them sat down, the governor and the attorney in their giltwood chairs, Hunt on the canapé the dogs had vacated.

"Tell me something, Governor," Hunt said. "Did Mother invite you tonight to do some political arm twisting?"

The governor was genuinely taken aback. "Not at all! And what's with this 'governor' crap, anyway?" Randle harrumphed. "You don't have to be so goddamn formal, Hunt. As you well know, I have a first name. My acquaintances call me Quentin. As for my friends, they call me Q."

Hunt met his eyes. "Are we friends?" he asked quietly.

Randle burst into rich peals of hearty laughter. "We better be, son. We can't afford to be enemies. Especially seeing as we're—"

"As we're what?" Althea asked brightly from the doorway.

The men all turned toward her and rose to their feet. Even Gloria flipped her cigarette out the open French door and quickly came forward.

Althea crossed the carpet briskly toward them. Everything about her was picture perfect, from her lacquered, artfully coiffed hair to her pale nail polish and black patent leather pumps. She was wearing a vermilion suit with large black buttons and a black, cowl-necked silk blouse with white polka dots. Her shapely legs were sheathed in minuscule-patterned black stockings and she had on simple gold earrings, a tiny gold watch, and a gold-link bracelet. Plus a twenty-carat pear-shaped diamond on her hand that Hunt hadn't seen before.

Violetta, her favorite Pekingese, padded regally beside her, glancing up from time to time with slavish devotion. The other two dogs wriggled happily toward their mistress, hindquarters pendulous, silken tails wagging.

Althea greeted the governor first. "Q," she said, placing her hands on his shoulders and turning her cheek to be kissed.

"Althea. As always, you're a vision for sore eyes."

"Flatterer!" she accused lightly, and focused her attention on the thin old attorney.

"Eli. Thank you so much for coming. Especially on such short notice."

He kissed her cheek also. "Wild dogs couldn't have kept me away," the veteran jurist said, with a glance down at the three Pekingese. "Not even yours."

"These pussycats!" Althea laughed. "I should hope not!"

She moved on to her son. "Hunt, darling." She took both his hands in hers and smiled and waited for his kiss.

"Hello, Mother," he said softly.

And finally it was Gloria's turn. For a moment the two women stared at one another in a silent battle of wills.

Gloria cracked first. "Mother Winslow," she managed truculently.

Althea proffered her cheek, and when no kiss was forthcoming, she raised her eyebrows in mock surprise. "What? No kiss?"

Gloria swallowed a rush of bile. *How like Althea!* she thought murderously. *Trust her to make me feel small and petty in front of company!*

She took a deep breath and girded her loins. Then gave her mother-in-law's proffered cheek a grudging, contactless kiss.

"Well, I suppose that's better than nothing," Althea said crisply, then turned and smiled brilliantly at the men. "Shall we sit?"

She hooked an arm through Quentin Randle's and led him to the plump goosedown-cushioned sofa directly facing the fire. Instead of sitting on the canapé with Hunt, Gloria opted for the giltwood chair beside Eli Drucker, where the governor had previously sat.

Althea picked up a little silver bell from the coffee table and tinkled it.

"Yes, madam?" Withams intoned.

"Be so good as to bring in the champagne, Withams, would you please?"

"Right away, madam."

"Champagne?" Hunt looked questioningly at his mother. "What are we celebrating? Did I miss somebody's birthday?"

"Not at all, darling," his mother assured him, and smiled.

Withams returned, a starched white linen napkin folded neatly across one arm. He was carrying a large silver tray with handles, which he deposited carefully on the coffee table.

The tray held a masterpiece of the silversmith's art: a George III wine cooler shaped like an urn. It was exuberantly baroque, and embellished with intricate, interlaced silver grapevines, bunches of silver grapes, and a ram's head at each end. It contained a bottle of chilled Dom Perignon nestled in a bed of crushed ice. There were also five magnificent champagne glasses, opulently long-stemmed and of paper-thin etched crystal.

Althea smiled at the questions in Hunt's, Eli's, and Gloria's eyes, but made them wait as Withams took the bottle, wrapped the napkin around it, and expertly, quietly, popped the cork. One by one, he filled the glasses and handed them round, the first to Althea, the second to Gloria, and the third to the governor. Eli Drucker and Hunt were last.

Once everyone was holding a glass Althea took one of the governor's hands in hers. "Governor Randle and I have an announcement to make," she said, her voice as clear as a bell. "He has decided not to seek another term in office."

"Hopefully not on my account," Hunt said. "I have no intention of running for governor."

"No, darling," Althea assured him, "it's not on your account. It's on mine."

"I don't understand."

"You will, in a moment," his mother said, her beautiful face surveying her audience like an arum lily turning toward the sun. "The diamond you see on my finger is an engagement ring. Governor Randle and I . . ."

She paused and began again. "That is to say, Q and I . . . have decided to get married."

Reactions are strange things. Eli Drucker blinked like an owl, momentarily at a loss for words. Hunt cocked one quizzical eyebrow, then raised his glass in a silent salute. And Gloria, stunned and shell-shocked, felt her fingers tightening on the champagne glass, tightening, tightening, until—

Snap!

—the delicate stem broke in half, champagne leaping out of the falling top half in Dali-esque slow motion. Then her fingers loosened and the bottom half of the glass fell to the carpet as well.

"Oh, *damn!*" she whispered.

She stared, wide-eyed, at the blood welling up on her hand.

"Withams?" Althea called out.

"Yes, madam?"

Althea's voice was calm. "I believe the younger Mrs. Winslow's glass was defective. Would you be so kind as to see to her hand and then bring her another glass?"

"Of course, madam."

But Gloria jumped to her feet, holding her injured hand by the wrist. "No!" She shook her head vehemently. "I—I'm leaving. I've got to *go*—"

She began to run from the room.

"*Gloria!*" Althea's raised voice stopped Gloria in her tracks.

Slowly Gloria turned around.

"This is a family celebration," Althea said mildly. "Granted, Hunt is filing for a divorce. But until then, you are still a member of this family. Now you can stop your histrionics, because you *will* stay for dinner and coffee. There are some important matters we must discuss."

Gloria stared at her.

"Come, Mrs. Winslow," Withams told Gloria gently. He started to lead her from the room. "I'll see to your hand. It looks far worse than it is. Cuts always do. Shouldn't take more than a Band-Aid."

"A toast," Hunt proposed. "To the future Governor and Mrs. Randle!"

"Hear, hear," Eli Drucker added.

They sipped their champagne.

Gloria had no appetite. She picked desultorily at her food, pretending to eat.

Not that the dinner wasn't delicious. Althea's chef had outdone himself with a marinated rack of spring lamb with rosemary sauce, lemon-thyme potato pie, and tiny baby eggplants stuffed with wild mushrooms. All accompanied by a Château Cheval Blanc 1947, a never-ending series of toasts, and plans for the future.

To Gloria, it was one interminable blur, a tedious bore she endured solely by going heavy on the wine and tuning everyone out. She kept sneaking furtive glances at her wristwatch, but time had slowed to a snail's pace.

She couldn't wait to split.

After Withams had attended to her cuts, which proved to be minor, she'd gone to the powder room to use the telephone.

Fortunately Christos was at home.

"I can't talk right now," Gloria whispered in a rush, her voice edged with hysteria. "We have a major problem—"

"Okay, calm down," Christos told her. "Keep your cool. We'll meet at the usual place. I'll be there. Okay?"

"I . . . I don't know when I'll be able to get away."

"That's cool. I'll wait for you."

Christos's levelheaded composure made her feel a little better. But not for long. As dinner dragged on, Gloria's mind grappled with the latest setback.

With Althea's plans to marry Governor Randle, Althea had, in effect, thrown yet *another* spanner into Gloria and Christos's best-laid plans. For even if Hunt *was* out of the way, and Gloria played the grieving widow, there would be Governor Randle to contend with. He had become yet one more obstacle standing between her and the Winslow billions.

So . . . Quentin Randle would have to be dealt with, too. And soon.

Christos can do it, Gloria told herself. *He'll make sure the wedding never takes place.*

And then it hit her.

Of course! Why even worry about the governor? If Hunt and Althea are both *out of the picture, the Winslow fortune automatically becomes mine.*

Yes. Hunt and Althea. Somehow Christos had to get rid of them *both.*

"Gloria? *Gloria.*"

Althea's voice jerked her out of her thoughts. Blinking, she looked blankly across the table. Her mother-in-law had risen to her feet.

"Well?" Althea said. "We're repairing to the library for coffee and brandy. Aren't you coming?"

Gloria nodded. She pushed back her chair and got up. She waited for the others to leave, then fell into step behind them. Althea, Governor Randle, and Violetta led the way down a long gallery. They were followed by Hunt and Eli Drucker.

Gloria felt like the caboose. A red caboose, flushed as she was from the potent mixture of wine, anger, anxiety, and misery. She couldn't understand why Althea had insisted she attend this . . . this farce.

It's obvious I'm no longer considered part of the family. So why put me through this torture?

Into the library they trooped. It was Cascades' concession to a gentleman's redoubt, a huge two-story double cube of a room. Three entire walls were built-in bookcases, and two sets of mahogany spiral stairs curled up to a balustraded gallery. The shelves and paneling were also mahogany, so that the overall effect was that of being inside a giant wooden box, the shelves gleaming with books bound in gilt-stamped Morocco.

The furnishings were in keeping with the masculine air—worn leather armchairs, such as one would expect to see in an Edwardian club. A giant billiard lamp casting two pools of light over a round mahogany table six feet in diameter. There was an enormous desk, and framed drawings on tilt-topped mahogany architect's tables, and a pair of big terrestrial and celestial globes.

They sat on leather-upholstered Regency chairs by the fire.

"Fetch the humidor, Withams, would you?" said Althea, with a lift of her well-bred chin. "Some of the gentlemen will want to enjoy an after-dinner cigar."

The cigars were offered from a Fabergé humidor of birchwood and blue enamel. The lid was inset with a round, gilt-edged picture frame containing an original sepia photograph of Tsar Nicholas holding the czarevitch Alexi. The cigars it contained were real Havanas, Flor de E Farach Extras.

Governor Randle and Eli Drucker lit up and Withams busied himself preparing the cognacs. It was a ritual nearly as reverential and dogmatic as a religious ceremony. First, he heated five huge snifters, after which he dribbled a mere teaspoon of cognac into each. Then he engergetically swirled that around to coat the inside of every glass. And finally, he poured a small portion of cognac into each snifter, loaded up a tray, and served.

Gloria took hers, gestured for Withams to wait a moment, and downed hers in a single gulp. It slid down her throat like velvet and exploded in her stomach.

There, that's better, she thought, and held the snifter out for a refill.

Althea cleared her throat noisily. If it was a warning intended for Gloria, she completely ignored it. Withams glanced at Althea, who hesitated, then gave a slight nod. When it was replenished, she took a tiny sip, then glanced over at her mother-in-law with a look of smug satisfaction.

Althea chose to ignore Gloria's self-indulgence and obvious lack of obeyance, and quickly became engrossed in conversation with Governor Randle, occasionally favoring Violetta with delicate strokes of her hand.

Hunt was discussing something with Eli Drucker, which Gloria could not overhear, not that she cared to anyway.

No. This after-dinner babble held no interest for her whatsoever.

She saw Governor Randle gently take Althea's hand in his and pat it. *Sweet,* she thought hatefully.

Gloria wanted to scream. Instead, she endured.

She took a gulp of her brandy and felt it go down her throat to her stomach, exploding again as before. Only this time it seemed to detonate in bileous, nauseating waves. Perspiration suddenly popped out on her forehead and upper lip, and a tremor ran through her.

Oh, God, she thought. *I've got to get out of this hellhole.* She sat for a moment, considering her options, and decided to leave.

"I'm really not feeling well," Gloria finally blurted out. "I think I'll have an early night."

Althea looked over at her and smiled. "What were you saying, my dear?" she asked.

The room was suddenly quiet, and the fire popping in the grate and the sound of cigar puffing became loud in Gloria's ears.

She looked at her mother-in-law and repeated herself. "I'm not feeling very well, and I think I'll call it a night."

"I do hope you're feeling better this Saturday," Althea said.

"This Saturday?" Gloria asked. What was the woman talking about?

"Don't tell me you've forgotten, Gloria," Althea said, as if she were addressing a wayward child.

Gloria stared at her. "Forgotten what, Mother Winslow?"

"There's a fund-raiser for the De Young Museum Saturday evening in Golden Gate Park," Althea said brightly. "I'm the chairperson, remember? And Hunt's giving a speech. So it is imperative that you be there, my dear."

Oh, God, Gloria thought miserably. *Does it never stop?* She said: "I really don't see—"

"Gloria," Althea broke in, using her most commanding tone of voice, "you are still Hunt's wife and my daughter-in-law. It is vital that you be there for the sake of appearances, if nothing else."

She paused and smiled, gently stroking Violetta. "It will probably be your last public commitment to us."

"Yo, babe," Christos greeted her as he opened the door to the house on Russian Hill. He kicked the door shut and grinned lecherously, his taut cheekbones two elongated, raised bony slashes.

"Am I glad to see you," Gloria said, without looking at him. She felt flushed and out of breath and was so self-absorbed she didn't notice the leer on his face. "Let's have a drink," she said. "Quick."

Christos wrapped his strong arms around her and started to kiss her deeply.

He wasn't quite prepared for her reaction. She jerked back and stared up at him.

"Christos," she protested. "Later. We have to talk. But first, I really need a drink. Vodka. Straight."

He dropped his arms to his side. "Sure, babe," he said. "Jeez. Just chill. I'll get us some drinks." He went into the tiny kitchen, where he poured vodka into two glasses and put in a few ice cubes. He came back out and handed Gloria hers, and she quickly slung it back, drinking nearly half of it in one gulp.

"Heeeeey," Christos said. "You're hittin' it pretty hard tonight." He smiled.

"I need it." Gloria finished off the drink and held it out for a refill. He took the glass back into the kitchen and poured more vodka in, then brought the bottle back out with him.

"Let's go spread out. Then you tell me what's goin' on, babe." Christos handed her the drink and took her arm and led her to the bedroom.

Gloria threw down her handbag and kicked off her heels. Then she shrugged out of her suit jacket and spread out on the bed, propping up the pillows behind her just so.

Christos sat down beside her. "Come on, Gloria," he said. "Talk to me." He pulled a marijuana joint out of a shirt pocket and lit it, then inhaled and held the smoke in his lungs before blowing out a plume of blue-gray smoke. He expected her to bitch and moan about the smell, but she surprised him again.

"We've got a problem," she said. "Not only does Hunt want a divorce, but now my mother-in-law is engaged to be married."

"The old broad?" Christos looked surprised. "Engaged?"

"Yes," Gloria said. "And to make matters worse, she's engaged to Governor Randle."

"*Governor* Randle?" Christos choked on smoke. "Whoa, babe. Shit. We're dealin' with some heavy hitters here."

"You bet we are," Gloria said. She took a sip of her drink. The vodka seemed to be clearing her head, straightening her out, and making her feel better now. "Even with Hunt out of the way, we'll have Althea and her new husband to deal with." She looked at him. "Which means," she finally said, "I'm just that much further away from the Winslow billions."

Christos moaned. "Ah, shit."

Gloria turned to him. "But I've figured out a solution," she said.

Christos stared at her quizzically, wondering what the crazy bitch had on her mind now. "If you're thinkin' about offin' the governor—" he began.

"*No,*" Gloria said firmly. "Not the governor." She stirred her drink with a finger, then licked it off. "Althea," she finally said and looked over at him. "My mother-in-law."

"Hey, wait a fuckin' minute, Gloria," He bounced to his feet and began pacing the floor, toking on the joint furiously. "Ya changin' the rules on me, Gloria," he said.

"Christos," she said calmly. "Come here. Sit down and listen." She patted the bed next to her and set her drink down.

He slowly walked over and sat down facing her. She put her arms around his neck and looked into his eyes. "Billions," she said. "Think of it, Christos. *Billions* of dollars. And it's going to be much simpler than I thought."

Christos pinched the marijuana joint between his fingers, putting it out, then put the roach in his shirt pocket. "Why ya say that?"

Gloria took her arms from around his neck and picked her drink up again. "Because Saturday night there is a party in Golden Gate Park." Gloria smiled, then continued. "There'll be a thousand people there, at least. All of them wandering around outdoors and in tents. And Althea and Hunt are both going to be there."

"That means a lotta security, Gloria," Christos said.

"It also means easy to disappear. It means chaos. It means both of them in the same place at the same time." She paused and took a sip of her vodka, then began slowly unbuttoning her blouse. "And it means there is *nothing* left between me and the Winslow billions. For me *and* you, Christos." She smiled up at him.

Christos was listening and watching her unbutton her blouse at the same time. He reached out and started running a hand over the tops of her smooth, pink breasts. "We gotta talk about this, Gloria. We gotta have a plan, you know?"

"I've got it all figured out," she said. She put a hand on his crotch, stroking the evident swelling she saw there. "It's going to be easy, and I'll even be there to watch."

He slid a hand up her skirt, working it between her thighs. "Saturday night, huh?" he said.

"That's right," Gloria gasped. "They'll both be there. Together."

"Whaddaya say we talk about this later, babe?" Christos said, pushing her skirt up and moving atop her.

"Yes," Gloria moaned. "Later."

"**O**y *vey*," Bernie Appledorf rasped. "*Golf!* She's pinnin' everything on this *goy* and his golf!"

"Great going, Owen!" Dorothy-Anne said enthusiastically, pointedly ignoring Bernie's sarcastic jibes. "Now keep up the good work."

"I'm off to Ponte Vedra this weekend," Owen said in his rich, plummy voice. "And I believe you can count on me to play to win. Golf and the contracts."

He was on his way out the office door, a smile on his perpetually boyish face.

"That's the spirit," Dorothy-Anne said. "Have fun in Florida."

"Will do," he answered, and was gone.

"A few games of golf," Dorothy-Anne said, shooting daggers at Bernie, "and Owen's convinced nearly all our airline catering clients not to defect."

"Golf smolf," Bernie Appledorf growled.

Dorothy-Anne eyed her comptroller critically. "Bernie Ever the Optimist Appledorf," she said sardonically. "What's on your bean-counting mind?"

He turned his sad, bloodhoundy, Walter Matthau eyes to her. They were half hidden by their Coke-bottle lenses and huge black frames. "Ya wanna know what's on my mind?" he rasped.

"Shoot," Dorothy-Anne said.

"Owen's piddlin' little victories with his golf buddies that use our airline catering is all just fine. But—"

"But what?" Arne Markoff, chief counsel, broke in.

"It's a drop in the proverbial bucket," Bernie said. "That's what."

"You're right, Bernie," Dorothy-Anne said. "There's no denying it. But all these 'piddlin' little victories,' as you call them, add up."

He ran a hand over the few thin strands of hair trained over his bald pate, then trained his thick-lensed glasses on her again.

"These Pan Pacific guys play rough," he said. "An' ya can't expect any good news from 'em."

"I'm not a fool, Bernie, Dorothy-Anne replied. "I certainly don't expect any."

"I never said ya were a fool. Far from it," Bernie rasped. "But ya won't cancel cruises. Ya won't lay off employees. Ya won't shut down Eden Isle. And I'm tellin' ya, ya gotta do something. My advice," he continued, "is sell something. Too bad ya can't dump Eden Isle. Ya kill two birds with one stone. That big suckin' sound is gone and that loan's paid off too."

Dorothy-Anne's eyes blazed. "No way," she said, her voice full of determination. "I wouldn't if I could. There has got to be another way."

"Eden Isle," Arne Markoff said, "is one of the properties held as collateral against the loan, so we might as well forget that. Even with our reorganizing, setting up umbrella companies, there is no *legal* way to make Eden Isle separate."

Dorothy-Anne stared at him, a lightbulb suddenly going off in her head. She abruptly jumped to her feet and began pacing the office, an animal on the prowl. She stopped and turned to Arne Markoff.

"Arne," she asked tentatively, "back up just a minute. FLASH is still separate, isn't it?"

"Yes, as of now," Arne said.

Dorothy-Anne continued pacing, then stopped again. "And FLASH hasn't been put under one of the umbrella companies yet?"

"Nothing's been finalized yet," Arne replied. "It's going to be weeks, maybe even longer, to iron out all the details and get all the paperwork done."

"Good," Dorothy-Anne said with mounting excitement in her voice. She whipped around to Arne again. "Don't do one single thing with FLASH," she said forcefully. "Leave it exactly like it is. On its own."

Bernie Appledorf was studying her, the semblance of a grin on his lips. "FLASH isn't part of the collateral for the loan, is it." It was a statement, not a question.

Dorothy-Anne looked at him, smiling now, "You got it, Bernie." There was triumph in her voice and fire in her eyes. For she knew deep down inside that the Hale Companies were going to be saved, and she knew how.

FLASH, the airline and hotel reservations system, was the chief rival of SABRE, the system owned by American Airlines. It was highly profitable, and she'd had several offers for it in the past. As of today, she knew it was worth at least a cool billion, possibly more.

"Arne," she said, staring at him, "I want FLASH put on the market. Yesterday. And I want the sale completed *this summer*. Got that?"

"I'll get right on it," Arne replied, jotting some notes on a pad.

"Now you're cookin' with gas," Bernie rasped.

"Okay," Dorothy-Anne said, looking at the two men seated in front of her. "Get busy. Time is awastin', as they say."

" 'Lo."

It was ten-thirty in the evening and Dorothy-Anne had started to doze when her private line chirruped her out of her slumber. The television set was on but she had the sound muted; she hadn't really been watching it, but studying some FLASH reports, which were now fanned out all around her on the bed. She brushed the hair out of her eyes and squinted at the Cartier Baignoir clock.

"Hey, beautiful, it's me."

Hunt's voice jolted her awake. Despite herself, she was excited to hear from him.

"Hunt," she said.

"Did I wake you?" he asked.

"It's okay," she yawned.

"I'm sorry," he said. "Hard as I try, I'm always forgetting the time difference."

"I'd just dozed off," Dorothy-Anne said. "Early for me, but I've been so busy since I got back, I practically passed out." She started gathering up the FLASH reports and making them into a stack.

"What's up?" he asked. "Is everything okay?"

"As a matter of fact," Dorothy-Anne said, "things couldn't be much better. The most incredible thing happened, Hunt."

"I'm all ears," he said.

She told him briefly about discovering Freddie's investment account and paying off the loan interest.

"You know," he said, "it's exactly the kind of luck you deserve. The best there is."

"Thanks, Hunt," she said. She glanced at the television and saw Joan Crawford's spooky face, all eyebrows, spidery lashes, and lipstick, silently screaming at her.

"Freddie must have been one helluva guy to do something like that," he said.

"He was," Dorothy-Anne said, and fell silent. She was reluctant to pursue this line of conversation any further. It was treading on ground that, right now, she felt was too personal and too painful.

"You okay?" Hunt asked. He had immediately sensed the hesitation in her voice and didn't want to risk upsetting her.

"Today," Dorothy-Anne said, quickly and adroitly changing the subject, "I decided to put FLASH on the market." All the while she was still sorting through the FLASH reports, trying to put them in some sort of order.

"You want to do that?" Hunt asked. "It's a real cash cow, isn't it?"

"It's not part of Great-Granny's legacy, so I don't mind so much," she answered. "Besides, it's not part of my loan collateral, so . . ."

"You are one brilliant lady," he said.

"Yeah?" Dorothy-Anne was pleased. She looked up and saw that Crawford, scarier than ever, was screaming at a child now.

"Yeah," he said. "Listen. I wanted to fill you in on what's up at this end."

"Oh?" Dorothy-Anne wasn't sure if she wanted to hear it.

"I've started divorce proceedings," Hunt confided. "It's all very quiet right now, but it's a beginning."

Dorothy-Anne's pulse seemed to quicken. She didn't know how to reply. Finally, she said, "I hope it works out for you, Hunt." She rubbed her temples with the fingers of one hand.

"It will, but it's not going to be easy," he said.

"How's your mother taking all this?" she asked.

"We discussed it with her," he said, "and I think she realizes our marriage is unsalvageable. But she insists that Gloria and I attend a fundraiser that's coming up." He sighed. "Together." He paused a beat. "She's always thinking of appearances."

"That must be very difficult for both of you," Dorothy-Anne said. Blue-gray light from the television flickered around the room as Joan Crawford started hitting the child. A little girl, Dorothy-Anne noticed.

"Yes," he said. He paused a moment. "Dorothy-Anne, I had to tell you. And no matter what you hear or see in the press, just remember. We're definitely splitting."

"Okay," she said, noncommittally. She got up, telephone nestled between ear and shoulder, and made a neat stack of the FLASH reports on the bedside table.

"I miss you," he said.

Dorothy-Anne resettled herself on the bed. "I miss you, too," she murmured.

"I don't want to sound pushy or come on too strong," Hunt continued, "but it was the best time I've had in years."

"I . . . I really enjoyed it, too, Hunt," Dorothy-Anne said.

"I'm glad you can say that, Dorothy-Anne," Hunt said. "Because I know you need time."

"Yes," she said. "Yes, I do."

"I'll let you get back to sleep now," he said softly. "I just had to tell you the news."

"Okay, Hunt," she said. "I know it will work out for the best." Suddenly, she realized it wasn't Joan Crawford on the television at all, but Faye Dunaway *playing* Crawford. *Mommie Dearest.*

"And Dorothy-Anne?" he said.

"Yes?"

"I love you," he said tenderly.

Dorothy-Anne felt the tears threatening to come now, and she couldn't trust herself to speak.

After a moment, Hunt said, "Good night, Dorothy-Anne."

" 'Night, Hunt," she whispered, and hung up the telephone.

And thought: *I love you, too.*

The party had begun.

Golden Gate Park was closed to through traffic from Cross Over Drive to Middle Drive East, and from John F. Kennedy Drive to Martin Luther King Drive. The only vehicles allowed access were the limousines and luxury cars bearing the formally attired guests, who had dished out anywhere from one hundred tax-deductible dollars per person for cocktails and dancing to twenty-five thousand dollars for a dinner table seating ten.

They alighted from their horseless carriages in front of the De Young Museum, the women in gowns and the gentlemen in black tie. Their limousines were directed to a parking area; the self-driven cars were turned over to valets.

Inevitably, the guests gasped in delight. For here, opposite the museum, the Music Concourse had sprouted a veritable Camelot of enchanted, open-sided tents with scalloped edges, raised wooden floors, and outdoor heaters. Inside each tent, airy chandeliers were swagged with garlands of fresh roses. And all around, as far as the eye could see, Tivoli lights glittered magically, made electrical bowers out of trees and shrubs and floral arbors.

There were tents for dancing, tents for dining, a separate tent for the caterers, another for coat check, and one for the chamber orchestra, whose strains of Vivaldi greeted the arrivals. Later, once the party was in full swing, the chamber musicians would exchange places with the dance band.

As chairperson of the event, Althea Netherland Winslow had been the first to arrive. She was wearing Dior, a bare-shouldered ballgown the precise shade of old-fashioned, dusty pink roses, with a simple silk bodice and a richly flaring skirt made of some fifty layers of overlapping, hand crafted lace.

Thus resplendent, she glided ornately among the tents, her seasoned perfectionist's eye ceaselessly on the lookout for the slightest flaw. She found countless faults, true, but saw to it that they were instantly rectified.

The turnout exceeded Althea's wildest expectations. This fund-raiser alone had raised in excess of one and a half million much needed dollars for the earthquake-damaged museum.

And so on this, her triumphant evening, Althea floated among the perfume-fragrant tides and eddies and whirlpools of the rich, the famous, the powerful, and the social climbing.

She was in her element, as always the center of the social universe, the guiding light who provided the gravitational pull for all the lesser planets and satellites. And, pro that she was, she graciously received the flattery that was her due, taking secret pleasure from every compliment, but dismissing them all with an airy, well-practiced gesture that indicated it was "nothing, nothing, darling, really," while the polished lump of diamond on her finger scintillated in the lights.

Yes, Althea allowed, *this is definitely an evening to remember.*

Which was why she had selected a few hand-picked photographers to record this party for posterity. *W, Town and Country,* and *Vanity Fair* were represented, along with a video team from the local ABC affiliate.

She thought: *This is one party that won't be forgotten.*

It was a thought she would soon regret.

Christos lay in wait. In the dark, under the groundsweeping boughs of a giant juniper. Beyond the reach of all those dazzling lights.

He was wearing a bulky black sweatsuit, size XX, but underneath it he had on a rented tux. The idea being, after he picked off his targets, there'd be turmoil and panic, people scattering in all directions, during which he'd do a Superman–Clark Kent number and lose himself among the likewise attired guests.

At least, that was the plan.

Beside him, the cello case was open, its lid folded back. Inside it, the Remington 700 was ready to be snatched up at a moment's notice. He'd prefocused the Unertl 10X scope so he'd have a clear view of the main tent, the one where a microphone stand had been set up.

He'd chosen this spot, back a ways and off to one side of the California Academy of Sciences, expressly for its location, this building and the De Young facing each other across the wide expanse of the Music Concourse. The entire area in between was lit up like a shooting gallery.

For the hundredth time, Christos ran through his mental checklist:

The Remington was loaded; weapon, bullets, and cello case wiped clean of prints.

The carbine and case were expendable; so was the sweatsuit. When he was done he'd strip, leave everything here, and walk away in black tie—real cool, the way James Bond might do it.

He was wearing surgical gloves. The only thing he had to remember was to strip them off and pocket them.

The Tercel, keys in the ignition, was hidden in a stand of bushes near Middle Drive East. It, too, had been carefully wiped clean, inside and out. Besides, he planned to use the car only as a last resort.

In the meantime, all he could do was wait. Lie here patiently until he could pick off the two of them—mother and son—*bam bam*, like that.

He was as prepared as he'd ever be . . . and glad he'd spent hours poring over the photographs Gloria had shown him of her husband and mother-in-law, so he could memorize what they looked like.

But shit and goddamn.

Wouldn't you know it? The more people that arrived, dressed up the way they were, the less you could tell one apart from another. The only reason he recognized the mother-in-law was because she arrived early, playing inspector general. And that Cinderella gown she was wearing was good: all those layers of lace on the skirt helped to make her stand out in the crowd.

But the husband, Hunt Winslow, was a lot harder to pick out. Especially now, with people packing the Music Concourse, the men all looking like penguins. As identical as nuns back in the old days, when they still had to wear wimples and veils.

Fortunately, Gloria had foreseen this problem. At some point, she was going to parade along the edge of the crowd with her husband. The way she planned it, she'd be carrying a glass of something—champagne or vodka or water, whatever—and "accidentally" drop it. Then go into a big production of wiping stains off the front of her dress, that being the signal the man was her husband.

Gloria had also shown him a fashion magazine, pointing to a model in the exact same dress she'd be wearing, a knee-length number made of orange and yellow and green feathers in a pattern, like she was a goddamn bird.

Looking at it, Christos said, "You wear it to bed, it would be like fuckin' a chicken."

To which Gloria responded, "That is an Yves St. Laurent." Pronouncing it Eve Saw Law-raw.

Christos pulled back the sleeve of his sweatshirt and pressed a button on his watch. Green LED numbers glowed brightly: 8:27.

He figured it was time for another look-see, find out what was happening. . . .

He picked up the carbine and squinted through the scope.

The distant, brightly lit people sprang into sharp focus, the magnification making him feel uneasy and vulnerable, as if he was right out there, face-to-face with everybody.

Taking his time, he swept the scope from left to right, slowly scanning the crowd. Then suddenly did a double take, quickly backtracking a couple of yards.

The fuck—?

What he saw was Gloria in that bird dress, the one she'd showed him in a magazine. Walking along the perimeter of the crowd, drink in hand, a tall, good-looking guy on her left.

Okay, that was the way they'd planned it. But what *wasn't* okay, what they *hadn't* planned, was the old buzzard in the Cinderella gown tagging along.

Shitfire and shinola!

Christos gnashed his teeth. Gloria wasn't supposed to lure them *both* into view. Just the husband . . .

As he watched, Gloria pretended to stumble. The glass flew out of her hand. When she regained her equilibrium, she looked down at herself with what appeared to be genuine consternation. Quickly she began brushing ineffectually at the feathers, making a big female to-do out of it.

Christos was in a pickle, unsure as to how to play this.

Does Gloria know something I don't? he wondered. *Is that why she's deviating from the script? Could it be the old broad's getting set to leave early?*

Maybe that's why Gloria had dragged her along. Because this was the only chance he'd get to take out the both of them, mother *and* son. Yeah, it could very well be . . .

His finger sought the smooth, cool curve of the trigger.

But how was he supposed to guess? Christ Almighty. This wasn't the way they'd planned for it to go down.

Was he supposed to shoot them now—or what?

C'mon, Glo, he projected. *C'mon. Give me some kinda . . .*

. . . *sign,* Gloria thought. *That's what I have to do. Signal Christos and let him know it's got to be* now.

Too late, she wished they'd worked out a variety of signals. They'd talked about it, but decided it was best to keep everything simple; the less complicated things were, the better.

One snag. Reality had a tendency of never being simple.

According to plan, it was supposed to go like this: once the dinner guests were seated, but before the food was served, Althea would take the microphone and thank the guests for the million and a half they'd helped raise for a good cause, blah-blah-blah. Then she'd call Hunt up on the dais. They'd josh a little, mother and son sharing a few society in-jokes, in the process drawing attention to the key people who had helped this event come about.

That had been the plan.

Hunt, unfortunately, had derailed it at the last minute.

It had been his bright idea—goddamn him!—that Althea substitute Governor Randle in his stead, thus giving his mother and future father-in-law the opportunity to announce their upcoming nuptials. The change was crucial in that it meant Althea and Hunt *weren't* going to be sharing the stage; *weren't* going to be standing side by side in the line of fire.

Having to do some quick improv, Gloria had drawn Hunt and Althea aside, hinting she had something important to tell them . . . in private. Could they take a little walk and hear her out?

Now here they were, Althea saying, "Really, Gloria. Your dress is fine. I don't see a single drop of liquid. If you'll just tell us what it is you wanted to say?"

Gloria fought down a wave of panic. *I have to get my message across to Christos,* she thought desperately. *But what if he isn't looking? What if his eyes are trained elsewhere? What then?*

Despite all the glittering lights, the mass of people, the voices competing with the music, the hired waiters circulating with trays, Gloria suddenly had the most peculiar sensation. It was as if she, Hunt, and Althea had crossed into a different dimension, one in which they were invisible to everyone but Christos, and where no one else existed . . . which was how she overlooked the security detail, two moonlighting cops in black tie, strolling toward them.

Turning in the direction where Christos was hidden, she put a hand over her heart, then made a gun with her fingers. Praying he'd interpret it correctly. Thinking: *Come on, come on! Why don't you—*

—shoot. Yeah, that's what she was trying to tell him. Christos sure of it now.

Atta baby . . .

Concentrating on lining up the husband in his sights, he swiftly swung the barrel over to the mother, then back at the husband again. A two-second practice drill, everything reduced to such a tight visual frame that he didn't notice the approaching security detail either.

Steady, Christos told himself. *Steady . . .*

And holding the husband in his crosshairs, he gently squeezed the trigger two times.

The rifle cracked and flashed twice, spitting spent brass and lighting up the shrubbery, the recoil kicking hard into his shoulder.

Both bullets found their target. The first slammed the husband backward through the air, arms flailing; the second whirled him around. Then, eyes wide with surprise, his legs gave out from under him and he collapsed like a grotesque puppet.

All right! *One down, one to go . . .*

Christos swung the barrel over to where the mother had been, but she'd moved, dammit!

Where . . . where . . . ?

And then suddenly all hell broke loose.

58

The sunset was a Hudson River School painting when Dorothy-Anne, Liz, and Fred cantered the yearlings back to Meadowlake Farm. The air had turned decidedly chill, and the yearlings Freddie had bought as their Christmas presents were gleaming with sweat and snorting plumes of vapor.

Dorothy-Anne pulled on the reins and looked back over her shoulder.

Simon Riley, the head groom, was following at a sedate trot. He was on Daddy's Girl, with Zack seated in front of him, the little boy's face flushed with excitement. Zack, naturally, trying his best to urge the horse on, kicking and bouncing around and yelling, "Giddy-yap! Giddy-yap!", while Simon held onto him and kept the thoroughbred reined in.

Dorothy-Anne smiled to herself. *What a perfect weekend it's turned out to be,* she thought, savoring the cold, moist, fresh country air. *We haven't been coming up here nearly enough.*

By the time they crested the hill, the sky was nearly as dark as the purple spines and ridges of the distant Catskills behind them. In front of them, lights glowed warmly in the windows of the big white eyebrow Colonial and in the lanterns on the white wooden lampposts in the yard.

As they returned to the stables, Venetia, who was not fond of horses, and who refused to ride, was out in the yard, waiting to intercept them. One look at her face in the lamplight, and Dorothy-Anne could tell that something was terribly wrong.

"Venetia?" she asked softly, dismounting at once.

"Oh, honey." Venetia's voice was mournful.

"Venetia!" Dorothy-Anne clutched her by the arms. "What is it?"

"It has been all over the news."

"*What* has? Don't tell me there's been another outbreak?"

"No, baby. It's Hunt. He . . . he has been shot."

Dorothy-Anne froze, rocked by the news. She stared at Venetia, her heart beating wildly.

Hunt? Shot?

"Nooooo . . ." she groaned aloud, recoiling as though from a snake. Dorothy-Anne felt the ground give way; the glowing lanterns starting to spin around her like some crazy Tilt-A-Whirl. She shut her eyes against the vertigo, and Venetia quickly reached out and held her. After a moment, the worst of the dizziness passed. Dorothy-Anne opened her eyes and pulled back. She looked at her friend questioningly.

"Is he—?" Dorothy-Anne could not put her fear into words.

"I don't know, honey," Venetia said gravely. "EMS rushed him to emergency. That is all I know. The last time I called, all the hospital would say is that he is in critical condition."

"Which hospital?" she asked shakily.

"California Pacific Medical Center."

Dorothy-Anne flinched and rubbed her face. She had the terrible sensation of history repeating itself. Her head swirled with fragmented memories. Her own recent stay at that very same hospital was still all too fresh in her mind.

Am I cursed? she wondered. *Is everyone whose life I touch doomed?*

Finally she drew a deep breath. "I . . . I need the plane," she said. "Have them bring it to Albany."

"It's already on its way. I figured you would want to fly out there."

"Yes . . . I . . . I've got to go now. Call the plane, tell them I'll be waiting at Albany airport. You'll see to it that the kids don't give Nanny a hard time?"

"Honey, maybe I should come along?"

Dorothy-Anne shook her head. "I appreciate the offer, really I do, but not this time."

I want to be alone, she thought. *I need to be alone.*

"Let me at least drive you to the airport," Venetia said.

But Dorothy-Anne wasn't listening. She was already running to the garage.

Please, God, she prayed, backing a Jeep Cherokee out in a spray of gravel. *You're not playing fair! You already took Freddie from me. You can't take Hunt too!*

An hour and a half later, Dorothy-Anne was over Lake Ontario on Hale One, headed for San Francisco.

The riverboat was new, but it would not last the night.

With beautifully varnished wood that gave it the appearance of some artifact from a colonial past, the boat had been styled to look like a turn-of-the-century Indo-Chinese river yacht. But the hundred-and-fourteen-foot *Jayavarman* had actually just been built, and this was its inaugural cruise. It had been intended for three-day luxury cruises on the Mekong River.

Two decks rose above its hull. On the lower one were eight cabins, all with a private bathroom and big outside windows. They each had a double bed built into a corner and decorated with intricate fretwork to resemble Chinese opium beds. At one end of the deck was a spacious dining room. The upper deck was large and entirely open. It was ideal for enjoying a view of the jungle that lined both banks of the Mekong River in this part of Laos. Travelers could rest in comfortable chairs and on daybeds, perhaps sipping a drink, with a view that was unobstructed by the sheer but effective mosquito netting that hung from the deck's roof, when needed.

But this evening's visitors onboard the *Jayavarman* weren't interested in the Mekong River or the pristine jungle in this part of Laos. The Mekong's palm-lined shores and the thatch-roofed villages that occasionally sprang into sight held no fascination for them.

They had come from various directions and at different times discreetly to board the boat at Pakse, in southern Laos. Some flew in from Vientiane, others from Bankgok or Ubon Ratchathani.

The few fishermen still plying the river's waters in their long, narrow boats at this hour did not see them. For they were all gathered in the dining room on the boat's lower deck, seated around a table in rattan

471

chairs, sipping tea from delicate cups. Their bodyguards, stationed out-side on the deck surrounding the dining room, ignored the setting sun as it turned a bloody red.

"Ayeeeeyah! The fornicating whore is a more competent adversary than we had anticipated," Honorable Tiger was saying. "She has given that round-eyed foreign devil Connery the fifty-million-dollar interest payment."

"Her strength has indeed surprised us," Honorable Snake affirmed.

"Bad joss for us," Honorable Dragon said, and the others nodded their heads and clucked their tongues.

"What is even worse," Honorable Horse said excitedly, "is that the eater of turtle shit has put FLASH on the market."

"*Fang-pi!*" Honorable Tiger spat out. "FLASH is highly esteemed. The gods of fortune may rain dollars on the mealy-mouthed whore."

"Forgive me for asking, Illustrious Elders," the ever-worried Honor-able Rooster asked with agitation in his voice, "but what are we to do if this barbarian pays off the loan in August, *heya*?"

The old *lung tao*, Kuo Fong, stroked his wispy beard, his dried-apple face a study in thoughtfulness as he listened. The Chiuchow took a sip of tea, then set down the lotus-shaped cup on the shiny wood table before speaking. He cleared his throat, and all heads turned to him, giving him their full attention. As Honorable Ox was the eldest, he was deemed the wisest.

"The interest payment is like the early spring flower," the old *lung tao* said. "Summer is nearly upon us, and the flowering is over. We must now turn our attention to the next season."

Heads nodded in assent around the table.

"In your superior wisdom," Honorable Rooster asked worriedly, "what must we do, Honorable Ox?"

The old *lung tao* sipped his tea fastidiously. Finally, he spoke: "The gods have seen fit to take her husband, is this not so, *heya*?"

All heads nodded in assent again.

"In the coming season," Honorable Ox continued, "Buddha may ne-glect this barbarian woman as he neglected her husband."

Honorable Dragon could barely conceal a smile. "Honorable Ox," he said, "can you suggest a path we should take so as to accommodate Buddha?"

"We had the *kwai lo,* Jimmy Vilinsky, buried like stinking manure," Honorable Snake chortled.

"Perhaps it is time," the old *lung tao* conceded, "to be of further assistance to the gods. Now that the round eye has put FLASH on the market, time is of the essence, *heya*?"

"*Ayeeyah!*" Honorable Tiger, as host, poured more tea for his guests. "It is time then to contact your wife's fifth cousin twice removed, *heya*?"

"Precisely," the old *lung tao* replied. "We must hurry now, and the one sure way to prevent the foreign whore's success is to treat her and her dog turd company as a snake."

"As a snake, Honorable Ox?" Honorable Horse asked.

The old *lung tao* stroked his wispy goatee. "Like the lowly snake," he said, "we chop off its head and dispatch it to its devils, then the body belongs to us to do with as we please."

"*Ayeeyah!* Illustrious Elder, you are most wise," Honorable Snake said.

"If we chop of the snake's head, then Pan Pacific will own the whore-strumpet's company," Honorable Ox said. The old *lung tao* paused dramatically and looked around the table with a gleam of triumph in his eyes. "And *we* are Pan Pacific."

Honorable Rooster, ever cautious, clucked his tongue. "We must make certain this turd-eating snake is dealt with at a great distance from us," he said worriedly.

"You are ever wise, Esteemed Rooster," the old *lung tao* said. "We must use my wife's fifth cousin twice removed to contact this Carmine."

"The Sicilian, *heya*?" Honorable Dragon asked.

"The Sicilian," Honorable Ox answered, nodding his head in agreement. "The time is nigh, Illustrious Elders." Then he paused again and glanced around the table, stroking his goatee once more. "Let us cast our votes. Those in favor of eliminating the devil-born whore, use the chop depicting the bird. Those opposed, use the fish."

As they usually did, each of six men opened his small teak box, picked up the chop he wished to use, and marked his choice on a square of rice paper. The folded squares were then dropped into the bowl in the center of the table.

"Honorable Tiger," said the old *lung tao*, "as our esteemed host, would you honor us by counting?"

The Laotian general who protected the rich upland poppy fields nodded, then picked up the bowl, emptied it on the table, and opened each piece of paper.

When he was finished, he looked up and glanced around the table, his eyes shining with evil malevolence. "There are six birds," he said, his voice expressing his satisfaction.

"It is decided," the old *lung tao* said. "Sonny Fong shall contact the Sicilian to send the pallid pink toad whore to her devils." He searched the eyes of his fellow conspirators. "Are there any further comments?"

There were none.

"Excellent. We shall depart as always. Honorable Tiger, your hospitality has been very gracious indeed," he said.

"Thank you, Esteemed Ox," Honorable Tiger said.

"Will you please remain until the rest of us have departed, then make certain that all evidence of our meeting is destroyed?"

"It will be my honor, Esteemed Elder," Honorable Tiger answered.

The old *lung tao* rose to his feet, and then the others followed suit. They bowed graciously to one another and each said: "May the gods of fortune attend you."

Their meeting was adjourned.

One half hour after Honorable Tiger had left the *Jayavarman*, the beautiful wooden riverboat inexplicably exploded into a sea of worthless rubble.

The cause was never determined, and an investigation was never made, due to the traditional payoff.

"It is good joss," the villagers nearby were heard to say. "The gods never intended that this boat transport tourists on the mighty Mekong."

BOOK THREE

SUDDENLY THAT SUMMER

60

Three in the afternoon, the streets baking outside, the below-street-level dining rooms at Mama Rosa's as cool as catacombs and as quiet, the last of the lunch crowd gone.

Sonny Fong, in full-throttle Armani, L.A. style—lightweight sports jacket and cuffed trousers with a black T-shirt and pricey shades—glanced around, hands in his pockets. The red-jacketed waiters and white-shirted busboys ignored him, too busy changing the table linens and setting up for dinner.

He acknowledged the arthritic, rheumy-eyed waiter who'd intercepted him on his first visit. Said, "How you doing?"

Getting a dead fish stare in return.

Sonny, unfazed, shot his cuffs, smoothed his lapels, and strutted past, headed to the kitchen in back. The gruesome, tortured saints on the walls didn't get so much as a glance, all of them old hat by now.

Outside the swinging door to the kitchen, he paused to steel himself against the heat. Then pushed his way through.

It was worse than a blast furnace, but the women working at the stainless steel counters, jabbering rapid-fire Italian while kneading, chopping, slicing, and dicing, didn't seem to mind.

One of them looked up and noticed him.

"Hey, *giovinettas!*" she called out to the others. "Look-a at what the cat dragged in-a! This-a must be Mama's lucky day!"

All ten of the women glanced over, the two good-looking ones shy and embarrassed, the rest—either scrawny old chickens or hefty mature oxen—cutting Fellini-esque poses, doing parodies of streetwalkers. A couple of them called out to Sonny in Italian.

Whatever it was they said, it set the others off, got them screeching hilariously. Even the two shy ones turned away, trying to hide their smiles.

Sonny, being cool about it, slipped off his shades and pocketed them. Took time to look around before seeing Mama Rosa.

She was at the far end, behind a long table between two giant sinks, busy at her big marble work surface.

He went over to her and placed his hands flat on the table.

Mama Rosa raised her head slowly, her black eyes cold.

"The hell were you?" he demanded quietly.

She had a big knife in her hand and pointed it at him, saying: "Don't curse in the presence of the Lord." She used the flashing blade of the knife to indicate the crucifix on the white-tiled wall, a dried frond from Palm Sunday stuck behind it. "It ain't respectful," she added.

He said, "I'm sorry. I'll try to watch my language. Okay?"

She gave him a long, hard stare. "Okay," she said grudgingly.

He watched as she resumed working, reminded of the women in Chinatown, the way she'd reach into a bucket of cold water and fish out handfuls of whole squid, slapping them down—smack, smack, smack—in perfectly aligned rows. Holding each saclike body with one hand, and with a single slice of the knife amputating the tentacles, all in the exact same spot, a hair's breath below the big protruding eyes. *Chop—chop—chop—chop—chop.* As skilled as any Asian cook he'd ever seen.

Sonny said: "For the past three weeks, I've been coming here every single day. Morning, noon, and night. And what do you think I found?"

She glanced at him, the knife flying. "What did you expect to find?" *Chop—chop—chop—chop—chop.*

"Well, I certainly didn't anticipate this place being closed, if that's what you mean."

She reversed the knife, using the flat side of the blade to scrape the tentacles to the left, the squid bodies to the right, then fished a few more handfuls out of the bucket, and slapped them down in neat rows.

"How do you think I felt, having to tell my superiors I couldn't get hold of Carmine?" Sonny continued softly. "When they wanted to know why, guess what I had to tell them?"

She shot him a needlelike look. "You should of said, because his mama's *ristorante* is closed."

"Well, that's what I said, yeah. It didn't exactly make me popular, you know?"

"That ain't my problem."

She attacked the squid bodies like a one-woman assembly line. Prick, squeeze, pop, pop, toss. Prick, squeeze, pop, pop, toss. Not a single eye missing the trash can. The ink she collected in the bowl slowly increased.

Sonny was tired of waiting, and wished she'd hurry up. He wanted to get business over and done with. A hot kitchen on a hot day was hardly his idea of fun.

His air-conditioned Lexus beckoned.

That was the trouble with using a go-between. *If I could deal with Carmine directly,* he thought, *my life would sure be a lot easier.*

"Anyway," Mama Rosa was saying, "we couldn't have stayed open." She motioned around the kitchen with her knife, the tip of the blade wet with purple ink.

"See?" she said. "Everything's been renovated."

Now that she'd pointed it out, Sonny saw she was right. The entire kitchen had been redone; everything was indeed shiny and brand new.

"See? All new everything. Ranges, grill, ovens . . . sinks, refrigerators, freezers. The works. It must have cost, I don't know." She shrugged. "Maybe two hundred thousand dollars? I'm not sure exactly."

Sonny thought: *I wonder how much of this fell off a truck? Or which restaurant supply dealer was burglarized?*

She smiled. "I had Carmine oversee it. He's real good at those kinds of things. Nobody dares pull a fast one over on him!"

Carmine! Sonny stared her. He couldn't believe it! All the times he'd dropped by, Carmine had been right here, overseeing the renovation!

Sonny said, "Jesus Christ, you shitting me! Right?"

Mama Rosa slammed down her knife and swiftly crossed herself, the Old World way, using her thumb to sketch a little cross on her forehead, another on her lips, and a third on her breast.

Sonny spread out his arms and turned a circle. "I don't fucking believe this!" he exclaimed. "You telling me Carmine was *here?*"

"What did I say about watching your mouth?" Mama Rosa's voice cut sharper than the knife she picked up again and waved threateningly.

He took a step backward, wishing she'd stop pointing it at him.

She glanced up at the crucifix on the wall. "I told you. I won't stand for *bestèmmia!* And I won't say it again!"

"Okay. Okay!" He held up both hands placatingly. "I'm sorry. I got a little carried away. It won't happen again."

Mama Rosa glared at him but lowered the knife. "It better not," she warned quietly.

"It's just that"—he shook his head in frustration—"all these weeks I've been coming around, I could have dealt with Carmine directly!"

"Unh-unh." Mama Rosa wagged a finger back and forth. "You know better than that. My Carmine, he don't deal directly with anybody. Not if it were the president. Not even if it were the . . . well, the pope, maybe."

"It sure would have sped things up, though," Sonny mused. "As it is, my people were starting to wonder."

"Oh, yeah? About what?"

"You know . . . they said things like, 'Maybe this Carmine's not reliable. Maybe the Sicilian's not everything he's jacked up to be.' "

Her beady little eyes, black and shiny as oil-cured olives, clicked in his direction.

"You better not let Carmine hear you," she advised. "For that matter, you'd better not talk about him like that around *me,* either."

Having finished emptying the squid sacs, she laid down the knife and pushed the bowl of ink aside.

"With calamari, you never wash the tentacles and the sacs together," Mama Rosa said. "If you mix them, the sacs turn purple. That's because the tentacles have ink in—"

She was about to pop another squid mouth, but suddenly paused and frowned.

"Ink. *Ink!* That reminds me—"

She slapped a pudgy red hand against her forehead—"Madonna! How could I forget!"

Sonny Fong said, "What?"

"The note I'm supposed to give you! From Carmine. He mentioned you might drop by."

"Yeah, and why's that?"

"Probably because he noticed you coming around all the time."

She quickly wiped her hands on a wet rag and dug around inside the front pockets of her apron, which she wore folded over, the top half hanging over the bottom. She came up empty, except for a wad of used Kleenex, which she stuffed back inside.

"Now where did I put it?" she muttered, pursing her lips and looking around. "He just gave it to me this morning."

Sonny was ready to throttle her. Why she couldn't have mentioned this right off the bat was beyond him. He wondered if she wasn't maybe losing it.

Carmine better find himself someone more reliable, he thought. *And soon.*

Those were his thoughts, but what he said was, "I hope you find it. We have an urgent job for him. One that can't wait. Otherwise, we'll have to hire someone else."

She didn't reply, her eyes searching the stainless steel shelves and counters. *Nothing there.* She burrowed her hands under the apron, checking the pockets of her blue floral housecoat.

More shredded Kleenex.

"Humph!" She put her hands on her hips. Licked her lower lip with the tip of her tongue. Turned a slow circle in place.

"Lemme see, now . . . I just got back from the fish market . . . Tony unloaded the truck, brought the seafood in on a dolly from the alley in back . . . I helped put it away . . .''

She nodded to herself, seeing it unroll like a mental film strip.

"Then Tony brought the trash cans in, yeah . . . and right after that was when Carmine—of course! *Stùpido!*"

She smacked her forehead once more.

"I must of thrown it out by mistake! Wait a moment."

She got on her knees, leaned over the trash can, and hitched her short sleeve higher up her right shoulder, exposing pale arms the consistency of cottage cheese, and armpits with damply matted grayish black hair. Without a second thought, she plunged her arm all the way down into the can, burrowing through layers of squid eyes and squid mouths, shrimp shells, wilted lettuce, coffee grounds, what have you. Huffing and puffing as she groped around.

Sonny, watching with distaste, wondered what Carmine would think if he saw her now.

He thought: *You'd have to pay me a million bucks to eat in this restaurant. And even then I'd probably pass it up.*

"Found it!" she announced at last.

There was a slurpy sucking sound as she pulled her arm out of the trash, a wadded-up ball of damp, fishy-smelling paper in her hand. Grabbing the edge of the trash can with both hands, she pushed herself heavily to her feet.

Breathing hard, but beaming triumphantly, she said, "See? What I tell you?"

She put the wadded-up paper on the counter and smoothed it, revealing a sealed envelope. She held it out to Sonny.

Jesus! he thought.

He didn't know which looked more disgusting—the envelope or her fleshy bare arm, slick with moisture and flecked with bits of tomato peel, coffee grounds, swordfish skin, pomegranate seeds, mint leaves, and carrot shavings.

He decided her arm won the gross-out contest hands down.

"Well?" she said. "Take it!"

He plucked the envelope gingerly from her hand, holding it delicately between two fingers.

"I'll read this later," Sonny said, not wanting to touch it more than necessary, thinking of his expensive threads.

"No. Carmine said you're to memorize what it says, and then I'm to burn it. That way, it don't fall into the wrong hands."

He sighed. Holding the envelope at arm's length, he tore it open.

Inside, a folded sheet of computer printout listed the routing instructions and account number of a bank in Luxembourg. There was also a separate blank sheet of paper.

As he committed the name of the bank and the numbers to memory, Mama Rosa lumbered over to one of the deep stainless steel sinks. She used the spray attachment to douse her arm, squirted it liberally with detergent, lathered herself, and then rinsed the soap off. She dried herself on a kitchen towel.

"You got it memorized?" she wanted to know.

Sonny nodded.

"Good." She took the papers out of his hand, then tried to hand him the blank sheet back. "You need to write your instructions down."

"Just give me a minute."

She waited while he went to the sink and washed his hands. He flicked the excess water off them, then reached into his breast pocket and took out a sealed envelope.

"I've been carrying this around with me for weeks," he said. "All the information Carmine needs is in here."

She accepted the envelope and slipped it into her apron pocket.

"Don't throw it away," he cautioned, only half jesting.

She wasn't amused. "There's no need to be a smart aleck."

"Who're you talking to?" He pretended to look to his left, then his right, and finally behind him. "*Me?*" He pointed to himself.

"Yeah. *You.*"

He flashed her his best smile, but it went to waste; she was immune to his charms. As he left, she was in the process of striking a match. She held the flame to a corner of Carmine's printout. The paper burned for a moment, then flared, and quickly began to curl.

61

"**L**ufthansa, Disney, ITT-Sheraton, TransAmerica, and Carnival Cruise Lines," Arne Mankoff said. "They're each willing to pay over a billion dollars."

"It's still on the low side," Dorothy-Anne said thoughtfully as she and Arne lunched at Le Cirque 2000, the new incarnation of New York's legendary restaurant. "What terms are we talking? Cash or stock swaps?"

"Basically half and half. Except for the Mouse," Arne said, referring to the Walt Disney Company. "They've got cash coming out of Mickey's ears."

Dorothy-Anne paused in the midst of cutting a bite-sized portion of salmon baked under a lemon-grass crust.

"I like cash," she said. "And as you're well aware, we *need* cash. Seven hundred and fifty million on or before the fifteenth of August. Preferably before, since I wouldn't put it past Pan Pacific to play real dirty and call in the loans early. Which, judging from the fifty-million-dollar interest payment, I fully expect them to do."

Arne nodded. "It pays to be ready."

Dorothy-Anne put down her cutlery and leaned across the table. "I want Pan Pacific out of my hair. ASAP."

"Then I'll call Michael Eisner. With the new Disney Cruise Line, their new holiday island in the Caribbean, and the various Magic Kingdoms, FLASH will pay for itself in no time."

Dorothy-Anne shrugged and picked up her fork and took a tiny bite of salmon.

"Are you sure you really want to do this?" Arne asked, looking worried. "You know the way FLASH is set up. Whoever owns the reservations system gets their product shoved to the top of the list. And that's at every other travel agent's on earth. I don't need to tell you the Mouse is going to be Eden Isle's main competitor.

Dorothy-Anne smiled bitterly. "I know all that, and I appreciate your concern, Arne. But we're talking *survival* here. Would you rather we sell FLASH, or do you want your paychecks coming from Pan Pacific?"

"Right," he said. "I'll get on it at once."

"Good." She nodded approvingly. "The sooner this is concluded, the better." She took a last bite of salmon, then put her fork and knife down.

The waiter asked if they wanted dessert. "No," Dorothy-Anne said, glancing at her watch. "Nor coffee. We don't have time." She smiled up at him. "Check, please."

On the way out, Sirio, the owner, came over to say hello.

"It was delicious, Sirio," Dorothy-Anne enthused. "As always."

"How do you like our new place?" Sirio asked.

"Heavenly," Dorothy-Anne said, pressing his hand. "Must dash. See you soon." Actually, she thought, though the food *was* fabulous, she wasn't certain she liked the ultramodern Milanese decor in the magnificent old Villard house. It was a little wacky.

At the curb, she turned to Arne. "I'll be at home," she said. "I hope you have good news for me soon."

"I'll try," Arne said, confidence in his voice.

"Good." Dorothy-Anne turned and slipped into her waiting black Infiniti.

She twisted around in her seat and looked back. Arne was climbing into a taxi. She turned back around.

This deal had better work out, she thought. *And quick.*

The traffic was bumper to bumper, and Dorothy-Anne wished she had walked. It was one of those rare, perfect, clear and sunny days in New York.

The car phone rang. She hoped whoever it was wouldn't take the shine off her day. "Yes?" she answered.

"Boss, it's me," said Cecilia Rosen, Dorothy-Anne's secretary.

"Don't tell me. Bad news?"

"Not bad, exactly. Just . . . potentially bad."

Dorothy-Anne sighed. "Okay. Hit me with it."

"There's a tropical storm brewing in the mid-Atlantic," Cecilia said. "They haven't upgraded it to hurricane status yet, but—"

"That's the third one already!" Dorothy-Anne exclaimed softly. "And the hurricane season's barely begun."

"That's right," Cecilia said. "*If* it develops into a full-blown hurricane, that is. Right now it's stalled at sea but picking up strength."

Dorothy-Anne sighed and stared out at the traffic. "Have all the Hale properties been notified?"

"You bet. We've already put them on alert in the Caribbean, Florida, and the Gulf Coast of Mexico."

"Does it seem to be headed for Puerto Rico?" Dorothy-Anne asked.

Her special concern was for Eden Isle. The construction site and its equipment were particularly vulnerable to a hurricane.

"It's too early to say."

"What about the Pacific?" Dorothy-Anne asked. "Anything brewing there?"

"Not at the moment."

"Keep me posted as the bulletins come in."

"Will do. But it'll be three hours before another one's due—unless something really significant happens."

Dorothy-Anne hit the End button and hung up.

It's the same every year, she thought as the car crept along.

Many Hale hotels and resorts lay in hurricane-prone areas, so she knew the drill by heart. First, evacuating the guests. Then, stocking up on emergency supplies—candles, batteries, canned goods, water, matches, and so on. Draining the pools. Hauling in the outdoor furniture. Securing the boats. And finally, if the storm got really serious, boarding up windows and doors and evacuating the staff—and hoping for the best.

Dorothy-Anne prayed that this time the storm would spend itself out at sea, or at least avoid the jewels of the Caribbean, and the gold coasts of the gulf and the Eastern Seaboard.

When Dorothy-Anne entered her town house, not a creature was stirring. Not yet. The children, she knew, should be home before too long. She decided to take advantage of the peace and quiet and call Hunt in California.

She went up to her bedroom, undressed, and threw on a comfortable silk bathrobe, then spread out on the bed. When she was settled, she dialed Hunt's number.

"Hi," she said, when he picked up. "It's me."

"Hi, me." he answered groggily.

"Were you asleep?" she asked, feeling a rush of emotion at the mere sound of his voice.

"Just dozing," he said. "We have a habit of waking each other, don't we?"

"Oh, Hunt, I'm sorry," she apologized. "I'll call back later. Just wanted to check up on you."

"No, don't hang up," he said anxiously. "It's okay. I just wish you were here to wake me up all the time." His voice was more awake now, with more than a hint of mischievousness. A very good sign, she thought.

"Down, boy, down," she laughed. "I guess you *are* feeling a little better." She twirled a strand of hair around a finger. His playfulness warmed her heart.

"I really am, Dorothy-Anne," he said. "This physical therapy is miraculous. But it wears you out."

"What do they say?" she asked. "Are you being a good patient and making progress?"

"Dr. Dempsey is very pleased, if I say so myself," Hunt said. "But he should be. Those gals of his really give me a workout."

"Are you doing the same exercises?" she asked. She got up from the bed and walked to her dressing table, the telephone cradled between her ear and shoulder. She picked up a monogrammed silver hairbrush and began stroking her hair as she walked back to the bed.

"Would you believe I'm up to forty-five minutes on the stationary bike? Pedaling to nowhere." He sighed. "The most boring bicycle ride in the world."

"Isn't there one of those stands on the bike, so you can read while you ride?" she asked. She stroked her hair languorously, enjoying the feel of the brush.

"The damn bike wobbles too much." He laughed. "After that it's all kinds of leg exercises with weights on my ankle. Then, get this. Walking with a giant rubber band around my ankles."

Dorothy-Anne laughed. "Sounds kinky!"

"I wish. But you know what?" he said. "It's working. I've already thrown away my crutches, and I'm using a cane. Very debonair."

"I wish I could see that," Dorothy-Anne said, brushing in long, even strokes.

"You're going to," he said. "I'm flying in to New York in a couple of days."

"You are!" Dorothy-Anne's eyes widened in surprise, and she dropped the brush now. The thrill of anticipation excited her. "Are you sure it's not too soon to travel, Hunt?"

"Don't you want to see me?" he asked.

"You know I do," she said softly. "It's just that I don't want to see you injure yourself. What does the doctor say?"

"Who cares?" Hunt laughed.

"I do," she replied.

"Actually," he said, "the doctor doesn't think it's a bad idea. As long as I do most of the exercises on my own." He paused and his voice dropped to a soft and tender whisper. "I can't wait to see you, Dorothy-Anne," he said. "I love you."

"I can't wait to see you, either, Hunt," she answered. Then she whispered, "And I love you, too."

After they had hung up, she picked up the brush, and began stroking her hair again, lost in though, remembering her trip to California to see him, a journey she would never forget.

Never. Not for as long as she lived . . .

Venetia had come to her with the news that Hunt had been shot.

The idea that she might lose this man who, despite her efforts to the contrary, she had fallen so deeply in love with was unbearable.

The flight out had been agony.

In San Francisco, she had rushed to the hospital, the very same hospital in Pacific Heights where she herself had been a patient not so long ago. She knew that Hunt's family might be there, but the urge, the *need*, to see him was so overwhelming that she felt she had no choice in the matter. If she had to confront the Winslows, so be it. She would try to appear to be a concerned friend who happened to be in town.

But as luck would have it, no one had been there. No one but the armed guards stationed at the door to his room.

She didn't think she would ever forget her first glimpse of him in that hospital room. Prone on the bed, his leg was encased in an enormous device that appeared to be attached with Velcro. He looked helpless as a child, but was trying so hard to be brave, to diminish the horror of what had happened to him.

She had approached the bed slowly, tentatively, full of trepidation at what she would find. Only then did she realize that she had been so fraught with worry she had come empty-handed. Without any sort of gift, only her own presence, to do what she could.

He had grinned up at her sheepishly, foggy from medication. "Hey, beautiful," he said.

"Hey, handsome," she answered. She leaned over and kissed him gently on the cheek.

"See the lengths I'll go to, just to get you to come see me?" he joked.

"Oh, Hunt," she said. "Shh. You need to rest."

"Naw," he said. "That's all I've been doing. Sleeping."

"Are you in any pain?" she asked. She pulled a chair over, to sit close to him. Its plastic cushions felt cool and somehow repulsive to her.

"Naw. I'm so full of painkillers I don't feel a thing." He held out a button device on a cord. "See this? I push the button and automatically get pain medication. Don't even have to call the nurse."

"Good," she replied. She remembered the same device from her own hospitalization.

He put the medication dispenser down and reached a hand out to her. She took it and held it in hers, gently stroking it, her heart filled with anxiety and, yes, love for this man.

For she now knew beyond a shadow of a doubt that she was in love with Hunt Winslow, and before her jet landed in San Francisco, she had made up her mind to give herself up to that love. The possibility of losing him had forced her to reckon with her feelings, and all other considerations—any obstacles to their love—had become secondary to Dorothy-Anne.

She has lost one great love, and she was determined that it would not happen again. Certainly not because she herself would stand in the way. She and Hunt were in love with each other and, come what may, they would have each other.

They discussed the events of the day. How he had been lucky the bullet got him in the leg, just above the knee. He told her that all they knew so far was the identity of the man who had shot him.

"It's weird," he said. "All we know is that he's this drifter. He has a Greek name, Christos something. Lots of Zs. I don't remember."

"Do you think it was political?" she asked.

"Don't know yet," he answered, "but what else could it be?"

"Could he be some kind of nut case?" she asked. "Just some crazy?"

"That's possible, of course." Hunt was silent for a moment, absorbed in his own thoughts. "The sad thing is," he finally said, "we'll never be able to find out from him, will we?"

Dorothy-Anne stared at him. "You certainly can't hold yourself responsible for that," she said.

"I know," he said. "But still. I can't help but wonder about him. Who he was. Why he did it. What made him tick."

How like Hunt, she thought, *to be concerned about the man who tried to kill him.*

He suddenly fell silent and looked into her eyes. "Will you give me a hug?" he asked.

And Dorothy-Anne had stood up and leaned over him, lying there prostrate on the bed, and she had held him in her arms, and they had kissed and kissed. . . .

Now the telephone's persistent chirrups jarred her from her reverie. She looked at it sitting there on the bedside table, and considered whether or not to answer.

What's if it's Hunt? He could be calling back for some reason.

She lunged for the phone and picked up. "Hello?"

"Mrs. Dorothy-Anne Cantwell?"

"Yes?" she said again. "Who is this?"

"Mrs. Cantwell, this is Harold J. Laughton," he said. "I'm with the National Transportation Safety Board."

Dorothy-Anne sucked in her breath. This was a telephone call that she had someday expected, but had relegated to a dark corner at the back of her mind.

"Yes, Mr. Laughton," she finally said. "What can I do for you?"

"I'm calling about our investigation into your husband's plane crash," he said. "As you know, we've recovered the aircraft and have been assembling it in a hangar in Denver."

Dorothy-Anne couldn't control the sudden quickening of her pulse, nor the tremor that abruptly gripped her voice. "Y-yes . . . ?"

"I hate to have to tell you this," he said, "but the lab reports are conclusive. C-4 explosives crippled the hydraulics *and* the backup systems. Is there anyone you know of who would have wanted to harm your husband?"

Harm my husband? What was he talking about? The room started to spin dizzily.

Dorothy-Anne finally found her voice. "Could you repeat what you just said, Mr. Laughton?" she asked.

Harold J. Laughton carefully repeated everything he had just told her.

Explosion?

Dorothy-Anne's mind reeled, and she felt a cold chill run up her spine. "An explosion," she finally said.

"Yes, ma'am," he said. "A C-4 explosion, to be precise."

C-4? What the hell is C-4? she wondered.

Harold J. Laughton kept talking, but she didn't hear anything he was saying. Slowly she replaced the receiver in the cradle.

My God, she thought, suddenly in the clutches of a terror she had never known existed. *Who would have tried to murder Freddie? What for? And what will they do now?*

62

6 6 I ve got some dignity left, you know," Gloria Winslow snapped. *Who does this old lizard think he is?* she asked herself. *Trying to get me to sign the divorce settlement?*

She got up from the couch, threw her shoulders back, and with the exaggerated caution of a drunk, made her way over to the kitchenette. It was still well stocked with bar supplies, she noted with a grim satisfaction. She'd made certain of that herself after taking this apartment at the Huntington Hotel on Nob Hill. She splashed some more vodka into her glass, added ice, and for the old lawyer's benefit, poured in some tonic water.

"You're sure you won't have anything, Mr. Mankiewicz?" she asked, making a big production of stirring her drink, then taking a tiny sip. Like most alcoholics, Gloria had begun to try to fool herself and everybody else about how much she really drank.

"No, thank you, Mrs. Winslow," the stringy old lawyer replied. He looked over his black-framed Ben Franklins at Gloria. He'd dealt with a lot of women like her in his day. Young, beautiful, rich, spoiled, bored, and more often than not, on booze or pills or both. Sometimes with a man or two on the side to service them. Not a good mix in the best of circumstances, he surmised. But add mad as hell, and you had a potentially lethal combination.

Gloria Winslow was no exception, he thought. What she ought to do, in his opinion, was take the money and run. Get on with her life. Which was what he was trying to tell her now.

Gloria returned to the couch and sat down, sipping her drink. She looked over at Raoul Mankiewicz. The wily old lawyer was immaculately groomed as always, in a pinstriped bespoke suit and custom-made shoes. His liver-spotted bald pate and eyeglasses shone in the light. Why, she asked herself, did the old reptile have to fly up from Los Angeles with these damn papers today? *I'm not ready for this shit,* she thought. *I just can't handle it right now.*

Raoul Mankiewicz cleared his throat. "I strongly suggest you sign the settlement, Mrs. Winslow," he said. "I think it would be in your best interest."

"I don't get it," Gloria said petulantly. "All that money and they expect me—*you* expect me—to take a measly ten million fucking bucks."

Uh-oh, the old lawyer thought, she's started cursing. A bad sign. I'd better hurry because she's really in her cups.

He looked at her with a neutral smile. "The offer is a considerable one, Mrs. Winslow," Mankiewicz pointed out patiently. "You have to take into consideration the penthouse apartment on Montgomery Street. That's worth a couple of million bucks. Plus all your jewelry. That's worth another couple of million."

"Yeah?" Gloria said. "Well, that's peanuts to the almighty Winslows and you know it." She took another sip of her vodka and set it down. *Jesus God,* she thought, *I'm getting a real buzz on.*

"You've got to remember that practically the entire Winslow fortune, everything, is in Althea Winslow's name." He paused a moment, clearing his throat again. "Your husband has virtually nothing, except his salary. Not even the house you lived in is in his name."

"I know all that shit," Gloria said truculently.

"If you go to court," the old lawyer continued, "you might end up with even less. Besides which, your legal bills would be astronomical."

Gloria knew that what he was saying was true, but she honestly didn't know what to do. Sign or not sign?

God, she thought, *if only Christos were here to help me. He would know what to do.*

But Christos was not here and never would be again, and Gloria felt as if she herself had signed his death warrant. In the meantime, she was confused, and didn't know which way to turn. Except to the bottle.

It's the only thing that kills the pain, she thought. *And the guilt and loneliness.*

What the hell was the old lizard saying now? Young and beautiful and rich? Get on with her life? *What life?* she wondered bitterly.

But before Gloria could ask Raoul Mankiewicz what he was talking about, the house phone rang. She picked up the extension on the table next to her. "What," she said impatiently.

"Mrs. Winslow," the manager said, "there are two police detectives here to see you."

Despite her alcoholic haze, Gloria felt an involuntary tremor run through her, and fought to control herself. "Send them up," she said. She slammed the receiver down and looked over at the old lawyer.

"Well," she said, "it's my lucky fucking day, I guess. First, you. Now, the cops." She barked an acidic laugh. "Would you do the honors, Mr. Mankiewicz?" She held out her glass for a refill.

She was now visibly drunk, even beginning to slur her words a bit, but Raoul Mankiewicz did not want an argument with her right now. No. Best to humor her. He got up, took her glass, and made her a weak vodka and tonic.

"Here," he said, bringing it back to her. "Don't worry about these policemen, Mrs. Winslow. I can handle this."

Gloria looked up at him and took the drink. "Not like you're handling the settlement, I hope," she said nastily.

He ignored the jibe and sat back down.

It was only moments before the doorbell rang. The old lawyer went to answer it. Gloria saw him return with a man and a woman, the same two who'd questioned her before.

Raoul Mankiewicz introduced them as Janie Yee, a slight, pretty, but strong-looking Asian woman, and Stanley Cohn, a once handsome and athletic man going to fat. Homicide detectives. "They just want to ask a few questions," he said.

Gloria looked up at them. "We've met," she snapped belligerently, "and I still don't know a damn thing." Then she took a sip of her drink.

"Why don't you take a seat," Mankiewicz asked them.

They took chairs facing the couch where Gloria sat. Janie Yee began the questioning. "Mrs. Winslow," she said, "there are just a few details we need to clear up. This is an ongoing investigation, as you know."

Gloria didn't bother responding.

"Mrs. Winslow . . . that is, Mrs. Althea Winslow," Janie Yee continued, "told us that on the night of the attempted murder you led her and your husband to the spot where the sniping occurred."

"So what?" Gloria sneered. "How was I to know somebody would try to shoot him?"

Stanley Cohn took over. "We're just wondering, Mrs. Winslow, why you took them to that spot. So is your mother-in-law."

"I don't think this line of questioning is relevant," Raoul Mankiewicz said, before Gloria could respond, "and I don't think Mrs. Winslow here is in a frame of mind to answer questions right now—"

"Mr. Mankiewicz," Janie Yee interrupted, "we would be glad to close this case. After all, the perp is dead. It's just that Mrs. Althea Winslow has indicated that . . . well, that until this divorce is over, she is going to continue to pursue this matter."

"That is *blackmail*, pure and simple," Raoul Mankiewicz said heatedly, "and you know it." He looked from one detective to the other. "I suggest that if you have any further questions for Mrs. Winslow you make an appointment. Right now we're discussing her divorce settlement."

"Uh-huh," Stanley Cohn said. "Well, maybe we'll come back another time, then." He motioned for Janie Yee to follow him as he started for the door. "Thanks for your time, Mrs. Winslow," he said. He turned to the old lawyer and nodded. "Mr. Mankiewicz."

Gloria swirled her finger around in her drink, and didn't look up at the departing detectives. Raoul Mankiewicz showed them out, then came back in and sat down.

He stared at Gloria. "Do you understand what's going on?" he asked her.

"Who gives a fuck," Gloria spat out, and returned his gaze.

"You'd better," the old lawyer retorted. "Those cops are not going to leave you alone until this divorce settlement is signed. That's what this is all about."

Mankiewicz paused, but Gloria didn't reply. She took her finger out of her drink and licked it off.

"Althea Winslow has obviously put a lot of pressure on the mayor's office and the police commissioner," he continued, "and she's not letting up until the divorce is over. If you sign, the cops disappear. If you don't, they are going to keep pestering you. Now I don't know whether or not you had anything to do with this attempt on your husband—"

"Go fuck yourself," Gloria snarled. "I didn't have a goddamn thing to do with it! Whose side are you on anyway?"

"Yours, Mrs. Winslow," the old lawyer said patiently. "That's why I say sign this settlement, take the money, and forget about the Winslows. Althea Winslow and the cops are not going to forget you until you do."

Gloria stared at him through her fog. *God, I'm so sick of this,* she thought. *I'm sick of this old lizard. I'm sick of hearing about that old bitch, Althea. I'm sick of the cops. I'm sick of everything.* And suddenly something went click in her head.

"Gimme a pen," she slurred.

Raoul Mankiewicz sighed with relief and handed her a fountain pen along with four copies of the settlement. "Sign each copy where I've indicate with an *X*," he said.

Gloria quickly scrawled her signature on all four copies, then slammed his pen on the coffee table. "There," she said. "Happy?"

"I think you've made the most intelligent decision considering the circumstances," the lawyer said, putting the papers in his briefcase. He retrieved his fountain pen and got to his feet. "It won't be long before all this is finalized. I'll be heading back to Los Angeles tonight, so if you need anything, you can get me there. In the meantime, I'll be in touch."

And he was gone.

Gloria looked around the living room, hoping to feel a sense of relief that this was finally over and the old lawyer was gone. But no relief came.

I'm sick of holing up in this fucking place, she thought. *I'm sick of the drinking. It's not fun anymore. Not without Christos.*

She grabbed her handbag and keys and left the apartment. Outside the hotel she began to walk. The vodka had done its trick, but it had also heated her up. She'd gone a few blocks without paying much attention to where she was when she realized she was on the fringes of the Tenderloin. Surrounded by low-life bars.

I met Christos in one of these dumps, she thought. *I think I'll just have a little celebratory drink in memory of him. Maybe I'll even luck out again.*

She opened the door to a grungy joint with lots of tacky neon signs. It reeked of stale beer. Ah, just the thing, she thought. Nobody I know would ever come to a place like this. She looked around in the dim interior and saw an empty booth. She walked over to it, and sidled into the side facing the front door, the better to see the clientele as they came in. The waitress came over and Gloria ordered a double vodka straight up, with ice.

She didn't notice the young woman at the long bar behind her. A young woman with long, straight, dark hair who was wearing a T-shirt that was too tight for her and exposed her navel.

While Gloria celebrated, the young woman watched her, a gleam of pure evil in her eyes.

63

The Big Apple seemed to have been polished expressly for Hunt's visit. The sky had been a cloudless, cerulean blue all day, with the skyline standing out with crisp, incredible clarity. The air was fresh, and the temperature rose no higher than the mid-seventies while the humidity remained low, a relief from the baking, steamy heat of the previous days.

Dorothy-Anne couldn't imagine a more perfect afternoon to be with Hunt.

Incandescent with joy and breathless with anticipation, she tore through the luxurious lobby of the Carlyle Hotel on Madison Avenue and Seventy-sixth Street, making a beeline for the concierge's desk. Hunt had wisely steered clear of the Hale Hotel, where the staff would instantly recognize Dorothy-Anne. And besides, the Carlyle was the one place in the city where the rich, the famous, and even the infamous could count on utter discretion.

Here their privacy would be respected and assured. Here her own staff would be unable to keep tabs on her, and gossip.

The chicly dressed young woman waited until Dorothy-Anne was inside the lobby before following her. She looked around, as if searching for someone, then pretended to consult her watch, craning her neck and looking around some more. She watched as the concierge greeted Dorothy-Anne and called upstairs to announce her. As Dorothy-Anne hurried over to the bank of elevators, the young woman went back outside, plucked a cell phone out of her purse, and punched a preprogrammed, automatically dialed number.

When a voice answered, she said, "Tell Carmine the woman's at the Carlyle Hotel. Ask if I should find out who she's visiting."

She was told to wait. Then the voice came back on the line. "Carmine says you're to do nothing. Keep a low profile and keep me posted."

Dorothy-Anne arrived at Hunt's suite flushed with excitement.

"Hello, beautiful," he said when he opened the door. He beamed at her, a golden radiance seeming to surround him.

Dorothy-Anne stepped into the entry hall, and Hunt closed the door. She turned around to face him.

"Hello, beautiful yourself," she said huskily, and he took her in his arms and they kissed passionately.

After a moment Dorothy-Anne pulled back. "Let me take a good look at you. I haven't seen you since you got out of the hospital."

Hunt stood back and threw his arms out theatrically. In one hand was an ebonized cane with a solid silver handle carved in the shape of a horse's head. "Well? Am I distinguished, or not?" he demanded, all smiling, pearly white teeth.

"*Very* distinguished," Dorothy-Anne responded, her heart choking with emotion at the sight of the cane, thinking of what he had so recently been through, of his close brush with death.

I'm so lucky that he's alive, she thought.

He saw the look on her face and took her in his arms again. He began peppering her with little kisses, all over her face and her neck, then nibbling tenderly at her ears.

"I'm so glad to see you," he whispered.

Dorothy-Anne pulled back again. "I'm glad to see you, too," she said. "But you really should have let me meet you at the airport."

"No," Hunt said. "I knew you were busy, and I had a limo pick me up." He grinned. "But now that I'm here, I want to dominate all of your time. From this moment till the time I leave."

"I'm all yours," Dorothy-Anne said.

Forever and ever, she thought, *as long as I have anything to say about it.*

She said, "We'll use my car and driver while you're here. It'll be easier to get around." She gave him a peck on the lips. "Come on, let's go sit down. You should take the weight off your leg."

He arched his eyebrows. "Bossing me around already?"

"Only for your own good."

They walked arm in arm to the chintz-covered sofa in the sitting room, which was elegantly furnished with formal but comfortable English and French pieces. Through the large, extravagantly draped window, Dorothy-Anne saw that the lights of the city were beginning to shimmer, like millions of stars being born. And on the coffee table, she noticed a silver tray holding two crystal flutes and a bottle of Louis Roderer Cristal in a silver bucket of ice.

They sat down, holding hands. Hunt spread his leg out in front of him, and laid his cane down.

"I see you've thought of everything," she said, indicating the champagne.

"To celebrate," Hunt said. "It isn't every day I get to see you. Here, I'll pop the cork."

"Nonsense," Dorothy-Anne said. "You sit still. I'm quite proficient at champagne corks."

She popped it expertly, filled the glasses, and handed one to Hunt.

He held his flute aloft, and she touched it with hers.

"To us," Hunt toasted, looking into her eyes.

"To us," Dorothy-Anne repeated, returning his gaze.

Dorothy-Anne took a sip. The champagne was bubbly and tasted delicious. She set her glass down and looked at him. "Have you thought about what you'd like to do while you're here?" she asked.

"You bet I have," he answered, grinning mischievously.

Hunt took Dorothy-Anne in his arms, and she melted against him, pressing her head to his chest, listening to the pounding of his heart. Then his lips sought hers and he kissed her mouth, her eyes, the throbbing pulse at the base of her throat.

Dorothy-Anne felt the sweetness of surrender. A shiver of anticipation ran through her and they began to undress, leaving a trail of shed clothing to the bedroom. They lay down together, side by side, facing each other in the middle of the big bed.

"Your leg," she said.

"What about it?"

She looked down at his knee, still in its brace.

"Can I?" she asked.

"Sure. Go ahead."

She touched it gingerly, frowning as she stroked her fingers ever so lightly across it.

She looked up at him. "Does this hurt?"

He shook his head and smiled. "Actually, that feels quite nice."

"But you're sure we should do this? I mean, I don't want to make your injury worse."

"Don't worry," he laughed. "This is the kind of injury I'd welcome."

She slid her hands smoothly up his legs to his hips and flat belly, and across his chest, her face not showing the slightest degree of embarrassment. He took her head in his hands and pressed her against him, burying his face in her hair. He inhaled deeply.

"Mmmmm," he murmured. "You smell like sugar and spice and everything nice."

"That," she said, lifting her head and tossing back her hair, "is because you're horny." She smiled, her hands feeling behind her and touching his tumescence. "Come to think of it, is there ever a time you're *not* horny?"

He gazed up her, his eyes deep and intense. "Oh, lots."

"And when might that be?"

"Whenever I'm not with you." He grinned. "But then I *think* about you and—*bing!* Old Johnson down there stands at attention."

"Then we'd better do something about poor Old Johnson," she said solemnly, bending over Hunt and covering his mouth with her own.

Their kiss was a passionate embrace that went beyond words. It said they had both shed their emotional baggage, and no longer had to hide their hunger. Finally guiltless and carefree, each of them surrendered body and soul to the other with a generosity of spirit that was unconditional, flexible, and deeply humbling because it knew no bounds.

Ever heedful of his injury, she whispered: "I'll do the acrobatics for us both. You just lie back and enjoy the ride."

Then, straddling him like a jockey, she placed him inside her and began moving herself up and down, up and down, her face knit in concentration.

His breath soughed from his lungs. She was warm and moist, and in no time he lost himself inside her. Then she felt him tense, and he begged her to stop.

"It's too soon!" he gasped.

But she shook her head. "There's no need to hold back, Hunt," she said softly. "We've waited for too long. Let it go. Let it *come!*"

And with a cry that was part joy and part agony, he exploded inside her, all the accumulated fears and anger and frustrations that had been throttled up inside him bursting like a geyser, darkness suddenly turning into brilliance, the poisons swallowed by the lust of her thighs, the tenderness of eyes, the love in her heart.

Afterward, as they lay in each other's arms, neither of them found it necessary to speak. They understood the potency and perfection of the love they shared.

When they partook of one another again, it was slower, and with less urgency and more concentration, allowing themselves time to linger and explore each other's bodies, reaching a plane of contentment so fulfilling, so sublime, and so precisely in tune, it seemed almost impossible.

I never believed I could feel like this about a man again, Dorothy-Anne thought blissfully. *Thank you, God. Thank you for answering my prayers.*

And that was when it dawned on her that the greatest gift of all had been bestowed on her: she felt no remorse for making love with Hunt. Absolutely none.

On the contrary, she felt rejuvenated, and knew from the depths of her heart that wherever Freddie was, this is what he would have wanted.

*   *   *

The tropical storm brewing off the coast of Africa had been on a feeding frenzy. It had picked up enormous strength in the heated waters of the Atlantic Ocean, and was now whirling savagely to the northwest, veering slowly but surely toward the Windward Islands, gathering power as it barreled across the water.

Its progress was being closely tracked. From out in space, weather satellites kept an eye on it. Closer to earth, a modified C-130, equipped as a flying weather station, was checking it out up close.

Since the storm was still out over open water, it was too early to predict either its course or its power.

It had not yet been upgraded to hurricane status.

Before long, it would be.

64

Through the concierge, Hunt had magically produced tickets for the musical *Titanic* at the Lunt-Fontanne Theater.

"Two tenth-row center orchestra seats for tonight," he said. "And we have reservations for pretheater dinner at Joe Allen."

"What!" Dorothy-Anne flew out of bed. "And me with nothing to wear! You stay in bed. I'll be right back."

"Where are you going?"

"Why, to get some clothes—what else?"

She popped over to the town house, where she stuffed more than she would need into a garment bag, put on what she and Venetia laughingly called her Little Red Riding Hooker raincoat with matching hood and umbrella, and then returned to the Carlyle.

"That the big bad wolf?" Hunt asked.

"Grrrr!" She made her fingers into claws. "Better watch it, buster, or I'll eat you."

"That a promise?" he said hopefully. "Or a threat?"

"Both," she said happily. "Just give me a minute to hang up my things."

"An obsessive-compulsive wolf!" he laughed. "That's a new one!"

The rain was still coming down steadily when it was time to go to dinner.

Hunt dressed for the occasion in a charcoal double-breasted suit, a white broadcloth shirt, and a reddish Hèrmes tie with tiny beige and white ostriches on it, alternating rows looking around and burying their heads in the sand. The display hankie in his breast pocket matched the tie, and his cufflinks were big reddish enamel ladybugs with black dots.

Dorothy-Anne was stylish in a crisp V-neck blouse of thick white lace

500

by Gianfranco Ferre. She had on very thin, very loose black silk pants, red patent leather Gucci penny loafers, and ruby cabochons on her ears. Her Little Red Riding Hooker raincoat with its dramatic cowled hood and matching umbrella completed the outfit.

On their way out, she took Hunt's arm and posed in front of the dressing mirror. "Well? Are we hot, or are we hot?"

He grinned at their reflection. "Hot enough to set the town on fire."

"Good. Then let's go start a conflagration!"

Dorothy-Anne's every move was relayed to Carmine, who was mobile and roving, and took the calls on a cellular phone.

"Subject, wearing red raincoat with red hood and matching umbrella, just left the Carlyle in a chauffeured black Infiniti. Said vehicle is heading north on Madison Avenue. I'm two cars behind. Subject's car now turning left on Sixty-ninth Street . . ."

"Car dropped the woman and a man off in front of Joe Allen's on Forty-sixth Street. That's between Eighth and Ninth Avenues."

Probably for a pretheater dinner, Carmine thought. *Enjoy your last supper.*

An hour later, the reports continued:

"Subject and her escort are leaving Joe Allen's. They're heading east on foot on the north side of Forty-sixth Street. . . . They're crossing Eighth Avenue. . . ."

"Subject is going into the Lunt-Fontanne Theater to see *Titanic.*"

Carmine's orders were specific: "Cease all surveillance until further notice. Repeat: Cease surveillance and clear the area."

Titanic, Carmine thought, with a smile. *What an appropriate choice.*

Mitzi Feinstein was not a New York City native. Sixteen years earlier, she had shuffled off from Buffalo with five hundred dollars and a dream.

She was going to become a Broadway star. A major Broadway musical star. She knew it. Her friends knew it. Everyone in Buffalo, New York, knew it. For Mitzi Feinstein possessed prodigious acting talent, a clear singing voice, great dancing legs, and knockout looks—for Buffalo.

Sad to report, in Manhattan she was just another face in an army of show biz wannabes.

Mitzi gave herself ten years to make it. During that time, she auditioned her heart out, waited on a lot of tables, turned a few tricks, and landed exactly four nonspeaking parts.

Clearly, it was time for a career change.

When her ten years were up, she stopped auditioning and found a job on the other side of the curtain. Earning union wages, and keeping a foot in the glamorous world of Broadway theaters—at the moment, the

Lunt-Fontanne—by working the bar. Only today, she was stuck with coat check because of the rain.

"Christ, I hate rainy days," she grumbled to Bea Weiss, who worked with her. "All I see are drenched raincoats and dripping umbrellas. I ask you? And me dying for a cigarette."

Bea, who was just hanging up a silklike red raincoat with a matching hood and umbrella, said, "Hey, Mitz! Take a look at this, would ya?"

She held the hanger aloft.

"This coat's identical to yours. Some coincidence, huh?"

Mitzi glanced at the coat and sighed. "That," she brooded, "is an original. Mine's a Canal Street knockoff."

"Well, to me it looks identical," Bea countered loyally, then both of them were suddenly too busy to chat. It was nearing curtain time, and a flurry of theatergoers was crowding the coat check counter.

Finally, the crowd thinned, then evaporated. They could hear the distant swell of music, then applause as the curtain went up. A few latecomers hurried in.

The lobby was quiet.

Mitzi said, "Cover for me, willya? I'm dying for a smoke and I'm out of cigarettes."

"I thought you quit."

"I said I'm *trying* to quit. Trying and doing are two different things."

Mitzi got her coat, slipped into it, and buttoned the front. She put up the hood, grabbed her purse, and rushed out.

Rain, propelled by gusts of wind, hit her head-on and she staggered momentarily. Quickly she pulled her hood tightly together under her chin and held it there. Keeping her head tucked down, she hurried down the nearly deserted street toward Eighth Avenue.

She never saw the dark shape looming out of the doorway beside her. One moment she was hurrying down the sidewalk, and the next she was being grabbed from behind. She tried to scream, but a gloved hand covered her mouth and she was whirled around and shoved into a doorway.

Mitzi stared, her eyes wild. *This can't be happening!* she thought. *Not to me! Not just outside the theater—*

Carmine plunged an eight-inch knife into her belly and then slashed the blade powerfully upward, disemboweling her and ripping her open to the bottom of her rib cage.

It was no longer necessary to keep her mouth covered, so Carmine stepped back and watched as she slid limply down, eyes wide with shock, into a sitting position. Blood was bubbling out of her mouth.

Shielding her by standing there, Carmine knotted a red tie around her hooded head, pulled off the military surplus poncho, and threw it over her. Making her look like just another homeless wretch in a doorway.

These are mean streets, Carmine thought, walking away without a backward glance. *Attractive women have no business walking them alone. Especially not at night.*

The next day's newspaper headlines screamed bloody murder.

The *New York Post:* MURDER ON B'WAY.

The *Daily News:* THEATER EMPLOYEE SLAIN.

Both articles speculated on motives. The woman's purse had not been stolen.

Dorothy-Anne did not read the articles nor watch the local televised news programs. It was her last day with Hunt, and they spent it together.

That evening, he flew back to San Francisco and she picked up where she'd left off—getting back to work, mothering the kids, and keeping track of the storm that was fast approaching the Caribbean.

The wrong victim.

Carmine stared incredulously at the newspapers, filled with disbelief and a growing rage that threatened to overwhelm.

The wrong victim . . .

No! Carmine thought. *It can't have been!*

But there it was, in black and white and read all over. Complete with a professional portfolio head shot that must have been ten, fifteen years old, judging by the hairstyle. Mitzi Feinstein, struggling actress—turned coat check clerk—dead.

Because of a red raincoat.

A damn red raincoat!

I should have known, Carmine thought, grabbing the newspapers and flinging them across the room. *It had been too easy.*

Well, it wasn't the end of the world.

I'll just have to try again. And this time, I'll succeed. Betcha ass I will!

During the past twenty-four hours, the storm had been upgraded to full-fledged hurricane status. It now had a name: Cyd.

It also had a projected destination. The entire chain of Windward Islands, from Trinidad up to Martinique, were heeding advisories and battening down the hatches.

Rated as a three on a scale of one to five, Hurricane Cyd, with winds of 120 miles per hour, was not to be trifled with.

Dorothy-Anne ordered the evacuation of guests from the Hale hotels on Trinidad, St. Lucia, and St. Vincent, and special charter flights were dispatched forthwith. The staff remained, busy boarding up windows and securing the resorts as best they could.

Dorothy-Anne's major worry, however, remained Eden Isle. At the construction site, there were no windows to board up, no hatches to batten down. Everything could simply be washed or blown away.

And there was nothing she could do except watch and wait.

65

Mama Rosa scraped the pile of chopped pork butt into a giant bowl. She pinched pieces of it between her fingers to check the texture, and eyed it critically. Then she nodded to herself. The meat was nice and pink, with lots of white fatty pieces to give it flavor. She smacked her lips. *Salsiccia al punto del coltello* was one of her favorite dishes. Hardly anyone made hacked sausage anymore. The secret was in the hand chopping, the generous proportion of fat, and the liberal amounts of fennel for flavor.

She hummed to herself while she worked. It was a Monday, and during the summer the restaurant was closed on Mondays, and she was alone in the kitchen. She liked these times by herself to indulge in making time-consuming specialties whose recipes she guarded jealously.

She set the bowl aside and went to flush out the hog casings under cold running water in the sink. Suddenly the door from the dining room was flung open.

Startled, Mama Rosa looked up. Then she heaved a sigh and shook her head. It was only that young man, the blade-thin Chinese-American.

She continued washing the casings as he marched over to where she was working.

"We need to talk," Sonny Fong told her quietly.

"Yeah? How did you get in? The front door is locked."

"It was only snap-locked, he said. I used my American Express card. You know what they say. 'Never leave home without it'?"

He smiled coldly, the whiteness of his teeth and his lean, cliffhanger cheekbones making for a chilly effect.

"So what do you want? If you're looking for my Carmine, he ain't here."

"According to you, he's never here."

She shrugged. "Carmine's a grown man. What do you expect me to do? Baby-sit him?" She had to smile at the idea.

"No, but I want to talk to him. Either face-to-face, or else you can deliver a message directly. And not on paper, either."

"Okay. I'm listening." She put the long, snakelike hog casings in a bowl of cold water. "What's the message?"

Sonny drew closer, his voice growing quieter. "Carmine *failed*!" he hissed. "He killed the wrong woman!"

She jerked back from him. "I don't know anything about no killing!" Swiftly she crossed herself. "My Carmine, he's—"

"Yeah, yeah. I know, an angel. And he loves his mother."

Her eyes narrowed. "Be careful what you say about him!"

"I'll say this. He failed, and now it's too late. You understand? My people want their three million dollars back. *Pronto.*"

"Three million dollars! Carmine?" She laughed. "Go on. You're crazy!"

"I am not crazy," he said tightly. "I'm dead serious. Carmine failed to fulfill a contract, and we want a refund."

She threw up her hands and waved them around in the air. "I refuse to listen to any more of this rubbish!"

"In that case, let me talk to Carmine."

Mama Rosa drew a deep breath, placed her hands on her hips, and puckered her lips. For a moment she puffed her cheeks and looked thoughtful, then nodded reluctantly to herself.

"All right," she sighed. "Here's the key to my apartment."

She reached under her folded-over apron and took a bunch of keys out of her housecoat.

"It's this silver one, here."

She handed him the entire key ring.

He waited.

"Go upstairs. Let yourself in and wait in the living room. Meanwhile, I'll call around and see if I can get hold of Carmine. If he can't drop by, I'll have him call you. So if my phone rings, answer it. Okay?"

Sonny was elated. *This is more like it,* he thought. *It's amazing how attitudes change when you apply a little pressure.*

"Now, listen carefully," Mama Rosa told him. "You sit in the big red chair in front of the TV. Facing *away* from the door. Got that. If you see Carmine's face . . . even accidentally . . ."

She let her shrug speak for itself.

Sonny grinned. "I hear you."

Then he executed a nifty about-face and strutted off, cocksure and confident. Jingling the keys. Tossing them up in the air and catching them underhand on their way down.

Her apartment upstairs was stifling. It faced south, and absorbed the sun's heat. Despite the open windows, there was no cross-ventilation.

While he stood there, he looked around. The living room was exactly as he remembered it—the upholstered pieces protected by clear, zippered vinyl covers. The tapestry of the Kennedy brothers hanging on the one wall; the one of the pontiff on the other. And there, in pride of place, the forty-inch Mitsubishi television with its screen aimed right at the red chair and ottoman.

He took a seat, put up his feet. Found the remote control for the TV, switched on the set, and tried some channel surfing.

He should have known. The reception sucked.

She's too cheap to spring for cable.

He didn't get it. Here she had the Cadillac of televisions, the set with the single largest picture tube on the market—and what for? Lousy, grainy reception, that's what.

Sonny unbuttoned his sports jacket and slipped the Glock 17 out of his shoulder holster. He checked for ammo. There was a round in every chamber. He slipped it back into the holster, then did a few practice draws, lining up people on TV as imaginary targets. Then he holstered the pistol but left the holster strap unsnapped and his sports jacket unbuttoned.

Keeping the gun within easy reach.

He tuned in to Ricki Lake, which was followed by Jenny Jones, mainly because Channel 9 came in the clearest.

Ricki Lake's guests were Kids Who Abuse Their Parents.

Jenny Jones's were white supremacists. A few wore pilly sheets that were supposed to pass for robes, and everybody seemed overweight, and was missing at least one crucial tooth. He had difficulty following the conversations—everyone was yelling, and most of the words were bleeped out.

Then he felt it. Halfway through Jenny Jones: a puff of air coming from behind him as the front door opened and closed.

Sonny sat up straighter. He knew he was no longer alone.

Carmine is here!

He resisted the instinctive habit of turning around.

I must do as Mama Rosa said. No one who could identify Carmine ever lived to tell about it.

Using his left hand, Sonny clicked the mute button on the remote.

"No!" Carmine's voice was a sibilant whisper. "Turn it back on."

Sonny hit the mute again. The Jenny Jones audience was waving its fists and jeering. With his right hand, he started to reach inside his jacket . . . slowly . . . very slowly . . . fingers creeping . . .

"Unh-unh." Carmine laughed softly. "You don't want to do that."

Sonny froze, then slowly withdrew his hand and placed it on the arm of the chair.

"That's better."

Carmine was standing right behind him now. Sonny could feel the assassin's breath on the back of his neck.

"Now close your eyes and lean your head back," Carmine whispered.

Sonny did as he was told, flinching as he felt something hard and round and cold pressing against his temple. He knew what it was. A gun.

"Now open your eyes," Carmine whispered.

"But . . . I-I'm not supposed to see you!" Sonny stuttered.

"No, but I want you to read my lips."

Sonny heard and felt the unmistakable click of the revolver's hammer. He clenched his teeth and gripped the arms of the chair. His fingernails dug into the vinyl covers like claws, and he was trembling violently.

"Open your eyes," Carmine whispered.

Sonny forced his eyes open and gasped.

"Now read my lips: I always guarantee a job. We clear on that?"

Sonny swallowed. He gave an almost imperceptible nod, afraid that too much movement might accidentally set off the gun.

Carmine eased up the pressure against Sonny's temple and began stroking Sonny's cheek with the revolver.

"That means if Plan A fails," Carmine continued, "then I go to Plan B. And if B doesn't work, I have Plan C in the works. *Capiche?*"

Sonny gave another little nod. He'd completely lost his cool. One of his eyelids was twitching wildly, and he was bathed in the cold, rank sweat of fear.

Carmine said, "In other words, the woman is unfinished business. She *will* die. Count on it."

The barrel was directly under Sonny's chin now. He barely dared breathe.

"You see," Carmine whispered. "I never give up. And I never give refunds. Ever."

Sonny nodded. "Okay," he croaked.

"So we got that straight?"

"Yes!"

"And one last thing."

Sonny waited.

Carmine squeezed the trigger and watched Sonny Fong's brains explode in a red mist.

"You're history," Carmine whispered.

On Monday, Hurricane Cyd slammed into Trinidad with winds topping 140 miles an hour, and was angling its way north by northwest. Dorothy-Anne caught the first broadcast of on-the-scene television footage on CNN. The swath of destruction Cyd had left behind was awesome.

The reporter, buffeted by what had *decreased* to sixty-mile-an-hour winds, could barely be heard above the roar of the wind blasting his microphone: ". . . in this, one of the worst hurricanes in recent history, much of the Delaware-size island is without power, and an estimated eight thousand people have been left homeless. . . ."

Additional footage showed people camped out in a shelter, thrashing palm trees, flying roofs, an airplane that had been tossed onto its back, wheels in the air, so that it looked like a dead insect, and a yacht the storm surge had left high and dry in the middle of a road.

Dorothy-Anne was shocked at the extent of the devastation. She immediately tried calling the Hale Hotel, located on the northern coast, but the lines were down. Next she tried several cellular numbers but was unable to get through on those, either.

The transmission towers are probably down, she thought.

At least, she hoped that was all it was.

Half an hour later, Cecilia burst into Dorothy-Anne's office. "Guess what, boss?"

Dorothy-Anne's nerves were frayed, and she was not in a good mood. "Don't tell me," she said with spicy indignation. "You decided you no longer have to knock before you enter?"

Cecilia's bubble was too optimistic to be burst. "Thanks to citizen's band radio, we're in contact with Trinidad!"

"What!" Dorothy-Anne jumped to her feet, her heart pounding. "And?"

"Oh, there's minor damage, but nothing that can't be fixed. The manager estimates fifty thousand dollars' worth, tops. It's so minor and cosmetic we can reopen immediately."

Dorothy-Anne felt weak with relief. She sank back down into her chair and offered up a silent prayer of thanks.

She spent the rest of that day tracking Cyd's course, ordering the evacuation of the Hale hotels on Monserrat, St. Kitts, and St. Croix, and ordering the staffs to batten down the hatches.

That evening, Cyd did the unpredictable. After slamming full force into St. Vincent and St. Lucia, the hurricane abruptly changed course and headed west, into the island-free center of the Caribbean.

Dorothy-Anne wondered if she hadn't jumped the gun. Was it possible she'd evacuated Monserrat, St. Kitts, and St. Croix prematurely?

Better safe than sorry, she reminded herself, and kept her fingers crossed.

If Cyd stayed on this new course—and Dorothy-Anne knew that nothing was more unpredictable than a hurricane—Eden Isle would be spared.

On Tuesday, she was feeling downright euphoric. St. Vincent and St. Lucia had both been hard hit, but Freddie's stringent construction codes were paying off. On islands where building codes were poor to nonexistent, Hale hotels had stood up to Hurricane Cyd's fury. Damage was minimal.

Better yet, Cyd was still moving west, avoiding the Lesser Antilles to the south, and the Greater Antilles to the north.

And then her day got even better. Arne Mankoff came into her office, leading an assistant who carried a two-foot stack of documents.

"I gather you can intuit what these are," the chief counsel said.

His assistant put the documents down on Dorothy-Anne's Regency desk and then left.

"Judging from the sheer magnitude of paperwork," Dorothy-Anne said, "I intuit they're the contracts for the FLASH sale."

She pressed the intercom switch on her desk.

"Cecilia."

"Boss?"

"I don't want any unnecessary interruptions. U.Y.B.J. Okay?"

U.Y.B.J. was their abbreviation for Use Your Best Judgment.

"You got it, boss. Only immediate family and a certain close friend."

"Cecilia?"

"Yes, boss?"

"Can the wiseass routine."

An hour passed, and Dorothy-Anne was still only halfway through initialing the third copy when her vision began to blur. She put her pen down, flexed the cramped fingers of her right hand, and briefly shut her eyes and gently massaged the lids.

Another hour and a half passed. They had just completed the last copy and Arne was stacking them when Cecilia buzzed. "Boss? Sorry to interrupt, but I *think* this falls under U.Y.B.J."

Dorothy-Anne was seized by a momentary panic. "Is it the children or the hurricane?"

"Neither."

"Dorothy-Anne was relieved. *Thank God,* she offered up silently.

"However, I believe it falls under the Certain Close Friend category," Cecilia said.

"What does?"

"You'll see in a minute."

Cecilia clicked off, and when the office door opened, Dorothy-Anne looked across the room. "Good heavens! What is *that?*"

Arne twisted around to look. "Seems like somebody sent you the entire Bronx Botanical Gardens," he said dryly.

Tottering through the door, seemingly under its own power, was the biggest floral arrangement either of them had ever seen. Only Cecilia's legs were visible; otherwise it hid her completely.

"Didn't realize it was your birthday," Arne said.

"It's not."

Venetia, carrying a round maple box tied with a red ribbon, followed Cecilia into the office.

"I was just coming down the hall and, *girl,*" she sang out, "let me tell you. I just *had* to follow the flowers!"

Venetia steered Cecilia toward one of the beautifully veneered round tables, where she swiftly moved a potted hydrangea from the center and made extra room by scooting aside stacks of books and gathering up silver-framed photographs.

With a grunt Cecilia set the arrangement on the table, then staggered to the nearest chair and sank gratefully down into it.

"I should have called one of the porters," she gasped. "I didn't realize it was that heavy."

Dorothy-Anne pushed back her ergonomic chairman-of-the-universe chair, got up, and went over to the table. She walked a slow circumference, investigating the king-size arrangement from all sides.

It was undeniably one of the most prodigal, opulent, and stunningly beautiful floral arrangements she had ever received. There were thick branches of creamy orchids; peonies of the palest pink, the size of dinner plates; clusters of white lilies; orange-hued poppies; blowsy old-fashioned roses; parrot tulips that looked as though they belonged in a Dutch still-life; and delicate, flesh-toned irises the likes of which she had never seen. All in a heavy glass cylinder and wrapped in see-through cellophane.

"Good golly," Dorothy-Anne exclaimed.

"Girlfriend," Venetia said. "Do you have any idea what this thing must have cost? When I saw it, I asked myself: Who is the lucky girl that has found herself an Arab prince? Well, I should have known."

Dorothy-Anne began to part the stapled cellophane.

"Oh, and Cecilia said this came with it." Venetia placed the round box tied with the red ribbon on the table.

"Where's the card?" Dorothy-Anne asked Cecilia. "I don't see one."

"I didn't, either," Cecilia replied. "Not on the flowers, nor the box."

"Maybe it's *in* the box?" Venetia suggested helpfully.

Dorothy-Anne picked it up. "Oh, how beautiful! It's one of those Shaker boxes they make up in the Berkshires," she said, turning it around. Then she set it back down and started to untie the bow.

"Hurry up, child," Venetia said impatiently from over her shoulder. "I am absolutely *dying* to find out what is inside that box. Yes. It cannot be jewelry. It is too heavy, and anyway it's hardly the kind of box you find at Bulgari or Van Cleef or—"

"This is strange," Dorothy-Anne murmured, her lips turning slightly downward.

"What is, sugar?"

"This ribbon. See? It's not really a ribbon. It's a red silk necktie!"

"A *neck*tie! Oooooo, baby!" Venetia laughed. "Kink-*yyyyy!* Sounds like You-Know-Who is sending you a not-so-subliminal message."

"Venetia!" Dorothy-Anne rolled her eyes. "Will you *stop?*" She had the tie loose and was lifting the lid off the box.

"Look!"

She held it out for the others to see.

The box was filled with small, golden-brown round cookies. Perfectly centered on each was half a maraschino cherry.

"Cookies?" Venetia sniffed. "I must say I am thoroughly disap-pointed. Yes. What sort of a man sends a woman *cookies?* I mean really! *Calories.* That's what they are."

Dorothy-Anne laughed. "Oh, come on. Here, take one."

Venetia leaned over the box. "Well, they do look rather tempting." Her thin nostrils flared. "And I must admit they smell delicious," she added, "but no." She shook her head. "I am on a strict diet."

"Be that way," Dorothy-Anne brought the box over to Cecilia. "Have one," she offered.

"Well," Cecilia said, momentarily undecided. "I'm on a diet too, but it's not quite *that* strict. Why not? *One* can't hurt me. Right?"

Her hand hovered over the box and then she plucked one out and immediately nibbled on it. "Mmm! *Very* good!"

"Arne?" Dorothy-Anne offered.

Arne reached in and grabbed a couple.

At that moment, Dorothy-Anne's personal phone line began to bleat. She thrust the box of cookies at Arne and hurried over to her desk. She grabbed up the receiver on the fourth ring. "Hello?" she answered breathlessly.

"Am I interrupting anything?" a familiar voice asked.

"Hunt!" she cried in delight. "The flowers and cookies just arrived. I must say, you've really outdone yourself this time. I've never *seen* so many flowers!"

"Flowers? Cookies? What are you talking about?" he said quietly.

Dorothy-Anne's forehead creased. "What do you mean?"

"I didn't send you any flowers or cookies. From your reaction, it makes me wish I *had.* . . ."

"But . . . If *you* didn't, then *who* . . . ?"

Dorothy-Anne frowned over at the massive floral arrangement. Cecilia had finished her cookie and was brushing crumbs off her skirt. Arne was standing there, holding the box with one hand, and trying to separate the two cookies he held in the other hand so he could eat them one at a time. And, towering nearly as high as the flowers, Venetia was removing the rest of the cellophane from around the arrangement, the three of them creating a perfect *tableau vivant* of the good life.

"The reason I called—not to alarm you," Hunt was saying, "is to see if you've been following the news."

"Oh, the hurricane," Dorothy-Anne said in a voice of tedious resignation. "I'm hurricaned up to my ears."

"This isn't about the hurricane."

"Then what news *are* you talking about?"

"Well, I get the major New York papers here—a day late, of course, and not that I have much of a chance to read them—but I do try and keep up with events—"

"Yes? And?"

"And, I just picked up a stack to toss out. You know how newspapers can accumulate? And what should be staring up at me but the *New York Post.* This past Sunday's issue."

"That's the day you returned to California," she murmured.

"That's right. The headlines read, and I quote, 'Murder on B'Way.' In four-inch letters."

Dorothy-Anne had to laugh. "Hunt! A murder, or more likely two or three or more murders, occur in this city every single day!"

"But not on Saturday night, the twenty-eighth of June," he said. "And not on the same block as the Lunt-Fontanne Theater."

"It happened on the block *we* were on?"

"That's right. Not only on the same block, but on the same side of the street."

"I see what you mean. The coincidence that we might have passed right by the body—"

No! You *don't* see what I mean!" There was a desperate urgency in his voice. "Darling, for God's sake, will you please *listen*?"

"I am listening."

"The woman who was murdered was wearing a *red raincoat*! A *red raincoat* with a *red hood*!"

Dorothy-Anne went stone cold, a sudden frisson rippling through her.

Could someone have thought it was me?

For a moment she felt a strident sense of menace, of events spinning out of control. Her hand shook, knocking the receiver against her ear.

Hunt was saying: "From the description, her coat was exactly like yours."

Dorothy-Anne quashed the feeling of imminent danger.

How ridiculous! she thought. *I mustn't overreact. If I let every newspaper headline spook me, then good night, nurse! I have enough problems without looking for more.*

"Hunt, I'm neck deep in this hurricane, and I've got to see Arne off with the FLASH contracts. We'll talk later?"

"Dorothy-Anne, *please*! Promise me you'll be careful!"

"I will. And stop *worrying* so much about—"

She broke off in midsentence, suddenly aware of the drama being played out halfway across the office. Something had gone terribly wrong with the *tableau vivant*.

Cecilia was leaning forward and starting to get to her feet. But Cecilia, bouncy Cecilia, energetic, acerbic, no-nonsense Cecilia, remained seated. Frowning and looking confused. Saying something that made Venetia and Arne exchange horrified glances.

Then Cecilia turned her head and stared over at Dorothy-Anne with huge, frightened eyes.

"Dorothy-Anne?" Hunt's voice was saying. "Darling, are you there?"

But she didn't hear him. The receiver slipped from her hand, and even before it hit the floor, she was rushing across the room. "Nooooooooo!" she cried. "God, noooooooooo!"

"Help me!" Cecilia screamed. "I can't get up! My legs won't move!"

"Call 911!" Dorothy-Anne shouted at Venetia.

Venetia stood there, frozen.

"Now!"

Venetia snapped out of it and lunged for the nearest phone. Dorothy-

Anne's arm blurred, knocking the box of cookies out of Arne's hand. The maple box and cookies went flying.

"What the—?" he began.

"Don't eat them!"

With dawning realization, Arne stared at the two cookies in his hand. Then he flung them away as though they were snakes.

"I-I'm . . . paralyzed," Cecilia whispered. She had broken out in a sweat and was having trouble breathing.

Dorothy-Anne dropped to her knees beside her chair and took her hand. "EMS is on its way," she told her. "You're going to be all right."

Cecilia tried to focus on Dorothy-Anne's face, but everything seemed blurred and out of focus. She shook her head, and struggled to get enough breath. "No. I'm going to die."

"You won't!" Dorothy-Anne said forcefully, but even as she said it, she knew she was lying. Tears streamed down her face. "I won't let you die, Cecilia! Hang in there! Damn it, stay with us! Help's on the way!"

Cecilia's breath rasped heavily and she leaned her head back against the chair. When she spoke, her lips twisted with the agony of effort. "I'm . . . sorry. I've . . . let . . . you down."

"You've never let me down," Dorothy-Anne sobbed. "Not once." She shook Cecilia's hand. "Do you hear me? Cecilia?"

But Cecilia was staring up at the ceiling with glazed, unseeing eyes. She was already dead.

In the distance, Dorothy-Anne could hear the wails of approaching sirens.

They're too late, she thought miserably. And she knew something else too. Cecilia wasn't supposed to die. *Those cookies were meant for me.*

Someone was trying to kill her.

H unt was not psychic. Nor did he need any of Dionne War-
wick's—ahem!—psychic friends to tell him something was terribly wrong in White Plains.

After Dorothy-Anne had dropped the phone, what he'd heard in the
background (he couldn't make out the words, exactly, but the tone was
enough to goose anybody), he sprang into action.

First, he paged Bob Stewart, the pilot of Winslow Communications'
Falcon 50 jet. Then, not bothering to pack a single suitcase, he jumped
into his Buick Park Avenue and headed out to the airport.

The pilot called him on the car phone. "You left a message, Mr.
Winslow?"

"Yes, Bob. I'm on my way to SFO. I need to fly to New York. ASAP."

When they arrived at the town house, Dorothy-Anne was shaking so
badly she fumbled and dropped her keys. Venetia picked them up and
unlocked the two dead bolts, then followed Dorothy-Anne inside.

The housekeeper, Mrs. Mills, was coming down the staircase. "Why,
Mrs. Cantwell!" she exclaimed. "We didn't expect . . ." Suddenly aware
of Dorothy-Anne's taut features and moist eyes, Mrs. Mills paused. "Is
something wrong?"

Yes. Everything.

Venetia started toward the living room, then backtracked when Dorothy-Anne remained in the foyer.

"Where are they?" Dorothy-Anne asked Mrs. Mills.

"Where are who, ma'am?"

Dorothy-Anne stared at her. *Who could I be talking about? My three
little Cantwelleers!*

"The children," she said impatiently.

The housekeeper frowned. "I'm not absolutely certain, ma'am, but I believe Liz and Fred are in their rooms. . . ."

Dorothy-Anne grasped hold of the newel post and leaned her head way back.

"Liz!" she called urgently up the stairwell. "Fred! Zack!"

Liz appeared on the third-floor landing, half hanging over the banister. "Hi, Mom!" she called down brightly. "What's up?"

Dorothy-Anne tottered and gasped, her hand flying to her breast. She could almost *see* the wood spindles splintering, could almost *hear* the banister railing crack as it gave way. And Liz, her precious daughter, plunging headfirst down the stairwell—to her death.

The vision was so appallingly vivid that something within Dorothy-Anne snapped.

"Elizabeth-Anne Cantwell!" she screamed. "How many times have I told you *not* to hang over the banister like that! You do that again and I'll . . . I'll . . ."

"Hey," Venetia said softly. "Ease up, honey."

Upstairs, Liz slowly unbent herself. "Jeez, mom. Like chill out."

Dorothy-Anne placed her fingertips against her forehead. *Dear God,* she thought, *I'm losing it.*

Then she pulled herself together.

I can't afford to lose it. I'm a mother with three children.

"Where's Fred?

"In his room," Liz said stiffly, from above. "Can't you, like, hear that bass beat? I bet they're complaining about it all the way over in Nanjing."

"And Zack? Where is he?"

Liz shrugged. "Beats me," she said loftily, and disappeared back into her room.

Dorothy-Anne spun around. "Mrs. Mills."

"Yes, ma'am?"

"Do you have any idea where Zack might be?"

"Let me think." Mrs. Mills tapped her lips with a finger and looked thoughtful. "The last I saw him, he was with Nanny Florrie. Yes. She was taking him to the park."

"At what time was this?" Dorothy-Anne's voice was pitched high. "Please, Mrs. Mills, *try* to remember! It's very important!"

"It was about . . . I remember now." Mrs. Mills nodded briskly. "Nine-thirty this morning."

"And they're not back yet? It's one o'clock, and they haven't had lunch?"

"Oh, dear," Mrs. Mills fretted. "I don't keep tabs on Nanny. . . ."

Dorothy-Anne pressed the back of a feverish, damp hand against her mouth. She stared at Venetia, who stared back at her.

"Girl? You're not thinking what I think you're thinking. Are you?"

"I have to," Dorothy-Anne said hoarsely. "Don't you see? After the murder outside the theater on Saturday . . . and now Cecilia . . . what better way is there to get to me but through one of the children?"

"Murder!" Mrs. Mills exclaimed. "What murder? Goodness gracious, what is going on?"

But neither Dorothy-Anne nor Venetia replied. They were already rushing back outside, racing down the front steps to the sidewalk, and then over toward Fifth Avenue and the green park beyond.

Central Park was the usual summer circus. RollerBladers in acid-hued Spandex flashed by at rocket speed. Bicyclists were out in full force, and ragamuffin skateboarders sported post-trendy grunge. Joggers in tights, sweatsuits, or combinations of the two ran laps, Walkmans on their hips and earphones on their heads.

Venetia, hands on her hips, did a panoramic eyesweep and shook her head. "Why," she moaned despairingly, "oh, *why* is it that when you're looking for someone specific, this place just seems to get bigger and bigger?"

"That's because it *is* big," Dorothy-Anne responded. "In this town, you're so used to everything being vertical that you lose your sense of perspective when it comes to open spaces."

"I suppose you're right," Venetia sighed. "Well? How do you want to work this? My idea is we split up."

Dorothy-Anne agreed. "I'll check north of here, where the British contingent of nannies usually congregate, and you check south. We'll meet back here in this spot in twenty . . ."

Dorothy-Anne paused in mid-sentence and pointed.

"Look! Way over there. Behind that copse of trees."

Venetia followed her hand. "You mean the police cars and that crowd of gawkers? Oh, baby! Surely you don't think—"

"Frankly, I don't know *what* to think anymore. But I have a bad feeling about this."

Venetia didn't waste any time. "Then let's go check that out first," she decided, and led the way.

Dorothy-Anne had to practically jog to keep up with Venetia's leggy stride. She wished she'd thought to change shoes, especially when they left the path and cut diagonally across the green. The moderate heels she and Venetia were wearing weren't made for the great outdoors; they sank into the grass, impeding their progress.

When they reached the crime scene, there were eight police blue-and-whites, each parked at a different angle; police band radios squawked from every car. The coroner's wagon was just arriving, and two uniforms cleared a path for it, holding aside a portion of the yellow crime scene tape that had been strung around trees, cordoning off the area.

With a blithe disregard for posted regulations, Venetia held up a section of the yellow tape.

"Quick!" she hissed. "Girl, what are you waiting for?"

Dorothy-Anne hesitated, then swiftly ducked underneath. Venetia followed.

"*Hey!* Hey, hey hey!" A gruff-voiced uniform cop came running. "Youse ladies! Can't ya read? Out. *Now!*"

The cop, cap pushed way back on his head, glared up at her. He was a good three inches shorter than Venetia, which put him at a distinct psychological disadvantage.

"Lady, you hard o' hearing?"

Venetia widened her stance, the better to stand her ground.

"Look, all I'm asking was if the victim was a plump Caucasian female. Large-bosomed, fleshy mouth, thinning fluff of red hair. Freckles . . . late forties . . . green eyes?"

The cop looked at her narrowly. "How do you know?" he asked suspiciously. "You the one called in this squeal?"

"I *don't* know," Venetia said calmly. "But the woman *we're* looking for fits that description. If it's her, she may be wearing a longish, dark, stitch-pleated skirt, probably blue or black or dark gray. A white, high-neck voile blouse with pearl buttons and a mock placket—"

"A mock *what?*"

A tall detective with a bald head and a little fringe of black hair had overheard them. He had a badge clipped to the lapel of his sport jacket and a bushy black mustache to compensate for the hair loss on his pate.

"I'll take over," he told the uniform. And to Dorothy-Anne and Venetia: "I'm Detective Passell."

He shoved his hands into his trouser pockets. First he looked thoughtfully at Venetia. Then he looked long and hard at Dorothy-Anne.

"One of you ladies know the victim?"

"That's what we're trying to find out," Venetia said.

"Mind identifying her? I've got to warn you, though. It's not a pretty sight."

Don't let it be Nanny Florrie, Dorothy-Anne prayed. *Please don't let it be anybody we know. Haven't we been through enough for one day?*

"I have one question," Dorothy-Anne said unsteadily. She took a deep, shuddering breath. "Was there . . . was there . . . anybody . . . with her?" She wanted to say, Was there a little boy, but was unable to voice her fears aloud.

"No, ma'am. The victim is alone."

"I'll do the identifying," Venetia decided. She took Dorothy-Anne's hand and squeezed it. "You stay right here."

Dorothy-Anne shook her head. "No. I have to see for myself. I won't rest until I do."

They followed Detective Passell, who said, "They're okay. They're with me." He led them to an immense shrub. A horseshoe of policemen stood around, staring down at a corpse.

"Excuse me, gentlemen," Passell said. "These ladies are here to identify the deceased."

The cops parted silently. Dorothy-Anne and Venetia drew close and looked down.

They were staring at Nanny Florrie. She looked heavier in death than in life. Her white blouse was dirty, her eyes were huge, and her head was at an odd angle. And then Dorothy-Anne realized why. She had very nearly been decapitated. The ground beneath her was soaked with blood, and a red necktie was loosely knotted around her throat.

"Ma'am?" Detective Passell said quietly.

Dorothy-Anne nodded and looked away and Venetia took her in her arms. "It's Nanny Florrie," Dorothy-Anne gasped. "Her full name is . . ." She swallowed and corrected herself. "Her full name *was* . . . Flora Dobbin Fergusson. She worked for me. She was my children's nanny."

He took out a small spiral-bound notebook and a Bic pen and jotted down the information.

"To the best of your knowledge, when was the last time anyone saw her alive?"

"When she . . . when she took my youngest son out this morning."

Dorothy-Anne fumbled in her purse, pulled out her wallet, and withdrew a recent wallet-size photograph of Zack. She thrust it at the detective. "Did you see him? Did anyone see my son?"

"Are you saying you son is missing?"

Dorothy-Anne nodded weakly.

Venetia said, "Detective, Mrs. Cantwell has suffered several bad shocks today. Could you come by the house? I think she'd better have a stiff drink and lie down."

Detective Passell nodded. "I'll have one of my men drive you both home. You'll be available?"

"Yes," Venetia said. She rattled off the address of the town house, which he wrote down in his notebook. "That was Mrs. Fergusson's address also."

Detective Passell clicked his fingers and a uniformed cop snapped to. "Drive these ladies home."

Dorothy-Anne nodded her thanks and followed the cop, Venetia holding onto her. The cop held open the rear door and they got in the backseat. Venetia gave him directions.

"It'll be okay," Venetia said softly. "We'll find Zack."

Dorothy-Anne slumped in the seat.

When they got out at the town house, Venetia thanked the cop and helped Dorothy-Anne up the front steps. The door was opened by Mrs. Mills.

"Mrs. Cantwell?"

Dorothy-Anne looked up slowly, her face weary.

Mrs. Mills said, "While I was checking around your office, a fax came in. It's still in the machine. I would have brought it down, but when I saw what it was, I thought I'd better not touch it."

Dorothy-Anne's voice was hoarse. "What is it?"

"Best you come upstairs and see for yourself, ma'am."

Dorothy-Anne and Venetia exchanged glances. "Is it about Zack?" Dorothy-Anne asked eagerly.

"I believe so. I'm not certain . . ."

Dorothy-Anne raced up the stairs and rushed into her office. The fax machine was on a table beside her desk, and she snatched up the paper. She let out a little cry.

The fax was a drawing executed by a child, and she recognized the artist at once. *Zack!* She knew, because she was his mother, and she'd seen and praised hundreds, probably thousands, of drawings he'd brought her over the years.

She held the fax with trembling fingers, staring at it. It was a drawing of . . . fish? No, sharks and a stingray! And a little boy watching them!

"Oh, *shit,*" Venetia exclaimed succinctly. "Do you recognize that place?"

"Of course I do. It's Eden Isle. He must have seen one of the planning videos or architectural photos or models."

"Oh, honey. Take a good look at the top line." Venetia ran a splendid wildberry-lacquered fingernail under it. "This one, that says where the fax originated."

Dorothy-Anne stared at the tiny print and her blood ran cold. She recognized the number at once. It was the fax number of Freddie's old office. The one in the Quonset hut on Eden Isle.

She felt the room blur and tilt and start to spin at a crazy angle. For a moment, she braced her arms on the desktop and shut her eyes. It was all she could do to fight the bile rising in her throat, and wait for the worst of the nausea to pass.

Someone had Zack . . . and that someone knew how to contact her.

As they stood there, the fax machine clicked on and hummed, breaking the silence. They all stared at is as another incoming message was received.

Dorothy-Anne snatched the paper out of the machine. It, too, originated from Eden Isle, and the hand-printed message was succinct.

IF YOU WANT TO SEE YOUR SON AGAIN
DO NOT INVOLVE THE POLICE

Downstairs, the front doorbell chimed. All three of them gave a start. Mrs. Mills started across the room to the second-floor intercom. "No!" Dorothy-Anne said urgently. "Don't answer that!"

"Honey, it's probably the police," Venetia said.

"I know! That's what I'm afraid of!"

"But you have to talk to them."

"No." Dorothy-Anne shook her head vehemently. "Don't you see? Zack is on Eden Isle! And the island's been evacuated!"

"And the hurricane . . ." Venetia smacked her forehead with the fleshy palm of her hand. "Oh, sweet baby Jesus. What are you going to do?"

"I'm going downstairs. I'll hide in the coat closet. . . . Mrs. Mills!"

"Ma'am?"

"When you let the police in, bring them up here, into the study. Have them wait while you ostensibly look for me."

Mrs. Mills fidgeted nervously. "I'm afraid I'm not very good at lying. Especially to the police."

"You won't be lying," Dorothy-Anne said. "You'll be procrastinating."

"And you?" Venetia asked. "What will you be up to?"

"As soon as the cops are upstairs, I'll slip out and hail a cab."

The door chimes sounded again, longer and more insistent.

"I've got to hurry," Dorothy-Anne said. "Don't tell anyone where I'll be. If Hunt calls, you can tell him where I'm headed."

"You're not thinking of flying to Eden Isle!"

"What do you expect me to do!" Dorothy-Anne snapped. "Let some killer do to Zack what he did to Nanny Florrie?"

68

In the taxi to the airport, Dorothy-Anne used her cellular phone to order Hale One to be prepared for immediate takeoff. She'd been specific about the crew: she wanted only the pilot and copilot.

When Captain Larsen asked her what flight plan to file, she'd simply said, "Miami." She would tell him their real destination once they were under way. Otherwise, air traffic control would never give them clearance to take off. Her biggest concern was that Captain Larsen might refuse to fly to Eden Isle. As the pilot of Hale One, he had the option to countermand any of her orders if it put the aircraft, its passengers, or its crew at risk.

When she boarded the 757-200, Captain Larsen gave her a weather update: "We'll have clear sailing the whole way."

She nodded, not about to burst his bubble . . . yet. "Could you please inform me when we reach cruising altitude?"

"Sure thing, ma'am."

"The sooner we take off, the better."

Dorothy-Anne made her way aft along the narrow portside corridor. She settled herself into the luxurious beige, brown, fawn, russet, and black cocoon that comprised the salon, buckled herself into a suede sofa, and for once didn't bother to activate the coromandel screens that would slide across the portholes at the touch of a button. Her fear for Zack far outweighed any anxiety she harbored for takeoffs.

Zack. She thought about him every single moment now. Zack, her youngest and sweetest. The most innocent and angelic of all three children.

And someone has snatched him, she thought. *Someone has taken him to Eden Isle, directly in the path of the hurricane, just to lure me there.*

Why? What possible reason could anybody have?

She never noticed the takeoff; the jet hurtling down the runway and climbing steeply up into the sky. She wasn't aware of anything until the intrajet intercom buzzer sounded.

She flipped a switch built into the cocktail table. "Yes?"

"It's Captain Larsen, ma'am. You asked to be notified when we reached cruising altitude."

"Thank you, captain. Could you have the copilot take over? I need to see you for a moment."

"Of course."

Less than a minute later, Captain Larsen knocked on the door of the salon and entered.

"We'll be landing in Miami in two hours and thirty-three minutes," he said.

"Captain Larsen, may I ask you a personal question?"

"Yes, ma'am."

"You're married, I know."

"Yes."

"Do you have any children?"

He smiled. "Four of them, two girls and two boys."

Dorothy-Anne looked at her hands. They were tightly curled in her lap. *Four children,* she thought. *And I want to put their father at such risk.* For a moment she was tempted to have him turn the plane around and go back.

Then she raised her head and looked at him directly. "I have three children, captain."

He smiled. "I know. It's been a pleasure to have them aboard."

"What I'm about to tell you is confidential, captain."

"I understand, ma'am."

"My youngest," she began, speaking with difficulty. She inhaled deeply. "My youngest, Zack, as been kidnapped."

"*What!*"

"Also, I'm sure you remember my children's governess, Nanny Florrie?"

"How could I forget?" He smiled faintly.

"Nanny Florrie was murdered sometime today. I identified the body."

"Ho-ly shit! Er, sorry about my language. It's just that—"

"I understand."

Dorothy-Anne unclasped her seat belt, got up, and began pacing the full-width cabin. "I have reason to believe that the person who kidnapped Zack and killed Nanny Florrie is after me."

She stopped at one of the portholes and leaned down. Far below,

New Jersey slid beneath the aircraft. When she straightened, she crossed the cabin and stood in front of Captain Larsen.

"What I am going to ask of you, captain, is probably a federal crime. I'll make it well worth your while. There's a million-dollar bonus in it for you, and a half a million for the copilot."

"What do you want to do? Have us fly you to Cuba?"

"Not quite. However, I want you to know several things. First, you have the option of refusing. Second, if you refuse, I won't think any less of you. And third, your employment will in no way be jeopardized, if you decide not to indulge me. Are we clear on that?"

"Yes, ma'am."

Dorothy-Anne held his gaze. "It's your choice, captain."

"Where do you want to go, Mrs. Cantwell?"

"Where Zack is being held. I just want to be dropped off there. You can continue on back."

"And where is this place?"

"Eden Isle," she answered quietly.

Hunt's Falcon 50 had been airborne for an hour and a half. He had tried calling Dorothy-Anne's office, and was told she'd left for the day. He'd tried her car phone, and nobody picked up. Now, somewhere over Rock Springs, Wyoming, he called the town house.

"Cantwell residence," a rich contralto answered.

"Venetia?" he said, surprised to hear her pick up.

"It is myself. Hunt, is that you?

"None other. Is the lady of the house in?"

Venetia hesitated. She was in Dorothy-Anne's study, and Detective Passell and another guy, his partner, a detective by the name of Finch, were both within earshot. Moreover, they were stewing mad—believing, correctly, that Dorothy-Anne had pulled a fast one on them.

"Look, Hunt," Venetia said carefully, "I really don't want us to date anymore."

"*Huh?*"

"You heard me. You want a lady to have a fling with? I suggest you go to that club . . . what's it called? Eden Isle?"

"You can't talk," Hunt guessed.

"Now you're turning into a regular Einstein."

His voice was incredulous. "Are you telling me that Dorothy-Anne is on her way to Eden Isle? Right *now?*"

"That is exactly what I am saying."

"But it's . . . it's directly in the path of Hurricane Cyd!"

"Don't talk to me. Tell that to your sweetheart at the Eden. You need the phone number?"

"It's the jet, right? The 757?"

"That's right," Venetia said sweetly. "And baby, do me a favor? Don't call *me* again. We're through. *Finito. Kaput!*"

She slammed down the receiver and looked at the detectives. "I guess you heard that." She shrugged. "Boyfriend trouble."

69

There the bitch is! Amber watched as Gloria Winslow, dressed in a bright citron pantsuit, exited the Huntington Hotel. She had on big dark sunglasses and was carrying a handbag. Looking very glamorous, chatting with a doorman.

Amber brushed strands of stringy hair out of her eyes. *What's she up to today?* she wondered.

Amber had been watching and waiting, watching and waiting.

Waiting for just the right moment to—*to get even!*

Today she'd borrowed Doreen and Roy's Jeep Wrangler. Doreen was a topless dancer she knew, and for gas money and a little extra, she and Roy let her use the Wrangler from time to time.

She jerked up when she saw Gloria's familiar Mercedes pull up in front of the hotel. A man got out and held the door open for Gloria, who slid into the car.

Good! Amber thought, starting the Jeep. *The bitch is driving someplace today. And I can follow her.*

She put the Jeep in first gear, and waited as Gloria slowly pulled out onto the street. Then Amber let out on the clutch, gave the Jeep gas, and eased up behind her. She didn't have to worry about being spotted. After all, the woman didn't even know she existed.

She followed her west on Sacramento a few blocks, then took a right just behind her onto Van Ness Avenue, heading north. Amber shifted up into third gear, then fourth, rolling along at a steady clip. Traffic on Van Ness wasn't too bad this afternoon. Rush hour hadn't started yet. But Amber was oblivious to everything but the Mercedes. She let Gloria get a couple of cars in front of her, but didn't let the glittering car get out of her sight.

After several blocks, she saw Gloria angle over into the left lane as they approached Richardson Avenue, Highway 101. Amber pulled up directly behind her when Gloria put on her turn signal at the traffic light. When the light changed, she took a left on Highway 101, Amber on her tail. Now Gloria picked up speed and Amber followed suit, giving the Jeep gas.

Cruising west along Highway 101 at a steady pace, then north as 101 curved toward the Golden Gate Bridge, Amber wondered: *Is she going to take the bridge? Going to Marin County somewhere?*

Only a few minutes later, she had her answer. Gloria was taking the approach to the Golden Gate, and Amber trailed along behind her, watching the Mercedes roll majestically along in front of her. The wind up here was powerful and buffeted the Wrangler, but Amber felt no fear. No. She felt exhilarated by the task at hand.

The end of the bridge neared, and she saw Gloria put on her right turn signal. *What? Right? Where the hell is the crazy bitch going now?* Amber wondered. She downshifted from fourth into third, put on her turn signal, then downshifted again as they approached the turnoff.

After the right turn, Amber realized what Gloria's destination was.

Jeezus! She nearly wet her pants with excitement. The old drunk was going up into the Marin Headlands. The perfect place to . . . *wipe her off the face of the earth!*

She watched the shiny metallic Mercedes curve up, up, up, into the vast hills overlooking San Francisco Bay and the city itself beyond. It was a sunny, clear day with almost no fog, but Amber didn't notice the spectacular scenery. Her eyes were glued to the car just ahead of her. There wasn't a single vehicle between them now. The Headlands were practically deserted.

Gloria was nearing the highest point of the brownish green hills, driving very slowly, apparently taking in the view. Two or three times, she nearly stopped, and Amber could see her take off her sunglasses, looking out over the bay to San Francisco.

She eased up directly behind her now and waited for Gloria to pick up a little speed. When she did, Amber caught up with her, then downshifted into second gear and gave the Jeep gas, revving it up as far as it would go in second.

She braced herself and rammed the rear end of the Mercedes, immediately letting off on the gas. The impact jerked Amber backward, then threw her forward. The seat belt kept her from slamming into the steering wheel.

Hot damn! she thought. *This is just like that time Christos took me to play bumper cars.*

Gloria slowed down the Mercedes and Amber could see her head jerk around. When she did, Amber put the Jeep in reverse and backed up a few feet. Then, shifting into first, up to second, she gave the Jeep gas again and rammed the Mercedes hard, on the left side of the rear. The Mercedes fishtailed toward the steep hillside, then jerked to a stop.

There! That'll give the crazy bitch something to think about!

She watched as the Mercedes started moving again, picking up speed. Gloria had obviously decided to get away from here. After a moment, Amber shifted up into second, then third, pulling to the left of the Mercedes, getting on the driver's side, up to the rear door. She could see the old bitch jerking around to try to see her. Could see that she still had her sunglasses off, her eyes real big. Then she floored the gas pedal, ramming the door hard. The car jerked to the right. Swerving off the road again, over the shoulder, then skidded to a stop. But Gloria quickly started moving forward again, angling up toward the road, picking up more speed.

Up ahead about seventy-five feet, Amber could see that a sharp curve—nearly ninety degrees!—to the left was coming up.

This is it! she thought. *This is where I pay the bitch back!*

She quickly caught up with the Mercedes and rammed into the rear end hard, giggling as she watched it jerk forward but keep on going, faster now.

Amber stayed right on its tail, giving the Jeep gas, then rammed it again, harder. And again, harder yet.

The Mercedes zigged, zagged, swung right, and bounced off the hillside. Then it plunged out of sight.

Amber stomped on the brakes, jumped out of the Jeep, and ran to the drop-off. She had to stand at the very edge to look down.

Far below, the Mercedes was rolling over and over until it smashed into the rocks along the shoreline and exploded.

The ground beneath Amber's feet shook, and a fireball enveloped the Mercedes.

Amber stared down for another minute, then walked slowly to the Jeep and drove off sedately.

You've got to be careful on this road, she thought. *It can be a real killer.*

70

Two hundred miles north of Puerto Rico, Captain Larsen turned on the seat belt sign.

"Better strap yourself in, Mrs. Cantwell," he said over the speaker system. "From here on in, things are liable to get bumpy."

Dorothy-Anne pressed the intrajet intercom. "Would you mind terribly if I joined you in the cockpit? Right now it's a little . . . quiet back here."

"If that's what you want, ma'am. It's your aircraft."

Dorothy-Anne hurried forward along the portside corridor. So far the skies were still clear, and the Atlantic Ocean far below looked deceptively calm.

When she appeared in the cockpit, Captain Larsen said, "Use that jump seat, there, Mrs. Cantwell. It folds down."

"Please," Dorothy-Anne said. "We're in this together, so let's drop the formalities, shall we? Call me Dorothy-Anne."

"And I'm Jim, as you know. And our copilot here is Pete."

Dorothy-Anne got the seat down, secured it, and strapped herself in.

"Did you get permission to change the route?" Dorothy-Anne asked.

Jim Larsen grinned. "We used the old noggin. Radioed in a change in our flight plan. Supposedly, we're headed to Caracas. Of course, San Juan will soon know we're off course. Can't fool radar."

"I hope this won't cost you your licenses. If it does, I'll think of something." She smiled humorlessly. "Maybe build some eco-resorts in the African veldt."

Jim Larsen grinned. "My boyhood dream always was to become a bush pilot."

"Get us through this alive, and your dream just might come true,"

Dorothy-Anne said wryly. Suddenly she leaned forward and squinted out the tinted windshield. "What in the name of God is *that*?"

A wall of looming, charcoal gray clouds extended from the surface of the ocean high into the sky, like a range of angry mountains on the move.

"That," said Jim Larsen, with admirable understatement. "is the leading edge of the storm. Say hello to Cyd."

"Holy Moses!"

"According to the latest reports, it's moving north at ten miles an hour and accelerating. Winds are exceeding one hundred fifty m.p.h., and it's been upgraded to a category five."

"If that's the leading edge, how far away is the storm proper?"

"About a hundred sixty miles south of Eden Isle."

"So it won't really hit for sixteen hours."

"Sooner. It's accelerating, which means it might hit full force as fast as eight hours from now. If it weren't for the clouds, we'd be seeing Puerto Rico."

"Then we're almost there."

At that moment, they hit a pocket of turbulence. The fuselage shook violently, and the aircraft dropped sickeningly straight down, as if it had lost its wings. After a few hundred feet it regained its forward momentum.

"Shit!" Dorothy-Anne whispered. "That was not fun."

"No," Jim Larsen agreed. "And the fun hasn't even begun. Once we hit the outer edge gales, you'll think you spent all day on a roller coaster."

The next winds to buffet the jet lifted it several hundred feet higher in one fell swoop. Jim Larsen fought with the controls.

"I think I know what they mean when people say 'bucking like a bronco,'" Dorothy-Anne said queasily. She was white as a sheet, and sick to her stomach.

"Actually, I've been in worse," Jim said calmly.

"I haven't," Pete said from the copilot's seat.

"Boeing 989 Charlie, this is San Juan Center," a voice crackled over the speakers. "We suggest you turn seven degrees west and skirt hurricane. Over."

"Negative, San Juan Center," Jim Larsen said steadily. "We only have enough fuel for a direct flight to Caracas. Over."

"Roger, Boeing 989 Charlie. Do you request permission to land at San Juan? Over."

"Negative, San Juan Center. Winds are too unpredictable. If landing is aborted we'll run out of fuel. Proceeding directly to Caracas at thirty-two thousand feet. Over."

"Roger, Boeing 989 Charlie. Proceed on course. Over and out."

"Won't they realize what we're doing when we descend?" Dorothy-Anne asked.

"They'll think it was an emergency. I'll radio back that we landed safely. And we're descending slowly already."

"I don't know much about these things, but how will you find the runway?"

"We'll execute an automatic instrument landing. Simply follow the Eden Isle beacon."

"But the island's been evacuated! Nobody's at the control tower."

"That doesn't matter. So long as there's electricity—and if that goes out, there's an automatic backup generator. It's good for up to four hours."

Jim put the 757 into a wide sweeping turn and ten minutes later, he began the descent. Soon they were no longer above the hurricane, but inside the gray clouds, buffeted by gale-force winds from all sides. Dorothy-Anne clenched her teeth and gripped her seat until her knuckles were white. She didn't know when she'd been so scared. Visibility was zero, with shreds of clouds whipping past.

Pete called out the altimeter readings: "Twenty-six thousand . . . twenty-five thousand, five hundred . . . twenty-five thousand feet . . ."

The lower their altitude, the more they were at the mercy of the winds. Dorothy-Anne wasn't sure how much more shuddering the fuselage or wings could take.

"Locked into automatic landing beacon," Jim said, glancing at the computerized screen. "Bringing her down to fifteen thousand feet."

Except for the shakes, rattles, and rolls, the cockpit was silent. Nobody spoke. The tension kept ratcheting up, notch after notch.

Eight thousand feet . . . seven thousand . . . six . . .

Visibility was zero, and wind-whipped rain blasted the aircraft. It wobbled and wavered, but Jim Larsen kept it on course, his eyes glued to the glowing green screen of a computer. The gridwork, with its perspective of a runway, kept shifting according to the plane's position, while the constantly changing readout tracked both the aircraft's true position and its ideal altitude and degree.

"Flaps are lowered," Jim said.

"Two thousand feet," Pete reported. "Fifteen hundred . . . one thousand . . ."

"Landing gear down," Jim announced.

Dorothy-Anne hardly felt the wheels descend and lock into place; it was as if they were in an earthquake.

What if the beacon is wrong? she thought in a sudden panic. *Or the computer that's guiding us if off a few degrees?*

"Decreasing airspeed," Jim said.

"Five hundred feet . . . four hundred . . ."

Jim fought to keep the nose of the jet up, and Dorothy-Anne noticed that both he and Pete were sweating profusely. Rain thrashed the windshield, drummed on the fuselage.

"One hundred feet," Pete read off. "Sixty feet . . ."

"According to the screen, the runway's below us . . . *now*," Jim said.

What if the construction crew made a mistake? Dorothy-Anne thought. *What if they made the runway too short?*

"Let's set her down," Jim said calmly.

Dorothy-Anne clutched her seat, prepared for the jet to land on its nose and begin flipping somersaults with its wings. Then she felt a familiar bump, a bounce, another bump, and the engines were screaming in reverse.

"Welcome to Eden Isle," Jim Larsen said.

Dorothy-Anne sat there, frozen to her seat. They were safe and on the ground, but it didn't register. Suddenly she was sick.

Jim handed her a bag, and she vomited into it. When her heaving stopped, she simply sat there, barely realizing the jet was not moving.

"I suggest you gear up for this weather," Jim told her.

She nodded and undid her seat belt and started aft. "I've got changes of clothes back in . . . in—"

Suddenly she vomited again.

"In my cabin," she said faintly.

Five minutes later, she had changed into khaki slacks, a long-sleeved shirt, lace-up hiking boots, and a heavy raincoat. Jim Larsen handed her two objects.

"First, here's a waterproof flashlight," he said. "And second, here's the gun we keep onboard."

It was a pistol in a plastic Zip-Loc baggie.

"I think you may need it more than we do. Careful, though. It's loaded. The chamber holds six shells. As a safety precaution, the first one's empty. That gives you five shots."

Dorothy-Anne pocketed the flashlight and the pistol both. "I can't express how grateful I am."

"There's time for that later. Sorry there's no jetway or boarding stairs. Pete and I will lower you down as far as we can. When we let go, cock your legs, try to land on the balls of your feet, and roll over."

She nodded, and on impulse hugged them both. Then Jim Larsen opened the cabin door and slid it aside.

The noise of the wind and rain was incredible, and Jim had to shout to make himself heard.

"You're on your own now. We'll be taking right off again. Otherwise there won't be much left of this plane." He paused. "Ready?"

As ready as I'll ever be, she thought, and nodded. Jim and Pete held her by the arms and lowered her. She nodded when she was ready for them to let go.

The fall seemed to take longer than she anticipated. She'd forgotten how high the jet stood of the ground.

Then her feet hit the tarmac, and she rolled.

I'm here, she thought in astonishment. *Even more amazing, I've made it here alive!*

After Hale One turned around and hurtled down the runway, engines screaming, and lifted off into the gray, almost maroon sky, Dorothy-Anne noticed another jet parked by the terminal building. Ducking forward to avoid the worst of the slashing rain, she ran over to the aircraft.

It was a small Citation I. Its door was open, and the folding boarding steps were down. She felt for the pistol in her pocket, seeking reassurance.

"Hello?" she yelled, approaching cautiously. *"Hello?"*

There was no reply. Carefully she moved up the steps. The pilot was in his seat.

But he would never fly again.

He had been shot in the back of the head.

71

Eden Isle was like Dante's inferno. What little sun leaked through the clouds gave them an ominous reddish cast, a surreal quality more suited to a Tim Burton film than a tropical paradise. The barometric pressure continued to plunge even lower, and the winds had risen to a steady forty-five miles per hour, with gusts of up to sixty.

And that's just the beginning, Dorothy-Anne knew. *Soon it will get worse. A whole lot worse.*

The approaching hurricane aside, Dorothy-Anne realized she had an even more dangerous enemy to worry about—namely, the faceless killer or killers who had gone through the trouble of luring her here. The same assassins, most likely, who had been responsible for a series of murders, from sabotaging Freddie's jet to murdering the woman in the red raincoat; from poisoning Cecilia to killing Nanny Florrie; and, most recently, who had shot the pilot of the Citation I.

She had to find out where Zack was being held captive—and fast. *Before* the full force of Hurricane Cyd hit the island.

Where the devil could they be keeping him?

Think! she told herself. *Think!*

The faxed drawing had depicted Predator's Lagoon. And the only inhabitable structures on Eden Isle—the temporary boomtown of Quonset huts, trailers, and RVs—the only real *shelters* were located just east of the lagoon, and north of the Oceanographic Institute.

That's got to be where they are.

Head tucked down, she struggled against the oncoming gusts of wind and made her way to the parking lot at the back of the terminal. Another squall of rain beat down at a crazy angle, each wind-driven drop stinging like a needle.

The first vehicle she came across she dismissed. This was no weather for a canvas-roofed Jeep Wrangler. She needed something heavier.

And there it was. One of the green Range Rovers.

Now this is more like it!

As expected, the vehicle was unlocked, and the keys were in the ignition. But when she opened the driver's side door, the wind tore it out of her hand. Soaked to the skin, she climbed inside, tugging the door shut with both hands.

She fell back against the seat, exhausted before she'd even begun. For a moment she just sat there, struggling to catch her breath. She was tense and cold and her teeth were chattering. The plunging barometric pressure, combined with the intense humidity, made her feel sluggish.

But sluggishness was not a luxury she could afford.

Switching on the windshield wipers, she put the Rover in four-wheel drive and backed out, then headed south, taking the shell-paved road that circled the perimeter of the island. Although it was several hours until sunset, it was eerily dark, and she switched on the brights.

Powerful gusts of wind thrashed the Rover, and Dorothy-Anne struggled to maintain a straight course. Shells, sand, and pebbles blasted the vehicle like hail. The palm trees along the road were bent in arcs, their fronds flapping sideways like shredded green flags, and the sea was angry: black as pitch and full of white-capped waves leaping in anticipation.

Holy shit! she thought. *And this is just the outer edge of the storm!*

What would it be like when it hit full force?

Carmine waited, the picture of calm and patience. It wouldn't be long now.

That good old maternal instinct. It works every time.

Carmine glanced over at the boy. Zack stared back from the chair to which he was duct-taped, his eyes huge and frightened. He was whimpering, a sound that was muffled by the tape across his mouth.

Something—a branch, or perhaps a piece of lumber—crashed onto the metal roof of the Quonset hut that served as the mess hall and kitchen. Zack's muffled whimper increased in volume.

What an idiot, Carmine thought. *He's more afraid of the storm than of me!*

Carmine didn't bother to look up, too busy chopping underripe tomatoes on the butcher block. Who would have thought? The storeroom had everything on hand for making some nice *pomodori alla Siciliana.*

Just because a hurricane was coming didn't mean you had to starve.

Hunt had gained time by changing the flight plan and cutting diagonally from Wyoming down to Baton Rouge. During the brief stopover, he'd dropped off his pilot and had the Falcon 50 refueled.

That done, he lost no time in taking off. He was flying the rest of this trip solo.

The final leg of his flight would cut another diagonal—across the Gulf of Mexico to the tip of Florida. From there, he planned to angle past the northern coast of Haiti and the Dominican Republic, and approach Eden Isle head-on from the west. Flying blindly and relying on an instrument landing.

At least, that was his plan.

It's suicide, the instinctive half of his brain told him.

But the cognitive half knew better. The alternative was worse. He could be doomed to a slower, and far more painful, death:

Life without Dorothy-Anne.

It wouldn't be worth living.

He wondered what she was doing now, this very minute. . . .

Driving the Range Rover as fast as she dared, that's what. The strident winds had risen to a steady fifty-five miles per hour, with howling gusts of up to seventy. Here and there, small trees and torn branches already littered the road. Loose palm fronds and leaves flew crazy loops through the air.

Thank God for four-wheel drive, Dorothy-Anne thought, blessing its unknown inventor. As she passed the skeletal Grand Victoria Hotel, she slowed and inched her window down to see how the structure was holding up. So far, so good. Its framework was wood, and wood was pliant. . . .

She drove past the giant free-form swimming pool, which was fast filling with rainwater, and on past Predator's Lagoon and the Oceanographic Institute. When she reached the outskirts of the temporary boomtown, she slowed down, killed the lights, and parked.

This was as far as she dared drive.

From here on, extreme caution was called for.

It was time to proceed on foot.

Dorothy-Anne opened the door of the Range Rover. Unprepared for the force of the wind, the door was torn from her grasp and swung wide.

Damn!

Well, at least she didn't have to worry about making noise. Everywhere, loose corrugated metal boomed like thunder, adding to the banshee shrieks of the wind and the snare drum staccato of rain hitting with the force of nails.

Each drop felt like a stinging barb.

She looked around, wondering where to begin her search. She had forgotten how many trailers and Quonset huts there were—literally blocks of them!

To save time, she decided to start with the main drag, the double-wide dirt road that divided the settlement in two. She would be exposed, true, but it might help narrow down her search.

Staying in the lee of the buildings to avoid the worst of the rain, she started walking, the sea of mud sucking at her boots, making every step an effort.

She shivered violently. There was something chilling and eerie about the settlement, like a ghost town from which everyone had inexplicably vanished.

She put her hand in the pocket of the raincoat where she kept the pistol. It felt heavy, but even through the baggie, the weight of the cold steel was oddly reassuring.

And the funny thing was, she hated guns.

"Falcon 618 Echo, this is San Juan Center." The crackling voice filled Hunt's ears. "We suggest you turn eighteen degrees south and skirt the hurricane. Over."

Hunt did not respond.

"Falcon 618 Echo. Repeat, this is San Juan Center. Do you copy? Over."

Hunt took off his headphones and tossed them aside. He switched off the radio.

Ahead and directly below, as far as the eye could see, stretched an angry, roiling sea of black clouds.

Hurricane Cyd.

From here on, he was flying straight into a nightmare. He would need his full powers of concentration. The least distraction could prove fatal.

As if to prove him right, he hit a pocket of turbulence. The small jet was tossed about like a toy.

And even as Hunt fought to regain control, the aircraft went into a nosedive. Engines screaming, it plunged toward earth.

72

On Eden Isle, the winds had risen to a steady fifty-eight miles per hour, with gusts of up to seventy-five.

Dorothy-Anne was on her own, and no one knew it better than she. It was too late to expect Hunt to come streaking to the rescue. The distance he had to travel was too far. The soonest he could possibly make it—and that was stretching things—was an hour from now. By then the winds would be too powerful for even a madman to attempt a landing.

Therefore, whoever was responsible for kidnapping Zack and killing the pilot of the Citation I—not to mention the murders of Nanny Florrie and Cecilia—would have to be dealt with by . . .

Dorothy-Anne flinched and heard her own sharp intake of breath.

. . . me.

It was the only option open to her. And if she died doing it, well, then so be it.

I'm Zack's mother. It's up to me to protect and rescue him from harm.

Her maternal flame burned brightly. Even brighter than—could it be?—was she hallucinating?—no—two lit windows!

There, on the flat side of the last Quonset hut on the left.

"Thank you, Lord!" she breathed.

Hurrying now, she sloughed through the squelching, deepening mud, oblivious to the spikes of rain hitting her face head-on. She dared feel a surge of hope.

In her rush, Dorothy-Anne tripped over a branch and fell. She caught herself at the very last moment by breaking her fall with one arm. When she scrambled back to her feet, she made a face of disgust. The mud was eight inches deep, and her right arm was filthy up to the elbow.

No matter. The rain would wash it off in no time.

And suddenly she was there. At the last Quonset hut. From up close, the lights inside shone brighter and more welcoming than she imagined. She was about to rush to the door and throw it open when some atavistic instinct slowed her.

Careful . . .

She crept up to the nearest window, pressed herself flat against the corrugated aluminum wall, and leaned her head slightly forward. Peering in from a sideways angle, so that she could look in, but wouldn't be noticed by anyone inside.

Just in case . . .

She glimpsed neat rows of utilitarian dining tables and stackable resin chairs. A long serving counter with steam tables. A big stainless steel restaurant range. And . . . were her eyes deceiving her?—a plump woman working at a counter! Cooking away as if nothing out of the ordinary were going on . . . as if the approaching hurricane were a mere inconvenience!

Dorothy-Anne heaved a deep sigh of relief. *There's nothing to fear,* she thought, feeling an immense burden lift from her shoulders. *I must really be getting paranoid.*

And without further ado, she went over to the door. Holding tightly to the doorknob, lest the wind flung the door out of her grasp, she turned the knob and pushed.

The door was locked.

Dorothy-Anne knocked, at once realizing the futility of such etiquette. Knocks couldn't be heard above the roar of the wind and the banging of torn tree limbs and the occasional unidentified flying object hitting a wall.

She pounded on the door with her fists, desperate to get in, away from the wind and pelting rain. Even more desperate to ask the woman if she knew where the men were. And whether or not she'd seen a young boy of ten.

The door opened. The fat woman was silhouetted in the rectangle of yellow light. She was dressed in black, with a white apron half-folded over her waist and a little gold crucifix gleaming around her neck.

"Oh, you poor thing!" she clucked. "You're all dirty and wet. If you stay out in this, you're liable to catch your death. Come in, come in."

She tugged Dorothy-Anne inside and used all her considerable weight, and a well-aimed thrust of her hip, to slam the door shut against the blasting wind. She turned the key and locked it.

"Otherwise it'll constantly fly open," the fat woman explained. "But you've arrived in plenty of time for a lovely supper. It'll still be a while. Here, let me help you off with your coat."

It was then that Dorothy-Anne saw what was in the corner. Strategically placed so he couldn't be seen from the windows outside.

Zack! Her precious ten-year-old angel—duct-taped to a chair, his eyes wide with terror. Trying to whimper out a warning from between duct-taped lips.

It came out sounding: *"Humpf! Hummmmmph! Huh! Uhhhhh! Humpf—"*

"Zack!" Dorothy-Anne screamed. She started to rush to him, but at that moment something hard connected with the back of her skull and the world went black.

Hunt didn't try to kid himself. He had cheated death by mere seconds.

They were, bar none, the longest twenty seconds of his entire life, and he knew he would never forget them. Even now he could hardly believe he'd managed to pull the jet out of its dive. He'd used every last trick in the book from his Top Gun days—and disaster had been narrowly averted.

Hunt's heart, however, had yet to receive the message. It continued to jackhammer, both from the scare and the exertion of wrestling with the controls. Ditto the adrenaline that flooded his system. He was still in overdrive.

Jesus, that was close! he thought, eyes stinging from the sweat that trickled down his forehead.

He was highly tempted to turn the jet around and head back for the mainland.

He thought: *I won't be much use to Dorothy-Anne if I'm dead.*

That was a given.

On the other hand, I'm Dorothy-Anne's last hope. If I chicken out, she won't survive—period.

He stayed on course.

"Hang in there, baby," he growled, wishing he could send Dorothy-Anne an ESP telegram. "Eden Isle, here I come!"

Dorothy-Anne's eyelids quivered, as though in sleep, then suddenly snapped open. Everything was out of focus, as though she were underwater.

She tried to lift her hand to rub her eyes, but no matter how hard she struggled, her arm refused to obey her brain's command.

Oh my God! Her first reaction was: *I'm paralyzed! I can't move!*

She shook her head, attempting to jiggle her vision into focus, and instantly regretted it. The movement sent splinters of pain shooting from the back of her skull through her entire head.

But the shock of pain cleared her vision. And her mind.

I'm not paralyzed, she realized, with a sinking feeling. *Oh, God. I'm captive.*

She cursed, but the only sound she could make was: "Uh! Sheeeee *eeeeee!*"

Her lips wouldn't move . . . because they *couldn't!* Her mouth had been taped shut!

Slowly, with dawning horror and realization, Dorothy-Anne stared down at herself—and saw herself seated on a resin armchair. Her arms were duct-taped to the chair's, her legs to its legs. A tight, mummifying swath of silver duct tape around her middle made her part of the chair back, and still more constricting strips across her thighs held her firmly down to the seat.

Widening her field of vision, she registered that she was seated at a formica table. And that directly across from her—*Oh, sweet Jesus! Sweet baby Jesus!*—was Zack. Shuddering violently. Still bound to his chair. Still gagged. His big eyes wide with terror.

The sight of him broke Dorothy-Anne's heart. If only she could talk to him, hold him in her arms, somehow soothe him. Reassure him that everything was going to be all right.

But of course, that was impossible.

Nor was everything going to be all right.

Slowly Dorothy-Anne turned her head to the left. The fat woman was still cooking. At the moment, sprinkling flour on the butcher block surface while rolling out dough with a rolling pin. Now and then stopping to rub her fleshy pink forearm across her sweaty brow, and then continuing.

Closer in, two items on the table caught Dorothy-Anne's attention. One was the flashlight; the other was the pistol, still in its waterproof baggie, which Captain Larsen had given her.

Dorothy-Anne eyed the firearm like a parched person lost in the desert might gaze upon an oasis. She moved her fingers, first tentatively, then briskly. She clenched and unclenched her hands. But when she tried to wiggle her arms, she realized it was futile. There was no slack. Nor would there be any, no matter how hard she struggled.

And the pistol so tauntingly close . . . yet so unreachable!

Goddammit! she thought. *Goddammit all to hell! The fat bitch obviously put it there on purpose. To tease me!*

"Mumph!" Zack was trying to communicate with her.

Dorothy-Anne quickly shook her head to hush him. It was a mistake. The movement sent new bolts of pain piercing through her skull.

"You say something?" At the counter, the fat woman had stopped rolling dough and was regarding Dorothy-Anne through narrowed eyes.

Dorothy-Anne nodded, careful not to move her head too suddenly.

The woman frowned, as if mulling it over. Then she heaved a deep sigh, clapped flour off her hands, and wiped her fingers on her apron. She waddled over to the table and stood there, hands on her hips. "Well? You wanna talk?"

Dorothy-Anne gave a tiny nod.

"You gonna give me trouble like him?" The woman glanced a scowl at Zack. "You gonna yell and scream your head off and beg and cry?"

Dorothy-Anne shook her head.

"Okay. But you give me any lip?" A fleshy pink forefinger was wagged in Dorothy-Anne's face. "The tape goes back on. Understood?"

Dorothy-Anne nodded again, and the woman reached out and yanked the duct tape off her mouth.

It hurt like hell, but Dorothy-Anne fought down the cry of pain.

"You got something to say, say it. But I ain't got all day. I don't want my cannoli dough to dry up."

"Who . . . who are you?"

The woman puffed up. "They call me Mama Rosa," she said proudly. "Others know me simply as Carmine."

Dorothy-Anne frowned. "I don't understand. I thought Carmine was a man's name."

"Carmine is a man's name. That's the whole idea. See, no one knows Carmine's identity, and they *think* he's a man. They believe he's my son."

"But . . . why would you want to be known as him?"

"Because it's what I do. Carmine is a contract killer."

Dorothy-Anne opened her mouth, closed it, and opened it again. She stared at the woman. "You mean . . . you're hired to *kill* people?"

"That's right."

"And someone paid you to kill *me?*"

"Three million dollars." Mama Rosa nodded. "Carmine doesn't come cheap."

Dorothy-Anne stared at her, barely able to breathe. "Who hired you? Do you know?"

Mama Rosa shrugged. "Some Chinese."

And suddenly all the missing pieces of the jigsaw puzzle came together.

Whoever really owns Pan Pacific, Dorothy-Anne thought. *That's who put the contract out on me. They wanted me dead so they could foreclose.*

"I'll pay you six million to spare us."

"You can offer me a billion, and I still wouldn't take it. A contract's a contract."

My God. She's serious!

There was another question that needed answering.

"Are you responsible for my husband's plane crash?" Dorothy-Anne asked.

Mama Rosa smiled. "That was Carmine's work. Yes."

"And you intend to kill my son, too? A child of ten?"

"That can't be helped."

"But there's no contract out on him! He's innocent!"

"He could identify me. Now, if you don't mind, I've got to finish cooking."

"Why don't you just kill us and get it over with?" Dorothy-Anne snapped. "Why torture us and make us wait?"

"Because cooking is what Mama Rosa does best. That's why."

"Yes, but what's the point? What are you preparing that's so important at a time like this?"

Mama Rosa stared at her.

"You really don't know?"

"No, I don't."

"Your last supper. What else?"

73

Hunt was flying blind, descending through the turbulent storm clouds, his eyes on the computer screen.

The electronic beacon from Eden Isle came in crystal clear, the runway a foreshortened perspective on the green electronic grid.

Sure, it was a computer landing. But that wasn't all it was. Take away the video game–like screen, the state-of-the-art electronics, the high-tech doodads, and fancy-schmanzy gizmos, and what did you have?

Why, good old-fashioned seat-of-the-pants flying—that's what!

Now, fighting the killer winds, and flying on pure instinct, Hunt felt absolutely no fear, only the same indescribable thrill he'd felt when he first started flying.

He would make it. He would land this baby perfectly. He *knew* it!

He was a man on a mission—not to mention one hell of a pilot!

The Quonset hut shook, creaked, and rattled. Rivets were popping loose and one wall kept undulating. The storm outside screamed like a thousand Furies.

Hurricane Cyd was intensifying. The wind had picked up tremendous velocity. One of the other structures or trailers lost its roof or a sheet of its siding, and a giant piece of metal flipped through the air and hit the hut with a thud. Metal screeched against metal, and Dorothy-Anne was sure the Quonset hut would collapse.

That it remained standing was miraculous.

Mama Rose either didn't notice, or didn't care. She had laid three place settings and was sitting at the head of the table, saying grace:

"O Lord, bless this, our daily bread, which we are about to receive."

She crossed herself the old-fashioned way, sketching a tiny cross on her forehead, her lips, and her beasts.

"In nomine patris et filii et spiritu sanctu. Amen."

Neither Dorothy-Anne nor Zack responded.

To Dorothy-Anne, this meal—or "Last Supper," as Mama Rosa called it—was utterly surreal. Seated around a wood-grained formica table—she and Zack without gags, and with one arm free so they could use their spoons (no knives or forks for the prisoners). With paper napkins carefully tucked into their collars like children. And a feast which, on any other occasion, would have been a mouth-watering spread.

At the moment, however, just the *idea* of food was enough to turn Dorothy-Anne's stomach.

Mama Rosa used a big serving spoon and the tip of a chef's knife to serve the antipasto. She placed two stuffed tomatoes on each plate.

"This is called *pomodori alla Siciliana.* You'll like it." She gestured. "Go ahead. Eat! *Mange! Eat!*"

Dorothy-Anne stared down at her plate. *One bite,* she thought, *and I'll throw up.*

"Hey! What's the matter?"

Mama Rosa shoveled half a tomato into her mouth and talked while she chewed. She gestured at Dorothy-Anne's plate with a fork.

"You know how much trouble I went through to cook this?"

"How do I know it's not poisoned?" Dorothy-Anne retorted dully.

" 'Cause I'm eating it, too. Anyway, what's the big deal about *how* you're gonna die?" Mama Rosa rolled her eyes to heaven. "You either die one way, or you die another. That's life."

No, that's crazy, Dorothy-Anne thought. *She's insane. She needs to be locked away.*

Thinking Mama Rosa wasn't looking, Dorothy-Anne slowly moved her hand off the table and down to her lap.

She thought: *Now, if I can only unwrap the tape and free my other arm . . .*

"Put your hand back up where I can see it," Mama Rosa warned quietly.

When Dorothy-Anne didn't obey quickly enough, a scream rent the air: *"Now!"*

Dorothy-Anne and Zack both jerked, and Dorothy-Anne quickly put her hand on the table.

Mama Rosa picked up the baggie with the pistol in it, then seemed to have second thoughts, and slid it aside. She grabbed the chef's knife instead. Lunging from her chair, she leaned across the table, pressed the point of the blade against Dorothy-Anne's throat, and pricked the skin.

Dorothy-Anne didn't dare breathe.

"You can die sooner," Mama Rosa said, "or you can die later. It's your choice."

Then she withdrew the knife, sat back down, and continued eating.

Dorothy-Anne sat there, shaking. She could feel a bead of blood trickling down her neck.

I might as well come to terms with this. Zack and I are going to die.

She could only pray that it would be painless.

And that was when she heard another sound, a soft sound which was all but masked by the rumbles and shrieks of the storm. Her heart gave a leap.

Could it be? Was it the sound of an approaching car engine?

She glanced over at the windows and saw the distant rise and dip of headlights. Mama Rosa was oblivious to them. She was busy eating, stuffing her face as though this might be her last supper, too.

"You don't know what you're missing," she told Dorothy-Anne. "But if you don't wanna eat"—she shrugged—"I ain't gonna force you."

Dorothy-Anne didn't hear a word she was saying. It was all she could do to conceal her excitement.

It's Hunt! she thought jubilantly. *It's got to be!*

"Maybe I will eat, after all," Dorothy-Anne decided, hastily making conversation in order to cover up the engine sounds. "*Pomodori alla* what Range did you say these are called?"

There was a deafening crash, as first the hood of a Range Rover, and then the entire vehicle, burst through the end wall of the Quonset hut. The wind, pounding at a steady seventy miles an hour, blasted in, scattering chairs and sending objects flying. Then the air pressure blew out the far end wall of the hut, and it turned into a wind tunnel.

Mama Rosa grabbed the baggie and tore it open. She had the pistol in her hand by the time Hunt dove out of the Range Rover.

She pressed the trigger.

Click.

She stared down at it. "Junk!" she screamed, slamming it back on the table.

She grabbed the chef's knife and leaped to her feet, leaning forward in a knife-fighting stance. There was an unholy glow in her eyes as she slashed the gleaming blade through the air.

"Hunt!" Dorothy-Anne shouted.

Whipped by the blizzard of wind, she struggled to unwrap her left arm, but it would take too long. The quickest way to free herself was to cut the tape, but she didn't have a knife. Only the pistol.

The pistol!

She remembered Jim Larsen's warning:

"It's loaded. The chamber holds six rounds. As a safety precaution, the first one's empty. That gives you five shots."

Dorothy-Anne stretched her arm across the table, grabbed the pistol, and aimed it at Mama Rosa.

The fat woman's big breasts heaved with laughter. "What are you planning to do?" she shouted above the roar of the wind. "*Scare* me to death?"

And Dorothy-Anne pulled the trigger.

The bullet slammed into Mama Rosa's shoulder. The fat woman was knocked backward off her feet, the knife clattering to the floor.

Seeing the venom in the glowing black eyes, Dorothy-Anne fired again. This time she got Mama Rosa in the leg.

And then Hunt was there, holding Dorothy-Anne in his arms. "Thank God you're alive!" he shouted. "Here. Let me get the knife."

Thinking he was after her, Mama Rosa pushed herself desperately backward with her hands, leaving a wide, wet smear of blood on the floor.

It took Hunt no time to cut Dorothy-Anne loose.

She flung her arms around his neck and clung to him. "Oh, Hunt. I can't *believe* it! You really are my knight in shining armor!"

He laughed and kissed her. "I knew I loved you, but you know something? It took this for me to know just how much. If anything had happened to you . . ."

He shook his head at the mere thought.

Dorothy-Anne noticed Mama Rosa struggling to her feet. Now, favoring her right leg and limping noticeably, the fat woman loped off into the storm.

Oh no, you don't, Dorothy-Anne thought.

"Cut Zack loose," she told Hunt. "And *stay* with him! I'll be right back."

"Where are you going?"

Dorothy-Anne snatched up the pistol. There were three rounds left. She looked around and found the flashlight on the floor.

"Taking care of some unfinished business," she said grimly, and was gone.

Dorothy-Anne had the advantage. She knew Eden Isle. And she knew exactly in which direction to chase the assassin.

Mama Rosa blundered south, past the rows of Quonset huts and trailers, bypassing the Oceanographic Institute, and heading for the sea.

Or so she thought.

But it wasn't the sea. It was Predators' Lagoon.

Dorothy-Anne fired a bullet, which missed its mark but had the desired effect. Mama Rosa rushed to the railing surrounding the lagoon, climbed over it, and dove in.

"*Buon appetito,*" Dorothy-Anne said wryly. Then she staggered back to the Quonset hut, where she found Hunt holding Zack.

"We've got to find shelter!" Hunt yelled. "*Now.* The wind's going to reach a hundred sixty, with gusts of up to two hundred miles an hour. Come *on!*"

Dorothy-Anne stared at him. "Where are we going?"

"The turbine room. Don't you remember it? It's built like a concrete bunker, and is far above sea level. We'll be safe in there."

"My hero," she laughed.

"My heroine," he shouted back.

"Hey!" Zack piped up. "Will you two lovebirds cool it? I want to get out of here."

74

Mama Rosa's head broke the surface of the lagoon, water sluicing off her. She spat out a stream of saltwater. The idiot! Didn't the woman realize Carmine could swim?

Well, she'd be sorry. Carmine would get them yet. The woman, the boy, *and* that meddlesome man. If not today or tomorrow, then next week, and if not then, the week after . . .

The blood leaking from her wounds spread in the water like a mushrooming pink cloud.

Mama Rosa was aware that she was bleeding, but it didn't concern her. *So I'm wounded. So I've lost a little blood.* It wasn't the first time.

Blood.

The sharks' sensory receptors were processing signals of food.

Sleek dark shapes, like lethal torpedoes, shot through the water from all around.

Blood.

Prey.

And suddenly Mama Rosa saw the fast-approaching fins cutting through the lagoon, and screamed, but it was too late.

The water became a furiously churning cauldron as the sharks struck, tearing off mouthfuls of flesh.

Mama Rosa died like her victims.

Wondering what had gone wrong.

EPILOGUE

The meeting was held in a houseboat on one of the lesser *klongs*, far from the heavily populated and highly trafficked areas of the Phrapinklao Bridge and the Klong Bangkok Noi. Here the canals were seemingly so infinite in number that they created a bewildering network, which offered both privacy and refuge.

All six of the elders arrived separately, and at different times. Their host was Honorable Rooster, the Thai chemist who converted opium to heroin.

While their bodyguards stood watch on deck, the elders sat inside around a table, their teak chop boxes in front of them. In the center of the table was a woven basket.

Honorable Ox was speaking: "There is an international fashion designer in Milan who has retail outlets in over one hundred countries. He is deeply in debt, and his shops would be ideal for laundering our money."

Excited murmurs greeted this news, and after more than an hour of discussion, Honorable Ox cleared his throat.

"It is time to cast our votes," the old *lung tao* said. "The bird signifies yes. The fish signifies no."

Each of the elders opened his teak box, selected the appropriate chop, pressed it into the ink pot, and stamped his mark on a sliver of rice paper. After the ballots were cast, Honorable Rooster emptied the basket and unfolded the votes.

"*Ayeeyah!*" he exclaimed. "See? It is unanimous! All are in favor of this action."

"It is decided," said Honorable Ox. "We shall depart as usual. Honorable Rooster, as our host, you shall be the last to leave. Please see to it that this boat is destroyed."